D0194846

TWO FACES OF LOVE

TWO FACES OF LOVE

Lust for Life

Immortal Wife

IRVING STONE

Garden City, New York
DOUBLEDAY & COMPANY, INC.

COPYRIGHT 1934, 1944 BY IRVING STONE
ALL RIGHTS RESERVED. PRINTED IN THE UNITED STATES OF AMERICA

Lust for Life

To the memory of my mother
PAULINE STONE

CONTENTS

PROLOGUE—*LONDON*

BOOK ONE—*THE BORINAGE*

PROLOGUE

LONDON

1

"Monsieur Van Gogh! It's time to wake up!"

Vincent had been waiting for Ursula's voice even while he slept.

"I was awake, Mademoiselle Ursula," he called back.

"No you weren't," the girl laughed, "but you are now." He heard her go down the stairs and into the kitchen.

Vincent put his hands under him, gave a shove, and sprang out of bed. His shoulders and chest were massive, his arms thick and powerful. He slipped into his clothes, poured some cold water out of the ewer, and stropped his razor.

Vincent enjoyed the daily ritual of the shave; down the broad cheek from the right sideburn to the corner of the voluptuous mouth; the right half of the upper lip from the nostril out, then the left half; then down the chin, a huge, rounded slab of warm granite.

He stuck his face into the wreath of Brabantine grass and oak leaves on the chiffonier. His brother Theo had gathered it from the heath near Zundert and sent it to London for him. The smell of Holland in his nose started the day off right.

"Monsieur Van Gogh," called Ursula, knocking on the door again, "the postman just left this letter for you."

He recognized his mother's handwriting as he tore open the envelope. "Dear Vincent," he read, "I am going to put a word to bed on paper for you."

His face felt cold and damp so he stuck the letter into his trouser pocket, intending to read it during one of his many leisure moments at Goupils. He combed back his long, thick, yellow-red hair, put on a stiff white shirt, low collar and a large knotted four-in-hand black tie and descended to breakfast and Ursula's smile.

Ursula Loyer and her mother, the widow of a Provençal curate, kept a kindergarten for boys in a little house in the back garden. Ursula was nineteen, a smiling, wide-eyed creature with a delicate, oval face, pastel colouring and a small, slender figure. Vincent loved to watch the sheen of laughter which, like the glow from a highly coloured parasol, was spread over her piquant face.

Ursula served with quick, dainty movements, chatting vivaciously while he ate. He was twenty-one and in love for the first time. Life opened out before him. He thought he would be a fortunate man if he could eat breakfast opposite Ursula for the rest of his days.

Ursula brought in a rasher of bacon, an egg, and a cup of strong, black tea. She fluttered into a chair across the table from him, patted the brown curls at the back of her head, and smiled at him while she passed the salt, pepper, butter and toast in quick succession.

"Your mignonette is coming up a bit," she said, wetting her lips with her tongue. "Will you have a look at it before you go to the gallery?"

"Yes," he replied. "Will you, that is, would you . . . show me?"

"What a droll person he is! He plants the mignonette himself and then doesn't know where to find it." She had a habit of speaking about people as though they were not in the room.

Vincent gulped. His manner, like his body, was heavy and he did not seem able to find the right words for Ursula. They went into the yard. It was a cool April morning, but the apple trees had already blossomed. A little garden separated the Loyer house from the kindergarten. Just a few days before, Vincent had sown poppies and sweet peas. The mignonette was pushing through the earth. Vincent and Ursula squatted on either side of it, their heads almost touching. Ursula had a strong, natural perfume of the hair.

"Mademoiselle Ursula," he said.

"Yes?" She withdrew her head, but smiled at him questioningly.

"I . . . I . . . that is . . ."

"Dear me, what can you be stuttering about?" she asked, and jumped up. He followed her to the door of the kindergarten. "My *poupons* will be here soon," she said. "Won't you be late at the gallery?"

"I have time. I walk to the Strand in forty-five minutes."

She could think of nothing to say, so she reached behind her with both arms to catch up a tiny wisp of hair that was escaping. The curves of her body were surprisingly ample for so slender a figure.

"Whatever have you done with that Brabant picture you promised me for the kindergarten?" she asked.

"I sent a reproduction of one of Caesar de Cock's sketches to Paris. He is going to inscribe it for you."

"Oh, delightful!" She clapped her hands, swung a short way about on her hips, then turned back again. "Sometimes, Monsieur, just sometimes, you can be most charming."

She smiled at him with her eyes and mouth, and tried to go. He caught her by the arm. "I thought of a name for you after I went to bed," he said. "I called you *l'ange aux poupons.*"

Ursula threw back her head and laughed heartily. "*L'ange aux poupons!*" she cried. "I must go tell it to Mother!"

She broke loose from his grip, laughed at him over a raised shoulder, ran through the garden and into the house.

2

Vincent put on his top hat, took his gloves, and stepped out into the road of Clapham. The houses were scattered at this distance from the heart of London. In every garden the lilacs and hawthorn and laburnums were in bloom.

It was eight-fifteen; he did not have to be at Goupils until nine. He was a vigorous walker, and as the houses thickened he passed an increasing number of business men on their way to work. He felt extremely friendly to them all; they too knew what a splendid thing it was to be in love.

He walked along the Thames Embankment, crossed Westminster Bridge, passed by Westminster Abbey and the House of Parliament, and turned into number 17 Southampton, Strand, the London quarters of Goupil and Company, Art Dealers and Publishers of Engravings.

As he walked through the main salon, with its thick carpets and rich draperies, he saw a canvas representing a kind of fish or dragon six yards long, with a little man hovering over it. It was called *The Archangel Michael Killing Satan*.

"There is a package for you on the lithograph table," one of the clerks told him as he passed.

The second room of the shop, after one passed the picture salon in which were exhibited the paintings of Millais, Boughton, and Turner, was devoted to etchings and lithographs. It was in the third room, which looked more like a place of business than either of the others, that most of the sales were carried on. Vincent laughed as he thought of the woman who had made the last purchase the evening before.

"I can't fancy this picture, Harry, can you?" she asked her husband. "The dog looks a rare bit like the one that bit me in Brighton last summer."

"Look here, old fellow," said Harry, "must we have a dog? They mostly put the missus in a stew."

Vincent was conscious of the fact that he was selling very poor stuff indeed. Most of the people who came in knew absolutely nothing about what they were buying. They paid high prices for a cheap commodity, but what business was it of his? All he had to do was make the print room successful.

He opened the package from Goupils in Paris. It had been sent by Caesar de Cock and was inscribed, "To Vincent, and Ursula Loyer: *Les amis de mes amis sont mes amis.*"

"I'll ask Ursula tonight when I give her this," he murmured to himself. "I'll be twenty-two in a few days and I'm earning five pounds a month. No need to wait any longer."

The time in the quiet back room of Goupils passed very quickly. He sold on an average of fifty photographs a day for the Musée Goupil and Company, and although he would have preferred to deal in oil canvases and etchings, he was pleased to be taking in so much money for the house. He liked his fellow clerks and they liked him; they spent many pleasant hours together talking of things European.

As a young chap he had been slightly morose and had avoided companionship. People had thought him queer, a bit eccentric. But Ursula had changed his nature completely. She had made him want to be agreeable and popular; she had brought him out of himself and helped him to see the goodness in the ordinary pattern of daily life.

At six o'clock the store closed. Mr. Obach stopped Vincent on his way out. "I had a letter from your Uncle Vincent Van Gogh about you," he said. "He wanted to know how you were coming on. I was happy to tell him that you are one of the best clerks in the store."

"It was very good of you to say that, sir."

"Not at all. After your summer vacation I want you to leave the back room and come forward into the etchings and lithographs."

"That means a great deal to me at this moment, sir, because I . . . I'm going to be married!"

"Really? This is news. When is it to take place?"

"This summer, I suppose." He hadn't thought of the date before.

"Well my boy, that's splendid. You just had an increase the first of the year, but when you come back from your wedding trip I dare say we can manage another."

3

"I'll get the picture for you, Mademoiselle Ursula," said Vincent after dinner, pushing back his chair.

Ursula was wearing a modishly embroidered dress of verdigris faye. "Did the artist write something nice for me?" she asked.

"Yes. If you'll get a lamp I'll hang it in the kindergarten for you."

She pursed her lips to a highly kissable *moue* and looked at him sideways. "I must help Mother. Shall we make it in a half hour?"

Vincent rested his elbows on the chiffonier in his room and gazed into the mirror. He had rarely thought about his appearance; in Holland such things had not seemed important. He had noticed that in comparison to the English his face and head were ponderous. His eyes were buried in deep crevices of horizontal rock; his nose was high ridged, broad and straight as a shinbone; his dome-like forehead was as high as the distance from his thick eyebrows to the sensuous mouth; his jaws were wide and powerful, his neck a bit squat and thick, and his massive chin a living monument to Dutch character.

He turned away from the mirror and sat idly on the edge of the bed. He had been brought up in an austere home. He had never loved a girl before; he had never even looked at one or engaged in the casual banter between the sexes. In his love for Ursula there was nothing of passion or desire. He was young; he was an idealist; he was in love for the first time.

He glanced at his watch. Only five minutes had passed. The twenty-five minutes that stretched ahead seemed interminable. He drew a note from his brother Theo out of his mother's letter and reread it. Theo was four years younger than Vincent and was now taking Vincent's place in Goupils in The Hague. Theo and Vincent, like their father Theodorus and Uncle Vincent, had been favourite brothers all through their youth.

Vincent picked up a book, rested some paper on it, and wrote Theo a note. From the top drawer of the chiffonier he drew out a few rough sketches that he had made along the Thames Embankment and put them into an envelope for Theo along with a photograph of *Young Girl with a Sword*, by Jacquet.

"My word," he exclaimed aloud, "I've forgotten all about Ursula!"

He looked at his watch; he was already a quarter of an hour late. He snatched up a comb, tried to straighten out the tangle of wavy red hair, took Caesar de Cock's picture from the table, and flung open the door.

"I thought you had forgotten me," Ursula said as he came into the parlour. She was pasting together some paper toys for her *poupons*. "Did you bring my picture? May I see it?"

"I would like to put it up before you look. Did you fix a lamp?"

"Mother has it."

When he returned from the kitchen she gave him a scarf of blue marine to wrap about her shoulders. He thrilled to the silken touch of it. In the garden there was the smell of apple blossoms. The path was dark and Ursula put the ends of her fingers lightly on the sleeve of his rough, black coat. She stumbled once, gripped his arm more tightly and laughed in high glee at her own clumsiness. He did not understand why she thought it funny to trip, but he liked to watch her body carry the laughter down the dark path. He held open the door of the kindergarten for her and as she passed, her delicately moulded face almost brushing his, she looked deep into his eyes and seemed to answer his question before he asked it.

He set the lamp down on the table. "Where would you like me to hang the picture?" he asked.

"Over my desk, don't you think?"

There were perhaps fifteen low chairs and tables in the room of what had formerly been a summer house. At one end was a little platform supporting Ursula's desk. He and Ursula stood side by side, groping for the right position for the picture. Vincent was nervous; he dropped the pins as fast as he tried to stick them into the wall. She laughed at him in a quiet, intimate tone.

"Here, clumsy, let me do it."

She lifted both arms above her head and worked with deft movements of every muscle of her body. She was quick in her gestures, and graceful. Vincent wanted to take her in his arms, there in the dim light of the lamp, and settle with one sure embrace this whole tortuous business. But Ursula, though she touched him frequently in the dark, never seemed to get into position for it. He held the lamp up high while she read the inscription. She was pleased, clapped her hands, rocked back on her heels. She moved so much he could never catch up with her.

"That makes him my friend too, doesn't it?" she asked. "I've always wanted to know an artist."

Vincent tried to say something tender, something that would pave the way for his declaration. Ursula turned her face to him in the half shadow. The gleam from the lamp put tiny spots of light in her eyes. The oval of her face was framed in the darkness and something he could not name moved within him when he saw her red, moist lips stand out from the smooth paleness of her skin.

There was a meaningful pause. He could feel her reaching out to him, waiting for him to utter the unnecessary words of love. He wetted his lips several times. Ursula turned her head, looked into his eyes over a slightly raised shoulder, and ran out the door.

Terror stricken that his opportunity would pass, he pursued her. She stopped for a moment under the apple tree.

"Ursula, please."

She turned and looked at him, shivering a bit. There were cold stars out. The night was black. He had left the lamp behind him. The only light came from the dim glow of the kitchen window. The perfume of Ursula's hair was in his nostrils. She pulled the silk scarf tightly about her shoulders and crossed her arms on her chest.

"You're cold," he said.

"Yes. We had better go in."

"No! Please, I . . ." He planted himself in her path.

She lowered her chin into the warmth of the scarf and looked up at him with wide, wondering eyes. "Why Monsieur Van Gogh, I'm afraid I don't understand."

"I only wanted to talk to you. You see . . . I . . . that is . . ."

"Please, not now. I'm shivering."

"I thought you should know. I was promoted today . . . I'm going forward into the lithograph room . . . it will be my second increase in a year . . ."

Ursula stepped back, unwrapped the scarf, and stood resolutely in the night, quite warm without any protection.

"Precisely what are you trying to tell me, Monsieur Van Gogh?"

He felt the coolness in her voice and cursed himself for being so awkward. The emotion in him suddenly shut down; he felt calm and possessed. He tried a number of voices in his mind and chose the one he liked best.

"I am trying to tell you, Ursula, something you know already. That I love you with all my heart and can only be happy if you will be my wife."

He observed how startled she looked at his sudden command of himself. He wondered if he ought to take her in his arms.

"Your wife!" Her voice rose a few tones. "Why Monsieur Van Gogh, that's impossible!"

He looked at her from under mountain crags, and she saw his eyes clearly in the darkness. "Now I'm afraid it's I who do not . . ."

"How extraordinary that you shouldn't know. I've been engaged for over a year."

He did not know how long he stood there, or what he thought or felt. "Who is the man?" he asked dully.

"Oh, you've never met my fiancé? He had your room before you came. I thought you knew."

"How would I have?"

She stood on tiptoes and peered in the direction of the kitchen. "Well, I . . . I . . . thought someone might have told you."

"Why did you keep this from me all year, when you knew I was falling in love with you?" There was no hesitation or fumbling in his voice now.

"Was it my fault that you fell in love with me? I only wanted to be friends with you."

"Has he been to visit you since I've been in the house?"

"No. He's in Wales. He's coming to spend his summer holiday with me."

"You haven't seen him for over a year? Then you've forgotten him! I'm the one you love now!"

He threw sense and discretion to the winds, grabbed her to him and kissed her rudely on the unwilling mouth. He tasted the moistness of her lips, the sweetness of her mouth, the perfume of her hair; all the intensity of his love rose up within him.

"Ursula, you don't love him. I won't let you. You're going to be my wife. I couldn't bear to lose you. I'll never stop until you forget him and marry me!"

"Marry you!" she cried. "Do I have to marry every man that falls in love with me? Now let go of me, do you hear, or I shall call for help."

She wrenched herself free and ran breathlessly down the dark path. When she gained the steps she turned and spoke in a low carrying whisper that struck him like a shout.

"Red-headed fool!"

4

The next morning no one called him. He climbed lethargically out of bed. He shaved around his face in a circular swash, leaving several patches of beard. Ursula did not appear at breakfast. He walked downtown to Goupils. As he passed the same men that he had seen the morning before he noticed that they had altered. They looked like such lonely souls, hurrying away to their futile labours.

He did not see the laburnums in bloom nor the chestnut trees that lined the road. The sun was shining even more brightly than the morning before. He did not know it.

During the day he sold twenty *épreuves d'artiste* in colour of the *Venus Anadyomene* after Ingres. There was a big profit in these pictures for Goupils, but Vincent had lost his sense of delight in making money for the gallery. He had very little patience with the people who came in to buy. They not only could not tell the difference between good and bad art, but seemed to have a positive talent for choosing the artificial, the obvious, and the cheap.

His fellow clerks had never thought him a jolly chap, but he had done his best to make himself pleasant and agreeable. "What do you suppose is bothering the member of our illustrious Van Gogh family?" one of the clerks asked another.

"I dare say he got out of the wrong side of bed this morning."

"A jolly lot he has to worry about. His uncle, Vincent Van Gogh, is half owner of all the Goupil Galleries in Paris, Berlin, Brussels, The Hague, and Amsterdam. The old man is sick and has no children; everyone says he's leaving his half of the business to this chap."

"Some people have all the luck."

"That's only half the story. His uncle, Hendrik Van Gogh owns big art shops in Brussels and Amsterdam, and still another uncle, Cornelius Van Gogh, is the head of the biggest firm in Holland. Why, the Van Goghs are the greatest family of picture dealers in Europe. One day our red-headed friend in the next room will practically control Continental art!"

When Vincent walked into the dining room of the Loyer's that night he found Ursula and her mother talking together in undertones. They stopped as soon as he came in, and left a sentence hanging in mid-air.

Ursula ran into the kitchen. "Good evening," said Madame Loyer with a curious glint in her eye.

Vincent ate his dinner alone at the large table. Ursula's blow had stunned but not defeated him. He simply was not going to take "no" for an answer. He would crowd the other man out of Ursula's mind.

It was almost a week before he could catch her standing still long enough to speak to her. He had eaten and slept very little during that week; his stolidity had given way to nervousness. His sales at the gallery had dropped off considerably. The greenness had gone from his eyes and left them a pain-shot blue. He had more difficulty than ever in finding words when he wanted to speak.

He followed her into the garden after the big Sunday dinner. "Mademoiselle Ursula," he said, "I'm sorry if I frightened you the other night."

She glanced up at him out of large, cool eyes, as though surprised that he should have followed her. "Oh, it doesn't matter. It was of no importance. Let's forget it, shall we?"

"I'd like very much to forget that I was rude to you. But the things I said were true."

He took a step toward her. She moved away.

"Why speak of it again?" Ursula asked. "The whole episode has quite gone out of my mind." She turned her back on him and walked down the path. He hurried after her.

"I must speak of it again. Ursula, you don't understand how much I love you! You don't know how unhappy I've been this past week. Why do you keep running away from me?"

"Shall we go in? I think Mother is expecting callers."

"It can't be true that you love this other man. I would have seen it in your eyes if you had."

"I'm afraid I've not got any more time to spare. When did you say you were going home for your holiday?"

He gulped. "In July."

"How fortunate. My fiancé is coming to spend his July holiday with me, and we'll need his old room."

"I'll never give you up to him, Ursula!"

"You'll simply have to stop this sort of thing. If you don't, Mother says you can find new lodgings."

He spent the next two months trying to dissuade her. All his early characteristics returned; if he could not be with Ursula he wanted to be by himself so that no one could interfere with his thinking about her. He was unfriendly to the people at the store. The world that had been awakened by Ursula's love went fast asleep again and he became the sombre, morose lad his parents had known in Zundert.

July came, and with it his holiday. He did not wish to leave London for two weeks. He had the feeling that Ursula could not love anyone else as long as he was in the house.

He went down into the parlour. Ursula and her mother were sitting there. They exchanged one of their significant looks.

"I'm taking only one grip with me, Madame Loyer," he said. "I shall leave everything in my room just as it is. Here is the money for the two weeks that I shall be away."

"I think you had better take all your things with you, Monsieur Van Gogh," said Madame.

"But why?"

"Your room is rented from Monday morning. We think it better if you live elsewhere."

"We?"

He turned and looked at Ursula from under the deep ridge of brow. That look made no statement. It only asked a question.

"Yes, we," replied her mother. "My daughter's fiancé has written that he wants you out of the house. I'm afraid, Monsieur Van Gogh, that it would have been better if you had never come here at all."

5

Theodorus Van Gogh met his son at the Breda station with a carriage. He had on his heavy, black ministerial coat, the wide lapelled vest, starched white shirt, and huge black bow tie covering all but a narrow strip of the high collar. With a quick glance Vincent took in his father's two facial characteristics: the right lid drooped down lower than the left, covering a considerable portion of the eye; the left side of his mouth was a thin, taut line, the right side full and sensuous. His eyes were passive; their expression simply said, "This is me."

The people of Zundert often remarked that the dominie Theodorus went about doing good with a high silk hat on.

He never understood to the day of his death why he was not more successful. He felt that he should have been called to an important pulpit in Amsterdam or The Hague years before. He was called the handsome dominie by his parishioners, was well educated, of a loving nature, had fine spiritual qualities, and was indefatigable in the service of God. Yet for twenty-five years he had been buried and forgotten in the little village of Zundert. He was the only one of the six Van Gogh brothers who had not achieved national importance.

The parsonage at Zundert, where Vincent had been born, was a wooden frame building across the road from the market place and *stadhuis*. There was a garden back of the kitchen with acacias and a number of little paths running through the carefully tended flowers. The church was a tiny wooden building hidden in the trees just behind the garden. There were two small Gothic windows of plain glass on either side, perhaps a dozen hard benches on the wooden floor, and a number of warming pans attached permanently to the planks. At the rear there was a stairway leading up to an old hand organ. It was a severe and simple place of worship, dominated by the spirit of Calvin and his reformation.

Vincent's mother, Anna Cornelia, was watching from the front window and had the door open before the carriage came to a full stop. Even while taking him with loving tenderness to her ample bosom, she perceived that something was wrong with her boy.

"*Myn lieve zoon,*" she murmured. "My Vincent."

Her eyes, now blue, now green, were always wide open, gently inquiring, seeing through a person without judging too harshly. A faint line from the side of each nostril down to the corners of the mouth deepened with the passage of the years, and the deeper these lines became, the stronger impression they gave of a face slightly lifted in smile.

Anna Cornelia Carbentus was from The Hague, where her father carried the title of "Bookbinder to the King." William Carbentus's business flourished and when he was chosen to bind the first Constitution of Holland he became known throughout the country. His daughters, one of whom married Uncle Vincent Van Gogh, and a third the well known Reverend Stricker of Amsterdam, were *bien élevées*.

Anna Cornelia was a good woman. She saw no evil in the world and knew of none. She knew only of weakness, temptation, hardship, and pain. Theodorus Van Gogh was also a good man, but he understood evil very thoroughly and condemned every last vestige of it.

The dining room was the centre of the Van Gogh house, and the big table, after the supper dishes had been cleared off, the centre of family life. Here everyone gathered about the friendly oil lamp to pass the evening. Anna Cornelia was worried about Vincent; he was thin, and had become jumpy in his mannerisms.

"Is anything wrong, Vincent?" she asked after supper that night. "You don't look well to me."

Vincent glanced about the table where Anna, Elizabeth, and Willemien, three strange young girls who happened to be his sisters, were sitting.

"No," he said, "nothing is wrong."

"Do you find London agreeable?" asked Theodorus. "If you don't like it I'll speak to your Uncle Vincent. I think he would transfer you to one of the Paris shops."

Vincent became very agitated. "No, no, you mustn't do that!" he exclaimed. "I don't want to leave London, I . . ." He quieted himself. "When Uncle Vincent wants to transfer me, I'm sure he'll think of it for himself."

"Just as you wish," said Theodorus.

"It's that girl," said Anna Cornelia to herself. "Now I understand what was wrong with his letters."

There were pine woods and clumps of oaks on the heath near Zundert. Vincent spent his days walking alone in the fields, gazing down into the numerous ponds with which the heath was dotted. The only diversion he enjoyed was drawing; he made a number of sketches of the garden, the Saturday afternoon market seen from the window of the parsonage, the front door of the house. It kept his mind off Ursula for moments at a time.

Theodorus had always been disappointed that his oldest son had not chosen to follow in his footsteps. They went to visit a sick peasant and when they drove back that evening across the heath the two men got out of the carriage and walked awhile. The sun was setting red behind the pine trees, the evening sky was reflected in the pools, and the heath and yellow sand were full of harmony.

"My father was a parson, Vincent, and I had always hoped you would continue the line."

"What makes you think I want to change?"

"I was only saying, in case you wanted to . . . You could live with Uncle Jan in Amsterdam while you attend the University. And the Reverend Stricker has offered to direct your education."

"Are you advising me to leave Goupils?"

"Oh no, certainly not. But if you are unhappy there . . . sometimes people change . . ."

"I know. But I have no intention of leaving Goupils."

His mother and father drove him to Breda the day he was to leave for London. "Are we to write to the same address, Vincent?" Anna Cornelia asked.

"No. I'm moving."

"I'm glad you're leaving the Loyers," said his father. "I never liked that family. They had too many secrets."

Vincent stiffened. His mother laid a warm hand over his and said gently, so that Theodorus might not hear, "Don't be unhappy, my dear. You will be better off with a nice Dutch girl, later, later, when you are more established. She would not be good for you, that Ursula girl. She is not your kind."

He wondered how his mother knew.

6

Back in London he took furnished rooms in Kensington New Road. His landlady was a little old woman who retired every evening at eight. There was never the faintest sound in the house. Each night he had a fierce battle on his hands; he yearned to run directly to the Loyer's. He would lock the door on himself and swear resolutely that he was going to sleep. In a quarter of an hour he would find himself mysteriously on the street, hurrying to Ursula's.

When he got within a block of her house he felt himself enter her aura. It was torture to have this feel of her and yet have her so inaccessible; it was a thousand times worse torture to stay in Ivy Cottage and not get within that penumbra of haunting personality.

Pain did curious things to him. It made him sensitive to the pain of others. It made him intolerant of everything that was cheap and blatantly successful in the world about him. He was no longer of any value at the gallery. When customers asked him what he thought about a particular print he told them in no uncertain terms how horrible it was, and they did not buy. The only pictures in which he could find reality and emotional depth were the ones in which the artists had expressed pain.

In October a stout matron with a high lace collar, a high bosom, a sable coat, and a round velvet hat with a blue plume, came in and asked to be shown some pictures for her new town house. She fell to Vincent.

"I want the very best things you have in stock," she said. "You needn't concern yourself over the expense. Here are the dimensions; in the drawing room there are two uninterrupted walls of fifty feet, one wall broken by two windows with a space between . . ."

He spent the better part of the afternoon trying to sell her some etchings after Rembrandt, an excellent reproduction of a Venetian water scene after

Turner, some lithographs after Thys Maris, and museum photographs after Corot and Daubigny. The woman had a sure instinct for picking out the very worst expression of the painter's art to be found in any group that Vincent showed her. She had an equal talent for being able to reject at first sight, and quite peremptorily, everything he knew to be authentic. As the hours passed, the woman, with her pudgy features and condescending puerilities, became for him a perfect symbol of middle-class fatuity and the commercial life.

"There," she exclaimed with a self-satisfied air, "I think I've chosen rather well."

"If you had closed your eyes and picked," said Vincent, "you couldn't have done any worse."

The woman rose to her feet heavily and swept the wide velvet skirt to one side. Vincent could see the turgid flow of blood creep from her propped-up bosom to her neck under the lace collar.

"Why!" she exclaimed, "why, you're nothing but a . . . a . . . country boor!"

She stormed out, the tall feather in her velvet hat waving back and forth.

Mr. Obach was outraged. "My dear Vincent," he exclaimed, "whatever is the matter with you? You've muffed the biggest sale of the week, and insulted that woman!"

"Mr. Obach, would you answer me one question?"

"Well, what is it? I have a few questions to ask, myself."

Vincent shoved aside the woman's prints and put both hands on the edge of the table. "Then tell me how a man can justify himself for spending his one and only life selling very bad pictures to very stupid people?"

Obach made no attempt to answer. "If this sort of thing keeps up," he said, "I'll have to write to your uncle and have him transfer you to another branch. I can't have you ruining my business."

Vincent moved aside Obach's strong breath with a gesture of his hand. "How can we take such large profits for selling trash, Mr. Obach? And why is it that the only people who can afford to come in here are those who can't bear to look at anything authentic? Is it because their money has made them callous? And why is it that the poor people who can really appreciate good art haven't even a farthing to buy a print for their walls?"

Obach looked at him queerly. "What is this, socialism?"

When he reached home he picked up the volume of Renan lying on his table and turned to a page he had marked. "To act well in this world," he read, "one must die within oneself. Man is not on this earth only to be happy, he is not there to be simply honest, he is there to realize great things for humanity, to attain nobility and to surpass the vulgarity in which the existence of almost all individuals drags on."

About a week before Christmas the Loyers put up a dainty Christmas tree in their front window. Two nights later as he walked by he saw the house well lighted and neighbours going in the front door. He heard the sound of laughing voices inside. The Loyers were giving their Christmas party. Vincent ran home, shaved hurriedly, put on a fresh shirt and tie, and walked back as fast as he could to Clapham. He had to wait several minutes at the bottom of the stairs to catch his breath.

This was Christmas; the spirit of kindliness and forgiveness was in the air. He walked up the stairs. He pounded on the knocker. He heard a familiar footstep come through the hall, a familiar voice call back something to the people in the parlour. The door was opened. The light from the lamp fell on his face. He looked at Ursula. She was wearing a sleeveless green polonaise with large bows and lace cascades. He had never seen her so beautiful.

"Ursula," he said.

An expression passed over her face that repeated clearly all the things she had said to him in the garden. Looking at her, he remembered them.

"Go away," she said.

She slammed the door in his face.

The following morning he sailed for Holland.

Christmas was the busiest season for the Goupil Galleries. Mr. Obach wrote to Uncle Vincent, explaining that his nephew had taken a holiday without so much as a "with your leave." Uncle Vincent decided to put his nephew into the main gallery in Rue Chaptal in Paris.

Vincent calmly announced that he was through with the art business. Uncle Vincent was stunned and deeply hurt. He declared that in the future he would wash his hands of Vincent. After the holidays he stopped washing them long enough to secure his namesake a position as clerk in the bookshop of Blussé and Braam at Dordrecht. It was the very last thing the two Vincent Van Goghs ever had to do with each other.

He remained at Dordrecht almost four months. He was neither happy nor unhappy, successful nor unsuccessful. He simply was not there. One Saturday night he took the last train from Dordrecht to Oudenbosch and walked home to Zundert. It was beautiful on the heath with all the cool, pungent smells of night. Though it was dark he could distinguish the pine woods and moors extending far and wide. It reminded him of the print by Bodmer that hung in his father's study. The sky was overcast but the night stars were shining through the clouds. It was very early when he arrived at the churchyard at Zundert; in the distance he could hear the larks singing in the black fields of young corn.

His parents understood that he was going through a difficult time. Over the summer the family moved to Etten, a little market town just a few kilometres away, where Theodorus had been named dominie. Etten had a large, elm-lined public square and a steam train connecting it with the important city of Breda. For Theodorus it was a slight step up.

When early fall came it was necessary once again to make a decision. Ursula was not yet married.

"You are not fitted for all these shops, Vincent," said his father. "Your heart has been leading you straight to the service of God."

"I know, Father."

"Then why not go to Amsterdam and study?"

"I would like to, but . . ."

"There is still hesitation in your heart?"

"Yes. I can't explain now. Give me a little more time."

Uncle Jan passed through Etten. "There is a room waiting for you in my house in Amsterdam, Vincent," he said.

"The Reverend Stricker has written that he can secure you good tutors," added his mother.

When he received the gift of pain from Ursula he had inherited the disinherited of the earth. He knew that the best training he could get was at the University at Amsterdam. The Van Gogh and Stricker families would take him in, encourage him, help him with money, books, and sympathy. But he could not make the clean break. Ursula was still in England, unmarried. In Holland he had lost the touch of her. He sent for some English newspapers, answered a number of advertisements, and finally secured a position as teacher at Ramsgate, a seaport town four and a half hours by train from London.

7

Mr. Stokes's schoolhouse stood on a square in the middle of which was a large lawn shut off by iron railings. There were twenty-four boys from ten to fourteen years of age at the school. Vincent had to teach French, German, and Dutch, keep an eye on the boys after hours, and help them with their weekly ablutions on Saturday night. He was given his board and lodging, but no pay.

Ramsgate was a melancholy spot but it suited his mood. Unconsciously he had come to cherish his pain as a dear companion; through it he kept Ursula constantly by his side. If he could not be with the girl he loved, it did not matter where he was. All he asked was that no one come between him and the heavy satiety with which Ursula crammed his brain and body.

"Can't you pay me just a small sum, Mr. Stokes?" asked Vincent. "Enough to buy tobacco and clothes?"

"No, I will certainly not do that," replied Stokes. "I can get teachers enough for just board and lodging."

Early the first Saturday morning Vincent started from Ramsgate to London. It was a long walk, and the weather stayed hot until evening. Finally he reached Canterbury. He rested in the shade of the old trees surrounding the medieval cathedral. After a bit he walked still farther until he arrived at a few large beech and elm trees near a little pond. He slept there until four in the morning; the birds began to sing at dawn and awakened him. By afternoon he reached Chatham where he saw in the distance, between partly flooded low meadows, the Thames full of ships. Towards evening Vincent struck the familiar suburbs of London, and in spite of his fatigue, cut out briskly for the Loyer's house.

The thing for which he had come back to England, the contact with Ursula, reached out and gripped him the instant he came within sight of her home. In England she was still his because he could feel her.

He could not quiet the loud beating of his heart. He leaned against a tree, dully aching with an ache that existed outside the realm of words or articulate thought. At length the lamp in Ursula's parlour was extinguished, then the lamp in her bedroom. The house went dark. Vincent tore himself away and stumbled wearily down the road of Clapham. When he got out of sight of the house he knew that he had lost her again.

When he pictured his marriage to Ursula he no longer thought of her as the wife of a successful art dealer. He saw her as the faithful, uncomplaining wife of an evangelist, working by his side in the slums, to serve the poor.

Nearly every week-end he tried tramping to London, but he found it difficult to get back in time for the Monday morning classes. Sometimes he would walk all Friday and Saturday night just to see Ursula come out of her house on the way to church on Sunday morning. He had no money for food or lodgings, and as winter came on he suffered from the cold. When he got back to Ramsgate in the dawn of a Monday morning he would be shivering, exhausted and famished. It took him all week to recover.

After a few months he found a better position at Mr. Jones's Methodist school in Isleworth. Mr. Jones was a minister with a large parish. He employed Vincent as a teacher but soon turned him into a country curate.

Once again Vincent had to change all the pictures in his mind. Ursula was no longer to be the wife of an evangelist, working in the slums, but rather the wife of a country clergyman, helping her husband in the parish just as his mother helped his father. He saw Ursula looking on with approval, happy that he had left the narrow commercial life of Goupils and was now working for humanity.

He did not permit himself to realize that Ursula's wedding day was coming closer and closer. The other man had never existed as a reality in his mind. He always thought of Ursula's refusal as arising from some peculiar shortcoming on his part, a shortcoming which he must somehow remedy. What better way was there than serving God?

Mr. Jones's impoverished students came from London. The master gave Vincent the addresses of the parents and sent him there on foot to collect tuition. Vincent found them in the heart of Whitechapel. There were vile odours in the streets, large families herded into cold, barren rooms, hunger and illness staring out of every pair of eyes. A number of the fathers traded in diseased meat which the government prohibited from sale in the regular markets. Vincent came upon the families shivering in their rags and eating their supper of slops, dry crusts and putrid meat. He listened to their tales of destitution and misery until nightfall.

He had welcomed the trip to London because it would give him the chance to pass Ursula's house on the way home. The slums of Whitechapel drove her out of his mind and he forgot to take the road through Clapham. He returned to Isleworth without so much as a brass farthing for Mr. Jones.

One Thursday evening during the services the minister leaned over to his curate and feigned fatigue. "I'm feeling frightfully done in this evening, Vincent. You've been writing sermons straight along, haven't you? Then let's hear one of them. I want to see what kind of minister you're going to make."

Vincent mounted to the pulpit, trembling. His face went red and he did not know what to do with his hands. His voice was hoarse and halting. He had to stumble through his memory for the well-rounded phrases he had set down so neatly on paper. But he felt his spirit burst through the broken words and clumsy gestures.

"Nicely done, Vincent," said Mr. Jones. "I shall send you to Richmond next week."

It was a clear autumn day and a beautiful walk from Isleworth to Richmond along the Thames. The blue sky and great chestnut trees with their load of yellow leaves were mirrored in the water. The people of Richmond wrote Mr. Jones that they liked the young Dutch preacher, so the good man decided to give Vincent his chance. Mr. Jones's church at Turnham Green was an important one, the congregation large and critical. If Vincent could preach a good sermon there, he would be qualified to preach from any pulpit.

Vincent chose as his text, Psalm 119:19, "I am a stranger on the earth: hide not Thy commandments from me." He spoke with simple fervour. His youth, his fire, his heavy-handed power, his massive head, and penetrating eyes all had a tremendous effect on the congregation.

Many of them came up to thank him for his message. He shook their hands and smiled at them in a misty daze. As soon as everyone had gone, he slipped out the back door of the church and took the road to London.

A storm came up. He had forgotten his hat and overcoat. The Thames was yellowish, especially near the shore. At the horizon there was a dash of light, and above it immense grey clouds from which the rain poured down in slanting streaks. He was drenched to the skin, but he tramped on at an exhilarated speed.

At last he was successful! He had found himself. He had a triumph to lay at Ursula's feet, to share with her.

The rain pelted the dust on the little white path and swayed the hawthorn bushes. In the distance was a town that looked like a Durer engraving, a town with its turrets, mills, slate roofs and houses built in the Gothic style.

He battled his way into London, the water streaming down his face and sopping into his boots. It was late afternoon before he reached the Loyer house. A grey, murky dusk had fallen. From some distance he heard the sound of music, of violins, and wondered what was going on. Every room in the house had its lamp burning. A number of carriages stood out in the sheets of rain. Vincent saw people dancing in the parlour. An old cabby was sitting on his box under a huge umbrella, huddled away from the rain.

"What's going on here?" he asked.

"Weddin', I fancy."

Vincent leaned against the carriage, rivulets from his red hair streaming down his face. After a time the front door opened. Ursula and a tall, slim man were framed in the doorway. The crowd from the parlour surged out on the porch, laughing, shouting, throwing rice.

Vincent slunk around to the dark side of the carriage. Ursula and her husband got in. The cabby flicked his whip over the horses. They started slowly. Vincent took a few steps forward and pressed his face against the streaming window. Ursula was locked tight in the man's arms, her mouth full on his. The carriage drew away.

Something thin snapped within Vincent, snapped neat and clean. The spell was broken. He had not known it could be so easy.

He trudged back to Isleworth in the slashing rain, collected his belongings, and left England for ever.

BOOK ONE

THE BORINAGE

I

Vice-Admiral Johannes Van Gogh, highest ranking officer in the Dutch Navy, stood on the *stoep* of his roomy, rent-free residence at the rear of the Navy Yard. In honour of his nephew's coming he had donned his dress uniform; a gold epaulet perched on each shoulder. Above the ponderous Van Gogh chin jutted a strong, straight-ridged nose that met the convex cliff of the forehead.

"I'm glad to have you here, Vincent," he said. "The house is very quiet, now that my children have married out of it."

They mounted a flight of broad, angular stairs and Uncle Jan threw open a door. Vincent entered the room and set down his bag. A large window overlooked the Yard. Uncle Jan sat on the edge of the bed and tried to look as informal as his gold braid would permit.

"I was pleased to hear that you had decided to study for the ministry," he said. "One member of the Van Gogh family has always done God's work."

Vincent reached for his pipe and loaded the bowl carefully with tobacco; it was a gesture he often made when he needed an extra moment to think. "I wanted to be an evangelist, you know, and get right to work."

"You wouldn't want to be an evangelist, Vincent. They're uneducated people, and Lord knows what sort of garbled theology they preach. No, my boy, the Van Gogh dominies have always been University graduates. But no doubt you would like to unpack now. Dinner is at eight."

The broad back of the vice-admiral had no sooner gone out of the door than a gentle melancholy descended upon Vincent. He looked about him. The bed was wide and comfortable, the bureau spacious, the low, smooth study table inviting. But he felt ill at ease, as he did in the presence of strangers. He snatched up his cap and walked rapidly across the *Dam*. There he found a Jewish book-seller who offered beautiful prints in an open bin. After a good deal of searching, Vincent selected thirteen pieces, stuck them under his arm and walked home along the waterfront, breathing in the strong odour of tar.

As he was pinning up his prints lightly, so as not to injure the fabric of the walls, there was a knock on the door. The Reverend Stricker entered. Stricker was also Vincent's uncle, but he was not a Van Gogh; his wife and Vincent's mother were sisters. He was a well-known clergyman in Amsterdam and by general admission a clever one. His black suit was of good material, smartly cut.

When the greetings were over the dominie said, "I have secured Mendes da Costa, one of our finest scholars of the classical languages, to tutor you in Latin and Greek. His home is in the Jewish quarter; you are to go there Monday afternoon at three for your first lesson. But what I came for was to ask your company at tomorrow's Sunday dinner. Your Aunt Wilhelmina and Cousin Kay are anxious to see you."

"I would like that very much. At what time shall I come?"

"We dine at noon, after my late morning service."

"Please present my compliments to your family," said Vincent, as the Reverend Stricker picked up his black hat and folio.

"Until tomorrow," said his uncle, and was gone.

2

The Keizersgracht, on which the Stricker family lived, was one of the most aristocratic streets in Amsterdam. It was the fourth horseshoe boulevard and canal which starts from the south side of the harbour, runs around the centrum and back to the harbour again on the north. It was clean and clear, far too important a canal to be covered with *kroos*, the mysterious green moss which for hundreds of years has laid a thick surface on the canals in the poorer districts.

The houses that line the street are pure Flemish; narrow, well built, tightly fitted together, a long line of prim Puritan soldiers standing at attention.

The following day, after listening to Uncle Stricker preach, Vincent set out for the dominie's house. A bright sun had waved away the ash-grey clouds that float eternally across the Dutch skies, and for a few moments the air was luminous. Vincent was early. He walked at a meditative gait and watched the canal boats being pushed upstream against the current.

They were largely sand boats, oblong except for the tapering ends; a water-worn black in colour, with great hollow spaces in the centre for the cargo. Long clothes-lines extended from prow to stern, on which hung the family wash. The father of the family thrust his pole into the mud, propped it against his shoulder, and struggled down the catwalk at twisted, tortuous angles while the boat slipped out from under him. The wife, a heavy, buxom, red-faced woman, sat immutably at the stern and worked the clumsy wooden tiller. The children played with the dog, and every few minutes ran down into the cabin hole that was their home.

The Reverend Stricker's home was of typical Flemish architecture; narrow, three-storied, with an oblong tower at the top containing the attic window, and decorated with flowing arabesques. A beam stuck out from the attic window with a long iron hook at the end of it.

Aunt Wilhelmina welcomed Vincent and led him into the dining room. A portrait of Calvin by Ary Scheffer hung on the wall, and a silver service gleamed on a sideboard. The walls were done in dark wood panelling.

Before Vincent could get used to the customary darkness of the room, a tall, lithe girl came out of the shadows and greeted him warmly.

"Of course you wouldn't know me," she said in a rich voice, "but I'm your cousin Kay."

Vincent took her outstretched hand and felt the soft, warm flesh of a young woman for the first time in many months.

"We've never met," the girl went on in that intimate tone, "and I think it rather curious, since I'm twenty-six, and you must be . . . ?"

Vincent gazed at her in silence. Several moments passed before he realized that an answer was necessary. In order to make up for his stupidity, he blurted out in a loud, harsh voice, "Twenty-four. Younger than you."

"Yes. Well, I suppose it's not so curious after all. You have never visited Amsterdam and I have never been in the Brabant. But I'm afraid I'm being a poor hostess. Won't you sit down?"

He sat on the edge of a stiff chair. With one of the swift, strange metamorphoses that changed him from an awkward, country boor to a polished gentleman, he said, "Mother often wished you would come to visit us. I think the Brabant would have pleased you. The country-side is very *sympatica*."

"I know. Aunt Anna wrote and invited me several times. I must visit there very soon."

"Yes," replied Vincent, "you must."

It was only a remote portion of his mind that heard and answered the girl. The rest of him was soaking up her beauty with the passionate thirst of a man who has drunk too long at a celibate well. Kay had the hardy features of the Dutch women, but they had been filed down, chiselled away to delicate proportions. Her hair was neither the corn blond nor the raw red of her country-women, but a curious intermingling, in which the fire of one had caught up the light of the other in a glowing, subtle warmth. She had guarded her skin against the sun and wind; the whiteness of her chin crept into the flush of her cheek with all the artistry of a little Dutch master. Her eyes were a deep blue, dancing to the joy of life; her full-lipped mouth was slightly open, as though for its acceptance.

She noticed Vincent's silence and said, "What are you thinking about, Cousin? You seem preoccupied."

"I was thinking that Rembrandt would have liked to paint you."

Kay laughed low and with a ripe lusciousness in her throat. "Rembrandt only liked to paint ugly old women, didn't he?" she asked.

"No," replied Vincent. "He painted beautiful old women, women who were poor or in some way unhappy, but who through sorrow had gained a soul."

For the first time Kay really looked at Vincent. She had glanced at him only casually when he came in and noticed his mop of rust-red hair and rather heavy face. Now she saw the full mouth, the deep set, burning eyes, the high, symmetrical forehead of the Van Goghs, and the uncrushable chin, stuck slightly out toward her.

"Forgive me for being stupid," she murmured, almost in a whisper. "I understand what you mean about Rembrandt. He gets at the real essence of beauty, doesn't he, when he paints those gnarled old people who have suffering and defeat carved into their faces."

"What have you children been talking about so earnestly?" asked the Reverend Stricker from the doorway.

"We have been getting acquainted," Kay answered. "Why didn't you tell me I had such a nice cousin?"

Another man came into the room, a slender chap with an easy smile and charming manner. Kay rose and kissed him eagerly. "Cousin Vincent," she said, "this is my husband, Mijnheer Vos."

She returned in a few moments with a tow-headed boy of two, a vivacious child with a wistful face and the light blue eyes of his mother. Kay reached down and lifted the boy. Vos put his arms about the two of them.

"Will you sit on this side of the table with me, Vincent?" asked Aunt Wilhelmina.

Opposite Vincent, with Vos on one side and Jan propped up on the other, sat Kay. She had forgotten about Vincent now that her husband was home. The colour deepened in her cheek. Once, as her husband said something pointed in a low, guarded tone, she leaned over with a quick alertness and kissed him.

The vibrant waves of their love reached out and engulfed Vincent. For the first time since that fateful Sunday the old pain for Ursula arose from some mysterious source within him and flooded the outermost ramparts of his body and brain. The little family before him, with its clinging unity and joyous affection, brought him to a realization that he had been hungry, desperately hungry for love all these weary months, and that it was a hunger not easily destroyed.

3

Vincent arose just before sunrise each morning to read his Bible. When the sun came up about five o'clock he went to the window which overlooked the Navy Yard and watched the gangs of workmen come through the gate, a long uneven line of black figures. Little steamers sailed to and fro in the Zuider Zee and in the distance, near the village across the Y, he saw the swiftly moving, brown sails.

When the sun had fully risen and sponged the mist from the pile of lumber, Vincent turned from his window, breakfasted on a piece of dry bread and a glass of beer, and then sat down for a seven hour siege with his Latin and Greek.

After four or five hours of concentration his head became heavy; often it burned and his thoughts were confused. He did not see how he was going to persevere in simple, regular study after all those emotional years. He pounded rules into his head until the sun was already sliding down the other side of the heavens and it was time for him to go to Mendes da Costa for his lesson. On the way there he would walk along the Buitenkant, around the Oudezyds Chapel and the Old and South Church, through crooked streets with forges and coopers and lithograph shops.

Mendes reminded Vincent of the *Imitation of Jesus Christ* by Ruyperez; he was the classical type of Jew with profound, cavernous eyes, a thin, hollowed out, spiritual face, and the soft, pointed beard of the early rabbis. It was very close and sultry in mid-afternoon in the Jewish quarter; Vincent, gorged with seven hours of Greek and Latin, and more hours of Dutch History and Grammar, would talk to Mendes about lithographs. One day he brought his teacher the study of *A Baptism* by Maris.

Mendes held *A Baptism* in his bony, tapering fingers, letting the sharp stream of dusted sunlight from the high window fall upon it.

"It is good," he said in his throaty, Jewish voice. "It catches something of the spirit of universal religion."

Vincent's fatigue left him instantly. He launched into an enthusiastic description of Maris's art. Mendes shook his head imperceptibly. The Reverend Stricker was paying him a high price to instruct Vincent in Latin and Greek.

"Vincent," he said quietly, "Maris is very fine, but the time grows short and we had better get on with our studies, yes?"

Vincent understood. On the way home, after a two hour lesson, he would pause before the interiors of houses where the wood-choppers, carpenters, and ships' victualers were at work. The doors stood open before a big wine cellar, and men with lights were running to and fro in the dark vault.

Uncle Jan went to Helvoort for a week; knowing that he was alone in the big house behind the Navy Yard, Kay and Vos walked over late one afternoon to fetch Vincent for dinner.

"You must come to us every night until Uncle Jan gets back," Kay told him. "And Mother asks if you won't take Sunday dinner with us each week, after services?"

When dinner was over the family played cards, but since Vincent did not know how to play, he settled in a quiet corner and read August Gruson's "Histoire des Croisades." From where he was sitting he could watch Kay and the changes of her quick, provocative smile. She left the table and came to his side.

"What are you reading, Cousin Vincent?" she asked.

He told her and then said, "It's a fine little book, I should almost say written with the sentiment of Thys Maris."

Kay smiled. He was always making these funny literary allusions. "Why Thys Maris?" she demanded.

"Read this and see if it doesn't remind you of a Maris canvas, where the writer describes an old castle on a rock, with the autumn woods in twilight, and in the foreground the black fields, and a peasant who is ploughing with a white horse."

While Kay was reading, Vincent drew up a chair for her. When she looked at him a thoughtful expression darkened her blue eyes.

"Yes," she said, "it is just like a Maris. The writer and painter use their own medium to express the same thought."

Vincent took the book and ran his finger across the page eagerly. "This line might have been lifted straight from Michelet or Carlyle."

"You know, Cousin Vincent, for a man who has spent so little time in classrooms, you are surprisingly well educated. Do you still read a good many books?"

"No, I should like to, but I may not. Though in fact I need not long for it so much, for all things are found in the word of Christ—more perfect and more beautiful than in any other book."

"Oh, Vincent," exclaimed Kay, jumping to her feet, "that was so unlike you!"

Vincent stared at her in amazement.

"I think you are ever so much nicer when you're seeing Thys Maris in the 'Histoire des Croisades'—though Father says you ought to concentrate and not think of such things—than when you talk like a stuffy, provincial clergyman."

Vos strolled over and said, "We've dealt you a hand, Kay."

Kay looked for a moment into the live, burning coals under Vincent's overhanging brows, then took her husband's arm and joined the other card players.

4

Mendes da Costa knew that Vincent liked to talk to him about the more general things of life, so several times a week he invented excuses to accompany him back to town when their lesson was done.

One day he took Vincent through an interesting part of the city, the outskirts that extend from the Leidsche Poort, near the Vondel Park, to the Dutch railway station. It was full of sawmills, workmen's cottages with little gardens, and was very populous. The quarter was cut through with many small canals.

"It must be a splendid thing to be a clergyman in a quarter like this," said Vincent.

"Yes," replied Mendes, as he filled his pipe and passed the cone-shaped bag of tobacco to Vincent, "these people need God and religion more than our friends uptown."

They were crossing a tiny wooden bridge that might almost have been Japanese. Vincent stopped and said, "What do you mean, Mijnheer?"

"These workers," said Mendes with a gentle sweep of his arm, "have a hard life of it. When illness comes they have no money for a doctor. The food for tomorrow comes from today's labour, and hard labour it is, too. Their houses, as you see, are small and poor; they are never more than a stone's throw away from privation and want. They've made a bad bargain with life; they need the thought of God to comfort them."

Vincent lighted his pipe and dropped the match into the little canal below him. "And the people uptown?" he asked.

"They have good clothes to wear, secure positions, money put away against adversity. When they think of God, He is a prosperous old gentleman, rather well pleased with himself for the lovely way things are going on earth."

"In short," said Vincent, "they're a little stuffy."

"Dear me!" exclaimed Mendes. "I never said that."

"No, I did."

That night he spread his Greek books out before him, and then stared at the opposite wall for a long time. He remembered the slums of London, the sordid poverty and suffering; he remembered his desire to become an evangelist and help those people. His mental image flashed to Uncle Stricker's church. The congregation was prosperous, well educated, sensitive to and capable of acquiring the better things of life. Uncle Stricker's sermons were beautiful and comforting, but who in the congregation needed comfort?

Six months had passed since he first came to Amsterdam. He was at last beginning to understand that hard work is but a poor substitute for natural ability. He pushed aside his language books and opened his algebra. At midnight Uncle Jan came in.

"I saw the light under your door, Vincent," said the vice-admiral, "and the watchman told me he saw you walking in the Yard at four o'clock this morning. How many hours a day have you been working?"

"It varies. Between eighteen and twenty."

"Twenty!" Uncle Jan shook his head; the misgiving grew more perceptible on his face. It was difficult for the vice-admiral to adjust himself to the thought of failure in the Van Gogh family. "You should not need so many."

"I must get my work done, Uncle Jan."

Uncle Jan brought up his bushy eyebrows. "Be that as it may," he said, "I have promised your parents to take good care of you. So you will kindly get to bed, and in the future do not work so late."

Vincent pushed aside his exercises. He had no need for sleep; he had no need for love or sympathy or pleasure. He had need only to learn his Latin and Greek, his algebra and grammar, so that he might pass his examinations, enter the University, become a minister, and do God's practical work on earth.

5

By May, just a year after he came to Amsterdam, he began to realize that his unfitness for formal education would finally conquer him. This was not a statement of fact, but an admission of defeat, and every time one portion of his brain threw the realization before him, he whipped the rest of his mind to drown the admission in weary labour.

If it had been a simple question of the difficulty of the work, and his manifest unfitness for it, he would not have been disturbed. But the question that racked him night and day was, "Did he want to become a clever, gentleman clergyman like his Uncle Stricker?" What would happen to his ideal of personal service to the poor, the sick, the downtrodden, if he thought only of declensions and formulae for five more years?

One afternoon late in May, when he had finished his lesson with Mendes, Vincent said, "Mijnheer da Costa, could you find time to take a walk with me?"

Mendes had been sensitive to the growing struggle in Vincent; he divined that the younger man had reached a point where a decision was imminent.

"Yes, I had planned to go for a little stroll. The air is very clear after the rains. I should be glad to accompany you." He wrapped a wool scarf about his neck many times and put on a high collared, black coat. The two men went into the street, walked by the side of the same synagogue in which Baruch Spinoza had been excommunicated more than three centuries before, and after a few blocks passed Rembrandt's old home in the Zeestraat.

"He died in poverty and disgrace," said Mendes in an ordinary tone as they passed the old house.

Vincent looked up at him quickly. Mendes had a habit of piercing to the heart of a problem before one even mentioned it. There was a profound resilience about the man; things one said seemed to be plunged into fathomless depths for consideration. With Uncle Jan and Uncle Stricker, one's words hit a precise wall and bounced back fast to the tune of yes! or no! Mendes always bathed one's thought in the deep well of his mellow wisdom before he returned it.

"He didn't die unhappy, though," said Vincent.

"No," replied Mendes, "he had expressed himself fully and he knew the worth of what he had done. He was the only one in his time who did."

"Then did that make it all right with him, the fact that he knew? Suppose he had been wrong? What if the world had been right in neglecting him?"

"What the world thought made little difference. Rembrandt had to paint. Whether he painted well or badly didn't matter; painting was the stuff that held him together as a man. The chief value of art, Vincent, lies in the expression it gives to the artist. Rembrandt fulfilled what he knew to be his life purpose; that justified him. Even if his work had been worthless, he would have been a thousand times more successful than if he had put down his desire and become the richest merchant in Amsterdam."

"I see."

"The fact that Rembrandt's work brings joy to the whole world today," continued Mendes, as though following his own line of thought, "is entirely gratuitous. His life was complete and successful when he died, even though he was hounded into his grave. The book of his life closed then, and it was a beautifully wrought volume. The quality of his perseverance and loyalty to his idea is what was important, not the quality of his work."

They stopped to watch men working with sand carts near the Y, and then passed through many narrow streets with gardens full of ivy.

"But how is a young man to know he is choosing rightly, Mijnheer? Suppose he thinks there is something special he must do with his life, and afterwards he finds out he wasn't suited to that at all?"

Mendes drew his chin out of the collar of the coat, and his black eyes brightened. "Look, Vincent," he cried, "how the sunset is throwing a ruddy glow on those grey clouds."

They had reached the harbour. The masts of the ships and the row of old houses and trees on the waterfront were standing out against the colour and everything was reflected in the Zee. Mendes filled his pipe and passed the paper sack to Vincent.

"I am already smoking, Mijnheer," said Vincent.

"Oh yes, so you are. Shall we walk along the dyke to Zeeburg? The Jewish churchyard is there and we can sit for a moment where my people are buried."

They walked along in friendly silence, the wind carrying the smoke over their shoulders. "You can never be sure about anything for all time, Vincent," said Mendes. "You can only have the courage and strength to do what you think is right. It may turn out to be wrong, but you will at least have done it, and that is the important thing. We must act according to the best dictates of our reason, and then leave God to judge of its ultimate value. If you are certain at this moment that you want to serve Our Maker in one way or another, then that faith is the only guide you have to the future. Don't be afraid to put your trust in it."

"Suppose I am not qualified?"

"To serve God?" Mendes looked at him with a shy smile.

"No, I mean qualified to become the sort of academic clergyman that the University turns out."

Mendes did not wish to say anything about Vincent's specific problem; he wanted only to discuss its more general phases and let the boy come to his own decision. By now they had reached the Jewish churchyard. It was very simple, full of old headstones with Hebrew inscriptions, and elderberry trees, and covered here and there with a high, dark grass. There was a stone bench near the plot reserved for the da Costa family, and here the two men sat down. Vincent put away his pipe. The churchyard was deserted at this hour of the evening; not a sound was to be heard.

"Every person has an integrity, a quality of character, Vincent," said Mendes, looking at the graves of his father and mother lying side by side, "and if he observes it, whatever he does will turn out well in the end. If you had remained an art dealer, the integrity that makes you the sort of man you are would have made you a good art dealer. The same applies to your teaching. Some day you will express yourself fully, no matter what medium you may choose."

"And if I do not remain in Amsterdam to become a professional minister?"

"It does not matter. You will return to London as an evangelist, or work in a shop, or become a peasant in the Brabant. Whatever you will do, you will do well. I have felt the quality of the stuff that goes to make you a man, and I know that it is good. Many times in your life you may think you are failing, but ultimately you will express yourself and that expression will justify your life."

"Thank you, Mijnheer da Costa. What you say helps me."

Mendes shivered a little. The stone bench under him was cold and the sun had gone down behind the sea. He rose. "Shall we go, Vincent?" he asked.

6

The following day, as twilight was falling, Vincent stood at the window overlooking the Yard. The little avenue of poplars with their slender forms and thin branches stood out delicately against the grey evening sky.

"Because I am no good at formal studying," said Vincent to himself, "does that mean I can't be of any use in the world? What, after all, have Latin and Greek to do with the love of our fellow men?"

Uncle Jan passed in the Yard below, making the rounds. In the distance Vincent could see the masts of the ships in the docks, in front the *Atjeh,* quite black, and the red and grey monitors surrounding it.

"The thing I wanted to do all along was God's practical work, not draw triangles and circles. I never wanted to have a big church and preach polished sermons. I belong with the humble and suffering *Now, Not Five Years From Now!*"

Just then the bell rang and the whole stream of workmen began pouring toward the gate. The lamplighter came to light the lantern in the Yard. Vincent turned away from the window.

He realized that his father and Uncle Jan and Uncle Stricker had spent a great deal of time and money on him in the past year. They would consider it entirely wasted if he gave up.

Well, he had tried honestly. He could not work more than twenty hours a day. He was obviously unfitted for the life of the study. He had begun too late. If he went out tomorrow as an evangelist, working for His people, would that be failure? If he cured the sick, comforted the weary, consoled the sinner, and converted the unbeliever, would that still be failure?

The family would say it was. They would say he could never succeed, that he was worthless and ungrateful, the black sheep of the Van Gogh family.

"Whatever you do," Mendes had said, "you will do well. Ultimately you will express yourself and that expression will justify your life."

Kay, who understood everything, had already surprised in him the seeds of a narrow minded clergyman. Yes, that was what he would become if he remained in Amsterdam where the true voice grew fainter and fainter every day. He knew where his place was in the world, and Mendes had given him the courage to go. His family would scorn him, but that no longer seemed to matter. His own position was little enough to give up for God.

He packed his bag quickly and walked out of the house without saying good-bye.

7

The Belgian Committee of Evangelization, composed of the Reverends van den Brink, de Jong and Pietersen, was opening a new school in Brussels, where instruction was to be free and the students had to pay only a small sum for their board and lodging. Vincent visited the Committee and was accepted as a pupil.

"At the end of three months," said the Reverend Pietersen, "we will give you an appointment somewhere in Belgium."

"Providing he qualifies," said the Reverend de Jong heavily, turning to Pietersen. De Jong had lost a thumb in mechanical labour while a young man, and that had turned him to theology.

"What is wanted in evangelical work, Monsieur Van Gogh," said the Reverend van den Brink, "is the talent to give popular and attractive lectures to the people."

The Reverend Pietersen accompanied him out of the church in which the meeting had been held, and took Vincent's arm as they stepped into the glaring Brussels sunshine. "I am glad to have you with us, my boy," he said. "There is a great deal of fine work to be done in Belgium, and from your enthusiasm I should say that you are highly qualified to carry it on."

Vincent did not know which warmed him more, the hot sun or the man's unexpected kindness. They walked down the street between precipices of six-story stone buildings, while Vincent struggled to find something to reply. The Reverend Pietersen stopped.

"This is where I turn off," he said. "Here, take my card, and when you have a spare evening, come to see me. I shall be happy to chat with you."

There were only three pupils including Vincent at the evangelical school. They were put in charge of Master Bokma, a small, wiry man with a concave face; a plumb line dropped from his brow to his chin would not have touched his nose or lips.

Vincent's two companions were country boys of nineteen. These two immediately became good friends, and to cement their friendship turned their ridicule on Vincent.

"My aim," he told one of them in an early, unguarded moment, "is to humble myself, *mourir à moi-même*." Whenever they found him struggling to memorize a lecture in French, or agonizing over some academic book, they would ask, "What are you doing, Van Gogh, dying within yourself?"

It was with Master Bokma that Vincent had his most difficult time. The master wished to teach them to be good speakers; each night at home they had to prepare a lecture to deliver the following day in class. The two boys concocted smooth, juvenile messages and recited them glibly. Vincent worked slowly over his sermons, pouring his whole heart into every line. He felt deeply what he had to say and when he rose in class the words would not come with any degree of ease.

"How can you hope to be an evangelist, Van Gogh," demanded Bokma, "when you cannot even speak? Who will listen to you?"

The climax of Bokma's wrath broke when Vincent flatly refused to deliver his lectures *extempore*. He laboured far into the night to make his compositions meaningful, writing out every word in painstaking, precise French. In class the following day the two boys spoke airily about Jesus Christ and salvation, glancing at their notes once or twice while Bokma nodded approval. Then it came Vincent's turn. He spread his lecture before him and began to read. Bokma would not even listen.

"Is that the way they teach you in Amsterdam? Van Gogh, no man has ever left my class who could not speak *extempore* at a moment's notice and move his audience!"

Vincent tried, but he could not remember in the proper sequence all the things he had written down the night before. His classmates laughed outright at his stumbling attempts and Bokma joined their merriment. Vincent's nerves were worn to a biting edge from the year in Amsterdam.

"Master Bokma," he declared, "I will deliver my sermons as I see fit. My work is good, and I refuse to submit to your insults!"

Bokma was outraged. "You will do as I tell you," he shouted, "or I will not allow you in my classroom!"

From then on it was open warfare between the two men. Vincent produced four times as many sermons as was demanded of him, for he could not sleep at nights and there was little use in his going to bed. His appetite left him and he became thin and jumpy.

In November he was summoned to the church to meet with the Committee and get his appointment. At last all the obstacles in his way had been removed and he felt a tired gratification. His two classmates were already there when he arrived. The Reverend Pietersen did not look at him when he came in, but Bokma did, and with a glint in his eye.

The Reverend de Jong congratulated the boys on their successful work and gave them appointments to Hoogstraeten and Etiehove. The classmates left the room arm in arm.

"Monsieur Van Gogh," said De Jong, "the Committee has not been able to persuade itself that you are ready to bring God's word to the people. I regret to say that we have no appointment for you."

After what seemed a long time Vincent asked, "What was wrong with my work?"

"You refused to submit to authority. The first rule of our Church is absolute obedience. Further, you did not succeed in learning how to speak *extempore*. Your master feels you are not qualified to preach."

Vincent looked at the Reverend Pietersen but his friend was staring out the window. "What am I to do?" he asked of no one in particular.

"You may return to the school for another six months if you wish," replied Van den Brink. "Perhaps at the end of that time . . ."

Vincent stared down at his rough, square-toed boots and noticed that the leather was cracking. Then, because he could think of absolutely no word to say, he turned and walked out in silence.

He passed quickly through the city streets and found himself in Laeken. Without knowing why he was walking, he struck out along the towpath with its busily humming workshops. Soon he left the houses behind and came to an open field. An old white horse, lean, emaciated, and tired to death by a life of hard labour was standing there. The spot was lonely and desolate. On the ground lay a skull and at a distance in the background the bleached skeleton of a horse lying near the hut of a man who skinned horses.

Some little feeling returned to flood out the numbness, and Vincent reached forlornly for his pipe. He applied a match to the tobacco but it tasted strangely bitter. He sat down on a log in the field. The old white horse came over and rubbed his nose against Vincent's back. He turned and stroked the emaciated neck of the animal.

After a time there rose in his mind the thought of God, and he was comforted. "Jesus was calm in the storm," he said to himself. "I am not alone, for God has not forsaken me. Someday, somehow, I will find a way to serve Him."

When he returned to his room he found the Reverend Pietersen waiting for him. "I came to ask you to have dinner at my home, Vincent," he said.

They walked along streets thronged with working people on their way to the evening meal. Pietersen chatted of casual things as though nothing had happened. Vincent heard every word he said with a terrible clarity. Pietersen led him into the front room, which had been turned into a studio. There were a few water-colours on the walls and an easel in one corner.

"Oh," said Vincent, "you paint. I didn't know."

Pietersen was embarrassed. "I'm just an amateur," he replied. "I draw a bit in my spare time for relaxation. But I shouldn't mention it to my *confrères* if I were you."

They sat down to dinner. Pietersen had a daughter, a shy, reserved girl of fifteen who never once lifted her eyes from the plate. Pietersen went on speaking of inconsequential things while Vincent forced himself, for politeness' sake, to eat a little. Suddenly his mind became rivetted to what Pietersen was saying; he had no idea how the Reverend had worked into the subject.

"The Borinage," his host said, "is a coal mining region. Practically every man in the district goes down into the *charbonnages*. They work in the midst of thousands of ever-recurring dangers, and their wage is hardly enough to keep body and soul together. Their homes are tumble-down shacks where their wives and children spend most of the year shivering with cold, fever, and hunger."

Vincent wondered why he was being told all this. "Where is the Borinage?" he asked.

"In the south of Belgium, near Mons. I recently spent some time there, and Vincent, if ever a people needed a man to preach to them and comfort them, it's the Borains."

A gulp came into Vincent's throat, barring the passage of food. He laid down his fork. Why was Pietersen torturing him?

"Vincent," said the Reverend, "why don't you go to the Borinage? With your strength and enthusiasm you could do a great deal of fine work."

"But how can I? The Committee . . ."

"Yes, I know. I wrote to your father the other day explaining the situation. I had an answer from him this afternoon. He says he will support you in the Borinage until I can secure you a regular appointment."

Vincent jumped to his feet. "Then you will get me an appointment!"

"Yes, but you must give me a little time. When the Committee sees what splendid work you are doing it will surely relent. And even if it doesn't . . . De Jong and Van den Brink will come to me for a favour one of these fine days, and in return for that favour . . . The poor people of this country need men like you, Vincent, and as God is my judge, any means is justified in getting you to them!"

8

As the train neared the South a group of mountains appeared on the horizon. Vincent gazed at them with pleasure and relief after the monotonous flat country of Flanders. He had been studying them only a few minutes when he discovered that they were curious mountains. Each one stood utterly by itself, rising out of the flat land with a precipitate abruptness.

"Black Egypt," he murmured to himself as he peered out of the window at the long line of fantastic pyramids. He turned to the man sitting next to him and asked, "Can you tell me how those mountains get there?"

"Yes," replied his neighbour, "they are composed of *terril*, the waste material that is brought up from the earth with the coal. Do you see that little car just about to reach the point of the hill? Watch it for a moment."

Just as he said this, the little car turned over on its side and sent a black cloud flying down the slope. "There," said the man, "that's how they grow. I've been watching them go up into the air a fraction of an inch every day for the past fifty years."

The train stopped at Wasmes and Vincent jumped off. The town was located in the hollow of a bleak valley; although an anaemic sun shone at an oblique angle, a substantial layer of coal smoke lay between Vincent and the heavens. Wasmes struggled up the side of the hill in two winding rows of dirty, red brick buildings, but before it reached the top, the bricks ran out and Petit Wasmes appeared.

As Vincent walked up the long hill he wondered why the village was so deserted. Not a man was to be seen anywhere; an occasional woman stood in a doorway with a dull and stolid expression on her face.

Petit Wasmes was the miners' village. It could boast of only one brick building, the home of Jean-Baptiste Denis, the baker, which sat right on the crest of the hill. It was to this house Vincent made his way, for Denis had written to the Reverend Pietersen, offering to board the next evangelist to be sent to their town.

Madame Denis welcomed Vincent heartily, led him through the warm kitchen-bakery with its smell of rising bread, and showed him his room, a small space under the eaves, with a window facing the rue Petit Wasmes, and rafters coming down at an abrupt angle at the rear. The place had been scrubbed by Madame Denis's thick, competent hands. Vincent liked it immediately. He was so excited he could not even unpack his things, but rushed down the few rough, wooden stairs which led into the kitchen to tell Madame Denis that he was going out.

"You won't forget to come back to supper?" she asked. "We eat at five."

Vincent liked Madame Denis. He felt in her the nature that understands things without going to all the trouble of thinking about them. "I'll be here, Madame," he said. "I just want to look about a bit."

"We have a friend coming tonight whom you should meet. He is a foreman at Marcasse and can tell you many things you will want to know for your work."

It had been snowing heavily. As Vincent walked down the road he observed the thorn hedges around the gardens and fields that had been turned black from the smoke of the mine chimneys. On the east side of the Denis house was a steep ravine in which were located most of the miners' huts; on the other side was a great open field with a black *terril* mountain and the chimneys of the Marcasse *charbonnage*, where most of the Petit Wasmes miners descended. Across the field there was a hollow road grown over with thorn bushes and torn up by the roots of gnarled trees.

Although Marcasse was only one of a string of seven mines owned by the Charbonnages Belgique, it was the oldest and most dangerous pit in the Borinage. It had a bad reputation because so many men had perished in it, either in descending or ascending, by poison gas, explosion, flooding water, or by the collapse of old tunnels. There were two squat, brick buildings above the ground, in which the machinery was operated for bringing up the coal and where the coal was graded and dumped into cars. The tall chimneys, which once had been of yellow brick, spread tangible, black smoke over the neighbourhood twenty-four hours a day. Around Marcasse were poor miners' huts with a few dead trees, black from the smoke, thorn hedges, dunghills, ash dumps, heaps of useless coal, and towering above it all, the black mountain. It was a gloomy spot; at first sight everything looked dreary and desolate to Vincent.

"No wonder they call it the black country," he murmured.

After he had been standing there for some time the miners began to pour out of the gate. They were dressed in coarse, tattered garments with leather hats on their heads; the women wore the same outfit as the men. All were completely black and looked like chimney sweeps, the whites of their eyes presenting a strange contrast to the coal-dust covered faces. It was not without reason that they were called *gueules noires*. The glare of the feeble afternoon sunlight hurt their eyes after they had laboured in the darkness of the earth since before dawn. They stumbled out of the gate, half blinded, speaking among themselves in a swift, unintelligible patois. They were small people with narrow, hunched-in shoulders and bony limbs.

Vincent understood now why the village had been deserted that afternoon; the real Petit Wasmes was not the small cluster of huts in the ravine, but the labyrinth city which existed underground at a depth of seven hundred metres, and in which almost the entire population spent the majority of its waking hours.

9

"Jacques Verney is a self-made man," Madame Denis told Vincent over the supper table, "but he has remained a friend to the miners."

"Don't all the men who get promoted stay friends with the workers?"

"No, Monsieur Vincent, it is not so. As soon as they move from Petit Wasmes to Wasmes they begin to look at things differently. For the sake of money they take the part of the owners and forget they once slaved in the mines. But Jacques is faithful and honest. When we have strikes he is the only one with any influence over the miners. They will listen to nobody's advice but his. But, poor man, he hasn't long to live."

"What's the matter with him?" asked Vincent.

"The usual thing—lung trouble. Every man who goes down gets it. He probably won't last the winter out."

Jacques Verney came in a little later. He was short and stoop shouldered, with the deep set, melancholy eyes of the Borain. Antennae of hair shot out from his nostrils, from the ends of his eyebrows and from the concha of his ears. His head was bald. When he heard that Vincent was an evangelist come to better the lot of the miners, he sighed deeply. "Ah, Monsieur," he said, "so many people have tried to help us. But life here goes on just as it always has."

"You think conditions bad in the Borinage?" asked Vincent.

Jacques was silent for a moment and then said, "For myself, no. My mother taught me to read a little, and through that I have become a foreman. I have a little brick house on the road leading down to Wasmes, and we are never in want of food. For myself I have nothing to complain . . ."

He was forced to interrupt himself for a violent fit of coughing; it seemed to Vincent that his flat chest would surely burst under the pressure. After walking to the front door and spitting into the road several times, Jacques again took his seat in the warm kitchen and gently pulled on the hairs of his ear, his nose, and his eyebrows.

"You see, Monsieur, I was already twenty-nine when I became a foreman. My lungs were gone by then. Nevertheless it has not been so bad for me these past few years. But the miners . . ." He glanced over at Madame Denis and asked, "What do you say? Shall I take him down to see Henri Decrucq?"

"Why not? It will do him no harm to hear the full truth."

Jacques Verney turned back to Vincent apologetically. "After all, Monsieur," he said, "I am a foreman and I owe some loyalty to 'them.' But Henri, he will show you!"

Vincent followed Jacques out into the cold night and plunged immediately into the miners' ravine. The miners' huts were simple wooden hovels of one room. They had not been put up with any plan, but ran down the side of the hill haphazardly at crazy angles, creating a labyrinth of dirt laden alleys, through which only the initiate could find their way. Vincent stumbled after Jacques, falling over rocks, logs, and heaps of refuse. About half-way down they came to Decrucq's shack. A light shone through the tiny window at the rear. Madame Decrucq answered the knock.

The Decrucq's cabin was exactly the same as all the others in the ravine. It had an earthen floor, moss covered roof, and strips of burlap stuck between the planks to keep the wind out. In each of the rear corners there was a bed, one of them already occupied by three sleeping children. The furnishings consisted of an oval stove, a wooden table with benches, one chair, and a box nailed to the wall, containing a few pots and dishes. The Decrucqs, like most Borains, kept a goat and some rabbits so that they might have meat occasionally. The goat slept under the children's bed; the rabbits had a bit of straw behind the stove.

Madame Decrucq swung open the upper half of the door to see who was there and then bade the two men enter. She had worked in the same *couches* with Decrucq for many years before their marriage, pushing the little cars of coal down the track to the tally board. Most of the juice was gone out of her. She was faded, worn and aged, and she had not yet celebrated her twenty-sixth birthday.

Decrucq, who had been leaning his chair against the cold part of the stove, sprang up at the sight of Jacques. "Well!" he exclaimed. "It is a long time since you have been in my house. We are glad to have you here. And I bid your friend welcome."

It was Decrucq's boast that he was the only man in the Borinage whom the mines could not kill. "I shall die in my bed of old age," he often said. "They can't kill me, for I won't let them!"

On the right side of his head a large square of red scalp-skin glowed like a window through the thatch of his hair. That was a memento of the day when the cage in which he was descending had plunged a hundred metres like a stone in a well and killed his twenty-nine companions. When he walked he dragged one leg after him; it had been broken in four places when the timbers in his cell collapsed and imprisoned him for five days. His coarse, black shirt bulged on the right side over the mound of three broken ribs that had never been set after an explosion of fire-damp had hurled him against a coal car. But he was a fighter, a game-cock of a man; nothing could put him down. Because he always talked so violently against the company, he was given the very worst *couches,* where it was hardest to get out the coal and where the working conditions were the most difficult. The more he took, the higher he flamed up against "them," the unknown and unseen but ever present enemy. A dimple, set just off centre in his stubby chin, made his short, compact face seem slightly askew.

"Monsieur Van Gogh," he said, "you have come to the right place. Here in the Borinage we are not even slaves, we are animals. We descend Marcasse at three in the morning; for fifteen minutes we can rest while we eat our dinner, and then we work on until four in the afternoon. It is black down there, Monsieur, and hot. So we must work naked, and the air is full of coal-dust and poison gas, and we cannot breathe! When we take the coal from the *couche* there is no room to stand up; we must work on our knees and doubled in two. We begin to descend, boys and girls alike, when we are eight or nine. By twenty we have the fever and lung trouble. If we do not get killed by *grisou,* or in the cage (he tapped the red scalp-patch on his head), we may live until forty and then die of consumption! Do I tell lies, Verney?"

He spoke in such an excited patois that Vincent found difficulty in following him. The askew dimple gave his face an amused look, in spite of the fact that his eyes were black with anger.

"It is just so, Decrucq," said Jacques.

Madame Decrucq had gone to sit on her bed in the far corner. The faint glow of the kerosene lamp put her half in shadow. She listened to her husband while he spoke, even though she had heard the words a thousand times before. The years pushing coal cars, the birth of three children, and the succession of bitter winters in this burlap-stuffed hut had taken all the fight out of her. Decrucq dragged his bad leg from Jacques back to Vincent.

"And what do we get for all this, Monsieur? A one-room shack and just enough food to keep us swinging a pick. What do we eat? Bread, sour cheese, black coffee. Once or twice a year, perhaps, meat! If they cut off fifty centimes a day we would starve to death! We would not be able to bring up their *charbon;* that is the only reason they do not pay us less. We are on the margin of death, Monsieur, every day of our lives! If we get sick we are put out without a franc, and we die like dogs while our wives and children are fed by the neighbours. From eight to forty, Monsieur, thirty-two years in the black earth, and then a hole in that hill across the way so we can forget it all."

10

Vincent found that the miners were ignorant and untaught, most of them being unable to read, but at the same time they were intelligent and quick at their difficult work, were brave and frank and of a very sensitive temperament. They were thin and pale from fever, and looked tired and emaciated. Their skin was pasty and sallow (they saw the sun only on Sundays), marked with thousands of tiny black pores. They had the deep-set, melancholy eyes of the oppressed who cannot fight back.

Vincent found them attractive. They were simple and good natured like the Brabant people in Zundert and Etten. The desolate feeling of the landscape was gone too, for he perceived that the Borinage had character and that things spoke to him.

After Vincent had been there a few days he held his first religious meeting in a rough shed in back of the Denis bakery. He cleaned the place thoroughly and then carried in benches for the people. The miners came at five with their families, long scarfs wrapped about their necks and little caps on their heads to keep out the cold. The only light was from a kerosene lamp which Vincent borrowed. The miners sat in the dark on the rough benches, watched Vincent hovering over his Bible and listened attentively, holding their hands under their armpits to keep them warm.

Vincent searched very hard to find the most appropriate message for his opening sermon. He finally selected Acts 16:9, "A vision appeared to Paul in the night: there stood a man of Macedonia and begged him saying, 'Come over into Macedonia and help us.'"

"We must think of the Macedonian as a labourer, my friends," said Vincent, "a labourer with lines of sorrow and suffering and fatigue in his face. He is not without splendour or glamour, for he has an immortal soul, and he needs the food that does not perish, God's word. God wills that in imitation of Jesus Christ man should live humbly and go through life not reaching after lofty aims, but adapting himself to the lowly, learning from the gospel to be meek and simple of heart so that on the chosen day he may enter the Heavenly Kingdom and find peace."

There were many sick people in the village and each day he went the rounds like a doctor, bringing them whenever he could a bit of milk or bread, a warm pair of socks, or a cover to put over the bed. Typhoid and a malignant fever which the miners called *la sotte fièvre* descended upon the huts, giving the people bad dreams and making them delirious. The number of bedridden miners, emaciated, weak, and miserable, grew day by day.

The whole of Petit Wasmes called him Monsieur Vincent with affection, though still with a good bit of reserve. There was not a hut in the village to which he had not brought food and comfort, in which he had not nursed the sick and prayed with the miserable and brought God's light to the wretched. Several days before Christmas he found an abandoned stable near Marcasse, large enough to seat a hundred people. It was barren and cold and desolate, but the miners of Petit Wasmes filled it to the door. They listened to Vincent tell the story of Bethlehem and peace on earth. He had been in the Borinage only six weeks and had watched conditions grow more and more miserable with the passing of the days, but there, in an humble stable, lighted only by the smoky glow of a few small lamps, Vincent was able to bring Jesus Christ to the shivering blackjaws and warm their hearts with the promise of the Kingdom to Come.

There was only one flaw in his life, one factor to cause him any disturbance; his father was still supporting him. Each night he prayed for the time when he would be able to earn the few francs necessary for his humble needs.

The weather turned nasty. Black clouds overhung the whole region. Rain fell in torrents, making muddy creeks of the hollow roads and the earthen floors of the huts in the ravine. On New Year's day Jean-Baptiste walked down to Wasmes and returned with a letter for Vincent. The Reverend Pietersen's name was in the upper left-hand corner of the envelope. Vincent ran to his room under the eaves, trembling with excitement. The rain slashed away at the roof but he did not hear it. He tore upon the envelope with clumsy fingers. The letter read:

Dear Vincent:

The Committee of Evangelization has heard about your splendid work and is therefore giving you a temporary nomination for six months, to begin the first of the year.

If at the end of June everything has gone well, your appointment will be made permanent. In the meanwhile your salary will be fifty francs a month.

Write to me often and keep looking upward.

Yours, fondly,
Pietersen.

He threw himself flat on the bed, letter clutched tight in his hand, exultant. At last he was successful! He had found his work in life! This was what he had wanted all the time, only he had not had the strength and courage to go straight to it! He was to receive fifty francs a month, more than enough to pay for his food and lodging and he would never have to be dependent upon anyone again.

He sat down at the table and wrote a tumultuous, triumphant letter to his father telling him that he no longer needed his help, and that he meant from that time on to be a source of credit and gratification to the family. When he finished writing it was already twilight; thunder and lightning were smashing over Marcasse. He ran down the stairs, through the kitchen, and flung himself joyously into the rain.

Madame Denis came after him. "Monsieur Vincent! Where are you going? You've forgotten your hat and coat!"

Vincent did not stop to answer. He ran to a mound nearby. He could see in the distance a great part of the Borinage, with the chimneys, the mounds of coal, the little miners' cottages, and the scurrying to and fro like ants in a nest of the black figures that were just coming out of the *houillères*. In the distance there was a dark pine wood with little white cottages silhouetted against it, a church spire a long way off and an old mill. A haze hung over the whole scene. There was a fantastic effect of light and dark formed by the shadows of the clouds. For the first time since he had been in the Borinage it all reminded him of the pictures of Michel and of Ruysdael.

11

Now that he was an authorized evangelist, Vincent needed a permanent place to hold his meetings. After a good deal of searching he found at the very bottom of the ravine, on a little road through the pine woods, a rather large house that was called Salon du Bébé, where the children of the community had once been taught to dance. After Vincent put up all his prints the house took on an attractive air. Here every afternoon he gathered the children between the ages of four and eight, taught them how to read, and told them the elementary stories of the Bible. It was the only instruction most of them received in their entire lives.

"How are we going to get coal to heat the room?" Vincent demanded of Jacques Verney, who had helped him secure the Salon. "The children have to be kept warm and the meetings at night can last longer if the stove is going."

Jacques thought a moment and then said, "Be here at noon tomorrow and I will show you how to get it."

When Vincent arrived at the Salon the next day he found a group of miners' wives and daughters awaiting him. They had on their black blouses, long black skirts and blue kerchiefs over their heads. All were carrying sacks.

"Monsieur Vincent, I have brought a sack for you," cried Verney's young daughter. "You must fill one, too."

They climbed through the maze of circuitous alleys formed by the miners' huts, passed the Denis bakery at the top of the hill, struck out across the field in the centre of which sat Marcasse, and skirted the walls of the buildings until they reached the black *terril* pyramid at the rear. Here they deployed, each one attacking the mountain from a different angle, climbing up its sides like tiny insects swarming over a dead log.

"You must go to the top before you will find any coal, Monsieur Vincent," said Mademoiselle Verney. "We have been picking the bottom of the heap clean for years. Come along, I'll show you which is the coal."

She scrambled up the black slope like a young goat, but Vincent had to go up most of the way on his hands and knees, for the stuff under his feet kept sliding away from him. Mademoiselle Verney scrambled on ahead, squatted on her haunches, and threw little pieces of caked mud at Vincent teasingly. She was a pretty girl with good colour in her cheeks and an alert, vivacious manner; Verney had been made a foreman when she was seven, and she had never seen the inside of a mine.

"Come along, Monsieur Vincent," she cried, "or you will be the last to get your sack filled!" This was an excursion for her; the company sold Verney fair coal at reduced rates.

They could not go altogether to the top for the little cars were dumping their loads of waste, first down one side, then down the other with mechanical regularity. It was no easy task to find coal on that pyramid. Mademoiselle Verney showed Vincent how to scoop up the *terril* in his hands and let the mud, rocks, clay and other foreign substances slip through his fingers. The amount of coal that escaped the company was negligible. The only thing the miners' wives ever found was a sort of shale composite which could not be sold in the commercial market. The *terril* was wet from the snow and rain, and soon Vincent's hands were scratched and cut, but he managed to get a quarter of a sack full of what he hoped was coal by the time the women had nearly filled theirs.

Each of the women left her sack at the Salon and rushed home to prepare the family supper, but not before promising to come to services that night and bring her family. Mademoiselle Verney invited Vincent home to share their supper, and he accepted with alacrity. The Verney house had two complete rooms; the stove, cooking equipment, and tableware in one room, the family beds in the other. Despite the fact that Jacques was fairly well off there was no soap in the house, for as Vincent had learned, soap was an impossible luxury for the Borains. From the time that the boy begins to descend the *charbonnage* and the girl begins to ascend the *terril* until the day they die, the Borains never completely get the coal-dust off their faces.

Mademoiselle Verney put a pan of cold water out in the street for Vincent. He scrubbed up as best he could. He did not know how well he had succeeded, but as he sat opposite the young girl and saw the black streaks from the coal-dust and smoke still lining her face, he realized that he must look as she did. Mademoiselle Verney chatted gaily all through the supper.

"You know, Monsieur Vincent," said Jacques, "you have been in Petit Wasmes almost two months now, and yet you really don't know the Borinage."

"It is true, Monsieur Verney," replied Vincent in all humility, "but I think I am slowly coming to understand the people."

"I don't mean that," said Jacques plucking a long antenna out of his nose and looking at it with interest. "I mean you have only seen our life above ground. That is not important. We merely sleep above ground. If you would understand what our lives are like, you must descend one of the mines and see how we work from three in the morning until four in the afternoon."

"I am very eager to go down," said Vincent, "but can I get permission from the company?"

"I already have asked for you," replied Jacques, holding a cube of sugar in his mouth and letting the tepid, inky, bitter coffee pour over it and down his throat. "Tomorrow I descend Marcasse for safety inspection. Be in front of the Denis house at a quarter before three in the morning and I will pick you up."

The entire family accompanied Vincent to the Salon, but on the way over, Jacques, who had appeared so well and expansive in his warm house, shrivelled up with a violent cough and had to go home again. When Vincent arrived at the Salon he found Henri Decrucq already there, dragging his dead leg after him and tinkering with the stove.

"Ah, good evening, Monsieur Vincent," he cried with a smile as broad as his compact face would allow. "I am the only one in Petit Wasmes who can light this stove. I know it from old, when we used to have parties here. It is *méchant*, but I know all its tricks."

The content of the sacks was damp and only a small part of it was coal, but Decrucq soon had the bulging, oval stove sending out good warmth. As he hobbled about excitedly, the blood pounded to the bare spot on the scalp and turned the corrugated skin a dirty beet-red.

Nearly every miner's family in Petit Wasmes came to the Salon that night to hear Vincent preach the first sermon in his church. When the benches were filled, the neighbouring families brought in their boxes and chairs. Over three hundred souls crowded in. Vincent, his heart warmed by the kindness of the miners' wives that afternoon, and the knowledge that he was at last speaking in his own temple, preached a sermon so sincere and believing that the melancholy look on the Borains' faces fell away.

"It is an old belief and a good one," said Vincent to his blackjaw congregation, "that we are strangers on earth. Yet we are not alone, for our Father is with us. We are pilgrims; our life is a long journey from earth to Heaven.

"Sorrow is better than joy—and even in mirth the heart is sad. It is better to go to the house of mourning than to the house of feasts, for by sadness the countenance of the heart is made better.

"For those who believe in Jesus Christ there is no sorrow that is not mixed with hope. There is only a constantly being born again, a constantly going from darkness to light.

"Father, we pray Thee to keep us from evil. Give us neither poverty nor riches, but feed us with bread appropriate to us.

"Amen."

Madame Decrucq was the first to reach his side. There was a mist before her eyes and a quiver at the corner of her mouth. "Monsieur Vincent," she said, "my life was so hard that I had lost God. But you have given Him back to me. And I thank you for that."

When they were all gone, Vincent locked the Salon and walked thoughtfully up the hill to the Denis's. He could tell from the reception he had received that night that the reserve was completely gone from the attitude of the Borains, and that they trusted him at last. He was now fully accepted by the blackjaws as a minister of God. What had caused the change? It could not have been because he had a new church; such things mattered not at all to the miners. They did not know about his evangelical appointment because he had not told them in the first place that he had no official position. And although he had preached a warm, beautiful sermon, he had delivered equally good ones in the wretched huts and in the abandoned stable.

The Denises had already gone to sleep in their little cubbyhole off the kitchen, but the bakery was still redolent of fresh, sweet bread. Vincent drew up some water from the deep well that had been enclosed in the kitchen, poured it out of the bucket into a bowl, and went upstairs to get his soap and mirror. He propped the mirror against the wall and looked at himself. Yes, his surmise had been correct; he had taken off only a small portion of the coal-dust at the Verney's. His eyelids and jaws were still black. He smiled to himself as he thought of how he had consecrated the new temple with coal-dust all over his face, and how horrified his father and Uncle Stricker would have been if they could have seen him.

He dipped his hands into the cold water, worked up a lather from the soap he had brought with him from Brussels, and was just about to apply the suds vigorously to his face when something turned over in his mind. He poised his wet hands in mid-air. He looked into the mirror once again and saw the black coal-dust from the *terril* in the lines of his forehead, on the lids of his eyes, down the sides of his cheeks, and on the great ball of his chin.

"Of course!" he said aloud. "That's why they've accepted me. I've become one of them at last."

He rinsed his hands in the water and went to bed without touching his face. Every day that he remained in the Borinage he rubbed coal-dust on his face so that he would look like everyone else.

12

The following morning Vincent got up at two-thirty, ate a piece of dry bread in the Denis kitchen, and met Jacques in front of the door at a quarter to three. It had snowed heavily during the night. The road leading to Marcasse had been obliterated. As they struck out across the field toward the black chimneys and the *terril*, Vincent saw the miners scurrying over the snow from all directions, little black creatures hurrying home to their nest. It was bitterly cold; the workers had their thin black coats tucked up around their chins, their shoulders huddled inward for warmth.

Jacques first took him into a room where many kerosene lamps were hanging on racks, each under a specific number. "When we have an accident down below," said Jacques, "we can tell which men are caught by the lamps that are missing."

The miners were taking their lamps hastily and rushing across a snow-covered yard to a brick building where the hoist was located. Vincent and Jacques joined them. The descending cage had six compartments, one above the other, in each of which a coal truck could be brought to the surface. A compartment was just large enough for two men to squat comfortably on their haunches while going down; five miners were jammed into each of them, descending like a heap of coal.

Since Jacques was a foreman, only he and Vincent and one of his assistants crowded into the top compartment. They squatted low, their toes jammed up against the sides, their heads pushing against the wire top.

"Keep your hands straight in front of you, Monsieur Vincent," said Jacques. "If one of them touches the side wall, you will lose it."

A signal was given and the cage shot downward on its two steel tracks. The free way through which it descended in the rock was only a fraction of an inch larger than the cage. An involuntary shudder ran through Vincent when he realized that the blackness fell away for a half mile beneath him and that if anything went wrong he would be plunged to death. It was a sort of horror he had never known before, this rocketing down a black hole into the abysmal unknown. He realized that he had little to fear, for there had not been an accident with the hoist in over two months, but the shadowy, flickering light of the kerosene lamps was not conducive to reasoning.

He spoke of his instinctive trembling to Jacques, who smiled sympathetically. "Every miner feels that," he said.

"But surely they get used to going down?"

"No, never! An unconquerable feeling of horror and fear for this cage stays with them until their dying day."

"And you, Monsieur . . . ?"

"I was trembling inside of me, just as you were, and I have been descending for thirty-three years!"

At three hundred and fifty metres—half-way—the cage stopped for a moment, then hurtled downward again. Vincent saw streams of water oozing out of the side of the hole, and again he shuddered. Looking upward, he saw daylight about the size of a star in the sky. At six hundred and fifty metres they got out, but the miners continued on down. Vincent found himself in a broad tunnel with tracks cut through the rock and clay. He had expected to be plunged into an inferno of heat, but the passageway was fairly cool.

"This is not at all bad, Monsieur Verney!" he exclaimed.

"No, but there are no men working at this level. The *couches* were exhausted long ago. We get ventilation here from the top, but that does the miners down below no good."

They walked along the tunnel for perhaps a quarter of a mile, and then Jacques turned off. "Follow me, Monsieur Vincent," he said, *"mais doucement, doucement;* if you slip once, you will kill us."

He disappeared into the ground before Vincent's eyes. Vincent stumbled forward, found an opening in the earth, and groped for the ladder. The hole was just large enough to pass a thin man. The first five metres were not hard, but at the half-way point Vincent had to about-face in mid-air and descend in the opposite direction. Water began to ooze out of the rocks; mud slime covered the rungs of the ladder. Vincent could feel the water dripping over him.

At length they reached the bottom and crawled on their hands and knees through a long passage leading to *des caches* situated farthest from the exit. There was a long row of cells, like partitions in a vault, supported by rough timbers. In each cell a unit of five miners worked, two digging out the coal with their picks, a third dragging it away from their feet, a fourth loading it into small cars, and a fifth pushing the cars down a narrow track.

The pickers worked in coarse linen suits, filthy and black. The shoveller was usually a young boy, stark naked except for a burlap loin-cloth, his body a dull black, and the miner pushing the car through the three foot passageway was always a girl, as black as the men, with a coarse dress covering the upper part of her body. Water was leaking through the roofs of the cells, forming a grotto of stalactites. The only light was from the small lamps whose wicks were turned down low to save fuel. There was no ventilation. The air was thick with coal-dust. The natural heat of the earth bathed the miners in rivulets of black perspiration. In the first cells Vincent saw that the men could work standing erect with their picks, but as he advanced down the passageway, the cells became smaller and smaller until the miners had to lie on the ground and swing their picks from the elbow. As the hours went on, the bodily heat of the miners raised the temperature of the cells, and the coal-dust thickened in the air until the men were gasping great mouthfuls of hot, black soot.

"These men earn two and a half francs a day," Jacques told Vincent, "providing the inspector at the checking post approves the quality of their coal. Five years ago they were earning three francs, but wages have been reduced every year since then."

Jacques inspected the timber proppings that stood between the miners and death. Then he turned to the pickers.

"Your propping is bad," he told them. "It is working loose and the first thing you know the roof will cave in."

One of the pickers, the leader of the gang, let forth a volley of abuse so fast that Vincent could catch only a few words.

"When they pay for propping," the man shouted, "we will prop! If we take the time off to prop, how will we get the coal out? We might as well die here under the rock as at home of starvation."

Beyond the last cell there was another hole in the ground. This time there was not even a ladder to descend. Logs had been shoved in at intervals to keep the dirt from pouring down and burying the miners below. Jacques took Vincent's lamp and hung it from his belt. "*Doucement,* Monsieur Vincent," he repeated. "Do not step on my head or you will send me crashing." They climbed down five metres more, foot following foot into the blackness, feeling for its timber to stand on while hands clutched the dirt in the sides, to keep from hurtling into oblivion.

At the next level there was another *couche,* but this time the miners did not even have cells to work in. The coal had to be picked out of a narrow angle in the wall. The men crouched on their knees, their backs pressed against the rock roof and threw their picks at the corner from which the coal was being taken. Vincent realized now that the cells above had been cool and comfortable; the heat at this lower level was like that of a blazing oven, thick enough to be cut with a blunt instrument. The men at work were panting like stricken animals, their tongues hanging out, thick and dry, and their naked bodies covered with a plaster of filth, grime and dust. Vincent, doing absolutely nothing, thought he could not bear the fierce heat and dust another minute. The miners were doing violent manual labour and their gorge was a thousand times higher than his, yet they could not stop to rest or cool off for a minute. If they did, they would not get out the requisite number of cars of coal and would not receive their fifty cents for the day's work.

Vincent and Jacques crawled on their hands and knees through the passageway connecting these beehive cells, flattening themselves against the wall every few seconds to let a car go by on the tiny tracks. This passage was smaller than the one above. The girls pushing the cars were younger, none of them over ten years of age. The coal cars were heavy and the girls had to fight and strain to get them along the tracks.

At the end of the passage there was a metal chute down which the cars were lowered on cables. "Come, Monsieur Vincent," said Jacques, "I will take you to the last level, seven hundred metres, and you will see something not to be found anywhere else in the world!"

They slid down the metal incline some thirty metres and Vincent found himself in a wide tunnel with two tracks. They walked for a half mile back in the tunnel; when it came to an end they pulled themselves up on a ledge, crawled through a *communiqué,* and lowered themselves on the other side into a freshly dug hole.

"This is a new *couche,*" said Jacques, "the hardest place of any mine in the world to get the coal."

Leading out of this excavation was a series of twelve minute black holes. Jacques shoved himself into one and shouted, "Follow me." The opening was just large enough to pass Vincent's shoulders. He jammed his way into it and crawled on his stomach like a snake, digging his way along with his fingernails and toes. He could not see Jacques's boots, three inches ahead of him. The tunnel through the rock was only a foot and a half high and two and a half feet wide. The hole from which the passageway started had almost no fresh air, but it was cool compared to this stope.

At the end of the crawl Vincent came into a little dome-like hollow almost tall enough for a man to stand up. The place was pitch black and at first Vincent could see nothing; then he noticed four little blue glows along a wall. His body was wet with perspiration; the sweat from his brow brought the coal-dust down into his eyes, making them smart cruelly. He was panting for breath from the long crawl on his stomach and stood up with a feeling of relief to catch a little air. What he caught was fire, liquid fire that burned and choked him as it went down his lungs. This was the worst hole in all Marcasse, a torture chamber worthy of the Middle Ages.

"*Tiens, tiens!*" cried a familiar voice, "*c'est Monsieur Vincent.* Have you come to see how we earn our fifty cents a day, Monsieur?"

Jacques went quickly to the lamps and inspected them. The arc of blue was eating up the light.

"He shouldn't come down here!" Decrucq whispered in Vincent's ear, the whites of his eyes gleaming, "he will have a hemorrhage in that tunnel and then we will have to haul him out with blocks and a pulley."

"Decrucq," called Jacques, "have these lamps been burning this way all morning?"

"Yes," replied Decrucq carelessly, "the *grisou* is growing day by day. Once it will explode and then our troubles will be over."

"These cells were pumped out last Sunday," said Jacques.

"But it comes back, it comes back," said Decrucq scratching the black scar in his scalp with pleasure.

"Then you must lay off one day this week and let us clean it out again."

A storm of protest arose from the miners. "We have not enough bread now for the children! It is impossible to live on the wages, let alone give up a full day! Let them clean it out when we are not in here; we must eat like all the others!"

"It's all right," laughed Decrucq, "the mines can't kill me. They've tried it before. I shall die in my bed of old age. Speaking of food, what time is it, Verney?"

Jacques held his watch near the blue flame. "Nine o'clock."

"Good! We can eat our dinner."

The black, sweating bodies with the white eyeballs ceased their labours, and squatting on their haunches against the wall, opened their kits. They could not crawl out into the slightly cooler hole to eat because they allowed themselves only fifteen minutes respite. The crawl going and coming would have taken almost that long. So they sat in the stagnant heat, took out two pieces of thick, coarse bread with sour cheese, and ate hungrily, the black soot from their hands coming off in great streaks on the white bread. Each man had a beer bottle of tepid coffee with which he washed down the bread. The coffee, the bread, and the sour cheese were the prize for which they worked thirteen hours a day.

Vincent had already been down six hours. He felt faint from lack of air and choking with the heat and dust. He did not think he could stand the torture very many more minutes. He was grateful when Jacques said they must go.

"Watch that *grisou*, Decrucq," said Jacques before he plunged into the hole. "If it gets bad, you'd better bring your gang out."

Decrucq laughed harshly. "And will they pay us our fifty cents for the day if we don't produce the coal?"

There was no answer to this question. Decrucq knew it as well as Jacques. The latter shrugged, and crawled on his stomach through the tunnel. Vincent followed him, completely blinded by the stinging, black sweat in his eyes.

After a half hour of walking they reached the *accrochage,* where the cage took the coal and men to the surface. Jacques went into a cave in the rock, where the horses were kept, and coughed up black phlegm.

In the cage, shooting upward like a bucket in a well, Vincent turned to his friend and said, "Monsieur, tell me. Why do you people continue to go down into the mines? Why don't you all go elsewhere, find other employment?"

"Ah, my dear Monsieur Vincent, there is no other employment. And we cannot go elsewhere because we do not have the money. There is not a miner's family in the whole Borinage that has ten francs put away. But even if we could go, Monsieur, we would not. The sailor knows that all sorts of dangers await him aboard his ship, yet, ashore, he is homesick for the sea. So it is with us, Monsieur, we love our mines; we would rather be underground than above it. All we ask is a living wage, fair working hours, and protection against danger."

The cage reached the top. Vincent crossed the snow-covered yard, dazed by the feeble sunlight. The mirror in the washroom showed him that his face was pitch black. He did not wait to wash. He plunged across the field, only half conscious, drinking in the fresh air and wondering if he had not suddenly caught the *sotte fièvre* and been suffering from nightmare. Surely God would not let His children work in such abominable slavery? Surely he must have dreamed all the things he had seen?

He passed the prosperous, comparatively well-to-do house of the Denis's and without thinking stumbled down the filthy labyrinth of alleys in the ravine to Decrucq's hut. At first no one answered his knock. After a bit the six year old boy came. He was pale and anaemic and undersized, but he had something of Decrucq's fighting courage about him. In two more years he would be descending Marcasse every morning at three, shovelling coal into cars.

"Mother went to the *terril*," said the boy in a high, thin voice. "You must wait, Monsieur Vincent; I am taking care of the babies."

Playing on the floor with some sticks and a piece of string were Decrucq's two infants with nothing on but little shifts. They were blue with the cold. The oldest boy fed *terril* to the stove but it gave off very little heat. Vincent watched them and shivered. Then he put the babies to bed and covered them up to the neck. He did not know why he had come to this miserable shack. He felt that he must do something, say something to the Decrucqs, help them in some way. He must let them know that he at least realized the full extent of their misery.

Madame Decrucq came home, her hands and face black. At first she did not recognize Vincent through his filth. She ran to the little box that hid her provisions, and put some coffee on the stove. It was colder than tepid when she handed it to him, black, bitter and woody, but he drank it to please the good woman.

"The *terril* is bad these days, Monsieur Vincent," she complained. "The company lets nothing through, not even little grains. How am I to keep the babies warm? I have no clothes for them, only those little shirts and some sacking. The burlap gives them sores and rubs their skin off. If I keep them in bed all day, how will they grow?"

Vincent choked with unshed tears, but he could say nothing. He had never seen such abject personal misery. For the first time he wondered of what benefit prayers and the Gospel would be to this woman when her babies were freezing to death. Where was God in all this? He had a few francs in his pocket; he gave them to Madame Decrucq.

"Please buy woollen drawers for the children," he said.

It was a futile gesture, he knew; there were hundreds of other babies freezing in the Borinage. The Decrucq children would freeze again as soon as these drawers wore out.

He walked up the hill to the Denis's. The bakery kitchen was warm and cosy. Madame Denis heated him some water to wash in, and prepared him a nice lunch of the rabbit stew that had been left over from the night before. She saw that he was tired and overstrung from his experience so she put a trifle of butter out for his bread.

Vincent walked upstairs to his room. His stomach was warm and full. The bed was wide and comfortable; the sheets were clean, and on the pillow was a white pillow case. On the walls were prints by the great masters of the world. He opened his bureau and surveyed the rows of shirts, underclothes, socks, and vests. He went to the wardrobe and looked at his two extra pairs of shoes, his warm overcoat, and the suits of clothes hanging there. At last he realized that he was a liar and a coward. He preached the virtues of poverty to the miners but he himself lived in comfort and plenty. He was nothing more than a hypocritical slinger of words. His religion was an idle, useless thing. The miners ought to despise him and run him out of the Borinage. He pretended to share their lot, and here he had warm, beautiful clothes, a comfortable bed to sleep in, and more food in one meal than the miners had in a week. He did not even work for his ease and luxuries. He just went about telling glib lies and posing as a good man. The Borains ought not to believe a word he said; they ought not to come to his sermons or accept his leadership. His whole easy life gave the lie to his words. He had failed again, more miserably than ever before!

Well, he had only two choices; he could get out of the Borinage, run under the cover of night before they realized what a lying, weak-livered dog he was, or he could make use of the knowledge to which his eyes had been opened that day and really become a man of God.

He took all the clothes out of the bureau and packed them quickly into his bag. He also put in his suits, shoes, books, and prints, and closed the valise. He let it sit on the chair for the time being, and ran buoyantly out the front door.

At the bottom of the ravine there was a little creek. Just beyond that, the pine woods began the ascent of the other slope. In this woods there were scattered a few miners' cabins. After some inquiry, Vincent found one that was unoccupied. It was a board shanty without a window, built on a rather steep slope. The floor was the native earth trod down by long usage; the melting snow ran under the boards at the high end. Overhead there were rough beams holding the roof in place, and since the shack had not been used all winter, the knotholes and cracks between the boards let in icy blasts of air.

"Who owns this place?" Vincent demanded of the woman who had accompanied him.

"One of the business men in Wasmes."

"Do you know the rent?"

"Five francs a month."

"Very well, I'll take it."

"But Monsieur Vincent, you can't live here."

"Why not?"

"But . . . but . . . it is wretched. It is even worse than my place. It is the most wretched shack in Petit Wasmes!"

"That is exactly why I want it!"

He climbed up the hill again. A new feeling of peace had come into his heart. Madame Denis had gone to his room on some errand during his absence and had seen the packed valise.

"Monsieur Vincent," she cried when he came in, "what has gone wrong? Why are you going back to Holland so suddenly?"

"I am not going away, Madame Denis. I am staying in the Borinage."

"Then why . . . ?" A puzzled expression came over her face.

When Vincent explained, she said softly, "Believe me, Monsieur Vincent, you cannot live like that; you are not used to it. Times have changed since Jesus Christ; nowadays we must all live as best we can. The people know from your work that you are a good man."

Vincent was not to be dissuaded. He saw the merchant in Wasmes, rented the shack, and moved in. When his first salary check of fifty francs arrived a few days later, he bought himself a little wooden bed and a second-hand stove. After these expenditures he had just enough francs left to secure him bread, sour cheese, and coffee for the rest of the month. He piled dirt against the top wall of the cabin to keep the water out, stuffed the cracks and knotholes with sacking. He now lived in the same kind of house as the miners, ate the identical food, and slept in the identical bed. He was one of them. He had the right to bring them the Word of God.

13

The manager of the Charbonnages Belgique, which controlled the four mines in the vicinity of Wasmes, was not at all the sort of voracious animal that Vincent had been prepared to find. True, he was a bit stoutish, but he had kindly, sympathetic eyes and the manner of one who had done a little suffering on his own accord.

"I know, Monsieur Van Gogh," he said, after listening attentively while Vincent poured out the tale of woe of the miner. "It is an old story. The men think we are purposely starving them to death so that we can earn greater profits. But believe me, Monsieur, nothing could be farther from the truth. Here, let me show you some charts from the International Bureau of Mines in Paris."

He laid a large chart out on the table and indicated a blue line at the bottom with his finger.

"Look, Monsieur," he said, "the Belgian coal mines are the poorest in the world. The coal is so difficult for us to reach that it is almost impossible to sell it in the open market for a profit. Our operating expenses are the highest of any coal mine in Europe, and our profits are the lowest! For you see, we must sell our coal at the same price as the mines which produce at the lowest ton cost. We are on the margin of bankruptcy every day of our lives. Do you follow me?"

"I believe so."

"If we paid the miners one franc more a day our production costs would rise above the market price of coal. We would have to shut down altogether. And then they would really starve to death."

"Couldn't the owners take a little less profit? Then there would be more for the workers."

The manager shook his head sadly. "No, Monsieur, for do you know what coal mines run on? Capital. Like every other industry. And capital must receive its return or it will go elsewhere. The stocks of the Charbonnages Belgique pay only three percent dividends today. If they were reduced half of a percent the owners would withdraw their money. If they do that our mines will have to shut down, for we cannot operate without capital. And again the miners would starve. So you see, Monsieur, it is not the owners or managers who create this horrible condition in the Borinage. It is the unsatisfactory lay of the *couches*. And that condition, I suppose, we will have to blame on God!"

Vincent should have been shocked at this blasphemy. He was not. He was thinking of what the manager had told him.

"But at least you can do something about the working hours. Thirteen hours a day down there is killing off your whole village!"

"No, Monsieur, we cannot decrease the working hours because that would be equivalent to raising their wages. They would be turning out that much less coal for their fifty cents a day, and consequently our production cost per ton would be raised."

"There is one thing that certainly can be improved."

"You are going to speak of the dangerous working conditions?"

"Yes. At least you can decrease the number of accidents and deaths in the mines."

The manager shook his head patiently. "No, Monsieur, we cannot. We are unable to sell new stocks on the market because our dividends are too low. And we have absolutely no surplus of profit to invest in improvements. —Ah, Monsieur, it is a hopeless, vicious circle. I have gone around it many thousands of times. That is what has turned me from a firm, faithful Catholic to a bitter atheist. I cannot understand how a God in Heaven would purposely create such a condition and enslave a whole race of people in abject misery for century after century without one hour of providential mercy!"

Vincent could think of nothing to say. He walked home stunned.

14

The month of February was the most bitter one of the year. Naked winds swept through the valley and over the hilltop, making it almost impossible to walk through the streets. The miners' huts now needed the *terril* more than ever for warmth but the icy winds were so fierce that the women could not go out to the black mountain to search for it. They had nothing but their coarse skirts, blouses, cotton stockings, and kerchiefs to protect them against the biting winds.

The children had to stay in bed day after day to keep from freezing. Hot food was almost impossible to get because there was no coal for the stove. When the men came out of the blistering hot bowels of the earth they were plunged without a moment's preparation into the below zero weather, and had to struggle home across the snow-covered fields in the cutting wind. Deaths from consumption and pneumonia occurred every day of the week. Vincent read a great many funeral services that month.

He had given up trying to teach the blue-faced children how to read, and was spending his days on the Marcasse mountain collecting what little coal he could, to be distributed among the huts where the misery was worst. He had no need to rub coal-dust on his face these days; he was never free from the mark of the miner. A stranger coming into Petit Wasmes would have called him, ". . . Just another blackjaw."

He had gathered almost half a sack of *terril* after many hours of work up and down the pyramid. The blue skin of his hands was torn by the ice-covered rock. At a little before four he decided to stop and take back what he had to the village so that at least a few wives might prepare hot coffee for their husbands. He reached the gate of Marcasse just as the miners began streaming out. Some of them recognized him and muttered a *bojou,* but the rest walked along with their hands in their pockets, shoulders caved inward, and eyes rivetted to the ground.

The last one out of the gate was a little old man whose cough racked his whole body so badly that he scarcely could walk. His knees trembled, and when the freezing wind from the snow-covered fields hit him, he staggered as though from a smashing blow. He nearly fell on his face in the ice. After a moment he gathered courage and began to cross the field slowly, presenting his side to the blast. He had a piece of burlap sack wrapped around his shoulders, a sack he had somehow secured from a store in Wasmes. Vincent saw that something was printed on it. He strained his eyes to make out what it said and deciphered the letters: *FRAGILE.*

After leaving his *terril* at the miners' huts, Vincent went to his own shack and laid all his clothes out on the bed. He had five shirts, three suits of underwear, four pairs of socks, two pairs of shoes, two suits of clothes and an extra soldier's coat. He left one shirt, one pair of socks and one suit of underwear on the bed. Everything else he stuffed into the valise.

The suit of clothes he left with the old man who had *FRAGILE* written across his back. The underwear and shirts he left for the children, to be cut up and made into little garments. The socks were distributed among the consumptives who had to descend Marcasse. The warm coat he gave to a pregnant woman whose husband had been killed a few days before by a cave in, and who had to take his place in the mine to support her two babies.

The Salon du Bébé was closed, as Vincent did not wish to take the *terril* away from the housewives. In addition, the families were afraid to tramp through the slush and get their feet wet. Vincent held little services at each hut as he made the rounds. As time went on, he found it necessary to devote himself to the practical duties of healing, washing, rubbing down, preparing hot drinks and medicines. At last he left his Bible at home because he never found time to open it. The Word of God had become a luxury that the miners could not afford.

The cold abated a little in March but fever set in to take its place. Vincent spent forty francs of his February salary for food and medicine for the sick, leaving himself on starvation rations. He was growing thinner from lack of food; his nervous, jumpy mannerisms became more exaggerated. The cold sapped his vitality; he began to walk around with a fever. His eyes became two great fire holes in their sockets, and his massive, Van Gogh head seemed to shrink. Hollows appeared in his cheeks and under his eyes, but his chin stuck out as firmly as ever.

The oldest Decrucq child contracted typhoid; a difficult situation set in over the beds. There were only two of them in the house; the parents occupied one and the three children the other. If the two babies remained in the same bed with the boy, they might catch his disease. If they were put on the floor they would develop pneumonia. If the parents slept on the floor they would be unable to work the following day. Vincent realized immediately what must be done.

"Decrucq," he said when the miner came home from work, "will you help me a moment before you sit down to your supper?"

Decrucq was tired and ill from the pain in his scalp but he followed Vincent without question, dragging his dead leg after him. When they got to his hut Vincent threw one of the two blankets off the bed and said, "Take an end of this; we are going to move it up to your house for the boy."

Decrucq gritted his teeth. "We have three children," he said, "if God wills it so, we can lose one of them. But there is only one Monsieur Vincent to nurse the whole village, and I will not let him kill himself!"

He limped wearily out of the cabin. Vincent took the bed apart, loaded it on his shoulders, tramped to the Decrucq house and set it up. Decrucq and his wife looked at him over their supper of dry bread and coffee. Vincent transferred the child to his bed and nursed him.

Later that evening he went to the Denis's to ask if they had some straw he might take to his cabin to sleep on. Madame Denis was aghast when she heard what he had done.

"Monsieur Vincent," she exclaimed, "your old room is still unoccupied. You must come back here to live."

"You are very good, Madame Denis, but I cannot."

"I know, you are worrying about the money. But that does not matter. Jean-Baptiste and I make a good living. You can live here with us free, as a brother. Aren't you always telling us that all God's children are brothers?"

Vincent was cold, shivering cold. He was hungry. He was delirious with the fever he had been carrying about for weeks. He was weak from malnutrition, from lack of sleep. He was harassed and nearly insane with the cumulative grief and suffering of the village. The bed upstairs was warm and soft and clean. Madame Denis would give him food to wipe out that gnawing at the pit of his stomach; she would nurse his fever and fill him with hot, powerful drinks until the cold was driven from the marrow of his bones. He shivered, weakened, almost collapsed on the red tile floor of the bakery. Just in time he caught himself.

This was God's ultimate test. If he failed now, all the work he had done before would have been futile. Now that the village was at its most horrible stage of suffering and deprivation, was he to backslide, be a weak, contemptible coward and grasp comfort and luxury the first moment it was thrust under his nose?

"God sees your goodness, Madame Denis," he said, "and He will reward you for it. But you must not tempt me from my path of duty. If you do not find me some straw, I'm afraid I'll have to sleep on the ground. But don't bring anything else, please, for I can't accept it."

He dumped the straw into one corner of his hut, over the damp ground, and covered himself with the thin blanket. He did not sleep all night; when morning came he had a cough, and his eyes seemed to have retreated even farther into his head. His fever had increased until he was only half conscious of his movements. There was no *terril* in the shack for the stove; he did not feel he could deprive the miners of even a handful of the stuff he collected from the black mountain. He managed to swallow a few mouthfuls of hard dry bread, and set out for his day's work.

15

March pushed its way wearily into April and conditions improved a bit. The winds disappeared, the slant of the sun became a little more direct, and at last the thaw came. With the melting of the snow the black fields became visible, the larks were heard, and in the woods the buds began to sprout on the elder trees. The fever died down and with the coming of warmer weather the women of the village were able to swarm over the Marcasse pyramid to get *terril*. Soon the cabins were blazing with cosy fires in their oval stoves; the children were able to stay out of bed during the day, and Vincent reopened the Salon. The entire village crowded in for the first sermon. A touch of a smile was coming back to the melancholy eyes of the miners; the people dared lift their heads just a little. Decrucq, who had appointed himself official fireman and janitor of the Salon, was cracking jokes over the stove and rubbing his scalp vigorously.

"Better times are coming," cried Vincent exultantly from his pulpit. "God has tried you and found you true. The worst of our suffering is over. The corn will ripen in the fields, and the sun will warm you as you sit before your homes after a good day's work. The children will run out to follow the lark and gather berries in the woods. Lift up your eyes to God, for the good things in life are in store for you. God is merciful. God is just. He will reward you for your faith and vigilance. Offer up thanks to Him, for better times are coming. Better times are coming."

The miners offered up fervent thanks. Cheerful voices filled the room and everyone kept saying to his neighbour, "Monsieur Vincent is right. Our suffering is over. The winter is gone. Better times are coming!"

A few days later, while Vincent and a group of the children were gathering *terril* behind Marcasse, they saw little black figures scurrying out of the building in which the hoist was located, and go running across the fields in all directions.

"What has happened?" exclaimed Vincent. "It can't be four o'clock yet. The sun isn't even in mid-heaven."

"There's been an accident!" shouted one of the older boys. "I've seen them run away like that before! Something's broken below!"

They scrambled down the black mountain as fast as they could, ripping their hands and clothes on the rocks. The field surrounding Marcasse was thick with black ants running to cover. By the time they all got down, the tide of movement had changed and the women and children were running across the field from the village, coming from every direction at a frightened speed, babies in their arms and infants tagging along behind.

When Vincent got to the gate he heard excited voices crying, *"Grisou! Grisou!* The new *couche!* They're caught! They're trapped in!"

Jacques Verney, who had been laid up in bed during the intense cold, came dashing across the field at top speed. He had grown thinner, his chest more cavernous. Vincent caught him as he went by and said, "What is it? Tell me!"

"Decrucq's *couche!* Remember the blue lamps? I knew it would get them!"

"How many? How many are there? Can't we get at them?"

"Twelve cells. You saw them. Five men to a cell."

"Can't we save them?"

"I don't know. I'm taking a volunteer crew down immediately."

"Let me come along. Let me help."

"No. I need experienced men." He ran through the yard to the hoist.

The little cart with the white horse drew up to the gate, the same cart that had carried so many dead and injured to the cabins on the hillside. The miners who had run across the fields began returning with their families. Some of the women cried hysterically, others stared ahead of them, wide eyed. The children whimpered and the foremen ran about, shouting at the tops of their voices, organizing rescue crews.

Suddenly the noise stopped. A little group came out of the hoist building and walked slowly down the stairs, carrying something wrapped in blankets. The hush was eloquent for a moment. Then everyone began shouting and crying at the same time.

"Who is it? Are they dead? Are they alive? For God's sake, tell us their names! Show them to us! My husband is down there! My children! Two of my babies are in that *couche!*"

The group stopped at the little cart with the white horse. One of the men spoke. "Three of the carriers who were dumping coal on the outside have been saved. But they are terribly burned."

"Who are they? For the love of Jesus tell us who they are! Show us! Show us! My baby is down there! My baby, my baby!"

The man lifted the blankets off the seared faces of two girls of about nine and a boy of ten. All three were unconscious. The families of the children fell upon them with mingled cries of lament and joy. The three blankets were laid in the cart with the white horse and driven across the hollow road of the field. Vincent and the families ran alongside like panting animals. From behind him Vincent heard the wail of fear and anguish mount ever higher and higher. He turned his head while he ran, and looked behind him, seeing the long line of *terril* mountains on the horizon.

"Black Egypt!" he cried aloud, giving vent to his pain. "Black Egypt, with the chosen people enslaved again! Oh, God, how could you? How could you?"

The children were burned almost to death. The skin and hair was seared off every part that had been exposed. Vincent went into the first cabin. The mother was wringing her hands in anguish. Vincent undressed the child and cried, "Oil, oil, quick!" The woman had a little oil in the house. Vincent applied it to the burns and then cried, "Now, bandage!"

The woman stood there staring at him, terror in her eyes. Vincent became angry and shouted, "Bandages! Do you want your child to die?"

"We have nothing," she blubbered. "There is not a piece of white cloth in the house. There has not been all winter!"

The child stirred and moaned. Vincent grabbed off his coat and shirt, and tore his undershirt from his body. He replaced his coat, ripped the other garments to strips, and bandaged the child from head to foot. He took the can of oil and ran to the second child. He bandaged her as he had the first. When he reached the third child the shirt and undershirt had been used up. The ten year old boy was dying. Vincent took off his trousers and woollen drawers, replaced the trousers and cut the drawers into bandages.

He pulled his coat tightly over his bare chest and ran across the field to Marcasse. From far off he could hear the lament, the unending cry of the wife and mother.

The miners were standing about the gate. Only one relief crew could work down below at a time. The approach to the ledge was narrow. The men were waiting their turn. Vincent spoke to one of the assistant foremen.

"What are the chances?"

"They're dead by now."

"Can't we get to them?"

"They're buried under rock."

"How long will it take?"

"Weeks. Maybe months."

"But why? But why?"

"That's how long it took before."

"Then they're lost!"

"Fifty-seven men and girls!"

"Every one of them gone!"

"You'll never see them again!"

Crews relieved each other for thirty-six hours. The women who had husbands and children below could not be driven away. The men above kept telling them rescue was sure. The women knew they were lying. The miners' wives who had lost no one brought hot coffee and bread across the field. The stricken women would touch nothing. In the middle of the night Jacques Verney was brought up in a blanket. He had had a hemorrhage. He died the following day.

After forty-eight hours Vincent persuaded Madame Decrucq to return home with the children. For twelve days volunteer rescue crews worked without stopping. No mining went on. Since no coal was brought up, no wages were paid. The few francs surplus in the village was soon gone. Madame Denis went on baking bread and distributing it on credit. She exhausted her capital and had to shut down. The company contributed nothing. At the end of the twelfth day they told the rescue crews to stop. The men were ordered back to work. Petit Wasmes had not one centime between it and starvation.

The miners struck.

Vincent's wages for April arrived. He went down to Wasmes and bought fifty francs worth of food. He distributed it among the families. The village lived on it for six days. After that they went to the woods to collect berries, leaves, grass. The men went out of doors searching for things that lived; rats, gophers, snails, toads, lizards, cats, dogs. Anything that could be put into the stomach to stop the throbbing ache of hunger. At last there was nothing more to find. Vincent wrote to Brussels for help. No help came. The miners sat down to watch their wives and children starve under their eyes.

They asked Vincent to hold services for the fifty-seven lost souls in the mine, the ones who had gone before them. A hundred men, women, and children packed into Vincent's tiny hut. Vincent had had nothing but coffee for days. He had had almost no solid food since the accident. He was too weak to stand on his feet. The fever and despair had returned to his heart. His eyes were just two black pin pricks, his cheeks had been sucked in, the circular bones under his eyes protruded, a dirty, red beard matted his face. He had rough sacking wrapped around his body to take the place of underwear. Only one lantern illuminated the shack. It hung from a broken rafter, giving but a flickering glow. Vincent lay on the straw in his corner, holding his head up on one elbow. The lantern flung fantastic, flickering shadows over the rough planks and the hundred mutely suffering souls.

He began speaking in a parched, feverish voice, every word filling the silence. The blackjaws, thin, emaciated, wracked by hunger and defeat, kept their eyes on him as they would on God. God was a long way off.

Strange, loud voices were heard outside the shack, lifted in indignation.

The door was flung open and a child's voice cried, "Monsieur Vincent is in here, Messieurs."

Vincent stopped speaking. The hundred Borains turned their heads toward the door. Two well-dressed men stepped in. The oil lamp flared up for a brief moment. Vincent saw horror and fear written across the strange faces.

"You are welcome, Reverend de Jong and Reverend van den Brink," he said without rising. "We are holding funeral services for the fifty-seven miners who were buried alive in Marcasse. Perhaps you will say a word of comfort to the people?"

It took the Reverends a long time to find their tongues.

"Shocking! Simply shocking!" cried De Jong, giving his protuberant stomach a resounding smack.

"You would think you were in the jungles of Africa!" said Van den Brink.

"Heaven only knows how much harm he's done."

"It may take years to bring these people back to Christianity."

De Jong crossed his hands on his paunch and exclaimed, "I told you not to give him an appointment in the first place."

"I know . . . but Pietersen . . . who could ever have dreamed of this? This chap is absolutely mad!"

"I suspected he was insane all the time. I never did trust him."

The Reverends spoke in rapid, perfect French, not one word of which the Borains understood. Vincent was too weak and ill to realize the import of what they were saying.

De Jong stomached his way through the crowd and said to Vincent quietly but fiercely, "Send these filthy dogs home!"

"But the services! We haven't finished the . . ."

"Never mind the services. Send them away."

The miners filed out slowly, uncomprehending. The two Reverends faced Vincent. "What in the world have you done to yourself? What do you mean by holding services in a hole like this? What sort of a new barbarous cult have you started? Have you no sense of decency, of decorum? Is this conduct befitting a Christian minister? Are you utterly mad, that you behave like this? Do you wish to disgrace our Church?"

The Reverend de Jong paused for a moment, surveyed the mean, sordid shack, the bed of straw on which Vincent lay, the burlap wrapped around his body and his deep sunk, feverish eyes.

"It is a fortunate thing for the Church, Monsieur Van Gogh," he said, "that we have given you only a temporary appointment. You may now consider that appointment cancelled. You will never again be allowed to serve us. I find your conduct disgusting and disgraceful. Your salary is ended and a new man will be sent to take your place immediately. If I were not charitable enough to think you entirely mad, I would call you the worst enemy to Christianity that the Belgian Evangelical Church has ever had!"

There was a long silence. "Well, Monsieur Van Gogh, have you nothing to say in your own defense?"

Vincent remembered the day in Brussels when they had refused him an appointment. Now he could not even feel anything, let alone speak.

"We may as well go, Brother de Jong," said the Reverend van den Brink after a time. "There is nothing we can do here. His case is quite hopeless. If we can't find a good hotel in Wasmes, we'll have to ride back to Mons tonight."

16

The following morning a group of the older miners came to Vincent. "Monsieur," they said, "now that Jacques Verney is gone, you are the only man we can trust. You must tell us what to do. We do not wish to starve to death unless we have to. Perhaps you can get 'them' to grant our wishes. After you have seen them, if you tell us to go back to work, we will. And if you tell us to starve, we will do that, too. We will listen to you, Monsieur, and to no one else."

The offices of the Charbonnages Belgique had a funereal air. The manager was glad to see Vincent and listened to him in sympathy. "I know, Monsieur Van Gogh," he said, "that the miners are outraged because we did not bore through to the bodies. But what good would it have done? The company has decided not to reopen that *couche;* it doesn't pay for itself. We would have had to dig for perhaps a month, and what would have been the result? Simply to take the men from one grave and put them in another."

"Then what about the living? Can you do nothing to improve conditions down below? Must they work in the face of certain death every day of their lives?"

"*Oui,* Monsieur, they must. They must. The company has no funds to invest in safety devices. The miners are on the losing end of this quarrel; they cannot win because they have iron-clad economic laws against them. What is worse, if they don't return to work within another week, Marcasse will be shut down permanently. Then God knows what will happen to them."

Vincent walked up the long winding road to Petit Wasmes, defeated. "Perhaps God knows," he said to himself bitterly. "And then again, perhaps He doesn't."

It was clearly evident that he was of no more use to the miners. He had to tell them to go back to work for thirteen hours a day in the consumption pits, for starvation rations, with sudden death staring half of them in the face and a slow, coughing death all the others. He had failed to help them in any way. Not even God could help them. He had come to the Borinage to put the Word of God into their hearts, but what could he say further when faced by the fact that the eternal enemy of the miners was not the owners, but the Almighty Father Himself?

The moment he told the miners to go back to work, to take up their slavery again, he ceased to be of any value to them. He could never preach another sermon—even if the Committee would allow him—for of what good was the Gospel now? God had turned a stone deaf ear to the miners and Vincent had not been able to soften Him.

Then suddenly he realized something he had known for a long time. All this talk about God was childish evasion; desperate lies whispered by a frightened, lonely mortal to himself out in a cold, dark, eternal night. There was no God. Just as simply as that, there was no God. There was only chaos; miserable, suffering, cruel, torturous, blind, endless chaos.

17

The miners returned to work. Theodorus Van Gogh, who heard from the Committee of Evangelization, wrote, enclosing money and asked Vincent to return to Etten. Instead Vincent went back to the Denis's. He made a farewell trip to the Salon, took all the prints off the wall and put them up in his room under the eaves.

It was bankruptcy once again, and time to take stock. Only there was no stock. There was no job, no money, no health, no strength, no ideas, no enthusiasms, no desires, no ambitions, no ideals, and worst of all, no pivot upon which to hang his life. He was twenty-six, five times a failure, without the courage to begin anew.

He looked at himself in the mirror. His reddish beard covered his face in whorls. His hair was thinning out, his rich, ripe mouth had been squeezed down to a narrow line, and his eyes were lost somewhere in dark caverns. The whole personality that was Vincent Van Gogh seemed to have shrivelled, grown cold, almost died within itself.

He borrowed a little soap from Madame Denis and scrubbed himself from head to foot, standing up in a basin of water. He looked down at what had been a massive, powerful body and saw that it was thin and emaciated. He shaved carefully and neatly, wondering where all the strange bones in his face had come from so suddenly. He combed his hair in its old design for the first time in months. Madame Denis brought him up a shirt and suit of underwear belonging to her husband. He dressed and descended to the cheerful bakery kitchen. He sat down to dinner with the Denises; solid cooked food passed his lips for the first time since the catastrophe at the mine. It seemed curious to him that he should bother to eat at all. The food in his mouth tasted like warm wood pulp.

Although he had not told the miners that he had been forbidden to preach again, they did not ask him to, nor did they seem to care about sermons. Vincent rarely spoke to them any more. He rarely spoke to anyone. He exchanged only a *bonjour* in passing. He never entered their huts or engaged in their daily lives or thoughts. By some profound understanding and tacit agreement the miners refrained from discussing him. They adopted his attitude of formality but they never condemned the change. Mutely they understood. And life went on in the Borinage.

A note from home informed him that Kay Vos's husband had died suddenly. He was at too low an ebb of emotional exhaustion to do more than store the fact in some remote corner of his mind.

The weeks passed. Vincent did nothing but eat, sleep, and sit in a daze. The fever was slowly being driven out of his body. He was gaining strength and weight. But his eyes were two glass openings to a corpse-filled coffin. Summer came; the black fields and chimneys and *terrils* glistened in the sun. Vincent walked through the country-side. He did not walk for exercise or for pleasure. He never knew where he was going or what he passed along the way. He walked because he was tired of lying, sitting, standing. And when he got tired of walking, he sat or lay or stood.

Shortly after his money ran out he received a letter from his brother Theo in Paris, begging him not to idle away his time in the Borinage but to use the enclosed banknotes to take a decisive step and re-establish himself. Vincent turned the money over to Madame Denis. He did not remain in the Borinage because he liked it; he stayed because there was no place else to go, and it would take so much effort to get there.

He had lost God and he had lost himself. Now he lost the most important thing on earth, the one and only person who had always been instinctively sympathetic, and who understood him as he hoped to be understood. Theo abandoned his brother. All during the winter he had written once and twice a week, long, loving letters of cheer and interest. Now the letters stopped altogether. Theo, too, had lost faith; had given up hope. And so Vincent was alone, utterly alone, without even his Maker, a dead man walking in a deserted world and wondering why he was still there.

18

Summer thinned into fall. With the death of the meagre vegetation something came to life within Vincent. He could not yet face his own life, so he turned to the lives of others. He returned to his books. Reading had always been his finest and most constant pleasure, and now in the stories of other people's triumphs and failures, sufferings and joys, he found surcease from the ever haunting spectre of his own fiasco.

When the weather permitted he went out into the fields and read for the entire day; when it rained he either lay on his bed under the eaves or leaned a chair against a wall in the Denis kitchen, and sat there for hours, engrossed. With the passing of the weeks he absorbed the life stories of hundreds of ordinary people like himself, who strove, succeeded a little, and failed a great deal; and through them he slowly got a proper perspective on himself. The theme that ran through his brain: "I'm a failure. I'm a failure. I'm a failure," gave way to "What shall I try now? What am I best fitted for? Where is my proper place in the world?" In every book he read, he looked for that pursuit which might give his life direction again.

Letters from home described his existence as *choquant;* his father insisted that he was violating all decent social conventions by leading the life of an idler. When did he plan to get a job again, to support himself, to become a useful member of society and contribute his share to the world's work?

Vincent would have liked to know the answer to that himself.

At length he reached the saturation point in reading and could no longer pick up a book. During the weeks that followed his debacle, he had been too stunned and ill to feel anything emotionally. Later he had turned to literature to drown out his feelings, and had succeeded. Now he was almost completely well, and the flood of emotional suffering that had been stored up for months broke like a raging torrent and engulfed him in misery and despair. The mental perspective he had gained seemed to do him no good.

He had reached the low point in his life and he knew it.

He felt that there was some good in him, that he was not altogether a fool and a wastrel, and that there was a small contribution he could make to the world. But what was that contribution? He was not fitted for the routine of business and he had already tried everything else for which he might have had an aptitude. Was he always doomed to fail and suffer? Was life really over for him?

The questions asked themselves, but they brought no answers. And so he drifted with the days that slurred into winter. His father would become disgusted and stop sending money; he would have to give up eating at the Denis's and go on short rations. Then Theo would feel a little prick of conscience and send a few notes through Etten. By the time Theo lost patience, his father would once again feel his responsibility. Between them Vincent managed to eat about half the time.

One clear November day Vincent wandered over to Marcasse empty handed, empty minded, and sat on a rusty, iron wheel outside the wall. An old miner came through the gate, his black cap forward over his eyes, shoulders hunched over, hands in pockets, and knees jerking out bonily. Something about the man, he could not tell exactly what, attracted Vincent. Idly, without particular interest, he reached into his pocket, pulled out the stub of a pencil and a letter from home, and on the back of the envelope quickly sketched the little figure tramping across the black field.

Vincent opened his father's letter and saw that the writing covered only one side. After a few moments another miner came out of the gate, a young chap about seventeen. He stood taller, more erect, and there was a cheerful lift to the line of his shoulders as he struck out along the high stone wall of Marcasse toward the railroad tracks. Vincent had several full minutes to sketch him before he disappeared.

19

At the Denis's, Vincent found several sheets of clean, white paper and a thick pencil. He put his two rough sketches on the desk and began copying them. His hand was clumsy and stiff; he could not get the line he had in mind on the paper. He used the eraser far more than the pencil, but kept plugging to reproduce his figures. He was so intent that he did not notice darkness creep across his room. He was startled when Madame Denis knocked on his door.

"Monsieur Vincent," she called, "supper is on the table."

"Supper!" exclaimed Vincent. "But it couldn't be that late already."

At the table he chatted animatedly with the Denises and there was a faint gleam in his eye. The Denises exchanged a significant look. After the light meal, Vincent excused himself and went immediately to his room. He lit the little lamp and pinned the two sketches on the wall, standing as far away from them as he could to get a perspective.

"They are bad," he said to himself with a curious grin, "very bad. But perhaps tomorrow I shall be able to do a little better."

He went to bed, placing the kerosene lamp on the floor beside him. He gazed at his two sketches without thinking about anything in particular; then his eyes saw the other prints he had on the wall. It was the first time he had actually seen them since that day, seven months ago, when he had taken them off the walls of the Salon. Suddenly he realized that he was homesick for the world of pictures. There once had been a time when he knew who Rembrandt was, who Millet, Jules Dupré, Delacroix and Maris were. He thought of all the lovely prints he had possessed at one time or another, the lithographs and etchings he had sent to Theo and his parents. He thought of all the beautiful canvases he had seen in the museums of London and Amsterdam, and in so thinking, he forgot to feel miserable, but fell into a deep, restful sleep. The kerosene lamp sputtered, burned bluely, and went out.

The following morning he awoke at two-thirty, thoroughly refreshed. He sprang lightly out of bed, dressed, took his big pencil and writing paper, found a piece of thin board in the bakery, and set out for Marcasse. He seated himself on the same rusty, iron wheel in the darkness and waited for the miners to begin coming in.

He sketched hastily and roughly, as he simply wanted to record his first impression of each personality. An hour later, when all the miners had gone down, he had five figures without faces. He walked briskly across the field, took a cup of coffee up to his room with him and when the light finally came, copied his sketches. He tried to put in all the strange little quirks of Borain appearance which his mind's eye knew so well, but which he had not been able to catch in the dark, with his models walking out from under him.

His anatomy was all wrong, his proportions were grotesque, and his drawing was so outlandish as to be funny. And yet the figures came out as Borains and could have been mistaken for nothing else. Vincent, amused at his own clumsiness and *gaucherie,* tore up the sketches. Then he sat on the edge of the bed, opposite the Allebé of the little old woman carrying hot water and coals on a wintry street, and tried to copy it. He managed to suggest the woman, but he couldn't get her into relation with either the street or the houses in the background. He crumpled up the sheet, flung it into a corner and sat his chair before the Bosboom study of a lone tree against a cloudy sky. It all looked so simple; just a tree, a bit of loam, and clouds at the top. But Bosboom's values were precise and exquisite and Vincent learned that it is always the simplest piece of art which has practised the most rigid elimination and is therefore the most difficult to duplicate.

The morning passed outside the realm of time. When Vincent used up his last sheet of paper, he searched his belongings very thoroughly to see how much money he had. He found two francs, and believing he could get good paper and perhaps even a stick of charcoal in Mons, set out to walk the twelve kilometres. As he went down the long hill between Petit Wasmes and Wasmes he saw a few miners' wives standing before their doors. He added a cordial *comment ça va?* to his usual automatic *bonjour.* At Paturages, a little town half-way to Mons, he noticed a pretty girl behind a bakery window. He went in to buy a five centime bun, just to look at her.

The fields between Paturages and Cuesmes were a bright shade of green from the heavy rains. Vincent decided to come back and sketch them when he could afford a green crayon. In Mons he found a pad of smooth yellow paper, some charcoal, and a heavy lead pencil. There was a bin of old prints in front of the store. Vincent pored over them for hours although he knew he could buy nothing. The owner joined him, and they commented on one print after another just as though they were two friends going through a museum.

"I must apologize that I haven't any money to buy one of your pictures," said Vincent, after they had spent a long time looking at them.

The owner brought his hands and shoulders up in an eloquent Gallic gesture and said, "It doesn't matter, Monsieur; come again another time even though you have no money."

He walked the twelve kilometres home in a leisurely fashion. The sun was setting over the pyramid-dotted horizon and lit up the outer fringe of some floating clouds with a delicate shell pink. Vincent noticed how the little stone houses of Cuesmes fell into natural etching designs, and how peaceful the green valley lay below him when he gained the top of a hill. He felt happy, and wondered why.

The following day he went to the *terril* behind Marcasse and sketched the girls and women as they leaned over the slope, digging specks of black gold out of the mountainside. After dinner he said, "Please do not leave the table for a moment, Monsieur, Madame Denis. I wish to do something."

He ran to his room, brought back the drawing pad and charcoal, and quickly planted a likeness of his friends on the paper. Madame Denis came around to look over his shoulder and exclaimed, "But Monsieur Vincent, you are an artist!"

Vincent was embarrassed. "No," he said, "I am only amusing myself."

"But it is nice," said Madame Denis. "It almost looks like me."

"Almost," laughed Vincent, "but not quite."

He did not write home to tell them what he was doing because he knew they would say, and rightly, "Oh, Vincent is at one of his fads again. When will he settle down and do something useful?"

Besides, this new activity had a curious special quality; it was his and nobody else's. He could not bring himself to talk or write about his sketches. He felt a reticence about them that he had not felt for anything before, a disinclination to let strange eyes see his work. They were, in some crude and incomprehensible way, sacred, even though they might be wretchedly amateurish in every last detail.

Once more he entered the miners' huts, but this time he carried drawing paper and crayon instead of a Bible. The miners were not any the less glad to see him. He sketched the children playing on the floor, the wives bending over their oval stoves, the family at supper when the day's work was done. He sketched Marcasse with its tall chimneys, the black fields, the pine woods across the ravine, the peasants ploughing down around Paturages. If the weather was bad, he remained in his room, copying the prints on the walls and the rough drafts he had done the day before. When he went to bed at night, he felt that perhaps one or two of the things he had done that day were not so bad. He awakened the next morning to find he had slept off the intoxication of creative effort and that the drawings were wrong, all wrong. He threw them away without a qualm.

He had put down the beast of pain within him, and he was happy because he no longer thought of his unhappiness. He knew he ought to feel ashamed to keep on taking his father's and brother's money when he made no effort to support himself, but it did not seem to matter and he just went on sketching.

After a few weeks, when he had copied all the prints on the wall a great many times, he realized that if he was to make any progress he would have to have more to copy, and those of the masters. Despite the fact that Theo had not written to him for a year, he hid his pride under a pile of poor drawings and wrote to his brother.

Dear Theo:

If I am not mistaken you must still have "Les Travaux des Champs" by Millet.

Would you be so kind as to lend them to me for a short time and send them by mail?

I must tell you that I am copying large drawings after Bosboom and

Allebé. Well, perhaps if you saw them you would not be altogether dissatis-
fied.

Send me what you can and do not fear for me. If I can only continue to
work, that will somehow or other set me right again.

I write to you while I am busy drawing and I am in a hurry to get back
to it, so good night, and send me the prints as soon as possible.

With a hearty handshake in thought,

Vincent.

Slowly a new hunger grew upon him, the desire to talk to some artist
about his work, and find out just where he was going right and where he
was going wrong. He knew that his drawings were bad, but he was too close
to them to see exactly why. What he needed was the ruthless eye of a
stranger who was not blinded by the creative pride of the parent.

To whom could he go? It was a hunger more cogent than any he suffered
the winter before when he had lived for days on dry bread. He simply had
to know and feel that there were other artists in the world, men of his own
kind who were facing the same technical problems, thinking in the same
terms; men who would justify his efforts by showing their own serious concern with the elements of the painter's craft. There were people in the
world, he remembered, men like Maris and Mauve, who gave their whole
lives to painting. That seemed almost unbelievable here in the Borinage.

One rainy afternoon, as he was copying in his room, there flashed before
his mind the picture of the Reverend Pietersen standing in his studio in
Brussels and saying, "But don't tell my *confrères* about it!" He knew that he
had his man at last. He looked over the original sketches he had done, selected the figures of a miner, a wife bending over her oval stove, and an
old woman gathering *terril*. He set out for Brussels.

He had only a little over three francs in his pocket, so he could not afford
to take a train. The distance on foot was some eighty kilometres. Vincent
walked that afternoon, all that night, and most of the following day, getting
within thirty kilometres of Brussels. He would have gone straight on except
that his thin shoes had worn through and he had pushed his toes through the
top of one of them. The coat he had used all the previous year in Petit
Wasmes was covered with a layer of dust, and since he had not taken even a
comb or change of shirt with him, he could do little more than throw cold
water over his face the next morning.

He put cardboard inside the soles of his shoes and started out very early.
The leather began to cut him where his toes stuck through at the top; soon
his foot was covered with blood. The cardboard wore out, water blisters took
its place, changed to blood blisters, and then broke. He was hungry, he was
thirsty, he was tired, but he was as happy as a man could be.

He was actually going to see and talk to another artist!

He reached the outskirts of Brussels that afternoon without a centime in
his pockets. He remembered very distinctly where Pietersen lived and walked

rapidly through the streets. People moved aside quickly as he passed, and then stared after him, shaking their heads. Vincent did not even notice them, but made his way along as fast as his crippled feet would permit him.

The Reverend's young daughter answered the bell. She took one horrified look at Vincent's dirty, sweat streaked face, his uncombed, matted hair, filthy coat, mud caked trousers and black, bloody feet, and ran screaming down the hall. The Reverend Pietersen came to the door, peered at Vincent for a moment without recognizing him, and then broke into a hearty smile of recognition.

"Well, Vincent my son," he exclaimed, "how good it is to see you again. Come right in, come right in."

He led Vincent into the study and drew up a comfortable chair for him. Now that he had made his objective, the cable of will broke within Vincent, and all at once he felt the eighty kilometres that he had tramped in the last two days on bread and a little cheese. The muscles of his back relaxed, his shoulders slumped, and he found it curiously difficult to breathe.

"A friend of mine nearby has a spare room, Vincent," said Pietersen. "Wouldn't you like to clean up and rest after your journey?"

"Yes. I hadn't known I was so tired."

The Reverend took his hat and walked down the street with Vincent, oblivious to the stares of his neighbours.

"You will probably want to sleep tonight," he said, "but surely you will come to dinner tomorrow at twelve? We will have a great deal to talk about."

Vincent scrubbed, standing up in an iron basin, and although it was only six o'clock, went to sleep holding his empty stomach. He did not open his eyes until ten the next morning and only then because hunger was pounding implacably on some anvil within him. The man from whom the Reverend Pietersen rented the room lent Vincent a razor, a comb, and a clothes brush; he did what he could to make himself look neat and found everything repairable except the shoes.

Vincent was ravenous for food, and while Pietersen chatted lightly about the recent events in Brussels, piled it in unashamedly. After dinner the two men went into the study.

"Oh," said Vincent, "you've been doing a lot of work, haven't you? These are all new sketches on the walls."

"Yes," replied Pietersen, "I'm beginning to find a great deal more pleasure in painting than in preaching."

Vincent said smilingly, "And does your conscience prick you occasionally for taking so much time off your real work?"

Pietersen laughed and said, "Do you know the anecdote about Rubens? He was serving Holland as Ambassador to Spain and used to spend the afternoons in the royal gardens before his easel. One day a jaunty member of the Spanish court passed and remarked, 'I see that the diplomat amuses himself sometimes with painting,' to which Rubens replied, 'No, the painter amuses himself sometimes with diplomacy!' "

Pietersen and Vincent exchanged an understanding laugh. Vincent opened his packet. "I have been doing a little sketching myself," he said, "and I brought along three figures for you to see. Perhaps you won't mind telling me what you think of them?"

Pietersen winced, for he knew that criticizing a beginner's work was a thankless task. Nevertheless he placed the three studies on the easel and stood a long way off looking at them. Vincent suddenly saw his drawings through his friend's eyes; he realized how utterly amateurish they were.

"My first impression," said the Reverend, after some time, "is that you must be working very close to your models. Are you?"

"Yes, I have to. Most of my work is done in the crowded miners' huts."

"I see. That explains your lack of perspective. Couldn't you manage to find a place where you can stand off from your subjects? You'll see them much more clearly, I'm sure."

"There are some fairly large miners' cabins. I could rent one for very little and fix it up as a studio."

"An excellent idea." He was silent again and then said with effort, "Have you ever studied drawing? Do you block the faces on squared off paper? Do you take measurements?"

Vincent blushed. "I don't know how to do those things," he said. "You see, I've never had a lesson. I thought you just went ahead and drew."

"Ah, no," said Pietersen sadly. "You must learn your elementary technique first and then your drawing will come slowly. Here, I'll show you what's wrong with this woman."

He took a ruler, squared off the head and figure, showed Vincent how bad his proportions were, and then proceeded to reconstruct the head, explaining as he went along. After almost an hour of work he stepped back, surveyed the sketch, and said, "There. Now I think we have that figure drawn correctly."

Vincent joined him at the opposite end of the room and looked at the paper. There could be no doubt about it, the woman was now drawn in perfect proportion. But she was no longer a miner's wife, no longer a Borain picking up coal on the slope of her *terril*. She was just any perfectly drawn woman in the world, bending over. Without saying a word Vincent went to the easel, placed the figure of the woman bending over her oval stove beside the reconstructed drawing, and went back to join Pietersen.

"Hummmm," said the Reverend Pietersen. "Yes, I see what you mean. I've given her proportion and taken away character."

They stood there for a long time, looking at the easel. Pietersen said involuntarily, "You know, Vincent, that woman standing over her stove isn't bad. She isn't at all bad. The drawing is terrible, your values are all wrong and her face is hopeless. In fact she hasn't any face at all. But that sketch has got something. You caught something that I can't quite lay my finger on. What is it, Vincent?"

"I'm sure I don't know. I just put her down as I saw her."

This time it was Pietersen who walked quickly to the easel. He threw the sketch he had perfected into the wastebasket with a "You don't mind, do you, I've ruined it anyway," and placed the second woman there all by herself. He rejoined Vincent and they sat down. The Reverend started to speak several times but the words did not quite form. At last he said, "Vincent, I hate to admit it, but I really believe I almost like that woman. I thought she was horrible at first, but something about her grows on you."

"Why do you hate to admit it?" asked Vincent.

"Because I ought not to like it. The whole thing is wrong, dead wrong! Any elementary class in art school would make you tear it up and begin all over again. And yet something about her reaches out at me. I could almost swear I have seen that woman somewhere before."

"Perhaps you have seen her in the Borinage," said Vincent artlessly.

Pietersen looked at him quickly to see if he was being clever and then said, "I think you're right. She has no face and she isn't any one particular person. Somehow she's just all the miners' wives in the Borinage put together. That something you've caught is the spirit of the miner's wife, Vincent, and that's a thousand times more important than any correct drawing. Yes, I like your woman. She says something to me directly."

Vincent trembled, but he was afraid to speak. Pietersen was an experienced artist, a professional; if he should ask for the drawing, really like it enough to . . .

"Could you spare her, Vincent? I would like very much to put her on my wall. I think she and I could become excellent friends."

20

When Vincent decided he had better return to Petit Wasmes, the Reverend Pietersen gave him a pair of his old shoes to replace the broken ones, and railroad fare back to the Borinage. Vincent took them in the full spirit of friendship which knows that the difference between giving and taking is purely temporal.

On the train Vincent realized two important things; the Reverend Pietersen had not once referred to his failure as an evangelist, and he had accepted him on equal terms as a fellow artist. He had actually liked a sketch well enough to want it for his own; that was the crucial test.

"He has given me my start," said Vincent to himself. "If he liked my work, other people will, too."

At the Denis's he found that "Les Travaux des Champs" had arrived from Theo, although no letter accompanied them. His contact with Pietersen had refreshed him, so he dug into Father Millet with gusto. Theo had enclosed some large sized sketch paper, and within a few days Vincent copied ten pages of "Les Travaux," finishing the first volume. Then, feeling that he needed work on the nude, and being quite certain he could never get anyone to pose for him that way in the Borinage, he wrote to his old friend Tersteeg, manager of the Goupil Galleries in The Hague, asking him if he would lend the "Exercises au Fusain" by Bargue.

In the meanwhile he remembered Pietersen's counsel and rented a miner's hut near the top of the rue Petit Wasmes for nine francs a month. This time the hut was the best he could find, not the worst. It had a rough plank floor, two large windows to let in light, a bed, table, chair, and stove. It was sufficiently large for Vincent to place his model at one end and get far enough away for complete perspective. There was not a miner's wife or child in Petit Wasmes who had not been helped in some way the winter before by Vincent, and no one ever turned down his request to come and pose. On Sundays the miners would throng to his cabin and let him make quick sketches of them. They thought it great fun. The place was always full of people looking over Vincent's shoulder with interest and amazement.

The "Exercises au Fusain" arrived from The Hague and Vincent spent the next two weeks copying the sixty studies, working from early morning to night. Tersteeg also sent the "Cours de Dessin" by Bargue; Vincent tackled this with tremendous vitality.

All five of the former failures were wiped completely from his mind. Not even serving God had brought such sheer ecstasy and constant, lasting satisfaction as creative art could give him. When for eleven days he had not one centime in his pocket and had to live off the few loaves he could borrow from Madame Denis, he did not once complain—even to himself—of his hunger. What did the hunger of his belly matter, when his spirit was being so well fed?

Every morning for a week he went to the gate of Marcasse at two-thirty and made a large drawing of the miners: men and women going to the shaft, through the snow by a path along a hedge of thorns; shadows that passed, dimly visible in the crepuscule. In the background he drew the large constructions of the mine, with the heaps of clinkers standing out vaguely against the sky. He made a copy of the sketch when it was finished and sent it in a letter to Theo.

Two full months passed this way, drawing from dawn to dark and then copying by the light of the lamp. Once again there came over him the desire to see and talk to another artist, to find out how he was getting on, for although he thought he had made some progress, achieved a little more plasticity of hand and judgment, he could not be sure. But this time he wanted a master, someone who would take him under his wing and teach him slowly and carefully the rudiments of the great craft. There was nothing he would not do in return for such instruction; he would black the man's boots and sweep the floor of his studio ten times a day.

Jules Breton, whose work he had admired since the early days, lived in Courrieres, a distance of a hundred and seventy kilometres. Vincent rode on the train until his money ran out, and then walked for five days, sleeping in hay ricks and begging his bread in exchange for a drawing or two. When he stood among the trees of Courrieres and saw that Breton had just built a fine new studio of red brick and generous proportion, his courage fled. He hung about the town for two days, but in the end, the chilly and inhospitable appearance of the studio defeated him. Then, weary, abysmally hungry, without a centime in his pocket, and the Reverend Pietersen's shoes wearing dangerously thin beneath him, he began the hundred and seventy kilometre walk back to the Borinage.

He arrived at the miner's cabin ill and despondent. There was no money or mail waiting for him. He went to bed. The miners' wives nursed him and gave him what tiny portions of food they could spare from the mouths of their husbands and children.

He had lost many pounds on the trip, the hollows were in his cheeks again, and fever ignited the bottomless pools of his green-black eyes. Sick as he was, his mind retained its clarity, and he knew that he had reached the point where a decision was imminent.

What was he to do with his life? Become a school teacher, book-seller, art dealer, mercantile clerk? Where was he to live? Etten, with his parents? Paris, with Theo? Amsterdam, with his uncles? Or just in the great void wherever chance might dump him down, working at whatever fortune dictated?

One day, when his strength had returned a little and he was sitting propped up in bed copying "Le Four dans les Landes" by Theodore Rousseau, and wondering how much longer he would have to indulge in this harmless little pastime of drawing, someone opened the door without knocking and walked in.

It was his brother Theo.

21

The passage of the years had improved Theo. Only twenty-three, he was already a successful art dealer in Paris, respected by his *confrères* and family. He knew and practised all the social amenities of dress, manners and conversation. He wore a good black coat, crossing high on his chest with satin piping on the broad lapels, a high stiff collar, and a white tie with a huge knot.

He had the tremendous Van Gogh forehead. His hair was dark brown, his features delicate, almost feminine. His eyes were soft and wistful and his face tapered in a beautiful oval.

Theo leaned against the door of the shack and gazed at Vincent in horror. He had just left Paris a few hours before. In his apartment there was lovely Louis Philippe furniture to sit upon, a wash bowl with towels and soap, curtains on the windows, rugs on the floor, a writing desk, bookcases, soft lamps and pleasant wallpaper. Vincent was lying on a dirty, bare mattress, covered by an old blanket. The walls and floor were of rough plank, the only furnishings a battered table and chair. He was unwashed and unkempt, his coarse, red beard splashed all over his face and neck.

"Well, Theo," said Vincent.

Theo crossed hastily and leaned over the bed. "Vincent, what in God's name is wrong? What have you done to yourself?"

"Nothing. I'm all right now. I was sick awhile."

"But this . . . this . . . hole! Surely you don't live here . . . this isn't your home?"

"Yes. What's the matter with it? I've been using it for a studio."

"Oh, Vincent!" He ran his hand over his brother's hair; the lump in his throat prevented him from speaking.

"It's good to have you here, Theo."

"Vincent, please tell me what has been the matter with you. Why have you been sick? What was it?"

Vincent told him about Courrieres.

"You've exhausted yourself, that's what. Have you been eating properly since you're back? Have you been taking care of yourself?"

"The miners' wives have been nursing me."

"Yes, but what have you been eating?" Theo looked around him. "Where do you keep your stores? I don't see any."

"The women bring me in a little something every day. Whatever they can spare; bread, coffee, a little cheese, or rabbit."

"But, Vincent, surely you know you can't get your strength back on bread and coffee? Why don't you buy yourself some eggs and vegetables and meat?"

"Those things cost money here in the Borinage, the same as anywhere else."

Theo sat down on the bed.

"Vincent, for the love of God, forgive me! I didn't know. I didn't understand."

"That's all right, boy, you did all you could. I'm getting along fine. In a few days I'll be up and about again."

Theo ran his hand across his eyes as though to clear away some misty cobweb. "No. I didn't realize. I thought that you . . . I didn't understand, Vincent, I just didn't understand."

"Oh, come. It's all right. How are things in Paris? Where are you bound for? Have you been to Etten?"

Theo jumped up. "Are there stores in this forsaken town? Can I buy things here?"

"Yes, there are places down the hill in Wasmes. But draw up that chair. I want to talk to you. Lord, Theo, it's been almost two years!"

Theo ran his fingers lightly over his brother's face and said, "First of all I'm going to load you full of the best food I can find in Belgium. You've been starved, that's what's the matter with you. And then I'm going to give you a dose of something for that fever and put you to sleep on a soft pillow.

It's a good thing I got here when I did. If I had only had the slightest idea . . . Don't move until I get back."

He ran out of the door. Vincent picked up his pencil, looked at "Le Four dans les Landes," and went on copying. In a half hour Theo was back, two small boys following him. He had two sheets, a pillow, bundles of pots and dishes and packages of food. He put Vincent between the cool, white sheets and made him lie down.

"Now how do you work this stove?" he asked, peeling off his beautiful coat and rolling up his sleeves.

"There's some paper and twigs. Light that first and then put in the coal."

Theo gazed at the *terril* and said, "Coal! Do you call this coal?"

"It's what we use. Here, let me show you how to work it."

He tried to get out of bed, but Theo was on him with a leap. "Lie down, you idiot!" he cried, "and don't move again or I shall be forced to thrash you."

Vincent grinned for the first time in months. The smile in his eyes almost put the fever to rout. Theo put two eggs in one of his new pots, and cut up some string beans in another. In a third he warmed some fresh milk, and held a flat toaster over the fire, with white bread on it. Vincent watched Theo hovering about the stove in his shirt-sleeves, and the sight of his brother close to him once again did him more good than any food.

At length the meal was ready. Theo drew up the table alongside the bed and spread a clean, white towel from his bag. He put a nice cut of butter into the beans, broke the two soft boiled eggs into a dish, and picked up a spoon.

"All right, boy," he said, "open your mouth. You're going to have a square meal for the first time in Heaven knows how long."

"Oh, come off, Theo," said Vincent, "I can feed myself."

Theo filled the spoon with egg and held it up for Vincent. "Open your mouth, young fellow," he said, "or I'll pour it in your eye."

When Vincent finished, he put his head back on the pillow with a deep sigh of contentment. "Food tastes good," he said. "I had forgotten."

"You're not going to forget again in a hurry."

"Now tell me, Theo, everything that's been happening. How are things at Goupils? I'm starved for news of the outside world."

"Then you'll have to stay starved for a little while longer. Here's something to put you to sleep. I want you to be quiet and give that food a chance to work."

"But, Theo, I don't want to sleep. I want to talk. I can sleep any time."

"Nobody asked you what you wanted. You're taking orders. Drink this down like a good fellow. And when you wake up, I have a nice steak and potatoes that will set you right on your feet."

Vincent slept until sundown, and awoke feeling greatly refreshed. Theo was sitting under one of the windows, looking at Vincent's drawings. Vincent watched him for a long time before he made a sound, a feeling of peace in his heart. When Theo saw that he was awake, he jumped up with a broad smile.

"Well! And how do you feel now? Better? You certainly were sleeping."

"What did you think of the sketches? Did you like any of them?"

"Wait until I put that steak on. I have the potatoes all peeled, ready to boil."

He attended to things at the stove and brought back a basin of warm water to the bedside. "Shall I use my razor, Vincent, or yours?"

"Can't I eat the steak without getting shaved?"

"No, sir. Nor without getting your neck and ears washed, and your hair neatly combed. Here, tuck this towel under your chin."

He gave Vincent a clean shave, washed him thoroughly, combed his hair, and put him into one of the new shirts he was carrying in his bag.

"There!" he exclaimed, backing away to survey the job he had done. "You look like a Van Gogh now."

"Theo, quick! The steak's burning!"

Theo set the table and put out the meal of boiled potatoes and butter, a thick, tender steak, and milk.

"My word, Theo, you don't expect me to eat that whole steak?"

"I certainly do not. Half of it belongs to me. Well, let's pitch in. All we would have to do would be to close our eyes, and we could imagine we were home at Etten."

After dinner Theo loaded Vincent's pipe with some tobacco from Paris. "Smoke up," he said. "I oughtn't to allow you to do this, but I guess real tobacco will do you more good than harm."

Vincent smoked in contentment, occasionally rubbing the warm, slightly moist stem of his pipe against his smooth cheek. Theo looked over the bowl of his pipe, through the rough boards, and all the way back to his childhood in the Brabant. Vincent had always been the most important person in the world to him, far more important than either his mother or father. Vincent had made his childhood sweet and good. He had forgotten that the last year in Paris; he ought never to forget it again. Life without Vincent was somehow incomplete for him. He felt that he was a part of Vincent, and that Vincent was a part of him. Together they had always understood the world; alone it somehow baffled him. Together they had found the meaning and purpose of life, and valued it; alone he often wondered why he was working and being successful. He had to have Vincent to make his life full. And Vincent needed him, for he was really only a child. He had to be taken out of this hole, put on his feet again. He had to be made to realize that he had been wasting himself, and be jerked into some rejuvenating action.

"Vincent," he said, "I'm going to give you a day or two to get your strength back, and then I'm taking you home to Etten."

Vincent puffed in silence for many minutes. He knew that this whole affair had to be thrashed out, and that unfortunately they had no medium but words. Well, he would have to make Theo understand. After that, everything would come all right.

"Theo, what would be the good of my going home? Involuntarily I have become in the family a kind of impossible and suspect person, at least somebody whom they do not trust. That's why I believe the most reasonable thing for me to do is to keep at a distance, so that I cease to exist for them.

"I am a man of passions, capable of doing foolish things. I speak and act too quickly when it would have been better to wait patiently. This being the case, must I consider myself a dangerous man, incapable of doing anything? I do not think so. But the question is to try to put these selfsame passions to a good use. For instance, I have an irresistible passion for pictures and books, and I want continually to instruct myself, just as I want to eat my bread. You certainly will understand that."

"I do understand, Vincent. But looking at pictures and reading books at your age is only a diversion. They have nothing to do with the main business of life. It is almost five years now that you have been without employment, wandering here and there. And during that time you have been going down hill, deteriorating."

Vincent poured some tobacco in his hand, rubbed it between his palms to make it moist, and stuffed it into his pipe. Then he forgot to light it.

"It is true," he said, "that now and then I have earned my crust of bread, now and then a friend has given it to me in charity. It is true that I have lost the confidence of many, that my financial affairs are in a sad state, and that my future is only too sombre. But is that necessarily deterioration? I must continue, Theo, on the path I have taken. If I don't study, if I don't go on seeking any longer, then I am lost."

"You're evidently trying to tell me something, old boy, but I'm blessed if I can gather what it is."

Vincent lit his pipe, sucking in the flame of the match. "I remember the time," he said, "when we walked together near the old mill at Ryswyk; then we agreed in many things."

"But, Vincent, you have changed so much."

"That is not quite true. My life was less difficult then; but as to my way of looking at things and thinking, that has not changed at all."

"For your sake I would like to believe that."

"Theo, you must not think that I disavow things. I am faithful in my unfaithfulness, and my only anxiety is, how can I be of use in the world? Cannot I serve some purpose and be of some good?"

Theo rose, struggled with the kerosene lamp, and finally lit it. He poured out a glass of milk. "Here, drink this. I don't want you to exhaust yourself."

Vincent drank it down too quickly, almost choking on its richness. Without even waiting to wipe the cream off his eager lips, he went on. "Our inward thoughts, do they ever show outwardly? There may be a great fire in our soul and no one comes to warm himself by it. The passers-by see only a bit of smoke coming through the chimney and continue on their way. Now look here, what must be done? Mustn't one tend that inward fire, have salt in oneself, wait patiently for the hour when somebody will come and sit near it?"

Theo got up and sat on the bed. "Do you know the picture that just flashed into my mind?" he asked.

"No."

"The old mill at Ryswyk."

"It was a nice old mill, wasn't it?"

"Yes."

"And our childhood was nice, too."

"You made my childhood pleasant, Vincent. My first memories are always of you."

There was a long silence.

"Vincent, I do hope you realize that the accusations I have made come from the family and not from me. They persuaded me to come here and see if I couldn't shame you into returning to Holland and a job."

"It's all right, Theo, the words they say are perfectly true. It's just that they don't understand my motives and don't see the present in relation to my whole life. But if I have come down in the world, you, on the contrary, have risen. If I have lost sympathies, you have gained them. That makes me very happy. I say it in all sincerity, and it will always be so. But I should be very glad if it were possible for you to see in me something else than an idle man of the worst type."

"Let's forget those words. If I have not written to you all year, it was through negligence, not disapproval. I've believed in you and had implicit faith in you since the earliest days when I used to take your hand through the high, grass fields at Zundert. And I haven't any less faith now. I need only to be near you to know that everything you do will eventually come right."

Vincent smiled, a broad, happy, Brabantine smile. "That was good of you, Theo."

Theo suddenly became the man of action.

"See here, Vincent, let's settle this thing right here and now. I have a suspicion that behind all these abstractions you've been dealing in, there is something you want to do, something that you feel is ultimately right for you and that will finally bring you to happiness and success. Well, old boy, just name it. Goupil and Company have raised my wages twice during the past year and a half, and I have more money than I know what to do with. Now if there is something you want to do, and you will need help right at first, simply tell me that you have at last found your real life work, and we'll form a partnership. You'll supply the work and I'll supply the funds. After we've put you on a paying basis, you can return the investment with dividends. Now confess, haven't you something in mind? Hadn't you decided long ago that there was something you wanted to do with the rest of your life?"

Vincent looked over at the pile of sketches Theo had been studying under the window. A grin of amazement, incredulity, and at last awareness spread across his face. His eyes opened wide, his mouth opened, his whole personality seemed to burst open like a *tournesol* in the sun.

"Well I'll be blessed!" he murmured. "That's what I've been trying to say all along, and I didn't know it."

Theo's eyes followed his to the sketches. "I thought so," he said.

Vincent was quivering with excitement and joy; he seemed to have suddenly awakened from some profound sleep.

"Theo, you knew it before I did! I wouldn't let myself think about it. I was afraid. Of course there's something I must do. It's the thing I've pointed towards all my life, and I never suspected it. I felt a tremendous urge to sketch, to put down what I saw on paper while I was studying in Amsterdam and Brussels. But I wouldn't allow myself to. I was afraid it would interfere with my real work. *My real work!* How blind I was. Something has been trying to push itself out of me all these years and I wouldn't let it. I beat it back. Here I am, twenty-seven, with nothing accomplished. What an idiot, an utterly blind and stupid idiot I've been."

"It doesn't matter, Vincent. With your strength and determination you'll be able to accomplish a thousand times as much as any other beginner. And you've got a long life ahead of you."

"I have ten years anyway. I'll be able to turn out some good work in that time."

"Of course you will! And you can live wherever you like; Paris, Brussels, Amsterdam, The Hague. Just take your choice and I'll send you money to live on each month. I don't care if it takes you years, Vincent, I'll never give up hope if you don't."

"Oh, Theo, all these bitter months I've been working toward something, trying to dig the real purpose and meaning out of my life, and I didn't know it! But now that I do know, I'll never be discouraged again. Theo, do you realize what it means? After all these wasted years I HAVE FOUND MYSELF AT LAST! I'm going to be an artist. Of course I'm going to be an artist. I've got to be. That's why I failed at all my other jobs, because I wasn't meant for them. But now I've got the one thing that can never fail. Oh, Theo, the prison is open at last, and you're the one who unbarred the gates!"

"Nothing can ever estrange us! We're together again, aren't we, Vincent?"

"Yes, Theo, for life."

"Now, just you rest and get well. In a few days, when you're better, I'll take you back to Holland, or Paris, or wherever you want to go."

Vincent sprang out of bed with a leap that carried him half-way across the cabin.

"In a few days, hell!" he cried. "We're going right now. There's a train for Brussels at nine o'clock."

He began pulling on his clothes with furious speed.

"But Vincent, you can't travel tonight. You're sick."

"Sick! That's ancient history. I never felt better in my life. Come on, Theo, boy, we've got about ten minutes to make that railway station. Throw those nice white sheets into your bag and let's be on our way!"

BOOK TWO

ETTEN

1

THEO AND VINCENT spent a day together in Brussels, and then Theo returned to Paris. Spring was coming, the Brabantine country-side called, and home seemed like a magic haven. Vincent bought himself a workman's suit of rough black velvet, of the material known as *veloutine,* some unbleached, muslin coloured Ingres paper for sketching, and caught the next train home to Etten and the family parsonage.

Anna Cornelia disapproved of Vincent's life because she felt it brought him more pain than happiness. Theodorus disapproved on objective grounds; if Vincent had been someone else's son, he would have had nothing to do with him. He knew that God did not like Vincent's evil way of living, but he had a suspicion that He would like even less the casting off of a son by his father.

Vincent noticed that his father's hair had grown whiter and that the right lid drooped still lower over his eye. Age seemed to be shrinking his features; he grew no beard to make up for the loss, and the expression on his face had changed from "This is me," to "Is this me?"

In his mother Vincent found greater strength and attractiveness than before. Age built her up rather than tore her down. The smile engraved in curved lines between her nostrils and chin forgave one's errors before they were committed; the broadness and wideness and goodness of her face were an eternal "Yea" to the beauty of life.

For several days the family stuffed Vincent with revivifying food and affection, ignoring the fact that he had no fortune and no future. He walked on the heath among the cottages with the thatched roofs, watched the wood-cutters who were busy on a piece of ground where a pine wood had been cut down, strolled leisurely on the road to Roozendaal, past the Protestant barn with the mill right opposite in the meadow and the elm trees in the church-yard. The Borinage receded, his health and strength came back with a rush, and within a short time he was eager to begin his work.

One rainy morning Anna Cornelia descended to the kitchen at an early hour to find the stove already glowing red, and Vincent sitting before it, his feet propped up on the grate, with a half finished copy after "Les Heures de la Journée" in his lap.

"Why son, good morning," she exclaimed.

"Good morning, Mother." He kissed her broad cheek fondly.

"What makes you get up so early, Vincent?"

"Well, Mother, I wanted to work."

"Work?"

Anna Cornelia looked at the sketch in his lap, then at the glowing stove. "Oh, you mean get the fire started. But you mustn't get up for that."

"No, I mean my drawing."

Once again Anna Cornelia glanced over her son's shoulder at the copy. It looked to her like a child's efforts to reproduce something from a magazine during a play hour.

"You are going to work at drawing things, Vincent?"

"Yes."

He explained his decision and Theo's efforts to help him. Contrary to his expectations, Anna Cornelia was pleased. She walked quickly into the living room and returned with a letter.

"Our cousin, Anton Mauve, is a painter," she said, "and he makes a great deal of money. I had this letter from my sister only the other day—Mauve married her daughter Jet, you know—and she writes that Mijnheer Tersteeg at Goupils sells everything Anton does for five and six hundred guilders."

"Yes, Mauve is becoming one of our important painters."

"How long does it take to make one of those pictures, Vincent?"

"That depends, Mother. Some canvases take a few days, some a few years."

"A few years! Oh, my!"

Anna Cornelia thought for a moment and then asked, "Can you draw people so that it looks like them?"

"Well, I don't know. I have some sketches upstairs. I'll show them to you."

When he returned, his mother had on her white kitchen cap and was placing kettles of water on the broad stove. The shining blue and white tiles of the wall gave the room a cheerful air.

"I'm fixing your favourite cheese bake, Vincent," said Anna Cornelia. "Do you remember?"

"Do I remember! Oh, Mother!"

He threw his arm about her shoulder roughly. She looked up at him with a wistful smile. Vincent was her eldest child and her favourite; his unhappiness was the only thing in life that grieved her.

"Is it good to be home with your mother?" she asked.

He pinched her fresh, wrinkled cheek playfully.

"Yes, sweetheart," he answered.

She took the sketches of the Borains and studied them carefully.

"But Vincent, what has happened to their faces?"

"Nothing. Why?"

"They haven't any."

"I know. I was only interested in the figure."

"But you can draw people's faces, can't you? I'm sure lots of women here in Etten would like to have their portraits painted. There's a living in that."

"Yes, I suppose so. But I'll have to wait until my drawing is right."

His mother was breaking eggs into a pan of sour cheese she had strained the day before. She paused with half the shell of an egg in each hand and turned from the stove.

"You mean you have to make your drawing right so the portraits will be good enough to sell?"

"No," replied Vincent, sketching rapidly with his pencil, "I have to make my drawing right so that my drawing will be right."

Anna Cornelia stirred the yolks into the white cheese thoughtfully and then said, "I'm afraid I don't understand that, son."

"Neither do I," said Vincent, "but anyway it's so."

Over the fluffy golden cheese bake at breakfast, Anna Cornelia broke the news to her husband. They had been doing a great deal of uneasy speculating about Vincent in private.

"Is there a future in that, Vincent?" asked his father. "Will you be able to support yourself?"

"Not just at first. Theo is going to help me until I get on my feet. After my drawing becomes accurate, I should be able to make money. Draftsmen in London and Paris earn from ten to fifteen francs a day, and the men who do illustrations for the magazines make good money."

Theodorus was relieved to find that Vincent had something—anything in mind, and was not going to drift idly as he had all these years.

"I hope, if you begin this work, Vincent, you will keep on with it. You'll never get anywhere changing from pillar to post."

"This is the end, Father. I'll not change again."

2

After a time the rain stopped and warm weather set in. Vincent took his drawing material and easel out of doors and began exploring the country. He liked best to work on the heath, near Seppe, though he often went to a big swamp in the Passievaart to draw the water lilies. Etten was a small, closely knit town and its people looked at him askance. The black velvet suit was the first of its kind to be seen in the village; never before had the natives known a full grown man to spend his days in the open fields with nothing but pencil and drawing paper. He was courteous to his father's parishioners in a rough, disinterested sort of way, but they wanted to have nothing to do with him. In this tiny, provincial settlement he was a freak, a sport; everything about him was bizarre; his clothes, his manner, his red beard, his history, the fact that he did not work, his incessant sitting in the fields and looking at things. They mistrusted and were afraid of him because he was different, even though he did them no harm and asked only to be let alone. Vincent had no idea the people did not like him.

He was doing a large study of the pine wood that was being cut down, concentrating on a lone tree at the border of a creek. One of the labourers who was clearing away would come and watch him draw, looking over his shoulder with a vacant grin, and occasionally breaking into a loud snigger. The sketch took Vincent some time. Each day the peasant's guffaws grew louder. Vincent decided to find out just what amused the man.

"You find it funny," he asked politely, "that I draw a tree?"

The man roared. "Yes, yes, it is so funny. You must be *fou!*"

Vincent deliberated for a moment and then asked, "Would I be *fou* if I planted a tree?"

The peasant sobered up instantly. "Oh, no, certainly not."

"Would I be *fou* if I tended the tree and took care of it?"

"No, of course not."

"Would I be *fou* if I picked the fruit off?"

"*Vous vous moquez de moi!*"

"Well then, would I be *fou* if I chopped the tree down, just as they have done here?"

"Oh, no, trees must be cut down."

"Then I can plant a tree, tend it, pick it, and cut it down, but if I draw one I am *fou*. Is that right?"

The peasant broke into his broad grin again. "Yes, you must be *fou* to sit there like that. All the village says so."

In the evenings he sat with the rest of the family in the living room. Around the immense wooden table the entire family gathered, sewing, reading, writing letters. His young brother Cor was a quiet child who rarely spoke. Of his sisters, Anna had married and moved away. Elizabeth disliked him so thoroughly that she did her best to pretend he had never come home. Willemien was sympathetic; she posed for Vincent whenever he asked her, and gave him an uncritical friendship. But their relationship was tied to earthly things.

Vincent worked at the table too, comfortable in the light of the huge yellow lamp which sat impartially in the centre. He copied his exercises or the sketches he had made in the fields that day. Theodorus watched him do one figure over a dozen times and always throw away the finished product with dissatisfaction; at last the dominie could contain himself no longer.

"Vincent," he said, leaning across the broad expanse of table, "don't you ever get them right?"

"No," replied Vincent.

"Then I wonder if you aren't making a mistake?"

"I'm making a great many, Father. Which one do you refer to?"

"It seems to me that if you had any talent, if you were really cut out to be an artist, those sketches would come right the first time."

Vincent glanced down at his study of a peasant kneeling before a bag in which he was putting potatoes. He could not seem to catch the line of the beggar's arm.

"Perhaps so, Father."

"What I mean is, you shouldn't have to draw those things a hundred times without ever getting them right. If you had any natural ability, they would come to you without all this trying."

"Nature always begins by resisting the artist, Father," he said, without putting down his pencil, "but if I really take my work seriously, I won't allow myself to be led astray by that resistance. On the contrary, it will be a stimulus the more to fight for victory."

"I don't see that," said Theodorus. "Good can never grow out of evil, nor can good work grow out of bad."

"Perhaps not in theology. But it can in art. In fact, it must."

"You're wrong, my boy. An artist's work is either good or bad. And if it's bad, he's no artist. He ought to have found that out for himself at the beginning and not have wasted all his time and effort."

"But what if he has a happy life turning out bad art? What then?"

Theodorus searched his theological training, but he could find no answer to this question.

"No," said Vincent, rubbing out the bag of potatoes and leaving the man's left arm suspended stiffly in mid-air. "At bottom, nature and a true artist agree. It may take years of struggling and wrestling before she becomes docile and yielding, but in the end, the bad, very bad work will turn into good work and justify itself."

"What if at the end the work remains poor? You've been drawing that fellow kneeling down for days and he's still wrong. Suppose you go on drawing him for years and years and he keeps on being wrong?"

Vincent shrugged. "The artist takes that gamble, Father."

"Are the rewards worth the gamble?"

"Rewards? What rewards?"

"The money one gets. And the position in society."

Vincent looked up from his paper for the first time and examined his father's face, feature by feature, as though he were looking at some strange being.

"I thought we were discussing good and bad art," he said.

3

He worked night and day at his craft. If he thought of the future at all, it was only to bring closer in fancy the time when he would no longer be a burden on Theo, and when the finished product of his work would approximate perfection. When he was too tired to sketch, he read. When he was too tired to do either, he went to sleep.

Theo sent Ingres paper, pictures from a veterinary school of the anatomy of a horse, a cow, and a sheep, some Holbeins in "The Models from the Artists," drawing pencils, quill pens, the reproduction of a human skeleton, sepia, as many francs as he could spare, and the admonition to work hard and not become a mediocre artist. To this advice Vincent replied, "I shall do what I can, but mediocre in its simple signification I do not despise at all. And one certainly does not rise above that mark by despising what is mediocre. But what you say about hard work is entirely right. 'Not a day without a line!' as Gavarni warns us."

More and more he had the feeling that the drawing of the figure was a good thing, and that indirectly it had a good influence on the drawing of landscape. If he drew a willow tree as if it were a living being—and it really was so after all—then the surroundings followed in due course, if only he concentrated all his attention on that same tree and did not give up until he had brought some life into it. He loved landscape very much, but ten times more he loved those studies from life, sometimes of startling realism, which had been drawn so well by Gavarni, Daumier, Doré, De Groux and Felicien Rops. By working on types of labourers, he hoped eventually to be able to do illustrations for the magazines and newspapers; he wanted to support himself completely during the long hard years in which he would perfect his technique and go on to higher forms of expression.

One time his father, who thought he read for entertainment, said, "Vincent, you are always talking about how hard you must work. Then why do you waste your time on all those silly French books?"

Vincent placed a marking finger in "Le Père Goriot" and looked up. He kept hoping that some day his father might understand him when he spoke of serious things.

"You see," he said slowly, "not only does the drawing of figures and scenes from life demand a knowledge of the handicraft of drawing, but it demands also profound studies of literature."

"I must say I don't gather that. If I want to preach a good sermon, I don't spend my time in the kitchen watching your mother pickle tongues."

"Speaking of tongues," said Anna Cornelia, "those fresh ones ought to be ready by tomorrow breakfast."

Vincent did not bother to upset the analogy.

"I can't draw a figure," he said, "without knowing all about the bones and muscles and tendons that are inside it. And I can't draw a head without knowing what goes on in that person's brain and soul. In order to paint life one must understand not only anatomy, but what people feel and think about the world they live in. The painter who knows his own craft and nothing else will turn out to be a very superficial artist."

"Ah, Vincent," said his father, sighing deeply, "I'm afraid you're going to develop into a theorist!"

Vincent returned to "Le Père Goriot."

Another time he became greatly excited at the arrival of some books by Cassagne which Theo sent to correct the trouble with his perspective. Vincent ran through them lovingly and showed them to Willemien.

"I know of no better remedy for my ailment," he said to her. "If I am cured of it, I shall have these books to thank."

Willemien smiled at him with her mother's clear eyes.

"Do you mean to tell me, Vincent," asked Theodorus, who was distrustful of everything that came from Paris, "that you can learn to draw correctly by reading ideas about art in books?"

"Yes."

"How very odd."

"That is to say, if I put into practice the theory they contain. However, practice is a thing one cannot buy at the same time with the books. If that were so there would be a larger sale of them."

The days passed busily and happily into summer, and now it was the heat that kept him off the heath, and not the rain. He sketched his sister Willemien in front of the sewing machine, copied for a third time the exercises after Bargue, drew five times over a man with a spade, *Un Bêcheur,* in different positions, twice a sower, twice a girl with a broom. Then a woman with a white cap who was peeling potatoes, a shepherd leaning on his staff, and finally an old, sick farmer sitting on a chair near the hearth, with his head in his hands and his elbows on his knees. Diggers, sowers, ploughers, male and female, that was what he felt he must draw continually; he must observe and put down everything that belonged to country life. He did not stand altogether helpless before nature any longer; that gave him an exultation unlike any he had ever known before.

The townspeople still thought him queer and kept him at arm's length. Although his mother and Willemien—and even his father in his own way—heaped kindness and affection upon him, in those innermost recesses to which no one in Etten or the parsonage could ever possibly penetrate, he was frightfully alone.

In time the peasants grew to like and trust him. He found in their simplicity something akin to the soil in which they were hoeing or digging. He tried to put that into his sketches. Often his family could not tell where the peasant ended and the earth began. Vincent did not know how his drawings came out that way but he felt they were right, just so.

"There should be no strict line between," he said to his mother who asked about this one evening. "They are really two kinds of earth, pouring into each other, belonging to each other; two forms of the same matter, indistinguishable in essence."

His mother decided that since he had no wife, she had better take him in hand and help him become successful.

"Vincent," she said one morning, "I want you to be back in the house by two o'clock. Will you do that for me?"

"Yes, Mother. What is it you wish?"

"I want you to come with me to a tea party."

Vincent was aghast. "But Mother, I can't be wasting my time that way!"

"Why will it be wasting your time, son?"

"Because there's nothing to paint at a tea party."

"That's just where you're wrong. All the important women of Etten will be there."

Vincent's eyes went to the kitchen door. He almost made a bolt for it. After an effort he controlled himself and tried to explain; the words came slowly and painfully.

"What I mean, Mother," he said, "is that the women at a tea party have no character."

"Nonsense! They all have splendid characters. Never a word has been breathed against one of them."

"No, dear," he said, "of course not. What I mean is, they all look alike. The pattern of their lives has fitted them to a specific mould."

"Well, I'm sure I can tell one from the other without any difficulty."

"Yes, sweetheart, but you see, they've all had such easy lives that they haven't anything interesting carved into their faces."

"I'm afraid I don't understand, son. You draw every labourer and peasant you see in the fields."

"Ah, yes."

"But what good will that ever do you? They're all poor, and they can't buy anything. The women of the town can pay to have their portraits painted."

Vincent put his arm about her and cupped her chin in his hand. The blue eyes were so clear, so deep, so kind and loving. Why did they not understand?

"Dear," he said quietly, "I beg you to have a little faith in me. I know how this job has to be done, and if you will only give me time I will succeed. If I keep working hard on the things that look useless to you now, eventually I will be able to sell my drawings and make a good living."

Anna Cornelia wanted to understand just as desperately as Vincent wished to be understood. She brushed her lips against her boy's rough, red beard and in her mind travelled back to that day of apprehension and fear when this strong, hard man body she held in her arms had been torn from her in the Zundert parsonage. Her first baby had been still-born, and when Vincent announced himself by yelling lustily and long, her thankfulness and joy knew no bounds. In her love for him there was always mingled a touch of sorrow for the first child that had never opened its eyes, and of gratitude for all the others that had followed.

"You're a good boy, Vincent," she said. "Go your own way. You know what is best. I only wanted to help you."

Instead of working in the fields that day, Vincent asked Piet Kaufman, the gardener, to pose for him. It took a little persuasion, but Piet finally consented.

"After dinner," he agreed. "In the garden."

When Vincent went out later he found Piet carefully dressed in his stiff Sunday suit, hands and face scrubbed. "One moment," he cried excitedly, "until I get a stool. Then I'll be ready."

He placed a little stool beneath him and sat down, rigid as a pole, all set to have his daguerreotype taken. Vincent had to laugh in spite of himself.

"But, Piet," he said, "I can't draw you in those clothes."

Piet looked down at his suit in astonishment. "What's the matter with them?" he demanded. "They're new. I only wore them a few Sunday mornings to meeting."

"I know," said Vincent. "That's why. I want to sketch you in your old working clothes, bending over a rake. That's the way your lines come through. I want to see your elbows and knees and omoplate. I can't see anything now except your suit."

It was the word omoplate that decided Piet.

"My old clothes are dirty and patched. If you want me to pose, you'll have to do me as I am."

And so Vincent went back to the fields and did the diggers bending over the soil. The summer passed and he realized that for the moment at least he had exhausted the possibilities of his own instruction. Once again he had the keen desire to enter into relation with some artist and continue his study in a good studio. He began to feel it absolutely necessary to have access to things well done, to see artists at work, for then he could tell what he lacked, and learn how to do better.

Theo wrote, inviting him to come to Paris, but Vincent understood that he was not yet ripe for that great venture. His work was still too raw, too clumsy, too amateurish. The Hague was only a few hours away, and there he could get help from his friend Mijnheer Tersteeg, manager of Goupil and Company, and from his cousin, Anton Mauve. Perhaps it would be better for him to settle in The Hague during the next stage of his slow apprenticeship. He wrote, asking Theo's advice, and his brother replied with the railroad fare.

Before moving permanently, Vincent wished to find out whether Tersteeg and Mauve would be friendly and help him; if not, he would have to go elsewhere. He carefully wrapped up all his sketches—with a change of linen this time—and set out for the capital of his country in the true tradition of all young provincial artists.

4

Mijnheer Herman Gijsbert Tersteeg was the founder of The Hague school of painting, and the most important art dealer in Holland. People from all over the country came to him for advice on what pictures they should buy; if Mijnheer Tersteeg said a canvas was good, his opinion was considered as definitive.

When Mijnheer Tersteeg succeeded Uncle Vincent Van Gogh as manager of Goupil and Company, the rising young Dutch artists were scattered all over the country. Anton Mauve and Josef lived in Amsterdam, Jacob and Willem Maris were in the provinces, and Josef Israels, Johannes Bosboom and Blommers were wandering about from town to town without any permanent headquarters. Tersteeg wrote to each one in turn and said,

"Why should we not all join forces here in The Hague and make it the capital of Dutch art? We can help each other, we can learn from each other, and by our concerted effort we can bring Dutch painting back to the world eminence it enjoyed in the age of Frans Hals and Rembrandt."

The response of the painters was slow, but in the course of the years every young artist whom Tersteeg picked out as having ability settled in The Hague. There was at this time absolutely no demand for their canvases. Tersteeg had chosen them, not because they were selling, but because he saw in their work the possibility of future greatness. He bought canvases from Israels, from Mauve, and Jacob Maris six years before he could persuade the public to see anything in them.

Year after year he went on buying patiently the work of Bosboom, Maris and Neuhuys, turning their canvases to the wall at the rear of his shop. He knew that these had to be supported while they struggled toward their maturity; if the Dutch public was too blind to recognize its own native genius, he, the critic and dealer, would see that these fine young men were not lost to the world forever through poverty, neglect, and discouragement. He bought their canvases, criticized their work, brought them into contact with their fellow painters, and encouraged them through the hard years. Day after day he fought to educate the Dutch public, to open its eyes to the beauty and expression of its own men.

By the time Vincent went to visit him at The Hague, he had succeeded. Mauve, Neuhuys, Israels, Jacob and Willem Maris, Bosboom, and Blommers not only had everything they painted sold at high prices by Goupil and Company, but they were in a fair way to becoming classics.

Mijnheer Tersteeg was a handsome man in the Dutch tradition; he had strong, prominent features, a high forehead, brown hair combed straight back, a flat, beautifully rounded, full-face beard, and eyes as pellucid as a Dutch lake sky. He wore a full black jacket in the Prince Albert manner, wide, striped trousers that fell over his shoes, a high, single collar and ready made, black, bow ties that his wife attached for him every morning.

Tersteeg had always liked Vincent, and when the latter was transferred to the London branch of Goupil and Company, he had penned a warm note of commendation about the boy to the English manager. He had sent Vincent the "Exercises au Fusain" to the Borinage and had included the "Cours de Dessin Bargue" because he knew it would be helpful. While it was true that Goupil and Company in The Hague was owned by Uncle Vincent Van Gogh, Vincent had every reason to believe that Tersteeg was fond of him for his own sake. Tersteeg was not the man to cater.

Goupil and Company was located at number 20, Plaats, the most aristocratic and expensive square in all The Hague. Only a stone's throw away was the S'Graven Haghe castle which had been the beginning of the city, with its medieval courtyard, the moat that had been turned into a beautiful lake, and at the far end the Mauritshuis where hung Rubens, Hals, Rembrandt, and all the little Dutch masters.

Vincent walked from the station along the narrow, winding, busy Wagenstraat, cut through the Plein and Binnenhof of the castle, and found himself in the Plaats. It was eight years since he had last walked out of Goupils; the tide of suffering he had gone through in that short space of time welled over his body and mind, stunning him.

Eight years ago. Everybody had liked him and been proud of him. He had been his Uncle Vincent's favourite nephew. It was common knowledge that he would not only be his uncle's successor but his heir as well. He could have been a powerful and wealthy man by now, respected and admired by everyone he met. And in time he would have owned the most important string of art galleries in Europe.

What had happened to him?

He did not take the time to answer the question, but crossed the Plaats and entered Goupil and Company. The place was beautifully decorated; he had forgotten. He suddenly felt cheap and shoddy in his workingman's suit of rough black velvet. The street level of the gallery was a long salon hung in rich beige drapes; three steps above that was a smaller salon with a glass roof, and to the rear of that, a few steps higher still, a tiny, intimate exhibition room for the initiate. There was a broad staircase leading to the second floor where Tersteeg had his office and living quarters. The walls going up were pyramided with pictures.

The gallery smacked of great wealth and culture. The clerks were well groomed men with polished manners. The canvases on the walls were hung in expensive frames, set against costly hangings. Thick, soft rugs sank under Vincent's feet and the chairs, set so modestly in the corners, he remembered as priceless antiques. He thought of his drawings of the tattered miners coming out of the shaft, of their wives bent over the *terril*, of the diggers and sowers of the Brabant. He wondered if his simple drawings of poor, humble people would ever be sold in this great palace of art.

It did not seem very likely.

He stood gazing in awkward admiration at a sheep head by Mauve. The clerks who were chatting softly behind a table of etchings took one look at his clothes and posture and did not even bother to ask if there was something he wished. Tersteeg, who had been in the intimate gallery arranging an exhibition, came down the steps into the main salon. Vincent did not see him.

Tersteeg stopped at the bottom of the few steps and studied his former clerk. He took in the short cropped hair, the red stubble on his face, the peasant's boots, the workingman's coat buttoned up around his neck with no necktie concealed beneath it, the clumsy bundle he was carrying under his arm. There was something so altogether *gauche* about Vincent; it showed up cruelly, in high relief in this elegant gallery.

"Well, Vincent," said Tersteeg, walking noiselessly across the soft rug. "I see you are admiring our canvases."

Vincent turned. "Yes, they are fine, aren't they? How are you, Mijnheer Tersteeg? I bring you compliments from my mother and father."

The two men shook hands across the unbridgeable chasm of eight years.

"You are looking very well, Mijnheer. Even better than when I last saw you."

"Ah, yes, living agrees with me, Vincent. It keeps me young. Won't you come up to my office?"

Vincent followed him up the broad staircase, stumbling all over himself because he could not tear his eyes from the paintings on the wall. It was the first time he had seen good work since that brief hour in Brussels with Theo. He was in a daze. Tersteeg opened the door of his office and bowed Vincent in.

"Will you sit down, Vincent?" he asked.

Vincent had been gawking at a canvas by Weissenbruch, whose work he had never seen before. He sat down, dropped his bundle, picked it up again, and then crossed to Tersteeg's highly polished desk.

"I've brought back the books you so kindly lent me, Mijnheer Tersteeg."

He unwrapped his bundle, pushed a shirt and pair of socks to one side, took out the series of "Exercises au Fusain," and laid them on the table.

"I worked on the drawings very hard, and you have done me a great service by lending them to me."

"Show me your copies," said Tersteeg, getting to the point.

Vincent shuffled about in the pile of papers and extricated the first series he had drawn in the Borinage. Tersteeg maintained a stony silence. Vincent then quickly showed the second copies he had made when he settled at Etten. This group elicited an occasional "Hummmm" but nothing more. Vincent then showed the third copies, the ones he had finished shortly before leaving. Tersteeg was interested.

"That's a good line," he said once. "I like the shading," he contributed another time. "You almost got that!"

"I felt it wasn't bad, myself," said Vincent.

He finished the pile and turned to Tersteeg for judgement.

"Yes, Vincent," said the older man, laying his long, thin hands out flat on the desk, with the fingers tapering upward, "you have made a little progress. Not much, but a little. I was afraid when I looked at your first copies . . . Your work shows at least that you have been struggling."

"Is that all? Just struggle? No ability?"

He knew he shouldn't have asked that question, but he could not keep it down.

"Isn't it too early for us to speak of that, Vincent?"

"Perhaps so. I've brought some of my original sketches along. Would you care to see them?"

"I should be delighted."

Vincent laid out some of his sketches of the miners and peasants. Immediately that awful silence fell, the silence famous all over Holland for having broken the indisputable news to hundreds of young artists that their work was bad. Tersteeg looked over the entire lot without even a "Hummmm" escaping his lips. Vincent felt sick. Tersteeg sat back, looked out the window and over the Plaats at the swans in the lake. Vincent knew from experience that if he did not speak first, the silence would go on forever.

"Don't you see any improvement at all, Mijnheer Tersteeg?" he asked. "Don't you think my Brabant sketches better than the ones from the Borinage."

"Well," replied Tersteeg, turning back from the view, "they are better. But they are not good. There is something fundamentally wrong with them. Just what it is, I can't say offhand. I think you had better keep to your copying for a time. You're not ready to do original work yet. You must get a better grasp of elementals before you turn to life."

"I would like to come to The Hague to study. Do you think that a good idea, Mijnheer?"

Tersteeg did not wish to assume any obligations toward Vincent. The whole situation looked very peculiar to him.

"The Hague is a nice place," he said. "We have good galleries and a number of young painters. But whether it is any better than Antwerp, Paris, or Brussels, I'm sure I don't know."

Vincent left, not altogether discouraged. Tersteeg had seen some progress, and his was the most critical eye in all Holland. At least he was not standing still. He knew that his sketches from life were not all that they should have been, but he was confident that if he worked hard and long they would come right in the end.

5

The Hague is perhaps the cleanest and most well-bred city in all Europe. It is, in the true Holland manner, simple, austere and beautiful. The immaculate streets are lined with full-bosomed trees, the houses are of neat and fastidious brick, with tiny, lovingly kept gardens of roses and geraniums in front. There are no slums, poverty stricken districts, or careless eyesores; everything is kept up with that efficient asceticism of the Dutch.

Many years before, The Hague had adopted the stork as its official emblem. The population had grown by leaps and bounds ever since.

Vincent waited until the following day before calling on Mauve at his home Uileboomen 198. Mauve's mother-in-law was a Carbentus, a sister of Anna Cornelia, and since family ties were strong in those circles, he received Vincent warmly.

Mauve was a powerfully built man with sloping but tremendous shoulders and a large chest. His head, like that of Tersteeg and most of the Van Gogh family, was a more important factor in his appearance than the features of his face. He had luminous eyes, somewhat sentimental, a strong, straight bridged nose springing bonily from his brow without any declivity, a high, square forehead, flat ears, and salt-grey beard which concealed the perfect oval of his face. His hair was combed on the extreme right side, a great swash of it lying flat across the skull and parallel to his forehead.

Mauve was a man full of an energy which he did not dissipate. He painted, and when he got tired doing that he went on painting, and when that fatigued him he painted some more. By that time he would be refreshed and could go back to his painting again.

"Jet isn't home, Vincent," said Mauve. "Shall we go out to the atelier? I think we'll be more comfortable there."

"Yes, let's." He was eager to see the studio.

Mauve led him out to his large wooden atelier in the garden. The entrance was on the side near the house, but some little distance from it. The garden was walled in by hedges, giving Mauve complete isolation for his work.

A delicious smell of tobacco smoke, old pipes, and varnish greeted Vincent as he stepped in. The atelier was quite large, with pictures on easels standing about on a thick Deventer rug. The walls were warm with studies; in one corner was an antique table, and before it a small Persian rug. The north wall was half window. Books were scattered about, and on every available inch of flat space could be found the painter's tools. In spite of the life and fullness of the studio, Vincent could feel the definite orderliness that emanated from Mauve's character and dominated the place.

The formalities of family compliments engaged them only a few seconds; immediately they plunged into the only subject in the world that either of them cared a tinker's dam about. Mauve had been avoiding other painters assiduously for some time (he always maintained that a man could either paint or talk about painting, but he could not do both) and was full of his new project, a misty landscape in a minor key of twilight. He did not discuss it with Vincent, he simply poured it out to him.

Madame Mauve came home and insisted that Vincent remain for supper. He sat before the fireplace and chatted with the children after the pleasant meal, and thought of how fine it would be if he could only have a little home of his own, with a wife who loved him and believed in him, and children around to pronounce him Emperor and Lord by the simple title of father. Would that happy day never come for him?

It was not long before the two men were back in the studio again, pulling contentedly at their pipes. Vincent took out his copies. Mauve looked them over with the quick, discerning eye of the professional.

"They're not badly done," he said, "for exercises. But of what importance are they?"

"Importance? I don't . . ."

"You've only been copying, Vincent, like a schoolboy. The real creating had already been done by other men."

"I thought they might give me the feel of things."

"Nonsense. If you want to create, go to life. Don't imitate. Haven't you any sketches of your own?"

Vincent thought of what Tersteeg had said about his original studies. He debated whether or not to show them to Mauve. He had come to The Hague to ask Mauve to be his teacher. And if all he could show was inferior work . . .

"Yes," he replied, "I have been doing character studies right along."

"Good!"

"I have some sketches of the Borain miners and the peasants in the Brabant. They're not very well done, but . . ."

"Never mind all that," said Mauve. "Let me see them. You ought to have caught some real spirit there."

Vincent laid out his sketches to the accompaniment of a furious beating in his throat. Mauve sat down and ran his left hand along the great swash of hair, smoothing the grain of it on his head again and again. Soft chuckles escaped from behind his salt and pepper beard. Once he rammed his hand against the swash of hair, left it standing in a bush, and threw a quick look of disapproval at Vincent. A moment later he took the study of a labourer, rose and held it alongside of a rough draft figure on his new canvas.

"Now I see where I went wrong!" he exclaimed.

He picked up a drawing pencil, adjusted the light, and made a few rapid strokes, his eye on Vincent's sketch all the time.

"That's better," he said, stepping back. "Now the beggar looks as though he belongs on the land."

He walked to Vincent's side and put his hand on his cousin's shoulder.

"It's all right," he said. "You're on the road. Your sketches are clumsy, but they're authentic. They have a certain vitality and rhythm I haven't found very often. Throw away your copy books, Vincent; buy yourself a paint box. The sooner you begin working in colour, the better it will be for you. Your drawing is only half bad now, and you can keep improving it as you go along."

Vincent thought the moment auspicious.

"I am going to move to The Hague, Cousin Mauve," he said, "and continue my work. Would you be kind enough to help me sometimes? I need help from a man like you. Just little things, such as you showed me about your studies this afternoon. Every young artist needs a master, Cousin Mauve, and I will be grateful if you will let me work under you."

Mauve looked carefully at all the unfinished canvases in his studio. Whatever little time he took away from his work he liked to spend with the family. The warm aura of praise in which he had engulfed Vincent evaporated. In its place came withdrawal. Vincent, always highly sensitive to the changes in people's attitude, felt it instantly.

"I'm a busy man, Vincent," said Mauve, "and I have little opportunity to help others. An artist must be selfish; he must guard every second of his working time. I doubt if I could teach you much."

"I don't ask for a great deal," said Vincent. "Just let me work with you here sometimes and watch you build up a canvas. Talk to me about your work as you did this afternoon, so I'll see how a whole project is completed. And occasionally, when you are resting, you might look over my drawings and point out my mistakes. That's all I ask."

"You think you are asking only a little. But believe me, it is a serious matter, to take an apprentice."

"I wouldn't be a burden to you, I can promise that."

Mauve considered for a long time. He had never wanted an apprentice; he disliked having people about when he worked. He did not often feel communicative about his own creations, and he had never received anything but abuse for the advice he offered beginners. Still, Vincent was his cousin, Uncle Vincent Van Gogh and Goupils bought his canvases, and there was something about the crude, intense passion of the boy—the same crude, intense passion he had felt in the drawings—that appealed to him.

"Very well, Vincent," he said, "we'll have a try at it."

"Oh, Cousin Mauve!"

"I'm not promising anything, mind you. It may turn out very badly. But when you settle in The Hague, you come to the studio and we'll see if we can help each other. I am going to Drenthe for the fall; suppose you come at the beginning of winter."

"That is just when I wanted to come. I still need a few months more of work in the Brabant."

"Then it is settled."

A crooning voice sang inside of Vincent all the way home on the train. "I have a master. I have a master. In a few months I shall be studying with a great painter, and then I shall learn to paint, too. I will work, oh how I will work during the next few months, and then he shall see what progress I have made."

When he got home to Etten he found Kay Vos there.

6

Kay's great grief had spiritualized her. She had loved her husband devotedly and his death had killed something within her. The tremendous vitality of the woman, her high spirits, her enthusiasm and verve were completely gone. Even her warm, live hair seemed to have lost its sparkle. Her face had tapered down to an ascetic oval, her blue eyes had deep pools of brooding blackness in them, and the superb lustre of her skin had paled to a monotone. If she had less vitality than when Vincent knew her in Amsterdam, she now had in its place a more mellow beauty, a seasoned sadness which gave her depth and substance.

"It's nice to have you here at last, Kay," said Vincent.

"Thank you, Vincent."

It was the first time they had called each other by their Christian names without attaching the "Cousin." Neither knew quite how it had happened, nor for that matter did they even think about it.

"You've brought Jan with you, of course?"

"Yes, he's in the garden."

"It's the first time you've visited the Brabant. I'm glad I'm here to show it to you. We must take long walks over the heath."

"I would like that, Vincent."

She spoke kindly, but without enthusiasm. He noticed that her voice had deepened, become more vibrant. He remembered how sympathetic she had been to him in the house on the Keizersgracht. Should he speak to her about the death of her husband, offer his condolence? He knew that it was his duty to say something but he felt it would be more delicate not to throw her grief into her face again.

Kay appreciated his tact. Her husband was sacred to her and she could not discuss him with people. She, too, remembered those pleasant winter evenings on the Keizersgracht when she had played cards with Vos and her parents by the fire, while Vincent sat under a lamp in a far corner. Mute pain welled up within her and a mistiness covered her now black eyes. Vincent put his hand softly over hers and she looked up at him with a deeply pulsating gratitude. He saw how exquisite suffering had made her. Before, she had been only a happy girl; now she was a passionately suffering woman with all the richness that emotional misery can bring. Once again there flashed into his mind the old saying:

"From out of pain, beauty."

"You'll like it here, Kay," he said quietly. "I spend all day out in the fields sketching; you must come with me and bring Jan."

"I would only be in your way."

"Oh, no! I enjoy company. I can show you many interesting things as we walk."

"Then I'll be happy to come."

"It will be good for Jan. The air will make him sturdy."

She pressed his hand ever so slightly.

"And we'll be friends, won't we, Vincent?"

"Yes, Kay."

She released his hand and stared across the road at the Protestant Church, without seeing it.

Vincent went out into the garden, placed a bench nearby for Kay, and helped Jan make a little house of sand. He forgot for the moment the great news he had brought home from The Hague.

At dinner that night he told the family that Mauve had accepted him as a pupil. Ordinarily he would not have repeated any word of praise that either Tersteeg or Mauve might have given him, but the presence of Kay at the table made him want to appear in his best light. His mother was greatly pleased.

"You must do everything Cousin Mauve tells you," she said. "He is a successful man."

The following morning, Kay, Jan, and Vincent set out very early for the Liesbosch, where Vincent wanted to sketch. Although he never bothered to take anything with him to eat at midday, his mother packed a nice lunch for the three of them. She had an idea that it was some sort of picnic. On the way they passed a magpie's nest in the high acacia in the churchyard; Vincent promised to find an egg for the excited boy. They walked through the pine woods with its crunchy bed of needles, then across the yellow, white, and grey sand of the heath. At one spot Vincent saw an abandoned plough and wagon standing in the field. He set up his small easel, lifted Jan into the wagon, and made a quick sketch. Kay stood a little way off to one side, watching Jan romp. She was silent. Vincent did not wish to intrude upon her; he was glad enough just to have her company. He had never known it could be so pleasant to have a woman at his side while he worked.

They passed a number of cottages with thatched roofs, and then came to the road to Roozendaal. At length Kay spoke.

"You know, Vincent," she said, "seeing you before your easel reminded me of something I used to think about you in Amsterdam."

"What was that, Kay?"

"You're sure you won't be hurt?"

"Not at all."

"Then, to tell you the truth, I never did think you were cut out to be a clergyman. I knew you were wasting your time all along."

"Why didn't you tell me?"

"I didn't have the right to do that, Vincent."

She pushed several strands of red-gold hair under her black bonnet; a crooked furrow in the road threw her against Vincent's shoulder. He put his hand under her arm to help her regain her balance, and forgot to take it away.

"I knew you would have to work things out for yourself," she said. "No amount of telling would have done any good."

"Now I remember," said Vincent. "You warned me against becoming a narrow minded clergyman. That was a queer thing for a minister's daughter to say."

He smiled at her eagerly, but her eyes went sad.

"I know. But you see, Vos taught me a great many things I might not otherwise have understood."

Vincent dropped his hand to his side. The mention of Vos's name put a queer, intangible barrier between them.

After an hour's walk they reached the Liesbosch, and once again Vincent set up his easel. There was a bit of swamp he wanted to catch. Jan played in the sand and Kay sat behind him on a little stool he had brought along. She held a book in her hand but she did not read. Vincent sketched rapidly, with a certain *élan*. The study sprang up under his hand with more vigour than he had known before. He could not tell whether it was because of Mauve's compliments or Kay's presence, but his pencil had a surety of touch. He did several sketches in quick succession. He did not turn to look at Kay, nor did she speak to interrupt him, but her nearness gave him a glow of well-being. He wanted his work to be particularly good that day so Kay would admire it.

At lunch time they walked a short way to an oak grove. Kay spread the contents of the basket under a cool tree. The air was utterly still. The smell of the water lilies in the swamp mingled with the faint oak fragrance above them. Kay and Jan sat on one side of the basket, Vincent on the other. Kay served him. The picture of Mauve and his family, sitting about the homely supper table, came to his mind.

As he looked at Kay he thought he had never seen anyone so beautiful. The thick, yellow cheese was delicious and his mother's bread had its usual sweet tang, but he could not eat. A new and formidable hunger was awakening within him. He could not tear his gaze from Kay's delicate skin, the chiselled oval, the brooding, night-pool eyes, the full, sweet mouth that had been robbed momentarily of its ripeness, but which he knew would blossom again.

After lunch Jan went to sleep with his head pillowed in his mother's lap. Vincent watched her stroke the child's light hair, gazing down searchingly into the innocent face. He knew that she was seeing the face of her husband reflected in the child, that she was in their house on the Keizersgracht with the man she loved, and not on the Brabant heath with her Cousin Vincent.

He sketched all afternoon, part of the time with Jan on his lap. The boy had taken a liking to him. Vincent let him mark up several sheets of Ingres paper with black smudges. He laughed and shouted and ran about in the yellow sand, constantly returning to Vincent with questions, with things he had found, with demands that he be entertained. Vincent did not mind; it was good to have a warm, live little animal climbing over him affectionately.

Fall was coming on and the sun set very early. On the way home they stopped at the frequent pools to watch the sunset colourings settle on the water with butterfly wings, darken slowly, and disappear in the dusk. Vincent showed Kay his drawings. She saw them only slightly, and what she did see, she thought crude and clumsy. But Vincent had been good to Jan, and she knew only too well the nature of pain.

"I like them, Vincent," she said.

"Do you, Kay?"

Her praise released a locked flood-gate within him. She had been so sympathetic in Amsterdam; she would understand all the things he was trying to do. Somehow, she seemed the only one in the world who would. He could not talk to his family about his projects because they did not even know the vocabulary; with Mauve and Tersteeg he had to assume a beginner's humility which he did not always feel.

He poured out his heart in hurried, incoherent words. As his enthusiasm increased, he quickened his pace, and Kay had difficulty in keeping up with him. When he was feeling anything deeply, his poise fled and in its place came the old violent, jerky manner. Gone was the mannered gentleman of the afternoon; the provincial boor startled and frightened her. She felt his outburst to be so ill-bred, so immature. She did not know that he was paying her the rarest, the most valuable compliment that man can pay to woman.

He poured out to her all those feelings that had been bottled up within him since Theo had departed for Paris. He told her of his aims and ambitions, of the spirit with which he was trying to imbue his work. Kay wondered why he was getting so excited. She did not interrupt him, nor did she listen. She lived in the past, always in the past, and she found it slightly distasteful that anyone should live with so much joy and vigour in the future. Vincent was feeling his own effervescence too keenly to sense her withdrawal. He went on gesticulating until a name he spoke caught Kay's attention.

"Neuhuys? Do you mean the painter who lived in Amsterdam?"

"He used to. He's at The Hague now."

"Yes. Vos was his friend. He brought him home several times."

Vincent stopped short.

Vos! Always Vos! Why? He was dead. He had been dead over a year. It was time she forgot him. He belonged to the past, just as Ursula did. Why did she always have to bring the conversation back to Vos? Even in the Amsterdam days he had never liked Kay's husband.

Fall deepened. The carpet of pine needles in the woods turned to a crinkly rust-brown. Every day Kay and Jan accompanied Vincent into the fields while he worked. A touch of colour came into her cheeks from the long walks across the heath, and her step became more firm and confident. She took her sewing basket with her now and kept her fingers as busy as Vincent's. She began speaking more freely and liberally about her childhood, about the books she had read, and interesting people she had known in Amsterdam.

The family looked on with approval. Vincent's company was giving her an interest in life. Her presence in the house made Vincent far more amiable. Anna Cornelia and Theodorus thanked God for the opportune arrangement, and did everything they could to throw the two young people together.

Vincent loved everything about Kay; the slender, fragile figure encased so sternly in the long black dress; the perky, black bonnet she wore when she went into the fields; the natural perfume of her body in his nostrils when she bent in front of him; the way she puckered her mouth when she spoke rapidly; the probing glance of her deep blue eyes; the touch of her vibrant hand on his shoulder or arm when she took Jan from him; her throaty, enharmonic voice that shook him to the very depths of his nature, and which he heard singing in his head after he had gone to sleep; the live lustre of her skin, in which he burned to bury his famished lips.

He knew now that for many years he had been living only partially, that great funds of affection and tenderness in him had been dried up, the clear, cooling waters of love been refused to his parched palate. He was happy only when Kay was near him; her presence seemed to reach out and embrace him gently. When she went with him to the fields, he worked rapidly and with a flair; when she stayed at home, each line was drudgery. In the evenings he sat across the great wooden table from her in the sitting room, and although he copied his sketches, her delicate face was always between him and his paper. If occasionally he glanced up to see her sitting in the pale light of the huge yellow lamp and caught her eye, she would smile at him with a sweet passive melancholy. Often he felt he could not stay away from her for another moment, that he would have to spring up before the whole family and crush her to him fiercely, burying his hot, dry lips in the well of her cool mouth.

It was not only her beauty he loved, but her whole being and manner; her quiet walk, her perfect poise and bearing, the good breeding that she expressed with every slight gesture.

He had not even suspected how lonely he had been in the seven long years since he had lost Ursula. In all his life he had never heard a woman say one caressing word, look at him with the mist of tender affection in her eyes, run her fingers lightly over his face, and follow their trail with kisses.

No woman had ever loved him. That was not life, that was death. It had not been so bad when he had loved Ursula, for then—in his adolescence—he had only wanted to give, and it was the giving that had been refused. But now, in his mature love, he wanted to give and receive equally. He knew that life would be impossible unless his new hunger could be fed by Kay's warm response.

One night he was reading Michelet and he ran across the phrase, *"il faut qu'une femme souffle sur toi pour que tu sois homme."*

Michelet was always right. He had not been a man. Although he was twenty-eight, he was still unborn. The fragrance of Kay's beauty and love had been breathed upon him and he had become a man at last.

As a man, he wanted Kay. He wanted her desperately and passionately. He loved Jan, too, for the child was part of the woman he loved. But he hated Vos, hated him with all his strength, because nothing he could do seemed to drive the dead man from the foreground of Kay's mind. He did not regret her former love and marriage any more than he regretted the years of suffering that his love for Ursula had caused him. They both had been hammered on the forge of pain, and their love would be the purer for it.

He knew that he could make Kay forget this man who belonged to the past. He could make his love so burning in the present that the past would be wiped out. He was going to The Hague soon, to study under Mauve. He would take Kay with him, and they would set up a *ménage* like the one he had seen on the Uileboomen. He wanted Kay for his wife, to have her near him always. He wanted a home, and children who would bear the stamp of his features upon their faces. He was a man now, and it was time he stopped wandering. He needed love in his life; it would take the roughness out of his work, round off the crude edges, quicken it with the consciousness of reality that had been lacking. He had never known before how much of him had been dead without love; if he had known, he would have loved passionately the first woman he had come upon. Love was the salt of life; one needed it to bring out the flavour of the world.

He was glad now that Ursula had not loved him. How superficial his love had been then, how deep and rich it was now. If he had married Ursula he would never have known the meaning of true love. He would never have been able to love Kay! He realized for the first time that Ursula had been a shallow, empty headed child, with no fineness or quality. He had spent years of suffering over a *poupon!* One hour with Kay was worth a lifetime with Ursula. The road had been hard but it had led him to Kay, and that was its justification. Life would be good from now on; he would work, he would love, and he would sell his drawings. And they would be happy together. Every human life had its pattern that had to be worked out slowly to its ultimate conclusion.

In spite of his impulsive nature and impassioned state of mind, he managed to control himself. A thousand times, when he was alone with Kay in the fields and they were speaking of things that mattered not at all, he wanted to exclaim, "See here, let us drop all this pretense and casualness. I want to hold you in my arms, and kiss your lips over and over and over again! I want you to be my wife and stay with me forever! We belong to each other, and in our aloneness we need each other desperately!"

By some miracle he managed to restrain himself. He could not suddenly speak of love out of a clear sky; it would have been too crude. Kay never gave him the slightest opening. She always avoided the subjects of love and marriage. How and when was he to speak? He felt that he must soon, for winter was approaching and he had to go to The Hague.

At last he could bear it no longer; his will broke. They had taken the road toward Breda. Vincent had spent the morning sketching diggers at work. They ate their lunch by a little brook in the shadow of some elm trees. Jan was asleep on the grass. Kay was sitting beside the basket. Vincent knelt down to show her some drawings. While he spoke, rapidly, without knowing a word that he said, he could feel Kay's warm shoulder burning into his side; it was this contact that fired him beyond control. The sketches fell out of his hand, he caught Kay to him suddenly, fiercely, and a great wave of rough, passionate words broke from his lips.

"Kay, I can't bear not to tell you for another moment! You must know that I love you, Kay, better than I do myself! I've always loved you, from the first time I saw you in Amsterdam! I've got to have you near me always! Kay, tell me that you love me just a little. We'll go to The Hague to live, all by ourselves. We'll have our home, and we'll be happy. You love me, don't you Kay? Say you'll marry me, Kay dear."

Kay had made no effort to free herself. Horror and revulsion had sent her mouth all awry. She did not hear the words he said, but she caught their import, and a great terror arose within her. Her blue-black eyes stared at him cruelly and she raised a hand to mute the cry at her lips.

"No, never, never!" she breathed fiercely.

She wrenched herself free from his grasp, snatched up the sleeping child, and ran wildly across the field. Vincent pursued her. Terror lent speed to her legs. She fled before him. He could not understand what had happened.

"Kay! Kay!" he called out. "Don't run away."

The sound of his voice drove her on even faster. Vincent ran, waving his arms madly, his head bobbing about on his shoulders. Kay stumbled and fell in the soft furrow of the field. Jan whimpered. Vincent flung himself on his knees in the dirt before her and grasped her hand.

"Kay, why do you run away from me when I love you so? Can't you see, I've got to have you. You love me too, Kay. Don't be frightened, I'm only saying that I love you. We'll forget the past, Kay, and begin a new life."

The look of horror turned to hatred in Kay's eyes. She wrenched her hand away from him. Jan was now fully awake. The fierce, impassioned look on Vincent's face frightened the child, and the tumultuous words pouring from the strange man's lips put him into a terror. He flung his arms about his mother's neck and began to cry.

"Kay, dear, can't you say that you love me just a little bit?"

"No, never, never!"

Once again she ran across the field towards the road. Vincent sat there in the soft sand, stunned. Kay gained the road and disappeared. Vincent picked himself up and dashed after her, calling her name at the top of his voice. When he got to the road, he saw her a long way down, still running, the child clasped to her bosom. He stopped. He watched them vanish at a turning. He stood there quietly for a long time. Then he recrossed the field. He picked up his sketches from the ground. They were slightly dirty. He put the lunch things into the basket, strapped his easel to his back, and trudged wearily home.

The parsonage was thick with tension; Vincent felt it the moment he entered the door. Kay had locked herself in her room with Jan. His mother and father were alone in the sitting room. They had been talking, but stopped abruptly when he entered; he could feel half a sentence suspended in mid-air. He closed the door behind him. He saw that his father must be frightfully angry, for the lid of his right eye was almost closed.

"Vincent, how could you?" wailed his mother.

"How could I what?" He was not sure precisely what they were reproaching him for.

"Insult your cousin that way!"

Vincent could think of no answer to this. He unstrapped the easel from his back and placed it in a corner. His father was still too wrought up to speak.

"Did Kay tell you exactly what happened?" he asked.

His father loosened the high collar that was cutting into the red flesh of his neck. His right hand gripped the edge of the table.

"She told us that you threw your arms about her and raved like a madman."

"I told her I loved her," said Vincent quietly. "I don't quite see how that's an insult."

"Is that all you told her?" His father's tone was icy.

"No. I asked her to be my wife."

"Your wife!"

"Yes. What is so astonishing about that?"

"Oh, Vincent, Vincent," said his mother, "how could you even think of such a thing?"

"Surely you must have been thinking too . . ."

"But how could I ever dream you would fall in love with her?"

"Vincent," said his father, "do you realize that Kay is your first cousin."

"Yes. What of it?"

"You can't marry your first cousin. That would be . . . that would be . . ."

The dominie couldn't even bring himself to pronounce the word. Vincent went to the window and stared out over the garden.

"What would it be?"

"Incest!"

Vincent controlled himself with an effort. How dare they muck over his love with second-hand words?

"That is sheer nonsense, Father, and completely unworthy of you."

"I tell you it would be incest!" shouted Theodorus. "I won't allow that sinful relation in the Van Gogh family."

"I hope you don't think you're quoting the Bible, Father? Cousins have always been allowed to marry."

"Oh, Vincent, my dear," said his mother, "if you did love her, why didn't you wait? Her husband is dead only a year. She still loves him devotedly. And you know you have no money to support a wife."

"I consider what you have done," said his father, "as distinctly premature and indelicate."

Vincent recoiled. He fumbled for his pipe, held it in his hand for a moment, and then put it back.

"Father, I must ask you firmly and decidedly not to use such expressions any more. My love for Kay is the finest thing that has ever happened to me. I won't have you calling it indelicate and premature."

He snatched up his easel and went to his room. He sat on the bed and asked himself, "What has happened? What have I done? I told Kay that I loved her and she ran away. Why? Doesn't she want me?"

"No, never, never!"

He spent the night tormenting himself by going over and over the scene. Always he ended at the same spot. That little sentence sounded in his ears like his death knell and his doom.

It was late the following morning before he could bring himself to go downstairs. The air of tension had been cleared away. His mother was in the

kitchen. She kissed him when he came in, and patted his cheek sympathetically for a moment.

"Did you sleep, dear?" she asked.

"Where is Kay?"

"Father drove her to Breda."

"Why?"

"To catch a train. She's going home."

"To Amsterdam?"

"Yes."

"I see."

"She thought it would be better, Vincent."

"Did she leave a message for me?"

"No, dear. Won't you sit down to your breakfast?"

"No word at all? About yesterday? Was she angry with me?"

"No, she just thought she'd go home to her parents."

Anna Cornelia decided it would be better not to repeat the things Kay had
said; instead she put an egg on the stove.

"What time does that train leave Breda?"

"At ten-twenty."

Vincent glanced at the blue kitchen clock.

"It's that time now," he said.

"Yes."

"Then there's nothing I can do about it."

"Come sit down here, dear. I have some nice fresh tongue this morning."

She cleared away a space at the kitchen table, laid a napkin and spread
breakfast for him. She hovered over him, urging him to eat; she had the
feeling that if only he would put enough into his stomach, everything would
come all right.

Vincent saw it pleased her, so he swallowed everything she placed on the
table. But the taste of "No, never, never" was in his mouth to make bitter
every sweet bite he ate.

7

He knew that he loved his work far better than he did Kay. If he had
been forced to choose between one and the other, there would have been
not the slightest doubt in his mind. Yet his drawing suddenly went flat. He
could no longer work with any interest. He looked over the sketches of the
Brabant types on the wall and saw that he had made progress since his love
for Kay had awakened. He knew that there was still something harsh and
severe in his drawings, but he felt Kay's love could soften that. His love was
serious and passionate enough not to be chilled by many "No, never, nevers";
he considered her refusal as a block of ice that he would press to his heart
to thaw.

It was the little germ of doubt in his mind that prevented him from working. Suppose he could never change her decision? She seemed to have conscientious scruples even at the idea of a possible new love. He wanted to cure her of the fatal disease of burying herself too much in the past. He wanted to join his draftsman's fist with her lady's hand, and work for their daily bread and happiness.

He spent his time in his room, writing passionate, imploring messages to Kay. It was several weeks before he learned she did not even read them. He wrote almost daily letters to Theo, his confidant, strengthening himself against the doubt in his own heart and the concerted attacks of his parents and the Reverend Stricker. He suffered, suffered bitterly, and he was not always able to hide it. His mother came to him with a face full of pity and many comforting words.

"Vincent," she said, "you are only smashing your poor head against a stone dyke. Uncle Stricker says her 'No!' is quite decisive."

"I'll not take his word for anything."

"But she told him, dear."

"That she doesn't love me?"

"Yes, and that she will never change her mind."

"We shall see about that."

"It's all so hopeless, Vincent. Uncle Stricker says that even if Kay loved you, he would not consent to the marriage unless you earned at least a thousand francs a year. And you know you are a long way from that."

"Well, Mother, he who loves lives, he who lives works, and he who works has bread."

"Very pretty, my dear, but Kay was brought up in luxury. She has always had nice things."

"Her nice things don't make her happy now."

"If you two were sentimental and married, great misery would come of it; poverty, hunger, cold, illness. For you know the family would not help with a single franc."

"I've been through all those things before, Mother, and they don't frighten me. It still would be better for us to be together than not to be together."

"But my child, *if Kay doesn't love you!*"

"If only I could go to Amsterdam, I tell you I could change that 'No!' to 'Yes!' "

He considered it one of the worst *petites misères de la vie humaine* that he could not go to see the woman he loved, that he could not earn a single franc to pay his railroad fare. His impotence put him in a rage. He was twenty-eight; for twelve years he had been working hard and denying himself everything but the bare necessities of life, yet in all the world, he had no way to command the pitifully small sum to buy a ticket to Amsterdam.

He considered walking the hundred kilometres, but he knew he would arrive dirty, hungry and worn. He did not mind the strain of it all, but if he should enter the Reverend Stricker's house as he entered the Reverend

Pietersen's . . . ! After he had sent Theo a long letter in the morning, he sat down again in the evening and wrote another:

Dear Theo:

I am in desperate need of money for the trip to Amsterdam. If I have just enough I go.

I send along a few drawings; now tell me why they do not sell, and how I can make them salable. For I must earn some money for a railroad ticket to go and fathom that "No, never, never."

As the days went on he felt new, healthy energy arise. His love made him resolute. He had driven out the germ of doubt, and in his own mind he now knew that if he could only see Kay, help her to understand the sort of person he really was inside, he could change that "No, never, never" to "Yes! for ever, for ever!" He went back to his work with a new verve; although he knew that his draftsman's fist was still unwieldy, he felt a powerful confidence that time would wipe that out, just as it would Kay's refusal.

The following evening he sent a letter to the Reverend Stricker, stating his case clearly. He did not mince his words, and he grinned as he thought of the expletive that would be wrenched from his uncle's lips. His father had forbidden him to write the letter; a real battle was preparing in the parsonage. Theodorus saw life in terms of strict obedience and strict behaviour; he knew nothing of the vicissitudes of human temperament. If his son could not fit himself to the mould, then it was his son who was wrong, and not the mould.

"It's all the fault of those French books you read," said Theodorus across the evening table. "If you keep company with thieves and murderers, how can anyone expect you to behave like an obedient son and a gentleman?"

Vincent looked up from his Michelet in mild astonishment.

"Thieves and murderers? Do you call Victor Hugo and Michelet thieves?"

"No, but that's what they write about. Their books are full of evil."

"Nonsense, Father; Michelet is as pure as the Bible itself."

"I want none of your blaspheming here, young man!" shouted Theodorus in a righteous rage. "Those books are immoral. It's your French ideas that have ruined you."

Vincent rose, walked around the table, and placed "L'Amour et la Femme" before Theodorus.

"There is only one way for you to be convinced," he said. "Just read a few pages for yourself. You will be impressed. Michelet only wants to help us solve our problems and our little miseries."

Theodorus swept "L'Amour et la Femme" onto the floor with the gesture of a good man casting away sin.

"I don't need to read it!" he fumed. "We have a great-uncle in the Van Gogh family who was infected with French ideas and he took to drink!"

"*Mille pardons,* Father Michelet," murmured Vincent, picking up the book.

"And why Father Michelet, if I may ask?" said Theodorus icily. "Are you trying to insult me?"

"I hadn't thought of any such thing," said Vincent. "But I must tell you frankly that if I needed advice I would sooner go to Michelet than to you. It would be more likely to be in season."

"Oh, Vincent," implored his mother, "why must you say such things? Why must you break up family ties?"

"Yes, that's what you're doing," exclaimed Theodorus. "You're breaking up family ties. Your conduct is unpardonable. You had better leave this house and go elsewhere to live."

Vincent walked up to his studio room and sat down on the bed. He wondered idly why it was that whenever he received a tremendous blow he sat on the bed instead of a chair. He looked around the walls of his room at the diggers, the sowers, the labourers, the seamstress and the cleaning girl, the wood-choppers, and the drawings from Heike. Yes, he had made progress. He was going forward. But his work was not finished here yet. Mauve was in Drenthe and would not return for another month. He did not wish to leave Etten. He was comfortable; living elsewhere would be more expensive. He wanted time to crash through his clumsy expression and catch the true spirit of the Brabant types before he went away forever. His father had told him to leave the house, had actually cursed at him. But it had all been said in anger. If they really said, "Go!" and meant it . . . Was he really so bad that he had to be driven from his father's house?

The next morning he received two letters in the mail. The first was from the Reverend Stricker, an answer to his registered letter. There was also a note enclosed from the Reverend's wife. They summed up Vincent's career in no uncertain terms, told him that Kay loved someone else, that the other man was wealthy, that they wished his outlandish attacks upon their daughter to cease instantly.

"There are really no more unbelieving, hard hearted and worldly people alive than clergymen," observed Vincent to himself, crushing the Amsterdam letter in his hand with as much savage pleasure as though it had been the Reverend himself.

The second letter was from Theo.

"The drawings are well expressed. I will do my utmost to sell them. In the meanwhile I am enclosing twenty francs for that trip to Amsterdam. Good luck, old boy."

8

When Vincent left the Central railway station, night was beginning to close in. He walked rapidly up the Damrak to the Dam, past the King's Palace and the post office and cut across to the Keizersgracht. It was the hour when all the stores and offices were being emptied of their clerks and sales-men.

He crossed the Singel, and stopped for a moment on the bridge of the Heerengracht to watch the men of a flower barge eat their dinner of bread and herring at an open table. He turned left on the Keizersgracht, passed the long row of narrow Flemish dwellings, and found himself in front of the short, stone steps and black railing of the Reverend Stricker's house. He remembered the first time he had stood there, at the beginning of his Amsterdam adventure, and he realized that there are some cities in which men are forever ill-fated.

He had rushed all the way up the Damrak and across the Centre at top speed; now that he arrived he felt a fear and hesitancy about entering. He looked upward and noticed the iron hook sticking out above the attic window. He thought what an excellent opportunity it afforded for a man to hang himself.

He traversed the wide, red brick pavement and stood on the curb, looking down into the canal. He knew that the next hour would determine the whole course of his external life. If he could only see Kay, talk to her, make her understand, everything would work out. But the father of a young girl pos-sessed the key to the front door. Suppose the Reverend Stricker refused to admit him.

A sand barge came slowly upstream, being pushed to its nightly an-chorage. There was a trail of moist yellow sand over the black side where the cargo had been shovelled out of the hollow. Vincent noticed that there was no wash strung from stern to prow, and idly wondered why. A thin, bony man stuck the side of his chest to the pole, and leaning against it heavily, pushed his way down the catwalk while the thick, clumsy boat slipped upstream from under him. A woman in a dirty apron sat at the stern, like a piece of water-carved stone, the hand behind her guiding the clumsy tiller. A little boy, a girl, and a filthy white dog stood on top of the cabin and gazed at the houses along the Keizersgracht wistfully.

Vincent mounted the five stone steps and rang the bell. After a moment the maid came. She peered at Vincent standing in the shadows, recognized him and thrust her adequate bulk into the doorway.

"Is the Reverend Stricker at home?" asked Vincent.

"No. He's out." She had received her orders.

Vincent heard voices inside. He pushed the woman aside brusquely.

"Get out of my way," he said.

The maid followed him and tried to bar his entrance.

"The family is at dinner," she protested. "You can't go in."

Vincent walked down the long hall and stepped into the dining room. As he did so he saw the very end of a familiar black dress disappear through the other door. The Reverend Stricker, his Aunt Wilhelmina, and the two younger children were at the table. Five places had been laid. At the place where the empty chair was pushed back at a crooked angle, there was a plate of broiled veal, whole potatoes, and string beans.

"I couldn't stop him, sir," said the maid. "He just pushed his way in."

There were two silver candlesticks on the table, with tall white candles giving off the only light. Calvin, hanging on the wall, looked eerie in the yellow glow. The silver service from the carved sideboard gleamed in the darkness, and Vincent noticed the little high window under which he had first spoken to Kay.

"Well, Vincent," said his uncle, "you seem to have less manners every day."

"I want to speak to Kay."

"She's not here. She's visiting with friends."

"She was sitting in this place when I rang the bell. She had begun her dinner."

Stricker turned to his wife. "Take the children out of the room.

"Now, Vincent," he said, "you are causing a great deal of trouble. Not only I, but everyone else in the family has completely lost patience with you. You're a tramp, an idler, a boor, and as far as I can see, an ungrateful, vicious character. How dare you even presume to love my daughter? It is an insult to me."

"Let me see Kay, Uncle Stricker. I want to talk to her."

"She doesn't want to talk to you. She never wants to lay eyes on you again!"

"Kay said that?"

"Yes."

"I don't believe it."

Stricker was aghast. It was the first time he had been accused of lying since he had been ordained.

"How dare you say that I am not telling the truth!"

"I'll never believe that until I hear it from her own lips. And even then I won't."

"When I think of all the precious time and money I wasted on you here in Amsterdam."

Vincent sank wearily into the chair Kay had just vacated, and rested both his arms on the table.

"Uncle, listen to me a moment. Show me that even a clergyman can have a human heart under his triple steel armour. I love your daughter. I love her desperately. Every hour of the day and night I think of her and long for her. You work for God, then for God's sake show me a little mercy. Don't be so cruel to me. I know that I'm not successful yet, but if you'll give me a little time, I will be. Give me a chance to show her my love. Let me help her to understand why she must love me. Surely you must have been in love once, Uncle, and you know what agony a man can suffer. I've suffered enough; let me find a little happiness for once. Just give me a chance to win her love, that's all I ask. I can't bear this aloneness and misery another day!"

The Reverend Stricker looked down at him for a moment and then said, "Are you such a weakling and a coward that you can't stand a little pain? Must you be forever whimpering about it?"

Vincent sprang to his feet violently. All the softness was gone from him now. Only the fact that they were standing across the table from each other, separated by two tall candles in silver candlesticks kept the younger man from hitting the minister. A bruising silence hummed in the room while the two men stood staring at the sparkling points of light in each other's eyes.

Vincent did not know how much time passed. He raised his hand and placed it near the candle.

"Let me speak to her," he said, "for just as long as I can hold my hand in this flame."

He turned his hand over and placed the back of it in the flame. The light in the room dimmed. The carbon from the candle instantly made his flesh black. Within a few seconds it turned to a raw, burning red. Vincent did not flinch or take his eyes from his uncle. Five seconds passed. Ten. The skin on the back of his hand began to puff. The Reverend Stricker's eyes were wide with horror. He seemed paralysed. Several times he tried to speak, to move, but he could not. He was held in the grip of Vincent's cruel, probing eyes. Fifteen seconds passed. The puffed skin cracked open but the arm did not even tremble. The Reverend Stricker at last brought himself to consciousness with a violent jerk.

"You crazy man!" he shouted at the top of his voice. "You insane fool!"

He threw himself across the table, snatched the candle from under Vincent, and crushed the light with his fist. Then he leaned down to the candle nearest him and blew it out with a great puff.

The room was in utter darkness. The two men stood leaning on their palms, across the table from each other, peering into the darkness, unable to see, yet seeing each other only too clearly.

"You're mad!" cried the Reverend. "And Kay despises you with all her heart! Get out of this house and never dare to come back!"

Vincent picked his way slowly along the dark street and found himself somehow on the outskirts of the town. The familiar and pleasantly fetid odour of still water assailed his nostrils as he stood staring down into a brackish, dead canal. The gas lamp at the corner cast a light on his left hand—some deep instinct had kept his drawing hand at his side—and he saw that there was a black hole in the skin. He passed over a series of tiny waterways smelling faintly of a long forgotten sea. At last he found himself near the house of Mendes da Costa. He squatted down on the bank of a canal. He dropped a pebble on the heavy green blanket of *kroos*. It sank without even showing that there was water beneath.

Kay was gone from his life. The "No, never, never" had been wrung from the depths of her soul. Her cry had now become transposed, had become his property. It pounded through his head, repeating, "No, never, never shall you see her again. Never shall you hear the lilting croon of her voice, the smile in her deep blue eyes, the feel of her warm skin on your cheek. Never shall you know love, for it cannot live, no, not even for as long as you can hold your flesh in the burning crucible of pain!"

A great inarticulate surge of grief welled up in his throat. He raised his left hand to his mouth to stifle the cry, that Amsterdam and all the world might never know that he had been judged, and deemed unworthy. On his lips he tasted the bitter, bitter ash of unrequited desire.

BOOK THREE

THE HAGUE

1

MAUVE was still in Drenthe. Vincent searched the neighbourhood of the Uileboomen, and found a little place behind the Ryn station for fourteen francs a month. The studio—it had been known as a room until Vincent took it—was fairly large, with an alcove for cooking and a large window facing the south. There was a stove squatting low in one corner with a long black pipe disappearing in the wall up by the ceiling. The wallpaper was a clean, neutral shade; out of the window Vincent could see the lumber yard belonging to the owner of the house, a green meadow, and then a vast stretch of dune. The house was located on the Schenkweg, the last street between The Hague and the meadows to the southeast. It was covered with black soot from the engines that banged in and out of the Ryn station.

Vincent bought a strong kitchen table, two kitchen chairs, and a blanket to throw over himself while he slept on the floor. These expenditures exhausted his small fund of money, but the first of the month was not far off and Theo would send the hundred francs that had been agreed upon as his monthly allowance. The cold January weather would not permit him to work out of doors; since he had no money to pay models he had to sit by and wait for Mauve to return.

Mauve came back to the Uileboomen. Vincent went at once to his cousin's studio. Mauve was setting up a big canvas excitedly, the swash of hair across his forehead falling into his eyes. He was about to begin the big project of the year, a canvas for the Salon, and had chosen for his subject a fishing smack being drawn up on the beach at Scheveningen by horses. Mauve and his wife Jet had thought it extremely doubtful that Vincent would ever come to The Hague; they knew that nearly everyone has a vague prompting to become an artist at some time or other during his life.

"So you've come to The Hague after all. Very well, Vincent, we shall make a painter of you. Have you found a place to live?"

"Yes, I'm over at 138 Schenkweg, just behind the Ryn station."

"That's close by. How are you fixed for funds?"

"Well, I haven't the money to do a great deal. I bought a table and a couple of chairs."

"And a bed," said Jet.

"No, I've been sleeping on the floor."

Mauve said something in an undertone to Jet who went into the house and returned in a moment with a wallet. Mauve took out a hundred guilder note. "I want you to take this as a loan, Vincent," he said. "Buy yourself a bed; you must rest well at night. Is your rent paid?"

"Not yet."

"Then get it off your mind. How about the light?"

"There's plenty of it, but the only window has a southern exposure."

"That's bad; you had better get it fixed. The sun will change the light on your models every ten minutes. Buy yourself some drapes."

"I don't like to borrow money from you, Cousin Mauve. It's enough that you should be willing to teach me."

"Nonsense, Vincent; it happens once in every man's life that he has to set up housekeeping. In the long run it's cheaper to have things of your own."

"Yes, that's so. I hope to be able to sell a few drawings soon and then I'll pay you back."

"Tersteeg will help you. He bought my things when I was younger and just learning. But you must begin to work in water-colour and oil. There is no market for simple pencil sketches."

Mauve, in spite of his bulk, had a nervous manner of darting about at great speed. As soon as his eyes lighted on something he was looking for he thrust one shoulder out before him and flung himself in that direction.

"Here, Vincent," he said, "here's a painting box with some water-colours, brushes, palette, palette knife, oil, and turpentine. Let me show you how to hold that palette and stand before your easel."

He showed Vincent a few elements of technique. Vincent picked up the ideas very quickly.

"Good!" said Mauve. "I used to think you were a dullard, but I see it is not so. You may come here in the mornings and work on water-colours. I'll propose your name for a special membership of *Pulchri;* you can draw there several evenings a week from the model. Besides, it will give you some intercourse with painters. When you begin to sell you can take out a regular membership."

"Yes, I want to work from the model. I shall try to hire one to come in every day. Once I get the human figure, everything else will come of its own accord."

"That's so," agreed Mauve. "The figure is the hardest to get, but once you have it, trees and cows and sunsets are simple. Men who neglect the figure do so because they find it too hard."

Vincent bought a bed, drapes for the window, paid his rent, and tacked the Brabant sketches on the wall. He knew they were unsalable and he easily saw their defects, but there was something of nature in them; they had been made with a certain passion. He could not have pointed out just where the passion was, nor how it got there; he did not even realize its full value until he became friends with De Bock.

De Bock was a charming man. He was *bien élevé,* had pleasant manners and a permanent income. He had been educated in England. Vincent met him at Goupils. De Bock was the exact antithesis of Vincent in every way;

he took life casually, nothing ruffled or excited him, and his entire make-up was delicate. His mouth was exactly as long as his nostrils were wide.

"Won't you come have a pot of tea with me?" he asked Vincent. "I'd like to show you some of my recent things. I think I have a new flair since Tersteeg has been selling me."

His studio was located in Willemspark, the aristocratic section of The Hague. He had his walls draped off in neutral velvets. Lounging divans with luxurious cushions filled every corner. There were smoking tables, amply filled bookcases, and oriental rugs. When Vincent thought of his own studio, he felt like an anchorite.

De Bock lit the gas under a Russian samovar and sent his housekeeper for some cakes. Then he took a canvas out from a closet and placed it on the easel.

"This is my latest," he said. "Will you have a cigar while you're looking? It may help the picture; you never can tell."

He spoke in a light, amused tone. Since Tersteeg had discovered him, his self-confidence had gone sky high. He knew Vincent would like the picture. He took out one of the long Russian cigarettes for which he was famous in The Hague, and studied Vincent's face for a passing judgement.

Vincent scrutinized the canvas through the blue smoke of De Bock's expensive cigar. He felt in De Bock's attitude that horrible moment of suspense when the artist shows one of his creations to strange eyes for the first time. What was he to say? The landscape was not bad, but neither was it good. It was too much like De Bock's character: casual. He remembered how furious and ill it made him when some young upstart dared condescend to his work. Although the picture was the sort that could be seen in its entirety with one glance, he continued to study it.

"You have a feeling for landscape, De Bock," he said. "And you certainly know how to put charm in it."

"Oh, thanks," said De Bock, pleased at what he thought was a compliment. "Won't you have a cup of tea?"

Vincent clutched the teacup with both hands, fearing that he might spill it on the rich rug. De Bock went to the samovar and drew himself a cup. Vincent wished desperately not to say anything against De Bock's work. He liked the man and wanted him for a friend. But the objective craftsman arose within him and he could not put down his criticism.

"There's only one thing I'm not sure I like about this canvas."

De Bock took the tray from his housekeeper and said, "Have a cake, old fellow."

Vincent refused because he did not see how he was going to eat a cake and hold a cup of tea on his lap at the same time.

"What was it you didn't care for?" asked De Bock lightly.

"Your figures. They don't seem authentic."

"You know," confided De Bock, stretching out leisurely on a comfortable divan, "I've often meant to plug away at the figure. But I never seem to get around to it. I take a model and work a few days, and then I suddenly become interested in some landscape or other. After all, landscape is very definitely my medium, so I needn't let the figure bother me much, need I?"

"Even when I do landscapes," said Vincent, "I hope to get something of the figure into them. Your work is years ahead of mine; besides, you're an accepted artist. But will you permit me to offer just one word of friendly criticism?"

"Love to have you."

"Well then, I should say your painting lacks passion."

"Passion?" inquired De Bock, cocking one eye at Vincent as he leaned over the samovar. "Which one of the numerous passions are you referring to?"

"It's rather hard to explain. But your sentiment seems a trifle vague. In my opinion it could stand a little more intensity."

"But see here, old chap," said De Bock, straightening up and regarding one of his canvases closely. "I can't spew emotion all over the canvas just because people tell me to, can I? I paint what I see and feel. If I don't feel any bloody passion, how am I to get it on my brush? One can't buy it at the greengrocer's by the pound, now can one?"

Vincent's studio looked almost mean and sordid after De Bock's, but he knew there were compensations for its austerity. He pushed the bed back into one corner and hid his cooking utensils; he wanted the place to be a painter's studio, not living quarters. Theo's money for the month had not yet arrived but he still had a few francs left from Mauve's loan. He used them to hire models. He had been in his studio only a short time when Mauve came to visit him.

"It took me only ten minutes to walk over," he said, looking about. "Yes, this will do. You should have north light, but this will do. It will make a favourable impression on those people who have suspected you of amateurism and idleness. I see you've been working from the model today?"

"Yes. Every day. But it's expensive."

"And the cheapest way in the end. Are you short of funds, Vincent?"

"Thank you, Cousin Mauve. I can get along."

He did not think it wise to become a financial burden on Mauve. He had just a franc left in his pocket, enough to eat on for a day, but he wanted Mauve to give freely of his instruction; money was not really important.

Mauve spent an hour showing him how to daub in water-colours, and how to wash out again. Vincent made rather a mess of things.

"Don't let that disturb you," said Mauve cheerfully. "You will spoil at least ten drawings before you come to handle the brush well. Let me see some of your latest Brabant sketches."

Vincent brought them out. Mauve was such a master of technique that he could penetrate to the essential weakness of a piece of work in a very few words. He never said, "This is wrong," and then stopped. He always added, "Try it this way." Vincent listened closely, for he knew that Mauve spoke to him just as he would have spoken to himself if he had gone wrong in one of his own canvases.

"You can draw," said Mauve. "That year with your pencil will be of great value to you. I shouldn't be surprised to see Tersteeg buying your water-colours in a short time."

This magnificent consolation did Vincent little good two days later when he had not a centime in his pocket. It was already several days past the first of the month and the hundred francs had not yet arrived from Theo. What could be wrong? Was Theo angry with him? Could it be possible that Theo would go back on him now, at the very moment when he was on the threshold of a career? He found a stamp in his coat pocket; that enabled him to write to his brother and beg him to send on at least a part of the allowance so that he might eat and hire a model occasionally.

For three days he went without a bite of food, working at water-colour at Mauve's in the morning, sketching in the soup kitchens and third-class waiting rooms in the afternoons, and going either to *Pulchri* or Mauve's to work again at night. He was afraid that Mauve would discover his situation and become discouraged with him. Vincent realized that although Mauve had come to like him, his cousin would cast him aside without a second thought if his troubles began to have an effect upon Mauve's painting. When Jet invited him to dinner, he refused.

The low, dull ache at the pit of his stomach turned his mind back to the Borinage. Was he to be hungry all his life? Was there never to be a moment of comfort or peace for him anywhere?

The next day he swallowed his pride and went to see Tersteeg. Perhaps he could borrow ten francs from the man who supported half the painters of The Hague.

Tersteeg was in Paris on business.

Vincent developed a fever and could no longer hold the pencil. He went to bed. The following day he dragged himself back to the Plaats and found the dealer in. Tersteeg had promised Theo that he would look after Vincent. He lent him twenty-five francs.

"I have been meaning to look in at your studio for some time, Vincent," he said. "I shall drop around shortly."

It was all Vincent could do to answer politely. He wanted to get away and eat. He had thought on his way to Goupils, "If only I can get some money, I will be all right again." But now that he had the money he was more miserable than ever. He felt utterly and forlornly alone.

"Dinner will cure all that," he said to himself.

Food removed the pain in his stomach but not the pain of aloneness that lodged in some intangible spot within him. He bought some cheap tobacco, went home, stretched out on the bed and smoked his pipe. The hunger for Kay came back to him with terrific force. He felt so desperately miserable he could not breathe. He jumped up from the bed, opened the window and stuck his head out into the snow covered January night. He thought of the

Reverend Stricker. A chill ran through him, as though he had been leaning too long against the cold stone wall of a church. He closed the window, snatched up his hat and coat, and ran out to a wine café that he had seen in front of the Ryn station.

2

The wine café had an oil lamp hanging at the entrance and another over the bar. The middle of the shop was in semidarkness. There were a few benches against the wall with mottled, stone topped tables before them. It was a workingman's shop with faded walls and a cement floor; a place of refuge rather than joy.

Vincent sat down at one of the tables. He leaned his back against the wall wearily. It was not so bad when he was working, when there was money for food and models. But to whom could he turn for simple companionship, for a casual and friendly word about the time of day? Mauve was his master, Tersteeg a busy and important dealer, De Bock a wealthy man of society. Perhaps a glass of wine would help him over the bad spot. Tomorrow he would be able to work, and things would look better.

He sipped the sour red wine slowly. There were few people in the shop. Opposite him sat a labourer of some sort. In the corner near the bar sat a couple, the woman in gaudy clothes. At the table next to him was a woman alone. He did not look at her.

The waiter came by and said to the woman roughly, "More wine?"

"Haven't a sou," she replied.

Vincent turned. "Won't you have a glass with me?" he asked.

The woman looked at him for an instant. "Sure."

The waiter brought the glass of wine, took the twenty centimes and went away. The tables were close together.

"Thanks," said the woman.

Vincent surveyed her closely. She was not young, not beautiful, slightly faded, one over whom life had passed. Her figure was slender but well formed. He noticed her hand as it clasped the glass of wine; it was not a lady's hand like Kay's, but the hand of one who worked much. She reminded him, in the half light, of some curious figure by Chardin or Jan Steen. She had a crooked nose that bulged in the middle, and a shadowy moustache on her upper lip. Her eyes were melancholy but there was, none the less, a touch of spirit in them.

"Not at all," he replied. "I'm grateful for your company."

"My name is Christine," she said. "What's yours?"

"Vincent."

"Do you work here at The Hague?"

"Yes."

"What do you do?"

"I'm a painter."

"Oh. That's a hell of a life too, aint it?"

"Sometimes."

"I'm a laundress. When I have strength enough to work. But that aint always."

"What do you do then?"

"I was on the streets for a long time. I go back to it when I'm too sick to work."

"Is it hard to be a laundress?"

"Yes. They work us twelve hours. And they don't pay nothing. Sometime, after I washed all day, I got to find a man to earn food for the kids."

"How many children have you, Christine?"

"Five. I'm carrying another one now."

"Your husband is dead?"

"I got them all from strangers."

"That made it difficult, didn't it?"

She shrugged. "Jesus Christ. A miner can't refuse to go down because he might get killed, can he?"

"No. Do you know who any of the fathers are?"

"Only the first son of a bitch. I never even knew their names."

"What about the one you're carrying now?"

"Well, I can't be sure. I was too sick to wash then, so I was on the streets a lot. But it don't matter."

"Will you have another glass of wine?"

"Make it gin and bitters." She reached into her purse, took out the butt of a rough, black cigar and lit it. "You don't look prosperous," she said. "Do you sell any paintings?"

"No, I'm just beginning."

"You look pretty old to be beginning."

"I'm thirty."

"You look forty. How do you live then?"

"My brother sends me a little money."

"Well, it's no goddam worse than being a laundress."

"With whom do you stay, Christine?"

"We're all at my mother's."

"Does she know you go on the streets?"

The woman laughed uproariously but without mirth. "Christ yes! She sent me there. That's what she did all her life. It's how she got me and my brother."

"What does your brother do?"

"He's got a woman at the house. He pimps for her."

"That can't be very good for your five children."

"It don't matter. They'll all be doing the same some day."

"It's all a rum go, isn't it, Christine."

"Aint no good crying about it. Can I have another glass of gin and bitters? What did you do to your hand? You got a big black sore."

"I burned it."

"Oh, that must have hurt awful." She picked up his hand tenderly.

"No, Christine, it was all right. I wanted to."

She dropped his hand. "Why did you come in here all alone. Aint you got no friends?"

"No. My brother, but he's in Paris."

"Makes a guy feel lonesome, don't it?"

"Yes, Christine, horribly."

"I get like that, too. There's all the kids at home, and my mother and brother. And all the men I pick up. But you live alone anyhow, don't you? It aint people that count. It's having someone you really like."

"Hasn't there ever been anyone you cared for, Christine?"

"The first fellow. I was sixteen. He was rich. Couldn't marry me 'cause of his family. But he paid for the baby. Then he died, and I was left without a centime."

"How old are you?"

"Thirty-two. Too old to have kids. The doctor at the free ward said this one will kill me."

"It won't if you have proper medical attention."

"Where in hell am I going to get it? I aint got nothing saved up. The doctors at the free ward don't care; they got too many sick women."

"Have you no way at all of getting a little money?"

"Sure. If I stay on the streets all night for a couple of months. But that'll kill me quicker than the kid."

They were silent for several moments. "Where are you going when you leave here, Christine?"

"I been at the tubs all day and I come in here to get a glass because I'm dead. They were supposed to pay me a franc and a half, but they put me off 'till Saturday. I got to get two francs for food. I thought I'd rest before I found a man."

"Will you let me come with you, Christine? I'm very much alone. I'd like to."

"Sure. Saves me the trouble. Besides, you're kind of nice."

"I like you too, Christine. When you picked up my burned hand . . . that was the first kind word a woman has said to me in I can't remember how long."

"That's funny. You aint bad to look at. You got a nice way."

"I'm just unlucky in love."

"Yes, that's how it is, aint it? Can I have another glass of gin and bitters?"

"Listen, you and I need not make ourselves drunk to feel something for each other. Just put in your pocket what I can spare. I'm sorry it isn't more."

"You look like you need it worse than me. You can come anyway. After you go, I'll find some other guy for the two francs."

"No. Take the money. I can spare it. I borrowed twenty-five francs from a friend."

"All right. Let's get out of here."

On their way home, threading their way through the dark streets, they chatted easily, like old friends. She told him of her life, without sympathy for herself, without complaint.

"Have you ever posed as a model?" Vincent asked her.

"When I was young."

"Then why not pose for me? I can't pay you much. Not even a franc a day. But after I begin selling, I'll pay you two francs. It will be better than washing clothes."

"Say, I'd like that. I'd bring my boy. You can paint him for nothing. When you get tired of me you can have my mother. She'd like to make an extra franc now and then. She's a charwoman."

At length they reached her house. It was a rough stone building of one floor and a court. "You don't got to see anyone," said Christine. "My room's in front."

It was a modest, simple little room in which she lived; the plain paper on the wall gave it a quiet, grey tone, like a picture by Chardin, thought Vincent. On the wooden floor there was a mat and a piece of old crimson carpet. An ordinary kitchen stove was in one corner, a chest of drawers in another, and in the centre a large bed. It was the interior of a real working woman's home.

When Vincent awoke in the morning and found himself not alone, but saw there in the twilight a fellow creature beside him, it made the world look so much more friendly. The pain and aloneness were gone from him and in their place had come a deep feeling of peace.

3

In the morning post he received a note from Theo with the hundred francs enclosed. Theo had been unable to send it until several days after the first. He rushed out, found a little old woman digging in her front garden nearby, and asked if she wouldn't come and pose for him for fifty centimes. The old woman assented gladly.

In the studio he placed the woman against a drowsy background, sitting next to the chimney and stove with a little teakettle off to one side. He was seeking tone; the old woman's head had a great deal of light and life in it. He made three fourths of the water-colour in a green soap style. The corner where the woman sat he treated tenderly, softly, and with sentiment. For some time his work had been hard, dry, brittle; now it flowed. He hammered his sketch on the paper and expressed his idea well. He was grateful to Christine for what she had done for him. Lack of love in his life could bring him infinite pain, but it could do him no harm; lack of sex could dry up the well springs of his art and kill him.

"Sex lubricates," he murmured to himself as he worked with fluidity and ease. "I wonder why Papa Michelet never mentioned that."

There was a knock on the door. Vincent admitted Mijnheer Tersteeg. His striped trousers were creased painstakingly. His round, brown shoes were as bright as a mirror. His beard was carefully barbered, his hair parted neatly on the side, and his collar was of impeccable whiteness.

Tersteeg was genuinely pleased to find that Vincent had a real studio and was hard at work. He liked to see young artists become successful; that was his hobby as well as his profession. Yet he wanted that success to be arrived at through systematic and preordained channels; he found it better for a man to work through the conventional means and fail, than break all the rules and succeed. For him the rules of the game were far more important than the victory. Tersteeg was a good and honourable man; he expected everyone else to be equally good and honourable. He admitted no circumstances which could change evil into good or sin into salvation. The painters who sold their canvases to Goupils knew that they had to toe the mark. If they violated the dictates of genteel behaviour, Tersteeg would refuse to handle their canvases even though they might be masterpieces.

"Well, Vincent," he said, "I am glad to surprise you at work. That is how I like to come in on my artists."

"It is good of you to come all this way to see me, Mijnheer Tersteeg."

"Not at all. I have been meaning to see your studio ever since you moved here."

Vincent looked about at the bed, table, chairs, stove, and easel.

"It isn't much to look at."

"Never mind, pitch into your work and soon you'll be able to afford something better. Mauve tells me that you're beginning water-colours; there is a good market for those sketches. I should be able to sell some for you, and so should your brother."

"That's what I'm working toward, Mijnheer."

"You seem in rather better spirits than when I saw you yesterday."

"Yes, I was ill. But I recovered last night."

He thought of the wine, the gin and bitters, and Christine; he shivered at what Tersteeg would say if he knew about them. "Will you look at some of my sketches, Mijnheer? Your reaction would be valuable to me."

Tersteeg stood before the old woman in her white apron, standing out from the green soap background. His silence was not so eloquent as Vincent remembered it from the Plaats. He leaned on his walking stick for some moments, then hung it on his arm.

"Yes, yes," he said, "you're coming along. Mauve will make a water-colourist out of you, I can see that. It will take some time, but you will get there. You must hurry, Vincent, so that you can earn your own living. It is quite a strain on Theo to have to send you a hundred francs a month; I saw that when I was in Paris. You must support yourself as quickly as possible. I should be able to buy some of the small sketches very soon now."

"Thank you, Mijnheer. It is good of you to take an interest."

"I want to make you successful, Vincent. It means business for Goupils. As soon as I begin to sell your work, you will be able to take a better studio, buy some good clothes, and go out a bit into society. That is necessary if you want to sell your oils, later. Well, I must run on to Mauve's. I want to see that Scheveningen thing he is doing for the Salon."

"You'll look in again, Mijnheer?"

"Yes, of course. In a week or two. Mind you work hard and show me some improvement. You must make my visits pay, you know."

He shook hands and departed. Vincent pitched into his work once more. If only he could make a living, the very simplest living out of his work. He asked for nothing more. He could be independent. He would not have to be a burden on anyone. And best of all there would be no hurry; he could let himself feel his way slowly and surely toward maturity and the expression he was seeking.

In the afternoon mail there was a note from De Bock, on pink stationery.

Dear Van Gogh:

I'm bringing Artz's model to your studio tomorrow morning so that we can sketch together.

De B.

Artz's model proved to be a very beautiful young girl who charged one franc-fifty for posing. Vincent was delighted, as he would never have been able to hire her. There was a roaring fire in the little stove and the model undressed by it to keep warm. Only the professional models would pose naked in The Hague. This exasperated Vincent; the bodies he wanted to draw were those of old men and women, bodies that had tone and character.

"I've brought along my tobacco pouch," said De Bock, "and a little lunch that my housekeeper put up. I thought we might not want to disturb ourselves to go out."

"I'll try some of your tobacco. Mine is a trifle strong for the morning."

"I'm ready," said the model. "Will you pose me?"

"Sitting or standing, De Bock?"

"Let's try the standing first. I have some erect figures in my new landscape."

They sketched for about an hour and a half, and then the model tired.

"Let's do her sitting down," said Vincent. "The figure will be more relaxed."

They worked until noon, each bent over his own drawing board, exchanging only an occasional grunt about the light or tobacco. Then De Bock unpacked the lunch, and all three gathered about the stove to eat it. They munched the thin slices of bread, cold meats and cheese, and studied their morning's sketches.

"Queer, what an objective view you can get of your own work once you begin to eat," remarked De Bock.

"May I see what you've done?"

"With pleasure."

De Bock had put down a good likeness of the girl's face, but there was not even a faint suggestion of the individual nature of her body. It was just a perfect body.

"I say," exclaimed De Bock, looking at Vincent's sketch, "what's that thing you've got instead of her face? Is that what you mean by putting passion into it?"

"We weren't doing a portrait," replied Vincent. "We were doing a figure."

"That's the first time I ever heard a face doesn't belong on a figure."

"Take a look at your stomach," said Vincent.

"What's the matter with it?"

"It looks as though it were filled with hot air. I can't see an inch of bowels."

"Why should you? I didn't notice any of the poor girl's entrails hanging out."

The model went on eating without even a smile. She thought all artists were crazy, anyhow. Vincent placed his sketch alongside of De Bock's.

"If you will notice," he said, "my stomach is full of guts. You can tell just by looking at it that many a ton of food has wended its weary way through the labyrinth."

"What's that got to do with painting?" demanded De Bock. "We're not specialists in viscera, are we? When people look at my canvases, I want them to see the mist in the trees, and the sun setting red behind the clouds. I don't want them to see guts."

Every morning Vincent went out bright and early to find a model for the day. Once it was a blacksmith's boy, once an old woman from the insane asylum on the Geest, once a man from the peat market, and another time a grandmother and child from the Paddemoes, or Jewish quarter. Models cost him a great deal of money, money that he knew he ought to be saving for food for the end of the month. But of what good was it for him to be at The Hague, studying under Mauve, if he could not go full speed ahead? He would eat later, when he became established.

Mauve continued to instruct him patiently. Every evening Vincent went to the Uileboomen to work in the busy, warm studio. Sometimes he became discouraged because his water-colours were thick, muddy and dull. Mauve only laughed.

"Of course they're not right yet," he said. "If your work were transparent *now,* it would possess only a certain chic and would probably become heavy later on. Now you are pegging away at it and it becomes heavy, but afterwards it will go quickly and become light."

"That's true, Cousin Mauve, but if a man must earn money from his drawing, what is he to do?"

"Believe me, Vincent, if you try to arrive too soon, you will only kill yourself as an artist. The man of the day is usually the man of a day. In things of art the old saying is true, 'Honesty is the best policy!' It is better to take more trouble on a serious study than to develop a kind of chic that will flatter the public."

"I want to be true to myself, Cousin Mauve, and express severe, true things in a rough manner. But when there is the necessity of making one's living . . . I have done a few things I thought Tersteeg might . . . of course I realize . . ."

"Let me see them," said Mauve.

He glanced at the water-colours and tore them into a thousand pieces. "Stick to your roughness, Vincent," he said, "and don't run after the amateurs and dealers. Let those who like come to you. In due time you shall reap."

Vincent glanced down at the scraps of paper. "Thank you, Cousin Mauve," he said. "I needed that kick."

Mauve was having a little party that night, and a number of artists drifted in; Weissenbruch, known as the "merciless sword" for his fierce criticism of other men's work; Breitner, De Bock, Jules Bakhuyzen and Neuhuys, Vos's friend.

Weissenbruch was a little man with an enormous spirit. Nothing could ever conquer him. What he disliked—and that was nearly everything—he destroyed with a single lash of his tongue. He painted what he pleased and how he pleased, and made the public like it. Tersteeg had once objected to something in one of his canvases, so he refused to sell anything more through Goupil. Yet he sold everything he painted; nobody knew how or to whom. His face was as sharp as his tongue; his head, nose, and chin cutting. Everyone feared him and coveted his approbation. He had become a national character by the simple expedient of despising things. He got Vincent off into the corner by the fire, spat into the flames at frequent intervals to hear the pleasant sound of the hiss, and fondled a plaster foot.

"I hear you're a Van Gogh," he said. "Do you paint as successfully as your uncles sell pictures?"

"No. I don't do anything successfully."

"And a damn good thing for you. Every artist ought to starve until he's sixty. Then perhaps he would turn out a few good pieces of canvas."

"Tosh! You're not much over forty, and you're doing good work."

Weissenbruch liked that "Tosh!" It was the first time anyone had had the courage to say it to him for years. He showed his appreciation by lighting into Vincent.

"If you think my painting is any good, you better give up and become a *concierge*. Why do you think I sell it to the fool public? Because it's junk! If it was any good, I'd keep it for myself. No, my boy, I'm only practising now. When I'm sixty I shall really begin painting. Everything I do after that I shall keep by my side; when I die I'll have it buried with me. No artist ever lets go of anything he thinks is good, Van Gogh. He only sells his garbage to the public."

De Bock tipped Vincent a wink from the other side of the room, so Vincent said, "You've missed your profession, Weissenbruch; you ought to be an art critic."

Weissenbruch laughed and called out, "This cousin of yours isn't half as bad as he looks, Mauve. He's got a tongue in his head." He turned back to Vincent and said cruelly, "What in hell do you go around in those dirty rags for? Why don't you buy yourself some decent clothes?"

Vincent was wearing an old suit of Theo's that had been altered for him. The operation had not been successful, and in addition, Vincent had been wearing it over his water-colours every day.

"Your uncles have enough money to clothe the whole population of Holland. Don't they give you anything?"

"Why should they? They agree with you that artists should starve."

"If they don't believe in you they must be right. The Van Goghs are supposed to be able to smell a painter a hundred kilometres away. You're probably rotten."

"And you can go to hell!"

Vincent turned away angrily, but Weissenbruch caught him by the arm. He was smiling broadly.

"That's the spirit!" he cried. "I just wanted to see how much abuse you would take. Keep your courage up, my boy. You've got the stuff."

Mauve enjoyed doing imitations for his guests. He was the son of a clergyman, but there was room for only one religion in his life: painting. While Jet passed around tea and cookies and cheese balls, he preached the sermon about the fishing bark of Peter. Had Peter received or inherited that bark? Had he bought it on the installment plan? Had he, oh horrible thought, stolen it? The painters filled the room with their smoke and laughter, gulping down cheese balls and cups of tea with amazing rapidity.

"Mauve has changed," mused Vincent to himself.

He did not know that Mauve was undergoing the metamorphosis of the creative artist. He began a canvas lethargically, working almost without interest. Slowly his energy would pick up as ideas began to creep into his mind and become formulated. He would work a little longer, a little harder each day. As objects appeared clearly on the canvas, his demands upon himself became more exacting. His mind would flee from his family, from his friends and other interests. His appetite would desert him and he would lie awake nights thinking of things to be done. As his strength went down his excitement went up. Soon he would be living on nervous energy. His body would shrink on its ample frame and the sentimental eyes become lost in a hazy mist. The more he became fatigued, the more desperately he worked. The nervous passion which possessed him would rise higher and higher. In his mind he knew how long it would take him to finish; he set his will to last until that very day. He was like a man ridden by a thousand demons; he had years in which to complete the canvas, but something forced him to lacerate himself every hour of the twenty-four. In the end, he would be in such a towering passion and nervous excitement that a frightful scene ensued if anyone got in his way. He hurled himself at the canvas with every last ounce of his strength. No matter how long it took to finish, he always had will enough to the last drop of paint. Nothing could have killed him before he was completely through.

Once the canvas was delivered, he collapsed in a heap. He was weak, ill, delirious. It took Jet many days to nurse him back to health and sanity. His exhaustion was so complete that the very sight or smell of paint made him nauseated. Slowly, very slowly, his strength would return. In its wake would come his interest. He would begin to putter about the studio cleaning up things. He would walk in the fields, at first seeing nothing. In the end some scene would strike his eye. And so the cycle began all over again.

When Vincent had first come to The Hague, Mauve was just beginning the Scheveningen canvas. But now his pulse was rising day by day, and soon the mad, magnificent, most devastating of all deliriums would set in, that of artistic creation.

4

Christine knocked at Vincent's door a few nights later. She was dressed in a black petticoat and dark blue camisole, with a black cap over her hair. She had been standing at the washtub all day. Her mouth usually hung a little open when she was extremely fatigued; the pock-marks seemed to be wider and deeper than he had remembered them.

"Hello, Vincent," she said. "Thought I'd come see where you lived."

"You're the first woman to call on me, Christine. I bid you welcome. May I take your shawl?"

She sat down by the fire and warmed herself. After a moment she looked about the room.

"This aint bad," she said. " 'Cept that it's empty."

"I know. I haven't any money for furniture."

"Well, I guess it's all you need."

"I was just going to fix supper, Christine. Will you join me?"

"Why don't you call me Sien? Everyone does."

"All right, Sien."

"What was you having for supper?"

"Potatoes and tea."

"I made two francs today. I'll go buy a little beef."

"Here, I have money. My brother sent me some. How much do you want?"

"I guess fifty centimes is all we can eat."

She returned in a few moments with a paper of meat. Vincent took it from her and attempted to prepare dinner.

"Here, you sit down. You don't know nothing about cooking. I'm a woman."

As she leaned over the stove, the heat sent a warm glow to her cheek. She looked rather pretty. It was so natural and homelike to see her cutting potatoes into a pot, putting the meat in with them to stew and simmer. Vincent leaned a chair against the wall and watched her, a feeling of warmth in his heart. It was his home, and here was a woman preparing dinner for him with loving hands. How often he had dreamed of this picture with Kay as his companion. Sien glanced about at him. She saw the chair leaning against the wall at a perilous angle.

"Here, you damn fool," she said, "you sit up straight. Was you wanting to break your neck?"

Vincent grinned. Every woman with whom he had ever lived in the same house—his mother, sisters, aunts and cousins—every last one of them had said, "Vincent, sit up straight on that chair. You'll break your neck."

"All right, Sien," he said, "I'll be good."

As soon as her back was turned, he leaned the chair against the wall again and smoked his pipe contentedly. Sien put the dinner on the table. She had bought two rolls while she was out; when they finished eating the beef and potatoes, they mopped up the gravy with their bread.

"There," said Sien, "I bet you can't cook like that."

"No, Sien, when I cook, I can't tell whether I'm eating fish, fowl, or the devil."

Over their tea Sien smoked one of her black cigars. They chatted animatedly. Vincent felt more at home with her than he did with Mauve or De Bock. There was a certain fraternity between them that he did not pretend to understand. They spoke of simple things, without pretense or competition. When Vincent spoke, she listened; she was not eager for him to get through so that she could talk about herself. She had no ego that she wished to assert. Neither of them wished to impress the other. When Sien spoke of her own life, its hardships and miseries, Vincent had only to substitute a few words to make her stories describe perfectly his own. There was no challenge in their words, no affectation in their silences. It was the meeting of two souls unmasked, stripped of all class barrier, artifice and distinction.

Vincent got up. "What are you going to do?" she asked.

"The dishes."

"Sit down. You don't know how to do dishes. I'm a woman."

He tipped his chair against the stove, filled his pipe, and puffed contentedly while she leaned over the basin. Her hands were good with the soap suds on them, the veins standing out, the intricate network of wrinkles speaking of the labour they had done. Vincent got pencil and paper and sketched them.

"It's nice here," she said when she finished the dishes. "If only we had some gin and bitters . . ."

They spent the evening sipping the bitters, while Vincent sketched Sien. She seemed content to rest quietly in a chair by the warm stove, hands in her lap. The glow of the heat and the pleasure of talking to someone who understood gave her vivacity and alertness.

"When do you finish with your washing?" he asked.

"Tomorrow. And a good thing. I couldn't stand much more."

"Have you been feeling badly?"

"No, but it's coming, it's coming. The goddam kid wiggles in me now and again."

"Then you'll begin posing for me next week?"

"Is this all I got to do, just sit?"

"That's all. Sometimes you'll have to stand or pose naked."

"That aint so bad. You do all the work and I get paid."

She looked out the window. It was snowing.

"Wish I was home," she said. "It's cold and I aint got nothing but my shawl. It's a long walk."

"Do you have to come back to this neighbourhood again tomorrow morning?"

"Six o'clock. It's still dark then."

"You can stay here if you like, Sien. I'd be glad to have company."

"Won't I be in your way?"

"Not a bit. It's a wide bed."

"Can two sleep there?"

"Easily."

"Then I'll stay."

"Good."

"It's nice of you to ask me, Vincent."

"It's nice of you to stay."

In the morning she fixed him coffee, made the bed, and swept out the studio. Then she left him to go to her tubs. The place seemed suddenly empty when she was gone.

5

Tersteeg looked in again that afternoon. His eyes were bright and his cheeks red from the walk in the glowing cold.

"How does it go, Vincent?"

"Very well, Mijnheer Tersteeg. It is good of you to come again."

"Perhaps you have something interesting to show me? That is what I came for."

"Yes, I have some new things. Won't you sit down?"

Tersteeg looked at the chair, reached for his kerchief to dust it off, and then decided it might not be good manners. He sat down. Vincent brought him three or four small water-colours. Tersteeg glanced at them all hurriedly, as though he were skimming a long letter, then went back to the first and studied it.

"You're coming along," he said after a time. "These aren't right yet, they're a bit crude, but you show progress. You should have something for me to buy very soon, Vincent."

"Yes, Mijnheer."

"You must think about earning your living, my boy. It is not right to live on another man's money."

Vincent took the water-colours and looked at them. He supposed they were crude, but like every other artist, he was unable to see the imperfections in his own work.

"I would like nothing better than to support myself, Mijnheer."

"Then you must work harder. You must speed things up. I would like to have you do some things soon that I can buy."

"Yes, Mijnheer."

"At any event, I am glad to see you happy and at work. Theo has asked me to keep an eye on you. Do some good work, Vincent; I want to establish you in the Plaats."

"I try to make good things. But my hand doesn't always obey my will. However, Mauve complimented me on one of these."

"What did he say?"

"He said, 'It almost begins to look like a water-colour.'"

Tersteeg laughed, wrapped his wool scarf about his neck, said, "Plug on, Vincent, plug on; that is how great pictures are produced," and was gone.

Vincent had written to his Uncle Cor that he was established in The Hague, and had invited his uncle to visit him. Uncle Cor came often to The Hague to buy supplies and pictures for his art shop, which was the most important one in Amsterdam. One Sunday afternoon Vincent gave a party for some children with whom he had become acquainted. He had to keep them amused while he sketched, so he bought a bag of sweets and told them stories as he bent over his drawing board. When he heard a sharp knock on the door and a deep, booming voice, he knew that his uncle had arrived.

Cornelius Marinus Van Gogh was well known, successful and wealthy. For all that, there was a touch of melancholy about his wide, dark eyes. His mouth was a little less full than the other Van Gogh mouths. He had the family head; square across the wide, high brow, square across the strong jawbones, with a huge, rounded chin and a powerful nose.

Cornelius Marinus took in every last detail of the studio while giving the impression that he had not even glanced at it. He had probably seen the inside of more artists' studios than any man in Holland.

Vincent gave the children the rest of the sweets and sent them home. "Will you have a cup of tea with me, Uncle Cor? It must be very cold out."

"Thank you, Vincent."

Vincent served him and marvelled at how unconcernedly his uncle balanced the cup on his knee while chatting lightly about news of the day.

"So you are going to be an artist, Vincent," he said. "It's about time we had one in the Van Gogh family. Hein and Vincent and I have been buying canvases from strangers for the past thirty years. Now we'll be able to keep a little of the money in the family!"

Vincent smiled. "I have a running start," he said, "with three uncles and a brother in the picture selling business. Will you have a bit of cheese and bread, Uncle Cor? Perhaps you're hungry?"

C.M. knew that the easiest way to insult a poor artist was to refuse his food. "Yes, thank you," he said. "I had an early breakfast."

Vincent put several slices of thick, black bread on a chipped plate and then took out some coarse cheese from a paper. C.M. made an effort to eat a little.

"Tersteeg tells me that Theo is sending you a hundred francs a month?"

"Yes."

"Theo is young, and he should save his money. You ought to be earning your own bread."

Vincent's gorge was still high from what Tersteeg had said on the subject only the day before. He answered quickly, without thinking.

"Earn bread, Uncle Cor? How do you mean that? Earn bread . . . or deserve bread? Not to deserve one's bread, that is to say, to be unworthy of it, that certainly is a crime, for every honest man is worthy of his bread. But unluckily, not being able to earn it, though deserving it, that is a misfortune, and a great one."

He toyed with the black bread before him, rolling a piece of the inside into a round, hard pill.

"So if you say to me, Uncle Cor, 'You are unworthy of your bread,' you insult me. But if you make the rather just remark that I do not earn it always, that certainly is so. But what is the use in making the remark? It certainly does not get me any farther, if you say no more than that."

C.M. spoke no more about earning bread. They got along pleasantly enough until, quite by chance, Vincent mentioned the name of De Groux in speaking about expression.

"But don't you know, Vincent," said C.M., "that in private life De Groux has no good reputation?"

Vincent could not sit there and hear that said of the brave Father De Groux. He knew it would be far better to "Yes" his uncle, but he never seemed able to find a "Yes" when he was with the Van Goghs.

"It has always seemed to me, Uncle Cor, that when an artist shows his work to the public he has the right to keep to himself the inward struggle of his own private life, which is directly and fatally connected with the peculiar difficulties involved in producing a work of art."

"Just the same," said C.M., sipping the tea for which Vincent had offered him no sugar, "the mere fact that a man works with a paint brush, instead of a plough or a salesbook, does not give him the right to live licentiously. I don't think we ought to buy the pictures of artists who don't behave properly."

"I think it even more improper for a critic to dig up a man's private life, when his work is beyond reproach. The work of an artist and his private life are like a woman in childbirth and her baby. You may look at the child, but you may not lift her chemise to see if it is blood-stained. That would be very indelicate."

C.M. had just put a small bit of bread and cheese into his mouth. He spit it out hastily into the cup of his hand, rose, and flung it into the stove.

"Well, well," he commented. "Well well well well!"

Vincent was afraid that C.M. was going to be angry, but luckily things took a turn for the better. Vincent brought out his portfolio of smaller sketches and studies. He placed a chair by the light for his uncle. C.M. did not say anything at first, but when he came to a little drawing of the Paddemoes as seen from the peat market, that Vincent had sketched at twelve o'clock one night while strolling about with Breitner, he stopped.

"This is rather good," he remarked. "Could you make me more of these views of the city?"

"Yes, I make them for a change sometimes when I am tired of working from the model. I have some more. Would you care to see them?"

He leaned over his uncle's shoulder and searched through the uneven papers. "This is the Vleersteeg . . . this the Geest. This one is the fish market."

"Will you make twelve of them for me?"

"Yes, but this is business, so we must set a price."

"Very well, how much do you ask?"

"I have fixed the price for a small drawing of this size, either in pencil or pen, at two francs-fifty. Do you think that unreasonable?"

C.M. had to smile to himself. It was such a humble sum.

"No, but if they turn out well, I will ask you to make twelve of Amsterdam. Then I shall fix the price myself so that you will get a little more for them."

"Uncle Cor, this is my first order! I can't tell you how happy it makes me!"

"We all want to help you, Vincent. Just bring your work up to standard, and between us we'll buy everything you make." He took up his hat and gloves. "Give my compliments to Theo when you write."

Intoxicated with his success, Vincent snatched up his new water-colour and ran all the way to the Uileboomen. Jet answered the door. She seemed rather worried.

"I wouldn't go into the studio if I were you, Vincent. Anton is in a state."

"What's the trouble? Is he ill?"

Jet sighed. "The usual thing."

"Then I don't suppose he'll want to see me."

"You'd better wait until another time, Vincent. I'll tell him you were here. When he calms down a bit he'll come round to see you."

"You won't forget to tell him?"

"I won't forget."

Vincent waited many days, but Mauve did not come. In his place came Tersteeg, not once but twice. Each time the report was the same.

"Yes, yes, you have made a little progress, perhaps. But they are not right yet. I still could not sell them in the Plaats. I'm afraid you don't work hard enough or fast enough, Vincent."

"My dear Mijnheer, I get up at five o'clock and work until eleven and twelve at night. The only time I stop is for a bite of food now and then."

Tersteeg shook his head uncomprehendingly. He looked at the water-colours again. "I don't understand it. The same element of roughness and crudeness that I saw the first time you came to the Plaats is still in your work. You ought to be getting over that by now. Hard work usually does it, if a man has any ability at all."

"Hard work!" said Vincent.

"Goodness knows I want to buy your things, Vincent. I want to see you begin earning your own living. I don't think it right that Theo should have to . . . But I can't buy until your work is right, now can I? You're not looking for charity."

"No."

"You must hurry, that's all, you must hurry. You must begin to sell and make your own living."

When Tersteeg repeated this formula for the fourth time Vincent wondered if the man were playing some game on him. "You must earn your own living . . . but I can't buy anything!" How in the devil was he going to earn his living if no one would buy?

He met Mauve on the street one day. Mauve was walking at a furious clip with his head down, going nowhere, shoving his right shoulder out in front of him as he walked. He almost seemed not to recognize Vincent.

"I have not seen you for a long time, Cousin Mauve."

"I've been busy." Mauve's voice was cool, indifferent.

"I know; the new canvas. How is it coming?"

"Oh . . ." He made a vague gesture.

"May I drop into your studio some time for a moment? I'm afraid I'm not making progress with my water-colours."

"Not now! I'm busy, I tell you. I can't be wasting my time."

"Won't you come in to see me some time when you're out for a walk? Just a few words from you would set me right."

"Perhaps, perhaps, but I'm busy now. I must be going!"

He darted forward, thrusting his body before him, nervously propelling himself down the street. Vincent stood staring after him.

What in the world had happened? Had he insulted his cousin? Had he in some way estranged him?

He was utterly amazed a few days later to have Weissenbruch walk into his studio. Weissenbruch never bothered with the younger painters, or for that matter the accepted ones, except to give their work a hearty damning now and then.

"Well, well," he said, looking about, "this certainly is a palace. You'll be doing portraits of the King and Queen here pretty soon."

"If you don't like it," growled Vincent, "you can get out."

"Why don't you give up painting, Van Gogh? It's a dog's life."

"You seem to thrive under it."

"Yes, but I'm successful. You'll never be."

"Perhaps not. But I'll paint far better pictures than you ever will."

Weissenbruch laughed. "You won't, but you'll probably come closer to it than anyone in The Hague. If your work is anything like your personality . . ."

"Why didn't you say so?" demanded Vincent, taking out his portfolio. "Want to sit down?"

"I can't see when I'm sitting."

He pushed the water-colours aside with a "This is not your medium; water-colours are too insipid for the things you've got to say," and concentrated on the pencil sketches of the Borains, the Brabantines, and the old people Vincent had drawn since coming to The Hague. He chuckled to himself gaily as he gazed at one figure after another. Vincent prepared for a stiff volley of abuse.

"You draw confoundedly well, Vincent," said Weissenbruch, his sharp eyes twinkling. "I could work from these drawings myself!"

Vincent had set himself to catch a heavy weight; Weissenbruch's words were so light they almost broke his back. He sat down abruptly.

"I thought you were called the 'merciless sword.'"

"So I am. If I saw no good in your studies, I would tell you so."

"Tersteeg has scolded me about them. He says they are too rough and crude."

"Nonsense! That's where their strength lies."

"I want to go on with those pen sketches, but Tersteeg says I must learn to see things as water-colours."

"So they can sell, eh? No, my boy, if you see things as pen drawings, you must put them down as pen drawings. And above all, never listen to anybody—not even me. Go your own way."

"It looks like I'll have to."

"When Mauve said you were a born painter, Tersteeg said no, and then Mauve took your part against him. I was there. If it happens again, I will take your part also, now that I have seen your work."

"Mauve said I was a born painter?"

"Don't let that turn your head. You'll be lucky if you die one."

"Then why has he been so cool to me?"

"He treats everyone the same, Vincent, when he's finishing a picture.

Don't let it worry you; when the Scheveningen canvas is done he'll come round. In the meanwhile you may drop in at my studio if you want any help."

"May I ask you one question, Weissenbruch?"

"Yes."

"Did Mauve send you here?"

"Yes."

"Why did he do that?"

"He wanted to hear my opinion about your work."

"But why should he want that? If he thinks I'm a born . . ."

"I don't know. Perhaps Tersteeg put a doubt in his mind about you."

6

If Tersteeg was losing faith in him and Mauve was growing cooler every day, Christine was taking their place, and bringing into his life the simple companionship for which he longed. She came to the studio early every morning, and brought with her a sewing basket so that her hands might keep company with his. Her voice was rough and her choice of words unfortunate, but she spoke quietly, and Vincent found it easy not to hear her when he wanted to concentrate. For the most part, she was content to sit quietly by the stove, looking out the window or sewing little things for the new baby. She was a clumsy model and learned slowly, but she was eager to please. She soon fell into the habit of preparing his dinner before she went home.

"You mustn't bother about that, Sien," he told her.

"It aint no bother. I can do it better than you."

"Then of course you'll join me?"

"Sure. Mother's taking care of the kids. I like to stay here."

Vincent gave her a franc every day. He knew it was more than he could afford, but he liked her company; the thought that he was saving her from the tubs pleased him. Sometimes, if he had to go out during the afternoon, he would sketch her until late at night, and then she would not bother to go home at all. He enjoyed waking to the smell of fresh coffee and the sight of a friendly woman hovering over the stove. It was the first time he had ever had a *ménage;* he found it very comfortable.

Sometimes Christine would stay over for no reason at all. "I think I'll sleep here tonight, Vincent," she would say. "Can I?"

"Of course, Sien. Stay as often as you like. You know I'm glad to have you."

Although he never asked her to do anything, she acquired the habit of washing his linen, mending his clothes, and doing his little marketing.

"You don't know how to take care of yourselves, you men," she said. "You need a woman around. And I'm sure they cheat you at the market."

She was by no means a good housekeeper; the many years of sloth in her mother's house had destroyed most of the will to cleanliness and order. She took care of things sporadically, in sudden bursts of energy and determination. It was the first time she was keeping house for anyone she liked, and she enjoyed doing things . . . when she remembered them. Vincent was delighted to find that she wanted to do anything at all; he never even thought of reproving her. Now that she was no longer dead tired day and night, her voice lost some of its roughness: the vile words dropped out of her vocabulary one by one. She had learned to exercise very little control over her emotions, and when something displeased her, she would fly into a passionate rage, dropping back into her rough voice and using obscene words that Vincent had not heard since he was a young boy at school.

At such moments he saw Christine as a caricature of himself; he sat by quietly until the storm subsided. Christine was equally tolerant. When his drawing went all wrong, or she forgot everything he had taught her and posed awkwardly, he would burst into a fit of rage that fairly shook the walls. She let him speak his piece; in a very few moments calm was restored. Fortunately they never became angry at identical moments.

After he had sketched her often enough to become familiar with the lines of her body, he decided to do a real study. It was a sentence from Michelet that set him on the track: *Comment se fait-il qu'il y ait sur la terre une femme seule désespérée?* He posed Christine naked on a low block of wood near the stove. He turned the block of wood into a tree stump, put in a little vegetation, and transposed the scene to the out-of-doors. Then he drew Christine, gnarled hands on her knees, the face buried in the scraggy arms, the thin hair covering the spine a short way down, the bulbous breasts drooping to meet the lean shanks, the flat feet insecurely on the ground. He called it *Sorrow*. It was the picture of a woman from whom had been squeezed all the juice of life. Under it he wrote the line from Michelet.

The study took a week and exhausted his supply of money; there were still ten days to go until the first of March. There was enough black bread in the house to last for two or three days. He would have to stop working from the model altogether and that would set him back some more.

"Sien," he said, "I'm afraid I can't have you any more until after the first of the month."

"What's the matter?"

"I have no more money."

"You mean for me?"

"Yes."

"I aint got nothing else to do. I'll come anyway."

"But you must have money, Sien."

"I can get some."

"You can't do any washing, if you're here all day."

". . . well . . . don't worry . . . I'll get some."

He let her come for three more days, until his bread ran out. It was still a week to the first. He told Sien that he was going to Amsterdam to visit his uncle and that he would call at her house when he got back. He did some copying in his studio for three days on water without feeling much pain. On the third afternoon he went to De Bock's, hoping to be served tea and cake.

"Hello, old fellow," said De Bock, standing at his easel, "make yourself comfortable. I'm going to work straight through until my dinner engagement. There are some magazines over on the table. Just dig in."

But not a word about tea.

He knew Mauve would not see him, and he was ashamed to beg from Jet. He would rather have died of starvation than ask Tersteeg for anything after the latter had spoken against him to Mauve. No matter how desperate he became, it never occurred to him that he might earn a few francs at some craft other than his own. His old foe the fever came up, his knees developed rickets and he stayed in bed. Though he knew it was impossible, he kept hoping for the miracle that would send Theo's hundred francs a few days early. Theo did not get paid until the first.

Christine walked in the afternoon of the fifth day without knocking. Vincent was asleep. She stood over him, looking at the furrowed lines in his face, the paleness of the skin under his red beard, the parchment roughness of his lips. She placed a hand lightly on his forehead and felt the fever. She searched the shelf on which the supplies were usually kept. She saw that there was not a crumb of dry, black bread or a lone bean of coffee. She went out.

About an hour later Vincent began having dreams of his mother's kitchen in Etten and the beans she used to prepare for him. He awakened to find Christine mixing things in pots over the stove.

"Sien," he said.

She went over to the bed and put her cool hand on his cheek; the red beard was on fire. "Don't be proud no more," she said. "And don't tell no more lies. If we're poor, it aint our fault. We got to help each other. Didn't you help me the first night we met down the wine cellar?"

"Sien," he said.

"Now you lay there. I went home and got some potatoes and string beans. They're all ready."

She mashed the potatoes on the plate, put some green beans alongside, sat on his bed and fed him. "Why did you give me your money every day if you didn't have enough? It aint no good if you go hungry."

He could have stood the privation until Theo's money arrived, even if it had been weeks. It was always the unexpected piece of kindness that broke his back. He decided to see Tersteeg. Christine washed his shirt, but there was no iron to smooth it with. The next morning she gave him a little breakfast of bread and coffee. He set out to walk to the Plaats. One heel was off his muddy boots, his trousers were patched and dirty. Theo's coat was many sizes too small. He had an old necktie askew at the left side of his neck.

On his head was one of the outlandish caps that he had a perfect genius for picking up, no one knew where.

He walked along the Ryn railroad tracks, skirted the edge of the woods and the station where the steam cars left for Scheveningen, and made for town. The feeble sun made him sensitive to his own anaemia. At the Plein he caught sight of himself in the window glass of a shop. In one of his rare moments of clarity he saw himself as the people of The Hague saw him: a dirty, unkempt tramp, belonging nowhere, wanted by no one, ill, weak, uncouth and *déclassé*.

The Plaats opened on a broad triangle to meet the Hof-vijver alongside of the castle. Only the richest shops could afford to keep establishments there. Vincent was afraid to venture into the sacred triangle. He had never before realized how many millions of miles of caste he had put between himself and the Plaats.

The clerks in Goupils were dusting. They stared at him with unabashed curiosity. This man's family controlled the art world of Europe. Why did he go about so foully?

Tersteeg was at his desk in the upstairs office. He was opening mail with a jade handled paper knife. He noticed Vincent's small, circular ears that came below the line of his eyebrows, the oval of his face that tapered down through the jaws and then flattened out at the square chin, the head that was going smooth of hair above the left eye, the green-blue eyes that stared through him so probingly and yet without comment, the full, red mouth made redder by the beard and moustache in which it was set. He could never make up his mind whether he thought Vincent's face and head ugly or beautiful.

"You're the first customer in the shop this morning, Vincent," he said. "What can I do for you?"

Vincent explained his predicament.

"What have you done with your allowance?"

"I've spent it."

"If you have been improvident, you can't expect me to encourage you. There are thirty days to each month; you should not spend more than the proper share each day."

"I have not been improvident. Most of the money has gone for models."

"Then you should not hire them. You can work more cheaply by yourself."

"To work without models is the ruin of a painter of the figure."

"Don't paint figures. Do cows and sheep. You don't have to pay them."

"I can't draw cows and sheep, Mijnheer, if I don't feel cows and sheep."

"You ought not to be drawing people, anyway; you can't sell those sketches. You ought to be doing water-colours and nothing else."

"Water-colour is not my medium."

"I think your drawing is a kind of narcotic which you take in order not to feel the pain it costs you not to be able to make water-colours."

There was a silence. Vincent could think of no possible answer to this.

"De Bock doesn't use models, and he's wealthy. Yet I think you will agree with me that his canvases are splendid; the prices are going up steadily. I have been waiting for you to get some of his charm into your work. But somehow it doesn't come. I am really disappointed, Vincent; your work remains uncouth and amateurish. Of one thing I am sure, you are no artist."

Vincent's cutting hunger of the past five days suddenly severed the sinews in his knees. He sat down weakly on one of the hand carved Italian chairs. His voice was lost somewhere in his empty bowels, and he could not find it.

"Why do you say that to me, Mijnheer?" he asked, after a pause.

Tersteeg took out a spotless handkerchief, wiped his nose, the corners of his mouth, and his chin beard. "Because I owe it to both you and your family. You ought to know the truth. There is still time for you to save yourself, Vincent, if you act quickly. You are not cut out to be an artist; you ought to find your right niche in life. I never make a mistake about painters."

"I know," said Vincent.

"One great objection for me is that you started too late. If you had begun as a boy, you might have developed some quality in your work by now. But you are thirty, Vincent, and you ought to be successful. I was at your age. How can you ever hope to succeed if you have no talent? And worse yet, how can you justify yourself in taking charity from Theo?"

"Mauve once said to me, 'Vincent, when you draw you are a painter.' "

"Mauve is your cousin; he was being kind to you. I am your friend, and believe me, my kindness is of the better sort. Give it up before you find that your whole life has slipped out from under you. Some day, when you have found your real work and are successful, you will come back to thank me."

"Mijnheer Tersteeg, I have not had a centime in my pocket for a piece of bread in five days. But I would not ask you for money if it were only for myself. I have a model, a poor, sick woman. I have not been able to pay her the money I owe. She needs it. I beg you to lend me ten guilders until the money arrives from Theo. I will pay it back."

Tersteeg rose and stared out the window at the swans in the pond, all that was left of the original court water works. He wondered why Vincent had come to The Hague to settle, when his uncles owned art shops in Amsterdam, Rotterdam, Brussels, and Paris.

"You think it would be a favour if I lent you ten guilders," he said without turning about, his hands clasped behind his Prince Albert coat, "but I'm not sure that it wouldn't be a greater favour to refuse you."

Vincent knew how Sien had earned the money for those potatoes and string beans. He could not let her go on supporting him.

"Mijnheer Tersteeg, no doubt you are right. I am no artist and I have no ability. It would be very unwise for you to encourage me with money. I must begin earning my own living immediately and find my niche in life. But for the sake of our old friendship I ask you to lend me ten guilders."

Tersteeg took a wallet from the inside of his Prince Albert, searched for a ten guilder note, and handed it to Vincent without a word.

"Thank you," said Vincent. "You are very kind."

As he walked home along the well kept streets with the neat little brick houses speaking to him eloquently of security, comfort, and peace, he murmured to himself, "One cannot always be friends; one must quarrel sometimes. But for six months I will not go to see Tersteeg again, or speak to him, or show him my work."

He dropped in at De Bock's to find out just what this salable thing was, this charm that De Bock had, but he had not. De Bock was sitting with his feet up on a chair, reading an English novel.

"Hello," he said, "I'm in the doldrums. Can't draw a line. Pull up a chair and amuse me. Is it too early in the morning for a cigar? Have you heard any good stories lately?"

"Let me see some of your canvases again, will you, De Bock? I want to find out why your work sells and mine doesn't."

"Talent, old fellow, talent," said De Bock, getting up lazily. "It's a gift. Either you have it or you haven't. I couldn't tell you what it is myself, and I paint the blasted things."

He brought in half a dozen canvases still on their frames, and chatted lightly about them while Vincent sat there, poking holes through the thin paint and thin sentiment with burning eyes.

"Mine are better," he said to himself. "Mine are truer, deeper. I say more with a carpenter's pencil than he says with a whole paint box. What he expresses is obvious. When he gets all through he has said nothing. Why do they give him praise and money and refuse me the price of black bread and coffee?"

When he made his escape, Vincent murmured to himself, "There is a consumptive atmosphere in that house. There is something blasé and insincere about De Bock that oppresses me. Millet was right: *J'aimerais mieux ne rien dire que de m'exprimer faiblement.'*

"De Bock can keep his charm and his money. I'll take my life of reality and hardship. That is not the road on which one perishes."

He found Christine mopping the wooden floor of the studio with a wet rag. Her hair was tied up in a black kerchief and a faint dew of perspiration glistened in the pock holes of her face.

"Did you get the money?" she asked, looking up from the floor.

"Yes. Ten francs."

"Aint it wonderful to have rich friends?"

"Yes. Here are the six francs I owe you."

Sien got up and wiped her face on the black apron.

"You can't give me nothing now," she said. "Not 'till your brother sends that money. Four francs won't help you much."

"I can get along, Sien. You need this money."

"So do you. Tell you what we'll do. I'll stay here 'till you get a letter from your brother. We'll eat out of the ten francs like it belonged to both of us. I can make it last longer than you."

"What about the posing? I won't be able to pay you anything for that."

"You'll give me my bed and board. Aint that enough? I'm glad enough to stay here where it's warm and I don't got to go to work and make myself sick."

Vincent took her in his arms and smoothed back the thin, coarse hair from her forehead.

"Sien, sometimes you almost perform a miracle. You almost make me believe there is a God!"

7

About a week later he went to call on Mauve. His cousin admitted him to the studio but threw a cloth over his Scheveningen canvas hastily before Vincent could see it.

"What is it you want?" he asked, as though he did not know.

"I've brought a few water-colours. I thought you might be able to spare a little time."

Mauve was cleaning a bunch of brushes with nervous, preoccupied movements. He had not been into his bedroom for three days. The broken snatches of sleep he had managed on the studio couch had not refreshed him.

"I'm not always in a mood to show you things, Vincent. Sometimes I am too tired and then you must for goodness' sake await a better moment."

"I'm sorry, Cousin Mauve," said Vincent, going to the door. "I didn't mean to disturb you. Perhaps I may drop in tomorrow evening?"

Mauve had taken the cloth off his easel and did not even hear him.

When Vincent returned the following evening, he found Weissenbruch there. Mauve was verging on hysterical exhaustion. He seized upon Vincent's entrance to amuse himself and his friend.

"Weissenbruch," he cried, "this is how he looks."

He went off into one of his clever impersonations, screwing up his face in rough lines and sticking his chin forward eagerly to look like Vincent. It was a good caricature. He walked over to Weissenbruch, peered up at him through half shut eyes and said, "This is the way he speaks." He went off into a nervous sputtering of words in the rough voice that often came out of Vincent. Weissenbruch howled.

"Oh, perfect, perfect," he cried. "This is how others see you, Van Gogh. Did you know you were such a beautiful animal? Mauve, stick your chin out that way again and scratch your beard. It's really killing."

Vincent was stunned. He shrank into a corner. A voice came out of him that he did not recognize as his own. "If you had spent rainy nights on the streets of London, or cold nights in the open of the Borinage, hungry, homeless, feverish, you would also have ugly lines in your face, and a husky voice!"

After a few moments, Weissenbruch left. As soon as he was gone from the room, Mauve stumbled to a chair. The reaction from his little debauch made him quite weak. Vincent stood perfectly still in the corner; at last Mauve noticed him.

"Oh, are you still here?" he said.

"Cousin Mauve," said Vincent impetuously, screwing up his face in the manner that Mauve had just caricatured, "what has happened between us? Only tell me what I have done. Why do you treat me this way?"

Mauve got up wearily and pushed the swash of hair straight upward. "I do not approve of you, Vincent. You ought to be earning your own living. And you ought not go about disgracing the Van Gogh name by begging money from everyone."

Vincent thought a moment and then said, "Has Tersteeg been to see you?"

"No."

"Then you don't care to teach me any more?"

"No."

"Very well, let us shake hands and not feel any bitterness or animosity toward each other. Nothing could ever alter my feeling of gratitude and obligation to you."

Mauve did not answer for a long time. Then he said, "Do not take it to heart, Vincent. I am tired and ill. I will help you all I can. Have you some sketches with you?"

"Yes. But this is hardly the time . . ."

"Show them to me."

He studied them with red eyes and remarked, "Your drawing is wrong. Dead wrong. I wonder that I never saw it before."

"You once told me that when I drew, I was a painter."

"I mistook crudity for strength. If you really want to learn, you will have to begin all over again at the beginning. There are some plaster casts over in the corner by the coal bin. You can work on them now if you like."

Vincent walked to the corner in a daze. He sat down before a white plaster foot. For a long time he was unable to think or move. He drew some sketching paper from his pocket. He could not draw a single line. He turned about and looked at Mauve standing before his easel.

"How is it coming, Cousin Mauve?"

Mauve flung himself on the little divan, his bloodshot eyes closing instantly. "Tersteeg said today that it's the best thing I've done."

After a few moments, Vincent remarked aloud, "Then it was Tersteeg!" Mauve was snoring lightly and did not hear him.

After a time the pain numbed a little. He began sketching the plaster foot. When his cousin awoke a few hours later, Vincent had seven complete drawings. Mauve jumped up like a cat, just as though he had never been asleep, and darted to Vincent's side.

"Let me see," he said. "Let me see."

He looked at the seven sketches and kept repeating, "No! No! No!"

He tore them all up and flung the pieces on the floor. "The same crudity, the same amateurishness! Can't you draw that cast the way it looks? Are you unable to make a positive statement about a line? Can't you make an exact duplicate for once in your life?"

"You sound like a teacher at a drawing academy, Cousin Mauve."

"If you had gone to more academies, you might know how to draw by now. Do that foot over again. And see if you can make it a foot!"

He went through the garden into the kitchen to get something to eat, and returned to work on his canvas by lamplight. The hours of the night went by. Vincent drew foot after foot. The more he drew, the more he detested the poisonous piece of plaster sitting before him. When dawn sneaked gloomily in the north window, he had a great number of copies before him. He rose, cramped and sick at heart. Once again Mauve looked at his sketches and crumpled them in his hand.

"They're no good," he said, "no good at all. You violate every elemental rule of drawing. Here, go home and take this foot with you. Draw it over and over and over again. And don't come back until you get it right!"

"I'll be damned if I will!" shouted Vincent.

He flung the foot into the coal bin, shattering it to a thousand pieces. "Do not speak to me again about plaster, for I cannot stand it. I will draw from casts only when there are no more hands and feet of living people to draw from."

"If that's the way you feel about it," said Mauve icily.

"Cousin Mauve, I will not allow myself to be governed by a cold system, yours or anyone else's. I've got to express things according to my own temperament and character. I must draw things the way I see them, not the way you see them!"

"I care to have nothing more to do with you," said Mauve in the tone of a doctor speaking to a corpse.

When Vincent awoke at noon, he found Christine in the studio with her eldest son, Herman. He was a pale faced child of ten with fish-green, frightened eyes and a negligible chin. Christine had given him a piece of paper and pencil to keep him quiet. He had not been taught to read or write. He came to Vincent shyly, for he was wary of strangers. Vincent showed him how to hold the pencil and draw a cow. He was delighted and soon became friendly. Christine put out a little bread and cheese, and the three of them lunched at the table.

Vincent thought of Kay and beautiful little Jan. A lump arose in his throat.

"I aint feeling so good today, so you can draw Herman instead."

"What's the matter, Sien?"

"I dunno. My insides is all twisted."

"Have you felt like this with all the other children?"

"I been sick, but not like this. This is worse."

"You must see a doctor."

"It aint no use seeing the doctor at the free ward. He only gives me medicine. Medicine don't do no good."

"You ought to go to the state hospital at Leyden."

". . . I guess I ought."

"It's only a short ride on the train. I'll take you there tomorrow morning. People go from all over Holland to that hospital."

"They say it's good."

Christine stayed in bed all day. Vincent sketched the boy. At dinner time he walked Herman home to Christine's mother and left him. Early in the morning they took the train to Leyden.

"Of course you've been feeling sick," said the doctor after he had examined Christine and asked her innumerable questions. "The child is not in position."

"Can anything be done, doctor?" asked Vincent.

"Oh, yes, we can operate."

"Would that be serious?"

"Not at this time. The child would simply have to be turned with the forceps. However, that takes a little money. Not for the operation, but for the hospital expenses." He turned to Christine. "Have you anything saved up?"

"Not a franc."

The doctor almost allowed himself a sigh. "That's usually the way," he said.

"How much would it cost, doctor?" asked Vincent.

"Not more than fifty francs."

"And if she doesn't have the operation?"

"There's not a chance in the world of her pulling through."

Vincent thought for a moment. The twelve water-colours for his Uncle Cor were almost done; that would be thirty francs. He would take the other twenty francs off Theo's April allowance.

"I'll take care of the money, doctor," he said.

"Good. Bring her back on Saturday morning and I'll operate myself. Now just one thing more; I don't know what the relationship is between you two and I don't care to be told. That's not part of the doctor's business. But I think you ought to be informed that if this little lady ever goes back to walking the streets, she will be dead within six months."

"She'll never return to that life, doctor. I give you my word."

"Splendid. Then I'll see you on Saturday morning."

A few days later Tersteeg came in. "I see you are still at it," he said.

"Yes, I am at work."

"I received the ten francs you sent back in the mail. You might at least have come in to thank me for the loan personally."

"It was a long walk, Mijnheer, and the weather was bad."

"The walk was not too long when you wanted the money, eh?"

Vincent did not answer.

"It is just such lack of manners, Vincent, that turns me against you. It is why I have no faith in you and cannot buy your work."

Vincent sat himself on the edge of the table and prepared for another struggle. "I should think that your buying would be a thing quite apart from personal disputes and difference," he said. "I should think it would depend not on me but on my work. It is not exactly fair to let personal antipathy influence your judgement."

"Certainly not. If you could only make something salable, with some charm in it, I would be only too glad to sell it in the Plaats."

"Mijnheer Tersteeg, work on which one has plodded hard and into which one has put some character and sentiment, is neither unattractive nor unsalable. I think it is perhaps better for my work not to try to please everyone at first."

Tersteeg sat down without unbuttoning his topcoat or taking off his gloves. He sat with both hands resting on the knob of his cane.

"You know, Vincent, I sometimes suspect that you prefer not to sell; that you would much rather live off someone else."

"I would be very happy to sell a drawing, but I am happier still when a real artist like Weissenbruch says about a piece of work which you call unsalable, 'That is true to nature; I could work from that myself.' Although money is of great value to me, especially now, the principal thing is for me to make something serious."

"That might apply to a rich man like De Bock, but it certainly does not apply to you."

"The fundamentals of painting, my dear Mijnheer, have very little to do with a man's income."

Tersteeg put his stick across his knees and leaned back in his chair. "Your parents have written to me, Vincent, and asked me to do what I can to help you. Very well. If I cannot in full conscience buy your drawings I can at least give you a little practical advice. You are ruining yourself by going about in those unspeakable rags. You must buy yourself some new clothes and try to keep up appearances. You forget that you are a Van Gogh. Again, you should try to associate with the better people of The Hague, and not always go about with working people and the lower classes. You somehow have a penchant for the sordid and ugly; you have been seen in the most questionable of places and with the most questionable of companions. How can you ever hope to arrive at success if you behave that way?"

Vincent got off the corner of the table and stood over Tersteeg. If there was any chance to win back the man's friendship, this was the time and place. He searched about within himself to find a soft and sympathetic voice.

"Mijnheer, it is good of you to try to help me, and I will answer as sincerely and truthfully as I know how. How can I dress better when I have not a single franc to spare for clothes, and no way of earning one?

"To stroll on wharves, and in alleys and markets, in waiting rooms and even saloons, that is not a pleasant pastime, *except for an artist!* As such, one would rather be in the dirtiest place, where there is something to draw, than at a tea party with charming ladies. The searching for subjects, the living among working people, the drawing from nature on the very spot is a rough work, even a dirty work at times. The manners and dress of a salesman are not suitable for me, or for anyone else who does not have to talk with fine ladies and rich gentlemen to sell them expensive things and make money.

"My place is drawing diggers in a hole on the Geest, as I have been doing all day. There, my ugly face and shabby coat perfectly harmonize with the surroundings, and I am myself and work with pleasure. When I wear a fine coat, the working people I want to sketch are afraid of me and distrust me. The purpose of my drawing is to make people see things worth observing and which not everyone knows. If I sometimes have to sacrifice social manners to get my work done, am I not justified? Do I lower myself by living with the people I draw? Do I lower myself when I go into the houses of labourers and poor people, and when I receive them in my studio? I think my profession requires it. Is that what you call ruining myself?"

"You are very headstrong, Vincent, and will not listen to older men who can help you. You failed before, and you will fail again. It will be the same story all over."

"I have a draftsman's fist, Mijnheer Tersteeg, and I cannot stop drawing no matter how much you advise me! I ask you, since the day I began to draw have I ever doubted or hesitated or wavered? I think you know quite well that I pushed onward, and that little by little I am growing stronger in the battle."

"Perhaps. But you are battling for a lost cause."

He rose, buttoned the glove on his wrist, and placed the high silk hat on his head. "Mauve and I will take care that you do not receive any more money from Theo. That is the only way to bring you around to your senses."

Vincent felt something crash in his breast. If they attacked him from the side of Theo, he was lost.

"My God!" he cried. "Why should you do this to me? What have I done to you that you should want to destroy me? Is it honest to kill a man just because he differs from your opinions? Can't you let me go my own way? I promise never to bother you again. My brother is the only soul I have left in the world. How can you take him from me?"

"It is for your own good, Vincent," said Tersteeg, and went out.

Vincent grabbed up his money purse and ran all the way downtown to buy a plaster foot. Jet answered the doorbell at the Uileboomen. She was surprised to see him.

"Anton isn't at home," she said. "He's frightfully angry at you. He said he doesn't ever want to see you again. Oh, Vincent, I'm so unhappy that this has happened!"

Vincent put the plaster foot in her hand. "Please give this to Anton," he said, "and tell him that I am deeply sorry."

He turned away and was about to go down the steps when Jet put a sympathetic hand on his shoulder.

"The Scheveningen canvas is finished. Would you care to see it?"

He stood in silence before Mauve's painting, a large picture of a fishing smack being drawn up on the beach by horses. He knew that he was looking at a masterpiece. The horses were nags, poor, ill-treated old nags, black, white and brown; they were standing there, patient and submissive, willing, resigned and quiet. They still had to draw the heavy boat up the last bit of the way; the job was almost finished. They were panting, covered with sweat, but they did not complain. They had got over that long ago, years and years ago. They were resigned to live and work somewhat longer, but if tomorrow they had to go to the skinner, well, be it so, they were ready.

Vincent found a deep, practical philosophy in the picture. It said to him, "Savoir souffrir sans se plaindre, ça c'est la seule chose pratique, c'est la grande science, la leçon à apprendre, la solution du problème de la vie."

He walked away from the house, refreshed and ironically amused that the man who struck him the very worst of all blows should be the one to teach him how to bear it with resignation.

8

Christine's operation was successful, but it had to be paid for. Vincent sent off the twelve water-colours to his Uncle Cor and waited for the thirty francs payment. He waited many, many days; Uncle Cor sent the money at his leisure. Since the doctor at Leyden was the same one who was going to deliver Christine, they wished to keep in his good graces. Vincent sent off his last twenty francs many days before the first. The same old story began all over again. First coffee and black bread, then just black bread, then plain water, then fever, exhaustion, and delirium. Christine was eating at home, but there was nothing left over to bring to Vincent. When he reached the end of his rope, he crawled out of bed and floated somehow or other through a burning fog to Weissenbruch's studio.

Weissenbruch had plenty of money but he believed in living austerely. His atelier was four flights up, with a huge skylight on the north. There was nothing in the workshop to distract the man; no books, no magazines, no sofa or comfortable chair, no sketches on the walls, no window to look out of, nothing but the bare implements of his trade. There was not even an extra stool for a guest to sit down; that kept people away.

"Oh, it's you, is it?" he growled, without putting down his brush. He did not mind interrupting people in their own studios, but he was about as hospitable as a trapped lion when anyone bothered him.

Vincent explained what he had come for.

"Oh, no, my boy!" exclaimed Weissenbruch. "You've come to the wrong person, the very last man in the world. I wouldn't lend you a ten centime piece."

"Can't you spare the money?"

"Certainly I can spare it! Do you think I'm a goddam amateur like you

and can't sell anything? I've got more money in the bank right now than I
can spend in three lifetimes."

"Then why won't you lend me twenty-five francs? I'm desperate! I haven'
even a crumb of stale bread in the house."

Weissenbruch rubbed his hands in glee. "Fine! Fine! That's exactly wha
you need! That's wonderful for you. You may be a painter yet."

Vincent leaned against the bare wall; he did not have the strength to stand
up without support. "What is there so wonderful about going hungry?"

"It's the best thing in the world for you, Van Gogh. It will make you
suffer."

"Why are you so interested in seeing me suffer?"

Weissenbruch sat on the lone stool, crossed his legs, and pointed a red
tipped brush at Vincent's jaw.

"Because it will make a real artist out of you. The more you suffer, the
more grateful you ought to be. That's the stuff out of which first-rate painters
are made. An empty stomach is better than a full one, Van Gogh, and a
broken heart is better than happiness. Never forget that!"

"That's a lot of rot, Weissenbruch, and you know it."

Weissenbruch made little stabs in Vincent's direction with his brush. "The
man who has never been miserable has nothing to paint about, Van Gogh.
Happiness is bovine; it's only good for cows and tradesmen. Artists thrive
on pain; if you're hungry, discouraged and wretched, be grateful! God is
being good to you!"

"Poverty destroys."

"Yes, it destroys the weak. But not the strong! If poverty can destroy
you, then you're a weakling and ought to go down."

"And you wouldn't raise a finger to help me?"

"Not even if I thought you the greatest painter of all time. If hunger and
pain can kill a man, then he's not worth saving. The only artists who belong
on this earth are the men whom neither God nor the devil can kill until
they've said everything they want to say."

"But I've gone hungry for years, Weissenbruch. I've gone without a roof
over my head, walking in the rain and snow with hardly anything on, ill and
feverish and abandoned. I have nothing more to learn from that sort of
thing."

"You haven't scratched the surface of suffering yet. You're just a beginner.
I tell you, pain is the only infinite thing in this world. Now run on home
and pick up your pencil. The hungrier and more miserable you get, the
better you will work."

"And the quicker I'll have my drawings rejected."

Weissenbruch laughed heartily. "Of course they'll be rejected! They ough
to be. That's good for you, too. It will make you even more miserable. Then
your next canvas will be better than the one before. If you starve and suffer
and have your work abused and neglected for a sufficient number of years,
you may eventually—notice I say you may, not you will—you may eventually

urn out one painting that will be fit to hang alongside of Jan Steen or . . ."

". . . or Weissenbruch!"

"Just so. Or Weissenbruch. If I gave you any money now I would be obbing you of your chances for immortality."

"To hell with immortality! I want to draw here and now. And I can't do hat on an empty stomach."

"Nonsense, my boy. Everything of value that has been painted has been done on an empty stomach. When your intestines are full, you create at the wrong end."

"It doesn't seem to me that I've heard about you suffering so much."

"I have creative imagination. I can understand pain without going through t."

"You old fraud!"

"Not at all. If I had seen that my work was insipid, like De Bock's, I would have thrown my money away and lived like a tramp. It just so happens that I can create the perfect illusion of pain without a perfect memory of it. That's why I'm a great artist."

"That's why you're a great humbug. Come along, Weissenbruch, be a good fellow and lend me twenty-five francs."

"Not even twenty-five centimes! I tell you, I'm sincere. I think too highly of you to weaken your fabric by lending you money. You will do brilliant work some day, Vincent, providing you carve out your own destiny; the plaster foot in Mauve's dustbin convinced me of that. Now run along, and stop at the soup kitchen for a bowl of free broth."

Vincent stared at Weissenbruch for a moment, turned and opened the door.

"Wait a minute!" cried Weissenbruch.

"You don't mean to tell me you're going to be a coward and weaken?" asked Vincent harshly.

"Look here, Van Gogh, I'm no miser; I'm acting on principle. If I thought you were a fool, I'd give you twenty-five francs to get rid of you. But I respect you as a fellow craftsman. I'm going to give you something you couldn't buy for all the money in the world. And there's not another man in The Hague, except Mauve, that I'd give it to. Come over here. Adjust that curtain on the skylight. That's better. Have a look at this study. Here's how I'm going to work out the design and apportion my material. For Christ's sake, how do you expect to see it if you stand in the light?"

An hour later Vincent left, exhilarated. He had learned more in that short time than he could have in a year at art school. He walked some distance before he remembered that he was hungry, feverish, and ill, and that he had not a centime in the world.

9

A few days later he encountered Mauve in the dunes. If he had any hopes
of a reconciliation, he was disappointed.

"Cousin Mauve, I want to beg your pardon for what happened in your
studio. It was stupid of me. Can't you see your way clear to forgive me?
Won't you come and see my work some time and talk things over?"

Mauve refused point blank. "I will certainly not come to see you, that is
all over."

"Have you lost faith in me so completely?"

"Yes. You have a vicious character."

"If you will tell me what I have done that is vicious, I will try to mend
my ways."

"I am no longer interested in what you do."

"I have done nothing but eat and sleep and work as an artist. Is that
vicious?"

"Do you call yourself an artist?"

"Yes."

"How absurd. You never sold a picture in your life."

"Is that what being an artist means—selling? I thought it meant one who
was always seeking without absolutely finding. I thought it meant the contrary
from 'I know it, I have found it.' When I say I am an artist, I only mean
'I am seeking, I am striving, I am in it with all my heart.' "

"Nevertheless, you have a vicious character."

"You suspect me of something—it is in the air—you think I am keeping
something back. 'Vincent is hiding something that cannot stand the light!'
What is it, Mauve? Speak to me frankly."

Mauve went back to his easel and began applying paint. Vincent turned
away and walked slowly over the sand.

He was right. There *was* something in the air. The Hague had learned
about his relation to Christine. De Bock was the one to break the news. He
blew in with a naughty smile on his bud-like mouth. Christine was posing,
so he spoke in English.

"Well, well, Van Gogh," he said, throwing off his heavy black overcoat
and lighting a long cigarette. "It's all over town that you've taken a mistress.
I heard it from Weissenbruch, Mauve and Tersteeg. The Hague is up in arms
about it!"

"Oh," said Vincent, "so that's what it's all about."

"You should be more discreet, old fellow. Is she some model about town?
I thought I knew all the available ones."

Vincent glanced over at Christine knitting by the fire. There was a homely
sort of attractiveness about her as she sat there, sewing in her merino and

apron, her eyes upon the little garment she was making. De Bock dropped his
cigarette to the floor and jumped up.

"My God!" he exclaimed, "you don't mean to tell me *that's* your mistress?"

"I have no mistress, De Bock. But I presume that's the woman they're
talking about."

De Bock wiped some imaginary perspiration from his forehead and looked
Christine over carefully. "How the devil can you bring yourself to sleep with
her?"

"Why do you ask that?"

"My dear old chap, she's a hag! The commonest sort of a hag! What can
you be thinking about? No wonder Tersteeg was shocked. If you want a mistress, why don't you pick up one of the neat little models about town? There
are plenty of them around."

"As I told you once before, De Bock, this woman is not my mistress."

"Then what . . . ?"

"She's my wife!"

De Bock closed his tiny lips over his teeth with the gesture of a man
tucking a buttonhole around a button.

"Your wife!"

"Yes. I intend to marry her."

"My God!"

De Bock threw one last look of horror and repulsion at Christine, and
fled without even putting on his coat.

"What were you saying about me?" asked Christine.

Vincent crossed and looked down at her for a moment. "I told De Bock
that you are going to be my wife."

Christine was silent for a long time, her hands working busily. Her mouth
hung slightly open and her tongue would dart quickly, like the tongue of a
snake, to moisten the rapidly drying lips.

"You would really marry me, Vincent? Why?"

"If I don't marry you, it would have been kinder of me to let you alone.
I want to go through the joys and sorrows of domestic life in order to
paint it from my own experience. I was in love with a woman once, Christine.
When I went to her house, they told me I disgusted her. My love was true
and honest and strong, Christine, and when I came away I knew it had been
killed. But after death there is a resurrection; you were that resurrection."

"But you can't marry me! What about the children? And your brother
may stop sending the money."

"I respect a woman who is a mother, Christine. We'll keep the new baby
and Herman here with us, the others can stay with your mother. As for
Theo . . . yes . . . he may cut off my head. But when I write him the full
truth I do not think he will abandon me."

He sat on the floor by her feet. She was looking so much better than
when he had first met her. There was a little touch of happiness in her
melancholy brown eyes. A new spirit of life had come to her whole

personality. Posing had not been easy for her, but she had worked hard
and patiently. When he first met her, she had been coarse and ill and miserable; now her whole manner was more quiet. She had found new health and
life. As he sat there looking up into her crude, marked face into which a
slight note of sweetness had come, he thought once again of the line from
Michelet: *"Comment se fait-il qu'il y ait sur la terre une femme seule
désespérée?"*

"Sien, we'll skimp and be as saving as possible, won't we? I fear there
will come a time when I shall be quite without means. I shall be able to
help you until you go to Leyden, but when you come back I don't know how
you will find me, with or without bread. What I have I will share with you
and the child."

Christine slipped off the chair, onto the floor beside him, put her arms
about his neck and laid her head on his shoulder.

"Just let me stay with you, Vincent. I don't ask for much. If there's nothing but bread and coffee, I don't complain. I love you, Vincent. You're the
first man's ever been good to me. You don't got to marry me if you don't
want. I'll pose and work hard and do whatever you tell me. Only let me
stay with you! It's the first time I ever been happy, Vincent. I don't want
things. I'll just share what you have and be happy."

He could feel the swelling child against him, warm and living. He ran
his fingertips gently over her homely face, kissing the scars one by one.
He let her hair fall down her back smoothing out the thin strands with
tender strokes of his hand. She laid her flushed, happy cheek on his beard
and rubbed softly against the grain.

"You do love me, Christine?"

"Yes, Vincent, I do."

"It's good to be loved. The world may call it wrong if it likes."

"To hell with the world," said Christine, simply.

"I will live as a labourer; that suits me. You and I understand each other
and we do not need to mind what anybody says. We do not have to pretend
to keep up a social standing. My own class cast me out long ago. I would
rather have a crust of bread at my own hearth, however poor it may be,
than live without marrying you."

They sat on the floor, warmed by the red glow of the stove, entwined
in each other's arms. It was the postman who broke the spell. He handed
Vincent a letter from Amsterdam. It read:

Vincent:
*Have just heard of your disgraceful conduct. Kindly cancel my order for
the six drawings. I will take no further interest in your work.*

C. M. Van Gogh.

His whole fate now rested with Theo. Unless he could make Theo understand the full nature of his relationship with Christine, he too would be
justified in cutting off the hundred francs a month. He could do without his

master, Mauve; he could do without his dealer, Tersteeg; he could do without his family, friends, and *confrères* as long as he had his work and Christine. But he could not do without that hundred francs a month!

He wrote long, passionate letters to his brother, explaining everything, begging Theo to understand and not desert him. He lived from day to day with a dark fear of the worst. He did not dare to order more drawing material than he could pay for, or undertake any water-colours or push on.

Theo offered objections, many of them, but he did not condemn. He offered advice too, but not once did he infer that if his advice were not taken he would stop sending the money. And in the end, although he did not approve, he assured Vincent that his help would go on just as before.

It was now early May. The doctor at Leyden had told Christine she would be confined sometime in June. Vincent decided that it would be wiser if she did not move in with him until after the confinement, at which time he hoped to rent the vacant house next door on the Schenkweg. Christine spent most of her time at the studio, but her possessions still remained at her mother's. They were to be officially married after her recovery.

He went to Leyden for Christine's confinement. The child did not move from nine in the evening until half past one. It had to be taken with the forceps, but it was not injured at all. Christine suffered a great deal of pain, but she forgot it all when she saw Vincent.

"We will soon begin to draw again," she said.

Vincent stood looking down at her with tears in his eyes. It did not matter that the child belonged to another man. It was his wife and baby, and he was happy with a taut pain in his chest.

When he returned to the Schenkweg he found the landlord and owner of the lumber yard in front of the house.

"What about taking that other house, Mijnheer Van Gogh? It is only eight francs a week. I'll have it all painted and plastered for you. If you will pick out the kind of wallpaper you like, I will put it on for you."

"Not so fast," said Vincent. "I would like the new house for when my wife comes home, but I must write to my brother first."

"Well, I must put on some wallpaper, so pick the one you like best, and if you can't take the house, it won't matter."

Theo had been hearing about the house next door for several months. It was much larger, with a studio, living room, kitchen, alcove, and an attic bedroom. It was four francs a week more than the old place, but with Christine, Herman, and the baby all coming to the Schenkweg, they needed the new space. Theo replied that he had received another raise in salary and that Vincent could rely upon receiving a hundred and fifty francs a month for the present. Vincent rented the new house immediately. Christine was coming home in a week and he wanted her to find a warm nest upon her arrival. The owner lent him two men from the yard to carry his furniture next door to the new studio. Christine's mother came there to straighten things.

10

The new studio looked so real, with plain greyish-brown paper, scrubbed wooden floors, studies on the walls, an easel at each end, and a large, white, deal working table. Christine's mother put up white muslin curtains at the windows. Adjoining the studio was an alcove where Vincent kept all his drawing boards, portfolios and woodcuts; in a corner was a closet for his bottles, pots, and books. The living room had a table, a few kitchen chairs, an oil stove, and a large wicker chair for Christine near the window. Beside it he put a small iron crib with a green cover, and above it the etching by Rembrandt of the two women by the cradle, one of them reading from the Bible by the light of a candle.

He secured everything that was strictly necessary for the kitchen; when Christine came back she could prepare dinner in ten minutes. He bought an extra knife, fork, spoon, and plate against the day when Theo should come to visit them. Up in the attic he put a large bed for himself and his wife, and the old one with all the bedding in good order for Herman. He and Christine's mother got straw, seaweed, bedticking, and filled the mattresses themselves in the attic.

When Christine left the hospital, the doctor who treated her, the nurse of the ward, and the head nurse all came to say good-bye. Vincent realized more fully than before that she was a person for whom serious people might have sympathy and affection. "She has never seen what is good," he said to himself, "so how can she be good?"

Christine's mother and her boy Herman were at the Schenkweg to greet her. It was a delightful homecoming, for Vincent had told her nothing about the new nest. She ran about touching things; the cradle, the easy chair, the flower pot he had placed on the sill outside her window. She was in high spirits.

"The professor was awfully funny," she cried. "He said, 'I say, are you fond of gin and bitters? And can you smoke cigars?' 'Yes,' I answered. 'I only asked it,' he said, 'to tell you that you need not give it up. But you must not use vinegar, pepper, or mustard. And you should eat meat at least once a week.' "

Their bedroom looked a good deal like a hold of a ship, for it had been wainscotted. Vincent had to carry the iron cradle upstairs every night and down again to the living room in the morning. He had to do all the house work for which Christine was still too weak; making the beds, lighting the fire, lifting and carrying and cleaning. He felt as though he had been together with Christine and the children for a long time, and that he was in his element. Although she still suffered from the operation, there was a renewing and a reviving in her.

Vincent went back to work with a new peace in his heart. It was good to

ave a hearth of one's own, to feel the bustle and organization of a family
bout one. Living with Christine gave him courage and energy to go on with
is work. If only Theo did not desert him he was certain that he could
evelop into a good painter.

In the Borinage he had slaved for God; here he had a new and more
angible kind of God, a religion that could be expressed in one sentence:
aat the figure of a labourer, some furrows in a ploughed field, a bit of sand,
ea and sky were serious subjects, so difficult, but at the same time so
eautiful, that it was indeed worth while to devote his life to the task of
xpressing the poetry hidden in them.

One afternoon, coming home from the dunes, he met Tersteeg in front
f the Schenkweg house.

"I am glad to see you, Vincent," said Tersteeg. "I thought I would come
nd inquire how you are getting on."

Vincent dreaded the storm that he knew would break once Tersteeg got
pstairs. He stood chatting with him a few moments on the street in order
o gather strength. Tersteeg was friendly and pleasant. Vincent shivered.

When the two men entered, Christine was nursing the baby in her wicker
hair. Herman was playing by the stove. Tersteeg gaped at them for a long,
eng time. When he spoke, it was in English.

"What is the meaning of that woman and child?"

"Christine is my wife. The child is ours."

"You have actually married her!"

"We haven't gone through the ceremony yet, if that's what you mean."

"How can you think of living with a woman . . . and children who . . ."

"Men usually marry, do they not?"

"But you have no money. You're being supported by your brother."

"Not at all. Theo pays me a salary. Everything I make belongs to him.
Ie will get his money back some day."

"Have you gone mad, Vincent? This is certainly a thing that comes from
n unsound mind and temperament."

"Human conduct, Mijnheer, is a great deal like drawing. The whole
erspective changes with the shifted position of the eye, and depends not on
ae subject, but on the man who is looking."

"I shall write to your father, Vincent. I shall write and tell him of the
·hole affair."

"Don't you think it would be ridiculous if they received an indignant letter
om you, and soon after, a request from me to come and visit here at my
xpense?"

"You intend to write, yourself!"

"Can you ask that? Of course I will. But you must admit that now is a
ery untimely moment. Father is being moved to the vicarage at Nuenen. My
ife's condition is such that any anxiety or strain now would be murder."

"Then of course I shan't write. My boy, you're as foolish as the man
·ho wants to drown himself. I only want to save you from it."

"I don't doubt your good intentions, Mijnheer Tersteeg, and that is why I try not to be angry at your words. But this conversation is very disagreeable to me."

Tersteeg went away, a baffled look on his face. It was Weissenbruch who delivered the first real blow for the outside world. He drifted in nonchalantly one afternoon to see if Vincent was still alive.

"Hello," he said. "I notice you managed to get along without that twenty-five francs."

"Yes."

"Now aren't you glad I didn't coddle you?"

"I believe about the first thing I said to you, that night at Mauve's, was 'Go to hell!' I repeat my invitation."

"If you keep this up, you'll become another Weissenbruch; you've got the making of a real man in you. Why don't you introduce me to your mistress. I've never had the honour."

"Bait me all you like, Weissenbruch, but leave her alone."

Christine was rocking the iron cradle with its green cover. She knew that she was being ridiculed, and looked up at Vincent with pain on her face. Vincent crossed to the mother and child and stood by their side, protectively. Weissenbruch glanced at the group, then at the Rembrandt over the cradle.

"I say," he exclaimed, "you make a corking motif. I'd like to do you. I'd call it *Holy Family!*"

Vincent sprang after Weissenbruch with an oath, but the latter got out the door safely. Vincent went back to his family. There was a bit of mirror hung on the wall beside the Rembrandt. Vincent glanced up, caught the reflection of the three of them and in one horrible, devastating instant of clarity saw through the eyes of Weissenbruch . . . the bastard, the whore, and the charity monger.

"What did he call us?" asked Christine.

"The Holy Family."

"What's that?"

"A picture of Mary, Jesus, and Joseph."

Tears sprang to her eyes and she buried her head in the baby's clothes. Vincent went on his knees beside the iron cradle to comfort her. Dusk was creeping in the north window and threw a quiet shadow over the room. Once again Vincent was able to detach himself and see the three of them, just as though he were not a member of the group. This time he saw through the eyes of his own heart.

"Don't cry, Sien," he said. "Don't cry, darling. Lift up your head and dry your tears. *Weissenbruch was right!*"

11

Vincent discovered Scheveningen and oil painting at about the same time. Scheveningen was a little fishing village lying in a valley of two protective sand dunes on the North Sea. On the beach there were rows of square fishing barks with one mast and deep-coloured, weather beaten sails. They had rude, square rudders behind, fishing nets spread out ready for the sea, and a tiny rust-red or sea-blue triangular flag aloft. There were blue wagons on red wheels to carry the fish to the village; fisherwives in white oilskin caps fastened at the front by two round gold pins; family crowds at the tide's edge to welcome the barks; the Kurzaal flying its gay flags, a pleasure house for foreigners who liked the taste of salt on their lips, but not choked down their throats. The sea was grey with whitecaps at the shore and ever deepening hues of green fading into a dull blue; the sky was a cleaning grey with patterned clouds and an occasional design of blue to suggest to the fishermen that a sun still shines over Holland. Scheveningen was a place where men worked, and where the people were indigenous to the soil and the sea.

Vincent had been doing a good many street scenes in water-colour and he found that medium satisfactory for a quick impression. But water-colour did not have the depth, the thickness, the character to express the things he needed to say. He yearned for oil, but he was afraid to tackle it because he had heard of so many painters being ruined by going to oil before they learned to draw. Then Theo came to The Hague.

Theo was now twenty-six, and a competent art dealer. He travelled frequently for his house, and was everywhere known as one of the best young men in the business. Goupil and Company had sold out in Paris to Boussod, Valadon (known as *les Messieurs*) and although they had retained Theo in his former position, the art business was not what it had been under Goupil and Uncle Vincent. Pictures were now sold for the highest price obtainable —regardless of merit—and only the successful painters were patronized. Uncle Vincent, Tersteeg, and Goupil had considered it the very first duty of an art dealer to discover and encourage new and young artists; now only the old and recognized painters were solicited. The newcomers in the field, Manet, Monet, Pissarro, Sisley, Renoir, Berthe Morisot, Cezanne, Degas, Guillaumin, and the even younger men, Toulouse-Lautrec, Gauguin, Seurat and Signac, were trying to say something different from what Bouguereau and the academicians were repeating endlessly, but no one would listen to them. None of these revolutionists had ever had a canvas exhibited or offered up for sale under the roof of *les Messieurs*. Theo had developed a profound distaste for Bouguereau and the academicians; his sympathies were all with the young innovators. Every day he did what he could to persuade *les Messieurs* to exhibit the new paintings and educate the public to buy. *Les Messieurs* thought the innovators mad, childish, and completely without technique. Theo thought them the future masters.

Christine remained upstairs in the attic bedroom while the brothers met in the studio. When their first greetings were over, Theo said, "I had to come on business, too, but I must confess that my primary purpose in The Hague is to dissuade you from establishing any permanent relationship with this woman. First of all, what is she like?"

"Do you remember our old nurse at Zundert, Leen Verman?"

"Yes."

"Sien is that kind of person. She is just an ordinary woman of the people, yet for me she has something sublime. Whoever loves one ordinary, commonplace person, and is loved by her, is already happy, notwithstanding the dark side of life. It was the feeling of being of some use that brought me to myself again and made me revive. I did not seek for it, but it found me. Sien puts up with all the worries and troubles of a painter's life, and is so willing to pose that I think I shall become a better artist with her than if I had married Kay."

Theo walked about the studio and finally spoke while staring intently at a water-colour. "The only thing I can't understand is how you could fall in love with this woman while you were so desperately in love with Kay."

"I didn't fall in love, Theo, not immediately. Because Kay turned me down, should all my human feelings be extinguished? When you come here you do not find me discouraged and melancholy, but you come into a new studio and a home in full swing; no mysterious studio, but one that is rooted in real life—a studio with a cradle and a baby's high chair—where there is no stagnation, but where everything pushes and urges and stirs to activity. To me it is as clear as day that one must feel what one draws, that one must live in the reality of family life if one wishes to express intimately that family life."

"You know I never draw class distinctions, Vincent, but do you think it wise . . . ?"

"No, I don't think I've lowered or dishonoured myself," interrupted Vincent, "because I feel my work lies in the heart of the people, that I must keep close to the ground, grasp life to the quick, and make progress through many cares and troubles."

"I don't dispute all that." Theo crossed swiftly and stood looking down at his brother. "But why does it necessitate a marriage?"

"Because there is a promise of marriage between her and me. I don't want you to consider her as a mistress, or as somebody with whom I am having a liaison without caring for the consequences. That promise of marriage is twofold; firstly a promise of civil marriage as soon as circumstances will permit, but secondly, it is a promise meanwhile to help each other, to cherish each other as if we were already married, to share everything together."

"But surely you will wait a bit before you go into the civil marriage?"

"Yes, Theo, if you ask me. We will postpone it until I earn a hundred and fifty francs by selling my work, and your help will no longer be necessary. I promise you I shall not marry her until my drawing has progressed so far that I'm independent. By degrees, as I begin to earn, you can send me less each month, and at last I will not need your money any longer. Then we will talk about a civil marriage."

"That sounds like the wisest thing to do."

"Here she comes, Theo. For my sake, try to think of her only as a wife and mother! For that's what she really is."

Christine came down the stairs at the rear of the studio. She had on a neat black dress, her hair was carefully combed back, and the touch of colour in her face almost obliterated the pock marks. She had become pretty in a homely sort of way. Vincent's love had surrounded her with an aura of confidence and well-being. She shook hands with Theo quietly, asked if he wouldn't have a cup of tea, and insisted that he remain for supper. She sat in her easy chair by the window, sewing and rocking the cradle. Vincent ran excitedly back and forth across the studio, showing charcoal figures, street scenes in water-colour, group studies hammered on with a carpenter's pencil. He wanted Theo to see the progress of his work.

Theo had faith that some day Vincent would become a great painter, but he was never quite sure he liked the things Vincent had done . . . as yet. Theo was a discriminating amateur, carefully trained in the art of judging, but he never could make up his mind just what he thought of his brother's work. For him, Vincent was always in a state of becoming, never in the state of having arrived.

"If you begin to feel the need to work in oil," he said, after Vincent had shown him all his studies and spoken of his craving, "why don't you begin? What are you waiting for?"

"For the assurance that my drawing is good enough. Mauve and Tersteeg say I don't know how . . ."

". . . and Weissenbruch says you do. You're the one who must be the final judge. If you feel that you've got to express yourself in deeper colour now, the time is ripe. Jump in!"

"But, Theo, the expense! Those confounded tubes cost their weight in gold."

"Meet me at my hotel tomorrow morning at ten. The sooner you begin sending me oil canvases, the quicker I'll get my money out of this investment."

During supper Theo and Christine chatted animatedly. When Theo left, he turned to Vincent on the stairs and said in French, "She's nice, really nice. I had no idea!"

They made a strange contrast, walking up the Wagenstraat the following morning; the younger brother carefully groomed, his boots polished, linen starched, suit pressed, necktie neatly in place, black bowler hat at a jaunty angle, soft brown beard carefully trimmed, walking along with a well poised, even pace; and the other, with worn out boots, patched trousers that did

not match the tight coat, no necktie, an absurd peasant's cap stuck on the
top of his head, beard scrambling out in furious red whorls, hitching along
with jerky, uneven steps, waving his arms and making excited gestures as
he talked.

They were not conscious of the picture they made.

Theo took Vincent to Goupils to buy the tubes of paint, brushes, and
canvas. Tersteeg respected and admired Theo; he wanted to like and under
stand Vincent. When he heard what they had come for, he insisted upon
finding all the material himself and advising Vincent on the merits of the
various pigments.

Theo and Vincent tramped the six kilometres across the dunes to
Scheveningen. A fishing smack was just coming in. Near the monument
there was a little wooden shed in which a man sat on the lookout. As soon
as the boat came in view the fellow appeared with a large flag. He was
followed by a crowd of children. A few minutes after he had waved his
flag, a man on an old horse arrived to go and fetch the anchor. The group
was joined by a number of men and women who came pouring over the sand
hill from the village to welcome the crew. When the boat was near enough
the man on horseback went into the water and returned with the anchor
Then the fishermen were brought ashore on the backs of fellows with high
rubber boots, and with each arrival there was a great cheer of welcome
When they were all ashore and the horses had dragged the bark up on the
beach, the whole troop marched home over the sand hill in caravan style
with the man on the horse towering over them like a tall spectre.

"This is the sort of thing I want to do with my paints," said Vincent

"Let me have some canvases as soon as you become satisfied with your
work. I might be able to find purchasers in Paris."

"Oh, Theo, you must! You must begin to sell me!"

12

When Theo left, Vincent began experimenting with his pigments. He did
three oil studies; one a row of pollard willows behind the Geest bridge, an
other of a cinder path, and a third of the vegetable gardens of Meerdervoort
where a man in a blue smock was picking up potatoes. The field was of
white sand, partly dug up, still covered with rows of dried stalks with green
weeds between. In the distance there were dark green trees and a few roofs
When he looked at his work in the studio, he was elated; he was certain
that no one could possibly know they were his first efforts. The drawing, the
backbone of painting and the skeleton that supported all the rest, was ac
curate and true to life. He was surprised a little because he had thought his
first things would be failures.

He was busy painting a sloping ground in the woods, covered with
mouldered, dry beech leaves. The ground was light and dark reddish brown

made more so by the shadows of trees which threw streaks over it and sometimes half blotted it out. The question was to get the depth of colour, the enormous force and solidity of the ground. While painting, he perceived for the first time how much light there was still in that darkness. He had to keep that light, and keep at the same time the depth of rich colour.

The ground was a carpet of deep reddish brown in the glow of an autumn evening sun, tempered by the trees. Young birches sprang up, caught light on one side, and were sparkling green there, the shadowy sides of the stems were warm, deep black-green. Behind the saplings, behind the brownish red soil was a very delicate sky, bluish grey, warm, hardly blue, all aglow. Against it was a hazy border of green and a network of little stems and yellowish leaves. A few figures of wood gatherers were wandering around like dark masses of mysterious shadow. The white cap of a woman, who was bending to reach a dry branch, stood out brusquely against the deep red-brown of the ground. A dark silhouette of a man appeared above the underbrush; moulded against the sky, the figure was large and full of poetry.

While painting he said to himself, "I must not go away before there is something of an autumn evening feeling in it, something mysterious, something serious." But the light was fading. He had to work quickly. The figures he painted in at once by a few strong strokes with a resolute brush. It struck him how firmly the little tree stems were rooted in the ground. He tried to paint them in, but the ground was already so sticky that a brush stroke was lost in it. He tried again and again, desperately, for it was getting darker. At last he saw he was defeated; no brush could suggest anything in that rich loam-brown of the earth. With a blind intuition he flung the brush away, squeezed the roots and trunks on the canvas from the tubes of paint, picked up another brush, and modeled the thick, coloured oil with the handle.

"Yes," he exclaimed, as night finally claimed the woods, "now they stand there, rising from the ground, strongly rooted in it. I have said what I wanted to say!"

Weissenbruch looked in that evening. "Come along with me to *Pulchri*. We're having some tableaux and charades."

Vincent had not forgotten his last visit. "No, thanks, I don't care to leave my wife."

Weissenbruch walked over to Christine, kissed her hand, asked after her health, and played with the baby quite jovially. He evidently had no recollection of the last thing he had said to them.

"Let me see some of your new sketches, Vincent."

Vincent complied only too gladly. Weissenbruch picked out a study of Monday's market, where they were pulling down the stands; another of a line waiting in front of the soup kitchen; another of three old men at the insane asylum; another of a fishing smack at Scheveningen with the anchor raised, and a fifth that Vincent had made on his knees, in the mud of the dunes during a driving rain storm.

"Are these for sale? I'd like to buy them."

"Is this another of your poor jokes, Weissenbruch?"

"I never joke about painting. These studies are superb. How much do you want?"

Vincent said, "Name your own price," numbly, afraid that he was going to be ridiculed at any moment.

"Very well, how about five francs apiece? Twenty-five for the lot."

Vincent's eyes shot open. "That's too much! My Uncle Cor only paid me two and a half francs."

"He cheated you, my boy. All dealers cheat you. Some day they will sell for five thousand francs. What do you say, is it a deal?"

"Weissenbruch, sometimes you're an angel and sometimes you're a fiend!"

"That's for variety, so my friends won't get tired of me."

He took out a wallet and handed Vincent twenty-five francs. "Now come along with me to *Pulchri*. You need a little entertainment. We're having a farce by Tony Offermans. It will do you good to laugh."

So Vincent went along. The hall of the club was crowded with men all smoking cheap and strong tobacco. The first tableau was after an etching by Nicholas Maes, *The Stable at Bethlehem*, very good on tone and colour but decidedly off in expression. The other was after Rembrandt's *Isaac Blessing Jacob*, with a splendid Rebecca looking on to see if her trick would succeed. The close air gave Vincent a headache. He left before the farce and went home, composing the sentences of a letter as he walked.

He told his father as much about the story of Christine as he thought expedient, inclosed Weissenbruch's twenty-five francs, and asked Theodorus to come to The Hague as his guest.

A week later his father arrived. His blue eyes were fading, his step becoming slower. The last time they had been together, Theodorus had ordered his oldest son from the house. In the interim they had exchanged friendly letters. Theodorus and Anna Cornelia had sent several bundles of underwear, outer clothing, cigars, homemade cake, and an occasional ten franc note. Vincent did not know how his father would take to Christine. Sometimes men were understanding and generous, sometimes they were blind and vicious.

He did not think his father could remain indifferent and raise objections—near a cradle. A cradle was not like anything else; there was no fooling with it. His father would have to forgive whatever there might have been in Christine's past.

Theodorus had a large bundle under his arm. Vincent opened it, drew out a warm coat for Christine, and knew that everything was all right. After she had gone upstairs to the attic bedroom, Theodorus and Vincent sat together in the studio.

"Vincent," said his father, "there was one thing you did not mention in your letter. Is the baby yours?"

"No. She was carrying it when I met her."

"Where is its father?"

"He deserted her." He did not think it necessary to explain the child's anonymity.

"But you will marry her, Vincent, won't you? It's not right to live this way."

"I agree. I want to go through the legal ceremony as soon as possible. But Theo and I decided that it would be better to wait until I am earning a hundred and fifty francs a month through my drawing."

Theodorus sighed. "Yes, perhaps that would be the best. Vincent, your mother would like you to come home for a visit sometime. And so should I. You will enjoy Nuenen, son; it is one of the most lovely villages in all the Brabant. The little church is so tiny, and looks like an Eskimo's igloo. It seats less than a hundred people, imagine! There are hawthorn hedges around the parsonage, Vincent, and behind the church is a flower filled yard with sand mounds and old wooden crosses."

"With wooden crosses!" said Vincent. "White ones?"

"Yes. The names are in black, but the rain is washing them away."

"Is there a nice tall steeple on the church, Father?"

"A delicate, fragile one, Vincent, but it goes way, way up into the sky. Sometimes I think it almost reaches God."

"Throwing a thin shadow over the graveyard," Vincent's eyes were sparkling. "I'd like to paint that."

"There's a stretch of heath and pine woods close by, and peasants digging in the fields. You must come home soon for a visit, son."

"Yes, I must see Nuenen. The little crosses, and the steeple and the diggers in the field. I guess there will always be something of the Brabant about me."

Theodorus returned home to assure his wife that things were not so bad with their boy as they had imagined. Vincent plunged into his work with an even greater zeal. More and more he found himself going back to Millet: "*L'art c'est un combat; dans l'art il faut y mettre sa peau.*" Theo believed in him, his mother and father did not disapprove of Christine, and no one in The Hague disturbed him any more. He was completely free to go ahead with his work.

The owner of the lumber yard sent him as models all the men who came for work and could not get it. As his pocketbook emptied, his portfolio filled. He drew the baby in the cradle by the stove many, many times. When the fall rains came he worked outdoors on oil torchon and captured the effects he wanted. He quickly learned that a colourist is one who, seeing a colour in nature, knows at once how to analyse it and say, "That grey-green is yellow with black, and hardly any blue."

Whether he was drawing the figure or landscape, he wished to express not sentimental melancholy but serious sorrow. He wanted to reach out so far that people would say of his work, "He feels deeply, he feels tenderly."

He knew that in the eyes of the world he was a good-for-nothing, an eccentric and disagreeable man, someone who had no position in life. He wanted to show in his work just what there was in the heart of such an eccentric man, of such a nobody. In the poorest huts, in the dirtiest corners he saw drawings and pictures. The more he painted, the more other activitie lost their interest. The more he got rid of them the quicker his eye graspe the picturesque qualities of life. Art demanded persistent work, work i spite of everything, and a continuous observation.

The only difficulty was that oil pigments were so frightfully expensive, an he laid his colour on so thick. When he squeezed it out of the tube onto th canvas in rich deep masses, it was like pouring francs into the Zuider Zee He painted so fast that his canvas bill was enormous; he did at one sittin an oil that would have taken Mauve two months. Well, he could not pain thin, and he could not work slowly; his money evaporated and his studi became filled with pictures. As soon as his allowance arrived from Theo— who had arranged to send fifty francs on the first, tenth, and twentieth— he would rush down to the dealer and buy large tubes of ochre, cobalt, an Prussian blue, and smaller tubes of Naples yellow, *terra sienna,* ultramarine and gamboge. Then he would work happily until the paints and the franc were exhausted, usually five or six days after the allowance arrived from Paris, and his troubles set in again.

He was amazed to find that so many things had to be bought for the baby that Christine had to have constant medicines, new garments, special food that Herman had to buy books and supplies for the school he was sent to and that the household was a bottomless pit into which he was forever pouring lamps, pots, blankets, coal and wood, curtains, rugs, candles, sheets, silver ware, plates, furniture, and an endless stream of food. It was hard to know just how to apportion the fifty francs between his painting and the thre people who were dependent upon him.

"You look like a labourer rushing off to the wine shop the minute he get paid," remarked Christine one time when Vincent snatched the fifty franc out of Theo's envelope and began gathering up empty tubes.

He built a new perspective instrument with two long legs that would stand up in the sand of the dunes, and had the blacksmith make iron corners for the frame. Scheveningen, with the sea, the sand dunes, the fisherfolk, the barks and horses and nets, lured him most. He trudged across the dunes every day, loaded down with his heavy easel and perspective instrument, to catch the changing nature of the sea and sky. As fall deepened and othe artists began to hug their studio fires, he went out to paint in the wind, the rain, the mist and the storm. In the roughest of weather his wet paint often became covered with blowing sand and salt water. The rain drenched him the mist and wind chilled him, the sand got into his eyes and nose . . . and he loved every last minute of it. Nothing but death could stop him now

One night he showed Christine a new canvas. "But Vincent," she exclaimed "how do you make it look so real?"

Vincent forgot he was speaking to an illiterate woman of the people. H might have been talking to Weissenbruch or Mauve.

"I don't know myself," he said. "I sit down with a white board befor the spot that strikes me, and I say, 'That white board must become something!' I work for a long time, I come back home dissatisfied, I put it away in the closet. When I have rested a little I go to look at it with a kind of fear. I am still dissatisfied because I have too clearly in my mind the splendid original to be content with what I have made of it. But after all, I find in my work an echo of what struck me. I see that nature has told me something, has spoken to me, and that I have put it down in shorthand. In my shorthand there may be words that cannot be deciphered, there may be mistakes or gaps, but there is something in it of what the woods or beach or figure has told me. Do you understand?"

"No."

13

Christine understood very little of what he was doing. She thought his hunger to paint things a sort of costly obsession. She knew it was the rock upon which his life was built, however, and made no attempt to oppose him; the purpose, the slow progress and painful expression of his work were completely lost upon her. She was a good companion for ordinary domestic purposes, but only a very small part of Vincent's life was domestic. When he wished to express himself in words, he was forced to write to Theo; he poured out a long passionate letter almost every night, telling of all the things he had seen, painted, and thought during the day. When he wished to enjoy the expression of others, he turned to novels; French, English, German and Dutch. Christine shared only a fraction of his life. But he was satisfied; he did not regret his decision to take Christine to wife, nor did he attempt to force upon her the intellectual pursuits for which she was manifestly unqualified.

All this was very well during the long months of the spring, summer, and autumn, when he left the house as early as five and six in the morning, to be gone until the light of day failed completely and he had to trudge home across the dunes in the cool dusk. But when a terrific snowstorm served to celebrate the first anniversary of their meeting in the wine shop opposite the Ryn station, and Vincent had to work at home from morning until night, it became more difficult to maintain a satisfactory relationship.

He went back to drawing, and saved money on paints, but the models ate him out of house and home. People who would gladly work for next to nothing at the worst kind of menial labour would demand a large sum just to come and sit for him. He asked permission to sketch at the insane asylum, but the authorities declared they had no precedent for it, and besides they were laying new floors so he could not work there except on visiting days.

His only hope lay in Christine. As soon as she was well and strong he expected her to pose for him, work as hard as she had before the baby came. Christine had different ideas. At first she would say, "I'm not strong enough. Wait a bit. You aint in any hurry." When she was completely well again, she thought herself too busy.

"It's not the same now as it was, Vincent," she would say. "I got to nurse the baby. And I got to keep a whole house clean. There's four people to cook for."

Vincent arose at five in the morning to do the housework so that she would be free to pose during the day. "But I aint a model no more," she protested. "I'm your wife."

"Sien, you must pose for me! I can't afford to hire models every day. That's one of the reasons you're here."

Christine flared up into one of the unrestrained fits of temper that had been so common when she first met Vincent. "That's all you took me in for! So you could save money out of me! I'm just a goddam servant to you! If I don't pose you'll throw me out again!"

Vincent thought for a moment and then said, "You heard all those things at your mother's. You didn't think of them for yourself."

"Well, and what if I did? They're true, aint they?"

"Sien, you'll have to stop going there."

"Why? I guess I love my mother, don't I?"

"But they're ruining things between us. The first thing you know they'll have you back in their way of thinking. Then where will our marriage be?"

"Aint you the one tells me go there when there's no food in the house? Make some more money and I won't have to go back."

When he finally did get her to pose, she was useless. She committed all the errors he had worked so hard to eradicate the year before. Sometimes he suspected that she wiggled, made awkward gestures purposely so that he would become disgusted and not bother her to pose any more. In the end he had to give her up. His expense for outside models increased. Along with it, the number of days that they were without money for food also increased, and so did the amount of time that Christine was forced to spend at her mother's. Each time she came back from there he perceived a slight change in her bearing and attitude. He was caught in a vicious circle; if he used all his money for living, Christine would not go back to the influence of her mother; he could maintain their relationship on a wholesome plane. But if he did that, he would have to give up his work. Had he saved her life just to kill himself? If she did not go to her mother's several times a month she and the children would starve; if she did go she would eventually destroy their home. What was he to do?

Christine ill and carrying a child, Christine in the hospital, Christine recovering from the confinement, was one sort of person; a woman abandoned *désésperée*, on the verge of a miserable death, intensely grateful for a single kind word or helpful action; a woman who knew all the pain in the world and would do anything for a moment's surcease, who would make all sorts of fervent and heroic promises to herself and life. Christine well again, her body and face filled out with good food, medicine, and care, was another sort of woman. The memory of pain was receding, the resolution to be a good housewife and mother weakening; the thoughts and habits of her earlier life were coming back again slowly. She had lived loosely and on the streets, amid liquor, black cigars, vile language, and coarse men for fourteen years. With the strength of her body returning, the fourteen years of sloth overbalanced the one year of care and gentle love. An insidious change began to steal upon her. Vincent could not understand it at first; then slowly a consciousness of what was happening came over him.

It was just about this time, the beginning of the new year, that he received a curious letter from Theo. His brother had met on the streets of Paris a woman, alone, ill, despairing. She suffered from an ailment of the foot and could not work. She had been ready to kill herself. Vincent had taught Theo the way; he followed his master. He found a place for the woman in the home of some old friends. He secured a doctor and had examinations made. He paid for all the expenses of the woman's life. In his letters he called her his patient.

"Should I marry my patient, Vincent? Is that the best way for me to serve her? Should I go through the legal ceremony? She suffers much; she is unhappy; she was deserted by the only person she loved. What must I do to save her life?"

Vincent was deeply touched, and he wrote of his sympathy. But every day Christine was becoming more difficult. When there was only bread and coffee, she grumbled. She insisted that he leave off having models and use his money for the house. When she could not have a new dress, she neglected the old one and let it become covered with food and dirt. She stopped mending his clothes and linen. She fell once again under the influence of her mother, who persuaded her that Vincent would either run away or throw her out. Since a permanent relationship was impossible, what was the good of bothering about the temporary one?

Could he advise Theo to marry his patient? Was legal marriage the best way to save these women? Or was the most important thing a roof over their heads, good food to build their health, and kindness to bring them back to a love of life?

"Wait!" he cautioned his brother. "Do all you can for her; it is a noble cause. But the ceremony will help you not at all. If a love grows between you, then a marriage will grow, too. But see first if you can save her."

Theo was sending fifty francs three times a month. Now that Christine was growing careless in her housekeeping, the money did not last as long as it had before. Vincent was avaricious for models so that he could collect enough studies for some real canvases. He regretted every franc that had to be taken away from his drawing and sunk into the house. She begrudged every franc that had to be taken away from the house and sunk into the drawing. It was a struggle for their lives. The hundred and fifty francs a month could just have supplied him with food, shelter and materials; the attempt to make it provide for four people was heroic but impossible. He began owing money to the landlord, to the shoemaker, the grocer, the baker, and the colour dealer. To cap the climax, Theo went short on funds.

Vincent wrote imploring letters. "If you can please send the money just a little before the twentieth, at least not later. I have only two sheets of paper in the house and one last crumb of crayon. I have not a franc for models or food." Three times a month he wrote such letters; when the fifty francs arrived, he already owed it all to the tradesmen and had nothing to live on for the next ten days.

Theo's "patient" had to be operated on for tumor of the foot. Theo had her taken to a good hospital. At the same time he was sending money home to Nuenen, for the new congregation was small, and Theodorus's income was not always sufficient to meet the needs of the family. Theo was supporting himself and his patient, Vincent, Christine, Herman, Antoon, and the family at Nuenen. He was pushed to the last centime of his salary and could not send Vincent an extra franc.

At last it came about, in early March, that Vincent was left with one franc, a torn note that had already been refused by a tradesman. There was not a mouthful of food left in the house. The next money could not arrive from Theo for at least nine days. He was desperately afraid to put Christine into the hands of her mother for that length of time.

"Sien," he said, "we can't starve the children. You had better take them home to your mother's until Theo's letter arrives."

They looked at each other for a moment, thinking the same thoughts, but without the courage to utter them.

"Yes," she said, "I guess I got to."

The grocer gave him a loaf of black bread and some coffee for the torn bill. He brought models into the house and owed them their money. He became increasingly nervous. His work went hard and dry. He had been starving his body. The incessant financial worries were telling on him. He could not go on without working, yet every hour of work showed him that he was losing ground.

At the end of nine days, promptly on the thirtieth, the letter arrived from Theo with fifty francs. His "patient" had recovered from the operation and he had put her in a private home. The financial strain was telling on him, too, and he had grown despondent. He wrote, "I am afraid I cannot assure you of anything in the future."

That sentence almost drove Vincent out of his mind. Did Theo mean simply that he would not be able to send any more money? That in itself would not be so bad. But did it mean that from the almost daily sketches Vincent sent him to show the progress of his work, his brother had come to the conclusion that he was without talent and could hope for nothing in the future?

He lay awake at night worrying about it, wrote incessant letters to Theo begging for an explanation, and cast about desperately for some means of making his own livelihood. There were none.

14

When he went for Christine he found her in the company of her mother, brother, brother's mistress, and a strange man. She was smoking a black cigar and drinking gin. She did not seem at all pleased at the thought of going back to the Schenkweg.

The nine days at her mother's house had brought back the old habits, the destroying ways of life.

"I can smoke cigars if I want!" she cried. "You aint got no right to stop me if I get them myself. The doctor at the hospital said I could drink all the gin and bitters I wanted."

"Yes, as medicine . . . to improve your appetite."

She broke into a raucous laugh. "Medicine! What a —— —— you are!" It was an expression she had not used since the very first days of their acquaintanceship.

Vincent was in a ragged state of sensitivity. He flew into uncontrollable rages. Christine followed his example. "You aint taking care of me no more!" she shouted. "You don't even give me something to eat. Why don't you make more money? What in hell kind of man are you, anyway?"

As the hard winter slipped into a grudging spring, Vincent's condition went from bad to worse. His debts increased. Because he could not give his stomach the right food, it went back on him. He could not swallow a bite. The ills of his stomach went to his teeth. He lay awake at night with the pain. The ache from his teeth went to his right ear, and all day it twitched jumpily.

Christine's mother began coming to the house, smoking and drinking with her daughter. She no longer thought Christine fortunate to be married. Once Vincent found her brother there, but he dodged out of the door as soon as Vincent entered.

"Why did he come here?" demanded Vincent. "What does he want of you?"

"They say you are going to throw me out."

"You know I'll never do that, Sien. Not as long as you want to stay."

"Mother wants me to leave. She says it aint good for me to stay here without something to eat."

"Where would you go?"

"Home, of course."

"And take the children into that house?"

"It's better than starving here. I can work and earn my own living."

"What would you work at?"

"Well . . . something."

"As a charwoman? At the tubs?"

". . . I guess."

He saw immediately that she was lying.

"So that's what they're trying to persuade you to do!"

"Well . . . it aint so bad . . . you make a living."

"Listen, Sien, if you go back to that house you're lost. You know your mother will send you on the streets again. Remember what the doctor at Leyden said. If you go back to that life, it will kill you!"

"It aint going to kill me. I feel all right now."

"You feel well because you have been living carefully! But if you go back . . . !"

"Jesus Christ, who's going back? Unless you send me."

He sat on the arm of her wicker chair and put his hand on her shoulder. Her hair was uncombed. "Then believe me, Sien, I will never abandon you. As long as you are willing to share what I have, I will keep you with me. But you must stay away from your mother and brother. They'll destroy you! Promise me, for your own sake, that you won't see them any more."

"I promise."

Two days later, when he came back from sketching at the alms house, the studio was empty. There was no sign of supper. He found Christine at her mother's, drinking.

"I told you I love my mother," she protested when they got home. "I guess I can see her all I want. You don't own me. I got a right to do as I please."

She fell into all the familiar, slovenly habits of her former life. When Vincent tried to correct them and explain that she was estranging herself from him, she would answer, "Yes, I know it quite well, you don't want me to stay with you." He showed her how dirty the house was, and how neglected. She answered, "Well, I am lazy and good-for-nothing; I always was that way and it can't be helped." If he tried to show her to what ultimate end her slothfulness was taking her she would reply, "I'm nothing but an outcast, that's true, and I'll end up by throwing myself in the river!"

The mother came to the studio nearly every day now, and took from Vincent the companionship he had so valued in Christine. The house fell into chaos. Meals became fitful. Herman was allowed to go around ragged and dirty, and stay away from school. The less Christine did, the more she smoked and drank her gin. She would not tell Vincent where she got the money for these things.

Summer came. Vincent went out of doors to paint again. This meant new outlays for paints, brushes, canvas, frames, bigger easels. Theo reported improved condition on his "patient," but serious problems in his relationship with her. What was he to do with the woman, now that she was better?

Vincent shut his eyes to everything in his personal life and continued to paint. He knew that his house was crashing about his ears, that he was being drawn into the abysmal sloth that had recaptured Christine. He tried to bury his despair in his work. Each morning when he set out on a new project, he hoped that this canvas would be so beautiful and perfect that it would sell immediately and establish him. Each night he returned home with the sad realization that he was still many years from the mastery he longed for.

His only relief was Antoon, the child. He was a miracle of vitality, and swallowed all kinds of eatables with much laughing and cooing. He often sat with Vincent in the studio, on the floor in a corner. He would crow at Vincent's drawings and then sit quietly looking at the sketches on the walls. He was growing up to be a pretty and vivacious child. The less attention Christine paid to the baby, the more Vincent loved him. In Antoon he saw the real purpose and reward for his actions of last winter.

Weissenbruch looked in only once. Vincent showed him some of the sketches of the year before. He had become frightfully dissatisfied with them.

"Don't feel that way," said Weissenbruch. "After a good many years you will look back on these early pieces of work and realize that they were sincere and penetrating. Just plug on, my boy, and don't let anything stop you."

What finally did stop him was a smash in the face. During the spring he had taken a lamp to the crockery man to have it repaired. The merchant had insisted that Vincent take some new dishes home with him.

"But I have no money to pay for them."

"It doesn't matter. There is no hurry. Take them and pay me when you get the money."

Two months later he banged on the door of the studio. He was a burly chap with a neck as thick as his head.

"What do you mean by lying to me?" he demanded. "What do you take my goods for and not pay me when you got money all the time?"

"At the moment I am absolutely flat. I will pay you as soon as I receive money."

"That's a lie! You just gave money to my neighbour, the shoemaker."

"I am at work," said Vincent, "and I don't care to be disturbed. I'll pay you when I get the money. Please get out."

"I'll get out when you give me that money, and not before!"

Vincent indiscreetly pushed the man toward the door. "Get out of my house," he commanded.

That was just what the tradesman was waiting for. As soon as he was touched, he smashed over his right fist into Vincent's face and sent him crashing into the wall. He struck Vincent again, knocked him to the floor, and walked out without another word.

Christine was at her mother's. Antoon crawled across the floor and patted Vincent's face, crying. After a few minutes Vincent came back to consciousness, dragged himself up the stairs to the attic and lay over the bed.

The blows had not hurt his face. He felt no pain. He had not injured himself when he had fallen heavily to the floor. But those two blows had broken something within him and defeated him. He knew it.

Christine came home. She went upstairs to the attic. There was neither money nor dinner in the house. She often wondered how Vincent managed to keep alive. She saw him lying across the bed, head and arms dangling over one side, feet over the other.

"What's the matter?" she asked.

After a long time he found the strength to twist about and put his head on the pillow. "Sien, I've got to leave The Hague."

". . . yes . . . I know."

"I must get away from here. Out to the country somewhere. To Drenthe, maybe. Where we can live cheaply."

"You want me to come with you? It's an awful hole, Drenthe. What will I do when you aint got no money and we don't eat?"

"I don't know, Sien. I guess you won't eat."

"Will you promise to use the hundred and fifty francs to live on? Not to spend it on models and paints?"

"I can't, Sien. Those things come first."

"Yes, to you!"

"But not to you. Why should they?"

"I got to live too, Vincent. I can't live without eating."

"And I can't live without painting."

"Well, it's your money . . . you come first . . . I understand. Have you a few centimes? Let's go over to the wine café across from the Ryn station."

The place smelled of sour wine. It was late afternoon, but the lamps had not yet been lit. The two tables where they had first sat near each other were empty. Christine led the way to them. They each ordered a glass of sour wine. Christine toyed with the stem of her glass. Vincent remembered how he had admired her worker's hands when she made that identical gesture at the table almost two years before.

"They told me you'd leave me," she said in a low voice. "I knew it, too."

"I don't want to desert you, Sien."

"It aint desertion, Vincent. You never done me nothing but good."

"If you are still willing to share my life, I'll take you to Drenthe."

She shook her head without emotion. "No, there aint enough for two of us."

"You understand, don't you, Sien? If I had more, I'd give you anything. But when I must choose between feeding you and feeding my work . . ."

She laid her hand over his; he could feel the rough parchment of her skin. "It's all right. You don't got to feel bad about it. You done all you could for me. I guess it's just time we was through . . . that's all."

"Do you want us to be, Sien? If it will make you happy, I'll marry you and take you with me."

"No. I belong with my mother. We all got to live our own lives. It'll be all right; my brother's going to take a new house for his girl and me."

Vincent drained his glass, tasting the bitter dregs at the bottom.

"Sien, I've tried to help you. I loved you and gave you all the kindness I had in me. In return I want you to do one thing for me, just one thing."

"What?" she asked dully.

"Don't go back on the streets again. It will kill you! For the sake of Antoon, don't go back to that life."

"Have we enough left for another glass of wine?"

"Yes."

She swallowed half the contents in a single gulp and then said, "I only know that I can't earn enough, 'specially when I got to pay for all the children. So if I walk the street it will be because I must, not because I want to."

"If you get enough work you'll promise me, won't you, not to go back to that?"

"Sure, I promise."

"I'll send you money, Sien, every month. I'll always pay for the baby. I want you to give the little fellow a chance."

"He'll be all right . . . same as the rest."

Vincent wrote to Theo of his intention to go to the country and sever his connection with Christine. Theo answered by return mail with an extra hundred franc note to pay off his debts, and a strong word of approval. "My patient disappeared the other night," he wrote. "She's completely well now, but we couldn't seem to find any relationship to fit ourselves into. She took everything with her and left me no address. It's better that way. Now you and I are both unencumbered."

Vincent stored all the furniture in the attic. He wanted to come back to The Hague sometime. The day before he was to leave for Drenthe he received a letter and a package from Nuenen. In the package was some tobacco, and one of his mother's cheese bakes wrapped in oil paper.

"When are you coming home to paint those wooden crosses in the churchyard?" his father asked.

He knew at once that he wanted to go home. He was ill, starved, desperately nervous, fatigued and discouraged. He would go home to his mother for a few weeks and recover his health and spirits. A feeling of peace that he had not known for many months came over him when he thought of his Brabant country-side, the hedges and dunes and diggers in the field.

Christine and the two children accompanied him to the station. They all stood on the platform, unable to speak. The train came in and Vincent boarded it. Christine stood there with the baby at her breast, holding Herman by the hand. Vincent watched them until his train pulled out into the glaring sunlight, and the woman was lost forever in the grimy blackness of the station.

BOOK FOUR

NUENEN

1

THE vicarage at Nuenen was a two-story, whitewashed, stone building with a tremendous garden in the back. There were elms, hedges, flower beds, a pond, and three pollard oaks. Although Nuenen had a population of twenty-six hundred, only one hundred of them were Protestant. Theodorus's church was tiny; Nuenen was a step down from the prosperous little market town of Etten.

Nuenen was in reality only a small cluster of houses that lined both sides of the road from Eindhoven, the metropolis of the district. Most of the people were weavers and peasants whose huts dotted the heath. They were God fearing, hard working people who lived according to the manners and customs of their ancestors.

On the front of the vicarage, over the door, were the black iron figures A° 1764. The entrance door led straight off the road and admitted to a wide hall which split the house in two. On the left-hand side, dividing the dining room and kitchen, was a rude stairway which led up to the bedrooms. Vincent shared the one over the living room with his brother Cor. When he awoke in the morning he could see the sun rise over the fragile tower of his father's church, and gently lay pastel shades on the pool. At sunset, when the tones were deeper than at dawn, he would sit in a chair by the window and watch the colour being thrown over the pool like a heavy blanket of oil, and then slowly dissolving into the dusk.

Vincent loved his parents; his parents loved him. All three made desperate resolves that the relationship was to be kept friendly and agreeable. Vincent ate a great deal, slept a great deal, walked sometimes on the heath. He talked, painted, and read not at all. Everyone in the house was elaborately courteous to him, as he was to them. It was a self-conscious relationship; before they spoke they had to say to themselves, "I must be careful! I don't want to disrupt the harmony!"

The harmony lasted as long as Vincent's illness. He could not be comfortable in the same room with people who did not think as he thought. When his father remarked, "I am going to read Goethe's 'Faust.' It has been translated by the Reverend Ten Kate, so it cannot be so very immoral," Vincent felt his gorge rise.

He had come home only for a two week vacation, but he loved the Brabant and wanted to stay on. He wished to paint simply and quietly from nature, trying to say nothing but what he saw. He had no other desire than to live deep in the heart of the country, and paint rural life. Like good Father Millet, he wanted to live with, understand, and paint the peasants. He had the firm conviction that there were a few people who, having been drawn into the city and bound up there, yet retained unfading impressions of the country, and remained homesick all their lives for the fields and the peasants.

He had always known that he would come back to the Brabant some day and remain forever. But he could not stay in Nuenen if his parents did not want him.

"A door must be either open or shut," he said to his father. "Let us try to come to an understanding."

"Yes, Vincent, I want that very much. I see that your painting is going to come to something after all, and I am pleased."

"Very well, tell me frankly whether you think we can all live here in peace. Do you want me to stay?"

"Yes."

"For how long?"

"As long as you wish. This is your home. Your place is with us."

"And if we disagree?"

"Then we must not get upset about it. We must try to live calmly and abide with each other."

"But what am I to do about a studio? You don't want me working in the house."

"I have been thinking about that. Why not take the wrangle room, out in the garden? You can have it all to yourself. No one need bother you."

The wrangle room was just off the kitchen, but there was no connecting door. It was a cubicle of a room, with one small window, high up, looking out onto the garden. The floor was of clay, always damp in winter.

"We'll light a big fire in here, Vincent, and dry the place out. Then we'll put down a plank floor so that you can be perfectly comfortable. What do you say?"

Vincent looked about. It was a humble room, very much like the peasants' huts on the heath. He could turn it into a real rural studio.

"If that window is too small," said Theodorus, "I have a little spare money now and we can make it larger."

"No, no, it's perfect just as it is. I'll get the same amount of light on the model that I would get if I were doing him in his own hut."

They brought in a perforated barrel and lit a big fire. When all the dampness had dried out of the walls and roof, and the clay floor was hard, they laid down the wooden planks. Vincent carried in his little bed, a table, a chair and his easels. He tacked up his sketches, brushed a rough GOGH into the whitewashed wall next to the kitchen, and settled down to become a Dutch Millet.

2

The most interesting people around Nuenen were the weavers. They dwelt in little thatched, clay and straw huts, generally of two rooms. In the one room, with a tiny patch of window letting in just a sliver of light, the family lived. There were square recesses in the walls, about three feet off the ground, for beds; a table, a few chairs, a peat stove, and a rough cabinet for the dishware and pots. The floor was of uneven clay, the walls of mud. In the adjoining room, about a third the size of the living room, and with half its height cut off by sloping eaves, was the loom.

A weaver who worked steadily could weave a piece of sixty yards in a week. While he weaved, a woman had to spool for him. On that piece of cloth the weaver made a net profit of four and a half francs a week. When he took it to the manufacturer, he often got the message that not before one or two weeks had passed could he take another piece home. Vincent found that they had a different spirit from the miners of the Borinage; they were quiet, and nowhere was there to be heard anything resembling rebellious speeches. But they looked as cheerful as cab horses, or the sheep transported by steamer to England.

Vincent quickly made friends with them. He found the weavers to be simple souls, asking only for enough work to earn the potatoes, coffee, and occasional strip of bacon on which they lived. They did not mind his painting while they worked; he never came without a bit of sweet for the child of the family, or a bag of tobacco for the old grandfather.

He found a loom of old, greenish-brown oak, in which the date 1730 was cut. Near the loom, before a little window which looked out on a green plot, stood a baby chair. The baby in it sat gazing for hours at the flying shuttle. It was a miserable little room with a clay floor, but in it Vincent found a certain peace and beauty which he tried to capture on his canvas.

He rose early in the morning and spent the entire day in the fields, or in the huts of the peasants and weavers. He felt at home with the people of the field and the loom. It had not been in vain that he had spent so many evenings with the miners, the peat diggers, and peasants, musing by the fire. By witnessing peasant life continually, at all hours of the day, he had become so absorbed in it that he hardly thought of anything else. He was searching for *ce qui ne passe pas dans ce qui passe*.

He went back to his love of drawing from the figure, but along with it he now had another love; colour. The half-ripe corn fields were of a dark golden tone, ruddy and gold bronze, raised to a maximum of effect by contrast to the broken cobalt tone of the sky. In the background were women's figures, very rough, very energetic, with sunbronzed faces and arms, with dusty, coarse, indigo clothes, and black bonnets in the form of berets on their short hair.

When he came swinging vigorously along the main road, easel strapped to his back, and wet canvas under his arm, the blinds of every house would open just a crack from the bottom, and he would run the gauntlet of curious and scandalized feminine eyes. At home he found that the old saying, "A door must either be open or shut," was not altogether true when applied to family relationships. The door of domestic felicity at the parsonage had a habit of remaining in some mysterious position that was very definitely neither open nor shut. His sister Elizabeth loathed him; she was afraid his eccentricities would ruin her marriage chances in Nuenen. Willemien liked him but thought him a bore. It was not until later that he became friends with his younger brother Cor.

Vincent ate his dinner, not at the family table, but in one corner, his plate on his lap, and the sketches of the day propped up on a chair before him, scrutinizing his work with piercing eyes, ripping it to pieces for imperfections and poor values. He never spoke to the family. They rarely addressed him. He ate his bread dry because he did not want to get in the habit of indulging himself. Occasionally, if the name of some writer whom he liked came up for discussion at the table, he would turn to them and speak for a moment. But on the whole he found that the less they had to say to each other, the better off they all were.

3

He had been painting in the fields for about a month when he began to have the very curious feeling that he was being watched. He knew that the people of Nuenen stared at him, that the peasants in the field used to rest on their hoes occasionally and gaze at him in wonder. But this was something different. He had a sense that he was not only being watched, but followed. For the first few days he tried to shake it off, impatiently, but he could not get rid of the sensation that a pair of eyes was staring holes through his back. Many times he searched the field about him with his glance, but he could see nothing. Once he thought he saw the white skirt of a woman disappear behind a tree when he turned suddenly. Another time, as he came out of a weaver's house, a figure scurried quickly down the road. Still a third time, when he was painting in the woods, he left his easel and walked to the pond for a drink. When he returned, he found fingerprints in the wet paint.

It took him almost two weeks to catch the woman. He was sketching diggers on the heath; there was an old abandoned wagon not far from him. The woman stood behind it while he worked. He picked up his canvas and easel suddenly, and pretended that he was making for home. The woman ran on ahead. He followed without arousing her suspicion, and saw her turn in at the house next to the parsonage.

"Who lives next door on the left, Mother?" he asked as they all sat down to dinner that night.

"The Begeman family."

"Who are they?"

"We don't know much about them. There are five daughters and a mother. The father evidently died some time ago."

"What are they like?"

"It's hard to tell; they're rather secretive."

"Are they Catholic?"

"No, Protestant. The father was a dominie."

"Are any of the girls unmarried?"

"Yes, all of them. Why do you ask?"

"I just wondered. Who supports the family?"

"No one. They seem to be wealthy."

"You don't know any of the girls' names, I suppose?"

His mother looked at him curiously. "No."

The following day he went back to the same spot in the fields. He wanted to catch the blue of the peasant figures in the ripe corn or against the withered leaves of a beech hedge. The people wore a coarse linen which they wove themselves, warp black, woof blue, the result of which was a black and blue, striped pattern. When this faded and became somewhat discoloured by wind and weather, it was an infinitely quiet, delicate tone which just brought out the flesh colours.

About the middle of the morning he felt the woman behind him again. Out of the corner of his eye he caught a sight of her dress in a copse behind the abandoned wagon.

"I'll catch her today," he murmured to himself, "even if I have to stop in the middle of this study."

He was getting more and more into the habit of *dashing a thing off*, getting down his impression of the scene before him in one great splurge of passionate energy. What had struck him most about the old Dutch pictures was that they had been painted quickly, that the great masters dashed off a thing from the first stroke and did not retouch it. They had painted in a grand rush to keep intact the purity of their first impression, of the mood in which the motif had been conceived.

He forgot about the woman, in the heat of his creative passion. When he happened to glance around an hour later, he noticed that she had left the woods and was now standing behind the wagon. He wanted to jump up and catch her, ask her why she had been following him all this time, but he could not tear away from his work. After a while he turned around again and noted to his surprise that she was standing in front of the wagon, gazing at him steadily. It was the first time she had come out into the open.

He went on working at a fever pitch. The harder he worked, the closer the woman seemed to come. The more passion he poured out on the canvas, the hotter the eyes became that were staring through his back. He turned his easel a fraction to get the light and saw that she was standing in the middle of the field, half-way between the wagon and himself. She looked like a woman mesmerized, walking in her sleep. Step by step she came closer and closer, pausing each time, trying to hold back, coming steadily forward, impelled toward him by some power beyond her control. He felt her at his back. He whirled about and gazed into her eyes. There was a frightened, feverish expression on her face; she seemed caught up in some baffling emotion which she could not master. She did not look at Vincent, but at his canvas. He waited for her to speak. She remained silent. He turned back to his work and in a final burst of energy, finished. The woman did not move. He could feel her dress touching his coat.

It was late afternoon. The woman had been standing in the field for many hours. Vincent was exhausted, his nerves worked up to a fine edge by the excitement of creation. He got up and turned to the woman.

Her mouth went dry. She moistened the upper lip with her tongue, then the lower lip with the upper one. The slight moisture vanished instantly and her lips became parched. She had a hand at her throat and seemed to have difficulty in breathing. She tried to speak, but could not.

"I am Vincent Van Gogh, your neighbour," he said. "But I suppose you know that."

"Yes." It was a whisper, so faint he could hardly hear it.

"Which one of the Begeman sisters are you?"

She swayed a little, caught him by the sleeve and steadied herself. Again she tried to moisten her lips with a dry tongue, and made several attempts to speak before she succeeded.

"Margot."

"And why have you been following me, Margot Begeman? I've known about it for several weeks."

A muted cry escaped her lips. She dug her nails into his arms to support herself, then fell to the ground in a faint.

Vincent went on his knees, put his arm under her head, and brushed the hair back from her brow. The sun was just setting red over the fields and the peasants were trudging their weary way home. Vincent and Margot were alone. He looked at her carefully. She was not beautiful. She must have been well on in her thirties. Her mouth stopped abruptly at the left corner, but on the right a thin line continued down almost to the jaw. There were circles of blue with little flesh freckles under the eyes. The skin seemed just on the point of going wrinkled.

Vincent had a little water with him in a canteen. He moistened Margot's face with one of the rags he used to wipe off paint. Her eyes shot open suddenly, and he saw that they were good eyes, a deep brown, tender, almost mystical. He took a little water on the end of his fingers and ran them over Margot's face. She shivered against his arm.

"Are you feeling better, Margot?" he asked.

She lay there for a brief instant, looking into his green-blue eyes, so sympathetic, so penetrating, so understanding. Then, with a wild sob that seemed wrenched from her inmost core, she flung her arms about his neck and buried her lips in his beard.

4

The following day they met at an appointed place some distance from the village. Margot had on a charming, high necked, white cambric dress and was carrying a summer hat in her hand. Although still nervous in his company, she seemed more self-possessed than she had been the day before. Vincent laid down his palette when she came. She had not even a fraction of Kay's delicate beauty, but compared to Christine, she was a very attractive woman.

He rose from his stool, not knowing what to do. Ordinarily he was prejudiced against women who wore dresses; his territory was more those who wore jackets and petticoats. The so-called respectable class of Dutch women was not particularly attractive to paint or look at. He preferred the ordinary servant girls; they were often very Chardin-like.

Margot leaned up and kissed him, simply, possessively, as though they had been sweethearts for a long time, then held herself to him, trembling for a moment. Vincent spread his coat on the ground for her. He sat on his stool; Margot leaned against his knee and looked up at him with an expression that he had never seen before in the eyes of a woman.

"Vincent," she said, just for the pure joy of uttering his name.

"Yes, Margot." He did not know what to do or say.

"Did you think bad things of me last night?"

"Bad things? No. Why should I have?"

"You may find it difficult to believe, but, Vincent, when I kissed you yesterday, it was the first time I had ever kissed a man."

"But why? Have you never been in love?"

"No."

"What a pity."

"Isn't it?" She was silent for a moment. "You have loved other women, haven't you."

"Yes."

"Many of them?"

"No. Just . . . three."

"And did they love you?"

"No, Margot, they didn't."

"But they must have."

"I've always been unfortunate in love."

Margot moved closer to him and rested her arm on his lap. She ran the fingers of her other hand over his face playfully, touching his high ridged, powerful nose, the full, open mouth, the hard, rounded chin. A curious shiver ran through her; she took her fingers away.

"How strong you are," she murmured. "Everything about you; your arms and chin and beard. I've never known a man like you before."

He cupped her face in his hands roughly. The love and excitement that throbbed there made it appealing.

"Do you like me a little?" she asked anxiously.

"Yes."

"And will you kiss me?"

He kissed her.

"Please don't think ill of me, Vincent. I couldn't help myself. You see, I fell in love . . . with you . . . and I couldn't keep away."

"You fell in love with me? You really fell in love with me? But why?"

She leaned up and kissed him on the corner of the mouth. "That's why," she said.

They sat quietly. A little way off was the Cimetière des Paysans. For ages the peasants had been laid to rest in the very fields which they dug up when alive. Vincent was trying to say on his canvas what a simple thing death was, just as simple as the falling of an autumn leaf, just a bit of earth dug up, a wooden cross. The fields around, where the grass of the churchyard ended beyond the little wall, made a last line against the sky, like the horizon of the sea.

"Do you know anything about me, Vincent?" she asked softly.

"Very little."

"Have they . . . has anyone told you . . . my age?"

"No."

"Well, I'm thirty-nine. In a very few months I shall be forty. For the last five years I have been telling myself that if I did not love someone before I left my thirties, I should kill myself."

"But it is easy to love, Margot."

"Ah, you think so?"

"Yes. It's only being loved in return that is difficult."

"No. In Nuenen it is very hard. For over twenty years I have wanted desperately to love someone. And I never have been able to."

"Never?"

She glanced away. "Once . . . when I was a girl . . . I liked a boy."

"Yes?"

"He was a Catholic. They drove him away."

"They?"

"My mother and sisters."

She rose to her knees in the deep loam of the field, soiling her pretty white dress. She placed both elbows on his thighs and rested her face in her hands. His knees touched her sides, gently.

"A woman's life is empty if she has no love to fill it, Vincent."

"I know."

"Every morning, when I awakened, I said to myself, 'Today, surely, I shall find someone to love! Other women do, so why shouldn't I?' Then night would come and I would be alone and miserable. An endless row of empty days, Vincent. I have nothing to do at home—we have servants—and every hour was filled up with longing for love. With each night I said to myself, 'You might just as well have been dead today, for all that you have lived.' I kept bolstering myself up with the thought that some day, somehow, a man must come along whom I could love. My birthdays passed, the thirty-seventh, and eighth, and ninth. I could not have faced forty without ever having loved. Then you came along, Vincent. *Now I too have loved at last!*"

It was a cry of triumph, as though she had gained a great victory. She leaned up, holding her mouth to be kissed. He stroked her soft hair back from her ears. She flung her arms about his neck and kissed him in a thousand wandering nibbles. Sitting there on his little painter's stool, his palette at his side, and the Cimetière des Paysans just in front, holding the kneeling woman close to him, and engulfed in the flow of her welled-up passion, Vincent felt for the first time in his life the luscious, healing balm of a woman's outpoured love. And he trembled, for he knew that he was on sacred ground.

Margot sat on the earth between his legs, her head back on his knee. There was colour in her cheeks and lustre in her eyes; she was breathing deeply and with effort. In the flush of her love she looked not more than thirty. Vincent, unable to feel anything at all, ran his fingers over the soft skin of her face until she clasped his hand, kissed it, and held the palm against her burning cheek. After a time she spoke.

"I know that you don't love me," she said quietly. "That would be asking too much. I only prayed to God to let me fall in love. I never even dreamed it would be possible for anyone to love me. It's loving that's important, isn't it, Vincent, not being loved."

Vincent thought of Ursula and Kay. "Yes," he replied.

She rubbed the back of her head against his knee, looking up at the blue sky. "And you'll let me come with you? If you don't want to talk, I'll just sit by quietly and never say a word. Only let me be near you; I promise not to disturb you or interfere with your work."

"Of course you can come. But tell me, Margot, if there were no men in Nuenen, why didn't you go away? At least for a visit? Didn't you have the money?"

"Oh, yes, I have plenty of money. My grandfather left me a good income."

"Then why didn't you go to Amsterdam or The Hague? You would have met some interesting men."

"They didn't want me to."

"None of your sisters are married, are they?"

"No, dear, all five of us are single."

A flash of pain went through him. It was the first time a woman had ever

called him dear. He had known before how miserable it was to love and
not be loved in return, but he had never suspected the utter sweetness of
having a good woman love him with the whole of her being. He had looked
upon Margot's love for him as a sort of curious accident to which he was
no party. That one, simple word, spoken so quietly and fondly by Margot,
changed his entire mental state. He gathered Margot to him and held her
quivering body against his.

"Vincent, Vincent," she murmured, "I love you so."

"How queer that sounds, to hear you say you love me so."

"I don't mind now that I've had to go all these years without love. You
were worth waiting for, my very own dear. In all my dreams of love I
never imagined that I could feel about anyone the way I do about you."

"I love you too, Margot," he said.

She drew away from him slightly. "You don't have to say that, Vincent.
Maybe after a while you will come to like me a little. But now all I ask is
that you let me love you!"

She slipped out of his arms, put his coat off to one side, and sat down.
"Go to work, dear," she said. "I must not get in your way. And I love to
watch you paint."

5

Nearly every day Margot accompanied him when he went out to paint.
Oftentimes he would walk ten kilometres to reach the exact spot on the
heath that he wanted to work with, and they would both arrive tired and
exhausted by the heat. But Margot never complained. The woman had
undergone a startling metamorphosis. Her hair, which had been a mouse
brown, took on a live blond tint. Her lips had been thin and parched; now her
mouth went full and red. Her skin had been dry and almost wrinkled; now it
was smooth and soft and warm. Her eyes seemed to grow larger, her breasts
swelled out, her voice took on a new lilt, and her step became strong and
vigorous. Love had opened some strange spring within her, and she was
constantly being bathed in its elixir of love. She brought surprise lunches to
please him, sent to Paris for some prints that he had mentioned with admiration, and never intruded on his work. When he painted, she sat perfectly still at his side, bathing in the same luxuriant passion that he flung at
his canvases.

Margot knew nothing about painting, but she had a quick and sensitive
intelligence, and a faculty for saying the right thing at the right moment.
Vincent found that, without knowing, she understood. She gave him the
impression of a Cremona violin that had been spoiled by bungling repairers.

"If I had only met her ten years ago!" he said to himself.

One day she asked him, as he was preparing to attack a new canvas,

"How can you be sure that the spot you choose will come out right on the canvas?"

Vincent thought for a moment and then replied, "If I want to be active, I must not be afraid of failures. When I see a blank canvas staring at me with a certain imbecility, I just dash something down."

"You certainly do dash. I never saw anything grow as fast as your canvases."

"Well, I have to. I find paralysing the stare of a blank canvas which says to me, 'You don't know anything!' "

"You mean it's a sort of challenge?"

"Exactly. The blank canvas stares at me like an idiot, but I know that it is afraid of the passionate painter who dares, who once and for all has broken the spell of that 'you cannot.' Life itself turns towards a man an infinitely vacant, discouraging, hopelessly blank side on which nothing is written, Margot, no more than on this blank canvas."

"Yes, doesn't it."

"But the man of faith and energy is not frightened by that blankness; he steps in, he acts, he builds up, he creates, and in the end the canvas is no longer blank but covered with the rich pattern of life."

Vincent enjoyed having Margot in love with him. She never looked upon him with critical eyes. Everything he did she thought right. She did not tell him that his manners were crude, that his voice was rough, that there were harsh lines in his face. She never condemned him for not earning money, or suggested that he do anything but paint. Walking home through the quiet dusk, his arm about her waist, his voice soft from her sympathy, he told her of all the things he had done, of why he preferred painting the *rouwboerke* (peasant in mourning) to the Mayor, why he thought a peasant girl, in her dusty and patched blue petticoat and bodice, more beautiful than a lady. She questioned nothing and accepted everything. He was what he was, and she loved him completely.

Vincent was unable to get used to his new position. Every day he waited for the relationship to break, for Margot to become unkind and cruel, and confront him with his failures. Her love increased with the ripening of the summer; she gave him that fullness of sympathy and adoration which only a mature woman can bestow. Unsatisfied that she did not turn against him of her own accord, he tried to goad her into condemnation by painting his failures as black as he could. She saw them not as failures, but as simple accounts of why he did what he had to do.

He told her the story of his fiasco in Amsterdam and the Borinage. "Surely that was a failure," he said. "Everything I did there was wrong, now wasn't it?"

She smiled up at him indulgently. "The king can do no wrong."

He kissed her.

Another day she said to him, "My mother tells me you are a wicked man.

She has heard that you lived with loose women in The Hague. I told them it was vicious scandal."

Vincent related the tale of Christine. Margot listened with some of the brooding melancholy in her eyes that had been there before love dissipated it.

"You know, Vincent, there's something Christ-like about you. I'm sure my father would have thought so, too."

"And that's all you can find to say to me when I tell you I lived for two years with a prostitute?"

"She wasn't a prostitute; she was your wife. Your failure to save her was not your fault, any more than was your failure to save the Borains. One man can do very little against a whole civilization."

"It's true, Christine was my wife. I told my brother Theo, when I was younger, 'If I cannot get a good wife, I shall take a bad one. Better a bad one than none at all.' "

There was a slightly strained silence; the subject of marriage had not come up between them. "There is only one thing I regret about the Christine affair," said Margot. "I wish I could have had those two years of your love for myself."

He gave up trying to break her love for him, and accepted it. "When I was younger, Margot," he said, "I thought that things depended on chance, on small accidents or misunderstandings that had no reason. But getting older, I begin to see deeper motives. It is the plight of most people that by a kind of fatality they have to seek a long time for light."

"As I had to seek for you!"

They had reached the low door of a weaver's house. Vincent pressed her hand warmly. She gave him a smile of such sweet surrender that he wondered why fate had seen fit to keep love from him all these years. They entered the thatched hut. Summer had passed into fall and the days were growing dark. A suspension lamp hung over the loom. A piece of red cloth was being woven. The weaver and his wife were arranging the threads; dark, bent figures against the light, standing out against the colour of the cloth, casting big shadows on the laths and beams of the loom. Margot and Vincent exchanged an understanding smile; he had taught her to catch the underlying beauty in ugly places.

By November and the *chute des feuilles,* when all the leaves on the trees fell off in a few days, the whole of Nuenen was talking about Vincent and Margot. The village liked Margot; it distrusted and feared Vincent. Margot's mother and four sisters tried to break off the affair, but she insisted that it was only a friendship, and what harm could there be in walking in the fields together? The Begemans knew Vincent to be a drifter, and confidently expected him to leave any day. They were not greatly worried. The village was; it said over and over again that no good could come from that queer Van Gogh man, and that the Begeman family would regret it if they did not keep their daughter out of his hands.

Vincent could never understand why the people of the town disliked him so. He interfered with no one, injured no one. He did not realize what a strange picture he made in this quiet hamlet, where life had not changed in one word or custom for hundreds of years. It was not until he found that they thought him an idler that he gave up hope of making them like him. Dien van den Beek, a small shopkeeper, hailed him as he was passing one day, and threw down the gage for the village.

"Fall has come now and the nice weather is over, eh?" he asked.

"Yes."

"A man supposes you'll be going to work soon, eh?"

Vincent shifted the easel on his back to a more comfortable position. "Yes, I'm just on my way out to the heath."

"No, I mean work," said Dien. "Real work that you do all year."

"Painting is my work," said Vincent quietly.

"A man means work that you get paid for; a job."

"Going to the fields as you see me now is my job, Mijnheer van den Beek, just as selling goods is yours."

"Yes, but I sell goods! Do you sell what you make?"

Every soul to whom he had spoken in the village had asked that identical question. He was getting heartily sick of it.

"I sell sometimes. My brother is a dealer and he buys."

"You should go to work, Mijnheer. It is not good for you to idle this way. A man will grow old and he will have nothing."

"Idle! I work twice as long as you keep this store open."

"You call that work? Sitting and daubing? That's only play for children. Keep a store; plough in the fields; that's a real man's work. You're getting too old to be wasting your time."

Vincent knew that Dien van den Beek merely voiced the opinion of the village, and that to the provincial mind the words artist and worker were mutually exclusive. He gave up caring what the people thought, and ceased to see them when he passed them on the street. When their distrust of him had come to a positive climax, an accident happened that put him back in favour.

Anna Cornelia broke her leg on getting out of the train at Helmond. She was rushed home immediately. Although the doctor did not tell the family so, he feared for her life. Vincent threw aside his work without a second thought. His experience in the Borinage had made him an excellent nurse. The doctor watched him for a half hour and then said, "You are better than a woman; your mother will be in excellent hands."

The people of Nuenen, who could be as kind in times of a crisis as they could be cruel in times of boredom, came to the vicarage with dainties and books and comforting thoughts. They stared at Vincent in utter amazement; he changed the bed without moving his mother, bathed and fed her, took care of the cast on her leg. At the end of two weeks, the village had completely revised its opinion of him. He spoke to them in their own language when they came; they discussed how best to avoid bed sores, what foods a sick person should eat, how warm the room should be kept. Talking to him thus and understanding him, they decided that he was a human being after all. When his mother felt a little better and he could go out to paint for a short time each day, they addressed him with a smile, and by name. He no longer felt the blinds go up a tiny fraction from the bottom, one by one, as he walked through the town.

Margot was at his side at all times. She was the only one who was not amazed at his gentleness. They were speaking in whispers in the sick room one day, when Vincent happened to remark, "The key to many things is the thorough knowledge of the human body, but it decidedly costs money to learn it. There is a very beautiful book, 'Anatomy for Artists,' by John Marshall, but it is very expensive."

"Haven't you the money to spare?"

"No, and I shan't have until I sell something."

"Vincent, it would make me so happy if you would let me lend you some. You know I have a regular income, and I never manage to spend it."

"It's good of you, Margot, but I couldn't."

She did not press her point, but a couple of weeks later handed him a package from The Hague. "What is it?" he asked.

"Open it and see."

There was a little note tied on the cord. The package contained Marshall's book; the note read FOR THE HAPPIEST BIRTHDAY OF THEM ALL.

"But this isn't my birthday!" he exclaimed.

"No," laughed Margot, "it's mine! My fortieth, Vincent. You gave me a present of my life. Do be good and take it, dear. I'm so happy today, and I want you to be, too."

They were in his studio in the garden. No one was about, only Willemien who was sitting with her mother in the house. It was late afternoon, and the falling sun pasted a slight patch of light on the whitewashed wall. Vincent fingered the book tenderly; it was the first time anyone but Theo had been so happy to help him. He threw the book on the bed and took Margot in his arms. Her eyes were slightly misty with the love of him. During the past few months they had done very little caressing in the fields; they were afraid of being seen. Margot always gave herself to his caresses so whole-heartedly, with such generous surrender. It was five months now since he had left Christine; he was a little nervous about trusting himself too far. He wanted to do nothing to injure Margot or her love for him.

He looked down into her kind brown eyes as he kissed her. She smiled at him, then closed her eyes and opened her lips slightly to receive his. They held each other tightly, their bodies fitting from mouth to toe. The bed was only a step away. Together, they sat down. In that locked embrace each forgot the loveless years that had made their lives so stark.

The sun sank and the square of light on the wall went out. The wrangle room was bathed in a mellow dusk. Margot ran her hand over Vincent's face, strange sounds coming from her throat in the language of love. Vincent felt himself sinking into the abyss from which there is only one precipitate return. He tore himself from Margot's arms and jumped up. He went to his easel and crumpled a piece of paper on which he had been working. There was no sound but the call of the magpie in the acacias and the tinkling bells of the cows coming home. After a moment Margot spoke, quietly and simply.

"You can if you want, dear," she said.

"Why?" he asked, without turning about.

"Because I love you."

"It wouldn't be right."

"I told you before, Vincent, the king can do no wrong!"

He dropped on one knee. Her head lay on the pillow. He noticed again the line on the right side of her mouth, that ran down to her jaw, and kissed it. He kissed the too narrow bridge of her nose, the too full nostrils, and ran his lips over the skin of her face that had gone ten years younger. In the dusk, lying receptively with her arms about his neck, she looked again the beautiful girl she must have been at twenty.

"I love you, too, Margot," he said. "I didn't know it before, but now I do."

"It's sweet of you to say that, dear." Her voice was gentle and dreamy. "I know you like me a little. And I love you with all my heart. That satisfies me."

He did not love her as he had loved Ursula and Kay. He did not even love her as he had loved Christine. But he felt something very tender for this woman lying so passively in his arms. He knew that love included nearly every human relationship. Something within him ached at the thought that he could feel so little for the only woman in the world who loved him unrestrainedly, and he remembered the agony he had undergone because Ursula and Kay had not returned his love. He respected Margot's overwhelming love for him, yet in some inexplicable way he found it a trifle distasteful. Kneeling on the plank floor of the dark wrangle room, with his arm under the head of the woman who loved him just as he had loved Ursula and Kay, he at last understood why the two women had fled from him.

"Margot," he said, "my life is a poor one, but I should be very happy if you would share it with me."

"I want to share it with you, dear."

"We could stay right here in Nuenen. Or would you rather go away after we're married?"

She rubbed her head against his arm, caressingly. "What is it that Ruth said? 'Whither thou goest, I will go.'"

6

They were in no way prepared for the storm that arose the next morning when they broke the news to their respective families. With the Van Goghs

the problem was simply one of money. How could he take a wife when
Theo was supporting him?

"First you must earn money and make your life straight; then you can
marry," said his father.

"If I make my life straight by wrestling with the naked truth of my craft,"
replied Vincent, "the earning of money will come in due time."

"Then you must also marry in due time. But not now!"

The disturbance in the vicarage was only a little squall compared to what
was going on next door in the house of women. With five sisters, all unmarried, the Begemans could face the world in a solid front. Margot's marriage
would be a living proof to the village of the failure of the other girls.
Madame Begeman thought it better that four of her daughters be kept from
further unhappiness than that one of them be made happy.

Margot did not accompany him to the weavers that day. Late in the
afternoon she came to the studio. Her eyes were puffy and swollen; she
looked more her forty years than ever before. She held him close for a moment in a sort of desperate embrace.

"They've been abusing you frightfully all day," she said. "I never knew a
man could be so many bad things and still live."

"You should have expected that."

"I did. But I had no idea they would attack you so viciously."

He put his arm about her gently and kissed her cheek. "Just leave them
to me," he said. "I'll come in tonight after supper. Perhaps I can persuade
them that I'm not such an awful person."

As soon as he set foot in the Begeman house he knew that he was in
strange, alien territory. There was something sinister about the atmosphere
created by six women, an atmosphere never broken by a masculine voice or
footstep.

They led him into the parlour. It was cold and musty. There had not been
people in it for months. Vincent knew the four sisters' names, but he had
never taken the trouble to attach the names to the faces. They all seemed
like caricatures of Margot. The eldest sister, who ran the household, took it
upon herself to manage the inquisition.

"Margot tells us that you wish to marry her. May one presume to ask
what has happened to your wife in The Hague?"

Vincent explained about Christine. The atmosphere of the parlour went
several degrees colder.

"How old are you, Mijnheer Van Gogh?"

"Thirty-one."

"Has Margot told you that she is . . ."

"I know Margot's age."

"May one presume to ask how much money you earn?"

"I have a hundred and fifty francs a month."

"What is the source of that income?"

"My brother sends it to me."

"You mean your brother supports you?"

"No. He pays me a monthly salary. In return he gets everything I paint."

"How many of them does he sell?"

"I really couldn't say."

"Well, I can. Your father tells me he has never sold one of your pictures yet."

"He will sell them later. They will bring him in many times as much as they would now."

"That is problematical, to say the least. Suppose we discuss the facts."

Vincent studied the hard, unbeautiful face of the eldest sister. He could expect no sympathy from that quarter.

"If you don't earn anything," she continued, "may one be allowed to ask how you expect to support a wife?"

"My brother chooses to gamble a hundred and fifty francs a month on me; that's his affair, not yours. For me it remains a salary. I work very hard to earn it. Margot and I could live on that salary if we managed carefully."

"But we wouldn't have to!" cried Margot. "I have enough to take care of myself."

"Be quiet, Margot!" commanded her eldest sister.

"Remember, Margot," said her mother, "I have the power to stop that income if you ever do anything to disgrace the family name!"

Vincent smiled. "Would marrying me be a disgrace?" he asked.

"We know very little about you, Mijnheer Van Gogh, and that little is unfortunate. How long have you been a painter?"

"Three years."

"And you are not successful yet. How long will it take you to become successful?"

"I don't know."

"What were you before you took up painting?"

"An art dealer, teacher, book-seller, divinity student and evangelist."

"And you failed at all of them?"

"I gave them up."

"Why?"

"I was not suited to them."

"How long will it take you to give up painting?"

"He'll never do that!" exclaimed Margot.

"It seems to me, Mijnheer Van Gogh," said the old sister, "that you are presumptuous in wanting to marry Margot. You're hopelessly *déclassé*, you haven't a franc to your name, nor any way of earning one, you are unable to stick to any sort of job, and you drift about like an idler and a tramp. How could we dare to let our sister marry you?"

Vincent reached for his pipe, then put it back again. "Margot loves me and I love her. I can make her happy. We would live here for another year or so and then go abroad. She will never receive anything but kindness and love from me."

"You'll desert her!" cried one of the other sisters who had a shriller voice. "You'll get tired of her and desert her for some bad woman like the one in The Hague!"

"You just want to marry her for her money!" said another.

"But you won't get it," announced the third. "Mother will turn the allowance back into the estate."

Tears came to Margot's eyes. Vincent rose. He realized that there was no use wasting time on these viragoes. He would simply have to marry Margot in Eindhoven and leave for Paris immediately. He did not want to go away from the Brabant yet; his work was not finished there. But he shuddered when he thought of leaving Margot alone in that house of barren women.

Margot suffered in the days that followed. The first snow fell and Vincent was forced to work in his studio. The Begemans would not allow Margot to visit him. From the moment she got out of bed in the morning until she was permitted to feign sleep, she was forced to listen to tirades against Vincent. She had lived with her family for forty years; she had known Vincent only a few months. She hated her sisters, for she knew they had destroyed her life, but hatred is one of the more obscure forms of love and sometimes breeds a stronger sense of duty.

"I don't understand why you won't come away with me," Vincent told her, "or at least marry me here without their consent."

"They wouldn't let me."

"Your mother?"

"My sisters. Mother merely sits back and agrees."

"Does it matter what your sisters say?"

"Do you remember I told you that when I was young I almost fell in love with a boy?"

"Yes."

"They stopped that. My sisters. I don't know why. All my life they've stopped the things I wanted to do. When I decided to visit relatives in the city, they wouldn't let me go. When I wished to read, they wouldn't allow the better books in the house. Every time I invited a man to the house, they would rip him to pieces after he left so that I could never look at him again. I wanted to do something with my life; become a nurse, or study music. But no, I had to think the same things they thought, and live exactly as they lived."

"And now?"

"Now they won't let me marry you."

Much of the newly acquired life had gone out of her voice and carriage. Her lips were dry, and the tiny flesh freckles under her eyes stood out.

"Don't worry about them, Margot. We will marry and that will be the end of it. My brother has often suggested that I come to Paris. We could live there."

She did not answer. She sat on the edge of the bed and stared down at the floor planking. Her shoulders turned in a crescent. He sat beside her and took her hand.

"Are you afraid to marry me without their consent?"

"No." Her voice was without strength or conviction. "I'll kill myself, Vincent, if they take me away from you. I couldn't stand it. Not after having loved you. I'll kill myself, that's all."

"They wouldn't have to know. Do it first and tell them afterwards."

"I can't go against them. They're too many for me. I can't fight them all."

"Well, don't bother fighting them. Just marry me and that will be the end of it."

"It wouldn't be the end. It would be the beginning. You don't know my sisters."

"Nor do I want to! But I'll have another try at them tonight."

He knew it was futile, the moment he entered the parlour. He had forgotten the chilling air of the place.

"We've heard all that before, Mijnheer Van Gogh," said the sister, "and it neither convinces nor impresses us. We have made up our minds about this matter. We want to see Margot happy, but we don't want her to throw her life away. We have decided that if at the end of two years you still want to marry, we will withdraw our objections."

"Two years!" said Vincent.

"I won't be here in two years," said Margot quietly.

"Where will you be?"

"I'll be dead. I'll kill myself if you don't let me marry him."

During the flood of, "How dare you say such things!" and "You see the sort of influence he's had on her!" Vincent escaped. There was nothing more he could do.

The years of maladjustment had told on Margot. She was not nervously strong, nor was her health of the best. Under the frontal attack of the five determined women, her spirits sank lower and lower with each passing day. A girl of twenty might have fought her way out unscathed, but Margot had had all the resistance and will beaten out of her. The wrinkles showed on her face, the old melancholy returned to her eyes, her skin went sallow and rough. The line on the right side of her mouth deepened.

The affection Vincent had felt for Margot evaporated with her beauty. He had never really loved her or wanted to marry her; now he wanted to less than ever. He was ashamed of his callousness; that made him all the more ardent in his love making. He did not know whether she divined his true feelings.

"Do you love them more than you do me, Margot?" he asked one day when she managed to escape to his studio for a few minutes.

She shot him a look of surprise and reproach. "Oh, Vincent!"

"Then why are you willing to give me up?"

She cuddled into his arms like a tired child. Her voice was low and lost.

"If I thought you loved me as I love you, I would go against the whole world. But it means so little to you . . . and so much to them . . ."

"Margot, you're mistaken, I love you . . ."

She laid her finger gently on his lips. "No, dear, you would like to . . . but you don't. You mustn't feel badly about it. I want to be the one who loves the most."

"Why don't you break away from them and be your own master?"

"It's easy for you to say that. You're strong; you can fight anyone. But I'm forty . . . I was born in Nuenen . . . I've never been farther away than Eindhoven. Don't you see, dear, I've never broken with anyone or anything in my life."

"Yes, I see."

"If it was something *you* wanted, Vincent, I would fight for you with all my strength. But it's only something I want. And after all, it comes so late . . . my life is gone by now . . ."

Her voice sank to a whisper. He raised her chin with his first finger and held it with his thumb. There were unshed tears in her eyes.

"My dear girl," he said. "My very dear Margot. We could live a whole life together. All you need to say is the word. Pack your clothes tonight while your family is asleep. You can hand them to me out the window. We'll walk to Eindhoven and catch the early morning train to Paris."

"It's no use, dear. I'm part of them and they're part of me. But in the end I'll have my way."

"Margot, I can't bear to see you unhappy this way."

She turned her face to him. The tears went away. She smiled. "No, Vincent, I'm happy. I got what I asked for. It's been wonderful loving you."

He kissed her, and on her lips he tasted the salt from the tears that had rolled down her cheek.

"It has stopped snowing," she said a little later. "Are you going to sketch in the fields tomorrow?"

"Yes, I think so."

"Where will you be? I'll come to you in the afternoon."

He worked late the next day, a fur cap on his head and the linen blouse drawn tightly around his neck. The evening sky was of lilac with gold, over dark silhouettes of the cottages, between the masses of ruddy-coloured brushwood. Above, the spare black poplars rose; the foreground was of a faded and bleached green, varied by strips of black earth and pale dry reeds along the ditch edges.

Margot came walking rapidly across the field. She was wearing the same white dress in which he had first met her, with a scarf thrown over her shoulders. He noticed a faint touch of colour in her cheeks. She looked like the woman who had bloomed so beautifully under love only a few weeks back. She was carrying a small work-basket in her hands.

She flung her arms about his neck. He could feel her heart beating wildly against him. He tipped her head back and looked into the brownness of her eyes. The melancholy was gone.

"What is it?" he asked. "Has something happened?"

"No, no," she cried, "it's . . . it's just that I'm happy . . . to be with you again . . ."

"But why have you come out in this light dress?"

She was silent for a moment and then said, "Vincent, no matter how far away you go, I want you always to remember one thing about me."

"What, Margot?"

"That I loved you! Always remember that I loved you more than any other woman in your whole life."

"Why are you trembling so?"

"It's nothing. I was detained. That's why I was late. Are you nearly finished?"

"In a few moments."

"Then let me sit behind you while you work, just as I used to. You know, dear, I never wanted to be in your way, or hinder you. I only wanted you to let me love you."

"Yes, Margot." He could think of nothing else to say.

"Then go to work, my darling, and finish . . . so that we can go home together." She shivered a little, drew the scarf about her, and said, "Before you begin, Vincent, kiss me just once more. The way you kissed me . . . that time . . . in your studio . . . when we were so happy in each other's arms."

He kissed her tenderly. She drew her dress about her and sat behind him. The sun disappeared and the short winter gloaming fell over the flat land. The quiet of the country evening engulfed them.

There was the clink of a bottle. Margot rose to her knees with a half stifled cry, then sank to the earth in a violent spasm. Vincent jumped up and flung himself before her. Her eyes were closed; across her face was spread a sardonic smile. She went through a series of quick convulsions; her body went rigid and arched backwards, with the arms flexed. Vincent bent over the bottle that was lying in the snow. A white, crystalline residue had been left just inside the mouth of the bottle. It was odourless.

He picked Margot up in his arms and ran madly across the fields. He was a kilometre away from Nuenen. He was afraid she would die before he could get her back to the village. It was just before the supper hour. People were sitting out in front of their doors. Vincent came in the far side of town and had to run through the full length of the village with Margot in his arms. He reached the Begeman house, kicked the door open with a smash of his boot, and laid Margot on the sofa in the parlour. The mother and sisters came running in.

"Margot took poison!" he cried. "I'll get the doctor!"

He ran for the village doctor and dragged him away from his supper table. "You are sure it was strychnine?" the medical man demanded.

"It looked that way."

"And she was still alive when you got her home?"

"Yes."

Margot was writhing on the divan when they got there. The doctor bent over her.

"It was strychnine, all right," he said, "but she took something along with it to kill the pain. Smells to me like laudanum. She didn't realize it would act as an antidote."

"Then she will live, doctor?" demanded the mother.

"She has a chance. We must get her to Utrecht immediately. She will have to be kept under close observation."

"Can you recommend a hospital in Utrecht?"

"I don't think a hospital advisable. We had better take her to a *maison de santé* for a time. I know a good one. Order your carriage. We must make that last train out of Eindhoven."

Vincent stood in a dark corner, silent. The carriage was brought around to the front of the house. The doctor wrapped Margot in a blanket and carried her out. Her mother and four sisters followed. Vincent brought up the rear. His family was standing next door, on the porch of the vicarage. The whole village had gathered before the Begeman house. A hard silence fell when the doctor came out with Margot in his arms. He lifted her into the carriage. The women got in. Vincent stood beside it. The doctor picked up the reins. Margot's mother turned, saw Vincent, and screamed,

"You did this! You killed my daughter!"

The crowd looked at Vincent. The doctor flicked the horses with the whip. The carriage disappeared down the road.

7

Before his mother had broken her leg, the villagers were unfriendly toward Vincent because they mistrusted him and could not understand his way of life. But they had never actively disliked him. Now they turned against him violently, and he could feel their hatred surrounding him on all sides. Backs were turned when he approached. No one spoke to him or saw him. He became a pariah.

He did not mind for his own sake—the weavers and peasants in their huts still accepted him as their friend—but when people stopped coming to the parsonage to see his parents, he realized that he would have to move.

Vincent knew that the best thing for him to do was to get out of the Brabant altogether and leave his parents in peace. But where was he to go? The Brabant was his home. He wanted to live there always. He wished to draw the peasants and weavers; in that he found the only justification for his work. He knew that it was a good thing in the winter to be deep in the snow, in the autumn deep in the yellow leaves, in the summer among the ripe corn, and in spring amid the grass; that it was a good thing to be always with the mowers and peasant girls, in summer with a big sky overhead, in winter by the fireside, and to feel that it always had been so and always would be.

For him Millet's *Angelus* was the closest man had ever come to creating anything divine. In the crudeness of peasant life he found the only true and lasting reality. He wanted to paint out of doors, on the spot itself. There he would have to wipe off hundreds of flies, battle the dust and sand, and get the canvases scratched as he carried them for hours across the heath and hedges. But when he returned he would know that he had been face to face with reality and had caught something of its elemental simplicity. If his peasant pictures smelled of bacon, smoke, and potato steam, that was not unhealthy. If a stable smelled of dung, that belonged to a stable. If the fields had an odour of ripe corn or of guano or manure, that too was healthy—especially for people from the city.

He solved his problem in a very simple manner. A short distance down the road was the Catholic church, and next to it the house of the caretaker. Johannus Schafrath was a tailor; he followed that trade when he was not taking care of the church. His wife Adriana was a good soul. She rented Vincent two rooms, with a sort of pleasure at being able to do something for the man against whom the whole village had turned.

The Schafrath house was divided in the middle by a large hallway; on the right, as one entered, were the quarters of the family. On the left was a large sitting room overlooking the road, and a smaller room behind it. The sitting room became Vincent's studio, the one behind it his storeroom. He slept upstairs in the beamed attic, one half of which was used for hanging out the Schafrath wash. In the other half was a high bed with a *veeren bed,* and a chair. When night came, Vincent would throw his clothes over the chair, jump into bed, smoke a bowl of tobacco, watch the glow fade into the darkness, and fall asleep.

In the studio he put up his drawings in water-colour and chalk; heads of men and women whose negro-like, turned up noses, projecting jawbones, and large ears were strongly accentuated. There were weavers and weavers' looms, women driving the shuttle, peasants planting potatoes. He made friends with his brother Cor; together they built a cupboard and collected at least thirty different birds' nests, all kinds of moss and plants from the heath, shuttles, spinning wheels, bed warmers, peasants' tools, old caps and hats, wooden shoes, dishes, and everything connected with country life. They even put a small tree in one of the rear corners.

He settled down to work. He found that bistre and bitumen, which most painters were abandoning, made his colouring ripe and mellow. He discovered that he had to put little yellow in a colour to make it seem very yellow, if he placed it next to a violet or lilac tone.

He also learned that isolation is a sort of prison.

In March his father, who had walked a great distance over the heath to visit a sick parishioner, fell in a heap on the back steps of the parsonage.

When Anna Cornelia got to him he was already dead. They buried him in the garden near the old church. Theo came home for the funeral. That night they sat in Vincent's studio, talking first of family affairs, then of their work.

"I have been offered a thousand francs a month to leave Goupils and go with a new house," said Theo.

"Are you going to take it?"

"I think not. I have an idea their policy will be purely commercial."

"But you've been writing me that Goupils . . ."

"I know, *les Messieurs* are also after the big profits. Still, I have been with them for twelve years. Why should I change for a few more francs? Some day they may put me in charge of one of their branches. If they do, I shall begin selling the Impressionists."

"Impressionists? I think I've seen that name in print somewhere. Who are they?"

"Oh, just the younger painters around Paris; Edouard Manet, Degas, Renoir, Claude Monet, Sisley, Courbet, Lautrec, Gauguin, Cezanne, Seurat."

"Where did they get their name?"

"From the exhibition of 1874 at Nadar's. Claude Monet had a canvas there which he called *Impression: Soleil Levant*. A newspaper critic by the name of Louis Leroy called it an exhibition of *Impressionistes* and the name has stuck."

"Do they work in light or dark colours?"

"Oh, light! They despise dark colours."

"Then I don't think I could work with them. I intend to change my colouring, but I shall go darker instead of lighter."

"Perhaps you will think differently when you come to Paris."

"Perhaps so. Are any of them selling?"

"Durand-Ruel sells an occasional Manet. That's about all."

"Then how do they live?"

"Lord only knows. On their wits, mostly. Rousseau gives violin lessons to children; Gauguin borrows from his former stock exchange friends; Seurat is supported by his mother; Cezanne by his father. I can't imagine where the others get their money."

"Do you know them all, Theo?"

"Yes, I'm getting acquainted slowly. I've been persuading *les Messieurs* to give them a small corner for exhibition at Goupils, but they wouldn't touch an Impressionist canvas with a ten foot pole."

"Those fellows sound like the sort I ought to meet. See here, Theo, you do absolutely nothing to procure me some distraction by meeting other painters."

Theo went to the front window of the studio and stared out over the tiny grass plot that separated the caretaker's house from the road to Eindhoven.

"Then come to Paris and live with me," he said. "You're sure to end up there eventually."

"I'm not ready yet. I have some work to finish here, first."

"Well, if you remain in the provinces you can't hope to associate with your own kind."

"That may be true. But, Theo, there is one thing I cannot understand. You have never sold a single drawing or painting for me; in fact you have never even tried. Now have you?"

"No."

"Why not?"

"I've shown your work to the connoisseurs. They say . . ."

"Oh, the connoisseurs!" Vincent shrugged his shoulders. "I'm well acquainted with the banalities in which most connoisseurs indulge. Surely, Theo, you must know that their opinions have very little to do with the inherent quality of a piece of work."

"Well, I shouldn't say that. Your work is almost salable, but . . ."

"Theo, Theo, those are the identical words you wrote to me about my very first sketches from Etten."

"They are true, Vincent; you seem constantly on the verge of coming into a superb maturity. I pick up each new sketch eagerly, hoping that at last it has happened. But so far . . ."

"As for being salable or unsalable," interrupted Vincent, knocking out his pipe on the stove, "that is an old saw on which I do not intend to blunt my teeth."

"You say you have work here. Then pitch in and finish it. The sooner you get to Paris, the better it will be for you. But if you want me to sell in the meantime, send me pictures instead of studies. Nobody wants studies."

"Well, it's rather difficult to say just where a study leaves off and a picture begins. Let us paint as much as we can, Theo, and be ourselves with all our faults and qualities. I say 'us' because the money from you, which I know costs you trouble enough to procure for me, gives you the right to consider half of it your own creation."

"Oh, as for that . . ." Theo walked to the rear of the room and toyed with an old bonnet that hung on the tree.

8

Before his father's death Vincent had visited the parsonage only occasionally for supper or an hour of company. After the funeral his sister Elizabeth made it plain that he was entirely *persona non grata;* the family wished to keep up a certain position. His mother felt that he was responsible for his own life, and that it was her duty to stand by her daughters.

He was utterly alone in Nuenen now; in place of people, he put his study of nature. He began with a hopeless struggle to follow nature, and everything went wrong; he ended by calmly creating from his own palette and nature agreed with it and followed. When he was miserable in his aloneness, he thought of the scene in Weissenbruch's studio and the sharp-tongued painter's approval of pain. In his faithful Millet he found Weissenbruch's philosophy expressed more cogently: "I do not ever wish to suppress suffering, because often it is that which makes the artists express themselves most forcibly."

He became friends with a family of peasants by the name of De Groot. There were the mother, father, son, and two daughters, all of whom worked in the fields. The De Groots, like most of the peasants of the Brabant, had as much right to be called *gueules noires* as the miners of the Borinage. Their faces were negroid, with wide, dilated nostrils, humped noses, huge distended lips and long angular ears. The features thrust far forward from the forehead, the head was small and pointed. They lived in a hut of one room with holes in the walls for beds. There was a table in the centre of the room, two chairs, a number of boxes, and a suspension lamp that hung down from the rough, beamed ceiling.

The De Groots were potato eaters. With their supper they had a cup of black coffee and, perhaps once a week, a strip of bacon. They planted potatoes, dug up potatoes and ate potatoes; that was their life.

Stien de Groot was a sweet child of about seventeen. She wore a wide white bonnet to work, and a black jacket with a white collar. Vincent fell into the habit of going to visit them every evening. He and Stien laughed together a great deal.

"Look!" she would cry. "I'm a fine lady. I'm being drawed. Shall I put on my new bonnet for you, Mijnheer?"

"No, Stien, you're beautiful just as you are."

"Me, beautiful!"

She went off into gales of laughter. She had large cheerful eyes and a pretty expression. Her face was indigenous to the life. When she leaned over to dig potatoes in the field, he saw in the lines of her body a more authentic grace than even Kay had possessed. He had learned that the essential note in figure drawing was action, and that the great fault with the figures in the pictures of the old masters was that they did not work. He sketched the De Groots digging in the field, setting their table at home, eating steamed potatoes, and always Stien would peer over his shoulder and joke with him. Sometimes of a Sunday she would put on a clean bonnet and collar, and walk with him on the heath. It was the only amusement the peasants had.

"Did Margot Begeman like you?" she asked once.

"Yes."

"Then why did she try to kill herself?"

"Because her family wouldn't let her marry me."

"She was foolish. Do you know what I would have done instead of killing myself? I would have loved you!"

She laughed up into his face and ran to a clump of pine woods. All day long they laughed and played among the pines. Other strolling couples saw them. Stien had a natural gift for laughter; the smallest things Vincent said or did brought unrestrained shouts from her lips. She wrestled with him and tried to throw him on the ground. When she did not like the things he drew at her house, she would pour coffee over them or toss them into the fire. She came often to his studio to pose, and when she left, the place would be in chaos.

And so the summer and fall passed and winter came again. Vincent was forced by the snow to work in his studio all the time. The people of Nuenen did not like to pose and if it were not for the money, nobody would have come to him. In The Hague he had drawn almost ninety seamstresses in order to do a group picture of three. He wanted to paint the De Groot family at its supper of potatoes and coffee, but in order to get them right, he felt he first had to draw every peasant in the vicinity.

The Catholic priest had never favoured renting room in the caretaker's house to the man who was both heathen and artist, but since Vincent was quiet and courteous, he could find no reason to put him out. One day Adriana Schafrath came into the studio, all excited. "Father Pauwels wishes to see you immediately!"

Father Andreas Pauwels was a large man, red of face. He took a hurried look about the studio and decided he had never seen such mad confusion.

"What can I do for you, Father?" Vincent asked politely.

"You can't do anything for me! But I can do something for you! I shall see you through this affair, providing you do as you are told."

"What affair do you refer to, Father?"

"She is a Catholic and you are a Protestant, but I shall get a special dispensation from the Bishop. Be prepared to marry within a few days!"

Vincent came forward to look at Father Pauwels in the full light of the window. "I'm afraid I don't understand, Father," he said.

"Oh, yes you do. And all this pretense is of no use. Stien de Groot is with child! The honour of that family must be upheld."

"The devil she is!"

"You may well call on the devil. This is indeed the devil's work."

"Are you certain of this, Father? You're not mistaken?"

"I don't go about accusing people until I have positive proof."

"And did Stien tell you . . . did she say . . . I was the man?"

"No. She refused to tell us his name."

"Then why do you confer this honour on me?"

"You've been seen together many times. Doesn't she come often to this studio?"

"Yes."

"Haven't you gone walking with her in the fields on Sunday?"

"Yes, I have."

"Well, what further proof do I need?"

Vincent was silent for a moment. Then he said quietly, "I'm sorry to hear about this, Father, particularly if it is going to mean trouble for my friend Stien. But I assure you that my relations with her have been above reproach."

"Do you expect me to believe that?"

"No," replied Vincent, "I don't."

That evening, when Stien returned from the fields, he was waiting for her on the step of their hut. The rest of the family went in to eat supper. Stien sank down beside him.

"I'll soon have somebody else for you to draw," she said.

"Then it's true, Stien?"

"Sure. Want to feel?"

She took his hand and put it on her abdomen. He was conscious of the growing protuberance.

"Father Pauwels just informed me that I was the father."

Stien laughed. "I wish it had been you. But you never wanted to, did you?"

He looked at the sweat of the fields caked in her dark skin, the heavy, crooked, coarse features, the thick nose and lips. She smiled at him.

"I wish it had been too, Stien."

"So Father Pauwels said it was you. That's funny."

"What's funny about it?"

"Will you keep my secret?"

"I promise."

"It was the *kerkmeester* of his church!"

Vincent whistled. "Does your family know?"

"Of course not. And I'll never tell them. But they know it wasn't you."

Vincent went inside the hut. There was no change in the atmosphere. The De Groots accepted Stien's pregnancy in the same spirit that they would have the cow's in the field. They treated him as they had before, and he knew they believed in his innocence.

Not so the village. Adriana Schafrath had been listening at the door. She quickly communicated the news to her neighbours. Within the hour, twenty-six hundred inhabitants of Nuenen knew that Stien de Groot was to be brought to bed with Vincent's child, and that Father Pauwels was going to force them to marry.

November and winter had come. It was time to be moving. There was no use in his remaining in Nuenen any longer. He had painted everything there was to paint, learned everything there was to learn about peasant life. He did not think he could go on living in the recrudescence of village hatred. Clearly the time had come for him to leave. But where was he to go?

"Mijnheer Van Gogh," said Adriana sadly, after knocking on the door, "Father Pauwels says you must leave this house at once and take lodgings elsewhere."

"Very well; as he wishes."

He walked about the studio, looking at his work. Two solid years of slaving. Hundreds of studies of weavers and their wives, of looms, and peasants in the field, of the pollards at the bottom of the vicarage garden, and the old church tower; the heath and hedges in the heat of the sun and the cool of a winter dusk.

A great heaviness fell upon him. His work was all so fragmentary. There were bits of every phase of peasant life in the Brabant, but no one piece of work that summed up the peasant, that caught the spirit of his hut and his steaming potatoes. Where was his *Angelus* of the Brabantine peasant? And how could he leave before he had painted it?

He glanced at the calendar. There were still twelve days until the first of the month. He called Adriana.

"Tell Father Pauwels that I have paid until the first and will not leave before then."

He gathered up his easel, paints, canvas, and brushes and trudged off to the De Groot hut. No one was at home. He set to work on a pencil sketch of the inside of the room. When the family returned from the fields, he tore up the paper. The De Groots sat down to their steamed potatoes, black coffee, and bacon. Vincent set up his canvas and plugged on until the family went to bed. All that night he worked on the picture in his studio. He slept during the day. When he awakened he burned his canvas with savage disgust and set out again for the De Groots'.

The old Dutch masters had taught him that drawing and colour were one. The De Groots sat down to the table in the same positions as they had all their lives. Vincent wanted to make it clear how these people, eating their potatoes under the lamplight, had dug the earth with those very hands they put in the dish; he wanted it to speak of *manual* labour, and how they had honestly earned their food.

His old habit of throwing himself violently at a canvas came in handy now; he worked with tremendous speed and vitality. He did not have to think about what he was doing; he had drawn hundreds of peasants, and huts, and families sitting before their steamed potatoes.

"Father Pauwels was here today," said the mother.

"What did he want?" asked Vincent.

"He offered us money if we would not pose for you."

"What did you tell him?"

"We said you were our friend."

"He has visited every house around here," put in Stien. "But they told him they would rather earn a sou posing for you than take his charity."

The following morning he destroyed his canvas again. A feeling, half of rage and half of impotence, seized him. He had only ten days left. He had to get out of Nuenen; it was becoming insufferable. But he could not leave until he had fulfilled his promise to Millet.

Every night he went back to the De Groots'. He worked until they were too sleepy to sit up any longer. Each night he tried new combinations of colours, different values and proportions; and each day he saw that he had missed, that his work was incomplete.

The last day of the month came. Vincent had worked himself into a frenzy. He had gone without sleep and largely without food. He was living on nervous energy. The more he failed, the higher his excitement rose. He was waiting at the De Groots' when they came in from the fields. His easel was set up, his pigments mixed, his canvas stretched on the frame. This was his very last chance. In the morning he was leaving the Brabant, forever.

He worked for hours. The De Groots understood. When they finished their supper, they remained at the table, talking softly in the patois of the fields. Vincent did not know what he was painting. He dashed off the thing without any thought or consciousness coming between his hand and the easel. By ten o'clock, the De Groots were falling asleep and Vincent was exhausted. He had done all he could with the canvas. He gathered his things, kissed Stien, and bade them all good-bye. He trudged home through the night, unaware that he was walking.

In the studio he set the canvas on a chair, lit his pipe, and stood regarding his work. The whole thing was wrong. It missed. The spirit wasn't there. He had failed again. His two years of labour in the Brabant had been wasted.

He smoked his pipe down to the hot dregs. He packed his bag. He gathered all his studies off the wall and from the bureau, and placed them in a large box. He threw himself on the divan.

He did not know how much time passed. He got up, ripped the canvas off the frame, threw it into a corner, and put on a new one. He mixed some paints, sat down, and began work.

One starts with a hopeless struggle to follow nature, and everything goes wrong; one ends by calmly creating from one's palette, and nature agrees with it and follows.

On croit que j'imagine—ce n'est pas vrai—je me souviens.

It was just as Pietersen had told him in Brussels; he had been too close to his models. He had not been able to get a perspective. He had been pouring himself into the mould of nature; now he poured nature into the mould of himself.

He painted the whole thing in the colour of a good, dusty, unpeeled potato. There was the dirty, linen table cloth, the smoky wall, the lamp hanging down from the rough rafters, Stien serving her father with steamed potatoes, the mother pouring the black coffee, the brother lifting a cup to his lips, and on all their faces the calm, patient acceptance of the eternal order of things.

The sun rose and a bit of light peered into the storeroom window. Vincent got up from his stool. He felt perfectly calm and peaceful. The twelve days' excitement was gone. He looked at his work. It reeked of bacon, smoke, and potato steam. He smiled. He had painted his *Angelus*. He had captured that which does not pass in that which passes. The Brabant peasant would never die.

He washed the picture with the white of an egg. He carried his box of drawings and paintings to the vicarage, left them with his mother, and bade her good-bye. He returned to his studio, wrote *The Potato Eaters* on his canvas, put a few of his best studies with it, and set out for Paris.

BOOK FIVE

PARIS

1

"THEN you didn't get my last letter?" asked Theo the next morning, as they sat over their rolls and coffee.

"I don't think so," replied Vincent. "What was in it?"

"The news of my promotion at Goupils."

"Why, Theo, and you didn't tell me a word about it yesterday!"

"You were too excited to listen. I have charge of the gallery on the Boulevard Montmartre."

"Theo, that's splendid! An art gallery of your own!"

"It really isn't my own, Vincent. I have to follow the Goupil policy pretty closely. But they let me hang the Impressionists on the *entresol*, so . . ."

"Who are you exhibiting?"

"Monet, Degas, Pissarro and Manet."

"Never heard of them."

"Then you'd better come along to the gallery and have a good, long look!"

"What does that sly grin on your face mean, Theo?"

"Oh, nothing. Will you have more coffee? We must go in a few minutes. I walk to the shop every morning."

"Thanks. No, no, only half a cup. Deuce take it, Theo, boy, but it's good to eat breakfast across the table from you once again!"

"I've been waiting for you to come to Paris for a long time. You had to come eventually, of course. But I do think it would have been better if you had waited until June, when I move to the Rue Lepic. We'll have three large rooms there. You can't do much work here, you see."

Vincent turned in his chair and glanced about him. Theo's apartment consisted of one room, a tiny kitchen, and a cabinet. The room was cheerfully furnished with authentic Louis Philippes, but there was hardly space enough to move around.

"If I set up an easel," said Vincent, "we'd have to move some of your lovely furniture out into the courtyard."

"I know the place is crowded, but I had a chance to pick these pieces up at a bargain and they're exactly what I want for the new apartment. Come along, Vincent, I'll take you down the hill on my favourite walk to the Boulevard. You don't know Paris until you smell it in the early morning."

Theo put on the heavy black coat that crossed up high under his immaculate, white bow tie, gave a final pat of the brush to the little curl that stood up on each side of the part in his hair, and then smoothed down his moustache and soft chin beard. He put on his black bowler hat, took his gloves and walking stick, and went to the front door.

"Well, Vincent, are you ready? Good Lord, but you are a sight! If you wore that outfit anywhere but in Paris, you'd be arrested!"

"What's the matter with it?" Vincent looked down at himself. "I've been wearing it for almost two years and nobody's said anything."

Theo laughed. "Never mind, Parisians are used to people like you. I'll get you some clothes tonight when the gallery closes."

They walked down a flight of winding stairs, passed the *concierge's* apartment and stepped through the door to the Rue Laval. It was a fairly broad street, prosperous and respectable looking, with large stores selling drugs, picture frames and antiques.

"Notice the three beautiful ladies on the third floor of our building," said Theo.

Vincent looked up and saw three plaster of Paris heads and busts. Under the first was written, Sculpture, under the middle one, Architecture, and under the last, Painting.

"What makes them think Painting is such an ugly wench?"

"I don't know," replied Theo, "but anyway, you got into the right house."

The two men passed Le Vieux Rouen, Antiquities, where Theo had bought his Louis Philippe furniture. In a moment they were in the Rue Montmartre, which wound gracefully up the hill to the Avenue Clichy and the Butte Montmartre, and down the hill to the heart of the city. The street was full of morning sunlight, of the smell of Paris arising, of people eating croissants and coffee in the cafés, of the vegetable, meat, and cheese shops opening to the day's trade.

It was a teeming bourgeois section, crowded with small stores. Workingmen walked out in the middle of the street. Housewives fingered the merchandise in the bins in front of the shops and bargained querulously with the merchants.

Vincent breathed deeply. "It's Paris," he said. "After all these years."

"Yes, Paris. The capital of Europe. Particularly for an artist."

Vincent drank in the busy flow of life winding up and down the hill; the *garçons* in alternately striped red and black jackets; the housewives carrying long loaves of unwrapped bread under their arms; the pushcarts at the curb; the *femmes de chambre* in soft slippers; the prosperous business men on their way to work. After passing innumerable *charcuteries, pâtisseries, boulangeries, blanchisseries* and small cafés, the Rue Montmartre curved to the bottom of the hill and swung into the Place Chateaudun, a rough circle formed by the meeting of six streets. They crossed the circle and passed Notre Dame de Lorette, a square, dirty, black stone church with three angels on the roof, floating off idyllically into the blue empyrean. Vincent looked closely at the writing over the door.

"Do they mean this *Liberté-Egalité-Fraternité* business, Theo?"

"I believe they do. The Third Republic will probably be permanent. The royalists are quite dead, and the socialists are coming into power. Emile Zola was telling me the other night that the next revolution will be against capitalism instead of royalty."

"Zola! How nice for you to know him, Theo."

"Paul Cezanne introduced me to him. We all meet once a week at the Café Batignolles. I'll take you there next time I go."

After leaving the Place Chateaudun, the Rue Montmartre lost its bourgeois character and assumed a more stately air. The shops became larger, the cafés more imposing, the people better dressed, the buildings more prosperous looking. Music halls and restaurants lined the sidewalks, hotels made an appearance, and carriages took the place of trade wagons.

The brothers stepped along at a brisk pace. The cold sunlight was invigorating, the flavour of the air suggestive of the rich and complex life of the city.

"Since you can't work at home," said Theo, "I suggest you go to Corman's Studio."

"What's it like?"

"Well, Corman is just as academic as most masters, but if you don't want his criticism, he'll let you alone."

"Is it expensive?"

Theo tapped Vincent's thigh with his walking stick. "Didn't I tell you I was promoted? I'm getting to be one of those plutocrats that Zola is going to wipe out with his next revolution!"

At length the Rue Montmartre flowed into the wide, imposing Boulevard Montmartre, with its large department stores, arcades, and expensive shops. The Boulevard, which became the Boulevard des Italiens a few blocks farther on and led to the Place de l'Opéra, was the most important thoroughfare in the city. Although the street was empty at this hour of the morning, the clerks within the stores were preparing for a busy day.

Theo's branch of the Goupil Gallery was located at number 19, just one short block to the right of the Rue Montmartre. Vincent and Theo crossed the wide boulevard, stopped alongside of a gas lamp in the centre to let a carriage go by, and then continued on to the gallery.

The well groomed clerks bowed respectfully as Theo walked through the salon of his gallery. Vincent remembered how he used to bow to Tersteeg and Obach when he was a clerk. In the air was the same aroma of culture and refinement, a smell he thought his nostrils had forgotten. On the walls of the salon were paintings by Bouguereau, Henner, and Delaroche. Above the main salon was a small balcony, with a flight of stairs at the rear leading to it.

"The pictures you'll want to see are up on the *entresol*," said Theo. "Come down when you're through and tell me what you think of them."

"Theo, what are you licking your chops about?"

Theo's grin became all the broader. "*A toute à l'heure*," he said and disappeared into his office.

2

"Am I in a madhouse?"

Vincent stumbled blindly to the lone chair on the *entresol*, sat down and rubbed his eyes. From the age of twelve he had been used to seeing dark and sombre paintings; paintings in which the brushwork was invisible, every detail of the canvas correct and complete, and flat colours shaded slowly into each other.

The paintings that laughed at him merrily from the walls were like nothing he had ever seen or dreamed of. Gone were the flat, thin surfaces. Gone was the sentimental sobriety. Gone was the brown gravy in which Europe had been bathing its pictures for centuries. Here were pictures riotously mad with the sun. With light and air and throbbing vivacity. Paintings of ballet girls backstage, done in primitive reds, greens, and blues thrown next to each other irreverently. He looked at the signature. Degas.

There were a group of outdoor scenes along a river bank, caught with all the ripe, lush colour of midsummer and a hot overhead sun. The name was Monet. In all the hundreds of canvases that Vincent had seen, there was not as much luminosity, breath, and fragrance as in one of these glowing pictures. The darkest colour Monet used was a dozen times lighter than the lightest colour to be found in all the museums of Holland. The brushwork stood out, unashamed, every stroke apparent, every stroke entering into the rhythm of nature. The surface was thick, deep, palpitant with heavy globs of ripe, rich paint.

Vincent stood before a picture of a man in his woollen undershirt, holding the rudder of a little boat with the intense Gallic concentration characteristic of the Frenchman enjoying himself on a Sunday afternoon. The wife sat by, passively. Vincent looked for the name of the artist.

"Monet again?" he said aloud. "That's funny. There's not the slightest resemblance to his outdoor scene."

He looked again and saw that he was mistaken. The name was Manet, not Monet. Then he remembered the story of Manet's *Picnic on the Grass,* and *Olympia,* and how the police had had to rope off the pictures to keep them from being slashed by knives and spat upon.

He did not know why, but the Manet paintings reminded him of the books of Emile Zola. There seemed to be that same fierce quest after truth, the same unafraid penetration, the same feeling that character is beauty, no matter how sordid it may appear. He studied the technique closely, and saw that Manet put elemental colours next to each other without gradation, that many details were barely suggested, that colours, lines, lights and shades did not end with definite precision, but wavered into each other.

"Just as the eye sees them waver in nature," said Vincent.

He heard Mauve's voice in his ears. "Is it impossible for you to make a definite statement about a line, Vincent?"

He sat down again and let the pictures sink in. After a time he caught one of the simple expedients by which painting had been so completely revolutionized. These painters filled the air of their pictures solid! And that living, moving, replete air did something to the objects that were to be seen in them! Vincent knew that, for the academicians, air did not exist; it was just a blank space in which they placed rigid, set objects.

But these new men! They had discovered the air! They had discovered light and breath, atmosphere and sun; they saw things filtered through all the innumerable forces that live in that vibrant fluid. Vincent realized that painting could never be the same again. Photographic machines and academicians would made exact duplicates; painters would see everything filtered through their own natures and the sun-swept air in which they worked. It was almost as though these men had created a new art.

He stumbled down the stairs. Theo was in the main salon. He turned with a smile on his lips, searching his brother's face eagerly.

"Well, Vincent?" he said.

"Oh, Theo!" breathed Vincent.

He tried to speak, but could not. His eyes darted up to the *entresol*. He turned and ran out of the gallery.

He walked up the broad boulevard until he came to an octagonal building which he recognized as the Opera. Through the canyon of stone buildings he caught sight of a bridge, and made for the river. He slid down to the water's edge and dribbled his fingers in the Seine. He crossed the bridge without looking at the bronze horsemen, and made his way through the labyrinth of streets on the Left Bank. He climbed steadily upward. He passed a cemetery, turned to his right and came to a huge railway station. Forgetting that he had crossed the Seine, he asked a gendarme to direct him to the Rue Laval.

"The Rue Laval?" said the gendarme. "You are on the wrong side of the city, Monsieur. This is Montparnasse. You must go down the hill, cross the Seine, and go up again to Montmartre."

For many hours Vincent stumbled through Paris, not caring much where he went. There were broad, clean boulevards with imposing shops, then wretched, dirty alleys, then bourgeois streets with endless rows of wine shops. Once again he found himself on the crest of a hill on which there was a triumphal arch. To the east he looked down over a tree-lined boulevard enclosed on both sides by narrow strips of park, and ending in a large square with an Egyptian obelisk. To the west he overlooked an extensive wood.

It was late afternoon before he found the Rue Laval. The dull ache within him had been numbed by sheer fatigue. He went directly to where his pictures and studies were tied in bundles. He spread them all out on the floor.

He gazed at his canvases. God! but they were dark and dreary. God! but they were heavy, lifeless, dead. He had been painting in a long past century, and he had not known it.

Theo came home in the gloaming and found Vincent sitting dully on the floor. He knelt beside his brother. The last vestiges of daylight were blotted out of the room. Theo was silent for some time.

"Vincent," he said, "I know how you feel. Stunned. It's tremendous, isn't it? We're throwing overboard nearly everything that painting has held sacred."

Vincent's small, hurt eyes caught Theo's and held them.

"Theo, why didn't you tell me? Why didn't I know? Why didn't you bring me here sooner? You've let me waste six long years."

"Waste them? Nonsense. You've worked out your craft for yourself. You paint like Vincent Van Gogh, and nobody else in the world. If you had come here before you crystallized your own particular expression, Paris would have moulded you to suit itself."

"But what am I to do? Look at this junk!" He kicked his foot through a large, dark canvas. "It's all dead, Theo. And worthless."

"You ask me what you are to do? I'll tell you. You are to learn about light and colour from the Impressionists. That much you must borrow from them. But nothing more. You must not imitate. You must not get swamped. Don't let Paris submerge you."

"But, Theo, I must learn everything all over. Everything I do is wrong."

"Everything you do is right . . . except your light and colour. You were an Impressionist from the day you picked up a pencil in the Borinage. Look at your drawing! Look at your brushwork! No one ever painted like that before Manet. Look at your lines! You almost never make a definite statement. Look at your faces, your trees, your figures in the fields! They are your impressions. They are rough, imperfect, filtered through your own personality. That's what it means, to be an Impressionist; not to paint like everyone else, not to be a slave to rules and regulations. You belong to your age, Vincent, and you're an Impressionist whether you like it or not."

"Oh, Theo, do I like it!"

"Your work is known in Paris among the young painters who count. Oh, I don't mean those who sell, but those who are making the important experiments. They want to know you. You'll learn some marvellous things from them."

"They know my work? The young Impressionists know my work?"

Vincent got on his knees so that he could see Theo more clearly. Theo thought of the days in Zundert, when they used to play together on the floor of the nursery.

"Of course. What do you think I've been doing in Paris all these years? They think you have a penetrating eye and a draftsman's fist. Now all you need to do is lighten your palette and learn how to paint living, luminous air. Vincent, isn't it wonderful to be living in a time when such important things are happening?"

"Theo, you old devil, you grand old devil!"

"Come on, get off your knees. Make a light. Let's get all dressed up and go out for dinner. I'll take you to the Brasserie Universelle. They serve the most delicious *Chateaubriand* in Paris. I'm going to treat you to a real banquet. With a bottle of champagne, old boy, to celebrate the great day when Paris and Vincent Van Gogh were joined together!"

3

The following morning Vincent took his drawing materials and went to Corman's. The studio was a large room on the third floor, with a strong north light coming in from the street. There was a nude male model posed at one end, facing the door. About thirty chairs and easels were scattered about for the students. Vincent registered with Corman and was assigned an easel.

After he had been sketching about an hour, the door to the hall opened and a woman stepped in. There was a bandage wrapped around her head and she was holding one hand to her jaw. She took one horrified look at the naked model, exclaimed *"Mon Dieu!"* and ran.

Vincent turned to the man sitting beside him.

"What do you suppose was the matter with her?"

"Oh, that happens every day. She was looking for the dentist next door. The shock of seeing a naked man usually cures their toothache. If the dentist doesn't move he'll probably go bankrupt. You're a newcomer, aren't you?"

"Yes. This is only my third day in Paris."

"What's your name?"

"Van Gogh. What's yours?"

"Henri Toulouse-Lautrec. Are you any relation to Theo Van Gogh?"

"He's my brother."

"Then you must be Vincent! Well, I'm glad to know you. Your brother is the best art dealer in Paris. He's the only one who will give the young men a chance. Not only that, he fights for us. If we are ever accepted by the Parisian public, it will be due to Theo Van Gogh. We all think he's mighty fine."

"So do I."

Vincent looked closely at the man. Lautrec had a squashed down head, his features, the nose, lips, and chin, stuck far out from the flat head. He wore a full black beard, which grew outward from his chin instead of downward.

"What makes you come to a beastly place like Corman's?" asked Lautrec.

"I must have some place to sketch. What about you?"

"Damned if I know. I lived in a brothel all last month up in Montmartre. Did portraits of the girls. That was real work. Sketching in a studio is child's play."

"I'd like to see your studies of those women."

"Would you really?"

"Certainly. Why not?"

"Most people think I'm crazy because I paint dance hall girls and clowns and whores. But that's where you find real character."

"I know. I married one in The Hague."

"*Bien!* This Van Gogh family is all right! Let me see the sketch you've done of the model, will you?"

"Take them all. I've done four."

Lautrec looked at the sketches for some moments and then said, "You and I will get along together, my friend. We think alike. Has Corman seen these yet?"

"No."

"When he does, you'll be through here. That is, as far as his criticism is concerned. He said to me the other day, 'Lautrec, you exaggerate, always you exaggerate. One line in each of your studies is caricature.' "

"And you replied, 'That, my dear Corman, is character, not caricature.' "

A curious light came into Lautrec's black, needle-point eyes. "Do you still want to see those portraits of my girls?"

"I certainly do."

"Then come along. This place is a morgue, anyway."

Lautrec had a thick, squat neck, and powerful shoulders and arms. When he rose to his feet, Vincent saw that his new friend was a cripple. Lautrec, on his feet, stood no higher than when he was seated. His thick torso came forward almost to the apex of a triangle at the waist, then fell in sharply to the tiny shrivelled legs.

They walked down the Boulevard Clichy, Lautrec leaning heavily on his stick. Every few moments he would stop to rest, pointing out some lovely line in the juxtaposition of two buildings. Just one block this side of the Moulin Rouge they turned up the hill toward the Butte Montmartre. Lautrec had to rest more frequently.

"You're probably wondering what's wrong with my legs, Van Gogh. Everyone does. Well, I'll tell you."

"Oh, please! You don't need to speak of it."

"You might as well know." He doubled over his stick, leaning on it with his shoulders. "I was born with brittle bones. When I was twelve, I slipped on a dance floor and broke my right thigh bone. The next year I fell into a ditch and broke the left one. My legs have never grown an inch since."

"Does it make you unhappy?"

"No. If I had been normal I should never have been a painter. My father is a count of Toulouse. I was next in line for the title. If I had wanted to, I could have had a marshal's baton and ridden alongside of the King of France. That is, providing there was a King of France . . . *Mais, sacrebleu,* why should anyone be a count when he can be a painter?"

"Yes, I'm afraid the days of the counts are over."

"Shall we go on? Degas's studio is just down this alley. They say I'm copying his work because he does ballet dancers and I do the girls from the Moulin Rouge. Let them say what they like. This is my place, 19 *bis*, Rue Fontaine. I'm on the ground floor, as you might have guessed."

He threw open the door and bowed Vincent in.

"I live alone," he said. "Sit down, if you can find a place to sit."

Vincent looked about. In addition to the canvases, frames, easels, stools, steps, and rolls of drapery, two large tables encumbered the studio. One was laden with bottles of rare wines and decanters of multi-coloured liqueurs. On the other were piled up dancers' slippers, periwigs, old books, women's dresses, gloves, stockings, vulgar photographs, and precious Japanese prints. There was just one little space among all this litter where Lautrec could sit and paint.

"What's the matter, Van Gogh?" he asked. "Can't you find a place to sit? Just shove that junk on the floor and bring the chair over to the window. There were twenty-seven girls in the house. I slept with every one of them. Don't you agree that it's necessary to sleep with a woman before you can fully understand her?"

"Yes."

"Here are the sketches. I took them down to a dealer on the Capucines. He said, 'Lautrec, why have you a fixation on ugliness? Why do you always paint the most sordid and immoral people you can find? These women are repulsive, utterly repulsive. They have debauch and sinister evil written all over their faces. Is that what modern art means, to create ugliness? Have you painters become so blind to beauty that you can paint only the scum of the earth?' I said, 'Pardon me, but I think I'm going to be sick, and I shouldn't like to do it all over your lovely carpet.' Is that light all right, Van Gogh? Will you have a drink? Speak up, what do you prefer? I have everything you could possibly want."

He hobbled about the chairs, tables, and rolls of drapery with agile movements, poured a drink and passed it to Vincent.

"Here's to ugliness, Van Gogh," he cried. "May it never infect the Academy!"

Vincent sipped his drink and studied Lautrec's twenty-seven sketches of the girls of a Montmartre sporting house. He realized that the artist had set them down as he saw them. They were objective portraits, without moral attitude or ethical comment. On the faces of the girls he had caught the misery and suffering, the callous carnality, the bestial debauch and spiritual aloofness.

"Do you like portraits of peasants, Lautrec?" he asked.

"Yes, if they're not sentimentalized."

"Well, I paint peasants. And it strikes me that these women are peasants too. Gardeners of the flesh, so to speak. Earth and flesh, they're just two different forms of the same matter, aren't they? And these women till the flesh, human flesh that must be tilled to make it produce life. This is good work, Lautrec; you've said something worth saying."

"And you don't think them ugly?"

"They are authentic and penetrating commentaries on life. That is the very highest kind of beauty, don't you think? If you had idealized or sentimentalized the women, you would have made them ugly because your portraits would have been cowardly and false. But you stated the full truth as you saw it, and that's what beauty means, isn't it?"

"Jesus Christ! Why aren't there more men in the world like you? Have another drink! And help yourself to those sketches! Take as many as you like!"

Vincent held a canvas up to the light, cast about in his mind for a moment, and then exclaimed, "Daumier! That's who it reminds me of."

Lautrec's face lit up.

"Yes, Daumier. The greatest of them all. And the only person I ever learned anything from. God! how magnificently that man could hate!"

"But why paint things if you hate them? I paint only things I love."

"All great art springs from hatred, Van Gogh. Oh, I see you're admiring my Gauguin."

"Whose painting did you say that was?"

"Paul Gauguin. Do you know him?"

"No."

"Then you should. That's a native Martinique woman. Gauguin was out there for a while. He's completely *fou* on the subject of going primitive, but he's a superb painter. He had a wife, three children, and a position on the Stock Exchange that brought him thirty thousand francs a year. He bought fifteen thousand francs worth of paintings from Pissarro, Manet, and Sisley. He painted his wife's portrait on their wedding day. She thought it a delightful *beau geste*. Gauguin used to paint on Sundays; you know, the Stock Exchange Art Club? Once he showed a picture to Manet, who told him it was very good. 'Oh,' replied Gauguin, 'I am only an amateur!' 'Oh, no,' said Manet, 'there are no amateurs but those who make bad pictures.' That remark went to Gauguin's head like neat spirits and he's never drawn a sober breath since. Gave up his job on the Exchange, lived with his family in Rouen for a year on his savings, then sent his wife and children to her parents' home in Stockholm. He's been living off his wits ever since."

"He sounds interesting."

"Be careful when you meet him; he loves to torment his friends. Say, Van Gogh, what about letting me show you the Moulin Rouge and the Elysée-Montmartre? I know all the girls there. Do you like women, Van Gogh? I mean to sleep with? I love them. What do you say, shall we make a night of it sometime?"

"By all means."

"Splendid. I suppose we must go back to Corman's. Have another drink before you go? That's it. Now just one more and you'll empty the bottle. Look out, you'll knock that table over. Never mind, the charwoman will pick all that stuff up. Guess I'll have to move out of here pretty soon. I'm rich,

Van Gogh. My father is afraid I'll curse him for bringing me into the world a cripple, so he gives me everything I want. When I move out of a place I never take anything but my work. I rent an empty studio and buy things one by one. When I'm just about to be suffocated, I move again. By the way, what kind of women do you prefer? Blondes? Redheads?

"Don't bother to lock it. Notice the way the metal roofs flow down to the Boulevard Clichy in a sort of black ocean. Oh, hell! I don't have to pretend to you. I lean on this stick and point out beautiful scenes because I'm a God damned cripple and can't walk more than a few steps at a time! Well, we're all cripples in one way or another. Let's get along."

4

It looked so easy. All he had to do was throw away the old palette, buy some light pigments, and paint as an Impressionist. At the end of the first day's trial, Vincent was surprised and a bit nettled. At the end of the second day he was bewildered. Bewilderment was succeeded in turn by chagrin, anger, and fear. By the end of the week he was in a towering rage. After all his laborious months of experimentation with colour, he was still a novice. His canvases came out dark, dull, and sticky. Lautrec, sitting by Vincent's side at Corman's, watched the paint and curses fly, but refrained from offering any advice.

If it was a hard week for Vincent, it was a thousand times worse for Theo. Theo was a gentle soul, mild in his manners and delicate in his habits of life. He was an extremely fastidious person, in his dress, in his decorum, in his home and place of business. He had only a small fraction of Vincent's bruising vitality and power.

The little apartment on the Rue Laval was just large enough for Theo and his fragile Louis Philippes. By the end of the first week Vincent had turned the place into a junk shop. He paced up and down the living room, kicked furniture out of the way, threw canvases, brushes, and empty colour tubes all over the floor, adorned the divans and tables with his soiled clothing, broke dishes, splashed paint, and upset every last punctilious habit of Theo's life.

"Vincent, Vincent," cried Theo, "don't be such a Tartar!"

Vincent had been pacing about the tiny apartment, biting his knuckle and muttering to himself. He threw himself heavily into a fragile chair.

"It's no use," he groaned. "I began too late. I'm too old to change. God, Theo, I've tried! I've started twenty canvases this week. But I'm set in my technique, and I can't begin all over again. I tell you, I'm done for! I can't go back to Holland and paint sheep after what I've seen here. And I came too late to get in the main swing of my craft. God, what will I do?"

He jumped up, lurched to the door for some fresh air, slammed it shut, pried open a window, stared at the Restaurant Bataille for a moment, shut

he window so hard he almost smashed the glass, strode to the kitchen for a
drink, spilled half the water on the floor, and came back into the living room
with a trickle of water running down each side of his chin.

"Well, what do you say, Theo? Must I give it up? Am I through? It looks
hat way, doesn't it?"

"Vincent, you're behaving like a child. Do quiet down for a moment and
isten to me. No, no, don't pace the floor! I can't talk to you that way. And
for goodness' sake take off those heavy boots if you're going to kick that gilt
chair every time you pass it!"

"But, Theo, I've let you support me for six long years. And what do you
get out of it? A lot of brown-gravy pictures, and a hopeless failure on your
hands."

"Listen, old boy, when you wanted to draw the peasants, did you catch
the entire trick in a week? Or did it take you five years?"

"Yes, but I was just beginning then."

"You're just beginning with colour today! And it will probably take you
another five years."

"Is there no end to this, Theo? Must I go to school all my life? I'm thirty-
three; when in God's name do I reach maturity?"

"This is your last job, Vincent. I've seen everything that is being painted
in Europe; the men on my *entresol* are the last word. Once you lighten your
palette . . ."

"Oh, Theo, do you really think I can? You don't think I'm a failure?"

"I'm more inclined to think you're a jackass. The greatest revolution in
the history of art, and you want to master it in a week! Let's go take a walk
on the Butte and cool our heads. If I stay in this room with you another
five minutes I shall probably explode."

The following afternoon Vincent sketched at Corman's until late, and then
called for Theo at Goupils. An early April dusk had fallen, the long rows
of six-story stone buildings were bathed in a coral-pink glow of dying colour.
All of Paris was having its *apéritif*. The sidewalk cafés on the Rue Montmartre were crowded with men chatting with their friends. From inside the
cafés came the sound of soft music, playing to refresh the Parisians after
their day of toil. The gas lamps were being lit, the *garçons* were laying table
cloths in the restaurants, the clerks in the department stores were pulling
down the corrugated iron shutters and emptying the sidewalk bins of merchandise.

Theo and Vincent strolled along leisurely. They crossed the Place Chateaudun, with its flurry of carriages from the six converging streets, passed
Notre Dame de Lorette, and wound up the hill to the Rue Laval.

"Shall we have an *apéritif*, Vincent?"

"Yes. Let's sit where we can watch the crowd."

"We'll go up to Bataille's, on the Rue des Abbesses. Some of my friends
will probably drop by."

The Restaurant Bataille was frequented largely by painters. There were only four or five tables out in front, but the two rooms inside were comfortably large. Madame Bataille always led the artists to one room and the bourgeois to the other; she could tell at first glance to which class a man belonged.

"*Garçon!*" called Theo. "Bring me a Kummel Eckau OO."

"What do you suggest for me, Theo?"

"Try a cointreau. You'll have to experiment for a while to find your permanent drink."

The waiter put their drinks before them on saucers with the price marked in black letters. Theo lit a cigar, Vincent his pipe. Laundry women in black aprons passed, baskets of ironed clothes under their arms; a labourer went by, dangling an unwrapped herring by the tail; there were painters in smocks, with wet canvases strapped to the easel; business men in black derbies and grey checked coats; housewives in cloth slippers, carrying a bottle of wine or a paper of meat; beautiful women with long, flowing skirts, narrow waists, and tiny plumed hats perched forward on their heads.

"It's a gorgeous parade, isn't it, Theo?"

"Yes. Paris doesn't really awaken until the *apéritif* hour."

"I've been trying to think . . . what is it that makes Paris so marvellous?"

"Frankly, I don't know. It's an eternal mystery. It has something to do with French character, I suppose. There's a pattern of freedom and tolerance here, an easy going acceptance of life that . . . Hello, here's a friend of mine I want you to meet. Good evening, Paul; how are you?"

"Very well, thanks, Theo."

"May I present my brother, Vincent Van Gogh? Vincent, this is Paul Gauguin. Sit down, Paul, and have one of your inevitable absinthes."

Gauguin raised his absinthe, touched the tip of his tongue to the liqueur and then coated the inside of his mouth with it. He turned to Vincent.

"How do you like Paris, Monsieur Van Gogh?"

"I like it very much."

"*Tiens! C'est curieux.* Still, some people do. As for myself, I find it one huge garbage can. With civilization as the garbage."

"I don't care much for this cointreau, Theo. Can you suggest something else?"

"Try an absinthe, Monsieur Van Gogh," put in Gauguin. "That is the only drink worthy of an artist."

"What do you say, Theo?"

"Why ask me? Suit yourself. *Garçon.* An absinthe for Monsieur. You seem rather pleased with yourself today, Paul. What's happened? Sell a canvas?"

"Nothing as sordid as all that, Theo. But I had a charming experience this morning."

Theo tipped Vincent a wink. "Tell us about it, Paul. *Garçon!* another absinthe for Monsieur Gauguin."

Gauguin touched the tip of his tongue to the new absinthe, wetted the inside of his mouth with it, and then began.

"Do you know that blind alley, the Impasse Frenier, which opens on the Rue des Forneaux? Well, five o'clock this morning I heard Mother Fourel, the carter's wife, scream, 'Help! My husband has hung himself!' I leaped out of bed, pulled on a pair of trousers (the proprieties!) grabbed a knife downstairs and cut the rope. The man was dead, but still warm, still burning. I wanted to carry him to his bed. 'Stop!' cried Mother Fourel, 'we must wait for the police!'

"On the other side my house overhangs fifteen yards of market gardener's bed. 'Have you a cantaloupe?' I called to the gardener. 'Certainly, Monsieur, a ripe one.' At breakfast I ate my melon without a thought of the man who had hung himself. There is good in life, as you see. Beside the poison there is the antidote. I was invited out to luncheon, so I put on my best shirt, expecting to thrill the company. I related the story. Smiling, quite unconcerned, they all asked me for a piece of the rope with which he had hung himself."

Vincent looked closely at Paul Gauguin. He had the great, black head of a barbarian, with a massive nose that shot down from the corner of his left eye to the right corner of his mouth. His eyes were huge, almond shaped, protruding, invested with a fierce melancholy. Ridges of bone bulged over the eyes, under the eyes, ran down the long cheeks and across the wide chin. He was a giant of a man, with overwhelming brutal vitality.

Theo smiled faintly.

"Paul, I'm afraid you enjoy your sadism a little too much for it to be entirely natural. I'll have to be going now; I have a dinner engagement. Vincent, will you join me?"

"Let him stay with me, Theo," said Gauguin. "I want to get acquainted with this brother of yours."

"Very well. But don't pour too many absinthes into him. He's not used to them. *Garçon. Combien?*"

"That brother of yours is all right, Vincent," said Gauguin. "He's still afraid to exhibit the younger men, but I suppose Valadon holds him down."

"He has Monet, Sisley, Pissarro, and Manet on the balcony."

"True, but where are the Seurats? And the Gauguins? And the Cezannes and Toulouse-Lautrecs? The other men are getting old now and their time is passing."

"Oh, then you know Toulouse-Lautrec?"

"Henri? Of course! Who doesn't know him? He's a damn fine painter, but he's crazy. He thinks that if he sleeps with five thousand women, he'll vindicate himself for not being a whole man. Every morning he wakes up with a gnawing inferiority because he has no legs; every night he drowns that inferiority in liquor and a woman's body. But it's back with him again the next morning. If he weren't crazy he'd be one of our best painters. Here's where we turn in. My studio is on the fourth floor. Look out for that step. The board is broken."

Gauguin went ahead and lighted a lamp. It was a shabby garret, with an easel, a brass bed, a table, and a chair. In an alcove near the door Vincent saw some crude and obscene photographs.

"From these pictures I would say you don't think very highly of love?"

"Where will you sit, on the bed or the chair? There's some tobacco for your pipe on the table. Well, I like women, providing they are fat and vicious. Their intelligence annoys me. I have always wanted a mistress who was fat and I have never found one. To make a fool of me, they are always pregnant. Did you read a short story published last month by a young chap by the name of Maupassant? He's Zola's protégé. A man who loves fat women has Christmas dinner served in his home for two and goes out to find company. He comes across a woman who suits him perfectly, but when they get to the roast, she is delivered of a bouncing baby boy!"

"But all this has very little to do with love, Gauguin."

Gauguin stretched out on the bed, put one muscular arm under his head and blew clouds of smoke at the unpainted rafters.

"I don't mean to say that I am not susceptible to beauty, Vincent, but simply that my senses will have none of it. As you perceive, I do not know love. To say, 'I love you' would break all my teeth. But I have no complaints to make. Like Jesus I say, 'The flesh is the flesh and the spirit is the spirit.' Thanks to this, a small sum of money satisfies my flesh, and my spirit is left in peace."

"You certainly dismiss the matter very lightly!"

"No, whom one gets in bed with is no light matter. With a woman who feels pleasure, I feel twice as much pleasure. But I'd rather take the empty external gesture, and not get my emotions involved. I save them for my painting."

"I've been coming to that point of view myself of late. No, thanks, I don't think I could stand any more absinthe. Not at all, go right ahead. My brother Theo thinks highly of your work. May I see some of your studies?"

Gauguin jumped up.

"You may not. My studies are personal and private, like my letters. But I'll show you my paintings. You won't be able to see much in this light. Well, all right if you insist."

Gauguin went on his knees, pulled a stack of canvases from under the bed, and stood them one by one against the absinthe bottle on the table. Vincent had been prepared to see something unusual, but he could feel nothing but stunned amazement at Gauguin's work. He saw a confused mass of sun-drenched pictures; trees such as no botanist could discover; animals the existence of which had never been suspected by Cuvier; men whom Gauguin alone could have created; a sea that might have flowed out of a volcano; a sky which no God could inhabit. There were awkward and angular natives with the mystery of the infinite behind their naive, primitive eyes; dream canvases done in blazes of pink and violet and quivering red; sheer decora tive scenes in which wild flora and fauna burst with the heat and light of the sun.

"You're like Lautrec," murmured Vincent. "You hate. You hate with all your might."

Gauguin laughed. "What do you think of my painting, Vincent?"

"Frankly, I don't know. Give me time to think about it. Let me come back and see your work again."

"Come as often as you like. There is only one young man in Paris today whose painting is as good as mine; Georges Seurat. He, too, is a primitive. All the rest of the fools around Paris are civilized."

"Georges Seurat?" asked Vincent. "I don't believe I've heard of him."

"No, you wouldn't have. There's not a dealer in town will exhibit his canvases. And yet he's a great painter."

"I'd like to meet him, Gauguin."

"I'll take you up there later. What do you say we have dinner and go up to Bruant's? Have you any money? I've only about two francs. We'd better take this bottle with us. You go first. I'll hold the lamp until you're half way down, so you won't break your neck."

5

It was almost two in the morning before they got around to Seurat's house.

"Aren't you afraid we'll wake him up?" asked Vincent.

"Lord, no! He works all night. And most of the day. I don't think he ever sleeps. Here's the house. It belongs to Georges's mother. She once said to me, 'My boy, Georges, he wants to paint. Very well, then, let him paint. I have enough money for the two of us. Just so long as he is happy.' He's a model son to her. Doesn't drink, smoke, swear, go out nights, pursue the ladies, or spend money on anything but materials. He has only one vice; painting. I've heard he has a mistress and a son living close by, but he never mentions them."

"The house looks black," said Vincent. "How are we going to get in without waking the whole family?"

"Georges has the attic. We will probably see a light from the other side. We'll throw some gravel at his window. Here, you'd better let me. If you don't throw it just right it'll hit the third floor window and wake his mother."

Georges Seurat came down to open the door, put a finger to his lips, and led them up three flights of stairs. He closed the door of his attic behind him.

"Georges," said Gauguin, "I want you to meet Vincent Van Gogh, Theo's brother. He paints like a Dutchman, but aside from that he's a damn fine fellow."

Seurat's attic was of tremendous size, running almost the full length of the house. There were huge, unfinished canvases on the walls, with scaffolding before them. A high square table had been placed under the gas lamp; lying flat on this table was a wet canvas.

"I'm happy to know you, Monsieur Van Gogh. You'll pardon me for just a few moments, won't you? I have another little square of colour to fill in before my paint dries."

He climbed on top of a high stool and crouched over his canvas. The gas lamp burned with a steady, yellowish flare. About twenty tiny pots of colour formed a neat line across the table. Seurat touched the tip of the smallest painting brush Vincent had ever seen into one of the pots and began putting little points of colour on the canvas with mathematical precision. He worked quietly and without emotion. His manner was aloof and detached, like that of a mechanic. Dot dot dot dot. He held his brush straight up in his hand, barely touched it to the pot of paint, and then dot dot dot dot on the canvas, hundreds upon hundreds of minute dots.

Vincent watched him, agape. At length Seurat turned on his stool.

"There," he said, "I've got that space hollowed out."

"Would you mind showing it to Vincent, Georges?" asked Gauguin. "Where he comes from they paint cows and sheep. He didn't know there was a modern art until a week ago."

"If you'll sit on this stool, Monsieur Van Gogh."

Vincent climbed up on the stool and looked at the canvas spread out before him. It was like nothing he had ever seen before, either in art or life. The scene represented the Island of the Grande Jatte. Architectural human beings, made out of infinitely graduated points of colour, stood up like poles in a Gothic cathedral. The grass, the river, the boats, the trees, all were vague and abstract masses of dotted light. The canvas was done in all the brightest shades of the palette, lighter than those Manet or Degas or even Gauguin dared to use. The picture was a withdrawal into a region of almost abstract harmony. If it was alive, it was not with the life of nature. The air was filled with glittering luminosity, but there was not a breath to be found anywhere. It was a still life of vibrant life, from which movement had been forever banished.

Gauguin stood at Vincent's side and laughed at the expression on his face.

"It's all right, Vincent, Georges's canvases strike everyone that way the first time they look at them. Out with it! What do you think?"

Vincent turned apologetically to Seurat.

"You will forgive me, Monsieur, but so many strange things have happened to me in the last few days that I cannot find my balance. I trained myself in the Dutch tradition. I had no idea what the Impressionists stood for. And now I suddenly find everything I believed in, discarded."

"I understand," said Seurat quietly. "My method is revolutionizing the whole art of painting, so you could not be expected to take it all in with one glance. You see, Monsieur, up to the present, painting has been a matter of personal experience. It is my aim to make it an abstract science. We must learn to pigeonhole our sensations and arrive at a mathematical precision of mind. Every human sensation can be, and must be reduced to an abstract statement of colour, line, and tone. You see these little pots of colour on my table?"

"Yes, I've been noticing them."

"Each of those pots, Monsieur Van Gogh, contains a specific human emotion. With my formula they can be made in the factories and sold in the chemists' shops. No more haphazard mixing of colours on the palette; that method belongs to a past age. From now on the painter will go to the chemist's shop and simply pry the lids off his little pots of colour. This is an age of science, and I am going to make a science out of painting. Personality must disappear, and painting must become precise, like architecture. Do you follow me, Monsieur?"

"No," said Vincent, "I'm afraid I don't."

Gauguin nudged Vincent.

"See here, Georges, why do you insist upon calling this your method. Pissarro worked it out before you were born."

"It's a lie!"

A flush spread over Seurat's face. He sprang off his stool, walked quickly to the window, rapped on the sill with the ends of his fingers, then stormed back.

"Who said Pissarro worked it out before me? I tell you it's my method. I was the first to think of it. Pissarro learned his pointillism from me. I've been through the history of art since the Italian primitives, and I tell you, no one thought of it before me. How dare you . . . !"

He bit his lip savagely, walked to one of his scaffolds, and turned a hunched up back on Vincent and Gauguin.

Vincent was utterly amazed at the transition. The man leaning over his canvas on the table had had architectural features, perfect and cold. He had had dispassionate eyes, the impersonal manner of a scientist in a laboratory. His voice had been cool, almost pedagogic. The same veil of abstraction had been over his eyes that he threw over his paintings. But the man at the end of the attic was biting the thick, red underlip that stuck out from the full beard, and was angrily rumpling the mass of curly brown hair that had been so neat before.

"Oh, come, Georges," said Gauguin, winking at Vincent. "Everyone knows that it's your method. Without you there would have been no pointillism."

Mollified, Seurat came back to the table. The glow of anger died slowly out of his eyes.

"Monsieur Seurat," said Vincent, "how can we make painting an impersonal science when it is essentially the expression of the individual that counts?"

"Look! I will show you."

Seurat grabbed a box of crayons from the table and crouched down on the bare plank floor. The gaslight burned dimly above them. The night was completely still. Vincent knelt on one side of him, and Gauguin squatted on the other. Seurat was still excited, and spoke with animation.

"In my opinion," he said, "all effects in painting can be reduced to formulae. Suppose I want to draw a circus scene. Here's a bareback rider, here the trainer, here the gallery and spectators. I want to suggest gaiety. What are the three elements of painting? Line, tone and colour. Very well, to suggest gaiety, I bring all my lines above the horizontal, so. I make my luminous colours dominant, so, and my warm tone dominant, so. There! Doesn't that suggest the abstraction of gaiety?"

"Well," replied Vincent, "it may suggest the abstraction of gaiety, but it doesn't catch gaiety itself."

Seurat looked up from his crouching position. His face was in the shadow. Vincent observed what a beautiful man he was.

"I'm not after gaiety itself. I'm after the essence of gaiety. Are you acquainted with Plato, my friend?"

"Yes."

"Very well, what painters must learn to portray is not a thing, but the essence of a thing. When the artist paints a horse, it should not be one particular horse that you can recognize in the street. The camera can take photographs; we must go beyond that. What we must capture when we paint a horse, Monsieur Van Gogh, is Plato's *horsiness,* the external spirit of a horse. And when we paint a man, it should not be the *concierge,* with a wart on the end of his nose, but manness, the spirit and essence of all men. Do you follow me, my friend?"

"I follow," said Vincent, "but I don't agree."

"We'll come to the agreement later."

Seurat got off his haunches, slipped out of his smock, and wiped the circus picture off the floor with it.

"Now we go on to calmness," he continued. "I am doing a scene on the Island of the Grande Jatte. I make all my lines horizontal, so. For tone I use perfect equality between warm and cold, so; for colour, equality between dark and light, so. Do you see it?"

"Go on, Georges," said Gauguin, "and don't ask foolish questions."

"Now we come to sadness. We make all our lines run in a descending direction, like this. We make the cold tones dominant, so; and the dark colours dominant, so. There! The essence of sadness! A child could draw it. The mathematical formulae for apportioning space on a canvas will be set down in a little book. I have already worked them out. The painter need only read the book, go to the chemist's shop, buy the specified pots of colour, and obey the rules. He will be a scientific and perfect painter. He can work in sunlight or gaslight, be a monk or a libertine, seven years old or seventy, and all the paintings will achieve the same architectural, impersonal perfection."

Vincent blinked. Gauguin laughed.

"He thinks you're crazy, Georges."

Seurat mopped up the last drawing with his smock, then flung it into a dark corner.

"Do you, Monsieur Van Gogh?" he asked.

"No, no," protested Vincent, "I've been called crazy too many times myself to like the sound of the word. But I must admit this; your ideas are very queer!"

"He means yes, Georges," said Gauguin.

There was a sharp knock on the door.

"*Mon Dieu!*" groaned Gauguin, "we've awakened your mother again! She told me if I didn't stay away from here nights, she'd take the hairbrush to me!"

Seurat's mother came in. She had on a heavy robe and nightcap.

"Georges, you promised me you wouldn't work all night any more. Oh, it's you, is it, Paul? Why don't you pay your rent? Then you'd have a place to sleep at nights."

"If you'd only take me in here, Mother Seurat, I wouldn't have to pay any rent at all."

"No, thanks, one artist in the family is enough. Here, I've brought you coffee and brioches. If you must work, you have to eat. I suppose I'll have to go down and get your bottle of absinthe, Paul."

"You haven't drunk it all up, have you, Mother Seurat?"

"Paul, remember what I told you about the hairbrush."

Vincent came out of the shadows.

"Mother," said Seurat, "this is a new friend of mine, Vincent Van Gogh."

Mother Seurat took his hand.

"Any friend of my son's is welcome here, even if it is four in the morning. What will you have to drink, Monsieur?"

"If you don't mind, I'll have a glass of Gauguin's absinthe."

"You will not!" exclaimed Gauguin. "Mother Seurat keeps me on rations. Only one bottle a month. Take something else. Your heathen palate doesn't know the difference between absinthe and *chartreuse jaune*."

The three men and Mother Seurat sat chatting over their coffee and brioches until the dawning sun stuck a tiny triangle of yellow light on the north window.

"I may as well dress for the day," said Mother Seurat. "Come to dinner with Georges and me some evening, Monsieur Van Gogh. We shall be happy to have you."

At the front door Seurat said to Vincent, "I have explained my method rather crudely, I'm afraid. Come back often as you like, and we will work together. When you come to understand my method you will see that painting can never be the same again. Well, I must return to my canvas. I have another small space to hollow out before I go to sleep. Please present my compliments to your brother."

Vincent and Gauguin walked down the deserted stone canyons and climbed the hill to Montmartre. Paris had not yet awakened. The green shutters were

closed tight, the blinds were drawn in the shops, and the little country cart
were on their way home again after having dropped their vegetables, fruits
and flowers at the Halles.

"Let's go up to the top of the Butte and watch the sun awaken Paris,"
said Gauguin.

"I'd like that."

After gaining the Boulevard Clichy, they took the Rue Lepic which wound
by the Moulin de la Galette and made its tortuous way up the Montmartre
hill. The houses became fewer and fewer; open plains of flowers and tree
appeared. The Rue Lepic stopped short. The two men took a winding path
through the brush.

"Tell me frankly, Gauguin," said Vincent, "what do you think of Seurat?"

"Georges? I thought you'd ask that. He knows more about colour than
any man since Delacroix. He has intellectual theories about art. That's wrong
Painters should not think about what they are doing. Leave the theories to
the critics. Georges will make a definite contribution to colour, and hi
Gothic architecture will probably hasten the primitive reaction in art. But
he's *fou,* completely *fou,* as you saw for yourself."

It was a stiff climb, but when they reached the summit, all of Paris spread
out before them, the lake of black roofs and the frequent church spire
emerging from the mist of night. The Seine cut the city in half like a winding
stream of light. The houses flowed down the hill of Montmartre to the valley
of the Seine, then struggled up again on Montparnasse. The sun broke clear
and lit up the Bois de Vincennes beneath it. At the other end of the city the
green verdure of the Bois de Boulogne was still dark and somnolent. The
three landmarks of the city, the Opera in the centre, Notre Dame in the
east and the Arc de Triomphe in the west, stood up in the air like mounds
of variegated stone.

6

Peace descended upon the tiny apartment in the Rue Laval. Theo thanked
his lucky stars for the moment of calm. But it did not last long. Instead of
working his way slowly and minutely through his antiquated palette, Vin
cent began to imitate his friends. He forgot everything he had ever learned
about painting in his wild desire to be an Impressionist. His canvases looked
like atrocious copies of Seurats, Toulouse-Lautrecs, and Gauguins. He
thought he was making splendid progress.

"Listen, old boy," said Theo one night, "what's your name?"

"Vincent Van Gogh."

"You're quite certain it's not Georges Seurat, or Paul Gauguin?"

"What the devil are you driving at, Theo?"

"Do you really think you can become a Georges Seurat? Don't you realize
that there has only been one Lautrec since the beginning of time? And only

one Gauguin . . . thank God! It's silly for you to try to imitate them."

"I'm not imitating them. I'm learning from them."

"You're imitating. Show me any one of your new canvases, and I'll tell you who you were with the night before."

"But I'm improving all the time, Theo. Look how much lighter these pictures are."

"You're going downhill every day. You paint less like Vincent Van Gogh with each picture. There's no royal road for you, old boy. It's going to take years of hard labour. Are you such a weakling that you have to imitate others? Can't you just assimilate what they have to offer?"

"Theo, I tell you these canvases are good!"

"And I tell you they're awful!"

The battle was on.

Each night that he came home from the gallery, exhausted and nervously on edge, Theo found Vincent waiting for him impatiently with a new canvas. He would leap savagely upon Theo before his brother had a chance to take off his hat and coat.

"There! Now tell me this one isn't good! Tell me that my palette isn't improving! Look at that sunlight effect! Look at this . . ."

Theo had to choose between telling a lie and spending a pleasant evening with an affable brother, or telling the truth and being pursued violently about the house until dawn. Theo was frightfully tired. He could not afford to tell the truth. But he did.

"When were you at Durand-Ruel's last?" he demanded, wearily.

"What does that matter?"

"Answer my question."

"Well," said Vincent sheepishly, "yesterday afternoon."

"Do you know, Vincent, there are almost five thousand painters in Paris trying to imitate Edouard Manet? And most of them do it better than you."

The battleground was too small for either of them to survive.

Vincent tried a new trick. He threw all the Impressionists into one lone canvas.

"Delightful," murmured Theo that night. "We'll name this one, *Recapitulation*. We'll label everything on the canvas. That tree is a genuine Gauguin. The girl in the corner is undoubtedly a Toulouse-Lautrec. I would say that your sunlight on the stream is Sisley, the colour, Monet, the leaves, Pissarro, the air, Seurat, and the central figure, Manet."

Vincent fought bitterly. He worked hard all day, and when Theo came home at night, he was chastised like a little child. Theo had to sleep in the living room, so Vincent could not paint there at night. His quarrels with Theo left him too excited and wrought up to sleep. He spent the long hours haranguing his brother. Theo battled with him until he fell asleep from sheer exhaustion, the light still burning, and Vincent gesticulating excitedly. The only thing that kept Theo going was the thought that soon they would be in

the Rue Lepic, where he would have a bedroom to himself and a good
strong lock on the door.

When Vincent tired of arguing about his own canvases, he filled Theo's
nights with turbulent discussions of art, the art business, and the wretched
business of being an artist.

"Theo, I can't understand it," he complained. "Here you are the manager
of one of the most important art galleries in Paris, and you won't even
exhibit one of your own brother's canvases."

"Valadon won't let me."

"Have you tried?"

"A thousand times."

"All right, we'll admit that my paintings are not good enough. But what
about Seurat? And Gauguin? And Lautrec?"

"Every time they bring me new canvases, I beg Valadon to let me hang
them on the *entresol*."

"Are you master in that gallery, or is someone else?"

"Alas, I only work there."

"Then you ought to get out. It's degrading, simply degrading. Theo, I
wouldn't stand for it. I'd leave them."

"Let's talk it over at breakfast, Vincent. I've had a hard day and I want
to go to sleep."

"I don't want to wait until breakfast. I want to talk about it right now.
Theo, what good does it do to exhibit Manet and Degas? They're already
being accepted. They're beginning to sell. It's the younger men you have to
fight for now."

"Give me time! Perhaps in another three years . . ."

"No! We can't wait three years. We've got to have action now. Oh, Theo,
why don't you throw up your job and open an art gallery of your own? Just
think, no more Valadon, no more Bouguereau, no more Henner!"

"That would take money, Vincent. I haven't saved anything."

"We'd get the money somehow."

"The art business is slow to develop, you know."

"Let it be slow. We'll work night and day until we've established you."

"And what would we do in the meanwhile? We have to eat."

"Are you reproaching me for not earning my own living?"

"For goodness' sake, Vincent, go to bed. I'm exhausted."

"I won't go to bed. I want to know the truth. Is that the only reason you
don't leave Goupils? Because you have to support me? Come on, tell the
truth. I'm a millstone around your neck. I hold you down. I make you keep
your job. If it wasn't for me, you'd be free."

"If only I were a little bit bigger, or a little bit stronger, I'd hand you a
sound thrashing. As it is, I think I'll hire Gauguin to come in and do it. My
job is with Goupils, Vincent, now and always. Your job is painting, now and
always. Half of my work at Goupils belongs to you; half of your painting

belongs to me. Now get off my bed and let me go to sleep, or I'll call a *gendarme!*"

The following evening Theo handed Vincent an envelope and said, "If you're not doing anything tonight, we might go to this party."

"Who's giving it?"

"Henri Rousseau. Take a look at the invitation."

There were two verses of a simple poem and some hand-painted flowers on the card.

"Who is he?" asked Vincent.

"We call him *le Douanier*. He was a customs collector in the provinces until he was forty. Used to paint on Sundays, just as Gauguin did. He came to Paris a few years ago and settled in the labourers' section around the Bastille. He's never had a day of education or instruction in his life, yet he paints, writes poetry, composes music, gives lessons on the violin to the workers' children, plays on the piano, and teaches drawing to a couple of old men."

"What sort of thing does he paint?"

"Fantastic animals, largely, peering out of even more fantastic jungles. The closest he ever got to a jungle is the Jardin d'Acclimation in the Bois de Boulogne. He's a peasant and a natural primitive, even if Paul Gauguin does laugh at him."

"What do you think of his work, Theo?"

"Well, I don't know. Everyone calls him an imbecile and a madman."

"Is he?"

"He's something of a child, a primitive child. We'll go to the party tonight and you'll have a chance to judge for yourself. He has all his canvases up on the walls."

"He must have money if he can give parties."

"He's probably the poorest painter in Paris today. He even has to rent the violin he gives lessons on, because he can't afford to buy it. But he has a purpose in giving these parties. You'll discover it for yourself."

The house in which Rousseau lived was occupied by the families of manual labourers. Rousseau had a room on the fourth floor. The street was full of squalling children; the combined stench of cooking, washing, and latrines in the hallway was thick enough to strangle one.

Henri Rousseau answered Theo's knock. He was a short, thickset man, built a good deal on Vincent's lines. His fingers were short and stumpy, his head almost square. He had a stubby nose and chin, and wide, innocent eyes.

"You honour me by coming, Monsieur Van Gogh," he said in a soft, affable tone.

Theo introduced Vincent. Rousseau offered them chairs. The room was colourful, almost gay. Rousseau had put up his peasant curtains of red and white checked cloth at the windows. The walls were filled solid with pictures of wild animals and jungles and incredible landscapes.

Four young boys were standing by the battered old piano in the corner, holding violins in their hands nervously. On the mantel over the fireplace were the homely little cookies that Rousseau had baked and sprinkled with caraway seeds. A number of benches and chairs were scattered about the room.

"You are the first to arrive, Monsieur Van Gogh," said Rousseau. "The critic, Guillaume Pille, is doing me the honour of bringing a party."

A noise came up from the street; the cries of children's voices and the rumble of carriage wheels over the cobblestones. Rousseau flung open his door. Pretty feminine voices floated up from the hall.

"Keep going. Keep going," boomed a voice. "One hand on the banister and the other on your nose!"

A shout of laughter followed this witticism. Rousseau, who had heard it clearly, turned to Vincent and smiled. Vincent thought he had never seen such clear, innocent eyes in a man, eyes so free from malice and resentment.

A party of some ten or twelve people burst into the room. The men were dressed in evening clothes, the women in sumptuous gowns, dainty slippers, and long white gloves. They brought into the room the fragrance of costly perfume, of delicate powders, of silk and old lace.

"Well, Henri," cried Guillaume Pille in his deep, pompous voice, "you see we have come. But we cannot stay long. We are going to a ball at the Princess de Broglie's. Meanwhile you must entertain my guests."

"Oh, I want to meet him," gushed a slim, auburn-haired girl in an Empire gown cut low across the breasts. "Just think, this is the great painter of whom all Paris is talking. Will you kiss my hand, Monsieur Rousseau?"

"Take care, Blanche," someone said. "You know . . . these artists . . ."

Rousseau smiled and kissed her hand. Vincent shrank into a corner. Pille and Theo chatted for a moment. The rest of the party walked about the room in pairs, commenting on the different canvases with gales of laughter, fingering Rousseau's curtains, his ornaments, ransacking every corner of the room for a new joke.

"If you will sit down, ladies and gentlemen," said Rousseau, "my orchestra will play one of my own compositions. I have dedicated it to Monsieur Pille. It is called *Chanson Raval*."

"Come, come everybody!" shouted Pille. "Rousseau is going to entertain us. Jeanie! Blanche! Jacques! Come sit down. This will be precious."

The four trembling boys stood before a lone music rack and tuned their violins. Rousseau sat at his piano and closed his eyes. After a moment he said, "Ready," and began to play. The composition was a simple pastoral. Vincent tried to listen, but the snickers of the crowd drowned out the music. At the end they all applauded vociferously. Blanche went to the piano, put her hands on Rousseau's shoulders and said, "That was beautiful, Monsieur, beautiful. I have never been so deeply stirred."

"You flatter me, Madame."

Blanche screamed with laughter.

"Guillaume, did you hear that? He thinks I'm flattering him!"

"I will play you another composition now," said Rousseau.

"Sing us one of your poems to it, Henri. You know you have so many poems."

Rousseau grinned childishly.

"Very well, Monsieur Pille, I will chant a poem to it, if you wish."

He went to a table, took out a sheaf of poems, thumbed through them and selected one. He sat down at the piano and began to play. Vincent thought the music good. The few lines he could catch of the poem he also thought charming. But the effect of the two together was quite ludicrous. The crowd howled. They slapped Pille on the back.

"Oh, Guillaume, you are a dog. What a sly one you are."

Finished with his music, Rousseau went out to the kitchen and returned with a number of thick, rough cups of coffee, which he passed about to the guests. They picked the caraway seeds off the cookies and threw them into each other's coffee. Vincent smoked his pipe in the corner.

"Come, Henri, show us your latest paintings. That is what we have come for. We must see them here, in your atelier, before they are bought for the Louvre."

"I have some lovely new ones," said Rousseau. "I will take them off the wall for you."

The crowd gathered about the table, trying to outdo each other in the extravagance of their compliments.

"This is divine, simply divine," breathed Blanche. "I must have it for my boudoir. I just can't live another day without it! *Cher Maître,* how much is this immortal masterpiece?"

"Twenty-five francs."

"Twenty-five francs! Only imagine, twenty-five francs for a great work of art! Will you dedicate it to me?"

"I will be honoured."

"I promised Françoise I would bring her one," said Pille. "Henri, this is for my fiancée. It must be the very finest thing you have ever done."

"I know just the one for you, Monsieur Pille."

He took down a painting of some sort of weird animal peering through a fairy tale jungle. Everyone howled at Pille.

"What is it?"

"It's a lion."

"It is not, it's a tiger."

"I tell you, it's my washerwoman; I recognize her."

"This one is a little larger, Monsieur," said Rousseau sweetly. "It will cost you thirty francs."

"It's worth it, Henri, it's worth it. Some day my grandchildren will sell this exquisite canvas for thirty thousand francs!"

"I want one. I want one," several of the others exclaimed. "I've got to take one to my friends. This is the best show of the season."

"Come along, everyone," shouted Pille. "We'll be late for the ball. And bring your paintings. We'll cause a riot at the Princess de Broglie's with these things. Au revoir, Henri. We had a perfectly marvellous time. Give another party soon."

"Good-bye, *cher Maître*," said Blanche, flicking her perfumed kerchief under his nose. "I will never forget you. You will live in my memory forever."

"Leave him alone, Blanche," cried one of the men. "The poor fellow won't be able to sleep all night."

They trouped down the stairs noisily, shouting their jokes at each other, leaving a cloud of expensive perfume behind them to mingle with the stench of the building.

Theo and Vincent walked to the door. Rousseau was standing at the table, looking down at the pile of coins.

"Do you mind going home alone, Theo?" Vincent asked quietly. "I want to stay and get acquainted."

Theo left. Rousseau did not notice Vincent close the door and then lean against it. He went on counting the money on the table.

"Eighty francs, ninety francs, one hundred, a hundred and five."

He looked up and saw Vincent watching him. The simple, childlike expression returned to his eyes. He pushed the money aside and stood there, grinning foolishly.

"Take off the mask, Rousseau," said Vincent. "I, too, am a peasant and a painter."

Rousseau left the table, crossed to Vincent and gripped his hand warmly.

"Your brother has shown me your pictures of the Dutch peasants. They are good. They are better than Millet's. I have looked at them many, many times. I admire you, Monsieur."

"And I have looked at your pictures, Rousseau, while those . . . were making fools of themselves. I admire you, too."

"Thank you. Will you sit down? Will you fill your pipe with my tobacco? It is a hundred and five francs, Monsieur. I will be able to buy tobacco, and food, and canvas to paint on."

They sat on opposite sides of the table and smoked in friendly, ruminative silence.

"I suppose you know they call you a crazy man, Rousseau?"

"Yes, I know. And I have heard that in The Hague they think you are crazy, too."

"Yes, that's so."

"Let them think what they like. Some day my paintings will hang in the Luxembourg."

"And mine," said Vincent, "will hang in the Louvre."

They read the thought in each other's eyes and broke into spontaneous, whole-hearted laughter.

"They're right, Henri," said Vincent. "We are crazy!"

"Shall we go have a drink on it?" asked Rousseau.

7

Gauguin knocked on the door of the apartment the following Wednesday toward dinner time.

"Your brother asked me to take you over to the Café Batignolles this evening. He has to work late at the gallery. These are interesting canvases. May I look?"

"Of course. I did some of them in the Brabant, others in The Hague."

Gauguin gazed at the pictures for a long while. Several times he raised his hand, opened his mouth, and made as if to speak. He did not seem able to formulate his thoughts.

"Forgive me for asking, Vincent," he said, finally, "but are you by any chance an epileptic?"

Vincent was just slipping into a sheepskin coat which to Theo's dismay, he had found in a second-hand store and insisted upon wearing. He turned about and stared at Gauguin.

"Am I a what?" he demanded.

"An epileptic. One of those fellows who has nervous fits?"

"Not that I know of, Gauguin. Why do you ask?"

"Well . . . these pictures of yours . . . they look as though they were going to burst right out of the canvas. When I look at your work . . . and this isn't the first time it's happened to me . . . I begin feeling a nervous excitement that I can hardly contain. I feel that if the picture doesn't explode, I most certainly will! Do you know where your paintings affect me most?"

"No. Where?"

"In the bowels. My whole insides begin to tremble. I get feeling so excited and perturbed, I can hardly restrain myself."

"Perhaps I could sell them as laxatives. You know, hang one in the lavatory and look at it at a certain hour every day?"

"Seriously speaking, Vincent, I don't think I could live with your pictures. They'd drive me mad inside of a week."

"Shall we go?"

They walked up the Rue Montmartre to the Boulevard Clichy.

"Have you had dinner?" asked Gauguin.

"No. Have you?"

"No. Shall we go up to Bataille's?"

"Good idea. Got any money?"

"Not a centime. How about you?"

"I'm flat, as usual. I was waiting for Theo to take me out."

"Zut! I guess we don't eat."

"Let's go up and see what the *plat du jour* is, anyway."

They took the Rue Lepic up the hill, then turned right on the Rue des

Abbesses. Madame Bataille had an ink-scrawled menu tacked to one of her imitation potted trees in front.

"Uummm," said Vincent, "*côté de veau petits pois*. My favourite dish."

"I hate veal," said Gauguin. "I'm glad we don't have to eat."

"*Quelle blague!*"

They wandered down the street and into the little triangular park at the foot of the Butte.

"Hello," said Gauguin, "there's Paul Cezanne, asleep on a bench. Why that idiot uses his shoes for a pillow is beyond me. Let's wake him up."

He pulled the belt out of his trousers, doubled it up, and gave the sleeping man a whack across the stockinged feet. Cezanne sprang off the bench with a yowl of pain.

"Gauguin, you infernal sadist! Is that your idea of a joke? I shall be forced to crack your skull one of these days."

"Serves you right for leaving your feet exposed. Why do you put those filthy Provence boots under your head? I should think they'd be worse than no pillow at all."

Cezanne rubbed the bottom of each foot in turn, then slipped on his boots, grumbling.

"I don't use them for a pillow. I put them under my head so no one will steal them while I'm asleep."

Gauguin turned to Vincent. "You'd think he was a starving artist the way he talks. His father owns a bank, and half of Aix-en-Provence. Paul, this is Vincent Van Gogh, Theo's brother."

Cezanne and Vincent shook hands.

"It's too bad we didn't find you a half hour ago, Cezanne," said Gauguin. "You could have joined us for dinner. Bataille has the best *côté de veau aux petits pois* I've ever tasted."

"It was really good, was it?" asked Cezanne.

"Good? It was delicious! Wasn't it, Vincent?"

"Certainly was."

"Then I think I'll go have some. Come and keep me company, will you?"

"I don't know whether I could eat another portion. Could you, Vincent?"

"I hardly think so. Still, if Monsieur Cezanne insists . . ."

"Be a good fellow, Gauguin. You know I hate to eat alone. Take something else if you've had enough veal."

"Well, just to oblige you. Come along, Vincent."

They went back up the Rue des Abbesses to Bataille's.

"Good evening, gentlemen," said the waiter. "Have you chosen?"

"Yes," replied Gauguin, "bring us three *plats du jour*."

"*Bien*. And what wine?"

"You choose the wine, Cezanne. You know more about those things than I do."

"Let's see, there's Saint-Estephe, Bordeaux, Sauterne, Beaune . . ."

"Have you ever tried their Pommard?" interrupted Gauguin, guilelessly. "I often think it's the best wine they have."

"Bring us a bottle of Pommard," said Cezanne to the waiter.

Gauguin bolted his veal and green peas in no time, then turned to Cezanne while the latter was still in the middle of his dinner.

"By the way, Paul," he remarked, "I hear that Zola's 'L'Oeuvre' is selling by the thousands."

Cezanne shot him a black, bitter look, and shoved his dinner away with distaste. He turned to Vincent.

"Have you read that book, Monsieur?"

"Not yet. I just finished 'Germinal.' "

" 'L'Oeuvre' is a bad book," said Cezanne, "and a false one. Besides, it is the worst piece of treachery that has ever been committed in the name of friendship. The book is about a painter, Monsieur Van Gogh. About me! Emile Zola is my oldest friend. We were raised together in Aix. We went to school together. I came to Paris only because he was here. We were closer than brothers, Emile and I. All during our youth we planned how, side by side, we would become great artists. And now he does this to me."

"What has he done to you?" asked Vincent.

"Ridiculed me. Mocked me. Made me a laughing stock to all Paris. Day after day I told him about my theories of light, my theories of representing solids under surface appearances, my ideas of a revolutionary palette. He listened to me, he encouraged me, he drew me out. And all the time he was only gathering material for his book, to show what a fool I was."

He drained his wine glass, turned back to Vincent and continued, his small, sour eyes smouldering with passionate hatred.

"Zola has combined three of us in that book, Monsieur Van Gogh; myself, Bazille, and a poor, wretched lad who used to sweep out Manet's studio. The boy had artistic ambitions, but finally hanged himself in despair. Zola paints me as a visionary, another misguided wretch who thinks he is revolutionizing art, but who doesn't paint in the conventional manner simply because he hasn't enough talent to paint at all. He makes me hang myself from the scaffolding of my masterpiece, because in the end I realize that what I mistook for genius was only insane daubing. Up against me he puts another artist from Aix, a sentimental sculptor who turns out the most hackneyed, academic trash, and makes him a great artist."

"That's really amusing," said Gauguin, "when you remember that Zola was the first to champion Edouard Manet's revolution in painting. Emile has done more for Impressionist painting than any man alive."

"Yes, he worshipped Manet because Edouard overthrew the academicians. But when I try to go beyond the Impressionists, he calls me a fool and an idiot. As for Emile, he is a mediocre intelligence and a detestable friend. I had to stop going to his house long ago. He lives like a damned bourgeois. Rich rugs on the floor, vases on the mantelpiece, servants, a desk of carved and sculptured wood for him to write his masterpieces. Phew! He's more middle class than Manet ever dared to be. They were brother bourgeois under the skin, those two; that's why they got along so well together. Just because I come from the same town as Emile, and he knew me as a child, he thinks I can't possibly do any important work."

"I heard that he wrote a *brochure* for your pictures at the Salon des Refusées a few years back. What happened to it?"

"Emile tore it up, Gauguin, just before it was to have gone to the printers."

"But why?" asked Vincent.

"He was afraid the critics would think he was sponsoring me only because I was an old friend. If he had published that *brochure,* I would have been established. Instead he published 'L'Oeuvre.' So much for friendship. My pictures in the Salon des Refusées are laughed at by ninety-nine people out of a hundred. Durand-Ruel exhibits Degas, Monet, and my friend Guillaumin, but they refuse to give me two inches of space. Even your brother, Monsieur Van Gogh, is afraid to put me on his *entresol*. The only dealer in Paris who will put my pictures in his window is Père Tanguy, and he, poor soul, couldn't sell a crust of bread to a starving millionaire."

"Is there any Pommard left in that bottle, Cezanne?" asked Gauguin. "Thanks. What I have against Zola is that he makes his washerwomen talk like real washerwomen, and when he leaves them he forgets to change his style."

"Well, I've had enough of Paris. I'm going back to Aix and spend the rest of my life there. There's a hill rising up from the valley that overlooks the whole country-side. There's clear, bright sunlight in Provence, and colour. What colour! I know a plot of ground near the top of the hill that's for sale. It's covered with pine trees. I'll build a studio there, and plant an apple orchard. And I'll build a big stone wall around my ground. I'll mix broken bottles into the cement at the top of the wall, to keep the world out. And I'll never leave Provence again, never, never!"

"A hermit, eh?" murmured Gauguin into his glass of Pommard.

"Yes, a hermit."

"The hermit of Aix. What a charming title. We'd better be getting on to the Café Batignolles. Everyone will be there by now."

8

Nearly everyone was there. Lautrec had a pile of saucers in front of him high enough to rest his chin on. Georges Seurat was chatting quietly with Anquetin, a lean, lanky painter who was trying to combine the method of the Impressionists with that of the Japanese prints. Henri Rousseau was taking cookies out of his pocket and dipping them into a *café au lait,* while Theo carried on an animated discussion with two of the more modern Parisian critics.

Batignolles had formerly been a suburb at the entrance of the Boulevard

Clichy, and it was here that Edouard Manet had gathered the kindred spirits of Paris about him. Before Manet's death, the École des Batignolles was in the habit of meeting twice a week at the café. Legros, Fantin-Latour, Courbet, Renoir, all had met there and worked out their theories of art, but now the École had been taken over by the younger men.

Cezanne saw Emile Zola. He walked to a far table, ordered a coffee, and sat aloof from the crowd. Gauguin introduced Vincent to Zola and then dropped into a chair alongside of Toulouse-Lautrec. Zola and Vincent were left alone at their table.

"I saw you come in with Paul Cezanne, Monsieur Van Gogh. No doubt he said something to you about me?"

"Yes."

"What was it?"

"I'm afraid your book has wounded him very deeply."

Zola sighed and pushed the table out from the leather cushioned bench to give his huge paunch more room.

"Have you ever heard of the Schweininger cure?" he asked. "They say if a man doesn't drink anything with his meals, he can lose thirty pounds in three months."

"I haven't heard of it."

"It hurt me very deeply to write that book about Paul Cezanne, but every word of it is true. You are a painter. Would you falsify a portrait of a friend simply because it made him unhappy? Of course you wouldn't. Paul is a splendid chap. For years he was my dearest friend. But his work is simply ludicrous. You know we are very tolerant at my house, Monsieur, but when my friends come, I must lock Paul's canvases in a cupboard so he will not be laughed at."

"But surely his work can't be as bad as all that."

"Worse, my dear Van Gogh, worse. You haven't seen any of it? That explains your incredulity. He draws like a child of five. I give you my word, I think he has gone completely crazy."

"Gauguin respects him."

"It breaks my heart," continued Zola, "to see Cezanne waste his life in this fantastic fashion. He should go back to Aix and take over his father's position in the bank. He could make something of his life that way. As things are now . . . some day he will hang himself . . . just as I predicted in 'L'Oeuvre.' Have you read that book, Monsieur?"

"Not yet. I just finished 'Germinal.' "

"So? And what do you think of it?"

"I think it the finest thing since Balzac."

"Yes, it is my masterpiece. It appeared en feuilleton in 'Gil Blas' last year. I got a good piece of money for that. And now the book has sold over sixty thousand copies. My income has never been as large as it is today. I'm going to add a new wing onto my house at Medan. The book has already caused four strikes and revolts in the mining regions of France. 'Germinal' will cause a gigantic revolution, and when it does, good-bye to capitalism! What sort of thing do you paint, Monsieur . . . What did Gauguin say your first name was?"

"Vincent. Vincent Van Gogh. Theo Van Gogh is my brother."

Zola laid down the pencil with which he had been scribbling on the stone topped table, and stared at Vincent.

"That's curious," he said.

"What is?"

"Your name. I've heard it somewhere before."

"Perhaps Theo mentioned it to you."

"He did, but that wasn't it. Wait a minute! It was . . . it was . . . 'Germinal!' Have you ever been in the coal mining regions?"

"Yes. I lived in the Belgian Borinage for two years."

"The Borinage! Petit Wasmes! Marcasse!"

Zola's large eyes almost popped out of his rotund, bearded face.

"So you're the second coming of Christ!"

Vincent flushed. "What do you mean by that?"

"I spent five weeks in the Borinage, gathering material for 'Germinal.' The *gueules noires* speak of a Christ-man who worked among them as an evangelist."

"Lower your voice, I beg you!"

Zola folded his hands over his fat paunch and pushed it inward.

"Don't be ashamed, Vincent," he said. "What you tried to accomplish there was worth while. You simply chose the wrong medium. Religion will never get people anywhere. Only the base in spirit will accept misery in this world for the promise of bliss in the next."

"I found that out too late."

"You spent two years in the Borinage, Vincent. You gave away your food, your money, your clothes. You worked yourself to the point of death. And what did you get for it? Nothing. They called you a crazy man and expelled you from the Church. When you left, conditions were no better than when you came."

"They were worse."

"But my medium will do it. The written word will cause the revolution. Every literate miner in Belgium and France has read my book. There is not a café, not a miserable shack in the whole region, that hasn't a well-thumbed copy of 'Germinal.' Those who can't read, have it read to them over and over again. Four strikes already. And dozens more coming. The whole country is rising. 'Germinal' will create a new society, where your religion couldn't. And what do I get as my reward?"

"What?"

"Francs. Thousands upon thousands of them. Will you join me in a drink?"

The discussion around the Lautrec table became animated. Everyone turned his attention that way.

"How is 'ma methode,' Seurat?" asked Lautrec, cracking his knuckles one by one.

Seurat ignored the gibe. His exquisitely perfect features and calm, mask-like expression suggested, not the face of one man, but the essence of masculine beauty.

"There is a new book on colour refraction by an American, Ogden Rood. I think it an advance on Helmholtz and Chevral, though not quite so stimulating as De Superville's work. You could all read it with profit."

"I don't read books about painting," said Lautrec. "I leave that to the layman."

Seurat unbuttoned the black and white checked coat and straightened out the large blue tie sprinkled with polka dots.

"You yourself are a layman," he said, "so long as you guess at the colours you use."

"I don't guess. I know by instinct."

"Science is a method, Georges," put in Gauguin. "We have become scientific in our application of colour by years of hard work and experimentation."

"That's not enough, my friend. The trend of our age is toward objective production. The days of inspiration, of trial and error, are gone forever."

"I can't read those books," said Rousseau. "They give me a headache. Then I have to go paint all day to get rid of it."

Everyone laughed. Anquetin turned to Zola and said, "Did you see the attack on 'Germinal' in this evening's paper?"

"No. What did it say?"

"The critic called you the most immoral writer of the nineteenth century."

"Their old cry. Can't they find anything else to say against me?"

"They're right, Zola," said Lautrec. "I find your books carnal and obscene."

"You certainly ought to recognize obscenity when you see it!"

"Had you that time, Lautrec!"

"Garçon," called Zola. "A round of drinks."

"We're in for it now," murmured Cezanne to Anquetin. "When Emile buys the drinks, it means you have to listen to an hour's lecture."

The waiter served the drinks. The painters lit their pipes and gathered into a close, intimate circle. The gas lamps illuminated the room in spirals of light. The hum of conversation from the other tables was low and chordal.

"They call my books immoral," said Zola, "for the same reason that they attribute immorality to your paintings, Henri. The public cannot understand that there is no room for moral judgements in art. Art is amoral; so is life. For me there are no obscene pictures or books; there are only poorly conceived and poorly executed ones. A whore by Toulouse-Lautrec is moral because he brings out the beauty that lies beneath her external appearance; a pure country girl by Bouguereau is immoral because she is sentimentalized and so cloyingly sweet that just to look at her is enough to make you vomit!"

"Yes, that's so," nodded Theo.

Vincent saw that the painters respected Zola, not because he was successful—they despised the ordinary connotations of success—but because he worked in a medium which seemed mysterious and difficult to them. They listened closely to his words.

"The ordinary human brain thinks in terms of duality; light and shade, sweet and sour, good and evil. That duality does not exist in nature. There is neither good nor evil in the world, but only being and doing. When we describe an action, we describe life; when we call that action names—like depravity or obscenity—we go into the realm of subjective prejudice."

"But, Emile," said Theo. "What would the mass of people do without its standard of morality?"

"Morality is like religion," contributed Toulouse-Lautrec; "a soporific to close people's eyes to the tawdriness of their life."

"Your amorality is nothing but anarchism, Zola," said Seurat, "and nihilistic anarchism, at that. It's been tried before, and it doesn't work."

"Of course we have to have certain codes," agreed Zola. "The public weal demands sacrifices from the individual. I don't object to morality, but only to the pudency that spits upon *Olympia*, and wants Maupassant suppressed. I tell you, morality in France today is entirely confined to the erogenous zone. Let people sleep with whom they like; I know a higher morality than that."

"That reminds me of a dinner I gave a few years ago," said Gauguin. "One of the men I invited said, 'You understand, my friend, that I can't take my wife to these dinners of yours when your mistress is present.' 'Very well,' I replied, 'I'll send her out for the evening.' When the dinner was over and they all went home, our honest Madame, who had yawned the whole evening, stopped yawning and said to her husband, 'Let's have some nice piggy talk before we do it.' And her husband said, 'Let's not do anything but talk. I have eaten too much this evening.'"

"That tells the whole story!" shouted Zola, above the laughter.

"Put aside the ethics for a moment and get back to immorality in art," said Vincent. "No one ever calls my pictures obscene, but I am invariably accused of an even great immorality, ugliness."

"You hit it that time, Vincent," said Toulouse-Lautrec.

"Yes, that's the essence of the new immorality for the public," agreed Gauguin. "Did you see what the *Mercure de France* called us this month? The cult of ugliness."

"The same criticism is levied against me," said Zola. "A countess said to me the other day, 'My dear Monsieur Zola, why does a man of your extraordinary talent go about turning up stones just to see what sort of filthy insects are crawling underneath them?'"

Lautrec took an old newspaper clipping out of his pocket.

"Listen to what the critic said about my canvases at the last Salon des Independents. 'Toulouse-Lautrec may be reproached for taking delight in representing trivial gaiety, coarse amusements and "low subjects." He appears to be insensible to beauty of feature, elegance of form and grace of movement. It is true that he paints with a loving brush beings ill-formed, stumpy and repulsive in their ugliness, but of what good is such perversion?' "

"Shades of Frans Hals," murmured Vincent.

"Well, he's right," said Seurat. "If you men are not perverted, you're at least misguided. Art has to do with abstract things, like colour, design, and tone. It should not be used to improve social conditions or search for ugliness. Painting should be like music, divorced from the everyday world."

"Victor Hugo died last year," said Zola, "and with him a whole civilization died. A civilization of pretty gestures, romance, artful lies and subtle evasions. My books stand for the new civilization; the unmoral civilization of the twentieth century. So do your paintings. Bouguereau is still dragging his carcass around Paris, but he took ill the day that Edouard Manet exhibited *Picnic on the Grass,* and he died the day Manet finished *Olympia.* Well, Manet is gone now, and so is Daumier, but we still have Degas, Lautrec and Gauguin to carry on their work."

"Put the name of Vincent Van Gogh on that list," said Toulouse-Lautrec.

"Put it at the head of the list," said Rousseau.

"Very well, Vincent," said Zola with a smile, "you have been nominated for the cult of ugliness. Do you accept the nomination?"

"Alas," said Vincent, "I'm afraid I was born into it."

"Let's formulate our manifesto, gentlemen," said Zola. "First, we think all truth beautiful, no matter how hideous its face may seem. We accept all of nature, without any repudiation. We believe there is more beauty in a harsh truth than in a pretty lie, more poetry in earthiness than in all the salons of Paris. We think pain good, because it is the most profound of all human feelings. We think sex beautiful, even when portrayed by a harlot and a pimp. We put character above ugliness, pain above prettiness, and hard, crude reality above all the wealth in France. We accept life in its entirety, without making moral judgements. We think the prostitute as good as the countess, the *concierge* as good as the general, the peasant as good as the cabinet minister, for they all fit into the pattern of nature, and are woven into the design of life!"

"Glasses up, gentlemen," cried Toulouse-Lautrec. "We drink to amorality and the cult of ugliness. May it beautify and re-create the world."

"Tosh!" said Cezanne.

"And 'Tosh!' again," said Georges Seurat.

9

At the beginning of June, Theo and Vincent moved to their new apartment at 54, Rue Lepic, Montmartre. The house was just a short way from the Rue Laval; they had only to go up the Rue Montmartre a few blocks to the Boulevard Clichy, and then take the winding Rue Lepic up past the Moulin de la Galette, almost into the countrified part of the Butte.

Their apartment was on the third floor. It had three rooms, a cabinet and a kitchen. The living room was comfortable with Theo's beautiful old cabinet, Louis Philippes, and a big stove to protect them against the Paris cold. Theo had a talent for home-making. He loved to have everything just right. His bedroom was next to the living room. Vincent slept in the cabinet, behind which was his studio, an ordinary sized room with one window.

"You won't have to work at Corman's any longer, Vincent," said Theo. They were arranging and rearranging the furniture in the living room.

"No, thank heavens. Still, I needed to do a few female nudes."

Theo placed the sofa across the room from the cabinet and surveyed the room critically. "You haven't done a complete canvas in colour for some time, have you?" he asked.

"No."

"Why not?"

"What would be the use? Until I can mix the right colours . . . where do you want this armchair, Theo? Under the lamp or next to the window? But now that I've got a studio of my own . . ."

The following morning Vincent got up with the sun, arranged the easel in his new studio, put a piece of canvas on a frame, laid out the shining new palette that Theo had bought him, and softened up his brushes. When it was time for Theo to rise, he put on the coffee and went down to the *pâtisserie* for crisp, fresh croissants.

Theo could feel Vincent's turbulent excitement across the breakfast table.

"Well, Vincent," he said, "you've been to school for three months. Oh, I don't mean Corman's, I mean the school of Paris! You've seen the most important painting that has been done in Europe in three hundred years. And now you're ready to . . ."

Vincent pushed aside his half-eaten breakfast and jumped to his feet. "I think I'll begin . . ."

"Sit down. Finish your breakfast. You have plenty of time. There's nothing for you to worry about. I'll buy your paints and canvas wholesale, so you'll always have plenty on hand. You'd better have your teeth operated on, too; I want to get you into perfect health. But for goodness' sake, go about your work slowly and carefully!"

"Don't talk nonsense, Theo. Have I ever gone about anything slowly and carefully?"

When Theo came home that night he found that Vincent had lashed himself into a fury. He had been working progressively at his craft for six years under the most heartbreaking conditions; now that everything was made easy for him, he was faced with a humiliating impotence.

It was ten o'clock before Theo could get him quieted down. When they went out to dinner, some of Vincent's confidence had returned. Theo looked pale and worn.

The weeks that followed were torture for both of them. When Theo returned from the gallery he would find Vincent in any one of his hundred different kinds of tempests. The strong lock on his door did him absolutely no good. Vincent sat on his bed until the early hours of the morning, arguing with him. When Theo fell asleep, Vincent shook him by the shoulder and woke him up.

"Stop pacing the floor and sit still for a moment," begged Theo one night. "And stop drinking that damned absinthe. That's not how Gauguin developed his palette. Now listen to me, you infernal idiot, you must give yourself at least a year before you even begin to look at your work with a critical eye. What good is it going to do to make yourself sick? You're getting thin and nervous. You know you can't do your best work in that condition."

The hotness of a Parisian summer came on. The sun burned up the streets. Paris sat in front of its favourite café until one and two in the morning, sipping cold drinks. The flowers on the Butte Montmartre burst into a riot of colour. The Seine wound its glistening way through the city, through banks of trees and cool patches of green grass.

Every morning Vincent strapped his easel to his back and went looking for a picture. He had never known such hot, constant sun in Holland, nor had he ever seen such deep, elemental colour. Nearly every evening he returned from his painting in time to join the heated discussions on the *entresol* of Goupils.

One day Gauguin came in to help him mix some pigments.

"From whom do you buy these colours?" he asked.

"Theo gets them wholesale."

"You should patronize Père Tanguy. His prices are the lowest in Paris, and he trusts a man when he's broke."

"Who is this Père Tanguy? I've heard you mention him before."

"Haven't you met him yet? Good Lord, you mustn't hesitate another moment. You and Père are the only two men I've ever met whose communism really comes from the heart. Put on that beautiful rabbit-fur bonnet of yours. We're going down to the Rue Clauzel."

As they wound down the Rue Lepic, Gauguin told Père Tanguy's story. "He used to be a plasterer before he came to Paris. He worked as a colour-grinder in the house of Edouard, then took the job of *concierge* somewhere on the Butte. His wife looked after the house and Père began peddling colours through the quarter. He met Pissarro, Monet, and Cezanne, and since they liked him, we all started buying our colours from him. He joined the communists during the last uprising; one day while he was dreaming on sentry duty, a band from Versailles descended on his post. The poor fellow just couldn't fire on another human being. He threw away his musket. He was sentenced to serve two years in the galleys at Brest for this treachery, but we got him out.

"He saved a few francs and opened this little shop in the Rue Clauzel. Lautrec painted the front of it blue for him. He was the first man in Paris to exhibit a Cezanne canvas. Since then we've all had our stuff there. Not that he ever sells a canvas. Ah, no! You see, Père is a great lover of art, but since he is poor, he can't afford to buy pictures. So he exhibits them in his little shop, where he can live among them all day."

"You mean he wouldn't sell a painting even if he got a good offer?"

"Decidedly not. He takes only pictures that he loves, and once he gets attached to a canvas, you can't get it out of the shop. I was there one day when a well-dressed man came in, admired a Cezanne and asked how much it was. Any other dealer in Paris would have been delighted to sell it for sixty francs. Père Tanguy looked at the canvas for a long time and then said, 'Ah, yes, this one. It is a particularly good Cezanne. I cannot let it go under six hundred francs.' When the man ran out, Père took the painting off the wall and held it before him with tears in his eyes."

"Then what good does it do to have him exhibit your work?"

"Well, Père Tanguy is a strange fellow. All he knows about art is how to grind colours. And yet he has an infallible sense of the authentic. If he asks for one of your canvases, give it to him. It will be your formal initiation into Parisian art. Here's the Rue Clauzel; let's turn in."

The Rue Clauzel was a one block street connecting the Rue des Martyres and the Rue Henri Monnier. It was filled with small shops, on top of which were two and three stories of white-shuttered dwellings. Père Tanguy's shop was just across the street from an *école primaire de filles*.

Père Tanguy was looking over some Japansese prints that were just becoming fashionable in Paris.

"Père, I've brought a friend, Vincent Van Gogh. He's an ardent communist."

"I am happy to welcome you to my shop," said Père Tanguy in a soft, almost feminine voice.

Tanguy was a little man with a pudgy face and the wistful eyes of a friendly dog. He wore a wide brimmed straw hat which he pulled down to the level of his brows. He had short arms, stumpy hands, and a rough beard. His right eye opened half again as far as the left one.

"You are really a communist, Monsieur Van Gogh?" he asked shyly.

"I don't know what you mean by communism, Père Tanguy. I think everyone should work as much as he can, at the job he likes best, and in return get everything he needs."

"Just as simply as that," laughed Gauguin.

"Ah, Paul," said Père Tanguy, "you worked on the Stock Exchange. It is money that makes men animals, is it not?"

"Yes, that, and lack of money."

"No, never lack of money, only lack of food and the necessities of life."

"Quite so, Père Tanguy," said Vincent.

"Our friend, Paul," said Tanguy, "despises the men who make money, and he despises us because we can't make any. But I would rather belong to the latter class. Any man who lives on more than fifty centimes a day is a scoundrel."

"Then virtue," said Gauguin, "has descended upon me by force of necessity. Père Tanguy, will you trust me for a little more colour? I know I owe you a large bill, but I am unable to work unless . . ."

"Yes, Paul, I will give you credit. If I had a little less trust in people, and you had a little more, we would both be better off. Where is the new picture you promised me? Perhaps I can sell it and get back the money for my colours."

Gauguin winked at Vincent. "I'll bring you two of them, Père, to hang side by side. Now if you will let me have one tube of black, one of yellow . . ."

"Pay your bill and you'll get more colour!"

The three men turned simultaneously. Madame Tanguy slammed the door to their living quarters and stepped into the shop. She was a wiry little woman with a hard, thin face and bitter eyes. She stormed up to Gauguin.

"Do you think we are in business for charity? Do you think we can eat Tanguy's communism? Settle up that bill, you rascal, or I shall put the police on you!"

Gauguin smiled in his most winning manner, took Madame Tanguy's hand and kissed it gallantly.

"Ah, Xantippe, how charming you look this morning."

Madame Tanguy did not understand why this handsome brute was always calling her Xantippe, but she liked the sound of it and was flattered.

"Don't think you can get around me, you loafer. I slave my life away to grind those filthy colours, and then you come and steal them."

"My precious Xantippe, don't be so hard on me. You have the soul of an artist. I can see it spread all over your lovely face."

Madame Tanguy lifted her apron as though to wipe the soul of the artist off her face. "Phaw!" she cried. "One artist in the family is enough. I suppose he told you he wants to live on only fifty centimes a day. Where do you think he would get that fifty centimes if I didn't earn it for him?"

"All Paris speaks of your charm and ability, dear Madame."

He leaned over and once again brushed his lips across her gnarled hand. She softened.

"Well, you are a scoundrel and a flatterer, but you can have a little colour this time. Only see that you pay your bill."

"For this kindness, my lovely Xantippe, I shall paint your portrait. One day it will hang in the Louvre and immortalize us both."

The little bell on the front door jingled. A stranger walked in.

"That picture you have in the window," he said. "That still life. Who is it by?"

"Paul Cezanne."

"Cezanne? Never heard of him. Is it for sale?"

"Ah, no, alas, it is already . . ."

Madame Tanguy threw off her apron, pushed Tanguy out of the way, and ran up to the man eagerly.

"But of course it is for sale. It is a beautiful still life, is it not, Monsieur? Have you ever seen such apples before? We will sell it to you cheap, Monsieur, since you admire it."

"How much?"

"How much, Tanguy?" demanded Madame, with a threat in her voice. Tanguy swallowed hard. "Three hun . . ."

"Tanguy!"

"Two hun . . ."

"TANGUY!"

"Well, one hundred francs."

"A hundred francs?" said the stranger. "For an unknown painter? I'm afraid that's too much. I was only prepared to spend about twenty-five."

Madame Tanguy took the canvas out of the window.

"See, Monsieur, it is a big picture. There are four apples. Four apples are a hundred francs. You only want to spend twenty-five. Then why not take one apple?"

The man studied the canvas for a moment and said, "Yes, I could do that. Just cut this apple the full length of the canvas and I'll take it."

Madame ran back to her apartment, got a pair of scissors, and cut off the end apple. She wrapped it in a piece of paper, handed it to the man, and took the twenty-five francs. He walked out with the bundle under his arm.

"My favourite Cezanne," moaned Tanguy. "I put it in the window so people could see it for a moment and go away happy."

Madame put the mutilated canvas on the counter.

"Next time someone wants a Cezanne, and hasn't much money, sell him an apple. Take anything you can get for it. They're worthless anyway, he paints so many of them. And you needn't laugh, Paul Gauguin, the same goes for you. I'm going to take those canvases of yours off the wall and sell every one of your naked heathen females for five francs apiece."

"My darling Xantippe," said Gauguin, "we met too late in life. If only you had been my partner on the Stock Exchange, we would have owned the Bank of France by now."

When Madame retired to her quarters at the rear, Père Tanguy said to Vincent, "You are a painter, Monsieur? I hope you will buy your colours here. And perhaps you will let me see some of your pictures?"

"I shall be happy to. These are lovely Japanese prints. Are they for sale?"

"Yes. They have become very fashionable in Paris since the Goncourt brothers have taken to collecting them. They are influencing our young painters a great deal."

"I like these two. I want to study them. How much are they?"

"Three francs apiece."

"I'll take them. Oh, Lord, I forgot. I spent my last franc this morning. Gauguin, have you six francs?"

"Don't be ridiculous."

Vincent laid the Japanese prints down on the counter with regret.

"I'm afraid I'll have to leave them, Père Tanguy."

Père pressed the prints into Vincent's hand and looked up at him with a shy, wistful smile on his homely face.

"You need this for your work. Please take them. You will pay me another time."

10

Theo decided to give a party for Vincent's friends. They made four dozen hard-boiled eggs, brought in a keg of beer, and filled innumerable trays with brioches and pastries. The tobacco smoke was so thick in the living room that when Gauguin moved his huge bulk from one end to the other, he looked like an ocean liner coming through the fog. Lautrec perched himself in one corner, cracked eggs on the arm of Theo's favourite arm-chair, and scattered the shells over the rug. Rousseau was all excited about a perfumed note he had received that day from a lady admirer who wanted to meet him. He told the story with wide eyed amazement over and over again. Seurat was working out a new theory, and had Cezanne pinned against the window, explaining it to him. Vincent poured beer from the keg, laughed at Gauguin's obscene stories, wondered with Rousseau who his lady friend could be, argued with Lautrec whether lines or points of colour were most effective in capturing an impression, and finally rescued Cezanne from the clutches of Seurat.

The room fairly burst with excitement. The men in it were all powerful personalities, fierce egoists, and vibrant iconoclasts. Theo called them mono-maniacs. They loved to argue, fight, curse, defend their own theories and damn everything else. Their voices were strong and rough; the number of things they loathed in the world was legion. A hall twenty times the size of Theo's sitting room would have been too small to contain the dynamic force of the fighting, strident painters.

The turbulence of the room, which fired Vincent to gesticulatory en-thusiasm and eloquence, gave Theo a splitting headache. All this stridency was foreign to his nature. He was tremendously fond of the men in the room. Was it not for them he carried on his quiet, endless battle with Goupils? But he found the rough, uncouth clamour of their personalities alien to his nature. There was a good bit of the feminine in Theo. Toulouse-Lautrec, with his usual vitriolic humour, once remarked,

"Too bad Theo is Vincent's brother. He would have made him such a splendid wife."

Theo found it just as distasteful to sell Bouguereaus as it would have been for Vincent to paint them. And yet, if he sold Bouguereau, Valadon would let him exhibit Degas. One day he would persuade Valadon to let him hang a Cezanne, then a Gauguin or a Lautrec, and finally, some distant day, a Vincent Van Gogh . . .

He took one last look at the noisy, quarrelsome, smoke laden room, slipped out of the front door unnoticed, and walked up the Butte where, alone, he gazed at the lights of Paris spread out before him.

Gauguin was arguing with Cezanne. He waved a hard-boiled egg and a brioche in one hand, a glass of beer in the other. It was his boast that he was the only man in Paris who could drink beer with a pipe in his mouth.

"Your canvases are cold, Cezanne," he shouted. "Ice cold. It freezes me just to look at them. There's not an ounce of emotion in all the miles of canvas you've flung paint at."

"I don't try to paint emotion," retorted Cezanne. "I leave that to the novelists. I paint apples and landscapes."

"You don't paint emotion because you can't. You paint with your eyes, that's what you paint with."

"What does anyone else paint with?"

"With all sorts of things." Gauguin took a quick look about the room. "Lautrec, there, paints with his spleen. Vincent paints with his heart. Seurat paints with his mind, which is almost as bad as painting with your eyes. And Rousseau paints with his imagination."

"What do you paint with, Gauguin?"

"Who, me? I don't know. Never thought about it."

"I'll tell you," said Lautrec. "You paint with your genital!"

When the laugh on Gauguin died down, Seurat perched himself on the arm of a divan and cried, "You can sneer at a man painting with his mind, but it's just helped me discover how we can make our canvases doubly effective."

"Do I have to listen to that *blague* all over again?" moaned Cezanne.

"Shut up, Cezanne! Gauguin, sit down somewhere and don't clutter up the whole room. Rousseau, stop telling that infernal story about your admirer. Lautrec, throw me an egg. Vincent, can I have a brioche? Now listen, everybody!"

"What's up, Seurat? I haven't seen you so excited since that fellow spit on your canvas at the Salon des Refusées!"

"Listen! What is painting today? Light. What kind of light? Gradated light. Points of colour flowing into each other . . ."

"That's not painting, that's pointillism!"

"For God's sake, Georges, are you going intellectual on us again?"

"Shut up! We get through with a canvas. Then what do we do? We turn it over to some fool who puts it into a hideous gold frame and kills our every last effect. Now I propose that we should never let a picture out of our hands until we've put it into a frame and painted the frame so that it becomes an integral part of the picture."

"But, Seurat, you're stopping too soon. Every picture must be hung in a room. And if the room is the wrong colour, it will kill the picture and frame both."

"That's right, why not paint the room to match the frame?"

"A good idea," said Seurat.

"What about the house the room is in?"

"And the city that the house is in."

"Oh, Georges, Georges, you do get the damnedest ideas!"

"That's what comes from painting with your brain."

"The reason you imbeciles don't paint with your brains, is that you haven't any!"

"Look at Georges's face, everybody. Quick! We got the scientist riled up that time, all right."

"Why do you men always fight among yourselves?" demanded Vincent. "Why don't you try working together?"

"You're the communist of this group," said Gauguin. "Suppose you tell us what we'd get if we worked together?"

"Very well," said Vincent, shooting the hard, round yolk of an egg into his mouth, "I will tell you. I've been working out a plan. We're a lot of nobodies. Manet, Degas, Sisley, and Pissarro paved the way for us. They've been accepted and their work is exhibited in the big galleries. All right, they're the painters of the Grand Boulevard. But we have to go into the side streets. We're the painters of the Petit Boulevard. Why couldn't we exhibit our paintings in the little restaurants of the side streets, the workingman's restaurants? Each of us would contribute, say, five canvases. Every afternoon we would put them up in a new place. We'd sell the pictures for whatever the workers could afford. In addition to having our work constantly before the public, we would be making it possible for the poor people of Paris to see good art, and buy beautiful pictures for almost nothing."

"*Tiens,*" breathed Rousseau, his eyes wide with excitement, "that's wonderful."

"It takes me a year to finish a canvas," grumbled Seurat. "Do you think I'm going to sell it to some filthy carpenter for five sous?"

"You could contribute your little studies."

"Yes, but suppose the restaurants won't take our pictures?"

"Of course they will."

"Why not? It costs them nothing, and makes their places beautiful."

"How would we handle it? Who would find the restaurants?"

"I have that all figured out," cried Vincent. "We'll make Père Tanguy our manager. He'll find the restaurants, hang the pictures, and take in the money."

"Of course. He's just the man."

"Rousseau, be a good fellow and run down to Père Tanguy's. Tell him he's wanted on important business."

"You can count me out of this scheme," said Cezanne.

"What's the matter?" asked Gauguin. "Afraid your lovely pictures will be soiled by the eyes of workingmen?"

"It isn't that. I'm going back to Aix at the end of the month."

"Try it just once, Cezanne," urged Vincent. "If it doesn't work, you're nothing out."

"Oh, very well."

"When we get through with the restaurants," said Lautrec, "we might start on the bordellos. I know most of the Madames on Montmartre. They have a better clientele, and I think we could get higher prices."

Père Tanguy came running in, all excited. Rousseau had been able to give him only a garbled account of what was up. His round straw hat was sitting at an angle, and his pudgy little face was lit up with eager enthusiasm.

When he heard the plan he exclaimed, "Yes, yes, I know the very place. The Restaurant Norvins. The owner is a friend of mine. His walls are bare, and he'll be pleased. When we are through there, I know another one on the Rue Pierre. Oh, there are thousands of restaurants in Paris."

"When is the first exhibition of the club of the Petit Boulevard to take place?" asked Gauguin.

"Why put it off?" demanded Vincent. "Why not begin tomorrow?"

Tanguy hopped about on one foot, took off his hat, then crammed it on his head again.

"Yes, yes, tomorrow! Bring me your canvases in the morning. I will hang them in the Restaurant Norvins in the afternoon. And when the people come for their dinner, we will cause a sensation. We will sell the pictures like holy candles on Easter. What's this you're giving me? A glass of beer? Good! Gentlemen, we drink to the Communist Art Club of the Petit Boulevard. May its first exhibition be a success."

11

Père Tanguy knocked on the door of Vincent's apartment the following noon.

"I've been around to tell all the others," he said. "We can only exhibit at Norvins providing we eat our dinner there."

"That's all right."

"Good. The others have agreed. We can't hang the pictures until four-thirty. Can you be at my shop at four? We are all going over together."

"I'll be there."

When he reached the blue shop on the Rue Clauzel, Père Tanguy was already loading the canvases into a handcart. The others were inside, smoking and discussing Japanese prints.

"*Alors*," cried Père, "we are ready."

"May I help you with the cart, Père?" asked Vincent.

"No, no, I am the manager."

He pushed the cart to the centre of the street and began the long climb upward. The painters walked behind, two by two. First came Gauguin and Lautrec; they loved to be together because of the ludicrous picture they made. Seurat was listening to Rousseau, who was all excited over a second perfumed letter he had received that afternoon. Vincent and Cezanne, who sulked and kept uttering words like dignity and decorum, brought up the rear.

"Here, Père Tanguy," said Gauguin, after they wound up the hill a way, "that cart is heavy, loaded down with immortal masterpieces. Let me push it for a while."

"No, no," cried Père, running ahead. "I am the colour bearer of this revolution. When the first shot is fired, I shall fall."

They made a droll picture, the ill-assorted, fantastically dressed men, walking in the middle of the street behind a common pushcart. They did not mind the stares of the amused passers-by. They laughed and talked in high spirits.

"Vincent," cried Rousseau, "have I told you about the letter I got this afternoon? Perfumed, too. From the same lady."

He ran along at Vincent's side, waving his arms, telling the whole interminable story over again. When he finally finished and dropped back with Seurat, Lautrec called Vincent.

"Do you know who Rousseau's lady is?" he asked.

"No. How should I?"

Lautrec snickered. "It's Gauguin. He's giving Rousseau a love affair. The poor fellow has never had a woman. Gauguin is going to feed him with perfumed letters for a couple of months and then make an assignation. He'll dress up in women's clothes and meet Rousseau in one of the Montmartre rooms with peepholes. We're all going to be at the holes watching Rousseau make love for the first time. It should be priceless."

"Gauguin, you're a fiend."

"Oh, come, Vincent," said Gauguin. "I think it's an excellent joke."

At length they arrived at the Restaurant Norvins. It was a modest place, tucked away between a wine shop and a supply store for horses. The outside was painted a varnish-yellow, the walls of the inside a light blue. There were perhaps twenty square tables with red and white checked table cloths. At the back, near the kitchen door, was a high booth for the proprietor.

For a solid hour the painters quarrelled about which pictures should be hung next to which. Père Tanguy was almost distraught. The proprietor was getting angry, for the dinner hour was near and the restaurant was in chaos. Seurat refused to let his pictures go up at all because the blue of the walls

killed his skies. Cezanne would not allow his still lifes to hang next to
Lautrec's "miserable posters," and Rousseau was offended because they
wanted to stick his things on the back wall near the kitchen. Lautrec insisted that one of his large canvases be hung in the *lavabos*.

"That is the most contemplative moment in a man's day," he said.

Père Tanguy came to Vincent almost in despair. "Here," he said, "take
these two francs, add to it whatever you can, and hustle everyone across
the street to a bar. If only I had fifteen minutes to myself, I could finish."

The ruse worked. When they all trooped back to the restaurant, the exhibition was in order. They stopped quarrelling and sat down at a large
table by the street door. Père Tanguy had put signs up all over the walls:
THESE PAINTINGS FOR SALE, CHEAP. SEE THE PROPRIETOR.

It was five-thirty. Dinner was not served until six. The men fidgeted like
schoolgirls. Every time the front door opened, all eyes turned to it hopefully.
The customers of Norvins never came until the dot of six.

"Look at Vincent," whispered Gauguin to Seurat. "He's as nervous as a
prima donna."

"Tell you what I'll do, Gauguin," said Lautrec, "I'll wager you the price
of dinner that I sell a canvas before you do."

"You're on."

"Cezanne, I'll give you three to one odds." It was Lautrec.

Cezanne grew crimson at the insult, and everyone laughed at him.

"Remember," said Vincent, "Père Tanguy is to do all the selling. Don't
anyone try to bargain with the buyers."

"Why don't they come?" asked Rousseau. "It's late."

As the clock on the wall drew nearer six, the group became more and
more jumpy. At length all bantering stopped. The men did not move their
eyes from the door. A feeling of tension settled over them.

"I didn't feel this way when I exhibited with the Independents, before all
the critics of Paris," murmured Seurat.

"Look, look!" whispered Rousseau, "that man, crossing the street. He's
coming this way. He's a customer."

The man walked past Norvins and disappeared. The clock on the wall
chimed six times. On the last chime the door was opened and a labourer
came in. He was shabbily dressed. Lines of fatigue were written inward and
downward on his shoulders and back.

"Now," said Vincent, "we shall see."

The labourer slouched to a table at the other side of the room, threw his
hat on a rack, and sat down. The six painters strained forward, watching
him. The man scanned the menu, ordered a *plat du jour*, and within a
moment was scooping up his soup with a large spoon. He did not raise his
eyes from his plate.

"Tiens," said Vincent, *"c'est curieux."*

Two sheet-metal workers walked in. The proprietor bade them good evening. They grunted, dropped into the nearest chairs, and immediately plunged

into a fierce quarrel about something that had happened during the day.

Slowly the restaurant filled. A few women came in with the men. It seemed as though everyone had his regular table. The first thing they looked at was the menu; when they were served, they were so intent upon their food that they never once glanced up. After dinner they lighted their pipes, chatted, unfolded their copies of the evening paper, and read.

"Would the gentlemen like to be served with their dinner now?" asked the waiter, about seven o'clock.

No one answered. The waiter walked away. A man and a woman entered.

As he was throwing his hat on the rack, the man noticed a Rousseau tiger peering through a jungle. He pointed it out to his comrade. Everyone at the painters' table stiffened. Rousseau half rose. The woman said something in a low tone and laughed. They sat down, and holding their heads close together, devoured the menu voraciously.

At a quarter to eight the waiter served the soup without asking. Nobody touched it. When it had grown cold, the waiter took it away. He brought the *plat du jour*. Lautrec drew pictures in the gravy with his fork. Only Rousseau could eat. Everyone, even Seurat, emptied his carafe of sour red wine. The restaurant was hot with the smell of food, with the odours of people who had laboured and perspired in the heat of the sun.

One by one the customers paid their checks, returned the cursory *bonsoir* of the proprietor and filed out.

"I'm sorry, gentlemen," said the waiter, "but it's eight-thirty, and we are closing."

Père Tanguy took the pictures off the walls and carried them out into the street. He pushed the cart home through the slowly falling dusk.

12

The spirit of old Goupil and Uncle Vincent Van Gogh had vanished forever from the galleries. In their place had come a policy of selling pictures as though they were any other commodity, such as shoes or herring. Theo was constantly being harassed to make more money and sell poorer pictures.

"See here, Theo," said Vincent, "why don't you leave Goupils?"

"The other art dealers are just as bad," replied Theo wearily. "Besides, I've been with them so long. I'd better not change."

"You must change. I insist that you must. You're becoming unhappier every day down there. Let go of me! I can walk around if I like. Theo, you're the best known and best liked young art dealer in Paris. Why don't you open a shop for yourself?"

"Oh, Lord, do we have to go over all that again?"

"Look, Theo, I've got a marvellous idea. We'll open a communist art shop. We will all give you our canvases, and whatever money you take in, we'll live on equally. We can scrape together enough francs to open a little shop in Paris, and we'll take a house out in the country where we'll all live and work. Portier sold a Lautrec the other day, and Père Tanguy has sold several Cezannes. I'm sure we could attract the young art buyers of Paris. And we wouldn't need much money to run that house in the country. We'd live together simply, instead of keeping up a dozen establishments in Paris."

"Vincent, I have a frightful headache. Let me go to sleep now, will you?"

"No, you can sleep on Sunday. Listen, Theo . . . where are you going? All right, undress if you like, but I'm going to talk to you anyway. Here, I'll sit by the head of your bed. Now if you're unhappy at Goupils, and all the young painters of Paris are willing, and we can get a little money together . . ."

Père Tanguy and Lautrec came in with Vincent the following night. Theo had hoped Vincent would be out for the evening. Père Tanguy's little eyes were dancing with excitement.

"Monsieur Van Gogh, Monsieur Van Gogh, it is a wonderful idea. You must do it. I will give up my shop and move to the country with you. I will grind the colours, stretch the canvas, and build the frames. I ask only for my food and shelter."

Theo put down his book with a sigh.

"Where are we going to get the money to begin this enterprise? The money to open a shop, and rent a house, and feed the men?"

"Here, I brought it with me," cried Père Tanguy. "Two hundred and twenty francs. All I have saved up. Take it, Monsieur Van Gogh. It will help begin our colony."

"Lautrec, you're a sensible man. What do you say to all this nonsense?"

"I think it a damned good idea. As things go now, we are not only fighting all of Paris, but fighting among ourselves. If we could present a united front . . ."

"Very well, you are wealthy. Will you help us?"

"Ah, no. If it is to be a subsidized colony, it will lose its purpose. I will contribute two hundred and twenty francs, the same as Père Tanguy."

"It's such a crazy idea! If you men knew anything about the business world . . ."

Père Tanguy ran up to Theo and wrung his hand.

"My dear Monsieur Van Gogh, I beseech you, do not call it a crazy idea. It is a glorious idea. You must, you simply must . . ."

"There's no crawling out now, Theo," said Vincent. "We've got you! We're going to raise some money and make you our master. You've said good-bye to Goupils. You're through there. You're now manager of the Communist Art Colony."

Theo ran a hand over his eyes.

"I can just see myself managing you bunch of wild animals."

When Theo got home the next night he found his house crammed to the doors with excited painters. The air was blue with foul tobacco smoke, and churned by loud, turbulent voices. Vincent was seated on a fragile table in the middle of the living room, master of ceremonies.

"No, no," he cried, "there will be no pay. Absolutely no money. We will never see money from one year to the next. Theo will sell the pictures and we will receive our food, shelter, and materials."

"What about the men whose work never sells?" demanded Seurat. "How long are we going to support them?"

"As long as they want to stay with us and work."

"Wonderful," grunted Gauguin. "We'll have all the amateur painters in Europe on our doorstep."

"Here's Monsieur Van Gogh!" shouted Père Tanguy, catching a sight of Theo as he stood leaning against the door. "Three cheers for our manager."

"Hurrah for Theo! Hurrah for Theo! Hurrah for Theo!"

Everyone was enormously excited. Rousseau wanted to know if he could still give violin lessons at the colony. Anquetin said he owed three months rent, and that they'd better find the country house very soon. Cezanne insisted that a man be allowed to spend his own money, if he had any. Vincent cried, "No, that would kill our communism. We must all share and share alike." Lautrec wanted to know if they could have women at the house. Gauguin insisted that everyone be forced to contribute at least two canvases a month.

"Then I won't come in!" shouted Seurat. "I finish only one big canvas a year."

"What about materials?" demanded Père Tanguy. "Do I give everyone the same amount of colour and canvas each week?"

"No, no, of course not," cried Vincent. "We all get as much material as we need, no more and no less. Just like food."

"Yes, but what happens to the surplus money? After we begin selling our pictures? Who gets the profits?"

"Nobody gets the profits," said Vincent. "As soon as we have a little money over, we'll open a house in Brittany. Then we'll open another in Provence. Soon we'll have houses all over the country, and we'll be travelling from one place to another."

"What about the railroad fare? Do we get that out of the profits?"

"Yes, and how much can we travel? Who's to decide that?"

"Suppose there are too many painters for one house during the best season? Who gets left out in the cold, will you tell me?"

"Theo, Theo, you're the manager of this business. Tell us all about it. Can anyone join? Is there a limit to the membership? Will we have to paint according to any system? Will we have models out there at the house?"

At dawn the meeting broke up. The people downstairs had exhausted themselves rapping on the ceiling with broomsticks. Theo went to bed about four, but Vincent, Père Tanguy, and some of the more enthusiastic ones surrounded his bed and urged him to give Goupils notice on the first of the month.

The excitement grew in intensity with the passing of the weeks. The art world of Paris was divided into two camps. The established painters spoke of those crazy men, the Van Gogh brothers. All the others spoke endlessly about the new experiment.

Vincent talked and worked like mad all night and day. There were so many thousands of details to be settled; how they were to get the money, where the shop was to be located, how prices were to be charged, what men could belong, who would manage the house in the country and how. Theo, almost against his will, was drawn into the febrile excitement. The apartment on the Rue Lepic was crowded every night of the week. Newspaper men came to get stories. Art critics came to discuss the new movement. Painters from all over France returned to Paris to get into the organization.

If Theo was king, Vincent was the royal organizer. He drew up countless plans, constitutions, budgets, pleas for money, codes of rules and regulations, manifestos for the papers, pamphlets to acquaint Europe with the purpose of the Communist Art Colony.

He was so busy he forgot to paint.

Almost three thousand francs rolled into the coffers of the organization. The painters contributed every last franc they could spare. A street fair was held on the Boulevard Clichy, and each man hawked his own canvases. Letters came in from all over Europe, sometimes containing soiled and crumpled franc notes. Art loving Paris came to the apartment, caught the enthusiasm of the new movement, and threw a bill into the open box before they left. Vincent was secretary and treasurer.

Theo insisted that they must have five thousand francs before they could begin. He had located a shop on the Rue Tronchet which he thought well situated, and Vincent had discovered a superb old mansion in the forest of St. Germain-en-Laye that could be had for almost nothing. The canvases of the painters who wanted to join kept pouring into the Rue Lepic apartment, until there was no space left to move about. Hundreds and hundreds of people went in and out of the little apartment. They argued, fought, cursed, ate, drank, and gesticulated wildly. Theo was given notice to move.

At the end of a month the Louis Philippe furniture was in shreds.

Vincent had no time even to think about his palette now. There were letters to be written, people to be interviewed, houses to be looked at, enthusiasm to be kindled in every new painter and amateur he met. He talked until he went hoarse. A feverish energy came into his eyes. He took his food fitfully, and almost never found a chance to sleep. He was forever going, going, going.

By the beginning of spring, the five thousand francs were collected. Theo was giving notice to Goupils on the first of the month. He had decided to take the shop on the Rue Tronchet. Vincent put down a small deposit on the house in St. Germain. The list of members with which the colony would be opened was drawn up by Theo, Vincent, Père Tanguy, Gauguin and Lautrec. From the piles of canvases amassed at the apartment, Theo picked those he was going to show in his first exhibit. Rousseau and Anquetin had a bitter quarrel as to who was going to decorate the inside of the shop, and who the outside. Theo no longer minded being kept awake. He was now as enthusiastic as Vincent had been in the beginning. He worked feverishly to get everything organized so that the colony might open by summer. He debated endlessly with Vincent whether the second house should be located on the Atlantic or the Mediterranean.

One morning Vincent went to sleep about four o'clock, utterly exhausted. Theo did not awaken him. He slept until noon, and awoke refreshed. He wandered into his studio. The canvas on the easel was many weeks old. The paint on the palette was dry, cracked, and covered with dust. The tubes of pigment had been kicked into the corners. His brushes lay about, caked solid with old paint.

A voice within him asked, softly, "One moment, Vincent. Are you a painter? Or are you a communist organizer?"

He took the stacks of ill-assorted canvases into Theo's room and piled them on the bed. In the studio he left only his own pictures. He stood them on the easel, one by one, gnawing his hangnails as he gazed at them.

Yes, he had made progress. Slowly, slowly, his colour had lightened, struggled toward a crystal luminosity. No longer were they imitative. No longer could the traces of his friends be detected on the canvas. He realized for the first time that he had been developing a very individual sort of technique. It was like nothing else he had ever seen. He did not even know how it had got there.

He had strained Impressionism through his own nature, and had been on the verge of achieving a very curious means of expression. Then, suddenly, he had stopped.

He put his more recent canvases on the easel. Once he nearly cried out. He had almost, almost caught something! His pictures were beginning to show a definite method, a new attack with the weapons he had forged through the winter.

His many weeks of rest had given him a clear perspective on his work. He saw that he was developing an Impressionist technique all his own.

He took a careful look at himself in the mirror. His beard needed trimming, his hair needed cutting, his shirt was soiled, and his trousers hung like a limp rag. He pressed his suit with a hot iron, put on one of Theo's shirts, took a five franc note out of the treasury box, and went to the barber. When he was all cleaned up, he walked meditatively to Goupils on the Boulevard Montmartre.

"Theo," he said, "can you come out with me for a short time?"

"What's up?"

"Get your hat. Is there a café about where no one could possibly find us?"

Seated at the very rear of a café, in a secluded corner, Theo said, "You know, Vincent, this is the first time I've had a word alone with you for a month?"

"I know, Theo. I'm afraid I've been something of a fool."

"How so?"

"Theo, tell me frankly, am I a painter? Or am I a communist organizer?"

"What do you mean?"

"I've been so busy organizing this colony, I've had no time to paint. And once the house is started, I'll never catch a moment."

"I see."

"Theo, I want to paint. I haven't put in this seven years of labour just to be a house manager for other painters. I tell you, I'm hungry for my brushes, Theo, so hungry I could almost run away from Paris on the next train."

"But, Vincent, now, after all we've . . ."

"I told you I'd been a fool. Theo, can you stand to hear a confession?"

"Yes?"

"I'm heartily sick of the sight of other painters. I'm tired of their talk, of their theories, of their interminable quarrels. Oh, you needn't smile, I know I've done my share of the fighting. That's just the point. What was it Mauve used to say? 'A man can either paint, or talk about painting, but he can't do both at the same time.' Well, Theo, have you been supporting me for seven years just to hear me spout ideas?"

"You've done a lot of good work for the colony, Vincent."

"Yes, but now that we're ready to move out there, I realize that I don't want to go. I couldn't possibly live there and do any work. Theo, I wonder if I can make you understand . . . but of course I can. When I was alone in the Brabant and The Hague, I thought of myself as an important person. I was one lone man, battling the whole world. I was an artist, the only artist living. Everything I painted was valuable. I knew that I had great ability, and that eventually the world would say, 'He is a splendid painter.' "

"And now?"

"Alas, now I am just one of many. There are hundreds of painters all about me. I see myself caricatured on every side. Think of all the wretched canvases in our apartment, sent by painters who want to join the colony. They, too, think they are going to be great painters. Well, maybe I'm just like them. How do I know? What have I to bolster up my courage now? Before I came to Paris I didn't know there were hopeless fools who deluded themselves all their lives. Now I know. That hurts."

"It has nothing to do with you."

"Perhaps not. But I'll never be able to stamp out that little germ of doubt. When I am alone, in the country, I forget that there are thousands of canvases being painted every day. I imagine that mine is the only one, and that it is a beautiful gift to the world. I would still go on painting even if I knew my work to be atrocious, but this . . . this artist's illusion . . . helps. Do you understand?"

"Yes."

"Besides, I am not a city painter. I don't belong here. I am a peasant painter. I want to go back to my fields. I want to find a sun so hot that it will burn everything out of me but the desire to paint!"

"So . . . you want to . . . leave . . . Paris?"

"Yes. I must."

"And what about the colony?"

"I am going to withdraw. But you must carry on."

Theo shook his head. "No, not without you."

"Why not?"

"I don't know. I was only doing it for you . . . because you wanted it."

They were silent for some moments.

"You haven't given notice yet, Theo?"

"No. I was going to on the first."

"I suppose we can return the money to the people it belongs to?"

"Yes . . . When do you think you'll be going?"

"Not until my palette is clear."

"I see."

"Then I'll go away. To the South, probably. I don't know where. So that I can be alone. And paint and paint and paint. By myself."

He threw his arm about Theo's shoulder with rough affection.

"Theo, tell me you don't despise me. To throw everything up this way when I've put you through so much."

"Despise you?"

Theo smiled with infinite sadness. He reached up and patted the hand that lay on his shoulder.

". . . No . . . no, of course not. I understand. I think you are right. Well . . . old boy . . . you'd better finish your drink. I must be getting back to Goupils."

13

Vincent laboured on for another month, but although his palette was now almost as clear and light as that of his friends, he could not seem to reach a form of expression that satisfied him. At first he thought it was the crudity of his drawing, so he tried working slowly, and in cold blood. The meticulous process of putting on the paint was torture to him, but looking at the canvas afterwards was even worse. He tried hiding his brush work in flat surfaces; he tried working with thin colour instead of rich spurts of pigment. Nothing seemed to help. Again and again he felt that he was fumbling toward a medium that would not only be unique, but which would enable him to say everything he wanted to say. And yet he could not quite grasp it.

"I almost got it that time," he murmured one evening in the apartment. "Almost, but not quite. If I could only find out what was standing in my way."

"I think I can tell you that," said Theo, taking the canvas from his brother.

"You can? What is it?"

"It's Paris."

"Paris?"

"Yes. Paris has been your training ground. As long as you remain here, you'll be nothing but a schoolboy. Remember our school in Holland, Vincent? We learned how other people did things, and how they should be done, but we never actually did anything for ourselves."

"You mean I don't find the subjects here sympathetic?"

"No, I mean that you're unable to make a clean break from your teachers. I'll be awfully lonely without you, Vincent, but I know that you have to go. Somewhere in this world there must be a spot that you can make all your own. I don't know where it is; it's up to you to find it. But you must cut away from your schoolhouse before you can reach maturity."

"Do you know, old boy, what country I've been thinking a lot about of late?"

"No."

"Africa."

"Africa! Not really?"

"Yes. I've been thinking of the blistering sun all during this damnably long and cold winter. That's where Delacroix found his colour, and maybe I could find myself there."

"Africa is a long ways off, Vincent," said Theo, meditatively.

"Theo, I want the sun. I want it in its most terrific heat and power. I've been feeling it pull me southward all winter, like a huge magnet. Until I left Holland I never knew there was such a thing as a sun. Now I know there's no such thing as painting without it. Perhaps that something I need to bring me to maturity is a hot sun. I'm chilled to the bone from the Parisian winter, Theo, and I think some of that cold has gotten into my palette and brushes. I never was one to go at a thing half-heartedly; once I could get the African sun to burn the cold out of me, and set my palette on fire . . ."

"Hummmm," said Theo, "we'll have to think that over. Maybe you're right."

Paul Cezanne gave a farewell party for all his friends. He had arranged through his father to buy the plot of land on the hill overlooking Aix, and he was returning home to build a studio.

"Get out of Paris, Vincent," he said, "and come down to Provence. Not to Aix, that's my territory, but to some place near by. The sun is hotter and purer there than anywhere else in the world. You'll find light and clean colour in Provence such as you've never seen before. I'm staying there for the rest of my life."

"I'll be the next one out of Paris," said Gauguin. "I'm going back to the tropics. If you think you have real sun in Provence, Cezanne, you ought to come to the Marquesas. There the sunlight and colour are just as primitive as the people."

"You men ought to join the sun worshippers," said Seurat.

"As for myself," announced Vincent, "I think I'm going to Africa."

"Well, well," murmured Lautrec, "we have another little Delacroix on our hands."

"Do you mean that, Vincent?" asked Gauguin.

"Yes. Oh, not right away, perhaps. I think I ought to stop off somewhere in Provence and get used to the sun."

"You can't stop at Marseilles," said Seurat. "That town belongs to Monticelli."

"I can't go to Aix," said Vincent, "because it belongs to Cezanne. Monet has already done Antibes, and I agree that Marseilles is sacred to 'Fada.' Has anyone a suggestion as to where I might go?"

"Wait!" exclaimed Lautrec, "I know the very place. Have you ever thought of Arles?"

"Arles? That's an old Roman settlement, isn't it?"

"Yes. It's on the Rhône, a couple of hours from Marseilles. I was there once. The colouring of the surrounding country makes Delacroix's African scenes look anaemic."

"You don't tell me? Is there good sun?"

"Sun? Enough to drive you crazy. And you should see the Arlesiennes; the most gorgeous women in the world. They still retain the pure, delicate features of their Greek ancestors, combined with the robust, sturdy stature of their Roman conquerors. Yet curiously enough, their aroma is distinctly Oriental; I suppose that's a result of the Saracen invasion back in the eighth century. It was at Arles that the true Venus was found, Vincent. The model was an Arlesienne!"

"They sound fascinating," said Vincent.

"They are. And just wait until you feel the mistral."

"What's the mistral?" asked Vincent.

"You'll find out when you get there," replied Lautrec with a twisted grin.

"How about the living? Is it cheap?"

"There's nothing to spend your money on, except food and shelter, and they don't cost much. If you're keen to get away from Paris, why don't you try it?"

"Arles," murmured Vincent to himself. "Arles and the Arlesiennes. I'd like to paint one of those women!"

Paris had excited Vincent. He had drunk too many absinthes, smoked too many pipefuls of tobacco, engaged too much in external activities. His gorge was high. He felt a tremendous urge to get away somewhere by himself where it would be quiet, and he could pour his surging, nervous energy into his craft. He needed only a hot sun to bring him to fruition. He had the feeling that the climax of his life, the full creative power toward which he had been struggling these eight long years, was not so very far off. He knew that nothing he had painted as yet was of any value; perhaps there was a short stretch just ahead in which he could create those few pictures which would justify his life.

What was it Monticelli had said? "We must put in ten years of hard labour, so that in the end we will be able to paint two or three authentic portraits."

In Paris he had security, friendship, and love. There was always a good home for him with Theo. His brother would never let him go hungry, would never make him ask twice for painting supplies, or deny him anything that was in his power to give, least of all full sympathy.

He knew that the moment he left Paris his troubles would begin. He could not manage his allowance away from Theo. Half the time he would be forced to go without food. He would have to live in wretched little cafés, lacerate himself because he could not buy pigments, find his words choking in his throat because there was no friendly soul with whom he could talk.

"You'll like Arles," said Toulouse-Lautrec the next day. "It's quiet, and no one will bother you. The heat is dry, the colour magnificent, and it is the only spot in Europe where you can find sheer Japanese clarity. It's a painter's paradise. If I weren't so attached to Paris, I'd go myself."

That evening Theo and Vincent went to a Wagnerian concert. They came home early and spent a quiet hour conjuring up memories of their childhood in Zundert. The next morning Vincent prepared the coffee for Theo, and when his brother had left for Goupils, gave the little apartment the most thorough cleaning it had had since they moved in. On the walls he put a painting of pink shrimps, a portrait of Père Tanguy in his round straw hat, the Moulin de la Galette, a female nude seen from the back, and a study of the Champs Elysées.

When Theo came home that evening he found a note on the living room table.

Dear Theo:
  I have gone to Arles, and will write you as soon as I get there.
  I have put some of my paintings on the wall so that you won't forget me.
                                        With a handshake in thought,
                                                              Vincent

BOOK SIX

ARLES

1

THE Arlesian sun smote Vincent between the eyes, and broke him wide open. It was a whorling, liquid ball of lemon-yellow fire, shooting across a hard blue sky and filling the air with blinding light. The terrific heat and intense clarity of the air created a new and unfamiliar world.

He dropped out of the third-class carriage early in the morning and walked down the winding road that led from the station to the Place Lamartine, a market square bounded on one side by the embankment of the Rhône, on the other by cafés and wretched hotels. Arles lay straight ahead, pasted against the side of a hill with a neat mason's trowel, drowsing in the hot, tropical sun.

When it came to looking for a place to live, Vincent was indifferent. He walked into the first hotel he passed in the Place, the Hotel de la Gare, and rented a room. It contained a blatant brass bed, a cracked pitcher in a washbowl, and an odd chair. The proprietor brought in an unpainted table. There was no room to set up an easel, but Vincent meant to paint out of doors all day.

He threw his valise on the bed and dashed out to see the town. There were two approaches to the heart of Arles from the Place Lamartine. The circular road on the left was for wagons; it skirted the edge of the town and wound slowly to the top of the hill, passing the old Roman forum and amphitheatre on the way. Vincent took the more direct approach, which led through a labyrinth of narrow cobblestone streets. After a long climb he reached the sun-scorched Place de la Mairie. On the way up he passed cold stone courts and quadrangles which looked as though they had come down untouched from the early Roman days. In order to keep out the maddening sun, the alleys had been made so narrow that Vincent could touch both rows of houses with outstretched fingertips. To avoid the torturing mistral, the streets wound about in a hopeless maze on the side of the hill, never going straight for more than ten yards. There was refuse in the streets, dirty children in the doorways, and over everything a sinister, hunted aspect.

Vincent left the Place de la Mairie, walked through a short alley to the main marketing road at the back of the town, strolled through the little park, and then stumbled down the hill to the Roman arena. He leaped from tier to tier like a goat, finally reaching the top. He sat on a block of stone, dangled his legs over a sheer drop of hundreds of feet, lit his pipe, and surveyed the domain of which he had appointed himself lord and master.

The town below him flowed down abruptly to the Rhône like a kaleido-
scopic waterfall. The roofs of the houses were fitted into each other in an
intricate design. They had all been tiled in what was originally red clay, but
the burning, incessant sun had baked them to a maze of every colour, from
the lightest lemon and delicate shell pink to a biting lavender and earthy
loam-brown.

The wide, rapidly flowing Rhône made a sharp curve at the bottom of the
hill on which Arles was plastered, and shot downward to the Mediterranean.
There were stone embankments on either side of the river. Trinquetaille
glistened like a painted city on the other bank. Behind Vincent were the
mountains, huge ranges sticking upward into the clear white light. Spread
out before him was a panorama of tilled fields, of orchards in blossom, the
rising mound of Montmajour, fertile valleys ploughed into thousands of deep
furrows, all converging at some distant point in infinity.

But it was the colour of the country-side that made him run a hand over
his bewildered eyes. The sky was so intensely blue, such a hard, relentless,
profound blue that it was not blue at all; it was utterly colourless. The green
of the fields that stretched below him was the essence of the colour green,
gone mad. The burning lemon-yellow of the sun, the blood-red of the soil,
the crying whiteness of the lone cloud over Montmajour, the ever reborn
rose of the orchards . . . such colourings were incredible. How could he
paint them? How could he ever make anyone believe that they existed, even
if he could transfer them to his palette? Lemon, blue, green, red, rose;
nature run rampant in five torturing shades of expression.

Vincent took the wagon road to the Place Lamartine, grabbed up his
easel, paints, and canvas and struck out along the Rhône. Almond trees were
beginning to flower everywhere. The glistening white glare of the sun on the
water sent stabs of pain into his eyes. He had left his hat in the hotel. The
sun burned through the red of his hair, sucked out all the cold of Paris, all
the fatigue, discouragement, and satiety with which city life had glutted his
soul.

A kilometre down the river he found a drawbridge with a little cart going
over it, outlined against a blue sky. The river was as blue as a well, the
banks orange, coloured with green grass. A group of washerwomen in smocks
and many-coloured caps were pounding dirty white clothes in the shade of a
lone tree.

Vincent set up his easel, drew a long breath, and shut his eyes. No man
could catch such colourings with his eyes open. There fell away from him
Seurat's talk about scientific pointillism, Gauguin's harangues about primitive
decorativeness, Cezanne's appearances beneath solid surfaces, Lautrec's lines
of colour and lines of splenetic hatred.

There remained only Vincent.

He returned to his hotel about dinner time. He sat down at a little table
in the bar and ordered an absinthe. He was too excited, too utterly replete
to think of food. A man sitting at a nearby table observed the paint splashed

all over Vincent's hands, face, and clothing, and fell into conversation with him.

"I'm a Parisian journalist," he said. "I've been down here for three months gathering material for a book on the Provençal language."

"I just arrived from Paris this morning," said Vincent.

"So I noticed. Intend to stay long?"

"Yes, I imagine so."

"Well, take my advice and don't. Arles is the most violently insane spot on the globe."

"What makes you think that?"

"I don't think it. I know it. I've been watching these people for three months, and I tell you, they're all cracked. Just look at them. Watch their eyes. There's not a normal, rational person in this whole Tarascon vicinity!"

"That's a curious thing to say," observed Vincent.

"Within a week you'll be agreeing with me. The country around Arles is the most torn, desperately lashed section in Provence. You've been out in that sun. Can't you imagine what it must do to these people who are subject to its blinding light day after day? I tell you, it burns the brains right out of their heads. And the mistral. You haven't felt the mistral yet? Oh, dear, wait until you do. It whips this town into a frenzy two hundred days out of every year. If you try to walk the streets, it smashes you against the buildings. If you are out in the fields, it knocks you down and grinds you into the dirt. It twists your insides until you think you can't bear it another minute. I've seen that infernal wind tear out windows, pull up trees, knock down fences, lash the men and animals in the fields until I thought they would surely fly in pieces. I've been here only three months, and I'm going a little *fou* myself. I'm getting out tomorrow morning!"

"Surely you must be exaggerating?" asked Vincent. "The Arlesians looked all right to me, what little I saw of them today."

"What little you saw of them is right. Wait until you get to know them. Listen, do you know what my private opinion is?"

"No, what? Will you join me in an absinthe?"

"Thanks. In my private opinion, Arles is epileptic. It whips itself up to such an intense pitch of nervous excitement that you are positive it will burst into a violent fit and foam at the mouth."

"And does it?"

"No. That's the curious part. This country is forever reaching a climax, and never having one. I've been waiting for three months to see a revolution, or a volcano erupt from the Place de la Mairie. A dozen times I thought the inhabitants would all suddenly go mad and cut each other's throats! But just when they get to a point where an explosion is imminent, the mistral dies down for a couple of days and the sun goes behind the clouds."

"Well," laughed Vincent, "if Arles never reached a climax, you can't very well call it epileptic, now can you?"

"No," replied the journalist, "but I can call it epileptoidal."

"What the devil is that?"

"I'm doing an article on the subject for my paper in Paris. It was this German article that gave me my idea."

He pulled a magazine out of his pocket and shoved it across the table to Vincent.

"These doctors have made a study of the cases of several hundred men who suffered from nervous maladies which looked like epilepsy, but which never resulted in fits. You'll see by these charts how they have mapped the rising curve of nervousness and excitement; what the doctors call volatile tension. Well, in every last one of these cases the subjects have gone along with increasing fever until they reached the age of thirty-five to thirty-eight. At the average age of thirty-six they burst into a violent epileptic fit. After that it's a case of a half dozen more spasms and, within a year or two, good-bye."

"That's much too young to die," said Vincent. "A man is only beginning to get command of himself by that time."

The journalist put the magazine back in his pocket.

"Are you going to stop at this hotel for some time?" he asked. "My article is almost finished; I'll mail you a copy as soon as it's published. My point is this: Arles is an epileptoidal city. Its pulse has been mounting for centuries. It's approaching its first crisis. It's bound to happen. And soon. When it does, we're going to witness a frightful catastrophe. Murder, arson, rape, wholesale destruction! This country can't go on forever in a whipped, tortured state. Something must and will happen. I'm getting out before the people start foaming at the mouth! I advise you to come along!"

"Thanks," said Vincent, "I like it here. I think I'll turn in now. Will I see you in the morning? No? Then good luck to you. And don't forget to send me a copy of the article."

2

Every morning Vincent arose before dawn, dressed, and tramped several kilometres down the river or into the country to find a spot that stirred him. Every night he returned with a finished canvas, finished because there was nothing more he could do with it. Directly after supper he went to sleep.

He became a blind painting machine, dashing off one sizzling canvas after another without even knowing what he did. The orchards of the country were in bloom. He developed a wild passion to paint them all. He no longer thought about his painting. He just painted. All his eight years of intense labour were at last expressing themselves in a great burst of triumphal energy. Sometimes, when he began working at the first crack of dawn, the canvas would be completed by noon. He would tramp back to town, drink a cup of coffee and trudge out again in another direction with a new canvas.

He did not know whether his painting was good or bad. He did not care. He was drunk with colour.

No one spoke to him. He spoke to no one. What little strength he had left from his painting, he spent in fighting the mistral. Three days out of every week he had to fasten his easel to pegs driven into the ground. The easel waved back and forth in the wind like a sheet on a clothesline. By night he felt as buffeted and bruised as though he had been given a severe beating.

He never wore a hat. The fierce sun was slowly burning the hair off the top of his head. When he lay on his brass bed in the little hotel at night he felt as though his head were encased in a ball of fire. The sun struck him completely blind. He could not tell the green of the fields from the blue of the sky. But when he returned to his hotel he found that the canvas was somehow a glowing, brilliant transcription of nature.

One day he worked in an orchard of lilac ploughland with a red fence and two rose-coloured peach trees against a sky of glorious blue and white.

"It is probably the best landscape I have ever done," he murmured to himself.

When he reached his hotel he found a letter telling him that Anton Mauve had died in The Hague. Under his peach trees he wrote, "Souvenir de Mauve. Vincent and Theo," and sent it off immediately to the house on the Uileboomen.

The following morning he found an orchard of plum trees in blossom. While he was at work, a vicious wind sprang up, returning at intervals like waves of the sea. In between, the sun shone, and all the white flowers sparkled on the trees. At the risk every minute of seeing the whole show on the ground, Vincent went on painting. It reminded him of the Scheveningen days when he used to paint in the rain, in sandstorms, and with the storm-spray of the ocean dashing over him and his easel. His canvas had a white effect with a good deal of yellow in it, and blue and lilac. When he finished he saw something in his picture that he had not meant to put there, the mistral.

"People will think I was drunk when I painted this," he laughed to himself.

A line from Theo's letter of the day before came back to him. Mijnheer Tersteeg, on a visit to Paris, had stood before a Sisley and murmured to Theo, "I cannot help thinking that the artist who painted this was a bit tipsy."

"If Tersteeg could see my Arlesian pictures," thought Vincent, "he would say it was delirium tremens in full career."

The people of Arles gave Vincent a wide berth. They saw him dashing out of town before sunrise, heavy easel loaded on his back, hatless, his chin stuck forward eagerly, a feverish excitement in his eyes. They saw him return with two fire holes in his face, the top of his head as red as raw meat, a wet canvas under his arm, gesticulating to himself. The town had a name for him. Everyone called him by it.

"Fou-rou!"

"Perhaps I am a red-headed crazy man," he said to himself, "but what can I do?"

The owner of the hotel swindled Vincent out of every franc he could. Vincent could not get anything to eat, for nearly everyone at Arles ate at home. The restaurants were expensive. Vincent tried them all to find some strong soup, but there was none to be had.

"Is it hard to cook potatoes, Madame?" he asked in one place.

"Impossible, Monsieur."

"Then have you some rice?"

"That is tomorrow's dish."

"What about macaroni?"

"There was no room on the range for macaroni."

At length he had to give up all serious thoughts of food, and live on whatever came his way. The hot sun built up his vitality, even though his stomach was getting little attention. In place of sane food he put absinthe, tobacco, and Daudet's tales of Tartarin. His innumerable hours of concentration before the easel rubbed his nerves raw. He needed stimulants. The absinthe made him all the more excited for the following day, an excitement whipped by the mistral and baked into him by the sun.

As the summer advanced, everything became burnt up. He saw about him nothing but old gold, bronze and copper, covered by a greenish azure sky of blanched heat. There was sulphur-yellow on everything the sunlight hit. His canvases were masses of bright burning yellow. He knew that yellow had not been used in European painting since the Renaissance, but that did not deter him. The yellow pigment oozed out of the tubes onto the canvas, and there it stayed. His pictures were sun steeped, sun burnt, tanned with the burning sun and swept with air.

He was convinced that it was no more easy to make a good picture than it was to find a diamond or a pearl. He was dissatisfied with himself and what he was doing, but he had just a glimmer of hope that it was going to be better in the end. Sometimes even that hope seemed a Fata Morgana. Yet the only time he felt alive was when he was slogging at his work. Of personal life, he had none. He was just a mechanism, a blind painting automaton that had food, liquid, and paint poured into it each morning, and by nightfall turned out a finished canvas.

And for what purpose? For sale? Certainly not! He knew that nobody wanted to buy his pictures. Then what was the hurry? Why did he drive and spur himself to paint dozens and dozens of canvases when the space under his miserable brass bed was already piled nearly solid with paintings?

The desire to succeed had left Vincent. He worked because he had to, because it kept him from suffering too much mentally, because it distracted his mind. He could do without a wife, a home, and children; he could do without love and friendship and health; he could do without security, comfort, and food; he could even do without God. But he could not do without something which was greater than himself, which was his life—the power and ability to create.

3

He tried to hire models, but the people of Arles would not sit for him. They thought they were being done badly. They were afraid their friends would laugh at the portraits. Vincent knew that if he painted prettily like Bouguereau, people would not be ashamed to let themselves be painted. He had to give up the idea of models, and work always on the soil.

As the summer ripened, a glorious strong heat came on and the wind died. The light in which he worked ranged from pale sulphur-yellow to pale golden yellow. He thought often of Renoir and that pure clear line of his. That was the way everything looked in the clear air of Provence, just as it looked in the Japanese prints.

Early one morning he saw a girl with a coffee-tinted skin, ash-blond hair, grey eyes, and a print bodice of pale rose under which he could see the breasts, shapely, firm and small. She was a woman as simple as the fields, every line of her virgin. Her mother was an amazing figure in dirty yellow and faded blue, thrown up in strong sunlight against a square of brilliant flowers, snow-white and lemon-yellow. They posed for him for several hours in return for a small sum.

When he returned to his hotel that evening, Vincent found himself thinking of the girl with the coffee-tinted skin. Sleep would not come. He knew that there were houses in Arles, but they were mostly five-franc places patronized by the Zouaves, negroes brought to Arles to be trained for the French army.

It was months since Vincent had spoken to a woman, except to ask for a cup of coffee or a bag of tobacco. He remembered Margot's loving words, the wandering fingers over his face that she followed with a trail of loving kisses.

He jumped up, hurried across the Place Lamartine and struck into the black maze of stone houses. After a few moments of climbing he heard a great hubbub ahead. He broke into a run and reached the front door of a brothel in the Rue des Ricolettes just as the gendarmes were carting away two Zouaves who had been killed by drunken Italians. The red fezzes of the soldiers were lying in pools of blood on the rough cobblestone street. A squad of gendarmes hustled the Italians to jail, while the infuriated mob stormed after them, shouting,

"Hang them! Hang them!"

Vincent took advantage of the excitement to slip into the Maison de Tolérance, Numero I, in the Rue des Ricolettes. Louis, the proprietor, welcomed him and led him into a little room on the left of the hall, where a few couples sat drinking.

"I have a young girl by the name of Rachel who is very nice," said Louis.

"Would Monsieur care to try her? If you do not like the looks of her, you can choose from all the others."

"May I see her?"

Vincent sat down at a table and lit his pipe. There was laughter from the outside hall, and a girl danced in. She slid into the chair opposite Vincent and smiled at him.

"I'm Rachel," she said.

"Why," exclaimed Vincent, "you're nothing but a baby!"

"I'm sixteen," said Rachel proudly.

"How long have you been here?"

"At Louis's? A year."

"Let me look at you."

The yellow gas lamp was at her back; her face had been in the shadows. She put her head against the wall and tilted her chin up towards the light so that Vincent could see her.

He saw a round, plump face, wide, vacant blue eyes, a fleshy chin and neck. Her black hair was coiled on top of her head, giving the face an even more ball-like appearance. She had on only a light printed dress and a pair of sandals. The nipples of her round breasts pointed straight out at him like accusing fingers.

"You're pretty, Rachel," he said.

A bright, childlike smile came into her empty eyes. She whirled about and took his hand in hers.

"I'm glad you like me," she said. "I like the men to like me. That makes it nicer, don't you think?"

"Yes. Do you like me?"

"I think you're a funny man, *fou-rou.*"

"*Fou-rou!* Then you know me?"

"I've seen you in the Place Lamartine. Why are you always rushing places with that big bundle on your back? And why don't you wear a hat? Doesn't the sun burn you? Your eyes are all red. Don't they hurt?"

Vincent laughed at the naiveté of the child.

"You're very sweet, Rachel. Will you call me by my real name if I tell it to you?"

"What is it?"

"Vincent."

"No, I like *fou-rou* better. Do you mind if I call you *fou-rou?* And can I have something to drink? Old Louis is watching me from the hall."

She ran her fingers across her throat; Vincent watched them sink into the soft flesh. She smiled with her empty blue eyes, and he saw that she was smiling to be happy, so that he might be happy, too. Her teeth were regular but dark; her large underlip drooped down almost to meet the sharp horizontal crevice just above her thick chin.

"Order a bottle of wine," said Vincent, "but not an expensive one, for I haven't much money."

When the wine came, Rachel said, "Would you like to drink it in my room? It's more homey there."

"I would like that very much."

They walked up a flight of stone steps and entered Rachel's cell. There was a narrow cot, a bureau, a chair, and several coloured Julien medallions on the white walls. Two torn and battered dolls sat on top of the bureau.

"I brought these from home with me," she said. "Here, *fou-rou*, take them. This is Jacques and this is Catherine. I used to play house with them. Oh, *fou-rou*, don't you look droll!"

Vincent stood there grinning foolishly with a doll in each arm until Rachel finished laughing. She took Catherine and Jacques from him, tossed them on the bureau, kicked her sandals into a corner and slipped out of her dress.

"Sit down, *fou-rou*," she said, "and we'll play house. You'll be papa and I'll be mama. Do you like to play house?"

She was a short, thickset girl with swelling, convex thighs, a deep declivity under the pointed breasts, and a plump, round belly which rolled down into the pelvic triangle.

"Rachel," said Vincent, "if you are going to call me *fou-rou*, I have a name for you, too."

Rachel clapped her hands and flung herself onto his lap.

"Oh, tell me, what is it? I like to be called new names!"

"I'm going to call you *Le Pigeon*."

Rachel's blue eyes went hurt and perplexed.

"Why am I a pigeon, papa?"

Vincent ran his hand lightly over her rotund, cupid's belly.

"Because you look like a pigeon, with your gentle eyes and fat little tummy."

"Is it nice to be a pigeon?"

"Oh, yes. Pigeons are very pretty and lovable . . . and so are you."

Rachel leaned over, kissed him on the ear, sprang up from the cot and brought two water tumblers for their wine.

"What funny little ears you have, *fou-rou*," she said, between sips of the red wine. She drank it as a baby drinks, with her nose in the glass.

"Do you like them?" asked Vincent.

"Yes. They're so soft and round, just like a puppy's."

"Then you can have them."

Rachel laughed loudly. She raised her glass to her lips. The joke struck her as funny again, and she giggled. A trickle of red wine spilled down her left breast, wound its way over the pigeon belly and disappeared in the black triangle.

"You're nice, *fou-rou*," she said. "Everyone speaks as though you were crazy. But you're not, are you?"

Vincent grimaced.

"Only a little," he said.

"And will you be my sweetheart?" Rachel demanded. "I haven't had one for over a month. Will you come to see me every night?"

"I'm afraid I can't come every night, Pigeon."

Rachel pouted. "Why not?"

"Well, among other things, I haven't the money."

Rachel tweaked his right ear, playfully.

"If you haven't five francs, *fou-rou,* will you cut off your ear and give it to me? I'd like to have it. I'd put it on my bureau and play with it every night."

"Will you let me redeem it if I get the five francs later?"

"Oh, *fou-rou,* you're so funny and nice. I wish more of the men who came here were like you."

"Don't you enjoy it here?"

"Oh, yes, I have a very nice time, and I like it all . . . except the Zouaves, that is."

Rachel put down her wine glass and threw her arms prettily about Vincent's neck. He felt her soft paunch against his waistcoat, and the points of her bud-like breasts burning into him. She buried her mouth on his. He found himself kissing the soft, velvety inner lining of her lower lip.

"You will come back to see me again, *fou-rou?* You won't forget me and go to see some other girl?"

"I'll come back, Pigeon."

"And shall we do it now? Shall we play house?"

When he left the place a half hour later, he was consumed by a thirst which could be quenched only by innumerable glasses of clear, cold water.

4

Vincent came to the conclusion that the more finely a colour was pounded, the more it became saturated with oil. Oil was only the carrying medium for colour; he did not care much for it, particularly since he did not object to his canvases having a rough look. Instead of buying colour that had been pounded on the stone for God knows how many hours in Paris, he decided to become his own colour man. Theo asked Père Tanguy to send Vincent the three chromes, the malachite, the vermilion, the orange lead, the cobalt, and the ultramarine. Vincent crushed them in his little hotel room. After that his colours not only cost less, but they were fresher and more lasting.

He next became dissatisfied with the absorbent canvas on which he painted. The thin coat of plaster with which they were covered did not suck up his rich colours. Theo sent him rolls of unprepared canvas; at night he mixed the plaster in a little bowl and spread it over the canvas he planned to paint the following day.

Georges Seurat had made him sensitive to the sort of frame his work was to rest in. When he sent his first Arlesian canvases to Theo, he explained just what sort of wood had to be used, and what colour it had to be painted.

But he could not be happy until he saw his paintings in frames that he made himself. He bought plain strips of wood from his grocer, cut them down to the size he wanted, and then painted them to match the composition of the picture.

He made his colours, built his stretchers, plastered his canvas, painted his pictures, carpentered his frames, and painted them.

"Too bad I can't buy my own pictures," he murmured aloud. "Then I'd be completely self-sufficient."

The mistral came up again. All nature seemed in a rage. The skies were cloudless. The brilliant sunshine was accompanied by intense dryness and piercing cold. Vincent did a still life in his room; a coffee pot in blue enamel, a cup of royal blue and gold, a milk jug in squares of pale blue and white, a jug in majolica, blue with a pattern in reds, greens and browns, and lastly, two oranges and three lemons.

When the wind died down he went out again and did a view on the Rhône, the iron bridge at Trinquetaille, in which the sky and river were the colour of absinthe, the quays a shade of lilac, the figures leaning on their elbows on the parapet blackish, the iron bridge an intense blue with a note of vivid orange in the black background and a touch of intense malachite green. He was trying to get at something utterly heartbroken and therefore utterly heartbreaking.

Instead of trying to reproduce exactly what he had before his eyes, he used colour arbitrarily to express himself with greater force. He realized that what Pissarro had told him in Paris was true. "You must boldly exaggerate the effects, either in harmony or discord, which colours produce." In Maupassant's preface to "Pierre et Jean" he found a similar sentiment. "The artist has the liberty to exaggerate, to create in his novel a world more beautiful, more simple, more consoling than ours."

He did a day's hard, close work among the cornfields in full sun. The result was a ploughed field, a big field with clods of violet earth, climbing toward the horizon; a sower in blue and white; on the horizon a field of short, ripe corn; over all a yellow sky with a yellow sun.

Vincent knew that the Parisian critics would think he worked too fast. He did not agree. Was it not emotion, the sincerity of his feeling for nature, that impelled him? And if the emotions were sometimes so strong that he worked without knowing he worked, if sometimes the strokes came with a sequence and coherence like words in a speech, then too the time would come when there would again be heavy days, empty of inspiration. He had to strike while the iron was hot, put the forged bars on one side.

He strapped his easel to his back and took the road home which led past Montmajour. He walked so rapidly that he soon overtook a man and a boy who were dallying ahead of him. He recognized the man as old Roulin, the Arlesian *facteur des postes*. He had often sat near Roulin in the café, and had wanted to speak to him, but the occasion had never arisen.

"Good day, Monsieur Roulin," he said.

"Ah, it is you, the painter," said Roulin. "Good day. I have been taking my boy for a Sunday afternoon stroll."

"It has been a glorious day, hasn't it?"

"Ah, yes, it is lovely when that devil mistral does not blow. You have painted a picture today, Monsieur?"

"Yes."

"I am an ignorant man, Monsieur, and know nothing about art. But I would be honoured if you would let me look."

"With pleasure."

The boy ran ahead, playing. Vincent and Roulin walked side by side. While Roulin looked at the canvas, Vincent studied him. Roulin was wearing his blue postman's cap. He had soft, inquiring eyes and a long, square, wavy beard which completely covered his neck and collar and came to rest on the dark blue postman's coat. Vincent felt the same soft, wistful quality about Roulin that had attracted him to Père Tanguy. He was homely in a pathetic sort of way, and his plain, peasant's face seemed out of place in the luxuriant Greek beard.

"I am an ignorant man, Monsieur," repeated Roulin, "and you will forgive me for speaking. But your cornfields are so very alive, as alive as the field we passed back there, for instance, where I saw you at work."

"Then you like it?"

"As for that, I cannot say. I only know that it makes me feel something, in here."

He ran his hand upward over his chest.

They paused for a moment at the base of Montmajour. The sun was setting red over the ancient abbey, its rays falling on the trunks and foliage of pines growing among a tumble of rocks, colouring the trunks and foliage with orange fire, while the other pines in the distance stood out in Prussian blue against a sky of tender, blue-green cerulean. The white sand and the layers of white rocks under the trees took on tints of blue.

"That is alive, too, is it not, Monsieur?" asked Roulin.

"It will still be alive when we are gone, Roulin."

They walked along, chatting in a quiet, friendly manner. There was nothing of the abrasive quality in Roulin's words. His mind was simple, his thoughts at once simple and profound. He supported himself, his wife, and four children on a hundred and thirty-five francs a month. He had been a postman twenty-five years without a promotion, and with only infinitesimal advances in salary.

"When I was young, Monsieur," he said, "I used to think a lot about God. But He seems to have grown thinner with the years. He is still in that cornfield you painted, and in the sunset by Montmajour, but when I think about men . . . and the world they have made . . ."

"I know, Roulin, but I feel more and more that we must not judge God by this world. It's just a study that didn't come off. What can you do in a study that has gone wrong, if you are fond of the artist? You do not find much to criticize; you hold your tongue. But you have a right to ask for something better."

"Yes, that's it," exclaimed Roulin, "something just a tiny bit better."

"We should have to see some other works by the same hand before we judge him. This world was evidently botched up in a hurry on one of his bad days, when the artist did not have his wits about him."

Dusk had fallen over the winding country road. The first chips of stars poked through the heavy cobalt blanket of night. Roulin's sweet innocent eyes searched Vincent's face.

"Then you think there are other worlds besides this, Monsieur?"

"I don't know, Roulin. I gave up thinking about that sort of thing when I became interested in my work. But this life seems so imcomplete, doesn't it? Sometimes I think that just as trains and carriages are means of locomotion to get us from one place to another on this earth, so typhoid and consumption are means of locomotion to get us from one world to another."

"Ah, you think of things, you artists."

"Roulin, will you do me a favour? Let me paint your portrait. The people of Arles won't pose for me."

"I should be honoured, Monsieur. But why do you want to paint me? I am only an ugly man."

"If there were a God, Roulin, I think he would have a beard and eyes just like yours."

"You are making fun of me, Monsieur!"

"On the contrary, I am in earnest."

"Will you come and share supper with us tomorrow night? We have a very plain board, but we will be happy to have you."

Madame Roulin proved to be a peasant woman who reminded him a little of Madame Denis. There was a red and white checked cloth on the table, a little stew with potatoes, home-baked bread and a bottle of sour wine. After dinner Vincent sketched Madame Roulin, chatting with the postman as he worked.

"During the Revolution I was a republican," said Roulin, "but now I see that we have gained nothing. Whether our rulers be kings or ministers, we poor people have just as little as before. I thought when we were a republic everyone would share and share alike."

"Ah, no, Roulin."

"All my life I have tried to understand, Monsieur, why one man should have more than the next, why one man should work hard while his neighbour sits by in idleness. Perhaps I am too ignorant to understand. Do you think if I were educated, Monsieur, I would be able to understand that better?"

Vincent glanced up quickly to see if Roulin were being cynical. There was the same look of naive innocence on his face.

"Yes, my friend," he said, "most educated people seem to understand that state of affairs very well. But I am ignorant like you, and I shall never be able to understand or accept it."

5

He arose at four in the morning, walked three and four hours to reach the spot he wanted, and then painted until dark. It was not pleasant, this trudging ten or twelve kilometres home on a lonely road, but he liked the reassuring touch of the wet canvas under his arm.

He did seven large pictures in seven days. By the end of the week he was nearly dead with work. It had been a glorious summer, but now he was painted out. A violent mistral arose and raised clouds of dust which whitened the trees. Vincent was forced to remain quiet. He slept for sixteen hours at a stretch.

He had a very thin time of it, for his money ran out on Thursday, and Theo's letter with the fifty francs was not expected until Monday noon. It was not Theo's fault. He still sent fifty francs every ten days in addition to all the painting supplies. Vincent had been wild to see his new pictures in frames, and had ordered too many of them for his budget. During those four days he lived on twenty-three cups of coffee and a loaf of bread for which the baker trusted him.

An intense reaction set in against his work. He did not think his pictures worthy of the goodness he had had from Theo. He wanted to win back the money he had already spent in order to return it to his brother. He looked at his paintings one by one and reproached himself that they were not worth what they had cost. Even if a tolerable study did come out of it from time to time, he knew that it would have been cheaper to buy it from somebody else.

All during the summer ideas for his work had come to him in swarms. Although he had been solitary, he had not had time to think or feel. He had gone on like a steam-engine. But now his brain felt like stale porridge, and he did not even have a franc to amuse himself by eating or going to visit Rachel. He decided that everything he had painted that summer was very, very bad.

"Anyway," he said to himself, "a canvas that I have covered is worth more than a blank canvas. My pretensions go no further; that is my right to paint, my reason for painting."

He had the conviction that simply by staying in Arles he would set his individuality free. Life was short. It went fast. Well, being a painter, he still had to paint.

"These painter's fingers of mine grow supple," he thought, "even though the carcass is going to pieces."

He drew up a long list of colours to send to Theo. Suddenly he realized that not one colour on his list would be found on the Dutch palette, in Mauve, Maris, or Weissenbruch. Arles had made his break with the Dutch tradition complete.

When his money arrived on Monday, he found a place where he could get a good meal for a franc. It was a queer restaurant, altogether grey; the floor was of grey bitumen like a street pavement, there was grey paper on the walls, green blinds always drawn, and a big green curtain over the door to keep the dust out. A very narrow, very fierce ray of sunlight stabbed through a blind.

After he had been resting for over a week, he decided to do some night painting. He did the grey restaurant while the patrons were at their meal and the waitresses were scurrying back and forth. He painted the thick, warm cobalt sky of night, studded with thousands of bright Provençal stars, as seen from the Place Lamartine. He went out on the roads and did cypresses under the moonlight. He painted the Café de Nuit, which remained open all night so that prowlers could take refuge there when they had no money to pay for a lodging, or when they were too drunk to be taken to one.

He did the exterior of the café one night, and the interior the next. He tried to express the terrible passions of humanity by means of red and green. He did the interior in blood red and dark yellow with a green billiard table in the middle. He put in four lemon-yellow lamps with a glow of orange and green. Everywhere there was the clash and contrast of the most alien reds and greens in the figures of little sleeping hooligans. He was trying to express the idea that the café was a place where one could ruin oneself, run mad, or commit a crime.

The people of Arles were amused to find their *fou-rou* painting in the streets all night and sleeping in the daytime. Vincent's activities were always a treat for them.

When the first of the month came, the hotel owner not only raised the rent on the room, but decided to charge Vincent a daily storage fee for the closet in which he kept his canvases. Vincent loathed the hotel and was outraged by the voraciousness of the owner. The grey restaurant in which he ate was satisfactory, but he had sufficient money to eat there only two or three days out of every ten. Winter was coming, he had no studio in which to work, the hotel room was depressing and humiliating. The food he was forced to eat in the cheap restaurants was poisoning his stomach again.

He had to find a permanent home and studio of his own.

One evening, as he was crossing the Place Lamartine with old Roulin, he noticed a *For Rent* sign on a yellow house just a stone's throw from his hotel. The house had two wings with a court in the centre. It faced the Place and the town on the hill. Vincent stood looking at it wistfully.

"Too bad it's so large," he said to Roulin. "I'd like to have a house like that."

"It is not necessary to rent the whole house, Monsieur. You can rent just this right wing, for example."

"Really! How many rooms do you think it has? Would it be expensive?"

"I should say it had about three or four rooms. It will cost you very little, not half what the hotel costs. I will come and look at it with you tomorrow during my dinner time, if you like. Perhaps I can help you get a good price."

The following morning Vincent was so excited he could do nothing but pace up and down the Place Lamartine and survey the yellow house from all sides. It was built sturdily and got all the sun. On closer inspection Vincent found that there were two separate entrances to the house, and that the left wing was already occupied.

Roulin joined him after the midday meal. They entered the right wing of the house together. There was a hallway inside which led to a large room, with a smaller room opening off it. The walls were whitewashed. The hall and stairway leading to the second floor were paved with clean red brick. Upstairs there was another large room with a cabinet. The floors were of scrubbed red tile, and the whitewashed walls caught the clean, bright sun.

Roulin had written a note to the landlord, who was waiting for them in the upstairs room. He and Roulin conversed for some moments in a fast Provençal of which Vincent could understand very little. The postman turned to Vincent.

"He insists upon knowing how long you will keep the place."

"Tell him indefinitely."

"Will you agree to take it for at least six months?"

"Oh, yes! Yes!"

"Then he says he will give it to you for fifteen francs a month."

Fifteen francs! For a whole house! Only a third of what he paid at the hotel. Even less than he had paid for his studio in The Hague. A permanent home for fifteen francs a month. He drew the money out of his pocket, hurriedly.

"Here! Quick! Give it to him. The house is rented."

"He wants to know when you are going to move in," said Roulin.

"Today. Right now."

"But, Monsieur, you have no furniture. How can you move in?"

"I will buy a mattress and a chair. Roulin, you don't know what it means to spend your life in miserable hotel rooms. I must have this place immediately!"

"Just as you wish, Monsieur."

The landlord left. Roulin went back to work. Vincent walked from one room to another, up and down the stairs again, surveying over and over every inch of his domain. Theo's fifty francs had arrived just the day before; he still had some thirty francs in his pocket. He rushed out, bought a cheap mattress and a chair and carried them back to the yellow house. He decided that the room on the ground floor would be his bedroom, the top room his studio. He threw the mattress on the red tile floor, carried the chair up to his studio, and went back to his hotel for the last time.

The proprietor added forty francs to Vincent's bill on some thin pretext. He refused to let Vincent have his canvases until the money was handed over. Vincent had to go to the police court to get his paintings back, and even then had to pay half the fictitious charge.

Late that afternoon he found a merchant who was willing to give him a small gas stove, two pots, and a kerosene lamp on credit. Vincent had three francs left. He bought coffee, bread, potatoes and a little meat for soup. He left himself without a centime. At home he set up a kitchen in the cabinet on the ground floor.

When night closed over the Place Lamartine and the yellow house, Vincent cooked his soup and coffee on the little stove. He had no table, so he spread a paper over the mattress, put out his supper, and ate it sitting cross-legged on the floor. He had forgotten to buy a knife and fork. He used the handle of his brush to pick the pieces of meat and potato out of the pot. They tasted slightly of paint.

When he finished eating, he took the kerosene lamp and mounted the red brick stairs to the second floor. The room was barren and lonely, with only the stark easel standing against the moonlit window. In the background was the dark garden of the Place Lamartine.

He went to sleep on the mattress. When he awakened in the morning he opened the windows and saw the green of the garden, the rising sun, and the road winding up into the town. He looked at the clean red bricks of the floor, the spotlessly whitewashed walls, the spaciousness of the rooms. He boiled himself a cup of coffee and walked about drinking from the pot, planning how he would furnish his house, what pictures he would hang on the walls, how he would pass the happy hours in a real home of his own.

The next day he received a letter from his friend Paul Gauguin, who was imprisoned, ill and poverty stricken, in a wretched café in Pont-Aven, in Brittany. "I can't get out of this hole," wrote Gauguin, "because I can't pay my bill, and the owner has all my canvases under lock and key. In all the variety of distresses that afflict humanity, nothing maddens me more than the lack of money. Yet I feel myself doomed to perpetual beggary."

Vincent thought of the painters of the earth, harassed, ill, destitute, shunned and mocked by their fellow men, starved and tortured to their dying day. Why? What was their crime? What was their great offense that made them outcasts and pariahs? How could such persecuted souls do good work? The painter of the future—ah, he would be such a colourist and a man as had never yet existed. He would not live in miserable cafés, and go to the Zouave brothels.

And poor Gauguin. Rotting away in some filthy hole in Brittany, too sick to work, without a friend to help him or a franc in his pocket for wholesome food and a doctor. Vincent thought him a great painter and a great man. If Gauguin should die. If Gauguin should have to give up his work. What a tragedy for the painting world.

Vincent slipped the letter into his pocket, left the yellow house, and walked along the embankment of the Rhône. A barge loaded with coal was moored to the quay. Seen from above, it was all shining and wet from a shower. The water was of yellowish white, and clouded pearl grey. The sky was lilac, barred with orange to the west, the town violet. On the boat some labourers in dirty blue and white came and went, carrying the cargo on shore.

It was pure Hokusai. It carried Vincent back to Paris, to the Japanese prints in Père Tanguy's shop . . . and to Paul Gauguin who, of all his friends, he loved the most dearly.

He knew at once what he had to do. The yellow house was large enough for two men. Each of them could have his own bedroom and studio. If they cooked their meals, ground their colours, and guarded their money, they could live on his hundred and fifty francs a month. The rent would be no more, the food very little. How marvellous it would be to have a friend again, a painter friend who talked one's language and understood one's craft. And what wonderful things Gauguin could teach him about painting.

He had not realized before how utterly lonely he had been. Even if they couldn't live on Vincent's hundred and fifty francs, perhaps Theo would send an extra fifty francs in return for a monthly canvas from Gauguin.

Yes! Yes! He must have Gauguin with him here in Arles. The hot Provence sun would burn all the illness out of him, just as it had out of Vincent. Soon they would have a working studio going full blaze. Theirs would be the very first studio in the South. They would carry on the tradition of Delacroix and Monticelli. They would drench painting in sunlight and colour, awaken the world to riotous nature.

Gauguin had to be saved!

Vincent turned, broke into a dog-trot and ran all the way back to the Place Lamartine. He let himself into the yellow house, dashed up the red brick stairs, and began excitedly planning the rooms.

"Paul and I will each have a bedroom up here. We'll use the rooms on the lower floor for studios. I'll buy beds and mattresses and bedclothes and chairs and tables, and we'll have a real home. I'll decorate the whole house with sunflowers and orchards in blossom."

"Oh, Paul, Paul, how good it will be to have you with me again!"

6

It was not so easy as he had expected. Theo was willing to add fifty francs a month to the allowance in return for a Gauguin canvas, but there was the matter of the railroad fare which neither Theo nor Gauguin could provide. Gauguin was too ill to move, too much in debt to get out of Pont-Aven, too sick at heart to enter into any schemes with enthusiasm. Letters flew thick and fast between Arles, Paris, and Pont-Aven.

Vincent was now desperately in love with his yellow house. He bought himself a table and a chest of drawers with Theo's allowance.

"At the end of a year," he wrote to Theo, "I shall be a different man.

But don't think I'm going to leave here then. By no means. I'm going to spend the rest of my life in Arles. I'm going to become the painter of the South. And you must consider that you have a country house in Arles. I am keen to arrange it all so that you will come here always to spend your holidays."

He spent a minimum for the bare necessities of life, and sunk all the rest into the house. Each day he had to make a choice between himself and the yellow house. Should he have meat for dinner, or buy that majolica jug? Should he buy a new pair of shoes, or get that green quilt for Gauguin's bed? Should he order a pine frame for his new canvas, or buy those rush-bottom chairs?

Always the house came first.

The yellow house gave him a sense of tranquillity, because he was working to secure the future. He had drifted too much, knocked about without rhyme or reason. But now he was never going to move again. After he was gone, another painter would find a going concern. He was establishing a permanent studio which would be used by generation after generation of painters to interpret and portray the South. He became obsessed with the idea of painting such decorations for the house as would be worthy of the money spent on him during the years in which he had been unproductive.

He plunged into his work with renewed energy. He knew that looking at a thing a long time ripened him and gave him a deeper understanding. He went back fifty times to Montmajour to study the field at its base. The mistral made it hard for him to get his brush work connected and interwoven with feeling, with the easel waving violently before him in the wind. He worked from seven in the morning until six at night without stirring. A canvas a day!

"Tomorrow will be a scorcher," said Roulin one evening, very late in the fall. They were sitting over a bock in the Café Lamartine. "And after that, winter."

"What is winter like in Arles?" asked Vincent.

"It's mean. Lots of rain, a miserable wind, and a biting cold. But winter is very short here. Only a couple of months."

"So tomorrow will be our last nice day. Then I know the very spot I want to do. Imagine an autumn garden, Roulin, with two cypresses, bottle green, shaped like bottles, and three little chestnut trees with tobacco and orange coloured leaves. There is a little yew with pale lemon foliage and a violet trunk, and two little bushes, blood-red, and scarlet purple leaves. And some sand, some grass, and some blue sky."

"Ah, Monsieur, when you describe things, I see that all my life I have been blind."

The next morning Vincent arose with the sun. He was in high spirits. He trimmed his beard with a pair of scissors, combed down what little hair the Arlesian sun had not burned off his scalp, put on his only whole suit of clothes, and as a special fond gesture of farewell to the sun, wore his rabbit-fur bonnet from Paris.

Roulin's prediction had been right. The sun rose, a yellow ball of heat. The rabbit-fur bonnet had no peak, and the sun pried into his eyes. The autumn garden was a two hour walk from Arles, on the road to Tarascon. It nestled askew on the side of a hill. Vincent planted his easel in a furrowed cornfield, behind and to the side of the garden. He threw his bonnet to the ground, took off his good coat, and set the canvas to the easel. Although it was still early morning, the sun scorched the top of his head and threw before his eyes the veil of dancing fire to which he had become accustomed.

He studied the scene before him carefully, analysed the component colours, and etched the design on his mind. When he was confident that he understood the scene, he softened his brushes, took the caps off his tubes of pigments, and cleaned the knife with which he spread on his thick colour. He glanced once more at the garden, burnt the image on the blank canvas before him, mixed some colour on the palette, and raised his brush.

"Must you begin so soon, Vincent?" asked a voice behind him.

Vincent whirled about.

"It is early yet, my dear. And you have the whole long day to work." Vincent gaped at the woman in utter bewilderment. She was young, but not a child. Her eyes were as blue as the cobalt sky of an Arlesian night, and her hair, which she wore in a great flowing mass down her back, was as lemon-yellow as the sun. Her features were even more delicate than those of Kay Vos, but they had about them the mellow maturity of the Southland. Her colouring was burnt gold, her teeth, between the smiling lips, as white as an oleander seen through a blood-red vine. She wore a long white gown which clung to the lines of her body and was fastened only by a square silver buckle at the side. She had a simple pair of sandals on her feet. Her figure was sturdy, robust, yet flowing downward with the eye in pure, voluptuous curves.

"I've stayed away so very long, Vincent," she said.

She placed herself between Vincent and the easel, leaning against the blank canvas and shutting out his view of the garden. The sun caught up the lemon-yellow hair and sent waves of flame down her back. She smiled at him so whole-heartedly, so fondly, that he ran a hand over his eyes to see if he had suddenly gone ill, or fallen asleep.

"You do not understand, my dear, dear boy," the woman said. "How could you, when I've stayed away so long?"

"Who are you?"

"I am your friend, Vincent. The best friend you have in the world."

"How do you know my name? I have never seen you before."

"Ah, no, but I have seen you, many, many times."

"What is your name?"

"Maya."

"Is that all? Just Maya?"

"For you, Vincent, that is all."

"Why have you followed me here to the fields?"

"For the same reason that I have followed you all over Europe . . . so that I might be near you."

"You mistake me for someone else. I can't possibly be the man you mean."

The woman put a cool white hand on the burnt red hair of his head and smoothed it back lightly. The coolness of her hand and the coolness of her soft, low voice was like the refreshing water from a deep green well.

"There is only one Vincent Van Gogh. I could never mistake him."

"How long do you think you have known me?"

"Eight years, Vincent."

"Why, eight years ago I was in . . ."

". . . Yes, dear, in the Borinage."

"You knew me then?"

"I saw you for the first time one late fall afternoon, when you were sitting on a rusty iron wheel in front of Marcasse . . ."

". . . Watching the miners go home!"

"Yes. When I first looked at you, you were sitting there, idly. I was about to pass by. Then you took an old envelope and a pencil from your pocket and began sketching. I looked over your shoulder to see what you had done. And when I saw . . . I fell in love."

"You fell in love? You fell in love with me?"

"Yes, Vincent, my dear, good Vincent, in love with you."

"Perhaps I was not so bad to look at, then."

"Not half so good as you are to look at now."

"Your voice . . . Maya . . . it sounds so queer. Only once before has a woman spoken to me in that voice . . ."

". . . Margot's voice. She loved you, Vincent, as well as I do."

"You knew Margot?"

"I stayed in the Brabant for two years. I followed you to the fields each day. I watched you work in the wrangle room behind the kitchen. And I was happy because Margot loved you."

"Then you did not love me any more?"

She caressed his eyes with the cool tips of her fingers.

"Ah, yes, I loved you. I have never ceased to love you since that very first day."

"And you weren't jealous of Margot?"

The woman smiled. Across her face went a flash of infinite sadness and compassion. Vincent thought of Mendes da Costa.

"No, I was not jealous of Margot. Her love was good for you. But your love for Kay I did not like. It injured you."

"Did you know me when I was in love with Ursula?"

"That was before my time."

"You would not have liked me then."

"No."

"I was a fool."

"Sometimes one has to be a fool in the beginning, to become wise in the end."

"But if you loved me when we were in the Brabant, why didn't you come to me?"

"You were not ready for me, Vincent."

"And now . . . I am ready?"

"Yes."

"You still love me? Even now . . . today . . . this moment?"

"Now . . . today . . . this moment . . . and for eternity."

"How can you love me? Look, my gums are diseased. Every tooth in my mouth is false. All the hair has been burnt off my head. My eyes are as red as a syphilitic's. My face is nothing but jagged bone. I am ugly. The ugliest of men! My nerves are shattered, my body gone sterile, my insides poisoned from tip to toe. How can you love such a wreck of a man?"

"Will you sit down, Vincent?"

Vincent sat on his stool. The woman sank to her knees in the soft loam of the field.

"Don't," cried Vincent. "You'll get your white gown all dirty. Let me put my coat under you."

The woman restrained him with the faintest touch of her hand.

"Many times I have soiled my gown in following you, Vincent, but always it has come clean again."

She cupped his chin in the palm of her strong white hand, and with her fingertips smoothed back the few charred hairs behind his ear.

"You are not ugly, Vincent. You are beautiful. You have tormented and tortured this poor body in which your soul is wrapped, but you cannot injure your soul. It is that I love. And when you have destroyed yourself by your passionate labours, that soul will go on . . . endlessly. And with it, my love for you."

The sun had risen another hour in the sky. It beat down in fierce heat upon Vincent and the woman.

"Let me take you where it is cool," said Vincent. "There are some cypress trees just below on the road. You will be more comfortable in the shade."

"I am happy here with you. I do not mind the sun. I have grown used to it."

"You have been in Arles long?"

"I came with you from Paris."

Vincent jumped up in anger and kicked over his stool.

"You are a fraud! You've been sent here on purpose to ridicule me. Someone told you of my past, and is paying you to make a fool of me. Go away. I'll not talk to you any more!"

The woman held his anger with the smile of her eyes.

"I am no fraud, my dear. I am the most real thing in your life. You can never kill my love for you."

"That's a lie! You don't love me. You're mocking me. I'll show your game up."

He seized her roughly in his arms. She swayed inward to him.

"I'm going to hurt you if you don't go away and stop torturing me!"

"Hurt me, Vincent. You've hurt me before. It's part of love to be hurt."

"Very well then, take your medicine!"

He pressed her body to him. He brought his mouth down on hers, hurting her with his teeth, crushing his kiss upon her.

She opened soft, warm lips to him and let him drink deeply of the sweetness of her mouth. Her whole body yearned upward to him, muscle to muscle, bone to bone, flesh to flesh, in complete and final surrender.

Vincent thrust her away from him and stumbled to his stool. The woman sank down on the ground beside him, put one arm on his leg, and rested her head against it. He stroked the long, rich mass of lemon-yellow hair.

"Are you convinced now?" she asked.

After many moments Vincent said, "You have been in Arles since I came. Did you know about *Le Pigeon?*"

"Rachel is a sweet child."

"And you don't object?"

"You are a man, Vincent, and need women. Since it was not yet time to come to you and give myself, you had to go where you could. But now . . ."

"Now?"

"You need to no longer. Ever again."

"You mean that you . . . ?"

"Of course, Vincent dear. I love you."

"Why should you love me? Women have always despised me."

"You were not meant for love. You had other work to do."

"Work? Bah! I've been a fool. Of what good are all these hundreds of paintings? Who wants to own them? Who will buy them? Who will give me one grudging word of praise, say that I have understood nature or portrayed its beauty?"

"The whole world will say it one day, Vincent."

"One day. What a dream. Like the dream of thinking that I will one day be a healthy man, with a home and a family and enough money from my painting to live on. I have been painting for eight long years. Not once in all that time has anyone wanted to buy a picture I've painted. I've been a fool."

"I know, but what a glorious fool. After you are gone, Vincent, the world will understand what you have tried to say. The canvases that today you cannot sell for a hundred francs will one day sell for a million. Ah, you smile, but I tell you it is true. Your pictures will hang in the museums of Amsterdam and The Hague, in Paris and Dresden, Munich and Berlin, Moscow and New York. Your pictures will be priceless, because there will be none for sale. Books will be written about your art, Vincent, novels and plays built around your life. Wherever two men come together who love painting, there the name of Vincent Van Gogh will be sacred."

"If I could not still taste your mouth on mine, I would say I was dreaming or going mad."

"Come sit beside me, Vincent. Put your hand in mine."

The sun was directly overhead. The hillside and valley were bathed in a mist of sulphur-yellow. Vincent lay in the furrow of the field beside the woman. For six long months he had had no one to talk to but Rachel and Roulin. Within him there was a great flood of words. The woman looked deep into his eyes, and he began to speak. He told her of Ursula and the days when he had been a Goupil clerk. He told her of his struggles and disappointments, of his love for Kay, and the life he had tried to build with Christine. He told her of his hopes in painting, of the names he had been called, and the blows he had received, of why he wanted his drawing to be crude, his work unfinished, his colour explosive; of all the things he wanted to accomplish for painting and painters, and how his body was wracked with exhaustion and disease.

The longer he talked, the more excited he became. Words flew out of his mouth like pigments from his tubes. His whole body sprang into action. He talked with his hands, gesticulated with his arms and shoulders, walked up and down before her with violent body contortions. His pulse was rising, his blood was rising, the burning sun sent him into a passion of feverish energy.

The woman listened quietly, never missing a word. From her eyes, he knew she understood. She drank in all he had to say, and still was there, eager and ready to hear more, to understand him, to be the recipient of everything he had to give and could not contain within himself.

He stopped abruptly. He trembled all over with excitement. His eyes and face were red, his limbs quivering. The woman pulled him down beside her.

"Kiss me, Vincent," she said.

He kissed her on the mouth. Her lips were no longer cool. They lay side by side in the rich, crumbly loam. The woman kissed his eyes, his ears, the nostrils of his nose, the declivity of his upper lip, bathed the inside of his mouth with her sweet, soft tongue, ran her fingers down the beard of his neck, down his shoulders and along the sensitive nerve-ends of his arm pit.

Her kisses aroused in him the most excruciating passion he had ever known. Every inch of him ached with the dull ache of the flesh that cannot be satisfied by flesh alone. Never before had a woman given herself to him with the kiss of love. He strained her body to him, feeling, beneath the soft white gown, the heat of her life flow.

"Wait," she said.

She unbuckled the silver clasp at her side and tossed the white gown away from her. Her body was the same burnished gold as her face. It was virgin, every beating pulse of it virgin. He had not known that the body of a woman could be so exquisitely wrought. He had not known that passion could be so pure, so fine, so searing.

"You're trembling, dear," she said. "Hold me to you. Do not tremble, my dear; my sweet, sweet dear. Hold me as you want me."

The sun was slipping down the other side of the heavens. The earth was hot from the beating rays of the day. It smelled of things that had been planted, of things that had grown, been cut away and died again. It smelled of life, rich pungent smells of life ever being created and ever returning to the stuff of its creation.

Vincent's emotion rose higher and higher. Every fibre of him beat inward to some focal core of pain. The woman opened her arms to him, opened her warmth to him, took from him what was the man of him, took into herself all the volcanic turbulence, all the overwhelming passion that hour by hour wracked his nerves and burst his body, led him with gentle caressing undulations to the shattering, creative climax.

Exhausted, he fell asleep in her arms.

When he awoke, he was alone. The sun had gone down. There was a solid cake of mud on one cheek, where he had buried his perspiring face in the loam. The earth was coolish and smelled of buried, crawling things. He put on his coat and rabbit-fur bonnet, strapped the easel to his back, and took the canvas under his arm. He walked the dark road home.

When he reached the yellow house, he threw the easel and blank canvas on the mattress in his bedroom. He went out for a cup of coffee. He leaned his head in his hands on the cold stone topped table and thought back over the day.

"Maya," he murmured to himself. "Maya. Haven't I heard that name somewhere before? It means . . . it means . . . I wonder what it means?"

He took a second cup of coffee. After an hour he crossed the Place Lamartine to the yellow house. A cold wind had come up. There was the smell of rain in the air.

He had not bothered to light the kerosene lamp when he had dropped his easel. Now he lit a match and set the lamp on the table. The yellow flare illumined the room. His eye was caught by a patch of colour on the mattress. Startled, he walked over and picked up the canvas that he had taken with him that morning.

There, in a magnificent blaze of light, he saw his autumn garden; the two bottle green, bottle shaped cypresses; the three little chestnut trees with tobacco and orange coloured leaves; the yew with pale lemon foliage and a violet trunk; the two blood-red bushes with scarlet purple leaves; in the foreground some sand and grass, and over all a blue, blue sky with a whorling ball of sulphur-lemon fire.

He stood gazing at the picture for several moments. He tacked it lightly on the wall. He went back to the mattress, sat on it cross-legged, looked at his painting and grinned.

"It is good," he said aloud. "It is well realized."

7

Winter came on. Vincent spent the days in his warm pleasant studio. Theo wrote that Gauguin, who had been in Paris for a day, was in vile frame of mind, and was resisting the Arlesian idea with all his strength. In Vincent's mind the yellow house was not to be simply a home for two men, but a permanent studio for all the artists of the South. He made elaborate plans for enlarging his quarters as soon as he and Gauguin put the place into working order. Any painter who wished to stay there would be welcome; in return for his hospitality he would be obliged to send Theo one canvas a month. As soon as Theo had enough Impressionist pictures on hand, he was to leave Goupils and open an Independent Gallery in Paris.

Vincent made it very clear in his letters that Gauguin was to be the director of the studio, master of all the painters who worked there. Vincent saved every franc he could in order to furnish his bedroom. He painted the walls a pale violet. The floor was of red tile. He bought very light, greenish lemon sheets and pillows, a scarlet covering, and painted the wooden bed and chairs the colour of fresh butter. The toilet table he painted orange, the basin blue, the door lilac. He hung a number of his pictures on the wall, threw away the window shutters, and then transferred the whole scene to canvas for Theo, so that his brother might see how restful his room was. He painted it in free flat washes, like the Japanese prints.

With Gauguin's room it was another matter. He was not willing to buy such cheap furniture for the master of the studio. Madame Roulin assured him that the walnut bed he wanted for Gauguin would come to three hundred and fifty francs, an impossible sum for him to muster. Nevertheless he began buying the smaller articles for the room, keeping himself in a constant state of financial exhaustion.

When he had no money for models, he stood before a mirror and did his own portrait over and over. Rachel came to pose for him; Madame Roulin came one afternoon a week and brought the children; Madame Ginoux, wife of the owner of the café where he took his drinks, sat for him in her Arlesienne costume. He slashed the figure onto the canvas in an hour. The background was pale lemon, the face grey, the clothes black, with raw Prussian blue. He posed her in a borrowed armchair of orange wood, her elbows leaning on a green table.

A Zouave lad with a small face, the neck of a bull, and the eye of a tiger agreed to sit for a small sum. Vincent did a half length of him in his blue uniform, the blue of enamelled saucepans, with braid of a faded reddish orange, and two pale lemon stars on his breast. There was a reddish cap on the bronzed, feline head, set against a green background. The result was a savage combination of incongruous tones, very harsh, common and even loud, but fitting the character of the subject.

He sat at his window for hours with pencil and drawing paper, trying to master the technique which would enable him with a few strokes to put down the figure of a man, a woman, a youngster, a horse, a dog, so that it would have a head, body, and legs all in keeping. He copied a good many of the paintings he had made that summer, for he thought that if he could turn out fifty studies at two hundred francs each within the year, he would not have been so very dishonest in having eaten and drunk as though he had a right to it.

He learned a good many things during the winter: that one must not do flesh in Prussian blue, for then it becomes as wood; that his colour was not as firm as it should have been; that the most important element in southland painting was the contrast of red and green, of orange and blue, of sulphur and lilac; that in a picture he wanted to say something comforting as music is comforting; that he wished to paint men and women with that something of the divine which the halo used to symbolize, and which he sought to give by the actual radiance and vibration of his colouring; and lastly, that for those who have a talent for poverty, poverty is eternal.

One of the Van Gogh uncles died and left Theo a small legacy. Since Vincent was so keen to have Gauguin with him, Theo decided to use half the money to furnish Gauguin's bedroom and send him to Arles. Vincent was delighted. He began planning the decorations for the yellow house. He wanted a dozen panels of glorious Arlesian sunflowers, a symphony of blue and yellow.

Even the news of the free railway fare did not seem to excite Gauguin. For some reason which remained obscure to Vincent, Gauguin preferred to dawdle in Pont-Aven. Vincent was eager to finish the decorations and have the studio ready when the master arrived.

Spring came. The row of oleander bushes in the back yard of the yellow house went raving mad, flowering so riotously that they might well have developed locomotor ataxia. They were loaded with fresh flowers, and heaps of faded flowers as well; their green was continually renewing itself in strong jets, apparently inexhaustible.

Vincent loaded the easel on his back once again and went into the country-side to find sunflowers for the twelve wall panels. The earth of the ploughed fields was as soft in colour as a pair of sabots, while the forget-me-not blue sky was flecked with white clouds. Some of the sunflowers he did on the stalk, at sunrise, and in a flash. Others he took home with him and painted in a green vase.

He gave the outside of his house a fresh coat of yellow, much to the amusement of the inhabitants of the Place Lamartine.

By the time he finished his work on the house, summer had come. With it came the broiling sun, the driving mistral, the growing excitement in the air, the tortured, tormented, driven aspect of the country-side and the stone city pasted against the hill.

And with it came Paul Gauguin.

He arrived in Arles before dawn and waited for the sun in a little all-night café. The proprietor looked at him and exclaimed, "You are the friend! I recognize you."

"What the devil are you talking about?"

"Monsieur Van Gogh showed me the portrait you sent him. It looks just like you, Monsieur."

Gauguin went to rouse Vincent. Their meeting was boisterous and hearty. Vincent showed Gauguin the house, helped him unpack his valise, demanded news of Paris. They talked animatedly for several hours.

"Are you planning to work today, Gauguin?"

"Do you think I am a Carolus-Duran, that I can get off the train, pick up my palette, and turn you off a sunlight effect at once?"

"I only asked."

"Then don't ask foolish questions."

"I'll take a holiday, too. Come along, I'll show you the town."

He led Gauguin up the hill, through the sun-baked Place de la Mairie, and along the market road at the back of the town. The Zouaves were drilling in the field just outside the barracks; their red fezzes burned in the sun. Vincent led the way through the little park in front of the Roman forum. The Arlesiennes were strolling for their morning air. Vincent had been raving to Gauguin about how beautiful they were.

"What do you think about the Arlesiennes, Gauguin?" he demanded.

"I can't get up a perspiration about them."

"Look at the tone of their flesh, man, not the shape. Look at what the sun has done to their colouring."

"How are the houses here, Vincent?"

"There's nothing but five franc places for the Zouaves."

They returned to the yellow house to work out some sort of living ar-rangements. They nailed a box to the wall in the kitchen and put half their money into it—so much for tobacco, so much for incidental expenses, in-cluding rent. On the top of the box they put a scrap of paper and a pencil with which to write down every franc they took. In another box they put the rest of their money, divided into four parts, to pay for the food each week.

"You're a good cook, aren't you, Gauguin?"

"Excellent. I used to be a sailor."

"Then in the future you shall cook. But tonight I am going to make the soup in your honour."

When he served the soup that night, Gauguin could not eat it.

"How you mixed this mess, Vincent, I can't imagine. As you mix the colours in your pictures, I dare say."

"What is the matter with the colours in my pictures?"

"My dear fellow, you're still floundering in neo-impressionism. You'd better give up your present method. It doesn't correspond to your nature."

Vincent pushed his bowl of soup aside.

"You can tell that at first glance, eh? You're quite a critic."

"Well, look for yourself. You're not blind, are you? Those violent yellows, for example; they're completely disordered."

Vincent glanced up the sunflower panels on the wall.

"Is that all you find to say about my sunflowers?"

"No, my dear fellow, I can find a good many things to criticize."

"Among them?"

"Among them, your harmonies; they're monotonous and incomplete."

"That's a lie!"

"Oh, sit down, Vincent. Stop looking as though you wanted to murder me. I'm a good deal older than you, and more mature. You're still trying to find yourself. Just listen to me, and I'll give you some fruitful lessons."

"I'm sorry, Paul. I do want you to help me."

"Then the first thing you had better do is sweep all the garbage out of your mind. You've been raving all day about Meissonier and Monticelli. They're both worthless. As long as you admire that sort of painting, you'll never turn out a good canvas yourself."

"Monticelli was a great painter. He knew more about colour than any man of his time."

"He was a drunken idiot, that's what he was."

Vincent jumped to his feet and glared at Gauguin across the table. The bowl of soup fell to the red tile floor and smashed.

"Don't you call 'Fada' that! I love him almost as well as I do my own brother! All that talk about his being such a drinker, and off his head, is vicious gossip. No drunkard could have painted Monticelli's pictures. The mental labour of balancing the six essential colours, the sheer strain and calculation, with a hundred things to think of in a single half hour, demands a sane mind. And a sober one. When you repeat that gossip about 'Fada' you're being just as vicious as that beastly woman who started it."

"*Turlututu, mon chapeau pointu!*"

Vincent recoiled, as though a glass of cold water had been thrown in his face. His words and tense emotion strangled within him. He tried to put down his rage, but could not. He walked to his bedroom and slammed the door behind him.

8

The following morning the quarrel was forgotten. They had coffee together and then went their separate ways to find pictures. When Vincent returned that night, exhausted from what he had called the balancing of the six essential colours, he found Gauguin already preparing supper on the tiny gas stove. They talked quietly for a little while; then the conversation turned to painters and painting, the only subject in which they were passionately interested.

The battle was on.

The painters whom Gauguin admired, Vincent despised. Vincent's idols were anathema to Gauguin. They disagreed on every last approach to their craft. Any other subject they might have been able to discuss in a quiet and friendly manner, but painting was the meat and drink of life to them. They fought for their ideas to the last drop of nervous energy. Gauguin had twice Vincent's brute strength, but Vincent's lashing excitement left them evenly matched.

Even when they discussed things about which they agreed, their arguments were terribly electric. They came out of them with their heads as exhausted as a battery after it has been discharged.

"You'll never be an artist, Vincent," announced Gauguin, "until you can look at nature, come back to your studio and paint it in cold blood."

"I don't want to paint in cold blood, you idiot. I want to paint in hot blood! That's why I'm in Arles."

"All this work you've done is only slavish copying from nature. You must learn to work extempore."

"*Extempore!* Good God!"

"And another thing; you would have done well to listen to Seurat. Painting is abstract, my boy. It has no room for the stories you tell and the morals you point out."

"I point out morals? You're crazy."

"If you want to preach, Vincent, go back to the ministry. Painting is colour, line, and form; nothing more. The artist can reproduce the decorative in nature, but that's all."

"Decorative art," snorted Vincent. "If that's all you get out of nature, you ought to go back to the Stock Exchange."

"If I do, I'll come hear you preach on Sunday mornings. What do you get out of nature, Brigadier?"

"I get motion, Gauguin, and the rhythm of life."

"Well, we're off."

"When I paint a sun, I want to make people feel it revolving at a terrific rate of speed. Giving off light and heat waves of tremendous power. When I paint a cornfield I want people to feel the atoms within the corn pushing out to their final growth and bursting. When I paint an apple I want people to feel the juice of that apple pushing out against the skin, the seeds at the core striving outward to their own fruition!"

"Vincent, how many times have I told you that a painter must not have theories."

"Take this vineyard scene, Gauguin. Look out! Those grapes are going to burst and squirt right in your eye. Here, study this ravine. I want to make people feel all the millions of tons of water that have poured down its sides. When I paint the portrait of a man, I want them to feel the entire flow of that man's life, everything he has seen and done and suffered!"

"What the devil are you driving at?"

"At this, Gauguin. The fields that push up the corn, and the water that rushes down the ravine, the juice of the grape, and the life of a man as it flows past him, are all one and the same thing. The sole unity in life is the unity of rhythm. A rhythm to which we all dance; men, apples, ravines, ploughed fields, carts among the corn, houses, horses, and the sun. The stuff that is in you, Gauguin, will pound through a grape tomorrow, because you and a grape are one. When I paint a peasant labouring in the field, I want people to feel the peasant flowing down into the soil, just as the corn does, and the soil flowing up into the peasant. I want them to feel the sun pouring into the peasant, into the field, the corn, the plough, and the horses, just as they all pour back into the sun. When you begin to feel the universal rhythm in which everything on earth moves, you begin to understand life. That alone is God."

"*Brigadier,*" said Gauguin, "*vous avez raison!*"

Vincent was at the height of his emotion, quivering with febrile excitement. Gauguin's words struck him like a slap in the face. He stood there gaping foolishly, his mouth hanging open.

"Now what in the world does that mean, 'Brigadier, you are right?' "

"It means I think it about time we adjourned to the café for an absinthe."

At the end of the second week Gauguin said, "Let's try that house of yours tonight. Maybe I can find a nice fat girl."

"Keep away from Rachel. She belongs to me."

They walked up the labyrinth of stone alleys and entered the Maison de Tolérance. When Rachel heard Vincent's voice, she skipped down the hallway and threw herself into his arms. Vincent introduced Gauguin to Louis.

"Monsieur Gauguin," said Louis, "you are an artist. Perhaps you would give me your opinion of the two new paintings I bought in Paris last year."

"I'd be glad to. Where did you buy them?"

"At Goupils, in the Place de l'Opéra. They are in this front parlour. Will you step in, Monsieur?"

Rachel led Vincent to the room on the left, pushed him into a chair near one of the tables, and sat on his lap.

"I've been coming here for six months," grumbled Vincent, "and Louis never asked my opinion about his pictures."

"He doesn't think you are an artist, *fou-rou.*"

"Maybe he's right."

"You don't love me any more," said Rachel, pouting.

"What makes you think that, Pigeon?"

"You haven't been to see me for weeks."

"That was because I was working hard to fix the house for my friend."

"Then you do love me, even if you stay away?"

"Even if I stay away."

She tweeked his small, circular ears, then kissed each of them in turn.

"Just to prove it, *fou-rou,* will you give me your funny little ears? You promised you would."

"If you can take them off, you can have them."

"Oh, *fou-rou*, as if they were sewed on, like my dolly's ears."

There was a shout from the room across the hall, and the noise of someone screaming, either in laughter or in pain. Vincent dumped Rachel off his lap, ran across the hall and into the parlour.

Gauguin was doubled up on the floor, convulsed, tears streaming down his face. Louis, lamp in hand, was gazing down at him, dumbfounded. Vincent crouched over Gauguin and shook him.

"Paul, Paul, what is it?"

Gauguin tried to speak, but could not. After a moment he gasped, "Vincent . . . at last . . . we're vindicated . . . look . . . look . . . up on the wall . . . the two pictures . . . that Louis bought from Goupils . . . for the parlour of his brothel. *They are both Bouguereaus!*"

He stumbled to his feet and made for the front door.

"Wait a minute," cried Vincent, running after him. "Where are you going?"

"To the telegraph office. I must wire this to the Club Batignolles at once."

Summer came on in all its terrific, glaring heat. The country-side burst into a riot of colour. The greens and blues and yellows and reds were so stark they were shocking to the eye. Whatever the sun touched, it burnt to the core. The valley of the Rhône vibrated with wave after wave of billowy heat. The sun battered the two painters, bruised them, beat them to a living pulp, sucked out all their resistance. The mistral came up and lashed their bodies, whipped their nerves, shook their heads on their necks until they thought they would burst or break off. Yet every morning they went out with the sun and laboured until the crying blue of night deepened the crying blue of day.

Between Vincent and Gauguin, the one a perfect volcano, the other boiling inwardly, a fierce struggle was preparing itself. At night, when they were too exhausted to sleep, too nervous to sit still, they spent all their energy on each other. Their money ran low. They had no way to amuse themselves. They found an outlet for their pent up passions in mutual exacerbation. Gauguin never tired of whipping Vincent into a rage and, when Vincent was at the height of his paroxysm, throwing into his face, *"Brigadier, vous avez raison!"*

"Vincent, no wonder you can't paint. Look at the disorder of this studio. Look at the mess in this colour box. My God, if your Dutch brain wasn't so fired with Daudet and Monticelli, maybe you could clean it out and get a little order into your life."

"That's nothing to you, Gauguin. This is my studio. You keep your studio any way you like."

"While we're on the subject, I may as well tell you that your mind is just as chaotic as your colour box. You admire every postage stamp painter in Europe, and yet you can't see that Degas . . ."

"Degas! What has he ever painted that can be held up alongside of a Millet?"

"Millet! That sentimentalist! That . . . !"

Vincent worked himself into a frenzy at this slur at Millet, whom he considered his master and spiritual father. He stormed after Gauguin from room to room. Gauguin fled. The house was small. Vincent shouted at him, harangued him, waved his fists in Gauguin's powerful face. Far into the tropical, oppressive night they kept up their bruising, battering conflict.

They both worked like fiends to catch themselves and nature at the point of fructification. Day after day they battled with their flaming palettes, night after night with each other's strident egos. When they were not quarrelling viciously, their friendly arguments were so explosive that it was impossible to summon sleep. Money came from Theo. They spent it immediately for tobacco and absinthe. It was too hot to eat. They thought absinthe would quiet their nerves. It only excited them the more.

A nasty, lashing mistral came up. It confined the men to the house. Gauguin could not work. He spent his time scourging Vincent into a continuous ebullition. He had never seen anyone grow so violent over mere ideas.

Vincent was the only sport Gauguin had. He made the most of it.

"Better quiet down, Vincent," he said after the fifth day of the mistral. He had baited his friend until the storm within the yellow house had made the howling mistral seem like a mild and gentle breeze.

"What about yourself, Gauguin?"

"It so happens, Vincent, that several men who have been a good deal in my company, and in the habit of discussing things with me, have gone mad."

"Are you threatening me?"

"No, I'm warning you."

"Then keep your warnings to yourself."

"All right, but don't blame me if anything happens."

"Oh, Paul, Paul, let's stop this eternal quarrelling. I know that you're a better painter than I am. I know that you can teach me a great deal. But I won't have you despising me, do you hear. I've slaved nine long years, and by Christ, I have something to say with this beastly paint! Now admit it, haven't I? Speak up, Gauguin."

"*Brigadier, vous avez raison!*"

The mistral died down. The Arlesians dared go out in the streets again. The blistering sun came back. An uncontainable fever settled over Arles. The police had to cope with crimes of violence. People walked about with a smouldering excitement in their eyes. No one ever laughed. No one talked. The stone roofs broiled under the sun. There were fights and knife flashes in the Place Lamartine. There was the smell of catastrophe in the air. Arles was too engorged to stand the strain any longer. The valley of the Rhône was about to burst into a million fragments.

Vincent thought of the Parisian journalist.

"Which will it be?" he asked himself. "An earthquake or a revolution."

In spite of it all, he still painted in the fields without a hat. He needed the white, blinding heat to make fluid within him the terrific passions he felt. His brain was a burning crucible, turning out red-hot canvas after canvas.

With each succeeding canvas he felt more keenly that all his nine years of labour were converging in these few surcharged weeks to make him, for one brief instant, the complete and perfect artist. He was by far surpassing his last summer's work. Never again would he produce paintings that so utterly expressed the essence of nature and the essence of himself.

He painted from four in the morning until night stole the scene from him. He created two, and sometimes even three complete pictures a day. He was spilling out a year of his life blood with every convulsive painting that he tore from his vitals. It was not the length of his stay on earth that mattered to him; it was what he did with the days of his life. For him time would have to be measured by the paintings he poured out, not by the fluttering leaves of a calendar.

He sensed that his art had reached a climax; that this was the high spot of his life, the moment toward which he had been striving all these years. He did not know how long it would last. He knew only that he had to paint pictures, and more pictures . . . and still more and more pictures. This climax of his life, this tiny point of infinity, had to be held, sustained, pushed out until he had created all those pictures that were gestating in his soul.

Painting all day, fighting all night, sleeping not at all, eating very little, glutting themselves with sun and colour, excitement, tobacco and absinthe, lacerated by the elements and their own drive of creation, lacerating each other with their rages and violence, their gorges mounted higher and higher.

The sun beat them. The mistral whipped them. The colour stabbed their eyes out. The absinthe swelled their empty bowels with turgescent fever. The yellow house rocked and throbbed with the tempest in the tropical, plethoric nights.

Gauguin did a portrait of Vincent while the latter was painting a still life of some ploughs. Vincent stared at the portrait. For the first time he understood clearly just what Gauguin thought of him.

"It is certainly I," he said. "But it is I gone mad!"

That evening they went to the café. Vincent ordered a light absinthe. Suddenly he flung the glass and the contents at Gauguin's head. Gauguin dodged. He picked Vincent up bodily in his arms. He carried him across the Place Lamartine. Vincent found himself in bed. He fell asleep instantly.

"My dear Gauguin," he said very calmly the next morning, "I have a vague memory that I offended you last evening."

"I forgive you gladly and with all my heart," said Gauguin, "but yesterday's scene might occur again. If I were struck I might lose control of myself and give you a choking. So permit me to write to your brother and tell him that I am coming back."

"No! No! Paul, you can't do that. Leave the yellow house? Everything in it I made for you."

During all the hours of the day the storm raged. Vincent fought desperately to keep Gauguin by his side. Gauguin resisted every plea. Vincent begged, cajoled, cursed, threatened, even wept. In this battle he proved to be the stronger. He felt that his whole life depended upon keeping his friend in the yellow house. By nightfall Gauguin was exhausted. He gave in just to get a little rest.

Every room in the yellow house was charged and vibrating with electrical tension. Gauguin could not sleep. Toward dawn he dozed off.

A queer sensation awakened him. He saw Vincent standing over his bed, glaring at him in the dark.

"What's the matter with you, Vincent?" he asked sternly.

Vincent walked out of the room, returned to his bed, and fell into a heavy sleep.

The following night Gauguin was jerked out of his sleep by the same strange sensation. Vincent was standing over his bed, staring at him in the dark.

"Vincent! Go to bed!"

Vincent turned away.

At supper the next day they fell into a fierce quarrel over the soup.

"You poured some paint into it, Vincent, while I wasn't looking!" shouted Gauguin.

Vincent laughed. He walked to the wall and wrote in chalk,

> *Je suis Saint Esprit*
> *Je suis sain d'esprit*

He was very quiet for several days. He looked moody and depressed. He hardly spoke a word to Gauguin. He did not even pick up a paint brush. He did not read. He sat in a chair and gazed ahead of him into space.

On the afternoon of the fourth day, when there was a vicious mistral, he asked Gauguin to take a walk with him.

"Let's go up to the park," he said. "I have something to tell you."

"Can't you tell me here, where we're comfortable?"

"No, I can't talk sitting down. I must walk."

"Very well, if you must."

They took the wagon road which wound up the left side of the town. To make progress they had to plunge through the mistral as though it were a thick, leathery substance. The cypresses in the park were being swayed almost to the ground.

"What is it you want to tell me?" demanded Gauguin.

He had to shout into Vincent's ear. The wind snatched away his words almost before Vincent could catch them.

"Paul, I've been thinking for the past few days. I've hit upon a wonderful idea."

"Forgive me if I'm a little leery of your wonderful ideas."

"We've all failed as painters. Do you know why?"

"What? I can't hear a word. Shout it in my ear."

"DO YOU KNOW WHY WE'VE ALL FAILED AS PAINTERS?"

"No. Why?"

"Because we paint alone!"

"What the devil?"

"Some things we paint well, some things we paint badly. We throw them all together in a single canvas."

"Brigadier, I'm hanging on your words."

"Do you remember the Both brothers? Dutch painters. One was good at landscape. The other was good at figures. They painted a picture together. One put in the landscape. The other put in the figures. They were successful."

"Well, to bring an interminable story to its obscure point?"

"What? I can't hear you. Come closer."

"I SAID, GO ON!"

"Paul. That's what we must do. You and I. Seurat. Cezanne. Lautrec. Rousseau. We must all work together on the same canvas. That would be a true painter's communism. We would each put in what we did best. Seurat the air. You the landscape. Cezanne the surfaces. Lautrec the figures. I the sun and moon and stars. Together we could be one great artist. What do you say?"

"*Turlututu, mon chapeau pointu!*"

He burst into raucous, savage laughter. The wind splashed his ridicule into Vincent's face like the spray of the sea.

"Brigadier," he cried, when he could catch his breath, "if that's not the world's greatest idea, I'll eat it. Pardon me while I howl."

He stumbled down the path, holding his stomach, doubled over with delight.

Vincent stood perfectly still.

A rush of blackbirds came out of the sky. Thousands of cawing, beating blackbirds. They swooped down on Vincent, struck him, engulfed him, flew through his hair, into his nose, into his mouth, into his ears, into his eyes, buried him in a thick, black, airless cloud of flapping wings.

Gauguin returned.

"Come on, Vincent, let's go down to Louis's. I feel the need of a celebration after that priceless idea of yours."

Vincent followed him to the Rue des Ricolettes in silence.

Gauguin went upstairs with one of the girls.

Rachel sat on Vincent's lap in the café room.

"Aren't you coming up with me, *fou-rou?*" she asked.

"No."

"Why not?"

"I haven't the five francs."

"Then will you give me your ear instead?"

"Yes."

After a very few moments, Gauguin returned. The two men walked down the hill to the yellow house. Gauguin bolted his supper. He walked out the front door without speaking. He had almost crossed the Place Lamartine when he heard behind him a well known step; short, quick, irregular.

He whirled about.

Vincent rushed upon him, an open razor in his hand.

Gauguin stood rigid and looked at Vincent.

Vincent stopped just two feet away. He glared at Gauguin in the dark. He lowered his head, turned, ran towards home.

Gauguin went to a hotel. He engaged a room, locked the door and went to bed.

Vincent entered the yellow house. He walked up the red brick stairs to his bedroom. He picked up the mirror in which he had painted his own portrait so many times. He set it on the toilet table against the wall.

He looked at his red-shot eyes in the mirror.

The end had come. His life was over. He read that in his face.

He had better make the clean break.

He lifted the razor. He felt the keen steel against the goose-flesh of his throat.

Voices were whispering strange tales to him.

The Arlesian sun threw a wall of blinding fire between his eyes and the glass.

He slashed off his right ear.

He left only a tiny portion of the lobe.

He dropped the razor. He bound his head in towels. The blood dripped onto the floor.

He picked up his ear from the basin. He washed it. He wrapped it in several pieces of drawing paper. He tied the bundle in newspaper.

He pulled a Basque beret down over the thick bandage. He walked down the stairs to the front door. He crossed the Place Lamartine, climbed the hill, rang the bell of the Maison de Tolérance, Numero I.

A maid answered the door.

"Send Rachel to me."

Rachel came in a moment.

"Oh, it's you, *fou-rou*. What do you want?"

"I have brought you something."

"For me? A present?"

"Yes."

"How nice you are, *fou-rou*."

"Guard it carefully. It is a souvenir of me."

"What is it?"

"Open, and you will see."

Rachel unwrapped the papers. She stared in horror at the ear. She fell in a dead faint on the flagstones.

Vincent turned away. He walked down the hill. He crossed the Place Lamartine. He closed the door of the yellow house behind him and went to bed.

When Gauguin returned at seven-thirty the following morning, he found a crowd gathered in front. Roulin was wringing his hands in despair.

"What have you done to your comrade, Monsieur?" asked a man in a melon shaped hat. His tone was abrupt and severe.

"I don't know."

"Oh, yes . . . you know very well . . . he is dead."

It took Gauguin a long time to gather his wits together. The stares of the crowd seemed to tear his person to pieces, suffocating him.

"Let us go upstairs, Monsieur," he said stammeringly. "We can explain ourselves there."

Wet towels lay on the floor of the two lower rooms. The blood had stained the stairway that led up to Vincent's bedroom.

In the bed lay Vincent, rolled in the sheets, humped up like a guncock. He seemed lifeless. Gently, very gently, Gauguin touched the body. It was warm. For Gauguin, it seemed as if he had suddenly got back all his energy, all his spirit.

"Be kind enough, Monsieur," he said in a low voice to the police superintendent, "to awaken this man with great care. If he asks for me, tell him I have left for Paris. The sight of me might prove fatal to him."

The police superintendent sent for a doctor and a cab. They took Vincent to the hospital. Roulin ran alongside of the carriage, panting.

9

Doctor Felix Rey, young interne of the hospital of Arles, was a short, thickset man with an octagonal head and a weed of black hair shooting up from the top of the octagon. He treated Vincent's wound, then put him to bed in a cell-like room from which everything had been removed. He locked the door behind him when he went out.

At sundown, when he was taking his patient's pulse, Vincent awoke. He stared at the ceiling, then the whitewashed wall, then out of the window at the patch of darkening blue sky. His eyes wandered slowly to Doctor Rey's face.

"Hello," he said, softly.

"Hello," replied Doctor Rey.

"Where am I?"

"You're in the hospital of Arles."

"Oh."

A flash of pain went across his face. He lifted his hand to where his right ear had once been. Doctor Rey stopped him.

"You mustn't touch," he said.

". . . Yes . . . I remember . . . now."

"It's a nice, clean wound, old fellow. I'll have you on your feet within a few days."

"Where is my friend?"

"He has returned to Paris."

". . . I see . . . May I have my pipe?"

"Not just yet, old fellow."

Doctor Rey bathed and bandaged the wound.

"It's an accident of very little importance," he said. "After all, a man doesn't hear with those cabbages he has stuck on the outside of his head. You won't miss it."

"You are very kind, Doctor. Why is this room . . . so bare?"

"I had everything taken out to protect you."

"Against whom?"

"Against yourself."

". . . Yes . . . I see . . ."

"Well, I must go now. I'll send the attendant in with your supper. Try to lie perfectly still. The loss of blood has made you weak."

When Vincent awoke in the morning, Theo was sitting by his bedside. Theo's face was pale and drawn, his eyes bloodshot.

"Theo," said Vincent.

Theo slipped off the chair, went on his knees beside the bed, and took Vincent's hand. He wept without shame or restraint.

"Theo . . . always . . . when I wake up . . . and need you . . . you're by my side."

Theo could not speak.

"It was cruel to make you come all the way down here. How did you know?"

"Gauguin telegraphed yesterday. I caught the night train."

"That was wrong of Gauguin to put you to all that expense. You sat up all night, Theo."

"Yes, Vincent."

They were silent for some time.

"I've spoken to Doctor Rey, Vincent. He says it was a sunstroke. You've been working in the sun without a hat, haven't you?"

"Yes."

"Well, you see, old boy, you mustn't. In the future you must wear your hat. Lots of people here in Arles get sunstroke."

Vincent squeezed his hand gently. Theo tried to swallow the lump in his throat.

"I have some news for you, Vincent, but I think it had better wait a few days."

"Is it nice news, Theo?"

"I think you'll like it."

Doctor Rey walked in.

"Well, how's the patient this morning?"

"Doctor, may my brother tell me some good news?"

"I should say so. Here, wait a minute. Let me look at this. Yes, that's fine, that's fine. It'll be healing fast, now."

When the Doctor left the room, Vincent begged for his news.

"Vincent," said Theo, "I've . . . well, I . . . I've met a girl."

"Why, Theo."

"Yes. She's a Dutch girl. Johanna Bunger. She's a lot like mother, I think."

"Do you love her, Theo?"

"Yes. I've been so desperately lonely without you in Paris, Vincent. It wasn't so bad before you came, but after we had lived together for a year . . ."

"I was hard to live with, Theo. I'm afraid I showed you a bad time."

"Oh, Vincent, if you only knew how many times I wished I could walk into the apartment on the Rue Lepic and find your shoes on the sideboard, and your wet canvases all over my bed. But we mustn't talk any more. You must rest. We'll just stay here with each other."

Theo remained in Arles two days. He left only when Doctor Rey assured him that Vincent would make a rapid recovery, and that he would take care of his brother, not only as a patient but as a friend.

Roulin came every evening and brought flowers. During the nights Vincent suffered from hallucinations. Doctor Rey put camphor on Vincent's pillow and mattress to overcome his insomnia.

At the end of the fourth day, when the Doctor saw that Vincent was completely rational, he unlocked the door of the room and had the furniture put back.

"May I get up and dress, Doctor?" asked Vincent.

"If you feel strong enough. Come to my office after you have had a little air."

The hospital of Arles was of two stories, built in a quadrangle, with a patio in the center, full of riotously coloured flowers, ferns, and gravel walks. Vincent strolled about slowly for a few minutes, then went to Doctor Rey's office on the ground floor.

"How does it feel to be on your feet?" asked the Doctor.

"Very good."

"Tell me, Vincent, why did you do it?"

Vincent was silent for a long time.

"I don't know," he said.

"What were you thinking of when you did it?"

". . . I . . . wasn't . . . thinking, Doctor."

Vincent spent the next few days recovering his strength. One morning, while he was chatting with Doctor Rey in the latter's room, he picked up a razor off the washstand and opened it.

"You need a shave, Doctor Rey," he said. "Would you like me to give you one?"

Doctor Rey backed into a corner, the palm of his hand out before his face.

"No! No! Put that down!"

"But I'm really a good barber, Doctor. I could give you a nice shave."

"Vincent! Put that razor down!"

Vincent laughed, closed the razor, and put it back on the washstand. "Don't be afraid, my friend. That's all over now."

At the end of the second week Doctor Rey gave Vincent permission to paint. An attendant was sent down to the yellow house to get the easel and canvas. Doctor Rey posed for Vincent just to humour him. Vincent worked slowly, a tiny bit each day. When the portrait was finished he presented it to the Doctor.

"I want you to keep this as a souvenir of me, Doctor. It is the only way I have of showing my gratitude for your kindness."

"That is very nice of you, Vincent. I am honoured."

The Doctor took the portrait home and used it to cover a crack in the wall.

Vincent stayed at the hospital two weeks longer. He painted the patio, baking in the sun. He wore a wide straw hat while he worked. The flower garden took him the full two weeks to paint.

"You must drop in to see me every day," said Doctor Rey, shaking hands with Vincent at the front gate of the hospital. "And remember, no absinthe, no excitement, and no working in the sun without that hat."

"I promise, Doctor. And thank you for everything."

"I shall write your brother that you are now completely well."

Vincent found that the landlord had made a contract to turn him out and give the yellow house to a tobacconist. Vincent was deeply attached to the yellow house. It was his sole root in the soil of Provence. He had painted every inch of it, inside and out. He had made it habitable. In spite of the accident, he still considered it his permanent home, and he was determined to fight the landlord to the bitter end.

At first he was afraid to sleep alone in the house because of his insomnia, which not even the camphor could overcome. Doctor Rey had given him bromide of potassium to rout the unbearable hallucinations that had been frightening him. At length the voices that had been whispering queer tales in his ears went away, to come back only in nightmares.

He was still far too weak to go out and work. The serenity returned but slowly to his brain. His blood revived from day to day and his appetite increased. He had a gay dinner with Roulin at the restaurant, quite cheerful and with no dread of renewed suffering. He began working gingerly on a portrait of Roulin's wife, which had been unfinished at the time of the accident. He liked the way he had ranged the reds from rose to orange, rising through the yellows to lemon, with light and sombre greens.

His health and his work picked up slowly. He had known before that one could fracture one's legs and arms, and after that recover, but he was rather astonished that one could fracture the brain in one's head and recover after that, too.

One afternoon he went to ask after Rachel's health.

"Pigeon," he said, "I'm sorry for all the trouble I caused you."

"It's all right, *fou-rou*. You mustn't worry about it. In this town things like that are not out of the way."

His friends came in and assured him that in Provence everyone suffered either from fever, hallucinations or madness.

"It's nothing unusual, Vincent," said Roulin. "Down here in Tartarin's country we are all a trifle cracked."

"Well, well," said Vincent, "we understand each other like members of the same family."

A few more weeks passed. Vincent was now able to work all day in the studio. Thoughts of madness and death left his mind. He began to feel almost normal.

Finally he ventured out of doors to paint. The sun was burning up the magnificent yellow of the cornfields. But Vincent could not capture it. He had been eating regularly, sleeping regularly, avoiding excitement and intense enthusiasm.

He was feeling so normal he could not paint.

"You are a *grand nerveux,* Vincent," Doctor Rey had told him. "You never have been normal. But then, no artist is normal; if he were, he wouldn't be an artist. Normal men don't create works of art. They eat, sleep, hold down routine jobs, and die. You are hypersensitive to life and nature; that's why you are able to interpret for the rest of us. But if you are not careful, that very hypersensitiveness will lead you to your destruction. The strain of it breaks every artist in time."

Vincent knew that to attain the high yellow note which dominated his Arlesian canvases he had to be on edge, strung up, throbbingly excited, passionately sensitive, his nerves rasped raw.

If he allowed himself to get into that state, he could paint again as brilliantly as he had before. But the road led to destruction.

"An artist is a man with his work to do," he murmured to himself. "How stupid for me to remain alive if I can't paint the way I want to paint."

He walked in the fields without his hat, absorbing the power of the sun. He drank in the mad colours of the sky, the yellow ball of fire, the green fields and bursting flowers. He let the mistral lash him, the thick night sky throttle him, the sunflowers whip his imagination to a bursting point. As his excitement rose, he lost his appetite for food. He began to live on coffee, absinthe, and tobacco. He lay awake nights with the deep colours of the country-side rushing past his bloodshot eyes. And at last he loaded his easel on his back and went into the fields.

His powers came back; his sense of the universal rhythm of nature, his ability to smash off a large canvas in a few hours and flood it with glaring, brilliant sunshine. Each day saw a new picture created; each day saw a rise in his emotional gauge. He painted thirty-seven canvases without a pause.

One morning he awoke feeling lethargic. He could not work. He sat on a chair. He stared at a wall. He hardly moved all through the day. The voices came back to his ears and told him queer, queer tales. When night fell he walked to the grey restaurant and sat down at a little table. He ordered soup. The waitress brought it to him. A voice rang sharply in his ear, warning him.

He swept the plate of soup to the floor. The dish smashed in fragments.

"You're trying to poison me!" he screamed. "You put poison in that soup!"

He jumped to his feet and kicked over the table. Some of the customers ran out the door. Others stared at him agape.

"You're all trying to poison me!" he shouted. "You want to murder me! I saw you put poison in that soup!"

Two gendarmes came in and carried him bodily up the hill to the hospital.

After twenty-four hours he became quite calm and discussed the affair with Doctor Rey. He worked a little each day, took walks in the country, returned to the hospital for his supper and sleep. Sometimes he had moods of indescribable mental anguish, sometimes moments when the veil of time and of inevitable circumstance seemed for the twinkling of an eye to be parted.

Doctor Rey allowed him to paint again. Vincent did an orchard of peach trees beside a road, with the Alps in the background; an olive grove with leaves of old silver, silver turning to green against the blue, and with orange-coloured ploughed earth.

After three weeks, Vincent returned to the yellow house. By now the town, and especially the Place Lamartine, was incensed against him. The severed ear and the poisoned soup were more then they could accept with equanimity. The Arlesians were firmly convinced that painting drove men mad. When Vincent passed they stared at him, made remarks out loud, sometimes even crossed the street so as to avoid passing him.

Not a restaurant in the city would allow him to enter the front door. The children of Arles gathered before the yellow house and made up games to torment him.

"*Fou-rou! Fou-rou!*" they cried out. "Cut off your other ear."

Vincent locked his windows. The shouts and laughter of the children drifted through.

"*Fou-rou! Fou-rou!*"

"Crazy man! Crazy man!"

They made up a little song which they sang beneath his window.

> Fou-rou *was a crazy man*
> *Who cut off his right ear.*
> *Now no matter how you shout,*
> *The crazy man can't hear.*

Vincent tried going out to escape them. They followed him through the streets, into the fields, a jolly crowd of singing and laughing urchins.

Day after day their number increased as they gathered before the yellow house. Vincent stuffed his ears with cotton. He worked at his easel, making duplicates of his pictures. The words of the children came through the cracks and the walls. They seared into his brain.

The young boys became more bold. They clambered up the drain pipes like little monkeys, sat on the window sills, peered into the room and shouted at Vincent's back.

"*Fou-rou*, cut off your other ear. We want your other ear!"

The tumult in the Place Lamartine increased. The boys put up boarding on which they could climb to the second floor. They broke the windows, poked their heads in, threw things at Vincent. The crowd below encouraged them, echoed their songs and shouts.

"Get us the other ear. We want the other ear!"

"*Fou-rou!* Want some candy? Look out, it's poisoned!"

"*Fou-rou!* Want some soup? Look out, it's poisoned!"

> Fou-rou *was a crazy man*
> *Who cut off his right ear.*
> *Now no matter how you shout,*
> *The crazy man can't hear.*

The boys perched on the window sill led the crowd below in a chant. Together, they sang with an ever rising crescendo.

"*Fou-rou, fou-rou*, throw us your ear, throw us your ear!"

"*FOU-ROU, FOU-ROU*, THROW US YOUR EAR, THROW US YOUR EAR!"

Vincent lurched up from his easel. There were three urchins sitting on his window sill, chanting. He lashed out at them. They scampered down the boarding. The crowd below roared. Vincent stood at the window, looking down at them.

A rush of blackbirds came out of the sky, thousands of cawing, beating blackbirds. They darkened the Place Lamartine, swooped down on Vincent, struck him, filled the room, engulfed him, flew through his hair, into his nose and mouth and eyes, buried him in a thick, black, airless cloud of flapping wings.

Vincent jumped onto the window sill.

"Go way!" he screamed. "You fiends, go way! For God's sake, leave me in peace!"

"*FOU-ROU, FOU-ROU*, THROW US YOUR EAR, THROW US YOUR EAR!"

"Go way! Let me alone! Do you hear, let me alone!"

He picked up the wash basin from the table and flung it down at them. It smashed on the cobblestones below. He ran about in a rage picking up everything he could lay his hands on and flinging them down into the Place Lamartine to be hopelessly smashed. His chairs, his easel, his mirror, his table, his bedclothing, his sunflower canvases from the walls, all rained down on the urchins of Provence. And with each article there went a flashing panorama of his days in the yellow house, of the sacrifices he had made to buy, one by one, these simple articles with which he was to furnish the house of his life.

When he had laid the room bare, he stood by the window, every nerve quivering. He fell across the sill. His head hung down toward the cobblestone Place.

10

A petition was immediately circulated in the Place Lamartine. Ninety men and women signed it.

To Mayor Tardieu:
We, the undersigned citizens of Arles, are firmly convinced that Vincent Van Gogh, resident at Place Lamartine, 2, is a dangerous lunatic, not fit to be left at large.
We hereby call upon you as our Mayor to have this madman locked up.

It was very close to election time in Arles. Mayor Tardieu did not wish to displease so many voters. He ordered the superintendent of police to arrest Vincent.

The gendarmes found him lying on the floor below the window sill. They carried him off to jail. He was put in a cell, under lock and key. A keeper was stationed outside his door.

When Vincent returned to consciousness, he asked to see Doctor Rey. He was refused permission. He asked for pencil and paper to write Theo. It was refused.

At length Doctor Rey gained entrance to the jail.

"Try to restrain your indignation, Vincent," he said, "otherwise they will convict you of being a dangerous lunatic, and that will be the end of you. Besides, strong emotion can only aggravate your case. I will write to your brother, and between us we will get you out of here."

"I beg you, Doctor, don't let Theo come down here. He's just going to be married. It will spoil everything for him."

"I'll tell him not to come. I think I have a good plan for you."

Two days later Doctor Rey came back. The keeper was still stationed in front of the cell.

"Listen, Vincent," he said, "I just watched them move you out of your yellow house. The landlord stored your furniture in the basement of one of the cafés, and he has your paintings under lock and key. He says he won't give them up until you pay the back rent."

Vincent was silent.

"Since you can't go back there, I think you had better try to work out my plan. There is no telling how often these epileptic fits will come back on you. If you have peace and quiet and pleasant surroundings, and don't excite yourself, you may have seen the last of them. On the other hand, they may recur every month or two. So to protect yourself, and others about you . . . I think it would be advisable . . . to go into . . ."

". . . A *maison de santé?*"

"Yes."

"Then you think I am . . . ?"

"No, my dear Vincent, you are not. You can see for yourself that you are as sane as I. But these epileptic fits are like any other kind of fever. They make a man go out of his head. And when a nervous crisis comes on, you naturally do irrational things. That's why you ought to be in a hospital, where you can be looked after."

"I see."

"There is a good place in St. Remy, just twenty-five kilometres from here. It's called St. Paul de Mausole. They take first, second, and third-class patients. The third class is a hundred francs a month. You could manage that. The place was formerly a monastery, right up against the base of the hills. It is beautiful, Vincent, and quiet, oh, so quiet. You will have a doctor to advise you, and sisters to take care of you. The food will be plain and good. You will be able to recover your health."

"Would I be allowed to paint?"

"Why, of course, old fellow. You'll be allowed to do whatever you wish . . . providing it doesn't injure you. It will be just like being in a hospital with enormous grounds. If you live quietly that way for a year, you may be completely cured."

"But how will I get out of this hole?"

"I have spoken to the superintendent of police. He agrees to let you go to St. Paul de Mausole, providing I take you there."

"And you say it is really a nice place?"

"Oh, charming, Vincent. You'll find loads of things to paint."

"How nice. A hundred francs a month isn't so much. Perhaps that's just what I need for a year, to quiet me down."

"Of course it is. I have already written to your brother, telling him about it. I suggested that in your present state of health it would be inadvisable to move you very far; certainly not to Paris. I told him that in my opinion St. Paul would be the very best thing for you."

"Well, if Theo agrees . . . Anything, just so long as I don't cause him more trouble . . ."

"I expect an answer any hour. I'll come back when I get it."

Theo had no alternative. He acquiesced. He sent money to pay his brother's bills. Doctor Rey took Vincent in a carriage to the station where they boarded the train for Tarascon. At Tarascon they took a little branch line that wound up a green, fertile valley to St. Remy.

It was two kilometres up a steep hill, through the sleeping town, to St.

Paul de Mausole. Vincent and Doctor Rey hired a carriage. The road led straight to a ridge of black, barren mountains. From a short way off Vincent saw, nestled at their base, the sod-brown walls of the monastery.

The carriage stopped. Vincent and Doctor Rey got out. On the right of the road there was a cleared, circular space with a Temple of Vesta and a Triumphal Arch.

"How in the world did these get here?" demanded Vincent.

"This used to be an important Roman settlement. The river, which you see down there, once filled this whole valley. It came right up to where you're standing. As the river receded, the town crawled lower and lower down the hill. Now nothing is left here except these dead monuments, and the monastery."

"Interesting."

"Come, Vincent, Doctor Peyron is expecting us."

They left the road and walked through a patch of pines to the gate of the monastery. Doctor Rey pulled an iron knob which sounded a loud bell. After a few moments the gate opened and Doctor Peyron appeared.

"How do you do, Doctor Peyron?" said Doctor Rey. "I have brought you my friend, Vincent Van Gogh, as we arranged by mail. I know that you will take good care of him."

"Yes, Doctor Rey, we will take care of him."

"You will forgive me if I run, Doctor? I just have time to catch that train back to Tarascon."

"Of course, Doctor Rey. I understand."

"Good-bye, Vincent," said Doctor Rey. "Be happy, and you will get well. I will come to see you as often as I can. By the end of a year I expect to find you a completely well man."

"Thank you, Doctor. You are very kind. Good-bye."

"Good-bye, Vincent."

He turned and walked away through the pines.

"Will you come in, Vincent?" asked Doctor Peyron, stepping aside.

Vincent walked past Doctor Peyron.

The gate of the insane asylum locked behind him.

BOOK SEVEN

ST. REMY

1

THE WARD in which the inmates slept was like a third-class waiting room in some dead-alive village. The lunatics always wore their hats, spectacles, canes, and travelling cloaks, just as though they were on the point of leaving for somewhere.

Sister Deschanel brought Vincent through the long corridor-like room and indicated an empty bed.

"You will sleep here, Monsieur," she said. "At night you will pull the curtains for privacy. Doctor Peyron wishes to see you in his office when you are settled."

The eleven men sitting about the unlit stove neither noticed nor commented upon Vincent's arrival. Sister Deschanel walked down the long narrow room, her starched white gown, black cape, and black veil standing out stiffly behind her.

Vincent dropped his valise and looked about. Both sides of the ward were lined with beds sloping downward at an angle of five degrees, each surrounded by a framework on which were hung dirty cream-coloured curtains. The roof was of rough beams, the walls were whitewashed, and in the centre was a stove with an angular pipe coming out of its left side. There was a lone lamp in the room, hung just above the stove.

Vincent wondered why the men were so quiet. They did not speak to each other. They did not read or play games. They leaned on their walking sticks and looked at the stove.

There was a box nailed to the wall by the head of his bed, but Vincent preferred to keep his belongings in his valise. He put his pipe, tobacco, and a book in the box, shoved the valise under the bed and walked out into the garden. On the way he passed a row of dark, dank looking rooms, locked tight and abandoned.

The patio cloister was utterly deserted. There were large pines beneath which grew tall and unkempt grass mixed with rampant weeds. The walls enclosed a square of stagnant sunlight. Vincent turned to his left and knocked on the door of the private house in which Doctor Peyron and his family lived.

Doctor Peyron had been a *médecin de marine* at Marseilles, after that an oculist. A severe case of gout had caused him to search for a *maison de santé* in the quiet of the country.

"You see, Vincent," said the Doctor, gripping a corner of the desk with each hand, "formerly I took care of the health of the body. At present I take care of the health of the soul. It is the same *metier*."

"You have had experience with nervous diseases, Doctor. Can you explain why I cut off my ear?"

"That is not at all unusual with epileptics, Vincent. I have had two similar cases. The auditory nerves become extremely sensitive, and the patient thinks he can stop the hallucinations by cutting off the auricle."

". . . Oh . . . I see. And the treatments I am to have . . . ?"

"Treatments? Well . . . ah . . . you must have at least two hot baths a week. I insist upon that. And you must stay in the baths for two hours. They will calm you."

"And what else am I to do, Doctor?"

"You are to remain perfectly quiet. You must not excite yourself. Do not work, do not read, do not argue or get upset."

"I know . . . I am too weak to work."

"If you do not wish to participate in the religious life of St. Paul, I will tell the sisters not to insist upon it. If there is anything you need, come to me."

"Thank you, Doctor."

"Supper is at five. You will hear the gong. Try to fit into the pattern of the hospital, Vincent, as quickly as you can. It will speed your recovery."

Vincent stumbled through the chaotic garden, passed the crumbling portico at the entrance to the third-class building, and walked by the row of dark, deserted cells. He sat on his bed in the ward. His companions were still sitting about the stove in silence. After a time he heard a noise from another room. The eleven men rose with an air of grim determination and stormed down the ward. Vincent followed them.

The room in which they ate had an earthen floor and no window. There was just one long, rough, wooden table with benches about it. The sisters served the food. It tasted mouldy, as in a shoddy boarding house. First there was soup and black bread; the cockroaches in the soup made Vincent homesick for the restaurants of Paris. Next he was served a dish of chick peas, beans, and lentils. His companions ate with all their might, brushing the crumbs of black bread from the table into their hands, and then licking them off with their tongues.

The meal finished, the men returned to the identical chairs about the stove and digested their food with intense concentration. When the supper had gone down, they rose one by one, undressed, pulled the curtains and went to sleep. Vincent had not as yet heard them utter a sound.

The sun was just setting. Vincent stood at the window and looked over the green valley. There was a superb sky of pale lemon, against which the mournful pines stood out in designs of exquisite black lace. The sight moved Vincent to nothing, not even the faint desire to paint it.

He stood at the window until the heavy Provençal dusk filtered through the lemon sky and absorbed the colour. No one came into the ward to light the lamp. There was nothing to do in the darkness but think of one's life.

Vincent undressed and went to bed. He lay there wide-eyed, staring at the rough beams of the ceiling. The angle of the bed pitched him downward toward the base. He had brought Delacroix's book with him. He fumbled in the box, found it and held the leather covering against his heart in the darkness. The feel of it reassured him. He did not belong with these lunatics who surrounded him, but with the great master whose words of wisdom and comfort flowed through the stiff binding and into his aching heart.

After a time he fell asleep. He was awakened by a low moaning in the bed next to his. The moans became louder and louder, until they broke into cries and a flood of vehement words.

"Go away! Stop following me! Why do you follow me? I didn't kill him! You can't fool me. I know who you are. You're the secret police! Well, search me if you like! I didn't steal that money! He murdered himself on Wednesday! Go way! For God's sake, leave me alone!"

Vincent jumped up and pushed aside the curtain. He saw a blond haired young boy of twenty-three, tearing at his nightgown with his teeth. When the boy saw Vincent, he sprang to his knees and clasped his hands fervently before him.

"Monsieur Mounet-Sully, don't take me away! I didn't do it, I tell you! I'm not a sodomist! I'm a lawyer! I'll handle all your cases, Monsieur Mounet-Sully, only don't arrest me! I couldn't have killed him last Wednesday! I haven't the money! Look! It isn't here!"

He tore the covers off him and began ripping up the bed in a paroxysm of maniacal frenzy, crying out all the while against the secret police and the false accusations against him. Vincent did not know what to do. All the other inmates seemed to be sleeping soundly.

Vincent ran to the next bed, slipped aside the curtain and shook the man in it. The fellow opened his eyes and stared at Vincent stupidly.

"Get up and help me quiet him," said Vincent. "I'm afraid he will do himself some harm."

The man in bed began to dribble at the right corner of his mouth. He let out a stream of blubbering, inarticulate sounds.

"Quick," cried Vincent. "It will take two of us to hold him down."

He felt a hand on his shoulder. He whirled about. One of the older men was standing behind him.

"No use bothering with this one," said the man. "He's an idiot. Hasn't uttered a word since he's been here. Come, we'll quiet the boy."

The young blond had dug a hole in the mattress with his fingernails and was crouched on his knees above it, pulling out the straw and stuffing. When he saw Vincent again, he began shouting legal quotations. He beat his hands against Vincent's chest.

"Yes, yes, I killed him! I killed him! But it wasn't for pederasty! I didn't do that, Monsieur Mounet-Sully. Not last Wednesday. It was for his money! Look! I have it! I hid the wallet in the mattress! I'll find it for you! Only make the secret police stop following me! I can go free, even if I did kill him! I'll cite you cases to prove . . . Here! I'll dig it out of the mattress!"

"Take his other arm," said the old man to Vincent.

They held the boy down on the bed, but his ravings rang out for over an hour. Finally, exhausted, his words sank to a jarred mumbling and he dropped off in a feverish sleep. The older man came around to Vincent's side.

"The boy was studying for the bar," he said. "He overworked his brain. These attacks come on about every ten days. He never hurts anyone. Good night to you, Monsieur."

The older man returned to his bed and promptly fell asleep. Vincent went once again to the window that overlooked the valley. It was still a long time before sunrise and nothing was visible but the morning star. He remembered the painting Daubigny had made of the morning star, expressing all the vast peace and majesty of the universe . . . and all the feeling of heartbreak for the puny individual who stood below, gazing at it.

2

The next morning after breakfast the men went out into the garden. Beyond the far wall could be seen the ridge of desolate, barren hills, dead since the Romans first crossed them. Vincent watched the inmates play lackadaisically at bowls. He sat on a stone bench and gazed at the thick trees covered with ivy, then at the ground dotted with periwinkle. The sisters, of the order of St. Joseph d'Aubenas, passed on their way to the old Roman chapel, mouse-like figures in black and white, their eyes drawn deep into their heads, fingering their beads and mumbling the morning prayers.

After an hour at mute bowls, the men returned to the cool of their ward. They sat about the unlit stove. Their utter idleness appalled Vincent. He could not understand why they did not even have an old newspaper to read.

When he could bear it no longer, he went again into the garden and walked about. Even the sun at St. Paul seemed to be moribund.

The buildings of the old monastery had been put up in the conventional quadrangle; on the north was the ward of the third-class patients; on the east Doctor Peyron's house, the chapel, and a tenth century cloister; on the south the buildings of the first and second-class inmates; and on the west, the courtyard of the dangerous lunatics, and a long, dead-clay wall. The locked and barred gate was the only exit. The walls were twelve feet high, smooth and unscalable.

Vincent returned to a stone bench near a wild rose bush and sat down. He tried to reason with himself and get a clear idea of why he had come to St. Paul. A terrible dismay and horror seized him and prevented him from thinking. In his heart he could find neither hope nor desire.

He stumbled toward his quarters. The moment he entered the portico of the building he heard the queer howling of a dog. Before he reached the door of the ward, the noise had changed from the howl of a dog to the cry of a wolf.

Vincent walked down the length of the ward. In the far corner, his face to the wall, he saw the old man of the night before. The man's face was raised to the ceiling. He was howling with all the strength of his lungs, a bestial look on his face. The cry of the wolf gave way to some strange jungle call. The mournful sound of it flooded the room.

"What sort of a menagerie am I a prisoner in?" Vincent demanded of himself.

The men about the stove paid no attention. The wails of the animal in the corner rose to a pitch of despair.

"I must do something for him," said Vincent, aloud.

The blond boy stopped him.

"It is better to leave him alone," he said. "If you speak to him, he will fly into a rage. It will be over in a few hours."

The walls of the monastery were thick, but all through lunch Vincent could hear the changing cries of the afflicted one straining through the vast silence. He spent the afternoon in a far corner of the garden, trying to escape the frenetic wails.

That night at supper, a young man whose left side was paralyzed, grabbed up a knife, sprang to his feet, and held the knife over his heart with his right hand.

"The time has come!" he shouted. "I shall kill myself!"

The man on his right side rose wearily and gripped the paralytic's arm.

"Not today, Raymond," he said. "Today is Sunday."

"Yes, yes, today! I won't live! I refuse to live! Let go of my arm! I want to kill myself!"

"Tomorrow, Raymond, tomorrow. This isn't the right day."

"Let go of my arm! I shall plunge this knife into my heart! I tell you, I've got to kill myself!"

"I know, I know, but not now. Not now."

He took the knife from Raymond's hand and led him, weeping in a rage of impotence, back to the ward.

Vincent turned to the man next to him, whose red-rimmed eyes were watching his trembling fingers anxiously as he tried to carry the soup to his mouth.

"What is the matter with him?" he asked.

The syphilitic lowered his spoon and said, "Not a day has passed for a whole year that Raymond has not tried to commit suicide."

"Why does he try it here?" asked Vincent. "Why doesn't he steal the knife and kill himself when everyone has gone to sleep?"

"Perhaps he does not wish to die, Monsieur."

While Vincent was watching them play bowls the following morning, one of the men suddenly fell to the ground and went into a convulsive paroxysm.

"Quick. It's his epileptic fit," shouted someone.

"On his arms and legs."

It took four of them to hold his arms and legs. The writhing epileptic seemed to have the strength of a dozen men. The young blond reached into his pocket, pulled out a spoon, and thrust it between the prostrate man's teeth.

"Here, hold his head," he cried to Vincent.

The epileptic went through a rising and falling series of convulsions, their peaks mounting ever higher and higher. His eyes rolled in their sockets and the foam lathered from the corners of his mouth.

"Why do you hold that spoon in his mouth?" grunted Vincent.

"So he won't bite his tongue."

After a half hour the shuddering man sank into unconsciousness. Vincent and two of the others carried him to his bed. That was the end of the affair; no one mentioned it again.

By the end of a fortnight, Vincent had seen every one of his eleven companions go through his own particular form of insanity: the noisy maniac who tore his clothes off his body and smashed everything in sight; the man who howled like an animal; the two syphilitics; the suicidal monomaniac; the paralytics who suffered from excess of fury and exaltation; the epileptic; the lymphomaniac with a persecution mania; the young blond who was being pursued by secret police.

Not a day went by without some one of them having a seizure; not a day passed but that Vincent was called to calm some momentary maniac. The third-class patients had to be each other's doctors and nurses. Peyron looked in but once a week, and the guardians bothered only with the first and second-class residents. The men stayed close together, helped each other in the moments of affliction, and had endless patience; each of them knew that his turn was coming again, soon, and that he would need the help and forebearance of his neighbours.

It was a fraternity of *fous*.

Vincent was glad that he had come. By seeing the truth about the life of madmen he slowly lost the vague dread, the fear of insanity. Bit by bit he came to consider madness as a disease like any other. By the third week he found his comates no more frightening than if they had been stricken by consumption or cancer.

He often sat and chatted with the idiot. The idiot could only answer with incoherent sounds, but Vincent felt that the fellow understood him and was pleased to be talking. The sisters never spoke to the men unless it was imperative. Vincent's portion of rational intercourse each week consisted of his five minute conversation with Doctor Peyron.

"Tell me, Doctor," he said, "why do the men never talk to each other? Some of them seem intelligent enough, when they are well."

"They can't talk, Vincent, for the minute they begin to talk, they argue, get excited, and bring a seizure upon themselves. So they've learned that the only way they can live is by remaining utterly quiet."

"They might just as well be dead, mightn't they?"

Peyron shrugged. "That, my dear Vincent, is a matter of opinion."

"But why don't they at least read. I should think that books . . ."

"Reading starts their minds churning, Vincent, and the first thing we know, they have a violent attack. No, my friend, they must inhabit the closed world of their own. There is no need to feel sorry for them. Don't you remember what Dryden said? 'There is pleasure, sure, in being mad, which none but madmen know.'"

A month passed. Not once did Vincent have the least desire to be elsewhere. Nor did he notice in any of the others a definite wish to get away. He knew this came from the feeling that they were all too thoroughly shattered for the life outside.

And over the ward hung the fetid odour of decaying men.

Vincent held the spirit of himself together rigidly, against that day when the desire and strength to paint should return to him. His fellow inmates vegetated in idleness, thinking only of their three meals a day. In order to discipline himself against this surrender, Vincent refused to eat any of the stale and slightly spoiled food. He swallowed only a little black bread and soup. Theo sent him a one-volume edition of Shakespeare; he read "Richard II," "Henry IV," and "Henry V," projecting his mind to other days and other places.

He fought valiantly to keep grief from gathering in his heart like water in a swamp.

Theo was now married. He and his wife Johanna wrote to Vincent often. Theo's health was poor. Vincent worried more about his brother than he did about himself. He begged Johanna to give Theo wholesome Dutch food once more, after ten years of restaurant fare.

Vincent knew that work distracted him infinitely better than anything else, and that if he could only throw himself into it with all his strength, it might possibly be the best remedy. The men in the ward had nothing to save them from a rotting death; he had his painting which would take him out of the asylum a well and happy man.

At the end of the sixth week, Doctor Peyron gave Vincent a little room for a studio. It was done in greenish-grey paper, and had two curtains of sea-green with a design of very pale roses. The curtains, and an old armchair covered with an upholstery splashed like a Monticelli, had been left behind by one of the wealthier inmates who had died. The room looked out on a slanting cornfield, and freedom. There were thick black bars across the window.

Vincent promptly painted the landscape that he saw from the window. In the foreground was a field of corn ruined and dashed to the ground after a storm. A boundary wall ran down a slope, and beyond the grey foliage of a few olive trees were some huts and hills. At the top of the canvas Vincent put a great grey and white cloud drowned in the azure.

He returned to the ward at supper time, exultant. His power had not left him. He had come face to face with nature again. The feeling for work had held him and forced him to create.

The insane asylum could not kill him now. He was on the road to recovery. In a few months he would be out. He would be free to return to Paris and his old friends. Life was beginning for him once more. He wrote Theo a long, tumultuous letter, with demands for pigments, canvas, brushes, and interesting books.

The next morning the sun came out, yellow and hot. The cicadas in the garden began to sing with a harsh cry, ten times stronger than that of the crickets. Vincent took his easel out and painted the pine trees, the bushes and the walks. His ward mates came to look over his shoulder, but remained perfectly silent and respectful.

"They have better manners than the good people of Arles," murmured Vincent to himself.

Late that afternoon he went to see Doctor Peyron. "I am feeling perfectly well, Doctor, and I should like your permission to go outside the grounds to paint."

"Yes, you are certainly looking better, Vincent. The baths and quiet have helped you. But don't you think it a bit dangerous to go out so soon?"

"Dangerous? Why, no. How?"

"Suppose you . . . had an attack . . . in the fields . . . ?"

Vincent laughed. "No more attacks for me, Doctor. I'm through with them. I feel better than I did before they began."

"No, Vincent, I'm afraid . . ."

"Please, Doctor. If I can go wherever I wish, and paint the things I love, don't you see how much happier I will be?"

"Well, if work is what you need . . ."

And so the gate was unlocked for Vincent. He loaded his easel on his back and went in search of pictures. He spent whole days in the hills behind the asylum. The cypress trees about St. Remy began to occupy his thoughts. He wanted to make something of them, like his sunflower canvases. It astonished him that they had not yet been painted as he saw them. He found them as beautiful in line and proportion as an Egyptian obelisk; splashes of black in a sunny landscape.

The old habits of the Arlesian days returned. Each morning at sunrise he trudged out with a blank canvas; each sundown saw it transcribed from nature. If there was any lessening of his power and ability, he could not perceive it. Every day he felt stronger, more sensitive, surer of himself.

Now that he was again master of his own destiny, he no longer feared eating at the asylum board. He devoured his food avidly, even the cockroach soup. He needed food for his working strength. He had nothing to fear now. He was in complete control of himself.

When he had been in the asylum three months, he found a cypress motif that lifted him out of his troubles, beyond all the suffering he had endured. The trees were massive. The foreground was low with brambles and brushwood. Behind were some violet hills, a green and rose sky with a decrescent moon. He painted the clump of brambles in the foreground very thick, with touches of yellow, violet and green. When he looked at his canvas that night he knew that he had come up out of the pit and was standing once more on solid earth, his face to the sun.

In his overwhelming joy he saw himself once again a free man.

Theo sent some extra money, so Vincent secured permission to go to Arles and recover his pictures. The people in the Place Lamartine were courteous to him, but the sight of the yellow house made him very ill. He thought he was going to faint. Instead of visiting Roulin and Doctor Rey, as he had planned, he went in search of the landlord, who had his pictures.

Vincent did not return to the asylum that night as he had promised. The following day he was found between Tarascon and St. Remy, lying face downward in a ditch.

3

Fever clouded his mind for three weeks. The men in the ward, whom he had pitied because their attacks were recurrent, were very patient with him. When he recovered sufficiently to realize what had happened, he kept repeating to himself.

"It is abominable. It is abominable!"

Toward the end of the third week, when he was beginning to walk about the barren, corridor-like room for a little exercise, the sisters brought in a new patient. He allowed himself to be led to his bed very docilely, but once the sisters were gone, he broke into a violent rage. He ripped all the clothes off his body and tore them to shreds, shouting at the top of his voice all the time. He clawed his bed to pieces, smashed the box nailed to the wall, pulled down the curtains, broke the frame, and kicked his valise into a shapeless mass.

The inmates never touched a newcomer. At length two guardians came and hauled the maniac away. He was locked in a cell down the corridor. He howled like a savage beast for two weeks. Vincent heard him night and day. Then the cries ceased altogether. Vincent watched the guardians bury the man in the little cemetery behind the chapel.

A terrible fit of depression came over Vincent. The more his health returned to normal, the more his brain could reason in cold blood, the more foolish it seemed to him to go on painting when it cost so much and brought in nothing. And yet if he did not work, he could not live.

Doctor Peyron gave him some meat and wine from his own table, but refused to let him go near his studio. Vincent did not mind so long as he was convalescing, but when his strength returned and he found himself condemned to the intolerable idleness of his companions, he revolted.

"Doctor Peyron," he said, "my work is necessary for me to recover. If you make me sit about in idleness, like those madmen, I shall become one of them."

"I know, Vincent, but it was working so hard that brought on your attack. I must keep you from that excitement."

"No, Doctor, it wasn't work. It was going to Arles that did it. I no sooner saw the Place Lamartine and the yellow house, than I became ill. But if I never go back there again, I'll never have another attack. Please let me go to my studio."

"I am unwilling to take the responsibility in this matter. I shall write to your brother. If he gives his consent, then we'll let you work again."

The return letter from Theo, urging Doctor Peyron to allow Vincent to paint, brought a revivifying piece of news. Theo was to become a father. The news made Vincent feel as happy and strong as he had before the last attack. He sat down immediately and wrote Theo a glowing letter.

"Do you know what I hope, Theo? It is that a family will be for you what nature, the clods of earth, the grass, the yellow corn, and the peasants are for me. The baby that Johanna is designing for you will give you a grip on reality that is otherwise impossible in a large city. Now certainly you are yourself deep in nature, since you say that Johanna already feels her child quicken."

Once again he went to his studio and painted the scene from the barred window, the cornfield with a little reaper and a big sun. The canvas was all yellow except for the wall, which ran down the slope at a steep, sharp angle, and the background of violet-tinted hills.

Doctor Peyron acquiesced in Theo's wish, and allowed Vincent to go outside the grounds to work. He painted the cypresses which flowed up out of the ground and poured into the yellow roof of sun. He did a canvas of women gathering olives; the soil violet, and farther off yellow ochre; the trees with bronze trunks and green-grey foliage; the sky and the three figures of the women a deep rose.

On his way to work he would stop and talk to the men labouring in the fields. In his own mind he considered himself below these peasants.

"You see," he told one of them, "I plough on my canvases, just as you plough in your field."

The late Provençal autumn came to a focal point of beauty. The earth brought forth all its violets; the burnt-up grass flamed about the little rose flowers in the garden; the green skies contrasted with the varying shades of yellow foliage.

And with the late autumn came Vincent's full strength. He saw that his work was getting on. Good ideas began to spring anew in his mind; he was happy in letting them develop. Because of his long stay he began to feel the country keenly. It was very different in character from Arles. Most of the

TWO FACES OF LOVE

mistral was stopped by the hills which overlooked the valley. The sun was far less blinding. Now that he had come to understand the country about St. Remy, he did not want to leave the asylum. In the early months of his stay he had prayed that the year would pass without breaking his mind. Now that he was wrapped in his work, he did not know whether he was staying in a hospital or a hotel. Although he felt entirely well, he thought it foolish to move to some chance place and spend another six months getting acquainted with strange terrain.

Letters from Paris kept him in high spirits. Theo's wife was cooking at home for him, and his health was recovering rapidly. Johanna was carrying the baby without difficulty. And every week Theo sent tobacco, chocolate, paints, books, and a ten or twenty franc note.

The memory of his attack after the Arlesian trip vanished from Vincent's mind. Again and again he reassured himself that if he had never gone back to that cursed city, he would have had six months of normal health to his credit. When his studies of the cypresses and olive groves dried, he washed them with water and a little wine to take away the oil in the *pâte*, then sent them to Theo. He received Theo's announcement that he was exhibiting a number of his canvases at the Independents with disappointment, for he felt that he had not yet done his best work. He wanted to hold off until he had perfected his technique.

Letters from Theo assured him that his work was going ahead at a remarkable pace. He decided that when his year was up at the asylum, he would take a house in the village of St. Remy and continue his painting of the Southland. He felt once again the exultant joy that had been his in the Arlesian days before Gauguin arrived, when he was painting his sunflower panels.

One afternoon, when he was working calmly in the fields, his mind began to wander. Late that night the guardians of the asylum found him, several kilometres away from his easel. His body was wrapped about the trunk of a cypress.

4

By the end of the fifth day his senses returned to normal. What hurt him most deeply was the way his fellow inmates accepted the seizure as being inevitable.

Winter came on. Vincent could not find the will to get out of bed. The stove in the centre of the ward now glowed brightly. The men sat about it in frozen silence from morning until night. The windows of the ward were small and high, letting in very little light. The stove heated and spread the thick odour of decay. The sisters, withdrawn even farther into their black capes and hoods, went about mumbling prayers and fingering their crosses. The barren hills in the background stood out like death heads.

Vincent lay awake in his slanting bed. What was it that Scheveningen picture of Mauve's had taught him? *"Savoir souffrir sans se plaindre."* Learn to suffer without complaint, to look on pain without repugnance . . . yes, but in that he ran the risk of vertigo. If he gave in to that pain, that desolation, it would kill him. There came a time in every man's life when it was necessary to fling off suffering as though it were a filthy cloak.

Days passed, each exactly like the last. His mind was barren of ideas and hope. He heard the sisters discuss his work; they wondered if he painted because he was crazy, or if he was crazy because he painted.

The idiot sat by his bedside and blubbered to him for hours. Vincent felt a warmth in the man's friendliness and did not chase him away. Often he talked to the idiot, for there was no one else who would listen.

"They think my work has driven me crazy," he said to the man one day, as two of the sisters passed. "I know that at bottom it is fairly true that a painter is a man too much absorbed by what his eyes see, and is not sufficiently master of the rest of his life. But does that make him unfit to live in this world?"

The idiot only drooled.

It was a line from Delacroix's book that finally gave him the strength to get out of bed. "I discovered painting," said Delacroix, "when I no longer had teeth or breath."

For several weeks he did not even have the desire to go into the garden. He sat in the ward near the stove, reading the books that Theo sent from Paris. When one of his neighbours was taken with an attack, he did not look up or get out of his chair. Insanity had become sanity; the abnormal had become the normal. It was so long since he had lived with rational people that he no longer looked upon his fellow inmates as irrational.

"I'm sorry, Vincent," said Doctor Peyron, "but I cannot give you permission to leave the grounds again. In the future you must stay within the walls."

"You will permit me to work in my studio?"

"I advise you against it."

"Would you prefer me to commit suicide, Doctor?"

"Very well, work in your studio. But only for a few hours a day."

Even the sight of his easel and brushes could not destroy Vincent's lethargy. He sat in the Monticelli armchair and stared through the iron bars at the barren cornfield.

A few days later he was summoned to Doctor Peyron's office to sign for a registered letter. When he slit open the envelope, he found a check for four hundred francs made out in his name. It was the largest sum of money he had ever possessed at one time. He wondered what on earth Theo had sent it for.

My Dear Vincent:

At last! One of your canvases has been bought for four hundred francs!

It was Red Vineyard, *the one you painted at Arles last spring. It was bought by Anna Bock, sister of the Dutch painter.*

Congratulations, old boy! Soon we'll be selling you all over Europe! Use this money to come back to Paris, if Doctor Peyron agrees.

I have recently met a delightful man, Doctor Gachet, who has a home in Auvers-sur-l'Oise, just an hour from Paris. Every important painter since Daubigny has worked in his home. He claims he understands your case thoroughly, and that any time you want to come to Auvers, he will take care of you.

I'll write again tomorrow.

Theo

Vincent showed Doctor Peyron and his wife the letter. Peyron read it thoughtfully, then fingered the check. He congratulated Vincent on his good fortune. Vincent walked down the path, the soft stuff of his brain springing to firm life again with feverish activity. Half-way across the garden he saw that he had taken the check with him but left Theo's letter in the Doctor's office. He turned and walked back quickly.

He was about to knock on the door when he heard his name mentioned inside. He hesitated for a moment, irresolute.

"Then why do you suppose he did it?" demanded Madame Peyron.

"Perhaps he thought it would be good for his brother."

"But if he can't afford the money . . . ?"

"I suppose he thought it was worth it, to bring Vincent back to normal."

"Then you don't think there's any chance of it being the truth?"

"My dear Marie, how could there be? This woman is supposed to be the sister of an artist. How in the world could a person with any perception . . . ?"

Vincent walked away.

At supper he received a wire from Theo.

NAMED THE BOY AFTER YOU   JOHANNA AND VINCENT FEELING FINE.

The sale of his picture, and the marvellous news from Theo made Vincent a well man over night. In the morning he went early to his studio, cleaned his brushes, sorted the canvases and studies that were leaning against the wall.

"If Delacroix can discover painting when he no longer has teeth or breath, I can discover it when I no longer have teeth or wits."

He threw himself into his work with a dumb fury. He copied *The Good Samaritan* after Delacroix, *The Sower* and *The Digger* after Millet. He was determined to take his recent misfortune with a sort of northern phlegm. The life of art was shattering; he had known that when he began. Then why should he take to complaining at this late date?

Exactly two weeks to the day after receiving the four hundred franc check, he found in the mail a copy of the January issue of the *Mercure de France*.

He noticed that Theo had checked an article on the title page called "Les Isolées."

That which characterizes all the work of Vincent Van Gogh [he read] is the excess of force, and the violence in expression. In his categorical affirmative of the essential character of things, in his often rash simplification of form, in his insolent desire to look at the sun face to face, in the passion of his drawing and colour, there lies revealed a powerful one, a male, a darer who is sometimes brutal, sometimes ingenuously delicate.

Vincent Van Gogh is of the sublime line of Frans Hals. His realism goes beyond the truth of those great little burghers of Holland, so healthy in body, so well balanced in mind, who were his ancestors. What marks his canvases is his conscientious study of character, his continuous search for the quintessence of each object, his deep and almost childlike love of nature and truth.

This robust and true artist with an illumined soul, will he ever know the joys of being rehabilitated by the public? I do not think so. He is too simple, and at the same time too subtle, for our contemporary bourgeois spirit. He will never be altogether understood except by his brother artists.

G.-Albert Aurier.

Vincent did not show the article to Doctor Peyron.

All his strength and lust for life came back to him. He painted a picture of the ward in which he slept, painted the superintendent of the buildings, and then his wife, made more copies after Millet and Delacroix, filled his nights and days with tumultuous labour.

By going carefully over the history of his illness, he saw clearly that his seizures were cyclical in nature, coming every three months. Very well, if he knew when they were to come, he would be able to take care of himself. When his next attack was due, he would stop work, go to bed, and prepare himself for a brief indisposition. And after a few days he would be up again, just as though he had been suffering from nothing more than a slight cold.

The only thing that now disturbed him at the asylum was the intense religious nature of the place. It seemed to him that with the coming of the dark winter, the sisters had suffered a hysterical seizure. Sometimes, as he watched them mumble their prayers, kiss their crosses, finger their beads, walk with their eyes glued to their Bibles, tiptoe into the chapel for prayer and services five and six times a day, he had difficulty in determining who were the patients in this insane asylum, and who the attendants. Since his days in the Borinage he had had a horror of all religious exaggerations. At moments he found the sisters' aberrations preying upon his mind. He drove himself more passionately into his work, trying to wipe the image of the black-hooded, black-caped creatures from his mind.

He gave himself forty-eight hours leeway before the end of the third month, going to bed in perfect health and spirits. He pulled the curtains of the bed about him so that the sisters, shaken by their ever rising religious exaltation, could not destroy his peace of mind.

The day arrived when his seizure was due. Vincent awaited it eagerly, almost with affection. The hours dragged by. Nothing happened. He was surprised, then disappointed. The second day passed. He still felt completely normal. When the third day drew to an end without mishap, he had to laugh at himself.

"I've been a fool. I've seen the last of those attacks, after all. Doctor Peyron was wrong. From now on I don't have to be afraid. I've been wasting my time, lying in bed this way. Tomorrow morning I'm going to get up and work."

In the dead of the night, when everyone was asleep, he climbed quietly out of bed. He walked down the stone floored ward in his bare feet. He made his way in the dark to the cellar where the coal was stored. He fell to his knees, scooped up a handful of coal-dust, and smeared it over his face.

"You see, Madame Denis? They accept me now. They know I am one of them. They did not trust me before, but now I am a *gueule noire*. The miners will let me bring them the Word of God."

The guardians found him there shortly after dawn. He was whispering chaotic prayers, repeating broken bits of scripture, answering the voices which were pouring queer tales into his ear.

His religious hallucinations continued for several days. When he came back to his senses, he asked one of the sisters to send for Doctor Peyron.

"I think I would have avoided this attack, Doctor," he said, "if it had not been for all the religious hysteria I am exposed to."

Doctor Peyron shrugged, leaned against the bed, and pulled Vincent's curtains behind him.

"What can I do, Vincent? It is just so, every winter. I do not approve but neither can I interfere. The sisters do good work, in spite of all."

"Be that as it may," said Vincent, "it is hard enough to keep sane among all the madmen, without being exposed to religious insanity in the bargain. I had passed the time for my attack . . ."

"Vincent, do not delude yourself. That attack had to come. Your nervous system works itself up to a crisis every three months. If your hallucinations had not been religious, they would have been of some other nature."

"If I have another, Doctor, I shall ask my brother to take me away."

"As you say, Vincent."

He returned to work in his studio on the first real day of spring. He painted the scene out of his window again, a field of yellow stubble being ploughed. He contrasted the violet-tinted ploughed earth with the strips of yellow stubble against the background of hills. The almond trees began to blossom everywhere, and once again the sky became pale lemon at sunset.

The eternal re-creation of nature brought forth no new life in Vincent. For the first time since he had grown accustomed to his companions, their mad babblings and periodic seizures tore his nerves and ripped into his vitals. Nor was there any escape from the mouse-like, praying creatures in black and white. The very sight of them sent shivers of apprehension through Vincent.

"Theo," he wrote to his brother, "it would make me unhappy to leave St. Remy; there is much good work to be done here yet. But if I have another attack of a religious nature, it will be the fault of the asylum, and not my nerves. It will only take two or three more of them to kill me.

"Be prepared. If I have another religious seizure, I shall leave for Paris the instant I am able to get out of bed. Perhaps it would be best for me to come north again, where one can rely on a certain amount of sanity.

"What about this Doctor Gachet of yours? Will he take a personal interest in my case?"

Theo replied that he had spoken to Doctor Gachet again, and shown him some of Vincent's canvases. Doctor Gachet was eager to have Vincent come to Auvers and paint in his house.

"He is a specialist, Vincent, not only in nervous diseases, but in painters. I am convinced that you could not be in better hands. Any time you wish to come, just wire me and I will catch the first train for St. Remy."

The heat of early spring came on. The cicadas began to sing in the garden. Vincent painted the portico of the third-class ward, the walks and trees in the gardens, his own portrait in the mirror. He worked with one eye on his canvas and the other on the calendar.

His next seizure was due in May.

He heard voices shouting at him in the empty corridors. He answered them, and the echo of his own voice came back like the malignant call of fate. This time they found him in the chapel, unconscious. It was the middle of May before he recovered from the religious hallucinations that went twisting through his brain.

Theo insisted upon coming to St. Remy to get him. Vincent wanted to make the trip alone, with one of the guardians putting him on the train at Tarascon.

Dear Theo:

I am not an invalid, nor yet a dangerous beast. Let me prove to both you and myself that I am a normal being. If I can wrench myself away from this asylum with my own strength, and take up a new life in Auvers, perhaps I shall be able to conquer this malady of mine.

I give myself one more chance. Away from this maison des fous, I feel confident that I can become again a rational person. From what you write me, Auvers will be quiet and beautiful. If I live carefully, under the eyes of Doctor Gachet, I am convinced that I will conquer my disease.

I shall wire you when my train leaves Tarascon. Meet me at the Gare de Lyon. I want to leave here Saturday, so that I can spend Sunday at home with you and Johanna and the little one.

BOOK EIGHT

AUVERS

1

THEO could not sleep all that night for anxiety. He left for the Gare de Lyon two hours before Vincent's train could possibly arrive. Johanna had to stay home with the baby. She stood on the terrace of their fourth floor apartment on the Cité Pigalle and peered through the leaves of the great black tree that covered the front of the house. She eagerly watched the entrance of the Cité Pigalle for a carriage which would turn in from the Rue Pigalle.

It was a long distance from the Gare de Lyon to Theo's house. To Johanna it seemed an endless time of waiting. She began to fear that something had happened to Vincent on the train. But at length an open *fiacre* turned in from the Rue Pigalle, two merry faces nodded to her, and two hands waved. She strained to catch a glimpse of Vincent.

The Cité Pigalle was a *rue impasse,* blocked off at the end by a garden court and the jutting corner of a stone house. There were only two long buildings on either side of the prosperous and respectable looking street. Theo lived at number 8, the house nearest the impasse; it was set back from a little garden and had a private *trottoir* all its own. It took the *fiacre* but a few seconds to draw up before the big black tree and the entrance.

Vincent bounded up the stairs with Theo at his heels. Johanna had expected to see an invalid, but the man who flung his arms about her had healthy colour, a smile on his face, and an expression of great resoluteness.

"He seems perfectly well. He looks much stronger than Theo," was her first thought.

But she could not bring herself to look at his ear.

"Well, Theo," exclaimed Vincent, holding Johanna's hands and looking at her approvingly, "you certainly picked yourself a fine wife."

"Thanks, Vincent," laughed Theo.

Theo had chosen in the tradition of his mother. Johanna had the same soft brown eyes as Anna Cornelia, the same tender reaching out in full sympathy and compassion. Already, with her child but a few months old, there was the faint touch of the coming matriarch about her. She had plain, good features, an almost stolid oval face, and a mass of light brown hair combed back simply from a high Dutch brow. Her love for Theo included Vincent.

Theo drew Vincent into the bedroom, where the baby was sleeping in his cradle. The two men looked at the child in silence, tears in their eyes. Johanna sensed that they would like to be alone for a moment; she tiptoed to the door. Just as she put her hand on the knob, Vincent turned smilingly to her and said, pointing to the crocheted cover over the cradle,

"Do not cover him too much with lace, little sister."

Johanna closed the door quietly behind her. Vincent, looking down at the child once more, felt the awful pang of barren men whose flesh leaves no flesh behind, whose death is death eternal.

Theo read his thoughts.

"There is still time for you, Vincent. Some day you will find a wife who will love you and share the hardships of your life."

"Ah, no, Theo, it's too late."

"I found a woman only the other day who would be perfect for you!"

"Not really! Who was she?"

"She was the girl in 'Terre Vierge,' by Turgenev. Remember her?"

"You mean the one who works with the nihilists, and brings the compromising papers across the frontier?"

"Yes. Your wife would have to be somebody like that, Vincent; somebody who had gone through life's misery to the very bottom . . ."

". . . And what would she want with me? A one-eared man?"

Little Vincent awakened, looked up at them and smiled. Theo lifted the child out of the cradle and placed him in Vincent's arms.

"So soft and warm, like a little puppy," said Vincent, feeling the baby against his heart.

"Here, clumsy, you don't hold a baby like that."

"I'm afraid I'm more at home holding a paint brush."

Theo took the child and held him against his shoulder, his head touching the baby's brown curls. To Vincent they looked as though they had been carved out of the same stone.

"Well, Theo boy," he said resignedly, "each man to his own medium. You create in living flesh . . . and I'll create in paint."

"Just so, Vincent, just so."

A number of Vincent's friends came to Theo's that night to welcome him back. The first arrival was Aurier, a handsome young man with flowing locks and a beard which sprouted out of each side of his chin, but conjured up no hair in the middle. Vincent led him to the bedroom, where Theo had hung a Monticelli bouquet.

"You said in your article, Monsieur Aurier, that I was the sole painter to perceive the chromatism of things with a metallic, gem-like quality. Look at this Monticelli. 'Fada' achieved it years before I even came to Paris."

At the end of an hour Vincent gave up trying to persuade Aurier, and presented him instead with one of the St. Remy cypress canvases in appreciation for his article.

Toulouse-Lautrec blew in, winded from six flights of stairs, but still as hilarious and ribald as ever.

"Vincent," he exclaimed, while shaking hands, "I passed an undertaker on the stairs. Was he looking for you or me?"

"For you, Lautrec! He couldn't get any business out of me."

"I'll make you a little wager, Vincent. I'll bet your name comes ahead of mine in his little book."

"You're on. What's the stake?"

"Dinner at the Café Athens, and an evening at the Opéra."

"I wish you fellows would make your jokes a trifle less macabre," said Theo, smiling faintly.

A strange man entered the front door, looked at Lautrec, and sank into a chair in a far corner. Everyone waited for Lautrec to present him, but he just went on talking.

"Won't you introduce your friend?" asked Vincent.

"That's not my friend," laughed Lautrec. "That's my keeper!"

There was a moment of pained silence.

"Hadn't you heard, Vincent? I was *non compos mentis* for a couple of months. They said it was from too much liquor, so now I'm drinking milk. I'll send you an invitation to my next party. There's a picture on it of me milking a cow from the wrong end!"

Johanna passed about refreshments. Everyone talked at the same time and the air grew thick with tobacco smoke. It reminded Vincent of the old Paris days.

"How is Georges Seurat getting along?" Vincent asked Lautrec.

"Georges! Mean to tell me you don't know about him?"

"Theo didn't write me anything," said Vincent. "What is it?"

"Georges is dying of consumption. The doctor says he won't last beyond his thirty-first birthday."

"Consumption! Why, Georges was strong and healthy. How in the . . . ?"

"Overwork, Vincent," said Theo. "It's been two years since you've seen him? Georges drove himself like a demon. Slept two and three hours a day, and worked himself furiously all the rest of the time. Even that good old mother of his couldn't save him."

"So Georges will be going soon," said Vincent, musingly.

Rousseau came in, carrying a bag of home-made cookies for Vincent. Père Tanguy, wearing the same round straw hat, presented Vincent with a Japanese print and a sweet speech about how glad they were to welcome him back to Paris.

At ten o'clock Vincent insisted upon going down and buying a litre of olives. He made everyone eat them, even Lautrec's guardian.

"If you could once see those silver-green olive groves in Provence," he exclaimed, "you would eat olives for the rest of your life."

"Speaking of olive groves, Vincent," said Lautrec, "how did you find the Arlesiennes?"

The following morning Vincent carried the perambulator down to the street for Johanna so that the baby might have his hour of sunshine on the private *trottoir*. Vincent then went back to the apartment and stood about in his shirt sleeves, looking at the walls. They were covered with his pictures.

In the dining room over the mantelpiece was *The Potato Eaters,* in the living room the *Landscape From Arles,* and *Night View on the Rhône,* in the bedroom, *Blooming Orchards.* To the despair of Johanna's *femme de ménage,* there were huge piles of unframed canvases under the beds, under the sofa, under the cupboard, and stacked solid in the spare room.

While rummaging for something in Theo's desk, Vincent came across large packages of letters tied with heavy cord. He was amazed to find that they were his own letters. Theo had carefully guarded every line his brother had written to him since that day, twenty years before, when Vincent had left Zundert for Goupils in The Hague. All in all, there were seven hundred letters. Vincent wondered why in the world Theo had saved them.

In another part of the desk he found the drawings that he had been sending to Theo for the past ten years, all ranged neatly in periods; here were the miners and their wives from the Borinage period, leaning over their *terril;* here the diggers and sowers in the fields near Etten; here the old men and women from The Hague, the diggers in the Geest, and the fishermen of Scheveningen; here the potato eaters and weavers of Nuenen; here the restaurants and street scenes of Paris; here the early sunflower and orchard sketches from Arles; and here the garden of the asylum at St. Remy.

"I'm going to have an exhibition all my own!" he exclaimed.

He took all the pictures off the walls, threw down the packages of sketches, and pulled piles of unframed canvases from under every piece of furniture. He sorted them out very carefully into periods. Then he selected the sketches and oils which best caught the spirit of the place in which he had been working.

In the foyer, where one entered from the hallway of the house, he pinned up about thirty of his first studies, the Borains coming out of the mines, leaning over their oval stoves, eating supper in their little shacks.

"This is the charcoal room," he announced to himself.

He looked about the rest of the house and decided that the bathroom was the next least important space. He stood on a chair and tacked a row of Etten studies about the four walls in a straight line, studies of the Brabant peasants.

"And this, of course, is the carpenter's pencil room."

His next selection was the kitchen. Here he put up his Hague and Scheveningen sketches, the view from his window over the lumber yard, the sand dunes, the fishing smacks being drawn up on the beach.

"Chamber three," he said; "water-colour room."

In the little spare room he put up his canvas of his friends the De Groots, *The Potato Eaters;* it was the first oil in which he had expressed himself fully. All about it he pinned dozens of studies of the weavers of Nuenen, the peasants in mourning, the graveyard behind his father's church, the slim, tapering steeple.

In his own bedroom he hung the oil paintings from the Paris period, the ones he had put on Theo's walls in the Rue Lepic the night he left for Arles.

In the living room he crowded every last blazing Arlesian canvas he could fit on the walls. In Theo's bedroom he put up the pictures he had created while in the asylum at St. Remy.

His job finished, he cleared the floor, put on his hat and coat, walked down the four flights of stairs, and wheeled his namesake in the sunshine of the Cité Pigalle, while Johanna held his arm and chatted with him in Dutch.

Theo swung in from the Rue Pigalle at a little after twelve, waved to them happily, broke into a run, and scooped the baby out of the perambulator with a loving gesture. They left the carriage with the *concierge* and walked up the stairs, chatting animatedly. When they came to the front door, Vincent stopped them.

"I'm going to take you to a Van Gogh exhibition, Theo and Jo," he said. "So steel yourself for the ordeal."

"An exhibit, Vincent?" asked Theo. "Where?"

"Just shut your eyes," said Vincent.

He threw the door open and the three Van Goghs stepped into the foyer. Theo and Johanna gazed about, stunned.

"When I was living in Etten," said Vincent, "father once remarked that good could never grow out of bad. I replied that not only it could, but that in art it must. If you will follow me, my dear brother and sister, I will show you the story of a man who began crudely, like an awkward child, and after ten years of constant labour, arrived at . . . but you shall decide that for yourselves."

He led them, in the proper chronological sequence, from room to room. They stood like three visitors in an art gallery, looking at this work which was a man's life. They felt the slow, painful growth of the artist, the fumbling toward maturity of expression, the upheaval that had taken place in Paris, the passionate outburst of his powerful voice in Arles, which caught up all the strands of his years of labour . . . and then . . . the smash . . . the St. Remy canvases . . . the crucial striving to keep up to the blaze of creation, and the falling slowly away . . . falling . . . falling . . . falling . . .

They looked at the exhibit through the eyes of casual strangers. Before them they saw, in a brief half hour, the recapitulation of one man's stay on earth.

Johanna served a typical Brabant lunch. Vincent was happy just to taste Dutch food once again. After she had cleared away, the two men lit their pipes and chatted.

"You must be very careful to do everything Doctor Gachet tells you, Vincent."

"Yes, Theo, I will."

"Because, you see, he's a specialist in nervous diseases. If you carry out his instructions, you are sure to recover."

"I promise."

"Gachet paints, too. He exhibits each year with the Independents under the name of P. Van Ryssel."

"Is his work good, Theo?"

"No, I shouldn't say so. But he's one of those men who has a genius for recognizing genius. He came to Paris at the age of twenty to study medicine, and became friends with Courbet, Murger, Champfleury, and Proudhon. He used to frequent the café La Nouvelle Athens, and soon was intimate with Manet, Renoir, Degas, Durante, and Claude Monet. Daubigny and Daumier painted in his house years before there even was such a thing as Impressionism."

"You don't say!"

"Nearly everything he has was painted either in his garden or his living room. Pissarro, Guillaumin, Sisley, Delacroix, they've all gone out to work with Gachet in Auvers. You'll find canvases of Cezanne, Lautrec and Seurat on the walls, too. I tell you, Vincent, there hasn't been an important painter since the middle of the century who wasn't Doctor Gachet's friend."

"Whoa! Wait a minute, Theo, you're frightening me. I don't belong in such illustrious company. Has he seen any of my work yet?"

"You idiot, why do you suppose he's so eager to have you come to Auvers?"

"Blessed if I know."

"He thought your Arlesian night scenes in the last Independents the best canvases in the whole show. I swear to you, when I showed him the sunflower panels you painted for Gauguin and the yellow house, the tears came to his eyes. He turned to me and said, 'Monsieur Van Gogh, your brother is a great artist. There has never been anything like the yellow of these sunflowers before in the history of art. These canvases alone, Monsieur, will make your brother immortal.'"

Vincent scratched his head and grinned.

"Well," he said, "if Doctor Gachet feels that way about my sunflowers, he and I shall get along together."

2

Doctor Gachet was down at the station to meet Theo and Vincent. He was a nervous, excited, jumpy little man with an eager melancholy in his eyes. He wrung Vincent's hand warmly.

"Yes, yes, you will find this a real painter's village. You will like it here. I see you have brought your easel. Have you enough paints? You must begin work immediately. You will have dinner with me at my house this afternoon, yes? Have you brought some of your new canvases? You won't find that Arlesian yellow here, I'm afraid, but there are other things, yes, yes, you will find other things. You must come to my house to paint. I will give you vases and tables that have been painted by everyone from Daubigny to Lautrec. How do you feel? You look well. Do you think you will like it here? Yes, yes, we will take care of you. We'll make a healthy man out of you!"

From the station platform Vincent looked over a patch of trees to where the green Oise wound through the fertile valley. He ran a little bit to one side to get a full view. Theo spoke in a low tone to Doctor Gachet.

"I beg of you, watch my brother carefully," he said. "If you see any symptoms of his trouble coming, telegraph to me at once. I must be with him when he . . . he must not be allowed to . . . there are people who say that . . ."

"Tut! Tut!" interrupted Doctor Gachet, dancing from one foot to the other and rubbing his little goatee vigorously with his index finger. "Of course he's crazy. But what would you? All artists are crazy. That's the best thing about them. I love them that way. I sometimes wish I could be crazy myself! 'No excellent soul is exempt from a mixture of madness!' Do you know who said that? Aristotle, that's who."

"I know, Doctor," said Theo, "but he is a young man, only thirty-seven. The best part of his life is still before him."

Doctor Gachet snatched off his funny white cap and ran his hand through his hair many times, with no apparent purpose.

"Leave him to me. I know how to handle painters. I will make a well man of him in a month. I'll set him to work. That will cure him. I'll make him paint my portrait. Right away. This afternoon. I'll get his mind off his illness, all right."

Vincent came back, drawing big breaths of pure country air.

"You ought to bring Jo and the little one out here, Theo. It's a crime to raise children in the city."

"Yes, yes, you must come on a Sunday and spend the whole day with us," cried Gachet.

"Thank you. I would like that very much. Here comes my train. Good-bye, Doctor Gachet; thank you for taking care of my brother. Vincent, write to me every day."

Doctor Gachet had a habit of holding people at the elbow and propelling them forward in the direction he wished to go. He pushed Vincent ahead of him, kept up a nervous flow of talk in a high voice, scrambled up his conversation, answered his own questions, and deluged Vincent in a sputtering monologue.

"That's the road to the village," he said, "that long one, straight ahead. But come, I'll take you up this hill and give you a real view. You don't mind walking with the easel on your back? That's the Catholic church on the left. Have you noticed that the Catholics always build their churches on a hill, so that people will look up to them? Dear, dear, I must be getting old; this grade seems steeper every year. Those are lovely cornfields, aren't they? Auvers is surrounded by them. You must come and paint this field some time. Of course it's not as yellow as the Provençal . . . yes, that's the cemetery on the right . . . we put it up here on the crest of the hill, overlooking the river and the valley . . . do you think it makes much difference to dead people where they lie? . . . we gave them the loveliest spot

in the whole Oise valley . . . shall we go in? . . . you get the clearest view
of the river from inside . . . we'll be able to see almost to Pointoise . . .
yes, the gate is open, just push it . . . that's right . . . now isn't this pleasant?
. . . we built the walls high to keep the wind out . . . we bury Catholics and
Protestants alike here . . ."

Vincent slipped the easel off his back and walked a little ahead of Doctor
Gachet to escape the flow of words. The cemetery, which had been laid at the
very crest of the hill, was a neat square in shape. Part of it ran downward on
the slope. Vincent went to the back wall, from where he could see the
whole Oise valley flowing beneath him. The cool green river wound its way
gracefully between banks of brilliant verdure. To his right he saw the
thatched roofs of the village, and just a short distance beyond, another slope
on the top of which was a chateau. The cemetery was full of clean May
sunshine and early spring flowers. It was roofed by a delicate blue sky. The
complete and beautiful quiet was almost the quiet from beyond the grave.

"You know, Doctor Gachet," said Vincent, "it did me good to go south.
Now I see the North better. Look how much violet there is on the far
river bank, where the sun hasn't struck the green yet."

"Yes, yes, violet, violet, that's just what it is, vio . . ."

"And how sane," murmured Vincent. "How calm and restful."

They wound down the hill again, past the cornfields and the church, and
took the straight road on their right to the heart of the village.

"I regret I cannot keep you at my house," said Doctor Gachet, "but alas!
we have no room. I will take you to a good inn, and every day you will come
to my house to paint, and make yourself at home."

The doctor took Vincent by the elbow and propelled him beyond the
Mairie, down almost to the river bank, where there was a summer inn.
Gachet spoke to the proprietor, who agreed to give Vincent room and
board for six francs a day.

"I will give you a chance to get settled now," cried Gachet. "But mind
you come to dinner at one o'clock. And bring your easel. You must do my
portrait. And let me see some of your new canvases. We will have a grand
chat, yes?"

As soon as the doctor was out of sight, Vincent picked up his belongings
and stalked out the front door.

"Wait a moment," said the proprietor. "Where are you going?"

"I am a labourer," replied Vincent, "not a capitalist. I cannot pay your six
francs a day."

He walked back to the Place and found a little café exactly opposite the
Mairie, called Ravoux's, where he could get room and board for three francs-
fifty a day.

Ravoux's café was the meeting place of the peasants and labourers who
worked around Auvers. Vincent found a little bar on the right as he walked
in, and all the way down the side of the dark, dispirited room, rough
wooden tables and benches. At the rear of the café, behind the bar, was a

billiard table with a soiled and torn green covering. It was the pride and joy of Ravoux's. A door at the rear led to the back kitchen; just outside this door was a flight of stairs winding up to three bedrooms. From his window Vincent could see the steeple of the Catholic church, and a small patch of the cemetery wall, a clean, crisp brown in the mild Auvers sunlight.

He took his easel, paints and brushes, a portrait of the Arlesienne, and set out to find Gachet's. The same road which came down from the station, and led past Ravoux's, sneaked out of the Place again on the west and climbed another grade. After a short walk, Vincent came to a spot where three roads forked. He saw that the one on his right led up the hill past the chateau, and the one on his left wandered down through fields of peas to the river bank. Gachet had told him to take the centre road, which continued along the contour of the hill. Vincent walked slowly, thinking of the doctor to whose care he had been committed. He noticed how the old thatched houses were being replaced by prosperous villas, and the whole nature of the country-side was changing.

Vincent pulled a brass knob stuck in a high stone wall. Gachet came running to the tinkle of the bell. He led Vincent up three flights of steep stone steps to a terraced flower garden. The house was of three stories, solid and well built. The doctor flexed Vincent's arm, seized the joint of the elbow and pushed him around to the back yard, where he kept ducks, hens, turkeys, peacocks, and a retinue of ill-assorted cats.

"Come into the living room, Vincent," said Gachet, after giving a complete life history of each of the fowls in the yard.

The living room at the front of the house was large and had a high ceiling, but there were only two small windows looking out on the garden. In spite of the size of the room it was so crammed full of furniture, antiques, and bric-a-brac that there was hardly enough space for the two men to move about the table in the centre. The room was dark from lack of window space, and Vincent noticed that every last piece in it was black.

Gachet ran about picking up things, thrusting them into Vincent's hands, taking them away again before Vincent had a chance to look at them.

"See. See that bouquet on the wall? Delacroix used this vase to hold the flowers. Feel it. Doesn't it feel like the one he painted? See that chair? Courbet sat in it by the window when he painted the garden. Aren't these exquisite dishes? Desmoulins brought them back from Japan for me. Claude Monet put this one into a still life. It's upstairs. Come with me. I'll show it to you."

At the dinner table Vincent met Gachet's son, Paul, a vivacious and handsome young lad of fifteen. Gachet, who was a sick man with a poor digestion, served a five course dinner. Vincent was accustomed to the lentils and black bread of St. Remy; he became distressed after the third course and could go no further.

"And now we must go to work," cried the doctor. "You will paint my portrait, Vincent; I will sit for you just as I am, yes?"

"I'm afraid I must come to know you better, Doctor, or it won't be an understanding portrait."

"Perhaps you are right, perhaps you are right. But surely you will paint something? You will let me see how you work? I am eager to watch you."

"I saw a scene in the garden I would like to do."

"Good! Good! I will set up your easel. Paul, carry Monsieur Vincent's easel into the garden. You will show us where you want it, and I will tell you if any other painter has done that exact spot."

While Vincent worked, the doctor ran about him in little circles, gesticulating with rapture, consternation and amazement. He poured a constant stream of advice over Vincent's shoulder, interspersed with hundreds of sharp exclamations.

"Yes, yes, you caught it that time. It's crimson lake. Look out. You'll spoil that tree. Ah, yes, yes, now you've caught it. No. No. No more cobalt. This isn't Provence. Now I see. Yes, yes, it's *épatant*. Careful. Careful. Vincent, put a little spot of yellow in that flower. Yes, yes, just so. How you make things live. There's not a still life in your brush. No. No. I beg of you. Be careful. Not too much. Ah, yes, yes, now I catch it. *Merveilleux!*"

Vincent stood the doctor's contortions and monologue as long as he could. Then he turned to the dancing Gachet and said, "My dear friend, don't you think it bad for your health to get yourself so excited and wrought up? As a medical man, you should know how important it is to keep calm."

But Gachet could not be calm when anyone was painting.

When he finished his sketch, Vincent went inside the house with Gachet, and showed him the portrait of the Arlesienne he had brought. The doctor cocked one eye and looked at it quizzically. After a long and voluble discussion with himself as to its merits and faults, he announced,

"No, I cannot accept it. I cannot fully accept it. I do not see what you have tried to say."

"I haven't tried to say anything," replied Vincent. "She is the synthesis of the Arlesiennes, if you like. I simply tried to interpret her character in terms of colours."

"Alas," said the doctor mournfully, "I cannot fully accept it."

"Do you mind if I look about the house at your collection?"

"But of course, of course, go look your fill. I will stay here with this lady and see if I cannot come to accept her."

Vincent browsed through the house for an hour, led from room to room by the obliging Paul. Thrown carelessly in one corner he found a Guillaumin, a nude woman lying on a bed. The canvas had obviously been neglected, and was cracking. While Vincent was examining it, Doctor Gachet came running up excitedly and poured out a string of questions about the Arlesienne.

"Do you mean to tell me you have been looking at her all this time?" demanded Vincent.

"Yes, yes, it is coming, it is coming, I am beginning to feel her."

"Forgive my presumption, Doctor Gachet, but this is a magnificent Guillaumin. If you don't have it framed soon, it will be ruined."

Gachet did not even hear him.

"You say you followed Gauguin in the drawing . . . I do not agree . . . that clash of colours . . . it kills her femininity . . . no, not kills, but . . . well, well, I will go look again . . . she is coming to me . . . slowly . . . slowly . . . she is jumping out of the canvas to me."

Gachet spent the rest of the long afternoon running about the Arlesienne, pointing at her, waving his arms, talking to himself, asking and answering innumerable questions, falling into a thousand poses. By the time night fell, the woman had completely captured his heart. An exulted quiescence fell upon him.

"How difficult it is to be simple," he remarked, standing in peaceful exhaustion before the portrait.

"Yes."

"She is beautiful, beautiful. I have never felt such depth of character before."

"If you like her, Doctor," said Vincent, "she is yours. And so is the scene I did in the garden this afternoon."

"But why should you give me these pictures, Vincent? They are valuable."

"In the near future you may have to take care of me. I will have no money to pay you. So I pay you in canvases instead."

"But I would not be taking care of you for money, Vincent. I would be doing it for friendship."

"*Soit!* I give you these pictures for friendship."

3

Vincent settled down once again to be a painter. He went to sleep at nine, after watching the labourers play billiards under a dull lamp in Ravoux's café. He arose at five. The weather was beautiful, with gentle sunshine and the fresh verdancy of the valley. His periods of illness and enforced idleness in St. Paul had taken their toll; the paint brush slipped in his hand.

He asked Theo to send him Bargue's sixty charcoal studies to copy, for he was afraid that if he did not study proportion and the nude again, he would be badly caught out. He looked about Auvers to see if he could find a little house in which he might settle permanently. He wondered if Theo had been right in thinking that, somewhere in the world, there was a woman who would share his life. He laid out a number of his St. Remy canvases, anxious to retouch and perfect them.

But his sudden activity was only a momentary gesture, the reflex of an organism that was yet too powerful to be destroyed.

After his long seclusion in the asylum the days seemed to him like weeks. He was at a loss to know how to fill them, for he did not have the strength to paint all the time. Nor did he have the desire. Before his accident in Arles no day had been long enough to get his work done; now they seemed interminable.

Fewer scenes in nature tempted him, and when he did begin work he felt strangely calm, almost indifferent. The feverish passion to paint in hot blood every minute of the day had left him. He now sketched in what was for him a leisurely fashion. And if he did not finish a canvas by nightfall . . . it no longer seemed to matter.

Doctor Gachet remained his only friend in Auvers. Gachet, who spent most of his days at his consulting office in Paris, often came to the Café Ravoux at night to look at pictures. Vincent had often wondered at the look of utter heartbreak in the doctor's eyes.

"Why are you unhappy, Doctor Gachet?" he asked.

"Ah, Vincent, I have laboured so many years . . . and I have done so little good. The doctor sees nothing but pain, pain, pain."

"I would gladly exchange my calling for yours," said Vincent.

A rapt eagerness lighted up the melancholy in Gachet's eyes.

"Ah, no, Vincent, it is the most beautiful thing in the world, to be a painter. All my life I wanted to be an artist . . . but I could spare only an hour here and there . . . there are so many sick people who need me."

Doctor Gachet went on his knees and pulled a pile of canvases from under Vincent's bed. He held a glowing yellow sunflower before him.

"If I had painted just one canvas like this, Vincent, I would consider my life justified. I spent the years curing people's pain . . . but they died in the end, anyway . . . so what did it matter? These sunflowers of yours . . . they will cure the pain in people's hearts . . . they will bring people joy . . . for centuries and centuries . . . that is why your life is successful . . . that is why you should be a happy man."

A few days later Vincent painted a portrait of the doctor in his white cap and blue frock coat, against a cobalt blue background. He did the head in a very fair, very light tone, the hands also in a light flesh tint. He posed Gachet leaning on a red table on which were a yellow book and a foxglove plant with purple flowers. He was amused to find, when he finished, that the portrait resembled the one he had done of himself in Arles, before Gauguin arrived.

The doctor went absolutely fanatical about the portrait. Vincent had never heard such a torrent of praise and acclaim. Gachet insisted that Vincent make a copy for him. When Vincent agreed, the doctor's joy knew no bounds.

"You must use my printing machine in the attic, Vincent," he cried. "We'll go to Paris, get all your canvases, and make lithographs of them. It won't cost you a centime, not a centime. Come, I will show you my workshop."

They had to climb a ladder and push open a trap door to get into the attic. Gachet's studio was piled so high with weird and fantastic implements

that Vincent thought he had been plunged into an alchemist's workshop of
the Middle Ages.

On the way downstairs, Vincent noticed that the Guillaumin nude was
still lying about, neglected.

"Doctor Gachet," he said, "I simply must insist that you have this framed.
You are ruining a masterpiece."

"Yes, yes, I mean to have it framed. When can we go to Paris and get
your paintings? You will print as many lithographs as you like. I will supply
the materials."

May slipped quietly into June. Vincent painted the Catholic church on the
hill. He wearied in the middle of the afternoon and did not even bother to
finish it. By dint of great perseverence he managed to paint a cornfield while
lying flat on the ground, his head almost in the corn; he did a large canvas of
Madame Daubigny's house; another of a white house in the trees, with a night
sky, an orange light in the windows, dark greenery and a note of sombre
rose colour; and lastly, an evening effect, two pear trees quite black against a
yellowing sky.

But the juice had gone out of painting. He worked from habit, because
there was nothing else to do. The terrific momentum of his ten years of
colossal labour carried him still a little farther. Where scenes from nature
had thrilled and excited him before, they now left him indifferent.

"I've painted that so many times," he would murmur to himself as he
walked along the roads, easel on his back, looking for a motif. "I have nothing new to say about it. Why should I repeat myself? Father Millet was right.
'J'aimerais mieux ne rien dire que de m'exprimer faiblement.' "

His love for nature had not died; it was simply that he no longer felt the
desperate need to fling himself at a scene and recreate it. He was burned
out. During the whole month of June he painted only five canvases. He was
weary, unspeakably weary. He felt empty, drained, washed out, as though the
hundreds upon hundreds of drawings and paintings that had flowed out of
him in the past ten years had each taken a tiny spark of his life.

At last he went on working only because he felt he owed it to Theo to
capitalize on the years of investment. And yet, when he realized, in the very
middle of a painting, that Theo's house was already jammed with more canvases than could be sold in ten lifetimes, a gentle nausea would arise within
him, and he would push away his easel with distaste.

He knew that another seizure was due in July, at the end of the three
month period. He worried for fear he would do something irrational while
the attack was upon him, and ostracize himself in the village. He had not
made any definite financial arrangements with Theo when he left Paris, and
he worried about how much money he was going to receive. The alternating
heartbreak and rapture in Gachet's eyes was driving Vincent's gorge up, day
by day.

And to cap the climax, Theo's child became ill.

The anxiety over his namesake almost drove Vincent frantic. He stood it as long as he could, then took a train to Paris. His sudden arrival in the Cité Pigalle heightened the confusion. Theo was looking pale and ill. Vincent did his best to comfort him.

"It isn't only the little one I'm worrying about, Vincent," he admitted at last.

"What then, Theo?"

"It's Valadon. He has threatened to ask for my resignation."

"Why, Theo, he couldn't! You've been with Goupils for sixteen years!"

"I know. But he says I've been neglecting the regular trade for the Impressionists. I don't sell very many of them, and when I do, the prices are low. Valadon claims my shop has been losing money for the past year."

"But could he really put you out?"

"Why not? The Van Gogh interest has been completely sold."

"What would you do, Theo? Open a shop of your own?"

"How could I? I had a little money saved, but I spent it on my wedding, and the baby."

"If only you hadn't thrown away those thousands of francs on me . . ."

"Now, Vincent, please. That had nothing to do with it. You know I . . ."

"But what will you do, Theo? There's Jo and the little one."

"Yes. Well . . . I don't know . . . I'm only worrying about the baby now."

Vincent stayed around Paris a number of days. He kept out of the apartment as much as possible, so as not to disturb the child. Paris and his old friends excited him. He felt a slow, gripping fever arise within him. When little Vincent recovered somewhat, he took the train back to the quiet of Auvers.

But the quiet did him no good. He was tormented by his worries. What would happen to him if Theo lost his job? Would he be thrown out into the streets like some vile beggar? And for that matter, what would happen to Jo and the baby? What if the baby died? He knew that Theo's frail health could never stand the blow. Who was going to support them all while Theo searched for a new job? And where was Theo going to find strength for the search?

He sat for hours in the dark café of Ravoux's. It reminded him of the Café Lamartine, with its odours of stale beer and acrid tobacco smoke. He jabbed around aimlessly with the billiard cue, trying to hit the discoloured balls. He had no money to buy liquor. He had no money to buy paints and canvases. He could not ask Theo for anything at such a crucial moment. And he was deathly afraid that when he had his seizure in July, he would do something insane, something to cause poor Theo even more worry and expense.

He tried working, but it was no good. He had painted everything he wanted to paint. He had said everything he wanted to say. Nature no longer stirred him to a creative passion, and he knew that the best part of him was already dead.

The days passed. The middle of July came, and with it the hot weather. Theo, his head just about to be chopped off by Valadon, frantic with worry over his baby and the doctor bills, managed to squeeze out fifty francs to send to his brother. Vincent turned them over to Ravoux. That would keep him until almost the end of July. And after that . . . what? He could not expect any more money from Theo.

He lay on his back under the hot sun in the cornfields by the little cemetery. He walked along the banks of the Oise, smelling the cool water and the foliage that lined its banks. He went to Gachet's for dinner and stuffed himself with food that he could neither taste nor digest. While the doctor raved on excitedly about Vincent's paintings, Vincent said to himself,

"That's not me he's talking about. Those can't be my pictures. I never painted anything. I don't even recognize my own signature on the canvas. I can't remember putting one single brush stroke on any of them. They must have been done by some other man!"

Lying in the darkness of his room he said to himself, "Suppose Theo doesn't lose his job. Suppose he is still able to send me a hundred and fifty francs a month. What am I going to do with my life? I've kept alive these last miserable years because I had to paint, because I had to say the things that were burning inside of me. But there's nothing burning inside me now. I'm just a shell. Should I go on vegetating like those poor souls at St. Paul, waiting for some accident to wipe me off the earth?"

At other times he worried about Theo, Johanna, and the baby.

"Suppose my strength and spirits return, and I want to paint again. How can I still take money from Theo when he needs it for Jo and the little one? He ought not spend that money on me. He ought to use it to send his family to the country, where they can grow healthy and strong. He's borne me on his back for ten long years. Isn't that enough? Shouldn't I get out and give little Vincent a chance? I've had my say; now the little one ought to have his."

But at the base of everything lay the overwhelming fear of what epilepsy would eventually do to him. Now he was sane and rational; he could do with his life what he wished. But suppose his next attack should convert him into a raving maniac. Suppose his brain should crack under the strain of the seizure. Suppose he became a hopeless, drivelling idiot. What would poor Theo do then? Lock him in an asylum for the lost ones?

He presented Doctor Gachet with two more of his canvases and wormed the truth out of him.

"No, Vincent," said the doctor, "you are all through with your attacks. You'll find yourself in perfect health from now on. But not all epileptics are that fortunate."

"What eventually happens to them, Doctor?"

"Sometimes, when they have had a number of crises, they go out of their minds completely."

"And is there no possible recovery for them?"

"No. They're finished. Oh, they may linger on for some years in an asylum, but they never come back to their right minds."

"How can they tell, Doctor, whether they will recover from the next attack, or whether it will crack their brains?"

"There is no way of telling, Vincent. But come, why should we discuss such morbid questions? Let's go up to the workshop and make some etchings."

Vincent did not leave his room at Ravoux's for the next four days. Madame Ravoux brought him his supper every evening.

"I'm well now, and sane," he kept repeating to himself. "I am master of my own destiny. But when the next seizure catches me . . . if it cracks my skull . . . I won't know enough to kill myself . . . and I'll be lost. Oh, Theo, Theo, what should I do?"

On the afternoon of the fourth day he went to Gachet's. The doctor was in the living room. Vincent walked to the cabinet where he had put the unframed Guillaumin nude some time before. He picked up the canvas.

"I told you to have this framed," he said.

Doctor Gachet looked at him in surprise.

"I know, Vincent. I'll order a stick frame from the joiner in Auvers next week."

"It must be framed now! Today! This minute!"

"Why, Vincent, you're talking nonsense!"

Vincent glared at the doctor for a moment, took a menacing step toward him, then put his hand in his coat pocket. Doctor Gachet thought he saw Vincent grip a revolver and point it at him through the coat.

"Vincent!" he exclaimed.

Vincent trembled. He lowered his eyes, pulled his hand from his pocket, and ran out of the house.

The next day he took his easel and canvas, walked down the long road to the station, climbed the hill past the Catholic church, and sat down in the yellow cornfield, opposite the cemetery.

About noon, when the fiery sun was beating down upon his head, a rush of blackbirds suddenly came out of the sky. They filled the air, darkened the sun, covered Vincent in a thick blanket of night, flew into his hair, his eyes, his nose, his mouth, buried him in a black cloud of tight, airless, flapping wings.

Vincent went on working. He painted the birds above the yellow field of corn. He did not know how long he wielded his brush, but when he saw that he had finished, he wrote *Crows Above a Cornfield* in one corner, carried his easel and canvas back to Ravoux's, threw himself across the bed and went to sleep.

The following afternoon he went out again, but left the Place de la Mairie from the other side. He climbed the hill past the chateau. A peasant saw him sitting in a tree.

"It is impossible!" he heard Vincent say. "It is impossible!"

After a time he climbed down from the tree and walked in the ploughed field behind the chateau. This time it was the end. He had known that in

Arles, the very first time, but he had been unable to make the clean break.

He wanted to say good-bye. In spite of all, it had been a good world that he had lived in. As Gauguin said, "Besides the poison, there is the antidote." And now, leaving the world, he wanted to say good-bye to it, say good-bye to all those friends who had helped mould his life; to Ursula, whose contempt had wrenched him out of a conventional life and made him an outcast; to Mendes da Costa, who had made him believe that ultimately he would express himself, and that expression would justify his life; to Kay Vos, whose "No, never! never!" had been written in acid on his soul; to Madame Denis, Jacques Verney and Henri Decrucq, who had helped him love the despised ones of the earth; to the Reverend Pietersen, whose kindness had transcended Vincent's ugly clothes and boorish manners; to his mother and father, who had loved him as best they could; to Christine, the only wife with which fate had seen fit to bless him; to Mauve, who had been his master for a few sweet weeks; to Weissenbruch and De Bock, his first painter friends; to his Uncles Vincent, Jan, Cornelius Marinus, and Stricker, who had labeled him the black sheep of the Van Gogh family; to Margot, the only woman who had ever loved him, and who had tried to kill herself for that love; to all his painter friends in Paris; Lautrec, who had been shut up in an asylum again, to die; Georges Seurat, dead at thirty-one from overwork; Paul Gauguin, a mendicant in Brittany; Rousseau, rotting in his hole near the Bastille; Cezanne, a bitter recluse on a hilltop in Aix; to Père Tanguy and Roulin, who had shown him the salt in the simple souls of the earth; to Rachel and Doctor Rey, who had been kind to him with the kindness he needed; to Aurier and Doctor Gachet, the only two men in the world who had thought him a great painter; and last of all, to his good brother Theo, long suffering, long loving, best and dearest of all possible brothers.

But words had never been his medium. He would have to paint good-bye.

One cannot paint good-bye.

He turned his face upward to the sun. He pressed the revolver into his side. He pulled the trigger. He sank down, burying his face in the rich, pungent loam of the field, a more resilient earth returning to the womb of its mother.

4

Four hours later he staggered through the gloom of the café. Madame Ravoux followed him to his room and saw blood on his clothes. She ran at once for Doctor Gachet.

"Oh. Vincent, Vincent, what have you done!" groaned Gachet, when he entered the room.

"I think I have bungled it; what do you say?"

Gachet examined the wound.

"Oh, Vincent, my poor old friend, how unhappy you must have been to do this! Why didn't I know? Why should you want to leave us when we all love you so? Think of the beautiful pictures you have still to paint for the world."

"Will you be so kind as to give me my pipe from my waistcoat pocket?"

"But certainly, my friend."

He loaded the pipe with tobacco, then placed it between Vincent's teeth.

"A light, if you please," said Vincent.

"But certainly, my friend."

Vincent puffed quietly at his pipe.

"Vincent, it is Sunday and your brother is not at the shop. What is his home address?"

"That I will not give you."

"But, Vincent, you must! It is urgent that we reach him!"

"Theo's Sunday must not be disturbed. He is tired and worried. He needs the rest."

No amount of persuasion could get the Cité Pigalle address out of Vincent. Doctor Gachet stayed with him until late that night, tending the wound. Then he went home for a little rest, leaving his son to care for Vincent.

Vincent lay there wide-eyed all night, never uttering a word to Paul. He kept filling his pipe and smoking it constantly.

When Theo arrived at Goupils the following morning, he found Gachet's telegram awaiting him. He caught the first train for Pontoise, then dashed in a carriage to Auvers.

"Well, Theo," said Vincent.

Theo dropped on his knees by the side of the bed and took Vincent in his arms like a little child. He could not speak.

When the doctor arrived, Theo led him outside to the corridor. Gachet shook his head sadly.

"There is no hope, my friend. I cannot operate to remove the bullet, for he is too weak. If he were not made of iron he would have died in the fields."

All through the long day Theo sat by his bed, holding Vincent's hand. When nightfall came, and they were left alone in the room, they began to speak quietly of their childhood in the Brabant.

"Do you remember the mill at Ryswyk, Vincent?"

"It was a nice old mill, wasn't it, Theo?"

"We used to walk by the path along the stream, and plan our lives."

"And when we played in the high corn, in midsummer, you used to hold my hand, just as you're doing now. Remember, Theo?"

"Yes, Vincent."

"When I was in the hospital at Arles, I used to think often about Zundert. We had a nice childhood, Theo, you and I. We used to play in the garden behind the kitchen, in the shade of the acacias, and Mother would make us cheese bakes for lunch."

"That seems so long ago, Vincent."

". . . Yes . . . well . . . life is long. Theo, for my sake, take care of yourself. Guard your health. You must think of Jo and the little one. Take them into the country somewhere so they can grow strong and healthy. And don't stay with Goupils, Theo. They have taken the whole of your life . . . and given you nothing in return."

"I'm going to open a tiny gallery of my own, Vincent. And my first exhibition will be a one-man show. The complete works of Vincent Van Gogh . . . just as you laid it out in the apartment . . . with your own hands."

"Ah, well, my work . . . I risked my life for it . . . and my reason has almost foundered."

The deep quiet of the Auvers night fell upon the room.

At a little after one in the morning, Vincent turned his head slightly and whispered,

"I wish I could die now, Theo."

In a few minutes he closed his eyes.

Theo felt his brother leave him, forever.

5

Rousseau, Père Tanguy, Aurier and Émile Bernard came out from Paris for the funeral.

The doors of the Café Ravoux were locked and the blinds pulled down. The little black hearse with the black horses waited out in front.

They laid Vincent's coffin on the billiard table.

Theo, Doctor Gachet, Rousseau, Père Tanguy, Aurier, Bernard, and Ravoux gathered about, speechless. They could not look at each other.

No one thought of calling in a minister.

The driver of the hearse knocked at the front door.

"It is time, gentlemen," he said.

"For God's sake, we can't let him go like this!" cried Gachet.

He brought all the paintings down from Vincent's room, then sent his son Paul running home to get the rest of his canvases.

Six of the men worked putting up the paintings on the walls.

Theo stood alone by the coffin.

Vincent's sunlight canvases transformed the drab, gloomy café into a brilliant cathedral.

Once again the men gathered about the billiard table. Gachet alone could speak.

"Let us not despair, we who are Vincent's friends. Vincent is not dead. He will never die. His love, his genius, the great beauty he has created will go on forever, enriching the world. Not an hour passes but that I look at his paintings and find there a new faith, a new meaning of life. He was a colossus . . . a great painter . . . a great philosopher. He fell a martyr to his love of art."

Theo tried to thank him.

"...I...I..."

The tears choked him. He could not go on.

The cover was placed on Vincent's coffin.

His six friends lifted it from the billiard table. They carried it out of the little café. They placed it gently in the hearse.

They walked behind the black carriage, down the sunlit road. They passed the thatched cottages and the little country villas.

At the station the hearse turned to the left and began the slow climb up the hill. They passed the Catholic church, then wound through the yellow cornfield.

The black carriage stopped at the gate of the cemetery.

Theo walked behind the coffin while the six men carried it to the grave.

Doctor Gachet had chosen as Vincent's last resting place the spot on which they had stood that very first day, overlooking the lovely verdant valley of the Oise.

Once again Theo tried to speak. He could not.

The attendants lowered the coffin into the ground. Then they shovelled in dirt and stamped it down.

The seven men turned, left the cemetery, and walked down the hill.

Doctor Gachet returned a few days later to plant sunflowers all about the grave.

Theo went home to the Cité Pigalle. His loss pushed out every aching second of the night and day with unassuageable grief.

His mind broke under the strain.

Johanna took him to the *maison de santé* in Utrecht, where Margot had gone before him.

At the end of six months, almost to the day of Vincent's death, Theo passed away. He was buried at Utrecht.

Some time later, when Johanna was reading her Bible for comfort, she came across the line in Samuel:

> *And in their death they were not divided.*

She took Theo's body to Auvers, and had it placed by the side of his brother.

When the hot Auvers sun beats down upon the little cemetery in the cornfields, Theo rests comfortably in the luxuriant umbrage of Vincent's sunflowers.

THE END

NOTE

THE reader may have asked himself, "How much of this story is true?" The dialogue had to be reimagined; there is an occasional stretch of pure fiction, such as the Maya scene, which the reader will have readily recognized; in one or two instances, I have portrayed a minor incident where I was convinced of its probability even though I could not document it, for example, the brief meeting between Cezanne and Van Gogh in Paris; I have utilized a few devices for the sake of facility, such as the use of the franc as the unit of exchange during Vincent's trek over Europe; and I have omitted several unimportant fragments of the complete story. Aside from these technical liberties, the book is entirely true.

My main source was Vincent Van Gogh's three volumes of letters to his brother Theo (Houghton, Mifflin 1927–1930). The greater part of the material I unearthed on the trail of Vincent across Holland, Belgium, and France.

It would be ingratitude indeed if I did not acknowledge my debt to the host of Van Gogh friends and enthusiasts in Europe who gave unsparingly of their time and material: Colin Van Oss and Louis Bron of the Haagshe *Post;* Johan Tersteeg of the Goupil Galleries in The Hague; the family of Anton Mauve in Scheveningen; M. and Mme. Jean Baptiste Denis of Petit Wasmes; the Hofkes family of Nuenen; J. Bart de la Faille of Amsterdam; Dr. Felix Rey of Arles; Dr. Edgar Le Roy of St. Paul de Mausole; Paul Gachet of Auvers-sur-l'Oise, who remains Vincent's stanchest friend in Europe.

I am indebted to Lona Mosk, Alice and Ray C. B. Brown, and Jean Factor for editorial assistance. Lastly, I wish to express my profoundest gratitude to Ruth Aley, who first saw the book in the manuscript.

I. S.

June 6th, 1934

Immortal Wife

THE BOOKS

For
JEAN
in whom I found my Jessie

BOOK ONE

DAWN COMES EARLY

1

SHE SWEPT into the reception room of Miss English's Academy, her hazel eyes bright with anger, the rustle of her taffeta gown raised from a crisp whisper to a cry by the vigor of her movements. Looking neither to right nor left Jessie Benton stormed up to her father and said in a low voice:

"I won't stay in this school another day. I'm going home with you tonight!"

Without trying to rise, her father asked, "What has happened?"

"I had Harriet Williams elected May Queen. She's the prettiest girl in the school, and the best dancer. But at breakfast this morning Miss English announced that we had to have a different queen."

Thomas Benton gazed into his daughter's enormous eyes.

"I trust you accepted the decision philosophically?"

She threw back her head with a spirited gesture of denial.

"I jumped to my feet and cried, 'This decision is unjust and unfair. The first choice of Harriet was honestly made!'"

"What happened then?"

"Miss English called me to the head of the dining room, put her hand on my forehead and said, 'Miss Jessie, you seem feverish. Please report to the infirmary.'"

Tom Benton chuckled at the mimicked severity of his daughter's voice.

"How was the hot senna tea?"

"Dreadful, thank you. They kept me in solitary all day. But I used the time to good advantage, planning a mutiny. On May Day all the girls will complain of a headache, and we'll be sent to bed with senna tea. The tea won't be half so bitter as watching that other queen try to dance. They only appointed her because she's a Fitzhugh, and Harriet's father is a government clerk . . ."

"Jessie dear," broke in her father, "Mother didn't feel well enough to come to the musicale, so I've brought a friend. May I present Lieutenant John Charles Fremont?"

A young man in army uniform who had been standing a few steps behind Tom Benton's chair came forward into the light of the candelabrum. The red wine of Jessie's anger, which she had been storing since breakfast, drained from her mind as suddenly as if someone had pulled the stopper of a vat. Her first thought was, At last I've met a man who is better-looking than my cousin Preston. I'm glad I wasn't too mad to wear my new pink candy-stripe with the rose sash instead of the dotted muslin with the blue.

She extended her hand, and instantly it was clasped in his. The young man had not moved with abruptness, nor was he now gripping her hand tightly; but here was a hand and a grasp that matched her own. She sensed what it was about a handshake that made it more than an empty social gesture: this brief embrace of the flesh.

The presentiment passed. She heard her father speaking to her.

". . . May Queen was supposed to be the best student in the school. Was Harriet at the top of her class?"

Only with the greatest reluctance could she bring herself back to the discussion. This morning seemed far away and long ago. In her dislike of the school she had seized upon the injustice to Harriet as a means of escape.

"No," she conceded, "Harriet was at the top of the mulberry tree more often than at the top of her class. We can climb into the tree from the window of my room, and the teachers can't hear us talking and laughing."

"You were vulnerable," pronounced Senator Thomas Hart Benton in his most pontifical tone; "when you decided that you were going to have Harriet elected, you should have managed her studies as well as shepherded her votes. Isn't it true, Lieutenant Fremont," he continued, "that in politics as well as war we must never permit ourselves to be vulnerable?"

"True," murmured the lieutenant, "in war, politics and love. But not always easy to live up to."

Jessie gazed at the young man admiringly. She thought, He outflanked Father neatly.

"As for that May Day uprising," her father went on, "mutiny is dangerous business; a little of it goes a long way."

Jessie turned to Lieutenant Fremont a cameo face, the delicate oval accentuated by the long brown hair parted in the center and combed over the temples to conceal all of the ear except the tip of the lobe. For so slender a face, her mouth was startlingly full and red-lipped, high-lighted by the smooth creamy texture of her skin. When she was thinking fast the color pounded into her cheeks, just as now, when she murmured:

"My father is really not qualified to preach that sermon, Lieutenant Fremont; he brought me up on stories of how he and Andrew Jackson mutinied against the War Department."

Her father made a ducking gesture of pleased acceptance of defeat; their years of close association had taught Jessie how to pull the sting out of any impending parental rebuke.

"However, I'll give up the idea," she agreed. "It wouldn't do any good, anyway: Harriet's mother took her out of school this afternoon. Come, gentlemen, let us go into the auditorium; the music will start any moment."

She sat between her father and the lieutenant while her older sister Eliza opened the program with a faithful but uninspired playing of a Bach fugue. There were perhaps a hundred guests in the assembly room; the small stage was lighted by guarded footlight candles, and the deep blue draperies were pulled over the side rows of windows to blot out the early February dusk. Because of her tale about Harriet they had come in late and were seated in a far corner on a button-back chaise. She was glad it had happened that way, for it gave her a chance to study John Fremont's face in the semidarkness.

She was astonished to see that he was a little man, certainly not much bigger than she, for their shoulders came to precisely the same height against the green silk of the sofa; their eyes too were on a level.

Why, he's small, she thought. Exactly my size, and I'm only five feet two. How odd I didn't notice that when we were standing. He doesn't have the feel of a little man.

She turned to look at her father, who towered above her, an enormous fellow with a big-boned frame, shoulders that sloped sharply as did her own, but heavy and powerful from years of outdoor living.

She was not greatly interested in music, and particularly not in this fugue which Eliza had been dinning into her ears for a solid week. Her eyes wandered over the backs of her schoolmates, seated between their parents. She had not wanted to come to Miss English's Academy in Georgetown, a suburb of Washington. She remembered the scene with her father when he had first told her that she must attend.

"What can I learn there that will be of as much value as studying at home?" she had demanded. "What will I find to read in their juvenile textbooks after I've been over most of the world's literature with you? Who is going to help you with your reports and speeches, who is going to calm you when you stomp up and down this room crying out at the stupidity of your opponents? By the Eternal, Tom Benton, I am not going to that girls' finishing school."

"Yes, you are, Jessie," he had said, his head down, eyes averted. "If it were ever to happen that anyone should accuse you of lacking in manners or grace or anything you can get at that school, I would never forgive myself. I'm afraid that you have become old before your time by associating with me so much. Mother accuses me of robbing you of your childhood."

"But that's not true," she had exclaimed, hurt at her mother's blindness. "I've had a magnificent childhood with you: we went quail hunting each autumn in the country, and lunched on biscuits and apples while you read to me the stories your friend Audubon wrote; we spent whole weeks in the saddle riding through Missouri while you campaigned; we . . ."

"Mother says you're undisciplined. She thinks you need classroom work; she says you need to learn to play girls' games."

"But damme, Father," she had answered, "I don't want to play games. And will you tell me why I need classroom discipline when every time we went out on a picnic you would make me take my copy of Homer's *Odyssey* and read from it in Greek? If I'm not better educated than any girl you will find at Miss English's Academy, I'll eat the twenty volumes of your *British State Trials*."

Her father had not even listened to her.

"I know my duty, Jessie, and I'm a hard man to divert."

Later that evening she had come back to his library and stood before him on the thick rug, her eyes red and swollen, her brown hair cut off at the shoulders.

"What in heaven's name have you done to yourself, Jessie?" her father had cried in anguish.

"I've cut off my hair so I'll be ugly," she announced through her tears; "now I won't need any classrooms or discipline, or to go out in society. Father, all I want to do is stay here and be your companion."

Tom Benton had remained firm. "I can't take the responsibility for anything lacking in your life. You are fourteen years old, you are already late in entering. Now stop the sniveling and go out with your mother and Eliza and order some new clothes."

As she had turned to leave the room he had called, "Maybe the school will only be half as bad as it sounds. I promise to save all of my important speeches for when you will be home on week ends."

That was two years ago; her hair had grown long again, but her dislike for the school had persisted.

Eliza finished her number, acknowledged the polite applause. Jessie looked to John Fremont, waiting for him to project himself, create the impression which the hundreds of men who crossed the threshold of the Benton home in Washington had sooner or later set out to create. The young lieutenant returned her gaze with friendly interest, but said nothing.

Words always had been beautiful to Jessie Ann Benton, but as she sat in the comfortably poised silence, feeling keenly the presence of the army officer beside her, she sensed that words were not the sole measure of communication, nor perhaps even the best. John Fremont did not speak; yet some inward ear, hitherto unsuspected, heard him speaking to her.

"What branch of the service are you in, Lieutenant Fremont?" she asked.

"The Topographical Corps. I'm working with Mr. Nicollet and Mr. Hassler on the map of the Minnesota country."

"Nicollet and Hassler? Why, they are two of Father's closest friends."

"That's how I met Senator Benton. He came to Mr. Hassler's house, where I am plotting the material we gathered on our expedition to the upper Missouri."

"Were you on that expedition with Nicollet?" she demanded excitedly.

"Yes, I've been his assistant for four years now; most of that time we've spent in the northern wilderness, in the Indian country."

An exclamation came from Jessie's full lips.

"Is it true, Miss Benton," asked the lieutenant, "that your father has never been west of Missouri? I can hardly believe it: he knows more about the West than any man I've met."

Jessie was warmed by the tribute to her father; she felt a companionable glow come over her.

"He has never been west of Missouri, but his mind has lived in those regions ever since he was a boy. His closest friends are the explorers and hunters who outfit in St. Louis and work their way to the Rockies; they stay at our home in St. Louis when they return from their expeditions." She made a half-turn to include her father in the conversation. "Father had it all planned for me to be a son. I was to be trained for the Army, join the Topographical Corps, and explore the West. Isn't that so, Father?"

"Something of the sort," he grumbled.

A string quartet began to play, and they again fell silent. At the intermission Thomas Benton introduced Lieutenant Fremont to Eliza. While Eliza and the lieutenant exchanged greetings, Senator Benton suggested to Jessie that they take a turn about the garden. Though it was only seven o'clock they found the air cool and sharp as they walked along the gravel path between Miss English's rows of trimmed hedges.

"Do you think Eliza will like Lieutenant Fremont?" asked Tom Benton.

"He's tremendously exciting," Jessie replied, her wide-set hazel eyes flashing.

Tom glanced quickly at his daughter.

"I asked if you thought Eliza would like him, not if you liked him. Young ladies who are still two months short of being seventeen aren't supposed to find strange men exciting."

Jessie looked amusedly at her father in the darkness.

"Would you mind citing your authority for that statement, Senator?" she asked, mimicking the tone which he reserved for his opponents on the floor of the United States Senate.

When they came back into the auditorium Jessie's eyes quickly caught the wiry figure of Lieutenant Fremont silhouetted against the blue draperies. He seemed surcharged with energy, yet he had the sensitive face of the intellectual. He's terribly young to be so close to the top of his profession, she thought.

As her sister and Lieutenant Fremont joined them, she felt a wave of resentment at her own romantic foolishness. Now I am behaving like a sixteen-year-old, she said to herself. If I can't do any better than this, Father is right to keep me in a girls' school.

She raised her sloping shoulders, tensed her diaphragm, concentrated on the group of ballads being sung. The music was diverting, her shoulders slowly slipped, and she sat relaxed. As the song reached a crescendo she had a feeling that the young man was speaking to her. She glanced about at him; his lips were quiet.

"Yes?" she asked softly.

His voice, deep for so small a person, said, ". . . nothing important; just that—I've been watching . . . your pearl earrings . . . gleam in the candlelight. The lights and shadows were keeping rhythm with the music."

Jessie lifted her hand to where the rich brown hair was combed tightly over her ear, took his finger and touched it lightly to the tiny circle of white lobe which she left exposed. Then she laughed, her laughter leaping forward; his laughter came forth strong, meeting her halfway, mingling with hers, seizing it. Happily the music had reached its climax, and no one heard them; but Jessie heard, and she asked herself in wonderment:

What does this mean?

2

She sat before the mirror of her dressing table, alternately gazing at her reflection and out the window at the back garden. This was the moment for which she had been waiting since her father had announced casually, after the Wednesday evening musicale, that she would meet Lieutenant Fremont again at dinner on Sunday. The intervening days had passed in stops and rushes; with Harriet gone from school, and the young lieutenant having pre-empted her place in Jessie's mind, Miss English's Academy for Young Ladies seemed more childish than ever.

Her father's friends and associates who habituated the Benton drawing room called her the prettiest girl in Washington; at Cherry Grove, her mother's home in Virginia, the family would put her on exhibition every summer when she visited, turning her about slowly, commenting on her lithe figure, the deep brown hair, the magnificently soft and sensitive hazel eyes and the delicacy of her face, which they declared to be in the genteel tradition of the McDowells.

Jessie had never been impressed by these comments; she had taken for granted that she was an attractive girl, as were all the girls about her; it was part of being young to be pretty.

Now for the first time as she scrutinized herself with what she insisted was objective detachment, she realized that her family and friends had been flattering her. Her eyes were too large and wide-spaced for so slender an oval. I'm all eyes, she thought, like a cat at night. The rest of my face drowns in them. No, not my nose; unfortunately I've got Father's nose. He has always loved his long Roman nose because it makes him look like a senator, but I don't want to be a senator, and I have no use for it. And if nature meant for me to have slender cheeks, why wasn't the design carried through? Why do I have a chin that looks like Senator Benton's when he's got it stuck out pugnaciously demanding free land for the settlers of the West?

Her interest in her own face passed abruptly as she swung about on the low dressing-table stool and tried to conjure up instead the face of Lieutenant John Charles Fremont. A feeling of disappointment came over her: she could not remember what the man looked like. How can this be? she asked herself. How is it possible that I cannot remember what color his eyes are, or the shape of his mouth, or how he combs his hair?

Hearing the sound of a carriage drawing up to the front entrance, she quickly adjusted the coral collar and cuffs on her white spencer blouse, grateful for the sheen of color with which they brushed the pallor of her skin. I wouldn't want him to think me delicate, she mused as she rose, pushed back a

strand of hair which insisted upon wandering down over her brow, and seized
a coral lace handkerchief from her bureau drawer. As she passed the door
of her mother's bedroom she stopped for a moment to look in.

Elizabeth Benton was stretched out on a satin-covered chaise; her black
hair was streaked with gray, her once beautiful face deeply lined. Though she
was only forty-seven, twelve years younger than her husband, she always
had seemed to Jessie to be incomparably older, perhaps because she had
spent most of her waking hours on this chaise, not bedridden, but with both
her body and spirit immobile. Mrs. Benton had made it understood that her
bedroom was her sanctuary, that no one might enter without permission. The
floor was covered with a deep rose carpeting, the curtains were of fine lace
encrusted with small medallions, two fragile gilt chairs stood before the windows, and next to the small bed was a tilt-top table with pink roses painted
on its mahogany surface. It was all very elaborate and delicate, unlike the
rest of this house which had been built by a wealthy English merchant and
had been both designed and furnished in the most massive masculine taste. It
was as unlike the rest of the house, the girl thought, as Elizabeth McDowell
Benton was unlike Thomas Hart Benton . . . or Jessie Ann Benton.

As her mother beckoned, Jessie walked quickly to her side, smoothed the
quilted chaise robe. "How are you feeling?" she asked.

"Fairly well, thank you."

"You're not coming down to dinner?"

"No . . . o, I'm comfortable here. Maylee will bring my tray. Father told
me everyone who was coming; there will be an interminable argument, Jessie.
I'm just not up to it; you know how ill the noise makes me."

Jessie knew that her mother was suffering from some intermittent ailment,
but its source was obscure to her. No doctors came to the house; Mrs.
Benton took no medicines or treatments; no symptoms ever were described.
Yet several years before she had stepped down from active management of
the household, leaving it in the hands of the trained servants she had brought
with her from Cherry Grove. She now joined the family for dinner only on
those rare occasions when there were no guests present. She seemed to her
young daughter to take part in no active life whatever, for she did not read,
her hands lay idle, she had abandoned her circle of women friends, and no
serious matter could be discussed in her presence.

Yet it had not always been so: Jessie could remember when her mother
had sat with them before the bright winter fire, her father at one side reading
one of an endless succession of books, Mrs. Benton sitting at a smaller table
opposite her husband, knitting or embroidering; Jessie and her sisters and
brother working at their lessons at a heavy, square desk under the front
windows.

Even now, during their yearly vacations at her mother's home in Virginia,
where both Elizabeth McDowell and Jessie Benton had been born, the illness
seemed to vanish, the lines in her mother's face to recede, her vigor return,

so that she appeared again the happy woman whom Jessie remembered from her childhood.

As she went to the windows and drew the blinds, then put a few drops of fresh eau de cologne on her mother's lace handkerchief, these early memories of her mother were pleasant to recall, even though there never had been a complete love or understanding between them. It had been largely her own fault, Jessie knew: she had loved her father and the work he had trained her to do so devotedly that she had been unable to hide her preference. And always in her mind there had been a resentment that her mother did not work with her father, that she did not assist him in formulating his plans, help him write his speeches and articles, did not discuss with him the unendingly exciting issues and causes of the contemporary world.

Though her father never had said anything to her, though she was given daily, even hourly evidence of how utterly Tom Benton was devoted to his Elizabeth, Jessie felt that he missed her sorely in his work. It was only by the implications of the philosophy on which he had raised his second daughter that she had come to understand this:

"Don't be content to be a housewife; don't be content to think only of manners and charm and dilettantish conversation; don't be content to have your mind and personality obliterated by your husband. Prepare yourself, develop your thinking powers, grow accustomed to conflict and the clash of ideas. Then when you grow up you will be able to make a contribution to the society in which you live, you will never weaken in the face of personal warfare."

Jessie wished her mother a pleasant dinner, then hurried on down the stairs. She paused on the threshold of the drawing room to listen to the relaxed hum of Sunday afternoon conversation, while her eyes roamed the room to identify their friends. Sitting in the bow of the window overlooking C Street, and framed by floor-length curtains of starched white lace, she saw her father and Senators Linn and Crittenden, his fellow battlers for western expansion, dressed in the conventional white waistcoat, black coat with square-stubbed tails, and black trousers which fitted tightly over their Wellington boots. Sprawled before them on a velvet love seat with curlicue arms were their two most savage opponents in the House, bantering the senators on the legislation they had blocked the week before.

At the back of the room Jessie saw her large, rather plain-faced sister Eliza playing softly on the piano. It had not surprised her that Eliza had been uninterested in the young lieutenant from the Topographical Corps. Eliza was quiet, slow-spoken and inclined to be literal-minded. She had inherited her father's rawboned physique and heavy features. If she were a man she would have been a lawyer, for she liked the precise and methodical thinking of the legal mind. Eliza had been ill during most of her childhood; she was not strong and she greatly feared the ravages of personal emotion. Jessie had thought at first that Eliza had no feelings, until she had learned that her sister was avoiding personal involvement in order to spare her limited strength.

Leaning against the piano was Mrs. Linn, dressed in a new white India muslin redingote lined with a pale blue silk. She was telling Mrs. Crittenden and Mrs. King, the Bentons' next-door neighbor, about the glass-blowing exhibition she had seen at the circus the day before. Seated in the far corner at a round, marble-topped table, and sipping sherry, was Nicholas Nicollet, the greatest scientist of exploration and map making in America. He was describing to Colonel J. J. Abert, head of the Topographical Corps, and Colonel Stephen Watts Kearny, one of the oldest and dearest friends of the Benton family, a new invention of a rubber boat which the next expedition could use for shooting the rapids of the Des Moines River.

Skimming quickly over the familiar surface of these faces and conversations, Jessie's eyes sought the tall rectangular mirror over the massive fireplace, in which she saw reflected three faces: that of Samuel Morse in his shiny black clothes, sallow and ill with the ravages of disappointment; Anne Royall, a bony, sharp-featured woman in her seventies, dressed in a stiff calico gown wrapped around the waist with a cord and tassel; and Lieutenant John Charles Fremont, in his blue army uniform with shining gold braid. The first feminist to invade Washington, Mrs. Royall was talking passionately about an article in her magazine, *Paul Pry,* while Samuel Morse stood unhearing, chewing his own bitter thoughts, and the lieutenant, in a most unmilitary manner, was trying to ward off the avalanche of words by gazing head down at the carpet and following a leaf pattern with the toe of his boot.

A quickening ran through Jessie. Now, before he sees me, she thought, before I get too close to him, I'll take a long, careful look. She gazed steadfastly at the reflection in the mirror, but the harder she looked the faster her breath came and the more blurred became the vision. It's like those first daguerreotypes Sam Morse made, she told herself; they catch an imprint, but faintly, through a haze.

Her eyes went first to his hair, which she saw with a start was parted in the center. Just like mine, she exclaimed to herself. It was black, and with a twinge of envy she noted its soft wave as it came a little forward on his high brow before sweeping backwards over the top of his ears. His black eyebrows slanted angularly downward at the corner of his eyes; his dark eyes were grave, sympathetic, his bone-ridged nose short and slender, his black mustache as straight as his stiffly pressed uniform.

Yet even as she enumerated to herself his separate features she realized that no such physical description could engrave an ineradicable picture of Lieutenant Fremont on her mind: for the look of the man was something over and above the component parts of the features with which he confronted the world. There appeared to be promise behind that slow, enigmatic smile: he radiated an aura of confidence.

Samuel Morse had begun to tell a story in a low hoarse tone, and as Lieutenant Fremont listened to the inventor with an expression of interest and sympathy, Jessie perceived that until she came to grips with this young man, until she understood the spirit which motivated him, she never could have a clear perception of what he looked like. She recalled how radically she had had to change her estimate of many of the men she had met through her father's work; some of those whom she had thought handsome had proved to be men of small souls, grasping, fickle, without the stamina to do a job that was so necessary in a full man. As their characters unfolded she had come to think of them as unattractive, while others, whose noses or eyelids curved in queer patterns, had grown not only increasingly attractive with the passage of the years but as beautiful in her mind as their qualities of integrity and devotion.

She was aware of how acutely Lieutenant Fremont stimulated her; there could be no escape from that realization. Would he continue to remain handsome and exciting as she traveled the mysterious road to knowledge of him? Or would he become dull-looking, perhaps downright ugly?

As though conscious that he was being studied, Lieutenant Fremont threw up his head sharply. In the mirror their eyes met. He smiled a boyish smile. Quickly she went forward to greet him.

3

Only the Sunday before, Jessie had heard their good friend James Buchanan characterize the Benton dining table as a place where lost causes mingled with unborn causes, and no one could tell them apart. As she waited for Joshaam, half of a pair of handsome Negro twins, to swing open the heavy wooden doors leading to the dining room, she reflected on what a considerable portion of American history had been rehearsed across its long mahogany table since her father had been elected senator from the state of Missouri and moved from St. Louis to Washington City in 1821. Every president since Madison: James Monroe, John Quincy Adams, Andrew Jackson, Martin Van Buren and William H. Harrison, had tucked his boots under this table and eaten heartily, along with the majority of cabinet officers and ambassadors, the changing panorama of congressmen, army officers, explorers and trappers of the western wilderness.

The doors opened, she stepped inside for a quick inspection before summoning the guests. It was a pleasant room, with paneled mahogany walls, high ceiling and tall windows, a simple Federal fireplace, its frame set flat into the wall, the mantel a narrow, tailored shelf. Her roving eyes took in the shining chandelier, hanging by its four highly polished chains, the deep burgundy rug with its border outlined in squares, the portraits of Thomas Benton's mother and father on the broad wall over the serpentine-front buffet, and the lovely portrait of Elizabeth McDowell Benton, painted many years before by Samuel Morse.

The table was covered with a damask cloth; in the center were the twisted candlesticks Elizabeth McDowell had brought with her from Cherry Grove, and on either side exquisite crystal cut-glass stands filled with fruits and flowers. At both ends of the table a monster salmon rested on waves of clear jelly, while at each place there was a cold broiled lobster, and before it metal cups of bubbling butter and rum over tiny charcoal braziers.

Satisfied that everything was as her father would wish it, she sent Joshaam to announce that dinner was served. She had arranged to have Lieutenant Fremont at her right, and in recompense to the remainder of the guests for what she considered a pre-empting of the most desirable dinner partner, she put Anne Royall on her left. When they were all seated, Jessie counted noses and saw that there were twenty-two at the table.

She poured the hot butter and rum over her lobster, then turned to her newest guest and asked, "Do you like to argue while you eat, Lieutenant?"

"Not unless the food is poor."

"Then I suggest that you enjoy the first three courses, for that is the extent of Father's indulgence. By the time the roast comes in, you won't be able to hear yourself think."

It was her task to guide the early conversation, to keep it entertaining, to see that the table did not break into circles of private discussion. Long practice had taught her the technique: she led Anne Royall into telling the story of how the editor of the Washington *Globe* had called her a petticoat editor, and how she had replied that a petticoat patriot was better than a trouserloon traitor. Having caught a snatch of Mrs. Crittenden's story in the drawing room about the production of *Richard III* at the National Theatre, she cued the lady into telling how the actor, Mr. Hackett, had handed out a program in which he attacked every other actor's interpretation of Richard. Mrs. King excoriated Congress for being too stingy to appropriate money to have the main streets of Washington City paved, or the lamps turned on at night.

"Why, only last week," she exclaimed, "poor Mrs. Spingarn, all dressed up in her new lace-cuffed evening gown, tried to walk to the National Theatre to hear the great Celeste, and fell headlong into a tremendous mudhole on B Street."

There was a deep-toned Chinese gong fastened to the right leg of the table, and by giving it a backward kick with the heel of her pump Jessie was able to summon the servants when she wanted them. While the twins padded about the table in their short black coats and trousers rolled above the ankles, replacing the lobster dishes with blue Wedgwood plates for the cold salmon, and then deep dishes for the oyster stew, Jessie encouraged Samuel Morse to tell what he knew of the stinginess of the Congress. Morse, his gloom unrelieved, portrayed the obtuseness of the committee to which he had demonstrated his telegraph: the congressmen had refused him the small appropriation necessary to build an experimental line to Baltimore.

But when the sides of rare roast beef were brought in, flanked by kidney pies, Jessie saw her father, who had hardly touched his food up to this point, cut himself generous helpings and then promptly launch into an argument with the congressmen from New England on the need to explore the country between Illinois, Missouri and the Rockies, so that one day the United States would extend from ocean to ocean. To the New Englanders this was the sheerest lunacy, and they had not the slightest hesitancy in telling their host so.

As the clamor at the table rose, Jessie laid down her knife and fork and sat back in her chair.

"Appetite gone, Miss Jessie?" asked John Fremont.

"Father eats best when he is arguing the hardest. I'm just the opposite: I can't eat when there is strong argument about. Father never expresses himself better than when in the midst of a heavy dinner . . ."

"I've been noticing," he remarked, glancing up the table at Senator Benton with amused admiration.

". . . though you would imagine he has not the slightest idea of what he is eating when he is thinking so hard. Once I teased him by asking how he enjoyed the mallards and frozen pudding. He replied, 'We haven't had duck since Tuesday, and the frozen pudding was last Sunday.' "

John laughed. "I guess that chided you."

"Indeed it did. Later tonight he will call me into the library, sit me down at my desk and dictate a whole speech for the Senate tomorrow, based on the material he is formulating right now with his mouth apparently full of candied yam."

"I've heard that the senator has the finest private library in Washington. Will you show it to me sometime?"

Jessie eyed her father's guests, then thought how pleasant it would be to have Lieutenant Fremont alone for a few moments. There was nothing she wanted to say to him that could not be heard by the others, yet she knew that their relationship would change subtly if their words could be flavored with privacy.

"When the others go to the drawing room for coffee," she said, "we can slip upstairs."

Before bringing in the pastries, Josheem and Joshaam removed the damask cloth, revealing a second one equally fresh and lovely; and then when the fruits and sweets were ready to be passed, they took off this second cloth, to leave the silver candlesticks, cut glass and crystal gleaming on the highly polished mahogany surface.

At last she suggested that her guests retire to the drawing room for coffee. She stood aside while her father, his arms linked through those of Mrs. Linn and Mrs. Crittenden, escorted the two ladies across the hall. When everyone had left the room, she murmured to Lieutenant Fremont:

"No one will miss us if we go upstairs for a few moments."

She entered the open door of the library, motioning for him to stand beside her. The lamps had been lighted, the Venetian blinds closed; the room had a feeling of warm evening intimacy. It was a large room, running

the full width of the house, with a row of windows overlooking C Street
and the open fields beyond; small windows were spaced intermittently along
the walls of shelves freighted with books of every color, age and nationality,
with full sets of Shakespeare, Racine, Molière, Voltaire. Along the east wall
was a long oak table almost completely covered with maps and atlases.
In front of the fireplace, facing each other, were two great leather chairs,
and alongside of them two tables which could be swung around to form
writing desks. Scattered about were comfortable chairs to drop into for the
length of a paragraph or a page; a well-worn rocker with curlicue arms
stood beneath Tom Benton's beloved *British State Trials,* and an Empire
armchair before the Duncan Phyfe table with its chessboard by the front
windows.

Seeing the library suddenly through a stranger's eyes, it became new and
fresh to her, bringing back sharply her years of comradeship with her father.

"What a beautiful room!" Lieutenant Fremont murmured, so softly that
she hardly heard.

He seemed no longer conscious of her presence, going to the tight-packed
shelves and pulling down the rare and beautiful volumes with the touch of
tenderness native to the man who loves books.

"Lieutenant Fremont, your eyes light at the sight of a beautiful book
the way other men's do when they see a pretty girl!"

He flashed her an eager smile.

"Must they be mutually exclusive tastes, Miss Jessie?" he asked shyly.

She laughed, then picked up a copy of Henry Schoolcraft's *Expedition
to the Upper Mississippi.* "Do you know this book? Father taught me to
read from it. I think he did it purposely, so that an interest in exploration
would come as natural to me as reading itself."

John Fremont was nodding his small dark head approvingly.

"I didn't know that men were constantly exploring the frontier until I
was almost nineteen." He opened the copy of the *Journals.* "I stumbled
onto this book the first day I went to work at the Apprentices' Library in
Charleston. It was like a new world to me. Until that time I hadn't the
faintest notion of what I wanted to do with my life. I read all night, and
when dawn came I knew what I was going to be. I spent the next six months
devouring the books you have here: General William Ashley, Jedediah Smith,
Zebulon Pike, John Jacob Astor, Lewis Cass."

Jessie indicated the two chairs by the fireplace. "Here, take my chair,
I'll take Father's."

She sat facing him as she had for so many years sat facing her father.
"This library, and the chair in which you are sitting, were my schoolroom.
Father taught me to read when I was four, and to draw and trace the maps
of the United States when I was five. Before I knew that Paris was the
capital of France, I knew there was a great river which flowed from the
Salt Lake to the Pacific Ocean."

"Which there may not be!" he exclaimed almost sternly. "Yes, I know that Jedediah Smith reported it, but Mr. Nicollet and I have gone over the reports of the topography of the country, and we can't find any possible route for a river from Salt Lake to the Pacific."

"And one day you will prove it," she added quietly.

He looked at her, both pleased and surprised.

"How did you know?"

"You would have a hard time concealing the fact that you are an explorer."

"I was not as fortunate as you, Miss Jessie," he continued, aroused; "I had no father to go to school to. I went to Charleston College for a couple of years, took languages and mathematics, which interested me, but I could never see any purpose behind my studies."

She followed his quick gestures as he told her of his childhood, of his father, an itinerant French teacher and painter who had died while his son was a small boy; of his mother's struggles to support her three children; of his friendship with Joel Poinsett, who had secured him his first job as an instructor in mathematics on the American warship *Natchez,* which sailed to Rio de Janeiro and Buenos Aires. His voice was low and musical and caused an excited tremor to run through her. Her mind caught the overtones of his early struggles and the joy in finding himself as he related his work on the survey for the proposed route of the Louisville, Cincinnati and Charleston railroad, and later as civilian assistant to Captain Williams of the United States Topographical Corps in surveying the Cherokee country.

She had rarely had any desire to talk about herself, but now she found the idea pleasurable.

"There isn't a great deal to tell," she started self-consciously. "My greatest happiness has always been working with Father. Before he sent me to that dreadful school, I used to sit in the chair where you are now, with that table across my knees, and write down his speeches for the Senate, while he paced the floor and dove into books for the references he wanted. When I was six I began to walk with Father up to the Capitol every morning where he would stake me out in the Congressional Library. Old Mr. Meehan would bring me Mr. Audubon's books on birds, or a collection of prints from the Louvre Gallery, and other books of old French engravings. When I grew tired of looking at the books I would go out onto the broad, recessed gallery and look at the wonderful view of the Potomac and the green hills opposite. By the time I was eight, Father decided I was old enough to listen to the Senate debates."

She walked to the oaken table with its profusion of maps, the bright reds, greens and yellows of the colored plates lending a touch of gaiety to the room. Her voice was serious.

"I think Father would forget that I was a girl, for he wanted to teach me everything there was to know about exploration and travel and the country of the unsettled West. He taught me Spanish so that I could read the reports of Cortez, Balboa, Magellan and De Soto. It was because he so desperately needed a companion in his work."

Reaching out to her with eagerness, John Fremont exclaimed, "I too studied Spanish in order to read Coronado and Cortez. Like you, I also know the geography of the wilderness far better than I do New York or Boston. Your father wanted you to be a son and to go into the Topographical Corps; from the first day I set out with Captain Williams on the railroad survey, I was determined that I would become an officer of the Topographical Corps, and explore the Far West for the government. While you were sitting in this library, I was in those very forests and mountains and prairies you were reading about, drawing maps, collecting botanical specimens, shooting the stars."

As he paused, Jessie turned her face full toward him, her eyes ablaze.

"Actually, Lieutenant Fremont, we were together out there in the wilderness!"

Then she blushed fiercely.

4

She was sitting at her desk in the small, characterless bedroom allotted to her at Miss English's Academy when she heard the throaty voice of a colored mammy singing a plodding spiritual; it was the song that announced the presence of the washerwoman below. All laundry was delivered up the side of the building by means of a rope and pulley attached to each of the window sills; Jessie never could figure why, except that it saved tracking through the schoolhouse. She left the desk, a fragile one designed to hold only light books and light thoughts, and walked to the open window where she could watch the woman tie the rope through the cross-handles of the basket and slowly haul it up to the rhythm of her song.

Leaning over the sill to take in her own basket, she was surprised to see a piece of writing paper resting on top of the crisply ironed clothes. She read, "I couldn't seem to wait until next Sunday. Isn't there some place we can talk? J.C.F."

Once again she looked out the window. This time she saw John Fremont standing beside the mulberry tree.

"Hello," she said, "this is a surprise."

"Can you come down?"

"No, but you can come up."

"Up?"

He gazed in bewilderment.

"Yes, up the mulberry tree. I'll come out from here and meet you in the top branch. That is, if you're not afraid of ripping those lovely blue breeches."

His delighted laughter drifted up to her as she watched him catch a high branch and swing himself onto it. She gathered her skirts tightly about her and climbed over the window sill onto a crisscross of sturdy limbs which formed a platform beneath her. She had no sooner seated herself than John Fremont's head appreared through the green leaves; with quick, graceful movements he was seated beside her. He had left his hat on the ground, and his hair was tousled from pushing upward through the foliage. They overlooked the rolling lawns of the school and the dark green forests along the Potomac. Sitting in the tree swinging her legs through the branches, Jessie Benton would have had difficulty convincing anyone she was almost seventeen.

"Isn't this a mild case of mutiny, Lieutenant Fremont," she asked, her eyes sparkling, "interfering with the curriculum of a girls' school? And how does it happen that the Army lets you wander around loose of a Wednesday afternoon?"

He smiled broadly.

"Messieurs Nicollet and Hassler held a conference over me at lunch today and decided that I had an acute attack of spring fever. That was the only way they could figure why I should be drawing girls' faces on my maps, instead of mountains and rivers."

"But it seems perfectly normal for a young man to draw girls' faces," she answered. "Haven't you ever done that before?"

"Oh, yes, but not for a number of years. Not since I was suspended from Charleston College."

To herself she said, I'm not going to like this, but it will be better to hear it now than later. Aloud she asked, "Who was the girl, Lieutenant Fremont?"

His dark eyes became serious. "Cecilia. She was the oldest daughter of a Creole family that escaped to Charleston in the midst of the San Domingo massacres. I grew up with her brothers; when we were sixteen, Cecilia and I decided we were in love."

"And were you?" she interrupted.

He hesitated for a moment, then said softly, "It wouldn't be right to disavow Cecilia; yes, I loved her as a boy loves his first sweetheart. She was beautiful with flashing eyes and a magnificent smile."

Completely jealous, Jessie struggled with herself not to ask, Was she prettier than I? She said instead, "But why did being in love cause you to be suspended from school?"

"I'm an impetuous man, Miss Jessie . . ."

". . . or you wouldn't be at the top of a mulberry tree at three o'clock . . ."

". . . and I just couldn't stay in the classrooms when there were green hills covered with wild flowers, and a boat to take out into the harbor to fish and swim from in secluded lagoons. And that was why I was never graduated. You see, Miss Jessie, I'm not one to take love lightly. When I fall in love, I throw over everything for it."

"I think I approve of that, Lieutenant. I have never been in love, but I should feel much the same way about it." She hesitated, embarrassed, then deciding to brave it through, added quickly, "Speaking of love, I had the most exciting news this morning: my friend Harriet Williams is going to marry Count Bodisco, the Russian minister."

"Count Bodisco?" he asked, with a puzzled, almost pained expression. "Isn't he the pretentious one who drives to his Embassy every day in a snow-white barouche drawn by four black horses?"

"Yes, I suppose he is pretentious, but in a kindly sort of way that does no one any harm. He's just trying to maintain the dignity of the Russian aristocracy in what some of the other ambassadors call a mudhole capital."

"But," he exclaimed angrily, "he's an old man. He must be past sixty!"

"Just sixty. And Harriet is just sixteen. But he is so terribly kind, the Count Bodisco. He has been most generous to her parents, who are having a difficult time with their large family. The count is going to educate the children and see that they have a brilliant future. Just think, Lieutenant, last week Harriet wasn't good enough to be the May Queen at this school, and in a couple of weeks she will be Countess Alexander de la Bodisco, cousin to the Czar, with a state wedding and President Harrison giving away the bride."

He did not reply. Not a muscle of his face twitched, but she felt a withdrawing, as though he were sorry he had come out to the school today, as though the spirit of the man had flown from the mulberry tree back to the workroom of the Hassler home. When he spoke his voice had a metallic edge.

"You seem to approve all this, Miss Benton."

She put a finger lightly as a falling leaf on his sleeve. "I would not want it for myself, Lieutenant Fremont," she said quietly. "But do you think it fair of us to judge Harriet Williams? The count is an entirely charming and cultivated man, one whom everyone respects. I know that Harriet likes him and is grateful to him. She's being generous, Lieutenant; don't you think that we might be equally generous to her?"

He picked up the finger resting on his sleeve and kissed it. "Forgive me, Miss Jessie; it was boorish of me, but I turned cold when I thought that you . . . might approve—that is you yourself . . ."

"No, Lieutenant, not I myself. I will marry a young man, one whom I can love with all my heart. A man at the very beginning of his career, who has an uphill fight to attain the ends he wants, and who will let our marriage be a partnership in the fullest sense of the term."

He did not answer, looking instead toward the west where the sun was setting behind an early spring heat haze which streaked the sky with flaming horizontal stripes ranging from light rose to deep purple. Jessie's eyes followed his gaze; they sat quietly in their bower taking in the beauty of the spring sunset and the fragrance of the budding foliage about them. She was the first to speak.

"Lieutenant, would you come to Harriet's wedding? I am sure it will be very gay."

"But I don't know Count Bodisco . . ."

"I was in the middle of a letter to Harriet when your note came up in the basket. Won't you let me ask her to have the count invite you? There will be a ball after the wedding supper. Do you like to dance, Lieutenant Fremont?"

On the day of the wedding Jessie was the center of attention in the Benton household, for this was to be her first state affair. She enjoyed the dressing up enormously, surrounded by her mother, two younger sisters and Maylee, who had raised her. Her gown of white figured satin with blonde lace about the neck and sleeves had been built by Mrs. Abbott, the fashionable mantua maker from London.

In midafternoon she entered the family carriage with her father and mother, who had stirred herself to make this effort for the sake of Harriet's family and social position. It was a gentle day, the air soft and intoxicating. The road for a mile before Bodisco's estate was swarming with carriages, for the entire Diplomatic Corps was there, as well as the upper circle of army and navy officers, with General Winfield Scott leading the procession of magnificent uniforms; the president and his Cabinet attended, as well as most of the older members of Congress and the Supreme Court.

Jessie was ushered to the bridesroom on the second floor where she found Harriet in a paroxysm of gaiety. She was a lighthearted, vivacious child who got the most fun from everything.

"Darling," she cried to Jessie, "here's a pearl ring the count wants you to have."

She ran to the window, peeped through the blinds. "Jessie, look at this carriage with the satin rosettes on the horses. It must be the French ambassador. I'm so excited, I haven't been able to eat for three days. The count says I can't have anything until the wedding supper."

Jessie smiled quietly; a feeling of release from anxiety came over her; Harriet would love every minute of her marriage: the jewels, the gowns, the coaches, the travel, state dinners and balls and ceremonies. She would take the happiness from her own bubbling nature, from the excitement of passing events and her family's well-being, and she would never stop long enough to tell herself that her husband was old and ugly.

Soon the bridal party was shepherded down a back stairway to the drawing room, which faced the loggia. The doors were thrown open and the seated guests watched the ceremony performed. Jessie scanned the room in a flash, her eyes finding Lieutenant Fremont, handsome in his full-dress uniform, a smile on his face. During the elaborate dinner she felt miles away from him, for he was more than halfway down the long table. But later when the orchestra began to play behind its screen of palms in the ballroom, and she had danced the first waltz with James Buchanan, and a Bohemian polka with Count Bodisco, she was free to join him on the open piazza overlooking the capital.

The music of the soft-stringed instruments floated out to them from the ballroom, where a large number of couples were already dancing, their jewelry and gold braid and lace glittering under a thousand lighted candles. Jessie, her cheeks flushed with the day's excitement, smiled in the growing darkness as the lieutenant slipped his arm under the frill of lace which fell over her elbow and murmured, "You may have come here for the wedding ceremony, but I came to dance with you."

They stepped onto the dance floor; for a moment they stood unmoving, tense, questioning, as though the beginning of this dance might be the start of something which they themselves might never be able or willing to stop. For Jessie it was a moment out of time, indistinct, yet caught forever. Then she was in his arms whirling about to the strains of Johann Strauss's *Brillante Vienne*.

For the first time since sitting next to him at the musicale she realized that he was a little man; she had never before danced with someone so short, so slender-limbed and -torsoed. At first it seemed strange, almost unpleasant, this not being able to look up to a man, to feel his bigness towering over you, his width and breadth making you seem small and delicate. With a start she recoiled at the emptiness of her quantitative evaluation.

Her thoughts and her feelings raced on, their impact so overpowering that she became frightened, began suddenly to feel faint. She was glad when the music stopped and they made their way to the end of the ballroom where she sank into a deep chair.

As suddenly and incomprehensively as weakness had come, there came anger over her, and a touch of awe. Who is he, she asked, this strange man who can do these things to me? A few weeks ago I had never heard of him, and now I can hardly stand on my own feet! It wasn't like this before: I thought about him, I pictured his face, and listened to the music of his voice; I liked him because he was the handsomest man I had ever seen, and because he also had a wistful quality; it seemed miraculous that he loved the books I loved, that he had decided to make a career of exploration and the settling of the West just as my father had, and I too, in my own small way. All these things seemed delightful and coincidental and exciting; but there was no wild force inside me to tell my knees that they couldn't sustain me!

5

On a warm Sunday morning early in March, after they had attended services at the Presbyterian church, Jessie and her father set out for Hassler's house, where Nicollet and Hassler had planned a conference to provide the senator with live ammunition with which to bombard the Senate into authorizing a series of expeditions to open the western wilderness. Tom Benton was a prodigious walker. His long, shambling legs carried him along at so fast a clip that Jessie had to do double time at his side to keep up with him. But it had always been so. Her father had never slowed his pace to suit the size, age or gait of his growing daughter. From the very beginning he had treated her as an adult, speaking to her with the same vocabulary and intensity as he did to his constituents in St. Louis or his confreres on the floor of the Senate. Jessie had groped slowly, many times painfully, toward understanding; but with the passage of the years the ideas he stood for became clearer and more firmly entrenched in her mind. The child born to Elizabeth Benton after Jessie had been a boy, but he had died, binding Tom Benton in his grief still closer to Jessie. By the time her brother Randolph had been born it had been too late to break her father's attachment to his most promising daughter, in whose mind and spirit he had found the desired reproduction of his own.

James Buchanan had remarked that Jessie was the square root of Tom Benton. Both father and daughter were delighted with the characterization; and both knew it to be true. Listening to Jessie talk about western expansionism, the need for a national road from St. Louis to Santa Fe, the listener could close his eyes and see Thomas Hart Benton before him, his tone, his vocabulary, his rolling out of incisive phrases.

Yet no one had ever dreamed of calling Jessie Benton an echo of her father. She had a mind of her own, and a good one; it just so happened that, coming from the frontier of St. Louis, having been raised with the hunters, trappers, guides, fur dealers and merchants who saw before them the great unexplored stretches of land where lay fortunes, she too had become convinced that the United States was now only a small fragment of what it must become. She even used terms like "manifest destiny," which sounded pompous in the mouth of a young girl, but Tom Benton had been preaching manifest destiny since she was five; since she was eight she had been listening to him battle for it on the floor of the Senate, seen him work with his companions in the library of the Benton home; she had read or had had read to her all those facts of history and biography which Tom Benton believed proved his case that no young nation can stand still, that it must conquer the wilderness which lies about it, that it must make of its physical flesh an organic unity. In the many speeches that she had written down for him in his library, and in the comments she had come to make during their discussions, she had even gone beyond Tom Benton in her thinking, for being younger by a generation she dared more by a generation.

As they walked along briskly in the spring sunshine, Jessie's mind went back to the earliest recollections of her childhood. Her first vivid memory was from the age of three; in 1828 her father had campaigned like a hurricane for the election of Andrew Jackson, his old commander and friend. For months she had heard the cry of "Hurrah for Jackson!" One morning she and Eliza went into the library dressed in their velvet pelisses and bonnets, prepared to take a walk around Lafayette Square with their father. Tom had been working that morning on a blistering attack on the isolationists of New England, who were not only content to have America stay as it was with twenty states, but were grimly determined that there must be no more territory acquired, neither in the South, the West, nor the Midwest, since it would upset the political balance in Congress, and weaken their influence over the control of national affairs. The week before Senator Foote had spoken for New England when he advocated that all public lands be removed from the market except those already owned by settlers, that the borders and boundaries of the United States be frozen forever at their existing latitudes.

Jessie and Eliza had found themselves alone in the library; they sat quietly in a chair for a few moments, then seeing the sheets of writing paper spread about, had gotten a box of crayons and begun to draw designs around Senator Benton's writing. A few minutes later when their father came into the room and saw what they had done, he demanded roughly, "Who did this?" Eliza burst into tears, but Jessie looked up, her face streaked with crayon, and announced:

"A little girl that says hurrah for Jackson!"

Tom gazed at his daughter incredulously for a moment, then burst into laughter. "Jessie, you're a chip off the old block; you know how to wriggle out of tight places."

Picking up his sheets of manuscript he had inspected the damage, let out a hearty exclamation as his eyes traced the twisting lines of her blue crayon. He read aloud, "The West is my country, not his. I know it; he does not. It is an injury to the human race to preserve the magnificent valley of the Mississippi for the haunts of wild beasts instead of making it the abode of liberty and civilization, an asylum for the oppressed of all nations."

Hassler's house was on Capitol Hill, overlooking the Potomac; they turned north past the Coast Survey building where Hassler directed the country's geodetic surveys, and continued up Pennsylvania Avenue. Nicholas Nicollet, looking old and ill from the remnants of jungle fever, led them up to the second floor of the rambling house and into a large front room which was entirely bare of furniture. Two long boards mounted on horses were covered with a profusion of maps, papers, charts, notes, journals, atlases, logarithms, tracing paper, crayons. As Jessie stepped into the room she caught a picture: Lieutenant John Charles Fremont on a high stool leaning over the table, a heavy drawing pencil in his right hand, the widespread fingers of his left hand holding down the pages of a journal; his shirt sleeves rolled high, his plain army shirt open at the throat, his dark hair rumpled and falling slightly over his brow, his face filled with the intensity of the man who is devoted to the job on hand.

"He was only twenty-four when I took him with me," Nicollet had told her; "he had had some training under Captain Williams on the two earlier expeditions, but he was really only a beginner in the craft of living harmoniously with the wilderness. Yet he sopped up training and experience like an impassioned one."

Looking intently at him as he sat concentrating on his work, synthesizing rough, hand-drawn maps, notes jotted down beside campfires, checking them against the published notes and maps of the wilderness they had explored, Jessie had the feeling that here was a first-rate man. A flutter at the pit of her stomach told her so, and told her in a way different from the way his hand had grasped hers that first evening at the Georgetown school; different from the way his laughter had engulfed and possessed hers; different from her feeling in the library when he had held her father's books and talked of them; different from that night at the Bodisco wedding; different from all these, something quite apart from them and over and above them. Here was a man who would be admired and respected by his associates, who would go forward in his work, a man who would have the substance and solidity of the job to which his life would be bent, who would make a valuable and permanent contribution to his times.

She stepped into the room, followed by her father and Nicollet. John looked up swiftly, disturbedly; then, seeing her, leaped off his stool and came forward to bid her welcome.

Tom Benton hurried to the big map in the making, ran his finger over the sections in which he was most interested.

"Yes, yes," he said, "that's what we need . . . but I am disappointed, it all comes so . . . so slowly."

Jessie watched Lieutenant Fremont as he turned to her father to say in a patient tone, "Yes, it is slow work, Senator, for we must achieve the utmost precision. The tiniest error on this map may mean danger to caravans expecting water or provision at a designated spot . . ."

"True, true," Tom murmured, "but our time is so short: England is scheming to take over the Pacific coast. This whole vast area has to be cut open with roads, dotted with forts and farm settlements. We've got to push expeditions through to the Columbia River Valley so that it can be settled by Americans."

"I agree, Senator Benton," John replied, his face aglow. "We must push our expeditions through every mile of the wilderness. But we cannot expose unprotected immigrant trains to hostile Indians and deserts and snow-covered mountain ranges until we can assure them that these maps are accurate."

Jessie felt a hand on her shoulder. She turned to find Nicollet beaming at his protégé.

"He is right, the young lieutenant," he whispered. "Think of it, Miss Jessie, in that tremendous map of the Missouri for which he himself gathered most of the material, and which he drew entirely by himself, he made only two small errors in calculation. That is good workmanship."

Watching her father and John Fremont with their heads together she saw how they stimulated each other. Yes, she thought, as she gazed at his tapering fingers which were sketching rapidly even while he talked: good workmanship. Only good men can turn out good work. Most of the young men I know are lighthearted; they seem inconsequential compared to a man like this. I could never love anyone who was not a good workman, who was not as devoted to that work as he was to me.

6

Knowing that Lieutenant Fremont had been invited, Jessie had asked Maylee to prepare a specially delicious dinner, but this time her warning to him to stay clear of the argument was to no avail; he had regretfully to lay down his knife and fork when Tom Benton called on him to persuade two newspaper editors, a cabinet officer and several congressmen that the land between the Mississippi and the Rockies was fertile and good for homesteading.

The first warmth of impending summer was in the drawing room, a hint of the intense heat that soon would settle over Washington City. Jessie had put on a cool gown of lawn. After the demitasse she suggested to John that they go into the back garden for a breath of air. Scarlet trumpet vines covered the high, enclosing walls. Just outside the porch they passed a small, improvised shed with two wooden barrels suspended over its top. At John's inquiring glance Jessie explained, "That's Father's shower bath. He takes it icy cold at dawn and sunset, part of his old army regime; he says he enjoys it, but Father loves hardship. I sometimes think he likes it for its own sake."

"Quite so!" exclaimed the lieutenant understandingly. "I enjoy the hardship of the trail and the danger of the unknown for its own sake. Frankly, the only hardship I find painful is that of being obliged to live in a big city, with crowds of people."

"Really, Lieutenant?" she asked, a trifle archly. "I've recently heard reports that you are one of the gayest young men in the capital, that never a dance takes place but you're still there at three o'clock in the morning."

He blushed.

"Ah well, Miss Jessie, I'm young, only twenty-eight. There are times when I like pretty girls and music, and if I must live in civilization to complete my work I might as well have the most fun of it. But give me a stampeding buffalo herd, a three-day forced march across the desert, our canteens empty; give me a prairie of blue wild flowers that no white man's eyes ever gazed upon before; or an unknown, unnamed river stream rushing by in the night while I lie on the ground and gaze up at stars."

Her ear caught the poetry of his words, mitigating the jealousy she had felt when thinking of him as part of the capital's society from which, because of her youth, she was still excluded. They walked along the hedge-lined path to the summerhouse. It was shaded by tall sycamores and much of it was covered by a deep green ivy. They sat side by side on the hard white bench, the air filled with the fragrance of honeysuckle, and chatted lightly about the people at the dinner table.

"I'm not greatly interested in politics," he commented absently. "I can hardly wait for the day when I can start out again on a new expedition."

"Father always said that politics and science make uncongenial bedfellows, but how is there any escape from it? You can do nothing without the help and authorization of Congress, and you can do nothing with Congress unless you do play mighty smart politics."

He nodded agreement with the well-turned argument, then leaned back against the latticework, his face set, his eyes serious. The coolness of the arbor seemed to magnify his detachment. She was hurt and baffled by his need for escape. Despite his openness and candor she had a sense of being unable to come into contact with the core of him. Her first reaction in the darkened music room of Miss English's school had been that there was in his character something mysterious, something submerged. This feeling of elusiveness, of withdrawal behind the poise and lovability frightened her.

She turned a little to face him. "Whatever happened to Cecilia?"

"I don't know," he answered. "I left Charleston and she stayed there. Why do you ask?"

"Because I'm interested in love, and it suddenly strikes me that I don't know a blessed thing about it."

"I'm afraid you've come to the wrong man," he grinned. "I don't know much about the subject myself. A topographer who spends most of his time in the wilderness doesn't get much chance at love."

They smiled, conscious of each other, of the sharp smell of the night earth, the scent of late spring. The words were all gone. They moved close. Their hands touched, her hair touched his lips as she leaned her head on his shoulder.

Suddenly she looked up to see her father and Nicollet standing on the path. Nicollet smiled, murmured something to Thomas Benton. Her father stiffened. There was a hostile pause, then he came to the door of the summerhouse and announced in a cold voice:

"Jessie, come into the house."

She rose and, with John Fremont at her side, trailed her father and Nicollet up the garden path. In the light of the foyer she saw that her father's face had frozen, that Nicollet was apologetic. Ignoring Lieutenant Fremont's presence, Tom Benton said, "Jessie, will you excuse yourself, please? It is growing late."

In the strained silence the unspoken words of these four leaped out to each other and clashed and were withdrawn. Lieutenant Fremont spoke out in a small voice. "I too must excuse myself. Thank you for your hospitality, Senator Benton, and for your excellent dinner."

He bowed formally, took his hat from a corner stand and left the house.

Tom Benton and his daughter stood gazing at each other. Nicollet murmured his adieus and left.

Jessie trailed her father up the stairs to the library, watching his broad, angry back. After he had slumped far down in his chair, his hand covering his face, she asked softly, "What have I done?"

He looked at her, his face seeming haggard and old.

"Jessie," he said, "I'm stunned."

"What is it that you feel so strongly about?" she queried.

"That is a silly and evasive question," he replied harshly. "You were so obvious that even Nicollet commented on it. I've been so absorbed in my work that I failed to notice . . ."

Her voice too became firm. "I've done nothing but enjoy Lieutenant Fremont's company. You've done as much yourself. What is it you are accusing me of?"

"Of falling in love with him," he shot back.

There it is, she thought, out in the open at last. I have never let myself think it, and now Father has put it into words.

"You may be right," she answered quietly. "I had not let that word come into my consciousness. I knew that Lieutenant Fremont was the most delightful and sympathetic young man I had ever met. But you never approved of romantic novels, and there is very little in the literature of exploration to tell a young girl when she is in love. Now that you face me with it, I think I am in love with him."

With a tight voice Tom Benton pronounced, "Lieutenant Fremont will not come to this house any more; he will not be invited; and you will not see him again."

"But why are you punishing him?" she demanded.

"He has made you fall in love with him."

"Made me!" Her face was as taut and pale as his. "Have I no mind of my own? Really, Father, that's unworthy of the years of training you have given me; you know that I am not a weak or silly child . . ."

"Nevertheless he is not coming here any more. You will not see him! It's far too advantageous a marriage to tempt the young lieutenant with."

"Lieutenant Fremont is no adventurer. He is one of the most talented and promising men in Washington. You said so yourself."

"Perhaps. But he is not so promising that he can't see the benefits of a marriage to Senator Benton's daughter."

Jessie's eyes flashed her indignation. She walked to the window, put aside the draperies and stared out over the dark green fields.

"So you think you have produced a daughter so unattractive and so unstimulating that the lieutenant could not fall in love with me for my own sake?"

Tom Benton said more quietly, "Forgive me, my dear, I did not mean to disparage your charms or your worth." But the coldness did not leave his voice. "Jessie, it is my job to protect you. You are too young to know . . ."

"Senator," she said deliberately, "that's the worst piece of sophistry you've ever been guilty of: Did you think I was too young at four to learn how to read, or too young at five to spend my days in the Congressional Library, too young at seven to go on hunting and camping trips with you, too young at eight to watch you from the Senate galleries, to read these heavy, serious books with you; too young at ten to begin writing down your speeches, too young at fourteen to become your adviser and confidante, to walk the streets of Washington at night while you were thrashing out your problems, using me as a sounding board? And now suddenly you thrust a calendar in my face, tell me that I am undeveloped, not quite seventeen, a child who doesn't know what she is doing."

She did not pause to give him an opportunity to answer, but pursued her advantage ruthlessly, even as Tom Benton did when his own desires were at stake.

"I've never questioned your judgment; when you praised me for some good work I had done, I worked ten times harder to earn more praise, until you have said that you'd soon be going to school to me. And now, at the first turn of events that displeases you, you become heavy-handed, the outraged father laying down the law."

Tom eyed her calmly. "That was quite a speech, Jessie; perhaps you should be the senator from Missouri."

She walked quickly to her father's side, her manner conciliatory.

"I don't want to be the senator from Missouri; I want to be the daughter of the senator. You know how much I love you, Father; we have never had to talk about that. You've led me gently by the hand through all these happy years; you can't suddenly put a ring through my nose on the pretext that it's for my own good."

"What has Lieutenant Fremont said to you?"

"Nothing . . . not with his lips anyway. Perhaps I've been reading his mind, but that kind of evidence isn't admissible in a court of law, is it?"

"I am not amused."

"Lieutenant Fremont has been very circumspect," she continued. "You are forcing issues, Father, and it has never been your tactic to bludgeon your way through delicate situations."

"I've taught you too well," he moaned.

"Come now, Tom," she chided. "You gave me weapons with which to fight; did you think I was not going to use them whenever my happiness was threatened?"

"Your happiness! But this is fantastic, Jessie! It is the first time you have had a romantic attachment, and you talk to me about your happiness! Lieutenant Fremont simply will not be invited to this house any more."

They stood in silence staring at each other, two pairs of brooding eyes, as alike as a reflection in a gold-backed mirror. Their wills met too, their stubbornness. Then Jessie turned and went to her room.

Maylee was waiting for her with a tray of food. "You must be starved, child," said the old colored woman, "I seed your plate when it come out the kitchen. You never even mussed it round."

"Thank you, Maylee, but I'm not hungry."

The woman looked at her in blank astonishment.

"You ain't hungry! What's the matter with you, child, you sick?"

"Father would say so."

"What you catch? You want I bring you some hot senna tea?"

Jessie smiled wryly.

"Thank you, no, Maylee, senna tea never cures anything, much less what I've got."

7

If not for the presence of Grandmother McDowell, who had arrived for her annual spring visit with the Bentons, the following weeks would have been unendurable for Jessie. Both at school and at home she suffered the agonizing experience of having Lieutenant Fremont's face fade from her mind. Though she was unhappy at being separated from him she did not despair, for she felt certain that the forces which had brought them together were too strong to be broken because Thomas Hart Benton thought her too young for love. She had wanted to talk to her father about Lieutenant Fremont, to show him that his arbitrary method was having the opposite effect to what he desired. If he would let him come to dinner again on Sundays, she would promise to keep the conversation in hand, to behave casually.

But on her second week end at home she was unable to discuss the subject with him, for he was preparing to make a speech in the Senate which he estimated would consume seven hours, and was maintaining an absolute silence for several days so that his voice would hold out. Jessie decided that she would wait until the day after his speech, giving him the night to rest, before pleading for a frank discussion. When she joined him in the library the following morning, and found him still suffering from the rawness of his throat, she had only compassion for him. She resolved to be patient.

The separation had been the more painful because there was no one in the Benton home with whom she could talk about John Fremont. That was why she had been happy to see Grandmother McDowell again.

Grandmother McDowell had been born in Cherry Grove, Virginia, eighty years before. She had lived through the Indian Wars and the War of the Revolution; on her forehead she carried a scar caused by an Indian's knife thrown at her in her childhood, an Indian in the British service. She called this scar King George's Mark. When Grandmother was ill or troubled or her children or grandchildren were in difficulty the scar seemed to grow larger; when she was feeling well and the family prospered it receded to almost unnoticeable proportions. Grandmother McDowell's growing old had proved an anomaly: instead of becoming thin in her advancing age, she had grown pleasingly plump; instead of becoming cantankerous because of her slowed gait and accumulated ills, she grew increasingly mellow; instead of growing fatigued with the love affairs and marriages of her children, grandchildren, nieces and nephews, she maintained a keen zest in seeing each of them in turn go through the process. Jessie had not needed to say more than a few sentences about Lieutenant Fremont before Grandmother McDowell had nodded her head and commented:

"So it has come to my Jessie at last. I was getting worried about you; by the time I was your age I already had a daughter."

The death of President William H. Harrison only one month after his inauguration furnished Jessie with her first opportunity to see John. The funeral cortege was to make its way up Pennsylvania Avenue to the Capitol; since the Benton home was a block off the main street, and the members of the family would not be able to watch the procession from their own windows, Tom Benton had announced to Grandmother McDowell that she might view the cortege from Mr. Hassler's house on Capitol Hill. To Jessie's sharply interrogating look he replied, "Mr. Hassler made the offer today when I met him in Colonel Abert's office. Yes, you may accompany your grandmother."

The morning of the funeral dawned cold and rainy. Though Grandmother McDowell wore a black silk dress with a wadded black cape, Jessie's mother permitted her to wear a dress and coat of dark green velvet. Tom Benton dropped his daughter and mother-in-law outside the Hassler house, then hurried on to the Senate for the official ceremonies. When the front door was opened by Lieutenant Fremont dressed in his full regimentals, Jessie exclaimed:

"Lieutenant, why aren't you with your regiment?"

"I developed a cold. The doctor at the armory did not consider it wise for me to march in this rain."

They stood smiling at each other, an eager smile. Then Jessie turned to her grandmother.

"This is the young lieutenant I have been telling you about."

"I'm glad to meet you, young man. I must confess I came more to see you than to get a better view of the funeral. At my age one is not overly partial to funerals."

"But Grandmother," Jessie exclaimed, "you couldn't have known that Lieutenant Fremont would be here. He was supposed to be marching with his regiment."

"Do tell!" murmured Grandmother McDowell.

John bent over to kiss the old woman's hand, then led them up to the second-floor workroom which had been cleared of its tables and working paraphernalia. He had placed potted azaleas on the window sills and there were many vases filled with geraniums and roses. A bright fire was burning in the fireplace, the cedar wood giving off a pungent fragrance. Before the fireplace a low table had been set for tea; comfortable chairs had been placed in front of the windows overlooking Pennsylvania Avenue. Jessie watched John as he received Colonel Abert's wife and Mrs. Crittenden, who also had been invited to this vantage spot. She sat at the big windows with the other women listening to stories about William Henry Harrison, but John was standing behind her chair and her head was spinning; the feeling that ran between them was strong and certain.

In the distance could be heard faintly the dirge of the funeral march; in another moment six white horses could be seen pulling the plumed hearse which was carrying the body of President Harrison up the slope of Capitol Hill. As two more women were ushered into the room, Jessie quickly rose to offer her chair, and John led her to the fireplace. Here they sat opposite each other over the tea table gazing into the yellow-red flames. The women assembled at the windows had their eyes on the solemn scene below; Jessie could not have felt their privacy more complete had they been alone.

"I've been to the Senate twice while Senator Benton was speaking," he said. "I hoped I might catch a glimpse of you there."

"But I am still attending Miss English's Academy."

"I knew our separation was only temporary. I knew that nothing could keep us apart, not even—forgive me—Senator Benton."

Jessie did not speak; she could not have uttered a word if her life had been at stake. He took her hand between his.

"Miss Jessie, perhaps a funeral procession is not the best possible background to speak of love, but I am so full of the subject that I am afraid I would find any moment and any background a good one."

"Always the impetuous one," she murmured.

"You have a way of reading my eyes," he said. "I think you've read what I feel for you."

"No," she mocked gently, "when it comes to love, I'm illiterate. Or so Father thinks."

"Do you know the first thing I said to Mr. Nicollet when I returned from the musicale at Georgetown? I said, 'I have fallen in love at first sight.' When you stormed into the reception room, indignant because an injustice had been done to your friend, I knew at once that something important was happening to me; when you laughed and your laughter enveloped me with its warmth I knew that the rest of my life would be barren unless I could be with you always. My one thought was how and where I might meet Miss Jessie again. I love you," he said very quietly. "I loved you from that very first instant. I think you love me too."

Her eyes glowed.

"Surely you too believe that it's all part of a design, that if we searched the world, both of us, spent years looking for the one man or woman who would be our most perfect mate . . ."

"Yes, I believe that," she replied softly.

"Mr. Benton is telling the truth when he says I am a penniless lieutenant with only modest prospects . . ."

"Modest prospects! You have the most brilliant prospects of any young man in America: you will do great things . . ."

"We will do them together, Jessie."

She withdrew her hand from his, sat up stiffly in her chair, her slight body rigid.

"You are serious about that?" she demanded. "I must warn you, I can't live without work to do. I could not marry a man who would not let me work by his side as an equal and his partner. Call me Anne Royall if you will, my mother has done that a hundred times, but I am not a feminist, you will never hear me cry for equal rights for women. I believe that the greatest job a woman can do in the world is to be a good wife, but I believe that to be a good wife a woman must stand shoulder to shoulder and brain to brain alongside her husband." Her voice faltered. "I simply must have a man who will have faith in my judgment, who will make me his confidante, who will not try to exclude me because I am a woman, tell me to go out into society and amuse myself."

She relaxed in her chair, but her hazel eyes were still intense.

"I will never embarrass you, John Fremont; I want no credit or limelight or public acclaim; I will never stalk the street with a bundle of causes in my hand so that my friends will duck down side alleys when they see me coming. But I want to help you, I want to make my own small contribution to your work, I want to extend your reach by just a little bit, that little bit of which I am capable."

She cast down her eyes and sat laving her small hands as though in anguish.

"There, I've said it all. I hope it hasn't repulsed you, that you will not think it unwomanly of me."

She looked up at him. His eyes were closed, his twenty-eight-year-old face had lines in it, his forehead was furrowed.

"I hope I'm not being romantic about this," she said. "I know that from the viewpoint of the outside world it is an unwanted task. I know that most men prefer an amusing and charming wife who will bear their children and manage their houses and be there when they come home from a day's or a year's work. It is a full-time task to bear children and raise them and watch after the health of the family and keep the home beautiful and peaceful so that they can grow up to be fine human beings. It is enough for any one woman. But can you understand, Lieutenant, that it is not enough for me? I am my father's daughter; if I were a man I would be deep in a profession already. Since I am a woman I must work through my husband, and so I must find a husband who will let me achieve this ambition, who will allow me to become as indispensable in his work as in his life."

The slowly dying dirge of the funeral procession could be heard in the room; several of the women at the window were weeping quietly. Lieutenant Fremont had started to speak.

"I love you, Jessie," he was saying. "I would not want an Anne Royall, but your radiance and charm dissipate my fears. Jessie, I will always love you, of that you may be sure. I may make other mistakes, I may fail you in other things, I may never come up to your full expectations, but I will always love you."

A flicker of tender amusement came into her eyes, and she was glad to feel her spirit lighten; she did not want this sacred moment which she would never forget, no matter how old she grew, to be too deadly in earnest.

"Spoken as a true French poet, Monsieur Fremont," she said with a twinkle.

"I will confess I have been writing verse to you. Bad verse, Miss Jessie, astonishingly bad verse, considering how deep a love it sprang from."

"I am not marrying you as a poet, Lieutenant Fremont, and I will not hold your bad verses against you."

With one of those lightning changes to which she had not yet grown accustomed, his eyes clouded.

"You really ought not to accept me, you know," he said sternly. "I am suspect in this affair. You can see how it would be a marriage of convenience: being Senator Benton's son-in-law would be of tremendous help to me in my career; the senator would use his influence in the Congress and the War Department to get me promoted quickly, put in command of expeditions . . ."

Jessie answered with mock seriousness:

"Yes, of course, but then you realize, Lieutenant Fremont, that I am too young to know what I am doing."

"Quite! At sixteen you are an irresponsible child."

". . . it will be several years yet before I will be old enough to make up my mind."

His dark mood had vanished.

"Since you are not marrying me as a poet," he asked eagerly, "when can I expect that you will marry me as a second lieutenant in the Topographical Corps?"

"That is the one answer I don't know. You must promise me to keep this secret until I can talk with Father."

"Will we have to wait long? You will forgive me if I appear impatient."

"We won't have to wait as long as he waited: Mother kept refusing him for six years. She said, 'I'll never marry a redhead, an army man or a Democrat.' Father replied, 'I can't change the color of my hair and I can never be anything but a Democrat, but I will get out of the Army: I only went into it to lick the British.' Let us allow circumstances to precipitate the right moment for telling him."

"I will keep our engagement a secret," he smiled; "what a beautiful word, engagement. My darling Jessie, now we are engaged to be married, and all our lives we will be engaged, engaged in valuable work, engaged in being happy and loving each other."

The funeral procession had passed out of view. Lieutenant Fremont threw another log on the fire, brought the chairs from the windows and made his guests comfortable. The air had grown warmer; the rain was beautiful as it slanted angularly over Pennsylvania Avenue. He disappeared for a moment, returning with a tray of ices, French *gateaux* and a Russian samovar. He chatted happily as he poured the tea.

Heavens, thought Jessie, is my happiness that apparent too? If it is, our secret will be all over Washington within an hour.

"How was the funeral cortege?" she asked her grandmother.

"I would say that it served its purpose," Grandmother McDowell replied.

8

The next morning she awoke and burst into song, then realized that she might as well tell her father everything that had happened as go into his presence unable to contain her happiness. She put on a blue flannel robe, combed her hair, tied it on top of her head with a ribbon and went downstairs.

She had no sooner joined the family at the breakfast table than Josheem and Joshaam came in, each carrying two potted azalea plants. Tom Benton looked at the card which accompanied them, failing to note that it had been addressed to Mrs. Benton. He laid down his knife and fork, pushed aside the cutlet he had been vigorously dispatching and stared at his daughter.

"Was Lieutenant Fremont at home yesterday, by any chance?"

"Yes," admitted Jessie, "he was."

"Why wasn't he marching in the procession?"

"He had a cold."

"Did you know when you went to Hassler's that Lieutenant Fremont would be there?"

"No, Father, I don't enjoy second sight. But to be quite honest with you, I did hope . . ."

"I don't like this kind of deception, Jessie, even when it seems so innocent on the surface. I forbade you to see Lieutenant Fremont, and you have disregarded my wishes."

The rest of the family had silently finished breakfast and slipped out of the room. Jessie and her father were alone.

"Will you kindly tell me what took place at Hassler's yesterday? For it is apparent that something did take place."

She was unwilling to tell a deliberate lie. Since she saw that she must expose her hand, she played it the bold way.

"I'll let you in on a secret, Father, if you promise not to tell anyone."

"A secret from whom?"

"From you, darling. I am engaged to Lieutenant John Charles Fremont!"

When Thomas Benton's anger was red hot he could get off the most profane diatribes to be heard in Washington; but when his anger was icy he held his emotion in leash and chose his words fastidiously.

"So you are engaged! Without my knowledge, without my consent, and against my express orders that you were not to see Lieutenant Fremont."

She could think of no reply, but only hung her head.

"Do you think your life is going to end that you must rush precipitately into clandestine arrangements? What has happened to your sense of perspective, Jessie?"

She realized with a shock that this was her first major difference with her father. She didn't like it, she didn't want to create a change in their relationship, but neither could she avoid this scene. Should her father gather that she was heavyhearted at quarreling with him, he would bludgeon her emotionally until she gave in. She had to keep the contest in the mood in which she could best and most effectively oppose him.

Pushing aside the plate before her, she stretched out her arms across the table.

"If I felt that my marriage to Lieutenant Fremont would separate me from you, Father, or in any way hurt you, I would do what you ask: I would give him up. I would give up whoever it might be, without your asking. But John Fremont is the fulfillment of your own ambitions. He will explore and conquer the wilderness. He will open the West, create the empire you have been tracing on maps and have had me tracing since I was five."

Joshaam padded in with a ham steak, grits baked in a casserole with orange honey, and a silver pitcher of chocolate. Jessie let him put the food down, then pushed her chair back from the table. Her young face was sober.

"Tom Benton, you should be the one pleading for this marriage, and I should be the one holding out: for I know what your dreams and plans will do to him, I know of the hardships and ever present dangers that will face him; I know of the long and bitter separations which your collaboration will bring about. It's a hard and painful future to think about, Father, but I rush out to meet it with open and loving arms."

"The first thing I know, you'll be telling me you are marrying him for my sake." After a pause, he cried, "Jessie, would you really set yourself up against my wishes? Would you oppose me in anything so critical?"

"If I let you deprive me of the most important thing in my life, Papa, my love for you might turn to hatred. I want you to protect and counsel me, but in the end it must be I and not you who determine my life. Surely you can see the justice of that?"

Thomas Benton alone had taught her to respect logic instead of people, to form her opinions on the basis of fact, and then stand by them through hell and high water. But Tom Benton shouted in his rage:

"And who is this sixteen-year-old that dares to defy her father?"

"A little girl who cries, 'Hurrah for Jackson!' "

His anger was caught up, stopped short by the summoning of their past.

Jessie drew her chair to the table, helped herself to the breakfast. She spoke quietly.

"All I can say, Tom Benton, is that you underestimate yourself. If I am a misguided fool and romantic idiot at seventeen, then your efforts and work are wasted, and I shall still be a fool at twenty-seven or sixty-seven. Let us say instead that I matured early owing to the fact that my father was a maturing influence, owing to the fact that his intensive education had a sobering influence on me. Perhaps if during those years I had been thinking about nothing but pretty manners and conquering the hearts of young men, instead of wildernesses, lost rivers and hostile Indian tribes, I would not have found it only natural to fall in love with the one man who I think is going to do more to open that West than anyone alive today."

Her voice carried a touch of bitterness. "Perhaps you should have let me have a normal childhood of dolls and games and giggling. Perhaps that would have been better for me."

Tom passed a heavy hand over his eyes.

"Jessie, my dear, have I really robbed you of your childhood? Your mother . . ."

With a tinkling laugh she dropped her fork, ran around the table and sat herself on her father's lap.

"For heaven's sake, Papa, don't let me take you in with my ridiculous feminine logic. By this time tomorrow you would know I had tricked you out of your opposition. You gave me the most wonderful and exciting childhood any girl ever had. All I'm trying to say is that I don't feel like a child, that you didn't leave much for the finishing school to finish. That it is possible for some people to live more and learn more and enjoy and suffer more, within the passage of time, than others."

"Yes, of course."

But when he looked up at her with hurt eyes, she realized that he was not thinking along with her; that he was feeling the impending loss not only of his favorite daughter, but as he himself often had told her, of his favorite human being. Intuitively she understood by imagining what her world would be like with Thomas Hart Benton gone out of it. She stroked his hot brow.

"You don't understand, child," he groaned; "a man needs time to prepare in his mind for changes as important as this. In the back of my head there was always the idea that when you fell in love and wanted to marry, I would be ready for it. It wouldn't descend upon me when I was unprepared."

"But, Father, we have no control over when we will meet the person we love: it might be at fifteen or fifty—or never. Would it be better to wait until I was eighteen or nineteen or twenty, when your mind would be prepared, and marry someone with whom you had little in common, than to marry a bit earlier than you had anticipated, and make a perfect marriage?"

She walked to the window and stood leaning against the sill, the sun warming her back.

"Whenever I have thought of marriage, it was to a man whose work I could be excited about. I have always believed that the woman who is excluded from a man's work has no contact with the best part of her husband's life. Where could I find anyone better suited to me than Lieutenant Fremont?"

Her father grunted, "Jessie, you have too many answers."

9

Thomas Benton's reply to the potted azaleas arrived a few days later in the form of Nicholas Nicollet, looking very old and muttering to himself, "There has been devil's work down there." To Jessie he reported, "They are taking him away from our map making; they are sending him on a survey of the Des Moines River in Iowa territory. Your father persuaded Secretary of War Poinsett to send him out immediately."

Half a dozen thoughts sprang simultaneously to Jessie's mind.

"On another expedition! But surely not without you?"

"I have work to do here, Miss Jessie. Besides, the lieutenant knows the Iowa territory; he will not need me."

She flushed with pride.

"In charge of the expedition! That is a promotion, is it not?"

"Most certainly; and it is the position for which I have been training him these four years." The full circle of wrinkles radiating out from the old man's eyes made his dark pupils look like water at the bottom of a well. "But I cannot spare him now; I need him to finish the maps; the original drawings are his . . ."

She was doing her best to listen to Nicollet, but there were insistent voices in her ears.

Why has this happened exactly at this moment? Will it be dangerous? Who is responsible for it? How am I to pass the months without him?

"He will be gone six months," Nicollet continued. "Do not mistake me, Jessie, it is a work that needs doing. But it comes suddenly; and I am so grieved that I cannot go . . ."

Tears came to her eyes.

"We can wait for him six months, you and I, for it will be the beginning of important things for him. He will do his work well, and when Father's plans for the great expeditions to the Rockies and to the Oregon country are approved in Congress, Lieutenant John C. Fremont will be the man they will turn to for leadership."

Nicollet rose. "Ah, it is good to be young, for then you are master of time." He embraced her gently.

She did not mention Nicollet's visit to her father. One thought kept whirling about in her mind: Will I see him before he leaves?

During dinner there was a sharp knocking of the door clapper. Joshaam came in and whispered something to Mr. Benton. He flushed, left the table.

A moment later the twin returned for Jessie. When she reached the hallway she saw Lieutenant Fremont, his military hat under one arm.

"I leave tonight for St. Louis," he said. "I have asked your father's permission to say good-by to you."

She could not speak, but stood there, all eyes. Looking up quickly she saw John too was all eyes. The yearning of two people in love and about to be separated filled the little hallway. Thomas Benton could endure it no longer.

"Very well," he said not unkindly, "at the end of a year, if you two feel as you do now, I will give my consent to your marriage."

He turned to John with his hand extended, "Good luck to you, and do a good job."

"That I will, sir," he grinned, as Jessie stood by, happy and proud of him. "I thank you for this opportunity to head my own expedition, and I assure you that I will bring back material which will make future and longer expeditions inevitable."

"I could almost permit myself to envy your summer out of doors," said Tom, "sleeping under the stars, shooting your own food, plunging at dawn into a mountain stream. It is a healthy life, Lieutenant."

"Very healthy, sir," John agreed with a twinkle in his eye, "but not likely to cure my particular ailment."

Tom Benton chuckled silently, then walked into the dining room and closed the door behind him. Jessie and John were alone.

During the long months of separation she would try to remember the moment that followed. She did not know what look had been exchanged, or what word had been said; she did not know who had moved first, or what the signal had been that united them in their first embrace. Suddenly she was in his arms and her lips were on his. There was no breath in her body or thought in her head, for his arms crushed her against him; his mouth covering hers was speaking not words, words that could be obscure or retracted, but the vitalizing kiss which could tell to both whether this mating was a lie or an ultimate truth.

The following morning her father called her into the library to tell her that she no longer had to attend Miss English's Academy.

"Thank you, darling, it is good of you to understand. Will you drive to Georgetown with me this morning and help me make a formal exit?"

She packed her possessions in her school bedroom quickly, then joined her father, who was making his apologies to Miss English. Miss English commented, "Miss Jessie is intelligent, Senator, but she lacks the docility of the model student. Moreover she has had the objectionable manner of seeming to take our assignments under consideration, to be accepted or disregarded by some standard of her own."

Jessie and her father exchanged a glance. Miss English understood the quick look, for she added:

"In a man this trait might be a praiseworthy attribute. But not in a young woman. It can only lead to trouble and heartbreak. I'm afraid Miss Jessie has strange ideas about a woman's place in modern society."

Turning to Jessie, she continued, "If you take nothing else from your two years at my school, Miss Jessie Benton, I hope you will remember that we tried to teach you to be a fine lady: to be quiet, to remember that fine manners are the most important thing in a woman's life, that without them she loses all charm and beauty; and that there is nothing more obnoxious than a pushing, self-assertive woman who refuses to remain within the sphere of her own influence: her home and her children. Senator Benton, I trust you will not allow your daughter to become a pioneer in this radical feminist movement; it can bring her nothing but unhappiness."

With the barest twitching of his lips, he replied, "It is true, Miss English, the life of a pioneer is a hard one; in my own modest way I have tried to do a little pioneering too; you are right in saying that the path is stony." Turning to his daughter he concluded, "Please remember what we have said here, Jessie; and when you get all through ignoring our strictures, don't say we didn't tell you so."

10

Jessie had expected to spend the next months working with her father, but word came from Cherry Grove that one of her young cousins was about to be married. Her mother decided that they would go south for the wedding. She could not help but see that her parents were delighted with the opportuneness of the trip, that they hoped the excitement of travel and gaiety of the wedding party might dissipate her memories of Lieutenant Fremont.

Her father escorted them onto the narrow river steamboat which would carry them down the Potomac to Fredericksburg, while Joshaam loaded their strapped and bulging bags up a rear gangplank. After the farewells had been said, Jessie and her mother stood in the prow and watched the little boat cut a clean swath through the placid blue water.

As their boat drew away from Washington City, as the miles began to intervene, Jessie noted that her mother seemed to grow younger; her eyes cleared, a little color came to her pallid cheeks, she stood up straighter. When she began to talk to her daughter about her childhood at Cherry Grove, about its beauties and peacefulness, it seemed to Jessie that a full ten years dropped from her mother's shoulders, that she once again was the beautiful woman she remembered from her childhood.

She was glad to be taking this trip with her mother, for her romance with John had seemed to separate them even farther. Though she loved her mother, Jessie deeply resented the fact that Elizabeth Benton was no longer interested in her husband's campaigns and battles, did not flush with gratification at the news that Senator Benton had won a victory for the national road or the gold bullion theory; that she did not suffer when he was attacked, or sit up nights working with him, giving him the best efforts of her heart and head to assure him of victory.

From aunts, uncles and former admirers, and particularly from Grandmother McDowell, she learned that her mother had been a soft-spoken, genteel southern girl, the favorite of Cherry Grove. Her room had been the sunniest of the large estate, her dressing table adorned with silver candelabra, her four-poster piled high with feather beds. She had a sweet, small voice and entertained her suitors with the popular ballads of the day, accompanying herself prettily at the pianoforte.

Jessie had at first been amused by the stories of how her mother, for six years and on six separate occasions, had rejected her father's proposal of marriage; but slowly this amusement had turned to indignation. In the small places of her heart she wondered why her mother had rejected Thomas Hart Benton when he was a young lawyer from St. Louis, but accepted him when he was the first senator from Missouri and started on an important career. She could not understand how one could not love a man or woman for six years, and then suddenly decide one loved him enough to marry him. For her, as for Thomas Benton, there could be no long line of suitors, no long line of years of doubts or hesitations, no wavering allegiance for man or cause.

Her father had met her mother at the home of her uncle, Governor James Preston of Virginia. It was on one of the many occasions when she drove to Richmond accompanied by her own maid and manservant in her English coach, painted a brilliant yellow and lined with scarlet morocco. He had fallen in love instantly; the following morning had declared himself. As she gazed at her mother now, at the face from which youth and beauty and serenity had fled, Jessie recalled her telling the story of how she had thought Tom Benton a boring young man who had fallen in love in a bovine fashion, and who suffered by comparison with her entourage of handsome Virginia cavaliers. At the time, Elizabeth McDowell, member of one of America's oldest and most important families, seemed to have all the advantages over Tom Benton: wealth, social position, beauty, breeding. Yes, Jessie thought, Mother had all the advantages, except one: intellect. She had been courted by one of the best minds in America, and yet for six years she kept saying:

"Papa and Mama admire and respect you; I respect you, but I have decided I can never marry you."

Nor, having her choice of the cream of southern aristocracy, had she accepted one of the Virginia blades. Elizabeth McDowell was having too good a time to select any one man and settle down. She liked the courting too well, the being surrounded by flattering males; she enjoyed the parties and the balls and the gaiety and complete lack of responsibility. Yet when she had married Senator Benton and come to Washington with him, she had become a thoughtful wife and mother; no one could doubt that she loved Tom Benton.

Suddenly her mother turned to her with unwonted intensity:

"Jessie, your cousin, Preston Johnson, will be at the wedding. You always said he was the handsomest man you ever met. Preston is a darling, he could give you such a pleasurable life. He comes into his inheritance of Blue Ridge Farm when he is twenty-one; it's every bit as beautiful as Cherry Grove. You could have such a fine life there, so free from the turmoil of Washington."

Jessie gazed at her mother incredulously.

"Are you suggesting that I marry cousin Preston?" she asked.

"You could love him, Jessie, very easily."

Mrs. Benton leaned against the curved railing of the prow. "Oh, Jessie, darling, I want to save you from what I've been through. Please believe me, my little girl, there is peace and tranquillity in Virginia. You can live a life of ease and charm. You don't have to fight and struggle and be called names, and have your private life spread over the vile newspapers. You don't have to be part of that pushing, grasping crowd of opportunists who always are trying to throw someone over, who use any means to get ahead."

"Then you never have liked Washington?"

"I have hated it more bitterly than anyone could know. I was brought up in peaceful country, I know nothing of wars and vendettas; I came out of the amiability of Cherry Grove and I was deposited into a cesspool of politics. In Virginia, at least among the Whigs, it was a gentleman's game. But since that dreadful day of Andrew Jackson's inaugural, when the mob broke into the White House, pushed the invited guests around, tore my lovely white gown . . . all politics is like that: the uninvited, unwashed, pushing around their superiors, ripping handmade lace gowns and handmade traditions."

She turned from her daughter, her excitement gone, gazed down into the white foam of water. "Do you think I liked it when my husband was called names, addressed as Old Rhinoceros Hide?"

"But Mother," exclaimed Jessie, "there is nothing bad about that. The name calling and abuse have never hurt Father, he took them in his stride. How much worse it would be for him if he lived under a king or a tyrant and neither he nor his opponents could speak their mind."

"But what about me?" wailed Mrs. Benton. "There is nothing I loathe in this world more than controversy. I could not come down to dinner without finding a group of your father's henchmen or opponents ready to thrash out their differences over the dinner table; for years if I went to a party there was no room for dancing or conversation or laughter, but only for argument and quarreling and plans about how to beat a person or a party into line. Wherever we went, wherever we traveled, the quarrels and the differences, the constant strife and sordid bickerings of public life followed us . . ."

". . . because they were part of Father's work."

"Jessie," her mother pleaded, "please try to understand. I do not criticize your father's work, nor do I mean to minimize its importance. I am only trying to say that that life could never be for me. I like quiet, pleasant,

amusing people, people without troubles or conflicts, the easy-going kind who
would hurt no one, like those I knew in Cherry Grove. Jessie, I want to
save you from what I have gone through: I should have married one of
those charming boys who had a plantation near to ours; then I could have
continued the kind of life that I was raised for, that I knew and loved. I
knew this when I was young, that was why I refused your father for six
years. I love your father; he will be the first to tell you that I have been a
faithful and loving wife, but I knew all the time that his way of life could
never be mine. Wherever he went he carried with him turbulence; I never
wanted these things, I detest them as vulgar, as destructive of the real and
permanent values. I tried hard; in the early years I went everywhere with
your father, I listened to his dreams, tried to share his defeats, but always
it was against my nature and always it sickened me . . . until I could no
longer face these people, I could no longer stomach their eternal vehemence.
It made me ill, Jessie, as ill as though I had contracted a disease."

"I understand," said Jessie gently. "I'm sorry, Mother, terribly sorry."

"But that is not the reason I have told you this," said her mother softly.
"I vowed that I would go to my death without telling anyone, because I
would never want Tom Benton to think that he had hurt me. I have broken
my resolve for you, Jessie. My darling, I know that something has come
between us; I know that in the last few years I have not been with you
enough, that I have withdrawn from your life and problems . . ."

"I have been all right, Mother; I have been happy and well."

". . . but now I must urge you, I must do everything that a mother can
do for her daughter to save her."

Jessie gazed at the gentle green hills.

"Save me from what?"

"From Lieutenant Fremont! Don't misunderstand me, Jessie. I like the
young man, but he is dynamic and pushing—like your father! He always
will be striving and battling his way uphill, spreading about him with a vast
club, as Tom Benton has; for that reason he will have enemies, he will
never be free of them. You will live with wrangling and dissension, the
interminable struggle mixed into the very food you eat. That is not good for
a woman. It destroys that inner spirit which must give her a sense of
relaxation and security if she is to live happily and raise her children."

She took Jessie's hand in hers and held it tightly.

"That is why I urge you to think seriously about your cousin Preston: he
comes from the best family in Virginia; he is wealthy and secure, he has no
ambition except the very proper ambition that his plantation be run well and
prosperously; he is full of laughter and he loves all the little things. How
beautifully you could live with him, Jessie; what a serene life you could
enjoy."

Seeing that her mother looked faint, Jessie insisted upon helping her to
their tiny cabin, where she made her comfortable on the combination berth-
bed and wiped her brow with cologne. At first she thought her mother would

sleep, but she felt Elizabeth's eyes following her every move, silently demanding an answer. She sat on the edge of the bed and stroked her mother's thin white arm.

"Mother, do you think Father could have lived without this constant conflict which has been so unpalatable to you?"

"No," replied Mrs. Benton, "what was the breath of life to him was poison to me."

"You have often said that I am Father's daughter; then you will understand, dear, that I too am ambitious, and I am not afraid of conflict. I understand and accept the turmoil of politics because I have grown up with it. Like you, I cannot eat dinner with arguments going on about me. But one can eat at any time, and it only sometimes happens that one can be with robust minds. I like Father's way of life, Mother; it comes as natural to me as it does to him. I would find it difficult to settle at Blue Ridge Farm, to spend my time in riding and dancing and hunting. I would die under that way of life. It would poison me as the turbulence of the life in Washington has poisoned you."

Mrs. Benton's tired, faded eyes looked at her daughter without comprehension.

"Jessie, you are so like me, your face is like mine, your figure is delicate like mine, it will not take all this hammering, it will sicken you, wither you . . ."

"You are wrong, Mother, you will see that you are wrong. I love John Fremont and I feel that he will leave his mark on history. I want to be part of that struggle and contribution."

". . . it would be so easy for you to love cousin Preston," her mother persisted. "He's handsome, charming . . ."

They were met at the wharf at Fredericksburg by the high-swung yellow family coach which the children had long since nicknamed the Pumpkin. Jessie clambered onto the hard leather seat beside her mother. After a few moments of bumpy riding she perceived that Elizabeth Benton had not yet given up the attempt to influence her.

"I can't tell you how it grieves me, Jessie, because I see nothing of the Cherry Grove tradition in you, but only your Father's tradition of a brawling, squawling frontier. I did not love your Father less because he became embroiled in those uncouth quarrels, but it created barriers between us. It is hard to separate a man from his work, Jessie, and when his work is a dirty one, when he brings in the vulgar trappings of his job with him, then one's whole way of life is disrupted."

"The best of a man is in his work," announced Jessie, categorically.

"Your father taught you that."

"Does that make it any the less true?"

Tears rolled down Elizabeth Benton's cheeks; but this time she made no effort to gather her daughter to her.

"My poor baby, how I pity you! How much misery and suffering you are rushing out to embrace."

As the tall oaks of Cherry Grove loomed into sight, Elizabeth Benton made a futile, fluttering gesture with her slender white hands which admitted defeat.

"I came into your father's life too late to change him, nor would it have been decent, or even sensible, to try. But you are so young . . . No one listens to me; everyone goes his cocksure way."

11

Cherry Grove had been paid in grant to Jessie's great-grandfather by the King of England in return for his military services in the colonies. It had been built in the manner of the Arlington Colonial, with the pillared portico and stately white wings, the great drawing room and dining room on either side of the lofty, spacious hall.

They were escorted into the house by Colonel McDowell, her uncle with the florid face and long silken mustaches. In addition to her grandmother McDowell and Eliza, who had returned with her in the spring, Jessie found herself exclaimed over and embraced by thirty-five aunts, uncles and cousins, the complete gathering of the clan: there were still-English cousins from Smithfield, the aunt from Richmond who had descended from Patrick Henry, the uncles from Abington who owned the salt works there; Uncle McDowell, whom the family claimed to be the most profound scholar in all Virginia, their cousin, the Reverend Robert Breckinridge, who was known all over the South for his fire and eloquence in the pulpit.

And her cousin, Preston Johnson, was there, home on his first vacation from West Point. He seized upon the opportunity in the crowded hallway to join in the embraces and kiss her enthusiastically. Preston was a tall, blond, blue-eyed boy, one of the most daring and skillful riders in Virginia. He was Jessie's second cousin. She had no sooner been ushered into the drawing room than the aunts and uncles insisted that she stand side by side with Preston so that they could exclaim over how amazingly she looked like Preston's mother and comment, in soft but audible undertones, what a beautiful couple they made.

While the elders collected in the library each morning for what she considered to be an endless recounting of family history, Jessie and her cousins escaped by going horseback riding in the hills. Preston was an incorrigible tease who kept them laughing.

"But Preston, have you no ambition beyond having fun?" she asked one morning.

She saw him grow sober and mature for the first time in the years she had known him, and for the last time until they would bring home his shrapnel-torn body from the plains of Cherubusco.

"I pity people with ambition," he said, measuring his words carefully. "They tear themselves apart so; and everyone around them, too. They never have any pleasure or peace; ambition feeds on itself; the greater the accomplishment, the greater the appetite. No, thank you, Jessie, no ambition for me; I want to live graciously; ambition is for the upstarts, for those who hope to leave off where I begin."

Jessie liked her young cousin better because he had revealed something of himself. At the same time she knew how wide was the bridge that separated them.

At dusk she wandered alone through the oak-lined park. The cherry trees were in rampant bloom, the maples and sycamores were in flower. While her serious attachments always had been for Washington City and Grandmother Benton's home in St. Louis, the spacious beauty of Cherry Grove never failed to awaken a nostalgia in her. While walking through the stately grounds, crossing the large stretches of lawn and gardens with square-boxed hedges, she understood a little the startling revelation her mother had made. Her mother had called her headstrong. Could it be that her dream of marriage as a joint career for husband and wife was an impossible one? That her love for the man who not only inflamed her senses, but whose work she considered important and valuable, was misplaced? She thought of her cousin Preston and of how different she felt when she was in the company of John Fremont, who served as a heady stimulant, who excited her to her deepest thinking and sharpest expression.

A woman had to work through a man; she must choose a good vessel into which to pour herself.

When she returned to the house she found her grandmother sitting quietly in the library with a book on her lap.

"Come here, child," she called.

Jessie sank onto the soft blue rug with her feet tucked beneath her and looked up at her grandmother.

"I shall make your wedding here at Cherry Grove," she said. "I will live that long, though I am getting very old and tired." She stroked Jessie's head gently. "It is you who make me realize how indestructible things are: my mother came here as a young bride a hundred years ago, in 1743. Her life was rich, but it was also full of hardships. She carried her scars from the Indian wars, just as I do: her first child was killed in a night raid. You will have your battles too, Jessie, after you marry that young man of yours; and you will carry scars, but you will carry them the way my mother did, like medals bestowed for bravery."

12

Four months had passed, and there were two more months of days in which, for the first time in her life, she found herself avoiding the company of her father. Her sister was the only one with whom she could talk about John, and talking about him somehow filled the hours of waiting.

She was reading in the family's small upstairs sitting room the evening Joshaam entered and announced that Lieutenant Fremont wished to pay his respects. No one moved: her mother looked hard at her multicolored afghan; Thomas Benton glared at his young son as though he were responsible for Lieutenant Fremont's not having been permanently lost among the Sioux; Jessie gazed at her father, her face hot and her heart cold with anxiety. Only Eliza seemed able to do the natural thing; she rose, went downstairs and returned with Lieutenant Fremont in tow. Jessie wanted to rise when she saw him in the doorway, his face bronzed, his hair long, making him look like the Indians among whom he had spent the summer.

Still unable to rise or speak, Jessie thought Mrs. Crittenden was right when she said he was the handsomest officer ever to walk the streets of Washington.

It seemed to her as though a very long time passed in awkward silence, but actually it was only a moment before Thomas Benton remembered his manners, clasped the young lieutenant firmly by the hand and welcomed him home. John presented the girls with gifts of Indian jewelry, young Randolph with a tomahawk. For Mrs. Benton, Jessie, and Eliza he had brought handsomely carved turquoise necklaces, and for Tom Benton a picturesque Indian pipe of peace. Jessie sat stiffly in her chair while Randolph demanded stories of the Indians. Then Tom Benton said, "I would like to hear something of your findings; suppose we go into the library where I have my maps."

Up to this moment Jessie had exchanged no word with her betrothed. She had not been invited into the library with the two men, but she knew that no matter what Senator Benton said later, she would go in with them.

The library was cool and dark, the heavy Venetian blinds having been closed all day against the hot sun. As her father lighted his astral lamp Jessie stood awkwardly on one foot, her eyes on John, wanting to be in his arms. But as Tom Benton moved about the room laying out his own rough charts she could feel his disapproval, the lack of understanding in the way he held his head.

She stood with her back to the worktable watching John as he bent over his maps, listening as he answered her father's questions in a deep voice. She watched his eyes, the glow of excitement on his dark face; though the fingers of his left hand gripped hers under the table, crushing them, she knew that he had forgotten her presence, that he was living again those hours of exploration. And she was not jealous.

But when Tom Benton went to put away his papers, they turned to each other; not knowing how they had overcome their restraint before him, or their reluctance in the face of his hunched-up disapproval, they were in each other's arms. In the distance they heard a voice; it was Senator Benton.

". . . very well, you love each other; I am not blind. But you still have six months to wait . . ."

Somewhere in the process of walking out of the library, going down the stairs and bidding him good night, always with her father at her elbow, she managed to murmur, "Tomorrow afternoon at Mrs. Crittenden's. Three o'clock."

The next afternoon she rang the doorbell of the senator from Kentucky. Mrs. Crittenden had always been fond of Jessie Benton; in addition she was a woman who liked to gather the world and its troubles to her.

"He's here, my dear," she said. "I sent him out to the garden; it's cool and quiet there and you can be alone. Really, I envy you, Jessie: that man grows more exciting every time he comes back from an expedition. If I were you I'd marry him fast."

Her teeth chattering, Jessie could only reply, "By the Eternal, Mrs. Crittenden, I'm trying! If only something could convince Father . . . The next six months sound to me like six decades; I'm certain I'll never survive them."

"You'll survive them," replied Mrs. Crittenden, "but you'll be on the point of death at least a hundred times."

Jessie tried to smile in response to the little joke.

"I think Father is planning to have him sent on another expedition before the six months are up. This time he may send him away for a year, or even two. Oh, he can do it, never fear," she said swiftly as Mrs. Crittenden appeared to protest, "he can persuade Secretary Poinsett again; there is endless work to be done. But not now, Mrs. Crittenden, not until we're married. I can't let Father send him away again!"

"No," agreed Mrs. Crittenden slowly, "I don't think you should."

She put her arm around Jessie's slender shoulders and walked with her out to the garden. "Do exactly as you think best, Jessie, though heaven knows I have interfered with my own children enough."

As she saw John Fremont sitting placidly in a low wicker chair, waiting for her, Jessie knew that she would do nothing, that she could not make herself bold. She would have to wait until he spoke his mind.

They sat in a shaded swing and talked about the past six months; she told him of the wedding festivities at Cherry Grove, of the riding and hunting on the estate, the talk of the elders about how many colonial and American governors they had contributed; of the death of Grandmother McDowell just two days after the ceremony.

The next afternoon when she met him at Mrs. Crittenden's, she saw that he was nervous and ill at ease.

"Let's take a walk," he announced brusquely. "I want to talk to you."

It was a crisp fall day, one of the few times in the year that one could take a real walk in Washington, for the early rains had been sufficient to settle the dust, but not heavy enough to create vast mud puddles. He struck out along the rough cobblestones of F Street, then lifted her over a rail fence, crossed a grazing field and a number of ditches and once again lifted her over a stile to come to the Navy Yard, where Christ Church stood in the center of a cluster of small cottages. From here they turned east past the city workhouse and the congressional cemetery. She was glad she had worn her walking dress of rose satin, for its long skirt puffed out with hoops swished back and forth rhythmically as she kept up with the lieutenant's pace. She buttoned her Brussels-lace gloves, then grasped his arm firmly to keep from tripping on the rough ground outside the Navy Barracks.

As they swept along she glanced at his profile and noted uneasily that his skin seemed darker than she had known it; his features heavier; she wondered if something was upsetting him. She enjoyed striding by his side, the feel of her shoulder touching his lightly. Then slowly their harmony was broken: he slowed his pace, in an instant he had stopped without giving her warning, his figure stiffened. He whirled about to block her passage, a look of resolution on his face, the charm and surety gone, so that she almost did not recognize the man who stood confronting her. Nor did she recognize his voice when he finally spoke, for it was hoarse and off key.

"I've waited—yes, I know it's almost too late . . . but please believe me, Jessie, it wasn't because I wanted to . . . to . . . conceal . . ."

"What is it, my darling?" she asked softly.

"I simply could not, Jessie, I dared not leave it for you to find out by yourself . . . later by accident . . . and then have it be something you would hold against me, because I did not tell you the full truth."

Jessie took his arm. "Let's walk over past Duff Green Row; it will be easier for you to talk."

They started out again, but his pace was slow, almost dragging.

"Jessie, I couldn't let you marry me until I told you . . ."

He was silent for another moment, then stopped dead in his tracks and said in a flat tone, "I never told you about my mother, did I?"

They were in front of the large brick building where Congress had held its first meetings. The air was utterly still.

"Only that she had a difficult time supporting her three children after your father died."

"Yes. Well. My mother's maiden name was Anne Beverley Whiting. Her father was Colonel Thomas Whiting, who was a large landowner in Virginia and one of the leaders in the House of Burgesses. My mother was the youngest of twelve children; the family was prosperous, but when her father died her mother married a man who dissipated the entire estate. Her mother died soon after, and my mother was brought up by a married sister."

He paced back and forth, talking faster.

"She never spoke about those days much; she was kept almost as a slave in her sister's house. My mother was a beautiful young girl—I will show you her picture one day. When she was only seventeen an elderly man by the name of John Pryor began courting her; he had fought under Washington, was wealthy, owned the biggest livery stable in Virginia, and the Haymarket Gardens. He was past sixty, but he wanted my mother. John Pryor offered security, a place in Richmond society, an escape from my aunt's household. She married him when she was only seventeen, and she spent twelve unhappy years with him."

Jessie took her eyes from his harassed face; she glanced down at her shoes, idly noting that the patent leather about the toe was hopelessly scuffed. Free from her observing eyes, John increased the tempo of his short staccato steps, and his story gained momentum.

"When my mother was twenty-seven she met a young schoolteacher in Richmond by the name of Charles Frémon. My father—he became . . . my father had been a Royalist during the French Revolution and had fled to San Domingo during one of the uprisings. His ship was captured by the English, he was made a prisoner in the West Indies for several years. Finally he was released and came on to Virginia where he made a living teaching French and painting frescos. Here my mother met him, and they fell in love."

He stopped short and whirled about to confront her.

"Jessie, they could not endure to be without each other. For a year they found happiness in Richmond, and then John Pryor learned about it. He told my mother that he would kill Charles Frémon and that everyone in Virginia would not only approve his act but would help him if necessary. The next morning my mother and Frémon were gone from Richmond."

He stopped, announced, "Let us turn back!" took her roughly by the shoulder and began walking impetuously in the direction from which they had come.

"John Pryor went to the Virginia legislature and asked for a divorce from my mother. My mother knew about this."

They circled the buildings of a brickworks, watching its blazing kiln. "Did my mother and father have a marriage ceremony performed? My mother said they did. But she never showed me the wedding certificate. It would have made little difference, in any event, for the Virginia legislature had turned down John Pryor's request, and he never did secure a divorce. I was born in Savannah on January 21, 1813. So . . . you see, I was . . . yes, I am . . ."

Jessie stood looking at him, feeling the deepest sympathy she had ever known.

"I am . . . an illegitimate child, Jessie. I can try to forget it or pretend it doesn't matter, I can tell myself that my mother did have a ceremony performed, that John Pryor's appeal to the Virginia legislature was as good as a divorce, but when I am all through I still come up against the cold fact of my illegitimacy."

John Fremont appeared to shrink until she seemed taller than he and had to look down into his eyes. She spoke out quickly.

"It has hurt you, it has made you bitter, I can see that; but surely you do not blame your mother?"

"No, no," he said fiercely, "I have always been happy that she found love and had the courage to take it."

"Then I must ask you, has all this made any difference to you?"

"No . . . o," he replied hesitantly, as though realizing that he was telling only a fraction of the truth, "except that it has made me more determined to make good, to show them that Anne Beverley Whiting's son is as good as the rest of them."

"Then why must you torment yourself so?"

"Because I'm afraid," he whispered.

"Afraid? You, who live in the face of imminent death every moment you are in the wilderness?"

"I live in terror . . . of the day when someone . . . will call me a . . . bastard!"

Jessie thought, There, it is out: it is better for him to have said it; now perhaps it won't fester in the dark places of his mind.

"You are the finest man I have ever known," she murmured softly, "as fine and wonderful as my own father. I love you completely. It wasn't necessary to tell me this, it's not of the slightest importance, and I know how much it cost you in the telling."

". . . the most painful . . . difficult . . . moment of my life."

"Be comforted, John; we will never discuss it again." She wrapped her long cashmere shawl tighter around her shoulders. "Come, let us go to Mrs. Crittenden's. A cup of hot tea will be good for both of us."

"One thing more, Jessie: I want you to know what has precipitated this. It was the stories you told me of Cherry Grove and the McDowell family that goes back two hundred years in American history. Imagine how outraged your family at Cherry Grove would be if they learned that a McDowell had married a bas . . . an illegitimate child. For they will find out, Jessie; far too many people in the South know, not to tell them. Behind your back they'll say, 'Are the children of an illegitimate man illegitimate?' "

Again she tried to reassure him, more by her manner than her words, for she knew that he had already told himself all the possible answers.

"My dear, you have made your own way and established a place for yourself; your ability and your reputation are growing, nothing can harm you . . ."

"Jessie, your position is impregnable: no one can ever challenge it. You could never know how this insecurity can poison a man, though he puts on a bold and charming front. Oh Jessie, if you could only know how I've wanted to belong, to be invulnerable, so that no one could possibly point out any difference! How I've wanted to belong to the majority, not to a despised minority; how I've wanted to have the security of knowing that I am thinking what everyone else is thinking . . ."

They walked on awkwardly, past the Old Glasshouse where some of the country's best glass was made. About a hundred men and boys were working in the big shop. Jessie and John watched them for a few moments, then wandered through their settlement of freshly painted cottages with wide verandas, covered by vines and shaded by tall trees.

So his strength was born of weakness, thought Jessie. Her father too would not have had to become a reckless and courageous fighter, but would have been a simple and ordinary man, like all other ordinary men, if he had not been a consumptive, if he had not been on the very verge of death. Adversity had made Tom Benton strong, as it had John Fremont.

She told him of Tom Benton's father, who had died of consumption while the children were still young, of how her father's three sisters had died of consumption, and within another year, two of his brothers. Then Tom had studied law in Nashville, been admitted to the Bar and elected to the Tennessee legislature. When war broke out in 1812 he had volunteered and become a colonel under Andrew Jackson. Going home to say farewell to his mother, he had had to admit to her that he too was in the early stages of the disease, for he had a fever, was coughing, and she could tell from his thin, racked frame that he had been having sleepless nights. The pioneer woman saw that her last and most promising child would be taken from her.

"This is the end of all my hope," she had cried. "Tom, stay home, let me put you to bed, let me take care of you."

"No, Mother," he had replied, "with this disease we have no chance. If I'm doomed, then it is better to give the last few months of my life fighting for my country."

Tom Benton had joined his regiment and made his way south to meet the British. But he had not given himself up to death. An iconoclast by nature, with a mind open to any radical thought that seemed to make sense, he had recalled that he felt best when he was outdoors in the sunshine, when he was subjecting his body to rigors which everyone told him would be fatal. He bathed at dawn and sunset in cold streams, rubbed down his body with coarse towels, stripped off his clothes when there was even a moment's time to stretch out naked in the sun; he foreswore alcohol and tobacco, made Herculean efforts to find eggs and milk to drink every day; and instead of pampering his sick body he had pushed it beyond its outermost limits on forced marches. By the end of the summer he had put on twenty pounds of hard flesh.

"Fear did that for my father," she said. "That fear has never abated, never for a day of his life, and consequently he has never given up his discipline. All this not only saved his life, but made a fighter of him. Think of how valuable a man he has become through that courage; think of the great work he has done, how he has stood up against his enemies and never given up to despair. Fear is good, my dear, it made a strong man of my father. It can make a great man of you."

Gratefully John murmured, "You are kind, Jessie; there are no walls that close in your understanding."

Jessie smiled wistfully. "I too have used weakness to build with. I was afraid that I might not measure up, that being a woman I would find myself weak, my mind unable to grasp the real issues and struggles of the day. That is why I studied and worked so hard, because I didn't want to fail, because I didn't want my father or my husband to feel that I didn't have the brains or the courage or the training to serve as his companion."

Some of the darkness receded from John's face, a little warmth came into his eyes, his figure seemed to regain its height. And Jessie felt her own blood sing through her veins. She stopped at the edge of the marsh along which they had been wandering, locked her arms around him, her open palms pressing his back tightly, and kissed him full on the mouth, a kiss of love and faith and affirmation, so strong, so indelible that all other words died in his throat.

13

The crisp wind of autumn was flurrying the leaves from the sycamores and poplars when Jessie and John, together with Mr. Nicollet and Mrs. Crittenden, met at an appointed hour at the home of the Presbyterian minister whose church Jessie attended.

Her fear that Senator Benton would have John sent off again was heightened by the sense of insecurity from which the lieutenant suffered and which imperiled their relationship. He had commented to her, "Confidence is the greatest gift that one human being can give to another." What greater token of confidence could she bestow upon him than immediate marriage?

They found the minister in his study, a tall white-haired man with a lean, esthetic face and an enormous mouth, reputed to be the largest in the contemporary service of the Lord. He looked at the unannounced assemblage and asked, none too cordially, "What can I do for you?"

It was Mrs. Crittenden who answered without hesitation, "Jessie Benton and Lieutenant Fremont wish to be married. Since Miss Jessie is a member of your congregation, we have naturally come to you to perform the ceremony."

"Ah, splendid, splendid," murmured the clergyman, his mouth smiling, but his eyes glancing swiftly and uncertainly from person to person. "And when can we expect your mother and father, Miss Jessie?"

"You can't," replied Nicollet shortly; "they're not coming."

"Not coming!" exclaimed the clergyman. "But I don't understand. Surely they will want to be at Miss Jessie's wedding . . . ?"

"They would and they wouldn't," replied Jessie. "You see, sir, this is a secret—er—marriage, that is, Father doesn't exactly . . . he wants us to wait another six months."

"You mean your mother and father don't know about this?"

"No, sir."

Pulling himself up to his full six feet the clergyman closed his lips so tightly his mouth appeared almost small.

"Did you really think I would incur the wrath of Senator Benton? Did you imagine that I would perform a secret ceremony knowing that the senator disapproved? Have you all taken leave of your senses?"

There was a dull pause before he continued, "I will not expose your secret, Miss Jessie. Come back with your mother and father, and it would be my great happiness to marry you to Lieutenant Fremont. Good day to you all."

A little stunned and very much disconcerted, the would-be wedding party trudged down the front stairs of the minister's house.

"What do we do now?" asked Lieutenant Fremont.

"We try another clergyman," replied Mrs. Crittenden; "whom do you recommend, Mr. Nicollet?"

"Let's try that new Methodist minister; he seems to have gumption."

The Methodist minister had discretion. He asked very politely, "Are you not a Presbyterian, Miss Benton? Why do you not go to your Presbyterian clergyman?"

"We've been," replied Jessie.

"And?"

"He won't marry us unless my mother and father are along."

"That sounds like uncommonly good sense," observed the minister with a twinkle in his eye. "Never let it be said that a Methodist rushed in where a Presbyterian feared to tread."

Once again the wedding party trooped out of the house. They tried the Lutheran minister, who was rehearsing his choir in a little wooden church. The Lutheran must have read defeatism in their faces, for he replied, "Quite unthinkable; however, if you are of the same opinion tomorrow, I will come to your home, Miss Benton, and perform the ceremony."

They had started out in high spirits and high hopes; now they stood in the brisk October sunshine looking at each other guiltily.

"Well," drawled Nicollet, "better luck next time; come along, Lieutenant, if you can't be married, you might as well go back to work."

Jessie walked Mrs. Crittenden home and then continued wearily onward to her own house. First she had been bewildered, then hurt, but now she was mad. What has the world come to, she asked herself, when a young couple in love can't get married? Surely there must be some way . . . ?

There was, but she spent three agonizing days before the answer turned up. Mrs. Crittenden arrived on the afternoon of October 19 for a visit with Mrs. Benton. She asked Mrs. Benton if Jessie might spend the night with her, as she was giving a party for her young niece. There could be but one purpose to this proposal: Jessie packed an overnight bag, jumped into Mrs. Crittenden's carriage as though the world had been reborn.

"It's all arranged," said Mrs. Crittenden. "I went yesterday to Father Van Horseigh, the Catholic priest, and persuaded him to perform the marriage. He is coming this afternoon. I've already sent word to Lieutenant Fremont.

Nicollet and Hassler will be there, Harriet Bodisco, and several other of your young friends. I have pledged them to secrecy."

When they arrived at the Crittenden home they found Lieutenant Fremont waiting. He was wearing his full-dress uniform, the same one in which he had proposed to her eight months before. Jessie was presented to Father Van Horseigh, a plump little Dutch priest with a moonlike face, a shock of red hair and a bubbling gift of laughter. Though Jessie and John Fremont were Protestants, they saw no reason why they should not be married by a Catholic priest: Jessie had been raised with the French of Catholic St. Louis; John had been taken by Nicollet for a vacation to St. Mary's College at the Sulpician Seminary in Baltimore after their second expedition.

The service was short and simple. Only once did Jessie Benton's determination almost fail her, and the tears well up behind her eyes: where were the beauties of Cherry Grove, the hundreds of friends and relatives who would gather; where was the magnificent Paris gown of blonde lace over satin, where the mahogany dining table laden with wines and wondrous foods, and the bridecake embedded in a wreath of ivy and geranium leaves cut from the candied rind of watermelon; where were the linens and cambrics, the muslins and lace, every stitch of delicate needlework sewn by friends and relatives? She would be the first of Cherry Grove to be married in "paid-for" sewing. Where were the saddle horses and barouches and London carriages gathered at the hitching shed, and all the countryside of Virginia alive and glowing because Miss Jessie Ann Benton was being married?

As a tear rolled down her cheek, Jessie Benton paralleled the traditional words the priest was speaking with her own prayer: I give up the traditions of Cherry Grove, I give up the Empire gown, I give up the lovingly sewed linens, I give up the bridecake; I can give up everything so long as I have you, John Fremont.

She came up from the depths of her thinking to find a quiet in the room; the ceremony was over, she had not even heard herself and John pronounced man and wife; nor had she need of the corroboration.

Mrs. Crittenden served a wedding supper, after which the servants offered claret, cheeses, fruits, candies, and as a grand climax a silver platter of ice cream which Jessie saw had been made with the expensive vanilla bean. There was the music of a violin, guitar and accordion, but Jessie left her food untouched and danced only a little, for her head felt feverish and her feet uncertain. At ten o'clock Mrs. Crittenden beckoned to John and herself and walked them out into the cold of the garden.

"Attention, my children," she said, "I will be responsible to Tom Benton only for the marriage ceremony. Kiss your bride good night, Lieutenant Fremont, for you are returning home to your bachelor quarters."

And so Jessie walked up the Benton steps the following morning, trembling with joy because she was Mrs. John Charles Fremont, and trembling at the thought of her father's rage when he should learn what had happened. Each day she and her husband saw each other for a few moments, but never alone, always there were Nicollet or Mrs. Crittenden, who played chaperon far more ardently than she had before the ceremony. Occasionally too Tom Benton found it awkward to exclude from his house the rising young star of the western expeditions.

The oval mirror on Jessie's dressing table told her that she was becoming peaked and hollow-eyed. It was growing increasingly difficult for her to stand looking at John, talking politely and restrainedly of impersonal things. Eliza knew of the marriage and urged her sister to reveal it. Nicollet also urged it. He was eager for them to get on with their normal life and work. "I'm growing older and more ill every hour, *mes enfants*," he would say, "it won't be long before I'll be studying celestial maps. Before I go, I would like to see this affair settled."

When at last John pleaded, "I have never liked this secrecy. We have been precipitous but not criminal. Let me go to the senator and explain," Jessie said firmly: "We will explain tomorrow morning. I will ask the senator for an early interview."

A little more than a month after their marriage ceremony, Jessie led John to the upstairs library. Tom Benton was sunk in his chair, his high domelike forehead creased with four deep lines, his mouth and chin set grimly, his gray eyes tired. They stood before him.

"We are married, Father," said Jessie in a low tone. "The ceremony was performed on October nineteenth."

She was frightened. She wanted the two men to be friends. Could her father understand that she did not love him the less because she had acquired a husband?

A bellow came up from the depths of Tom Benton's chair; the outburst was directed at John Fremont.

"Get out of my house and never cross this door again! Jessie shall stay here."

Quietly, and without hesitation, Jessie linked her arm through her husband's. Her voice was calm and clear.

"Father, do you remember Ruth's pledge from the Bible? 'Whither thou goest, I will go . . .'"

Tom Benton rose slowly and towered above them. He would give in, but in his own peculiar way. Her hope was that it would not be too peculiar for her husband's understanding.

"Go collect your belongings and return at once to the house," he ordered the lieutenant, his tone suggestive of the colonel commanding a subaltern.

There was a stillness in the room. It was broken by a brusque knock on the door. Two newspaper reporters stood on the threshold.

"Senator Benton," said the man from the *National Intelligencer*, "we hear there is news about Miss Jessie."

Tom Benton glared at the man, then growled, "Yes. I have the pleasure of announcing the marriage of my daughter, Jessie Ann Benton, to Lieutenant John Charles Fremont."

The reporter from the New York *Globe* grinned. "Isn't that an unusual way of putting it, Senator? Families generally announce the marriage of the man to their daughter."

Tom Benton looked sharply at his daughter, then said, unsmilingly, "If ever I saw a woman do her damnedest to get married to a man, it's my daughter Jessie. But if you print that I'll sue you for libel. Good day, gentlemen."

BOOK TWO

A WOMAN WAITS

1

SHE LAY QUIETLY in her high bed, the air cold from the window above the garden, the quilt tucked under her chin. In a few hours it would be New Year's Day. Lieutenant and Mrs. John Charles Fremont had been invited by President John Tyler to a reception at the White House.

It was now two o'clock in the morning; her husband lay sleeping peacefully beside her. It amused her to see that this man who held himself so erect while in public now lay curled up like a child, all need for defense vanished. She thought, Who but a wife can know all about a man, see him and feel him whole, understand his sudden flights and equally sudden withdrawals?

They had talked for a long time with the darkness of the bedroom like a sheltering canopy, and only an occasional burst of laughter from some incongruous idea broke the silence. She liked these hours the best, the comradely periods when she could lie with a protecting arm about her, nestled against the man she loved.

From her earliest days she had wanted to create a fine marriage. She had been born with the idea, but it also had been nurtured by her father, who had talked to her about the "great marriage," which would be the highest aim she could achieve, of equal importance with the children she would bear. Marriage was to be her proving ground, the combined art and science with which she could most truly express herself. It would be different from the fragmentary unions she saw about her; it would show that in the accomplishing two human beings could reach their completest fulfillment. Her father had told her how valuable her mother's judgment had been to him; of how tremendous his loss had been when she was taken ill. Jessie sometimes watched her mother and father together in the hope of catching a glimpse of their early relationship; she was heartbroken to see how little was left. In the arrogance of her youth she was certain that she would be equal to the task in which her mother had failed.

As she gazed at her husband's dark face on the pillow, pushed a lock of hair off his brow, she was overcome by a sense of elation that she had found not only the top man in the profession into which she had felt she must marry, but also a man who excited her now every moment she was with him. She might have married a man whom she admired but never loved with this sense of ardency; or she might have loved and married a doctor, an architect, a lawyer, and thus robbed the second half of her dual personality of its ambition.

She had never allowed anyone to know she was thinking these thoughts, for they would have accused her of being an Anne Royall. But as she ran a fingertip along the faint lines in her husband's forehead, down the small-boned nose, and across the warm lips, there was joined to her feeling of elation a sense of awe that she could have been so fortunate as to find one of those exceedingly rare men who would permit his wife to work by his side. She had never assumed marriage to be a relationship from which she would take, but rather a relationship to which she could give.

She was delighted with what marriage had done for John. Before this he had been a homeless one, a man without a family. Now the Benton loyalty and confidence had reached out to envelop him; their marriage seemed to dissipate the last fragment of uncertainty at the back of his eyes.

They had spent their honeymoon in the big house on C Street; their blue-tinted bedroom and sitting room faced south, overlooking the garden, and was flooded with gentle winter sunshine. The family disturbed them not at all; Maylee or one of her twins served breakfast in their rooms; the children stayed out of the garden as much as possible. She had let their friends in Washington City know that they did not want to be entertained by formal dinners or receptions. Her only visitor was the Countess Bodisco, who dropped in frequently with a box of imported Russian or French candy under her arm, amusing chatter on her lips.

"I laugh," said Harriet, "when I remember what one of my uncles told my father. I eavesdropped and heard him say, 'Don't let Harriet marry that old man; he can never give her a complete married life.' My dear, I'll wager that within five minutes of the time the count first closed that bedroom door behind him, I was *enceinte*. That old Russian has me down to skin and bones."

Jessie glanced at Harriet's tall figure, which was filling out rapidly.

"You seem to be thriving under it," she retorted.

She took pleasure in murmuring to herself: my husband. There was nothing possessive in the phrase except in the sense that she belonged; since John Fremont was now her husband, she belonged to him as his wife. Because of her Anne Royall idea of equal work and equal responsibility she found it difficult to call her sweet and lovable husband Mister Fremont. Her mother still called her father Mister Benton after all these years. In public Jessie referred to her husband as Lieutenant Fremont; when they were alone she called him John.

Tonight they had enjoyed several hours of talk before he had at last dropped off to sleep in the middle of a sentence, the room in friendly darkness, the bed soft beneath them, the air cool and spiked with the scent of night-blooming jasmine. At the height of their physical union she had felt that there was no further enigma, no possible withholding. But once it was over, though their love was as great in its ebbing peacefulness, the connecting rod had been snapped like a brittle twig; and dimly she perceived that this probing, onrushing fever of understanding could not be constant or sustained:

that it must ebb and flow, that it must now be hard and strong and compulsive within her, and now recede, be withdrawn entirely, be extinguished as a light is extinguished, leaving her abandoned, and yet exhilarated at having even for so short a climax possessed him whole.

Perhaps that is what marriage means, she thought, the spending of a lifetime trying to understand your mate, trying to evolve the mysteries of character which even he may not suspect are there. Perhaps that's what success in a marriage means: not the establishment of a place in society, not the acquiring of a fortune, no, not even the creating of children; but the full understanding of another human soul, the most difficult and at the same time the most beautiful task of all.

2

When Lieutenant and Mrs. John Fremont reached the White House shortly after noon on January 1, 1842, Pennsylvania Avenue was jammed with private carriages, public hacks, broad-beamed omnibuses and a hundred horses tethered to hitching posts. Hassler had urged them to use his imported English carriage for the New Year's call. The carriage was famous up and down the Atlantic seaboard as Hassler's Ark, for he had had it built large enough to house his sleeping and cooking equipment, his scientific instruments, books and journals. Jessie made a last critical appraisal of her dark blue velvet gown with its full straight skirt over narrow hoops, the close-fitting bodice outlined at the neck and sleeves with frills of Mechlin lace. In her strapped slippers she stepped lightly to the ground, leaned on her husband's arm, took an approving glance at his blue-and-gold dress uniform, then gave an adjusting hitch to her blue velvet cape. As they reached the front door she turned to her husband with an inquiring glance which asked, Am I all right? John touched the white lobe of ear which she had not covered with her tightly drawn hair and said:

"What lovely pearl earrings you wear, Madame."

They passed the Marine Band which was playing in the vestibule and were welcomed by Senators Linn and Crittenden. Linn exclaimed:

"My dears, you are positively radiant. I know you are going to captivate President Tyler."

"Captivate him thirty thousand dollars' worth," said Senator Crittenden. "If he'll sponsor the bill in Congress, we'll get that appropriation, and you'll be off for South Pass."

"We'll do our best," promised Jessie.

The senators escorted them into the reception room and presented them to President Tyler: high-domed and hollow-cheeked, with a bony nose which curved sharply in an outward arc and seemed to be a continuation of the outward curve of his high forehead. It was the arresting, characterful face of the incorrigibly independent man.

As a former senator from Virginia, President John Tyler had long known the Bentons. He congratulated the young couple upon their marriage, then said to Lieutenant Fremont, "Young man, I understand that you are aching to get off into the wilderness on an expedition."

"That's right, Mr. President," John replied.

"I have reason to believe you won't be disappointed," said President Tyler, "though if I were in your place, just married to Miss Jessie, nothing could persuade me to leave Washington."

"But I plan to wait for him, Mr. President," she replied, smiling.

President John Tyler's lean, hard-bitten face became serious; he said in a low tone: "We need detail maps of all the country from St. Louis to the Rockies so our immigrant trains will settle there. But see that you don't go west of the Rockies, young man; we already have more than a hundred Americans in Oregon; if many more of our settlers reach the Columbia, there will be danger of a war with England."

On a cold gray morning in mid-January they walked up to the Senate Building with Thomas Hart Benton: this was the day for which the expansionists had been working for twenty years. A bill was before the Senate to appropriate thirty thousand dollars for an expedition "intended to acquaint the government with the nature of the rivers and country between the frontiers of Missouri and the base of the Rocky Mountains, and especially to examine the character, and ascertain the latitude and longitude of the South Pass, the great crossing place to these mountains on the way to Oregon."

Jessie sat in the first row of the visitors' gallery watching the scene in the red-plush amphitheater below them. Both she and John knew that on the passage of this appropriation rested their future, for Nicollet was certain to be named to command the expedition and he in turn would name Lieutenant Fremont as his second in command. They waited breathlessly while the roll was called; when the last senator had voted aye and the expedition was authorized, husband and wife turned to each other with happy eyes.

That evening there was a party at the Benton home to celebrate the victory. Jessie, who had been talking with Colonel Abert and Colonel Stephen Watts Kearny about how jubilantly this news would be received in St. Louis and the Southwest, saw Nicholas Nicollet beckoning to her.

"Put on a wrap, my child," he said, "I want to talk to you."

As they walked down the garden path Nicollet commented, "It was here I first saw you sitting with Lieutenant Fremont. I said to your father, 'How beautiful is young love.' And because of my congenital Gallic romanticism, I got poor John banished from the house."

"If you hadn't precipitated that crisis," laughed Jessie, "we might not yet have been married."

They sat side by side on the garden bench. Nicollet said, "Miss Jessie, I have something to tell you."

For an instant the words stopped revolving in her mind. "But surely you are taking Lieutenant Fremont as your second in command?"

"No, Jessie. He will be the commander of the expedition. I am not going, I am too ill."

"But that's not possible," she exclaimed, her sympathy for the white-faced old man overcoming her first flash of joy. "This is the most important expedition sent out by the federal government since Lewis and Clark, an expedition for which you have been working for twenty years!"

"I am an old man," said Nicollet doggedly, "I have done my job. Tomorrow morning I shall inform Colonel Abert that I am unable to command the expedition and that I nominate my successor, Lieutenant Fremont."

By the next afternoon all Washington rang with the news that Nicholas Nicollet had retired, that Lieutenant John Fremont was to head the expedition to South Pass.

The months that followed were the gayest of Jessie's life. Countess Bodisco gave a glittery ball in their honor for the Diplomatic Corps in her Georgetown home. Nancy Polk collected the young people of Washington City for a dinner and dance. Senators Linn and King gave dinners at which astonishingly large groups of the Congress came to be wined and dined and tell Lieutenant Fremont, on a full stomach, how to map the barren West. Samuel Morse gave a masquerade ball to which everyone came dressed as either a painter or one of his subjects; Anne Royall had a tea for the feminists of Washington with Jessie as her guest of honor. Colonel Abert entertained at Army Headquarters for the Topographical Corps, Stephen Kearny gave them a dinner at the Metropolitan Hotel, to which he invited the high-ranking army officials. James Buchanan bought out the house of the National Theatre, inviting Jessie's friends to a performance of *The Conscript, or the Maiden's Vow*. To climax the whirling, happy weeks, President John Tyler entertained them at an informal dinner in the White House.

But if there was a round of parties, there also was work to be done. John had his expedition to assemble, his equipment to purchase. In addition it appeared that half of America wanted to help map the South Pass. Mail poured into the Benton home from every hamlet in the country, from every walk of life, from men young and old, asking if they might go along; they came in person to the house on C Street bearing letters of introduction; and with them came the inventors with new instruments and weapons, the manufacturers with products they wanted to sell.

Almost without either of them noticing it, Jessie slipped into the role of secretary. Each morning she rose at six, had chocolate in her sitting room, answered the basket of mail which had accumulated the day before; each afternoon she set aside an hour to talk to the eager ones who came knocking at the front door. In the late afternoon when John returned from the Topographical Office she wrote down the notes and outlines he had been formulating during the day. In early March she rode with him to the Baltimore & Ohio station to see him off to New York where he would spend two weeks buying equipment. He returned excited by several new inventions he had discovered there, chief among them a collapsible rubber boat which Nicollet had had a hand in conceiving.

"We'd better take it out on an open porch to unwrap it," he told the family. "The manufacturer in New York said the chemicals might smell bad."

When the oilcloth paper was unwrapped on the open loggia they were enveloped in an overpowering stench which quickly spread through the house. Jessie turned green. When she was able to walk, Maylee said:

"The lieutenant want you in your sittin' parlor, honey. From the look of him I think he know."

While Joshaam and Josheem heated two big shovels in the kitchen stove, filled them with coffee beans and walked through the house, letting the burning coffee dissipate the noxious odors, Maylee helped her to the doorway of her bedroom, gave her shoulder a reassuring pat. Jessie saw her husband half leaning against, half sitting on a window sill. There was a perplexed and at the same time chiding look in his eyes.

"Confound it, John," she said, "I've been looking for a delicate way to tell you. But you would bring home that newfangled rubber boat. During the weeks you were gone I had so much fun figuring out picturesque ways of revealing . . . We would be sitting by a fire, and suddenly you would notice that I was crocheting baby things . . ."

He crossed the room, picked her up and kissed her. Then with stumbling fervor he told her of his hunger for a son, this disinherited one who had lived without the security of a family name. He had changed his father's name of Frémon to the anglicized Fremont, yet he knew that no matter what the change or what the form, the name was not legally his. But if he spent a lifetime establishing it, passed it on to a son, the process of carrying forward would also carry back to the very moment when he himself had taken it.

Hosts of friends and well-wishers jammed the Benton house on the afternoon before he was to leave. At three o'clock Jessie served tea and little cakes to a hundred guests. By five o'clock, when dinner was ready, some fifty of them remained. After dinner there was laughter and storytelling, and Jessie's heart was full; it seemed that everybody in the world loved and admired her husband and was confident of his success.

By ten o'clock the last of the guests had gone. Jessie made her way to their bedroom. She was tired, yet these were the hours she had looked forward to; the last moments when she could have her husband to herself, taste the last kiss, hear the last word of love.

"You wouldn't want me to stay, to have someone else head the expedition?" he asked.

She bolted upright in the bed, her tears dried miraculously.

"Heavens, no. If that happened, I would cry ten times louder and a hundred times longer."

In the darkness she felt rather than saw him smile.

"Ah, my dear," she murmured, "you are being tactful with me. Well, never mind, it worked. I always thought I would make a good wife; at least I always wanted to: that was my ambition, just as yours was to be an explorer and topographer. I thought of marriage as a career, the way a man does. I'll shed a few tears, but it's part of my job to send you out into the wilderness and to represent you in Washington while you are gone; make you divisible into two, half of you on the trail and the other half here."

"That's quite a speech, Senator," he mocked gently.

"Wasn't it? But you would be astonished how much better it made me feel. And now you really must go to sleep, my darling, you have a hard day tomorrow, getting started."

He took her at her word; almost in a flash she felt his rhythmical breathing and knew he was asleep. For an instant she was hurt: this was their last night together, when they should have talked until dawn of their plans and their child, and yet at her first suggestion he had fallen into a sound sleep. Then she remembered that it must be well past midnight, and he had been up since five that morning. For just one moment longer she let the warmth and breathing of his body reassure her, then she too was sunk in deep slumber.

3

The next evening she was sitting in the library before the fire when her father returned to tell her that John had gotten off successfully. He dropped into his chair and said matter-of-factly:

"Jessie, I've let my work pile up. Do you think you will feel well enough in the morning to help me?"

"Help you? Of course I'll feel well enough."

"Good!" he exclaimed brusquely. "I need a copy of the Treaty of 1818; the one which establishes our joint sovereignty with England over the Oregon country."

"Yes, Papa."

She rose from her chair, sank to the red carpet at his feet and leaned her head against his knee.

"So many times when I've had little problems you sat in this chair opposite me and blew them into thin air. You're sure you're not giving me this work just to take my mind off . . . ?"

"Yes, of course I am," he replied harshly to conceal his feelings. "Work is good for you. But at the same time I need the results of that work. Surely there is nothing wrong in combining your needs with mine."

"Always the able tactician," she exclaimed. "It is good to know that you need me: I need to be needed just now."

"It will be a sad day for you, my dear, when you no longer need to be needed. Come along now, it's time for bed."

She left word for Maylee to bring her breakfast at five-thirty and got quickly into bed, though she was sure she would lie awake all night thinking of John, visualizing his trip to Baltimore on the slow, smoke-filled train. That thought was the last she had until there was a knock on the door and Maylee brought in a silver pitcher of chocolate, two croissants, a pat of butter and a tiny glass dish of blackberry jam.

By five minutes to six she entered the library, thinking to surprise her father by being there before him, but Tom Benton had arisen an hour earlier than usual; he had set up her movable desk in front of her deep chair. There were six new Perry-point steel pens and fifty sheets of satin-finish foolscap on the desk, lighted by her father's own candelabrum invention which he used for early morning work: four spermaceti candles burning on a square of white blotting paper which reflected the light. She slipped into her chair silently.

In his youth someone had told Thomas Hart Benton that he looked like a Roman senator. Jessie had never been able to figure out whether Tom had become a senator because he looked like one, or that he looked like one because he had made himself so completely the apotheosis of the senator. He had a long bony nose which started at the very level of his bold eyebrows, but where it passed his wide-set hazel eyes the skin was curiously wrinkled. He had a great head, and his brow was so high that his face seemed to jut backward. He carried it at an aggressive angle, his chin stuck up in the air as though the whole of him were ready to spring into intellectual action on the slightest provocation. His cheekbones were high and strong, but his mouth was small in proportion to the nose and chin. He wore his sideburns low, almost to his upper lip line, and brushed forward; it was a stubborn face, not handsome but attractive, showing the strain of warfare.

"I didn't follow orders last night, Jessie," he said. "I lay awake for an hour or so evolving a plan: no one has put together the story of American exploration . . ."

"Lewis and Clark and Pike and Cass all wrote about their expeditions . . ."

"Yes! Each man has told of his own adventures, but their journals are technical. I think the American people would enjoy the story, Jessie, if you could put it together."

Her eyes shone with excitement.

"You know, Papa, this fits in with a curious idea I have. When John showed me his provisional maps, trying to give me an idea of how many miles his party would cover each day, I thought I might set up a duplicate map, drawing to scale all the country between St. Louis and South Pass. We know what day he expects to leave St. Louis; I could start him off on that date, drawing a line for the extent of ground he might cover in that day, then put a red dot where they would camp for the night and build their fires."

Her father was nodding his head, so she took courage to continue.

"I had thought I would read the available accounts of what the country is like for each day's march: what wild life is there, what kind of animals they will be shooting for their food. I would draw my map to show the plains and forests and rivers and mountains, and dotted through the map, I would paint in what I imagined the country looked like, with a small field of wild flowers, a patch of pine forests, a few buffaloes roaming across a plain . . ."

"You've set quite a task for yourself," said her father, amused.

"But don't you see, Father," she cried passionately, "in that way he never leaves me, I'll never be alone, I'll be with him on the trail every hour."

Her father left for the Senate. There was a split second in which the sudden loneliness of living through the next six months without her husband seemed to press down on her heart and cut off the breath at her throat. She made a deliberate gesture to throw off the hysteria, sat down quickly in her chair and bent over the pile of papers which her father had left on her desk. At first she could see no word of the writing that lay before her, then she perceived that he had written her a note. It read:

Jessie, my dear, I wanted to leave you this one line from Marcus Aurelius. "Be not disturbed about the future, for if you ever come to it, you will have the same reason for your guide which preserves you at present."

She unbuttoned the top of her tight-sleeved robe, folded her father's note, pinned it securely to her petticoat, buttoned up the robe again with lightning fingers, and plunged into her work.

4

Nicollet and Hassler thought it little more than an amusing idea, but they indulged her. They set up a rectangle of thin wood, four feet high by nine feet long, covering it with large sheets of white paper. For several days the two old men showed her how to reduce to scale and organize the outlines of the big map.

Joshaam and Josheem carried the map down Capitol Hill the next morning, installing it in the library, where her father had made space for it on the back wall. At four-thirty Nicollet and Hassler arrived in the Ark, making their way quickly up to the library. Jessie had estimated how many days it would take her husband to reach South Pass, plotting her map into these fifty-five daily vertical divisions. She had then ruled a sharp black line horizontally across the center of the map, dividing it into the journey out and the journey back. Toward the end of the trip home she put a small symbol which only she would understand; somewhere around that time her first child would be born.

Hassler took some notes out of his black coat and began to sketch in part of the terrain of the Colorado. Nicollet said, "You're using Major Long's map for that material, and you know perfectly well Long has been discredited as a scientific observer."

"This material is not out of Long," exclaimed Hassler heatedly; "I put it together myself from trappers' reports."

Her map began to cause interest in Washington. General Winfield Scott, who had gone out to Detroit to fight the Blackhawk Wars, insisted upon putting down everything he knew about the territory around the Great Lakes, while General Lewis Cass, the first governor of Michigan Territory, came in a few nights later to sketch in the country between Detroit and Chicago, a trail over which he had been the first white man to pass. Colonel Kearny, who had planned several of his military expeditions into the Southwest on the porch of Senator Benton's St. Louis home, did a water-color sketch of that terrain. A professor of botany from Harvard suggested some of the wild life. Colonel Abert, who fancied himself as an astronomer, came to dinner and could hardly finish his chocolate mousse in his impatience to draw in the heavenly bodies.

Each morning she joined her father in the library until it was time for him to walk up to the Senate. The bookcase at her right elbow was now filled with some thirty-four volumes, in addition to copies of the official reports made to the United States government in the form of House and Senate executive documents. On the bottom shelf she assembled the notes her father had written in his large, bold, almost undecipherable script on the wide porch of their St. Louis home during the many years when the French, Spanish, Mexican and American hunters, trappers, traders and merchants had come back from their voyages to Mexico and the Pacific coast.

Starting with the date of 1836, when she had been twelve years of age, the reports were in her own handwriting, for Tom Benton had hated to write while he was listening, had turned the job over to her as soon as he had thought her handwriting legible. At first she had written furiously, trying to get down every last syllable, but slowly she found her own mind editing more and more these alfresco discussions. Each had a kernel of fresh and applicable material, but much of them was pointless repetition.

One day her father asked her for the material on the Santa Fe Trail, read her extract of a five-hour conversation, and said to his daughter:

"Well thought out, Jessie. This will save me endless work." He looked at her curiously out of the corner of his eye and over one shoulder. "Jessie, I always thought I would make a great educator. Now I am convinced of it."

"Of course it doesn't hurt you to have good material to work with, does it, Senator?"

"Tush, tush, child," he said, "never let yourself get bitten by the virus of conceit." He took her in his arms. "Look what an old fool it's made of your father."

Both in St. Louis and in Washington she had continued her practice of sharp editing. The intensity of this training had an inevitable but almost tragic result: she soon began to edit Thomas Hart Benton.

In the early years she had thought everything her father said to be God-given and perfect; but as she listened to his comrades and opponents on the floor of the Senate, to Clay, Hayne, Webster and Calhoun, she perceived that her father had limitations: he was sometimes repetitious where a straight attack would have been more effective, he leaned too heavily on Marcus Aurelius, the Caesars and Plutarch, sometimes favored the high-flown phrase where simplicity would have won the day. At first when he dictated to her she would simply leave out a word or a phrase; later, she condensed paragraphs, eliminating the weaknesses and redundancies.

A fierce storm raged when Tom Benton learned what his daughter had been doing. For several days he had not talked to her . . . not until she had secured the *Congressional Record,* copied on one piece of paper what Tom Benton had said in the Senate, and on an opposite piece what he had actually dictated to her. After much persuasion and a few tears she succeeded in getting him to look at the two papers side by side. She watched his face as he sat huddled in his deep chair studying the sheets, knowing that her future was at stake; that he must approve what she had done or she would never be able to work with him again.

At length he had raised his head, his face still flushed.

"By the Eternal, Jessie," he exclaimed, "you had no right to do this. It is the damnedest piece of presumption I ever heard of . . . but having done it, I am glad to see you did it so well!"

5

She was at her desk in the library every morning from eight until eleven. After luncheon she would take a long slow walk through Washington with her sister Eliza, Harriet Bodisco or Nancy Polk. She called for her father at the Senate building at four and walked him home for dinner. In the evening she busied herself making baby clothes, crocheting their thread edgings, cutting out sacques and nightgowns to be given to the Negro seamstress.

She was stimulated to learn from her reading that American exploration of the West had begun just a decade before her father settled in St. Louis in 1815, that the West had been opened to migration at almost precisely the hour of her own birth: by the discovery of a pass over the Rockies which brought the Oregon Trail into being.

When the United States made the Louisiana Purchase in 1803, doubling the extent of its territory, no man knew more than the tiniest fraction of what had been bought for the fifteen million dollars. For this reason President Jefferson had sent out Meriwether Lewis and William Clark to traverse the country and map a possible trail. Lewis and Clark had been the first white men to cross the Continental Divide of the Rocky Mountains, had made their way down the west slopes of the Rockies into the Columbia River country. They had no sooner returned to Washington in 1806 with their report than the government sent Zebulon Pike to explore that part of the Louisiana Purchase which ran southwest of St. Louis. Pike made his way to Mexico, establishing the Santa Fe Trail, which quickly became a well-traveled route for traders and trappers.

By 1811 John Jacob Astor's hunters and trappers had begun crossing the Rockies through Idaho, and by 1814 the trappers of the Northwest Company and the Hudson's Bay Company were crossing the Rockies every year. They built up a tremendous lore about the wilderness in their rovings to find better furs, yet they were largely uneducated frontiersmen who drew no maps and wrote no journals; consequently their knowledge was of little value to the thousands of families in the East who were eager and poised for western migration, but unwilling to strike out without accurate descriptions of the country.

Then General William Ashley had founded the Rocky Mountains Fur Company and persuaded such frontiersmen as Andrew Henry, James Bridger and Jedediah Smith to join with him. It was a fateful moment in western exploration: for in their wide-swinging movements in search of game, Jim Bridger discovered Salt Lake in 1823, and within a year South Pass had been discovered. When Jessie was only one year old, Jedediah Smith had discovered the Humboldt, followed that stream to the Sierra Nevadas, which he crossed into the Sacramento Valley. Yet neither Ashley nor Smith nor Fitzpatrick nor Henry had made their discoveries available to the American public; the information had been elicited only by the efforts of men like Senator Benton, who had asked that the material be submitted in reports to the Congress.

Then about 1832 the government began sending out army surveyors to map specific localities for railroad sites and Indian relocations. Among the most important of these were the two expeditions under Captain Williams, and the two under Nicholas Nicollet, in all four of which Lieutenant John Fremont had participated. Prior to these four expeditions the maps that had been drawn had been fragmentary and often erroneous; now Lieutenant Fremont was to draw the first scientific and comprehensive map of the region between St. Louis and South Pass. He would not be exploring in the way that Lewis and Clark, Pike, Cass and Schoolcraft had been exploring, for his avowed job was that of pathmarker rather than pathfinder. Yet before he had left he had told his wife:

"I want to do some exploring before this expedition is over; I want to traverse some new ground that no one ever reported on."

"Will there be time for that?" she had asked.

"I most urgently hope so; after all of our topographical work has been done I should still have several weeks for exploration. I want to show them that I can blaze new trails as well as map old ones."

"Yes," she had agreed, "you must do that if you can; then the War Department will give you more latitude on future expeditions."

The days passed, and the nights; the feeling of life inside her grew more insistent and pushed itself outward as she grew bigger in body and heavier in step. She never mentioned to anyone how achingly she missed her husband during these months while her child grew within her. Already the baby gave her companionship, even in those dark hours after she had gone to bed, for those were the hours in which she missed John most, in which she longed to clasp her hand in his, to feel his arms about her, protecting her from the deep-lying anxieties of impending childbirth. She passed many sleepless hours in repeating the child's name, John Charles Fremont, for she was positive that it would be a son, a son whom they would raise to be an explorer.

As important to her as the company of her child was the delightful game which half of official Washington was playing on her giant map. Not only did Nicollet and Hassler come in three or four times a week to protest that in her enthusiasm for her husband's abilities she was letting him make far too rapid progress each day, but everyone joked with her about it. She laughed when Samuel Morse said:

"What a wife you are, Jessie; your hapless husband can't even escape your surveillance by going into the wilderness." Or when James Buchanan commented, "Those are pretty large campfires; you are keeping the lieutenant warm, Jessie, only I hope you don't start forest fires," she would be moved to answer:

"Never you mind, James Buchanan, some day cities will spring up on the sites of Lieutenant Fremont's campfires."

During the months of preparation for the expedition, Mrs. Benton had joined in the family life more than she had in several years; she had even seemed to take a sense of pride in the fact that her son-in-law was to command the expedition. Then Jessie noticed that her mother's resurgence of strength was ebbing. One evening she was horrified to perceive that one half of her mother's face was pulling against the other, that the corner of her right eye and right temple arched upward, while the left corner of her mouth and lower cheek were pulling downward. When she went to her mother's bedroom to say good night she saw some of this pulling and twisting reflected in the terror of her mother's eyes.

The following morning Maylee could not awaken Mrs. Benton. She ran screaming for Senator Benton. Joshaam hurried for the doctor, who came at once and stumblingly informed Tom Benton that his wife had had a paralytic stroke. Thomas Benton stood as though clubbed, his eyes bloodshot, his big face sagging.

The three days that followed were an agony to Jessie. Her father never left her mother's bedside, trying to rub life back into her white, motionless hands, speaking to her, kissing her lips. On the evening of the third day

Jessie entered the dark and forsaken library, saw her father facing the front windows, weeping silently. She went to him and put her arm about him; after a moment he quieted.

"Jessie, you can't know what it's like . . . not to be able to fight back. It's like being hit in the dark: you don't know who your adversary is— you don't know where to turn, what to say or do. I've never felt helpless before, but now . . ."

The words and the look of her father were cut deep in her memory.

The next morning Mrs. Benton's eyes fluttered open; she lay without moving. Then she achieved a little smile, a smile which told her family that her life would be spared. Eliza took over the management of the household; Jessie remained most of the day with her mother, sometimes reading to her from the Bible. On the tenth day Mrs. Benton indicated that she wanted to talk to her daughter. Jessie waited for several moments before Mrs. Benton could summon her strength.

". . . not your father's fault . . . I couldn't . . . enjoy . . . not father's fault . . ."

She rested for several moments, closed her eyes, then opened them again. "I was . . . ill . . . you must not . . . blame your father . . . Remember, Jessie, not . . . his fault."

Her head down, tears swimming in her eyes, Jessie realized that the only words her mother had striven to achieve since her stroke was an attempt to eradicate from her daughter's mind any reproach or bitterness that might have been left from their discussions on the trip to Cherry Grove.

And she began to realize how far she had to go on the long uphill road to becoming a good wife.

6

She was well into her ninth month when word came that John and his party had returned safely to St. Louis.

"I hope the lieutenant gets here in time for the birth of your baby," her father commented.

"He will."

"How can you be so sure?"

"Because I'm going to wait," she replied doggedly.

It was the twenty-eighth of October when John bounded up the front stairs of the Benton home, his black hair falling over the collar of his uniform. After he had been welcomed by the family, had gone to Mrs. Benton's room to kiss her cheek and let her know that he was happy she was better without intimating that she had ever been ill, Jessie led him to their sitting room where they sat down together in the roomy armchair by the fireplace.

"I'm sorry I'm so bumpy, darling. It would be nice to be ravishingly beautiful for your return."

"If you hadn't been so ravishing before I left, you wouldn't be so bumpy now. Don't be worried, I can wait for our second honeymoon."

She got a comb, brush and scissors, called him to sit on the edge of the bed and then knelt behind him. She wrapped a towel around his shoulders, brushed out the long hair. After she had cut off as much as she dared, she stood in front of him saying: "There, now you're my beautiful lieutenant once again," and kissed him gently. He pulled her down on the bed beside him.

"You look hungry," she said, running her fingers over his sunken cheeks. "We'll have to fatten you up with terrapin and sides of roast beef."

"You just want to make me as fat as you."

The next day she slept late, able to rest with a tranquillity she had not known in the months he had been away. She opened her eyes to find the fall sunlight flooding high in the room and her husband gone from her side. She found him in the library, stretched out on his stomach with a pencil and crayons in his hand, working on her big map, which he had taken down from the wall. He looked up, aware of her presence.

"When I first walked in here and saw that map on the wall," he said, "I thought I had taken leave of my senses. I don't know how long I stood in front of it before I realized it was your work."

"Mine," laughed Jessie, "and everyone else's in Washington: Nicollet, Hassler, Colonel Abert, General Clark, Colonel Kearny, General Scott, Senators Benton, Linn, Crittenden, King, that botanist friend of yours at Harvard, and half the amateur astronomers in the capital."

He led her back to the map and drew up a chair for her.

"You've made a lot of errors: you pushed our party ahead much too fast, you didn't give us a fraction of the time we needed in the Rockies; you've left out dozens of small ranges, canyons and streams that you couldn't possibly know about. But look how close your line runs to mine."

Jessie pointed with her finger to a campfire on the Big Sandy.

"That was the night I missed you most. Since I couldn't be there, I made you comfortable: I put you alongside of a cool river so that you could have a swim after the day's march; with plenty of game at hand . . ."

Joshaam padded in with a broad grin, his short black trousers rolled just below the knee. He set up a table and served John's favorite dishes: grilled lamb chops with creamed potatoes, a fluffy egg soufflé, cornbread with blackberry jam, a large pot of coffee with thick cream. When her husband had loaded his pipe with fresh tobacco Jessie said:

"You are going to have to tell all the stories of your expedition; by this afternoon the house will be crowded. But I would like to hear the first story and the best."

He was silent for a moment. "You remember how we agreed that I should try to do some exploring after we had South Pass mapped?"

"Yes."

"Well, we struggled up the Sweetwater Valley, and on August eighth

reached South Pass. It was such a broad opening, and we reached it by
such a gradual ascent, that I had difficulty in fixing the precise point of
the Continental Divide. There was no gorge. Instead we found a wide sandy
road which followed a slow and regular grade to the summit, about seven
thousand feet above sea level. We continued up to the headwaters of the
Green River and followed this to the Colorado. Then there rose up before
us the greatest sight I have ever seen: the Wind River chain of mountains
tumbling backward pile upon pile, with their icy caps glittering in the bright
light of the August day."

"Has anyone recorded any material on the Wind River chain?"

He sprang from his chair and began pacing back and forth.

"Darling, what do you think I found? The highest point in the central
Rockies! I scaled a peak that no one has ever seen before, let alone reached
the summit! You remember that flag I had made in New York with the
pipe of peace in the eagle's mouth to show the Indians we were friendly?"

"Of course I remember."

"I took five of my companions with me. It was a rough ascent, with the
five of us riding beneath a nearly perpendicular wall of granite. We could
look straight up three thousand feet to endless lines of broken, jagged cones.
We left our horses and climbed hand over hand up this wall. After we got
up about a thousand feet we found three little lakes of emerald lying in a
chasm below us. At one point I had to work my way across a vertical
precipice by clinging to the crevices. I sprang upon the summit, but if I
had gone another half-foot I would have fallen into an immense snow
field five hundred feet below. For I was on the very edge of a sheer icy
precipice."

Her eyes reflected his excitement.

"Jessie, it was magnificent: a bright and sunny day, to the west a vast
shining network of lakes and streams, on the east the deep, forested trough
of the Wind River Valley with the faint gleam of streams which flow into
the Yellowstone and down to the Missouri. To the far northwest we could
pick out the snowy peaks of the Three Tetons which mark the sources of
the Snake and the Columbia. I fixed a ramrod in the gneiss, unfurled our
flag and planted it on the summit."

"That is a lovely story," she murmured.

The welcome-home party that had gathered by five in the afternoon was
much like the farewell party except that it was more hilarious. Everyone
wanted stories. Colonel Kearny, in his usual blunt manner, got in the first
demand:

"We heard reports that the Sioux, Blackfeet and Cheyennes had combined and might block your route from Laramie to South Pass. Did you
have any trouble with them?"

John stood with his back to the fireplace. Jessie sat watching her husband, thinking how handsome he looked.

"We reached Fort Laramie just as Jim Bridger came in from the North

Platt trail with a company of traders. He told us about the Sioux and Black-feet being done up in war paint and spoiling for a fight. The traders and the Indians at the fort advised us to wait for a few weeks until the raids were over and the Indians had gone home, but that didn't sound like a wise idea to me."

"We're having trouble enough with them now," grunted the colonel. "If they ever get the idea they could keep us out of their country simply by putting on war paint . . ."

"That's exactly the way I figured it, Colonel Kearny: one of the purposes of this reconnaissance was to find the best spots for the Army to establish forts; but no amount of forts would be any protection against Indians who had succeeded in frightening us."

General Winfield Scott wanted to be shown exactly where on the map John recommended that army forts be built; the western senators wanted to know about the nature of the soil, whether there was water available, how much of the land was tillable and how large a population it could support; several eastern congressmen demanded to know whether farm and laboring families really could take covered wagons over the South Pass.

The party lasted late, almost too late; Jessie did not know whether it was the joy of having her husband home again or the excitement of the party, but before dawn her first child was born. When the doctor told her she had a daughter she burst into angry tears. She had failed her husband; had not fulfilled her part of the relationship. She knew how keenly disappointed he would be. When he entered the room she could not meet his eyes.

"No, don't console me," she said. "If you try to turn me off with platitudes, I shall never forgive you."

John had already had two hours in which to become reconciled. He wore a too bright smile as he came to the side of her bed.

"Very well, no platitudes; but might I suggest two thoughts: at eighteen you are not exactly too old to bear more children; nor has six months in the wilderness slaked my desire to sire them."

A tiny gleam appeared in her tired eyes.

"Neatly put, Lieutenant. Now go away and let me sleep."

She slept straight through until noon of the following day. When she awakened and had been washed, her hair combed and tied with a pink velvet ribbon, her husband came in holding a cloth bundle bunched under his left arm.

"Darling, you remember the flag I told you I planted on Fremont's Peak?"

Jessie's eyes said yes, wonderingly.

"It's a little faded now, and the wind whipped a few holes in it; but it's the first American flag to be raised on the highest peak of the Rocky Mountains. I brought it back for you, my dear."

He shook out the flag and laid it across her bed. Jessie was touched.

"Always the romantic poet," she whispered, holding out her arms for the embrace which her disappointment of the night before had denied her.

7

At the end of two weeks she could be carried to a chaise in their living room, which was directly in the path of the early winter sun, and here John would entertain her with stories from the trail. She listened to his narrative to see how it fitted into the history of exploration, and what contribution Lieutenant Fremont might be able to make to the tradition of Rogers and Clark, Pike, Ashley, Smith, Cass, Long or Captain Bonneville.

During the succeeding days he unrolled a panorama of his voyage in a kind of continuous serial, a portion of it related in bed, portions over the breakfast table, portions in his pajamas walking up and down the bedroom, in his underwear as he shaved, in his rough dungarees and faded khaki shirt sorting specimens on the floor, in his blue-and-gold uniform waiting to go to an appointment with a War Department official.

She watched him ford the Kansas River a hundred miles from its mouth, trying out Nicollet's India-rubber boat on the swollen yellow current. She advanced with him into hostile Indian country where powder was distributed to each of the men in the early morning; she met up with a party of immigrants going to the Columbia, who gave them mail to be taken back to the States; she crossed the Big Vermilion and encamped on the Big Blue, where antelope overran the hills and Amorpha bent beneath the weight of its purple clusters; she traveled on the fresh traces of Oregon immigrants, which relieved the loneliness of the road; she found the earth more sandy as she traveled westward, with rain coming at night and thousands of mosquitoes biting hungrily; she went thirsty for two days because the creeks at Big Trees were inexplicably dry, but when she reached the Little Blue she and the men and horses together all drank and bathed in the clear cool stream; she mounted guard every night but safely reached the Platte, where the party divided at the forks, Kit Carson leading half the men over the regular Oregon Trail to Fort Laramie while her husband took the other party by way of Fort Saint Vrain. There were the dramatic hours at Fort Laramie when Jim Bridger told of the Sioux, Blackfeet and Cheyennes combining on the warpath, and the determination to push forward in the face of the danger, the long ascent up Sweetwater Valley, and then at last the great day on August 8 when the party mounted South Pass, making maps and sketches and voluminous notes to document the trail for future immigrants to Oregon.

Jessie asked her husband if he had any objections to her reading his journal. She was delighted by much of his poetry and imagery, but she soon saw that the diary consisted of brilliant fragments. Lieutenant Fremont had reported faithfully and picturesquely what he had seen, but he had set up no organizational plan which would have enabled him to fit all the parts into a design. His journal was much like the raw material published by Lewis and Clark, by Cass or Schoolcraft. As such it would be read by scientists, explorers and students, but not by the general public. In order to accomplish the most good for western migration, Lieutenant Fremont's report must be vastly more readable than its predecessors; it must include everything of beauty and fact from his notes, and yet somehow in the process of transcription become literature.

She knew she must exercise the utmost tact, find a subtle method of leading him to conclusions about what his written report to Congress must be. When she was up and around again she showed him the work she had been doing on the history of exploration; in the process of telling him about it she was able to make many of her points as to why former accounts of expeditions had not been widely read.

John appeared interested, yet he gave no indication of whether he would do any part of the job she suggested. She set up a desk for him in their sitting room, laying out pens and pencils and foolscap; she arranged for quiet and privacy. She kissed him, said, "Good luck, my dear, I know your report will come out well," and closed the door behind her.

At dinner she found him in an unhappy state of mind; he had not been able to put one word on paper. She comforted him by saying that the first page was harder than the next ninety-nine put together, that the story would come with a rush once he had started. At the end of the second day she found their sitting room a mass of crumpled papers, the ink spilled over the desk, her husband so grouchy she could not talk to him. When she knocked lightly at dinnertime of the third day, she found him in the midst of a nosebleed. She stretched him out on the floor, washed his face and put cool cloths on his brow.

"I just can't understand it, Jessie," he growled; "when I tell you stories of what happened on the trip I am stimulated and excited, the words flow and the scenes are vivid in my mind. But once I sit down to write on paper, the words become cold and dead."

Jessie had a moment of panic in which she demanded of herself, What have I done? Have I imposed such pressure on him, have I put the report in such a light that he can no longer work with it?

The panic passed; she said quietly to her husband, while holding a cold towel over his face, "Perhaps it is just the mechanics of writing that disturb you. Perhaps your mind works too fast for your fingers to record what you are thinking."

"No, I think it's something your presence does to me, Jessie: you stimulate me so that I think and talk swiftly; everything comes alive in the air between us."

With her pulse bumping in her throat she asked, "Then perhaps, my dear, I could serve as your amanuensis? You tell me the stories just the way you did before, and I'll write them down for you."

She had been uneasy at making the suggestion; she shuddered lest he think she was trying to intrude, gain a voice and an importance through collaborating with him. He jumped up from the floor, threw his arms about her and began dancing her around in circles.

"Jessie, my love, I've been sitting here in misery for three days wondering how long it would take you to offer your services. Confound it, I've been lonely in here; you gave me such complete privacy I felt like a hermit locked in a cell."

It was on New Year's Day of 1843, just a year after they had gone to President Tyler's reception, that she sat down at the desk in her sitting room, with John agitatedly walking the floor behind her. Her father had protested her going to work so soon after the birth of her child.

"But Father, I feel entirely well. This report to Congress is as important to you as it is to John; the better we make it, the more ammunition it gives you."

"That's entirely true," he agreed, unsmiling; "if this report comes out well, a second expedition, this time as far as California, may be authorized. It's only that I feel you need another month or two . . ."

She found that her husband needed her help in organizing his material; she rejected a number of dullish starts and got him off to a beginning which would not only excite the reader but pull him out of his chair and send him on the trail across the swollen Kansas River. In the first rush of his enthusiasm she was unable to write down everything, so she selected the most germane of what he said and let the rest go. She began joining bits of narrative together while he talked, shaping a sentence a little more roundly than he had, using a more explicit or precise word when he stumbled.

"Let me see what you've done."

When he had finished reading, he commented, "No man is fool enough not to enjoy being made to look his best."

And so their story grew, sometimes at the rate of five finished pages a day. She had heard these stories before; she had retold them to herself, frequently in her own terse and direct language. When she found his prose too flowery or poetic, she related the episode with something of her own lean style and pacing. This last experiment she was frankly frightened to tell him about. She remembered the violent scene when her father had discovered that she was not only editing him but had had the presumption to be collaborating in his speeches for the Senate.

When she went into the sitting room the next morning she found her husband reading their previous day's work. He had a strained, somewhat puzzled expression on his face.

"Jessie, when did I say this sentence? I don't remember it."

She gulped, replied, "You didn't say it. Shall we tear up these sheets and do this section over again?"

He walked to the window overlooking the garden. She stayed awkwardly by the desk, unable to guess what was going on in her husband's mind. After what seemed an interminable length of time, he came back to the desk, expressionless, and asked:

"May I read those pages again?"

She handed him the five clipped pages. When he had finished reading, he returned them to her.

"It was only the strangeness of those sentences that bothered me the first time over." After a pause he continued, "I agreed the day I proposed to you that our marriage was to be a collaboration. Each of us has fractional talents. If you have the fraction that is missing from mine, then how fortunate I am."

Jessie sat down weakly.

They labored for three months to complete the hundred-page report. During the last few weeks she worked alone, revising and rewriting. They both agreed that Tom Benton must be the first to see the manuscript.

"It's good," her father declared when he had finished; "it will not only start a wave of immigration to Oregon, but we'll have no trouble getting an appropriation for a second expedition."

Three days later her father returned from the Senate with good news: Congress had been highly pleased with both the report and the map, had ordered a thousand extra copies to be printed, the major newspapers of the country were asking for permission to reprint. The second expedition had been ordered, the money appropriated, and Lieutenant Fremont was once again to command. They would all leave for St. Louis within the month, Tom Benton to mend his political fences and prepare for the coming election; John to assemble his expedition; Jessie to live in the Benton home while he was away.

These were happy days for her: her baby girl, whom they had named Lily, was growing strong and pretty; it seemed as though everyone in the country were talking about Lieutenant Fremont, his expedition, his report and map. He was praised in the press, the pulpit, the schools. The War Department and the Topographical Corps assured him that he had made an important contribution.

Lieutenant Fremont wore his new honors with modesty and decorum.

And Jessie Fremont sat quietly in the background, glowing with love and pride, utterly content.

8

The many suitcases, trunks and boxes were taken down to the Baltimore & Ohio station the evening before. The next morning Jessie, her mother, her father, her husband, Maylee with little Lily in her arms, and Randolph and the two younger girls, took the hard-benched, smoky cars to Baltimore, a trip which consumed much of the day. They passed the night at an inn on the waterfront, where their baggage could be transferred to the steamboat at dawn. The passage to Philadelphia was cool and pleasant. They spent a night and a day in Philadelphia before making connection with the mail coach, which bumped and jostled them up the length of the Susquehanna Valley to Harrisburg. There were canal boats plying between Harrisburg and Pittsburgh, but there was no regular schedule and they considered themselves fortunate to catch one on the second night. The high-pressure steamboats which operated between Pittsburgh and Cincinnati were among the fastest and most luxurious traveling inland in America. Jessie and John mingled with the passengers, listening to the conversation. There were hunters and trappers in their leather garments and coonskin caps; land speculators carrying sacks of gold and headed for the new townships in Illinois and Iowa; the ever present group of surveyors heading west to lay out new villages and roads; traveling salesmen from Louisville and Cincinnati with their boxes of wares; adventurous Englishmen taking their resources into the wilderness to get in on the ground floor; congenital frontiersmen moving west for a third or fourth time; merchants from the East with their wives and children, seeking independence in still another new world; and most conspicuous in noise and excitement, Irishmen and Germans just over from the old country, looking forward to the frontier as eagerly as to paradise.

The trip took between two and three weeks, according to one's luck and the connections. But Jessie was in no hurry. She had her husband with her and was greatly enjoying these days of his company, unharassed by work or demands on his time. She knew every foot of the road: she had first made the passage when she was ten months old, had been thrown out of a coach at the age of three, had stopped at nearly every inn and private home along the way in the fourteen round trips she had made in her nineteen years.

They crossed the Mississippi from Cairo on the bright and sparkling spring morning of May 16, the busiest period in St. Louis' life, with the roustabouts thronging the riverbanks, the Mississippi churned by steamboats, vessels and scows moored to the rough wooden docks, the levee crowded with Negro boat hands chanting rhythmically as they loaded up.

Tom Benton insisted upon driving the party up Main Street to see if the new rock pavements were still smooth, and to rejoice at the sight of new buildings. They passed the mansion of Colonel Auguste Couteau, fronting on Main Street, protected by a ten-foot-high, two-foot-thick stone wall with portholes through which to shoot Indians in case of attack. As their carriage continued along the locust-lined street they saw the few whitewashed aristocratic houses in St. Louis, the magnificent Cathedral and Bishop's Garden. After that, on the way out to the Benton home, there was little but alleys and a confusion of mean houses, for St. Louis had grown by accretion, everyone building how and where he pleased.

Jessie remarked how fast the city was growing: it was the great and last metropolis of the West, the fitting-out and jumping-off place for Mexico, California, Oregon and Canada and the vast stretches of wilderness that lay between. Gazing out of the carriage she saw the colorful, dramatic and heterogeneous scene on which she had been raised: hunters and trappers in the garb they wore on the trail; friendly Indians in their native costumes; adventurous and restless ones from every country in Europe, still wearing their native clothing and speaking their native tongue. There was always a sense of excitement pervading the air, for St. Louis was not a place where people stayed, but a spot where they outfitted and prepared to jump off into adventure. To her it was as though the city were the last outpost of civilization into which the whole world poured, eager to get away from that civilization, to plunge into the vastness of the unknown, only sometimes realizing that it was this very stream of plungers who must inevitably push civilization farther and farther west until it had eaten up the wilderness and all of America would be settled and civilized.

Tom Benton had built his home so far out of the business district of St. Louis, some twenty years before, that he was still on the outskirts and enjoyed a measure of quiet and privacy. When he had arrived in 1817 with four hundred dollars in his pocket he had invested three hundred dollars of it in ten acres of land just outside the tiny village. Two years later, so swiftly had the traffic in the Mississippi border port grown, so many had been the armed caravans of merchants which had assembled, so countless the number of traders, trappers and voyagers of the American Fur Company who had been outfitted, that Tom Benton began selling his land for two thousand dollars an acre.

The Benton home was shaded by acacias with their clusters of vanilla-scented blooms; built in the prevailing Creole fashion, there was a central courtyard paved with flagging, and a line of locust trees making a delicate green screen for the wide galleries which ran the length of the house on both sides. The floors were of black walnut, brilliantly waxed. Tom Benton had built to the south of the wharf and business district, on a slight rise overlooking the wide muddy torrent of the Mississippi.

Jessie settled herself in the south bedroom which looked out on what remained of Tom Benton's pear orchard and was furnished with the light cherrywood bed, bureaus and chairs which he had bought from the early French immigrants. Though there was the ever present knowledge that her husband would leave in a week or two, she felt happier that she would pass the time here in St. Louis where everyone was interested in western expansion, where one talked of little else; where any stranger she might stop on the street would be able to tell her approximately how far Lieutenant Fremont had progressed and why it was so important for him to find an easier crossing of the Rockies. In Washington she had enabled herself to be with him during the six months of the first expedition by keeping detailed maps; here in St. Louis she would need no artificial stimulus to keep her abreast. Within St. Louis lived every race, religion and philosophy to be found in the world; and if, she thought, it is one's fate to stay at home and wait for one's husband, then surely the best spot to wait is where all the world has assembled and where one ate, breathed, slept and dreamed expedition.

The only thing missing from her return was Grandmother Benton, who

had died five years before. Grandmother Benton's welcome on their trips
to St. Louis almost never varied. An invalid in her eighties, Anne Benton put
on her best black dress and waited in her rooms at the end of the lower
gallery to greet her son and his family. The first moments of greeting had
always perplexed Jessie, for despite her father's being so happy at coming
home, there were tears in his eyes when he bent to kiss Grandmother. When
it came her own turn to greet the silent old lady sitting on the couch, she
trembled as the white fingers motioned to her to draw near and she felt the
touch of dry lips upon her cheek.

There seemed to be no valid reason why Anne Gooch Benton should have
left her established home in Hillsborough, North Carolina, in 1798, where
she was surrounded by relatives and friends, where life was safe and secure.
But Mrs. Benton, after her young husband's death, had packed her belongings, children and slaves into a series of wagons and taken the long, dangerous, four-hundred-mile trail through the Carolina mountains and the dark
pine needle forests to Nashville. Her husband had been given a large grant of
land in Tennessee years before, worthless and uninhabitable land at the time
the King of England had granted it, and still overrun by hostile Indians. Here
she had set up the Widow Benton Settlement, built her own log cabin, a
church, school and general store. Widow Benton offered seven years of free
rent to the settlers who came along the trail, after which she either sold or
leased the land to the established families at moderate rates.

Anne Benton had wanted and deliberately chosen the wilderness; this urge
for the rough-hewn, the just-being-born, the pioneer opportunity had been
buried deep in Tom Benton. The tiny outpost of St. Louis, settled by the
French people he liked and felt so comfortable with, was in the process of
germination. He abandoned his law practice in Nashville, struck out for St.
Louis. Though he could speak little of their language, the French settlers liked
and trusted him. A few other Americans were beginning to come in and
settle, and Tom Benton had become the liaison between the two national
groups. By the end of the year he had been appointed to the school board,
was contributing political articles to the *Missouri Enquirer*, was named as
one of the editors, crusading for immediate exploration of the wilderness in
order to "place these vast lands forever under the domination of our people."

By 1820 he was in prosperous circumstances; he had built himself a big
house, brought his mother to St. Louis. He was active and important in making Missouri a state, was elected to the first legislature, helped to draw its first
constitution, and then been elected one of the state's two first senators. He
found Washington City a wretched scattering of houses alongside a river
and surrounded by marshes; most of the congressmen left their families behind them, lived in third-rate boardinghouses and escaped the capital at the
earliest opportunity with little but curses for its dampness, malaria and miserable life. But Tom Benton had seen in Washington a city just being born,
and he had loved it; he had brought his wife and children to Washington,
declared it to be his second home, rented the best house he could find until

he was able to buy one. He urged his fellow congressmen to bring their families with them so that they could set up schools and churches and develop Washington.

Jessie's days in St. Louis were full, for she now was secretary to both her father and her husband, and nothing could have persuaded her to give up any part of the work. The sun rose over the Mississippi at five in the morning; though she had closed the shutters tight, John was awake at the first touch of light. Within a half-hour he had dressed, breakfasted, and left the house. At six o'clock Jessie and her father had their light breakfast out of doors, on the long gallery of the parlor floor. This gallery was also Tom Benton's office, where he set up a settee, table and what he called a colony of chairs, for by six-thirty visitors began to arrive to get the latest news from Washington and to discuss the ever-growing problems of Missouri. She kept a record of these morning meetings so that her father would have his notes when he returned to Washington in the fall. At eleven o'clock her husband would return, his organizing for the day completed, and after their lunch would dictate to her on the setup of the expedition: the names of the sixty-odd hunters and trappers who were going with him; the one-dollar-a-day wage which each was to receive, the hundred dollars a month for Kit Carson, an unheard-of sum but one which he defended on the grounds that Kit Carson had no equal in America. There were the lists of materials that had been bought and how much they had cost, the scientific implements which were needed for a complete record of the journey: the compasses, telescopes, sextants, chronometers, barometers.

Dinner was at five, after which their many friends and cousins came in for music, dancing and laughter, for St. Louis was a lighthearted town in the French tradition, with a fiddle in every house.

Then all too soon her double stint came to an end; her father left for a barnstorming trip of the state, and John prepared to leave for Kaw's Landing, where the expedition would receive its final integration, the horses fattened and the long journey to Oregon begun. Several days before he was to leave he asked his wife:

"Could you invite Colonel Kearny to dinner? I have some special business I want to talk over with him alone."

"I'll arrange it."

Colonel Stephen Watts Kearny, commandant of the Jefferson Barracks just outside St. Louis, came to dinner on the intensely hot afternoon of June first. He was a hard-bitten soldier, with sandy hair, sandy of face as well as voice. He had distinguished himself in the War of 1812. He was fearless, never a brilliant strategist but an inexhaustible plodder who wore out rather than outsmarted his opponents. He had the blunt, ungraceful manner of the man who had spent the past thirty years in the wilderness and in army encampments.

After much pleasant talk, John asked, "Colonel Kearny, do you suppose it would be possible for you to lend me a cannon for the expedition?"

His guest took the cigar out of his mouth.

"A cannon! What ever do you want a cannon for?"

"I expect serious trouble with the Indians; their prestige fell last year when they failed to make an attack on us while on the warpath. I understand they are out for revenge."

"I see."

"Besides," John continued, "I think it about time we demonstrated that the Army can move its heavy equipment across the continent . . ."

"But you are not commanding an army expedition," interposed Colonel Kearny, "you are a scientific expedition. The sight of that cannon might lead the Indians, yes, and the English and Spanish also, to imagine that we are sending an army of conquest across the plains."

"All this with one small cannon, Colonel? My main reason is to show that we can take a heavy cannon across the new pass in the Rockies which I hope to find. If we can move a cannon over it, then the immigrant trains will know they can get their wagons over it."

"But in the heavy snows? Lieutenant, you would never make it. You'll beat out your strength trying to pull it over the mountains."

"You are doubtless right, Colonel," replied John, "but I should like a chance to try. Can you spare me a cannon? I promise to bring it back to Jefferson Barracks at the end of a year."

Colonel Kearny was silent for a few moments, puffing on his cigar.

"Very well, since you seem so keen on it. I don't anticipate that we will need it here in Missouri during the next year."

Three days later Jessie once again bade good-by to her husband. There were no tears this time. After his work was done of plotting the trail to Oregon, and finding a new pass over the Rockies which would be easier to traverse than South Pass, he was to drop down with his party into California, be careful not to alarm or antagonize the Mexican government, assure the local governors from Mexico City that this was purely a scientific expedition, but at the same time survey the ground, talk to the Americans who had ranches there, become acquainted with the Californios and get some idea of the military strength of the Mexican garrisons, learn what would be needed to enable California to fall into American hands: for no one could doubt any longer that Mexico was going to lose both Texas and California. The western people were grimly determined that the English must not own California.

"I want to go with you to California on the next expedition," said Jessie. "I want to settle there."

"But I doubt if there are half a dozen American women in the entire state."

"I wouldn't mind if I were the first," she answered. "In fact I would like it. We already have a Bentonville in the family. Now it's our turn to start a Fremontville."

John laughed. "I'm sure I can make Sutter's Fort, and that will give me a chance to investigate the Sacramento Valley. From what I hear it's fertile

land. I'll prospect around, see if I can find the exactly right spot for Fremontville. If I do, I'll stake it out."

"Excellent," said Jessie, "and as soon as California becomes a state, you
will be sent to Washington as its first senator."

9

She set up a rigorous program which she hoped would leave her little
time to be lonely. She awakened at six, went into the nursery for a play with
Lily. At seven she took coffee and rolls up to her mother. At eight she went
into the kitchen with Maylee to plan the day's marketing and menus, then
talked to old Gabriel about the work that needed doing around the grounds.
Having established a routine for the house, she organized a schedule of intellectual activity: four hours of reading every day, one in Spanish and one
in French to keep her hand in, two hours of reading and notetaking in her
father's books on history.

She had almost a year to endure without her husband. The first of the
fifty-two weeks passed quickly enough, for she found a kind of pleasure in
establishing her discipline.

At the end of the twelfth day the mail boat arrived. Gabriel brought her an
official-looking letter from the War Department addressed to Lieutenant
John C. Fremont. Having been instructed by her husband to open all mail in
order that she might be able to take care of whatever business arose, Jessie
put aside her sewing basket, inserted a long ivory opener under the flap and
slit the top of the envelope. She read:

LIEUTENANT JOHN C. FREMONT
U. S. Army Topographical Corps
St. Louis, Missouri

SIR:

*You are herewith ordered to turn over your expedition to your second in
command, and to repair at once to Washington. An explanation is required of
why you have taken a twelve-pound howitzer cannon on a peaceful, scientific
survey.*

*Another officer of the Topographical Corps will be dispatched to take
charge of the expedition.*

COLONEL J. J. ABERT

Her trembling fingers dropped the paper. Lieutenant Fremont recalled to
Washington? But that was impossible! The party must leave Kaw's Landing
within a few days if they were to get over the Rockies before snow fell.
Another officer in command! How could another officer take over John's
hand-picked party? He had organized every last detail of the expedition, he
had the journey laid out with scientific precision: the reorganizing would

take weeks, half the men would leave, it would become a haphazard, poorly integrated party which would accomplish only the smallest fraction of what was desired.

Then the paralyzing thought came to her: What would happen to her husband? Would they penalize him at the Topographical Corps in Washington, give him a routine job behind a desk, send him to some obscure fort? This second expedition, which was intended to go all the way to Oregon, was the most important since President Jefferson had sent Lewis and Clark to traverse the continent. If successful, John could go on to ever greater accomplishment. But if he were pushed aside now there would be no more expeditions for him, another man would take over, someone with only the smallest fraction of his genius for the wilderness.

She concealed the order at the bottom of her Martha Washington sewing basket, then went into the courtyard and stood with her face in the hot sun. I've been too much a part of the whole plan, she thought, to put it in peril now. I simply cannot fail John and his men; I can't fail my father and the westerners who have worked so many years for these expeditions. I've got to save this expedition! But how?

She knew that a duplicate of the War Department letter would be on the mail boat, which would deliver it to Kaw's Landing. Once John received his letter he would have no choice but to abandon the expedition and leave for Washington.

The answer came to her almost immediately: the duplicate must not reach him! The expedition must start on the trail without his learning that his command had been revoked!

She sent Gabriel to summon the French-Canadian DeRosier, to whom John had granted permission to remain an extra two weeks in St. Louis because of his wife's illness. DeRosier came within the half-hour, a tall, black-eyed trapper who had spent the better part of his life in the wilderness.

"DeRosier, I have an urgent message which must reach Lieutenant Fremont at once."

"I will take it, madame."

"How long will you need to get ready?"

"The time to get my horse."

"You know the country between here and Kaw's Landing?"

"Like my beard in the mirror."

"Can you get there before the mail boat?"

"But certainly, Madame Fremont. I know how to cut off the bends in the river. I can save the time the mail boat will lose lying at anchor by night on account of the river fogs."

"Good! I am relying on you, DeRosier. This message must reach Lieutenant Fremont before the mail boat gets there. Is that clear?"

"Perfectly, madame. May I suggest taking my brother along? Two horses travel together better, and my brother will bring back a letter from Lieutenant Fremont."

"An excellent idea. It will take me only a moment to write the message."

She went to her father's table on the enclosed porch where there were pen, ink and paper. Without hesitation she wrote:

My dearest: Do not delay another day. Trust me, and start at once.

She sealed the envelope, handed it to DeRosier. Unsmiling he said, "Have no uneasiness, madame. The message will be delivered in time."

"God bless you," said Jessie.

She went back to her father's table and sat down, the starch gone out of her. She could feel little but the devitalizing fear that something might happen to DeRosier on the ride to Kaw's Landing, that the duplicate order from the Topographical Corps would reach John before her note could get there.

The day hours and the night hours merged into each other in a sleepless confusion of hope and anxiety. Would her husband trust her judgment? Would he start on the trail at once, even though the party were not quite ready? Or would he dismiss her note as a hysterical outburst to which women were prone? This was the first real test of whether or not John Fremont had meant what he said when he had promised to accept her as full partner, with faith in her judgment.

She did not know how many days had passed, three, four, when DeRosier's brother came galloping up to the Benton house at top speed, slid off his horse and pounded on the front door. He took a now soiled and sweat-stained letter from his buckskin jacket. Handing it to her he said:

"Lieutenant Fremont sends this message to you, madame. I brought it as fast as my horse would travel."

"Thank you, DeRosier; you and your brother have been wonderfully kind."

She tore open the message and read:

Good-by. I trust, and go.

Standing in the doorway, feeling weak but triumphant, the thought flashed into her mind: There is no need for anyone to know about this! The De-Rosiers will never talk. We will simply let the War Department think that the letter reached Kaw's Landing too late.

She rejected the idea summarily; she was not afraid of her act or ashamed of it. Picking up the same pen with which she had written to her husband, she wrote a letter to Colonel Abert explaining what she had done; outlining the reasons why a cannon was needed to get through the Blackfeet country; why it would have been a tragic mistake either to recall Lieutenant Fremont at that moment and abandon the expedition or to put his picked body of men under the line-and-rule control of another officer. She ended by saying that she was entirely willing to stand for investigation and trial upon her return to Washington, but that she felt the results of this second expedition would be so gratifying to Colonel Abert and the Topographical Corps that her conduct would be vindicated.

She wrote in full blood and full confidence, but once Gabriel had taken the letter to the post, her courage abandoned her and she threw herself face down on her bed. That her husband would approve of her decision, she had no doubt. But what of her father? Tom Benton was a rigid disciplinarian. By what outrageous presumption did a nineteen-year-old girl rebel against the United States government? She was certain that she had been right, yet she was equally certain that if her father condemned her she could never endure the year of separation from her husband.

Early the next morning Colonel Stephen Kearny arrived, his face as bilious yellow as his eyeballs.

"I have just received a letter from the War Department," he said in a cold tone, "reproving me for having given Lieutenant Fremont a howitzer for his expedition. The affair is my fault; I did not stand firm in dissuading the lieutenant. I do not like being rebuked by the War Department, Jessie, but I will not be selfish enough to think only of my own humiliation; I'm sorry that Lieutenant Fremont has been recalled to Washington."

"He is not going back to Washington, Colonel Kearny," said Jessie, in a small but firm voice.

"Not going . . . ? My letter informed me that he has been ordered back."

"That order will never reach him. He started on the trail several days ago."

"I don't understand, Jessie. One copy of the letter must have reached you, since you know what is going on. Lieutenant Fremont was not scheduled to leave Kaw's Landing for another week. The mail boat would have been there by now with a duplicate copy of the order."

"That is why I had to act quickly, Colonel Kearny," she replied. "When the message from the Topographical Corps reached me, I sent a note to Lieutenant Fremont asking him to break camp at once. I gave no reasons. Yesterday afternoon I received a message that he had started on the trail."

She watched the blood come into the colonel's eyes, turning the yellowish fields to a vein-ribbed red. At the same time his lips became pale and bloodless. His voice too, when he spoke, was without warmth.

"And you had no thought that this action would fall upon my shoulders! That I will not only be condemned for lending Lieutenant Fremont the howitzer, but in the event its presence causes trouble with the Indians, the English or the Mexicans, I will be held to blame for the consequences."

"There will be no consequences; Lieutenant Fremont will use the cannon only in the event that he is attacked."

"That is not for you to say!" shouted Colonel Kearny. "We are on the verge of war with both Mexico and England. How can we explain away an army howitzer, under the command of an army officer, being taken into disputed territory? I tell you, Jessie, this affair can precipitate a war. What a fool I was to have let a rash and impetuous officer talk me into such an act of folly!"

She saw that his fears were genuine, not only for himself but for the country as well. When she spoke her voice was conciliatory.

"I'm truly sorry, Colonel Kearny, not that Lieutenant Fremont took a cannon with him, for that will protect his party against the marauding Indians. Nor am I sorry that I intercepted the command for Lieutenant Fremont to return to Washington. But I am deeply regretful over the trouble we have caused you. You have always been our good and dear friend; when I intercepted the order, I had no realization of how deeply you would be involved. I have already written to Colonel Abert telling him what I have done and taking the full responsibility. I will write again this very day and further assure him that the taking of the cannon was Lieutenant Fremont's responsibility and not yours, and that he will stand up to the consequences of any act of his."

Colonel Kearny's rigid figure softened a little.

"Ah, Jessie," he said with quiet exasperation, "you are mature in so many ways, and yet fundamentally such a child. Do you really think that a letter from you to the War Department can absolve me from responsibility if Lieutenant Fremont gets into trouble? And have you no comprehension of the terrible thing you have done in suppressing orders?"

"It was a question of comparative values, Colonel. I could either see the expedition destroyed, all of my husband's and my father's work wiped out; or I could take matters into my own hands. I met the situation as I saw right."

"Jessie, let us sit down. I must talk to you as a friend who knew your father many years before you were born. You know that I have your best interests at heart; that is why I must try to make you understand."

They sat side by side and there were a few moments of silence. Then Colonel Kearny began speaking in the plain language of the soldier.

"Jessie, there is no one who can disobey the War Department or his superior officer, no matter how right he may think himself or how completely wrong he may think the command."

"Under ordinary circumstances that would be true . . ."

"It is true under all circumstances. An army will fall apart without complete discipline, particularly a citizens' army. Mutiny breeds chaos; this is true not merely of the army but of the whole democratic government."

When Colonel Kearny used the harsh word, mutiny, Jessie was profoundly shocked, shocked to think that what she had done could be called mutiny. When her scattered thoughts came into focus she explained that what she had done had been only good common sense, carried out in the best interests of the expedition, the Army and the government.

"Then you demand the right to define mutiny according to your own terms?" queried the colonel. "Don't you realize that everyone accused of mutiny swears that it wasn't mutiny at all, but conduct justifiable under the circumstances?" He shook his head sadly. "No, I suppose women don't understand things like that. There isn't a man in the world who would approve of what you have done, Jessie."

"Lieutenant Fremont will approve."

"Then so much the worse for Lieutenant Fremont. If you were a man you would understand exactly what I mean. But don't think your being a woman constitutes your justification. I know of no other woman who would approve of your conduct."

She nodded her head in denial.

"I think there are many women who would have done for their husbands exactly what I did—if similar circumstances had arisen."

"Then I can only say that for everyone's sake I am glad wives are kept out of men's business. If all women were permitted to create the kind of chaos your temperament creates, the work that men do would soon stop. Anne Royall would probably call you a modern woman, but in my opinion an interfering woman is a retrogression and not an advance."

He paused for a moment, looking at her steadily.

"Jessie, many times our superior officers are wrong and mistaken; many times our elected officers are wrong and mistaken. But we do more damage by mutinying against them than we possibly can by carrying out a bad order. We have set up our own form of government; without the discipline of obedience which we have imposed upon ourselves we cannot sustain our way of life."

He rose, picked up his hat, put it under his left armpit and added, before leaving: "I regret this entire affair. I regret it even though I am as deeply interested in the expedition and in western expansion as you, Senator Benton or Lieutenant Fremont. I say that Colonel Abert was wrong in recalling Lieutenant Fremont. I say that the expedition would have failed without him in command; I say that the cause of western expansion would have been retarded. Yet in the light of all these things, I still regret most bitterly that you saw fit to set yourself up against established authority. For your sake I hope Colonel Abert will decide to do nothing. Good day, Jessie."

The interval before Senator Benton's return to St. Louis was the worst of all. She was positive she was right, that one cannot always obey blindly, that every rule must be broken under exceptional circumstances. And yet she knew that Colonel Kearny would answer, "Every man thinks his own case constitutes exceptional circumstances."

Her father returned several days later. Unable to contain herself for one moment longer than necessary, she blurted out the story without giving him even a chance to wash or rest after his long journey from the interior of Missouri. She watched his face while she talked, seeking some sign that he would approve her conduct. But Tom Benton's face was set. When she had finished telling everything Colonel Kearny had said, he sat uncertainly for a moment. Jessie was stricken with terror, for she saw that he was not instantly going to proclaim his agreement.

"I wish . . . I wish you had waited, Jessie, consulted me . . ."

"But there was no time, Father, it was a matter of hours, even minutes. I had no way of knowing whether DeRosier could beat the mail boat. It was a gamble, and I did not know until his brother came back . . ."

"Yes, yes!" he exclaimed, pulling himself up to his feet. "You did the right thing! Confound those idiots in Washington. Can't they understand that it's a dastardly mistake to break up an expedition that's about to start, with the whole country waiting eagerly for its results? Can't they understand that you don't just pull off a commanding officer and stick anybody in his place, that exploring is a difficult and complicated business? What would have happened to the English fleet if Lord Nelson hadn't held up his blind eye to the telescope when his admiral was issuing a stupid order? What would happen to the human brain and human soul if we never used our own judgment, if we behaved like machines even when we were facing destruction? That's the confounded military mind, Jessie; all it can understand is obedience and more obedience and never mind if you get killed for it."

"Then you don't feel that I have committed a mutinous act?"

"Most certainly not! You have done us all the greatest possible service. Colonel Abert will be the first to agree when the expedition returns triumphantly. A little mutiny goes a long way, but that little is the sometime genius of democracy. I mutinied against the War Department once myself; it was at the end of March 1813, when I was a colonel under General Andrew Jackson. We had moved our little army to Natchez when we received an order from the War Department to disband our troops then and there. When General Jackson showed me the dispatch, I advised him to disobey it. I said, 'This is dated February 6. The Secretary of War expected it to reach you before we were so far from home. We are now a full five hundred miles from Nashville. This is General Jackson's army. It should be marched home under Jackson. We can appeal to Governor Wilkinson for money to transport the sick, and treat with the merchants here for stores.' Our little insurrection saved the health and loyalty of the Tennessee army, so that when General Jackson went back into the field his troops fought with him in the battle of New Orleans and helped win the War of 1812.

"Get me ink and paper, Jessie, I'm going to write to Colonel Abert and take responsibility for the affair. You are to put it out of your mind, for you only acted as my agent; had I been here I would have done the exact same thing."

When her father had finished his letter, Jessie asked quietly: "What is the worst they can do to us?"

Tom Benton reread his letter without answering.

"Father, I asked you a question. What is the worst that the Army can do to Lieutenant Fremont?"

Without looking up, he said disinterestedly:

"They will do nothing. When John returns to Washington, and the second report is published, the Topographical Corps will thank you . . ."

"I want to face the last-ditch consequences of what I have done, so that I may be prepared. What is the worst they can do to my husband?"

Tom Benton gazed at his daughter, studied her delicate but resolute face, and in her eyes read that there was no use deluding her.

"Court-martial. Dismissal from the service."

10

She lay in her room off the shaded courtyard in air that was soft with perfume and which should have lulled her to sleep. But she tossed all night, convinced that her husband would be court-martialed and dismissed, that she had ruined his life, that he would be unable to forgive her and would cease loving her; that she had destroyed their marriage, that a woman should never mix in her husband's work but should remain aloof so that, even though the family suffered if the man were unsuccessful, it could never be the wife's fault: the husband could not hold it against their marriage relationship.

When she rose at dawn she expected to find herself pale and haggard-eyed. When she looked into the mirror she could find no trace of the night's unrest, except that her clear and soft skin was marred by a slight swelling under the left corner of her mouth.

She made no attempt to re-establish the discipline that had served as a connecting link for the hours before the fateful letter had arrived from Washington. Instead she drifted through the days, making no plans, never thinking past the moment at hand, watching over her mother and Lily. The days weren't so bad: there were several hours of work in the morning with her father, there were people in the house discussing trade and politics and exploration. But at night she would lie awake in her high four-posted French bed longing for her husband, for the chance to tell him what she had done, to know that he would condone her action.

One afternoon she took a walk along the Mississippi to the outskirts of the town, where in a wide meadow a number of immigrant caravans were resting and making their final preparations. Wagonmakers and vendors of oxen, mules and horses were selling their wares, representatives from the grocers, clothiers and gunmakers were displaying their goods. She was attracted to the large letters DELAWARE painted in bright blue on the canvas top of a prairie schooner. Seated on an overturned tub near the wagon was a young woman about her own age, nursing her baby. Her laughing blue eyes peeped up at Jessie from a pink-ruffled sunbonnet.

"I have a little girl just about your baby's age," said Jessie. "Won't you tell me its name."

"John, named for his father."

"My husband's name is John, too."

"Well, now, that's a coincidence, ain't it? Are you going to Oregon, too?"

"No. . . . That is, not yet."

"But it ain't dangerous no more. Look, I'll show you the map we got, it was drawn by that military officer."

The young woman climbed up onto the seat of her wagon and took a much-thumbed paper from an inside pocket of the canvas.

"You see here, it shows where there's plenty of grass for the horses and where we must stock up with water, and just how we get over the mountains at the pass. And the Indians ain't so bad if all the families stay together and fight together."

"I wouldn't be afraid," said Jessie. "My father taught me how to shoot a gun."

Stirred by the yearning in Jessie's voice, the young woman's eyes became serious.

"Wouldn't you and your folks like to come along? There are three wagons of us. Did you know you can get a whole section of good land to yourselves and save your children from a life of wages?"

Jessie was crying. Impulsively the woman seized her hand.

"Tell you what I'll do," she said. "Give me your name and address and when I get out to Oregon I'll write you a letter, all about the trail and how you can make it best. Next year maybe you could get your own wagon and join us out there. My name's Mary Algood. What's your'n?"

The long summer passed with no word from John. She was not worried about his welfare, yet always lurking at the base of her brain was the dagger of fear; it took only one small accident such as a rubber boat overturning on the Platte; one moment of relaxed vigil at night; one Indian arrow . . . All these images she managed to keep locked away during the active hours of the day, but the night weighed on her like a soggy blanket, and the hours from dark to dawn were a hundred times longer than those from dawn to dusk.

In the fall her father returned to Washington for the opening of Congress. It was a difficult parting for both of them.

"I know how endless it is for you," he said, "this waiting and uncertainty. But I beg of you not to grieve. Don't fight the hours, go along with them. Soon you will possess all those that have passed, and Lieutenant Fremont will be back."

As she moved slowly against time, she came upon the duality of her love for John and the duality of her own personality. She was the woman who loved him as a man, but also the wife who loved him as a partner in marriage. It was the wife who sent him forth on these long and hazardous expeditions, the wife who was ambitious, not for herself or for her husband, but for their marriage. It was the wife who was strong to the point of steel, who could endure privation and hardship; and it was the wife who frequently made the woman suffer, the woman who had no ambition whatever except to be with the husband she loved. She had made her important decisions as a wife who believed that marriage was the highest goal between a man and a woman, that to it everything had to be subjugated; but when the loneliness overwhelmed her she became convinced that the only imperative between a man and a woman was their love. It was their love which must be sustained, even at the expense of their marriage collaboration; and at such times she would have recalled him gladly to her arms, let the expedition and their career be forgotten.

Her father came home for Christmas. There had been no letter from John in all these six months, yet coupled with her uneasiness was a sense of elation that half of the year of separation was already gone. Tom Benton insisted that they have gaiety, so he borrowed a custom from St. Louis' German population and put up a Christmas tree for Lily. A few of their closest friends and cousins were invited to share the roast goose and plum pudding and to exchange gifts before the roaring log fire. Jessie was particularly pleased by her father's present, the three-volume set of Prescott's *Conquest of Mexico* which had been published only a few weeks before in New York.

When her father returned to Washington in the middle of January, she said to him in a far happier mood than she had been in when he had left that fall:

"Lieutenant Fremont must have been in California for some time now. I'm sure he'll be leaving very shortly and will come home by the southern route. I expect him by the end of March at the latest."

For an instant she thought she saw a cloud pass over his eyes, but he answered, "Captain Sutter will provision him in the Sacramento Valley, and that will make his trip home by the southern route a comparatively easy one."

It was not long after her father's departure that she began to notice a change in the attitude of the people around her. Her cousins and friends had shown her many kindnesses, yet their manner had been casual: after all, Lieutenant Fremont was off on a glorious mission, no man knew better how to command an expedition and bring it back safely, and while the year of separation was necessarily hard, it was a fate many wives shared. By the beginning of February she saw that her cousins were going out of their way to shower tenderness upon her, that some of her father's friends were coming to the house rather more often than they had, bringing little gifts, chatting animatedly.

She asked herself, Why are they so solicitous of me? What has happened to make them change their attitude? She searched the newspapers line by line for some communication from the Pacific coast, sent to Washington and New York for the major journals. She asked indirect questions, but her cousins and friends veered away from them. Unable to bear the added burden she went to her cousins, the Brants, and begged them to tell her what they knew that she didn't know. She saw the same withdrawal in her cousins' eyes that she had seen in her father's: they put her off with comforting speeches, and she felt trapped in a conspiracy of kindness.

That afternoon when she returned home she saw the reflection of her face in the rectangular mirror over the fireplace as she passed the downstairs parlor. Something drew her to the glass. During the months of the fall, whenever her anxieties would come to a momentary crisis, she had noticed that the little swelling under the corner of her mouth would come forth; when she had pushed the fears to the back of her mind, the blemish gradually disappeared. Now as she gazed into the mirror she saw that it had come out again, this time larger than before.

It's my King George's Mark, she thought, like Grandmother McDowell's mark on her forehead.

From the labyrinth of her brain a thought shot forth: *They think my husband is dead!* There could no longer be any doubt about it: even her father had known there was bad news when he had been home for Christmas. Nor did she imagine that these people were making up a story from whole cloth; somewhere, somehow, a report had come out of the West that Lieutenant Fremont was in trouble. But where had it come from? And how could she find out what it was?

If John were dead, then for her all the world was dead. She remembered the story of Grandmother Benton: she had been only thirty when her husband died. Young Tom was not allowed to see his mother for three months. When he had seen her last she had been a lovely, blue-eyed woman; when he was taken in to her again he found in place of the vivacious young woman he had known a thin white-haired old lady.

No one knew better than Jessie that the Bentons loved only once.

At last she cornered an old trapper who had not the guile to deceive her. He told her that a report had come out of Oregon that Lieutenant Fremont, after reaching the Columbia with his party intact, had then made the hazardous crossing from the Columbia to the Truckee River just east of the Sierras. Here he had disregarded the advice of the Indians that the Sierras were impassable, had plunged into the ice and snow, been enveloped by blizzards, and vanished completely. No word had come out of California of his arrival at Captain Sutter's, and so much time had passed in the interval that it would have been impossible for him not to have perished.

Having been separated from her husband for ten months, Jessie had imagined that she had learned all there was to know about the anatomy of loneliness. She imagined that loneliness had a traceable pattern, that once she had met the worst of it, she would recognize her old enemy when he arose the next time, and would have the technique with which to combat it. But she found that loneliness was a Hydra-headed monster who never appeared twice in the same shape or form; that it was an unslayable enemy who thrust himself upward in unexpected places and at unexpected times, just when one was beginning to feel some small measure of security. It could emerge in the middle of a page of print and make a superb piece of prose suddenly unendurable; it could burst forth when one was washing one's face or combing one's hair, and the brush would fall out of the hand and the soap drop into the basin and one's reflection in the mirror stare back like a lifeless mask; it could get into one's mouth while one was talking, and the words would die and the teeth would clench, and the lips would be bitten; it could crawl into bed at night when one lay half awake, half asleep, and bring with it the most excruciating torture of all, making of this one small bed a wide and empty world with no man to love, no husband to embrace, no arms to lock one safely against the darkness and the fatality of life.

Yet this kind of loneliness was endurable because the loved one would return; the first embrace of meeting would obliterate the wretched hours. But if the loved one is never to return?

For four days she went with little food or drink or sleep, walking through her duties with her feelings numbed. She did not accept the fact of John's death any more than she was able to repudiate it. She knew that if there was any man who could get through the Sierras in the face of blizzards, it was he. But if no human being could get through, what then?

Toward dawn of the fifth day, as she lay rigid on her bed, the cycle of anxiety broke; she fell into a sound sleep. When she awakened at noon she leaped out of bed, bathed, brushed and combed her long hair, donned a close-fitting blue silk dress which she had made almost daringly short in front, exposing her ankle, in order to get some comfort in walking the rough cobblestones of St. Louis. After luncheon she spent an hour with Lily, then put on a matching jockey cap of blue silk and set out for the Brants. To her cousins she said:

"You can stop your worrying. Lieutenant Fremont and his party are safe."

They betrayed their past concern when several of them exclaimed at once:

"Oh, Jessie, how wonderful, we are so happy for you, we are so relieved! When did the news come? How did he manage to survive in the mountains under those horrible conditions?"

"There has been no news. I have received no letter. I simply know that my husband is safe. Nothing could possibly persuade me otherwise. Lieutenant Fremont will be home in a very few weeks."

Her cousins were shocked. When she saw the frightened expression in their eyes, she smiled and said:

"No, my dears, I have not gone out of my mind. What I know, I know. It is almost a year now since Lieutenant Fremont left on his expedition. He will soon be back in St. Louis."

11

She threw herself into a happy fever of preparation for his return. Though the first of March was a little early for spring cleaning she turned the house upside down and had everything scrubbed, whitewashed, painted and waxed. Then she planned new outfits for herself and Lily, spending hours cutting out dresses and embroidering on them. She set a place each night at the table for John, and when the rest of the family had finished dinner, his setting was transferred to a small table by the fire. His food was left on the kitchen stove where it could be heated on short notice.

"A man must not feel unexpected," she said.

A log fire was kept burning brightly in the downstairs parlor, which she replenished just before she went to sleep. However, sleep was the last of her desires; she stayed up until midnight studying and perfecting her Spanish, which she felt would be a great asset when she returned to California with her husband. She then placed her reading lamp on a table by the window that faced toward town, a light which he must see from far off as he came down the riverbank to the Benton home. It was not that she thought he needed light to guide his steps, this man who had just crossed an uncharted continent, but only that it would stand for the light in her heart and for her great and burning desire for him to be back. She knew that he would understand.

Occasionally she would fall asleep in her chair by the fire, but she would awake with a start thinking she heard footsteps outside, those short, swift, staccato footsteps which distinguished him from every other man in the world just as surely as did his voice or his appearance. Some time after midnight she would go to bed and lie there certain that he would return before morning, catching only snatches of troubled, conscious sleep. By dawn she was up again to put away the lamp, to remove the setting from the table by the fireplace, to face another day of waiting, sustaining herself on faith and devotion, feeding off them because no other food was digestible.

March passed, and then April. Still there was no word from John. The population of St. Louis was positive that he and his party had perished in the snows of the Sierras. When her cousins learned that she was setting a place at the table for him each night, saving his food and lighting a lamp to guide his footsteps, they became concerned for her sanity.

She grew thinner and frailer. By June, one year from the day he had left, she was down to ninety pounds, her skin pulled taut over the bones, her eyes enormous and staring in her hollow-cheeked face, the King George's Mark flaming red below the corner of her mouth.

There was something about going into the second year of separation which broke down her discipline. She ceased reading altogether, almost ceased thinking. There were no longer any divisions in her mind between night and day, nor among the weeks or months. The heat of summer sapped her last strength as she drifted through the days of July and early August. It was five months since she had told her cousins that John was alive and well; she realized that by now she was the only one in the United States who thought so.

In the early morning of August seventh when she had fallen into that curious state she had known so many months of being a little asleep and yet terribly awake, she heard the sound of excited voices below her in the hallway. She jumped out of bed, put on a robe and ran downstairs. Maylee was talking to Gabriel, who was either excited or trembling with fear. She heard him say:

"I hear pebbles against my window . . . the coachhouse . . . I look out.

There Lieutenant Fremont. He ask can I let him in without I wake the family?"

Jessie confronted the old man.

"You say you saw Lieutenant Fremont? What time was it? Why didn't you bring him to me?"

"It must be three o'clock, Miss Jessie. He say he wait till morning, he don't want to wake nobody, he walk downtown till dawn."

Then she heard the sound for which her ears had been attuned for fourteen months; footsteps running up the front stairs; a sharp knock at the door, and John was in the hallway, had brushed past Gabriel and held her half fainting in his arms. He carried her to one of the larger chairs, sat down with her, covered her trembling face with kisses.

Word spread around town almost as fast as though a cannon had been fired. Friends began thronging into the Benton house. By eight in the morning it had turned into a full-scale reception, with people laughing and crying and everybody talking at once.

Jessie's happiness returned in a great rush. The waiting was over now, all the uncertainty gone. Beside her sat her husband, thinner than she, his cheeks sunken, his skin gray and blotched with stubble, his face engraved with heavy lines of fatigue, his eyes a little wild, his clothes threadbare. But here he sat beside her, his bony tired arm about her tired shoulder, his exhausted voice against her unhearing ear, his dry, cracked lips against her hollowed cheek. She knew that neither of them was beautiful to look at, but ah, how beautiful the world, how beautiful to be together again!

At noon the milling throng of friends departed.

"My poor darling," said Jessie, "you have no luck: when you came home from your first expedition I was big with child; and now I am as skinny as a starved cat."

"You never looked more beautiful," he replied, kissing her full on the mouth. The kindness broke the back of her resolve to be calm; she began blubbering like a child, and he had to hold her against him so hard that there was almost no breath left in her body.

Later she said, "I must tell you why I sent that message to Kaw's Landing. I hope you will approve of what I did, but if you do not approve, you must tell me so quite honestly so that I may use it as a guide for future conduct."

"If you told me to go, I knew there was sufficient reason to go," he said. "What happened?"

"A letter arrived from the Topographical Department calling you to Washington to explain the presence of a cannon on a peaceful expedition."

"A recall. But that would have meant . . ."

". . . another officer was being sent to take your place."

"Take my place!" He reared up like a balky horse, his face a dull, brick red. "It's that West Point clique! They're jealous of what I've accomplished."

"Then I did right to suppress the order?"

"Right!" He shouted at her as though she were the entire West Point aristocracy. "You would have been a fool if you hadn't. You saved the day for all of us."

"Good! What happened to the cannon? Was it valuable? Were you able to bring it back?"

"Yes and no: it staved off one major Indian attack; we could have survived it, but it might have cost us several men. We pulled that cannon from Kaw's Landing fifteen hundred miles to the Dalles on the Columbia, then another four hundred miles through the snow and icy passes going south from Oregon to the east side of the Rockies. We even got it halfway across the Sierras; there we lost it in snowdrifts twelve feet high. We were hard pressed to save our own lives, and the cannon had to be abandoned."

"I'm sorry you couldn't have brought it back to the Jefferson Barracks. But since it saved you from an attack you have justified its presence to both Colonel Abert and Colonel Kearny."

"Wait until they see our maps and reports, Jessie; we'll both be vindicated."

It was then she asked, "What happened in the Sierras? Why did the report get out that you and your party had perished? Did you have terrible hardships? Were you in serious danger?"

He rubbed his feet up and down on the cool wood floor. He had left her side, had gone back to the Sierras and the blinding snows.

"Hardships? Yes. Danger? Yes. Death? No. Only the weak die on the trail. Only those whose will power succumbs to a stronger force. I crossed the Sierras in midwinter, Jessie, when the Indians who had lived there all their lives said it was impossible. I am the first man to traverse the Sierras in winter. I found a pass over a fourteen-thousand-foot wall of ice when we were all nine-tenths dead and everyone except Carson and myself had abandoned hope. I forced that crossing, Jessie, right where my calculation told me it must be. And once we were over, we dropped straight down into the Sacramento Valley and Sutter's Fort. I found a straight route and a new pass to California; one day it will be as widely used as the Oregon Trail. If war comes with Mexico, we will take California by the Army moving in over the trail I blazed."

His voice rang with exultation. "Jessie, it was the greatest experience of my life! I was defeated; the Sierras had whipped me; it was impossible for humans to get through . . . we were only shadows of men, almost too weak to move; the snow lay so deep neither man nor horse could struggle forward; we were too blinded to see, too cold to feel, too hungry to move our legs. Never has a party been closer to death and destruction."

He paced up and down the room. "That's when a man lives at his height, when he is beaten, when all the world knows he's beaten, when he hasn't the slimmest chance, and yet he pushes through, he defeats and surmounts all the obstacles, when he is stronger than nature, when he is the strongest force on earth. For, Jessie, I found that pass! I found it without food or strength or eyesight or arms or legs. I crawled up over ten thousand feet and found our pass and went back and got the rest of the party and dragged them up with me, men and horses, both. Ah Jessie, such moments, such triumphs are vouchsafed but a few times in a man's life."

And Jessie, sitting there, intensely proud of his accomplishment, found her heart wrung in pity; pity for this unfortunate creature who must make himself a king because in his own mind he was not a whole man. In the icy passes of the Sierras the last could be first, John Fremont had vindicated himself: by making himself the conqueror of nature he had conquered his own illegitimacy. If only he could live forever in these icy passes, she thought, overcoming insurmountable obstacles, making impossible conquests, then always he would be a king, the fear and uncertainty would vanish, the enigma of John Charles Fremont would be solved and vanquished.

12

The next two weeks were delightful ones. Lingering over their late breakfast, Jessie heard her husband say in a ruminative voice:

"The man who has a good wife is a king; she sweetens every hour. There can be no real happiness or success in life for the man with a poorish wife, and there can be no genuine failure for the man with a good wife. What a stroke of pure genius I had when I recognized you, Jessie. I shall always think well of myself for that magnificent flash of wisdom."

She chuckled at the oblique compliment.

"And what about me?" she asked. "Don't I get any credit for recognizing you?"

"A relatively minor accomplishment, compared to mine. Do you know wherein the true greatness of your accomplishment lies?"

"Do tell me."

"In the fact that, search my memory as I will, I can find no scars on our marriage. I know that I have sometimes been difficult and unreasonable, that you are hard pressed not to become angry with me or lose patience. But you have been so unfailingly kind, you have kept our relationship so sympathetic and serene that, when I want to quarrel with you, my mind can find no dark spots around which to fester. I can't even conjure up a quarrel with you in my imagination. That is a great accomplishment, Jessie, and all the credit must go to you."

"A mere nothing," she mocked, to conceal her emotion. "All you need is love, and it's as easy as falling off a precipice."

At the end of two weeks they had completed their arrangements to leave for Washington. They took the steamboat to Wheeling, where they rented a carriage and drove the rest of the way along the now completed national road to Washington. It was good to be home again in Washington, but the crush of people was so great in the Benton house that it proved impossible for them to get to work on their report. At the beginning of October, when she was looking well and fresh again, she found a vacant two-storied cottage just a block away. She took John to see it, showing him through excitedly.

"Look, darling, we can have complete privacy here, for no one need know it is our workshop. We can turn these two upstairs rooms into writing rooms and give the downstairs quarters to Preuss and John Hubbard for their maps. Does it look good to you?"

"Rent it at once," he replied. "I'll move over our notes and journals first thing in the morning."

John and her father rose at dawn, had their showers, coffee and rolls at six, and John left for his cottage. Jessie was not allowed to appear until nine. From nine until one she worked with him on the report. Then Maylee would arrive with little Lily under one arm and a luncheon basket under the other and tell them stories of the baby while they ate cold chicken on cornbread and munched fresh fruit. After lunch Maylee would place Lily in the basket and take her back home, while the Fremonts went for a half-hour's walk along the Potomac before returning to the workshop.

John had done an even better job on his journals than he had on the previous expedition. There was a magnificent wealth of scientific observation, vivid descriptions of the trail, the mountains, the rivers and the forests; and of the greatest importance to her, the rich and natural poetry of his mind when, sitting by his campfire late at night, he had written unrestrainedly of everything he had seen and experienced. There was no hesitation in their collaboration now; each knew his own role and was respectful of the contribution of the other. She took the utmost pains to preserve the color and flavor and beauty of his rough notes, the sharp pungency of the stories he told, content to contribute form and organization, to burn out the dross and to leave John's work appearing at its best.

They labored for five months on the report, the most concentrated piece of work she had ever done. She knew her contribution to this document to be a modest one, and for that reason she felt secure in believing that it was to be one of the great books of exploration; here were descriptions of forest and mountain ranges, of sunrises over icy blue crags which had not been surpassed for beauty in any literature she knew; here was an entirely new fund of material about the Indians and their way of life; here were studies of the souls of men enduring excruciating agonies, bending under the burden but always snapping back; here was a fluid technique of exploration which utilized everything known to the minds of explorers, yet went beyond all precedent of daring ingenuity and resourcefulness in the face of hardships which staggered the imagination; here was a wealth of observation on botany, geology, the nature of mountain and snow and forest which had not been surpassed for scientific meticulousness or for the brilliance of poetic observation.

Colonel Kearny came to Washington on army business and was invited to dinner by Tom Benton. A blunt and earnest man, he was not one to allow a fractured relationship to limp along without splint or bandage. He found a moment alone with Jessie, saying to her in his slightly rough voice, "Do not mistake me, Miss Jessie, I am tremendously happy for your sake that everything has worked out so well. I am putting the entire incident out of my mind."

The following evening she and John were invited to Colonel Abert's home as guests of honor at a dinner for the officers of the Topographical Corps. She was slow and uncertain in her dressing; John urged her to hurry several times, but she could not seem to complete her coiffure.

"What are you fretting about?" he asked.

"I'm afraid. Colonel Abert's home is almost the last one in Washington I care to go into."

"Colonel Abert is a subtle man; he's not like Colonel Kearny. He will never mention that obstructed order, any more than he ever answered your letter."

"Nevertheless I'm nervous," she replied, "so nervous that I can't get this confounded part straight in the middle of my hair."

"Then leave it crooked. I don't want to be late."

But when she got to Colonel Abert's home, still a little pale, and without words to carry her over the difficult moment of meeting, the colonel welcomed her with warmth and charm, seated her at his right and was more delightful than she had ever known him. She couldn't touch the delicious bouillabaisse for fear that his charm was only a front, that the colonel would take the first opportunity to reprove her; but by the time the mallards and suckling pig arrived she saw that her little uprising had been forgiven.

The frequent meetings which took place in the Benton home showed Jessie and John that to official Washington the most interesting part of his trip was his brief sojourn in California: for war with Mexico over the annexation of Texas seemed to be growing closer every day, and nearly everyone in Washington was resolved that California must not fall into British hands. Senator Benton, as chairman of the Military Affairs Committee, had been receiving disquieting news.

"That magnificent coast and its harbors are going to fall into British hands like ripe fruit off a tree," he exclaimed. "The Mexican government has granted them thousands of acres in a huge tract, and the British are sending in a whole colony of Irish families. If that colony gets established, California will be lost to us."

No one in the capital had been in California except John, and his opinion was eagerly sought. There was material which Jessie had not been able to write into the report, for Mexico was still considered a friendly nation, but he had sketched for her the outlines of his findings: Mexico City's only interest in this vast country appeared to be the taxes it could extract; no Mexican colonizing was going on; the Mexican government kept a small army in California, inadequately equipped and officered. There were almost a hundred fast-shooting Americans in California, none of whom liked the Mexican rule and nearly all of whom would fight to join the United States.

"An army officer with a hundred men under him could capture California," said Lieutenant Fremont, "only they have to be there at the right moment."

When they had finished the report on February 20, just a year after he had crossed the Sierras, Jessie asked anxiously:

"Will Congress order a thousand extra copies to be printed again? That was such a tremendous help last time."

"I hardly think so, Jessie."

"Why not? This report is far superior to the last, and all the material from South Pass to the Pacific coast is new . . ."

"But it stretched to three hundred pages; Congress may find it too long and boring."

Before she could answer she saw that he had been teasing her. On March 3, 1845, the day before President James K. Polk was to be inaugurated, John came home flushed with pleasure.

"What do you think?" he exclaimed. "The Senate passed a resolution ordering five thousand extra copies of our report."

"Five thousand," exclaimed Jessie, "why, that's magnificent!"

"Only half as magnificent as what finally happened: James Buchanan praised me to the skies and carried a motion that the number be increased to ten thousand copies. And here, my dear, read what Secretary Buchanan said about your husband. I'm too modest to tell you."

Jessie made a mocking grimace, then read aloud Buchanan's statement to the Senate of John's progress: "He is a young gentleman of extraordinary merit, great energy and ability to serve his country. Lieutenant Fremont deserves encouragement." Hiding her pleasure under a little joke, she said, "I never found that you needed encouragement; you just sort of reach out and grab everything you want."

The next day Jessie did her hair in the new Polish fashion with a braid of nine strands, a small bunch of flowers and leaves hanging from the coil at the back, and on top of her head a small black muslin cap. Her new gown was black moire, with the bodice opening over a chemisette of white muslin. Her silk paletot wrap was trimmed with black lace and caught around the waist with a broad ribbon.

"I think I look uncommonly handsome," she remarked to her husband.

"Why do you always get dressed up in your best clothes and look so gorgeous when we go out?" he countered. "Why don't you get dressed up like that for me when we stay home?"

"You're supposed to love me for my spiritual values, dear, not for my new clothes."

"But even your spiritual values show up to better advantage in a black moire gown."

Driving up Pennsylvania Avenue, Jessie asked, "Do you remember the last reception we came to? We were newly married and President Tyler gave us the first clue that an expedition might be ordered."

"I hope that established a precedent for inaugurals," he replied. "I would like President Polk to give me an intimation today that he favors a third expedition to California."

"I'm sure he will, dear," she murmured. "Who could resist you when you look so beautiful in your new uniform?"

"True. But I'm afraid I don't stimulate the president quite as much as I do my wife."

They were welcomed on the reception line by Nancy Polk, Jessie's longtime friend. After the formalities were over, President Polk summoned them and, surrounded by a group of army officers and Cabinet members, asked Lieutenant Fremont for stories of the West. He chose a number of short and dramatic incidents which seemed to capture the president's imagination. Encouraged by his success, he became emboldened to say, "Mr. President, the entire Pacific coast could be of the utmost value to the United States. Geographically it belongs to us; there will be a continuous conflict if two or three nations own land on the Pacific."

Polk's face lost its interested expression; knowing that he faced four years of being importuned, he said, not unkindly, "Lieutenant Fremont, you suffer from two afflictions under which I labored not so long ago: youth and impulsiveness. I expect you will outgrow them both; in the meanwhile please accept my warmest congratulations on the accomplishments of your second expedition."

Lieutenant and Mrs. Fremont found themselves dismissed. On the way home in their carriage they were a little glum together.

"The precedent fell on its face," mourned John. "Mr. Polk has no intention of backing a third expedition."

"Maybe he just needs a little time. I do wish we could have told all this to Nancy. She is open to new ideas, and she would have known how to convince the president."

It was no surprise to Jessie that when Congress released the second report, Lieutenant Fremont became the popular hero of America. The newspapers reprinted substantial excerpts, featuring his picture on the front page. Several publishing houses rushed the book into print, and it sold like wildfire, in England almost as widely as in the United States. Honors poured in from scientific societies in England and Europe. General Winfield Scott, founder of America's professional army, six foot four of military brilliance, came to the Benton home with an official-looking document in his hand to announce to the delighted family in his most ceremonial fashion that President Polk had breveted John captain for "gallant and highly meritorious services in two expeditions commanded by himself."

Such popularity had not been seen in the capital since army generals had won important military victories in the War of 1812. Sermons were preached on the morals of the expedition, school children had parts of the report read to them in the classrooms; everywhere in the United States, on small farms, in crossroad stores, in hotels and bars and clubs, on the sidewalks of great cities people gathered to talk about the second Fremont report, to feel in their blood the stir of the westward movement, of the desire to experience these great adventures, to see these beautiful sights, to farm this new and rich land, to win property in this vast new country, to be once again movers, doers, breakers of trails, settlers, pioneers of new states as well as new lands: to be their own man.

And Jessie Benton Fremont was content; she had known her man the moment she had seen him; she had recognized him for the strength and greatness that were in him; she had helped him beat his road through the mountains; she had strengthened his sinews and extended his reach, made him a little bigger by lending that little talent which had been hers to contribute.

These were the things of which she had dreamed when her mind had turned to marriage.

13

The argument in Washington over the possibility of war with Mexico because of the annexation of Texas waged warmer every day. Much of it centered in the home of Chairman Benton, of the Senate Military Affairs Committee, and his son-in-law, Captain Fremont. Senator Benton was averse to war with Mexico, felt that Texas and the Southwest, including California, should be bought at a fair figure, just as the vast Louisiana Purchase had been made from France. There was neither ethics nor justice in forcing Mexico to sell, and even though this attitude of purchase was comparatively new on the international scene, Tom Benton realized that his government was on the difficult side of the situation. Mexico had no use for the land; it was a hang-over from the Spanish days, and there was little likelihood that the country could become prosperous or settled while being ruled from Mexico City. Nevertheless, it legally belonged to Mexico.

Captain Fremont, thinking as a military man, was more opportunistic in his attitude. He didn't care how the United States got California—by purchase, occupation, seizure, or even pure theft.

"My ethics may be a little obscure," he admitted to Jessie, "but my eyesight is perfect. I have been to California. I know that geographically it belongs to the United States. I should like to help in its acquisition. I can't shed any tears over the Mexicans; aside from the revenues they extract, they are as interested in California as we are in the moon."

One evening when she was browsing through a copy of the *United Science Journal*, published in London, she found a passage which considerably startled her. She exclaimed, "Father, John, listen to this:

" 'There is no doubt that we, the English, have three powerful rivals in France, Russia, and the United States, but of these three the Americans are the most important on account of their origin, their courage, and their even greater enterprise and activity than our own. They have raw material, workingmen, and sufficient merchant navy to arm as men-of-war when called upon to do so.'"

Senator Benton, who had disliked the British profoundly since the War of 1812, snatched up the newspaper, put on a hat and coat and walked to Senator Calhoun's house. Calhoun felt confirmed in his suspicion that England intended to wage war against the United States for the acquisition, first of Oregon, then of California. The two men marched militantly to Secretary of Navy George Bancroft's house. The next morning Secretary Bancroft had a long session with President Polk. Within a very few days the third expedition to the West had been authorized, the War Department had set aside fifty thousand dollars for its prosecution, and Captain Fremont had been named as commander.

The following days of confidential meetings were exciting for Jessie, but before long a tinge of uneasiness crept into her thoughts: everyone wanted to acquire California and would prefer to buy it at a reasonable figure, yet it was obvious that no one wanted to let it go by default to England if it couldn't be bought. Men spoke of how valuable and important California was, how it was manifest destiny that it belong to the United States; everyone was certain that Mexico would not sell or negotiate; everyone seemed to know that California would have to be seized if the United States were not to lose the territory to England. Yet no one would admit he thought this, no one was willing to be quoted to that effect, no one wanted to be held responsible for outlaw conduct or go down in the historic record as an instigator of an international theft.

Many of Captain Fremont's superior army officers, many Cabinet members, senators and congressmen assured him how happy they were that a scientific expedition was on its way to California; they agreed that it would be propitious to have an army officer present in the event that war should break; yet no one would lay out a definite course of conduct or give him specific authorization.

"Everybody knows what they would like you to do," said Jessie, "but no one is willing to take the responsibility for it."

"It's not difficult to understand," replied John. "We are still at peace with Mexico; no representative of our government can go on record as sponsoring aggression. That would make the United States government responsible for his acts. But I am not an official representative of the government. I am just a captain in the Topographical Corps. Anything I may do, aside from exploring, I do on my own responsibility. If I embarrass my government, they can disavow me."

"I do wish that you could get some kind of written authorization."

"It's not possible in such a delicate situation. It may be that Mexico will sell us California; it may be that the Americans out there will revolt and set up an independent republic, the way they did in Texas; it may be that the time is not yet ripe for annexation. In any of these instances it would be dangerous for me to have authorization to do anything but explore and make maps of the Pacific coast."

She planned to remain in the capital during her husband's absence, for the situation had changed so rapidly that Washington City rather than St. Louis would now be the hub of activity for the West. She knew that this separation would be the longest of all, that her husband would have to remain on the Pacific coast until the climax of events could release him. How long would he be away? A year, two years, three years! She had hoped to go with him the next time he went to California; instead she faced a staggering separation. Her only reassurance was that this would probably be the last time he would go west without her. They had agreed that he was to invest their savings in the most beautiful ranch he could find between Monterey and San Francisco. California would be an American state within a few years, and the Fremonts would be among its first settlers.

They spent their last evening together in their upstairs sitting room after a jolly family dinner at which Mrs. Benton had been the only one to break down and show how bad she felt about his leaving. To everyone's amazement, Eliza had asked permission to invite a young lawyer she had met recently, a tall, spindly, blond chap, quiet and dry-spoken.

The preparations for the expedition had gone smoothly, except that Preuss, the magnificent map maker, had had to withdraw because his wife had issued him an ultimatum: "Choose between your home and family and your instinct to wander."

While Jessie sat sewing a waterproof pocket on the side of John's canvas-and-leather jacket, in which he was to keep his valuable papers dry, her husband cried:

"Darling, how can I leave you here? I was gone for fourteen months last time; this time I will be gone longer. The days when I am with you go so fast, but when I am away from you they drag so terribly."

A tear splashed on the leather pocket.

"There," she said, "your jacket has been christened. Now it will bring you good luck." She ran her fingers through his short black hair. "It was good of you to say that, even though in its strictest sense it isn't true; you live at the height of excitement when you are on the trail. Your job is to go, my job is to let you go cheerfully."

"Confound it, Jessie, would you mind looking a little sad so that my ego can be inflated?"

"Like your India-rubber boat? You wouldn't want me to be a Mrs. Preuss. I decided long ago that you would tire of a pining wife. My dear, I don't want you to tire of me, I want you to love me all our long lives together."

When she awakened the next morning she saw Maylee's grinning black face before her, holding a copy of the *Union* for her to see. In the center of the front page was a large picture of Captain Fremont.

"How wonderful, Maylee, to be greeted by my husband's face when I cannot be greeted by his voice. Would you like to hear what they say?

" 'Captain Fremont has gone upon his third expedition, determined upon a complete military and scientific exploration of all the vast unknown region between the Rocky Mountains and the Pacific Ocean, and between the Oregon River and the Gulf of California. This expedition is expected to continue nearly two years, and its successful result is looked to with the highest degree of interest by all the friends of science in America and Europe. His life is a pattern and his success an encouragement to young men of America who aspire to honorable distinction by their own meritorious exertions.' "

She hardly had had time to adjust herself to his absence when Secretary of State James Buchanan dropped in unannounced, gratefully accepted her invitation to a cup of tea, and asked if he might speak to her privately. She led him to the library, closed the door behind them. James Buchanan had come to Washington to enter the House at the same time that Tom Benton had arrived to enter the Senate; thus Jessie had known him all her life. He was a good-looking man with an open face, almost round eyes, and what women thought an amorous mouth. He was a lonely man who had endured tragedy in his youth: the girl to whom he was devoted with the single-purposeness of his nature had become angry with him over a bit of gossip. Without giving him a chance to explain, she had terminated their engagement and boarded a train to visit some relatives in New York. She died while en route; he never was able to learn whether it had been a natural death, an accident, or suicide: nor had he ever ceased reproaching himself for not having prevented her from leaving. After the loss of his first love he had never loved again or married, though many women had tried to invade his bachelorhood.

James Buchanan never pretended to be brilliant, but he was conscientious and painstaking. A man of quiet charm who had developed an ironclad system of logic from his studies of the law, he had been respected as minister to Russia, his constituents in Pennsylvania had declared him to be a valuable senator. He lived an impeccable private life, taking pleasure from work well done; he was a man who loathed force, crudity, irregularity. If some people thought him too meticulous, too encased in an unassailable shell of formal manners, to spinsterish, these qualifications had enabled him for some twenty-five years to render valuable service to his state and his country.

Jessie noticed a curious thing about him: the front half of his full underlip, the exposed half, was always dry, apparently covered by a fine white powder. Anyone looking at him would think him to be a dry and powdery man. Yet when he opened his mouth to speak, the inner half of his lip was revealed to be red and moist and alive. This was the paradox of James Buchanan: inwardly he lived a rich intellectual and spiritual life; the side which he exposed to public view he allowed to appear dry and dead.

While she had been ruminating about his life and career, he had begun to speak.

". . . difficult to understand how a woman of her family background and breeding . . . I refused to believe it for some time until I felt obliged to make a test. There can be no doubt of it, Mrs. Greenhow is a spy, in the pay of the British government."

If the accusation had not come from the secretary of state himself, Jessie would have refused to believe it.

"Mrs. Greenhow a spy! Why, her family is one of the best in Washington!"

"We must spend our time not in trying to understand the lady's motives, but in undoing the harm she has accomplished. Do I remember rightly that your Spanish is good?"

"Quite good. Father brought me up with the language."

Secretary Buchanan placed his tongue tentatively on the dry half of his lip, moistening the white powder before speaking.

"You know how delicate our situation is with Mexico. I have private and confidential reports coming in every day. I never learned to read Spanish, and since the revelation about Mrs. Greenhow, I feel that I dare not trust anyone in my own office. Would you translate these confidential reports for me? Would you survey the Spanish newspapers and magazines and write me a report every few days on the tone and temper of the Mexican press?"

"Mr. Buchanan, I thank you with all my heart for this opportunity, and you may be sure that I will do a good job."

"Of that I am certain, Miss Jessie. You realize, of course, no part of the information you gather from the confidential reports may be passed on to your father. As secretary of state I am an officer of the executive branch of the government, while your father, as the chairman of the Senate Military Affairs Committee, is an officer of the legislative branch. While there can be no conflict between us over the national interest, there is sometimes a struggle between the executive and the legislative over the powers of government."

"I understand, Mr. Secretary. No word of my information will reach Senator Benton."

"Good! And now the last stricture: your husband is en route to the Pacific coast. There are certain people in our government who would be willing to encourage him to use force in taking California. To this attitude I am unalterably opposed. I shall have to ask that no part of your information be transmitted to Captain Fremont. I would be violating the function of my office if he were to secure advance and confidential information which might precipitate him into a conflict with the Mexicans."

"You will see, Mr. Secretary, that all American women are not irresponsible."

Secretary Buchanan rose, bowed stiffly.

"Thank you for the cup of tea, Miss Jessie. A page will bring you a pouch early tomorrow morning. Here is a key to the lock; never allow anyone in the room while you are working, and never leave the room without returning the papers to the pouch."

"Very good, sir."

He shook her hand, then bade her good day.

14

In her first batch of confidential papers from Mexico, Jessie learned that the Mexican government was negotiating with Great Britain to intercede in the event of hostilities with the United States. The trouble had arisen over Texas: when the United States annexed Texas, the Mexican government broke off diplomatic relations. When Texas accepted the American offer of annexation, Mexico reorganized its army. President Polk was preparing to send Joseph Slidell to Mexico City as minister, with an offer of forty million dollars for the peaceful purchase of Texas, when news of Mexico's war preparations flooded Washington. Since the United States and England still were quarreling over the Oregon territory, Jessie concluded from the dispatches that in the event of a war between England and the United States over Oregon, England would seize California with her Navy, having made an advance agreement with Mexico to do so.

When she went to Secretary Buchanan's office the next day to show him her synopsis of the news, he was distressed. He said:

"Mexico wants to go to war over Texas; England seems to want to go to war over Oregon; the United States seems to want to go to war over California. President Polk fears that the British will accept no compromise on the Oregon boundary, but I am convinced that they will. I am also convinced that Mexico will accept a cash settlement for Texas and California, since they have no legitimate use for them. When our minister goes to Mexico City, I am going to suggest that he offer twenty-five million dollars for California and New Mexico."

"Yes, Mr. Secretary, but the tone of the Mexican press indicates that they would not consider any price a fair one because they feel they are being forced to sell. Unless there is a sharp change of attitude, our minister may not even be received."

"Miss Jessie, I am determined to avert war with both England and Mexico; if either war comes about, I shall feel that I have failed in my office."

She rose, assured him that she would keep the information flowing to him, and returned home.

Her days were so crammed with duties and obligations that she found little time for pining. In addition to her work for Secretary Buchanan and her father, she managed the household and played hostess for unceasing dinner parties: one for Sam Houston, who had served under her father in the War of 1812, and who had just arrived in Washington as the first senator from Texas; one for Commander Robert S. Stockton of the United States warship *Princeton,* who was about to leave for California and would unquestionably see Captain Fremont when he got there; one for Secretary of the Navy George Bancroft, a dynamo of energy and a lion of courage, handsome, rugged-faced, virile and militant, young but already famous for his histories of the United States, the leader of the forces in Washington who were determined that all the Southwest, including California, must become American, even if it meant a bloody war with Mexico; one for John L. Stevens, author of the travel books on Arabia and Palestine which Jessie had read as a child; her own dinner party in honor of Samuel Morse, who at long last had been given a small appropriation by Congress, and from a Senate room had sent a message to Baltimore on the first thirty miles of telegraph line.

Her deepest gratification of the passing weeks was watching Eliza fall in love. She had been alarmed over her twenty-three-year-old sister, for it seemed that Eliza would never care to marry. Jessie watched her sister and William Carey Jones together at the Benton dinner table; they took each other casually, without personal interest. When the young lawyer asked Tom Benton's permission to marry Eliza, Jessie understood that that had been their manner of falling in love.

One afternoon at the beginning of November, Secretary of the Navy George Bancroft sent a message asking if he might come to tea. Jessie put on a wide-skirted silk dress that made her look rather like a petunia blossom. When George Bancroft arrived she led him to her sitting room, which was filled with the pleasant fragrances of potted rose geraniums, burning sassafras wood, Chinese tea and spice cake.

George Bancroft was as informal a man as James Buchanan was meticulous. He refused her invitation to a deep lounge chair, taking instead a hard seat, whirled it around so that he was sitting on it backwards, his elbows resting on the back while he looked at her over his own folded arms and half-clenched fists, studying her with magnificently alert wide-set blue eyes. He did not speak for several moments. Jessie took in the black hair combed back straight over his head, the sideburns chopped off toward the top of his ears, the long bony, curved, unbeautiful nose with hollows just above the nostrils; his uneven but rugged and eloquent mouth: a rough-hewn face, muscular, powerful, direct, the face of a man with a driving will and intellect.

She poured him a cup of tea, then lay back in her chaise against a nest of lace pillows, tired from the long day of work but curious about what he might want of her.

"You have been doing some translating for Secretary Buchanan," he said, after downing three slices of spice cake. "I only tell you that I know because it means we can go forward from this moment without discussing the background of the Mexican situation."

"Very well, Mr. Secretary."

"Miss Jessie, the British think they are going to capture California with their warships. They're mistaken; they can capture the ports, but they can't move those ships into the interior."

"Yes," agreed Jessie, not knowing what he was leading up to.

"But what holds true for the British warships holds equally true for ours: warships cannot take possession of a country. We need soldiers in California."

This time Jessie did not even bother to answer yes. She just sat up a little straighter on her chaise, waiting for Bancroft to declare himself.

"From the advice I have from Consul Larkin at Monterey and certain commanders of our ships that have put in at Monterey and San Francisco, I am certain that we would not need a large force to take California. But we are faced with a dilemma, Miss Jessie: we cannot send troops into the territory of a country with whom we are not at war. And if we don't send in troops before they declare war, we are going to lose California."

Again she did not interrupt, but rather said to herself: He knows as well as I do that Captain Fremont will soon be on the Pacific coast. He is an army officer. He has sixty well-armed men with him, men who are unquestionably willing and ready to fight.

"Things are touch and go, Miss Jessie. President Polk is right in saying that we cannot steal into another man's orchard, but if the fruit is ripe and is about to fall to the ground, where it will either be stolen or rot, why is it unethical to be standing under the bough with our hands open?"

"It is only unethical if all opportunism is unethical."

"Which is not necessarily true. As you know, I am a historian; I have watched the progress of our nation as it has unfolded year by year. I have always been in agreement with your father that this country must and shall extend to the Pacific Ocean. It would be criminal stupidity on our part to allow California and the Southwest to fall into the hands of a European nation, or even to lie dead and unused by Mexico. That is against our national character; that is against our national interests; and I am passionately convinced that it is against the entire flow of history. Do you agree with me?"

"I would not be Senator Benton's daughter if I did not," said Jessie.

"Good," exclaimed Secretary Bancroft, "then we understand each other."

"Yes," she replied, not knowing what it was that she was supposed to understand. The secretary of the navy had not come to her house to discuss a historical theory. Bancroft seemed to be waiting for her to make the next move. Seeing that she was not going to say anything, he began again, this time in a more tentative tone of voice.

"At first I thought President Polk was in error in not taking a more militant stand in California, for he is as eager to have California as I am, but as president of a peace-loving country his hands are tied. I have sent several of our ships of war to lie off Mexico and California ports to be on hand if anything happens, but beyond that point there is nothing I myself can do; as a Cabinet officer my hands too are tied."

Knitting her brows Jessie thought, He is trying to lead me to a conclusion without involving himself in it.

"Without official authorization," he continued, "nothing can be done in California." He was talking fast now. "That is, unless unofficial action is taken for which the government cannot be held responsible. If, for example, we had someone in California who could act swiftly and decisively at the right moment, Mexico would have no opportunity to call for British protection, and England could not take possession. What we desperately need, Mrs. Fremont, is what we will call for the moment an irresponsible man, someone whom we can honestly repudiate if things do not turn out well."

"I see your dilemma," said Jessie softly, and to herself, even more softly, she said, And I also see mine. He has just called me Mrs. Fremont for the first time; Mrs. Fremont has a husband by the name of Captain Fremont who at this very moment must be dropping down the Sierras into the Sacramento Valley with a well-trained party. Captain Fremont is an unofficial representative of the United States, not of the government or the Army, but of the scientific Topographical Corps. His rank and his reputation will win him support in California if he should need it, and yet as an "unofficial" of the government he could readily be repudiated.

Aloud she said: "A few moments ago you said to me, 'We understand each other.' I answered yes, but frankly I did not. Now I think I do. What is it precisely that you would like me to do?"

George Bancroft jumped up from his chair and began striding energetically about the room, picking up objects and laying them down, moving the lighter pieces of furniture around, raising the Venetian blinds, then lowering them again. Watching him, half amused, half frightened, Jessie poured herself a cup of tea and thought, I have put my finger on a sore spot. He can't tell me what he wants me to do. He has reached the climax of this scene and he quite frankly does not know where to go from here. But I can outsit him even if he wrecks the whole room.

After a few moments he came back to her chaise, dropped down beside her with a hard thud.

"Let me see if I can explain to you the kind of man we need in California: he must be willing to act on his own initiative, without orders. He must be willing to be an opportunist; what the outside world might call an adventurer. He must be hotheaded, impulsive, quick to action. He must be a man who is not afraid to face the consequences of rashness, failure and international censure."

"In other words," murmured Jessie, "he must have a fast trigger finger and a stout heart."

"Ah, Mrs. Fremont, a far stouter heart than you will be able to imagine. I am willing to take the responsibility of causing a war, but I will take that responsibility as secretary of the navy. The man who starts the war with Mexico in California, or seizes that country without a war, can expect no backing and no authorization. We would have to have his resignation in our pocket, dated considerably prior to any conceivable action, so that we could publish it if we thought it expedient to do so. If it became necessary for the United States government to save face, he would be thoroughly excoriated. The press would tear his reputation to shreds. He would become an entirely discredited man. If he were a naval officer, I as secretary of the navy would be obliged to call for his court-martial. He might never again be trusted, given a responsible position: his life and career could easily be smashed."

"That also I can understand," said Jessie slowly.

"It is tragic that we have no such man in California. Yet even if we had I could send him no written orders or authorization, nor could anyone else in the government. If at some future date he were to find it necessary to vindicate himself and were to try to present evidence, such as, let us say, this conversation, I would be obliged to deny that it ever took place. For obviously it never did take place, Mrs. Fremont; I have just come here to talk with you and unburden my mind."

He smiled warmly.

"And now I must bid you good night. It was extremely good of you to listen to my long harangue. Frankly, I have been quite jealous of Secretary Buchanan, and now I feel that in some small measure I have evened the score. Speaking of Secretary Buchanan, it is hardly necessary for me to tell you that he would agree with nothing I have intimated this evening. The secretary of state is a meticulous man, as indeed the secretary of state ought to be. The secretary of the navy is a man of action, even though he has been a historian; and a man of action is what the secretary of the navy needs to be. Good night, Mrs. Fremont; please don't trouble to take me down."

For several hours Jessie lay on the chaise dissecting Secretary Bancroft's statement of the problem. Though he had never once mentioned Captain Fremont's name, it was clear he had been talking about her husband all the time; there was no other army officer within two thousand miles of California, and no naval officer could possibly act without implicating his government. Secretary Bancroft wanted Captain Fremont to seize California for the United States when the proper moment arose; but he would give him no authorization, he would refuse to stand by him if the seizure miscarried; he might find it necessary to deny that any such plan for Captain Fremont had ever entered his mind. His description of the type of man needed in California, while not altogether complimentary, she had to admit was a fairly accurate description of her husband: impulsive, quick to action—like herself, something of an adventurer, more mindful of today's job than tomorrow's consequences.

Would Captain Fremont take this terrible risk? Would he put his career and future in danger? Would he stand the chance of having his government declare him an unscrupulous adventurer, cashier him from the service? Would he gamble his years of scientific training, his skill as an explorer and topographer, on one turn of the wheel?

Almost as important, Jessie knew, was the question of whether she could allow him to face these hazards. What would happen to him if he were to be retired from the Army in disgrace, with no one to back him or stand by him, his former work thrown into deep shadow? What would happen to the character and spirit and the pride of John Fremont if all the world thought him a disreputable man, one whom his government had been forced to repudiate? Could he stand up under such a blow? Could he carry such a burden, this man who had a canker of uncertainty already eating at his vitals, who had to make himself greater than all men in order to feel the equal of the least of them? Would not such a fate destroy him? Could he go through life content to know that he had done a service for his government, a service to which he had been directed, though only his president, his secretary of the navy, and his wife knew that he had been acting under orders?

Her heart beat wildly. What would happen to their life together, to their love, their marriage?

She was not able to answer for herself how well her husband could endure the consequences of failure, but she knew for a certainty that nothing could prevent him from taking the gamble. He was not afraid of the word adventurer; the thought of failure would never enter his mind; when the time came to seize California, he would lead his men to victory and take over the conquered state.

He would be willing to take the risk. She too was not only willing, but eager. History was on the march, and she wanted John to play an important role. Here was his chance; more accurately, since she was ambitious for him, here was their chance.

15

Jessie wondered what she was supposed to do. What action had Secretary Bancroft meant for her to take?

She was not left long in doubt. The following morning Marine Lieutenant Archibald H. Gillespie came to the Benton home to announce that he was leaving for California on the warship *Cyane*. He was carrying dispatches from the president, the State Department, and the secretary of the navy. He understood that Captain Fremont would be in or near Monterey about the time he would reach the Pacific coast. Would Mrs. Fremont care to send a letter to Captain Fremont in his charge? He could assure her it would be delivered safely.

She sought out her father and quickly gave him the gist of what had happened, without repeating Secretary Bancroft's words. Did he think Captain Fremont justified in using force against the Mexican Army and the Californios? Was he convinced this action would be in the best interests of the United States? Was it a gamble she could advise her husband to take? She waited impatiently while Tom turned his thoughts over. When he finally spoke it was in a tone from which he had consciously removed all emotion.

"Our people have moved from the Atlantic coast westward, ever westward," he said. "The movement will grow a hundred times stronger and swifter in the next few years because of Captain Fremont's expeditions, reports and maps. There is nothing that can stop this flood of immigration to new and rich and free lands. Our people will overrun them in the next few years, and what happened in Texas is certain to happen all over the West, spontaneously, without any help or even any encouragement from our government."

"That's an interesting generality, Father," she insisted.

"My dear," said Senator Benton softly, "I am eager to instruct Captain Fremont to go ahead with the conquest of California. But I must also protect you. You understand what this entails, perhaps another year of separation . . ."

"I understand," she replied firmly.

She must give John the signal for action. Everything he had said to her before he left indicated that he was willing to take these risks; they had agreed that the main purpose of the expedition was for him to be on hand in the event of war so that he and his party could take over California. They had even arranged a code for confidential communication. There could be no reason for him to have changed his mind.

She seated herself at her desk, fondled the long quill of her pen, smoothed her hand over the cool surface of the foolscap. For whom was she doing this? For John, because it was what he most wanted to do regardless of the risk involved? For Tom, because it would fulfill his lifetime ambition? For herself, because she was ambitious as a woman and wanted important things to come to her through her husband: power, prestige, prominence?

It was impossible to separate their interests, but as John's dark face and eager eyes glowed back from the paper before her, she knew that she would be doing it for her husband, who would never cease to reproach her if she failed to send him the word; for her husband, whom she must encourage to seize every important opportunity. As a woman in love she could only urge him to come home; he had done the work that had been assigned to him; he could return to make his maps, write the third report which would open the highway to California. But as his wife she would not be faithful to their marriage if she did anything less than help him achieve the full potential of his opportunity.

As always when she had her full strength, the wife dominated the woman in her. The marriage was more important than her momentary happiness.

She wrote most of the night, telling her husband stories of Lily and of the family, of Eliza's coming marriage, of the dinner parties and the politics that had been discussed, all the things that a husband who has been away from home for half a year wants to hear. She spoke of her love for him and how much she missed him, how resolutely she was carrying on in the full confidence that his work would be well done.

Using their code of reference to things in their past, she gave him a picture of the official status of American and Mexican relations, picking her way carefully among the bones of fact, for her original promise to Secretary Buchanan had been that she would reveal nothing of a confidential nature which might impel her husband to action. Then she told him that when the time came he must act, that he must not feel limited by lack of official authorization. She gave no explanation for this sentiment, any more than she had given it two years before when she had sent with DeRosier the order, "Do not delay another day. Trust me, and start at once." She knew that her husband's answer would be the equivalent of, "I trust, and go."

Lieutenant Gillespie came for the letter early the next morning, assured her that he would tell Captain Fremont how well the family appeared. She watched him until he turned the corner of C Street and disappeared up Pennsylvania Avenue; then she knew the die was cast, that before many months Captain Fremont would be involved in action of far-reaching consequences.

Christmas passed quietly; she had decorated a tree in the upstairs sitting room for Lily. When there was an occasional hour of fatigue or shapeless anxiety she would peer into the mirror to see if her King George's Mark had returned, but could find no trace of it, and so she knew that her mind was at peace.

When news reached her it was sudden and dynamic. Picking up the morning edition of the *Union*, she learned that Captain Fremont had set himself up against the Mexican Army. The Mexicans had been suspicious of him and his party of sixty men, but they had given him temporary permission to remain in California. Toward the end of February Captain Fremont had broken camp and moved, not back to Oregon and American territory as he had promised, but south, deeper into Mexican country. Within a couple of days a Mexican cavalry officer had dashed into Captain Fremont's camp with a dispatch from General Castro ordering the party out of California immediately, assuring them if they did not depart they would be arrested and forcibly expelled by the Mexican Army.

Captain Fremont had known that the Mexicans were within their legal rights, that actually he was an intruder on their soil. However, he had spent several months making friends with the Americans in California and sizing up the strength of the Mexican arms. He had come to the conclusion that if he accepted General Castro's order and departed hastily under the threat of expulsion, he would forfeit the respect and confidence of the Americans in California, all of whom would also have lost caste by his retreat.

Captain Fremont had decided that the historic moment had arrived. He moved his party to a natural fort on top of a peak overlooking the Santa Clara Valley; here he cut a tall slender tree and raised the first American flag in California. For three days he and his men had stood ready to defend their fort and their dignity. In the *Union* Jessie read her husband's letter to Consul Larkin:

From the heights where we are encamped, Hawk's Peak, we can see with the glass, troops mustering at St. John's. I would write you at length if I did not fear my letter would be intercepted. We have in no wise done wrong to any of the people, and if we are hemmed in and assaulted, we will die every man of us under the flag of his country.

She began to feel nervous spasms in her stomach as she read that toward evening of the second day a body of Mexican cavalry had come within a few hundred yards of the fort, that the Americans had waited in the thicket with their fingers on their triggers, ready to fire the first shots of the Mexican war. However, the Mexican cavalry had not attacked. At the end of the third day, convinced that they never would attack and confident that he had established his position and authority among the American settlers, Captain Fremont had withdrawn his party and moved slowly into Oregon.

The next morning when she went to Secretary Buchanan's office she found him looking harassed and pale.

"We should never have allowed Captain Fremont to go to the Pacific coast at such a delicate time," he said. "He has committed what amounts to a declaration of war on Mexico. He acted outside the pale of all legal and international rights. If his conduct starts a war with Mexico, he will have to take the full responsibility for it; he had no orders, no authorization . . . he has put the State Department in an embarrassing and painful position."

Jessie shriveled. All she could whisper faintly was, "Isn't it true that President Polk has ordered General Zachary Taylor into the disputed territory around Texas, that he is now only a few miles from the Rio Grande?"

"Yes, but . . ."

"I myself translated the dispatch for you which said that the Mexicans would consider this a declaration of war. The president's action is far more likely to begin the war with Mexico than Captain Fremont's resistance in California to what he called an insulting order."

"It is not Captain Fremont's prerogative to decide when the United States has been insulted. That is the privilege of the State Department!" He stopped abruptly, his round, doll-like eyes softened. "I am sorry, my dear Jessie: I did not mean to punish you for your husband's conduct; I know you are not responsible for what he does three thousand miles away. I think you will forgive me when I tell you that I am distraught, on the verge of resigning. I see war coming; everyone around me is doing his best to force this war on Mexico when I know it is a detestable thing to do and will create the first black blotch on American history. Thank you for coming. I shall communicate with you in a few days."

She walked over to Secretary Bancroft's office. Here she found an entirely different atmosphere, for Secretary Bancroft was delighted with the progress of events.

"Yes, yes, I read the *Union* article," he exclaimed. "I am glad Captain Fremont stood up to them. It was premature, it was indiscreet, and I assure you that I would not have had the courage to behave as he did without governmental orders in my pocket. Your husband is an impulsive man, Mrs. Fremont, perhaps even a little too impulsive; but it is a quality for which I greatly admire him. His three-day rebellion will teach the Mexicans that we are not in a docile frame of mind."

"Do you think that Captain Fremont's action will cause a war?"

"No, the war will start over Texas, and I am the one who must take the responsibility for that. If you want to know what the administration thinks about the California episode, I have just been informed that President Polk has promoted your husband to the rank of lieutenant colonel."

News from the West began to reach her more frequently. She watched the conquest of California unfold day by day, fitting the pieces of the story together from the American newspapers, the Mexican newspapers, the confidential dispatches to Secretary Buchanan, and the information which came to Senator Benton as chairman of the Military Affairs Committee. Because she had access to these combined sources of information, and because she saw much of this material before anyone else, she knew that she was keeping closer to the conflict in California than anyone east of the Sierras. This gave her a sense of being by her husband's side day by day.

Encouraged by Colonel Fremont, who was working behind the scenes, on June 14, 1846, the Americans in California staged the Bear Flag uprising and declared California a republic. When the settlers had their first battle with the Mexicans at San Raphael, Colonel Fremont stepped into command, but not before he had written out his resignation from the Army and dispatched it to Senator Benton to be published in the event his action embarrassed the government. He then captured San Francisco on July 4, formed the California Battalion of some three hundred men and, upon learning that war with Mexico had been declared some two months before, that fighting was going on in Texas and Mexico, seized all of central California. On July 10 Commodore Sloat of the United States Navy occupied Monterey, and Colonel Fremont moved his battalion in. Commodore Stockton, replacing the irresolute Commodore Sloat, swore Lieutenant Colonel Fremont and his battalion into the Navy and transported them to San Diego in the *Cyane*. From San Diego Colonel Fremont moved his men north toward Los Angeles, where a Mexican division was reported to be encamped, and rejoined Commodore Stockton near San Pedro. On August 13 they occupied Los Angeles without firing a shot or without encountering the Mexican Army. Stockton sent Colonel Fremont north to recruit another battalion and to command northern California. During his absence the Mexican Army defeated the small American garrison and recaptured Los Angeles.

There were several uneasy weeks while the Americans continued to be defeated in southern California, but Jessie was encouraged by the fact that John had been able to organize a strong army which was marching south, and that their old friend Colonel, now Brigadier General, Stephen Watts Kearny had left Santa Fe with three hundred volunteers, en route for southern California. By January 9, 1847, the Americans had once again taken Los Angeles. Colonel Fremont accepted the surrender of the Mexican general Pico, gave him generous terms, and the war was over in California.

Now assured of her husband's safety, Jessie was further delighted to learn that Commodore Stockton had named Colonel Fremont the first civil governor of California. Reports began to come through in the press of the generosity and efficiency of his rule, and everywhere people spoke with enthusiasm of the young colonel who was doing such a good job. From the notes and drawings which John had sent east after reaching California, cartographer Preuss had drawn a superb map of the comparatively safe route to California which he had just established. When Senator Benton presented the map to the Senate, he delivered a eulogy on Colonel Fremont which made Jessie, sitting in her accustomed seat in the gallery, swell with pride.

In the middle of February, some twenty-one months after John had left Washington, she wrote a letter to her cousin Sarah Brant. In it she tried to explain the innumerable devices, fill-ins and fortitudes which she had used to somehow pass the time, explaining also the sense of being only fractionally alive when one cannot hear the voice of a loved one, touch his hand, see a look of understanding flash into his eyes. She ended on a cheerful note which looked toward the future:

I feel that the honor to Colonel Fremont is but honor due for the arduous labors he has performed and for his conspicuous bravery, and it is little enough reward for his incalculable scientific contributions to his country. It is difficult, indeed, dear cousin, for me to express my own happiness. Its warmth and light have driven all the chill and dark foreboding from my heart. My happiness gives me renewed strength and patience.

Exactly a week later, when she was working at her desk in her sitting room, Josheem brought in a page from the State Department with a packet of Spanish letters.

"If you will return at five this afternoon," she told the page, "I will have the material ready for you."

She was skimming a long letter from Monterey which dealt largely with land grants when she suddenly sat bolt upright in her chair. The letter told of a quarrel which had arisen between Commodore Stockton of the Navy and General Kearny of the Army over the command and control of California. The letter ended with a sentence which the writer included as of only mild interest:

"Colonel Fremont has been removed as commandant of California."

16

She waited with impatience until Senator Benton returned at four o'clock. She expected that when she read the translation to him he would be as dumbfounded as she had been. Instead she saw her father flush, his eyes become watery. In a terrifying moment she thought, He knows about this; then it must be worse than it appears in this dispatch.

After a moment he said, "I heard of it in St. Louis when I was there last month."

"Why didn't you tell me?"

"I had hoped the trouble would blow over, Jessie. I had hoped that it was just a passing quarrel between General Kearny and Commodore Stockton."

"Has it blown over?"

"No."

She began pacing the room nervously.

"But what could possibly have happened? According to the reports John was doing a good job as governor. Why did they suddenly become dissatisfied?"

"It was not a question of his performance; your husband got himself caught in a contest between the Army and Navy for authority over California. Commodore Stockton had orders to take and hold California and to set up a civil administration. When the Mexicans surrendered, Commodore Stockton appointed Colonel Fremont as the governor. But General Kearny also had orders from Washington to assume the governorship of California, should he conquer and take possession of the country."

"But wouldn't Commodore Stockton's orders be considered the valid ones, since the fighting was practically over by the time General Kearny got there?"

"Kearny fought one battle, a battle which he lost, by the way. However, the problem revolves about the question of who had the latest orders from Washington, Kearny or Stockton."

"Who did?"

"We're not certain yet. In any event, General Kearny demanded that Colonel Fremont acknowledge him to be the commander in chief of California. John and his men were still serving under Stockton as part of the Navy, and so he declined to acknowledge Kearny's authority. Kearny then moved his headquarters to Monterey, where he set up a civil government and declared Colonel Fremont to be deposed as governor, with no further authority."

"Why can't President Polk put an end to this squabble?" she asked with a heavy heart. "The Army and Navy belong to the same government, don't they?"

Once again her father's manner was evasive. He had been honest with his daughter for so many years that he found the transition difficult.

"I have already spoken to the president."

"Yes?"

"He wants the men in California to settle this dispute among themselves."

"Do you think they will?"

"There is certainly nothing in the argument that can't be settled."

Her peace shattered, Jessie impatiently edged through the weeks that followed, waiting for some word of how her husband was faring in the conflict. Her only momentary diversion was Eliza's marriage; Eliza had been so helpful during her own troubled courtship that she was happy to be able to stage a beautiful wedding for her older sister in the drawing room of the Benton home. Eliza wanted the affair to be a quiet one, but before the imperative lists were completed Jessie saw that she must of necessity invite some two hundred people. The dinner which followed the ceremony was elaborate, for Jessie tried to duplicate for her sister the magnificent wedding dinner served at Cherry Grove. The preparations, the excitement, the visits to the dressmaker, the planning of the ceremony and dinner occupied her time for almost three weeks; she was glad to be so exhausted by the end of the day that she could fall into a troubled sleep.

She saw her sister and new brother-in-law off for a trip to New York, then bade good-by to her father, who was going to St. Louis on political business. At the front door he said to her:

"Be of good courage, and take care of your health."

"I'll do my best, Father, but it is this groping in the dark that has upset me. If only I could know what is going on out there . . ."

Thomas Benton had a saying that good news travels on the swiftest horse, but bad news rides the lightning. Jessie had not long to wait before the almost comfortable silence surrounding the events in California was split open. Her cousin Sarah sent her an anonymous letter published in the St. Louis *Republican* which mercilessly flayed Colonel Fremont for the part he had played in the conquest of California, challenged his motives, his character and his conduct, accused him of dictatorial methods, willful insubordination, usurpation of authority, and conduct detrimental to the welfare of the Army.

This then was what George Bancroft had intimated; the Army was in process of disavowing Colonel Fremont! John had waged war successfully and conquered central California . . . but without authorization.

The following day a similar clipping arrived from a friend who had cut it from the New York *Courier and Enquirer*. When practically the identical article arrived from the New Orleans *Picayune*, it became obvious to her that the indictments all had been written by the same hand. She now knew that the quarrel had not been settled in California, that affairs were growing worse. She sat down to write a letter to her father telling him what was contained in the articles, when Maylee knocked sharply on her sitting-room door and said:

"A packet just come from the colonel, Miss Jessie."

Without rising, she held out her hand for the letter, tore it open and was plunged into the reading before Maylee could close the door behind her. An enclosed dispatch to President Polk fell to the floor while she quickly scanned the opening paragraphs of affection, her eyes racing ahead to get to John's statement of his trouble, his assurance that everything was working out well. He warned her to be prepared for a severe attack in the eastern papers, for Lieutenant Emory, General Kearny's dispatch bearer to Washington, had left for the capital, and it was being rumored in California that he had been sent to undermine John's position.

She sat reading his description of how California had been in American hands before General Kearny arrived on the scene; during the final battles with the Mexicans, General Kearny had acknowledged that Commodore Stockton was commander of all American forces in California. However,

after John had signed the peace treaty with General Pico at Cahuenga
Rancho, and Commodore Stockton had set him up as governor of California,
General Kearny had established his own headquarters on the Plaza in Los
Angeles, proclaimed himself commander of all forces in California, ordered
both Commodore Stockton and John to step down, to issue no more orders
or appointments without his sanction. Commodore Stockton refused to accept General Kearny's authority; John also refused to be deposed. He had
gone to General Kearny's headquarters the next morning to tell him that
until the Army and Navy had adjusted their difficulties in California, and
the supreme authority had been established by word from Washington, he
would take his orders from Commodore Stockton and retain his position as
governor of California. The scene had been a bitter and violent one. General
Kearny had then moved his troops to Monterey. John was still governor in
southern California, but there was no one to sustain his authority.

She did not close her eyes all night, but lay awake in the candlelight
reading and rereading the letter from John, almost memorizing the words
of love. In her mind she formulated the best method of approach to President
Polk; perhaps from him she could get a written authorization for Colonel
Fremont to remain as governor of California.

Visitors were not permitted at the White House until one o'clock, so she
had ample time in which to make the most meticulous toilet. She donned a
green cashmere gown, spent a long while brushing her hair, and on top of it,
at a saucy angle, she perked a green corded hat.

President Polk received her promptly at one o'clock with assurances of his
pleasure in seeing her. He broke the seal on Colonel Fremont's dispatch
and read it quickly. As Jessie saw him lift his eyes from the last word, she
asked with a rush of emotion:

"Mr. President, doesn't Colonel Fremont's course seem reasonable under
the circumstances?"

There was no doubt in her mind that he would reply at once, "Entirely
reasonable, Mrs. Fremont; I shall send a dispatch which will clear up the
situation and leave Colonel Fremont in command as civil governor."

But no word came from President Polk. He dropped into a chair, glanced
at the letter again and then looked up at her with a noncommittal expression.

"The misunderstanding may be settled by now, Miss Jessie. In that case,
there would be no need for any of us to take sides."

She saw that the President had terminated the interview. A feeling of
frustration arose, then a calm seized her.

"Mr. President, I do not expect you to side against General Kearny. I
only beg you to assure me that Colonel Fremont will not be victimized by
the quarrel between the Army and Navy. General Kearny is threatening to
relieve him of command of his California Battalion."

"Miss Jessie, I think we can do that much to put your mind at ease,"
replied the president, slowly. "I will send a dispatch giving Colonel Fremont

the right to remain on duty in California or to join his original regiment of mounted rifles in Mexico if he prefers."

"Thank you, Mr. President. That is the fair and equitable thing to do."

President Polk smiled slightly at the thought of Jessie assuring the President of the United States that he was doing the fair and equitable thing. He then shook her hand, sent his compliments to her father and walked with her to the door of the reception room.

17

There was little she could do now but sit back and wait. A few days later her father returned from St. Louis and asked her to take a walk with him along the Potomac.

"I am sorry that I must be the one to break this to you, Jessie, yet as your father I suppose it is best. Things in California have come to a most unfortunate pass."

Jessie stopped. She turned to confront her father, who loomed big before her. Even in her anxiety she had time to notice how old he was looking: his thinning hair was completely silver, his eyes had a tired and commiserating expression, the flesh wrinkles at the bridge of his nose seemed tightly lined.

"General Kearny ordered John to bring his archives from Los Angeles to Monterey. Colonel Fremont took a wild horseback ride up to Monterey where a most unfortunate scene took place. General Kearny revealed the latest order giving him command, and Colonel Fremont went back to Los Angeles, followed by several of Kearny's officers, all of them antagonistic to your husband. There were quarrels and recriminations until finally . . ."

"Yes?"

One corner of Tom Benton's mouth fell loose, as it always did when he labored under heavy personal emotion.

"Colonel Fremont has been relieved of his command. He was ordered back to Washington."

A thin smile came over her tired face.

"Then he is coming home! At least I shall see him again. We will be able to work this out together, all of us."

Her father took her arm and began walking along the riverbank. Jessie tried to watch his eyes, but he was turned so she could not see him too closely.

". . . you don't understand, my dear: Colonel Fremont . . . is coming back to Washington . . . under arrest."

Jessie got home as quickly as possible, refused dinner and went straight to bed, lying as still and lifeless as a corpse. John coming home under arrest! After all his accomplishments, after all the magnificent promise for the future, he was being dragged across the continent like a prisoner, in disgrace!

George Bancroft had intimated that if the capture of California were successful, anything her husband might have been required to do would be forgotten. California was in American hands, war had been waged officially with Mexico, and there had been no international scandal. Then why were they visiting upon him the punishment which had been promised only if he failed and embarrassed his government?

She began to thrash about in the bed, turning, twisting, matching with her movements the turnings and twistings of her mind as she sought some way out of the hopeless trap. Why had John quarreled with General Kearny? Was it because he had started the war in California without authorization? Or was there something more personal involved? She pulled the covers up over her head and burst into weeping, giving vent to all of the fears and misgivings of the past months, months during which she had maintained her self-control with an iron discipline.

Suddenly she found herself picked up, the blanket over her head, and miraculously was sitting on her father's lap.

"Here, drink this," he said. "It is warm milk and rum. Do you know what time it is, child? Two in the morning. I went down into the kitchen and warmed the milk; drink this now. It will put you to sleep."

"And may I ask what you were doing until two in the morning?"

"You may ask. I was writing a stiff letter to President Polk, summarizing the case and demanding an investigation. I assure you there is nothing to worry about, Jessie. We will bring all the facts to the light, and when we have done so, Colonel Fremont will be vindicated."

"Thank you, Father. This warm milk and rum has made me drowsy. I think I can fall asleep now."

She spent the intervening weeks, before John could reach Washington, in a state of suspension, giving in neither to despair nor sanguinary hope. She knew that she and her husband faced a difficult time. She knew that they could not come out of the contest unscathed. She knew that the coming months would demand the most of their faith in themselves and their loyalty to each other.

At the end of August the long vigil was ended. She was sitting in the bow of the drawing-room windows watching out over C Street when she saw a carriage turn Pennsylvania Avenue on two wheels and dash up to the Benton home. Out sprang a young man in a faded blue army uniform. He turned and spoke to the driver about his luggage, giving Jessie time to run through the hall, fling open the door, and welcome home her husband after two years and three months of absence. Unashamedly in the open doorway she clung to him, wet his beard with her tears, kissing him many, many times.

But even at this first numb moment of joy she perceived that her husband was not responding. She took his hand and led him to the drawing room, then stood gazing at him. Her heart sank: this was only the shell of the man whom she had sent forth with such high hopes more than two years before. It was not merely that he was cadaverously thin, his hair long and unkempt; his eyes were those of a stranger, of a man desperately ill. The John Fremont she had sent away on his third expedition was a man of charm, of grace and poise, a man who knew his world and not only loved it but commanded it. This gray-haired and sunken-cheeked person before her stood awkwardly, his arms not seeming to fit into their sockets, his torso twisted at an ugly angle, his legs slumped within the discolored trousers, his face at war with itself, the mouth taut, awry, the features twisted. It was difficult to remember that this was the indestructible body and spirit that had forced a passage in the winter-locked Sierras where no other man could have survived; that this was the powerful yet quiet and graceful one who was beloved by Kit Carson and the frontiersmen of America.

For this man who stood before her was no leader, no strong one; this was a man profoundly hurt, caught at his most vulnerable spot, disorganized, frightened, unbeautiful and ineffective. His skin, his manner, his whole expression was bleak. Jessie remembered the night when John Fremont had put himself through the agony of revealing his illegitimacy to the woman he loved. Then, too, he had been awkward and disjointed. She could tell by every discordant line and knot of him that he felt humiliated, defeated. Above all, he was angrily and bitterly ashamed.

She brought him a drink, ran her fingers through his long, shaggy hair, smoothed the whorls of black beard with the gentlest touch of her finger tips; she kissed the bloodless lips and then buried her head on his shoulder and lay quietly.

She did not let him see that she was alarmed. Her task was to bring him back to himself, to revive his courage, his faith. It was a moment in their marriage that she must handle with sensitivity and tenderness; if she succeeded now she could serve at his side to the end of his days. What happened later was of little importance: he must be made whole and well again. If she could do that they could triumph over their difficulties.

She sensed that he was frightened of her reception, afraid that she might censure or condemn him, believe him to have been hotheaded, blundering, stupid. She knew that this would have been the worst blow of all to him, and from his withdrawal, his refusal to come to her, she saw that he had already built up his defenses of cynicism and indifference.

There had been no word from him, or any caress; he had not told her how happy he was to see her or how much he loved her. He was too bitterly unhappy to think in such terms.

"Why has General Kearny done this to us?" she asked. "What is the meaning behind it all?"

John did not reply to her question, but began talking disjointedly.

". . . refused to let me join my regiment in Mexico . . . didn't let me get my notes or journals in San Francisco . . . any of my scientific instruments or specimens that I collected for two years . . . had plans to arrest me for six months, but didn't give me five minutes' warning . . . made me trail behind him across the Sierras and Rockies like a servile Indian or a common criminal . . . heaped indignities . . . degraded me in front of my own men . . . deprived me of the privileges of my rank . . ."

"But now that you are back in Washington, what does General Kearny plan to do?"

John bolted to his feet and thrust his head upward belligerently.

"Court-martial."

"Court-martial! But on what charge?"

"Mutiny!"

Her breathing stopped. Her mind flashed back to the scene with Colonel Kearny four years before. At last her chickens had come home to roost. This court-martial was the logical culmination of the long line of events that had transpired since that fateful moment in St. Louis when she had torn open an order from the War Department and concealed it in her sewing basket.

BOOK THREE

COURT-MARTIAL

1

SHE DID NOT WANT ANYONE to see her husband while he was in his present condition, yet there were few places they could go where Colonel Fremont would not be recognized. She thought of Francis Preston Blair's estate, Silver Spring, which lay just outside the District of Columbia, but she had no desire to go there if the Blair family were present. While John was resting she sent Josheem by horseback to Silver Spring with a note. He returned later that evening with a letter from Mr. Blair saying that by a happy coincidence he and his family were leaving for St. Louis the following day, and he would be delighted to have her spend as much time at Silver Spring as she liked.

She now had the more difficult task of convincing her husband that for a short time at least he should step outside the arena, let the battle wait. She could tell by his every nervous gesture and intonation that he was spoiling for a fight; she also knew him well enough to realize that he would be least effective if he ventured forth now.

After a quiet dinner in their apartment she waited for a suitable moment and then said:

"Darling, the good book of matrimony preaches that when a husband and wife have been separated for twenty-seven months, they have a right to demand a honeymoon."

He was not amused by her oblique approach. He looked up sternly, muttering:

"Honeymoon! At a time like this? How can you even think, Jessie . . . We have a whole case to prepare . . ."

"I'm looking forward to working with you, John, but please, not just yet. Doesn't love have any rights?"

"There is a time for love, and there is a time for . . ."

"Why aren't you entitled to a couple of weeks' vacation after you have been in harness for two and a half years? Even the government wouldn't begrudge you that, hardhearted as it may be. You're so tired and worn, sweetheart; two weeks of rest and you would feel like a different man."

"I don't want to feel like a different man, I'm satisfied with the old one. Besides, I'm not tired and I'm not worn, I'm just determined to . . ."

She rested her head on her arms.

"Very well, if you insist on my telling the truth: I'm the one who is worn. I was brave when you came home from the other expeditions. I didn't cry on your shoulder or fill your ears with how much I had suffered or how tired I was. Now did I?"

"No, you've always been brave."

"But I don't feel brave right this moment. I feel exhausted after the long months of waiting for you. By the Eternal, if I don't have you to myself for a few days I just can't face the long ordeal. I know that it's weak of me, and that I shouldn't add my burdens to yours . . ."

His expression lightened.

"But what do you propose? Where could we go?"

"Francis Preston Blair has offered us refuge at Silver Spring. We won't tell anyone where we are going, and we'll have complete seclusion. It will be wonderful to become acquainted all over again."

Since Josheem had carried the note to Silver Spring the day before, they let him drive them in the carriage the next morning, warning him that he was to tell no one where he had been.

They rode through rows of tall pines, chestnuts and oaks, then crossed a stone bridge and drew up on a triangular roadway before a rambling house with a wide front porch. The servant who carried in their bags and made them comfortable in the guest suite assured them that they would have privacy.

Jessie did not wait for their suitcases to be unpacked but urged John to take her for a long walk through the estate. Francis Preston Blair had supported Van Buren for the presidency, arriving in Washington in 1836 with a family of three sons and a daughter. He founded the *Globe,* which became one of the outstanding newspapers in the country, rapidly becoming rich on its proceeds and on the benefits of governmental printing contracts. With his first affluence he had bought the wooded acres of Silver Spring.

Jessie and her husband walked past the Acorn summerhouse and vegetable gardens, turned down the Lovers' Walk which followed the stream almost to the Potomac, then entered the forest where the hot August sun was blocked out. They relaxed in the cool green darkness. They walked for almost three hours, resting frequently in the bowers and grottoes which Francis Blair had built along his many gravel-lined trails.

Determined as she was not to think about their troubles until she had nursed her husband back to balance, there was a complication she could not drive out of her mind; the War Department had decreed that the trial must be held at Fortress Monroe, an island off the coast of Virginia. John would be held almost incommunicado; it would be difficult to find a lawyer who would be able to isolate himself on the island for several months; in all likelihood the proceedings would be secret, and newspapermen barred from the fortress; there would be no way for the Fremonts to present their case to the public. Tom Benton was working with all his might to get the trial transferred to Washington. Time enough to tell her husband about Fortress Monroe, from which even she would be excluded, if the senator's efforts failed. When Josheem brought a letter from her father she scanned it eagerly for news of the removal of the trial to Washington, but there was none.

*I have a full view of the whole case, Kearny's as well as yours, and I am
perfectly at ease. Your husband will be justified and exalted; his persecutors
will be covered with shame and confusion. The process through which the
colonel has gone is bitter; but it will have its sweet. You both will realize
the truth of what Lord Palmerston said to Van Buren when he was rejected
by the Senate: "It is an advantage to a public man to be, in the course of
his life, the subject of an outrage."*

They had complete quiet, yet Jessie perceived that the beauty of Silver
Spring, its air of seclusion and peacefulness, was lost upon John. His spirit
was in turmoil and he did not know where he was. She talked to him
quietly, trying to analyze not the case itself nor the troubles in California,
but his feeling about them; for she had to know what he was thinking in
order to work with him. He was torn by humiliation and rage, but above
all she saw that his attitude was dominated by the idea that he was being
persecuted.

"They never wanted me," he muttered. "They were after me all the time,
that West Point clique. They were just waiting for the best hour to strike.
They let me get so far, and only so far, and then they conspired to knock me
down. I told you before we were married that they would never give me any
permanent peace, but only a truce. I signed more than half a million dollars'
worth of notes in California for horses and supplies, but General Kearny
laughed at the people who trusted my signature, told them my notes were
practically worthless. It is a conspiracy to keep me from returning to
California. We'll never to able to live on that beautiful Santa Cruz ranch
I bought with our savings."

While he recounted the indignities that had been heaped upon him she
slowly understood that these slights had come to have more importance
for him than the basic dispute in California. When she saw how ill he was
in his mind she cried to herself, What have they done to him? How am I
going to save him from them and from himself? How can I bring him back
to health so that no matter what the outcome of the court-martial he will be
strong and resolute in the face of it?

She thought shrewdly that everything that happens in a marriage, both for
good and evil, is not only implicit but actually revealed in the courtship.
There were no surprises in marriage, only the working out of everything one
has dimly perceived during the process of becoming acquainted. If she had
stopped to analyze things then she could have predicted not only the nature
of her happiness but the outlines of her troubles as well.

She approached the rebuilding of her husband scientifically. She had never
had any intention of being an amateur wife, for she had little enjoyment of
amateur talent; she had meant to be a professional wife; one who used the
same degree of skill as any serious practitioner of an art or science. Her
problems up to this moment had been comparatively simple: to sustain herself while her husband was on his long voyages; to protect his interests in

Washington while he was away; to help him turn out the reports which were so important in spreading knowledge of his work and of the West. The serious element now was the one that lay submerged and ever ready to spring: his obsession with his own illegitimacy and the danger it created because of the sense of insecurity it bred within him.

She spent sleepless hours during the long nights wondering what method she could best use to elicit the full story from him without causing a continuous uproar or protracting his bitterness as he relived the events. They were nerve-racking days, for no word or gesture could be accidental, spontaneous. Each step had to be planned, integrated, tested; any slip could tear down hours of work. She needed art in handling the situation, all the art that ever a wife needed, all the accumulated skill that wives the world over have needed to help their husbands. If the task seemed difficult, exhausting, she knew that it was not unselfishness on her part, but intelligent self-interest. Everything that happened to John must of necessity happen to her; when two people marry they cease to be purely themselves but step into a new and expanded character, the character of their marriage. It was not possible for either of them to do a misguided act without injuring the creation, the third being, which resulted from their having put their lives together: the child that was born of the mating of their temperaments before any child could be born of the mating of their loins.

It was too early for her to think logically about the facts; she went along with John emotionally, agreeing with his attitudes, accepting what he said as the truth, asking only those questions which would lead to the further sustaining of his position, using no method of analysis with which to achieve perspective. For she conceived it to be her function not to earn an acquittal of the charges, but to put her husband in a frame of mind to acquit himself to advantage in the courtroom, to appear at his best before the nation during the trial. For herself, she had not time yet to decide whether she was to believe only what he told her, or to hold her sympathies for her husband while keeping her mind open. What had been done in California had been done; although the action there could be interpreted in different ways, none of it could be changed. For the moment she could do a better job as a wife, acting as a complete partisan on her husband's side. As a wife she could only influence the result by working to keep her husband balanced, his poise unshatterable, his attitude toward the proceedings respectful but penetrating; later perhaps she could be the strategist seeking to set up the best possible case for her client.

In her sympathy for the man she loved she could not do otherwise.

She used every art and guile known to the heart of woman to nurse him to health. As they rode Francis Blair's spirited horses through the forests she challenged him to race with her, complimented him on how beautifully he sat the horse. Sitting before the warmth and bright red flames of the fireplace she played up the hours and episodes he had enjoyed most in their years together, in which he had appeared to the best advantage, filled him with her pride in his accomplishments. She showed him the accumulation of honors that had come to him while he was away: the Founder's Medal of the National Geographical Society of London, the gold medal from Baron Humboldt, awarded by the Prussian government for his contribution to science: read him articles from such magazines as the *Southern Literary Messenger,* the *Electric Review* and the *Democratic Review,* in which it was declared that the name of John Fremont was immortalized, that his accomplishments were greater than those of Lewis and Clark, that he should be compensated as they had, with large land grants and double pay. She turned the pages of her scrapbook in which she had pasted the stories of his achievements from the newspapers and magazines of Britain and Europe. She concurred with his motives even when she was not able to follow his reasoning. She played the temptress, wearing her loveliest gowns, using her most delicate perfumes, shamelessly arousing his sexual love for her, the love that always had been such a strong and potent force between them.

There were moments when she thought she was making headway, when a flash of humor would illuminate his remarks, but these successes were momentary and all too soon he slipped back into the pattern of his illness: his overstatement of his own importance, his conviction that everything he had done was right, that he couldn't possibly have made even one mistake during the harrowing circumstances; his lack of sympathy or tolerance for his opponents while decrying their lack of sympathy and tolerance for him; his discounting of his own impetuousness, his irritability with restraint, his tendency to act on his own.

When everything looked hopeless because, no matter how subtly she tried, she could not set his perspective straight, she indulged in a melodramatic scene in which she wept bitterly, showed herself to be weak and frightened. She did not have to pretend, for deep in her heart she felt weak and frightened.

Ashamed at last, realizing something of the agony he was putting her through, he wrapped his arms around her, kissed her tears upward along her cheeks, drying his lips in the hair of her temples.

"Don't cry, dear," he murmured, "it's not that bad. We'll work it out, we'll defeat them, now don't you worry about it."

One evening toward the end of the second week, knowing that they had only a few more hours on what she called their happy island surrounded by a sea of troubles, they had the horses saddled and rode over to Miss English's Academy. It was a full moonlit night, the countryside bathed in a white and powdery fluorescence. They tied the horses to the mulberry tree and stood holding hands while they gazed up at her window.

"Do you remember how you hid your first letter in the wash basket?"

"I remember."

"What would you have done if Mammy hadn't come along at just the right moment with that bundle of wash?"

"I would have wrapped the note around a rock and thrown it through your window. I was an irrepressible youth, Miss Jessie; I should have pursued you and thrown rocks through your window until you were eighty."

"How nice. Just think of all the time I was smart enough not to waste. Do you think you could climb up this mulberry tree without tearing your lovely breeches?"

Without waiting for an answer she pulled herself up into the tree, climbed quickly among the familiar branches and then sat in the nook where she and John had first talked. It was only an instant before she saw his head appear between the branches. The moonlight on his hair made it seem silvery; instead of being projected back to their first meeting, she saw how he would look thirty years hence when his hair and beard would be white. He pulled himself up and sat beside her.

"I have had exciting news this morning, Lieutenant Fremont: my roommate Harriet Williams is going to be married to Count Bodisco. Would you come to the wedding?"

"I'm not likely to receive an invitation."

"I was just writing to Harriet when your note arrived in the wash basket. I'll ask Harriet to have the count send you an invitation. Do you like to dance, Lieutenant Fremont?"

He put his arm about her and lifted her half out of the juncture of the limbs, until she was lying against his chest, her cheek on his, the corners of their mouths touching.

"Ah, Jessie," he whispered, "a good marriage is truly a miracle."

2

On the day her father was due back from St. Louis, Jessie donned one of her new house gowns which she wore high at the throat, finished with a small flat collar of lace, and went down to the drawing room to await his arrival. The hours passed and Senator Benton did not come home. Finally she saw him striding down C Street from Pennsylvania Avenue, his big frame swinging along quickly and confidently. She could tell by his manner that he bore good tidings. The first thing he said as he gave her a bearlike hug was:

"I've been to the War Department. The trial has been transferred to the Arsenal Building in Washington. I showed them what the public would think if they dragged a man all the way from the Pacific Ocean to a secret trial in the Atlantic Ocean. Now I'll be able to attend the trial myself."

A surge of relief swept over her. She kissed her father's cheek, commented on the fact that he needed a shave, and then said, "So far so good. Now there's just one more thing we need to do."

"What is that?"

"Have the court-martial stopped altogether. Colonel Fremont was acting under secret orders from President Polk: why else should Captain Montgomery of the S.S. *Portsmouth* have provided him with money, munitions and medical supplies to start the war in California, and Consuls Larkin and Leidesdorff help him to organize the campaign? If the president can't reveal these secret orders, then at least let him tell everybody involved to let bygones be bygones."

"No, no, Jessie," cried Tom Benton. "It's too late now to try to hush up the affair. Too many of General Kearny's officers have been writing articles in the newspapers attacking John. If we withdraw, everyone will say we're guilty. We want this court-martial; the best way to prove the colonel's innocence and justify him is a public trial here in Washington. We'll use it as an open forum to tell the whole world of his accomplishments. You will see, Jessie, he will emerge as a greater man than ever. The administration will back us . . ."

"Even if he were to win," she replied quietly, "I still wouldn't think it was the wise thing to do. Father, won't you go to President Polk and ask him to call off the trial?"

Her father looked at her long and hard, then replied: "I can't do that, Jessie, but if your husband wants to, that is another affair. From all Colonel Fremont has said, I don't think anything in the world could keep him from fighting this case in the open."

"I might be able to persuade him," she replied. "Is there no one who can intercede to stop this court-martial without anybody losing face?"

"Yes, General Kearny. He is the only one. If he would withdraw his charges . . ."

"Then if you'll excuse me, Father, I will dress at once and go to see him. Somebody must stop this dreadful quarrel."

She walked to the office which General Kearny occupied in the War Department on his trips to Washington, feeling as gray and barren as the grayish cubicle into which she entered. One look at the general's ill and aging face showed her that he too was suffering deeply. He rose from his chair, stiffly, no sign of recognition or friendliness coming over his sand-worn face, the eyes small and dull. She closed the door behind her and leaned against the hand which still gripped the knob.

"General Kearny, no matter what has happened or will happen, I want you to know that I regret this entire affair bitterly."

He made no reply; she felt that he was probing her intent and would make no move until he was sure of its nature.

"There have been mistakes made," she continued in a tight tone. "I have come to ask you not to multiply those errors into misfortunes for all of us."

After a painful pause he spoke:

"Then you can see that Colonel Fremont made serious mistakes."

"I grant that, General. The only ones who don't make mistakes in life are those who do nothing."

"Am I to understand that Colonel Fremont is prepared to make public apologies?"

Jessie flinched. She made her way uncertainly to a hard wooden chair, sat on its very edge. "I don't know, General Kearny; I am here without his knowledge."

"Then why did you come?"

"To ask you to put an end to this conflict. Nothing can come of it but grief for all of us."

"There will be no grief for me, Miss Jessie: I am the commanding officer whose orders have been thwarted. Your husband caused me untold difficulty in California. Now it is his turn to suffer."

She rose from the sharp edge of the chair, went close to him.

"He has already suffered; more than you could possibly imagine. This court-martial will be tragic for him, but it will be equally tragic for you and everyone concerned."

"There you are wrong; I have nothing to conceal; no discredit can possibly fall upon me."

"Please forgive me, General, if I am so presumptuous as to contradict you: I know the nature of the charges that will be hurled, both by you against my husband and by my husband against you."

In spite of her sincerity, General Kearny was offended.

"If you are so sure he is right and I am wrong, then why have you come to me?"

"Because I am convinced that in a case like this, even though everybody may be right and nobody wrong, everyone must lose and no one can win."

"Have you seen the case against Colonel Fremont? Do you know how completely we can crush him? Or have you been listening only to your husband's version?"

"I have been listening to my husband's version; I am prejudiced in his favor, but that prejudice has not blinded me. I know how right you were, and—forgive me—how wrong, no, not wrong, but intolerant you were. I also know how wrong Colonel Fremont was; no, not wrong, but rash and impetuous. But he is a younger man; because of your friendship for our family you could have been like a father to him. Senator Benton and I could have expected that much of you."

"My obligations to the Army come first, Mrs. Fremont. We play no favorites and allow no infractions for the sake of friendship."

"But surely you are exaggerating the importance of Colonel Fremont and his conduct."

"I know your father is outraged with me, Miss Jessie; and please believe that I have loved you almost like a daughter. I am deeply regretful of the pain I must inflict on you. But Colonel Fremont insulted me in the presence of other officers; he refused to obey my orders and quarreled with my representatives. Mutiny is a habit of mind with Colonel Fremont. If I let this mutiny go by I will so have undermined my position that I will never again be able to command. I owe it to myself and my long career to punish this conduct. Colonel Fremont must not be allowed to get away with this second mutiny successfully, or he will establish a precedent which will injure the morale of the Army."

"Second mutiny? What was the first . . . ?"

"When he left Kaw's Landing after having received the order to report back to Washington."

Jessie paled, began to feel faint.

"But that was my doing, General Kearny. My husband never knew that order had been sent out, not until I told him about it upon his return."

"Forgive me for being brutal," replied General Kearny with the devastating plainness of a sandstorm sweeping across the desert, "but I don't believe you. I think he is the one who received the order and arranged this scheme with you to avoid its implications."

She stumbled back onto her chair.

"How can you say that to me, when you have been a friend of the Benton family for forty years? When you have known me since the day I was born?"

"That is the very reason I say it. The Bentons have always been passionate partisans, putting the cause above the truth. I know that you would lie to defend your husband, Jessie: I know there is nothing in the world you wouldn't do to protect him. I don't speak critically when I say that you lie; it is a kind of compliment; every man's wife should lie to protect her husband. But that is no reason for me to be deceived. Your husband is a confirmed mutineer. The sooner we get him out of the Army, the better."

"Very well, then," said Jessie, hardly recognizing the metallic tone of the voice she somehow managed to project. "I am a liar and my husband is a congenital mutineer. Even so, must all the world hear our charges and countercharges? It will hurt the administration, it will hurt our government, it will hurt our army."

"I shall insist upon the court-martial," he replied hoarsely, "because I will allow no one to do this to me at the end of my career."

"Then I can answer with equal truth that you must not do this to yourself at the end of your long career! The bitterness of the trial, the accusations will make you enemies and obscure what you have done for your country."

"I will take my chances," he replied. "I would consider myself derelict in duty if I failed to prosecute this case."

There was an awkward silence. Finally Jessie pleaded, "Why must you revenge yourself on him because of me? I was responsible for Colonel Fremont's leaving with your cannon, against orders. If not for that trouble you would never have thought of him as a mutineer. You would have been more patient and kindly with him in California, forgiven his brashness and concealed his refusal to obey. But because of what I did in St. Louis you were already set in your mind to think of him as rebellious. I am the one who is responsible for your state of mind. And if my husband is retired from the Army in disgrace it will be my fault. Would you make me responsible for destroying my own husband? I cannot believe that of you. Submit your report to the War Department; let the War Department take whatever disciplinary action it sees fit; but don't make this a matter of public scandal. Give me time to reason with Colonel Fremont and I promise that sooner or later he will see what mistakes he made and will come to you with his apologies."

General Kearny turned from her and stared unseeing at the blank gray wall. When he turned back his eyes were as blank and gray as the walls at which he had been looking.

"I ordered Colonel Fremont to come to Monterey and bring his archives; this, after four months in which he kept himself in command in southern California against my direct and explicit orders. He came into my headquarters at Monterey unkempt and disheveled after a four-hundred-mile dash on horseback, still having disobeyed my orders and not having brought his records. Colonel Mason was with me. Your husband demanded that I dismiss Colonel Mason from our presence, so that he could talk to me privately. When I refused, he shouted, 'Did you bring him to spy upon me?' Please believe me, Mrs. Fremont, I know of no equivalent of that scene in all army history. Later, when I sent Colonel Mason to Los Angeles to take over Colonel Fremont's command, your husband had the effrontery to challenge his commanding officer to a duel! He was so arrogant and contemptuous of my command that he refused to return to me the two howitzers I had brought across the desert from Santa Fe, and which the Mexicans turned over to him when they surrendered. This is chaos, Mrs. Fremont. Can't you understand that? How could I do anything else but put him under arrest?"

Jessie dug her short nails into her palms. Now both of the mutinies of the Fremont family centered around howitzers; for it was obvious from General Kearny's critical attitude and tone of voice that he had been more deeply offended by Colonel Fremont's refusal to return the cannon than by anything else in their conflict.

"He was overwrought from the months of conquest. If he had been ill in his body you would have seen that he got the best medical care, you would have nursed him with your own hands. But he was tired in his mind, and for that kind of sickness you have neither understanding nor sympathy."

She rose from the chair, toyed with her gloves. "General Kearny, why must you be so cold and hardhearted? Why must you try to destroy Colonel Fremont? And me? Why should you want to injure the cause of western expansion, to hurt my father? You cannot harm people whom you love and not maim yourself along with them."

"If I had been afraid of mortal combat, Miss Jessie, I should never have become a soldier."

"But this is something infinitely worse than death: the same tar with which you will cover my husband will cover you."

"My conscience would no more permit me to withdraw from this battle than it would have to withdraw from a battle against the British, the Mexicans or the Indians. There are fundamental issues involved here, issues more important than any one person or group of persons. Good day, Mrs. Fremont."

After leaving General Kearny's office Jessie wandered slowly through the streets of Washington. An hour later she found herself in the Navy Yard and sat down on the wooden stairs of the barracks to let her head clear. Then she picked herself up wearily and trudged homeward, asking Maylee to heat her some water for a hot bath. While sitting in the big iron tub, her knees drawn up under her chin, she utilized the quiet and relaxation to review the morning.

Yes, John had overstepped himself, his attitude toward General Kearny appeared inexcusable; but she would not try to post-guess him. To herself she said: Living in the security and comfort of my Washington home, able to exercise the most beautiful hindsight, I could easily say that he should have done so and so. But in the heat of the excitement, with the future still an unwritten document, called on to make split-second decisions, what he did must have seemed right for him to do at that particular moment and under that particular set of circumstances. It is easy enough to have good judgment after all the facts are in, but a soldier is not a philosopher, he is a man of action. I am not going to be a blind and adoring wife, but I certainly shall not sit in Olympian calm and decide that I would have done it differently or better.

As the steam from the hot water rose about her head and enveloped her in its mist she thought, We both have incipient mutiny in our blood: I rebelled against the head of my school and her choice of a May Day Queen, leading my cohorts into the infirmary rather than letting them participate. Seven years later I mutinied against the War Department. My husband rebelled against discipline and was expelled from school because as a romantic youth he preferred to roam the hills with his sweetheart. Twelve years later he too mutinied against the War Department. We are too much alike; we double each other's weaknesses. He should have married a different kind of woman, one who would never have interfered . . . who would have been a better balance wheel . . .

In her own feeling of guilt she was not able to look too deeply into her husband's guilt. She remembered her father saying, "A little mutiny goes a long way." Yes, too frequent mutiny would ruin not only the American Army, but the American form of government which, resting upon the consent and co-operation of the governed, must also have the absolute obedience of the governed. It was very well for Vice-Admiral Nelson to raise his blind eye to the spyglass when his inadequate commanding officer was giving a stupid and disastrous command, but what would happen if every one of the thirty million Americans constituted himself a Lord Nelson, raising his blind eye to orders from Washington? A co-operative government could survive mistakes and blunders in particular events, but not consistent disobedience. The government was the parent, the particular affair on hand the child; if one child be lost, the fruitful parents can create more children; but if the child destroy the parent, the family is destroyed.

Thus she came to feel that although her revolt had been justified in everything John had accomplished, in the gathering of the scientific data and the further opening of the West, actually he had not been indispensable: someone else would have gathered the data; the historical forces, of which he was only an instrument, would have opened the West. She had struck a great blow for her husband and his work, but when a blow is struck for someone, it must be struck against someone as well. That someone had been the American form of government, for which her grandmother McDowell had carried a scar on her forehead all her life.

3

Eliza and William Carey Jones came in for dinner that night. That they were happy together Jessie knew from little hints that Eliza had let drop; but there was nothing in the undemonstrative manner of either to indicate that there had been any change in their lives. Jessie managed to keep the conversation away from the trial during dinner, but when they had adjourned to the drawing room for coffee, Thomas Benton launched into a legal analysis of Colonel Fremont's course in California, intermingled with a tirade against General Kearny.

Jessie found her eyes glued to William Jones's face. He rarely indicated what he was thinking, yet she felt that he disapproved of what was being said. She had been so preoccupied with her own troubles that she had paid little attention to her new brother-in-law, but now she found herself studying him intently. He was tall and slender, with cool green eyes, a turned-up nose, a shock of blond hair which stood up straight, and an ascetic, almost beardless face. He had a quiet and reserved manner of speaking: she admired his calm, unhurried, unemotional nature; she herself could never aspire to this type of temperament, yet she knew its worth. Mr. Jones's position in this family difficulty was not yet clear; she had not discussed the case with him, nor had he volunteered any opinions. She knew that he could be valuable to their cause, not only because he would remain quiet and logical in the face of her husband's and father's hurricanes, but also because he was a student of international law. John Fremont and Tom Benton would fight in terms of personal conflict, but in the courtroom the issues would have to be tried according to the legal imperatives. Her husband was no lawyer; her father had not practiced law for some twenty years.

Later in the evening, while Eliza went up to visit with her mother, Jessie created an opportunity to talk with her brother-in-law. She did not know whether she could speak to him frankly, for although he was now a member of the family, he had given no indication of affection for anyone beside Eliza. For all she knew he might be entirely disinterested in the dispute.

"Forgive me if I try to read your thoughts," she said, "but it did seem to me that while Father was discussing the case, something in the back of your mind was disagreeing."

After a moment of expressionless but not unfriendly silence, he replied, "There is an old saying that in a lawsuit nobody wins except the lawyers."

"And in this instance not even the lawyers can win! I feel that Colonel Fremont was right in what he did, that his conduct can be justified because of the complicated circumstances. However, I must tell you that my heart sinks at the very thought of a public squabble."

"I must agree with you, Jessie. Things will be said in a spirit of vindictiveness and revenge which will be impossible to expunge from the historic record."

"But do you see any way of stopping the trial? I've already been refused by Father and General Kearny."

William Jones glanced at the other end of the room where John and Tom had their heads together.

"I'm afraid we have to go through with it, Jessie."

"We?"

"Yes. I want to offer my services. I don't know that I can be of any great help, but I should be happy and honored if you will permit me to serve as co-counsel."

The welling up of her emotion was cut short by the matter-of-fact manner in which her brother-in-law had made his offer, an offer which would cost him months of hard work and neglect of his own practice. She was nonplussed to see that a man could make a considerable sacrifice in the same casual manner in which he would offer to bring her a demitasse.

"It is extremely kind of you," she said quietly. "My husband and father and I are all so emotional, we fly off the handle so easily. Won't you please try to hold us down? If only you will stay calm and logical, we will always have a solid legal base. Please don't pay us the compliment of sharing in our vices."

"I will be as I am, Jessie," he remarked. "I cannot be otherwise."

Senator Benton secured a second and last concession from the War Department, the postponement of the trial for another month so that Colonel Fremont might gather his witnesses from the frontiers.

Jessie was interested to watch the trial fought in miniature before the hearing opened: their army friends, who had been visiting the house for years, stayed away; naval officers with whom the Bentons had had only moderate contact became most friendly, called on the slightest provocation to assure Colonel Fremont that he had been entirely right in supporting the navy command in California. When Jessie went to the War Department to secure copies of papers needed for the defense, she was treated politely but coolly and given no assistance. At the office of the secretary of the navy she was received with warmth; the entire staff aided her not only in locating documents but in organizing and copying them. It was extreme bad fortune that Secretary of the Navy Bancroft had been sent abroad as minister to England. George Bancroft should have been in Washington to defend them, though she realized that he would have been able to do little: he had warned her that anything John might attempt in California would be his own gamble, that he would be obliged to deny that he had given encouragement to a campaign against the Mexicans; and in any event, the Army would vehemently have denied that any order from the secretary of the navy constituted a valid defense for an army officer.

The library of the Benton home was set up as a workshop. Jessie and her father used their regular tables in front of the fire, while her husband and brother-in-law spread their papers over the map table. The lawyer spent his day making a detailed study of the records of all courts-martial held in America up to that time; Jessie spent her hours in the Library of Congress securing data, her mind going back to the years when she had been "pastured" there by her father while he attended the Senate.

For her the most interesting period of the day was the evening, when they assembled in the library to instruct each other on their findings. John was concentrating on only one aspect of the trial: the fact that Commodore Stockton was the legal and rightful commander in California between January and May 1847; Tom Benton was concentrating on his legal authority for the conquest and governing of California; William Jones was concentrating on the trial framework and the laws of evidence. Jessie's task was to write the letters that had to go out to witnesses, to extract and copy the orders which each man wanted to include in his working brief, to reconcile the coldly legalistic approach of her brother-in-law with her father's hotheaded denunciation of General Kearny and every last one of his witnesses; and to somehow keep her husband's faith and confidence running strong and logical so that together they could build a foolproof case.

She awakened early on the morning of the trial, November 2, 1847, and ran quickly to the window to see what kind of a day she was to have. The sun was already up, bright but not hot; there was the crisp crackle of autumn in the air. She had slept little the night before, but over their light breakfast she assured her husband that she had slept the sleep of confidence. She kissed him good-by with a firm embrace, saying, "Everything is going to come out all right."

"There is not the slightest doubt of it in my mind," he replied, but she could see that he was sorely troubled.

The men left early in Hassler's Ark to round up the defense witnesses. Court was not to open until noon. Jessie sat before her dressing table anxious that she emerge from her preparations looking serene and confident. She had several obstacles to overcome: there were bluish rings under her eyes, her temples were a greenish white, and her King George's Mark was hard and prominent. She bathed her eyes with warm and then cold water, massaged her face for a long time to bring back some blood and color, then sat quietly brushing her hair. At ten-thirty she put on a warm, wine-colored dress with hat and shoes of the same color. While she was engrossed in her thoughts there was a light knock on the door, and Eliza came in. She had on a black gown. Jessie gazed at her sister for a moment.

"Eliza, my dear, this isn't an occasion for mourning."

"Then you don't approve of my black?"

"No, please put on your new dress, the lovely navy one."

At a little after eleven General Dix's spacious carriage arrived with Dix's two daughters, who had offered to take the Benton sisters to the Arsenal. They drove down C Street to Pennsylvania Avenue and then turned left. Since this was the calling hour in Washington there were many carriages abroad, some of them on their way to the Arsenal, others en route to friends' homes. Jessie saw a number of their family acquaintances walking, and she returned their bows with a series of forced smiles; with the hand that was out of sight she clung to Eliza.

"Your fingers are ice cold and trembling, Jessie. Here's the turn toward the Arsenal, you had better put on your gloves."

The Arsenal was a huge rambling wooden building painted a faded mustard color. As Jessie alighted she saw a large crowd of spectators gathered on either side of the entrance. A murmur went up as she stepped out of her carriage, one which she felt was sympathetic. This told her even better than had the friendly tone of the press for the past few days that the sympathies of the people were with Colonel Fremont.

The trial chamber was not overly large except that it had a high-domed ceiling with windows up toward the roof. There was room for only two hundred spectators, and guards were already barring the doors because every seat was occupied. Clasping Eliza's arm, Jessie walked down the center aisle with every pair of eyes fastened upon her. She took her seat in the front row of spectators just behind the railed enclosure inside of which, at a long mahogany table to the left, sat her husband, her father and her brother-in-law, and on the opposite side the prosecuting attorney and his assistants. Since there was to be no jury at this trial, a duplicate jury box had been built on the left side of the enclosure, and here sat Kit Carson, Alexander Godey, and a large number of John's California Battalion and associates in California who had come to testify. In the opposite box near the prosecutor sat a bolt-upright array of army officers banked silently behind their commanding officer, General Stephen Watts Kearny. In the front row across from Jessie was the phalange of newspaper reporters come to report what the *Union* called "the most dramatic army trial since General Wilkinson's, thirty years before."

The sympathy of those in the courtroom heartened her. Then the thirteen judges, comprised of generals, colonels, majors, a captain, filed in, their uniforms resplendent with gold braid. They took their seats on the high judges' bench which ran almost the full width of the courtroom, their position ranging downward from the general to the captain. The court was called to order, the preliminary ceremonials dispensed with and then, while she listened to the terrifying quiet of the courtroom, the charges were read against her husband. The critical hour of their lifetime had struck.

4

She studied her husband anxiously when the court demanded whether he had any objection to the judges. She had persuaded him to buy a new uniform for the trial and he appeared to her to be as trim and handsome as ever, with his flashing eyes and quick, expressive face, albeit more mature-looking because of his rapidly graying hair and the lines in his face. But most important she saw that he was poised and balanced for the long ordeal.

According to the rule of court-martial the defense attorneys could never address the court; they could work up the legal points, but Colonel Fremont alone could speak in the courtroom; he alone could read the arguments and papers that had been prepared during the arduous nights of work; he alone could cross-examine witnesses, make protests to the court. This was a hardship, for it not only obliged the defendant to function in a field in which he was not trained, but also put upon him the burden of appearing before the court with the legalistic phlegm of the lawyer who has only a single decision at stake.

She watched her husband rise and read in a clear, charged voice the paper on which they had worked the night before.

"Mr. President: In preferring the usual request to be allowed counsel in this case, I wish to state that it is no part of my intention to make a defense on any legal or technical point, but only to have friendly assistance in bringing out the merits of the case. With this view, no objection will be made to the relevancy or legality of any question proposed by the prosecution or the court; nor to any question which goes to show my motives, either by words or acts; nor to the authenticity of any evidence, written or printed, which I know or believe to be authentic. In this way I hope to facilitate the progress of the trial, and enable the court the sooner to obey the feelings which call them to a very different service. I name as the counsel allowed me the two friends who accompany me, Thomas H. Benton and William Carey Jones."

She flashed him an approving nod as he half turned to her while sitting down, but her heart was racing when the judge advocate rose to open his case by reading a letter from Colonel Fremont to General Kearny of the United States Army.

To Brig. Gen. S. W. Kearny, *United States Army*
Sir:

I have the honor to be in receipt of your favor of last night, in which I am directed to suspend the execution of orders which, in my capacity of military commandant of this territory, I had received from Commodore Stockton, governor and commander-in-chief in California. I avail myself of an early hour this morning to make such a reply as the brief time allowed for reflection will enable me.

I found Commodore Stockton in possession of the country, exercising the functions of military commandant and civil governor, as early as July of last year; and shortly thereafter I received from him the commission of military commandant, the duties of which I immediately entered upon, and have continued to exercise to the present moment. I found also, on my arrival at this place some three or four days since, Commodore Stockton still exercising the functions of civil and military governor, with the same apparent deference to his rank on the part of all officers, including yourself, as he maintained and required when he assumed in July last. I learned, also, in conversation with you, that, on the march from San Diego, recently, to this place, you entered upon and discharged duties implying an acknowledgment on your part of supremacy to Commodore Stockton.

I feel myself, therefore, with great deference to your professional and personal character, constrained to say that, until you and Commodore Stockton adjust between yourselves the question of rank, where I respectfully think the difficulty belongs, I shall have to report and receive orders, as heretofore, from the Commodore.

With considerations of high regard, I am your obedient servant,

> J. C. FREMONT, *Lt. Col. U.S.A.*
> *Military Commandant of the*
> *Territory of California.*

As simple and respectful as the letter sounded she felt with a quick flash that herein lay the crux of the case which the Army would present, the focal point around which the conflict and confusion would center: the court would decide who had been the legal commander of California! If it were Commodore Stockton, then Colonel Fremont would be declared innocent of the charges. If it were General Kearny, then he was guilty of disobeying the orders of the army officer. All of the thousands of words that would be spilled in this courtroom, many of them in anger, even more in hot blood, would revolve about this one point.

The prosecutor proceeded to charge Colonel Fremont with twenty-two "specifications" of mutiny, disobedience of lawful command and conduct to the prejudice of military discipline. For four solid hours she heard the case against her husband pile up until the prosecution had presented the most formidable body of charges brought against an officer since the trial of Aaron Burr for treason. As an ominous and crushing rehearsal for all that was to follow during the three feverish months of claims and counterclaims, accusations and counteraccusations, the judge advocate drove spikes into her consciousness by accusing her husband of: breaking his word to the Mexican authorities, cruelly and shamefully abusing the native Californios and antagonizing them against the American government; taking their horses and provisions and paying for them not in cash but in promissory notes; leading a body of well-armed troops into a country on the pretext of scientific survey and rising in arms against that country because it had ordered him out of its boundaries; instigating the American settlers to rise against their Mexican governors, declaring war against California in a series of surprise attacks, assuming full authority over northern California and the supplies and ammunitions of American battleships in San Francisco Harbor without written authority to do so; granting peace terms to the Mexicans without conferring with a superior in command. He had refused to return the two howitzers captured from General Kearny at San Pascual; refused to acknowledge the authority of General Kearny, giving orders to recruit more troops for his California Battalion after the general had commanded him to cease; he had tried to make a bargain with General Kearny for the governorship of California, had turned against him only when his demands were refused, instructing his civil officers in California to regard General Kearny's orders as obsolete. He had used insulting conduct to General Kearny before staff officers, illegally purchased supplies for his troops after having been suspended by General Kearny, illegally carried on a civil government and proclaimed himself to be governor.

By the time the court adjourned at four o'clock she was exhausted and numb with fear. How were they ever going to overthrow this tremendous body of accusation? What could they possibly do in the ensuing days to upset the dreadful charges, free John from them in the minds of the nation?

Official Washington suspected that there had been secret orders sent to Colonel Fremont, yet it would be as impossible to bring them up during this court-martial in vindication of her husband as it was to make them public at the time they had been sent to him through Lieutenant Gillespie. The trial could only be bathed in a fog of innuendo: while ostensibly trying Colonel Fremont for mutiny against General Kearny, the Army actually would be prosecuting him for presenting the United States Army as an implement of conquest. Since in their effort to clear the Army for the historic record they could call to trial neither Secretary Bancroft and the United States Navy nor the president and those of his Cabinet members who had sponsored the forcible pre-empting of California, they would visit upon Colonel Fremont the full strength of their outraged wrath, build up the strongest personal case they could expound against him, disown him, convict him on the only charges they dared make public.

Jessie could not touch her dinner. She noticed that only Eliza and her husband were eating theirs. After she had successfully downed a cup of hot black coffee, she broke the silence by asking:

"Why have they the right to convict a man before he is tried? Why is it just practice to throw up this terrifying screen of accusations before we can enter a defense?"

"Don't you worry about our defense," boomed Tom Benton, angrily pushing away his plate. "If you think their list of fabrications against us is terrifying, wait until you hear what we will do to them."

Jessie turned an anxious face to William Jones, who was dispatching the last of his baked ham and sweet potatoes. He continued uninterrupted until his plate was clean, then wiped the corner of his mouth meticulously with his napkin, pushed back his chair, crossed one long bony knee over the other and spoke in a quiet voice.

"It is entirely proper procedure. We cannot enter a defense until the case against us has been stated. Furthermore, from their point of view, all twenty-two of the specifications are rightfully lodged. If we grant the premise that Colonel Fremont was legally bound to obey General Kearny's order of January 17, then every move he made for the next ninety days was illegal."

"But he was not obliged to obey General Kearny," cried Jessie, her emotion, like her stomach, rising into her throat. "Commodore Stockton refused to allow him to resign from the Navy."

"Quite so," murmured Jones. "I was merely stating the case for the opposition. Now let us look at our case: if the colonel was right in obeying the orders of Commodore Stockton because he had been sworn into the Navy, then everything he did between January 17 and May 8, when he was permitted to see General Kearny's new and conclusive orders from Washington, was not only right and legal, but necessary to the fulfillment of his duties as governor. He would have been derelict in his duty had he done less. That is our case. We will be given every opportunity to present it."

While Jessie tried to quiet her feelings with a second cup of coffee, Tom Benton rose heavily from his chair and boomed:

"If the worst comes to the worst, who is the Army convicting here? Certainly not Colonel Fremont! They will be convicting the Navy, trying to chastise the Navy with a backhand slap at an army officer."

"They're not going to convict us," cried Jessie. "Every last charge in that dreadful bill of particulars happened before Kearny received his conclusive orders from Washington in May . . ."

William Jones, who had lighted a cigar and risen from the table, came to her side.

"Easy does it. We can only fight this case on the facts, not on our hypotheses of what lies behind those facts. I believe in our case."

She looked up at him with tears of gratitude in her eyes.

"Of course we believe in our case," said Tom Benton. "But we've got to make the world see it the way we see it. Come now, let us go to work. We can convince no one by merely reassuring ourselves."

"Please, not yet, Father," begged Eliza. "It's too soon after dinner. Come into the drawing room for an hour and let me play for you. Jessie, it will do you good to sing a few ballads."

"Eliza is right," announced her husband; "we should all rest for an hour and talk of other things."

Jessie saw that John and her father resented this cool good sense, that they wanted to go upstairs and plunge into work immediately, not because they were short of time and couldn't get everything done, but because it was intolerable to their impatient natures to be kept away even momentarily from a refutation of the charges. Nevertheless she knew that her sister was right, and she walked across the hall into the drawing room with an arm tucked under her husband's arm.

At eight o'clock they went up to the library to begin work. The wooden-pegged map table which had always stood by the bookshelves was brought to the center of the room and an astral lamp placed at each end. Here the notes from the day's proceedings were spread out, as well as the documents in John's possession and the copies of official papers which they had made during the day. Jessie and John sat facing the wall, Tom Benton and William Jones opposite. At midnight they had their paper completed, a statement which exonerated John on every charge made against him that day by the judge advocate.

Now, suddenly, they were hungry.

"We didn't have any dinner," exclaimed Jessie; "at least we didn't eat any. All I can remember is that wonderful chocolate cake. Come along, we'll ransack the kitchen; there should have been some ham left over, and I'll make a fresh pot of coffee."

"I feel considerably better," announced her father. "I feel like an avenging angel who has demolished the forces of evil."

Jessie glanced eagerly at her husband to see if he too were feeling the upsurge of emotion which had engulfed them.

"We have stated our case," he said heartily, "and we've stated it mighty well."

"Easy does it," cautioned William Jones, lighting his second cigar of the evening, now that he again had a few moments to relax. "We must beware of overoptimism, just as we had to beware of overpessimism at the dinner table."

"Oh come, William," cried Jessie, amused that she had used her brother-in-law's Christian name for the first time; "it's after midnight and we're all tired and hungry and exultant. For a few moments let's not be cautious, let's be confident and happy. Let's talk about that long row of gold braid that sits up on that bench: did you ever see so many gorgeous uniforms? They looked as though they were about to decide the strategy of Lundy's Lane or Waterloo."

"No," protested her father good-humoredly, "let's not be prejudiced against the court. I think we will get a fair trial."

"I'm sure of it," she cried, feeling carefree for the first time in days. "We're also going to get a fair amount of ham. Look, Maylee baked an extra one. John, you make the coffee; William, slice a French bread; Father, how about a little brandy to celebrate the successful conclusion of our first day's work?"

He returned with a bottle of brandy. When the glasses had been filled, Tom Benton raised his in a toasting gesture and said, "To us."

"Yes, to us," murmured Jessie. Going to her husband, she kissed him and said: "And to you, my dear."

5

The following days were bad ones: General Kearny, Lieutenant Emory and Colonel Cooke occupied the stand and built up detail by detail the edifice against Colonel Fremont. It was clear to Jessie that her husband had been headstrong, yet this process of unclothing a man in public seemed to her a vicious and senseless one. As the trial progressed it was apparent how his difficulties had pyramided; the moves he had made over a period of three months resulted from his first decision to conquer California for the United States and command as governor, and inevitably had to follow. Judged individually, without reference to the original reasoning which had prompted them, the acts looked hasty, misguided, rash and quarrelsome; anyone picking up a newspaper and reading a given set of charges made by General Kearny, Lieutenant Emory or Colonel Cooke would convict Colonel Fremont on the very face of things. Yet once the original premise was granted these acts followed logically; anyone reading the full story would see that Colonel Fremont's actions had to be judged as sequences rather than a group of isolated incidents.

In all fairness to General Kearny, she perceived that the same was true of him: anyone reading a single day's accusations against him would have had to pass severe judgment on him: he had been domineering, officious. He had arrived in California after indiscreetly sending back two thirds of his Mormon Battalion, had been defeated at San Pascual, had his two howitzers captured by the Mexicans, had to be rescued from annihilation by Commodore Stockton; he had played a subsidiary part in the last battles against the Mexicans in California; he knew that Commodore Stockton had orders from Washington to set up a civil government and had named Colonel Fremont as governor; despite this he had behaved like a martinet in brushing aside the commodore's accomplishments, Colonel Fremont's almost bloodless conquest of the territory and successful civil rule, and had suddenly decided that he would be the sole commander. Yet his conduct in relation to Colonel Fremont was inevitable if one granted the rightness of his original premise: that he had the latest order from Washington to rule California, that in refusing to accept his authority Colonel Fremont had committed an act of mutiny.

She spent a good deal of her time watching the faces of the judges to see how they were reacting; she stole quick glances at the spectators who thronged in each day at noon to enjoy this dramatic conflict between two famous men; she devoured the newspapers, cutting out the favorable articles to show to her husband, but feeling depressed at the condemnatory ones, which she destroyed before he could stumble across them.

On the morning of the twelfth day the judge advocate summoned General Kearny to the stand; Jessie saw that his leathery face was sallow. She thought how ill he looked, and had a moment of sympathy for this aging warrior who had chosen to fight in a court-martial instead of on a battleground. This sympathy was dispelled when he accused Colonel Fremont of destroying important papers. Jessie was glad to see her husband jump to his feet to protest. General Kearny apologized, said that he hadn't meant to use the word destroy, but in his first accusation the accuser had set the tone of the trial. General Kearny told of how he had led his troops across more than one thousand miles of desert, faced by hostile Indians, hunger and thirst, how he had played an important part in subduing California. Jessie extracted pencil and paper from her black handbag and began jotting down questions. After dinner she found that her husband, father and brother-in-law had engaged in the same process; for four hours they sat in the library framing a cross-examination which would lay bare a truer picture. When they went to bed that night she said to her husband:

"I can sleep easily for the first time since this trial opened, for I think General Kearny has exposed himself."

She had found that trouble and love were not amiable companions: from the moment they had left Silver Spring and plunged into the work of the trial, she and John had not been husband and wife, or even sweethearts, but business partners immersed in difficulties which threatened their association. Tonight because she genuinely felt the confidence she had been pretending, because he too felt hopeful, they could be lovers once again.

The next morning, refreshed and bright-eyed, they left the house a half-hour earlier and walked in the cool and invigorating air to the Arsenal. There were a few people standing outside the entrance, with its wide wooden overhang, and some of them spoke in a friendly tone.

"Good luck to you, Colonel. Don't be afeared of them, Mrs. Fremont, they can't hurt you."

The *Union* that morning had stated that Colonel Fremont would cross-examine General Kearny; there were whole periods of the California story to be gone over, hundreds of people would testify and a thousand documents be introduced, but everyone in Washington knew that this was the critical moment of the trial, when the two adversaries would come face to face. It was still a half-hour early when Jessie and John entered the courtroom, but every seat was taken. There was a hum of conversation, and quick looks were flashed at them as they walked down the aisle, an uncommonly handsome couple: twenty-three-year-old Jessie in a sea-green redingote with a brown velvet bonnet which matched her hair, her slender cheeks brushed with color from the walk in the sharp winter air, her eyes glistening from the confidence in which the people of the courtroom engulfed them, her mouth red and moist; and tightly gripping her arm, her thirty-four-year-old husband, his black hair combed forward a little over the brow and waving back across his ears, looking older and dignified because he was no longer shaving the beard which had grown during his third expedition and his year in California, walking erect and proud, his vitality evident beneath his full-dress uniform. For a moment he slipped into the spectators' seat beside the one which was reserved for Jessie and said quietly in her ear, so that no one could hear:

"After today, you won't be ashamed to be known as Mrs. Fremont. Today your name is going to be vindicated."

"Oh, darling," she murmured, "nothing that could ever happen in all this world would ever make me ashamed of my name. I carry it like that medal of honor Baron Humboldt awarded you."

"I'll confess that is what I hoped you would say," he replied with a wistful smile.

As he started to rise she took his hand and asked entreatingly, "Do be careful, dear; let General Kearny make the mistakes, let him be bitter and harsh and resentful. He had his day yesterday, today is yours: you can afford to be chivalrous."

He patted her hand.

"Trust me," he said. "My sword has such a fine edge this morning that the general won't know his throat is cut until he tries to turn his head."

It was not the answer for which she had hoped, but she had to be content with it. The court was opened, General Kearny sworn in and John rose, glanced at the papers before him, then addressed his commanding officer. Jessie was relieved to see that his voice was quiet and his manner courteous. She had been sitting tensed on the hard bench of the mustard-colored room; it was still cold and she had wrapped the coat of her green redingote over her bosom. The moment John began to speak her tension relaxed and the room felt warmer; she sat comfortably, while to her ears there came the cross-examination which seemed to her to vindicate her husband.

"General Kearny, did not William W. Russell, my secretary of state in California, come to your headquarters in Los Angeles on January 13 and tell you that I had sent him from the plains of Cahuenga where I had just accepted the surrender of the Mexican Army?"

"Yes."

"Did not Mr. Russell tell you that he had been sent for the purpose of ascertaining who was in chief command at Los Angeles, and after learning who this was, to make a report of the surrender of the Mexican Army and the armistice terms I had granted them?"

"Mr. Russell came to my headquarters on the thirteenth of January."

"Did not Mr. Russell ask you whether your arrival in the country had superseded Commodore Stockton's, who had before been recognized as chief commander?"

"He asked that question."

"Did you not tell him that Commodore Stockton was still in chief command, and tell him to make his report to the commodore?"

"Yes."

"And this was exactly four days before you ordered me to cease obeying Commodore Stockton and henceforth carry out your orders?"

"It was."

"Did you receive any orders from Washington between the fourteenth and the seventeenth of January, changing your status?"

"No dispatches reached me during that period."

A gasp went up from the audience; there came scattered applause. Jessie turned about in her seat gratefully; she saw that the spectators agreed that her husband had sincerely tried to find out who was the legal commander in chief; that General Kearny had contradicted himself. While the judge advocate threatened to clear the court, John asked that General Kearny be excused and put William W. Russell on the stand. Russell testified that he was a major in the California Battalion, had participated in the surrender of the Mexicans at Cahuenga, and had been instructed by Colonel Fremont to ride to Los Angeles and find out who was the commander in chief.

"Mr. Russell, when you talked to General Kearny at headquarters, before taking your report to Commodore Stockton, was my name mentioned?"

"It was. General Kearny expressed great pleasure at Colonel Fremont being in the country, and spoke of his eminent qualifications for the office of governor and his knowledge of the Spanish language and the manner of people. He told me that it was his intention to appoint Colonel Fremont governor of California if the instructions which he brought with him from the secretary of war were recognized in California."

"Did you then submit my reports to Commodore Stockton?"

"Yes, sir; I learned from the commodore that his relations to the territory as chief commander were in no wise changed by the arrival of General Kearny in the country."

"Did you then return to the California Battalion?"

"I did. I met Colonel Fremont at the head of his battalion on the morning of the fourteenth of January, about five miles from Los Angeles. I told him that I had had much conversation with both General Kearny and Commodore Stockton, touching their respective positions in the country; that I was satisfied, from what had occurred, that General Kearny was a better friend of his than Stockton; but, from Kearny's own admission, I regretted to have to give it as my opinion that we should have to look to Commodore Stockton still as commander in chief; that I found Stockton exercising the functions of commander in chief and submitted to implicitly, as I thought, by Kearny."

"Mr. Russell, did obedience to the command of Commodore Stockton in preference to that of General Kearny, when both were claiming the chief authority, present any advantages personal or military to Colonel Fremont?"

"I think not; General Kearny was known to have funds; and expected shortly an arrival of troops. He was, besides, known to be a warm friend of Colonel Fremont's family. I am satisfied that Colonel Fremont elected to obey Commodore Stockton alone from a conviction of duty."

Once again a murmur swept the courtroom. Jessie's spirits were rising rapidly. John then summoned General Kearny back to the stand.

"General Kearny, four days later when you ordered me to cease serving under Commodore Stockton and obey your commands, did I not inform you that Commodore Stockton had refused to cancel my appointment in the Navy and that he would consider me mutinous if I failed to recognize him as commander in chief?"

"As commander in chief of California I was not bound by Commodore Stockton's statements."

"But you knew that he threatened to use his sailors and marines to keep the California Battalion from being dismembered?"

"I was not convinced that Commodore Stockton would use his sailors against the California Battalion."

"Did you inform Commodore Stockton that he was no longer commander in chief of California, and that you were?"

"I so informed the commodore."

"And did he not refuse to step down from command?"

"He refused to acknowledge my command."

"Since I had been appointed governor of California, and was the next highest ranking officer to you and the commodore, were you not trying to use me to settle your dispute with Commodore Stockton?"

The judge advocate refused to allow the question. John turned, gazed at his wife for a long moment, then walked closer to the witness box.

"When I sent my first respectful letter declining to make any decisions until the question of rank was settled, did you not say that the man who carried my letter was a stranger to you?"

"I don't recall that I did."

"Then let me read it to you from your own testimony."

After he had read this bit from General Kearny's testimony, John continued, "That letter was brought to you at your headquarters by Christopher Carson. Did you not spend many weeks on the trail with Kit Carson, using him as your guide?"

"Mr. Carson served as our guide."

"Then how could you not recognize him a few weeks later when he brought you my letter?"

"The man who brought your letter was a stranger to me."

John Fremont called Kit Carson to the stand. Jessie exchanged a fragmentary smile with him as he came down the center aisle, having been summoned by a guard. After Carson was sworn in, John asked:

"Did you take a letter from me to General Kearny on the seventeenth of January 1847, saying that until General Kearny and Commodore Stockton adjusted between themselves the question of rank, where I thought the difficulty belonged, I should have to report and receive orders as hitherto, from the commodore?"

"I carried that letter to General Kearny."

"Did he recognize you?"

"Recognize me?" asked Carson, puzzled.

"Did he know that you were Christopher Carson?"

"We were on the trail together. How could he not know me?"

"Thank you, Mr. Carson. I should like to call General Kearny to the stand again.

"General Kearny, did you not inform the officers of your staff, immediately after my refusal of January seventeenth, that you were going to arrest me?"

"I may have mentioned it."

"When did you instruct me that I was to be placed under arrest? Was it not on the sixteenth of August, six months later, after we had reached Fort Leavenworth?"

"You were placed under arrest at Fort Leavenworth."

"Did you give me any chance to gather data for my defense in California? Was I able to inform my witnesses that I had need of them in Washington for the court-martial?"

"You were informed of your arrest in due time at Fort Leavenworth."

"When you ordered me to return to Washington, did you not refuse me the right to go to San Francisco and collect my journals, drawings, maps and specimens of the third expedition?"

"That was government property, unfit to be trusted to an officer derelict in his duty."

"Did you not refuse me permission to take my battalion to Mexico, to serve under General Taylor, even though General Scott had asked you to extend this privilege?"

"I know of no such advice from General Scott."

"When I asked for permission to return over a new route to complete my maps for the Topographical Corps, did you not oblige me to march behind your army under guard of the Mormon Battalion?"

"You marched behind the Mormon Battalion."

"Just one last question, General Kearny. Did you not attempt to prevent Lieutenant Gillespie and Midshipmen Beale and McLane from leaving California, even though they were overdue in Washington?"

"I have no authority over naval officers."

"But did you not go to Commodore Shubrick and ask that these men not be allowed to make the overland passage?"

"I informed Commodore Shubrick that I did not think Lieutenant Gillespie a responsible man to be wandering loose in California."

It was four o'clock. The court adjourned for the day. Jessie sat happy and almost complacent in her seat, waiting for the three men to gather up their papers inside the railing and go with her to the carriage. She felt that the trial was over, that it must be obvious to everyone that General Kearny had had a sudden change of attitude, had decided to assume command after informing everyone that Commodore Stockton was the commander; that John had been justified in not being able to understand this shift, since no new orders had arrived; that he was right in refusing to be responsible for deciding which of his superior officers was the commander in chief of California. General Kearny's motives and conduct had appeared in a bad light, he had shown himself overbearing while in California, and today on the stand had displayed such vindictiveness to the younger officer as to render his testimony invalid.

Early the next morning, when she was working in the archives of the War Department, she stumbled across the original report that General Stephen Watts Kearny had filed against Colonel John Fremont. Numbly she perceived that these were not the charges on which her husband was being tried, that the final bill of particulars had been drawn up by the War Department itself.

6

Her confidence of the day before vanished. The trial was by no means over, their gleeful confidence had been self-deception. Since the War Department had enlarged and elaborated the charges, since they had selected their own board of judges and were running the trial to suit themselves, nothing John could prove would make the slightest difference in the verdict.

She told no one of her discovery, but put on a gay face and tried to make a few jokes in the carriage when her father called for her. Her sense of impending disaster was magnified during the day when she found the court consistently ruling against her husband: refusing to allow Commodore Stockton to testify on the stand that he was the legal commander of California; refusing to admit to evidence reports of the secretary of the navy and the secretary of war which praised John's conquest of California; refusing to oblige Lieutenant Emory and Colonel Cooke to testify whether or not they were the authors of the anonymous letters in the newspapers prior to the trial; refusing to allow John to introduce material tending to prove that General Kearny had used his influence to retain on the Pacific coast all naval officers sympathetic to the defendant; refusing to allow any material to be presented which might impeach General Kearny as a witness.

The trial, which up to this point had proceeded quietly, broke into an unending series of wrangles. Every few moments the court was ordered cleared, and Jessie and the spectators were forced to stand for an hour in the vestibule, returning to the courtroom in time to hear, "the court cannot inquire into the refusal of General Kearny to grant Colonel Fremont . . . the court cannot inquire into the orders given to Colonel Fremont at Fort

Leavenworth . . . the court has read the documents submitted and finds they have nothing applicable to the case now on trial . . . the court decides that Colonel Fremont's objections to the course to be pursued cannot now be entertained . . ."

After working with John, her father and brother-in-law for five hours at night on a paper to prove that certain evidence could be introduced, she would lie wide-eyed in bed until dawn, then go up to the War or Navy Department to unearth the proper documents to buttress their brief—only to find their material challenged as irrelevant and inadmissible, to have the court cleared while she stood in the cold and drafty foyer waiting to be readmitted, and then to hear the crushing blow that the court had once again decided against them.

She was no longer able to reassure her husband that all would come out well; nor for that matter could John play the game any longer. William Carey Jones alone insisted that they were getting an unprejudiced trial, even though the judges almost never agreed with his penetrating analyses of the laws of evidence. They worked terribly hard, got along on too little sleep and too little food, lived half the time on black coffee. As their sense of frustration and injustice rose, their nerves became frayed. Jessie grew thin, dropped below a hundred pounds. She was alarmed over what was happening to her husband; her heart suffered compression pains when she saw how his black eyes were sinking deeper, becoming filled with a look of hatred and the sense of persecution. This was bad, it hurt their cause, yet when she tried to quiet him, to assure him they were getting a fair trial, she knew that within the hour a decision of the court would confound her, that they would become frenzied by learning that the questions which the judge advocate was asking General Kearny had been written beforehand by General Kearny himself!

Her father's wrath had been aroused as Jessie had never seen it during the years of his hardest battles. The attack on his son-in-law left him grieved and wildly partisan. At least half of his judgments had to be thrown out because he was indulging in illogical and violent reasoning.

Sitting beside him, emanating a chill which would have frozen any other man's turbulence, sat William Carey Jones, with cold green eyes, his light-skinned face expressionless, unruffled, dousing the fire of Tom Benton's emotions in icy legalistic thinking. Jessie frequently had to remember back to that one revealing moment when he had permitted himself to display his loyalty for the family, or she would have thought him so disinterested as to be worthless as counsel. Yet as she observed the means by which the briefs and arguments were prepared step by step so that not only before the court but in the daily press John would look his very best, she saw that the rapier-like brain of William Jones was their greatest asset.

She watched her husband at work, torn by the accusations and evidence piling up against him, realizing how much damage his enemies were doing to his reputation day by day, yet always and completely positive that he had been right, that there had been no other possible course of action for him, that General Kearny's entire motivation was one of revenge because of wounded dignity, the motivation of men like Emory and Cooke based on envy and jealousy, that of the War Department to re-establish its own pre-eminence when obliged to work in concert with the Navy.

It was neither the nerve strain nor the unceasing labor that got them down, but rather the feeling that they were batting their heads against a stone wall. The court seemed to be hearing the same words of defense that Jessie, the spectators and the newspaper reporters were hearing, yet no argument had any effect. The newspapers grew irritated with the court, asked in editorials why it was taking longer to settle their internecine squabble than to win the war in Mexico.

Thomas Hart Benton, the oldest and wisest among them, broke first under the strain. Shortly after the opening of the court one early December morning, General Kearny rose heavily to his feet and charged:

"I consider it due to the dignity of the court that I should here state that when I was answering the questions propounded to me by the court, the senior counsel of the accused, Thomas H. Benton, of Missouri, sat in his place, making mouths and grimaces at me, which I considered were intended to offend, to insult, and to overawe me."

There was a gasp in the courtroom. Jessie's cheeks flamed in embarrassment. The spectators craned to concentrate their gaze on Senator Benton. Over the sharp whisperings in the audience, Jessie heard the president of the court say that he had not observed the occurrence but regretted very much to hear of it. He then read the 76th Article of the Rules and Articles of War prohibiting the use of menacing words, signs or gestures in presence of the court-martial. There was an expectant hush when the president finished. All eyes were again turned on Senator Benton. He pulled himself to his feet, his face a dull brick red, and cried angrily:

"General Kearny fixed his eyes upon Colonel Fremont, looked insultingly and fiendishly at him. The judge advocate, by leading questions, led General Kearny into a modification of what he had previously sworn . . ."

A member of the court rose and said: "Mr. President, remarks reflecting upon the integrity of our proceedings are not, in my opinion, admissible . . ."

Tom Benton boomed out, "When General Kearny fixed his eyes on Colonel Fremont, I determined if he should attempt again to look down the prisoner, I would look at him. I did this today; and the look of today was the consequence of the looks in this court before. I did today look at General Kearny when he looked at Colonel Fremont, and I looked at him till his eyes fell—till they fell upon the floor!"

When Jessie reached home, after hearing her father reprimanded by the court, she flung herself into her big leather chair and wept unrestrainedly. This was the kind of blow for which she was not prepared. Whatever obloquy her husband might endure because of his conduct in the line of duty they could somehow face up to; but that her father should so completely forget himself . . . that he should leave himself open to bitter criticism, made her heartsick and guilty at the grief she was bringing upon him. Because of her he was profoundly hurting his name and the career he had so long cherished.

7

At the beginning of December, after having awakened with nausea three mornings in a row, she knew that she was pregnant again. With the knowledge came feelings compounded of elation and misgiving. This was the first time since the birth of Lily that she had become pregnant; that this time she would have a son she had not the slightest doubt. She knew what joy the arrival of a boy would bring to her husband, how much pride and renewed ambition. For all this she was happy, and yet if her husband were convicted and discharged from the service he would be lost, not know where to go or where to turn; their delight at the birth of their child would be submerged by their misfortune.

The very moment she was convinced that she was with child, Jessie made two resolutions: that she would tell no one until the trial was over; that they simply must not lose the case. She vowed that she would work her fingers to the bone, fight every last point to its uttermost extremity and beyond, that they would never give in. The early scenes of triumph, the clear-cut justification for her husband had to be brought out of this maze of quarrels and dusty documents. Her son must not be born into a world in which his father was an outcast. He must be born into a world in which the name of Fremont was honored.

She walked to her mother's room and, being preoccupied with her own thoughts, forgot to knock. Eliza was sitting on her mother's chaise; a fragment of a sentence hung in mid-air; the two women looked guilty. Jessie closed the door and, holding the knob in her tightly clenched fist, leaned against it, crushing her fingers. The physical pain drove out the pain of having come upon her mother and sister while they were discussing her. The three women maintained an awkward silence for a moment while Jessie asked herself what it was that they had been talking about. Had they been condemning her husband? Had they been criticizing her for her part in this drama? Were they ashamed of the scandal, resentful that their names had been dragged through the gutters of public gossip?

She left the door and came forward to her mother and sister; the intensity of her manner made them look up at her, and when she saw their eyes, soft and solicitous, she understood that only in her overwrought condition could she have accused her mother and sister of being disloyal. They had been pitying her, that was all; pitying her for her troubles and her burdens. She could imagine the dialogue between them, could hear them regretting that she had married a public figure, that she had gotten herself immersed in these questionable courses of action, pitying her for her misfortunes. She knew that her mother would be remembering the scene on the boat and in the carriage going to Cherry Grove, when she had cautioned her daughter against plunging her happy and protected life into conflict; would be remembering how positive Jessie had been that that was what she wanted, that her mother had been wrong to evade the important issues of life. Her mother probably thought that now she understood what a terrible mistake she had made, and wished that she had listened to older counsel.

She thought nothing of the sort; she did not regret her marriage or anything that happened in it, including the events that had led up to this trial. She was not afraid of life; she was not afraid of bold and vigorous action; she was not even afraid of this trial and its consequences. Having endured the worst that participation could bring about, she was qualified to speak; she wanted to cry out to her mother that she had not changed her mind, that she still believed in a life of action and conflict, in working by a man's side no matter how much mud splattered on the hem of her garment.

She did not want their pity; it was unendurable to her. They did not understand that they were pitying her for a suffering which she was not undergoing. If it were part of her job to have the fierce white light of publicity on her; if it were part of her job to endure public exposure as well as public acclaim; if it were part of her job to have her husband and her name smeared with abuse, then that was the price she would pay in order to carry forward an important work. No, she did not want their pity; it was misplaced. Let them rather pity weakness and withdrawal, the inability to endure the ravages of conflict and to come out of it with a serene heart and an ever increased faith in one's destiny.

She had forgotten why she had come into the room. She smiled a little too brightly, kissed her mother and her sister on the cheek, went out again without speaking.

On the night of December eighteenth Jessie, John, Tom Benton and William Jones worked straight through until dawn organizing a bill of particulars against the conduct of the court, summing up and analyzing every adverse decision and showing how their parallels had been decided affirmatively for General Kearny. They finished work at six, after which she had a cup of coffee, bathed, and was driven to the War Department to copy a number of paragraphs needed in the brief. The work occupied her until a few minutes before noon, allowing no chance to refresh herself or even to get a bite of food. She hurried to the Arsenal to provide her husband with the needed material.

She could not see him very clearly when he arose to present his brief, but she could not decide whether this was because the now unhappy, shrunken face of John Fremont was suffused in a haze of frustration or because there was a roaring in her head. The first words were the only ones that Colonel Fremont could speak out: the judge advocate challenged the admissibility of the brief, and the court was cleared. She went out into the bitterly cold vestibule, with icy drafts blowing in through the windows and he cracks under the doors. She stood still as long as she could, then walked ack and forth to generate warmth. By three o'clock she could no longer stand on her feet and had to ask an acquaintance to drive her home. She went to bed immediately. The room was swinging around, her body was burning as though a coal stove had been ignited inside her, her ears were pounding and her mouth felt filled with cotton. Only dimly did she hear her husband's words of comfort. But one word of the doctor's she heard distinctly before she lost consciousness:

"Pneumonia."

Her sister Eliza came back home to manage the household. Eliza was not very good at expressing herself in words, but when it came to expressing herself in deed, there was no one more eloquent. She kept Jessie's room at exactly the right temperature, no easy task in the middle of a raw December; either she or Maylee or a nurse was present every moment of the night and day; delicate and nutritious foods were prepared and kept warm over a brazier at the bedside. Mrs. Benton, who had taken to her bed altogether for the past two months to avoid the storms which were rocking the Benton household, had Maylee dress her each morning and, despite the fact that the left side of her face and body still were semiparalyzed, spent many hours by her daughter's side, holding her hand and telling bright stories from her childhood.

The most stricken was John, who felt that somehow he had brought this illness upon his wife. Jessie saw that he was reproaching himself unreservedly, even though when he visited her he kept a carefree smile on his face.

Tom Benton alone did not seem alarmed: Jessie had pneumonia? Well, lots of people had pneumonia! If he had been able to conquer the tuberculosis which had carried off the rest of his family, how could anyone doubt that Jessie would very quickly throw off anything so transitory as pneumonia?

Nor had it occurred to Jessie that her life was in danger; all of her nightmares had been woven around her husband and the trial. For four days she was very ill; at three o'clock of the fifth morning the fever broke. As soon as her strength returned she demanded news of each day's proceedings. She thought it sweet of her husband and father to take a light tone, to assure her that everything was going well. They did not know that she had bribed Josheem to bring her fresh copies of the *Union* and the *National Intelligencer* at noon after the men had left the house, and that she was following the case word for word. It was not good for her to read the proceedings when they contained bad news, but the anxiety of uncertainty was worse.

She spent Christmas and New Year's in bed propped up straight against a bank of cushions. Her father set up a small Christmas tree in the corner of her bedroom, and the doctor gave permission for the family gifts to be opened in her presence on Christmas morning.

John had run wild, spending almost the last of their rapidly diminishing funds on dozens of gifts for her, ranging all the way from pearl earrings to a sea-green silk lounging robe which she had to take off hastily because it made her face seem even greener than it was.

By the end of the third week she was out of bed trying a few experimental steps around the room, her legs feeling as weak as they had the first time she had tried to walk after giving birth to Lily. She leaned heavily on her husband's arm, rubbing her toes back and forth luxuriously on the soft, thick carpet. She had thought she would like to stay up for an hour or two, but at the end of five minutes she was grateful to be helped back to bed. Each day she ate everything Maylee put before her in an effort to recover quickly, put on a little weight, so that the men would let her resume work. By the third week in January she was remaining up all day. She did her best to conceal her pregnancy from the doctor; he complied with her tacit wish to keep the matter secret for just a little longer.

The hearing already had dragged through three months, exhausting the patience of the nation. By the last days in January the end finally came into sight. Though John refused her permission to attend court for the few remaining sessions, the men could not persuade her to keep away from the drawing up of the final statement for the defense. This summation proved to be their best collaboration of the trial, each of the four contributing his own particular analysis of the events. The document began with John's arrival in California, told of the ammunition, food, money and medical supplies given him by the Navy in order to help in the conquest, related the story of the war with Mexico and the surrender in California and the events leading up to the conflict over command. The testimony and documents submitted over a period of three months were sifted and analyzed, the discrepancies and irregularities set side by side.

On the face of it Jessie felt confident that although the court might bring in a guilty verdict on the two lesser charges of disobedience and conduct to the prejudice of military discipline, there could be no real basis for sustaining the charge of mutiny.

The next morning no one worked. The family assembled for a late breakfast: Jessie and her husband, Eliza and her husband, Thomas and Elizabeth Benton, her two younger sisters and brother. They dallied over their shirred eggs and coffee cake, dressed leisurely and departed en masse for the courtroom just a few moments before noon.

Jessie was proud of John when he rose to read his final summation in a well-modulated voice. Her confidence grew as he clicked off point after point, building a solid edifice of justification. At four o'clock, when it was time to adjourn, the court granted him permission to continue his presentation, and so he carried on for another hour, his voice growing a little throaty, but more resolute all the while. At the very end she sat almost unbreathing while he made the last eloquent plea which she and her husband had written in the same collaboration with which they had created the reports of the first two expeditions.

"My acts in California have all been with high motives, and a desire for the public service. My scientific labors did something to open California to the knowledge of my countrymen. My military operations were conquests without bloodshed; my civil administration was for the public good. I offer California, during my administration, for comparison with the most tranquil portions of the United States. I prevented civil war against Commodore Stockton, by refusing to join General Kearny against him; I arrested civil war against myself, by consenting to be deposed—offering at the same time to resign my place of colonel in the Army.

"I am now ready to receive the decision of the court."

The spectators broke into applause. Even the row of judges looked satisfied, as though this had indeed been a worthy presentation of a complicated case. Jessie relaxed; their tribulations were over, they had acquitted themselves in the best possible fashion. She started to rise, as had part of the audience, when suddenly, in a hard tone, in a manner become emotional and bitter, she heard her husband exclaim:

"Mr. President, I cannot rest my case without one final statement."

O dear God, thought Jessie, what has happened? What is he going to do now?

"Certainly the difficulties in California ought to have been inquired into," said John loudly, "but how? Not by prosecuting the subordinate, but the principals; not by prosecuting him who prevented, but him who would have made civil war. If it was a crime in me to accept the governorship from Commodore Stockton, it was a crime in him to have bestowed it; and, in either event, crime or not, the government which knew of his intention to appoint me, and did not forbid it, has lost the right of prosecuting either of us! I consider these difficulties in California to be a comedy of three errors: first, in the faulty orders sent out from this place; next, in the unjustifiable pretensions of General Kearny; thirdly, in the conduct of the government in sustaining these pretensions. And the last of these errors I consider the greatest of the three."

When he had finished he stood by his table awkwardly. Jessie felt herself grow limp. She rose and rushed down the center aisle of the courtroom blinded by tears. All of their good work had been overthrown. The uncertainty lodged in the deepest fragment of John Charles Fremont's heart had betrayed him.

8

When she reached home she suffered an hour of retching which produced little but yellow bile. The presence of Maylee with her strong arm clasped about her waist was all that kept her from slipping to her knees.

Maylee picked her up and put her into bed, where she lay white and weak and frightened. She pretended that she was asleep when her husband came up to the room several hours later; with her eyes shut she could see

his face: dark, twisted, unhappy, ashamed of his last outburst but preferring
to die before he would admit that he shouldn't have done it or that he had
hurt his own chances. She lay still while he slipped into the bed beside her.
She wanted to turn to him and take him in her arms, to comfort him, to kiss
the unshed tears from his eyes, to smooth away the gnarled lines that slashed
his face. But she dared not, for she feared she would herself break down and
cry, give an indication of how tragic she thought his mistake in antagonizing
the court and appearing before the nation in his last moment as an arrogant
and insolent man; having built a magnificent defense to prove that he had
not been guilty in California, then in a last shattering few minutes to reveal
the very temper and manner which General Kearny and the War Department
had been prosecuting these three months long.

She did not love him the less for his outburst; she loved him the more,
as a mother loves an errant and headstrong child whom she cannot control.
Nor could she reveal that she felt sorry for him and wanted to cradle his
confused, hot head on her breast. Better to let the moment go and face the
consequences than to injure their relationship by showing her husband that
she pitied him. Though he made not the slightest move, though he lay like a
man of stone at her side, she knew that he was not asleep, and she knew
the agonies he was enduring as once again he mentally recapitulated his
defense. Still she gave no sign that she was awake; better to let this cold
silence lie between them.

At last she heard the slow rhythmical breathing for which she had been
listening. For another few moments she lay quietly, then she rose, put on a
quilted robe and slippers, went down to the kitchen, where she made herself a
cup of strong coffee, then went up to her father's library. She had already
participated in the writing of the defense; now she must write the case for the
prosecution, reacquaint herself with the evidence against her husband. Once
she had drawn up the most formidable bill of particulars available, had put
them all down in black and white, they would furnish her with a means of
accepting the verdict of the court-martial, enable her to go on from there.
She was frightened at what might happen to John if a verdict of guilty on
all charges was brought in; she did not know whether he would have the
stamina to keep from further injuring himself in the intensity of his reaction.
She, for the both of them, must be prepared to accept the worst.

There were a number of glowing coals in the fireplace. She put on some
kindling from the woodbox, then added a walnut log and stood rubbing her
pale slim fingers before the flames. When they were warm she sat in her
old chair, drew her desk over her knees and began writing rapidly.

It was not difficult to build up a formidable case against Colonel Fremont,
for its particulars had been dinned into her ears in the courtroom for three
months. She recounted the twenty-two specifications, starting with his three-
day stand at Hawk's Peak, his assistance to the Americans in Mexico in
their "Bear Flag Rebellion," his share in the unauthorized conquest of California, his unauthorized acceptance of Mexican surrender, through to the

point where he refused to relinquish his command to an army officer sent by the War Department.

When John C. Fremont had converted his third expedition into the California Battalion, one of his men had refused to make the shift and be plunged into a war. John had ordered him locked in a dungeon below Sutter's Fort overnight. By morning the man had reconsidered, joined the California Battalion. This single act of coercion constituted the blackest deed of the California exploit: John Fremont demanded absolute obedience and ironclad discipline; had he not told her stories of how he preserved this discipline on his three expeditions? Had he not clapped one of his men into prison for failure to obey an unwarranted command? Why then had he himself not accorded the same strict obedience and the same ironclad discipline to his superior officer? If discipline were imperative for those below him in rank, was it not also imperative for those above him? And if he were going to use force on a member of his exploring expedition, why was General Kearny not justified in using the same force on Colonel Fremont?

She could answer this only by concluding that John knew that under his appointment from Commodore Stockton as civil governor he would be in command of the new territory, for the Navy would not rule on shore, Commodore Stockton would set out for sea and John Fremont would be left in complete charge. Under General Kearny's appointment he always would be a subordinate: General Kearny would appoint his own staff officers with whom he had worked for years, and who were superior to him in rank. The principal appointments would go to real army men, not to a Topographical engineer; after he had done the groundwork, played the most important role in the conquest, he would be ordered to pack up his maps and journals and report back to the Topographical office in Washington, his career in California ended. He would want to write up his third expedition, make his new maps, but once that was finished, what did he do next? Having caught an image of a greater part for himself on the stage of history, the function of topographer and map maker must have seemed limited. From now on he would be a conqueror of new territory, a governor of new states. All this he stood to lose if he acknowledged General Kearny over Commodore Stockton.

Jessie laid down her pen, walked once again to the fire and threw on another log. The hours of the night slipped away and she felt forlorn; for here, hidden in the mass of detail, was the most important point of the controversy, one which had been allowed to remain obscure: John was an army man, he had always been an army man, he had attained his rank, gained his honors and done his work as an army man; the Army had financed his expeditions, won him his respect and fame. It was very well for him to be a naval officer while there was no superior army man on hand, but the very instant a superior army officer arrived on the scene there could be no question as to his obligation; under any circumstances he had no alternative, no choice. When General Kearny ordered him to obey he had but one possible answer:

"Yes, sir."

If John had made that one answer, these troubles would never have happened, there would have been no court-martial.

With equal clarity there came to her the realization that from this viewpoint the procedure of the court-martial had not been prejudiced. John had not put the Army first, above everything, and particularly above himself. Now she understood why the West Point officer did not like the volunteer officer: what the regular army man had as a part of his equipage, John did not have: the discipline that no matter how good his work, or how important he had become on the spot, he surrendered his position to a superior officer immediately that he arrived with authority to take over . . . regardless of whether the subordinate officer felt himself to be more qualified than the officer coming to supplant him. All army officers had suffered such thwarting, but they had accepted it because it was part of their tradition.

John was not and never had been an army man; he had been a topographer and engineer. Nor had she accepted the Army's iron discipline as part of her husband's unbreakable duty. Why did her father not condemn her for her mutiny, send couriers after the second expedition to bring her husband back to stand charges in Washington? Why did he allow her to send John the signal to become involved in still another mutiny?

Because we are headstrong people! Because we are driven by emotion, are certain of our superior abilities, and are unable to put ourselves aside, to make the sacrifice of pride and individuality to our government. We are all equally guilty, myself, my father and my husband, but I am the most guilty because I had no extenuating circumstances.

She went back to her desk and continued writing. When she finished, dawn was just prying up the dark flooring of the eastern sky. As she walked down the long hallway she saw a light coming from under the crack of William Carey Jones's door. She knocked lightly. After a moment her brother-in-law came to the door, a blue flannel bathrobe wrapped around his thin frame, a pen clutched in his right hand, his fingers inky.

"Haven't you been asleep, William?" she asked.

"No, I . . . I was just making a few notes."

She saw that his desk was littered with sheets of paper, and asked if she might see what he had written. When he replied that she might, she walked past him into the bedroom; Eliza was sleeping with her face turned away from the light. A glance at the small, tight, precise writing showed her that it was about the trial, but she did not gather at once what its point was. She asked in a whisper, "Why have you written down all this material?"

"A good lawyer must never be taken by surprise," he replied with a minimum of voice. "He must know everything the opposition can bring to support its contention."

Jessie smiled wanly, handing him the batch of her papers. He read two pages, then looked up at her with a startled expression.

"You've been doing exactly the same thing."

"You know the old line about great minds," she murmured, trying to force a laugh; "would you care to compare our bills of particulars?"

"Let's go into the library where we won't disturb Eliza."

He sank into his father-in-law's chair before the fire and went back to the reading of her pages. After a few moments he shook his head.

"Yes," he agreed, "Colonel Fremont's commission in the Navy was automatically canceled when General Kearny took over."

"What are our chances today in that courtroom?"

He rose, put her papers on the map table, stalked about the room holding the flannel bathrobe around his tall, skinny figure.

"Light, William, light," she murmured, "I am prepared to hear the worst."

He made the best case he could, pointing out that neither President Polk nor the Cabinet nor the majority of the Senate wanted a conviction. He spoke of her husband's long and magnificent record of service. Jessie was not convinced. She replied so softly he almost could not hear:

"William, you don't believe your own arguments. If this case had not been your brother-in-law's, you would never have pled it. You feel it the duty of the court to bring in a verdict of guilty."

He denied her accusations. She did not press him. She kissed him lightly on the cheek, thanked him for all he had done for them. Just then her child moved inside her; her heart and stomach seemed to turn over, and she began to tremble.

"Whatever the law may be, I am not able to see it that way. I am his wife, and I know how he will suffer if the court declares him guilty. I know how it will wreck his life. I want my children to have a successful father, a man who can hold his head high. Oh, William, I am responsible: I led him into his first mutiny; I urged him into the action in California which led him to believe that he could disobey General Kearny. If only I could take the blame!"

William Jones put his arm about his sister-in-law and said quietly, "Come, Jessie dear, you are overtired: you should not have worked all night. You must go to bed now and get some sleep. You will want to be strong and rested when we leave for court."

She permitted herself to be led down the long hall to her room. At the doorway he patted her shoulder with his bony fingers. Jessie crawled exhausted to bed and fell into a black sleep.

9

Maylee had to wake her at ten o'clock when she brought up a hot breakfast. Jessie heard the torrents of rain sloshing against the outside windows.

It was a dark, depressing day. She put on a knitted tan wool dress with wide-bottomed sleeves over her white chemisette, and over her shoulders she gathered her new brown Cornelia wrap which she fastened in front with a cameo brooch. A last glance in the mirror showed her that her outfit looked much too somber, as though she were anticipating the worst, so she went to the top drawer of her bureau, rummaged through the jewelry and slipped a long chain of bright green beads around her neck. The beads were out of place, but they lightened her spirit.

She looked for the men and found each of them sitting alone and silent: her father in the library slumped down in his chair by the cold fireplace; her brother-in-law in his bedroom reading Plato's *Republic;* her husband in the drawing room hunched up on the divan before the bow window. She kissed him on the cheek and said, "We are all ready to go now," and gratefully took his proffered arm while he led her down to the carriage.

The courtroom was jammed with the hundreds of people come to hear the final verdict.

The judges filed in, took their places at the high tribunal. After what seemed an interminable silence, while her heart pumped hard and the child within her never stopped moving, Brigadier General George M. Brooke rose, spread out a paper before him and started to read:

"Of the first specification of first charge: Guilty. Of the second specification of first charge: Guilty. Of the third specification of first charge: Guilty."

She turned cold as he read all eleven of the first specifications, with a "Guilty" after each of them. He continued to read in a toneless voice:

"Of the first specification, second charge: Guilty. Of the second specification, second charge: Guilty," and continued to declare seven times "Guilty." Still carrying on in the clamped silence of the courtroom, he reiterated:

"Of the first specification, third charge: Guilty. Of the second specification, third charge: Guilty."

There was one last strangulating moment, and then the judge advocate rose before General Brooke and announced:

"The court finds Lieutenant Colonel Fremont guilty of mutiny; of disobedience of the lawful command of his superior officer; of conduct to the prejudice of good order and military discipline. The court does therefore sentence the said Lieutenant Colonel John C. Fremont, of the regiment of Mounted Riflemen, United States Army, to be dismissed from the service."

No one murmured or moved. Jessie did not dare to look at her husband or her father. Each sat alone, chewing the bitter herb of his thoughts. Then General Brooke once again rose and said in an easier tone: "The majority of this court after careful consideration wishes to make a final statement:

"Under the circumstances in which Lieutenant Colonel Fremont was placed between two officers of superior rank, each claiming to be commander in chief in California—circumstances in their nature calculated to embarrass the mind and excite the doubts of officers of greater experience than the accused—and in consideration of the important professional services rendered by him previous to the occurrence of those acts for which he has been tried, the undersigned, members of the court, respectfully commend Lieutenant Colonel Fremont to the lenient consideration of the President of the United States."

When they reached home John said: "You had better lie down at once, Jessie; I hope the verdict isn't going to make you ill."

She was surprised to find that instead of feeling ill she felt stronger than she had for several days; there was a time for being frightened, the waiting time, when one's fate hung in the balance and there was nothing one could do but suffer the tortures of uncertainty. Now she knew the worst; it had to be endured calmly and strongly; she had laid the groundwork for that endurance the night before when she had charted the objective case against her husband. She knew that this was the time for serenity and strength.

To her husband she replied, "Thank you, dear, but I feel all right. There is nothing those thirteen judges could have said that could have hurt me. That decision was arrived at before the case opened. Any civilian jury in a civil court would have acquitted you. I cannot be hurt by the determination of the War Department to put the Navy in its place. As the judges had the courage to say at the very end, you were the victim of a conflict over authority. I held before this trial opened, and I hold even more strongly now, that you did exactly right. If it means anything to you, my darling, I acquit you on all charges, and I say 'well done.'"

"It means a great deal to me," said John, not looking at her. "Your faith in me is the one rock that can never be shattered."

"Good then, let us go in to dinner. I am ravenous. It seems to me that I haven't eaten a hearty meal for weeks."

Later that evening she found her father in the library. She closed and locked the door behind her. He was having a difficult time repressing his anger.

"Very well," she said in a small voice. "The verdict is in. There is nothing we can do about the court-martial. Let us put all thoughts of it out of our minds. The important question now is: what will President Polk do?"

"He will overrule the decision of the court," growled Tom Benton.

"Are you certain of that?"

"He damned well better," he cried, "or I'll blast his administration. He knows that he and his Cabinet are responsible for the mess in California. They played careful and cautious; they wanted the credit for acquiring California, but they avoided the responsibility as though it were scarlet fever. They're avoiding the conflict of the Army and Navy in exactly the same fashion. If President Polk doesn't countermand that verdict, I'll start a senatorial investigation that will expose the whole regime."

Jessie felt the old sense of fear come over her. Why did men try to cover trouble with more trouble? Why didn't they know that the more deeply one became involved in exposure the more impossible it was to pull oneself up out of the morass? She did not want any more investigations; she did not want more charges and trials and hurt feelings and blasted reputations. She wanted only peace now, peace to go back to their work. She wanted her husband's hurts healed, as she knew that time alone could heal them. She wanted soft words now and quiet thinking, not threats and anger.

"I only want one thing, Father," she said. "I want President Polk to commute the sentence."

Her father sensed the tremulousness in his daughter's voice. He held out his big bearish arms to her and she sat on one knee hiding her face in his shoulder.

"I'm sorry, my little girl," he said softly. "I'm just dreadfully sorry. But don't feel too badly about it; most of the newspapers will protest the verdict, call it intergovernmental politics, nothing more."

Without lifting her head, Jessie asked in a muffled voice, "Will President Polk commute the sentence?"

"Yes. Of that I am certain. The court's recommendation for leniency makes it inevitable. That is why the judges put it in: it is their way of telling John that all is forgiven, and he can come home."

She lifted her head, speaking with all the intensity of her being:

"He must not leave the service. He has been in the Army for ten years. It's the only life he knows and the only life he loves. He has such pride in the Topographical Corps; he had plans for so many expeditions, and so much valuable work in carrying on the tasks of Nicollet and Hassler. If he must give up his uniform and his rank and his work, he will be like a man whose arms have been cut off . . ."

"I know, I know," interrupted her father sympathetically. "We cannot let him leave the Army. That is the one blow that would really cripple him. I will go to President Polk tomorrow, even though it is unnecessary. No one wants Colonel Fremont out of the service."

"If President Polk will order that the verdict be set aside, I won't regret anything that has happened or even condemn the court. We'll start fresh. I've talked to his fellow officers in the Topographical Corps; they want him back, they want him to continue his work. We'll get him sent out on another expedition, mapping the southwest trail to Los Angeles, perhaps. By the time he returns everything will be forgotten."

In her agitation she rose, walked to the long rough table and began opening atlases without seeing the maps. Her father came to her side.

"Everything you say is true, Jessie; true and sensible. Have no further fears. In another few days your husband will be back at work in the Topographical office drawing his maps of the third expedition."

Jessie turned about, a new vitality seizing her.

"That is the way it must be, Father; he must go back to work at once. I know that after he is plunged into his maps and his reports these bad memories will fade. After all, he did find a new trail to California, one which will replace the Oregon Trail. Thousands of people in the country are waiting to see his new map and read his report. And that is where he must go for his ultimate justification, to the people. They will sustain Colonel Fremont. But he must get back to his work; he must publish the results of his third expedition."

10

The next two days, while they waited for President Polk's decision, passed for Jessie in alternate rushes of hope and anxiety. She knew that when her father spoke in loud, blustering tones he could be wrong in his judgment, but he had assured her quietly that the president would commute her husband's sentence. She firmly believed this, but of it she said no word to John. She did not know what he was thinking, for he talked little, disappeared for long stretches each day, returning with his boots and the bottom of his trousers wet and mud-stained. That he had great hopes in President Polk, she knew, for had not President Polk sent him secret orders with Lieutenant Gillespie to take charge of the conquest in California? Had he not been Polk's confidential agent, superior in command to both General Kearny and Commodore Stockton? President Polk would not let him down. He would sustain Colonel Fremont, overthrow and dismiss the charges, praise him for his work in California and tell him to resume his sword. All these things Jessie learned were in her husband's mind from the scattered phrases he let drop as the weary hours spun themselves out.

At noon of the third day, just as they were about to sit down to a luncheon for which no one had any appetite, a courier arrived from the War Department. John jumped up from the luncheon table, ran into the foyer, snatched the letter when Jessie reached his side; together they read the lines that danced crazily before them:

Upon an inspection of the record, I am not satisfied that the facts proved in this case constitute the military crime of "mutiny." I am of the opinion that the second and third charges are sustained by the proof, and that the conviction upon these charges warrants the sentence of the court. The sentence of the court is therefore approved, but in consideration of the peculiar circumstances of the case, of the previous meritorious and valuable services of Lieutenant Colonel Fremont, and of the foregoing recommendations of a majority of the members of the court, the penalty of dismissal from the service is remitted.

Lieutenant Colonel Fremont will accordingly be released from arrest, will resume his sword, and report for duty.

JAMES K. POLK

Washington, February 14, 1848.

Relief and joy swept through her. President Polk had sustained her judgment, and that of the press and the people, by declaring her husband innocent of mutiny! It was unimportant that he upheld the court in decreeing that John had been guilty of conduct in the prejudice of military discipline. What was important was the fact that the president had praised her husband, spoken of his meritorious and valuable services. He had remitted the penalty of dismissal, ordered Colonel Fremont to resume his sword and report for duty.

She slid her arm about his shoulder and cried, "Oh, I am so happy, I knew it would come out all right. The president has vindicated you and praised you to the whole country."

John broke away from her embrace, stabbed her with a dark look of withdrawal, crumpled the president's paper to a pulp in his hand, flung it away from him and stormed out of her presence.

What have I done? she asked herself, numbly. Why does he behave like this?

After a moment she followed him up the stairs to their bedroom. He was standing at a window with his back to her, a back that had anger and hurt humiliation written across every hostile line. Jessie entered and stood in the center of the room.

"John," she said softly, "I'm sorry if I offended you. It was only that I was so happy and proud that President Polk had praised your work in California. It seemed to me that by praising you, he was telling the nation obliquely that this trial should never have been held."

Her words struck irresilience. Still groping in the dark, fearful lest she offend him further, she slid into a chair, was silent for a few moments, then continued:

"You see, my dear, I am being a little selfish in this affair: I know that in part they have been trying you for my act two years ago in St. Louis, when I suppressed the order summoning you back to Washington. And I sent you the first unauthorized instructions to act in California. If President Polk had declared you guilty of mutiny, he would have been convicting me as well. But the president said we are not guilty of mutiny. If he's unwilling to expose his own hand, to tell the world that he fomented the uprising in California through you, then we must suffer in silence. That is the part of the job we agreed to do when I suggested you move quickly and boldly. Who in the country is better able to vindicate you than our chief executive? The president has declared publicly how valuable you have been, and by ordering you back to your command, he is telling the country that you are indispensable."

John turned about quickly, his eyes blazing, his skin greenish beneath the black beard.

"I won't take his charity," he said in a cold, embittered voice. "He knows I'm innocent; that whole prejudiced court knows I'm innocent; but they turned against me, they slandered my character and minimized my contri-

bution. Then they throw me a bone with a few shreds of meat on it and
expect me to grovel before them in gratitude. President Polk has done a
cowardly thing; he is perpetuating the injustice of the court. Why didn't
he have the courage to declare me innocent . . . ?"

"He did, darling, he did," urged Jessie, trying to placate him. "Don't
you see how he told the court they were wrong when they declared you
guilty of mutiny?"

"Then why didn't he overthrow the other two convictions? Why does he
deal in half-measures . . . ?"

She interrupted, but quietly, so as not to antagonize him:

"It wouldn't be wise to hurt the War Department too severely, John. You
must be tolerant; you must understand that the president can't completely
disavow the Army. That would lead to ill feelings, to conflicts within the
government . . ."

"I see! It's better to commit still another injustice, to declare an innocent
man guilty, rather than incur the displeasure . . ."

"It goes deeper than that, John dear. Every day of his life the president
has to make a thousand compromises. In this affair he has to keep you satisfied, and the Army and the Navy satisfied as well. I think he leaned over
on your side considerably; he will suffer from it, never fear."

He took several steps toward her, demanding, "Then you approve his
decision? You approve his declaring me guilty of disobedience to my superior officers, of conduct prejudicial to good order and military discipline?
I never thought I would live to see the day when my wife . . ."

Sick at heart, Jessie jumped up, went to him and flung her arms about
his neck.

"No, no! I'm only saying that it was a sop the president had to throw
to the Army."

"Yet you approve the president's confirmation of the conviction," he flung
out at her. "What a miserable state of affairs this is: you say I am innocent
of the charges, yet you approve the guilty verdict! Really, Jessie, I am astonished! You're taking sides against me."

"Please don't say things like that. Can't you be generous enough to allow
this compromise? Then the affair will be settled to everyone's satisfaction . . ."

"To everyone's satisfaction!" he cried with irony. "To my satisfaction?
After I conquered a whole new territory for them, I have to be tried like
a criminal, have the court declare me guilty and the president sustain the
verdict, and my wife tells me that it should be to my satisfaction! Jessie,
what has come over you? How can you say these things to me?"

She realized that it would be unwise to continue. Instead she agreed that
President Polk had avoided his full duty. Since her opposition seemed only
to infuriate him, she understood that it would be better to go along with
him and by her agreement, her love, slowly soften his harsh anger, blur
the edges of his indignation, and let time come to her rescue. She must not

allow him to feel that she too was against him, that she was part of the conspiracy to persecute him. Only a few days before he had told her that her faith in him was the one rock that could never be shattered. Right or wrong, she must never allow that faith in her loyalty to be dissipated.

There was a knock at the door. Jessie called, "Come in." Her father entered the room. He carried the president's paper in his hand; he had smoothed it out, read the message and come up to congratulate John on the outcome.

"I told you that President Polk would stand by the colonel!" he exclaimed happily to his daughter. He walked to his son-in-law with his hand extended. "Ah John," he said kindly, "I'm happy for all our sakes that it's over. It will be good to see you come striding down the street again with your sword clanging at your side. I know how anxious you are to get back to your work . . ."

"I am not going back to my work," broke in John, sharply.

Tom Benton's hand dropped to his side, while his big bluff face bore an expression of bewilderment.

"Not going back . . ."

"No. I am resigning from the Army."

Tom screwed up his eyes until they were reduced to narrow slits, but he could perceive the meaning no better that way. He turned to his daughter, asking, "What is the meaning of this, Jessie?"

She was passionately convinced that John must not resign, both because she felt that his resignation would be in some small measure an admission of guilt, but mostly because she was horrified at the thought of his giving up the work for which he had trained himself, which he loved so ardently, and for which he was so well equipped. What would he do? After his expeditions and years on the trail, could he become a government clerk, go to work in a shop? To what did a man of his training turn? He could get a teaching job, but he was a man of action, not a man of theory and classrooms; he would wither in such an atmosphere. She was not worried about how good a living he could earn, that was unimportant; what concerned her was how her husband was going to find another place in the world which would enable him to be valuable, to hold his head high, to keep his flaming spirit, to be a man among men and a leader among men. He had deliberately and joyously chosen his role and prepared himself for it, just as her father had, and she knew how badly it would break Thomas Hart Benton if he could no longer be the senator from Missouri.

She must not let her husband resign from the Army! Yet he was utterly confident that she would agree with him and sustain his judgment: their years of happy marriage, the complete confidence and intimacy of their every plan had made it impossible for him to imagine that she would not uphold his decision.

Faced with a painful dilemma, she had to choose between the equally desperate alternatives of permitting John to wreck his brilliant career, or herself to wreck their marriage; for she sensed that their marriage would be irrevocably injured if she inflicted upon him the blow of contesting his judgment. Before she had accepted John's proposal of marriage she had asked for the right to collaborate with her husband in his work, and he had granted that right. It was a tragic mistake for him to resign; it was arbitrary of him to take this step without consulting with her. But there had been another covenant in the marriage agreement: she had promised to cherish him in sickness and in health, in misfortune and in prosperity, to go with him whither he went. These vows left no room for indecision: she had no right to cut the fabric of their marriage. His career would shift and change and vary, rise and fall, succeed and fail many times over the years. But the marriage relationship was more tenuous, more in need of protection: it must never fail, it must never shift and change and vary, it must not endure despair and renunciation.

She thought, There are no ugly or painful memories that either of us can evoke about our marriage, nor must there be any. Marriage is not only the most important relationship, but the one which can make all the rest of life seem beautiful and worthwhile, no matter how difficult its externals. If I sustain our marriage, I sustain all; if I fail in this and yet succeed in everything else, I shall have failed in my life.

She went to her husband's side, slipped her hand into his and held herself against his shoulder.

"It's very simple, Father," she said in a quiet, almost casual tone. "John is resigning from the Army."

"But why?" thundered Tom Benton. "He's been pardoned! He's been praised! Everyone expects him to go back . . ."

"I'm not going back to an army that could declare me guilty on twenty-two specifications, not even having the decency or comradely good will to declare that I had proved my innocence on at least one of the counts."

"Of course, of course," Tom boomed, "it was a miserable show. But seven of the judges signed the affidavit asking the president to commute the order."

John picked up a copy of the document lying on his desk, folded back the first page, then pointed to a paragraph on the second.

"Did you read this?" he demanded, harshly. "Do you really advise me to return to an army which says: 'The court has found nothing conflicting in the orders and instructions of the government; nothing impeaching the testimony of the part of the prosecution; nothing, in fine, to qualify, in a legal sense, the resistance to authority of which the accused is convicted . . .' The only way I can register a full protest is to resign."

Realizing the grave consequences, but not knowing what to do next, Tom Benton turned to his daughter for the help he was certain would be forthcoming.

"What do you say to all this, Jessie?" he demanded.

For a split second Jessie thought that her breath would stop coming. Her husband had been hurt anew by her father's stand; his pride already had suffered so deeply that there was danger of injuring his very fiber. He would never recover if they stood against him. Knowing that her father was absolutely right and her husband absolutely wrong, she nevertheless understood that she must stand by her husband, by this man who had never had a sense of security, a sense of the confidence of the world and his associates. She must accept his judgment and, more important, show him by every word and gesture that she agreed with him.

She caught hold of herself, drew breath in sharply and replied, her voice under full control:

"I agree with John."

Her father's face seemed to sag.

"You agree! But Jessie, that's impos . . . Only two days ago you . . ."

"Two days ago I did not know that President Polk would not dismiss all the charges."

"But don't you realize . . ."

"I realize that an injustice has been done to my husband. It is his right to register the severest possible protest."

All of the pomp and sternness went out of Tom Benton; to Jessie's blurred eyes it seemed that her father too was trapped.

He cried in despair, "I thought I had trained you in masculine logic. I thought I had made a man of you in straight thinking. And here you are, thinking like a woman!"

Jessie smiled a little plaintively, then replied, "Yes, Father, just like a woman."

There was a finality in her voice which prevented Tom Benton from persisting. She was unhappy at hurting him, at being obliged to conceal the truth behind her motives. But her first duty was to protect her husband; in marriage there was no right or wrong, logic or illogic, reason or unreason; there was only a man's nature to work with, a man's gifts and limitations, his emotion, his temperament, his personality, his character: these and these alone were the determinants of conduct. Marriage was the rock; all else was the foam which beat against the rock.

11

She went with him to select the best black broadcloth on the market, yet the first time she saw her husband in civilian clothes Jessie's heart sank. In the eight years that she had known him she had never seen John in any apparel but his army uniform, which he had always worn handsomely and with pride. His dark suit had been well made, it fitted him nicely, but he wore it awkwardly; he who had shown infinite grace beneath his plain army blue now evidenced by every stiff, resentful movement that he knew his stature had been lessened.

Despite the fact that his notes, journals and drawings still were in San Francisco, Jessie was convinced that they had to write the memoir of his third expedition. Even if nothing appreciable came of it, the work would be the best thing conceivable for him. It would be difficult to get him to begin work; yet there were important reasons why she must bring this third report into being: his salary, never a large one, had now stopped altogether. It was the first time that she had encountered an actual need for money: while her husband's salary had been modest, their expenses in the Benton home had been small, otherwise they could not have saved the three thousand dollars which he had handed over to the American consul Larkin in Monterey to buy a ranch in the Santa Cruz mountains over-looking the Pacific Ocean. They yearned to leave Washington behind them, to go out to California, build themselves a home on their ranch, set up a little community to be called Fremontville.

But they hadn't the money to book passage to California, for the voyage was an expensive one; they had no money to build themselves a house even if they could reach their ranch; most serious of all, they had no resources with which to buy horses, farm machinery, feed and livestock, or to pay for the necessary labor. Tom Benton had offered to lend them money; Harriet Bodisco had come to Jessie just before the trial with a jewel case of diamonds and sapphires and asked her to please sell them and use the money for their expenses; friends like James Buchanan had offered to lend them anything they might need.

She was not frightened at the lack of money, but she sensed how severely her husband might suffer if the burden of debt were added to the others. The memoir was a way out of their difficulties; it would set her husband back to work, help rid him of his concentration on himself. Its publication could perhaps earn them a sum of money adequate to get them to California and start work on their ranch. If the book were successful, then she was confident that the newspapers and magazines would buy their stories.

She worked on the assumption that eventually he would of course write his third report; she had known that he would refuse to do so, and had prepared her attack against this defeatism. It was a long, slow, uphill battle, but she was in no hurry. A good wife must be a leveler: when her husband was riding the crest it was her obligation to deflate his ego by placing his accomplishment in proper perspective, to keep him from growing inordinately fond of himself. This was a comparatively simple task for any woman who had a light touch and was gifted with humor; the more difficult task for a wife was when her husband was discouraged, unhappy, at loose ends, without a job or a purpose or a direction. It was then that the wife had to create a healthy setting for her husband, establish the right mood, bring out the best in him, buttress his confidence by keeping in the forefront his gifts and accomplishments.

Being a good wife was probably the most difficult achievement in the human agenda.

After a few weeks, in the early days of March, she saw that she almost had him convinced; she needed only one culminating stroke. That night she confided to her husband that she was pregnant, that this time she had the utmost confidence it would be their long-desired son, and she wanted to have the report finished before young John came into the world. She determined that by the time the child was born, sometime late in July, the memoir must be completed and published, her husband once again established.

Now more than ever she was grateful for the years of intensive training she had had with her father. She worked steadily, but not too long at a stretch. She was not carrying as well as she had with Lily; her youth and health had been eaten into. However, her main concern was with her husband. Though she had succeeded in reviving his energy and health sufficiently to begin work, he would go to no dinners or parties, he took the long walks and rides so necessary to his well-being only after dark, after he had put her to bed. At the dinner table it was obvious that he was unhappy, constrained. For once she did not regret it when Congress adjourned in the spring and her father returned to St. Louis. She thought that the work and her companionship were helping her husband a little, bringing him back slowly, enabling his eyes to look at people head on. Yet no one knew better than she what a slow process his recovery would be.

Then one day, as she was sitting before her desk in the library rewriting a section of geographic description, he burst into the room with his old-time enthusiasm, embraced her and cried:

"Darling, listen to this! Your father has arranged another expedition for me!"

Her eyes crinkled as she looked at his glowing face, spots of color bringing the warm flesh tones back to his cheeks, his eyes dancing.

"Another expedition," she said slowly. "But how . . . ?"

"Some of his friends in St. Louis want to build a railroad to the Pacific coast. They have the money and the backing; all they need is a southern route that the trains will be able to run over in winter."

"They are engaging you to find a railroad pass," exclaimed Jessie.

"But of course! Whom else could they turn to to find another pass?"

He pushed aside her little table with so much vitality that it fell over on the red carpet, the papers flying. He went on both knees before her, slipped his hands under her arms and, gripping her shoulder blades with powerful fingers, exclaimed in a voice she had not heard since he had left on his third expedition almost three years before:

"They are going to finance the expedition any way I want to put it together. And they are willing to pay me partly in railroad stock."

She gave him a kiss of affirmation.

"You see," she exclaimed, "you are going to be a railroad magnate! And after you find a new pass you will serve as engineer, lay out the whole route for the railroad, just as you helped Captain Williams before you came to Washington."

"God bless your father!" exclaimed John.

Amen, said Jessie to herself; he has saved our lives.

Aloud she said, "Let me see the letter. When must you go? Are you to buy your equipment in New York or St. Louis? How soon . . . ?"

"Not so fast, not so fast," he laughed gaily. "The details are to be worked out later. But here, you can see by the letter it is all settled. Ah, Jessie, I'm so happy at this chance . . ."

Jessie rubbed her cheek down the side of his soft beard.

"We must hurry and finish our report," she commented. "We must have it ready for the printer before you have to go to St. Louis. And while you are organizing your expedition and setting out on the trail for the coast for the fourth time, the country will be reading of your route to California . . . There, I'm crying all over your lovely beard. I am so happy for all of us. And particularly for your son; when he gets himself born his first sight of his father will be one of watching you prepare for the trail."

He combed his fingers through her long brown hair.

"I'm so happy I'll even take a second daughter and like it."

"You'll say as Father did," replied Jessie mockingly, " 'two daughters are a crown to any household.' But will you swear?"

"Just like General Scott," he grinned. "I thought you were so anxious to get on with this work? Come along, then, let's gather these papers together. I think I can dictate some good material: my mind is on fire; I can remember whole passages I wrote in my journal."

The old John returned in full measure. They worked together vigorously and well, pleased with the way the memoir was shaping up, excited over the early preparations he was making to assemble his comrades from the first three expeditions. During the last two weeks of May she did an extensive rewrite by herself to give the material greater readability. A publisher had been found who was enthusiastic at the prospects of a robust sale.

One evening toward the end of May when she had put in an extremely long day and had just about finished the last pages, she turned from her work and said to her husband, who was lying in front of the fire:

"John, you promised that there would be no more separations. The baby is due at the end of July. You don't expect to leave on the expedition until the end of September. I'll be strong enough by then; can't I come with you? I have always wanted to make the overland passage."

He turned over on his side, supported his head on one elbow and gazed at her admiringly.

"You have a lot of spunk, Jessie: you can sit there big with child and declare that only a few weeks after your baby is born you want to make the crossing over the Rockies in winter. No, my dear, not this time."

"But I can't bear the thought of being separated from you . . ."

He leaped to his feet, picked her out of her chair, and sat down with her on his lap.

"You're right, Jessie, no more long separations: you will come with me to the Delaware Indian Reservation on the Missouri, my last jumping-off place. While I head overland, you will return to New York and take a ship around Cape Horn. By the time I reach San Francisco you will be there with the two children. We will go to our ranch and build our home, and then we will never be separated any more."

Jessie rested securely with her head against his chest. She felt tired and weak from her labors of the day and from a sense of being stretched taut by the growing child within her.

"I suppose you're right," she said. "The boy would be too young to send with a wet nurse around the Horn. It won't be such a long time, and I'll be happy at the thought of our new home. Now, set me back in the chair so I can finish those last pages. I want you to be here when I write Finis."

He put her back in her chair, adjusted her desk, then went to the map table. After a moment or two she called:

"Don't move the lamp. It makes it too dark for me to write."

He turned swiftly.

"What did you say, Jessie?"

"I said don't move the lamp, it's growing dark. Oh, John, quick, I'm faint . . ."

He carried her to her bed, then summoned the doctor, who ordered her to remain there for the six or seven weeks until her baby should be born. She felt well again the next day, but was glad the doctor had restricted her. She would have a chance to rest and grow strong for her hour of trial. The memoir went to the printer, and in June the Senate ordered twenty thousand copies of John's map to California. The map was received with acclaim throughout the nation; this triumph, added to the fact that it was known he was organizing a fourth expedition, brought him back to himself. The bad days were behind them; they had survived and were going forward.

And so Jessie lay quietly in her blue bedroom with the windows overlooking the garden wide open, while her friends came to call, bringing her candy and light romantic novels.

At dawn of July 24, 1848, her son was born. It had taken her almost seven years to fulfill one of her husband's greatest needs, yet if she had had to wait so long, surely she could not have found a better moment to bear a male heir. Flushed with pride she said to her husband as he appeared in the doorway:

"You don't need a flag to put over my bed this time. You have a son. We're going to name him John Charles Fremont, after you."

He caressed her with the love and gratitude in his eyes, then went to her side, kissed the palm of each hand.

"Not John Charles Fremont," he said, generous in his joy. "Benton Fremont, after your father. He has done so much for us. I want my son to carry his name."

12

Toward the end of September she felt sufficiently strong to make the trip to St. Louis. They traveled together as a family of four now. Lily, who was almost six, was a quiet child, matter-of-fact, without any of the impetuousness of her parents, rather like her grandmother and her aunt Eliza. They had tried to keep most of the troubles of the trial away from Lily's small world, but she had seemed to understand what was going on, and Jessie had noted that her plain-faced and mild-mannered little girl had been solicitous of them during the bad months.

Lily seemed joyous about having a baby in the family; she was more affectionate with the little one than she ever had been with her mother or father. She hovered over the child, wanting to do little duties for him. Jessie occasionally would let her select the dress or wrapper he was to wear, which made her feel important.

"When will he be old enough for me to play with him, Mother?" she would ask.

"Soon," replied Jessie with a satisfied smile.

"But how soon? When we get to St. Louis? Will you let me dress him?"

She was nursing the baby herself. It was too early to know what he would be like, but she was sometimes a little disturbed at how quietly he lay in her arms, how much she had to urge him to suck the milk from her breast. He had been born with a patch of black hair coming over his ears and straggling down the back of his neck; in his features he looked like his father, even to the dark skin. She loved him wildly.

The early parts of the trip by stagecoach and train were pleasant in the early fall weather, with the leaves turning brown and the crops in the fields half through their harvest. They stood in the prow of the little river boat *Saratoga* making its way down the Ohio. Jessie held the baby in her arms, with Lily clinging to her skirt. Though she had borne two children her figure still was lithe and girlish; her eyes were a deeper hazel and more solicitous now, for they had come to know the nature of pain, but her face was happy once again, her skin smooth, flushed with health. John was wearing a mustache, but he had had his beard cropped close before leaving Washington, and he was carrying his civilian clothes with an air of familiarity.

With a start Jessie realized that they were in much the same position as Mary Algood, the young mother with whom she had talked on the outskirts of St. Louis and who had invited her to come along to Oregon. It was now the Fremonts' turn to go west to become free again. Her brain whirled at the thought of how far they had risen in so few years, and how far they had fallen in an even shorter time.

It was particularly good to be back home in St. Louis. Everyone received them cordially. The enclosed galleries around the patio were still warm and redolent of acacias. She was happy to slip into the slow, peaceful life of the Mississippi River port, content to do little but take care of her son while John scurried about to meetings, buying his supplies and interviewing the French voyagers who wanted to accompany him. He was disconcerted that only a few of his old-time companions of the trail were available; the others were scattered all over the Pacific coast and the Southwest; for the most part he had to accept new and untried men.

Her father was entranced by his first grandson, particularly because he had been named Benton. It seemed to Jessie that everybody wanted to fondle the infant. She had been told that she would leave with her husband for the Delaware Indian Reservation in October. A competent and reliable nurse was found so that Jessie was able to spend the last few days helping John and preparing her own clothing. Two days before they were to leave, John awakened at dawn, dressed and hurried out to meet his party of frontiersmen. Jessie was lying abed, half asleep and half awake when the nurse came running in, her eyes wide with terror.

"Mrs. Fremont," she cried, "come quick! We can't wake the baby."

Springing out of bed, Jessie ran next door to the nursery. Lily, still in her nightgown, was standing over the crib frantically rubbing young Benton's hand between hers.

"Mama," she cried, "the baby won't wake up. We've been shaking him and shaking him and he won't wake up."

Jessie took a quick look at her son, saw that his face was purple. She sent for the doctor, then picked the boy up, wrapped a blanket around him, carried him into her room and took him into bed with her, clasping him fiercely against her bosom, her eyes wide and unseeing, her heart like a stone in her chest.

She did not know how much time passed. Their family doctor, who had taken care of the baby since their arrival in St. Louis, came into the room. Gently he took the child from Jessie, unwrapped the blanket and made a quick examination. He then covered the child. It was several moments before he spoke.

"I'm terribly sorry, Mrs. Fremont," he said. "The boy is dead. I've been afraid all along that he had a defective heart. He must have been born with it."

Jessie's ears were shut to words and her mind to meaning. She held the child to her, his little head on her shoulder, her cheek on his.

"The baby is dead, Miss Jessie," said the doctor. "Do let me have him."

She made no move. After several moments she looked up at the doctor with a twisted smile and said without emotion: "I have had him such a little while. Please go away, all of you. We'll wait here until my husband comes."

She remained alone, still clasping the child. After a time John came up the stairs and into their room. She saw his sharp, worried look, his first concern for her and how she might be taking the loss. He leaned over her where she lay white-faced in the bed. She was grateful for his silence, and then she was grateful that he had begun to speak. His voice was compassionate.

"I won't try to comfort you, Jessie."

"No, please don't."

"The boy is gone. We will have to get used to the idea. It will be hard, but we can do it, together."

"You may take him now," she murmured.

John lifted the paper-light body of his dead son, took a last look at the boy's face, then covered his head with the blanket, stepped outside the door and gave him to the nurse. Quickly he returned to his wife's side, and with the blankets tucked under her back and legs picked her up and carried her to a deep chair by the window, where she held herself to him with the same fierceness with which she had just a moment before held her son.

"You can cry now, my dear," he said.

And so the tears came. All the tears she had not shed when her husband had returned from California a prisoner; all the tears she had not shed during the days of the trial when the man she loved was publicly lacerated until all of his pride was stripped from him; all the tears she had not shed when the court had declared her husband a malefactor, a traitor to his service; all the tears she had not shed when she had felt it imperative to support her husband against her father, to help him resign from the service and halt his career; all the tears she had not shed when she had seen her husband that first time in civilian clothes and realized how wounded he was and how profoundly his stature had diminished.

All these things somehow had not counted when her son had been born; this good fortune had made up for all they had undergone; she no longer had any hatred for General Stephen Watts Kearny, for the judges of the tribunal. In the depths of her gratitude she had freely forgiven them all, harbored no resentment.

As the hours passed, the bitterness flooded back. If not for General Kearny there would have been no arrest, no blasting of her husband's career in California, no court-martial. Her husband's return to Washington would have been one of triumph; she could have carried her child in health and serenity. Instead they had sapped her strength, made her undergo unending torment, and as her strength had fled, so had the strength of the child she was carrying. A defective heart? No wonder! How could she have carried a normal, healthy child during those miserable months? Now she could never forgive her husband's enemies: they had robbed him of his son.

Lily was sent to the Brants' so that she would not be exposed to the grief of the household. When she was brought back Jessie asked that she come up to her room. Lily was uneasy. Jessie took her daughter on her lap.

"I have something to tell you . . . about . . . the baby. You see Lily . . . he . . ."

"I know," interrupted Lily. "He'll never grow up to play with me."

On the evening before they were scheduled to leave for the reservation, while she was mechanically chewing the food which had been brought to her on a tray, John said, "My dear, it would be better if you don't come with me. Here you will have your father to watch over you, a good doctor and a nurse. Conditions are primitive on the Indian reservation . . ."

"Please," begged Jessie, "don't make me stay here. I'm not sick in my body, only in my heart. I feel better when you're by my side."

"It's lonely on the reservation; there is only one white couple. I won't be able to be with you much during the day, I will have to be working with the men."

She slipped her hand gently into his.

"Just to know that you are close by will be enough for me. If I am with you I won't need doctors and nurses. Please let me come. I need to be near you these next weeks."

He squeezed her hand reassuringly.

"All right, I'll take you with me on one condition: that you eat your dinner. You're getting so thin, I'm frightened for you."

She took the fork of potatoes which he held to her lips.

"Don't be frightened for me, John. I'll be all right. We'll have more sons. Being with you on the reservation will help me; when the time comes for you to leave, I will return to New York and take the ship around the Horn."

13

They reached the Indian reservation at dusk of the second day. On the clearing were a number of tepees of the Indian colony and two rough log cabins, one occupied by Major Cummins and his wife, the other for passing trappers, guides and army officers. Major Cummins and his wife were plain but kindly people to whom hospitality was the first law of the frontier. They had had no opportunity to hear of Jessie's loss; when the cabins came in sight, Jessie asked her husband if they might omit all mention of the boy.

The Cumminses had lived at this frontier point for thirty years, on the edge of the trailless prairie. Mrs. Cummins was a woman of about fifty, with all of the independence and matter-of-factness of the wives who follow their husbands to the outposts of the world. She settled Jessie in the one-room cabin with its hard-beaten earth floor, its open fireplace for both cooking and heating, hand-hewn log table and chairs, and one shop-built piece on the reservation, the bed that had been carted on horseback from St. Louis. Jessie had no wish to appear unresponsive to Mrs. Cummins.

John rose each day at dawn to join his men at camp. At midmorning Jessie would walk a mile or so over the prairie to sit in the shade of the cottonwoods and watch them put their wagons, animals, gear, scientific implements and foodstuffs into shape. It brought her comfort to watch her husband directing his men, supervising the details of work to insure their greatest possible safety. He appeared at his best at such moments: giving his orders in a low and gentle tone of voice, yet commanding the respect and instant attention of the men. She liked to watch the rhythmical way he moved about the camp, the bright gleam of his eyes as he gave a word of approval here, corrected an error or oversight there, the ease with which he operated because of his experience and skill; the feeling he gave of assurance, of joy in a well-loved task. And Jessie was grateful to her father for having secured this chance for him, grateful that Tom Benton should have invested several thousand dollars in a venture from which he was not likely to receive any return.

She walked back to the reservation at noon; John rode in about four o'clock to have a cup of hot tea with her and to chat quietly of the simple things that had happened during the day, or to lay their plans for the house they would build in California, with its windows overlooking the Pacific, the simple log-cabin school and church they would put up, much as Grandmother Benton had in Bentonville a half-century before.

The nights should have been the easiest, for her husband was at her side, falling asleep with his arms about her, but in the darkness the images came back, images which the sparkling sun diffused. At night, lying sleepless, her thin body curled up but her mind stiff and slablike, she saw the face of her infant before her; she felt the tugging of his gums at her breast; lived again the joy of those first hours when she realized she had given her husband a son to carry his name. At such moments she knew that there was no grief that could compare with the death of a son.

When she fell into a troubled sleep she would be awakened by a swift muted cry which would rend the silence of the night air, the cry of a momentary but mortal struggle as something outside the cabin was killed by an attacker. She mentioned these ghostly noises to no one, and it was not until the fourth day that she accidentally learned what they were, by going out with John at dawn one morning to find the usually quiet-spoken Major Cummins in a torrential rage.

"That blasted wolf killed another of our sheep," he cried. "She just had a litter of cubs and she drags our sheep back there to feed 'em. We've worked so hard and so long to raise these ewes; we can hardly last out the winter without fresh meat."

The merging nights and days passed all too quickly for her. At last the hour of parting struck. John's men had moved ten miles out to the edge of the prairie, the horses being fattened against the lean months of forage in the snow-covered mountains. They were to strike camp at sunrise the next morning. As he left the cabin John called that he would be back for four o'clock tea.

At noon Major Cummins knocked at her door.

"Come along with me, Mrs. Fremont," he exclaimed, a look of resolution on his grizzled face. "I'm about to prove the old adage that revenge is sweet."

Not knowing what he meant or what he wanted of her, Jessie thought it the courteous course to go along. The major had two horses in the small corral between the cabins; he helped her into the saddle and headed sharply west to a deep-gorged ravine. He dismounted, assisted Jessie off her horse, took her by the arm and led her at so fast a pace that she would have fallen were it not for his tight grip. The trail turned sharply, and just ahead Jessie saw a clump of oaks.

"Wait here, Mrs. Fremont," said the major, "you will be able to see all right."

She watched him drop silently to the oaks, take out his revolver and fire quickly five times. When the sound of the shots died away she heard death moans similar to the ones that had interrupted her sleep in the cabin. Major Cummins came up the trail, flushed.

"That will be the end of the sheep killing," he told her with grim satisfaction. "I just killed all five of the wolf cubs."

Jessie's head throbbed. Killing and death, death and killing. That's all there was in this world. Everyone and everything kills. Men kill each other, animals kill each other, men and animals kill each other. Death and bloodshed and misery.

She whispered, "Major, I am feeling ill. You had better take me on your horse and hold me, or I'll fall off."

Anxious, though not understanding, Major Cummins lifted her to his horse and carried her quickly back to the reservation. He summoned his wife, who put her to bed and made her a strong cup of coffee. Jessie thanked the woman, said that she thought she could go to sleep.

She lay abed in the most aching misery she had ever known, worse than that hour when she had held her dead son in her arms. What was left but death, continuous and senseless death? What did life hold but ugly and senseless and tragic destruction of one's hopes and plans and ideals? She was not bitter against any one person or any one thing: wolves had to kill sheep to live; men had to kill wolves to live. But did men have to kill men to live? Did they have to destroy each other to stay alive? Did Kearny have to kill her infant son in order to survive? Was this world nothing more than a cage of snarling beasts, with the rule of dog eat dog the only one that made survival possible? If everyone and everything had to kill to live, was life worth while?

She did not hold Major Cummins responsible for what she had just gone through; she did not even hold him responsible for what she knew the wolf mother would suffer when she came back to her lair and found her five cubs dead. Major Cummins had had no way of knowing what this sight would do to her; nor had he any way of knowing what this killing would do to the wolf mother. And even if he had known, could he have refrained from the butchering? Could he let the wolf take away the meat that he and his family needed to live on when they would be snowbound in winter?

Through all the years of her childhood, up to the last few months, she had believed that she lived in a good and beautiful world, a world in which ideals and kindness could survive, in which each person could determine the kind of life he wanted to live, where intelligence and training and industry led to accomplishment, where one could rest secure in the knowledge that he lived in an orderly universe.

What a sentimental child she had been, what a blind, stupid and misguided idiot! She had thought she could lay out the pattern of her days. She had thought she knew what she was doing, that she could control events and circumstance. She had not listened to counsel, taken the opinion or guidance of older and wiser people; she had been positive of what she wanted, of how she was going to get it; of exactly what she was going to do with her life as the accomplishments and rewards rolled up. And now the dream had given way to the reality. What was there but fire, the fire of greed and quarrelsomeness and lust for destroying?

She had thought before that her heart had been broken; now she knew that it had only been suspended, enduring in a kind of somnambulistic trance the misery of her loss. Always deep at the base of her brain had been the knowledge that time would cure this illness, that her strength would revive, that she would be able to go on, to conceive and bear more sons. She had known she could survive.

Now she felt no further chance for survival; now her heart and her brain and her spirit were truly broken by the unending, senseless and brutal tragedies of mankind.

And now she knew that she had been bitterly wrong; her mother had been right. Only a few months before when she had seen pity in her mother's eyes she had rejected it summarily, wanting and needing no pity, thinking her mother weak in failing to understand that her daughter had the stamina to brave the revolutions of fortune. But now her mind brought back line by line everything her mother had told her on her trip to Cherry Grove before her marriage:

"I like your young man, Jessie, don't misunderstand me, but he is like your father! He will always be striving and battling his way uphill, spreading about him with a vast club, just as Tom Benton always has, and for that reason he will have his enemies lurking around every corner, with daggers and foul names, ready to stab at every opportunity. You will never know quiet or tranquillity, Jessie. You will live forever in conflict and dissension, with struggle mixed into the very food you eat at your dinner table, poisoning the milk with which you feed your babies. That is not good for a woman, Jessie. It kills everything in her, destroys that inner spirit which must give her a sense of relaxation and security if she is to live happily and raise her children. A man's work is the least important part of him, the menial labor that he must do, and get done as fast as possible, in order to earn a living, and when he enters his home he should wipe off the stain of that labor as he wipes the mud from his shoes. My poor baby, how I pity you! How much misery and suffering you are rushing out to embrace."

A woman's position had truly been decreed by nature: to manage her home, bear her children, keep her house and children and husband well and cared for. Outside this realm she should never set foot. She should not go into the arenas of conflict, demand the right to work and fight by her husband's side, bear the blows and exhaustions and disillusionments of a man's world of conflict. She had been so very wrong: she should have married someone like her cousin Preston Johnson; no matter how much she had admired and loved John she should have known from what her mother had told her of the fighting and tempestuous male, she should have known from the revelations of his belligerent nature that trouble would arise, trouble so deep-cutting and critical that it would endanger them all, not only their health and position but their very lives as well.

Already it had cost the life of her son. And now it was costing her own life: for she knew that there was not the strength in her ever to believe again, ever to hope for peace or an orderly and sweet life. She was only twenty-four, but she had endured the sufferings of a hundred years; her heart had grown old and died within her breast. That breast was dead too, the milk within her had dried. Grandmother McDowell had told her that last time at Cherry Grove, "You will have your battles after you marry that young man of yours, and you will carry scars, but you will carry them the way my mother did, like medals bestowed for bravery." Grandmother McDowell had misjudged her, just as she had misjudged herself. She could endure no more battles, carry no more scars.

For all this she blamed no one but herself. She had been the aggressive woman, headstrong and determined; she had thought to change the status of a wife, to make of a wife something more than a housekeeper and a brood mare; she had thought to develop a husband's sinews and to further the world's work by the use of the training and brains that God had vouchsafed her sex. And now in seven years she had willfully and blindly destroyed them all: her son, herself, her husband. For how could John survive with a dead woman by his side, a woman whose love for him had vanished because love had been burnt out of her heart by human cruelty? She did not feel sorry for her little boy, he was dead and gone; she felt sorry only for those who were living and who would be hurt so deeply by her death: her husband, her daughter, her father and mother. If only she had not insisted upon working so hard at the trial, insisted upon going every day, exposing herself to the emotional turmoil, to the cold and fatigue, she would not have injured her baby. She had killed her son, just as deliberately as Major Cummins had killed the wolf cubs. Her husband should hate her for that. He does hate me, she thought, only he's too kind to let me see it. Why shouldn't he hate me, when I killed his career too, when I am responsible for his troubles, when I am the one who encouraged him to mutiny?

I wanted to be a good wife. I worked so hard to be a good wife; now I know that the best wife is the least wife. There can be no mixing of a man's world and a woman's world; if I had stayed out of his affairs they would not be in chaos. If only I had shown the same responsibility to the child I was carrying; if only I had said to myself, I am pregnant, I must not expose myself to this excitement . . . If only . . .

Ah yes, she thought with a terrifying clarity, if only. Two of the shortest words in the English language, and yet how long their implications. On what a long trail they have led me to this dreadful moment. A few hours ago I said that there is no grief that can compare with the death of a son. In this too I was wrong: even greater is the grief of knowing that you have come to the end of love and marriage with the man who was the fulfillment of your dreams. I cannot go out to California to meet him; I cannot endure the voyage; I cannot endure starting over again. I cannot endure the thought of making similar mistakes, of leading us both to the same unhappy ending in everything we start. I am no good for John. I have killed my love for him because I have killed everything inside me that can feel. What will living with a dead woman do to his tortured soul? Isn't it kinder to let him go to California and build a new life for himself there without me? I can only do him harm. But can I break my pledge to him, let him arrive and find that I am never coming? He called me the rock of his faith; with this last rock shattered, what will happen to him? O dear God, she murmured, what am I to do?

The long howls of the wolf, who was mourning her cubs, began to penetrate the log walls of the cabin, coming nearer and nearer until Jessie felt they were inside the cabin with her. The young dogs shut in the enclosure between the two cabins howled with fright and the prairie wind shrieked as it whipped around the lonely buildings.

She rose from the bed and began walking about the cabin, first longways, then sideways, brushing against the wooden table and benches and bed, hard bitter sobs welling in her throat with excruciating pain.

Before her rose the whipped figure of her father standing in the dark library, facing the drawn blinds of the front windows, weeping silently because his wife had been felled by paralysis. She heard his words clearly as they came to her between the howls of the she-wolf. "Jessie, you can't know what it's like not to be able to fight back. It's like being hit in the dark: you don't know who your adversary is—you don't know where to turn, what to say or do. I've never felt helpless before, but now . . . ." Now she too had been struck in the dark; she too felt helpless because there was no way to fight back. Who was her adversary?

She heard the sound of voices, her husband's among them. Quickly she poured some water from the earthen bowl into an enamel pan, splashing it into her feverish eyes and mouth, running it over her brow and into her hair. Her King George's Mark, swollen and red, throbbed fiercely. She dried her hands and face with a towel and ran a comb through her hair while she heard John's rapid footsteps approaching the cabin. She stirred the dead ashes of the fire, threw on some kindling and got the teakettle ready.

These were her final hours with her husband. She knew that as a last act of kindness she must not let him perceive what she was undergoing. She must not cripple him in this expedition which was to be the most important of them all, for he needed success most now, now that he was discredited, a man without a career. She must somehow give him the strength and the courage to go forward, to be successful and re-establish himself.

She saw by his face that he grasped something of what she had been suffering. She was relieved to learn that he misunderstood its source. He kissed her cheek, murmuring, "Courage, little lady. This will be the shortest separation of all. In two months, three at the most, we will be in San Francisco together. I will be showing you the beautiful strait which leads from the Pacific to San Francisco Bay. We will be buying lumber and furniture for our home overlooking the ocean."

Jessie smiled, then with a forced note of gaiety cried, "You came earlier than I had thought. I must be a sight. Give me a few minutes."

She retired to the corner of the cabin beyond the fire, took a little rouge from her handbag and applied it to her cheeks, then let down her hair, brushed it, straightened the part in the center, pulled the long brown strands over her ears and pinned them low and tight at her neck. She was surprised to see how easy it was to play this game, for when all is lost what more has one to lose; when all feeling is gone, what does it matter what feeling one pretends?

She went to her husband and asked, "There, isn't that better?"

"Much better," he agreed. "I want my memory of you to be beautiful and serene. And now where is that cup of tea you promised me if I would come home early?"

She fixed a cup of hot black tea for him, pretending to drink a little of her own, asking him questions about the last-minute arrangements for the expedition. Major Cummins and his wife had invited them for their farewell dinner in the settlement. Mrs. Cummins put out the few pieces of fine china that were left after her thirty years' sojourn in this wilderness. She had roasted a chicken, and there were colored candles lighted festively on the log table. The major triumphantly brought out one of his few remaining bottles of wine. Jessie talked of things of which she had no thought before, or memory after they left her lips, but the moments began to seem endless, and toward seven o'clock she thanked the Cumminses for their kindness and walked back to the cabin with her husband.

This was their last hour together. She prayed for the strength to carry it off. But when he took her in his arms, when he set her beside him on the edge of the bed, when he began speaking of how much he would miss her, of how he would think of her night and day until they could be together in San Francisco, all of the grim and sordid bleakness of death came over her again. She became pale and lifeless. Some part of her maintained its consciousness, continued to go through the motions of being kind, of pretending that nothing had happened between them, of fulfilling that moment of love so important to a couple that is to be separated by countless miles and minutes.

It was here at last that she failed, that her pretenses broke down. For her lips were dry and ashen, her body was dry and ashen. She knew that in death there could be no creating of life, not even the going through of the motions; that love can penetrate, love can be rhythmical, but in death the brain and the heart and the pulse and the womb are closed; there can be no entrance of life into death.

She lay on the bed silent, her eyes closed. He tried to talk to her: to comfort her over the loss of their child, to minimize the hardship and the extent of their coming separation, to hearten her by his enthusiasm for their fresh start in California, for the new life they would build, the new sons they would create. She heard the sound of his voice but none of the words; her strength had vanished. She was spent. This was the greatest of her failures: that she must send this unfortunate man out into the trackless snows of the Rockies, into hardship, privation and ever constant danger of death, send him out heavy of heart, beaten before he started.

She felt his kiss on her cheek, heard his murmured good-by, managed to pull herself up halfway to run her fingers down his silken beard, to wish him well. But the actual moment of his going, the closing of the door behind him, she did not know.

She was lying in a half-torpor when she heard Mrs. Cummins calling to her many times. She rose, wrapped a heavy shawl around her shoulders and opened the door. An army sergeant was standing beside Mrs. Cummins, his face caked with perspiration and dirt, his uniform crushed and ringed with sweat. While she stood staring at them blankly, she heard Mrs. Cummins say:

"This is Sergeant O'Leary, come with a message from St. Louis."

The sergeant stepped forward, opened a dispatch case at his side, and handed her a sealed letter.

"From General Kearny," he said. "I was ordered to deliver it in the fastest possible time."

She tore open the envelope, but was unable to read the message in the dark. She bade the sergeant enter. Then she went to the fire and read the message in the dying flames:

DEAR MISS JESSIE:

You were right, we cannot destroy our friends without destroying ourselves. The whole trial was a dreadful mistake. Please come back with this courier. I want to beg your forgiveness for the harm I have done you and your family. If you cannot come, won't you please send a message that you forgive me?

Your old and devoted friend,
STEPHEN WATTS KEARNY

Jessie reread the note, going from the last line to the first over and over again, uncomprehending. Why was General Kearny doing this? And why had he not done it before she left St. Louis? He had been there all the time at Jefferson Barracks, but he had sent no word, not even when her son had died. Why now . . . ?

She turned to the army officer who was standing stiffly, his cap crushed under his arm.

"Why had you to ride so hard?" she asked. "Why is General Kearny in such haste?"

The sergeant wiped the dust off his lower lip by running his left thumb roughly across it.

"The general be dying, mum. The doctor say he has only a few hours to live. The general ordered I should bring you back with me. He says he must see you before he die."

Jessie stood silently, the letter hanging loosely at her side. If only this had happened before, she thought, I could have felt there was some decency left in the world. But now it is too late. Stephen Kearny is frightened. He doesn't want to die with me on his conscience. After breaking my husband and killing my son, he wants a cheap and easy forgiveness.

To the sergeant she said, "I cannot go back with you. Tell General Kearny it is impossible."

"I don't know what's in the message, mum," he answered, "but the general told me if I couldn't bring you I was to bring an answer."

"There is no answer."

The man shifted from one foot to the other.

"Please," he said, "I been with the general many a year now. I fit with him agin the Indians, I was with him on the march to California. I been his dispatch bearer and he been my friend. He's terribly unhappy, mum, said, 'Just ask her to say those few words, O'Leary. Just ask her to say she forgive me.' "

Jessie stood cold and impassive.

"Tell the general I cannot forgive him. Tell him a grave stands between us."

The sergeant opened his mouth to speak, but the misery in her eyes stopped him. He pulled himself up slowly, awkwardly, then saluted, left the cabin.

She stood there, her brain as black as the starless night. After a time she put a log on the fire, then pulled an end of the heavy bench to the hearth and sat down, her bony elbows digging into her thighs, the palms of her hands holding her eyelids tight-closed and stretched wide apart, blotting out all memory. Here she sat while time passed, the minutes, the hours, the bleak black minutes and hours that stretched ahead endlessly.

She was aroused by the swift gallop of a horseback rider. The lightning beats thundered up to her doorstep, were pulled to an abrupt stop. There was a sound of something hitting the earth, the door of her cabin was thrown open. Jessie looked up to see John standing there, disheveled, grim. He threw the door shut hard behind him, rushed to her side, locked his arms fiercely about her.

"Jessie, I couldn't go. I couldn't leave you this way. I know how ill you are, and how wretched. You need me with you. I am not going away. I have given up the expedition. I put someone else in charge. They leave at dawn. Come, let us pack our things. We will go to St. Louis, and then on to New York. I promised you we would never be separated again, and we never will."

His voice was hoarse. She stared at him, unbelieving. This was the one sacrifice nobody could have asked or expected him to make; it left him once again without a rudder or a future. To one of his intense pride it would have been easier to throw away his life than to throw away this opportunity to re-establish himself. From the ravaged lines in his face she could tell something of the struggle he had undergone to achieve this unselfishness. But his love for her had been sufficiently strong: to save her from further suffering he had been willing to face contempt for his failure to carry through. He had known he could never explain or justify himself; he had known what his bruised pride would be forced to undergo. He was willing to face this punishment for her sake.

A little feeling crept back into her tired body and nerves.

"You would give up . . . the expedition . . . when it means so much to you?"

"It means nothing to me," he cried. "You are the only one who means anything to me. You are my love and my life. I cannot leave you alone now."

"But so much is at stake," she whispered. "If you are successful, you have a life to live again. Without it you have nothing . . ."

He ran his fingers roughly, supplicatingly over her face.

"How wrong you are, Jessie! I have you to turn to! You are my future, you are everything I want and need. With you I can rise again, I can do anything. Our love is more important than any expedition or any chance for success. Don't you understand that, darling? Don't you understand that we must go on together, always side by side?"

She took his dirt-lined hand and kissed the pocket of its warm, curved palm. If John were willing to make this sacrifice for her, then her love and marriage had not been a failure.

"You would do this for me?" she persisted. "You would give up the only thing that brought you back to life? You would let some other man command your party, find the new pass and lay out the railroad route? You would give up everything you hoped would grow out of this work because I am ill and unhappy and I need you?"

His face showed hurt astonishment.

"But of course, Jessie! How can you doubt it? Did my love seem such a shallow thing? Did you think there was any sacrifice I wouldn't gladly make to protect you? Ah, Jessie, how little you really know me! How little you have known of how much I love you, and what our marriage has meant to me."

She was crying now, she could feel the hot tears streaming down her cheeks; and these hot tears seemed like rivers of strength pouring courage and hope back into her body. She slipped off the edge of the bench onto the floor beside him. She wrapped her arms tightly and securely about his neck, her mouth clinging to his.

True love never died; it surmounted all obstacles, it was indestructible; all else perished: hopes, plans, dreams, illusions, ambition and accomplishment, kindness, good will, even sweet charity. Yet one was able to carry on because the greatest force of all survived. So often it seemed to have worn thin, to have turned sour, to have been beaten out of shape: yet, miracle of miracles, love survived; it could conquer death, achieve eternal rebirth.

"Yes, John," she murmured against his lips. "I understand. All is well. I love you too, more than I ever have before. You can go now, you can be happy and sure about me. I will be well again, quickly. I will be in St. Louis within two days, then go on to New York and catch the first ship for California. Yes, my darling, I will be in San Francisco before you, awaiting your arrival as eagerly as any woman ever waited for her love. You still have an hour to daybreak. You can make camp in time to give the order for the march. Good-by, and may God keep you."

She stood in the open doorway watching her husband gallop off into the blackness of the night. When the last reverberation of the hoofbeats had died away she turned back to the cabin and set about packing her bags. With the first light of dawn she mounted her horse and headed east into the rising sun on the first leg of the long journey to San Francisco.

BOOK FOUR

TO CONSECRATE A HEARTH

1

THE MID-MARCH WINDS were icy and the wooden planks of the wharf slippery under foot when Jessie and Lily boarded the S.S. *Panama*. Tom Benton had insisted upon bringing them to New York, had filled their cabin with the newest books, fruit and flowers. They were determined to be lighthearted about the parting, hustling about the cabin unpacking valises and trying to make it seem a little like home. They spoke in quick rushes of how soon California could become a state, what John's chances were of being elected the first senator; of the possibility that there really was a large quantity of gold, and how quickly a genuine gold rush would settle the new territory. But at last there was no more time for impersonal talk, and father and daughter embraced, murmuring words of farewell.

She stood alongside of the rail while orders were shouted; there were the noises of the hauling up of the gangplank, of winches being turned. The ship pulled slowly into the bay. When she could no longer see the little wharf in the blackness, she turned and went down to her cabin. The two kerosene lamps were swinging from their hooks in the ceiling beams. Lily was in her berth, lying wide-eyed.

"Haven't you gone to sleep yet, child?" Jessie asked.

"No, Mother, I'm frightened. Won't you come in bed with me?"

"Yes, dear, I'll undress immediately."

It took only a moment to slip out of her clothes and don a warm flannel nightgown. Outside the two square portholes a gale was raging as the ship pitched its way forward. She got into the berth with Lily; they comforted each other in the darkness with talk about the future. Jessie tried to imbue the child with her own excitement and impatience to reach California.

The first three days were stormy. When she dressed and went out on deck on the fourth morning off the coast of Florida, she found the sun shining brightly and the ocean tranquil.

Captain Schenck of the S.S. *Panama* had assured Senator Benton that everything would be done to keep her comfortable. She sat on deck in a wicker lounge chair with the sun beating strong on her face, while Lily went forward to watch the sailors paint the gear. The sun had a soothing quality; so did the quiet and the blue skies, the flight of gulls out from the coast of Florida and the Bahamas. In the heat of the day she took long naps; at sunset, with the skies flaming cerise and indigo, she walked for an hour about the deck, storing up strength for the difficult days ahead when she must cross Panama.

Though she had planned to go around Cape Horn on the S.S. *Fredonia* which had left in January, her father had insisted that she have more rest before she made the journey, that John could not be in California before March, and that it would be better if he arrived there first and prepared a place for them. In addition he wanted her to wait a few months so that she could travel on the newly proposed line of government steamships. Rumors that gold had been discovered in California had reached Washington toward the beginning of 1848, but no one in the East had given them any serious credence; in December of 1848 a tea caddy filled with gold nuggets was delivered to President Polk. This first concrete evidence of gold had excited the easily inflammable and congenitally adventuresome, who prepared to get to California as fast as they could and by any means available. Though most people in the East did not consider one tea caddy of gold to be proof of a gold strike, the government used the additional inducement of gold on the west coast to establish regular steamship connections with California. The S.S. *California* left to go around the Horn and was to remain on the west coast plying between San Francisco and Panama City. The S.S. *Panama* left New York on March 13, 1849, for Chagres, the port of entry to Panama on the Atlantic coast. Jessie, Lily and the other passengers would cross the Isthmus, which had just been opened to travel, and catch the S.S. *California*, which would come down from San Francisco to pick them up.

In the evenings she read from the volumes on agriculture she had bought in Washington in order to prepare herself to be a farmer's wife. She did not think that John should become a farmer; he lacked not only the training, but the temperament as well; yet the important thing was to establish a permanent home in California. When Elizabeth Benton had heard of her daughter's plans to erect a log cabin in the Santa Cruz mountains outside of San Francisco, she had taken Jessie's hand and murmured, "Remember that you were born on land that had never been bought or sold, a crown grant for military services to my grandfather's father. Not only should your home be inherited, Jessie, but your servants and money as well. 'The gods are slow to consecrate a new hearth.' You're not strong enough to endure the hardships of wild country like California. Let John complete his railroad expedition, return to Washington and find his life here. You would be a great deal happier."

On the ride to Cherry Grove eight years before, seventeen-year-old Jessie had shrugged off her mother's warnings as unimportant. But this was a chastened Jessie who had already endured much of the worst her mother had predicted.

"Someone has to build a hearth at the beginning, Mother," she had replied, "or the rest of us wouldn't be able to inherit it."

John would eventually find other activities more interesting to him than farming, but first their home place must be established. If her mother had been right in saying that "the gods are slow to consecrate a new hearth," then the more reason to begin at once.

At the end of two weeks of sailing, when she had her first sight of palm trees and the tropical growth of Chagres, it was another wrench to know that she would have to leave Captain Schenck, her last connection with home. She awakened while it was still dark, dressed herself by candlelight in the clothes she had laid out the night before. With Lily's hand clutched tightly in hers, she went on deck in time to watch the tropical sunrise, the sun bursting above the horizon as though it were shot out of a cannon, day breaking with the same roar with which the sea was breaking on the white beach of Chagres. It was her first view of the tropics; from a distance it looked friendly enough, with the palm trees fringing the sand bar and the heavy green growth along the river. When Captain Schenck came forward, Jessie turned a smiling face toward him.

"So the voyage is ended, Captain," she said. "You have made it pleasant for me and my little girl."

Captain Schenck did not return her smile. Anxiously he said, "Then let me perform one last service for Senator Benton and Colonel Fremont. Do not attempt to cross Panama. The country is rotten with Chagres fever. People are dying in the boats and on the trails. The food is abominable, the water is poisoned. That route should never have been opened."

The unexpected opposition to her continuing onward to meet John brought sharply to her mind the scene at the Delaware Indian Reservation where she had come so close to losing her love, her husband and everything that had meaning in her life. She valued it doubly now for having so nearly lost it. Any thought that she might fail in her efforts to join her husband in San Francisco brought back the intensity of those despair-fraught hours in Major Cummins' cabin.

"I am certain I will be able to stand the passage, Captain," she answered serenely.

The ship was rolling under them and she was anxious to get ashore. She returned to her cabin for her coat and purse. Having left her door ajar, she heard the heavy stomping of a man's boots. An unfamiliar voice cried:

"I ain't taking the responsibility for any Washington fine lady across Panama. She'll object to the Indians havin' no clothes on, she'll make trouble, she'll not be able to stand it."

She hadn't heard the phrase "fine lady" since the day she had left Miss English's Academy. She gave her hat a final touch, resolutely swished her long dark skirt out behind her, opened the door and faced the stranger. The man looked at her slender, ivory-tinted face, at her fragile figure, at the burning hazel eyes, and said stumblingly, "Why, you're not a fine lady at all; you're just a poor thin woman!"

She handed Lily to a sailor who carried her down the ship's rope ladder and placed her in the tender that was bobbing on the bay. Swinging from side to side Jessie manipulated the ladder, edged herself into the tender. The little boat made its way to shore.

2

At the waterfront she was almost overcome by the stench of stale fish, tea and cinnamon; but she felt at home with the throngs of men who were jamming the beach ready to start their journey overland, for it sounded like St. Louis in the early days, soft Spanish intermingled with the French patois, Indians and Negroes talking their own dialects, the American and English swearing at everybody in their haste to arrange for transportation. She thought with a smile, if one were going to be a world traveler, St. Louis was an ideal training ground.

Jessie and Lily and their baggage were to be transported up the first eight miles of the Chagres River in one of the deep-water boats with a number of Americans who had been wise enough to arrange for passage. Within two hours after landing she was on her way. The banks of the river were low and covered with jungle growth to the water's edge, where white and scarlet flowers rose from the tangled green. By midafternoon the chugging motor had covered the eight miles and swerved into shore; they had had no food, no tarpaulin to protect them from the fierce heat, no water which she felt safe in drinking, though they were painfully parched, no way to take care of their personal needs. She disembarked and was informed by the native boatman, in sign language, that they would be transferred to the narrow dugouts which were tied to the thick overhanging branches. Each of the dugouts was manned by naked Negroes and Indians. Jessie felt Lily's hand clutching her own.

"Don't be frightened by their noise," she reassured her, "they're laughing and yelling out of excitement. It is only a three-day voyage up the shallows, and then we will be out on the trail."

A man in uniform appeared in the clearing. He came to her and said, "I'm Captain Tucker; I received a letter that you were coming. I have the company's boat ready for you and your daughter. I'm sorry I can't go along; you will be the only woman aboard, but the native crew is reliable, they frequently carry my wife to company headquarters."

"You mean we won't have to travel in those dugouts?" asked Jessie, realizing how far her heart had sunk at the sight of the savages.

Captain Tucker laughed. "I don't blame you for your consternation. But I think we can keep you comfortable. The company has tent camps at regular intervals up the river and my carriers have informed them that you are coming. Will you get into the boat now; there is no time to lose if you are to make the first camp by nightfall."

She thanked him heartily. The Jamaica Negroes pushed out against the heavy current, poling slowly upstream while they chanted in rhythm. Sometimes they traveled in midstream where the sun was so hot it burned the skin like a fire, but more often they stayed close to the shore, gliding lazily under the arching trees and canopies of flowering vines. When they could go no further because of growths of jungle creeper, Jessie and her daughter would have to go ashore and sit in the midst of the dank green foliage while the boatmen jumped into the water and with their long knives cut a trail along the riverbank. Then they would come back for Jessie, and half pull, half push the boat through the clearing while their wild singings joined in with the screeches of the tropical jungle birds.

They made their first landing while the sun was still bright. In a small clearing a company tent with a wooden floor had been set up. She wondered why they had stopped so early, but she soon knew the answer, for night came upon them with the swiftness of a falling star. The native boys made a small fire outside the tent flaps as a protection against the animals and the deadly dews, then brought her some cooked food, but she preferred not to eat it, feeding Lily and herself a few cookies and an apple which she had brought from the ship. After the child had fallen asleep, Jessie lay awake in her narrow iron cot listening to the discordant night noises of the tropics, to what seemed an unceasing rush of sound all around the tent.

There was no sleep in her, for she was possessed by the irony that she whose husband had marked and broken more trails across the continent than any other living American should be denied the right to travel on one of them and be plunged instead into this aboriginal nightmare. All the time she had worked on the three reports, watched John's maps grow, she had had the intensest personal interest in each mile of the terrain, for she had always thought that she would one day travel these routes. She had not only been prepared over a number of years, but had been anxious to encounter the hazards of the covered wagon, the plains, the snowbound mountain passes, the hostile Indians, the moisture-parched deserts; all these images and the attendant hardships had been part of her thoughts since she had been a child. Yet here she was set down in the midst of country and hardship which she had never anticipated, and for which she was in no way prepared. Here she was on the first real voyage of her life, traveling without husband or friend by her side, in country so fantastic that not even the Spanish explorers had done it descriptive justice. This was land upon which no one she had ever known had laid eyes or foot; for perhaps the thousandth time she recalled Mary Algood, sitting by her blue-painted Delaware wagon, about to set off on the Oregon Trail. If only John's eyes had seen this country, John's drawing pencil sketched its character, she would have felt more at home.

The next morning they were off at the crack of dawn, being poled up the stiff current. She told Lily stories of how the first white men who had invaded Peru had carried their loot down this very river on their way to the Atlantic Ocean and back to Spain. The banks were brilliant with white and scarlet perch flowers; the native boys jumped into the river to cool off or cut food from the bank, but Jessie and Lily suffered agonies of heat, hunger, thirst and the other pressures to which the body is heir.

The nights were dank with mist; the cries of sudden death in the jungle gave the journey a mortal aspect. She was grateful for the floored tents and cots; without this barest of protection she doubted their chances of continuing. Though she had sympathized with her husband's privations on the trail, she now realized that her sympathy had been cerebral; her husband had suffered from the cold while she was suffering from the heat, he had been victim to the sparseness of vegetation while she was oppressed by its lushness, yet now that she was experiencing these momentary tortures with her own flesh she at last had an intimation of the agonies that must have racked the body of John Fremont.

On the morning of the fourth day they reached Gorgona, a little settlement where they transferred from the shallow Chagres to the trail over the mountains. Though it was only eight in the morning the sun was like a knife under the eyelids. The alcalde was down at the landing beach to invite her to his home for breakfast. His house was built on stilts with a thatched roof of palm fronds and wattled sides. They had no sooner seated themselves at the rattan table than native boys brought in two big baking dishes and popped off the covers. Jessie let out an exclamation of horror, for in the big casserole there was something that resembled a child.

"Special for the honored guests," said the alcalde, his eyes gleaming while he rubbed his hands in anticipation. "Baked ring-tailed monkey and boiled iguana lizard."

Her stomach slowly seemed to rise to her throat. One look at Lily's face told her that the child would not be able to eat the monkey. They needed strength for the arduous three-day trip over the mountains. She remembered how John had preferred the pangs and weakness of hunger to eating a portion of their pet dog. She decided that her husband was more fastidious than she. To her daughter she murmured:

"Remember what Sam Weller used to say: 'Weal pie ware a good thing when you knew it waren't made of kittens.'"

They both ate a little of the monkey, but the lizard was too much for them. Then the alcalde took them to the clearing which marked the beginning of the mule track to Panama. Part of Jessie's baggage was placed on a mule, the rest of it on a cow which was to head the procession. To the chief baggageman she said, "Will you please put my daughter on a mule immediately in front of mine, and make sure the animal is kept there?"

"He stay dere, lady," laughed the baggageman. "No place to go else."

There were fifty mules, a half-dozen cows and thirty men in the caravan. The native leader gave a fierce whoop which was echoed up and down the line, the mules began to move beneath them. The track followed the contour of the mountains, up to the top of a hill and down again into the valley on the twenty-one-mile pilgrimage to Panama City. The mule steps that had been cut by hand into the mountainside were rarely more than four feet wide, and at the edge one looked down a thousand feet into jungle growth. Mango trees and alders were packed solid along the trail, topped by towering palms and cocoanuts. In spite of the intense glare of the tropical sun, it was dark under the green roof; Jessie kept looking upward to find a ray of sunlight toward the top of the branches, then a few steps more and it would be dark green again, with a sudden burst of rain falling down through the matted foliage. There were no bridges across the narrow streams; the mules jumped them, and several of the travelers were dumped headfirst into the water. She was thankful that both she and Lily were experienced riders, and was proud, as she rode behind the slender form of her daughter, at the way the child was withstanding their travels, the constantly changing temperatures, the strange sights, steady hours of movement, the hardships of hunger, heat and personal discomfort.

The first night they slept in a tent with a wooden floor, but on the second night there was only a filthy Indian hut. Jessie took two blankets out of her boxes, rolled Lily in one and herself in the other and slept the sleep of exhaustion, impervious to the lizards, snakes and hundreds of insects which crawled across them in the course of the night. The sunrise was glorious: from the mountain top she looked down into a sea of blossoms, and beyond she saw as Balboa had seen from this very peak before her the Pacific Ocean at her feet. She ardently wished that Tom Benton could be sharing with her this first view of the Pacific.

Several hours before the sixth nightfall they reached Panama City. The trail came out of the mountains some distance from the walled city, with its ancient cathedral. Her first sight of the cathedral roof and spire of inlaid mother-of-pearl made her think that she had fallen victim of the Chagres fever, after all. At the trail's end there were Indian carriers, one of whom took her on his back, and another Lily, and carried them over the shallow water of the bay and across the sand reef to the entrance of Panama City. She walked on the ancient roadway through the railed gate, entered the walled town with its weather-stained old houses and wide balconies leaning out so far they almost closed over the narrow passages. In the streets were trotting donkeys carrying bundles of leaves and water jars, dusky Indian women wearing a single white garment.

Instead of finding a sleepy little Spanish town with a few natives wandering the streets, she found the place a bedlam of stranded Americans, several hundred of them camping on the hillside above the city, others hustling and jostling through the streets. While waiting for the Indian carriers to bring her baggage to the Cathedral Square, from which point she would seek a hotel, she inquired of the group of Americans who were wearing the western garb she knew so well from St. Louis:

"Why are so many of you men here?"

A lean, gray-haired man in a leather jacket and buckskin pants stepped forward and said, "Ain't you heard the news, ma'am, the ship ain't coming back to Panama."

Stupefied, having visions of Lily and herself camping endlessly on the hills above Panama, she could only gasp: "Ship not coming back? But why? What do you mean?"

A young man dressed in a black business suit much the worse for wear replied, "Don't you know what's happened in California, ma'am? All the ships' crews have deserted and gone into the gold fields. The *California* was due a month ago, but it never got here."

She looked from face to face anxiously, then asked, "Deserted their ships?"

There was a moment of silence while the men looked at each other. Then everyone began talking at once. "Yes, ma'am! All the rumors was true! Millions of dollars' worth of gold! People picking it up on the mountainside in sacks! Getting rich overnight! Here we're rottin' in Panama City, and millions of dollars of gold laying all over California just waiting to be picked up."

The verification that there was gold in California meant little to her except that she and Lily would be marooned in Panama City. She asked the first man who had spoken, the gray-haired one, if he knew anything about the hotels in Panama. He assured her that they were vermin-infested, that there were no rooms anyway. Night was drawing on when she saw coming toward her a Spanish woman with white hair under a black mantilla. Trailing her were several native boys. She came to Jessie and said:

"I am Madame Arce, cousin of the American minister from New Granada, General Herran. He wrote to me that you were coming and told me of the many happy hours he had spent in your home in Washington. It is now my privilege to return that hospitality. Will you come with me, Madame Fremont?"

She followed Madame Arce across the square to a great barrack of a house with twenty-foot ceilings, and windows as big as barn doors. When she was led to her bedroom she found it furnished with a lounge covered in a blue damask, two hammocks, and crystal chandeliers with wax lights. Madame Arce made available to her a velvet-footed girl with a soft laugh, named Candelarias. Jessie's relief at being rescued was so great that she murmured to Lily, "Now I know how your father must have felt when he found that pass across the Sierras."

Madame Arce's house was a tropical version of Tom Benton's home overlooking the Mississippi, built around an enclosed patio, with the floors redtiled. She stepped out onto the wide gallery which surrounded the house and overlooked the cathedral. A few moments later there was a knock at her door and Candelarias asked if she would like to have a bath before dinner. Jessie called to Lily and they walked to an outside bathhouse much like her father's shower on C Street, for on a high ledge there were containers, ranging from small vases to four-foot-high jars filled with water from the well. The smaller jars were dumped on them by three grinning young girls, then the larger jars were overturned as they became accustomed to the coldness of the water.

The days passed, a week, two weeks, three weeks. Jessie spent many hours with Madame Arce in the coolness of the back garden speaking in the Spanish they both loved, walking along the ramparts of the old town at sunset and watching the twenty-foot tide crashing over the reefs. In the evening she strolled about the Cathedral Square talking to the men whom she knew from her own ship and those with whom she had become acquainted during her first hour in Panama. They were growing more desperate with each passing day. There was no food to be bought, they were living on the salted foods they had carried with them, and death from disease was an everyday occurrence in the camps that dotted the hillsides.

A month passed and still there was no ship and no news of any; the men were becoming frightened that they would all die here in Panama, that there would be no chance for them to escape.

Jessie was well cared for, yet she too was growing uneasy. There had been no word from John since he had left her side that early morning on the Delaware Indian Reservation. Some five months had passed since then; if all had gone well, her husband and his party should be safely in San Francisco. He would be waiting for her, scanning the sea for her arrival. He would be fearful lest she had encountered difficulties, or had been too delicate to withstand the rigors of Panama, where strong men were stricken and died within a few hours. She knew the heartbreak of worrying about a loved one; that had been her lot over the years; she did not want her husband to undergo this slow torture. And yet there was nothing she could do but sit and wait and let the days succeed each other as painlessly as possible.

3

The rainy season came down like a thunderclap, filling the streets of the little town as though they were shallow pools. Madame Arce's house was wet, the floors, ceilings wet; lanes of damp ooze trickled down the twenty-foot walls, while outside the rains filled the air with sickening inhalations. Jessie caught cold, and with it a racking cough. Madame Arce insisted that she remain in bed, while Candelarias kept a fire lighted in the room in a vain attempt to dry out the walls. She lay in the hammock, her dreams shattered by grotesque pictures of screaming, naked savages dancing around her, taunting her with being a fine lady, the hallucinations dissolving into pictures of the snow-locked Sierras where freezing men fell forward into the snow.

Another month passed, and then one night she was awakened by the booming of a cannon which told her, even as the noise tore her from her dream, that an American ship had arrived. She rushed out on the balcony to behold a wild scene. It was a bright moonlight night and every trail leading down from the hills was filled with singing and shouting Americans who were crying out with joy as they hurried toward the ramparts. The Indians too had been awakened, and they were singing and dancing in sympathy. On the balcony of every house were shrouded figures in their night clothes watching the scene. Even before she could return to her room to begin dressing and packing, there was another boom from a cannon; a second American ship had dropped anchor in the harbor.

Breathlessly she dressed Lily and herself, began throwing clothes into her suitcases, then went out on the balcony again to search for the ship as the light of day began to filter through. She saw a man in the uniform of the United States Navy stride across the square. She rushed down the patio stairs, across the red tile, and threw open the heavy door. With a glad cry she grasped the hand of Lieutenant Fitzhugh Beale, who had been a friend of Colonel Fremont's in California, fought with him in the conquest, testified for him at the court-martial and been their guest in the Benton home in Washington.

"Ah, Mrs. Fremont!" he cried. "I had surmised you were stranded here, waiting for the *California*. I've just come down on her, with naval dispatches and samples of gold dust."

"Have you heard news of Colonel Fremont?"

"No."

She led him to the back garden, then told him of her voyage while he sipped a warm drink. Lieutenant Beale was blue-eyed, blond, about thirty, with a long, horselike face. He loved danger and movement and an ever changing panorama: a congenital bachelor, he had been at sea since he was twelve; among his intimates he was known as "Beale of the steady hands and wandering feet." Jessie saw that he was uneasy, that he had something to tell her. He asked permission to light a cigar, gazing at the burnt match for a moment before speaking.

"I must hurry on to Chagres and deliver my papers to the next ship leaving for New York. Every possible facility has been given me to make the Panama crossing as quickly and easily as possible. Mrs. Fremont, you look ill; I don't think you should expose yourself to more hardship. I urge you to return to Chagres with me; there will be a fast ship for New York, and I will arrange for you to be taken care of."

Her thoughts colliding, she asked:

"But why should I return to New York now, when there is a ship to take me to San Francisco?"

"Mrs. Fremont, San Francisco has gone crazy wild. The original settlers have rushed off for the gold fields; the new arrivals are insane with excitement to get away and find their millions in gold. The hotels are dirty and cold and jammed, there is no help to be had except Indians and Chinese, and people will tell you that their time is worth fifty dollars a minute. San Francisco isn't a town, it isn't even a village, it's just a settlement of delirious maniacs living in shanties and knock-together cabins, waiting for the moment when they can get away to the gold fields. There is no water, no adequate food, no sanitary equipment. The streets are flowing mud streams impossible to cross. Why, I have seen men try to pave them with bales of cotton and bags of flour. There is no lumber available, no brick or stone, nothing with which you and the colonel could build a house. The shanty towns are full of fever and cholera, and the death rate is terrifying. Mrs. Fremont, I beg you not to risk arriving alone in the hysterical hamlet; there can't be more than two or three white women there."

She watched the young lieutenant puff animatedly on his cigar, feeling a familiar paralyzing fear clutch at her heart.

"Please tell me the news, Lieutenant Beale," she murmured. "You said that you had not heard from Colonel Fremont."

The lieutenant took the cigar out of his mouth. "It is true, I have not heard from him. But I have heard about him. There has been trouble, Mrs. Fremont. Your husband's expedition never got over the Rockies. The fur traders and the Indians warned them not to go in, told them that the snow and the cold had never been so intense, that it was impossible to cross the Rockies at that point. But Colonel Fremont insisted. He said there must be a pass on the thirty-eighth parallel . . . and he ran into the most impenetrable part of the Rockies, in the worst winter within the memory of anyone who knows that country."

Her body as cold as though she herself had plunged into the frozen Rockies, she asked, "My husband, is he safe?"

After a barely imperceptible pause, Lieutenant Beale replied, "We don't know. The colonel engaged Bill Williams to guide him. Williams wanted to take a southerly route, but your husband felt that would defeat the purpose of the expedition, that he had to find a central pass for the railroad. The colonel and Williams quarreled; they never found a pass. They pushed deeper and deeper into the snows until they could go no farther. Then they turned back . . . they lost their mules and supplies . . . The men began to die along the trail . . ."

"But my husband. What about Colonel Fremont?"

His head down, Lieutenant Beale repeated, "We don't know, Miss Jessie."

"Some of the party must have gotten out. Else how would you know?"

"The colonel sent out a relief party with Williams, Brackenridge, King and Creutzfeldt to get help in New Mexico and rush it back. King starved to death, but Williams, Brackenridge and Creutzfeldt got through. From them we learned about the disaster to the expedition."

Twisting her lace handkerchief between her taut fingers, Jessie cried, "If the relief party got out, then surely they must have sent back supplies. The rest of the men must be safe?"

Lieutenant Beale shook his head slowly. "The three men were almost dead before they reached a settlement. They did not have the strength to take back relief, and there was no one at the settlement who could go into the mountains. A runner carried the news to Kit Carson at Taos, but it would have taken too long for Carson to organize relief and get up into the Rockies. The rest of the expedition would have had to get out on its own resources."

"Then there is no word about Colonel Fremont?"

"None."

"He was still alive when the Williams party was sent out for relief?"

"It was the colonel who sent them."

"What was his condition then?"

"His leg was badly frozen."

"There has been no word from anybody left in the mountains?"

"None. Williams says they could not have lived more than a few days . . ."

She stalked agitatedly about the patio.

"My husband could not have perished in the snows! He faced greater hardships when he crosed the Sierras in '44. If Williams could get out with a relief party, then Colonel Fremont can get out with the rest of the expedition. Neither the snows nor the mountains could ever kill him. There is no man in the world better equipped to survive . . ."

Lieutenant Beale put his arm about her.

"The expedition is ended, Miss Jessie; the equipment was abandoned, no one got over the mountains and no one got through to California. Those who survived are returning east to St. Louis. If Colonel Fremont came out of the Rockies, he will be in St. Louis by now. I have made all arrangements to take you back across Panama. There are merchantmen in the harbor at Chagres; they will not be leaving before we reach there. Miss Jessie, I want you to pack your things and return with me. I will put you on a ship for New York."

Pale now, and coughing, she faced Lieutenant Beale determinedly. "You believe that my husband is dead?"

He did not answer.

"No, don't be afraid for me. I have gone through this before. Tell me if you think there is any chance that my husband is alive."

When Lieutenant Beale could not garner the courage to speak, she said, "Very well, you think he is dead."

He took her hand between his. "Please prepare to leave with me for Chagres. You will be in New York almost by the time your husband is in St. Louis. Within a few weeks you will be reunited."

Though he maintained that the reason he wanted her to leave was that her husband would have returned east, she knew that his real reason was that he believed she was going on to San Francisco to meet a man who was buried in the glacial snows of the highest Rockies.

"I thank you for your kindness, Lieutenant; I know how much you have my interest at heart; but you are mistaken. Colonel Fremont must be in San Francisco by now; he will be waiting; I promised I would meet him there."

He bowed. "Please think it over, Miss Jessie."

After he had left she sat rocking in a chair. So the fourth expedition had failed! For her own part she did not suffer too greatly over the failure: the men had met insuperable obstacles, that was all; they had done their best, but it had not been enough in the face of the unscalable Rockies. But how would John take it: the loss of the money that his admirers in St. Louis had invested, the loss of his opportunity to re-establish himself as an explorer and trail blazer? Would he not consider it a matter of personal inadequacy, count the failure his own, be stricken by it? Would he not fear the criticism and the disgrace of having some of the men perish under his leadership? Would this make it impossible for him ever to start out again?

And here again was the phantom of her husband's death. She could believe it this time no more than the last, but in the closeness of the warm spring morning she was gripped by the terrifying realization that John might have been seriously injured. Bill Williams had reported him suffering from a badly frozen leg. The mules had frozen to death or been killed for food; there was no way for him to come down the vastness of the Rockies except on his own feet, for his men would be too weak to carry him. What then if he could no longer drag that frozen leg? He was not stronger than the forces of nature: because he had forced the Sierras, there was no reason to believe he was an imperishable one.

Her mind would not allow her to conceive that her beloved was dead, yet there might be no way for him to get through to California. He would return to St. Louis or Washington to recoup his health. By what token should she go up to San Francisco, pestilential mudhole caught in the hysteria of the gold rush, where she had neither friend nor relative, where she would be alone with her daughter, with no place to go and nothing to do, and no husband to meet her?

She was so homesick that the tears coursed unrestrainedly down her cheeks. Would anyone blame her if she let herself be persuaded that there was no sense in going on to San Francisco? True, she had promised to meet her husband there; but if he had been unable to reach San Francisco, if he were even now on his way to St. Louis, what possible sense could there be in her going on? Why persist in this cruel voyage? They would have no way of communicating with each other, to tell whether she should once more take ship to Panama, or whether John would come overland in the summer to join her. The best that could happen would be confusion and heartbreak and more months of separation.

She got out of the chair and walked upstairs to the balcony. The cooler air refreshed her a little. The Cathedral Square was abandoned but the spire gleamed with oriental splendor. And standing there, feeling desperately alone, wanting her husband's arms about her as she had never wanted them before, not even in the darkest hours in St. Louis when everyone had thought he was dead, she knew that she could not return to New York. She had not said, "I'll meet you in San Francisco if circumstances permit," or "providing I'm sure you will be there to meet me," or "if I can make it." She had made a categorical promise, and promises were made to be kept, the hard ones as well as the easy ones. If she kept this promise, under these almost unendurable circumstances, then not only would John know that she always would keep her promises, but even more important, she herself would know that she could keep them.

4

She finished her packing. Madame Arce came to her bedroom to express her happiness that she would at last go on to her own country and her own people. Jessie embraced the older woman, murmuring softly, "If not for you I might have died here. How am I to repay your kindness?"

Madame Arce replied, smiling, "In the Spanish language we do not have the word repay."

They were still murmuring gracious words to each other when another clamor arose in the town. A new party of Americans had just come off the trail from Chagres. With them had arrived a carefully guarded United States mail sack, its destination San Francisco. A portion of the mail would surely be addressed to the Americans who had been detained in Panama City these several months.

The head baggageman turned the sack over to the American representative in Panama City, a Central American consul who had no authority to do otherwise than to deliver it to the first ship headed north for San Francisco. When the Americans learned that mail had come in they thronged the official's office demanding that he open the pouch. Jessie rushed through the courtyard to join the excited group in front of the consul's office. The consul kept repeating, "I decline to usurp functions. It is locked. It cannot be opened until it reaches San Francisco. Do you not see it is marked, 'Destination San Francisco'? I have no authority . . ."

The Americans had no intention of waiting several weeks for news of their families while the locked mail sack accompanied them to San Francisco. "We'll take the responsibility!" they shouted. "We'll sign a petition! Every last one of us will sign for his letter!"

If John had come down from the mountains alive there would be a letter from him in that sack. She was positive the letter was there, and she was determined to have it. She pushed her way through the crowd. The men cried, "Here's Mrs. Fremont! She wants news of the colonel. Open that blasted sack and give us our mail."

The consul took one last look at the men's faces, then gazed into Jessie's eyes and said quickly, "Very well, but I do not take responsibility. I do not cut open this sack! You must appoint a committee and the committee must take responsibility."

The pouch was torn open before the consul had his last words out. Someone cried, "For you, Mrs. Fremont!" With tears half blinding her, Jessie saw that she had a fat envelope from Taos addressed in her husband's handwriting, another from her father in Washington. She stumbled across the square, ran up the patio stairs, tore open John's envelope and read:

Taos, New Mexico
January 27, 1849

MY VERY DEAR WIFE:

I write to you from the house of our good friend Kit Carson. This morning a cup of chocolate was brought to me, while yet in bed. While in the enjoyment of this luxury, I pleased myself in imagining how gratified you would be in picturing me here in Kit's care, whom you will fancy constantly endeavoring to make me comfortable . . .

She could read no further, for tears were falling on the familiar and dearly beloved handwriting. He was safe! He had not perished in the snows! If she had yielded to her own weakness, if she had given in to the persuasiveness of Lieutenant Beale, she would have passed this mail sack on the trail to Gorgona, she would not have known that her husband was alive until she had reached New York.

She stretched out on the lounge and buried her face in the damask, unable to think or read, knowing only overwhelming relief at his safety. After some time she picked up the letter again. There were ten tightly packed pages of handwriting, for John had put them into journal form, making his letter to her serve as a record of the harrowing and tragic events of the fourth expedition. She paled as she read on: eleven men had perished out of the thirty-three, died of cold and hunger and insanity on the trail; those who had been saved had emerged as emaciated shadows, half out of their minds with grief and suffering. Everyone in the party was blaming, criticizing and hating everyone else; John blamed Williams for the tragedy; Williams blamed John for interference, for guiding the party into hopeless tracks. John was blamed for ordering the men to try to save the baggage instead of themselves, an act which had cost perhaps nine lives; Williams was accused of cannibalism while on his way out with the relief party. Both men were blamed for not having gone back to save the balance of the party after they had made their way out. John's own life had been saved only by meeting the son of an Indian chief with whom he had been friends years before. He had reached Kit Carson's home unable to drag his leg behind him, a scarecrow, sick in body and despairing of heart.

Yet in spite of his misfortunes, he ended the letter on a cheerful note, saying that he did not consider the expedition a failure, for he had learned much about that mountainous region, was convinced that a railroad pass could be found close by, and that he would one day find it under more favorable circumstances.

When I think of you, I feel a warm glow at my heart, which renovates it like a good medicine, and I forget painful feelings in strong hope for the future. We shall yet, dearest wife, enjoy quiet and happiness together—these are nearly one and the same to me now. I make frequently pleasant pictures of the happy home we are to have, and oftenest and among the pleasantest of all I see our library with its bright fire in the rainy stormy days, and the

*large windows looking out upon the sea in the bright weather. I have it all
planned in my own mind.*

She had been right, she thought exultantly. She had kept her pledge and
they would meet in San Francisco!

But when? He had written this letter while in bed, unable to move about;
there was no way for him to get to California except on foot or horseback,
and he could not risk the hazardous journey until he was strong again. How
long might that be? Perhaps months. Perhaps never! She had known frontiersmen whose legs had been frozen, and who had lost them. If John's leg did
not heal he would need medical care; if it could not be provided in Taos,
Kit Carson would have to take him back to St. Louis for hospitalization.
Yes, she would meet her husband in San Francisco; but when?

She opened the letter from her father; in it he told her the bad news of the
expedition, including an article he had written for the eastern papers. He told
her how ill her husband was in Taos, how badly his leg and side had been
affected. He was altogether certain there would be no way for John to make
the crossing to California without seriously endangering his life. He told his
daughter that he was sending dispatches to Taos urging John to return to
St. Louis as fast as his health would permit; and he now urged his daughter
with equal vehemence to return to New York, whence she could go to St.
Louis to join her husband.

Jessie put aside the letter and stared at the high ceiling of Madame Arce's
bedroom; yes, her father would urge John to return to St. Louis, just as
Lieutenant Beale had urged her to return to New York. Sick as she was, she
had refused to turn back; sick as he might be, John would refuse to turn back.

A sailor from the S.S. *Panama* knocked at Madame Arce's door to inform
them that the captain wanted Mrs. Fremont and her daughter to come
aboard. Two Indian boys carried her luggage to the waterfront. She was
rowed in a small boat to the ship and then hauled up to the deck in a wooden
tub suspended by ropes at the end of a boom. Captain Schenck welcomed
her. The S.S. *Panama* had returned to New York after leaving Jessie at
Chagres, and had now come around the Cape with another shipload of
voyagers for California. As she gazed at the hundreds of Americans crowded
into every spare inch, she asked, "Where will all of us stay?"

"I don't know, Madame Fremont," replied the captain, with a wistful smile.
"But we dare not refuse anyone as long as there is standing room."

Within a few hours both the S.S. *Panama* and the S.S. *California* set sail for
San Francisco. Jessie's ship, which had cabin accommodations for eighty
passengers, carried four hundred men. There was no cabin available, but
Captain Schenck put two iron cots under the spanker boom, covering the
space with a large American flag. Everyone was so happy to be en route to
San Francisco that no one complained, theatricals were performed on deck,
Jessie and the passengers exchanged the few books in their possession, read-
ing aloud in the clear sunshine off the coast of Mexico.

She was delighted to meet several companionable American women, chief among them Mrs. Matilda Gray, a youngish but matronly soul who was going out to San Francisco to join her husband; and Mrs. William Gwin, one of Louisiana's most famous hostesses. Her husband was William McK. Gwin, with a leonine head topping his superb six-foot-two figure, the voice of the professional orator, the carriage of the politician. Gwin's father had fought with Tom Benton in the War of 1812 and the families had been acquainted ever since; Gwin had no hesitancy in speaking frankly to Jessie. He had a great deal of political experience, having been a congressman from Mississippi.

"I left the most lucrative political job in the United States to migrate to California," he said. "Within a year I'll be back in Washington as the first senator from the new state."

Jessie felt a sense of amused shock, as though someone had read her thoughts aloud in public meeting.

"You seem quite certain of that, Mr. Gwin."

"I am not the only one," boomed Gwin. "Before I left Washington I told Stephen A. Douglas that by this time next year I would ask him to present my credentials to the Senate. Douglas exclaimed, 'God bless you, I believe you will.'"

To herself Jessie said, I can believe that, too; but there are only two senators from a state; how many men are headed for California with that identical ambition in mind?

When the ship reached San Diego she put Lily in the care of Mrs. Gray and locked herself in the other woman's cabin, fearful of the news that was coming, unwilling to be seen when she received it. Above the noise and shouts of the passengers who were disembarking at San Diego she heard the sound of running feet, then someone pounded on her door and a man cried, "Mrs. Fremont, the colonel's safe; he's riding up to San Francisco to meet you! He didn't lose his leg, only a bad frostbite."

Jessie unlocked the door and flung it open.

"Are you sure?" she cried.

"Yes, ma'am! He was here only a few days ago."

The last two days at sea passed swiftly in the anticipation of being reunited with her husband. On the morning of June 4 the S.S. *Panama* swung eastward toward shore. As she moved through the Golden Gate Strait into the bay, with the sandy beaches of San Francisco to the south and the rocky promontories and little islands to the north, Jessie had the impression that this channel in the curvilineal coast of California was not a strait at all, but rather a canal leading into the fertile womb of the bay, with the ship carrying the seeds of men, machinery, tools and ideas to give birth to a new civilization.

Anchored in the bay were a number of ships, their wooden masts standing up bare as winter orchards, several of them abandoned. She could see a small level square flying the flag of the California Republic, and around the sides a few wooden buildings. For the rest, there was little but unpainted shacks and cabins and miners' tents dotting the hills which rose immediately back of the square. The S.S. *Panama* fired a salvo of guns to inform San Francisco that she had arrived. A heavy anchor was dropped, and Jessie watched a number of small boats being rowed out to meet them. Once again she and Lily climbed down the side of a rope ladder and were rowed to shore. Since there was no place for the small boats to dock, the sailors had to carry them over the surf. There were hundreds of men on the beach, many of them shouting words of welcome. The cold and the fog set Jessie coughing again. She was glad this was the end of the voyage: she would need the comforts of her own home and the protection of her husband to nurse her back to vigor after the grueling months.

But as she stood uncertainly at the edge of the surf and then walked up among the red-shirted, bearded men, she caught no sight of John. Once again her heart sank. He had not yet arrived in San Francisco. She was here alone. Perhaps he had not reached California at all, and the reports in San Diego had been merely encouragement by kindhearted men. As she stood on the edge of Portsmouth Square holding Lily by one hand, Mrs. Gray came to her side.

"Never you mind, dearie," she said, "the colonel's been delayed a day or two. This is my husband; Harry, meet Mrs. Fremont. Let us take you to the Parker House."

Appreciating the kindness, Jessie let Mr. and Mrs. Gray lead her to a hotel room at the Parker House and light a fire in the grate. The Grays took Lily for a walk to see the little mining village while Jessie slept soundly, awakening after dark to the clamor of men's voices. By looking out the window she saw that she was next door to the Eldorado gambling hall and that a brawl was apparently in process. She lay down on the bed again, but a few minutes later Mrs. Gray returned with Lily and a tray of food.

For five days she remained in bed, the cough she had contracted in Panama growing increasingly worse. From the conversation outside her window and from the information vouchsafed by her few visitors, she learned that San Francisco was almost deserted, that everyone had spent whatever money he had for supplies and miners' tools and rushed to the gold fields. Aside from the small amount of trade and the gambling casinos where the men spent the night in order to keep warm, there was no life in San Francisco. As a community it had hardly been born. She thought how greatly her father would have enjoyed this rawness, and was shamed that she could not be more wholeheartedly her father's daughter.

She had grown thin again, her King George's Mark throbbed unceasingly. There were several men in town who knew Colonel Fremont from Washington or his expeditions, and they made sure she had sufficient food and firewood for the grate. They kept assuring her that her husband would arrive any hour, but with the passage of the days she realized that although the trip from San Diego was a long and hard one by horseback, and the weather had been bad, if John had been there he would have had plenty of time to reach San Francisco by now.

There were days of heavy rains, converting the earthen surface of Portsmouth Square into a muddy bog. The nights were bitterly cold, for a penetrating wind came over the bay, seeping through the walls and the ill-fitted windows of the hastily constructed hotel. The brushwood fagots smoked, making her eyes smart, and she and Lily lay huddled in the narrow iron bed, comforting each other with hopeful words and bodily warmth. This cold, bare shacklike room was her first home and her first hearth in California. She wondered if her grandmother Benton had lived thus with her children when she had first reached Tennessee; she wondered if her grandmother had suffered the despair that was gnawing at her own heart. If only she could be sleeping on the hard cold ground of the Santa Cruz ranch, for that would be her own land and her home, and the open campfire would be a truer hearth than this acridly smoking grate which choked their lungs even while it warmed their flesh.

At dusk of the tenth day as she was sitting before the fire, her thin hands clasped in her lap, she heard men's voices outside her window. Someone cried, "Your wife's inside the house, Colonel." She moved out of the chair to open the door. Before she could do so, it was flung open and John had taken her in his arms and was crushing her against him.

Neither could speak. He led her back to her chair, threw some fresh fagots on the fire, then sat on the floor by her side holding her two hands in his, gazing up at her.

"You have been ill; you are ill now, my darling."

"No . . ."

The door opened and Lily entered. John embraced his daughter, then took her on his knee. Lily said, sober-faced:

"You didn't come. Mother almost died. A lady downstairs says she will die."

He rose before Jessie, put his arms about her waist and gazed into her face. His eyes were dark, self-accusing. She ran her fingers lightly through his long gray hair, then laid her cheek on his.

"In her innocence, Lily is partly right. Being away from you is a kind of a death. Only with you am I fully alive and well."

5

The next morning she propped a small mirror against a straight-backed chair and sat before it combing out her hair and massaging her face, interested in her appearance for the first time in months. John brought a breakfast of hot coffee and bread up to the room, then left for the office of the American consul to pick up the deed to the Santa Cruz ranch which had been deposited there by Consul Larkin of Monterey. Several hours passed before she heard his footsteps in the hall; her quick ear perceived that something was wrong: this was not the fast springy step of her husband who could not bear to move slowly; this was the plodding step of a man who had suffered a blow. She seized this last instant to tie a blue ribbon about her hair with a small bow on top and to cast a quick look at her blue quilted robe in the pocket mirror. She forced a smile to her face.

"John, what has happened?"

He did not answer for a moment, then said:

"Larkin didn't get our ranch."

She waited for him to continue, but when he did not, she demanded, "Didn't buy . . . ? But he's had a full year."

"He bought all right," John moaned, "but not the magnificent ranch with the beautiful vines and orchards that I told him to acquire; he used our three thousand dollars to buy a wild tract of land somewhere up in the mountains called the Mariposa." He took an official-looking document from his inside coat pocket and flung it angrily on the bed. "The Mariposa," he repeated, "several hundred miles from here, a hundred miles from the ocean or the nearest settlement, high up in the Sierras, impossible to farm, overrrun with Indians, so we couldn't even set up a cattle ranch . . ."

She picked up the document from the bed, opened it and gazed unseeing at the title grant. "But what does it mean?" she asked. "You didn't tell Larkin to buy the Mariposa. You told him to buy the Santa Cruz ranch. Is it possible that he confused your orders?"

"No, no! When I handed him the three thousand dollars I gave him written instructions. He had been over the land with me. There was no possibility of an error." He jumped up from his chair, striding about the cramped little room. "I'll have to borrow a horse and ride down to Monterey."

"Is the Santa Cruz ranch still available?" asked Jessie. "Has no one else bought it?"

John's eyes fell. "Our consul thinks the land has been sold. He has heard . . . Jessie, it's just coming to me. Larkin must have bought that land for himself!"

"But if that's the case, John, we can sue him; we can recover, it's a fraudulent transaction."

"How? This is not the United States. This is the Republic of California. They have no courts, no legal system, no judges, no police. It's the law of the frontier. Every man for himself . . ."

Shrewdly she asked, "Who was the previous owner of the Mariposa? Did Larkin own it, or did he buy it from someone else?"

John took the deed from her hand, glanced at it and replied, "According to this paper, Larkin bought the Mariposa from former governor Alvarado of California, who had been given it in a grant from Spain. It's a vast tract of mountains and valleys, freezing cold in winter; no one can live there. What good is a lot of land if it's valueless?"

She put her fingers lightly on his shoulder.

"I shall loathe being left here alone again, but there can be no doubt that you must see Larkin. We want either our land or our three thousand dollars!"

It had always been their intention that John should play a role in making California a state. But how could he do this if he suddenly were deprived of his property, if he were without a means of livelihood or position to buttress him? She did not want him to be known as a former explorer; that would be doubly unfortunate since the failure of his fourth expedition. In order to play a full-voiced part in the forming of the state, to be elected senator, he must be important in California while the state was being founded. But what was this job to be? Even now the delegates of the Constitutional Convention were being elected; William Gwin had thrown his hat into the ring while he was still wading ashore. John would have to move fast if he wanted to be sent to Monterey as a delegate.

She was awakened one night by a clangor in front of the hotel and saw that the sky outside her window was vividly red. The warehouse on the waterfront, where her trunks and heavy boxes were stored, was in flames. It burned all night; all night she sat by the window in her robe watching the last of her possessions go up in smoke: her clothing, her linens, blankets, books, silver, ornaments, beautiful and familiar things she had brought to make herself a home in California. First they had lost the Santa Cruz ranch, and now her only possessions were those in her small suitcases in the hotel room. Fortunately she had her money box with her; these gold coins were her last link to family and security. When they were gone, they would really be pioneers, starting from scratch like everyone around them.

John returned to the hotel after five days to tell her of his interview with Larkin.

"There's something strange about the entire transaction," he said with a baffled expression. "Thomas Larkin was always straightforward and honest, a shrewd Yankee trader, but one to be trusted. Now his answers are evasive . . ."

"But does he admit he took the three thousand dollars? Does he acknowledge that you instructed him to buy the Santa Cruz ranch?"

"Yes, he acknowledges all that, but he has a hundred strange reasons for what he did; reports came to him that the Santa Cruz soil wasn't good; he didn't think I wanted to be a farmer; he had a chance to buy the Mariposa from Alvarado and thought I would prefer to live in the mountains, since I loved them so much; he thought I would rather be a cattle rancher; he felt that he had the right to use his own judgment in my best interests."

"How much does he say he paid for the Mariposa?"

"The same three thousand dollars."

"Did you tell him we want either our land or our money?"

"Yes. He said it was impossible, that I had appointed him as my agent, with discretionary powers, and I had to accept the results of his judgment. He was sorry if I was disappointed, but . . ."

They sat in silence in the mean little room, the future staring them down. She knew that John was grieving mostly over the loss of the beautiful ranch and his opportunity to earn a living as a farmer. For her the blow was of a different and more subtle nature: she had been deprived of her opportunity to create a home. Perhaps the gods were not only slow to consecrate a new hearth, but actually reluctant to see one laid. If Consul Larkin had bought any piece of land other than the Mariposa, even though it might have been inferior to the Santa Cruz ranch, she would not have felt so bad, for they still would have had their chance to make a home place. But the Mariposa was wild and frozen mountainous country, overrun by hostile Indians; it would be impossible for them to settle there.

What were they to do next? John was not the kind to grasp a pick and basin and rush to the gold fields; nor was there any business he could enter into in San Francisco. Perhaps in time he might receive a government appointment, but that was months off. She had brought with her one thousand dollars in gold loaned to her by her father to buy lumber and farm equipment, but her husband had borrowed twice that sum in Taos in order to bring the remnants of his party through to California.

"What do you think we ought to do?" she asked, curled up crossways on the bed. He too curled himself across the bed, running his fingers gently over her sunken cheeks.

"I'm sorry you got the starved-cat wife again, John."

"I'll confess I was hoping to find the bumpy one."

"Be patient, my dear."

"You asked what we should do first," he cried. "We are going to cure that cold of yours and get some weight back on you. I'm going to show you the beauties of California: all you've seen so far is this mudhole, but down on the peninsula there are bright sunshine and rolling hills and lovely valleys. I'm going to take you where it's warm and the countryside is beautiful. When we have had a month's vacation, we will face the future."

She snuggled closer into his arms, murmured, "Thank you, darling. But shouldn't you spend that month campaigning? The elected delegates are to meet in Monterey in September to adopt a constitution."

He had a way of welding firmness with tenderness. "My first task is to nurse you back to health. You are more important to me than politics. Besides, I'm not . . . I'm not a campaigner. Most of the people in the state know me, or know of me. There's little I could say from a stump that they don't already know."

Her mind went back to the spring evening in the summerhouse on C Street when Tom Benton had perceived that his daughter was in love with Lieutenant Fremont. John had said, "I am not much interested in politics."

"But surely you want to participate in the Constitutional Convention?"

"Not as a delegate. As a friend and adviser of the delegates, as an influence behind the scenes. I think I can do more good that way."

She did not see how, but she thought it wiser not to press the point. Instead she closed her eyes to embrace the vision of a month of leisure in warmth and beauty, with her husband at her side.

Gregorio, an Indian boy who had stuck with John through the worst rigors of the cold and starvation and had accompanied him from Taos, joined them on their trip down the peninsula. Also old Knight, who had been with John on an earlier expedition and was one of the sharpest frontiersmen of the West.

The following morning John disappeared early, telling her to be in front of the Parker House in an hour. Jessie dressed in her black silk, with the silk bonnet that matched. She did not think it a proper costume in which to go camping, but it was the only one she had left. After an hour she and Lily went down to the entrance of the Parker House. Within a few moments her husband came driving across Portsmouth Square in a six-seated surrey, the first she had seen in California. John whoaed the horses, jumped out and helped his wife into the new and luxurious interior, with its upholstered cushions of Spanish leather, compartments for storage of suitcases and foodstuffs.

"Where ever did you find this in San Francisco?" she asked in awe, caressing the beautiful upholstery.

"I had it made for you in New Jersey before I left. It's been standing here in a storehouse for two months. It's guaranteed to ride as smooth as a boat, and look, it has reversible seats that make a bed. You can sleep in here as comfortably as you would at home. Lily will have plenty of space in this large boot to stretch out."

"Oh, darling," she murmured, "this is the first piece of good luck we've had in California."

"There's another piece of good luck waiting around the corner, afraid to come to you, but I have convinced him that all is forgiven."

Jessie saw Lieutenant Beale come striding toward her with a sheepish grin on his long face. He said, "Madame Fremont, I am a fool! I do not deserve your forgiveness! If you had followed my wretched advice you would now be in the East while your husband would be here. When I think how hard I tried to persuade you . . ."

"These are things that only women understand, Lieutenant," she replied gaily. "There's nothing to forgive; I was touched by your concern for me in Panama."

"Then may we take him along on our junket?" asked her husband. "He makes an excellent *pot-au-feu* when he doesn't throw too much pepper into it; and he's the one who begged, borrowed or stole these beautiful white horses."

They followed the trail down the peninsula, leaving behind the fog and cold of San Francisco, and within a couple of hours had emerged into warm clear sunlight, with the ripe fields of oats moving gently on the hillsides, and the wild cattle grazing under the trees. The countryside was like a park with mile after mile of beautiful grasses, wild flowers and magnificent trees. When the air grew a little cool, John threw his faded blue army cape over her shoulders.

They made camp in midafternoon by the side of a brook. While Jessie refreshed herself and Lily in the cold water the men rode off in search of a neighboring ranch house, returning with half a sheep and some fresh corn which they barbecued over live coals of the fire. The Morocco carriage cushions were piled in front of the fire for Jessie and Lily, who ate their meat from the ends of long twigs. John had brought along claret and tea and a box of French bonbons for Lily. Under the deepening cloudless sky the air was soft and warm. Supper was finished by dusk. Fresh logs were put on the fire, the men began telling stories of other camps on the frontiers of South America, the Orient, and this wide American continent. Gregorio told of his childhood with the Indian tribe. Beale told sea stories and little jokes to make Jessie laugh. Old Knight, tall and gnarled as a mountain pine, ageless, with a long white beard which seemed somehow transplanted from his bald and shiny head, spun yarns of the days when the frontier had been only a hundred miles west of Washington.

As the night skies deepened, the campfire lighted the trees and brook, then the stars came out and to Jessie it was a scene of great beauty. This is my first hearth, she said to herself, just the kind we should have in a new country. May all of my hearths be as serene.

By nine o'clock she and Lily were comfortably settled in the carriage. The men had tied their hammocks to the trees and fallen asleep. Jessie listened to the crackling of the logs on the fire, the mules munching their wild oats, the half-muted cry of a coyote who had not the courage to come in and steal her supper. At dawn John awakened her with a cup of hot tea, then made a dressing tent for her by the side of the brook from a pair of blankets. She took her tin basin, towels, French soap and cologne to the running water, scrubbed Lily and then gave herself a leisurely bath. A doctor might have told her that bathing in a cold stream at dawn was dangerous; they had told that to her father forty years before. By the time she had dressed and returned to the campfire the carriage was ready, with most of the gear packed. After a cup of tea and a couple of old Knight's hot muffins, she said to John:

"Now what is my share of the duties?"

"To eat with all the appetite you can gather, to be happy."

"That's all, no work?"

"No work," replied the men. "This is your holiday. Women are useless on the trail, anyway."

The sun was bright and warm when they started toward San José. There weren't any roads, but the sturdily built carriage could go anywhere that wheels could go, and so they drove through the dry fertile valleys, climbed up the hills to overlook the ocean, followed bridle paths among the pines ever southward into warmer country, the men holding back the carriage with their riatas on steep grades. Knight and Gregorio would walk ahead of the two pack mules, which carried leather panniers loaded with clothing, cans and bottles of food, hammocks, pots and pans. John and Beale took turns driving the horses. At noon they stopped for luncheon and a siesta, throwing into the *pot-au-feu* large Spanish onions, sweet red peppers and whatever the men had shot that morning. They also scoured the countryside for eggs and fruits. When Jessie awakened from her nap they would drive on until time to make camp. For the first week her cough persisted; she began taking sun baths during the noon halt and by the end of the second week the pain in her chest was easing.

And so she moved through the balmy days, having no interest in time, regaining her joyousness with each passing hour. Sometimes in an inland valley behind the coast range the sun was burning hot, sometimes the air from the sea was soft and cool. When they put into a village they had their linens washed by the Indian women; sometimes they stopped at the ranches of the Californios where Jessie had proof that General Kearny's charges against her husband of maltreating the natives had been false. The Californios welcomed the party, staged fiestas in their honor, while Jessie and the women talked of clothes and babies. They had the good fortune to participate in a three-day wedding celebration, riding in the parade amidst the satin dresses and slippers of the women and the short velvet jackets and colorful velvet trousers of the men. Jessie's carriage was a matter of great interest to the Californios, who had nothing but solid wooden wheel carts pulled by oxen.

On the last night of July, while they were camped in the Santa Cruz mountains overlooking the sea, not far from the ranch which was supposed to have been their home, a sudden gust of rain swept across the ridge. John said, "I think your vacation is over, madame. We must decide now where we are going to settle down."

Jessie sighed reluctantly. "This has been a wonderful month. But I'm ready to set up our home. Where shall it be? How far are we from the Mariposa?"

"About two hundred miles, I should guess."

"Would it be difficult for us to see the land? I'm curious about it."

"It's a long journey on horseback across mountain trails and unbridged streams."

"What route would we take? Tell me how we get in."

His eyes lighted as he thought of the journey. "We'd go up the San Joaquin Valley, then straight into the Sierras."

"Would we pass the gold fields?"

"Yes, we'd go straight through the gold country."

They looked at each other, an expression of incredulity coming over their faces.

"By the Eternal, Jessie," whispered John, "I never thought of it before. We own the largest tract of mountain country in California. Men are washing out fortunes in gold dust only a hundred miles away . . ."

Her eyes wide with wonderment, she whispered too, "Darling, is it possible? Could there be gold on the Mariposa?"

He sprang to his feet. "It's the same mountain range; it would have the same rock formations, the same mineral deposits. It would have the same kind of rushing mountain steams to carry the gold dust down."

A slow, warm smile lighting her face, she said, "Could we start for San Francisco tomorrow morning? Could we buy picks and shovels and join the gold rush?"

"It's a risk, you know," said John. "Once we occupy the Mariposa, even to hunt gold on it, we will be making a legal acceptance of the land. We can never get our three thousand dollars from Larkin."

"We have no way of getting it back, anyway."

"How much cash do we have left out of your father's thousand dollars?"

"About five hundred."

"Then why don't we plunge the rest of our resources in a real gamble?"

"How do you mean?"

"While I was coming out from Taos I encountered a party of Sonorans from Mexico, en route to the gold fields. I rode with them for several days. When I was in Monterey I met them again; they were exhausted from the long march and planned to rest before starting into the mountains. I think I can make a deal with them: if I outfit them with food and tools and offer them half of all the gold they find on the Mariposa, they'll bring us down a fortune—if there is a fortune to be brought down. If there's no gold in the Mariposa, we will be broke."

"I'm not scared, John. Besides, I think it is futile to arrive in California at the height of the greatest gold strike the world has ever known and not take part in it. I'd like to wade up a mountain stream myself with a dishpan in my hands and see if I couldn't collect some gold dust . . ."

Exhilarated, he chuckled, "That's the mercenary streak in you, Jessie; let me be the luster after wealth in this family, it doesn't become you. I'll take the Sonorans up to the Mariposa. When we return you will be a rich man's lady."

"Just so long as I'm not a Washington fine lady," she retorted.

6

The next afternoon they reached the plateau above Monterey, with the little village nestling in the pines beneath them, and still farther down, the rocky shore of the crescent-curved bay. Jessie stood among the pines, watching the gulls flash white across the sun; she said to her husband, "Why couldn't we make our permanent camp here within sight and sound of all this beauty? It is warmer and quieter than San Francisco."

"Yes, I think you would be happy in Monterey. I will go into town to see if I can find us a house."

He was gone only an hour when she saw him swinging up the little trail from the village.

"There are no houses available," he announced, "but I've found two lovely rooms in the house of the wife of the Mexican general Castro, who was exiled to Mexico City after our conquest. She does not hold this against us. We will be comfortable there."

He helped her into the carriage and drove it down the winding path to the village. Madame Castro's house was the former Mexican governor's home: a huge ballroom fronted the bay, two adobe wings ran back from the water to meet a garden enclosed in soft-colored adobe walls; the roof was of rough red tile, the floors of smooth red tile, and there were hedges of pinks lining the garden walls and walks.

The ballroom was now rented as a warehouse for a flour merchant; Jessie was ushered into one of the wings which contained two rooms, high-ceilinged, the adobe walls whitewashed. They were innocent of furniture except for a wood stove in a small anteroom. Jessie presented her compliments to Madame Castro, who loaned them two cots and two chairs, several pots and pans, a few dishes and some flatware.

Leaving her to survey her new home, and to wonder how she was going to get it furnished, John went out to find his Sonorans, returning at lunchtime.

"The Mexicans have agreed to my proposition," he told her excitedly. "I must leave for San Francisco with them at once."

At her crestfallen expression, he added quickly, "I will be back in a couple of weeks, just as soon as there is news."

"Very well," said Jessie, "but since you are going up to San Francisco, you must use part of our funds to buy furniture and linens and dishes and silverware. This is the first time I shall be a housewife, and I am afraid I can't do very well with a few borrowed dishes. Let me give you a list; and you had better buy materials so that I can make some clothes for Lily and myself. Our two outfits are threadbare."

He left by midafternoon, assuring her that the first ship to reach Monterey would carry everything needed to make them happy at Madame Castro's. Jessie was delighted when Gregorio asked permission to remain behind as houseboy. She set about her duties as housewife, but the gold seekers had swept the country clean of every vestige of chicken, eggs, milk, meat, vegetables, fruits, canned goods and the wheat and grain staples. She could find little to buy but rice and beans, a little flour and sugar. She had never cooked anything more than a pot of coffee, and now she was thrust into the position of feeding herself, Lily and Gregorio on a few crude staples. Occasionally when she came back from a brisk walk in the hills with Lily she would find Gregorio squatting before the fire, a broad red sash around his waist and a red silk handkerchief tied around his jet-black hair, cooking a *guisado*, a compound of birds, squirrel, dried red peppers and rice stewed together.

Gregorio liked to picture himself in the role of houseboy, as he had been for the Mission Fathers, but he had preconceived notions of what a man might and might not do: he would light the fire in the open hearth in the living room, but a man did not chop wood, that was a squaw's work, so Jessie chopped her own firewood. Men shot food, but they did not cook over a stove, that was squaw's work, and so Jessie did the cooking.

"It's a good thing Gregorio is ornamental," she laughed to Lily, "with that red band around his straight Indian hair, because he really isn't useful. You and I do more cooking for him than he does for us."

"When he shoots a partridge or quail," answered Lily, "he cooks it over the open fire and brings it to us on a stick."

"Yes," agreed Jessie with a wry smile, "whether it's three in the afternoon or three in the morning! We have to eat it whether we're hungry or not, so that we won't offend him. I wonder if I'll ever be able to teach him the quaint American custom of cooking and serving food at mealtimes?"

"I don't think so," replied Lily, straight-faced. "You see, Mother, the Indians never had clocks and so they didn't know when it was mealtime. They ate when they got hungry, or they had shot something."

At the end of two weeks a ship arrived from San Francisco, and a number of sailors began bringing crates up to the Castro house. When everything had been assembled Jessie found that her husband had sent her two high, roomy New England bedsteads, plenty of sheets and blankets, woven East Indian wicker chairs, a beautiful inlaid teakwood table, enough Chinese matting to cover the tile floors, white lace material for curtains, Chinese satins and French damasks for draperies, two exquisitely shaped English pottery punch bowls to be used as washbasins, colorful French and Chinese satin-cushioned bamboo couches and chairs; two big grizzly-bear skins to be thrown over the matted floor in front of the fireplace; tin candlesticks and tall white spermaceti candles under whose light she and her father had worked for so many hours in their library in Washington. Wrapped as though it were the prize of the shipment, she found a copy of Lane's translation of *The Arabian Nights,* the only book in her possession.

With help from Madame Castro, and with Gregorio doing the heavy work, Jessie tacked the lovely white curtains over the windows, spread the matting on the floor, set out the beds in the rear room and the teakwood table with the wicker chairs in the living room. When the place began to look warm and homelike, she had Gregorio bring in the last big package and open it in front of the fire. For a moment she believed she was dreaming, for someone had sold to her husband as "very durable for a lady's winter clothes" harsh merinos, thick muslins and cotton-back satins in loud and garish patterns. After her first shock, she had to laugh.

"It serves me right," she said to Lily, "for letting a man buy cloth for women's clothes; but never mind, we'll make the best of it. Here we go for a winter wardrobe."

She carefully ripped up her one remaining set of cambric underclothes to use as a pattern, also the one faithful black silk dress which remained of her

Washington wardrobe. She did the same for Lily, laying out the patterns on the living-room floor as a guide, attempting to copy their lines in these new and strangely intractable stuffs. She pinned, measured, and remeasured herself and Lily before daring to put scissors to cloth. She had grown so thin since the black silk dress had been made that the first fitting showed the need for drastic alterations. She told her daughter the story of the old lady in St. Louis who never shaped stockings, but knitted them straight to the heel, saying, "It's a mighty poor leg that can't shape its own stocking." She built Lily's wardrobe and her own on this plan, playing a game in which she became Mrs. Abbott of London, fashionable mantua maker, and Lily her wealthy and imperious client, having elegant gowns built for Washington society. The game had added piquancy, for John had taken nearly all their money to San Francisco to outfit the Sonorans, and Jessie was getting down to her last few dollars for food. Their furnishings, she surmised with a crooked smile as she gazed about her, had been bought on credit.

With her husband away, Lily became her companion. She took her daughter for long walks among the pine-covered hills overlooking the bay, spent several hours each day teaching her arithmetic, geography and history, gave the seven-year-old a feeling of participation in their communal life by letting her do her share of the housework. Although these separations from her husband gave her the opportunity to devote herself to her daughter, they also brought Jessie closest to Lily during those periods when the light was gone from her eye and the sparkle from her brain and spirit. Lily was an observant child, she commented on what a different person her mother was when Father was present, how much more gay she was then, her step and her words fast and strong. Jessie felt conscience-stricken and redoubled her efforts to make Lily feel her love, but the light, the inner warmth and glow went out when John left, and all that was available for her daughter was the shell of a woman, wishing away her days until her husband would return.

She was perplexed by Lily's unfolding nature; by some strange twist of fate she found her daughter unimaginative in everything except this suffering of her mother's while her father was away. While she knew that the child must resent her father's dominating her mother's love and interest, yet when loneliness overcame her, it was Lily who served as comforter, stroking her hair the way John did, speaking her father's words of endearment exactly in her father's tone. She could discover no way in which Lily was like herself or John. She was a great deal like her aunt Eliza: biggish and awkward in figure, with plain features, literal-minded, practical in a way that neither Jessie nor John could ever be. Jessie had once remarked to her husband that Lily was a demon for the unvarnished truth; the daughter frequently punctured the romantic imaginings of her parents. There were occasions when Jessie was grateful, for the Fremont family had no more room for romantics, and a practical nature at the family board could be a blessing.

Late one afternoon, about a month after John had left for San Francisco, while she was sewing before the hearth in the living room, with Gregorio and Lily squatting on their haunches before the fire toasting quail, the door was thrown open and John burst into the room, his face and clothing soiled from the long ride, but a fiery glow in his eyes. He was at her side before she could rise, had laid a heavy sack at her feet. She did not open it but only gazed up at him. He quickly untied the thongs about the neck of the sack, scooped his right hand into it and with his left hand grasping her wrist tightly, poured a slow, bright stream of powder into her palm.

"Gold!" she cried.

"Yes, my darling, gold. Do you know how much gold is in this sack? One hundred pounds! Worth almost twenty-five thousand dollars!" He left her side and ran to the door, crying over his shoulder, "Wait there, don't move." In a moment he returned with another heavy sack in each hand, the weight far more than he could ordinarily have borne. He dropped the two sacks in front of her on the hearth, untied the thongs and spilled out a handful of gold from each.

"Every creek is lined with gold. The Sonorans washed out seventy-five thousand dollars' worth in three weeks!"

This turn of events was more than Jessie could comprehend. She had been reduced to her last few dollars for provisions, and now suddenly she had hundred-pound sacks of gold dust dumped at her feet. When she at last found her tongue, all she could stutter, unbelievingly, was:

"It's . . . all . . . ours?"

"No, only half is ours; you remember, I promised the Sonorans half the gold they found. But there are millions of dollars' worth of gold in there. It's richer than anything yet found in California. But that's not the most important part: I think the Mother Lode runs through our Mariposa!"

"Mother Lode?" she repeated meaninglessly, still too stunned to think.

"Yes. While crossing our land I saw geological formations that I thought gave promise of containing precious minerals. Then I found a large piece of gold-bearing quartz. Do you know what that means, Jessie? All the gold that we wash out of the rivers comes originally from the gold-quartz rock formations. A thousand men swarming over the streams of the Mariposa could wash out all the gold that the water has carried down for centuries; that supply can be exhausted within a few months. But if we have the original source, the deep layers of gold quartz that might run across a whole mountain range, then literally there are millions of dollars in the Mariposa!"

She didn't know whether to laugh or cry; there certainly was no disputing these three heavy sacks of gold, or the piece of quartz with the strong gold streak through it.

Money had never been important in her life, but that was because she had never wanted for it. Having arrived in a strange country, only to find themselves dispossessed of their ranch, several thousand dollars in debt, and with no means of earning a livelihood, she felt this discovery to be providential. This gold through which she ran her fingers in the open mouths of the sacks was to her more a symbol of happiness than of wealth, for she knew how much it could mean to her husband: in success, in accomplishment, while at the height of his powers and in the midst of overwhelming praise, John was modest, reserved, unassuming, warmhearted, generous, lovable. He was built to withstand success; the greater the success, the finer John Fremont shone forth. But he was not equipped to withstand failure or defeat; these brought out the very worst in him. They made him suspicious, vindictive, intolerant, mean-spirited and small-souled. That was why she had been so stricken in Panama at the news of the collapse and destruction of the fourth expedition; that was why the loss of the Santa Cruz ranch, even though she had never thought that he should be a farmer, had been such a serious blow: she had feared it might turn her husband bitter, start him thinking in terms of conspiracy and persecution.

But now he would be rich. This was a kind of success everyone could understand and no one could dispute. Even more important than being rich, he would have become the darling of the gods: for he had discovered gold on his own land, not merely the gold that had been washed down by the streams, but the very source of that gold. She knew that when word of this discovery reached the East it would wipe out the criticism of his failure to find a new railroad pass, his failure to keep his party alive and return them all to safety. The news that John Fremont had discovered part of the Mother Lode on his Mariposa estate would sweep the East with as wild an excitement as had any of the reports of his first three expeditions—and it would do as much to intensify the ever growing migration to California! She uttered thanks to God, grateful that her man had once again been set on his feet.

7

By the following morning, when he had dashed off for the mines, it all seemed like a fantastic dream; every once in a while she would have to return to the sacks and run her fingers through the shining dust to reassure herself that she had not been dreaming. Yet the presence of the gold in the house brought little material change, for there was no additional food available, and there were no men left in Monterey to perform any kind of service; everyone had rushed to the gold fields, and the Indian women would do no work. One day a strapping Texan knocked at her door with a healthy young mulatto girl in tow.

"I hear you are in need of a servant, Mrs. Fremont," he said. "I come to sell you this slave girl. I'm going into the gold fields and I don't need her no more. I'll make a reasonable bargain."

"Would you allow her to work for me for wages?"

"No, ma'am," replied the Texan, "I want to sell her and get rid of her for good."

"I don't want to buy her," replied Jessie firmly.

"But why not, ma'am? I'm not even naming the price. I can collect from the colonel any time."

"I thank you for your kindness, sir," she replied, "but you don't understand. I don't believe in buying and selling persons."

"Why should you keep yourself from living in comfort?" asked the Texan. "Everybody buys and sells niggers."

"Colonel Fremont and I do not. We don't believe in slavery. We have always had colored people in our home, but they have been freemen, free to go when they wished."

And so she continued to scrub her own floors, pushing aside the gold sacks under the bed so that she could wash where they had been standing.

In addition to the gracious Spanish women with whom she could spend a neighborly hour now and then, she found that the United States Army officers were moving their headquarters to Monterey because living in San Francisco had grown too expensive. Generals James Benton Riley and P. T. Smith were there with their wives, and young William T. Sherman, with a consumptive cough but an inexhaustible supply of good stories. During August, Monterey became excited and busy, for it was to be the first state capital and within a few weeks the delegates would assemble to organize their government and draw up a constitution. Colton Hall, which the Reverend Samuel Wiley had been using as a school, was turned into a convention hall; a hotel had been started for the delegates, but since the mechanics had departed for the mines, there were few carpenters to work on it.

By the first of September the delegates began to ride into Monterey. For the most part they were a rough-hewn group of frontiersmen, all of whom carried weapons; some of them Jessie knew from Washington and St. Louis, with most of the others John was acquainted from his former stays in California. Six-foot-six Robert Semple, who had been important in forming the Bear Flag Republic, was chosen chairman; William G. Marcy, son of the secretary of war, was appointed secretary; J. Ross Browne, a traveling journalist, was made shorthand reporter; W. E. P. Hartnell, an Englishman, was engaged as interpreter for the Californios. There were early settlers, professional politicians, Englishmen, Irishmen, Frenchmen, Spaniards: America in microcosm.

Two days before the convention opened the hotel owner abandoned all hopes of getting his building completed, announcing, "The weather will hold good; the delegates can roll up in their serapes and sleep under the pine trees." However, there was not a restaurant in town; some of the men brought their own food in packs, but others came totally unprepared. Hospitality was for Jessie as natural as breathing, and she held open house every afternoon. While she could serve no varied menus, she had become good at making rice puddings, and the delegates were expert with their guns and fishing lines. Few came to dinner without a bird or a fish in hand.

She and Gregorio set up a long wooden table in the big garden. Here every afternoon ten or fifteen delegates would gather to talk politics and discuss the coming convention. Of the thirty-six American delegates, twenty-two came from the North and only fourteen from the South; nevertheless, the contest over slavery was sure to be hotly waged. There were three other American women in Monterey, Mrs. Larkin, Mrs. Riley and Mrs. Smith, all pleasant and hospitable women who did their share in entertaining the delegates; however, because Jessie and John had already been friends with some thirty out of the thirty-six delegates, their home became the informal star chamber of the convention, and here many of the issues were rehearsed. Long experience in the clash of political theories had taught Jessie how to sustain an atmosphere in which these ideas could be fought to their logical conclusions. Her two rooms were small; the furnishings were bizarre and ill-fitted; the outdoor table was of rough wooden planks; but her warmth, her delight in participating in the creation of the new state kept the glow on her cheeks, her eyes sparkling, her tongue witty and welcoming.

As she looked about the rough board table with its covering of unbleached muslin brier-stitched with red thread, the oddly assorted silverware and unmatched Chinese and Mexican dishware; as she looked at the unshaven, roughly garbed frontiersmen eating the fish which they had caught themselves in Monterey Bay, and she had baked over the outdoor fire, with big bowls of rice pudding in the center of the table to finish off the repast, her mind went back to the highly polished mahogany table in the Benton dining room in Washington, with its shining damask cloths, gleaming silver and cut-glass bowls of fruits and candies, with Joshaam and Josheem padding about silently, passing the sides of rare roast beef, the terrapin, the roast duck and turkey, the beef and kidney pies.

Incongruous as were the furnished two rooms at Madame Castro's house, she developed a genuine love for them. Visited by men who spent most of the year sleeping on the ground or living in improvised shacks, tents or wretched boardinghouses, Jessie's rooms seemed like a breath of home. One Sunday evening when the weather suddenly turned cold, and they were eating indoors, William Gwin, John Sutter, Robert Semple, and Henry W. Halleck made an inspection of the rooms, and then Semple said: "Mrs. Fremont, we were saying among ourselves how surprising it was that you could achieve such comfort in a queer place like Monterey."

Jessie looked about her critically, trying to see the rooms with the eyes of a stranger. On the floor were the two grizzly-bear skins, their glass eyes lighted by the fire; the windows were draped with elegant Chinese brocade, the adobe walls were crudely whitewashed, and on the Chinese rattan furniture were cushions covered with exquisite French silks. The only wall decoration was a colored print of St. Francis, while on the Chinese teakwood table was the representative of another great religion, a bronze Buddha; alongside were a two-year-old copy of the London *Punch* and her Martha Washington sewing basket, the same one in which she had concealed the letter from Colonel Abert. She took the stance of a professional lecturer, raised one arm in the air for silence, and announced in her father's sometime pontifical tone:

"Gentlemen, at first glance you might think this room incongruous, but having made close study of it, I find it true to the period, Pioneer Forty-nine, worthy elements from all over the world, guarded by a California grizzly."

Her one disappointment was that her husband was not at home to join in the hospitality, the discussions, and the formulation of policy. She felt that John should have been a member of this convention, that even now he should be having serious talks with every delegate, helping to set official state policy. But word of the tremendous findings on the Mariposa had spread over central California and already several thousand prospectors were placer mining on the Fremont land. Their land grant did not give them exclusive mineral rights; anyone was entitled to wash out and pick up the gold lying in the Mariposa streams. John had felt that at that particular moment he should be with the Sonorans, helping them find the best streams in which to work, taking out their gold nuggets and gold dust before another several thousand prospectors flooded over the land. Jessie had not thought it so necessary to get out the last possible bag of gold dust; they had not come to California to be gold miners or to become rich; they had come to enter into the local politics; why then allow the accidental discovery of gold on the Mariposa to upset their plans and to keep John away from the California Constitutional Convention?

She had suggested all this to her husband, but he had declared that as long as he was not a delegate there was no proper place for him; that most of the delegates knew his stand and his politics from years of contact; that no one could blame him for making gold while the sun shone. Later, when they opened their regular quartz mines, their property would be safe and he would not have to be on the ground. It was unfortunate that the convention and the Mariposa gold rush were taking place at the same moment, but he felt he owed it to all of them to get out as much gold as he could and let Jessie be his representative in Monterey as she had been in Washington.

One evening Delegate Lippincott of Philadelphia brought fifteen delegates in to dinner. They watched Jessie standing over the stove cooking the food; they watched her cover the rough planks with the strips of unbleached muslin brier-stitched together; they watched her serve, with Gregorio's help, twenty-four guests; they saw her sit at the head of the table and with high spirits guide the political discussions so that they included everyone about the table; they saw her gather up the soiled plates, then wash the dishes and silver while William Sherman, the Reverend Wiley and Robert Semple stood about drying them, everyone keeping up a rapid-fire repartee. When the work was done and they had assembled in the living room, several of the lanky frontiersmen sprawling on the floor in front of the fire, one of the delegation said:

"Mrs. Fremont, we heard in town that you were offered a young slave girl to do your work and you refused to buy her. Is that true?"

"Quite true," replied Jessie. "Neither Mr. Fremont nor I believe in buying and selling human beings. I would never consent to use or own a slave."

"Not even if it meant you would have to scrub your own floors and wash your own dishes for the rest of your life?"

"Not even," said Jessie with a quiet smile.

"The women in San Francisco are crying for suv-vents, but if you, a Washington fine lady, can get along without, they shan't have them. We'll keep clear of slave labor."

Hallelujah! thought Jessie. At last that title "fine lady" may accomplish some good. Aloud she said:

"Colonel Fremont has called California the Italy of America. Isn't it an ideal place for small homes and well-tended acreage? If we keep slave labor out, we will have the wealthy and comfortable middle class, but no poor."

"That's a fine sentiment," replied William Steuart, head of the proslavery leaders, "but the aristocracy will always have slaves."

"How about you joining the aristocracy of emancipators, Mr. Steuart?" she shot back. "My father freed all his slaves in St. Louis before he went to Washington twenty-five years ago."

"But who's going to do all the hard and dirty labor?"

"You are," flashed Jessie, "and I am! I am raising a child in California, and before long you men will be bringing your wives out here or marrying and raising families. It isn't a pretty sight in a free country for a child to see and hear chain gangs clanking through the streets or to watch officers chasing a fugitive slave and putting him in irons. Is that what we're founding a new state for? If so, it would be better if we all returned east and left this beautiful country alone."

On the day before the convention was to open, John rode in from the Mariposa, unable to stay away. There was a gala party in the Fremont rooms that night, with every American in Monterey assembled, even Consul Larkin, looking sheepish, but wanting to be friends again.

The next morning the convention opened. Jessie and John sat behind the rough wooden railing which had been stretched across the middle of the hall. Using the constitutions of New York and Iowa as models, the delegates pushed forward rapidly in a series of sharp discussions, debates which seemed to Jessie to be on a high plane of intelligence and integrity. She remembered the story her father told her of the Constitutional Convention of Missouri, which much of the California procedure now duplicated.

William Gwin dominated the convention with his magnificent figure, leonine head and orator's voice. He was a sincere man, honest according to his lights, an able tactician in parliamentary procedure. Jessie saw that the delegates not only admired him but had faith in his judgment. As the days passed and Gwin directed more and more of the discussion, she became convinced that his boast in Washington would be carried out, that he would be returned by the legislature as one of the first two California senators. That left only one berth open. To whom would it go? To her husband, sitting quietly beside her, for some reason best known to himself never rising to his feet, never asking for permission to participate, content to exercise his influence at home over the dinner table in quiet and friendly chats?

After the convention had been in session for a week, and it was evident that California would become a free state, John could contain himself no longer. He rode south to buy several big cattle ranches which he had admired since he had first seen them during the conquest, then returned to San Francisco to invest some of his rapidly accumulating gold in tracts of land lying about a mile west of Portsmouth Square. He sent word not to expect him for a considerable time, as the Sonorans wanted to go home for Christmas and he thought he ought to stay on the Mariposa as long as possible. Gregorio went up to the mountains to be with him, leaving Jessie and Lily alone. With the last of the delegates gone, Monterey seemed quiet and lonely.

8

In October slashing rains were whipped against the windows by strong winds off the Pacific. The streets became the same kind of mudholes Jessie remembered from the early days of Washington, and there could be little visiting back and forth. One large window overlooked the bay, the deserted beach and the rocks beyond. She thought, With the sea one is never alone. Yet with the sea, as with everything else, its joys are enhanced a hundredfold when you have a loved one by your side to share in its rich variety. After supper Lily would get into her nightgown and then stretch out on the grizzly rug before the fire, where she would burn the resinous pine cones which crackled and made ever changing flame pictures.

The days and the nights were long, for she had too little to do, and her library consisted of exactly the one book which John had found in San Francisco while buying furniture. She read one story from *The Arabian Nights* to Lily each Sunday night, Lily calling it their Sunday dessert, for she wanted to make the book last as long as possible. Fortunately the flour merchant who had taken over the ballroom at the front of the house found five bound volumes of the London *Times* and a number of volumes of the *Merchant's Magazine*, which he gave to her. She had not much interest in commerce, but for want of something better to read she persisted and finally grew interested: for a lover of books is like a lover of women, he would rather have an interesting book than a dull one, but he would rather have a dull one than none at all. Then General Riley stumbled across a volume of Lord Byron's poems, and these brought her many hours of beauty as she sat before her fireplace while the winter surf boomed across the rocks and the night was filled with cold and rain.

Every week or two Gregorio or a trusted Sonoran would arrive with more sacks of gold dust, which she stored in trunks and boxes under the beds. One day in November, General Riley's wife was visiting when Gregorio came in with two of the heavy buckskin sacks. Mrs. Riley, who had been in the Army since she was nineteen, living on low-scale army pay, said:

"I really must congratulate you on your growing riches."

The well-meant remark, said without any apparent envy, threw Jessie's weeks of loneliness into focus. She did not enjoy being separated from her husband for the sake of making money; they had already been separated too much and too cruelly. Nor did she enjoy the thought of sitting in two rain-swept rooms with nothing to do but feed herself and her child, while the weeks and the months passed, and she had no part to play, no job to do. John would be obliged to spend a considerable portion of his time on the Mariposa; he thought it too remote and too dangerous for his wife to come there and make their home. What then was she to do? Sit here in Madame Castro's two rooms while they accumulated more and more wealth? To what end? She asked only a few simple things of life: the company and love of her husband; important work to do at his side; sons to bear his name. Turning to Mrs. Riley she murmured:

"Gold isn't much as an end, is it? It can't conjure comforts or an ounce of brain rations. I am simply famished for the taste of a good book. I'd give every last one of those buckskin sacks to have my husband here with me now."

As the long months of winter spun themselves out, and John managed to get home only for a day or two, Jessie realized that this was almost the same as his being out on another expedition. She counted back over the memories of her marriage, realizing that more than half the time she had been alone, prey to illness, anxiety and uncertainty over his welfare. She did not think that the quantity of money involved should have any influence on her feelings; she could not have felt more keenly a sense of life in abeyance if John had been earning single dollars instead of tens of thousands.

Toward the end of November she received in the mail a long envelope addressed to Colonel John C. Fremont, which proved to be a questionnaire relating to her husband's political beliefs. The committee that had written the letter wished to assure Colonel Fremont that if he would answer the questions satisfactorily, they would back him for the United States Senate.

She engaged an Indian to ride to the Mariposa and summon John, for an immediate answer was expected, and both letters would be published in the California newspapers. She made a copy of the letter to send with the messenger, so that he could be formulating his reply on the long ride home. He arrived at the end of the fourth day, tired and overwrought: there were now some three thousand prospectors pouring over the Mariposa; the Sonorans figured that they had enough money to last the rest of their lives in Mexico and would work no longer; there was no labor available at any price to take their place. Jessie saw that her husband was less than ever interested in politics. She boiled an iron tub of water over the outside fire in order that he might have a brisk scrub-up, then they had tea and biscuits.

"You see," she said, "I'm a better visionary than I am a cook: I predicted when you left on the second expedition five years ago that you would be one of the first senators from California."

He did not look as pleased at her outburst of confidence as she had hoped. His dark eyes could peer as fiercely inward as they could peer outward, and she saw that her husband had been undergoing several days of intense soul searching.

"If I am elected, Jessie," he said, "what do we do with the Mariposa and our mines? All the surface gold will be gone very shortly. We'll have to buy machinery, bring in a competent labor supply and follow the gold quartz into the sides of the mountains. If we don't start this work very soon, others will, and we will lose possession; under existing law we have no mineral rights even inside our land unless we set up permanent equipment to mine it. If I were to be elected and we left for Washington, how do we know when we would get back? Our dream of wealth will be gone; others will have preempted it."

She did not think this a serious problem; even after they had paid the Sonorans their half of the gold dust, there still would be about two hundred thousand dollars in gold for them. This was a great deal of money; it was a lifetime's money; why did they need millions, particularly if the cost of those millions was a seat in the United States Senate?

She knew it would not be wise to argue thus to her husband; it would seem that she was trying to force her peculiar values on him, as though she would oblige him to think that because in the Benton family a United States senator was the world's most important dignitary, John Charles Fremont, who had never shown any appetite for the Senate, should give up the opportunity to become one of the world's richest and most powerful men, an opportunity neither remote nor fanciful, but at his very finger tips.

"I don't want to influence you," she said—"that is, not too strongly. I've always dreamed of seeing you in the Senate, but there's no reason why you should shackle yourself with my ambitions. After all, it is you who will have to do the work, and so you should decide for yourself. If you want to go to the Senate, then we should write the strongest polemic on your political philosophy we can create; if you would prefer to stay here and start to mine on a big scale, then we will forget about Washington, and Lily and I will move up to the Mariposa with you and build our home there. You say you will need labor for the mines; the best way to attract it is to have a going community with comfortable cabins and a store and a school for the children."

"Yes, those are our alternatives."

"Then it's purely a case of values. Which means the more to you?"

He was silent for a long time, his chin resting on his chest, his eyes staring inward, not seeing the strained and hopeful expression on his wife's face.

"I should like to try to do both," he finally said; "I think we can work it out. I will stand for the election, and we will leave for Washington immediately if I am successful. When our ship arrives in New York, I will buy the mining equipment and send it out here. I will also try to hire mining engineers and have them accompany the equipment and install it. At the end of the congressional session we will come back to California for as long as we can, long enough to supervise the mines and set up a system."

He looked toward her hopefully. "Do you think we can do them both, Jessie, or am I being overly ambitious?"

"We can try, darling. Shall we begin work now on the answer to this letter?"

"No, I'm too tired. I need a night's sleep; besides, though it's difficult to keep track of time in the mountains, it seems to me that it has been a month since I embraced my wife."

"Only a month?" she murmured. "I would say it was a year."

They spent the next day drafting his free-state, Democratic stand, and his answer to the questions affecting California. The following day he returned to the mines, promising to be back for Christmas.

Once again Jessie was alone in her rooms overlooking the Pacific. Christmas approached slowly through a succession of dark and wind-swept days. Neither Jessie nor Lily could venture forth in such weather, and so Jessie would light a half-dozen candles in the tin holders John had sent down from San Francisco with the furnishings and go over the pictures in an illustrated London *Times*. Just two days before the holiday her door was wrenched open, rain swept into the room, then the door was slammed shut. She turned quickly from the fire to see John leaning against a now wet door, panting for breath, his sombrero, face and native jacket drenched, the water running off his high boots in rivulets onto the floor.

"Jessie, I couldn't wait, I have ridden from San José to greet the first senator's lady from California."

She cried from her chair, "John, you've been elected!"

"On the first ballot," he exulted. "I received twenty-four votes out of thirty-six. William Gwin was elected on the third ballot. We sail for New York on New Year's Day."

She sprang out of her chair, ran to him and flung her arms about him, kissing him joyfully.

"You'll get wet," he laughed. "I'd better not walk across the room, I'd make it a pool of water."

"Drop out of those clothes right where you stand, then come to the fire and get warm. I'll have dry clothes for you in a minute. You must be tired. It's a seventy-mile ride from San José."

After a gay supper of coffee, cold beef and bread, and a bottle of champagne to celebrate their victory, they sprawled out on the warm bear rugs facing the fire, their chins cupped in the palms of their hands, their fingers framing the ovals of their excited faces.

"Ah, my dear," she murmured, "it will be a happy day for me when I see you in the Senate. I will have that exact seat in the visitors' gallery where Father first put me to listen to him speak when I was only eight."

"It will be a happy day for me," rejoined her husband, "when I see Maylee serving you morning tea in bed."

Later, in the glow of the burned-down eucalyptus logs, they fell asleep on the rugs. At dawn, after a cup of hot coffee, Jessie embraced her husband and he left to ride the seventy miles back to San José.

In festive mood she had Gregorio cut them an evergreen from the hills above the bay and set it in a corner of her living room. Having no ornaments for the tree, she searched through her possessions until she found some old tin foil, rolled it into soft balls and stuck them on the ends of the branches. The tin candleholders she tied to the stronger branches, putting in red and yellow candles. Having opened a can of sardines for lunch, she had Gregorio cut up the tin into odd shapes and make little holes in them so they could be strung onto the tree, then sent him out to the hotel where she had seen pieces of sheet metal thrown down from the now finished roof. Gregorio cut this metal roughly into shapes of stars and crescents, which Jessie painted blue and red before hanging on the tree.

John returned on Christmas Eve with gifts for everyone, a beautiful doll just off the boat from China for his daughter, a soft red cashmere shawl for Jessie, and the first box of candy manufactured in California.

The week between Christmas and New Year's was crowded and exciting. John was busy making arrangements for agents to handle the mines. The Sonorans came down from the Mariposa and took their half of the gold. Jessie had a great deal of packing to do, the furniture had to be stored so that they could have it again when they returned to build a home on the Mariposa. She took a last sentimental walk through the empty rooms, remembering how uncertain their future had been when first they had moved in five months before.

The S.S. *Oregon* came into the harbor at Monterey on New Year's night, firing its guns to notify the passengers ashore. In the most torrential rain she had ever seen, and with the streets pouring rivers of mud down to the sea, they trudged to the waterfront followed by Gregorio and another Indian boy carrying their luggage. John lifted her into a rowboat, Gregorio carried Lily. They sat in the downpouring torrents while the two Indian boys rowed them out through the blackness of the night.

"Don't cry so hard, Gregorio," said Jessie, "you're waterlogging the boat. We promise to come back soon."

Once again she climbed up a ship's rope ladder, swaying from side to side as the wind-swept rain buffeted her. The S.S. *Oregon* stopped at Mazatlan to coal. Consul Parrott, who had fought with Colonel Fremont and the California Battalion, came aboard to invite them to his thick-walled Mexican house for dinner. The weather was warm off the coast of Mexico and Jessie had found her Monterey clothes too heavy for comfort. Searching through her bags she discovered a white, ruffled morning sacque to wear with her rough merino skirt.

By the time they returned to their ship the night air had turned cool.

Jessie realized too late that she had made a serious error; her cough returned and she was confined to her bunk for the rest of the voyage to Panama. John too was stretched flat on his back, his left side and frostbitten leg gripped with rheumatism. Both were taken off the ship on stretchers, with Lily, white-faced with worry, watching over them. Again Madame Arce came to Jessie's rescue. She took the Fremonts to her home and installed them in the same bedroom Jessie had occupied eight months before. She and her servants devoted their full time to nursing the sick couple, concealing from them the fact that Lily was down with Chagres fever, as ill as her parents.

They had been scheduled to catch the ship which left Chagres five days after they had reached Panama City. Instead they lay in their hammocks in Madame Arce's house for a month. During the last week John was able to hobble around the room, and Jessie's fever went down. John L. Stephens, who was building the Panama Railroad, came in late each afternoon, murmuring, "I have come to take my chill with you."

When the last day arrived which they could possibly catch the next steamer to New York, Jessie insisted that she was strong enough to travel. John limped out of the room and went aboard a United States man-of-war in the harbor. When he returned he said, "We can leave in the morning; I've borrowed a ship's hammock; we'll rig an awning over it to keep out the sun, and hire Indian bearers to carry you across Panama."

The next morning John Stephens brought four of his best Indian carriers. Jessie was taken out to her palanquin and lifted into it. Madame Arce settled a crimson silk, lace-trimmed pillow under her head and filled the flat canvas pockets with handkerchiefs and flasks of cologne. John and Lily each had a mule to ride. Lily was recovering, but all of her hair had been shaved off during the fever, and her face was pinched and white. Jessie had quite a start when she first saw her daughter, but the stolid Lily assured her that she was well again and perfectly able to ride the mule to Gorgona. As the Indian bearers moved through the streets of Panama, the natives came out from their houses to see the strange cortege.

After two days and nights on the trail, and two days in the boat going down the Chagres River, during which Jessie stoked herself regularly with quinine and coffee, she at last caught sight of the masts of the steamer. Once in their cabin, she sat on the edge of the berth, ran her hand over her husband's forehead with her fingers, combed the hair back from his brow. Then she lay down in the berth alongside of him, motioning Lily to come into her arms. She lay quietly, one arm about her husband, the other about her daughter; the bunk was crowded with the three of them in it, but Jessie did not care; she was happy to have them all together again.

From the docks in New York they drove direct to the Irving House. The manager told them they would have the suite just vacated by Jenny Lind. They walked into the sitting room and stood in the middle of the room in front of a long French mirror in which Jessie had an opportunity to survey her family. First came Lily; she had eaten steadily for two weeks aboard ship, was now plump and red-cheeked; her brown merino dress was too small for her and she seemed to be bursting out of it both fore and aft; it was also too short, revealing the unbleached muslin panties. She had on a pair of Indian buckskin shoes presented to her by Gregorio, and since her hat had blown overboard, her shaved head was wrapped in a black silk handkerchief, making her look like one of the immigrant children off the boats from Europe.

In the middle was her husband, dressed in knee-high miner's boots and his California outfit of miner's trousers, buckskin jacket, open-throated shirt and handkerchief tied around his neck, his gray-shot beard untrimmed, his hair as long as when he had come home from his expeditions. Then her eyes fell upon herself: emaciated, her pale skin made to look a jaundiced yellow by the rough-fitting, brown satin basque blouse. The dark skirt she had cut out of her riding outfit hung straight and shapeless to her ankles, and out of it peeped rusty black satin slippers, the only pair of shoes she had left; held on to her head with a China crepe scarf was a leghorn hat whose color clashed with the brown blouse and blue skirt.

To herself she murmured, The senator's lady from the Golden West! Miss English should see me now!

She had been away a year, six months of it spent in California, the rest in travel. She had made no home there, made no real indentation upon the country; she did not belong, yet she wanted to belong. In the back of her mind she knew that the reason she had failed had been that, in spite of her lifetime ambition to go west to the frontier, she had not set out for California with a wholehearted desire to settle there permanently and make it her life. She had gone with the idea that she and her husband would very soon return to Washington as Senator and Mrs. Fremont. In a sense she had been disloyal to the new land; perhaps that was why the gods had refused to consecrate her hearth. If she wanted a hearth in California, she would have to go there with the idea of remaining forever, loyal and devoted, and enduring of hardship. In spite of the battered apparition of the three of them in the glass, she knew that she did want to go back to California. Perhaps next time she could become part of the country, indigenous to its life.

9

They spent two days getting their land legs, buying clothes, preparing for the train trip to Washington. She had been able to send a telegram to her father announcing their safe arrival in New York, a telegram over the wires that Samuel Morse had begged Congress to build for the five lean years during which he had come so often to the Bentons' to show why the telegraph was practical.

Tom Benton met them at the station, looking old and harassed but happy at welcoming them home. It was the first time she had been away from the family, and it seemed to her that the year had made more than its proportion of changes: her sisters had grown into young ladies; Randolph had developed into a tall, pleasant lad with her mother's finely chiseled features and her father's slightly hoarse voice; her mother's face and body had grown frail; her father's battle-scarred features reflected his heavy burdens.

She walked about the house enjoying the smell of rose geraniums in the drawing room, looking with joy at the damask-covered dining table and silver service set out for dinner; she moved about the library touching the leather-bound books, the arms of comfortable chairs, her writing desk in front of the fireplace.

Their friends came in to welcome them and congratulate John on his election. James Buchanan gave a formal dinner in their honor. Jessie ordered a new gown of soft brocade with lace frills. As they sat down to the table flanked by friendly Cabinet officers, congressmen, army and navy officers, ambassadors and a considerable portion of Washington society, Jessie and John exchanged a meaningful glance: they remembered how Washington had treated them when they left, with few people calling, the Army wanting no part of their indicted brother, the Cabinet officers remaining away for fear of embarrassing the administration, the congressmen unwilling to take sides. Now they were the darlings of Washington society, rich with the fabulous California gold, John the first senator from what would soon be the first state of the Far West. As Jessie gazed at her husband she saw that he wore his new dinner clothes with poise and dignity but that he looked thin, his gray hair and weather-beaten face making him seem far older than his thirty-seven years. When John looked at his wife he saw a young woman of twenty-six with flashing hazel eyes, brown hair a little thinner than when he had first known her but gleaming richly as it was combed over her ears and gathered low at the back of her neck; her skin as clear as a child's in spite of the rigors of Panama and California, her delicate sloping shoulders white and firm and warm to the eye above her Empire gown of deep blue brocade. Simultaneously they recalled that moment in the Irving House when they had first seen themselves in their crude, garish and ill-fitting clothes.

Jessie was delighted to be back in cultivated society. She laughed gaily, more intoxicated by the swift flow of conversation than by the many toasts she drank to California and its admission as a state. John too had a gleam in his eye while he told about the possibility of a railroad to California, of the wealth and beauty of the state; but mostly their eyes sought each other, for they could not believe that they were back in Washington, just as though nothing had happened to them.

James Buchanan leaned over and murmured to her, "Miss Jessie, I don't think you should engage in flirtation with your husband while sitting next to me."

"Flirtation?"

"I would describe it as such," he replied, "a mental wink, a flash of the eye, a fleeting smile . . . I am beginning to suspect that your husband loves you."

"An unwarranted hypothesis," laughed Jessie. "He is so stunned at seeing me in an evening gown, after my unbleached muslins and black merinos, that he can hardly believe his eyes."

There was a week of parties and dinners and fun, and then they settled down to work. Behind the closed door of the library, Thomas Hart Benton admitted to his young daughter that his position in the Senate was in danger. His long fight to prevent the extension of slavery had consolidated the slavery men of Missouri against him, and after thirty years of service it was growing apparent that they had a chance to defeat him in the coming election. The focal center of the slavery battle was now California: since its own legislature had declared California to be a free state, the slavery men in the Congress were determined that California must not be admitted to the Union.

Tom Benton thus faced a painful dilemma: for thirty years he had been working to bring the Pacific coast into the United States; he had always been opposed to the extension of slavery beyond the existing southern states; but if he fought for the admission of California as a free state, his waging of the battle would afford the last round of ammunition needed to put him out of the United States Senate.

John was a senator-elect from California, but California was not yet a state and so actually he had no job. Officially there was little he could do to hasten the admission, but unofficially the Fremonts served as goodwill ambassadors and an information service on the topography, climate and general future of that territory. Through the Benton home on C Street moved a large section of official Washington. Many of those who had been skeptical about the distant land left at the end of the evening having caught some of their enthusiasm. Neither Jessie nor John had anticipated a serious struggle over the admission of California: Why wage a war over a territory, pour thousands of settlers into its boundaries, and then refuse to incorporate it within the nation? Nevertheless the weeks and the months passed, the beautiful spring merged into the hot summer and the hot summer spent itself into an early fall while the slavery faction maneuvered to gain ever increased concessions as the price of admitting California.

John utilized some of his leisure to buy mining equipment which he shipped out to San Francisco. After the third of his buying junkets, during which he laid out a great deal of cash, he informed Jessie that he was going to have to capitalize the Mariposa, issue leases on certain of the mines, and sell stock in them. This would provide the capital to build dams, roads and buy other expensive equipment so necessary for large-scale mining. She was disturbed at the idea, for it meant setting up in business; there would be stockholders, managers and boards, control would eventually be taken from John's hands, he would be responsible to a great many people. She asked her husband if he did not think it would be better to mine on a small scale and remain the master of his mines. He laughingly replied:

"Jessie, you sound as though you didn't want us to take too much gold out of the Mariposa. Don't you like money?"

"Yes, I love money," she exclaimed. "But like every other vice, it should be indulged in moderately. Besides, I think you're meant for more important things than just making money. Did I ever tell you what Nicollet said about money? He said that the accumulation of money was a period of affliction, like adolescence, which we had to pass through before we could reach maturity. I'd like to take just a modest amount of gold out of the Mariposa, John, enough to buy you the freedom and financing for whatever work may appeal to you: further expeditions, mapping a railroad route to California, building wagon roads to the West. I don't think the Mariposa gold should be an end, I think that it should be a means: a means of fulfilling your life and your work. Or do I sound like a moralistic schoolteacher?"

"You sound like a schoolteacher . . . and you sound right. However, one cannot fly in the teeth of fate; the gods dumped a Mother Lode into my lap; to do less than exploit it to its fullest, to refuse to extract the millions of gold from those quartz lodes would be like refusing to accept the gifts of the gods."

"Yes," she agreed thoughtfully, "I can see that point of view. But did it ever occur to you that the gods might also appreciate a bit of restraint? That it might be the better part of virtue not to gobble up their gifts? When the slavery men at Monterey told you that you could be the richest man in the world if you would use slave labor in your mines, you said that that was too high a price to pay for wealth. Then why isn't giving your own life to digging out gold too high a price to pay? I would rather have you a free workman than a bounden mine owner."

John did not agree, and so an English agent by the name of Hoffman was given the right to sell leases on the Ave Maria, West Mariposa and East Mariposa mines. The agreement signed, Hoffman took the next ship to England to set up stock companies, the proceeds of which were to be sent to John to turn the three mines into major producing units. A few weeks later she learned that her husband was dealing with a second agent by the name of Thomas Sargent, giving him the right to sell leases for half of the vast Mariposa tract. Sargent also planned to go to England to sell stock in the company. She had no wish to intrude upon her husband's business arrangements, and she was reassured by the fact that her father approved of Sargent and the granting of the additional leases.

On the morning of September 10, 1850, when John Charles Fremont was to be presented to the United States Senate, Jessie rose early, took a leisurely bath, creamed her face, dressed partially, then sat before her dressing table to brush her long brown hair and coil it low on her neck. When she tried to rise to put on her gown there swept over her the same wave of nausea that she had suffered while carrying her son. She laughed gaily to herself as she thought, California may be fertile country, but Washington is the better conceiving ground!

She rode with her husband and her father up to the Senate; they were as gay as children, laughing at silly jokes, yet there was an undertone of fatality about it, for Tom Benton knew that the South was rapidly losing its temper, growing angry and frightened, that this might well be his last session. He had always wanted to die in the seat behind his Senate desk, in the midst of a fiery debate; yet if he had to be dispossessed now, go down to defeat as one of the first casualties of the threatening conflict between the North and the South, it was a good feeling to know that his daughter's husband would take his place, that California from 1840 to 1870 would be the frontier of freedom and the capital of the West, just as Missouri had been during his thirty years from 1820 to 1850.

Jessie took her accustomed seat in the front row of the visitors' gallery across from the eagle poised on top of the canopy which covered the Speaker's chair. Below were seated the senators from thirty-one states, in their long, tight black trousers held down by straps under the heels of their boots, their long-tailed, square-cut black coats and the wide lapels which framed the bow tie and white shirt.

She believed that her husband was the youngest man on the floor. She also thought him the handsomest. She glowed with pride as she watched him being sworn in as a United States senator.

In the three weeks that remained of the session she worked hard as John's secretary. Her experiences as a traveler, housewife and mother enabled her to help her husband. Yet John needed little help: she had never seen his mind work with greater clarity or comprehensiveness. Although he was no lawyer, he dictated bills to extend the laws of the judicial system of the United States to California, bills to grant public lands for purposes of education and the building of universities, asylums for the deaf and dumb, the blind and the insane, bills to record land titles, settle land claims, to negotiate the working of mines, for a system of post roads and national roads to California. She saw that California was indeed being well represented. His eighteen bills to facilitate the migration of the people westward, and for the internal developments of California, were all passed by the Senate. At the end of the session even those southerners who had so bitterly opposed the introduction of California, Barnwell, Davis, Calhoun, Clay, congratulated Senator Fremont on his legislative program.

Jessie carried the new child well, strong and happy and hopeful about the future. She indulged herself not at all, went for long walks, danced at the frequent balls. On the afternoon that the Senate adjourned, she asked, "When is Gwin going back to California to stand for re-election?"

After a moment of hesitation John replied. "He isn't going. At least, not yet . . ."

She blinked uncomprehendingly. "He isn't going to stand for re-election?

But that's not like Gwin. He told me himself he's determined to remain a senator from California."

"Yes, that's true. But you know, Jessie, we have a long term and a short term."

"You were elected to the long term. You have another five years . . ."

John shook his head. "Neither of us was elected to the long term. I know you have been assuming all along, Jessie, that I had the long term, and you were so happy about it I just hated to put any doubts in your mind."

Her cheeks flamed.

"But why should I have had any doubts? You received an overwhelming majority of votes. That makes you the man they want in the Senate, that gives you the six-year term."

"The election laws don't say so. Gwin and I have to draw lots for it."

She lost her temper.

"It's too utterly preposterous, John, that you should agree to gamble over a seat in the Senate. What about fighting for your rights? I don't understand you, this is out of character; two thirds of the people in California meant for you to have the long term. Gwin has no real stake in California: he went out there as a political adventurer, determined to pull the prize plum out of the pie! What does he know about California? What part did he play in making California an American state, except trying to get it to go proslavery at the convention? Your expeditions and reports are responsible for half the families that are now living out there. You played a critical role in the conquest of the state; kept it from falling into British hands. You know every valley and mountain range. You know what the people are like and what their needs are, they trust you to do important things for them here in Washington . . ."

She slumped down into her chair, her anger burnt out.

"I'm sorry I shouted at you, dear, but it just seems so incongruous for the first citizen of California to gamble over a senatorial seat with a political adventurer. There is no rhyme or reason in it."

He sat beside her and brushed the tears from her eyes with a hard circular motion of his palm.

"There's nothing I can do, Jessie; what you suggest would cause a scandal. People would say that it was another of John Fremont's uprisings, a mutiny against established tradition. Don't you see, there's no law to sustain me; it has always been a gentlemen's agreement that two senators elected from a new state must draw lots for the long and short terms."

His reference to another John Fremont uprising quieted her.

"Your stand against slavery has earned you powerful enemies here in Washington," she pleaded; "at the end of a six-year term you will have made friends with them, you will have done so much good work for California that you will be re-elected again and again for thirty full years, the way Father has from Missouri. But if you go back now after only three weeks in the Senate, the slavery group will fight you tooth and nail."

John's black eyes peered at her unhappily.

"We have to take our chances; we have to draw lots. Wish me luck, dear. I'm going to draw the long term."

She smiled a little wistfully, kissed the niche in the corner of his mouth.

"Of course you will," she said.

There was no need for John to tell her the next day when he returned home, his face a polite but withdrawn mask, that he had drawn the short term. The thirty-year career in the Senate had evaporated to three short weeks! Another turn of the wheel of fortune: when they were down, the wheel spun, they found gold, they were elected, they returned to Washington triumphant. Then the wheel turned again, thousands of gold seekers flooded their lands; they had to incorporate and give away control over their property; the senatorial career was ended almost as it began.

10

She occasionally accompanied John to New York to buy the modern mining equipment with which to dig their tunnels into the sides of the Mariposa. He decided to spend the New Year holiday in Washington, then take the ship that left New York on January 2, 1851.

She had a long session with herself in which she weighed the comparatives of her problem: she was six months with child; though the roughness of the sea voyage was not too formidable a danger, the crossing of Panama might be. Having lost young Benton, this coming child meant twice as much to both of them; on the other hand she could not bear the thought of another long separation from her husband. She knew that with John to watch over her she would be well cared for on the trail across Panama; nor was there fear in her heart: this was the opportunity to demonstrate that she had the makings of the pioneer wife, that she meant to create a home and a hearth in California. This was her challenge, more serious and more important than her first lonely trip had been: to carry inside her the new generation of the frontier, to give birth to her baby in the almost unborn community.

"I won't be gone so very long, Jessie," he assured her, "just long enough to stand for re-election and to see that the mine machinery is installed. I will be back in Washington by July."

"You mean we will be back in Washington by July," she replied calmly. "I'm going with you."

A look of terror flashed into his eyes.

"But you can't . . . We can't risk the child. The rigors of crossing Panama . . ."

She stood resolutely before him, tossing her hair free from her head with a spirited gesture.

"We have nothing to fear," she said. "I never felt stronger, and I am positive that this is a healthy child I am carrying. If you are going to California, the children and I are going with you. Your son is going to be born in California."

"But Jessie," he protested, "the ocean is rough in winter. You have to go over the Gorgona trail by muleback . . ."

"No, no," she cried, "I will go over the trail in my palanquin. I had a comfortable ride last time. I've learned many things about Panama: I'm taking my own tea things, canned foods that are easy to prepare and digest. The passage will be swifter now, with so many thousands of Americans having made the crossing. Please, let's not discuss it. There's confidence in my heart, and that is the best protection our child could have."

They sailed on January 3 for Chagres. The first few days were rough, so Jessie stayed in her berth and slept through them. Lily kept her father company on deck. At Chagres a little wharf had been built, and she did not have to bob around in a tender. John had sent money and instructions ahead, so there was a boat to convey them up the Chagres to Gorgona. She got bumped around a little in her canopied hammock over the mountain trail, but she laughed at the hardship and felt not the slightest worry. They arrived in San Francisco early in April. When she landed at the broad wooden pier and caught her first glimpse of the town she was glad she had made her decision, for the city had grown miraculously, many homes had sprung up, hundreds of workmen were sawing and pounding, there were wooden sidewalks and Market Street was an imposing area of white-front hotels and business firms.

She did not want her child to be born in a hotel, she wanted him to be born at her own hearth, so they set out at once to buy a house. The only one they could find was an ugly wooden frame structure high up on Stockton Street overlooking the Portsmouth Square. There was no interior decoration, the walls were bare, but the rooms were large and the furnishings comfortable. They bought the house and moved in. On the morning of April 15 she gave birth to a son, whom they promptly named John Charles.

Gregorio had come running to join his family again. When the nurse announced that she would leave at the end of the first week, Gregorio said laughingly, "My mother had ten babies, I helped raise seven of them. I know everything to do. I take care of Charlie when the nurse go."

Jessie remained in bed while John went about San Francisco hiring mechanics for the mines, buying supplies, checking the homes and shops that had been built on the land he had bought before leaving for Washington. A committee of Australians who had established a colony on the Fremont holdings came to the house and presented to her a petition asking that they be allowed to buy their land so that they could feel permanently settled. She promised to urge their request on her husband. That evening she asked John to sell the Australians the property, pointing out that these people were as anxious for their own hearths as they were.

When the baby was fifteen days old, and she was rocking him in an improvised crib, she heard alarmed shouts below her. A few moments later she smelled smoke. Sending for Gregorio, she demanded to know what was happening.

"There's a fire on the south side of the square."

"Is it coming this way?"

Gregorio went to the bedroom window and called back, "I can't tell where the fire come, but the wind come this way."

At that moment John rushed in with extra blankets and a grass hammock.

"There's nothing to be alarmed about," he said reassuringly, "but we must be prepared. The houses below us on the hill are catching. If the fire rises much higher Gregorio and I will carry you and the baby to Russian Hill. The sand dunes will keep the fire from reaching there. I've already sent over our silverware and papers."

"I've ridden in hammocks before," she replied calmly; "just give me two minutes' notice to prepare Charlie."

By nightfall all of San Francisco was aglow, the air filled with smoke and flying ash. From her bed Jessie could watch the night sky grow redder and redder. Friends thronged up the hill to help John hang wet canvas and soaked carpet over the side of the house to prevent sparks from setting it aflame. Below her she could hear the shouts of the men fighting the fires; by the growing intensity and the heat she knew that the flames were coming ever higher on the hill. The sidewalks, made of wooden planks, carried the flames, and the crackling fires of the wooden houses mingled with the sounds of the fire bells and shouts of the men dashing through the streets trying to save their properties.

At midnight there was a sharp veering of the wind. The fire began racing south again across the square. Their home was saved.

The next morning, leaning on the arm of her husband, Jessie circled the house to survey the damage. Below her most of the city lay in ashes. The paint was blistered on her own home, but there was no other damage. It wasn't until she had gone back into the house and climbed into bed again that she realized her calm of the night before had been the same kind of protection with which she had insulated herself for the trip across Panama.

At the end of a month, when her strength had returned, and the machinery had arrived for the mines, John left for the Mariposa to begin the installation work. He was standing for re-election, yet he would do nothing to promote his candidacy. Jessie wondered why her husband declined to strive as mightily for the political office he wanted as he had striven to make himself a successful engineer. Electioneering demanded that a man get out on the stump, that he tour the state, speaking to every group that assembled, that he keep a steady stream of articles flowing to the press, that he treat politics as though it were a business or a profession and throw himself into it wholeheartedly if he expected to achieve the desired result. But John would not electioneer and would not campaign. As he had in Monterey, he said quietly to his wife:

"Everyone in this state knows me and knows whether or not he wants me to continue being senator. Shaking a few thousand hands won't change the results of the election; if the majority of the people in this state are in favor of slavery, then I'll be defeated; if the majority are in favor of freedom, then I'll be sent back to the Senate. No one is going to change the mind of a slavery man by making a speech at him; and besides I'm not a good speech-maker."

She respected his reticence, his refusal to fight for his seat in the Senate. Nevertheless she wished that there were some way to campaign for him. She would have been entirely willing to take her carriage and the team of horses and stump the state, speaking in every hamlet and village, debating with the slavery faction. But alas, there was nothing she could do; a wife could not campaign for her husband, and surely a wife could not urge that a man plunge himself into public conflict if it was against his temperament to do so.

And once again she was puzzled by the riddle of her husband's character. Why, under one set of circumstances, did he grasp more power and authority than he was entitled to, then in another field be modest, self-effacing, refuse to play the critical part which everyone expected of him? Was he behaving this way because the court-martial had declared him to be a usurper, a man seeking personal power and fame—and he wanted to live down the accusa-tion? Or did this contradiction in his temperament arise from the various components within his mind: the components dealing with politics enclosing one set of attitudes; those dealing with war and the Army another and very different set? Only she knew how many dozens of separately locked com-partments there were, and how divergent their contents.

She remembered how in the first days of her honeymoon she had dimly perceived that marriage might mean the spending of a lifetime trying to understand her mate, evolving the mysteries of character which even he didn't know were there. She had said to herself then, I would not want a man who would be obvious. It will be an exhilarating pursuit, trying to understand what will come next, fitting all the pieces together. And what a great hour it will be, ten years from now, fifty years from now, when I finally understand John. She had now been married for ten years, she understood many fragments of her husband's behavior, and yet she had to confess to herself that she was no closer to a solution of his character than she had been the day she married him.

San Francisco was growing at an amazing rate; she liked to walk down into the business district and shop for rare art objects or furnishings from the Orient, wines or sweets from Paris, woolens from England. On one of her trips she was delighted to find two sets of violet-colored muslin curtains, which she tied back with pink ribbons to brighten the parlor and dining room. There were a flourishing newspaper and theater; thousands of people were coming in from overland trails and by ship from Australia and the Orient. They were a conglomerate crew: along with the eastern farmers and settlers, the staid businessmen and the gold seekers, there was a large crowd of British criminals released from Botany Bay in Australia, as well as the irresponsible *Guarde Mobile* which had been shipped over from Paris for the greater safety of France; there were the wild ones, the professional adventurers and gamblers, the thieves, embezzlers, swindlers, murderers from all over America who had thronged to this fabulously rich and exciting frontier.

Despite the fact that Senator Fremont's bills for the setting up of courts and a legal structure had been passed in Washington, the machinery for these was not yet working in San Francisco. Violence flared everywhere; bands of armed thieves roamed the streets at night, plundering and shooting. Anyone who tried to protest had his house or business set on fire; women could not leave their homes after nightfall, and no man's property was safe from their depredations. The respectable merchants and settlers in San Francisco were organizing to put an end to the lawless element which, it was claimed, had started the fire. When the citizens' committee, who named themselves the Vigilantes, threatened to take the law into their own hands and punish the miscreants, civil war broke out in the town. One warm June afternoon as she was sitting in her back garden overlooking the bay, a handbill was thrown over the fence. She read:

If the people of San Francisco carry out their threatened intentions, we will fire the city. We will make your wives and families suffer for your acts.

She knew how fast fires could carry in the wind-swept city, and she was afraid that her own wooden structure would go up in flames before she could get the two children out to safety. From then on she did no more sleeping of nights, but read, wrote letters home and to her husband, kept a vigilant eye out of the windows which faced in three directions. In the morning, after Gregorio and his cousin, who had become Charlie's nursemaid, were awake, she would draw the blinds in her room and sleep until noon.

One Sunday morning after Gregorio and his cousin had gone to church, and just as the bells began to toll ten o'clock, the hour when the summer winds swept across San Francisco, she saw fire break out simultaneously in several parts of the residential district below her. She picked up little Charlie naked and wet from the bath and wrapped him in the skirt of her dressing gown. Lily came in with her two pet hens, asking, "Mother, could you find me ribbons to tie their legs?"

"Go up the hill to Mrs. Fourgeand's house on Clay Street and stay there until I come for you."

Lieutenant Beale came running, bareheaded, his face already black with soot, led her out of the house in her slippers and gown and up the several blocks of steep rough hill to Mrs. Fourgeand's. Here she found dozens of women and children gathered in this one spot of safety. Lily threw herself into her mother's arms, but Lieutenant Beale relieved the tension by exclaiming, "Look, the baby is still asleep on my shoulder."

Jessie went into the front room, which overlooked the burning city. A Frenchwoman was kneeling before the window, laughing hysterically as she watched her house go up in flames. After a few moments she turned to Jessie, recognized her and cried, "Madame Fremont! Your house goes next. Here, take my place. It is the best seat in the house, you can see your place burn up!"

Sympathetic women led the afflicted one away. Jessie stood by the window for a long time, while her heart cried out at the sight of her home, her baby's birthplace, catching like dry tinder, almost every part of it roaring into flames at once. At the end of an hour there was nothing left but the gaunt red brick chimney pointing up to the sky like an accusing finger. At dusk most of San Francisco had once again been burned to the ground. Lieutenant Beale returned to Mrs. Fourgeand's and said, "I have a place where you and the children can rest tonight; it is not very elegant, but at least we have food and blankets there. Come along, we'll pretend we're camping on the Monterey peninsula again."

That night she lay on a cot in a tent on the sand dunes, the baby sleeping in the crook of her arm, Lily and her two chickens with blue ribbons around their legs on a mattress on the floor. She spent the night alternately weeping and trembling over the loss of this first home of her own. Bitterly she remembered, "The gods are slow to consecrate a new hearth." Imaginary fire bells clanged in her ears; behind her feverish and tightly closed eyelids she once again watched the city burn, each succeeding house catching fire and going up in flames, until the whole world outside of her eyelids was blazing.

The next morning Lieutenant Beale came back to tell her that he and Gregorio had worked all night on a former army barrack several miles out in the dunes, scrubbing it and putting it in condition so that she could have a place to live until her new home could be built. Since there were no horses or carriages available, she trudged through the sand, her water-soaked slippers heavy with mud, her dressing gown trailing. When she reached the barrack she found that the men had assembled fresh clothing, some books, candles for lighting and boxes of foodstuffs. After the children fell asleep, she sat through the long night reading Donald Mitchell's *Reveries of a Bachelor* by candlelight. She was too nervous to go to bed; she had a feeling of despair at ever becoming settled in such a wild community. The baby woke at dawn, demanding its breakfast. The Indian girl announced, "Gregorio, he find a white goat with lots of milk . . ."

Jessie smiled and thanked her, but the girl did not move.

"Some people come see you," she exclaimed. "Please you talk to them?"

She washed her hands and face, combed her hair and slipped into a dress. She walked through the front room of the barrack and opened the door. Before her stood a middle-aged Australian and his wife; she recognized them as the spokesmen for the tenants who had asked for permission to buy their land. Looking over their shoulders she saw a long procession of people coming across the dunes, all of them carrying parcels and bundles and some of them pulling carts.

"What is it?" she asked, stupefied.

"It is like this, Mrs. Fremont," replied the Australian, "when the fire began on Sunday morning we decided the wind would carry it up to your house. All of us rushed up to your home to see if we couldn't save it. You and the little ones were already gone."

"We saw we couldn't save your house, Madame Fremont," broke in the wife, "so we did the next best thing: we saved everything inside your walls." She turned and indicated the trail of people. "We carried out all of your clothing, your furniture, mirrors, china, silverware and glasses, rugs, and your books. Madame Fremont, you lose the building, nothing else."

Jessie watched the tenants come up one by one to the front porch, deposit all of her valuables: her jewelry and personal effects, her dishes and perfume bottles, her dresses and lingerie, the children's clothing, and the toys they had brought from Washington, foods and cases of wine, even the violet curtains with the pink tie-backs. The Australians knocked the furniture together, set up two beds in the back room; moved the bookcase into the front room and arranged the books on its shelves; they put the curtains on the windows, hung her pictures on the walls, and on the floors laid her carpets and rugs. Within an hour the lonely barrack in the sand dunes had been transformed into the Fremont household. The leader then brought forth a heavy parcel tied in a red silk handkerchief.

"We knew the colonel was from home," he said, "and since there was a young baby in the house, we thought money might come in handy. We brought a quarter's rent in advance."

He untied the handkerchief and let fall onto a table a heap of coins. In her excitement Jessie could not control her tears. She shook hands with every last one, thanking them warmly.

Several days passed. Though she was comfortable, surrounded by her own possessions, she longed ardently to have her husband by her side. There was no regular mail service to the Mariposa and she was unwilling to send a courier after him. She would simply have to wait until he learned of the new fire that had swept the city.

It was almost a week later when, sitting on the front porch in the warm June sunshine, she saw his familiar figure trudging over the dunes. She jumped up and ran across the sand hillocks to meet him. When she could tear herself from his embrace she asked: "But how did you know where to find us?"

"I came by the night boat from Stockton," he replied. "I practically ran up the hill from the square, but when I got to our house there was nothing left but the chimney with the sun shining on it. I asked a passer-by if he knew where you were, and he replied, 'Near Grace Church.' From the front porch of the church I surveyed the landscape, and I saw this little house with violet curtains fluttering out the windows. When I saw the pink ribbons, I was sure it was you."

That afternoon Jessie sent for the Australian tenants. John had been writing busily at his desk. When they arrived he thanked them heartily, then picked up a stack of papers.

"These are your deeds of sale. You now own your land."

There was a moment of silence, during which the men looked over the deeds. Their spokesman murmured:

"Colonel Fremont, it is better than we expected. We could pay a little more."

"You have already paid that little more," he replied. "Good luck to you, and God bless you."

When each had clasped his hand and thanked him in turn, and they had left, Jessie kissed her husband sedately and said:

"Thank you, dear. That was a special gift to me."

That evening as they walked the hills above the burned city that was already again rebuilding on its ashes, John told her of his many difficulties on the Mariposa: serious quarrels had arisen with mining groups who claimed that they had located their mines before he arrived, that he had purposely staked out his boundaries to include their holdings. They had refused to abandon their mines and were threatening warfare if anybody tried to put them off. The machinery he had bought in New York was proving costly and inefficient; only a bare portion of the available gold was being secured. The mining engineers he had hired, and whose expenses he had paid to California, had left him and were staking out their own claims. In order to operate the mines he needed dams, roads, mills, but no money had arrived from England, and trouble had arisen in London over the stock companies based on the Mariposa leases. Hoffman, his first choice, had proved to be an honest and conscientious worker, but Sargent had placed fraudulent advertisements in the London newspapers, soliciting the sale of stock, and his manipulations had cut the ground out from under Hoffman's feet; banks and investors originally interested in Mariposa leases had withdrawn their subscriptions, while Sargent was collecting funds on a basis which could dispossess the Fremonts of the entire holdings.

Nor was that all. The Indians, who had not quarreled with the whites up to this time, were on the warpath because the miners had deprived them of their hunting grounds, killed and eaten their wild cattle, and driven them so deep into the mountains that the tribes could not secure enough food. They had met in common council, decided to kill and eat the white men's cattle, and then drive the white men out of the region. There had been shootings and killings; the mining on the Mariposa would have to be stopped unless the Indians could be placated. The United States commissioners had been treating with the Indians, attempting to move them out of the gold country and on to other hunting grounds; the Indians had agreed to move on, provided they would be furnished with beef during the time it would take to move their tribes and set up on the new lands. The small quantities of cattle available were being held for extortionate rates, and the commission had been unable to secure enough to guarantee the treaty. The Indians were preparing to wage open warfare in order to drive the white men out of the gold country.

"What about your cattle, John? Have you enough to take care of their needs?"

"Yes. But the commission has no funds with which to buy—hold on now! I'm perfectly willing to let them have the cattle on credit, but you know that I don't come off very well when I spend money for the government. My notes for a half-million dollars' worth of provisions taken during the conquest have never been paid . . ."

"But if you make a bona fide offer to the commission," said Jessie, "and they make a written acceptance . . . ?"

"Then when do we get our money? The commission doesn't return to Washington for a year. If the Department of the Interior refuses to believe that the Indians were in desperate straits and ready to pillage, they can disavow their own commission, just as they disavowed me. No one can sue the federal government, so I'll once again be in the awkward positon of petitioning the Congress to get our money for the cattle. It isn't that I mind so much running the risk of never being repaid, or even of the trouble and weeks of work it will involve; what I don't like is being obliged to appear before the American people as someone trying to make money off the government."

"Then don't make money off them," she replied calmly. "Go down to the commission and give them an offer which will meet your costs. That will save the government money and avert warfare with the Indians. As long as you have the cattle available, can you do less?"

"No, Senator Benton, I can't do less. Confound it; it means I'll have to be away from the mines for a solid month, and then I'll probably never get my money back. But I can't do less."

The next morning he went to Commissioner Barbour and made him an offer. Barbour replied, "Your offer is the lowest and best yet made by a respectable man. I'll take it."

John reported to Jessie; she watched as he was once again in the saddle, off for Southern California to drive up the cattle himself.

11

September was a lovely month. The fogs disappeared, the sun came out bright and warm; each day Jessie roamed the hills and sand dunes with Lily and little Charlie, the baby carried papoose fashion by either Gregorio or his cousin. The bay and the strait sparkled in the early fall. The children thrived, grew strong and red-cheeked.

Jessie had talked to John about their home: whether they should buy one of the few remaining residences at no matter how extortionate a price, whether they should build their new house on their lot on Stockton Street, whether they should perhaps buy a farm near by on the peninsula where it would be warm. John had been uncertain. He had told her she could do anything she wanted, but had evidenced no enthusiasm for any of the alternatives. Nor had she been able to derive any idea of his plans for the future; he spoke of going back to Washington to try to push through some mining laws, returning to New York to design and build more modern ore-crushing equipment, going to London to straighten out the financial mess, of moving the entire family up to the Mariposa. As long as his mind was suspended she did not feel free to move in any direction, and so she remained in the little barrack on the dunes.

The winter before she had spent in Madame Castro's two rooms, watching the rain pour in from the sea; the November rain swept windwise across San Francisco, and once again she was isolated in two rooms. The senatorial election came and went without John uttering one word or making a single gesture toward succeeding himself. The organized groups beat the drums for their candidates; ever-growing slavery factions decried his political experience; his friends and supporters were scattered throughout the county, busy with their own affairs. There was nothing she could do with him away, apparently disinterested in the result, and so she had to sit back and watch her husband be beaten.

She had been well trained in the history and literature of exploration, but the work of exploring had worn out; she had read books on agriculture and done what she could to prepare herself to be a farmer's wife, but the farm had never materialized. She had hoped to be a senator's wife, had been equipped by both training and temperament to fill that job; now their seat in the Senate had vanished. There was no part she could play in gold mining, and she frankly had little interest in it.

Her mind went back as it so often did to her few moments of conversation with Mary Algood on the outskirts of St. Louis. Mary's lot was the hard one; she had had to cross the plains in her covered wagon, break ground in the Oregon wilds, live the life of unrelenting toil. Yet frequently Jessie found herself envying Mary: she had been free to go to Oregon in her covered wagon with her husband by her side; she had been free to stumble across stubble fields behind the plow to break the Algood acres; she had been free from public censure and the aggravations that follow the collapse of high ambition. Jessie knew that at each point the world would have said she was the more fortunate of the two: her husband was the famous explorer whose map the Algoods were using in their passage across the plains, yet being his wife meant that she had had to endure endless months of aloneness and agony over her husband's safety; she had a thousand times more money than Mary Algood would ever see after a lifetime of back-breaking toil, and yet that money only meant that she was separated from her husband for months at a time.

John seemed no longer to need her; the same accidental discovery of gold on the Mariposa which had removed him from any field of creative work had also removed her opportunity to collaborate with him. It seemed to her that before long she would be in her mother's position: mistress of a large home, children to raise, entertaining to be done, a background to be created for her husband—and nothing more. For the hundredth time she wished that Larkin had kept his Mariposa and left them in possession of the Santa Cruz ranch with its old vines and peaceful orchards and lovely view over the sea. She remembered what Nicollet had told her: "Any accident or scoundrel can take your money—and usually does—but no one can deprive you of the skill to turn out good work. The finest and most durable possession in all the world is good workmanship."

In proportion as they amassed gold, their marriage, that individual entity which was a third being created by their union, had deteriorated into routine. It was no longer something greater than the sum total of the two of them, but rather something less. She sat in the forlorn barrack on the sand dunes with her two children, prey to loneliness, while her husband remained away for months at a time extracting wealth from the earth. Their marriage could be a beautiful thing when they were apart for a purpose, such as an expedition; then it could glow with a sustaining light. Geographic separation did not detract from the stature or intensity of the marriage, but separation in ultimate desires, separation in one's conception of the good and valuable life could slash away at the stature of a marriage until this third being which was created by the meeting of two minds and two hearts had died, and there was little left but a husband and a wife.

This was the reverse of the shield of her despair on the Delaware Indian Reservation, but this could be the profounder tragedy of the two: either of the two mates might die, grow weary or calloused with the ideals of their relationship, become indifferent, disillusioned. Yet even when this happened, the other could maintain the marriage by tenderness, sympathy and patience, by hanging grimly on and fighting, by enduring difficult periods; the marriage would maintain its fundamental strength, would come back to robust life when the temporary derangement had passed. One had to refuse to think in terms of disruption or defeat or possible ending: one had to forgive transgressions, have an iron-willed, incorruptible faith in the permanence of the relationship: for a marriage, like a human life, must endure all manner of vicissitude; the weak mortal, the weak relationship went down to destruction at the first ill wind; the stalwart marriage survived all gales, even though sometimes it had to plunge blindly through black and mounting seas.

But if the marriage were dead! If it had slowly crumbled into meaninglessness, then everything was gone.

She knew that her plight was no one's fault, but rather a piling up of accidental circumstance. Yet accidental circumstance must not be allowed to be the master, or their lives would be buffeted by every changing wind. She did not want these gold mines, she did not want wealth; the gold had come into their hands only by an ironic twist of fate. Was John right in saying that if fate dumped a fortune down into your lap you were a fool not to take it? Perhaps they were the more fools in the taking!

She knew she could not impose this reasoning on John, for that would be obliging him to accept her standards. He had to reach that conclusion by himself, come to the point where he realized that the mines were costing him more in companionship and love and accomplishment than they were producing in other precious metals. She did not doubt that he would one day come to this conclusion; but how long and how far away? How many weary miles would they have to retrace their steps to find again that partnership which had characterized their earlier years?

Once again she was confronted by the unsolvable character of her husband: how could a man who was so indifferent to money and its trappings, who had worked for years in a field in which he could hope to earn nothing but the most modest army salary, suddenly devote his life to making money? How did one ever come to understand the enigma of another man's soul?

Her one joy during these long and troubled days was her love for little Charlie, which was multiplied in intensity because in it there was included the love for her lost son, Benton, and her profoundest gratitude for demonstrating that she could again bear healthy children. She insisted upon bathing the boy herself, in feeding him his morning and evening meal, so that they would grow close together, know and love each other's every move. Charlie was full of laughter, and Jessie whiled away many an hour playing games to make her son giggle.

The day before Christmas she roamed the hills with Lily looking for a Christmas tree. She rolled tin foil and made spur-of-the-moment ornaments. Friends came during the afternoon to bring gifts and extend the holiday greetings: some of the delegates to the Monterey convention who had known the warmth of her fireside and the hospitality of her table; army officers and their wives to whom she had brought memories of their homes in the East; the Australians, whose property they had made available on generous terms; their old friends Beale and Knight, to whom she and her children were like family; old acquaintances from St. Louis and Washington who had come straight from the wharf to their home on Stockton Street for a welcome to California; miners whom they had grubstaked, merchants from whom they had bought even though the wares were not yet satisfactory; the son of an Indian chief whose tribe had been rescued with John's cattle; the Saunders family, Negroes who had been saved from slavery because John had taken the man up to the Mariposa with him and helped him wash out seventeen hundred dollars in gold, enough to buy his freedom.

But by dark they had all gone, gone to join their families and friends for Christmas dinner. Jessie was left alone with her two children, for Gregorio

and his cousin had ridden south for the holidays. After she fed Lily and
Charlie and put them to sleep, she sat in a rocker by the Christmas tree,
longing for her husband, for a roaring fire, for her parents and Eliza, for
her young sisters and brother and the friends and relatives who gathered in
the warm and brightly lighted rooms in their home on C Street. She fell to
musing about the years that had passed and the years that were to come.
There was no fireplace in this little two-room barrack, no hearthstone, yet
in the mellowness of spirit engendered by Christmas she perceived that a
hearth is not merely a fireplace: a hearth can also be a fire kindled in the
hearts of other people, a kindness done here, a service done there, a man
or woman given happiness on a frontier thousands of miles from home. It
was a year and a half since they had first come to California; she had been
almost the first white woman to cross Panama, hers had been one of the
first American homes in Monterey; by her refusal to buy or use slaves she
had played a small but significant role in keeping California free; by their
discovery of gold on the Mariposa and their importing of machinery to set
up permanent mines, they had quickened the migration of easterners to
California, increased the buying power abroad of the new state; by John's
willingness to provide beef for the Indians they had kept peace in the mining
regions; by his comprehensive program in the Senate they were slowly bringing the United States to California; by their own return to California, by
their steadfastness in remaining in San Francisco after the fires and violence
and destruction, they had helped create a sense that this frontier would
survive and be permanent; by making the long, hazardous trip by sea, by
crossing Panama while heavy with child and by giving birth to her son in the
primitive conditions of San Francisco, she had created a home of flesh and
blood rather than wood and glass.

It was not much to have done, she knew, and not at all what she had
planned. Yet some sixty years had passed since Grandmother Benton had
set out for the frontier of Tennessee; times had changed, this new frontier
was unlike any other the country had known; each one played his part
according to the contour of the times and the nature of the need. If she
could not duplicate Grandmother Benton's performance, it was perhaps not
altogether her fault; she had done the best she could, had gone through
much for her efforts. She was only twenty-seven, yet at moments like these
she felt as though she had lived as long as Grandmother Benton or Grandmother McDowell.

She glanced at the clock and saw that it was an hour from midnight.
She decided that she would remain awake long enough to see the Christmas
Day in and would then go to her cold and lonely bed. But the wish was
stronger than the will, and in a few moments she fell asleep, her head on
her chest, her breathing quiet in the still house. She dreamed that she heard
the swift beat of a horse coming over the dunes, of a man springing from
its back and rushing across the wooden porch. The image went back to
that moment on the Delaware Indian Reservation when John had returned

in just this fashion to offer his sacrifice, to bring her new courage and new life. She dreamed that the door was flung open, that heavy sacks were dropped on the rough wooden floor, that she was swooped up in her husband's arms, her face covered with kisses, that she was seated again in the same chair, but this time on John's lap with his arms about her and her head on his shoulder and her lips on his lips: and at last she knew it was no dream.

"My dear," she murmured, "you did come home for Christmas."

"Could you doubt it? Are you all right? Are the children well?"

He listened quietly, his dark eyes scanning her face, while she told him of the commonplaces of her routine, led him to the bedroom to show him how well his son and daughter looked. Then he brought the two sacks into the candlelight and began showing her the gifts he had managed to purchase in his hasty flight for home.

"They aren't much," he said, "most of the stores were closed. But how would you like a trip to Paris as a Christmas gift?"

"Splendid," she replied tartly; "let's also give Charlie a peep at the man in the moon."

He chuckled, took a wallet from his back trouser pocket, opened a brightly colored envelope and dangled two long steamship tickets before her unbelieving eyes, his index finger underscoring the lines.

"Read them, Miss Jessie. We're going to have a full year in Europe."

In a whisper she read, "San Francisco to Chagres. Chagres direct to Liverpool. Folkstone to Boulogne, France."

As the tears began to roll down her cheeks, he caught them in his palm and brushed them away. Her thoughts went back ten full years to the rainy afternoon when they had sat before the fire in Hassler's workroom, with Grandmother McDowell at the front window watching the funeral procession of President Harrison, and the ardent, dark-eyed young man sitting across the tea table from her had said, "I will always love you, Jessie, of that you can be sure. I may make mistakes, I may fail you in other ways, I won't come up to your expectations, but I will always love you."

How true it was that marriage required patience rather than logic, that it must not be disrupted at every unforeseen twist of fortune, but allowed time to work out its fundamental and organic pattern.

"Can you leave the mines?" she asked.

"The mines have already separated us too long. Let's spend our time and money together while we still have them, before I prove that Nicollet was right about a fool and his funds. It will be your first real vacation in ten years. The first since you spoke those fateful words, 'Whither thou goest I will go.' Do you remember, Jessie?"

BOOK FIVE

FIRST LADY

1

THEY CROSSED THE ATLANTIC on the Cunard sidewheeler, the *Africa;* since she was the only woman on board, the captain gave her the Ladies' Parlor as her stateroom. Two sofas were bound together to make a wide bed for herself and Charlie. Jessie and John spent the rainy gale-swept days relaxing and reading. When the weather was fair they tied little Charlie on a four-foot line to the pole in the center of the room, and although Lily declared that the baby spent as much time on his head as on his feet, he seemed to enjoy himself.

When they reached London they found everything in readiness for them, including their hotel suite with its chintz hangings and cheery wood fire. Mr. Abbott Lawrence, the American minister to England, had been a friend of Tom Benton's for many years, and so the Fremonts were taken under official chaperonage. Jessie went twice to what the English called "authorities of toilette," where she was measured and fitted, her preference in fabric and color noted. For each social engagement a new and beautiful outfit would be delivered to her hotel. She was haunted by the specter of the Jessie Fremont of Monterey who had worn a cut-off, faded blue riding skirt and an unbleached muslin sacque. It was fun to lie in bed at the Clarendon Hotel in a violet morning robe and have breakfast served, while one remembered rising at dawn in the two-room barrack on the dunes of San Francisco to light a fire in a coal stove and prepare warm cereal for one's children.

Their first night in London she and John dined at Sion House, the town residence of the Duke of Northumberland; here she met Lady Bulwer, whom she had known in Washington when her husband had been minister to the United States. Lady Bulwer took Jessie and John to an old man who was moving about the lavishly furnished rooms sunk in thought; she murmured, "This is my uncle, the Duke of Wellington," and speaking very distinctly, presented the Fremonts. The Iron Duke bowed mechanically and was about to pass on when a gleam of memory came into his watery eyes.

"I remember that name," he said. "Fremont, the great American traveler."

He shook hands with John. Later Jessie said to her husband, "You have shaken the hand that proved the hand of fate to Napoleon."

Her friends decreed that they would be doing less than their simple duty if they allowed her five minutes of any day without an affair in her honor. When Jessie remarked to the Marchioness of Wellesley, who had been one of the Caton girls from Maryland, that she would like to visit Westminster

Abbey, her friend replied, "Monuments live forever, people pass away."

Jessie thought how much her mother would have enjoyed the life in London, the capital from which the traditions and ideals of Cherry Grove had sprung. If Elizabeth McDowell could have married a member of the English Parliament instead of the American Congress, she would have been perfectly at home and completely happy; it was just bad luck that she had been plunged into a raw and crude capital, creating its own history, instead of this venerable seat of tradition. But it was to her father that her mind turned a few nights later at the opera, when she was introduced to an Englishwoman of high birth as "Mrs. Fremont from North America." "From North America," exclaimed the woman, examining Jessie through her lorgnette, "I thought all North Americans were Indians." Jessie laughed to herself while she thought, Thank heavens Tom Benton wasn't here to hear that remark. He would have declared war on the whole British Empire!

Now, at Easter, she stood before the mirror in their suite at the Clarendon in London, surveying herself in her presentation gown. The gown itself was of lace, adorned with artificial roses, from deep red to white. Her dark brown hair was piled on top of her head and her light hazel eyes were glowing with excitement. She picked up her bouquet of roses and turned to John, who was sitting in a lounging robe watching the ritual of his wife's dressing.

"Will I do justice to California?" she asked.

"You were more indigenous in your unbleached muslins."

"I am not trying to be indigenous, dear, I am trying to appear beautiful and sophisticated."

"Let me see the curtsy that Ambassador Lawrence's wife took a week to teach you."

"That's because Father always had an aversion to seeing a lady bow like a man or duck like a servant."

There was a knock at the door. "That must be my carriage," she exclaimed. "I'm sorry you are not a bride, or at least a lady, so that you could be presented to the queen. However, I will meet you at the Duchess of Bedford's for tea at four o'clock."

It was only a few moments before her carriage turned into the courtyard of Buckingham Palace. She was escorted directly to the room where the ladies of the diplomatic corps were waiting. Mrs. Lawrence had gone early in order to reserve a place for her in one of the deep windows where she might see the queen drive up. The royal carriage arrived at the palace for the Easter presentation drawn by cream-colored horses. After a time the doors of the throne room were opened; Mrs. Lawrence made her curtsy, then presented Jessie, who did her best not to bow like a man or duck like a servant. After she had been presented to Prince Albert and the queen's mother, she took her place in the queue and for two hours watched the procession of English noblewomen as they made obeisance, kissed the queen's hand then backed out from the royal presence. She was struck by the contrast between this scene and the position of the First Lady in the United States, who got a four-year lease on a White House which was forever in need of repairs, and a grudging, sometime courtesy from the voters.

After tea at the Duchess of Bedford's, Jessie and John went to the home of Sir Roderick Murchison, president of the Royal Geographical Society, who was giving a dinner for John's fellow medalists. This evening, spent among the bronzed travelers and explorers, was the most enjoyable she had in London, for here John was among his own kind. These men had read with great interest all three of their reports, had studied the Fremont maps; they in turn had sent him the accounts of their travels. They were truly friends and brothers, bound by the indestructible kinship of profession. It was a joy to watch her husband in this group, for here John was at his best; his eyes flashed, he spoke with the easy charm and sure authenticity of the man who is a sound artisan. More than ever she felt that it had been a misfortune for him to withdraw from his craft, that he must get back into it, that his talents must not be wasted.

One night in April as they were about to step into a carriage to go to a dinner party being given in their honor, four constables from Bow Street surrounded them and informed John that he was under arrest.

"Under arrest?" he demanded. "What for?"

A nervous little fellow who identified himself as a clerk from a solicitor's office cried rudely, "You'll jolly soon find out! Haul him off to jail, my boys, the mighty colonel will soon learn that in England a man has to pay his drafts."

More perplexed than frightened, Jessie asked, "John, do you know what this is about?"

"Probably the Mariposa affair. Sargent sold stock. I haven't been able to locate him."

"But you're not responsible for Sargent . . ."

"Come along now, Colonel," said one of the constables.

As they started down the street, she called, "Don't worry, dear, I'll go straight to Mr. Lawrence's house; he'll get you out."

But when she reached the minister's house she learned that he had gone to the dinner party in their honor. Once again she entered her carriage. Her host was waiting for them. She explained what had caused her delay; Abbott Lawrence excused himself from the party and went with her at once to Bow Street. The police headquarters seemed dismal, but the words of the officer in charge were still less pleasant: he informed them that Colonel Fremont's bail was a high one, that he could not release the colonel without the cash being deposited. She returned with Mr. Lawrence to the dinner, but the guests did not have enough money on them to secure John's release.

It was midnight when she left the party; she knew that John would be wondering why he was still sitting in the Bow Street jail when a fair portion of the bankers and statesmen of London were at a dinner being given in his honor. The Lawrence family took her to the Clarendon, where she found that a sleepless night in a strange hotel room, with one's husband in jail, makes an excellent time for unvarnished thinking.

While she had been driven through the parks in the mornings, been entertained at luncheons and teas, John had spent his days trying to iron out the muddle created by the conflicting and sometimes fraudulent Mariposa sales companies in London. From his reluctance to discuss the London stock promotion, she suspected that he hoped to straighten matters before relating the details. The Mariposa was a rich strike, they could extract a good deal more gold from it, yet as the complexities grew she became ever more convinced that they should have mined the gold on a small scale, or sold their rights for a flat sum. The American courts had not yet confirmed purchases made from Mexican grants, and at any moment their ownership of the Mariposa might be invalidated. Her husband was no businessman: he hadn't the temperament for it. It was unlikely that a man with his particular set of gifts could also be good at business. She had no head for business either; no one in her family had had any interest in commerce, or any heart for it. Even though she was grateful for the money they had taken out of the Mariposa, she feared lest the wealth cost more than it was worth, lest it continue to put the emphasis of their lives in the wrong place. The Mariposa mines were affording them large sums of money, yet the legal situation was so tenuous that it could snap without an instant's notice, leaving them rich in little but litigation.

The next morning, when their host of the night before went bail for John and delivered him to the Clarendon, she learned that he had not been arrested for the Mariposa financing after all, but rather for four drafts amounting to nineteen thousand dollars, which he had issued during the conquest of California. Secretary of State Buchanan had been unwilling to make good these drafts on the grounds that this would give the conquest official backing; bills introduced into Congress to pay them had never passed; and now a Californian by the name of Huttman was suing John in England, hoping to recover from his personal funds.

She did not feel that her reasoning about the Mariposa of the night before had been any the less valid because this particular difficulty had a different origin; she was certain that if the confused financing were allowed to continue they could fall into serious trouble. John agreed that the English venture had come to an unfortunate impasse; by ten o'clock he had left the hotel to visit the bankers and terminate all investments in the Mariposa. She was considerably relieved, but she found herself troubled by the thought that British investors, so frequently widows and aged people living on pensions, might have lost money on the unauthorized issue. If there had been victims of Sargent's shady sales, she would have liked to repay them: some of those who had invested had doubtless done so on the strength of John Fremont's name, feeling secure because he owned the property. But to advertise for such people would bring an avalanche of claimants down upon her, many of them fraudulent; it would also convict her husband of being responsible for Sargent's acts. She shrugged her shoulders with distaste and despair.

Toward the end of April, as she walked past the desk of the Clarendon, a clerk handed her a letter from her father. She tore open the envelope and began reading phrases that made no sense. There was a line about how her brother Randolph had delivered the Kossuth oration in St. Louis and been favorably received; then suddenly she read, ". . . cholera . . . quickly set his bowels on fire with inflammation . . . delirious by the second day, died without realizing his torment . . . so young for him to die . . . we were just beginning to be friends . . ."

Like her father, she too was just beginning to be friends with her young brother. For a time she wept, then the memories of Randolph began flooding back, memories that hurt. She had made no strong effort to know the boy: her life had been dominated by her relationship with her father and her husband. She had had no time or emotion or even interest for anyone else. Only her mother had given him the patient kindness he had needed.

She had known how precious every moment was in a marriage, that tomorrow was too late to be loving and kind, that the relationship must be kept at its finest pitch every moment; yet she had never understood these simple truths in her relationship with her brother or her mother. She had been a good daughter to her father; she believed she was a good wife; was she being a good mother as well? Or were the hours and the years slipping by, while she failed Lily and Charlie the way she had failed Randolph?

She had never consciously said, I put my husband above my children, yet that decision had long since been made. As much as she loved her children, they would always come after her husband in her own mind. John had had her deepest love before there had been any children; he would still be there, still have her deepest love when the children had gone their separate ways. There was no way to conceal this fundamental of her nature from herself; nor, as she was to learn, could that knowledge be withheld from her children.

When John returned at teatime and saw how red her eyes were, he picked up the letter from the bureau and scanned it quickly. He drew the blinds against the late afternoon sun, dipped a hand towel in cold water, laid it over her feverish face. Several hours later she said, "Are your affairs well enough settled for us to leave London? Do you think we could move to Paris? We'll never find any of the tranquillity we have been seeking in this social whirl."

"We can leave within a day or two," he replied. "I have stopped all exploitation of the Mariposa in England. The stock issues will be handled by a bank in San Francisco from now on. I've also succeeded in having that Huttman suit transferred back home."

They found a small place in Paris on the Champs Elysées, an elegant little house in the Italian style, with a courtyard and large garden in the rear where the ground fell away rapidly towards the Seine, giving a fine view of the dome of the Invalides on the opposite bank. They settled in the villa for what was to be the most peaceful fourteen months of their turbulent half-century of marriage.

Almost immediately upon their arrival Jessie found she was going to have another child. She thought how fine it would be to spend the time in the quiet beauty of this villa. She was feeling lazy, but John kept in shape with fencing lessons. He would sometimes ask an instructor from the school to come to the house so she could observe his progress. As she watched the fencing she recalled the description of him sent from Monterey to the New York *Herald* by Bayard Taylor: "I have seen in no other man the qualities of lightness, activity, strength and physical endurance in so perfect an equilibrium." He was also attending the school where his beloved Nicollet had taught, studying astronomy and mathematics as well as the works of the French geologists on quartz mining.

They both spoke excellent French, which helped them to feel at home in Paris. Once a week they would drive through the park of St. Cloud to Versailles, spend the day walking through the grounds and galleries, and return home the following evening. On warm afternoons they followed their own grounds down to the Seine, where they would lie on the bank with open but unread books, watching small boats sail by; in the evenings there were delicious dinners, then an hour on the balcony overlooking the city, the air beneficently soft and quiet. Half a dozen times a day she found herself rejoicing that she not only had her husband constantly by her side, but that she also had him to herself. In the early fall they bought tickets for the grand tour of Europe, packed their bags and prepared to leave, only to decide at the last moment that it was folly to wear themselves out voyaging, they who had spent so many heartbreaking months in travel.

Having had their fill of social life in London they did little entertaining until the winter season came on; then they went regularly to the Théâtre Français and to hear Rachel at the Italian Opera. Lady Bulwer came over for the Paris season and introduced them to the diplomatic corps. They were invited to a *thé dansant* at St. Cloud given by the Prince President; they spent a dramatic day watching Louis Napoleon ride into Paris to be crowned emperor; and from their own house they watched the bridal procession of the emperor and his empress as it left the Tuileries and came up the Champs Elysées. The Count de la Garde, who had been a member of the Bonaparte family, became attached to Jessie; he would stop by at eleven after his airing in the Bois de Boulogne to recount stories of French history. The Fremont salon became popular without Jessie intending that it should.

The winter months slipped by. Though her baby was due within a week or two, she decided that she wanted to give her husband a party for his fortieth birthday. John had been troubled in his mind about reaching this milepost; he had told her that a good explorer was a young explorer. She thought that the best way to ease him into the birthday would be to invite to dinner the friends they had made during their nine months' stay, in par-

ticular the French scientists, astronomers and explorers. A few days later
her second daughter, Anne, was born. The attending physicians assured her
that the child was sound and healthy; the Count de la Garde named her
"the little Parisienne."

At John's insistence she treated herself to a leisurely recovery, for both
had the feeling that their vacation was nearly over and that they soon would
be returning to the United States. The exact provocation came in the form
of a letter from Tom Benton, telling them that three new railroad expeditions were being organized by the government to find the pass over the
Rockies which John had failed to locate on his fourth expedition. Her father
told them that a number of the leading newspapers were saying that Colonel
Fremont, who was the most experienced pathfinder of the West, should be
in charge of an expedition.

She had had many long talks with her husband during the reposeful winter
months. They agreed that even though his studies of mining in Paris had
shown him how to set up the quartz mines at the Mariposa so that they
could derive continuing wealth from them, this soliciting of gold from the
earth could not be an end in itself, but only a means. She had persisted in
her theory that their wealth should be used to implement his further exploring, map making and writing of books on new wildernesses and frontiers.

"That's all very true," he had replied, his dark eyes thoughtful, "but
no man can be an explorer in a void. In exploring, as in love, one wants
to be the pursued as well as the pursuer; a man has to wait until a set of
circumstances arise in which there is a need for him to explore. I can't
just say, 'I'll now explore in Central America' or 'I'll now explore in Canada.' That kind of thinking would never bring any worth-while results."

"Your field is the western part of the United States," replied Jessie. "No
one man is more closely identified with it than you. Surely there is a great
deal of work still to be done there?"

"Yes, but the specific purpose has to come to a head."

Just as, after the court-martial, the arrival of Tom Benton's letter from
St. Louis telling John of the proposed fourth expedition had brought her
husband back to life, now once again her father's letter threw his career
into focus.

"I'll return to America on the next boat," he exclaimed. "I'll wait just
long enough to buy the latest scientific equipment here in Paris. You can
close the house at your leisure and then come on with the children."

Her hard-won period of tranquillity between storms was over.

"Yes, you must get back to Washington as quickly as possible," she agreed.
"They'll need your help in organizing the expeditions; you will want time
to plan your route and collect your party."

2

When she reached C Street at the end of June with her three children, she found that official Washington had passed John by. Secretary of War Jefferson Davis was determined that the first transcontinental railroad should have a southern route, whereas John had published his views on the advisability of a central route. The War Department, which hitherto had conducted all expeditions, wanted the commands to go to the young engineers of the Topographical Department.

She rented a modestly furnished bungalow close to her father's house, settled her family comfortably, then tackled the problem of what John was to do about the rebuff. To accept this ostracism was to admit that he had exhausted his usefulness, that his days as a trail blazer were over. She had watched him sketch rough maps and indicate where he was going to find the pass that he had failed to discover in 1849; she had seen him depart from Paris wild with excitement, shepherding his newly acquired instruments as his most valuable possessions. For the first time she had seen him planning to convert the wealth of the Mariposa into a creative project: once he had charted this path across the Rockies, he intended to use the gold to lay out the railroad line and build it himself, the iron road which would fulfill her father's dream.

She was relieved to find that her husband was wistful rather than angry.

"I could organize my own party," he said; "Preuss and Kern are eager to start out with me again. But it's hard to readjust . . . I had visions of an army expedition . . . I even had hopes that they would restore my commission . . ."

He ended lamely, watching her face to see if she would show astonishment or disapproval. But she had always known how terribly he wanted the Army to solicit his rejoining; for her own part she would never rest content until she saw him in uniform again, working with the service in which he had begun his professional life.

"When President Polk commissioned you a lieutenant colonel, I prophesied that you would be a general before you were forty. My chronology is off, but when the right circumstances combine, the Army will urge you back into service. In the meanwhile you are surely not going to give up your plans for a fifth expedition? That railroad pass is so important; you are the man to find it and chart it."

"You mean we ought to finance it ourselves?"

"What better use could we put our money to? You've already spent several thousand dollars for your scientific equipment; surely you didn't ever hope to get that money back from the government?"

When John grimaced she continued, "Very well then, let's use our resources to organize the men and buy supplies. If you find the pass, the country will want to help finance your railroad; if you don't find it, we've lost nothing except a lot of gold. We can still go back and build our cabin on the Mariposa. Paris was a long way from Fremontville. Or don't you want a Fremontville any more?"

His eyes gleamed. "It will be a main stop on our railroad. I'll run it right past your front door."

The next morning, when they told her father that they were going to finance an independent expedition, Tom nodded his approval, wrote out a check for his contribution, and sent letters to his friends in St. Louis. By return mail there arrived a series of modest checks, not enough to take the financial burden off the Fremonts, but by the very gesture of faith and confidence on the part of those who had lost their money on the fourth expedition, sufficient to provide the last necessary impetus for John to work with his old-time enthusiasm.

As always it felt good to Jessie to be in Washington, even though she had returned to a disappointment. She found pleasure in the companionship of her sisters. Sarah had moved to Boston with her husband, but Eliza and Susie were still in Washington. The coming of Eliza's first child had brought her not only the health she had never enjoyed, but by filling out her tall, awkward figure and heavy-featured face, had brought her a kind of attractiveness. She and William Carey Jones had built themselves a conservative brick house on H Street, only a few blocks from the Benton home; on the wings of her first real energy Eliza had begun the study of law so that she might better understand her husband's affairs.

Jessie and Eliza frequently lunched together, either at Eliza's home or at Jessie's, where they found an hour of companionship: for marriage, children and a serious interest in their husbands' careers afforded them much common ground. The most delightful hours, however, were those spent with her youngest sister, Susie, who was now twenty. Susie had abandoned the piano after years of onslaught and was devoting her time to bedeviling the young men of Washington. She had her mother's face, the delicate features, the high coloring, the sparkling blue eyes. When Jessie had last seen Susie, two and a half years before, she had been all arms and legs and high-pitched laughter; she was now beautiful in the way that Elizabeth McDowell had been beautiful in her youth, a lighthearted child who bewitched her cavaliers. She was at the center of much of the young social life of Washington, and was dangling half a dozen men at the end of her affections, unwilling to come to any serious decision because she was having far too pleasant a time in the courting. Though Jessie was only nine years older than Susie, she felt temperamentally old enough to be her mother. Susie brought her the stories of her romances, of the music and dancing and theaters and young men who filled her life. When she was to be out late she stayed with Jessie instead of going home and waking their parents.

She went to the funeral of Count Bodisco, returning with Harriet to her home in Georgetown. Harriet was now twenty-eight, full blown, with round red cheeks and a buxom figure.

"Jessie," she said with a look of affectionate bewilderment in her eyes, "the Russians are a wonderful people. The count showed me his will a few days before he died. He willed me every last dollar of his estate, with the provision that I marry a young man who will give me the pleasure he says I gave him during the twelve years of our marriage!"

The hot weather came on. Jessie put her three children in a screened loggia just off the garden, the coolest spot in the house. Lily and Charlie seemed to enjoy the heat; they turned on a hose in the back yard and kept themselves wet all day, pretending the spray was one of the fountains of Paris. But little Anne, now five months old, did not fare so well. She was refusing her food, tossing fretfully at night. Jessie spent many anxious hours in the darkness rocking the baby's crib, singing soft lullabies.

An epidemic spread through Washington. Four babies died of colic within two days. On the morning of July tenth, Anne fell ill. Once again Jessie sent Josheem to Silver Spring to ask Francis Blair if she might have refuge there. Blair returned with his carriage, bundled Jessie and the baby into it and hastened them out to the coolness and isolation of his estate. When John arrived at dinnertime, the pain around Jessie's heart had eased a little, for the baby seemed better. The next morning while she was holding Anne against her bosom, and her doctor was assuring her that the child would grow well here at Silver Spring, she felt a tiny spasm sweep over the baby. Anne grew rigid against her breast. Her second daughter was dead.

Too numb at the suddenness of the shock to feel any articulated pain, she gazed into the child's face. Their year in Paris was over now. She had lost young Benton because she had been exhausted and tortured during the court-martial, but she had carried the little Parisienne in health and calm. She had crossed Panama while carrying Charlie, borne him without proper medical safeguards in San Francisco. Yet Charlie was bursting with energy and health, while little Anne was gone. How could one understand life, make any kind of recognizable sense of it?

Even before she could cry, sharp thoughts stuck into her heart like pointed knives: she had borne four children and two were dead; half of life was wasted; half of all that one tried to do failed tragically and disappeared. It had been that way with John, too; he had been on four expeditions; the first two had been glorious successes, the last two had brought conflict, failure and death.

As the doctor took the baby from her she remembered that moment in St. Louis when her first son had died, when the doctor had tried to take young Benton and she had been unable to give him up. Then her grief had been more for herself and her husband than for the lost boy; but Anne had been so sweet and fragile, with such a disarming smile; she had wanted the child to grow up to be a lovely girl. Deep within her was a sorrow for the child's sake.

She was still sitting immobile in her chair, dry-eyed, feeling hard and cold, when John reached her. He buried his head on her lap and wept. The little Parisienne had meant much to him; he could not restrain his grief. Jessie thought, When young Benton died, and I could not endure my pain, he comforted me, he was calm and resolute. Now it is my turn to comfort him: I must not weep, I must not be bitter, I must help my husband. When one is weak, the other must be strong. When one is ill, the other must be well. When one is heartbroken, the other must be calm and hopeful. Neither can be the strong one, the well one, the brave one all the time; the roles must change, they must reverse as health and courage flag or revive. Living together did not mean that each mate was always at his strongest or that the two of them together were always twice as wise or resolute; but that through love, through tenderness, through sympathy, even through pity, their acceptance of life and their journey through the years could be enhanced. This was collaboration; this was marriage.

She lifted his head from her lap, gripped his face tightly between her fingers, kissed away the tears.

3

It was only a few days after John and his party had left St. Louis that she received a telegram telling her that he was unable to hobble along on his left leg and had been obliged to return to St. Louis for medical treatment.

She caught the next train for St. Louis, remembering that when she and John had first made this trip ten years before, they had used stages, canal boats and steamboats, the voyage taking over two weeks. Now she made the trip in three days and nights.

He was in their old room in the Benton house overlooking the pear orchard. "They were right, the War Department, to pass me by," he growled when she came into the room. "They knew I could never drag this confounded leg over the Rockies."

She stood in the doorway, noting how the lines of his face were visible even under the dark beard.

"You didn't get that leg dancing at Washington parties," she retorted; "you got it because you tried to blaze a railroad trail over the Rockies in the dead of winter. If you can't go on, you can't go on, but don't wear that leg like a curse; wear it the way Grandmother McDowell would say you should, like a medal bestowed for bravery under fire."

Her caustic tone had its salutary effect. He limped to her side and embraced her.

"I'm sorry I barked at you, dear. It's just that I've gone soft, and I don't like it. After a year of sleeping on lace and down in Paris, I no longer find a wet saddle the most comfortable pillow." He held her at arm's length, scanning her face. "Forgive me, Jessie, for being selfish and talking about myself. You look tired."

"Yes, I am tired," she admitted. "But that's not why I look pale. I started out on my fifth expedition just about the same moment you did on yours." She threw her head back sharply. "Like you, I find a wet saddle hard to sleep on after a soft pillow; it was easy carrying Anne because Charlie was so strong and healthy. Now . . ."

He drew her close to him and, with his arms locked about her, rocked from side to side.

"I'm afraid," she admitted, "but not too much. I seem to do all right on the odd numbers. My first and third children are as strong as tigers; my second and fourth were weak and died. I am due for a healthy child again this time."

"When will you have the baby?"

"About the middle of May."

"Good. I am rejoining my party at the Saline Fork of the Kansas River. I should be on the other side of the Rockies by February; from there we'll push on to San Francisco, and I'll come back across Panama. I'll be in Washington by the beginning of May."

On the first morning after her return to Washington she had tea and rolls at six, then walked up to the house on C Street. By six-thirty she was in the library. It was not yet light out; she saw her father's shaggy head bent over the papers on his desk, the spermaceti candles taking her mind back to that morning, twelve years before, when she was carrying her first child, her husband had just left on his first expedition, and she had joined Tom Benton in the library to help him with his work. Now she was to help her seventy-two-year-old father write his memoirs, *Thirty Years in the United States Senate*. Impulsively she went to him, leaned her head over his shoulder and kissed him on the cheek.

"It's good to be here with you again, Father," she said fondly, "working on your papers in this beautiful library as I did for so many years."

Tom Benton reached up and patted the hand resting on his shoulder.

"I've missed you, Jessie, more than you can know. This house is so empty without you. So often I needed your help, started to call out your name . . . But you had your own life to lead, your own work to do. I want you to know I'm proud of the fine things you've accomplished with John."

"Whatever I've been able to accomplish has been because of your training and help. But I think we ought not to be separated any more. I think we all ought to stay together and work out our problems together. If John and I have to go to California again, then you must come with us. How you would love the West, Papa! It is even richer and more colorful than you dared to dream."

Tom's eyes gleamed with excitement. "Yes, Jessie," he exclaimed, "next time you go to California I shall make the trip. I've wanted to for years now. It is the one last adventure I want to enjoy before I die."

Through the fall, mail from John reached her frequently, for he was on a well-traveled route; where she had once plotted his journey through sheer wilderness, twelve years of westward movement had brought hundreds of villages, farms, forts, and a two-way stream of wagons. It was not until after the turn of the year, when she had been without a letter for several months, that amorphous fears began to press upon her. On an early February afternoon as she sat in the living room of her rented cottage, with Lily and Charlie playing at her feet, she felt sudden pangs of hunger, where only an instant before she had felt no hunger at all. With this hunger gnawing at her insides as though she had not eaten for days, her formless anxieties took shape: John was starving; the last of the supplies had long since been eaten, the last of the animals killed and dispatched; the countryside was buried under snow and there was no morsel to sustain them.

That night at dinner she could not touch her food. When her father asked what the matter was, she replied, "John is starving. I can't eat with him desperately hungry."

"You didn't tell me you heard from John today!"

"I've had no communication. I just know he is hungry."

Tom Benton was thoughtful for several moments; he had no choice but to believe that his daughter was suffering from some oppressive force. He had to contend with the actuality of her pain rather than the improbability of her knowledge.

"It may be true that John is hungry," he agreed gently; "there has frequently been a shortage of food on his expeditions. But there is nothing to worry about. He has always come through."

She sat silent, her head down, all appetite gone. When the second day passed and she had had nothing but water, Tom Benton became angry.

"This is the sheerest nonsense I ever encountered. If John were starving there would be no possible way for him to communicate that information to you. Even if he could, he would refuse to do so. I will not allow you to endanger the baby you are carrying."

"You're right, Father," she whispered.

Two nights later, February 6, 1854, she was sitting in a robe before the fire in the living room, her hair down her back, her hands clasped in her lap, trying to perceive through the flames the true picture of what her husband was enduring at that moment. She heard the front door close noisily and the sound of young laughter on the staircase. Her sister Susie and a Benton cousin, who had been to a wedding at General Jessup's, came in to spend the night. She welcomed the two girls and urged them to make themselves comfortable before the fire after their drive over the rough and frozen streets. They slipped out of their ball gowns, put on loose woolen robes, then settled at her feet to tell her of the fun and gaiety of the wedding while they brushed their hair and sipped hot tea.

The fire burned down. Jessie said, "Let me get another log or two," and went into the dining room where there was a feeder box from an outside porch. She had just knelt beside the box when she heard a voice which in all the world could be only John's whisper, "Jessie."

She did not move or even breathe; half kneeling in the darkness, a wave of intense relief swept across her brain. She knew that her husband was safe.

She rose and carried the wood into the living room. Susie, who was standing with her back to the fire, met Jessie's glance as she entered the room. "Why, Jessie dear, what has happened? Your eyes are glowing as though you had received the most wonderful news."

"I have," replied Jessie serenely, "John is safe."

Tom Benton arrived late the next morning, shaking his head disapprovingly. "All this is a piece with your being so positive he was starving. I don't like it, Jessie. It's a dangerous kind of game, more dangerous than anything John himself is facing on the trail."

"Don't be frightened," she replied softly. "I'm happy now because I know John is safe. You'll have no more trouble with me, you'll see."

"Never look a gift horse in the mouth," he said *sotto voce*. "I don't like mysticism, but if it serves to restore your appetite, I'll accept it."

She was as good as her word; relieved of anxiety over her husband, she slipped quickly through the weeks. Toward the end of March she received a letter from Parowan, in Utah, brought in by a Mormon elder who had come to Washington on business. As she tore open the envelope and folded the pages upright so that she could read, one word stood out, one word repeated in nearly every line: *hunger*. Even before she saw the salutation of "My darling wife" she had seen the word hunger, and breathlessly she was reading:

Our food supplies disappeared steadily. There was no chance to replenish them with game. We could think of little else but our hunger. We lived for nearly fifty days on our horses, until the last one was killed. Three days later as I was trudging up the mountain, hunger overcame me so completely that my strength vanished and I almost fell. I told no one of my condition, but merely said that this was an excellent spot to camp, and turned in at once. The next morning I was able to continue. I called my men together, told them that a small group on my last expedition had been guilty of eating one of their number, and cried, "If we are going to die of hunger, let us die like men." Late the following day we encountered a band of Utes, one of whom remembered me from my journey through here in 1844. They gave us a dog . . .

When she had finished the letter she leaned weakly against the edge of the fireplace. Her mind flashed to another year and another house; she saw herself lying upon her four-posted cherrywood bed in the Benton home in St. Louis, with all the world thinking John dead; she recalled that one night while the cycle of dread was revolving in her mind, somehow the circuit had broken, she had fallen into an untroubled sleep, had awakened carefree, knowing that her husband was safe.

She went to her father's house to inform him joyously that all was well with John and his party. She did not mention the word hunger.

An early March spring came to Washington. Tom Benton felt tired after the intense work of the winter and visited Silver Spring to rest for a short time. Jessie planned to spend these days in the house on C Street with her mother. She took Elizabeth her tray the first night; there was nothing on it but a cup of tepid milk and a piece of buttered toast.

When she had returned from Paris she had been able to see how much her mother had faded. Yet in the day-by-day contact with her now there was little change discernible. Her eyes were withdrawn, her face white. During the last few years Elizabeth McDowell Benton had remained alive because she knew of no way to die until her time came.

Jessie ran a warm cloth over her mother's hands, dried them, brushed her hair a little. After a few moments had passed, Elizabeth said:

"Jessie, help me . . . out . . . bed."

Jessie slipped the robe around her mother's shoulders and put warm slippers on her feet.

She supported Elizabeth, with an arm around her back, down the long hallway as her mother headed for the library. She followed closely as her mother moved about the room, touching Tom's desk, the books on the shelves, the chessboard on the Duncan Phyfe table by the windows. When she came back to the door, Jessie saw that there were tears in her eyes. She half carried, half supported her mother down the broad flight of stairs. Summoning her strength, Mrs. Benton went from room to room, gazing at the portraits of her parents in the drawing room, touching one high note on Eliza's and Susie's piano, then walked across the entrance hall to the dining room, where, leaning against the table, she gazed up at the portrait of herself as a young woman painted by Samuel Morse when portrait painting had been his career. She sat down in Tom Benton's big chair at the head of the table. Across the gleaming mahogany the two women faced each other in the rapidly falling dusk. As Jessie watched her mother's face, she saw her eyes clear, a spot of color come into the white cheeks.

"I had much happiness here . . . but it was never my home . . . in the way . . . it is your home. You grew up here . . . you have roots here. You have loved it. This home will be yours . . . what Cherry Grove was to me. Your father has willed it to you . . . it will become your inherited home . . . the inherited home of your children. I am happy . . . you will have it, Jessie, you and your family . . ."

"Father said you made this home the little White House of Washington. For years everyone of importance who came to the capital sat at this table and enjoyed your hospitality. You entertained Andrew Jackson and his Rachel here the first time they came to Washington, when no one else would receive Mrs. Jackson because she had been divorced."

Elizabeth smiled faintly. Jessie knew that in her own way her mother had been a martyr to marriage; she had said, I cannot endure this kind of life so

I will quietly withdraw, but I will never hurt my husband by telling him that this has always been the wrong life for me, that it was a fatal error for me to have married him. If she could not be strong enough to stand up to a life that was against her own instincts, at least she could be strong enough to protect her husband against the knowledge of what was killing her. Elizabeth Benton too had borne a King George's Mark. Another woman would have left her husband, gone back to Cherry Grove to live, renounced her marriage as a mistake. Elizabeth McDowell Benton had paid for her mistake with her life, yet no one but her daughter knew it. There had been a chasm between them, a chasm of temperament, of values, of natures; but now Jessie felt closer to Elizabeth than she ever had before.

She perceived that courage, like loneliness, has many faces; that nothing she might ever do would require more courage than had been shown by Elizabeth of the charming and amiable background.

That night her mother slipped so quietly and gently out of life that Jessie could feel almost no transition. Her eyes seemed closed only a trifle tighter, the face only a little paler, the fragile, bony hand in her hand only a little colder. When her daughter raised the blinds to let in the first light of dawn, she saw that the ordeal of Elizabeth McDowell Benton was over.

She was lunching with her children a few weeks later when Josheem came running to the house, his eyes wild, panting, "Miss Jessie, come quick—house burning down!"

She ran through the streets of Washington; from several blocks away she could see the mounting flames. She turned down C Street, stopped running; her feet began to drag. There was a crowd already assembled in front of the Benton home; firemen were working hand hoses, attempting futilely to put out the flames. Her eyes closed and behind the lids she saw again the two great fires in San Francisco, which she had blamed on the lawlessness of the frontier community. She stood on one foot, her shoulders sagging, breathing short, labored breaths, watching her home with its memories and hopes go up in flames. This then was her inheritance; a home built, a life made, then nothing left but a bare and forlorn chimney against the sky.

Her father's carriage turned in from Pennsylvania Avenue. She helped him down. They stood with arms about each other while Tom murmured:

"My manuscript of _Thirty Years in the Senate_. It's gone."

The crowds grew more dense. Sympathetic words were spoken. She heard someone say the Senate had adjourned when they heard the news, then she saw many of the senators with whom Tom Benton had spent his working years offering their condolences, the hospitality of their homes, while the roof of the Benton house caved in and the wooden walls seemed to blaze all at once.

She asked someone to help her lead her father to her own house. Here Tom Benton sank into a big chair in the living room, his head on his chest, all life gone out of him. After a few moments there was a knock on the front door.

Maylee announced President Franklin Pierce. Pierce had been a congressman from New Hampshire for some twenty years before an unkind fate had
precipitated him into an office for which he had neither talent nor appetite.
He was a kindly man who knew the nature of suffering: his wife had lost her
mind when their young son had died, and there could be no happiness for
Franklin Pierce in the White House. He went up to Tom Benton, put his
hand roughly on his shoulder and said, "Senator, this is a miserable piece of
fortune. I was riding when the news met me. I hurried here, stopping only
long enough at the White House to give the necessary orders. You will find
everything ready for you; the library and the bedroom next to it. You must
stay there until you rebuild your house."

Jessie recalled what her father had said about the president: "It is Pierce's
head that is wrong—his heart is always right." They were touched by his
kindness, but even while they thanked him they knew that Tom could not
move into the White House, for it too was a house of mourning.

True to his promise, John was back in Washington by the middle of May.
In the course of their quick revelations of all that had happened in the seven
months they had been separated, she hesitantly told her husband of how she
had known of his hunger and been unable to eat, of how he had come to her
to assure her that he was well. They had never talked of these things before;
she was uneasy lest he ridicule her or even reprove her for indulging in the
occult. Instead he turned searching eyes upon her and asked:

"Do you happen to remember what night that was?"

"Yes, it was February sixth."

He went to the weatherproofed duffel bag and brought forth his journal.
Thumbing through it, he opened to the entry of February sixth.

"That's the very night we reached Parowan," he said in a curiously hushed
voice. "We were all of us so feeble we could barely drag ourselves down the
trail, but the Mormons took us in, one or two of us in each house, and they
fed us and nursed us back to health." He was silent for a moment, reading
his notes, then looked up at her again.

"What time of the night was it that you heard me speak to you?"

"The girls came home from the wedding about one o'clock. They slipped
into gowns and settled before the fire. It must have been almost an hour
later when I was kneeling by that woodbox . . ."

"Listen to this entry in my journal," he said. "After those good Mormon
folk had fed me and showed me to my room, I sat down at once and wrote,
'If I could only tell Jessie that I am safe now, tell her how happy I am that
we have all been saved.' "

"What time did you make that entry?"

"My notes say eleven-thirty."

"Then your message reached me, but it took two and a half hours to get
here. I suppose I shouldn't complain; even Samuel Morse's telegraph couldn't
do better."

John took her face in his hands. "You are a good wife, but a poor astrono-

mer. Utah is two and a half hours earlier in time than Washington. The
message I wrote to you in my journal was flashed over a quicker and more
accurate wire than a Samuel Morse could ever invent."

4

Two days later she gave birth to a boy. They named him Frank. They
were happy with their son, and with the new trail over the Central Rockies
where John hoped to build his railroad. Together they wrote a short account
of his travels over the pass, accompanying it with a map to indicate the
proposed line to California.

They now had to give much of their time to the practicalities of business:
the banking house of Palmer, Cook & Company in San Francisco had successfully floated a stock issue and John had brought bank drafts which he
planned to use to straighten out his affairs in Washington. The representatives
from California finally put through the Congress the bills which would pay
them the hundred and eighty thousand dollars they had spent in beef cattle
for the Indians; Huttman won the case which John had had transferred from
London, but Congress voted to pay both the principal and the interest, and
so they did not have to meet the forty-three-thousand-dollar judgment with
their personal funds. Huttman's success led others in California who held
John's notes from the conquest to file suit. John grumbled to Jessie that
affairs were getting more complicated every hour: the government would
not honor the seven hundred thousand dollars' worth of drafts he had drawn,
but they were apparently willing to pay all court judgments levied against
him for these obligations . . . after he had spent months defending the suits
and a fortune for lawyers!

While in California he had learned that several of the best sites he had
staked out for quartz mining had been claim-jumped by squatters who could
not be put off the Mariposa except by force. Much of his work in Washington was with the Department of the Interior, where he was attempting to get
laws passed which would protect mineral rights under the still unconfirmed
land grants in California. He had no success, and with each ship that reached
New York there came disquieting news from Palmer, Cook and his managers
on the Mariposa, telling him that if some action were not taken the squatters
would be in possession of all the mines. Jessie agreed reluctantly that he
would have to make another trip to California. He could then return east to
begin promotion of the central railroad line for which they hoped Congress
might appropriate funds. As soon as their many affairs could be settled satisfactorily in the East, the family would move on to the Mariposa.

At the moment Jessie was loath to leave her father. Tom Benton's wife
was dead, his job in the Senate gone, his house burned down, and with it his
manuscript and his papers; his son was dead, his three daughters were busy
raising their own families and caring for their own husbands. With the house

on C Street still standing he had had his work, his books, his roots, his own roof, his friends who could come to call; he could entertain, be the master of a home, a man with a place in the world. With the burning of his home the last of his possessions had gone up in smoke, and though she kept him comfortable, in his own mind he was dispossessed. She wept for him; he had lived just a little too long, everything in his life had died before him—everything except the slavery issue.

She encouraged him to begin rewriting his book, not only because she wanted the permanent record but because the work would keep him occupied. By dint of assembling a number of documents from senatorial friends and helping him sketch the early chapters, her father's energy renewed and he threw himself forcibly into the task. With the quickening of his mental strength and courage, Old Rhinoceros Hide proved that he had justly earned his title, for at seventy-two he not only began the rewriting of his book, but plunged as well into a last great struggle to keep the slavery issue from splitting the Union.

For Jessie there was no escape from the maelstrom over slavery, for she and her husband had taken a definite stand: that the extension of slavery must be prohibited. With both the northern and southern interests trying to use the federal government as an instrument to further their beliefs, Washington became a battlefield in miniature. Discussions in the Congress were no longer restrained; they were waged in bitterness; physical blows were struck. The atmosphere was poisoned with a deadly virus, for the Fugitive Slave Law had aroused the people of the North to flaming indignation, and the Kansas-Nebraska Act, which had opened to slavery new territories from which it had been prohibited since the Missouri Compromise of 1820, had given rise to civil war in Kansas. There seemed to be no other issue on all the vast American panorama except slavery: it cut across friendships, family ties, every aspect of politics, economics, religion and ideology. Their oldest friends, intimates of the Benton and McDowell families for half a century, no longer came to the house, refused to receive the Fremonts in their homes, abused them both publicly and privately. Angry letters arrived from their friends and relatives in the South with whom they had had the closest bonds. Tom Benton, his shoulders bent, his big head covered by only a few wisps of white hair, was starting out on a lecture tour to warn the public that the South was working itself toward dissolution of the Union by force, that the moderate-thinking people in every section of the land must awaken to the dangers involved, must work together to prevent disunity.

She had not realized before how southern a city Washington was; despite the fact that there were representatives from every section of the United States, the proslavery element dominated the city: its tone, its manner, its thinking, even its press. The air was filled with hatred, vituperation and impending violence; no home could be kept free from it; few discussions, no matter how peaceably they started, but ended in curses and bad blood. After a particularly harsh outburst, she held a conference with her husband.

"John, is there any particular reason why we must remain in Washington? Do you have important business here that necessitates our living in the capital?"

"On the contrary, Jessie," he replied, "it seems to me that there is no business being transacted here at all except the war over slavery."

"Then could we go somewhere else to live? A northern city, where the people feel as we do? I haven't wanted to complain, but neither the walls of this bedroom nor the walls of this little cottage have been stout enough to keep out the quarrels."

"Don't think I haven't worried about that, Jessie," he answered. "There isn't a square inch in Washington where you can avoid them. I always loved this city, but now I am uneasy here."

"We have so little left, the city is so changed, our home has burned down, so many of our old friends hate us now . . ."

"How soon do you think you could move, and where would you like to live?"

"I would like to move tomorrow, and I'd like to live in New York. That seems the most cosmopolitan of our cities; there we can be with our own kind of people and at least avoid the more personal aspects of this controversy."

She was astonished to see how few possessions they had. It took only two days to pack them in trunks and move to New York. They rented a house on Ninth Street, near Fifth Avenue. It was three stories high with a parlor overlooking the street and a good-sized dining room behind. Going up from the entrance hall was a rather narrow flight of stairs which led to three bedrooms. Jessie considered herself fortunate in the furnishings, for they were light and cheerful maple pieces, with marine oil paintings on the walls.

Lily attended the neighboring public school. Charlie, now four years old, was sent to a day nursery. Maylee came along ostensibly to cook for Jessie and John, but actually because she had lost her heart to little Frank. Joshaam joined the family, but his twin remained with Eliza and Tom Benton in Washington. Just as she had taken special joy in Charlie because that love encompassed her love for Benton who was gone, Jessie now found that her love for hazel-eyed, robust little Frank had an added intensity because she wanted to lavish on him all the love that would have gone to the little Parisienne.

She found that New York was not as peaceful as she had expected, but at least the agitation came from people with whom she agreed. In the late spring of 1855 she took a cottage at Siasconset, Nantucket, in order to escape the summer heat of the city. John left on his trip to the Mariposa, certain that he would be back by September. Her father accepted her invitation to spend some months in the seaside cottage with his three grandchildren.

The afternoons were spent on the beach; each evening they worked together on the *Thirty Years*. But the hour Jessie found the most vital of the day was at four o'clock when Maylee served tea on the porch overlooking the road. Tom had the leading New York, Boston, Washington, St. Louis and Charleston papers delivered to the cottage; he was greatly exercised at the growth of the new Republican party, which had been started in Wisconsin almost a year before and was sweeping the country with an evangelical fervor, bringing into its midst former Whigs, whose party was now dead, as well as great blocks of northern Democrats who had watched Franklin Pierce permit the Democratic party to serve the southern slave interests.

"Why are you so incensed at the Republicans, Father?" she queried. "Our government is based on a two-party system, and everyone knows that the Whigs are completely disorganized."

"Granted, granted," boomed Tom, whose voice had not subsided with the passage of the decades. "We need a second party, but it should be national in character, not geographic and factional. The Republicans will become a purely northern party, a solidly anti-slavery party . . ."

". . . that sounds strange coming from as old an opponent of slavery as you, Papa."

". . . which will set the North and South solidly against each other. Once this split becomes political as well as geographic, nothing will stop a civil war."

Jessie poured her father a third cup of tea, but it had grown so cold that Tom took one sip and then laid down the cup. She sorted her thoughts carefully before speaking. "It will be the slavery issue that will cause the war, Papa, not the formation of the new party."

"Again granted, but you know, Jessie, it has been my lifelong hope to settle this slavery question without force or violence. The Republican party will throw the quarrel so sharply into focus that, should they win the election in 1856, the South would secede from the Union."

He rose, feeling chilled now that the sun had gone down, started for his room, his big head sunk on his chest. Before he reached the door he turned around and said with almost resigned quietness, "Ah, Jessie, we are in for bad times. My only hope is that this Republican party will die out as fast as it came in."

"Frankly, Father," she said brusquely, "I don't follow your reasoning. You know perfectly well that the Democratic party is dominated by the southern politicians. They will never nominate anyone who does not favor slavery or who will not fight for its extension."

"Then we lifetime Democrats must try to get control of the party; we must not burn down the barn just to get rid of the rats."

She smiled at the astuteness of the political phrase. "I don't think the Republicans are barn burners, Father; if they will nominate a real anti-slavery candidate, I think John will vote for him."

In August, S. N. Carvalho arrived with a present for Jessie, a copy of the book that had just come off the press about his trip with Colonel Fremont on the fifth expedition. Carvalho, the first photographer to accompany a transcontinental expedition, had produced many wonderful and accurate plates. He stayed for luncheon, after which the talk turned to politics.

"Did you know, Mrs. Fremont," asked Carvalho, "that the men of the fifth expedition have already picked their next candidate for president?"

"Really? Who is the unfortunate man?"

"Colonel Fremont."

"Colonel Fremont!" she exclaimed in astonishment. "How ever did that happen?"

"Very simply. We were camping on the Saline Fork of the Kansas River waiting for the colonel to rejoin us after his bad leg had taken him back to St. Louis. One evening while eating buffalo steaks around the campfire, we were discussing who the next president should be; the thought suddenly came to me: Colonel Fremont! I put him in nomination right then and there."

Amused, Jessie asked, "How was the nomination received?"

"With acclamation! He was the first choice of every man in that camp."

She sat up that night reading Carvalho's book, touched by the tribute paid to John:

In all the varied scenes of vicissitude, of suffering and excitement, during a voyage when the natural character of a man is sure to be developed, Colonel Fremont never forgot he was a gentleman; not an oath, no boisterous ebullitions of temper . . . Calmly and collectedly he gave his orders, and they were invariably fulfilled to the utmost of the men's abilities. The greatest etiquette and deference were always paid to him, although he never ostensibly required it. Yet his reserved and exceptionable deportment demanded from us the same respect with which we were always treated and which we ever took pleasure in reciprocating.

In early September Tom Benton returned to Washington to open a tour at the National Theatre in the capital. Some ten days later Jessie received a telegram from John telling her that he had returned safely to New York and would remain there only long enough to take care of imperative business.

Four months after he had left for California, she saw her husband walking briskly up the road. She was sitting on the front porch having midafternoon tea with her children; John stopped for a moment as though to survey the scene, then hastened to her. From the bottom of the five wooden steps he said, "You all make a very lovely picture; I think I'll just gaze at it for a while and let it sink in."

But Lily and Charlie scrambled out of their chairs and down the stairs to throw themselves upon him; he came up with one child under each arm to embrace her. Jessie noted that there was something unusual about his demeanor, something over and above his joy and excitement at being home with his family again. There was a glint behind his eyes, his mouth seemed to want to laugh. He sat bemused in his chair, answering the children's rapid-fire questions, interweaving stories of his trip with conditions at the Mariposa.

It was almost five when they had finished tea. Lily and Charlie ran around

to the ocean side of the house to play in the sand. The words for which
Jessie had been waiting almost an hour at last came from his lips.

"Could you put on a wrap and walk with me up the beach? We might go
as far as the lighthouse."

5

They left the house by the back door, tried the dry sand first but found it
too yielding, then went down to the water's edge and walked along the damp
hard-packed sand from which the tide had just receded. They were bareheaded, the offshore breeze blowing their hair. Jessie slipped her hand into
his, the hand into which hers fitted so intimately; she could feel the thoughts
pounding through his head, yet she made no attempt to hurry him. They
turned a sharp curve of the beach; the sinking sun glared full in their eyes.
He chose this moment to begin.

"Jessie," he murmured, "I've been offered the nomination for the presidency."

She stopped in her tracks, feeling the dampness of the cold sand through
the soles of her shoes.

"That's what Carvalho said!"

"Carvalho?"

"Yes, he was here the other day to leave a copy of his book. He told me
that your men nominated you for the presidency while encamped on the
Kansas River."

"This second nomination is more official; I've just come from a conference
at the St. Nicholas Hotel with the recognized leaders of the Democratic party.
They strongly urged me to accept the nomination, and are positive we can win
the election."

Impulsively she flung her arms around her husband. When she disengaged
herself her eyes were sparkling with joy and gratification.

"Would you like to be First Lady, Jessie?" he asked softly. "You would
be the most charming mistress the White House has had since Dolly Madison."

"Of course I would like the opportunity," she cried. "What woman
wouldn't? I'm even conceited enough to think I might fill it rather well. I
have watched the White House grow from a cold, water-logged, miasmic
little house in a swamp, where the president had to pay for his own heating
and lights, until it has become the beautiful mansion that it is today. During
the eight years that Jackson lived there we used to have dinner *en famille*
and romp through the rooms playing games. When Martin Van Buren was
elected I always went to his son's birthday parties and his first dances. Nancy
Polk and I had been friends during all the years that her husband was a
senator, and when she moved into the White House we went calling just as we
had when she was in her own home."

John took a quick glance at her flushed face, then said: "We've had bad luck with our First Ladies: poor Rachel Jackson was slandered to death by Henry Clay in that filthy campaign of 1828; she never got a chance to reign over the White House; Mrs. Van Buren was so terribly formal that the White House ceased to be what Jackson called it, 'The People's House.' Nancy Polk was pleasant as First Lady, but poor Franklin Pierce's wife has been mentally ill and has never received anyone. It's high time we had a First Lady who could carry on Anne Royall's work. There is a great deal you could do for the women of this country, Jessie; fight for their causes, help them progress, fulfill the modern ideas of a woman's place."

"It is good of you to put the emphasis on me, John, but the committee is not nominating me; it is nominating you. You will make a splendid president; I can see an era of building for this country the like of which we've never had. I can see railroads pushing out to the west coast, national roads, new cities rising on the ashes of your campfires."

The sun had gone down. Darkness was falling rapidly. Up ahead they could see the revolving beam of the lighthouse which stood on the edge of a promontory.

"Yes, it would be wonderful," he agreed. "But there are costs."

"Costs?" She quickened her pace, as though this would quicken the tempo of their discussion. "What are they asking of you?"

"We must approve the Fugitive Slave Law. We have to work for the extension of the Kansas-Nebraska Act."

The wind went out of her sails; her feet began to drag along the cold sand.

"Ah," she murmured. "We must approve of slavery! We must work for the spread of slavery in what are now free states and territories!"

"The Whigs are dying on their feet; the Republicans are too new to count; the Democratic nominee must certainly win. But no man can be nominated by the Democratic party who will not protect slave interests."

It was dark now. The sea air grew cold. Jessie wrapped her coat more securely about her to lock out the chill.

"How did they happen to choose you, John? The southern Democrats know that you're a free-soiler, that you fought for the admission of California as a free state. Why do they choose you to protect their slave interests?"

"Apparently because I would be a good compromise candidate, both geographically and ideologically. You and I were born in the South, we have strong connections there. We are also well known in the West. The free-soilers and many of the Whigs would vote for me because they know I helped to get California admitted as a free state; they would assume that I would work for free soil in the new territories. At the same time, if I publicly avow the Fugitive Slave Law and the Kansas-Nebraska Act, the slavery factions have nothing to fear from me because I have committed myself to work for their interests."

"In other words, in voting for you both factions would be voting for mutually exclusive hopes."

"Quite."

They had reached the beginning of the rocky promontory; they climbed over the sharp, ragged stones and paused at the base of the lighthouse tower. Just beneath them lay the wooden hulk of a submerged wreck; above, the circular light flashed out its message to warn all seafarers. They selected two of the flatter rocks and sat huddled together, two small, quiet figures merging into the darkness and the rocks behind them. She waited for her husband to declare himself, but he remained quiet.

"How do you feel about all this, John," she asked. "The burdens of a country facing a civil war would fall on your shoulders."

He turned and smiled his wistful, poignant smile.

"I want you to be First Lady," he said. "I would like to see you mistress of the White House. It is a role for which you have been preparing all your life. There is no woman in America today so qualified to do a glorious job." He took her hand and laid it alongside his cheek. "You have gone through a great deal for me, Jessie. You have endured agonies of the mind and the flesh. I have dragged you through quarrels and scandals and disease-ridden frontiers. Always you have stood by my side, backed me even when I have been wrong. Yes, my dear, I've known for a long time how wrong I was to resign from the Army after the court-martial; now that I have the opportunity of becoming president I have the courage to confess to you how utterly headstrong I was, how dominated by false pride. But you did not fight me, you did not force me to go your way, even though it was the right way, even though you knew how much we would have to endure if I resigned. It was I who cost you your first son. I know all you endured in San Francisco in those lonely months while I left you in the sand dunes and tried to hack out enough gold from the Mariposa to give me security for the rest of my life, a security which would have defeated those promises and hopes set in motion that day in Hassler's workroom. I know that in the past few years I have been giving my time and energy to a business which you thought purposeless. Yet you've been patient, you've gone along with me when I've been wasteful of our years and our dreams . . ."

"Because I always had confidence that eventually . . ."

"Could this serve as the eventuality you've been hoping for, Jessie? I can be president of the United States and you can be First Lady. I owe you that for everything you've been through; I owe it to you for the love you've given me. I have never given you a real home; the White House could be your home. I haven't given you the position in society you deserve; this could be my way of letting the rest of the world know you are truly the first lady of your times."

She was quiet for several moments, breathing deeply, feeling unfathomable emotion, watching the slow-moving light as it illumined for a moment the succeeding spokes of dark water.

"In order to see me First Lady," she said almost hoarsely, "you would go against your lifetime principles? You would issue the orders through which runaway slaves would be dragged back in chains to their bondage? You would permit slavery to extend to free Kansas and all the thousands of miles of free land between there and southern California?"

He did not reply.

"John," she cried, "I want to be the president's wife. Looking back now, I guess I've always hoped I would be. Maybe there is some way we can work this out: if they don't nominate you, they'll nominate an out-and-out slavery man, won't they? Surely it would be better to have a free-soiler in the White House, though he made temporary concessions, than to have a slavery man who will work every hour to extend the borders of slave territory."

"There is logic in what you say."

"We know how angry the North and South will grow, John, and how bitter; perhaps only a compromise candidate can keep the country from civil war. Perhaps you are the man to do that; you have friends in the South as well as the North and the West. You can pour oil on troubled waters, keep the North and South from each other's throat. Father says that no cotton can be grown in Kansas or any of the other states in the Midwest and Southwest, that the southerners who take slaves there will be obliged to send them back. As for the Fugitive Slave Law, the Underground Railroad is growing so effective that the South will find it too difficult and too expensive to retrieve its runaways. The Democrats have picked you as a compromise candidate; perhaps you too can make a compromise, John, and spend the next four years in the White House keeping the country at peace."

"You make a good case, Jessie," he said softly; "those are compromises I could make. Will you stand by that attitude? Can you continue to justify it? Your father would say that it would be the wise thing to do. Do you agree with him? Or have you built this case to make it easy for me to compromise?"

She turned full face to him; even in the darkness they could see each other plainly. Should she not sacrifice her own feelings for his sake, brave the storms of criticism and abuse which would be hurled at them by their former comrades? Would there not be compensations, advances she could make for the women of the country which would recompense for such compromises? Her main ambition had always been to help her husband achieve his highest potential; where better to achieve it than as president of the United States, a president who loved both the North and the South, who would bind up the wounds of the nation, strive for peace and friendship?

As a woman in love, she must help her man reach the uttermost peak of position and achieve the highest attainable goal. But as a wife creating a marriage which would survive even after their deaths, which would go on even longer than their children or grandchildren, must she not help her husband realize his greatest spiritual potential? Must marriage be baldly opportunistic, crawling ever upward on its hands and knees over dead rocks and dead timber, dead ideals and dead friends? Or was marriage an intense flame which devoured the dross in the husband and wife, leaving only what was pure and fine?

"I could be willing to make these compromises, John, only if you wanted them made. I won't try to conceal from you that I want to see you inaugurated president of the United States . . ."

"You scrubbed your own floors and washed your own dishes in Monterey rather than buy a slave . . ."

" . . . you refused to buy slaves to work your mines even though you could have become a millionaire by doing so and found that security you were so frantically seeking. During those early days in Monterey when the delegates were arguing slavery over our dinner table, I won sympathy for freedom by demanding how they would like to have their children watch fugitive slaves being returned in irons. Can we support a slavery law in 1856 which we utilized to support freedom in 1850?"

They sat silently in the darkness. She knew how much it meant to him to become president, for then the last would be the first, the bastard would be king. It would be a thousand times more difficult for him to give up this opportunity than for any other man. But the price he must pay to become president was critically high: for approving the Fugitive Slave Law and the Kansas-Nebraska Act the abolitionists and all those against slavery would despise him as a turncoat, one who had sold out for the highest possible offer. The Democrats would despise him as a weakling, an opportunist whom they could use for their own purposes.

She wanted to be First Lady; but even more she wanted to remain true to the fundamental beliefs and convictions of their lifetime.

She felt that John would be wrong, terribly wrong, in accepting the nomination under these conditions. Yet if he had his heart set on becoming president, how could she thwart him? He had said that he wanted her to be First Lady, that he would pay almost any price to see her mistress of the White House. But it was a price she did not want him to pay.

She knew that just as she had sustained him when he had determined to resign from the Army, she must sustain him now if he wished to resign from his fight against slavery. Resolutely she turned to her husband and said, "You must speak frankly to me. You have had many hours in which to think things over and resolve your doubts. I will approve of your decision whichever way you make it. But you must not put the burden of the decision on me. It is you who must either decide to be president or renounce the opportunity."

"Very well, Jessie, you have asked for a categorical answer, and I shall give it to you. Coming up on the train I asked myself, 'Does every man have his price? Have I reached the breaking point?' "

She watched him stare out to sea for a moment, then he said, "We have a clear choice: we can either serve as this beacon light, flashing a message of freedom to all those at sea, or we can smash our ideals against the rocks, like that battered hulk of a ship beneath us."

"Then you are willing to forego the opportunity?"

"There has never been any doubt in my mind. I would have taken the nomination for your sake, my dear, but I never wanted it."

"John," she murmured, "do you know what picture comes to my mind? It is of your second expedition, when you were trapped in the Sierras, when nothing but death awaited you, and yet you had the courage to force a passage where lesser men would have fallen. This crossing tonight was even more hazardous for you, yet you have made it safely and blazed a new trail. If you had been willing to pay the price to be president, I would have gone along with the case for compromise; but, my dear, you have been of greater value to your country in this last hour, you have done more for the cause of freedom than you could have in four years in the White House. I am proud of you, and I love you very much. I am ready now to go back to those two rooms at Madame Castro's in Monterey, or to the barrack on the sand dunes in San Francisco. I can be perfectly happy and contented."

She was cold and cramped from their awkward position. Her husband helped her along the rocks to the shore. They walked back in the soft, dry sand, slowly, not speaking, not touching, yet in complete union. Just before they reached the house, he stopped and took her in his arms.

"The Democratic chairman at the St. Nicholas Hotel said that no woman could refuse the presidency. That is why I did not want to deny it to you. But he was wrong; he didn't know my Jessie."

6

On the first of October they moved back to their house on Ninth Street in New York City. The air was sharp and invigorating, but even more invigorating was the temper of the times. She was intensely interested in watching the mass meetings against slavery, the growing partisanship of the press, but above all the spontaneous growth of the Republican party in all parts of the North and West. The leaders of the Republican party knew that they could not elect either a platform or an idea in the 1856 campaign. They would have to elect a man. Since their party was young, they wanted a young candidate; since their entrance into politics was new, they wanted a candidate new to national politics; since they were an exploring party which must blaze new trails across the wilderness of political confusion, they wanted a trail blazer; since their platform was to be based on the romantic notion of universal freedom, they needed a romantic figure; since their fight for freedom was to be heroic, they needed a heroic figure; since they were so little known, they would need a universally known figure; and finally, since this election would create in embryo a geographic and ideological war, they needed a man of indomitable courage, one whose spirit and will to conquer would not flag in the most desperate passes.

Though neither John nor Jessie had publicized their rejection of the Democratic nomination, word of this dedication to principle made its way through political circles. John was young, only forty-three. He was new to national politics; he had few passionate enemies, was not beaten and battered by years of political quarrels. He was a trail blazer, nationally known and admired, a man of superb courage, a romantic figure. Yet all these seemingly obvious virtues might have remained hidden had not the Democrats offered him the nomination first; by so doing they virtually set up their opposition: if the Democrats had been so positive that John Fremont could win, why could he not win for the Republicans as well?

The intimation that John might become the Republican nominee was first brought to them when a committee composed of Francis Blair and his son, Frank, Nathaniel P. Banks, Senator Henry Wilson of Massachusetts, Joseph Palmer, head of Palmer, Cook & Company, and Senator John P. Hale of New Hampshire called at the house on Ninth Street. While Jessie, in a violet-colored silk gown with a flattering cowled neck, served tea and cinnamon toast, the unofficial delegation urged John not to take his family to California, but to remain in New York for a series of conferences with the Republican leaders of other states who were traveling back and forth in the intense excitement surrounding the birth of a new and radical movement. When the gentlemen had finished their discussion and had left the Fremont parlor heavy with bluish cigar smoke, Jessie asked, "Can the Republicans win?"

"I didn't think so a few days ago. But if the enthusiasm of those men is indicative of the feeling in the North and West, they have a chance."

"Are you willing to take this nomination even if they have no chance?"

"I don't think we have any right to demand a guarantee of success. If this is our fight, then we must participate in it. It's the waging of the battle that is important. Even if the Republicans lose in 1856, it may be a victory for them in that they will have established their party and created a real chance to win in 1860. No battle can be viewed by itself, but only in relation to an entire campaign; sometimes battles that were lost in the beginning are the very ones which insure victory in the end. Our refusal to join battle last month when the Democrats offered us the nomination has put us in a strategic position today."

"Father always said that the office should seek the man, not the man the office. Since the nomination is seeking you, you can take it with a full heart and with full confidence. Your name would help the growth of the party. If anyone can win for the Republicans, you can."

In quiet times, party agitation began only a couple of months before the conventions; but these were troubled times, and by November of 1855, a whole year before the election, the newspapers were full of political maneuvers and potential candidates. Jessie subscribed to the newspapers of every major city in the North and the West; she was able to show her husband that the idea of his leading the Republican party was spreading like a prairie fire. Other candidates were mentioned, veterans like William H. Seward, Salmon P. Chase, Judge John McLean, who had worked long and hard against slavery; but this very fact made them unavailable: they had made too many enemies, there was too much that could be charged against them.

At a national committee meeting held at Silver Spring in December, Francis Preston Blair and such other important national figures as Charles Sumner, Preston King, Nathaniel P. Banks, Salmon Chase, Dr. Bailey and a host of others agreed that John Fremont was the one and only man who could lead the Republican party to victory. Francis Blair said that he would take full charge of the campaign if John were nominated; his dynamic son, Frank, vowed that he would organize a speakers' bureau which would carry John's name to every hamlet in America.

With the turn of the year the Fremont home on Ninth Street became the semiofficial headquarters of the Republicans in New York City; hardly a day went by but there were ten or twenty guests at luncheon, tea or dinner. Seeing Joshaam adding wooden horses and planks to the moderate-sized dinner table brought a glow to Jessie's eyes as she thought back to the best years in the Benton home, when so many of the political issues were formulated over its long mahogany dining table. This unceasing ferment in her household was meat and drink to her; she kept her thirteen-year-old daughter in the midst of things so that she would have the same training she had had in Washington. Joshaam served Lily only the tiniest portions, for the daughter, like the mother, could not eat while arguments were obscuring the beef or the chicken pies. After the last of the company had left, Jessie and Lily would go into the kitchen, rewarm the food that Maylee had left for them, and discuss the politics that had been reviewed during the course of the evening.

At the end of the first week in March, after a number of confidential meetings, John assured his wife there could be little doubt about his receiving the nomination. Jessie turned her mind to the one problem she had been avoiding: Tom Benton was making a last-ditch stand against the Republican party, as he had told her that he would at Siasconset the summer before. What would he say now that it was his son-in-law who would be named to head the new party? Surely this would make matters appear in a different light, cause him to change his viewpoint?

She went alone to Washington to reveal the news to her father. Eliza had made him comfortable in a combination bedroom and study, where he was surrounded by books and papers loaned by his former colleagues. Tom Benton was seventy-four years of age. Neither the spirit nor the will had flagged, but his physical empire, which he had all but lost when he was twenty, was crumbling under the ravages of time. The pleasure in Tom Benton's face at seeing her made her errand the more difficult.

She closed the door of the library behind her and said abruptly, "Father, John has been assured of the Republican nomination for the presidency."

His jaw set and his face solidified into the stubborn mask she knew so well from the days when he was fighting with all his strength against Biddle's Bank of the United States. He walked to a leather armchair which Eliza had bought for him, sat down heavily and shaded his eyes with the great paw of his left hand, a hand which only lately had become marked with brownish spots. She stood before him, uncertain.

"Aren't you glad, Father?" she asked. "You were so proud of John when he turned down the Democratic nomination. Why aren't you proud when he is chosen by the freedom party?"

Tom Benton dropped his hand wearily to his lap; as the daughter and father looked deep into each other's eyes there passed before both of them the panorama of their years together.

"I am proud that John has become one of the outstanding figures of his time," he said hoarsely; "but he must not accept the Republican nomination. That would be even worse than taking the Democratic offer."

She could only exclaim, "But why, Papa? There is no one in the country more ardently opposed to the extension of slavery than you. The Republicans will keep slavery from spreading."

"If that were all they were going to do, I would back them with my remaining strength. But they are purely a geographical party, Jessie; they will split the nation in two."

"It is a geographical party because the slaveholding states won't join it. They'll never be anything but Democratic. New England, the East, the Middle West, and the West are against slavery; they'll vote for John and the Republican party."

"If they do, Jessie, they'll be voting not for John but for civil war. Mark my words, if John accepts the Republican nomination and is elected, he will be responsible for plunging the nation into bloodshed. I know that neither he nor you want to do this. If you were determined to become First Lady at any price, then you should have accepted the Democratic offer: you would have had to endorse slavery, perhaps even extend it a little, but you would not have caused the secession of the South."

There was a knock at the door. Josheem came in with coffee, scones and the blackberry jam which he knew Jessie liked. She shook hands with the tall and lanky Negro, glad to see him again.

"We miss you in Washington, Miss Jessie," he said with a wide grin. "When you all comin' back here to live?"

"About the fourth of next March," she replied with a half-smile as she glanced at her father.

"You goin' to take a house here, Miss Jessie?"

"I understand the White House is for rent, Josheem. But Father doesn't think I ought to take a lease on it; he says the water still gathers in the kitchen during the rainy season, and everybody who lives there gets miasma."

His eyes wide with wonder, Josheem murmured, "Why, Miss Jessie, there ain't been no water in the kitchen in the White House since President Jackson left, and the swamps was all drained years ago. If'n you got a chance to move into that White House, don't you be afeared of anything: Mammy Maylee, Joshaam and I will keep it warm and dry."

Tom Benton dismissed him with a wave of his hand.

"You are right, Jessie," he said harshly. "The White House will be filled with miasma if the Republicans get in. I most strongly advise you not to let John accept the nomination."

"And if he does accept?"

"Then I'll oppose his election. I'll stump the country warning people that they must not put a factional party into the White House."

She was aghast. "You mean you would campaign against your own son-in-law?"

"I would be obliged to. It would not be easy, Jessie, but then, not many things in my life have been easy."

She picked up her coffee cup, walked to the front window and stood staring out, not seeing the houses opposite but rather the face of her husband, visualizing how she would have to tell him that her father was renouncing him. She gulped the coffee, hot and black, and thought numbly how the tables had turned: When John resigned from the Army, Father expected my support; he had every right to expect it, but I failed to say that John must not do so. Now that I have every right to expect him to support me, he refuses to do so. I had my reasons eight years ago; Father has his reasons now; how miserable it is when a daughter and father must oppose each other.

She went to her father's chair and, with an affectionate gesture, brushed back with her fingers the remaining strands of his white hair.

"Will the country interpret this as a political gesture, Papa, or will they feel it a personal repudiation on the part of Tom Benton towards his son-in-law?"

"I long ago gave up the futile pursuit of trying to determine in advance what people will think."

"Won't the public be right in saying, 'If a man's father-in-law is against him, how can you expect strangers to be for him?' "

"Frankly I don't know," he replied with a touch of coolness. "John has had no political training aside from his three weeks in the Senate; his background has been scientific; it would be a tremendous gamble to put in the White House a man as innocent of political experience as he. I believe in his integrity; I know his capacity for work, and I am convinced there is no more courageous man in America today. I don't know whether he would make a good president in these bitterly partisan and angry times. But even if I did know, I would not vote for him or anyone else, no matter what genius he might have for the presidency, if he were running on a divisionist ticket. If John had taken the Democratic nomination, I would have campaigned for him."

"I see; even though he would be committing himself to a program in which none of us believed, you would have campaigned for him! You would have backed a man who had sold himself for a high offer."

"My dear," her father replied, shrugging, "your husband's idealism is a luxury to me. I care only about the peace of the nation, of the North and South getting along in friendship, and the Union being preserved. If John had been elected as a Democrat, there would be no fear of civil war. If he is elected as a Republican . . ."

She came behind her father's chair, put her arms about his neck, laid her cheek on the white hairs over his temple. "Father, you always said no matter what happened, we must stand together. Please don't desert me now."

Something in her voice, something overstrained, caught his ear. He reached up, took one of her hands, drew her around to him. Then he searched her face carefully, trying to read what lay behind her eyes.

"I know you're not doing all this for yourself," he said softly. "If you had wanted to be First Lady, you could have persuaded John to accept the Democratic nomination. Then why are you doing it now? What is there in the situation that goes beyond politics? You owe me full honesty, Jessie."

For a moment her eyes wavered, her head sunk down. Then she said, "I thought I would never tell this to anyone, but now I know I must. You see, Father, John is not . . . not exactly . . . like other men. He has scars across his mind. Those scars are why he sometimes does things that you cannot understand, and they are why I have sometimes agreed with his judgments even against your superior reasoning . . ."

". . . such as the time you let him resign from the Army?"

"Yes. John's mother was married at seventeen to a man over sixty . . . After twelve years of unhappiness, she met John's father, Charles Frémon, and ran away with him. She told John there was a marriage ceremony performed, but her husband was apparently unable to secure a divorce from the Virginia legislature—and so the Frémon marriage would have been illegal in any event. John was a . . . a natural child."

Tom stared at his daughter, dumbfounded.

"Illegitimate," he murmured. "Why, I had no idea . . . Jessie, how long have you known this?"

"John told me before we were married. He thought I might want to break our engagement."

"By the Eternal," he whispered to himself. "How has this been kept from me all these years? Why has no one ever told me?"

"Because they would have been frightened for their lives."

"Does anyone else know? How common is this knowledge?"

"It's well known in the South," she replied frankly. "It would have been impossible to conceal . . . Now you can see, Father, why I don't want to inflict any more scars upon him. Another man, perhaps, might understand it as a purely political question; John may take it personally; it may embitter his relationship with you."

Tom began stalking the small, crowded room.

"Then I am a thousand times more right than before, Jessie," he exclaimed. "You must not allow John to expose himself. This campaign is going to be the bitterest and most violent since Andrew Jackson beat Henry Clay in '28. When people are on the verge of a civil war, they care nothing about personal feelings. His illegitimate birth will be spread from one end of the nation to the other; it will create a frightful scandal. Think of the slander and the mud that will be flung."

"John will know why the Democrats are slinging mud at him; he can rise above the tumult because he will understand its objective. But he has loved you and you have loved him; if you abandon him there will be no way for him to understand."

"Jessie, even if you are willing to expose yourself to this scandal, have you no consideration for your three children? Are you willing to have them go through life bearing the burden of your political ambitions?"

"I know that you love Lily and Charlie and Frank. If you are fearful lest these charges hurt their position in the world, then back John in this fight, help put him in the White House. The children of a president need never fear for their social position."

Tom Benton sat down heavily. Jessie knew that she had taken an unfair advantage. After a pause, he dropped the hand that had been veiling his eyes; she saw that he had been crying in the peculiar way in which old men cry without shedding tears.

"Jessie, my dear," he said, "nothing but the death of your mother and your brother has hurt me as much as this: but I still must turn against you. I don't have long to live now, and I can't go to my grave feeling that I played a part in bringing on civil war. You have me caught in the dilemma between loyalty to my family and loyalty to my country; it's a miserable and painful decision for any man to have to make, particularly for a man who has loved you as devotedly as I have. As deeply as I have loved you, Jessie, I also loved my seat in the United States Senate. I don't need to tell you that it was the backbone of my life, the justification of my existence. Yet I gave it up to fight for the admission of California as a free state. I can break, Jessie; I am almost at the breaking point now, but I cannot bend. I want to see you in the White House; that would bring joy and solace to my last years, seeing my little Jessie as the First Lady of the land. It's hard to give up, perhaps even harder than giving up my desk in the Senate four years ago. But I can't approve the election of John as a Republican, even though it will put you in the White House, for I know that it will disrupt the Union. Please forgive me, my dear. I am an old and stubborn man, but I must stand by my lifetime faith. You would not ask me to do otherwise."

When she returned to New York and related her father's decision to her husband, John said softly: "Your father has fought so many fights for me, he is entitled to wage one against me. I wish he hadn't chosen this particular time and issue, but Tom Benton was always one to pick his own battles."

They were pleased when the Democrats nominated James Buchanan on the seventeenth ballot: he was a northerner, had never owned a slave, never publicly favored slavery, had a superb background of training in the federal government; no one knew better than Jessie his scrupulousness of ethic. They agreed that he was a good choice, for as an experienced diplomat, a born compromiser, he would strive to find new and effective means of appeasing the firebrands of both factions.

She went alone to the Republican convention in Philadelphia because John did not consider it proper for a potential candidate to mingle with the delegates. She arrived by train on the afternoon of June 16, and was at Musical Fund Hall by eleven o'clock the next morning. As she took her seat in the front row of the visitors' gallery she was struck by the evangelical nature of the assembly, for this was no routine, prearranged party machine politicking. The thousand delegates milling about on the floor of Musical Fund Hall were dominated by a religious fervor; in their eyes was the gleam of the crusader for freedom. It was a heterogeneous throng, clothed in everything from the striped trousers of northern society to the buckskin pants of the western frontier. To Jessie it seemed nothing less than a miracle that a single idea could pervade and dominate this assemblage, yet when David Wilmot mounted the platform and enunciated the dominant issues of the Republican platform—unalterable opposition to the extension of slavery, denial of the power of Congress to legalize slavery within the new territories, the continuance of the Missouri Compromise, the admission of Kansas as a free state—the convention rose as one man, shouting its tremendous faith in freedom for all the peoples of America. As Jessie watched the newspaper reporters writing at top speed to carry the news of this revolutionary convention to the country, she remembered the reporters who had sat each day at the court-martial carrying the account of John's trial to the nation. She recognized a number of these men as the same ones who had covered the Washington assignment, and who were now going to tell the nation of the choice of the young, vigorous, progressive Republicans.

She expected that John would be unanimously nominated on the first ballot; however, he gathered only 359 votes, while Judge McLean of Ohio had 196 votes. She was astonished at the strength shown by McLean; for a moment her confidence faltered. But David Wilmot, who had won over the convention by his reading of their platform, sprang up and made a mighty plea for unanimity behind John Fremont. The pandemonium that followed almost drowned out the count of votes, but she saw by the pad in her lap that her husband now had 529 votes and was the first presidential nominee of the new party. While the band played its loudest, the thousand delegates and the visitors in the gallery roared their cheers and acclamations deafeningly. The clamor reached its height when a huge banner was strung across the platform reading:

FREE SPEECH, FREE PRESS, FREE SOIL, FREE MEN,
FREMONT AND VICTORY

She sat quietly in her seat in the midst of the impassioned ones about her who were throwing their hats and handkerchiefs and newspapers into the air, while the tears rolled down her cheeks. She supposed it was unworthy of her, but her happiness at this moment of wild acclaim bore little relation to politics, elections or even to such profound issues as slavery and the impregnability of the Union. While the thousand zealots about her saw in the nomination of John Fremont the end of slavery in the United States, Jessie Fremont could feel only as a woman and a wife. The fact that her husband was the outstanding figure in the United States justified not only her original judgment and faith in him, but the design of their marriage. In fifteen years he had risen from an obscure second lieutenant in the Topographical Corps to become the leader of the greatest movement in America since the Revolution. His prominence, his importance, his success were not due solely to his accomplishments, nor were they attributable to anything she had done to help him; they had come about as a result of their collaboration, they were symbolic of the strength and solidity and intelligence of the marriage the two of them had created. Either of them alone might have achieved interesting results; the two of them together in an ordinary marital relationship doubtless would have prospered; but it was their dedication to this marriage that had inspired them to good work, preserved them under desperate difficulties, enabled them to strive ever upward. They had made errors of overzealousness, but never had their failures or shortcomings arisen from a lack of faith or interest in each other, the task at hand, or their marriage. To her intensely feminine mind it was this marriage which was now being nominated to serve as president, to reside in the White House.

As she watched the delegates marching with frenzied joy, chanting, "Free Speech, Free Press, Free Soil, Free Men, Fremont and Victory!" she knew that by the grace of God she had succeeded far better than she had envisaged in her wildest dreams.

Only the year before, they had left Washington believing they no longer belonged there. Now they would move back with bands playing and flags flying; the hearth she had failed to create in Monterey, or in the sand dunes of San Francisco, would be lighted triumphantly in the White House.

7

She was interested to find out what kind of a campaign John planned to wage, whether he would make speeches only in the key cities or would spend the months on the long swing through the country, reaching as many people as he could with his personal message. When she returned home she glowingly related every detail of the convention to her proud family. But when she asked her husband what his plans were, he replied, "I have none."

"But don't you intend to . . . ?"

"I have nothing to tell people that they don't already know, Jessie. I am against the further extension of slavery. In those few words rests the entire

campaign. The people of this country know me, they know what I think
and what I stand for. There is nothing I could tell them that would bring
them any more enlightenment or give them any more cause to vote for
me than they have now."

"California!" exclaimed Jessie. "That's exactly what you said in California when you were running for the Senate."

"Is it?"

"I guess you must have meant it the first time, if you're still holding to
it six years later."

"I didn't seek the office, Jessie; the office sought me. Then why is it either
right or necessary for me to travel through the country making rash promises or inciting the people? I can't promise them anything, and I certainly
can't fool them. Those who want to vote for me will vote for me; the others
won't."

"Very well," she agreed resignedly. "If that's the way you feel the campaign must be waged . . ."

"Now that you've brought the subject up, I can tell you further that I
don't want to become emotionally involved. I don't think that's the function
of a candidate. I think it's his job to be quiet and dignified."

"If you can do that, you're a marvel," replied Jessie, laughing; "what can
I do to help you accomplish it?"

"Act as my aide-de-camp, just as you always have while I was preparing
the expeditions, and in Washington while I was on the trail. Be my spokesman. Interview the newspaper reporters when they come, help me write the
special articles that are needed, answer the political mail . . . I'll work with
the Republican board of strategy, but I'd rather not appear in public. I don't
want to enter into a thousand arguments and quarrels, get the hysteria of
mass meetings in my blood. I think I can make my best contribution by
trying to keep tempers down, since nearly everybody else will be in a blood-
thirsty mood."

Francis Blair, who was the Republican campaign chairman, yielded to
Jessie's urging that he occupy the spare bedroom in her house. Blair was
sixty-five years old, bald except for a fringe of black and gray hair which
ran around the base of his head and stopped over his ears. He had big
bushy eyebrows which hung over and concealed much of his eyes; his
mouth and jowls had begun to break with age, but even at sixty-five he was
a gamecock of a man, an adroit strategist and last-barricade fighter. He had
been important in presidential elections ever since he had helped put Martin
Van Buren into the White House in 1836. He had frequently been called
a president maker; this time, he told John and Jessie, he was really going
to earn the title.

His younger son Frank, who had practiced law in St. Louis as a protégé
of Tom Benton's, became the roving chairman. Frank was tall, lean, fiery,
smart, with a shock of black hair, a bold black mustache which he wore
long and down the sides of his chin. Tom Benton had frequently said that

Frank Blair was like his own son, for Frank was a man of fanatical loyalties, without a shred of fear; he had fought slavery since the day he could talk, and like his father and brother Montgomery, he had written, lectured and canvassed for the development of the West. He had served in the Missouri legislature for the past four years as a Free-Soil Democrat, working hard for the formation of the Republican party in Missouri.

There had been a time when Tom Benton had hoped that Jessie would marry Frank Blair, but Frank had been only eighteen when Jessie met John Fremont.

She was delighted with her job as aide-de-camp; it was one she had been trained to fulfill, and for which she had the greatest enthusiasm. She consulted with John constantly, doing little of importance on her own responsibility, but the major burden of the work fell on her shoulders. Mail poured in from all over the country, from individuals demanding to know how John felt about every last issue. Each letter had to be answered honestly and to the point, for when it returned to Michigan or Kentucky or California it would be shown to everyone within a radius of twenty miles and would engender countless discussions. Newspaper editors would pose a list of questions at John Fremont, challenging him to answer. A frank, direct and closely reasoned statement would have to be prepared at once, to be published in the paper within a week in order that its readers might be satisfied, and no one would have an opportunity to say that candidate Fremont was afraid or unable to meet issues.

The most pleasant part of the work was the daily interviews with women reporters, the literary descendants of Anne Royall who were now taking a firm place in American journalism, beginning to wage their intensive campaigns for woman suffrage and equal rights. Though these ladies were reporting for the women's magazines and the women's pages of the newspapers, she knew the importance of the articles they would write, for few men voted for a candidate whom their wives disliked. She encouraged the women reporters to come in at teatime, and over her favorite combination of sassafras tea, spice cake, scones and blackberry jam she would answer questions about her life in California, the travels across Panama, her early years with Senator Benton of Missouri, her stay in Europe, how she envisaged the family life of the White House. For the most part these tea sessions were amiable, but occasionally there was a spirited contretemps. Unsympathetic interviewers snarled at her for serving tea in the English fashion, for wearing a loose-fitting silk housecoat instead of a black silk dress, for having two colored servants. She turned aside their brusqueness by telling how she had cooked over an open fire in her rooms in Monterey, of the year when she and Lily had only unbleached muslins of their own sewing.

Across her desk came both the plans and the evidences of the Republican fervor sweeping the nation. Campaign biographies of John, written by John Bigelow, Horace Greeley and Charles Upham, sold by the tens of thousands and were serialized in the Republican newspapers; lithographs showing his dark, serious, sensitive face could be seen in home and store windows in the North and West. The northern and western newspapers were filled with glowing accounts of the Fremont expeditions, of his qualities as a leader, with the tributes of the men who had suffered so greatly with him on the trail. Testimonials from every part of the Union sang his praises as a man of courage and character, as a leader, a student, a thinker. English and European scientists spoke of his accomplishments; university presidents, poets, clergymen, sprang forth to battle for "Free Speech, Free Press, Free Soil, Free Men, Fremont and Victory!"

Each day brought her fresh gratifications and fresh disappointments: Millard Fillmore and his Free-Soilers, who had formed a third party, were using the Republican campaign material to publicize their own party. William L. Dayton, who had been given the vice-presidential nomination against John's expressed wish, contributed nothing to the campaign. The sons of Daniel Webster and Henry Clay came out against John Fremont for fear of southern secession; important Whig leaders, such as Rufus Choate and Caleb Cushing, campaigned arduously among their fellow Whigs to vote for the long-detested Democrats on the grounds that Tom Benton had been right when he told the Missouri voters that the South would never submit to Fremont and the Republican platform. But on the same day there arrived a poem from John G. Whittier, which read:

> Rise up, Fremont, and go before;
> The hour must have its man;
> Put on the hunting shirt once more,
> And lead in Freedom's van!

Then a poem arrived from Walt Whitman, and another from Henry W. Longfellow. Most of the literary figures of the age extolled him in public print: Washington Irving, Edward Everett Hale, Ralph Waldo Emerson. So many songs were written that two musical pamphlets were published. Many of the songs stressed the differences between the gray, aged Buchanan and the youthful Fremont. The take-off on Stephen Foster's *Camptown Races* was the most popular:

> *The Mustang Colt is strong and young, Du da, du da,*
> *His wind is sound and his knees not sprung, Du da, du da day.*

> Chorus: *We're bound to work all night,*
> *We're bound to work all day,*
> *I'll bet my money on the Mustang Colt,*
> *Will anybody bet on the Gray?*

There passed over their dining-room table hundreds of letters from life-time friends and relatives in the South renouncing them forever. "Traitor" was one of the least offensive of the names called. Of these disappointments Jessie told little to John; the disavowing letters she showed him not at all. If he were to be elected, she did not want him to go into the White House with this burden of hatred and disavowal in his soul.

During the weeks of July, while the campaign machinery was beginning to roll, the opposition press restrained itself. Then, about the first of August, the one story appeared which she knew must come; it was published simultaneously in almost every Democratic paper in the country: John was publicly labeled a "French bastard." The story of his illegitimacy was spread over hundreds of columns. She would have found it bad enough had the papers been content to tell the truth, but ever new fodder was needed, and so the facts of his birth were cruelly distorted, his mother's character and life made scandalous, his father described as a French pseudo-artist and adventurer. The fury of the charges mounted day by day; the country was asked by the Democratic press if it wanted a bastard ruling over the White House; it was asked what would happen to the morals and family life of America if this tragedy should befall them, declaring that the United States would become the butt of obscene European laughter. As a climax the press suggested that the kindest thing that could be done for John Fremont would be to ship him, along with his ridiculous French beard, back to the gutters of Paris where he belonged.

Frantic at the intensity of this attack, she did her best to conceal the papers from John's eyes. When Francis Blair or his son Frank came in waving the sheets with murderous expressions on their faces, Jessie persuaded them not to discuss the matter with John, but to ignore the mudslinging. She remembered only too well her father's warning as the Democrats appeared momentarily to have abandoned the issue of slavery and to have determined to settle the election on the basis of John's paternity. She suffered most keenly over what Lily and Charlie would think when they saw the charges, for it was impossible to keep them from seeing the newspapers, and she did not feel that she could deceive them by denying the story. For a few days she thought she saw a look of reproach and unhappiness in her daughter's eyes, yet it was not long before the hardheaded and capable Lily somehow settled the matter to her own satisfaction and to her brother's. To Jessie's intense relief, neither child ever mentioned the matter to her.

One afternoon John returned from a walk with copies of several southern newspapers he had picked up on a Broadway newsstand. Her heart sank at the sight of him; though it was fifteen years later, the expression on his face was the same as he had worn when he had first told her of this illegitimacy. His skin was dark, his eyes small and hurt and withdrawn, his gestures were fraught with pain and awkward as he moved about the room; this was how he had carried himself when he had returned from California under arrest, for his torso was twisted at an ugly angle, his arms did not seem to fit their sockets.

She said in as quiet a tone as she could muster, "Surely this doesn't take you by surprise? You knew that the Democrats were desperate, that they would utilize any means at hand . . ."

"I know who started this," he replied fiercely. "It was the editor of the Charleston paper. He has provided the others with the material. Jessie, I'm going to put an end to this campaign of slander, not for my sake but for yours and the children."

"That's what they're trying to do, dear, get you so wrought up that you'll be indiscreet and provide them with more campaign ammunition. But they don't know you, John; they don't know that you're above vicious backbiting."

"I'm used to a fight in the open," he replied, partially mollified, "not one filled with innuendo and recrimination. I'll meet them on any grounds if they'll stand up and be men."

"You know, John," she continued in an impersonal tone, "I couldn't fully understand why it was that you wanted to remain aloof from the campaign; I am not sure that in the beginning I altogether approved. But now I see how completely right you were. You have the surest method of defeating them: let them expose themselves to the country in their full venality; every time they do so, they make votes for us."

His tenseness eased, the hate faded from his eyes. He sank into a chair, motioning for her to come to him.

"I've frequently heard that the aide-de-camp was a more capable strategist than his commanding officer. It's a fortunate thing that I encountered you first, Jessie, and not a southern editor . . ."

"The fault is partly yours, for you disobeyed your own orders. Why did you buy those southern papers? They won't publish your answers, and nothing you could say would change a slave vote anyway. Since there is nothing to be gained, why don't you avoid the campaign material?"

"Heaven knows I'm willing," he groaned. "I don't want to see another newspaper for a year."

"As aide-de-camp," she replied, "I will blue-pencil the newspapers, giving you only the genuinely important material. Then you can preserve your full energy for the work that needs doing."

He looked up at his wife, shaking his head in affectionate amazement.

"Do you realize what punishment you're going to take?" he asked. "In order to blue-pencil the vicious material you have to read it all first. Once those lines get into your head you can never get them out. Since when are you stronger than I, more able to endure a whipping?"

"I am not stronger, John; I'm just better able to relegate personal attacks on you to their proper place. I know they're false, I know they are intended solely to turn people against you; I will not react to them emotionally, I will be objective about their vituperation, and the wilder they grow the more frightened I will know they are becoming."

"Very well then, I will go back to my original conception: I shall read nothing except what you have edited. I shall remain calm and aloof and dignified"—he gave her a wistful smile—"even if it kills you!"

8

As in the Benton home in Washington, they occupied the back bedroom overlooking a small garden, where they occasionally found an hour of quiet and privacy. John took the front room on the second floor for his study. Three times a week a fencing master came in; the books and furniture were moved to one side and here he kept in physical form by matching rapiers with the instructors.

Instead of spending his days and weeks making campaign speeches, he assembled an extensive library on American government: there were books on the constitutional powers of the three branches, accounts of the Revolution and the convention that followed, George Bancroft's histories, biographies of the men who had played key parts in the formation of the government. He told Jessie that he needed this study to compensate for Buchanan's long experience. In the evening, if there were no guests, a big lamp would be placed in the center of the table after the dishes had been cleared, and under its light John and Lily would study their books, John annotating the margins, while Jessie answered personal letters and supplied information to newspaper editors, her pen, scratching through the hours, dipping into the inkwell with a steady motion, filling the pages of foolscap.

With the passing of the weeks the Republican cause gained momentum. Abraham Lincoln sang John's praises to ten thousand enthusiasts at Princeton and to thirty thousand at the State Fair at Alton. Demonstrations gathered: twenty-five thousand at Massillon, thirty thousand at Kalamazoo, thirty thousand at Beloit. The Tabernacle in New York was rocked by the oratory of William Cullen Bryant, Carl Schurz, Charles A. Dana, Horace Greeley, Hannibal Hamlin, Franz Sigel. Gigantic mass meetings in every city roared their approval of "Free Speech, Free Press, Free Soil, Free Men, Fremont and Victory!" Torchlight processions fired the nights, the men wearing black oilcloth hats and raincapes to catch the running paraffin of their candle lamps. Bands and military parades stretched for miles, almost a hundred thousand people marching in a Fremont parade in Indianapolis, kept in time by the blaring of fifty bands. Hundreds of orators toured the country, and many others who had never been speakers before and never would be again.

Early tests indicated that Francis Blair had been right, that given the proper man to head the movement, the Republicans could sweep the nation. However, as the Republican forces gathered strength, the southern Democrats became more desperate; Jessie was sickened by the intensity of the personal vilification. John was declared to be an habitual drunkard, to have been seen sprawling in the gutters; of being not only a slaveowner but a slave merchant, buying and selling slaves on a commercial basis for profit; of carrying on a clandestine affair with the maid in his household; of making himself a millionaire during the California conquest by buying great blocks of land, thousands of horses and cattle with government notes; of defrauding the English public through his agent Sargent; of working secretly with Palmer, Cook & Company, the San Francisco bankers, to leave Americans holding worthless mining stock.

Day by day the violence mounted. Jessie saw that there was almost no name in the language too foul to be levied against her husband. He was called a brigand, a horse thief, a despoiler of innocent Spanish women, a braggart, a cheat, a hypocrite. All the material of the court-martial supplied by General Kearny, Colonel Cooke and Lieutenant Emory was divorced from its text and spread throughout the land in anonymously printed brochures. Putting together the body of accusation, there could be little doubt that John Fremont was the lowest human creature ever spawned.

Fifteen years before, when her mother had told her on their ride to Cherry Grove how wretched it was to live in the midst of incessant public name calling, Jessie had assured her that this practice was an innocent part of the game of politics and could do no real harm. Now that her husband was being administered a more severe lashing than even her father had been obliged to endure, she realized how much truth there had been in her mother's observations. Slowly she came to perceive that one of the greatest accomplishments of the democratic form of government, the freedom of the press, was in process of destroying democracy because it was destroying the validity of popular elections. The press was misnamed; these scandalmongering sheets were not newspapers, they were prejudice papers, political lie factories. They cared less about the news than an incendiary does about the house he burns down; news was something to be thrown into the wastebasket if it hurt the paper's cause, something to be twisted and perverted to keep a political party and a special group of interests in power. The Republican press, she knew, was as bad; it was not slandering Buchanan's personal character, but it was inciting the North and the West to sectional hatred and violence. She posed this dilemma to Francis Blair, commenting that although the elimination of the freedom of the press would destroy democracy, the press was doing its best to destroy democracy anyhow. Blair, who had started one of the nation's earliest newspapers, replied quietly:

"Very few of our papers were begun to disseminate the news, Jessie. They were begun to promote a political party or a political candidate, and they have never changed their character. Some day, if elections become quieter and more civilized, papers will content themselves with reporting the news and leave the hysteria to the voters. Right now, however, the main task is to defeat their opponent at any cost."

"Yes," she agreed bitterly, pushing a batch of clippings across the table toward him. "At any cost . . . to the nation."

It was not until late September that the most devious blow of all was struck: John Fremont was charged with being a Catholic. The Know-Nothing or anti-Catholic party was strong, and had been for a number of years; anti-Catholicism was one of the most dangerous political issues of the day, filling the air with almost as much poison as the slavery issue. Now all of the incipient tragedy of religious intolerance was dragged into the campaign by the simple device of labeling John Fremont a Catholic; for once it had been established that he was a Catholic, all the anti-Catholic charges that had been circulating underground for the past twenty years could be brought into the open and made public. If John Fremont were an emissary of the Pope and were put in the White House, Catholicism would dominate American life, all Protestants would be obliterated by fire and the sword, the United States would become a Catholic country, the Pope would move the Vatican to Washington!

It was claimed that John's father was a French Catholic; that John had lived in a monastery in Baltimore; that he had carved a cross upon Rock Independence on his first expedition. To buttress the charge, documents were published showing that John Fremont and Jessie Benton had been married by a Catholic priest. Upon this one fragment of meaningless truth, the Democrats were arousing the hatred of anti-Catholics throughout the country. Jessie felt bad about this because it was her fault: if she had been willing to wait for her parents' consent, they could have been married by a Presbyterian or Episcopalian minister, and this most dangerous of all issues, that of religious intolerance, might never have been raised.

Nor was it possible to keep this conflagration from John, for an important Republican committee arrived at the Fremont home to settle the matter. Francis Blair said, "John, we know that you are an Episcopalian. The charge that you are a Catholic is costing us vast blocks of votes. You will have to publish a denial; we will have to prove that you have always been an Episcopalian."

Jessie watched her husband while he sat in the armchair by the front window overlooking the street. Since the day when she had quieted him over the attack on his parentage, he had preserved his calm and dignity, had met everyone who came to him with courtesy; and he had never uttered or written one word of anger or vilification. He looked from face to face of the committeemen and then said resolutely:

"No, gentlemen; I shall make no denial."

Everyone began talking at once.

"No denial? But you must! Silence gives assent. People will think . . . You'll convict yourself . . ."

"All of what you say is true," he replied. "They are hurting us greatly. But if I acknowledge the attack by denying it, I thereby admit that religion is a matter of political issue in this country, that people have a right to quarrel about it and refuse office to one religion or another. If I publicly deny that I am a Catholic, it will appear that I am repudiating the Catholics, that I am agreeing that no Catholic can become president of this country, that I am indifferent to the venal slanders that are being told about them. I will not dignify their campaign by participating in it. We have religious tolerance in this country. A man's religion is his private affair. My religion is my own, and I shall make no public statement on it."

He had spoken gently but his voice rang true. There was a moment of silence while the committeemen examined the floor, their shoes, the walls and the ceilings. James Gordon Bennett of the New York *Herald* finally rose and exclaimed, "Follow those convictions, Colonel, and I will sustain you." The other committee members accepted his decision, some of them with misgivings, others with pride in their candidate.

To Jessie it seemed that her husband had achieved at this moment a greatness equal to his rejection of the Democratic nomination. In his refusal to allow Catholicism to enter the campaign as an issue, she saw another instance of his philosophy of *noblesse oblige*.

Her months of thoughtful labors were having their effect. Magazines and newspapers began to run sympathetic articles about her; stories of her courtesy and hospitality began to circle the country. She was declared to be the most fitting First Lady the White House would have had since Dolly Madison; stories of her intelligence and integrity were told to the country in terms of her collaboration with her husband. As a result the Republican ticket was slowly changed to read: FREMONT AND JESSIE rather than FREMONT AND DAYTON. By October the Republicans had become as proud of Jessie as they were of John, and had jettisoned their vice-presidential candidate.

For the first time in American history a political party was bragging about their candidate's wife, intimating to the voters that the First Lady was important to the welfare of the people. The Democratic nominee's bachelordom was cited as a liability, an idea which James Buchanan sustained by making a surprise visit to the house on Ninth Street. It was eleven in the morning, and the house was empty except for the servants. Even before she could express her surprise at the visit, Jessie noted how old and puffy James Buchanan looked, as though he were unhappy at the thought that he might be elected. The white powder which seemed to cover the exposed half of his underlip had spread over his face, leaving nothing alive but the round virginal eyes.

"Why, Mr. Buchanan!" she exclaimed. "What a wonderful treat to see you in the midst of battle!"

"Ah well, Jessie," murmured Buchanan, "there is little we can do to stop them from fighting. John and I are the innocent bystanders . . . I had a spare hour during my New York visit, and so I have come to tell you that you should be First Lady."

Astonished, Jessie laughed, "Does that mean that you are going to vote for us, Mr. Buchanan?"

"Much as I don't think John ought to be president," he replied with a twinkle, "I am sorely tempted to vote for him just to get you into the White House."

"That, Mr. Buchanan, is about the sweetest compliment anyone ever paid me. I am going to feel very badly at defeating you, after you have been so nice."

Buchanan took the chair by the window which Jessie indicated for him. "You can't defeat me, Jessie, because too many people in this country know that the election of a Republican will bring on civil war. You will recall how I worked for peace with England over the Canadian-boundary dispute, and how I tried my utmost to keep us out of war with Mexico . . ."

". . . while Mr. Fremont and I did our best to get us into a war."

James Buchanan smiled. "Quite so. The American people know that I won't be particularly ornamental in the White House, they know I can't bring a Miss Jessie with me, but they believe that I will work for peace, peace at any price. Please believe me, Miss Jessie, any price is a good price to pay for peace. That's why I can't vote for John, even to see you First Lady: he would use force to restrain the South, and that would precipitate a war almost immediately."

"You are too good a candidate for your party, Mr. Buchanan; just as you are tempted to vote for me, my admiration might very well tempt me to vote for you. In the remote possibility that you should beat John," she continued, "your niece will make a charming mistress for the White House."

Buchanan rose, picked up his hat, made his way toward the front door. "Quite so, Miss Jessie," he said, "but the White House needs more than a charming mistress. Next time I run for president I'm going to have you nominated as my running mate. My compliments to your good husband."

In spite of the tremendous amount of work to be done and the excitement and pressure surrounding it, she had the time of her life. It was like that period when she had been at the core of American-Mexican relations, with material flowing in to her from every source, making her a kind of editor in chief of the impending war. In her position in the dining room on Ninth Street where she worked she was a kind of editor in chief of the campaign, for into this room all the information flowed, and out of it went many of the major articles and decisions of the hectic months. As the campaign gained momentum John began to make brief, friendly speeches to the crowds which assembled outside their house nearly every afternoon at five o'clock; he wrote many of the important letters himself and began to lay out the newspaper articles with her.

When the people in front of the Fremont house, after calling for John and listening to his short speech, would cry, "Fremont and Jessie!" she became uneasy lest he conclude that this was something of her doing, lest he suspect that she was unwilling to play a secondary role, that she wanted to be the equal of the presidential nominee. She began concealing some of the articles in which she was the main topic. She had exercised the utmost tact in all of her interviews and writing to play down her own part in her husband's life, to show that it had always been subsidiary. When John had proposed to her at Hassler's, she had promised, "I will never embarrass you, I want no credit or public acclaim; I will never stalk the street with a bundle of causes in my arm so that my friends will duck down side alleys when they see me coming." She was relieved to find that no one knew of her collaboration on the three Fremont reports, of the part she had played in the preparation of the court-martial defense, or of her political sessions in Monterey while John was on the Mariposa. It would take only one hint of all this to start the Democratic press crying that John Fremont was led by his wife; she was uneasy at what such a barb might do to their collaboration.

Walking up Broadway one morning she heard a group of young men singing lustily, "We go for our country and Union, and brave little Jessie forever." Soon copies of other campaign songs began arriving in the mails. There was one that was sung to the tune of "Comin' through the Rye," which was called, "O, Jessie is a Sweet Bright Lady" and went:

> We'll with Johnny, give 'em Jessie,
> 'Neath the White House roof;
> From brave Johnny and sweet Jessie,
> Need Southron hold aloof?

Then there was another which made it seem that, if she were not running for vice-president, most surely she must have been running for assistant president:

> She's wise and she's prudent; she's good as she's bonnie;
> For virtue and Freedom she takes a brave stand;
> For the Chieftain's White Mansion she's better than onie;
> So give her "God speed!" there, the flower o' the land.

Francis Blair was delighted with her services: he felt that she was playing an important part in enlisting the aid of northern and western women in the Republican party. He told her that up to this time women's influence in politics had been negligible, but that his son Frank's letters, coming in from every important station in the Republican campaign, indicated that women were pleased and excited at the prospect of having a representative in the White House, that their political excitement was having a strong effect on their men. He urged Jessie to redouble her efforts. When she protested that she had to be discreet, that some people might not think it seeming for a woman to play too active a part in a national election, Francis Blair expressed astonishment at what he called her sudden reversal of a lifetime philosophy, generously confiding that if John were elected, an important portion of the credit must go to her.

"Wait until you see the new banners that are being made for our big parades," he told her with his eyes twinkling; "they read: JESSIE BENT-ON BEING FREE. It will make every woman in the North insist that she too is Bent-On being free."

It was Lily who finally got her into difficulty, but at the same time allayed her fears. Lily found a batch of suppressed articles and songs about her mother in a desk drawer. Pleased, she took them to her father. John asked his wife why she hadn't shown them to him. Jessie blushed, said with a side-ward toss of her head, "Oh, they're just trivia from the women's papers, gossip about what kind of food I would serve in the White House if you were elected. They have nothing to do with the campaign."

John laid out the articles on the dining-room table, read bits of them here and there, hummed aloud a song:

> *Freedom's star shall brightly shine,*
> *And Plenty's horn shall bless ye,*
> *When in the White House we enshrine*
> *Fremont and gentle Jessie.*

When he had finished, he looked into his wife's embarrassed face. "They have a great deal to do with the election," he answered. "There are a lot of people who are going to vote for you who wouldn't vote for me. It's the first time in the history of our nation that a candidate's wife has been of importance in the election. People know you and like you, Jessie. They know how hard you've worked for me for fifteen years. They admire you for that, and they'll vote for you . . ."

"Really, John . . ."

"So take the tribute as an indication of how successful our marriage has been. People know that you are my full partner, that by electing me they'll be getting two Fremonts for the price of one. You told me in Hassler's work-room the day I asked you to marry me that the one thing you wanted in life was a good marriage collaboration; you've achieved it so well that you will be the first First Lady to be elected by popular ballot."

9

With the mounting enthusiasm of the Republicans, the steady growth in the party's strength and the rapidity with which it absorbed segments of the old Whig party, it became evident that John Fremont had an excellent possibility of becoming the fifteenth president of the United States. The Free-Soil party was a small cloud on the horizon which might cut into John's freedom vote, but Millard Fillmore did not seem a strong candidate, and the Republicans were not much concerned. With the rise in optimism Jessie found herself unable to refrain from planning the redecoration of certain portions of the White House, in particular the old-fashioned bedrooms, the rather darkish family dining room, and the nursery, which had not heard childish laughter for far too many years. She decided to reintroduce some of the informal customs of Andrew Jackson's regime; she would abolish the formal receiving lines and the rigid dinner parties to which only those who were invited might come; the line of formally gowned ladies who assisted at receptions would be replaced by an open door. Dinner would be served *en famille;* their friends could drop in any night, those who were going through

Washington would always be welcome. The White House dinner table would become an elaborate version of the Benton dinner table, where all of national politics would be rehearsed. She remembered the first time she had ever seen the White House; her father had taken her there just before a big reception and supper. The wood fires flamed brightly in each room, the wax lights burned in soft profusion, the rooms were decorated with rows of camellias and laurestinus. In the state dining room the horseshoe-shaped table, covered in the center with berries, candies, nuts and fruits, groaned under every kind of delicious food the French chef could conjure, climaxed at either end by her father's favorite Sunday dish, whole iced salmons lying in waves of meat jelly.

She would bring those days back to the White House. Every American would feel it was his second home.

The campaign was fraught with a thousand implications, yet it became evident by October that it would be decided on one fundamental: would the election of John Fremont cause the South to secede? From a hundred stumps in Missouri, Tom Benton was proclaiming that the South would secede immediately if a "Black Republican" were elected. Voters in the North began to ask, "What good will it do to elect John Fremont if it is going to cost us a civil war?"

Election day dawned sharp and clear. The Fremont family rose early, put on their best clothes, and Jessie, Lily and Charlie accompanied John while he cast his ballot. Then they went to campaign headquarters on Broadway, where by noon the election results were already coming in over Samuel Morse's telegraph. By dinnertime it became evident that John was carrying majorities in New York, Ohio, Michigan, Wisconsin, Iowa, Connecticut, Maine, Massachusetts, New Hampshire, Rhode Island and Vermont. He began to fall behind in Pennsylvania, Illinois and Indiana, all three of which states the Blairs and the Fremonts had expected to go Republican. The severest personal blow to Jessie was that Missouri yielded to Tom Benton's arguments and voted Democratic. Little Charlie and John did well by the dinner that was brought in on trays, but neither Jessie nor Lily could touch a bite: it was becoming evident that Millard Fillmore and his Free-Soilers were taking enough Republican votes to swing doubtful states into the Democratic camp.

For Jessie the excitements of the day were framed in gratifications as well as disappointments: the loyalty of the volunteer campaign workers around her, most of them young and fired by the cause of freedom; their unwillingness to concede defeat until the last possible moment, and the courage with which they kept repeating, "We may be beaten this time, but we'll elect John Fremont in 1860"; the disappointment of such men as Dana and Greeley, who came in during the evening to shake hands with them and tell them they had put up a magnificent fight; John's reserved, unemotional reaction to the growing indications of defeat; all these were compensations for the fact that they had run almost half a million votes behind James Buchanan.

They remained at headquarters until dawn, shaking hands with each departing campaigner, then dissecting the election results scientifically with Francis and Frank Blair: Fillmore and his Free-Soilers had drawn eight hundred thousand ballots, votes which would have been Republican if the North had not been split. Three hundred thousand Whigs had voted for Buchanan to avoid secession, rather than for Fremont and the party which more closely represented their own convictions. Jessie thought, If only those Whigs and northern Democrats who believed in the Republican cause had not been frightened by the threats of southern secession, John would have been elected; if only the Republicans had selected the man from Pennsylvania whom they had originally wanted for vice-president, he might have defeated Buchanan in his own state; if only Tom Benton hadn't come out against his son-in-law; if only the new party had had campaign funds to match their youthful enthusiasm; if only . . .

Ah yes, she whispered to herself as the first rays of the sun came into the now cold and forlorn campaign headquarters, if only . . .

They walked home through the deserted streets. Jessie and her daughter went into the kitchen to fry eggs and ham steaks. She served breakfast on the dining-room table across which the material of the campaign had flowed for almost five months. In the middle of his meal Francis Blair suddenly broke down; the tears began dropping into his plate.

"Forgive an old man," he said, "but I cannot contain my disappointment. I was so sure we were making a new political party, a new president and a new era. Now that it is all over we have accomplished nothing . . . nothing . . . We also ran!"

Encouraged by this breakdown, Lily began to whimper. "I had so many plans made to spend the next four years in the White House. I was going to give a lot of wonderful parties and all the boys and girls in Washington would be my friends . . ."

"I had even redecorated the White House," said Jessie with a wry smile, "put new French wallpaper in the reception room. I had set up buffet suppers for a thousand guests. Lily, stop that blubbering. Go put on your coat and walk around Washington Square until you can control yourself. If you can't take disappointments better than this, you're going to make yourself miserable through half your life."

Lily put on her coat and went out the front door. Francis Blair excused himself and went up to his bedroom. Their appetites gone, Jessie and John sat looking at each other across the table.

"Don't you think we ought to try to get some rest?" she asked.

"Yes, we should try."

They trudged wearily upstairs to their bedroom. Jessie turned down the candlewick cover. They did not undress, but slipped out of their heavy outer garments and put on robes. They were too tired to talk and too tired to sleep; they lay rigidly side by side, each thinking his own thoughts.

For the first time since she had spent the lonely and meaningless months in the sand dunes of San Francisco, five years before, she was overcome by despondency. She had always had the utmost faith in their accomplishments, yet she now had to admit that their career could best be described by what the French so aptly called *génie manqué:* they almost achieved so many magnificent results, but nothing actually came to its final and complete fruition. They started upward on so many promising cycles, rode superbly to the top—and immediately began sliding down the other side. They could not seem to make anything last, to continue in a straight line of achievement. Where did they go next, and what did they do? Would they be able to sustain the next role? Or would they once again rise to great heights, only to fall and be cast out?

She realized that this was hardly fair: John had achieved greatly as an explorer, had played a critical role in the settling of the West, had done good work as a conqueror, a civil governor, a senator, a presidential candidate. But in none of them had he been anything more than momentarily successful; the roles changed so fast as to make one dizzy! What was the matter with her husband, that this should happen? What was the matter with her? What was the matter with their marriage? She had so often concerned herself with the enigma of John Fremont, but now she saw that it was the riddle of their marriage that was truly perplexing. She found herself wondering why it was that no matter how great the difficulty or the crisis, neither of them failed in their personal relationship to each other, and yet this solid and successful marriage encountered defeat at almost every turn of its external and worldly career. Why did not a good marriage lead to an equally good career? Was there something in the one which excluded the other? Or were those gifts which enabled a man and woman to live together in love and harmony the very attributes which precluded worldly success? They failed for valid reasons, sometimes even for heroic reasons, but always in the last analysis they had failed.

Or had they? Was it because she was thinking of the end as more important than the means? Actually John had been wonderfully successful as a presidential candidate. He had been faithful to the finest elements in his own character and to the finest traditions of American statesmanship. Only she and her husband would know that; the rest of the country would consider them as having failed; but since when had this kind of knowledge between them been insufficient? Had they not been willing to risk censure and ostracism for the conquest of California? Though this eventuality had not materialized in precisely the form for which they had been prepared, had they not suffered because they could not reveal the complete picture to the nation? This time they had been working under their own secret orders: refusal to accept the Democratic nomination; refusal to order a campaign of viciousness, to enter a campaign of religious intolerance. They could not go to the public and cry, "We insisted upon winning under ideal conditions!"

No, they could not parade their virtue. They had lost, and that was the end. But between them, between man and wife, they would always know they could have been president and First Lady had they been willing to pay the price. Such confidences were good for a marriage: they gave it meaning, they gave it dimension.

John got out of bed and went into his study. She heard him opening and closing books, moving furniture around. She rose, went to his doorway and saw him standing among his papers and notes, gazing down at them with a surfeited expression. He looked up, said over his shoulder, without moving, only his dark, withdrawn eyes seeming alive:

"Can you keep a secret?"

"Now that the newspaper reporters have evaporated, I daresay I can."

"Then I will have to confess that I regret deeply having thought it necessary to be so confounded noble. I should never have turned down the Democratic nomination! Or, having taken the Republican nomination, I should have campaigned wildly, threatened civil war if I weren't elected, allowed the religious issue to be introduced. Yesterday there were thousands of people thronging in front of our house; today we are alone, not even one newspaper reporter to find out how a loser feels. I tell you, Jessie, we were idiots! We should have played the game according to the rules of politics! The rules were made for us, years ago. If we had been sensible and practical, you could be out this morning buying violet-colored curtains with pink tie-backs for the White House, instead of talking alone with your husband in a cheerless room full of useless memories!"

Having gone through her own peculiar form of despondence, she was better able to understand her husband's regrets.

"You're entitled to grumble, John," she said sympathetically; "an overdose of idealism, like a too-rich pastry, leaves a slightly sickish-sweet taste in one's mouth. But you couldn't have done otherwise, my dear, and I'm proud of you. I prefer being alone in this little room with you, in the midst of all the work and the memories that now seem useless, to buying violet-colored curtains with pink tie-backs, if I had to prostrate myself to get them. You remember what you told me that night when we first knew it was possible for you to have the Republican nomination: sometimes a lost battle contributes to the winning of a campaign. You and the Republican party have been defeated in your first national election, but you have both conducted yourself so well that it must inevitably lead to victory. Perhaps that victory will be under you in 1860; perhaps it will be under some other Republican; but whoever may win will owe you a great debt. Your candidacy brought to the Republican party almost a million and a half votes; it has established the Republicans as the permanent second party. You have preserved the dignity of the electoral process in a year of blood and passion when you could have easily inflamed your followers. This was your contribution, my dear, as important as any that James Buchanan will be able to make in the White House."

They stood looking at each other in the dark room, with the world very quiet and shut out, two forlorn figures who had been rejected, yet not disgraced; who had lost everything and yet lost nothing; to whom the cost had been tremendous, yet who now had more than they had started with. A few hours before they had been two of the three most important individuals in their nation; today, they felt like the least important within its borders, with little to do but lick their wounds.

She did not know who made the first move, or whether either of them spoke, or how they reached each other, yet like that first embrace in the foyer of her home in Washington, they were suddenly and miraculously in each other's arms. Words, almost any words at this moment, could have lied, lied tenderly, pityingly; but this kiss could not lie, it told them both that there was neither failure nor unhappiness in their world, whatever might happen, so long as they loved and worked together.

From the fullness of her heart, she murmured:

"Story writers say that love is concerned only with young people, that the excitement and glamor of romance end at the altar. How blind they are; the best romance is inside marriage; the finest love stories come after the wedding, not before."

BOOK SIX

GENERAL JESSIE

1

THEIR COTTAGE WAS LOCATED in the center of twelve parklike acres which their manager had fenced in several years before, surrounded by white oaks and colorful California mountain shrubbery. There was a mining village named Bear Valley eleven miles away, but for the most part Fremontville had to be self-sufficient. Their meat and vegetables, eggs and milk had to be imported from San Francisco, for the miners were content with canned food and rice. Jessie brought up the two rooms of furnishings which had been stored by the flour merchant at Madame Castro's in Monterey. She missed the outlook on the sea, but the mountains were covered with a compensating carpet of golden poppies. By climbing to the crest above them they could see for a hundred miles in all directions, the San Joaquin River with its broad belt of trees, the Stanislaus and Tuolumne rivers flashing across the broad plain like metallic ribbons.

Jessie, John and their three children had driven eighty miles from Stockton in an open carriage to settle on the Mariposa. They found a number of small wooden buildings inside their enclosure; a barn was converted into a store-room, a lean-to into a kitchen. Jessie gave their cabin a coat of whitewash on the outside, put up plank walls on the inside. When the furniture arrived from Monterey she put the white lace curtains on the windows, the Chinese matting on the floor, the high New England bedsteads in the bedroom. In the living room she laid the grizzly-bear skins before the fireplace, then placed the East India wicker chairs and the Chinese satin-cushioned bamboo couches. Lily put in a yard of chickens, geese and ducks. An Italian neighbor who was struggling to raise a vegetable garden was given the overflow supply of water from John's mines, in return for which he shared his precious crop.

The mail steamer arrived in San Francisco every two weeks, and the mail was delivered by wagon to the village of Bear Valley. When Lily rode to town on horseback she would return with panniers loaded with letters, canned goods, packages of books and magazines, fresh food and candy from San Francisco. Bear Valley was a typical Sierra mining village, with one block of saloons and general stores on either side of a deeply rutted dirt road. Miners' cabins dotted the hills behind it. There were a number of respectable and congenial families here with young wives and children, but much of the town was made up of adventurers. They made their living by claim jumping, having banded together for this purpose into what they called the Hornitas League.

John now had some forty men working for him. At the Princeton mine he had set up twenty-four stamps and a mill driven by steam which enabled him to get seventy dollars' worth of gold out of each ton of rock. The Pine Tree and Josephine mines were being tunneled and were yielding around seventy thousand dollars' worth of gold a year; the Mariposa mine was the richest, with rock of white ribbon quartz. Most of John's workers had cabins in Bear Valley or immediately around the Fremont enclosure. There were Cornish families whom he had sent over when he was in England, a number of southerners who had come in to make their fortune but had gone to work at good wages instead, drifters of all kinds who worked for a week or a month and disappeared.

Jessie set out to make the acquaintance of her neighbors: her storeroom, in which she kept the foodstuffs that were brought from Stockton by wagon, became an emergency larder for the district; she found herself summoned as an emergency doctor when the Calhoun baby had a fit because he had swallowed a piece of salt pork. Their former manager had left behind some memoirs on the French Revolution, an illustrated set of Shakespeare, three volumes of medical jurisprudence. In the months before Jessie's cases of books reached her from the East, she used the texts on hand to train her little brood.

"It's going to be an irregular course," she told John. "Just what use they will be able to make of medical jurisprudence I don't know, but any study is good for their minds."

With the nucleus of her own three children, she soon found that she was conducting a school, for a half-dozen of John's miners' wives, as well as others among their Sierra neighbors, brought in their children several times a week to participate.

And so at last Fremontville came into existence. They had a store and a school. They built log cabins for the miners who came to work, and enjoyed a kind of community life. There was no church as yet; Jessie had always envisaged a log-cabin church, but somehow they did not get around to building it.

Her only real disappointment was in not having her father at Fremontville. Tom Benton had planned for more than a year to come with them, but almost at the last moment he had begged off: there was still so much work to be done in the East; he wanted to finish the second volume of his *Thirty Years' View;* he could not desert his fight against the break in the Union. He promised to come out later, when the second volume was finished, when he had completed his lecture series. She had tried to convince him that he had already done several lifetimes of work, that a year in the out of doors of the West would renew his strength. She was never really convinced of the validity of his reasons for staying. She wrote to him on every mail that went east, long letters describing their life in the mountains. Tom Benton never failed to send her several packets of news, as well as the newest books being published on the Atlantic seaboard.

Lily, who was now a tall sturdy girl of fifteen, liked best to roam the mountains. Her father gave her a pale cream-colored horse with a silver mane and tail whom she named Chiquita; she spent the major part of her day, when Jessie was not training her in history and poetry and reading, riding the trails and valleys of the Sierras, bringing home great armfuls of wild flowers. She frequently rode to the various mines with her father, standing in the entrance to watch the liquid gold pour from the retorts.

Jessie was fortunate in securing the services of an Irishwoman by the name of Rose, whom they quickly dubbed Irish Rose, to do the cooking; and a gnarled, bitter, mountain man by the name of Isaac, part Indian and part Negro, to take care of the horses, the grounds, and to drive the carriage. Isaac was small, dark, silent as deep night and distrustful of all the world. Neither Jessie nor John could understand why he was willing to work for them, but they soon found the answer in the manner in which Isaac lavished his love on Charlie and three-year-old Frank, teaching them to ride and handle guns.

The Sierras were full of Indian settlements; there were constant quarrels and killings between the wandering miners and the tribes. However, John had a genius with Indians: his Delaware scouts had accompanied him on four of his expeditions; the delivery of his cattle five years before to the Sierra Indians had kept them from starvation and won their gratitude; he saw to it that they were not disturbed at the springs or in their settlements. The Indian women, returning to their camps from their berry and fagot gathering, would squat under the shade of a tall pine tree that stood in front of Jessie's cottage. Since their favorite repast was a helping of turnip peelings and suet between two pieces of bread, Irish Rose saved her scraps for them, and Charlie and Frank would play with the Indian children while the squaws ate. The Indian men returning from a hunt would drop off fresh meat.

Jessie began to notice that the Indians had a name for her house. When she asked what it meant they told her: "White House." Standing under the pine tree with a group of squaws, their papooses lashed to their backs in woven baskets, Jessie turned to look at her two-room whitewashed cabin.

It's a bit different from that other White House, she thought. That evening she told her husband of the name their house had earned. John replied, "Everyone in this part of the mountains calls it that."

"Do they mean it ironically?"

"I don't think so. It's just that a coat of paint is so rare in the Sierras."

"Do you ever have any regrets, John?" she asked softly. "We would have been entertaining ambassadors instead of Indian squaws . . ."

"I don't believe in mourning the gold ore that escapes through the slough," he replied. "This is what we have."

Though he did his best to conceal his business worries from her, she knew that he had ample cause to be disturbed. According to the ruling just handed down by a California court, anyone could enter and take possession of an unoccupied mine, even though it had been occupied five minutes before, and thousands of dollars had been invested in it. John had put almost thirty thousand dollars in the Pine Tree mine, only to have his guard bribed while the miners were home in their beds. When John arrived the next morning the Hornitas League was working his mine and was legally entitled to keep it. There was no way to recover the thirty thousand dollars he had invested or to claim any part of the gold they were gathering with his equipment.

When Jessie and John had returned to Mariposa after their two years' absence, the mines were almost a half a million dollars in debt. At first she tried to understand how the mines could have run so deeply in debt when so much gold was being taken out. John assured her that the business was on a sound basis because the half-million dollars represented investments in heavy machinery, stamping mills, smelters, roads, which cost a great deal to install but would pay back their costs many times over.

With her husband taking full charge she imagined that the debts would be paid off. Instead they continued to grow. John was a good engineer and had a daring mind: he built a huge storage dam on the Merced River to give them water power, probably the first power dam built in California. He imported hundreds of Chinese workmen from San Francisco to build a railroad around the contour of the mountain so that the ore could be brought down speedily to the smelters in town. He installed new ore-crushing apparatus at the Benton Mills, where twelve stamps were in continuous operation. All this cost large sums of money, but he was confident that he would have a hundred stamps in operation in another year or so; by that time they would be clearing ten thousand dollars a week and could easily meet their obligations.

Despite his assurance, Jessie knew that he was restless. He rose while it was still dark and left for the mines, returning after the sun had gone down. Every week he was off to Stockton or Sacramento or San Francisco to see his lawyers, to try to buy new equipment, to hunt for respectable miners. He was constantly making plans for a quick trip to New York, to cross to Europe for more modern equipment, to float new stock issues, engage more Cornish miners. She knew that for some of these things there was a need, but for the most part his desire for locomotion was mental. None of his plans for a railroad to the West had yet materialized; he was now a gold miner and nothing more. There was really little else on hand for him to do: a man is not always master of his fate; there were frequent fill-in periods, hiatuses, years when he could only do what was at hand.

For her own part the founding of Fremontville had come almost a decade too late, catching her at a time when she would have preferred the cosmopolitan life of New York or San Francisco. The years since she had first arrived in San Francisco aboard the S.S. *Panama*, afire to create her own hearth, had brought deep-lying changes. The naïveté was gone from her concept of building a township. What at twenty-five years of age would have been a gay adventure had to be accomplished at thirty-three by a conscious effort.

After almost having been First Lady of the United States it was difficult to throw oneself heartily into being First Lady of Fremontville. Under her guidance the settlement on the Mariposa became homelike and enjoyable for her husband and her children and her neighbors, but for Jessie Benton Fremont the ambition to pioneer had been achieved too late to vouchsafe its full flavor.

They had arrived on the Mariposa in the spring, the most beautiful time of the year in the Sierras, when the air is crystal clear and tangy with the perfume of pine, oak and chaparral. Though John was away much of the time, she was not too lonely, for a stagecoach line had been established between St. Louis and San Francisco which took only three weeks to complete the journey, and there were frequent visitors at Fremontville. A number of their old friends from San Francisco came through on hunting and prospecting trips, including Fitzhugh Beale and old Knight. An English family they had known in London sent out their seventeen-year-old son Douglass, a six-foot, spindly, towheaded boy who had been studying too hard and who needed a spell of outdoor life. Richard Henry Dana, who had seen California ten years before John first reached there, and whose book, *Two Years Before the Mast,* had made him famous, arrived for what developed into an exhilarating visit.

Then summer came. The sun beat down into Bear Valley all day, the surrounding ravines and mountains holding the heat in, clamping it down like an iron roof upon the Fremont cottage. The dust made the air almost unbearable; the ground was so burnt that the children had to make leather shoes for the dogs to keep their feet from blistering.

She was awakened early one morning by a knock at the door. A man's voice called, "Colonel, the Hornitas League has jumped the Black Drift."

As John quickly got out of bed she asked, "What does that mean?"

"Only mine work," he replied.

She lay awake for a few moments enjoying the brief coolness which came before dawn. When she rose the sun was up, hot and fiery. She had breakfast with Lily and Douglass, after which they devoted an hour to reading about the French Revolution. Ordinarily Isaac took Charlie and Frank to the barn for their play hours because it was cooler there, but today he would not let them out of the cottage. Jessie noticed that neither Lily nor Douglass had any interest in their lesson, that everybody about the place seemed jumpy. It did not take her long to conclude that the predawn visitor had brought bad news. When she demanded of Isaac what had happened, he told her plainly that the Hornitas League was attempting to take possession of their Black Drift mine. Six of John's Cornish miners were at work inside, a fact which the League had not known. Since they could not take immediate possession, the mine jumpers decided to starve the men out. If they could force the miners from the Black Drift, within a few weeks they would have taken possession of every mine on the Mariposa.

The boys climbed into an oak from where they could see past the steam mill and up the yellow road which glared in the hot sunshine. Jessie took her usual place at the front-room window. Just as the sunset sky was flaming crimson the boys caught sight of their father, his horse showing black against the sky. "Father's coming!" shouted Charlie.

"Have they got into the Black Drift?" she demanded at once.

"No," replied John, unbuckling his revolver belts, "and they're not going to. Those six Cornish miners will never be frightened out."

"John, we've got to get a message down to the governor."

"They have every pass and road blocked off with armed men. I tried to send three different expresses through today, but they were all shot at."

They did not sleep much that night, preferring to talk in the coolness of possible ways of ending this blight on the mining region. John vowed that once he got rid of the Hornitas crowd he would go to San Francisco and have his lawyers appeal the claim-jumping law.

He left at four in the morning for the Black Drift. Jessie rose when the sun came up, to find Lily missing. No one knew where she had gone. An hour later Douglass returned to tell them that Lily was riding to the governor, that she had made her way up dry creek beds and through thickets of manzanita and chaparral which concealed her horse until she got across the summit, and was already down the opposite side of the range, having eluded the Hornitas guards. Jessie flushed with pride in her daughter's courage.

Shortly before noon, Mrs. Caton, wife of the foreman in the Black Drift mine, arrived from her cabin about a mile beyond the clearing. She had a luncheon basket on her arm.

"I'm taking Caton's dinner in to him, Mrs. Fremont."

"The Hornitas League will never let you through."

"I've got Caton's revolvers strapped under my dress," the woman replied grimly. "I wish I could wear one of your Paris crinolines, then I could take in a whole arsenal."

Since she could not dissuade Mrs. Caton, Jessie decided to go with her. Mrs. Caton unstrapped one of her revolvers and put it under the napkin which covered the luncheon basket; then they walked the two miles up the narrow trail leading to the Black Drift. As they came to the sharp bend, Mrs. Caton said, "Wait here, Mrs. Fremont, where the Leaguers can't see you."

Jessie concealed herself behind a rock and watched her storm up to the entrance of the mine. The Leaguers blocked her way. Mrs. Caton reached into her basket, took out her revolver and exclaimed, "You wouldn't like to be shot by a woman! You've just got to let me carry his supper in to Caton. You have your quarrel with the colonel about mines and lands and you can fight that out with him. But I'm a poor woman that's got only my husband, and five children for him to work for. I stand by Caton."

Her uplifted revolver waved like a fan toward one and then another; they fell back and let her enter the mine. A few moments later Jessie saw her emerge from the tunnel.

"They didn't dare to shoot a woman," she said with a quick laugh when she had rejoined Jessie. "I put enough food in the basket for all six of the men in there."

When John returned that afternoon Jessie informed him of Lily's exploit. She also told him about Mrs. Caton. "She was superb, John: the picture of everlasting woman, determined to feed her man or die in the attempt! I don't know where she got the courage."

"Each of us has his own way of showing courage," replied John with a half-smile; "look at Lily. I think we've got them licked, Jessie. The hundred-degree heat up at the tunnel opening is burning out their enthusiasm. If we could hold them off for another day . . ."

Early the next morning a message was brought to Jessie which read:

Resolved at Bates Tavern that Mrs. Fremont be allowed twenty-four hours to leave her house. An escort will see you across the mountain and down to the plain. You can take your children and clothes, no harm will be done to you. If you are not gone within twenty-four hours, the house will be burned and you must take the consequences. We will kill the colonel. Signed for all present.

DENNIS O'BRIEN, President.

She thought quickly, If the men at the Bates Tavern start drinking they will never allow us the twenty-four hours' grace, but will fire our house just as they twice fired San Francisco. Going to her closet she selected her prettiest Paris muslin, with gay ribbons, and summoned Isaac to drive her to the Bates Tavern in Bear Valley. A number of the Hornitas Leaguers were lounging on the front veranda. Isaac drove up to the front steps.

Jessie rose to her feet and eyed the men in cold silence. After a moment she exclaimed in Tom Benton's senatorial voice:

"The White House and the land it stands on is ours. We intend to remain upon it. If you burn the house, we will camp there in tents. If you kill the colonel, you will have to kill me too and my three children. You are a pack of worthless cowards! If there was a real man among you, he would be out finding his own gold instead of trying to steal from others. Good day to you all."

With this she sat down, crying in the same tone she had used so many times in Washington, Paris and London, "Home, Isaac!"

When John returned at noon and learned what she had done, he whispered against her ear, "I'm a poor woman that's got only my husband and five children for him to work for. I stand by Caton!"

By this time they were seriously concerned about Lily, for if she had gotten through safely, she should have been home by now. An hour later the boys, who were holding down their observation post in the oak tree, shouted, "Here she comes!"

Lily was tired but calm. She couldn't understand why everyone was making such a fuss over her, or why Mama should shed tears of relief. She had followed a steep descent to the river, along which she had ridden behind granite boulders, then guided herself by the stars until she reached a rope ferry, where she found an old friend of Colonel Fremont's. He had dashed off for Stockton to send the alarm.

All night Jessie heard the sound of shots reverberating in the hills and the wild gallop of horses' hooves, but no one came near the White House. By noon a hundred men of the Coulterville Home Guard had arrived and were scattering through the mountains. At nightfall five hundred troops arrived under the state marshal, accompanied by a convoy of twenty-mule teams from Stockton, carrying arms and ammunition. The troops were bivouacked on the twelve acres surrounding the White House, and by the following day the Hornitas League had vanished from the Sierras.

Late that afternoon Jessie received a delegation of wives who lived in the mountains between the White House and Bear Valley. She invited them to stay for tea. The women were picturesque in their blue merino dresses, wide knitted collars and hats loaded down with flowers and ribbons. The storeroom, which had been all but exhausted by the state troops and the Coulterville Guard, was ransacked for boxed cookies, candy and Chinese tea. One of the women announced, "Had you left the cottage, Mrs. Fremont, our hills would have run blood."

A second woman, young and with golden hair, who reminded Jessie of Mary Algood, exclaimed enthusiastically, "We're going to celebrate the defeat of the Hornitas League with a regular ball: printed invitations and a ball committee and dancing in the Odd Fellows Hall."

A week later Jessie, John and Lily drove into Bear Valley to attend the first formal affair of the Sierras. The women were excited and happy-faced, the men dressed in their Sunday-best. Behind the ballroom was a room with two beds in which were put the half-dozen young babies who had to be brought. The hall was decorated with native evergreens and well lighted with candles, the fiddler and guitar player sitting back to back in the center of the room. Jessie danced twice with John, then watched her daughter be the belle of the ball, for Lily's feat was known throughout the mountains. Bemused, she remembered that she had been only a year older than Lily when she had danced at Harriet Bodisco's state wedding with young Lieutenant Fremont, amidst the jewels and lace gowns, the gold braid and thousand lighted candles, with the European orchestra playing behind its screen of palms in the ballroom.

Toward the end of the evening Lily came to her with two high points of color in her cheeks to confess that she had just received a proposal of marriage. Jessie was shocked, for she still thought of Lily as a child. For the first time in sixteen years she understood why her father had fought so hard against her precipitate marriage to Lieutenant Fremont when she had been only seventeen.

Poor Father, she mused. I surely gave him a difficult time. But even so,

I was right. If Lily finds a nice young man in these mountains, I shan't stand in her way.

2

Now that peace descended upon the Sierras, Jessie asked if they might not build themselves a more adequate home.

"You know, John," she said, "you can calculate to a fraction the displacement caused by a man-of-war, but there is no calculating the displacement caused by two small boys."

John laughed at the phrase. "You won't find it easy building up here. It's a long haul for materials from San Francisco and Stockton."

"I have no intention of erecting a two-story brick house."

"Then go ahead, but don't spend more than five thousand dollars. That is all the cash we can spare now. I have to go down to San Francisco; are there some things I could order for you and bring back with me?"

"No," she replied with an enigmatic smile. "I can handle everything from here. You'll be back for Christmas Eve, of course?"

"Of course."

As soon as her husband left, Jessie set about bringing her new house into being: several pine trees were cut down and the trunks trimmed so that they made smooth rollers. The five detached buildings on the twelve acres, including the barn, storeroom, kitchen, office and a far cottage were hoisted onto the rollers by a grizzled old man from Maine and his three sons, who had done all the hauling of the logs to make John's mills and dams. Ox teams pulled them to the White House, where they were joined together.

She spread word throughout Bear Valley that she wanted to have her home completed in two weeks, in time for Christmas Eve; because the countryside had just come through a harrowing time together, the men and their wives laid aside more pressing tasks to help her. Carpenters joined the six buildings together and built a broad veranda across the full length of the house. The roof was covered with uniform shingles, the front with neat planking. A competent bricklayer came for three days to the White House to build a sturdy chimney. She scoured the countryside for all the windowpanes she could find, running them in a solid line across the front and back of the rooms and achieving a Queen Anne effect, with a magnificent view of Bear Valley.

At the end of the first week the house had been put together, the wide veranda built, the heavy mechanical work completed; she now had another week in which to finish the interior. On no other frontier could she have found the luxurious furnishings that were available in Bear Valley, for miners made their money unexpectedly and fast, and when they had it to spend they wanted the world's finest goods. In the crude, unpainted plank stores of Bear Valley she discovered imported French wallpapers, as lovely as any she had seen in Paris, the most expensive carpeting and rugs imported from the Orient and Europe, rolls of Chinese silks from which to make curtains. She bought matting for the wide veranda, cane furniture and hammocks, then enclosed it with green Venetian blinds. She framed the windows with full straight woolen draperies with a deep frill atop; they could be closed at night to shut out the darkness and give a sense of intimacy to those sitting before a wood fire reading or chatting by waxlight.

One of the miners had been a scene painter for the St. Charles Theatre in New Orleans; he took charge of the delicate wallpapers. The parlor was done in cream-white and gold with deep borders of dull red, Jessie's bedroom in pale blue with white roses. The dining room was made the formal chamber of the house, being hung with walnut and oak papers, which gave it the air of a great house in the East. The men who sewed sacks for the ore of the mines came down with their needles and thread to sew the carpeting. An old piano was found in Stockton and brought up by twenty-mule team; Jessie located some strings in the store at Bear Valley and summoned the blacksmith, Manuel, a Virginia Negro, who wound on the new strings with a winch, tightening them until Jessie, who was tapping at the keyboard, would exclaim, "Stop!"

By the end of the tenth day the fireplace was finished and she lit a fire in the hearth. It drew perfectly. On the twelfth day the painters finished giving the outside and the roof a coat of white paint, for she was unwilling to give up the name by which the Fremont home was known throughout the mountains.

Charlie and Frank were sent with Isaac up the side of the mountain to select a fir tree. Jessie trimmed it to the right size, then brought it into the dining room. She and Lily brushed the long cones with glue and covered them with gilt paper. The tree was set in the corner by the brick fireplace with a gold star resting on the top dark green spire. A Vienna baker who had recently opened his shop in Bear Valley made candles of beeswax for her, coloring them with gold leaf. For a month she had been ordering her Christmas candies, fruits, picture books, toys and games, as well as inexpensive colored jewelry for the Indians; the gifts were now wrapped separately and placed beneath the tree. The boys distributed wreaths of ground pine about the house and hung up the wild-rose haws which had to take the place of holly berries.

A heavy mist rolled down the mountains before dusk on Christmas Eve, a mist which Jessie knew would delay John. Lily and Douglass were sent down the trail on their horses with lighted torches to cheer him on the last few miles. By dark she saw the torches coming back toward the house; she refreshed the lights in the Queen Anne windows. When John dismounted, walked through the wide veranda and into a house that had not been there two weeks before, he was stupefied. Jessie led him in this dazed condition from room to room, while she pelted his unhearing ears with descriptions of the scene painter who had hung the wallpapers, the blacksmith who had tuned the piano, the sack sewers who had laid the carpets. At the end of the tour she exclaimed in final triumph, "and it cost me only one fifth of what you said I might spend."

She had invited everyone who had worked on the house to see the tree on Christmas Day, and to receive their gifts of appreciation. They came on horseback, in carriages and prairie schooners all during the afternoon, but the guests were by no means confined to those who had thrown up her house and painted and decorated it. Wives and mothers who had been in the Sierras for almost ten years without having seen a Christmas tree came with their husbands and children to ask if they could not have just one look. The Bear Valley committee arrived, bringing their husbands, and along with them many of the wives and mothers who had been at the Odd Fellows ball, wanting nothing more than to see a lighted Christmas tree again. The miners came in from the Fremont mines, the bachelors in groups, the married men with their families. The Indian women arrived with their papooses; they could not be persuaded to come indoors, but sat in their regular seats under the trees gazing through the windows.

By dusk Jessie began to count noses and saw that she had almost a hundred friends and neighbors thronging her home. Many of these people, who had ridden for hours to get to the White House, had had no food since morning. Irish Rose was equal to the task: platters of cold meats and hard-boiled eggs, crackers and rolls and cakes were circulated among the guests; even Isaac thawed out for the occasion and consented to pass the glasses of wine. There were beads and necklaces for the Indians, toys for each of the mining children. At seven o'clock, when everyone had crowded into the parlor and the adjoining dining room, Jessie lit the candles on the tree.

A hush fell over the group. There were tears in many eyes. The old father from Maine, whom Jessie had named Kriss Kringle, fell to his knees before the tree, offering up a fervent prayer of thankfulness to God. One by one the miners, their wives and their children went on their knees and joined in the prayer. Jessie and John knelt with Lily at their side and their two sons before them. When the old man's prayer came to an end there was a moment of silence; John whispered to his wife: "You told me that if only we had a church, Fremontville would be complete. Here is your church."

3

The boys played in the winter snows and came in bright-eyed and rosy-cheeked. An old friend from New York, Hannah Kirsten, who had come out to visit her brother in San Francisco, journeyed up to the Mariposa for a month's visit with Jessie. Hannah was young, with a happy disposition and a fine musical talent. The White House was filled with the beautiful music of her songs and piano playing.

One day when Jessie and Hannah were sitting on the veranda facing the long draw up Bear Valley, they saw a strange-looking creature coming along the trail, wobbling from side to side on a small horse, his feet almost touching the ground.

"By the Eternal," exclaimed Jessie, "it's Horace Greeley!"

Greeley, founder of the New York *Tribune,* was tall, skinny, angular; neither his head, torso nor limbs seemed to bear much relation to each other, as though all three had been sired by different parents and stuck together with mucilage. His head was round, with a bulging forehead, his hair worn long and around his face. One trouser leg was stuffed inside his high boot, the other was hanging out. The rest of his costume consisted of a string necktie which hung over one shoulder, a white linen suit, a tall white hat and a bulging umbrella.

After three weeks of being bumped around in a stagecoach, of putting up in frontier cabins and inns, Horace Greeley was as dumbfounded at Jessie's home as John had been. That evening as they lingered late over dinner in the oak-and-walnut-papered dining room, he complimented Jessie on her gift for getting things done.

"You have executive ability, Jessie," he said wistfully; "my wife has none at all. Our servants come in the front door and go out the back. For years now I have really had no home. My wife cares nothing about food; the rooms are a boar's nest of confusion and discomfort. It's impossible for me to bring friends home. When she grows angry at my preoccupation she will seize the manuscript on which I am working and fling it into the fire. Ah well, I love my Mary, but if only she had a little executive ability . . ."

Jessie and John had talked little national politics since their arrival at Mariposa, for John had no intention of going through another presidential campaign. Greeley, whose trip west had been prompted by his desire to test the political temper of the times, gave them a brilliant survey of the increasing struggle between the North and the South. He was incensed at President James Buchanan, speaking of the "curse of the good man, the honest man, the man who compromises for peace at any price"; for Buchanan was permitting the South to arm itself, to deplete the northern store of munitions, to talk openly of rebellion, while at the same time he kept the North from preparing for war by decrying preparedness as an attitude which might provoke the South to rebellion. Greeley insisted that if John had been elected he would have thrown cold water on talk of rebellion by arming the North, by strengthening national forts and garrisons in the South, by allowing the South no opportunity to prepare itself for a conflict.

Jessie asked, "Can we use force to keep the South in the Union?"

"Yes," replied John. "Just as we use force to keep one man from murdering another; or, more apposite, from committing suicide."

It was only a few days after Greeley's departure that Jessie received a letter from Eliza telling her of her father's death in Washington. She was totally unprepared for the blow; though Tom Benton's strength had been failing, he had seemed hardy when she left him a year before. He had been promising to come out to California that spring.

When John returned from the mines, he explained that Tom Benton had died of cancer; that her father had known of his sickness when he bade her farewell the year before. That was why he had not come out to California with them.

"Your father swore me to secrecy; he said he didn't want you grieving or spending your days with the anxiety of his death hanging over you. Now you know how hard it was for him to let you go . . . He went to bed the day we left, and he never got up again."

Through her tears Jessie said, "He wanted to die with his hand in mine; he told me that after Mother's death. Yet he let me go, knowing that he would never see me again . . ."

By June the fierce summer heat came again to Bear Valley; there was no breath of air, nor were the nights long enough for the hotness to rise out of the valley. John had been going into San Francisco every few weeks. In the middle of July he suggested that she accompany him, for it was cool in the city. They crossed the Tuolumne and Stanislaus rivers by ferry, then took the night boat from Stockton, putting their carriage and horses on board. In the morning John drove her along Golden Gate strait, stopping the horses before a promontory which projected out into the bay, pointing straight at Alcatraz Island. A house sat primly in the midst of mountain laurel and small trees whipped by the ocean winds. Standing on the edge of the bluff, with the bay and the strait just ahead of her, the mountains of Contra Costa beyond and the blue Pacific to the west, Jessie exclaimed, "What a heavenly spot. Whose is it?"

"Yours."

It was now her turn to be speechless.

"I bought the house and twelve acres from a San Francisco banker for forty-two thousand dollars. We always said our California home must overlook the Pacific. Do you like it? It's called Black Point. We can spend as much of the year as we want here, and go up to the White House for the spring and fall months. I've deeded it in your name, Jessie. It will always belong to you and the children."

Breathlessly happy and excited, she cried, "May I see the inside of the cottage?"

The house was simple but sturdily built. As she walked through the empty rooms she exclaimed, "We'll build a glass veranda all around the seaside: that'll cut off the winds and leave us free to watch the ships go in and out at all seasons of the year. I'll build a summer house 'way out there on the edge of the bluff for the warm weather. We'll bring in paint and wallpaper and within a few weeks you won't recognize the place."

She spent an active month redecorating and furnishing her new home, surrounding it on three sides with a glass veranda on which she placed lounging chairs and writing tables, enlarging the parlor to twice its size, with a native stone fireplace filling one whole wall. She laid out paths among the roses and fuchsia, while John built a stable for their horses and carriages. She knew it was extravagant to buy all new furniture, rugs and draperies when she had so many beautiful things in the White House, but they would spend many months of the year at the mines and she did not have the heart to upset it in any way.

When the children's bedrooms had been freshly wallpapered and carpeted she sent a message to the Mariposa. Irish Rose and Isaac brought the two small boys and Lily down in safety.

It was nine years since she had climbed down the sides of the S.S. *Panama* and been carried over the shallow surf by a sailor. Then there had been only a few crude buildings bordering Portsmouth Square; today San Francisco was a city with rows of well-built homes, a prosperous business district and small factories springing up on the outskirts. Trade with the Orient kept the harbor full of ships, while the overland stage and the pony express were bringing in settlers and mail across the mountains and plains in thirteen days from New York and ten days from St. Louis. Samuel Morse's telegraph had been completed to San Francisco; there was a steam railroad on Market Street, omnibuses to the Presidio, horsecars in the business district. A literary magazine, the *Golden Era,* had been established to serve as the counterpart of Boston's *Atlantic Monthly.* The best plays and concert artists included San Francisco in their itineraries; there was a full season of opera.

Jessie enjoyed San Francisco: it was young enough to be awkward in its growing pains, yet full of an impetuous vitality which kept events so rapidly on the march that each day the city was born anew. Her big parlor and glassed-in porch, overlooking the strait, the ocean and the bay, became San Francisco's first literary and political salon. With her father dead, she had no desire to return east to live. The children loved Black Point, they found playmates on the settlement overlooking the strait and spent their hours wandering the dunes and the beaches below. The fog bell clanged in a low friendly tone, the circular light on Alcatraz Island reminded her of the light-house at Siasconset.

She was now thirty-four, no longer young, but maturity had brought its own kind of beauty. Her hazel eyes seemed deeper in color and more compassionate; her mouth was more understanding than resolute. A touch of gray was beginning to show at the center part in her hair. The fragile oval had filled out a little. There were adaptations too in her temperament: she no longer fought so hard for every next hour, every next month; she had developed a kind of rugged acceptance, if not of every twist and turn of their fortune, at least of their over-all pattern. She no longer was so determined to rush out and confront fate in its lair; she was willing to wait a little, to let fate meet her halfway. Nor did she feel that every hour not spent in the pursuit of one's major aim was an hour wasted; she had come to accept the fact that their professional career, like their marriage, had its own pace and rhythm; now it moved slowly, seemed mired in the morass of petty activity; now it rushed forward to some momentous achievement. She no longer had the desire to be forever rushing forward; it was good to renew one's strength, to evaluate the past, gain perspective.

Yet if she were maturing in some ways, in others she could not feel that she was a day older than when she had driven to Mrs. Crittenden's house to be married by Father Van Horseigh. Her external life might wear a little thin, sometimes pull at the seams, but the miracle of her marriage never faded. Even after seventeen years, her sense of excitement at John's physical presence had not abated. The touch of his hand, his kiss, his embrace were as magically joyous and delightful as they had been in those early weeks of their honeymoon in the back bedroom of the house on C Street. On the Mariposa she had been obliged to use the twin New England bedsteads which had been stored in Monterey all these years; there had been no chance to reach out a hand for the reassuring touch of his presence should she awaken during the night. Now in San Francisco she bought a big cherrywood bed similar to the one they had had in St. Louis, and here, during the long cool nights, they listened to the fog bell and the gentle lapping of the waters at the base of the cliff, talking of their plans.

After nearly two decades of marriage, and the bearing of five children, her passion for her husband ran as strong as in the earliest days. Before she had met John she had gathered that the physical side of marriage was a burden women carried in order to bear children, and to accommodate their husbands. Any concept of fulfillment was unthinkable to a respectable wife. Jessie had known this to be a monstrous lie from the first moment she had encountered John Fremont; it had proved to be a lie during the rapturous days of their honeymoon; and it was more than ever a lie today. The years might grow old, and the world, but never a good marriage.

And now, even as on that New Year's morning of 1842, she lay by her husband's side, listening to his steady breathing, ruminating over the enigma of John Fremont which she had never solved: she felt in him an aloneness, a seeking for something that can never be found, a last hidden rampart of self-defense. His life had fallen from its sublime heights to mediocre routine; at the back of his brain was the compulsion to unceasing expedition, though it might be only up to the Mariposa. Dimly she perceived that he was longing for that ultimate moment of triumph, that single greatest moment of his life, from which all the rest had been a falling away: when he had so divinely risen above human strength and forced the crossing of the Sierras. In her love for him there was mixed this fine leaven of pity, pity at the unceasing urges that pushed him forward and made no place his home, no hearth his undying fire. Nothing that could ever happen to John could make him secure: all his life he would be the pursuer and the pursued, pursuing legitimacy, pursued by all the phantoms to which the insecure mind falls prey.

For herself she had learned that the future must inevitably arrive, that they were not likely to pass the rest of their lives serenely in some uneventful corner; that was neither in their own character nor in the character of the times. Even here, living in her lovely and secluded home, several thousand miles from the core of the slavery controversy, they had been caught up in the struggle that was being waged to take California out of the Union in the event of secession.

Their companion in the fight against the growing number of slavery sympathizers in California was the Reverend Thomas Starr King. Former minister of the Hollis Street Church in Boston, King had come to San Francisco to be pastor of the Unitarian church. He was a man of wide learning, a passionate warrior for freedom and a mesmeric speaker in the manner of Henry Ward Beecher and Theodore Parker. He was young, slender, beardless, with yellow hair which hung down over his collar and a powerful, open face, with great burning eyes. Jessie and King became friends, for they had much in common: the love of liberty, books and writing, the exciting march of ideas. They differed only in one particular, their devotion to San Francisco. King never got over being astonished at the lack of grace and elegance of the frontier, the houses which seemed to be chasing each other up hill and down dale, the throngs of Chinamen on the streets.

One Sunday he complained that it was impossible for him to get his work done because all San Francisco thought it could walk up to his front door, knock, and spend the rest of the day discussing politics or religion with him. "I can't even salvage sufficient time or privacy to write my sermons, Mrs. Fremont. I declare, I shall have to take pencil and paper and hide in the dunes."

"Why not use the little summerhouse we've built on the bluff?" asked Jessie. "No one need know you're working there."

He accepted with alacrity. Each day at one o'clock he arrived with his papers and set himself up in the arbor to read, study and write the articles which appeared in the Boston *Transcript* and the *Atlantic Monthly*. By late afternoon he came up the trail, his tawny hair blowing in the breeze, his slender body swinging along jerkily. Over his several cups of tea he would read Jessie the sermons, articles and stories he had written, ask for her criticism, defend volcanically everything he had done, only to incorporate many of her suggestions in his work the following day. Once in passing he mentioned the name of Bret Harte.

"Bret Harte," murmured Jessie. "Isn't he the one whose stories I read in the *Golden Era?*"

"Yes, he's a printer on the *Golden Era*. He writes his pieces in the composing room, not with pencil but with galley type."

"Think how strong the writing force must be within him if he can set up whole stories in type! I should like to meet him. Won't you bring him here sometime?"

King said hesitantly, "He's so dreadfully shy . . . he won't go anywhere

. . . particularly when there are ladies present. Among other reasons, he's poor; he has only that miserable printer's wage; his clothes are worn thin."

"Very well," she replied, "if he is too proud to come to me, I am not too proud to go to him. We need vigorous young writers who can dramatize the West."

The next afternoon she went to the office of the *Golden Era* and asked if she might speak to Mr. Bret Harte. After ten minutes a young man of about twenty-four came down. He was of medium height, slight of build, with a black mustache and a thatch of intensely black hair parted sharply on the left side. He was dark-complexioned, one eye seemed larger than the other; he gave the impression of a turbulent young man, wanting to be pleasant, yet not knowing how.

"Forgive me for intruding upon you, but the Reverend Thomas King has talked of you and I have read several of your stories in the *Golden Era*. I liked them very much, in particular one in which your central character was like an old innkeeper Colonel Fremont knows in Tuolumne, who has good within him, behind a perfectly abominable front."

Bret Harte relaxed a little.

"Won't you come to dinner this Sunday? We should all be friends."

On Sunday he appeared in a long cutaway black coat, wide gray trousers, a low-fitting wide collar and a beautiful gray cravat.

He has spent his last dollar for a new outfit, mused Jessie; but it will do him good, for it will make him feel more at ease.

She led him out to the glass-enclosed veranda. Of his own writing he would say nothing. However, by the end of the afternoon, after John had told him stories of the Hornitas League, young Harte lost a little of his self-consciousness. He even seemed to accept with eagerness John's invitation to dinner the following Sunday.

During the week she had a note asking if he might come an hour earlier to discuss a story. She walked with him along the cliff, with the sun sparkling on the water. He talked about the character of the miners he was describing. She told him of her husband's experiences. He dropped in unexpectedly the following Thursday to read her the new story and to ask for her criticism. When she had finished he sat staring down at the carpet.

"Do you know, Mrs. Fremont," he said, "this is the first constructive criticism I have had. I find it very good to be able to talk about my stories, to treat my characters as living beings, capable of modification and change."

From then on Bret Harte came every Sunday to dinner, reading them the result of his week's work. She thought the stories imitative and precious, but they showed a constantly growing power. She and Thomas King sent his stories east with recommendations to the newspaper and magazine editors.

One rainy afternoon, when the rest of the company was late in arriving, Jessie said, "You have told me so little about yourself, Mr. Harte. Where did you come from? What brought you to San Francisco?"

There was an awkward silence before Harte began in a constrained voice to tell how his widowed mother had come to California to marry a Colonel Williams in Oakland; how he had followed her when he was eighteen; worked in apothecary shops, been a private tutor, an expressman, taught school in a small town and worked on mining-camp newspapers. He was now twenty-four, determined to have a literary career, but with no idea of how he could earn his bread and at the same time keep enough free time to write his stories.

"What is the name Harte?" she asked. "We knew a family of Hartes in London, but you don't look English. You look more like one of the Latin races, Spanish perhaps?"

His skin became darker than she had seen it before.

". . . Harte is not really my name; the *e* on the end was placed there accidentally by a printer, and I've never had the courage to take it off. You see, Mrs. Fremont . . . my name is Hart; my grandfather was a Jewish merchant in New York. I've never concealed the fact that I was a Jew, but that accidental *e* on the end of my name enabled me to find a job with the *Golden Era* . . . and to have my stories published."

He leaned toward her, exclaiming, "Mrs. Fremont, you can't understand what it is to be a minority of one, to be despised, not because you are inferior but because you are different."

Jessie's heart ached for the young man.

"My dear Mr. Harte, since I first met Mr. Fremont I have known that everybody is a minority of one, that nobody truly belongs and that every human soul is a lonely stranger."

"But how could you know that?" Harte exclaimed. "You who come from one of the most prominent families in America?"

She told him the story of her mother, who had been a tragic minority of one, living in a world which everyone else had thought magnificent; of her husband who had first revealed to her the terrors of insecurity; and finally something about herself, how in trying to follow the implications of Anne Royall's philosophy, she had so often stood alone.

"I take courage from what you have told me, Mrs. Fremont, and I thank you," said Harte. "If it is my lot to bear intolerance, then it is different in detail from every other man's burden, but no different in degree."

"Continue to write your stories, Mr. Harte," she urged. "Perfect your craft, make our West known to all the world."

Hesitantly he replied, "That is not so easy to do. My work as a printer leaves me little time to write. I have agreed to take a job on an Oregon newspaper; the wage is higher . . ."

Charlie and Frank were attending public school, in addition to which Jessie gave poetry and literature classes for the youngsters of the neighborhood three afternoons a week in her parlor. Lily had no interest in Jessie's poetry, nor did she care for the theater or opera, but at seventeen she was slowly taking over the management of the household. She liked to do the shopping, the paying of the bills and balancing of the books. She began edging her way into John's confidence about the mines and Mariposa business, trying to understand what was going on, proclaiming that if she were a man she would become a mining engineer and run the Mariposa for her father.

Even as Lily was making a stubborn effort to understand her father's business, its status and logic were growing more obscure to Jessie with each passing day. She knew that they had made a good deal of money from the increased values of their San Francisco real estate and the cattle ranches in southern California; she also knew that the mines were turning out some twenty thousand dollars' worth of gold dust a week. She was therefore taken by surprise when John told her that he was obliged to sell half of the Mariposa. To her startled inquiries he explained that the Mariposa was in debt for one million two hundred thousand dollars; that they had solid assets to show for this indebtedness, but that they could never pay it off from current income. When he explained that it would be a load off his mind if he could sell half of their holdings, pay their debts and be out in the clear, she agreed that it was wise to buy such freedom from worry. He thought that the best way to sell would be by floating stock issues in France, and told her that after the presidential election in November they would go to France to complete the arrangements, then take the grand tour of Europe for which they had made plans while Jessie was carrying the little Parisienne.

The Fremonts played a quiet but determined part in the election of Abraham Lincoln. They had never met him, but they had followed his debates with Stephen A. Douglas on the slavery issue two years before with intense interest, and had felt that Mr. Lincoln had the best of the argument. Jessie spent the months between the nomination and the election writing articles for the California newspapers, holding meetings in her home to establish Republican clubs. She organized mass rallies and parades and sometimes spoke with Thomas King to audiences of several thousand people. John made no public appearances, but devoted his time to combating a plot to force California to secede if Lincoln were elected.

When the final count was taken, Jessie saw that Abraham Lincoln had better fortune than they had had four years before. Douglas and Breckinridge were Democrats who split their party even as the Free-Soil Party had split the Republicans in 1856. Had there been but one Democrat running, Mr. Lincoln would have been hopelessly swamped. He had received a million votes less than a majority; comparatively, John had done better against Buchanan than Lincoln had done against Douglas and Breckinridge. She was struck by the twist of fate which placed one man in the White House in Washington, D.C., and another man in the White House in Bear Valley, California.

With the election over, and a loyal Union general arrived from Washington to command the strengthened federal garrisons, California was safe. John completed their preparations for the journey. The steamship tickets were purchased, plans were made to leave the children with Eliza and Susie. Everything was in readiness for what was to be a combination business and pleasure trip. Jessie was looking forward to the days of uninterrupted companionship with her husband.

Three days before they were to sail she had to make a hurried trip to Palmer, Cook & Company. She had always been terrorized by the steepness of the San Francisco hills and avoided them whenever possible. This day she told Isaac to follow the most direct route. Isaac had taken horses and carriages down far steeper hills in the Sierras, but he had no understanding of paved streets; in the middle of Russian Hill one of the horses fell to its knees and the carriage overturned. Jessie was thrown out. When she awakened in her own bed at home she found that her left arm had been broken. John prepared to cancel their trip until she was well, but Jessie knew that the business plans were arranged for immediate negotiation, that if they were set aside now they might never go through as he wanted them.

"You go ahead, John," she urged. "Take care of your business and come back as fast as you can."

He waited for two days before making up his mind. At the last moment he yielded to her persuasions, hurriedly packed his suitcases and sailed for Panama.

Lily was an excellent nurse; the girl was so delighted at not having to leave San Francisco that Jessie sometimes thought her daughter believed the carriage accident to have been the working of divine providence. She drifted through the days, missing her husband but not too unhappy, content to read, to visit with her friends, to gaze out over the waters. When Fitzhugh Beale was installed as surveyor general of the Land Office she persuaded him to appoint Bret Harte as a clerk at one hundred dollars a month. Beale did not take to the idea of having a writer use the Land Office for his private Bohemia, but she assured him that Harte would do his full share of the work and still have time and energy for his writing. In gratitude Bret Harte exclaimed, "If I were to be cast away on a desert island, I should expect a savage to come forward with a three-cornered note from you to tell me that, at your request, I had been appointed governor of the island at a salary of two thousand four hundred dollars."

She had a letter from John telling her that he had spent an hour with Abraham Lincoln at the Astor House in New York. Mr. Lincoln still had strong hopes that all differences could be settled without reverting to war, but John wrote to his wife in confidence, "With the inflammatory press and inflammatory conversations on every hand, I am convinced that actual war is not far off." He had offered his services to Mr. Lincoln, and the president-elect had assured him that if war should break out, he would be named to an important command.

In her enforced leisure Jessie had time to wonder why John couldn't have sold half of the Mariposa right here in San Francisco, or in St. Louis, Washington or New York. Why must he go to the farthest possible place to float a stock issue? Why France, of all places? Was it because the farthest place took the longest to reach, and it was the journey rather than the arrival that he wanted?

She did not hear from him again until the end of March, at which time she received a discouraging note telling her that the French were so frightened at the impending war in the United States that it was impossible to sell half of the Mariposa. He did not know what he was going to do next, but he promised to write in a few days and tell her of his decision.

Then things began to happen so fast that she was hardly able to keep them in proper sequence. On April 12 Fort Sumter was fired on. President Lincoln immediately called for volunteers. Next she heard from Postmaster General Montgomery Blair that John had been commissioned a major general. He was to be one of the four major generals of the regular Army, the highest post available in the United States. His headquarters were to be in St. Louis, where his command would include not only Illinois and Missouri but all the states and territories between the Mississippi River and the Rockies, that vast expanse which John Fremont had been the first to map and open to organized immigration. Both the press and the public received the announcement with jubilation, for no man in America knew this country, foot by foot and trail by trail, as well as General Fremont.

With a quick rush of joy she realized that John once again would be back in the uniform he loved. He had passed twelve years as a civilian, and now that they were over she could admit how directionless those years had been. It was tragic that it had taken a civil war to fulfill her prediction that John would one day be a general, but when the war was over he would remain in the Army, perhaps in command of the Presidio right here in San Francisco!

In an astonishingly quick time she received a letter from her husband to the effect that he was buying arms and guns as wildly as his own credit and the backing of Ambassador Adams in England would permit: that as soon as he had bought everything he could snatch from under the hands of the prosperous Confederate agents, he would catch a fast ship for New York. He gave Jessie her marching orders: lock up the house and come east.

After the first shock had passed she knew that her contentment in San Francisco and in their home on Black Point had grown out of her prescience that this period was but another calm between storms, that she had wanted it to last a little longer before they were plunged once again into the unknown. Now that the time for action had come, she was ready and willing to throw off the mantle of the gold miner's wife, to live in an atmosphere where dollars and accounts and stock issues were not the first object, where John would have an opportunity to do an exciting and important work.

But if she were so willing and ready to go now, she found that her daughter's allegiance to Black Point and San Francisco was far deeper grained. When she told Lily that they would have to close the house and go east, Lily's outbreak, for so phlegmatic a girl, was ferocious.

"I don't want to leave San Francisco," she cried. "Black Point is my home. I love it. I protest against being forever dragged around the world, never allowed to settle anywhere, to feel as though we belonged. I just don't think it's respectable to move from one house to another year after year, never to have a place to rely on or to call home. You and Father are old enough to settle down now; it's time you became conventional and ordinary folks like everybody else."

She quieted her daughter, rented their house to Fitzhugh Beale, then packed her trunks and a big suitcase for each of the three children.

Friends saw them off at the boat. The steamer weighed anchor and made its way carefully out of the bay and into the strait. Jessie stood on deck with Lily and the two boys, watching Black Point and their home disappear from view. The two boys were wide-eyed and glum, but unspeaking. Lily broke into uncontrollable crying and ran down to her stateroom to lock herself in. Jessie stood on deck until the ship veered south. In her heart she was sad to leave her home, but the sadness was lightened by the knowledge that she soon would be playing a part in the fight for freedom and the Union.

4

She left the children with her sister Susie in Boston, then spent three weeks with John in New York trying frantically to buy arms and supplies for the recruits of the West. They reached St. Louis on a desperately hot summer morning.

Francis Blair, who with his sons Montgomery and Frank had secured John's commission, had urged her not to go to war-torn St. Louis, but to make her headquarters in Washington, where she could serve as a liaison officer for her husband. She preferred to be by John's side, yet she had seen the sense of what Francis Blair was saying. She had left the decision to John.

"You're coming with me," he replied. "I am going to step into a crushing volume of work, much of which I will have to delegate to men I have never met and of whose capabilities and loyalties I know nothing; I will want you to take care of all confidential matters. To anyone else I would have to dictate the thousands of letters, orders and reports verbatim. After twenty years of working with you, I have only to give you the barest idea of what I want to say. Should I dismiss you now because you are my wife, at the precise moment when your services can be of the most value?"

"That is a nice speech, General," she said with a warm smile, knowing how happy he was to be back in uniform, with two stars on his shoulder.

Her entry into St. Louis had always been a joyous homecoming. On this morning of July 25, 1861, she found the stores locked, house shutters drawn, few people in the streets. The fiddle in every home had been exchanged for a musket, no one knew who was friend and who enemy. St. Louis was a border town, partly northern, partly southern. Recruiting for the Confederate Army was going on publicly. The North had just lost the battle of Bull Run, Washington was in danger of being captured, Union morale was at its lowest ebb, the Confederacy was claiming it would terminate the war in a matter of months.

While John rode out to the Jefferson Barracks, from which General Kearny had provided him with a howitzer for his second expedition, Jessie tackled the problem of setting up headquarters for the general staff. She drove directly to her cousin Sarah Brant's house, a three-story edifice with a marble front and some seventeen rooms in its rambling interior. Most of the family had died or moved away; Sarah was living there alone. Jessie caught her in the midst of packing her bags and storing everything movable. She welcomed Jessie, but an anxiety overlay her greeting: she felt certain that, with Missouri's governor and legislature sympathetic to the Confederacy, Missouri would secede from the Union and St. Louis be captured by the rebels. Jessie made a quick survey of the house and offered six thousand dollars a year rental if she could move General Fremont and his staff into the building. Sarah refused the offer on the grounds that the army would ruin the home, but Jessie assured her cousin that she would watch over the premises, that the rental would cover all ordinary costs of repair. By noon, when John returned from Jefferson Barracks, Sarah Brant was on her way north and Jessie had begun to move the Brant furniture out of the two lower floors.

With a company of soldiers delegated to work under her orders, she set up the printing press, telegraph office and an emergency arsenal in the basement, as well as a room for the newspaper correspondents. The first-floor foyer she turned into a reception room; in the spacious drawing room and dining room desks were arranged for the lower-ranking officers who would have to interview the hundreds of visitors. The large front bedroom on the second floor she made into John's office; the two bedrooms adjoining it were stripped of furniture, and long plank-surfaced tables set up on horses for maps and diagrams. She then moved three desks into the second-floor hallway, one for herself in an alcove just outside John's door, the other two for Lieutenants John Howard and William Dorsheimer, John's young aides-de-camp. On the third floor there were a number of small dormer-window bedrooms which had formerly been used by the governess, tutor and bookkeeper of the Brant family. Jessie took the smallest of the rooms for herself, with John on one side and Lieutenants Howard and Dorsheimer, who were routed out of bed at all hours of the night, on the other.

The first to arrive for a conference was young Frank Blair, flaming with eagerness to help the Union gain control of Missouri. In the five years since Frank had stumped the country campaigning for John and Jessie, he had made important strides toward achieving his father's ambition of seeing him in the White House. Elected to Congress from Missouri, he had taken his place as one of the most intelligent and dynamic of the young legislators. Frank had especially endeared himself to the North for his superb daring and almost fanatical loyalty during the past troubled months: helping to form home-guard companies out of the Republican Wide Awake clubs; harassing the War Department to send in loyal troops in charge of Captain

Nathaniel Lyon; working with Lyon to muster four regiments of loyal citizens into the Missouri volunteers; preserving the arsenal for the North and capturing Camp Jackson.

Jessie was alone in John's front office, tacking up regional maps, when a sentry ushered Frank in. He approved of her establishment of general headquarters; in return she thanked him for the Blair family's efforts in securing John's appointment as commander of the West.

"He was a natural selection," replied Frank quickly. "His knowledge of the West, its people and terrain, the fact that the inhabitants know and respect him, will be of great advantage to the Union cause. But I must tell you quite frankly, Jessie, that I tried to get Nathaniel Lyon appointed because I believe that he is going to become the greatest of all the Union generals in the field. However, I quickly came to see that Father and my brother Montgomery were right: General Lyon's place is not at headquarters, but on the battlefront; General Fremont is by far the wisest choice for commanding officer."

John came in, the two men clasped hands fervently, then plunged at once into a discussion of strategy, working with the maps that lay strewn over the rough plank tables. Jessie listened carefully while Frank urged that John reinforce General Lyon immediately, and John informed him that he had orders from President Lincoln and Secretary of War Cameron to use all available troops to hold Cairo. John turned the conversation from strategy to supply, urging Frank to send him the best supply merchants in St. Louis, in particular the men whom he knew to be trustworthy.

Jessie rose at dawn of her second day in St. Louis and rode out to the Jefferson Barracks, where the fever patients and the wounded were quartered. The Union Sanitary Commission was in process of formation, but it had not yet begun to function in the West. As she walked down the long barrack aisles she saw that there were no shades on the windows to keep the blazing sun off the sick men, no nurses to tend them, no tables or medical accessories. Mugs of black coffee and pieces of salt pork were laid on the chests of the sick and dying men, but most of them were too ill to raise the food to their lips.

Horrified, she returned to St. Louis and made a round of the stores, banging her fist on the locked doors until her flesh was bruised, begging, pleading, demanding supplies for the boys in the hospital. The Union sympathizers gave freely; those sympathetic to the Confederacy were determined to give her nothing. Jessie cried at the owner of one store, whom she had known for years: "If you want to abandon the Union, that's your own business, but you cannot take it out on a sick boy who has probably been in and out of your store since he was a child. Once a soldier is wounded he ceases to be a Yankee or a Rebel, he's just a sick boy who will die if you don't help him."

"Very well," replied the storekeeper, "I'll give you what you ask, but remember—I'm doing this for Senator Benton's daughter, not General Fremont's wife."

By noon she had assembled blinds, pillows, mattresses, blankets, dishware, tables, soap, disinfectants, paint. She rode on the seat of the lead supply wagon, anxious to convert the ugly barracks into a hospital before another day dawned.

She had no authority to issue orders to the wagon drivers or their helpers, yet she pressed them into service, charging about the building like one possessed, supervising a hundred tasks at once: the scrubbing of floors, whitewashing of walls, installation of window coverings, putting the sick men between white sheets, with tables to hold their food and medicine. At first the soldiers demurred: they were afraid of the disease inside the hospital.

"She's got no right to give us orders," she heard one soldier mumble. "Who does she think she is, anyway?"

"She's the general's Jessie."

"Well . . . something tells me we'd better do what General Jessie says."

In the cool of evening, after they had had a light supper, Jessie and John went to his office, lit the lamps and settled down to a five-hour stretch of work. As the hours passed and John's plans became clear to her, she was thrilled by the bold stratagems which had taken shape in his mind. He had established a Union depot which combined all of the outlying railroad stations, saving countless hours in the moving of troops in and out of the city; he had ordered five river boats converted into mortar boats, assigning to army engineers the task of iron-plating the ships; ordered a fortification of St. Louis which would relieve forty thousand men for the battlefield; declared martial law in the city, putting an end to Confederate recruiting. Because his ninety-day volunteers had threatened to leave for want of their pay, he seized one hundred and fifty thousand dollars which the quartermaster had refused to relinquish; he commissioned foreign officers available in St. Louis, delegating them to train their own regiments for immediate battle service; laid out a campaign which would clear the Mississippi all the way to New Orleans.

At one in the morning John went to bed, asking Jessie to finish the written orders by the time he got up at five. She found it pleasant to work in the cool stillness of the night, with no sound to be heard except the slow movement of the sentries on guard below. Shortly after four in the morning she finished the orders, then went up to her room under the eaves and unpacked the simple clothes she had brought with her. As she lay in her narrow cot her mind went back to those wondrous, untroubled days when she was first married and had worked with her husband on the reports of the early expeditions.

5

Within a week after John's arrival some of the confusion had been eradicated, and results were beginning to show: St. Louis was now a Union city, the crescent-shaped fortifications were going up fast, Frank Blair's supply merchants were beginning to deliver food and clothing, a spirit of hopefulness and faith had been instilled into the troops, the officers were studying books on military science, such foreign officers as Zagonyi had trained several companies to a fighting pitch, the five gunboats had been completed.

But to Jessie conditions still seemed desperate: General Lyon was sending daily telegraphic messages for reinforcements. General Prentiss was making frantic appeals for fresh troops at Cairo. The War Department in Washington was not only unable to provide money or arms or men, but was insisting that General Fremont dispatch his trained companies to protect the capital. No part of the arms he had so farsightedly bought in France or England had been shipped to his command.

On August first General Fremont took his gunboat flotilla down the river to save Cairo from Confederate General Pope, who was advancing on it from the south. The next morning Dorothea Dix arrived in St. Louis. Jessie spent the following days working with the Union superintendent of women nurses, signing up women from the city and its environs for hospital work.

At the end of five days she received a telegram from John that he had beaten General Pope to Cairo, had relieved General Prentiss' depleted troops, moved the sick onto the gunboats. Jessie released the dispatch to the newspaper reporters; General Fremont's gunboat flotilla and relief of Cairo were acclaimed by a victory-starved North.

But when John returned to St. Louis she had no opportunity either to welcome or congratulate him, for Frank Blair had been waiting impatiently for hours, waving distress telegrams from General Nathaniel Lyon, who had fallen back almost as far as he could go and was now supplicating John for reinforcements. Frank was pleased with the success of the Cairo flotilla, but he was bitterly unhappy over General Lyon's plight, feeling that the failure was his own, for he had promised his friend that once General Fremont was in command there would be well-trained troops forthcoming.

John listened attentively to Frank's passionate pleas, studied the latest reports on his desk, and finally said, "Frank, I will send instructions to General Lyon at once. It is clear to me now what he must do, and I am sure he will do it skillfully and with success."

"Thank you!" exclaimed Frank heartily. "I knew you would not fail me."

When Frank Blair had departed, Jessie murmured, "I don't understand; how are you going to reinforce Lyon? You have no available troops."

"Quite so. It is impossible for me to reinforce him. Instead I shall order him to continue to fall back. That will extend the Rebel supply lines and make them more vulnerable. The delay will give me time to train the necessary troops; perhaps the Zagonyi Guard will be ready . . . When I order Lyon to fight, he will have an adequate army, he will defeat the Rebels and chase them out of Missouri."

Misgivings arose at once in Jessie's mind. Frank would feel that he had been misled; he would become angry when he learned that he had been put off with an oblique promise. She started to say as much, then decided that it was not part of her function to contest her husband's judgment.

She found that her work increased with each passing day, for St. Louis was one of the most feverish war centers in America. No matter how often John instructed her to write or telegraph to President Lincoln, Secretary of War Cameron or Postmaster General Montgomery Blair for "money and arms without delay and by the quickest conveyance," the best that Montgomery could answer was, "I find it impossible now to get any attention to Missouri or western matters from the authorities here. You will have to do the best you can and take all needful responsibility to defend and protect the people over whom you are specially set." John was on his own, he had to raise food and equipment from the surrounding country, enlist the men of the neighboring territories, somehow get them armed, trained, put into uniform and equipped to fight a war. To Jessie's eyes it seemed an impossible feat, and since she was unofficial chief of staff for supply, she worried over the fact that General Lyon's men had never been paid, were traveling on inadequate rations, without the proper clothing or tents or replacements for their horses or arms.

Hundreds of men thronged in and out of general headquarters each day, all wanting something: contracts, commissions, information, favors. To her dismay Jessie found that every last word, decision or act made enemies at the same time that it accomplished results. When she set up a guard system to keep out the hordes of visitors who wanted to see John each day, she heard complaints that General Jessie was being autocratic and keeping people away; yet John had begged her to keep his working hours free at any cost. When Jessie and John found that many of the contractors recommended by Frank Blair were victimizing the Union soldiers, that the guns didn't shoot, the supply wagons broke down on the road because the wood in them had rotted, that the soldiers' shoes lasted only a week because they were made of paper, that some of the canned food was poisoned and the critically needed horses fell lame a few days after being delivered, they lost faith in Frank's friends and gave out supply contracts to their own friends from the West whom they had known to be honest men. Men who were refused an audience became their personal enemies. Missourians who were refused contracts began working for John's removal by the time they had reached the bottom step of the Brant house. She was accused of having paid an exorbitant rental for the Brant house, of living in luxury and splendor, amidst fine furnishings, silver and linens. When John used his Zagonyi Guard to impress upon belligerent Missouri the fact that he had a well-organized fighting force, criticism arose on the grounds that he was acting like a European monarch.

However, these troubles became as nothing when their first real blow fell. General Lyon, fearful lest his harrowed army be disorganized and destroyed in its retreat, made a heroic attack against McCulloch's vastly superior forces at Wilson's Creek. His troops were defeated. General Lyon was shot through the breast and killed.

Headquarters was stunned by the news; where battles are fought, men die, but John had issued orders to General Lyon not to fight. The Union needed generals, particularly a general of Lyon's long experience; they needed victories, not defeats. And now John would be responsible for this serious setback.

When the first shock had passed, Jessie asked, "Perhaps General Lyon didn't get your orders?"

"He received them," answered John quietly. "But he thought I was wrong. He thought it would be irreparable to give up that part of Missouri; he reasoned that I couldn't know the full facts sitting here at headquarters."

"But in a war, can every officer make his own decisions? Mustn't he obey orders and fit into a major campaign?"

"You and I are not the right ones to ask that question, Jessie," said John ruefully. "Have you forgotten about Lord Nelson and his blind eye? From our point of view, sitting here at headquarters, trying to evolve an over-all strategy, Lyon was wrong; from his point of view, urged to retreat from a battlefield which he felt he could not spare, General Lyon thought he was right. And there the case will have to rest."

"But at least the country will not blame you for Lyon's death. You did order him to fall back."

"No one will ever know that."

"What do you mean?"

"Lyon died a hero's death. Nothing must be said or done to detract from it."

"But you know what the press will say, the War Department . . ."

"Nothing must detract from General Lyon's heroic death."

She left her husband's office and made arrangements for the body to lie in state on the side veranda, putting up the flags and arranging the flowers herself. When Lyon was brought in, she had the plain wooden coffin placed in the center of the room and draped it with his regimental colors.

At five the next morning, while she was having coffee with John at his desk, an orderly announced that Frank Blair was downstairs. Jessie and John went quickly to the veranda. Frank came in, his face sallow with grief. He walked to the head of the coffin and stood staring down into his friend's face. After a moment he looked up, took in the flowers and flags; to Jessie he said, "I thank you for these last kindnesses to my friend."

Jessie did not answer. She stood quietly, uneasily, while Frank and John gazed at each other.

"He was a good general and a good friend," Frank murmured softly.

"It's tragically cruel that he should have died before he had a chance to engage in a major campaign."

There was no criticism in his voice, only grief. John said, "I am sorry, Frank. I did what I could, but there was so little time . . ."

"It is not your fault, John. I only say that it would have been better in the long run to lose Cairo than to lose Lyon. We could retake Cairo, but we can never find another General Lyon."

John put his hand on Frank's shoulder. "I know that you have lost one of your dearest friends, Frank, but I have also lost my ablest commanding officer. We will miss him sorely, but you will see, his heroic death will thrill and unite the North."

Frank did not answer. John excused himself, went back to his office. Frank took a last look at his friend's face, then left the veranda, his head down.

Two days later he arrived in midafternoon with a friend whom he introduced as a clothing manufacturer, assuring John that his products would be good, then drawing forth from his pocket a contract which he put on John's desk for his signature. John had several times been criticized for signing contracts without reading or fully understanding them. As he had once explained to Jessie, he could either read the legal contracts or fight a war, but it was impossible to do both. As he sat looking blankly at the closely filled pages, Jessie asked quietly:

"How many outfits is this for, Frank?"

"Forty thousand."

Still trying to read the contract, John asked, "Forty thousand? When we have fewer than ten thousand troops in all Missouri?"

Frank's face reddened.

"Of course," he said coldly, "if you'd rather give the contracts to your California friends . . . They're the only ones who are permitted to provide for your army now. All the men in Missouri who fought this war before you ever got here aren't good enough to get contracts any more!"

"Now, Frank," pleaded Jessie. "John didn't say any such thing. He only said the number was too high . . ."

"Make the contract for ten thousand, Frank," said John; "that's all we'll need for the time being, and I'll be hard pressed to scrape together the money even for that amount."

He rose, excused himself on the basis of urgent business, and left his office. The clothing manufacturer walked out behind him. Jessie watched Frank's face to see whether the offer of a compromise had mollified him, but the young man began a passionate tirade which included all the criticism that had been levied against John since their second week in St. Louis. Keeping her temper under control, she replied, "Frank, you know perfectly well why he had to do these things. You and John must not quarrel; you have too important a job to do together."

"That's not what the high and mighty general thinks," cried Frank. "He thinks he doesn't need me any more now that I got him his command. He wants to get rid of me, me and all my friends who fought for months to keep Missouri in the Union. Once he gets rid of all of us there will be no one here to challenge his power. Then he can go on holding military parades and dazzling the city with his European uniforms . . ."

Sadly, Jessie answered, "You don't mean all these things, Frank. You wouldn't be saying them if it were not for the death of Nathaniel Lyon. You mustn't let Lyon's death warp your judgment."

"Lyon's death," exclaimed Frank. "You mean Lyon's murder! Your husband had plenty of troops and plenty of arms; he could have reinforced Lyon at any time he had wanted to—but he was afraid of Lyon, afraid Lyon would win brilliant victories, be given John Fremont's command!"

Aghast at these accusations, Jessie could only cry, "Frank, you must not say these horrible things! You will do everyone terrible harm. I will not allow you to start circulating this kind of rumor."

"You won't allow," snorted Frank, his face contorted with rage, "General Jessie will not allow! Don't you know what a ridiculous figure you are making of yourself? Don't you know how everyone resents your intrusion and wants you to go home, get out of a man's war? Don't you know how ridiculous you're making your husband look, with people saying that you wear the stars in the family and your husband takes the orders?"

She somehow managed to say, "Please go away. You've said enough."

Frank Blair replied, "Almost enough, but not quite: until John arrived here, I was the political commander of the state. But your husband decided that Missouri was too small for two commanders, that one of us had to be driven out. He thought that one was going to be me, but that's where he made his mistake. He is the one who is going to be driven out, and I am the one who is going to do the driving."

She left the office and slowly climbed the narrow stairs to her little bedroom, gazing out the dormer window over the roofs of St. Louis, seeing nothing, feeling deeply this moment of decision. Had she made a mistake in coming to St. Louis with John? Was Frank Blair right in charging that she had made both herself and her husband ridiculous in the eyes of the world? Was she exaggerating the worth of her contribution, doing more harm than good by being here? How would John react to the charge that she wore the stars?

For the first time she realized that in war no one achieves a quick and easy success. There would be many failures before a victory was achieved, there would be dreadful quarrels; everyone engaged in the fight would suffer from the quarrels, would fight two wars instead of one.

If she returned home now, if she stepped down from the work and responsibility, then no matter what happened in the war and the Department of the West, it could not be her fault, it could not hurt her marriage. Once before she had learned that the best wife was the least wife, yet here she was immersing herself in fields where a woman did not belong. She sensed from Frank's attack the intensity of the campaign that would

be waged against her. She knew that, working in confusion, she must inevitably make errors, mistakes. Suppose these had serious consequences?
Suppose they hurt her husband, his position, his status, his hold on his
command? Would he not charge this against her; would it not cause a strain
on their marriage? She had almost ruined him once before by this kind of
participation. She knew that she was impulsive, strong-willed, disliking
authority or restraint. Might she not do something that once again would
lead to disgrace, court-martial? They were older now; they would not be
able to endure trouble as they had when they were young. Would it not be
the better part of wisdom to go away, to Washington perhaps, as Francis
Blair originally had suggested, and let her husband fight this war without her?

In her most fanciful dreams she had never anticipated that their collaboration would involve co-operation in a war; yet that was the way it had
worked out, and, startling as it seemed, now that she stopped and saw it
through Frank Blair's eyes, she knew that she could not abandon her work
merely because it was a war which was calling forth this collaboration. She
was aware of the fact that she could get hurt, seriously hurt, just as she had
been hurt after the conquest of California. She could go back to New York
or Siasconset, but John had said he needed her. She thought, If my reasoning is good and my organizational work sound, if they help to win battles
and end the war, who is going to say later that the work was invalid and
objectionable because it stemmed from a woman rather than a man, from a
marriage relationship rather than that of officer and subordinate?

How then could she run away? These were the hours and the periods
for which she lived, the hours of crisis and extreme effort. These were the
periods for which she enjoyed months of calm and quiet such as she had spent
on the Mariposa and in the house at Black Point, resting, storing up her
strength.

She walked to the chiffonier to gaze at herself in the mirror. What she saw
reflected there was not the gentle face she had known. All beauty was gone,
and all softness. It was impersonal, hard-set, with nothing feminine about it.
Her King George's Mark had already begun to show beneath the left corner
of her mouth. This was a mask that could have been fitted onto a soldier
and not have seemed incongruous; the harsh black dress she wore day after
day might easily be a uniform.

Resolutely she patted her hair into place, kicked out her skirt behind her,
and left the room for her next conference with General Fremont.

6

John had little time to deal with anything but military strategy and policy
making; it was up to her to fill in the vast gaps with detail. Horace Greeley
had complimented her on being an executive housewife. In this emergency,
general headquarters was not unlike a home, and the plans for military

supply an elaboration of the countless details one had to fulfill in order to keep a home and family functioning successfully.

Her attitude involved only a desire to extend her husband. She was proud of the manner in which he instilled a fighting spirit into the troops and prepared them for battle. She marveled at how he kept his poise and patience when Washington commandeered the arms he had bought in Europe, refusing to send any part of them to the Western Command, when General Meigs canceled his order for Canadian horses without even informing him of the cancellation. To her ever watchful eyes he showed no lessening of spirit in the chaos that surrounded him.

The days were full of worries and frustrations, for the worst blight of all had descended upon the Department of the West: southern guerrilla forces were laying waste Missouri, burning the farms and the homes and driving the Union supporters out of the state. The guerrillas operated in small bands, apparently unorganized, yet striking so suddenly and doing so much quick damage in the night that they had the effectiveness of an army. John sent out heavily armed parties in search of the guerrillas; they could not be found, let alone stopped. But one thing he did learn: the bands were composed of men from plantations who were able to leave their homes because their Negro slaves remained behind to do the work. After battering his head against this problem through the hot days of August, he commented to Jessie, "There is only one way to beat these guerrillas, but it's a drastic action . . ."

"What is it?"

"I can liberate the slaves in my department."

"Emancipation! But, John, have you the power? Have you the right?"

"You're asking two questions in one, Jessie. As military commander, I have the power; as to whether or not I have the moral right, that is something every man will have to decide for himself. If I issue an emancipation proclamation for all slaves whose owners have gone to war against us, it will serve two important purposes: it will send these guerrilla plantation owners scurrying back to their homes to protect their property; and it will make them unwilling to risk the loss of their slaves. If they persist in fighting, they will release thousands of Negroes to the Union forces."

"It will change the nature of the war," cried Jessie. "Up to now we've been fighting to keep the South from dissolving the Union; too many people in the North think we ought to let the southern states go, that they are only a source of trouble anyway. But this proclamation would convert the war into a crusade for freedom."

He ran his hands wearily over his eyes. "I don't know," he mumbled. "When I think of this emancipation from a military point of view it looks clear and logical; then when I start thinking of the political implications . . . I am no politician, Jessie; all I want to do is defeat the secessionists in the Western Command. The closer I get to the war the less I understand what the North is fighting for. Is it to punish the South for firing on Sumter? To force them back into the Union? Or to abolish slavery, so that the nation will be able to think about something else?"

"Each group in the country has its particular reason, depending on where the people live and what they believe."

"And may I ask why you are fighting the war, Mrs. Fremont?"

"I can answer that simply and directly: to abolish slavery." She came to her husband's side. "Don't you think we should talk it over with Frank Blair?" she asked. "He will understand the political implications . . ."

"No, no!" broke in John. "This issue must be settled on its military necessity, not politically. Frank would begin to talk about its effect on the doubtful border states, whether it might not drive some of them into the Confederacy, and what its effect would be in official Washington. I would want it to be a local military maneuver, applicable to Missouri alone. Its effectiveness will depend upon its suddenness and surprise; Frank would have it in the newspapers by the next day."

There was silence in the room while they both carried forward the train of thought. Jessie found herself studying her husband. He no longer parted his hair in the middle, but wore it brushed forward in rather a short and flat line, still moderately curly. His hair and beard were more gray than black, his forehead higher because of the receding hairline; his expression was the strongest and most positive she had seen it since the days of the earliest expeditions: his eyes large, boldly analytical, determined to action. Conscious of the two stars of the major general in the epaulets on either shoulder, he gave the impression of a man of vigor and action, entirely able to emerge victorious.

Aware of her searching scrutiny, he said quietly, "What do you say, Chief of Staff? Would you approve?"

Jessie threw back her head with a defiant gesture.

"Yes, General, I approve heartily: it will show the South that we mean business, it will keep many slaveholders from waging war against us."

The next morning she was awakened at dawn by a sharp knock at her door. When she answered, the voice of an orderly called out, "Mrs. Fremont, the general wants you at his desk immediately." She dressed as quickly as she could and went down the stairs to John's office on the second floor. She did not speak, but one look at her husband showed her that he had done little sleeping, if any, that night.

"Jessie, I have decided that there is no time to be lost. We must clear Missouri of the guerrillas. This order will do it."

He picked up the sheet of tight handwriting, gave it to his wife and asked her to read it aloud. She read:

In order to suppress disorder, to maintain the public peace, and to give security and protection to the persons and property of loyal citizens, I do hereby extend and declare established martial law throughout the state of Missouri. The property, real and personal, of all persons in the state of

Missouri who shall take up arms against the United States, or who shall be
directly proven to have taken an active part with their enemies in the field,
is declared to be confiscated to the public use, and their slaves, if any they
have, are hereby declared freemen.

When she had finished she was breathing hard. John said firmly, "The time
has come for decisive action. I have been given the power to crush rebellion
in the department, and I will bring the penalty of rebellion home to every
man striving against the Union."

She laid the order down on the desk, saying excitedly, "This is the most
important document that has yet appeared in the war; giving freedom to the
slaves of the Rebels will make it impossible for the South to continue
fighting."

He asked her to transcribe his order so that it would be legible for the
printer, and then have it set up on the press. After taking it down to the
printer in the basement, she stood by his side while he ran proof. She then
took a copy over to the St. Louis *Democrat,* and returned to the newspapermen's quarters to give them the full story.

Neither she nor John was prepared for the enthusiasm and almost hysterical acclaim with which his emancipation proclamation was greeted in the
North. Jubilant crowds marched and sang in the streets of New England;
young men who had been holding back in uncertainty as to what the war
was about rushed to the recruiting offices. A member of Congress announced
that "it stirred and united the people of the loyal states far more than any
other event of the war." The great newspapers of the North, including the
New York *Herald* and the Chicago *Times,* which had been sympathetic
toward the South, joined in the praise. The emancipation proclamation,
with accompanying editorials, was splashed across the front pages of the
New York *Times* and *Tribune,* the Washington *National Intelligencer,* the
Boston *Post,* the Chicago *Tribune. Harper's Weekly* declared it "the beginning of the end," a feeling shared by a majority of those in the loyal states.
In the Midwest people cried, "At last we know what we're fighting for, and
now we'll get it over with fast."

While sitting in the basement telegraph office, organizing the hundreds of
congratulatory messages that were pouring in, Jessie found one from Secretary of War Cameron. She rushed it upstairs to John, for this constituted
official administrative approval of his action.

But on the morning of September first, Frank Blair arrived at headquarters. John received him courteously; Jessie exchanged only a quick
piercing glance. They had been careful to give him no further affront, had
leaned over backwards to grant contracts of supply to several of his less
unreliable friends, but the chasm between them had grown wider over conflicts in authority. Although they had had no further personal differences,
their quarrel had been carried on with ever mounting intensity in the press.
The *Democrat* was lavishing praise on John for his swift organization of the

department; where once it had lauded Frank Blair for saving Missouri, it now urged him to go back to Washington and leave the West in the more capable hands of General Fremont. Outraged, Frank launched a violent counteroffensive in the St. Louis *Evening News,* with scathing articles on the failure of General Fremont to carry through any of the preparations so carefully laid by Blair and Lyon.

Coming into their presence now, he castigated John roundly for having usurped his authority, for having done something which would embarrass President Lincoln, the administration and the northern cause.

"This act was done behind my back!" he declared vehemently. "You had no right to make such a move without my knowledge and consent. I am the political leader here and am responsible for Missouri. Our political war is as important as the military! Had you consulted with me, I could have shown you the folly of your act."

Jessie was glad that she had not revealed to her husband Frank's quarrel with her: It would make it easier for John to keep his temper. When he denied that he was obliged to consult Frank, or get his consent before making a military move, Jessie was reassured to find his voice not only courteous but friendly.

"Then you repudiate my authority in Missouri?" Frank demanded.

"No," replied John, "I recognize your political leadership. But I am the military leader, and the emancipation proclamation was a military measure."

Outraged, Frank leaned over John's desk and said in a hoarse but intense tone, "I was grossly deceived about your capabilities. You issued your emancipation proclamation, not for military purposes, but as a political maneuver to regain the confidence of the North which you lost because of your failure to reinforce Lyon. You have made a hopeless failure and confusion of your command. I am going to admit my mistake in recommending you by filing charges with President Lincoln, asking for your recall."

He stormed out of the office. Jessie sprang up and followed, overtaking him on the broad staircase leading to the foyer.

"Frank," she said quietly, so that no one in the downstairs offices might hear, "do you realize that you've accused John of issuing his emancipation proclamation as a charlatan would, seeking political support at any cost? I know you couldn't believe that possible of John, but if you make the accusation it is going to have unfortunate implications. For the sake of our friendship, and the friendship of our families, don't let us come to a breaking point. If you disagree with the wisdom or effectiveness of the emancipation proclamation, that is your privilege, but please come back with me and tell John that you don't think him a political adventurer, endangering the cause of the Union and the war for his private purpose."

With his eyes flashing, his body taut, Frank replied, "That is precisely what I do mean. That's exactly what John Fremont is. He has failed and weakened our position in the West; now he is using the most dangerous weapon within his reach to pull himself out of the chaos. But he shan't get away with it, Jessie; I'll convict him before the world for the bungler he is."

The anxiety and tremulousness within her died. She could see no further hope in placation. In a voice as furious as Frank's she said, "Very well, Frank, if it is your purpose to declare war on us, we will treat you as we would treat a Rebel caught within the lines with a gun in his hand. If you want us for enemies, you shall have us!"

The encounter with Frank should have warned them that they might not face as clear sailing as the first outbursts of enthusiasm had indicated, but they were completely unprepared when a letter arrived by special messenger from Abraham Lincoln, six days after the publication of the emancipation proclamation, requesting that General Fremont withdraw it. They were stunned and a little ill.

"But why has President Lincoln done this," exclaimed Jessie, "when the North has approved so heartily?"

"Francis and Montgomery Blair have gotten to him: Lincoln says that the emancipation proclamation will alarm our southern Union friends and ruin our prospects in Kentucky . . ."

"And you are ordered to revoke the emancipation proclamation!"

"Yes. But it is suggested that I do it on my own authority, so that it will not appear that I have been rebuked."

"What do you intend to do? In only six days we have seen important progress against the guerrillas . . ."

"I must either admit I was wrong . . . or refuse the president's suggestion."

"Why not write Mr. Lincoln as strong a letter as you can, explaining the reasons for your action and the good it is already accomplishing?"

"First I must dictate my official reply and give it to the dispatch bearer. I am not going to take Mr. Lincoln's suggestion. If he wants the emancipation rescinded, he will have to do it by his own order. However, in a personal letter I think I can convince him to let the order stand."

He rose from his desk and paced the room. "If only I could speak to Mr. Lincoln, I could show him the merciful nature of our measure. Letters are cold things at best; Mr. Lincoln may be too busy or involved to read ours carefully, there will be no one on hand to interpret or answer questions. I wish I could go to Washington and explain the situation, but it is impossible for me to leave here."

"Isn't there anyone on your staff whom you could trust to speak for you?"

"Yes, there is one."

"Who?"

"You. You were my representative in Washington during the years I was away. You'll have to take that job again."

The request came as a surprise, yet never for an instant did she doubt that she would be received at the White House as one qualified to speak for her husband. Former presidents had always received her in this capacity; certainly Mr. Lincoln would be the more friendly, since he had campaigned so arduously for Fremont and Jessie in 1856 and they had helped win California for him in the election of 1860.

John walked to the window, raised the green blind and stood staring down into the glare of the street below. She noted how sharp and precise his profile was, how white his trim, close-cropped beard had become. He turned to her, his eyes grave, almost brooding.

"We must reach Mr. Lincoln with our private letter first and with your interpretation and presentation of the full case. That is the most important thing, Jessie, do you understand? You must get to him with this informal letter before he has had a chance to see my official dispatch or write the rescinding order. A matter of a few minutes one way or the other may make all the difference. The dispatch bearer will be on the same train . . ."

"Trust me," replied Jessie. "I know the shortest cut to the White House from any given point in Washington. It's a good deal like Colonel Abert's letter: if I had waited until the next morning, or even nightfall, a duplicate letter would have reached you by the mail boat, before DeRosier could have covered the ground on horseback."

A sudden despair came over her when she realized what she had said. Quickly she murmured, "John, have you ever regretted my decision at that moment? If I had not withheld that order there never would have been a court-martial."

"Nor would there have been a second or third expedition," he replied in a dry voice, without smiling. "We would have been robbed of our most important opportunity and would have failed to make our most important contribution. I regret nothing from those years, Jessie, except my personal quarrel with General Kearny. I don't say I was wrong in what I did, but only that I wish it could have been avoided."

"I never told you," she murmured; "after you left the Delaware Indian Reservation, an aide reached me from General Kearny begging me to come to him with my forgiveness before he died. I sent the courier back with a message that I could not forgive him, that a grave stood between us. General Kearny died the next day. I was wrong, John, I should have forgiven him . . ."

The memories of the Delaware Indian Reservation, of the loss of their first son and the tragedy that almost engulfed their marriage, swept over them both. They were quiet in the hot, bare room, reliving for a swift instant the pain of that difficult time, yet rejoicing that they had come through it unscathed, that they had other sons, that John was now a general as she had predicted he would be on the day that he was appointed a lieutenant colonel. For a moment there fell away from them their burdens, their responsibilities, their labors, the ominously threatening future, and they were cut out of time and place and crisis, were once again a husband and wife whose chief sustainer, the only thing that never failed them, was their love. For this one brief instant, cut out of a world at war, a world in flames, they were locked in embrace.

Then Jessie thanked John for his confidence, told him that she would prepare to leave on the night train and that she would do her best to represent him in Washington.

With a fragment of a smile John replied, "I am sure your campaign will be successful, General Jessie."

She reddened, not having realized that John knew of the title. He touched her shoulder reassuringly, said, "I will want to know the results of your interview at the earliest possible moment. However, you had best not send it on the regular telegraph routes, as the Blair faction undoubtedly have spies here at headquarters. Take along this cipher code and send a message to Lieutenant Howard, signing the name of his fiancée."

Jessie picked up the code book. "I'll telegraph immediately after my first interview with the president. I will do my best to make it good news."

7

At six o'clock that night she left the Union Depot. The train was jammed with soldiers, with civilians on private and governmental business, and with families from the interior of Missouri fleeing northward from the guerrillas. Though the war was only five months old the rolling stock was already deteriorating, carrying three times its normal capacity on each journey. She found a seat in one of the coaches. It was a hot September night, and by the time the train pulled out the aisles and platforms were filled with standing men, with women sitting on their suitcases.

She did not close her eyes all night: the heat, the noise of the wheels beneath her, the swaying and jostling of the train, made sleep impossible. Knowing that there would be little food available, she had packed an oilcloth bag of victuals. There was no chance to wash or change her clothing, the few facilities being overtaxed and rapidly going out of commission. She passed the hours as best she could, dropping off to sleep now and then when exhaustion overcame her, awakening stiff and sore from the hard wooden bench.

The train reached Washington a little before eight o'clock on the evening of the second day. She was met by Judge Coles, an old friend from New York, who had worked with them during the 1856 campaign. He had a carriage waiting and a room reserved for her at the Willard Hotel. Two hours before completing the journey she had felt at the end of her strength, but now that she was in Washington, so close to the task on hand, she had no patience with her own fatigue, but only a desire to accomplish what she had planned minutely a thousand times during the fifty hours on the train.

When they reached the hotel, and Jessie had washed her hands and face, she said to Judge Coles, "I must send a message to Mr. Lincoln, urging an immediate audience."

"But surely you don't intend to go to the White House this evening?"

"Yes. It is urgent that I see the president at once."

Quietly he suggested, "Wouldn't it be better if you had a night's sleep first? You must be exhausted from your train trip. In the morning you will be refreshed, your suitcase will be here and you will be able to dress . . ."

"No, no," she interrupted. "Tomorrow morning may be too late."

Judge Coles stared at her steadfastly for a moment. "As an old friend, may I ask why? What can you possibly accomplish tonight in your exhausted condition that can't be better done tomorrow morning?"

"There was a courier on my train with a dispatch for the president. It is part of my purpose in coming here to reach the president before he acts on the basis of that dispatch."

"Mr. Lincoln may not receive your message this evening. He is harassed and overworked; it may be sometime tomorrow before he will summon you."

"I will ask him to see me at once," replied Jessie; "if the message reaches him, I think he will grant my wish."

"As you see fit, Mrs. Fremont," replied the judge rather formally. "I will find a reliable messenger while you write the note."

It seemed to Jessie that the messenger had hardly had time to reach the White House, when he was back and delivered a card. It read:

A. LINCOLN

Now

Before leaving the hotel room Jessie took a quick glance in the dresser mirror. She noted that her hair was dusty from the long train ride and that it made her seem older. She noted too that her white collar was considerably more soiled than the rest of the white lawn gown, which was badly rumpled and discolored from the train. An image replaced that in the glass, the picture of herself in her court gown standing before the dresser mirror at the Clarendon Hotel in London, her hair piled on top of her head in the nine braids of the Polish fashion, her face aglow with the excitement of the Easter presentation to the queen. Dimly, at the back of her mind, she realized that it was neither good taste nor good manners to go to the president looking so soiled and worn, yet surely the kindhearted and simple-mannered Abraham Lincoln would not take offense, any more than he would take offense at any other soldier-courier being ushered into his presence with dispatches from the front lines.

She asked Judge Coles to accompany her to the interview, then took the short cut from the Willard to the White House. As she entered the front door she said to herself, All my life I've been at home in the president's house; but now most of all I must be received well.

They were ushered into the red parlor. The page told them that the president would be there shortly. She stood awaiting President Lincoln's entrance, not wanting to be seated when he entered the room. However, the moments passed in an agony of suspense and fatigue; it seemed to her a very long time before the far door was opened and Abraham Lincoln appeared against the brighter kerosene lamps of the dining room. He stopped for an instant to close the dining-room door behind him, but as he advanced slowly toward her Jessie saw the door opened again, and behind it she caught a glimpse of Mary Todd Lincoln.

She searched the president's face intently for a clue to her reception. Mr. Lincoln's expression was noncommittal. He did not speak but only bowed slightly. After Jessie had thanked him for receiving her, she introduced Judge Coles as a member of the New York Bar. President Lincoln said nothing, nor did the expression on his face change. Upset by the coolness, she reached into her bag, drew forth John's sealed letter and said:

"General Fremont asked me to deliver this letter into your hands, Mr. President. The general felt the subject to be of so much importance that he sent me to answer any points on which you might want further information."

President Lincoln held out his hand for the letter. As he broke open the seal and moved closer to the light of the chandelier, Jessie thought in terror, His mind is already turned against John; he has been listening to our enemies. That is why he has given me such a cold reception, why he is so neglectful of me. Why has he not offered me a seat, when I must look as tired as I feel? Mr. Lincoln has already decided to discourage me and to take a stand against John. I must do my best to change his mind. I must not appear nervous or overwrought. I must sit down, the better to conceal my feelings, even though the president has not offered me a chair.

Judge Coles had discreetly withdrawn to the blue parlor, where Jessie occasionally caught a glimpse of him walking up and down before the open doorway. For a moment she watched the president while he stood beneath the chandelier reading the long letter; then she drew out one of the row of chairs and seated herself.

After a time President Lincoln finished his reading of the letter. He came to her side, pulled a second chair out of the row along the wall and sat at an angle, facing her. The long arm which held the letter seemed to be resting the sheet on the red carpet.

"Mrs. Fremont," he said, "I have written to the general and he knows what I want done."

"Mr. Lincoln, may I ask if you have revoked the general's emancipation proclamation?"

"Yes, I have just finished writing a draft of the order. It will be copied and sent tomorrow morning."

"Mr. President," she cried, "before that message is sent out, before it is too late, let me give you a full picture of what is happening in Missouri, let me show you why the general's emancipation proclamation can help materially in winning the war."

When she saw a frown come over the president's face, she continued more quickly. "That is why I have come, Mr. President, because General Fremont thought it would be advantageous if I could explain fully. The general feels that he is at the great disadvantage of being opposed by people in whom you have every confidence."

"Whom do you mean," demanded President Lincoln, "persons of different view?"

Jessie knew that she had been rebuked. She said, "The general's conviction is that it will be long and dreadful work to conquer by arms alone, that there must be other considerations to get us the support of the West. An idea sometimes can be as effective as a gun: if we convince the South that every Rebel will lose his slaves, the secessionist leaders will have an internal war on their hands, and that will seriously hamper their efforts to recruit and fight . . ."

"You are quite a female politician," remarked the president.

Jessie recoiled as though she had been struck. In the few seconds that passed as she sat in silence before the president, she reflected that he had not heard what she had said; he had rejected her reasoning summarily because she was a woman. As General Kearny had told her, women could do no good in a man's world; they would only make for chaos. And now here was Abraham Lincoln, who had campaigned so ardently for FREMONT AND JESSIE, this man who had every reason to be her friend and admirer, looking down upon her and despising her, calling her a female politician.

Her eyes reflected some of her hurt; President Lincoln's expression softened and he said in a firm but kindly manner, "The general ought not to have done it; he never would have done it if he had consulted Frank Blair. I sent Frank there to advise him and to keep me advised about the work, the true condition of things there, and how they were going."

"But, Mr. President, you gave the general *carte blanche* in the Western Department. You told him to do whatever he thought necessary for victory."

"Military victory, Mrs. Fremont." The president went on in a tone which she could only interpret as angry. "The general should never have dragged the Negro into the war! It is a war for a great national object. The Negro has nothing to do with it."

"General Fremont has strong influence and followers in Missouri; if it was his determination to carry through the emancipation order, he could do so . . ."

Mr. Lincoln frowned, said, "Mrs. Fremont, we have no independent commanders in the Union army; they are all under the command of the War Department."

She knew that the time of her interview was short, and she pushed forward to another phase of the problem.

"We were not aware that Frank Blair represented you," she said. "He did not do so openly. We had been led to believe that General Fremont was the sole commander of his department."

"Nothing has been done to limit or contravene the general's authority.

Quarrels do our cause much injury, Mrs. Fremont; they should not be permitted."

He rose. Jessie looked up to where he towered above her. She saw that she had been dismissed without accomplishing any portion of the task for which she had been sent. The president had not once referred to John's long letter or asked for any further information. Apparently his mind was made up about General Fremont and the emancipation proclamation. She must make one last effort to persuade him.

She rose and began talking, swiftly. She reviewed the full history of the Western Command, the chaos in which John had found it, his work to protect St. Louis, to drill the troops, to find equipment on his own account when it could not be provided by Washington; how he had saved Cairo, inspired confidence in the men. She outlined the guerrilla warfare, the hundreds of interlocking problems and how the emancipation proclamation would settle so many of them. She made the point of which she was profoundly convinced, that this was not a war of defense on the part of the North, or a war of revenge for firing on Sumter, or even a war to force the South back into the Union. It was a war to end slavery, and if it did not end slavery, even though the southern states might be whipped back into the Union, this war would rise again and again.

She was thinking and speaking at top speed and with the utmost precision now, but at the same time her mind took in all of the externals: President Lincoln's wife was listening at the door of the dining room; Judge Coles was listening at the door of the blue room; Abraham Lincoln was towering above her, dark, brooding, wanting to stop her and not knowing how. She did not know how long she spoke, ten minutes, perhaps fifteen; she did not even know all the things she said, for her mind was racing ahead wildly, trying to use these last few precious seconds to turn the tide of the president's repudiation of her husband. She stated the full and imposing case of all that John Fremont had done, beseeching the president not to listen to John's enemies, not to withdraw his confidence, not to undermine his position by rebuking him before the nation as an impetuous and headstrong man, one who took authority into his own hands.

But suddenly her voice and her mind stopped in mid-sentence, for she perceived that Mr. Lincoln was offended: offended at her coming to the White House in her soiled gown, her hair dusty with the soot of the train and the road; offended that she had not accepted her dismissal when she had been dismissed, offended because she was intruding into a man's world where she did not belong, offended that she was trying to force her judgment upon him when the results of any serious action must be his responsibility, and his alone.

There was a harsh silence while she and the president stood looking at each other. Then, in a voice so soft she hardly knew whether the words could be heard, she thanked him for his kindness in receiving her. He did not reply.

"When could I have the answer to General Fremont's letter?" she asked.
"I have a great deal to do. Tomorrow, if possible, or the next day."
"Thank you, Mr. President. I will come for it."
"No, I will send it to you tomorrow or the day after. Where are you staying?"
"At Willard's, Mr. President. I shall wait there for your answer. Good night, sir, and thank you."

As they walked through the grounds, Judge Coles said, "Mrs. Fremont, the general will be deprived of all his part in the war; there is a faction which plans the affairs of the North, and they are against the general."

Too crushed and despondent to answer, Jessie bade the judge good night at the entrance to the hotel, went to her room and wrote out a cipher message to John. She gave him the tone of what had happened, but did not allow herself to appear too pessimistic, telling him instead that she would stay in Washington until she had fulfilled her mission. Almost ill with fatigue now, she fell out of her soiled clothes and into bed. Deep in her heart was the crushing knowledge that she had bungled, done everything exactly wrong, so thoroughly antagonized the president that there could be no possible hope of winning him back to their side.

She had wanted to be the strongest possible wife; now that it was too late, she realized that General Kearny, Frank Blair and President Lincoln had been right: the least wife is the best wife.

8

She slept late the next morning, awakening after eight o'clock, took a hot bath, washed her hair carefully, and was greatly relieved to be able to don clean linens and a fresh gown. She had no sooner dressed than Francis Blair knocked sharply at the door. Five years had elapsed since he had campaigned for the Fremonts; even the fringe of hair around his bald head had now disappeared, and his eyes seemed only half open. They embraced in the manner of people acknowledging the past, yet angry and ready to fight about the future.

"Well," said Francis Blair, "who would have expected you to do such a thing as this, to come here and find fault with the president? What sense was there in antagonizing Mr. Lincoln?"

"I didn't antagonize him. On the contrary, the president was hard and cold to me. He had made up his mind against me before I got there, and did not even pay me ordinary courtesy."

"Don't you understand the staggering burden the president is laboring under?" exclaimed Blair. "You had no right to take a belligerent tone towards him; no man would have presumed to do so. If you want to play a man's game, you should not lean on your prerogatives as a woman to break the rules."

Thoroughly alarmed, she asked faintly, "Why do you charge me with these things?"

"Because the president says you taxed him so violently that he had to exercise all his tact to avoid quarreling with you. He also said you intimated that if General Fremont should decide to try conclusions with him, he could set up for himself."

Jessie was struck dumb at the last accusation. She sat down abruptly on the edge of a chair. "Try conclusions with the president! But I said no such . . . What led Mr. Lincoln to believe . . . ?"

"Didn't you tell the president that if General Fremont determined to carry through the emancipation order, he could do it without . . ."

Her heart sinking, Jessie exclaimed, "So that was why Mr. Lincoln said what he did about independent commanders! But I didn't mean that John could set himself up against the president! I only meant that Mr. Lincoln need not be afraid of John's success with the emancipation order in Missouri."

"Why did you come to Washington at all? Why couldn't you let Frank handle things in St. Louis, with Montgomery handling them here at the capital? Why do you have to quarrel with Frank, try to push him out of the picture in Missouri?"

Summoning her strength, Jessie replied, "We tried our best not to quarrel with Frank. We tried in every way to propitiate him. But from the moment of Nathaniel Lyon's death he seemed to lose confidence in us."

"Frank told me the very opposite. He wrote me that he was trying to avoid quarreling with you, but that you seemed to want to quarrel as an excuse to get rid of him."

"No, no! That isn't true, Mr. Blair, you know we have always loved Frank."

"Before you went to St. Louis I urged you to come to Washington, I showed you how you could help your husband here—told you that it was not fitting for a woman to go with an army. If you had stayed in Washington you could have had everything you wanted. But you disregarded me, and now, of all times that you should not have come, you go into the presence of the president in an unkempt condition . . ."

"There were reasons for my going to the president at the first possible moment, and my fresh linens had not arrived from the depot. We know that Frank sent the president an angry letter filing charges against John. That's true, isn't it?"

"Frank wrote to Mr. Lincoln," admitted Blair, "but it was not an angry letter. It merely surveyed the situation in the West."

". . . and asked for John's recall?"

"The president is going to give John every opportunity; he has faith in John's impulses and integrity, but no faith in him as a military leader. After all, John was a topographical engineer, not a military man. That is why the president has sent Montgomery and General Meigs to investigate the Western Command."

Jessie sprang up to confront Blair.

"John has accomplished miracles in Missouri in the six weeks of his command. Show me one Union general who has done better! His men are fighting every day, fighting without food, without supply wagons, without artillery . . ."

"You have done John no good. We've heard reverberations about General Jessie . . ."

"Have you heard the term used disparagingly?"

Blair took a gentler tack. "There has been no severe criticism, in fact Dorothea Dix has complimented you on your work with the sick. But the fact that the name is used is a criticism in itself. Can't you see how incongruous it is? Are you an amazon, a leader of a woman's army, that you should be called General Jessie? Since when do women become generals? It's bad taste, Jessie; it's pushing oneself in where a woman doesn't belong, no matter how good a job she may do."

"That is the sheerest sophistry, Mr. Blair. It was only five years ago that you complimented me on the part I was playing in the election, making the women of America interested in politics, helping to bring in the family vote. When a woman is serving your purpose, you approve her activities; when what she is doing seems to conflict with your interests, then you drag in the extraneous matter of sex. That's not consistent, Mr. Blair, and inconsistency is reputed to be a feminine attribute."

Francis Blair picked up his hat from the chiffonier, then put his hands on her shoulders. "Jessie, I'm too old a man now to quarrel with the children I helped raise. You know how deeply I love Frank, you know what high ambitions I hold for him. That is why it racks me so to have you two quarrel. But whatever happens, you and I must not cease loving each other: Tom Benton would insist on that, Jessie."

She kissed his leathery cheek. Blair went out, closing the door behind him. She thought how like her meeting with General Kearny over the howitzer this meeting with Francis Blair had been; she recalled what tragic results had evolved from her contretemps with Kearny, and had the gravest misgivings lest the parallel be carried out.

She waited through the hours for Mr. Lincoln's letter, hoping against hope that it would be friendly and reassuring. As she passed the small mirror she noted to her surprise that, though she had washed her hair early that morning, the dust of the train trip was still sprinkled through it. She leaned closer to the mirror and took a carefully scrutinizing look.

It isn't dust at all, she murmured, half aloud. My hair has turned gray. It must have happened last night.

For a moment she was stunned, then her eyes filled with tears.

At five in the afternoon, no longer able to endure the cramped hotel room, feeling that she would go out of her mind with anxiety if she did not get an hour's release, she put on her hat and left the hotel. She did not know where she was going, but she soon found herself turning into C Street. She stood in front of the Benton lot, which was still owned by the family, though no one had built on it. The brick chimney had been pulled down, the ground was overgrown with weeds. As she stood there, it came over her how alone she was in Washington now, and how hostile a city it had become. Eliza was away with her husband on war business. Her two younger sisters lived elsewhere, the great host of southern cousins and friends had gone home, hating the Fremont name. She had known every house and stile and meadow and stream, and nearly every face that walked the streets of the capital; now she knew no one. The city had grown past her and beyond her, she was no longer wanted here; for the first time she had been unwelcome in the White House.

Above all of her heartbreak and anxiety there was one emotion which engulfed her: if only her father could be here, if only Senator Thomas Hart Benton of Missouri had taken her arm as they mounted the steps of the White House, everything would have worked out well. But Tom Benton had lived his life, conducted his campaign, and now he was gone; she would have to fight her own battles. She recalled the words that Thomas Starr King had written to a friend about her: "Jessie Fremont carries guns enough to be formidable to a whole Cabinet: she is a she-*Merrimac*, thoroughly sheathed and carrying fire in the genuine Benton furnaces."

At this moment, tired, discouraged, uneasy at the president's long silence, her King George's Mark throbbing painfully, not knowing what to do next or where to turn, she did not feel like a she-*Merrimac*; the fires had been pretty well banked by her meetings with Mr. Lincoln and Mr. Blair. At the moment she felt only one desire, to be able to run, to run fast and far away from these scenes of conflict in Washington and St. Louis, to go back to her cottage on Black Point overlooking San Francisco Bay and the strait, where she could hear the sails flapping in the wind as the ships came into the harbor.

Early the second morning, after passing a sleepless night, she wrote Mr. Lincoln a letter:

To the President of the United States:

I was told yesterday by Mr. Francis Blair that five days since, a letter was received from his son Frank Blair, and laid before you by his son Postmaster Montgomery Blair, containing certain statements respecting General Fremont and his military command in the Western Department.

I was further told by Mr. Blair that on the basis of that letter, you sent Postmaster Blair and General Meigs to St. Louis to examine into that Department, and report.

On behalf of, and as representing General Fremont I have to request that I be furnished with copies of that letter, and any other communications,

*if any, which in your judgment have made that investigation necessary.
I have the honor to be*

Yours very respectfully,
JESSIE BENTON FREMONT.

By midafternoon she had a reply from the president.

MRS. GENERAL FREMONT.
MY DEAR MADAM:

*I answered the letter you bore me from General Fremont, on yesterday,
and not hearing from you during the day, I sent the answer to him by mail.
I do not feel authorized to furnish you with copies of letters in my possession,
without the consent of the writers. No impression has been made on my mind
against the honor or integrity of General Fremont, and I now enter my
protest against being understood as acting in any hostility towards him. Your
obedient servant,*

A. LINCOLN.

Seeing that there was nothing further she could do in Washington, she took
the night train back to St. Louis. The following morning, as the train was
leaving Harrisburg, a middle-aged gentleman who had been sitting opposite
her with his wife rose, came to her side, bowed respectfully, and said,
"Madame Fremont, I am going to ask you a question; my wife and I want the
answer to it. Is it true that the president is going to refuse to use emancipation as a weapon in the war?"

"It is true."

The woman threw up her hands and cried, "Oh, my son! My son! I had
given him willingly! I gave him to the Lord, but now it's for nothing."

Upon her return to St. Louis she found that John had achieved a strategic
victory: two weeks before he had appointed Ulysses S. Grant a brigadier
general, putting him in charge of southeastern Missouri and southern Illinois,
with headquarters at Cairo. General Grant had acted with speed and vigor,
moving into Paducah just ahead of the Confederate General Polk, thus insur-
ing to federal troops passage down the Mississippi when the major campaign
began. Grant had waited in General McClellan's outer office for four days,
hoping for an appointment, and had been ignored; John had selected him,
as he told Jessie, for "qualities I could not find combined in any other man,
for General Grant has dogged persistence and an iron will."

She determined to forget about the unfortunate episode in Washington,
confident that the means would soon be available for John to start on his
full-strength campaign. The reaction in the newspapers and among the public,
when President Lincoln rescinded John's emancipation proclamation, was almost as intense as it had been ten days before when they had news of it:
enlistments fell off, people declared themselves no longer interested in the
war, the outcry in such states as Indiana and Illinois was so pain-fraught that
the war effort was seriously injured.

She found it increasingly difficult to make any progress in the field of supply; Frank Blair had been provided with a complete account of her meetings in Washington with Mr. Lincoln and with his father, and was more determined than ever to secure John's removal. He organized the dissident elements in Missouri, waged a campaign against John in the *Evening News,* began spreading the impression throughout the West that since General Fremont must very soon be deposed there was consequently little sense in helping to fulfill his purposes or obeying his commands. John's former imperturbable poise was slowly being shattered by the effectiveness of Frank's campaign.

"Now I know what General Winfield Scott meant in the Mexican War," he commented, "when he complained about 'a fire in front from the Mexicans, and a fire upon my rear from Washington.'"

Jessie was no longer capable of judicious thinking about the youngest of the Blair family. "Doesn't Frank's conduct amount to treason?" she asked. "If he is doing everything in his power to obstruct the formation and supply of your army, then surely that is giving aid and comfort to the enemy? If you caught anyone else giving aid and comfort to the enemy, you'd soon put an end to his activities. Then why can't you stop Frank?"

"Because I don't know what to do with him."

During the next few days Blair's campaign for the removal of General Fremont broke into the open and was published in the northern press as well as the local western papers. The results were nearly disastrous to John's preparations. Once again husband and wife went into conference. As they sat in the bare front office, the light of the kerosene lamps flickering on the wall maps, regarding each other in gloom and misgiving, John's skin darkened, his eyes became angry. He muttered, "The simplest solution would be to shoot him; the next best thing would be to lock him in jail."

"You can't shoot him," she replied, coldly, "but you certainly can lock him up. It would be the greatest service you could perform for the northern cause."

"He belongs in jail, but . . ."

"Then put him there! You are hoping to leave for the southern battle front in a week or two. You will have no chance to be equipped if he is allowed to remain loose and oppose you. Lock him up; at least until you have won your victory in the south."

"Yes," replied John, "I think I'll do it."

He wrote out an order for the arrest, summoned the guard and sent it to Blair's home. They sat up until late that night drawing the formal charges. The next day Jessie learned that the nation was aghast at the arrest, for to the North it meant dissension and disunity and the weakening of the Union forces. A telegram arrived from Montgomery Blair which read, "I will send Frank's letter. It is not unfriendly, release him. This is no time for strife except with the enemies of the country."

The furor in the northern press shook her; she regretted their action, not because Frank had not deserved imprisonment at the Jefferson Barracks, but because John already had a sufficient number of wars on his hands. She considered the blunder to have been hers. Instead of keeping John's judgment calm in the midst of the furies, she had betrayed him, doubled his weakness by doubling his anger and counseling him to rash action. Twice within one week she had made serious errors, not only of judgment but of taste. Instead of helping her husband, she was hurting him immeasurably: she overheard one angry officer exclaim about the now notorious Blair Case: "That was General Jessie's doing!" Her husband had not reproved her for the fiasco in Washington; he had assured her that she had done her best. Yet encouraging him to imprison Frank Blair was inexcusable.

She locked herself in her bedroom to gain a few uninterrupted moments in which to think. She sat down heavily on the corner of her army cot. Didn't these two ghastly failures mean that she had exhausted her usefulness? Wouldn't it be the better part of kindness to go away now, to leave John alone to fight his war? Wouldn't it have been far better if she had accepted Frank Blair's first angry dictum that she would hurt her husband and make him ridiculous? No matter how many details she had taken off John's shoulders in the past two months, no matter how many supply trains had reached the battle fronts, no matter how many wounded had been routed to newly organized hospitals, how could these accomplishments compensate for her overzealousness?

She went out onto the tiny balcony and stood looking down into the street, watching the movement of the Zagonyi Guard on its way to the parade grounds. It was not only that she could not admit how sadly she had failed her husband, but that she must not demonstrate by public flight how misguided General Fremont had been in bringing his wife to the war. No, she must stand her ground, continue with her work, wait for the opportunity to make good her failures.

9

Her first act was to ask John to release Frank, but Blair refused his freedom, demanding a public trial and preferring formal charges against General Fremont with the War Department. However, within a few days, despite the condemnation of the North, the imprisonment began to have beneficial results. The general staff was co-operating more heartily, supplies and equipment were coming in faster, a new vitality spread through the troops. She was beginning to breathe easier when Colonel James A. Mulligan, who was being pursued by a superior Confederate force under General Price, determined to make a stand at Lexington, threw up hasty fortifications and sent urgent telegrams to General Fremont asking for reinforcements. Though the newspapers were saying that John had forty thousand trained troops available, Jessie knew that there were at his disposal something under seven thousand men, including the Home Guard, barely enough to defend St. Louis. Yet she also knew that if Colonel Mulligan suffered a severe defeat, this last blow might be the culminating stroke against John's command. When she went to his office to urge him to send Colonel Mulligan every last man available, John handed her two telegrams. The first from Secretary of War Cameron read:

THE PRESIDENT ORDERS 5000 WELL ARMED INFANTRY TO BE SENT HERE WITHOUT A MOMENT'S DELAY.

The second was from General Winfield Scott:

DETACH 5000 INFANTRY FROM YOUR DEPARTMENT TO COME HERE WITHOUT DELAY. THE PRESIDENT DICTATES.

"But can't you expostulate with them?" Jessie demanded. "Can't you telegraph and tell them you need the men to reinforce Colonel Mulligan?"

For the first time in many years she saw that there were tears in his eyes. "No," he said, "that would be insubordination, with which I have been unjustly charged. The capital must be again in danger, and must be saved, even if Missouri falls and I sacrifice myself."

Three days later Colonel Mulligan suffered the worst defeat the Western Command had yet known, with three thousand, five hundred men captured, as well as large quantities of munitions and commissary stores. The North went into mourning, for Missouri was supposed to be a loyal state, controlled by General Fremont, and here they were still suffering major setbacks. Jessie was obliged to report to her husband that the chief complaint of the northern press was that General Fremont was steadily losing battles and had still to win his first major victory. Many of the papers called for a new general, one who could win.

"This simply means that you must hasten your plans, John," she said. "You will have to strike before your preparations are complete. No one ever is going to reach any degree of perfection in this war: battles will have to be fought without sufficient men, guns or supplies. They'll have to be won with substitutes like daring and courage."

". . . which the South has in equal measure. I had hoped to wait until we had a superior quantity of guns, since the North obviously has greater resources for supply. But if the North is starved for victories, if it needs them for morale, then I shall have to get a victory at any price."

Within a few days he had moved out at the head of his troops. Jessie remained behind to serve as liaison officer for supply. A continuous stream of messages came in by courier making known John's wants: "Tell the Sanitary Committee that the whole surgical department here is in a very bad condition, and gives me great anxiety . . . Our difficulty consists absolutely and only in the want of transportation; ask Captain McKeever to do all that is humanly possible to get wagons, mules, harness and drivers sent forward . . . We must have sabers and guns; send such things forward as best you can

. . . Hurry up Constable's Battery if it is in any way possible to get him, and a thousand of the Austrian altered muskets would be most acceptable if we could have them sent at once . . . We want all the revolvers that can be spared . . . Hurry up the Guards and have the requisition for their clothing filled . . . Have Captain McKeever send up the Fitz H. Warren Regiment to me, all of it if possible . . . Order up instantly Colonel Crafts-Wright's Regiment . . ."

There were few officers left in St. Louis, and most of those on hand were sick. Jessie had no authority to sign orders or requisition goods; she spent half her time trying to locate the arms and supplies, the other half trying to get officers to sign the requisitions so that they would be legal. She worked with a demoniacal intensity which surpassed her own strength and abilities; for she knew how hard pressed John was, and how dangerous his position. She let no slight possibility escape her to send him a word of encouragement: to tell him how loyal the people of St. Louis were to him, of how certain they were of a smashing victory; of the tribute that Horace Greeley had paid him in the New York *Tribune,* of what a congressman had said on the floor the day before about the energy and the determination of General Fremont. She kept her letters cheerful, confident, loving; and always there would come back the reply, "I read your note to get its good, bright color."

On September twenty-ninth she received a telegram telling her that since he would be obliged to remain for a number of days in Jefferson City, she was to leave at once for his camp. She knew there was no special work for which she was wanted in Jefferson City; in addition to wanting to see her one last time before going into battle, this telegram-summons was a gesture of love and affirmation.

John met her at the railroad station in Jefferson City. She spent five days watching him whip the army into its final fighting form. There were still many things lacking: several of his officers had failed to bring up their regiments from other parts of Missouri; it was impossible to keep a continuous chain of supply wagons flowing to the camps. Yet she saw that none of these difficulties deterred John or his men: they were living off the countryside, were in the highest health and spirits and spoiling for the battle which would establish the Army of the West as one of the great fighting forces of the nation.

On the day before they were to break camp and move southward in pursuit of Confederate General Price, Secretary of War Simon Cameron arrived in camp unannounced. Secretary Cameron had long been an admirer of the Fremonts, had campaigned for them in 1856 and had supported their emancipation proclamation before Lincoln had turned the administration against it. Simon Cameron was tall, slender, with friendly gray eyes, a high brow, a magnificent stand of hair, and an ever youthful manner. He had been a newspaper editor as a youth, had joined journalism to politics, made a fortune out of state printing, gone on to railroad building and banking. Enormously successful as a businessman and a boss politician in Pennsylvania, he had scrambled for the Republican nomination in 1860, withdrawing in favor of Abraham Lincoln after Lincoln's manager had promised him the office of secretary of war. He gave war contracts only to his friends, and then blinked at their defrauding of the Union armies, a condition which had brought such an avalanche of criticism that President Lincoln was already casting about for a European appointment with which to get rid of him.

He said as bluntly as his genial manner would permit, "General, I have taken the liberty of inspecting your camp. I find things in confusion: the organization of the companies is bad, the troops are in need of clothing . . ."

"We are in need of many things, Secretary Cameron," replied John. "Supplies for which we have been begging Washington frantically for two months, and no part of which we have received. Though the men's uniforms may not be in fighting trim, their hands and hearts are."

"Please understand me, General," cried Secretary Cameron. "This investigation is not of my choosing."

"Then may we ask of whose choosing it is?" said Jessie.

"President Lincoln ordered me to investigate the general's department."

"Did you confer with Blair in St. Louis?"

"Yes, Mrs. Fremont, I went over the affairs of the department with Frank Blair."

There was an awkward moment of quiet, during which Jessie almost had to bite her tongue to keep from replying; but she had learned a bitter lesson in the past months, and so she kept silent, waiting for John to speak. It was Secretary Cameron who broke the silence.

"I have in my pocket a recall order signed by President Lincoln. He asked me to use my own judgment: if I did not find you ready to open the long-awaited campaign, I was to relieve you of your command."

Jessie had to admire the courtesy of John's manner.

"Secretary Cameron," he said, "let us not waste our time discussing Frank Blair or his charges against me in St. Louis. May I show you our plans for the offensive? We are ready to strike. In another thirty to sixty days we will have swept the Confederates out of Missouri, and our gunboat flotilla will have opened the Mississippi River all the way to New Orleans."

He launched into a vigorously detailed presentation of his campaign plans. Jessie watched Secretary Cameron; she was relieved to see the grimness ease out of his face as he became interested in John's swift maneuvers on the strategy maps before them. The sun had sunk behind the western hills and long shadows were creeping into the tent. An officer entered, saluted and said, "The troops are ready for the evening service, sir."

John looked up from his maps. "Mr. Secretary, would you pay us the honor of attending our last services?"

Secretary Cameron nodded, took Jessie's arm, went out of the tent and into the large open square. The Zagonyi Guard in its dark blue uniforms was drawn up at attention before the flag bearer, with troops solidly banking the square. The band played the hymn "Old Hundred" while the several thousand young soldiers sang the words of the simple prayer. To Jessie it was a beautiful and stirring sight, this army standing bareheaded against the setting sun as the chaplain gave the benediction. Then she heard the drumbeat which sent the companies back to their camps; as darkness overcame the square the fires were lighted on the hillsides, and they could hear the soldiers singing.

Jessie, John and Secretary Cameron stood quietly in the now deserted square until John finally said, "You have seen the Army of the West; you can see that there is no confusion in their hearts. They are ready and eager to fight for the Union."

Secretary Cameron turned to Jessie. "I will admit that Mrs. Fremont was right in her deduction. After my visit with Frank Blair in St. Louis I had decided to serve President Lincoln's removal order. But now I have changed my mind: I have seen your plans, I am impressed by your vitality, and if ever I have seen a unified body of men, ready to fight, this army which received its benediction tonight is ready. I am going to withhold the recall order until my return to Washington; this will give you a chance, General, to fulfill your hopes of routing the enemy."

"How much time will I have?"

"As much as I can earn for you. Strike hard and fast, let nothing deter you. We are starved for a victory: northern morale is shattered. Enlistments have fallen off, the administration is losing the confidence and support of the people, England and Europe expect our defeat and are planning to support the Confederacy. If you give us a victory now, at no matter what immediate cost, you may save the Union cause."

John's eyes flashed as he said, "You shall have your victory."

"Believe me, General Fremont, I myself would put no time limit on you, but your enemies in Washington are hounding Mr. Lincoln, giving him no peace, trying to force his hand . . . I can hold them off for only a few more weeks. Should you have failed by that time, you can understand that you must give place to some other officer."

"Should I fail," replied John gravely, "I will resign at once."

The next morning Jessie returned to general headquarters in St. Louis. On her maps, during the weeks following, she watched her husband push ever deeper south in pursuit of the enemy, Tipton, Warsaw, the Osage River, while General Price retreated, burning everything behind him. John had confided to her in code message that the enemy could not fall back farther than Springfield; he was confident that he could overtake them there and inflict a defeat.

Then on October twenty-sixth came news which thrilled both her and the nation: the Zagonyi Guard, numbering only one hundred and fifty men, had attacked and routed General Price's garrison of two thousand men at Springfield. This heroic action disproved the months of charges against John and the Zagonyi Guard: that they were bedecked autocrats whose only function it was to serve as a staff of honor to their general. It was the first good news Jessie had had in weeks, and she blessed the foolhardy, valiant men who had achieved the victory.

The next day, though the press still rang with praise of the Zagonyi charge, a secret message reached her from Washington. John's weeks of grace were up: President Lincoln had recalled him. The official order had already been dispatched by courier to General Hunter, in St. Louis. General Hunter was to relieve General Fremont, taking over his army and his command. After all John's work and plans, now, on the eve of his major attack, he was to be relieved, under conditions which implied that all charges against him were true.

She sat bolt upright in her chair: General Hunter was here in St. Louis. It would take two full days for President Lincoln's dispatch bearer to reach St. Louis by train. Her telegraphic message would have given her a day's start. What then, if she beat General Hunter to John's camp, gave him the word which would send him into action and bring about such a decisive victory that the recall order could never be served?

This was the opportunity she had been awaiting so eagerly, the chance to do John a service over and above the line of duty, of such outstanding importance that it would compensate for her failing with Abraham Lincoln and Frank Blair.

10

She sprang up and went to the map of Missouri hanging on the wall. John was camped just south of Springfield, about two hundred and fifty miles away. A train was due to leave for Rolla in two hours. Rolla was halfway to Springfield; from there she could hire fast carriages, and when these failed, saddle horses. That would still give her several hours' lead on General Hunter. She quickly packed a few toilet articles in a small handbag and by four o'clock was on the train that left the Union Station. The cars were crowded with troops, the roadbed was bad, the train made long stops every few miles for purposes which the passengers never ascertained.

She rode all night in the dark, cold car, almost beside herself with impatience at the fact that the train stood still in the middle of prairie darkness as often as it moved forward. She sat with her eyes closed, but her thoughts were racing at tremendous speed, recapitulating everything they had done since the first hour they reached St. Louis, all that could be done in the future if only John's drive to the south were successful.

She relived the agonies she had endured while waiting for DeRosier's brother to return from Kaw's Landing with word from John that he had started on the trail with his second expedition before Colonel Abert's recall order could reach him. Then, she had just turned nineteen; today she was going on thirty-eight; then she had stood up against Colonel Stephen Watts Kearny; today she had stood up against Abraham Lincoln. She knew that reverberations of her session with the president had done her serious injury, that Mr. Lincoln's closest friends were publicly labeling her a virago and a fishwife, calling her a dangerous woman because of her fanatical loyalty to her husband. Was there any other kind of loyalty? If she were not passionately prejudiced in her husband's favor, what kind of a wife was she, what kind of a marriage had she created? If a wife were unwilling to dash through the night to save her husband, even though she knew from years of deep-bitten experience the suffering and hardship which might ensue, was she being the most possible wife?

At six in the morning she had coffee and a roll in the station at Rolla, then found a livery stable, engaged a carriage and two horses. The driver was old and unused to hurrying, but something in her manner persuaded him to urgency. During the long hours of the morning she was jostled and bumped along the stagecoach road; at noon they exchanged horses at an inn where she was able to get a hot meal; within the hour they were on their way again. The driver knew his road, but in the failing light of dusk, outside Lebanon, one of the wheels struck a deep rut, broke and threw the carriage over on its side. Jessie crawled out unhurt, but she could not persuade the tired driver to do anything about getting a new wheel or patching the carriage.

Leaving her suitcase behind, she walked the seven miles to Lebanon as fast as she could. She had not slept for almost forty-eight hours, she had been jostled and scrambled and thrown out on the road and was near exhaustion, but her driving will pushed her forward. In Lebanon she hoped to find a fresh carriage.

It was dark by the time she reached the public square. The town was locked up for the night. She saw that it would be almost impossible to get even a saddle horse at this hour; simultaneously she realized that she was spent, that she would not be able to ride the remaining fifty miles to John's camp without a few hours of rest. Three men were talking at one side of the square; she went to them and asked if they could direct her to an inn. An elderly man studied her carefully, then motioned for her to follow him. He led her up the hill to a large house, opened the door and showed her in. His wife and daughters took her into a large family room; she saw at once from their faces, the violins and guitars, the high pile of music books, the too tightly plaited light hair of the women, that this was a bit of Germany transplanted to Missouri.

She explained that she wanted a room in which to rest for a few hours, and some kind of conveyance to take her to Springfield. The mother showed her to a small bedroom. She slept until she heard the sound of a cart coming up the hill. She dressed quickly, found that it was four in the morning and that her hosts could locate only a plow horse and a country cart without springs. The young son went along to drive for her, but the progress was so slow that she seized the first opportunity to rent a riding horse from a farmer along the road.

It was night when she reached John's camp. The sentry took her quickly to the general's tent, before which a fire was burning. As she opened the flap and stepped in, she saw John sitting at the end of a long wooden table, poring over his maps. He sprang up, an alarmed expression on his face, asked her a hundred questions, why she had come, how she had gotten there, what had happened. It was not until she had bathed her hands and face in cold water and rested for a few moments that she could speak.

"John," she said, "President Lincoln has recalled you. General Hunter is on his way here to take over your command."

His face became a polite mask of withdrawal as he asked, "When will General Hunter arrive?"

"I don't know. I have been dreading all along that I would be too late, that he would get here before me."

"We are attacking at dawn," he said quickly. "All the plans have been laid. The Rebels are determined to make their stand at Wilson's Creek. In another few hours we will reach the culmination of our month's work . . . and avenge Nathaniel Lyon's death."

"General Hunter may be only an hour or two away."

"I will double the guard." He summoned an officer, issuing orders that no one was to be admitted through the lines for any reason whatever. When the officer had left, John said, "Come, sit here with me at the table." She sat quietly while he sketched for her with darting fingers the strategy by means of which he intended to defeat General Price's army and drive it before him. She heard little of what he said. She knew that he would lead his troops into action, that what had happened to Nathaniel Lyon at Wilson's Creek could happen to John Fremont, that many men must fall. He might be one of them. After a time John saw that she was not listening. He studied the anxiety in her eyes, then pushed aside his papers and maps, taking her hand in his.

"You would not have me be a haystack general?"

"I was just thinking: we had a twentieth anniversary a few days ago. You were in camp near the Osage River. Neither of us thought of it. We were too busy and preoccupied. So, my darling, this is a kind of anniversary party for us."

John held the palm of her hand to his cheek, saying, "We will have a celebration tomorrow—when the battle is over and the victory is won. But you have brought me a real anniversary present, Jessie: a chance to make good before it is too late. You have always given me my chance to make good, and always it has been at some critical moment like this."

They sat in the cool quiet of the tent, on either side of a corner of the rough table, while their minds went back over the twenty years; each knew that this might be the end. The tent was filled with their unspoken thoughts, their recollections of their happy years as well as the trials and difficulties they had come through. Slowly, almost painfully, Jessie said: "It's easy to speak of love in ordinary times—when there is no crisis at hand. But now, when your life is in danger, when we face a possible separation, I am so filled with gratitude for our twenty years of companionship that I have almost nothing to tell you; nothing but what I have told you so many times before: that I love you, that I loved you from the first moment you stepped from behind Father's chair at Miss English's Academy and took my hand, that you have been my whole life, and you have made my life beautiful and happy."

He did not move, but only watched her.

"I promised you that rainy afternoon, when we sat over the tea table before the blazing fire, that I would always love you. It is that love that has kept me ever striving to meet your hopes. I don't know what will happen tomorrow, Jessie; war is uncertain. A hundred unforeseen things can take place which will keep us from a real victory. But I will go onto that battlefield at dawn knowing that I must win . . ."

There was a sharp rap on the outside supporting pole of the tent. A courier pushed aside one flap and stepped in, his face streaked where the lines of perspiration had cut through the dust of the road. He saluted, asked, "General Fremont?" then ripped open his coat lining, took out a document that had been sewed in, and handed it to John.

John slammed the paper down on the table and cried, "Sir, how did you get admission into my lines?"

"I was ordered by General Hunter to deliver this message to you, sir." He saluted and disappeared.

11

Jessie studied her husband's face anxiously while he looked first at the superscription, then at the signature at the bottom of the page. He then handed her the dispatch. She read the order, signed by President Lincoln, relieving General Fremont of his command. They sat in bitter silence for several moments, until John said, "The attack cannot be made at dawn. Everything that has been planned must be thrown aside."

"What is the hour now?"

"Almost midnight."

"Aren't you in command here until General Hunter arrives to supersede you?"

"Technically, yes."

"Then if General Hunter does not arrive by dawn, are you obliged to countermand your orders to this army? Everything has been prepared for a great victory. The Army of the West has the right to prove that it can fight and play its part in this war. You have that right too, John. If that messenger had been held outside the lines until morning . . ."

Seeming small and disheartened now, he could only reply, "You are right, Jessie, the attack should be made. This order will cost the North an important victory. Tomorrow will be a hundred days since we arrived in St. Louis; everything we have done since then, every move that has been made, has been pointed to this moment. It would be cruel to the northern cause to throw away this opportunity . . ."

"Then you will attack?"

"No, I cannot. Any other officer might—any other officer should. With my background, I cannot."

"But why, John?"

"I cannot commit mutiny."

Her thoughts stopped dead, for here was the enemy, their ever present companion, the one word in all the world which paralyzed their brain and courage as well, the symbol of their unhappiness. She walked quickly to her husband's side. They must not be defeated now by tortuous shadows from the past. She knew the chagrin that lay in store for him if he were deposed now, at this very instant of climactic action; if only she could persuade him to take the bold and brave course, her mission would be fulfilled. In the aftermath of John's great victory she would be able to step down with dignity, return north to her children because her task had been completed. John would go on to greater victories. She faced her husband resolutely.

"That is what you said when I urged you to send your troops to reinforce Colonel Mulligan, instead of obeying orders and sending your five thousand men to Washington so that General McClellan could parade them up and down Pennsylvania Avenue. Everything you've achieved, John, has come through independent action rather than blind obedience. It is the word we are afraid of, and not the act, for that cursed word mutiny has come to haunt our dreams. When you needed money to pay the troops, troops that were about to leave at the end of their ninety-day enlistment, you seized the necessary money from the quartermaster. That was illegal, but even the president approved of it. It may be illegal to start such a battle at dawn, but to end it victoriously would never be considered mutinous."

He shook his head despairingly.

"Ah, Jessie, the Army has a long memory: if I make a charge in the morning and the enemy is not there, or they flee and refuse to fight, or if they stand up and fight and we do not achieve an outstanding victory, there will be a frightful hue and cry. It will be 'Fremont the Mutineer' once again, the man who refuses to acknowledge authority, who is ruining the discipline of the Army, who leads his troops into battle not to help the Union but to save his own command and commission."

"Secretary Cameron told you how desperately a victory was needed; he ordered you to secure it at any cost . . ."

"Mr. Lincoln is commander in chief. His recall order supersedes Secretary Cameron's instructions."

"John, did you ever regret that I suppressed the order from Colonel Abert and sent you word which started you out on the second expedition?"

"No, Jessie, the result justified the act."

"Then why is that reasoning not equally valid now? You have reached the critical hour, the hour toward which you have been working for a hundred days. You have a decisive victory within your grasp. Will General Hunter be able to carry out your plans?"

"He will want to lay his own plans and determine his own campaign. This expedition will have been wasted."

"No victory is illegal, John, only defeats are illegal. Don't you owe it to the preparations you have made to fight this battle in the morning? You have never refused to accept the implications of bold and independent action. Is it fear of another court-martial? We have endured one such trial, we can endure another."

He sat at the end of the long wooden table, holding his face in his hands.

"I can't do it, Jessie," he murmured. "Your father once said that a little mutiny is the sometime genius of democracy. I have already indulged in that sometime genius. To that extent General Kearny was right. Consistent mutiny is more dangerous than any beneficial result it may achieve. I cannot make myself out an habitual mutineer."

She did not have the right to push him further. For herself, she was not afraid of the consequences; whether it were called mutiny, or any one of a hundred other names, she would have attacked at dawn. She had seen the men turn from raw recruits into a finely organized fighting unit; she had watched the laborious methods by means of which John had assembled sufficient guns and artillery to make this attack possible. Like Napoleon, they had spent one hundred days in a great campaign. But now it was all over, their efforts were for nothing, they would be denied any further place in this cause and this war for freedom for which they had long been preparing and had already made many sacrifices.

She knew that if the attack failed in the morning, Jessie and John Fremont would be called the "congenital mutineer and the female politician." She wondered why she, who once had been convinced by General Kearny that one cannot rise against one's own government, should now be willing to start on that rocky road all over again.

There was the sound of voices in the distance; they grew stronger by the moment and seemed to be converging from many directions. Jessie and John stepped outside the tent to learn the cause of the commotion. Word of John's removal had reached the officers' mess, and they had come to inquire. They stood about the tent in a semicircle, six deep; then there came a second movement of sound, of running feet and excited voices, and the soldiers began to pour into the open square until, in the quarter light of the moon, it seemed to Jessie that there were thousands of them stretching back to the very edge of the darkness.

One officer cried out, "Is it true, General Fremont, that you have been removed?"

"Yes," replied John quietly, "it is true." After a time he continued, "We have grown up together as an army. I have become familiar with the brave and generous spirit which you bring to the defense of your country. Continue as you have begun, and give to my successor the same cordial and enthusiastic support with which you have encouraged me. Soldiers, I regret to leave you."

There was a sharp cry of protest from the front rank of the officers. As Jessie stood to one side, she heard a unified wave of protest arise from the men, each saying something different, but each meaning the same. She could hear the officers threatening to resign, the soldiers demanding that he remain in charge, swearing that they would fight under no one else, that they would throw away their guns, that they had a right to fight as they had so long planned and been promised.

The men quieted. Everyone looked to John for his answer. He told them that no one could protest the act of the president, that it was a soldier's first duty to obey orders, that he was no longer their commanding officer, that they were not fighting for any one officer but for the great Union cause.

He asked the soldiers to return to their quarters. No one moved; this was not the answer they wanted or would accept. He turned and gazed at his wife. The air was charged with tension. She saw that he was undergoing a difficult struggle. She did not speak. It was now up to John, facing the army he had brought into existence, to make his final decision. He turned back to his men.

"Prepare for the attack!"

There was a spontaneous cry of joy; officers and men dispersed at once, shouting and singing in the wildest of enthusiasm. Jessie went inside the tent and sat at the long wooden table. After a few moments John came in and dropped down beside her. They sat with an arm about each other, these two companions of the Hundred Days. They had been plunged into a maelstrom of confusion and chaos, they had worked like people possessed, they had given the very best of their hearts and their brains to the cause they had loved for so many years. True, they had made mistakes: they had tried to fight the war, not the least expensively in dollars, but the least expensively in men. They had been fooled, cheated, defrauded—but always by northerners who were enriching themselves off war contracts. Combined with John's daring in the realm of military strategy, they had tried to utilize equal daring in the field of political maneuver, but President Lincoln had not been willing to emancipate the slaves, and so their independent action had been charged up to their record of impetuousness, to the uncontrollable passion to exceed their own authority. They still thought they were right about the emancipation of the Negroes; they still thought that that was what the war was about; they still thought that the slaves would have to be emancipated before the war could be ended, and they took comfort from the fact that half of the North sustained them in this belief. Yet here they were after only a hundred days, already disavowed and recalled. Only two or three hours, and then they must strike once again, without the legal right to do so, but with every need of their nature and of their cause crying out, even as it had in the second expedition and the California conquest, for bold and decisive action.

Once again their silence and their resolution were shattered: horses' hooves pounded in the distance, growing louder by the moment. While Jessie and

John sat looking at each other in the darkness, their hands clasped, the horses galloped up to the front of the tent. The riders quickly dismounted. There was the sound of boots on the small wooden platform outside the tent. Jessie and John rose as General Hunter entered, presented his compliments to General Fremont, and took command of the Army of the West.

Their train was due in St. Louis at nine in the morning, but it did not get in until nine in the evening. When they reached the Brant house they found the street and all the open space around the house filled with women and children, with young boys and old men who had been standing there since early morning. When they got out of their carriage they heard cheers and shouts. As the crowd opened to let them through, she saw that their doorposts were garlanded and the steps covered with flowers. The wives and children of their soldiers in Springfield spoke to them as they went by, words of encouragement and praise and love. One old woman said resolutely as they passed:

"Never you mind, General Fremont and Jessie, we stand by you in your hour of disgrace."

John stood in the doorway facing the crowd below him, trying to speak, to express some word of gratitude or encouragement. Jessie did not want all these good people to see her crying; she went into the house and climbed resolutely to her tiny bedroom where, from the dormer balcony, she could gaze on the scene below. Far down the side street she saw the crowds part and horsemen come through, carrying torches. It was the Zagonyi Guard, many of them bandaged, their horses and their uniforms bullet-torn. They halted before the Brant house, wheeled front, drew their sabers and gave their last salute to their commander.

For Jessie it was such a moving sight that the tears streamed down her cheeks: these officers of the Zagonyi Guard had been dismissed from the service with John, their commissions nullified; the wounded and dead among them had been repudiated, the dead who had fought so valiantly at Springfield had died in vain.

A feeling much like the one at the Delaware Indian Reservation came over her. She sat down on the edge of her iron bed and buried her face in her hands. She knew that the war, which had hardly begun, was already over for them. All that would be left would be investigations and trials, charges and accusations, the bitterness of frustration and defeat. Yet in a sudden flash of clarity she saw that this would be true for everyone involved in this dreadful war, that few would achieve more than defeat, despair and death.

She heard the last round of cheers from the crowd below; she heard the horses wheel and go down the long cobbled street; she heard the people move away and the night grow silent; she heard her husband's weary footsteps on the stairs.

What did they do now? Where did they turn? How did they face the days ahead?

Standing there, suffering mutely, her heart hurting, scarcely able to breathe, she remembered a moment twenty years before: she was carrying her first child, and John had left that very morning on his first great expedition to the West. She would have to live without him for the next six months. She had gone very early into her father's library to help with some work. When they had organized their tasks, and her father had departed for the Senate, an overwhelming loneliness had risen out of the early morning darkness, just as now. And then she had seen that her father had left a note on her desk with a quotation from Marcus Aurelius:

Be not disturbed about the future, for if you ever come to it, you will have the same reason for your guide which preserves you at present.

She heard John's steps coming up the last few stairs. She turned from the window, a slow smile on her lips, and crossed the room quickly to throw open the door for her husband.

BOOK SEVEN

GOOD TIMES WILL COME AGAIN

1

WHEN SHE COULD ENDURE NO LONGER the pain of war, when death was all about her, death of their former comrades on the battlefield, death of the sons of their closest friends, when it seemed as though the whole nation would destroy itself, her mind turned for asylum to the little cottage at Black Point, so simple, so clean with the wind and the sun and the rain of the West keeping everything fresh and alive. She had three enthusiastic allies, Lily, Charlie and Frank, who were more homesick than she for San Francisco. Yet she knew that they could not go home: they had to defend themselves before a congressional investigating committee; once exonerated, there might be another command or an important position inside the government, where John could use his skill and experience to help put an end to the hostilities.

She tried to rent a furnished home in New York, but the city was crowded with war activities and the thousands of people who had flocked there from all over the North. She could find nothing livable and so, to rescue her family from hotels and to get them all under one roof again, she bought a furnished house on Nineteenth Street. John moved his papers into a small downstairs study where he devoted the days to working on his defense. Jessie spent her mornings helping to write his brief, assembling the documents that he needed to substantiate his case. They both worked hard and earnestly, discussing little else when they were in each other's presence; but John was frequently summoned to Washington to provide the investigators with information, and so part of Jessie's time was released for the task that touched her the most deeply. The sick and wounded of the Union armies were streaming into the big cities, where there were inadequate facilities to care for them. The Sanitary Commission was doing what it could, but just as on that first day at the Jefferson Barracks, when she had found men lying mortally ill with cups of coffee and slabs of salt pork resting on their chests, so now there were insufficient hospitals to provide beds for the wounded, a dire lack of doctors, nurses, medical and sanitary supplies: the government had money on hand to buy the implements of war with which to injure men, but rarely enough to buy the remedies with which to make them well again.

After settling her family in the house on Nineteenth Street and putting the children into their various schools, she gave her afternoons and evenings to the task of raising funds. From old friends she elicited money by loving means; from others she extracted by any method she could contrive: persuasion or flattery, by shaming some, as she had in St. Louis, or conveying to others who had seen no part of the war, who had never clapped eyes on a stricken soldier, the greatness of the need and the value of the contribution. Between fund-raising campaigns she began one of the first drives to stock the hospitals with books and magazines; persuaded women to go into the sickrooms each day to write letters for the wounded; kept the wards brightened by the color and fragrance of home-grown flowers. Any day which gave one moment of happiness to a stricken man or brought him one step closer to recovery was a day superbly spent. There were letters from nearly every state in the North and West, letters from mothers thanking her for a last kindness to a boy, far away from home, before he died; letters from wives and sisters whose young men had returned to them because of an arrangement she had made for their medical care; letters from the men now back in service with the Army who had not forgotten the hour of kindly talk, the bringing of a specialist who was able to save an arm or an eye.

One of her greatest heartbreaks was the sorry condition of the wounded officers of the former Zagonyi Guard. Ill, destitute, not even entitled to government hospitalization, the plight of these men and their families was a desperate one. To Jessie's mind they had not only earned full hospitalization and financial help until they could get on their feet again, but were entitled to credit for one of the great charges of the war. One day she perceived a way to achieve both of these ends: she went to Boston to see Ticknor & Fields, a publishing company, and suggested that she write a book called *The Story of the Guard*. Mr. Ticknor advanced her six hundred dollars on the idea, all of which she spent on medical care for the suffering officers. She then settled herself in the dining room of her home with the correspondence from the Guard while they were en route to Springfield, and John's records of their early formation. She worked for eleven consecutive days, from seven in the morning until it was time to clear away her papers for dinner. Ticknor & Fields rushed *The Story of the Guard* into print. It sold widely among a northern public avid for stories of heroism and victory. Jessie earned several thousand dollars with which to aid the Zagonyi officers.

She found it salutary to be doing a non-controversial labor of love: on the political front there were no hospitals, no doctors or nurses, no books, flowers or acts of mercy. Her reputation was now at as low a point as it had been at a high in 1856, when almost half of the nation had cried out for "Fremont and Jessie." Her interview with President Lincoln had been spread abroad, without any of its extenuating circumstances. People only knew that she had come into the presence of Mr. Lincoln soiled and unkempt, that Mr. Lincoln had said, "She taxed me so violently that I had to exercise all my clumsy tact to avoid quarreling with her"; that she had belligerently told Frank Blair that she had just as much right at the war front as any man. The Army was criticizing her for having usurped the position of chief of staff; the echoes of the unfortunate forty-eight hours in Washington were being repeated from mouth to mouth, altered with each telling, exaggerated, twisted and sometimes even perverted; and this picture of herself as an ambitious, pushing, dictatorial, vainglorious and unnatural female was something that shocked her to the very core. How much finer and sweeter to walk into a hospital room with a gift for a sick boy than to walk into general headquarters and be plunged into a quarrel over the military power versus the political.

With spring, Jessie and John went down to Washington for the formal hearing before the joint committee of both houses of Congress. Once again, as with the court-martial fourteen years before, their reputation and personal standing were at stake. Yet this could not be a scientific trial: it was to be conducted by civilians who would be obliged to form opinions about elements of battle strategy which General Fremont had not been given sufficient time to bring to completion. General Jessie too would be on trial here, for although she had no official standing or commission of which she might be deprived, the investigation had the power to condemn both her presence and her activities in St. Louis, and to convict her husband on the basis of her performance.

Instead of being uneasy and worried at the frequent postponements of the hearing, Jessie did what she could to delay further the opening of the investigation. True, John was being held inactive, he was spoiling for the fight with his adversaries in the War Department, but a cooler judgment showed her that every passing day brought them closer to vindication; the ever onrushing failures and tragedies of the war had already enveloped so many other departments and commanders that her husband was no longer the most important general to have been broken. Had not President Lincoln removed General George B. McClellan as commander of the Army of the Potomac because he was impotent to give the order which would send his superbly trained and equipped army into action? The North was coming to understand the complexity of waging a war without trained soldiers, without rifles or artillery, without food or clothing, and she saw that public sympathy was slowly swinging back to General Fremont, that the obloquy which had blanketed them when they first had reached New York was lightening, withdrawing to cover other Union commanders, continuing defeats and political frustrations in Washington.

Jessie and John stayed at the home of Eliza and William Carey Jones during the weeks of the hearing. Though no one referred back to the burdened days of the court-martial, the memory of those sorely troubled times was heavy upon them when John asked William Carey Jones for a few suggestions as to proper procedure before the Committee on the Conduct of the War.

Late in March, Jessie, Eliza and John walked up Pennsylvania Avenue in the cool spring sunlight, standing for a moment on the steps of the Congressional Building before going into the committee room. When the investigators filed in and took their places around a long table, she was relieved to find that for the most part they were men who had been sympathetic to the Fremont cause: Ben Wade of Ohio, Zachariah Chandler of Michigan, John Covode of Pennsylvania and George W. Julian of Indiana.

By checking the more important northern newspapers she saw that they were reproducing the solicitor general's charges in full, but that their sting was being pulled by accompanying editorials which pictured the chaos into which the Fremonts had been plunged in July, and told of how much more they had accomplished, under incredible hardships, than had been accomplished in most other fields of operation.

When John rose to face the commission it was with quiet assurance; his voice as he began to read his prepared defense was calm. She made no attempt to follow his argument point by point; she had been over this manuscript countless times. Instead her mind wandered back to the court-martial of fourteen years before. This too was a court-martial, though it was being held under more polite guise: what good to try a man after he had already been publicly condemned and punished? The court-martial had terminated John's career in the Topographical Corps, rung down the curtain on the first half of his professional life. Was this committee meeting then the final act in their drama? Would this investigation terminate the second half of their career, send them out to face another thirteen or twenty-three years of wandering?

She was awakened from her reverie by the mention of her own name and the revelation of material which her husband had put in the brief without her knowledge: stories of her service in St. Louis, affidavits from his general staff on her success in assembling supplies when there were simply no supplies to be had; the tribute paid to her by Dorothea Dix for setting up the hospital at Jefferson Barracks, testimonials from the Sanitary Commission which praised her work in gathering nurses and medical equipment. He testified that he had sent her to Washington, instructed her to go straight to the White House from the railroad station, that she not leave until Mr. Lincoln had a full accounting of the Western Command. She was grateful and touched when John apologized to the president by assuring Mr. Lincoln that his wife had gone to him with the fullest respect for his person and his office, that any untoward word that had been uttered had come as the result of great tension and fatigue for which he, General Fremont, alone was responsible.

It took him two and a half days to present his case; it then took the commission another two and a half days to reach its decision. Generals Fremont and Jessie were not only cleared, but given high praise for their conduct of the war. Their mistakes and failures were not glossed over, but were set down as the results of energy and purpose in trying to accomplish in a few months what would have required a year in the careful doing. John was commended for the gunboat flotilla, the Unionizing of St. Louis, the warfare against the guerrillas, the appointment and instructions to General Grant, the building of fighting morale into the Army of the West, the pursuit of General Price, who had been determined even in the face of impending defeat to take a stand against General Fremont's superior forces beyond Springfield at the dawn of the day that General Hunter took over the command.

The newspapers of the East and West were almost unanimous in their praise of the commission's decision, agreeing with its final statement that John Fremont's command of the West "was eminently characterized by earnestness, ability, and the most unquestionable loyalty." At a giant meeting at the Cooper Institute some of the North's best loved leaders, Charles Sumner, Schuyler Colfax, David Dudley Field, Charles King, William Evarts endorsed John's now repudiated doctrine of emancipation. Henry Ward Beecher urged them to come to his Plymouth Church one Sunday morning, and in his sermon contrasted John with Daniel Webster, saying that Webster had died and would remain dead because he had compromised with slavery, but that John Fremont's name would live and forever be remembered when the United States was a nation of free men. Reports came in from Cincinnati, Andover, Gallipolis and from the farm lands of Iowa that among the families who were fighting the war, the love of John Fremont and his emancipation proclamation remained deep and constant, that his removal had undermined the people's faith in their government.

She was happy that they had been exonerated, yet it was the happiness of relief and thanksgiving rather than of promise for the future. These public avowals of faith could not bring back those hours just before the dawn of November third when John and his army stood ready to score one of the first major victories for the North. The commission had justified John Fremont, the country's faith in him had been reborn, yet there were other men, younger men who would come up to take his place, men who were fresh and enthusiastic and full of fight, men with confidence because the war in all its ramifications had not yet rolled over them. They had had their chance to make a contribution to the Union cause and had somehow failed; failed, as always, for good reasons, even for heroic reasons, but nonetheless failed.

2

The war years had a special quality for Jessie: an ever present nervous tautness, a lean brittle hardness, the sense of living not in the hateful present, which one repudiated with each battle, but in the passionately desired and far away future.

The year 1863 opened so auspiciously that she genuinely believed its end might also see the end of the war: for on New Year's Day Abraham Lincoln gave the country an emancipation proclamation. Only fifteen months before he had cried at her, "The general should never have dragged the Negro into the war. The Negro had nothing to do with it." Now Mr.

Lincoln's acceptance of emancipation had vindicated them politically, as the congressional investigators had vindicated them militarily.

Her work with the Sanitary Commission was almost done, for there was an adequate supply of nurses and hospitals, and the country had been awakened to the need of supplying funds for the wounded soldiers. Just as on that unhappy night in Washington when she had stood before the weed-grown Benton lot and yearned to be back in her home at Black Point, away from the strife and warfare which were tearing her apart, so now her thoughts went with increasing frequency to their glassed-in gallery where they watched the ships in the Golden Gate strait, where she rode horseback over the dunes with her three children and sailed the bay with them in an open boat. She yearned for peace and privacy, for the touch of her intimate possessions, for the literary discussions with Thomas Starr King and Bret Harte, for the sense of living on a frontier where people were too busy growing and building to participate in personal feuds or political vendettas. With a start she realized that she was longing for the amiable and tranquil life; if she was not yearning for the stately traditions of Cherry Grove she was at least hungering for the security and tradition of Black Point, more fitted to her own temperament than Cherry Grove, but nonetheless the beautiful refuge against controversy for which Elizabeth McDowell Benton had yearned so many years.

"I know how terribly you want to go home, Jessie," John said sympathetically, "but there would be nothing for me to do in San Francisco."

". . . Not even your plans for the transcontinental railroad?"

"All railroad projects originate here, in the East. I'm beginning to feel my way about; the prospects look good . . . Patience, my dear, and courage," he murmured, as he kissed her cheek. "In a few years you will have your own private railroad car, and you will travel between your New York and San Francisco homes every month."

She returned his kiss, then cried, "Of course! I am trying to chase a rainbow across a whole continent. Home is where your work lies! Could anyone know that better than I?" She paused pensively. "It's only that those months at Black Point were so beautiful; they stay as vivid in my memory as though they happened yesterday. When your railroad is built, we will go back home."

Suspended in mid-air, with no real job or desire but to see this horrible war ended, she carried on a correspondence with Thomas Starr King, exchanging news of the East for King's reportage of the spirit and temper of San Francisco; she succeeded in getting one of Bret Harte's poems in the *Atlantic Monthly;* and she and John became the close friends and confidants of the poet, John Greenleaf Whittier, who had written during their presidential campaign, "Rise up, Fremont, and go before; the hour must have its man"; who had given the Fremont supporters throughout the nation a rallying point when he had written, after John's removal, "Thy error, Fremont, simply was to act a brave man's part, without the statesman's tact." John clung to Whittier's judgment and friendship because of what he described to Jessie as the poet's spiritual incorruptibility. Seeing how much of insight and perspective Whittier was able to bring to her husband, she frequently invited the poet to their home for a several days' visit; she and John went to Amesbury to spend the week end with Whittier among his flowers and books.

Then the war struck at her from yet another angle: she received a telegram from the War Department informing her that the government had taken over Black Point, that a fort was to be built on the site of her home. She read the telegram several times, unable to grasp its meaning. Why should the government want Black Point? Why must they have this particular tiny piece of land? They could not take away a family's home. A home was private property!

But when she showed the telegram to her husband, he stumblingly told her that her deductions were wrong: the government could confiscate any property it needed for the national safety. Black Point was only a mile away from Alcatraz; with cannons mounted at both these points, no enemy ship could enter San Francisco Bay. It was cruel, it blasted their dream of returning to Black Point, but he could see the War Department's justification. No, there was nothing they could do about it except send on their title and receipt for payment, and wait for the government to return the cost of their land.

Her eyes swimming in tears, Jessie asked, "But what about our house? They have no need for our cottage."

"It's too big to be moved, and the War Department is in too much of a hurry. They'll tear it down to make way for gun emplacements."

"Tear it down!" she cried in agony. "Why do other people have the right to tear down our possessions and our lives? Why did they have the right to tear us down in St. Louis and dismiss you from your command, only to have the investigating committee and now President Lincoln acknowledge that you were right all the time? Why do they have the right to tear down our home on Black Point and then in a year or two acknowledge apologetically that they were wrong, that they didn't need the land after all? Aren't we human beings, with hearts and souls and feelings? Don't we have any rights? Can we be stripped of everything we own and everything we hold sacred? Have we no defense against them . . . ?"

"I can't answer your questions, my dear," he said, heavyhearted, "for there is no 'them.' Today it's the War Department that has deprived us of our home; yesterday it was the Blairs and Mr. Lincoln who deprived us of our command; the day before that it was the venality of the press and lack of restraint in the slanderings of a political party that lost us the presidency and the White House; the day before that it was the negligence of an election law which did not guarantee to the most widely desired senator the long term, which deprived us of our career in the Senate; the day before that it was General Kearny, Colonel Cooke and Lieutenant Emory who robbed us of our commission. You see, my dear, there is no 'them': with each turn of fortune it's another person, another reason, another force."

"Then there is nothing we can do—no protest we can make . . . ?"

"None. This telegram from the War Department does not ask your permission to take over Black Point; its purpose is to inform you that they have already done so. Now listen to me, my darling; no, no, don't turn your head away. Let me see your face. Yes, I know you're crying and that you don't like me to see you when your eyes are red; I'm even foolish enough to think that you're beautiful when you're crying, for you always cry for the right reasons. I know that San Francisco and the cottage on Black Point have been your mind's haven. We must simply find another haven . . ."

She shook her head sadly.

"It was our first real home and hearth, a way of life, a tradition to go back to. Our last refuge has been taken from us."

But she was wrong: there were other refuges, refuges of the mind, deep recesses of comfort and faith that could be stripped from her. The first came in the news of the Reverend King's death in San Francisco, death from overwork and exhaustion, from the burning out of his flaming spirit for the Union cause. On the heels of this blow, Eliza died suddenly in Washington, died from the illnesses that had plagued her during her youth. William Jones was in California on a war mission, and so Jessie went to Washington to bury her older sister in the Benton plot, at the foot of her mother and father. Along with her grief at the early passing of Eliza, who was forty-one, Jessie was stricken at how fast the Benton family was disappearing. She was only thirty-nine, and yet she had already lost her mother and her father, her brother and her sister. Now there were only herself and the two younger girls left.

Death must be my friend, she thought; he so rarely leaves my side.

She was sitting in the window of her home on Nineteenth Street one mid-afternoon of June 1863 when she saw John come bounding up the steps, his face wreathed in smiles. Proudly he thrust a copy of the New York *Tribune* into her hand, his eager finger circling an announcement that he had formed a partnership with Samuel Hallet, a respected promoter, and had been elected president of a proposed railroad which they were going to build across the state of Kansas. She tried to continue reading the article, which told of how General Fremont had opened offices on Beaver Street, but John was too impatient to let her finish; he took the paper from her, noisily turned the page and showed her his advertisement, which asked for bids on several thousand tons of iron rails to be delivered to Kansas City, the Kaw's Landing of his early expeditions. Even in the excitement her eyes caught the accompanying diagram and she saw that the route he had laid out for his railroad followed very closely the original trail he had mapped through the mountains and plains, that his major stations were to be built at towns which had grown up on the ashes of his early campfires.

They had lived largely on the hopes of starting their railroad, but up to this moment there had been nothing but disappointment. The blows had fallen from every side: they had necessarily neglected the Mariposa and it was sold out from under them, with John losing both ownership and control, but still holding three eighths of the profits; the federal government was disinterested in railroading and would give them no assistance; their opponents in Washington, in particular the Blair family, still made it impossible for John to secure any co-operation from the administration. He complained to Jessie, "I am completely *persona non grata* in the capital; you would think I was a fire-eating Democrat who had opposed their election. I can't build my railroad without a right of way and land grants. As Tom Benton could have told you, you can't get a right of way through Congress without being a tactical politician."

"And Lord knows we've had enough politics," she sympathized.

But now the difficult days were over: John was on the main track again, fulfilling a lifetime ambition of their family. His eyes sparkled and his proper love of self seemed to have been born again with the setting up of the new project. The newspapers carried thrilling accounts of his plans for an iron road to California; the country became railroad conscious and even the reluctant Congress began to see that they would eventually have to play some part in this expansion to the west. Taking his position as a bold and resourceful railroad builder, a man fulfilling still another dream of western expansion, John rose rapidly in favor and was restored to the position of respect he had so long enjoyed.

Once again they would be able to start a new life and work at a valuable job; all that had gone before would be forgotten in the vigor and joy of accomplishment. For the first time since General Hunter had taken over their command in the lamp-lit tent beyond Springfield, eighteen months before, she felt the promise of personal happiness and security.

3

She had intimated to her husband that she was through with politics, but she soon learned that politics was not through with her. Though she no longer visited Washington, much of official Washington was in and out of her home in New York. Over her dinner table Richard Henry Dana told them that it was almost impossible to find loyalty to the president in Washington, that the general conviction of Lincoln's incompetence had taken such a firm hold that if a convention were to be held that night he could not be renominated. It was reported that only two members of the Thirty-Seventh Congress supported Mr. Lincoln, that no one in Washington except Lincoln's inner group wanted his renomination. William P. Fessenden wrote in a letter, "Never was such a shambling set of incapables collected in one government; we went in for a rail-splitter, and we have got one." Senator Sherman of Ohio charged Lincoln with responsibility for the war chaos. Reverberations came of a movement in New York to force the president to resign because he was "fickle, careless and totally unqualified."

For a long while Jessie followed the political furor simply as part of the war scene, but by the time 1863 was half over she was obliged to report to her husband that the critics of Mr. Lincoln were not baying in a hollow: they wanted Abraham Lincoln replaced by General John C. Fremont. They went to hear Wendell Phillips tell an audience of abolitionists jammed into the Cooper Institute that peace could not be restored until General Fremont manned the guns. She showed her husband cuttings from the Boston *Pioneer*, which proclaimed him to be the imperative candidate for the presidency in '64, and supporting editorials from such German newspapers as the Springfield *Staats Anzeiger* and the Mississippi *Blatter* which had begun a campaign for Fremont for president. Fremont clubs were formed in Illinois, Ohio, Wisconsin and New York. By the end of the year, as faith in President Lincoln declined, confidence in the ability and character of John Fremont began to rise to the fervor which had earned him the nomination in 1856.

Jessie did not know whether to be alarmed or pleased at these developments. Her thoughts raced on in confusion, for whenever she felt a twinge of regret that this deplorable criticism of the president was impeding the war effort, she would remember in the very same sentence the humiliation her husband had suffered at the hands of the administration. How magnificent it would be for John to replace Lincoln as the Republican nominee, to be elected to the presidency on a wave of popular acclaim—but how distasteful to go through another presidential campaign, to endure the insults and venom that had darkened their days in 1856!

But if there was uncertainty in her mind, she soon saw that there was none in her husband's: he wanted the nomination, he wanted the campaign, he wanted the election and the presidency and the White House. The slights and injustices he had suffered since the day of his appointment to the Western Command could be wiped out in one bold stroke: he would become commander in chief. He would dispossess his adversaries, the self-seeking men who had locked the borders of Washington against him; he would wage the war efficiently and decisively, end it quickly, then bend every effort of the government toward the rehabilitation of the South.

All of these things he told her, the secret hopes, revenges and gratifications which a husband confides only to a wife. When she saw how strongly he felt, how overwhelmingly he wanted the presidency, a thousand times more now than he had in 1856, she silenced the doubts and confusion in her own mind.

"Apparently you can once again have the Democratic nomination, if you want it," she commented, as she handed him a batch of clippings. "New York elected a Democratic governor in Horatio Seymour last year, and seven of the northern states went Democratic in Congress. If the temper of the people is the same in November 1864 as it is today, you could defeat Mr. Lincoln."

"No," replied John firmly, "we cannot injure the party we helped form. I am a Republican. I will never be anything else. If the war is still dragging on next spring, and I am offered the nomination of our own party . . ."

By a close survey of the newspapers in the early months of 1864, she was able to assure her husband that the popular swing to his support was gaining momentum. There was hardly a city in the North or West that did not have a Fremont club or a Fremont paper. The *New Nation* was founded to advance his candidacy. A convention of radical Republicans was called in Cleveland on May thirty-first, backed by the Fremont clubs and the many newspapers which supported him. When Jessie went to Cleveland, as she had gone to Philadelphia eight years before, she found some four hundred delegates gathered, representing practically all of the states of the North. The convention criticized President Lincoln for suspending the freedom of the press and freedom of speech, as well as the writ of habeas corpus, for being too lenient toward the South and, most important, of being incapable of terminating the conflict. While she sat, small and disheartened at the rear of the hall, convinced that John should not traffic with these malcontents and divisionists, she heard her husband nominated for the presidency.

When she had returned home from the Philadelphia convention in 1856 she had come back to her husband bursting with pride; this time she returned a little sick at her stomach. She had not been back in the house on Nineteenth Street for more than a day before she learned that John's nomination by the radical Republicans had become a serious threat to the Lincoln administration and that powerful weapons were being forged against him. Those portions of the Republican press which had been lukewarm toward Mr. Lincoln struck out boldly because their candidate had been put in jeopardy. The Cleveland *Herald* declared that the Cleveland nominating convention had been made up of "sly politicians from New York, impetuous hare-brained Germans from St. Louis, abolitionists, and personal friends and parasites of Fremont." She was further concerned to find that John's nomination greatly encouraged the South by evidencing a split in the Republican ranks; that the New York *Times* and other solidly Union papers were declaring that Mr. Lincoln had to be re-elected because any defeat now would be an admission that he should not have been elected in the first place.

Jessie found the campaign of 1864 to be even more maleficent than the one of 1856; for now, with the actualities of war, death and destruction everywhere, the voters and their press went berserk, reaching heights of name calling and personal vilification never before known. Few of the leading Republicans believed Lincoln could defeat the Democratic nominee, General George B. McClellan; his campaign managers lost all hope. Mr. Lincoln himself was resigned to defeat. It was then that the administration supporters began filing through the Fremont home to persuade John to step out of the race, offering him, through his wife, an important command in the war, the unseating of his enemies.

Jessie saw that her husband was adamant. He would not withdraw; he would strike no bargain. He told her a hundred times over that he was certain he could win. She knew that he had sufficient provocation to be sickened with idealism and to feel that the end justified the means, yet she found herself in the same position she had occupied in 1856 when John had told her about the Democratic nomination: she had wanted to become First Lady, but not at the cost of endorsing slavery. Now more than ever, after the harsh criticism that had been levied against her, she wanted to move into the White House. But if she had to risk destroying the Republican party, put a Democrat into the presidency, end the war by appeasement, with slavery still intact, was that not too high a price to pay for the chance of success? They had won two victories for idealism in 1856; for her part they must now somehow win another.

Toward the beginning of September she packed a bag and went to see John Whittier at Amesbury. Now fifty-seven, tall, with dark eyes that pierced one's intent, Whittier had suffered both physically and mentally at the hands of organized mobs that had pursued him for his fanatical loyalty to abolition. Though his poetry had a strong religious conviction, he did not hesitate to fall back on his practical experience as a political campaigner and founder of the Republican party. Jessie knew that the man who had edited anti-slavery newspapers throughout the forties and published the stirring *Voices of Freedom* poems in 1846 would give her advice that would be in season. Whittier lived alone in a small ivy-covered house, a bachelor, working as steadily as his ill health would permit at the three loves of his life: poetry, politics and freedom.

"I have come to ask what you think about the political situation, Mr. Whittier," she said. "I know how long and ardently you have supported General Fremont."

Whittier was thoughtful for a moment as he cleared away stacks of old newspapers and magazines, making room for Jessie on a wicker chair before a fireplace stuffed with discarded manuscripts. After pouring two glasses of sherry and seating himself on a hassock at her feet, he answered, "I still support the general, but I feel that his candidacy on the third party is a tragic error."

"Why do you think so?"

"Because its sole effect will be to elect General McClellan and bring about a compromise peace with the South; the rebellion will not have been put down, slavery will not have been affected, and all those thousands of young men who died will have died for no purpose and for no accomplishment."

"My husband thinks he can win . . ."

Whittier shook his head violently. He rose and gazed at her with kindly but stubborn eyes.

"No, no, my dear Mrs. Fremont, please believe me. I would be the first to plead his cause if I thought he had a chance. But he has none. If the general persists in his candidacy and helps McClellan defeat the Republicans, his motives will be charged to personal anger against Mr. Lincoln and a desire for revenge. The effect will be disastrous for our nation. Mr. Lincoln is so tied into the secession, the war, the fight for the Union and for freedom that we cannot change horses in midstream. No one knows better than I General Fremont's magnificent faith in the cause of Union and Freedom, and how much he has already suffered for it. He must make one more sacrifice, then; he must withdraw and help Mr. Lincoln be re-elected."

"That will be bitter medicine."

"He has swallowed bitter medicine before. You came to me for an honest opinon: the people want Mr. Lincoln re-elected."

"Then you are not afraid that General McClellan will win?"

"Not if General Fremont withdraws."

Jessie smoothed the folds of her long velvet dress, then unconsciously fingered the recalcitrant strand of hair from her brow.

"Thank you, Mr. Whittier, for telling me the truth. You have given me the means to persuade General Fremont to withdraw."

The old man's eyes flashed approval.

"You will be doing your country a great service, Mrs. Fremont."

She returned to New York. When she told John the result of her interview with John Greenleaf Whittier, he asked darkly, "Then you are both convinced that I have no chance?"

". . . You have a great chance: you can prove your faith in the Republican party by refusing to help it be defeated; you can prove that your objective is and always has been the Union cause."

"But don't you see," exclaimed John, "that by withdrawing now I maintain in office the man who relieved me of my command, who has kept me out of an important position either in the Army or the government? . . . And you are asking me to turn the other cheek!"

She cast about in her mind for the most subtle approach.

"Aren't you the one who taught me that a battle lost in the beginning may win the campaign in the end? You lost the immediate battle for the White House in 1856, but you helped create a victorious Republican party. You lost the Hundred Days in Missouri, but you contributed to the winning of the war. By stepping down from your nomination and helping Mr. Lincoln to win you will be losing still another battle, but your candidacy has already achieved important results: Mr. Lincoln has been forced to take a stronger stand against slavery; he has called for the resignation of Montgomery Blair and put the southern appeasers out of his Cabinet; the regular Republican platform was practically copied from the platform you endorsed when you accepted the nomination of the radicals."

She poured herself a glass of water from the decanter on the sideboard. Her voice, when she resumed, was low and resonant.

"I believe, John, that by refusing to accept the Democratic nomination you brought the Republican party into existence, and that that was more valuable than anything James Buchanan did in the White House from 1856 to 1860. Your emancipation proclamation created such a public demand for emancipation that Mr. Lincoln was finally forced to the point last year; your demand today for the freedom of all Negroes and a more powerful prosecution of the war will help bring them about. You have already achieved magnificent results, my dear, and they may be more important than anything Mr. Lincoln will do in Washington in the next four years. Perhaps that is your role in life, John, always to lose the opening battle, thereby laying the stage for the ultimate triumph of your cause."

John stood in hostile silence for several moments, then put his hands on her shoulders and shook her a little. He growled with affectionate gruffness, "Now that you have made me out such a hero, how can I refuse to step down? Get a pencil and paper, we'll write out a statement for the press announcing my withdrawal."

4

Generals Grant, Sherman and Sheridan finally brought in smashing victories for the Union cause; President Lincoln was re-elected. In the early spring of 1865 Generals Lee and Johnston surrendered to Grant, and the war was over.

Now that the restraints against railroad building were lifted, Jessie warmly approved the investment of their resources, some two hundred thousand dollars in savings, in the construction of the Kansas Pacific and the Missouri Pacific railroads. Always with his eye on the California terminus, John sold his interest in the two lines after they were partly constructed and bought the proposed Memphis & El Paso Railroad, which brought with its charter from the Texas legislature some eighteen million acres of land along the right of way. He next purchased land for a terminal in San Diego and drew up plans for the San Diego-Fort Yuma Railroad. For Jessie there was the old-time thrill in watching her husband function at the top of his form: bold and daring in his schemes to push the iron rails across the Rockies. At fifty-two John had a white beard and a head of white hair, but he was still as exciting as he had been in the days before their marriage, when Mrs. Crittenden had called him "the handsomest officer to walk the streets of Washington."

As the four war years had been taut, so now the years from 1865 to 1870 were wondrously slack, the most delightful period she had yet known. She decided that she must be growing old, for she was content to live peacefully, providing a gracious home and a cultivated life for her family and friends. She thought how amused her mother would be if she could see her now, living much in the manner of Cherry Grove, at long last the "fine lady" that Miss English had been so intent upon making her. Because she had never ceased to grieve over the loss of Black Point, John had insisted that in addition to their town house they should have a country place where they would find the natural beauty they had loved so much in San Francisco. The government had not yet returned the forty-two-thousand-dollar purchase price of the San Francisco property, but they were in no hurry, for it was now true that Jessie and John Fremont were millionaires.

They bought a magnificent estate of a hundred rolling acres and a gray stone mansion on the hills above the Hudson, called Pocaho. Into a mahogany-lined library, which gave a superb view of the Tappan Zee, Jessie placed the library they had bought from the Humboldts after the baron's death. Here too she assembled John's collection on military science and on political government, as well as all the books she had loved through her life, from the early Audubon volumes in the Library of Congress through the latest fiction pouring off the Boston and New York presses. The dining room, which overlooked the flower garden, and where Jessie served the finest foods her French chef could concoct, was always filled with guests. The broad, forty-foot living room which stood across the hall from the library was gay with the music and laughter of her three children and their friends. There were fine riding horses, and a handsome sailing boat for Charlie, now a young man with his father's dark, grave eyes and black hair parted in the center. Charlie was eighteen and wanted to become an admiral; he was entering Annapolis in the fall. For young Frank, now fifteen, with his mother's warm hazel eyes, slender sensitive face and brown hair, there was a grand piano which the boy often played at one and two in the morning. She educated her children by exposing them to all kinds of people, philosophies, books and the various arts, but she did not take advantage of her position by forcing them into fields for which they had neither interest nor liking. She said in effect, Here is the world; take from it what you will. My job is to open doors for you, not to push you into cold, dark rooms. Later you will decide for yourself which of the ideas and arts you wish to discard, and which you want for your lifetime friends.

She was constantly baffled by the differences in her three children, by the startling contrasts, not only between Lily and her two volatile brothers, but between the boys themselves. Charlie, open-faced, candid, was not happy unless he was on or near the water; the only books he cared for were those on travel and science. Frank was quiet and moody, uninterested in the out of doors, not seeming to come alive until darkness fell, and then spending his hours reading novels and poetry and playing the piano. She thought it odd that neither boy had as yet evidenced personal ambition.

These were years without uncertainties. They knew all the world, and all the world seemed to know and like them. There were luxurious trips to Europe, where she was presented to Queen Louisa of Denmark and became friends with Hans Christian Andersen. Her salon, which she built around the quiet but commanding personality of her husband, not only attracted the finest minds and talents in the country but served as an introduction to America for their many European friends.

She still felt that she was only the chatelaine of her wealth, supporting generously the charities of the day, in particular the funds to help the wounded soldiers of the war. At one time, in 1868, she was putting thirteen young people through college, nine young men and four young ladies. Everyone came to her for help: scientists, inventors, explorers, writers, painters, all those who needed money for any reason whatsoever. She contributed to university endowments, symphony-concert funds, art collections. She kept no track of how much money she gave away, for she had learned that John was making no attempt to keep track of how much was coming in; there was just too inexhaustible a supply to spend one's days in bookkeeping.

For their own part she and John lived unostentatiously; their clothes and pleasures were simple, Jessie wore no jewelry or furs. Aside from their travels, their money was spent in their two homes, entertaining their friends. Thirty years of marriage had deepened rather than exhausted their sense of pleasure in each other: the delight at a new hair style, the way a dress or suit fitted, the adroit expression of an idea, the slow, warm, approving smile on a face whose every expression was better known than one's own image in the mirror. In three decades of marriage they had gone through so much together, both of success and failure, that they were carved into each other's memory; there was gratitude here, but gratitude would not have been enough to engender the closeness and delight of their spirits. During the harassed and unhappy war years they had relearned that trouble and passion are poor bedfellows; now, in the easy, joyful comfort of creative years, when their last ambitions were pushing forward toward completion, their physical love flared anew.

John persuaded her to let Fagnani paint her portrait; when after many sittings the artist permitted her to gaze at the canvas she saw reflected the interesting things that had happened to her in these last years, of which she herself had been but dimly aware. She had filled out, so that her always delicate shoulders were now rounded and firm, her bosom deep. She wore her graying hair still parted in the center, but instead of combing it low at the back of her neck she let it fall in two long rich curls down the side of her head and shoulders. Her eyes seemed larger than in her early years, a far darker hazel, mellow, accepting, at peace with the world. Her mouth, always rich and red, had deepened and widened, which made her long Roman nose seem shorter and more delicate. In the painter's objective portrait she was no longer a young woman: at forty-five she was a matron, the most active part of her life behind her, but with long years to enjoy the tranquillity of middle life.

Gazing at herself as the artist Fagnani saw her, she thought about the oddness of perspective. When she stood on a hilltop overlooking a valley, the immediate foreground, the first few miles of ranches, orchards, houses and plowed fields were seen in the most vivid detail; but beyond them the landscape ran together, so that nothing was seen clearly and in detail, but rather was merged in an obscuring haze. With the years of their marriage it was the early ones that stood out now in her mind with the starkest of clarity: she could recall every hour, every ache of loneliness, every pain of disappointment and failure, every aspiration, every moment of work, every tiny, joyous success. But these later years, these years far away from youth, from the freshness of beginning, the haze of long-range perspective had covered with an obscuring veil. She could not recall or even feel the separate hours and days now: they merged into each other, grouped themselves so closely and genially that there were no sharp divisions in time. Everything passed so quickly, the months, the years, so quickly that there was no way of counting them, let alone holding them back.

She hoped that they would be able to live out their lives in this pastoral, in which they used their money for good and generous purposes while John helped lay the trails for transcontinental railroads. Yet deep in her heart she had a prescience that this could not last; nothing so far had lasted, nothing had been permanent, secure or unchangeable; they had gone through many and violent cycles. She sensed storms ahead, but she did not let this intuition detract from her enjoyment and happiness of the good years. Instead she used them, as she had always used the tranquil periods, to fortify herself against the day when they would be obliged to go to the wars again. The thought sometimes came to her that she should not spend money so lavishly, but should try to save some portion of it, invest it in land or stocks or bank vaults. And yet she had an even stronger certainty that this subterfuge could do no possible good: when the change of circumstances came, all of these thousands that she was spending now would inevitably have been lost with everything else. Better to use them, to make them serve high purposes.

The happiest day of these years of contentment was when she and John went to St. Louis to participate in the unveiling of a statue of Senator Thomas Hart Benton. Forty thousand spectators crowded into Lafayette Park to witness the ceremony, while school children in white stood about the pedestal, a band played martial music, and the westbound train stopped on the Pacific railroad tracks to blow its whistles. As Jessie pulled a cord and the white drapery slipped down from the bronze statue, there stood the Old Roman, facing westward, his slightly hoarse voice seeming to cry out the lines which were inscribed at the base: *"There is the East. There lies the road to India."* A salute of thirty guns, one for each year of his service in the Senate, was fired by order of the secretary of war. While the Missouri dignitaries were making fine speeches about Thomas Hart Benton's life and work and the things he had done for education and freedom, Jessie turned to her husband with tears in her eyes and whispered, "What a shame that Father couldn't be here for the unveiling. He would have enjoyed it so."

Her one disquietude was centered around Lily. Her daughter was now twenty-six years old; to the best of Jessie's knowledge the girl had never been in love. She had countless friends, was well liked, she would ride, hunt, fish, sail or work for a worth-while cause with the young sons of their friends and their neighbors at Pocaho or in New York. Yet she rarely accepted invitations to mixed parties, cared little for dancing, preferred the company of her family. Jessie was not able to tell whether any young men had fallen in love with her daughter, for Lily was completely uncommunicative on the subject. On numerous occasions she had tried to draw her out. She was able to learn that at least Lily was not pining over an unrequited love; and she came to the conclusion that Lily had no intention of ever falling in love! Up to this point Jessie had thought her daughter might be maturing late, that like her aunt Eliza she was waiting for precisely the right man to come along. Now she saw that Lily did not believe in such romantic notions as the right man, that instead of giving him a chance to fall in love, should he come along, Lily would ride him half to death up the valley of the Hudson, or involve him in a fund-raising campaign for a new clinic which would wear out his energy even as it burned out his romantic interest.

Unable to bear the uncertainty any longer, she determined to have matters out with Lily. It took a lot of doing, for Lily was either disinterested or elusive. Jessie cornered her one wintry night in the mahogany-lined library and locked the door behind them. Standing with her back to the fire she gazed at Lily's heavy brows and jaw and the resolute cast of her features.

"Lily," she said, "you'll have to forgive me for intruding where I'm obviously not wanted, but I am seriously upset about you."

"Why so, Mother?" Lily asked, "I'm in perfect health, I eat three wonderful meals a day, I'm out in the air in the roughest weather . . ."

"I think you know that I did not mean it literally, Lily," replied Jessie engagingly. "I am not talking about your creature comforts, nor am I discussing the state of your health."

Her gray eyes unemotional, Lily replied, "I'm perfectly happy. You're perfectly happy . . ."

Jessie pulled up a small wooden chair beside her daughter. She said in a firmer tone, "No, my dear, I am not perfectly happy, because I see the years going on, and I find you growing farther and farther away from the most important thing in a woman's life: marriage."

"Why is it the most important, Mother?" asked Lily, with equal firmness. "Merely because you find it so? Isn't there room for difference of opinion on that subject?"

Jessie shook her head several times as though she could not believe what she had just heard.

"Difference of opin . . . What are you talking about, child? What is there in life for a woman if she doesn't have a husband and children and a home?"

"Many, many things, Mother dear. Your belief that an unmarried woman is a tragic and useless figure is old-fashioned. The Lord only knows how many females were bullied into marriages they didn't want, on those very grounds. There are lots of young women who don't want to marry, who want to live a different kind of life . . ."

"The life of a spinster?" demanded Jessie, horror-stricken.

"Don't make the word sound so ugly, darling. Don't you see, my heart is so full of love for you and Father and the boys that there just isn't room for anyone else."

"Then in your own best interests," cried Jessie, "I think your father and I ought to pack your belongings and put you out of the house. We could never forgive ourselves if we thought that you loved us so much . . ."

Lily rose from her deep chair and began striding about the room, energetically picking up objects and putting them down again; Jessie's mind flashed across the years to her meeting with George Bancroft in her sitting room at the rear of the Benton home. Lily came back and stood towering over her mother, looking down at her with assured and fearless eyes.

"Very well, Mother, you shall have blunt speaking. I shall never marry for the very simple reason that I dislike heartily the whole idea of marriage."

Aghast, Jessie could only whisper, "You dislike . . . ? But why? It isn't normal to dislike marriage. How can you possibly feel that way when you've grown up with your father and me, when you've seen how much we have loved each other over the years, when you've seen how much we have suffered and struggled, yes, and achieved too, for our marriage?"

"That is exactly what I am talking about," said Lily in a plain voice.

Coldly Jessie asked, "What are you trying to tell me, Lily?"

"I am trying to tell you, Mother dear—and apparently you will give me no peace until I do—that for twenty years I have seen what marriage has done to you and Father. I have seen how dreadfully your ambitions for that marriage have made you suffer. I was too young to understand much about the court-martial, but even at the age of six I could see the agonies you endured. I don't want to endure such things, or expose myself to them. For years, in Monterey and on the sand dunes of San Francisco, I watched you creep about the house like a stricken creature because you could not have your husband by your side. In the years when Father was away on his expeditions your existence became a still-life; when he was reported dead, I saw how near dead you were at the prospect, and how completely you would have been killed had the news been true. I don't want to be stricken that way. I don't want to be dependent on any other human being for my happiness, and my very life as well. I know what you underwent during the years of the Civil War after Father was deprived of his command; I know how many evil tongues there are in this country calling you unfortunate names because you dared to battle with President Lincoln for your husband's sake. I don't want to battle with people; I don't want to grow angry and wage wars and violate my own character for the sake of a man. I want to live on my own two feet, complete inside my own body and my own brain. To you and to Father your love and marriage are great and beautiful. But that way of life is not for me."

She paused for a moment, her voice growing quiet.

"Perhaps if I had grown up in the midst of a mild or mediocre marriage, I could have accepted the idea. The intensity of my reaction is in direct proportion to the intensity of your relationship. Please believe me, dear, and please leave me in peace on the subject: I shall never marry."

For a long time there was no sound in the room but that of the rain slashing across the library windows. Jessie made no attempt to hide or restrain the tears that coursed down her cheeks. This then was the failure of her marriage: that she had created an antipathy for it in her daughter. Now the cycle was complete. Her philosophy of marriage had been formulated as a reaction to her mother's concept of the "least marriage"; now, twenty-eight years later, in a new time and a new generation, her daughter was reacting even more violently than had she: the daughter had seen so much of the "most marriage" that she wanted no part of it for herself.

As wrong as she thought Lily was, as desperately as she regretted her daughter's decision, she knew that she could do nothing to oppose it. Time would work out its pattern. Perhaps circumstance would change Lily's mind; but in any event her daughter had a right to live her own life, free of her mother's interference and direction, just as she herself had insisted with Elizabeth McDowell Benton that, wrong, desperately wrong as her mother might believe her to be, she had the right to marry Lieutenant John C. Fremont and fulfill her own destiny.

She rose, kissed Lily lightly on the forehead and said, "At the opening of this discussion I asked you to forgive me for intruding, but that was merely a politeness. Now, at the end, I urge you most deeply to forgive me for trespassing upon your private life and your private convictions. I will never bring up the subject again. I think you are wrong, but that is apparently the prerogative of mothers. Go your own way, my dear; your father and I want only one thing for you: that you be happy. I shall make no further attempt to influence you to be happy according to my definition of the term. Good night, Lily."

5

Though John told her little about the complicated financing of his railroad structures, she knew that his ten-million-dollar bond issue had sold well, providing money to order locomotives, grade many miles of track in Texas, and send surveyors into New Mexico to stake out the Rocky Mountain pass. However, the money from American investors came in too slowly to suit his purposes, and in the summer of 1869 he confided to Jessie that he was at last going to achieve his plan of almost ten years before: instead of floating a stock issue for the sale of the Mariposa, which had been prevented at the last moment by the threat of civil war in the United States, he was now going to put through a bond issue in France for his Memphis & El Paso Railroad. This time his idea was eagerly seized upon, and more than five million dollars' worth of securities were sold to French investors, many of whom bought because of their faith in General Fremont.

The five-year period of tranquillity and prosperity drew to its close. She began to notice that her husband was growing worried, that his absences were longer than usual, that when he returned he was jumpy and taut once again. She had to piece together the fragments to learn that his difficulties were compounded of the mechanical and the financial: the House of Representatives had given his railroad a right of way through the territories, but the Senate defeated the bill, and without this grant there would be no way of connecting the eastern and western halves of his line. The cost of grading the land on which to lay track was everywhere higher than had been anticipated; his engineers were having recurrent troubles in the mountains due to landslides, washouts and unexpected steepness of grades; materials could not be transported to points of construction because rivers overflowed and the boats carrying railroad equipment were tied up. Nowhere was the task of building a railroad across wild and virgin territory easier or less expensive than had been anticipated; often the cost rose to three and four times its estimate. As for the financial upsets, too large a percentage of the money from French investors had been taken by the Paris banks for floating the loan; the balance of the money was provided not in cash but in supplies and rolling stock. When the equipment reached the United States from France there was no grading or roadbed ready to use it.

But the most serious blow, which came late in 1869, was a close repetition of the Sargent affair in London. John had worked through the French consul general at New York, who had introduced him to reputable French financiers and engineers; however, when the bond issue was put through the Paris Bourse, the bonds stated that they were guaranteed by the United States government in terms of munificent land grants. When John went on record to the French public with the true facts, the sale of bonds stopped immediately and a series of civil and criminal law suits were instituted. Charges were brought in Paris against General John C. Fremont as a participant in the fraud. Senator Howard of Michigan, who originally had defeated the bill to grant the railroad right of way across the territories, used the Franch scandal to block John's further attempts to secure federal co-operation.

After a three-week business trip, during which she received only the barest hurried notes from him, he arrived at Pocaho one evening looking pale and ill. Jessie's heart sank at the sight of him. She had a bath prepared for him, laid out a fresh suit and then had a supper tray brought to the library. John sank into a low-lying leather seat facing the Hudson. Jessie sat quietly on the arm of his chair, her hand lightly on his shoulder. When at last he could bring himself to speak she surmised the enormity of the misfortune he had suffered by the hoarse and twisted quality of his voice.

"It's gone, Jessie, everything's gone. I came to the very end of our funds three weeks ago . . . I have been rushing about frantically trying to raise money . . . They gave me one small extension . . . Now we're through . . . I couldn't meet the payments. The mortgage holders have taken over our railroad, Jessie—we have been thrown into receivership."

She hesitated for a moment to make sure that her voice would be calm: her main concern now was to make certain that their loss be confined to metallic dollars and rails.

"But how can they take over your railroad, John? It's yours, isn't it? Your money and ability went into building it . . . Five years of your life . . . thousands of your dollars . . ."

Staring out unseeing over the river, he replied, "All of that is gone, it was swept away by floods and washouts, by hard grades and harder rock; I took tools and equipment and rails from manufacturers on credit; they have to be paid. If I can't give them the cash, I must give them the railroad."

"Surely they're not entitled to more than is owed to them? After they have been paid their debts, what is left belongs to you."

John shook his head wearily, trying to rub the exhaustion out of his eyes.

"There will be nothing left over, Jessie. As it stands now, only one-quarter laid, the line is useless—no money can be earned on it until it is completed." He looked up at her, his eyes small, dark and hurt. "Don't you understand, Jessie, we're wiped out! I've lost not only the physical property, but the control of the railroad as well."

As he poured out in an almost inarticulate rush of broken words the story of deception and betrayed friendship which were the underlying cause of his troubles, she slowly fitted together the pattern of misplaced confidence and financial intrigue with which the business end of his venture had been honey-combed. Once again, as she had that night in the Clarendon Hotel, with John in jail, she saw that neither of them had any business sense, that they were trusting souls who had never defrauded anyone and consequently knew little of how money can persuade old companions to lie and cheat and work at cross-purposes behind one's back. John was an engineer and a visionary, a rare combination of talents that had enabled him to break and map trails to the West, and now to lay iron rails along these former paths through the wilderness. Could he also be a sharp and shrewd businessman?

She was certain that her husband had done the best he could. She was equally certain that there was nothing she could have done that would have changed matters, even if she had been as close to his business transactions as she had been to his early exploring expeditions. Nor, as in the days of the court-martial, did she think it loyal or decent of her to try to postguess her husband. John had had to carry the burden of heavy responsibility in a difficult and pioneering field. What he had done had seemed the right and necessary thing to do at that moment, and so she would accept it as having been right. If one benefited from a man's accomplishments over a long period of years, it was fair play to accept philosophically the results of those judgments which turned out badly. That was what was meant by partnership; no partnership could survive on any other basis.

She kissed the corner of his mouth.

"You ran into difficulties and complications that were impossible to foresee. Who should know better than you that the pioneer in any field, the one who has the courage to fight the obstacles and hardships, is never the one to reap the benefits? Let them have this railroad; you will plan another; next time we'll get government help . . ."

"People are saying that a transcontinental railroad is an impossible dream," he broke in harshly, "that the idea should be abandoned."

". . . We'll use the rest of our assets to get started again. You can't let yourself be discouraged by a first failure."

His eyes held hers steadily.

"Assets?" he asked dully. "What assets?"

"Our interest in the Mariposa. Our lands and ranches in California. The house in New York . . ."

A convulsion swept over John as he told her in broken phrases, ". . . You haven't really understood. I borrowed up to the hilt on the Mariposa . . . It's gone . . . Our gold mines are gone. So is our property in California . . . I mortgaged it all to push ahead with the railroad."

Aghast, she could only cry, "But not our homes, John? Not the New York house? Not Pocaho?"

". . . The New York house, but not Pocaho; that is in your name. Everything in it belongs to you. Thank God I could not mortgage it; we have this, our home—nothing more, nothing, darling—not a cent."

He rose, walked to a far corner of the library and stood by Baron Humboldt's books. He had aged ten years in the past six months; she had seen him angry, bitter, resentful, vengeful, fighting mad, but never before had he been as crushed as he looked now, his shoulders bent over, the white hair on his bowed head standing out against the dark leather bindings.

For herself, she was momentarily disheartened, but neither stunned nor broken by these developments. Had John not been the conqueror and governor of California, only to be dragged across the continent like a criminal; had he not been America's most valuable trail blazer, map maker and opener of the West, only to be court-martialed and cast out of the Army in disgrace; had he not been the standard bearer of a new and great political movement, only to be defeated and forgotten; had he not been the commander of the Army of the West, only to be ignominiously removed without an opportunity to prove his worth? For five years they had been among the world's richest people, had been pushing through the most valuable contribution to western expansion since the Oregon Trail; now they were penniless, their railroad bankrupt, the idea of a transcontinental line proven impractical. Everything they touched they built almost to a pinnacle, then the hand of fate or the hand of man brushed them aside. Their projects went on; their ideas matured and flourished; their conquests became part of the main stream of American life; but they, the pioneers, were deprived of participation or recompense.

Very well, then, if this were their pattern, if this were their life, there was little they could do but put up with it. She was not frightened about their living, even though she had two sons to educate. Nor was she disturbed over the prospect of returning to an austere life; she would not mind cooking and cleaning in Madame Castro's rooms in Monterey or in the sand dunes of San Francisco, providing her husband were by her side. She could go back to that life, or forward to any other life that might lie ahead; recurrent adversity and disappointment had not weakened her fiber, for Jessie Benton Fremont was like a deeply built ship that drove best under a stormy wind. She had only one problem, to safeguard her husband's health and peace of mind, reconcile him to his losses, help him make his adjustments, plan with him for new directions, new activities, a new start. Surely, at fifty-seven, he was not finished? Six months before he had been at the height of his powers; today he was saddened, bewildered. Tomorrow he would rest, recoup his strength and confidence, and the day after tomorrow they would begin anew.

6

She dismissed all the servants except one general maid. Lily helped with the housework, young Frank took over the gardening. In her safe-deposit vault in New York she had some stocks and bonds which John had given her as gifts; these were cashed and used for living expenses. Baron Humboldt's former library sold for a substantial sum; their horses and carriages and Charlie's sailboat brought sufficient to pay the more pressing debts. Part of the big house was closed off; all entertaining was stopped, except for their few intimate friends, chiefly Hannah Kirsten.

Jessie worked constantly, with a desperation she had never been conscious of before, sending out letters and petitions to get Congress to return the forty-two-thousand-dollar purchase price of their confiscated Black Point; to secure for John a government appointment which would afford them a modest living. Although the passing of the months lessened his bitterness, though he was able to busy himself for some little time in straightening out the tangled accounts of the Memphis & El Paso Railroad, actually there was no work for him to do, no position for him to occupy. She watched as he chafed at idleness, yet something inside him seemed to have died, and try as she might, with every means she had developed in thirty years of a loving marriage, she could not bring back to life his inner flame.

The years of opulence and Mariposa gold had weakened her habits of thrift. She became confused because the bills were still large, though they appeared to be living at a minimum, and there just was no cash with which to meet them. Without telling her family about it, she took a substantial bank loan on Pocaho, thinking that the money would earn them the months necessary to bring John a business opening, a government appointment perhaps. The stratagem was only a half-success; a personal note of John's came due, one he had forgotten in the collapse of his affairs; he was so despondent at not being able to meet the payment that Jessie handed over her bank loan, telling him that she had had the money hidden in her vault for just such an emergency.

They were without funds for the simple necessities. It was at this point that Lily took over, decided which paintings and *objets d'art* should be sold, began collecting a few of the sums owed to them. She handled their slim and often disappearing bank account, purchased the supplies, paid the bills, judged which part of the grounds should be allowed to run to weeds and which part kept up.

Jessie was grateful to her daughter for taking this burden off her shoulders; it released her full time and energies for John. They took long walks along the river; they spent the wintry nights before the log fire in the library; they made their plans to move back to San Francisco as soon as Congress paid for Black Point, and to build a little cottage overlooking the strait. She kept him encouraged by news from friends in Washington who were confident that the Black Point bill would go through, who had assured her that General Fremont was sorely needed at this post or in that position in the West, that the appointment would soon be made by President Grant or the War Department. Yet nothing came through, nothing; Congress would not pay for Black Point; President Grant ignored all requests to help his former commander.

Between them, Jessie and Lily managed the miracle of hanging on at Pocaho for almost two years. The women had a tacit agreement never to tell John what had been sold or how straitened were their circumstances. But at length the time came when Lily had to confide to her mother that there was no more money or salable assets, that in order to buy food, in order to keep Charlie at Annapolis and Frank at West Point, they would have to borrow still further on Pocaho. They knew that this was the beginning of the end, for they had been unable to meet the interest payments on the first loan; if they did not meet the new indebtedness they would lose Pocaho and be without a roof over their heads.

"I don't think we should do it that way, Mother," said Lily. "Father would be terribly distressed if we lost the house. I have one alternative, but I am not sure you will approve . . ."

"What do you suggest, Lily?"

"That I find a position in New York. A lot of girls are going into business today who never did before. I am good at business, you know, or at least Father always says I am. Then why can't I take a job in some office?"

Something in her mother's eyes stopped her.

"You are good and you are brave, Lily," she murmured. "But don't you see, we can't do this to Father. As long as we live here at Pocaho quietly, the world knows nothing of our affairs. But once you take a job we publish to all the world that we are destitute, that our daughter must support us. I would like to take a job at a desk beside you, but you know how proud your father is; he would take it as a personal token of failure. We must spare him that humiliation. Give me a little more time; something is certain to come through, an appointment, some money for Black Point . . ."

"I understand, Mother," replied Lily, her face somber.

And so they borrowed again on Pocaho. There were unexpectedly heavy expenses in the winter of '73; new debts had a way of popping up, debts of

several years' standing which Jessie and Lily had not known about, but which
John said had to be acknowledged. Fighting against time, fighting against
hope, they fell further and further behind in their interest, and at last, toward the end of 1873, the bank foreclosed the mortgage and took over the
house.

Her courage unfailing, but her heart almost broken at what this was doing
to her now white-faced husband, Jessie packed their clothes and moved into
New York. With their few remaining dollars they rented a small, ugly frame
house on Eighth Street, the paint coming off the outside walls, the inside
shabby and dirty. Jessie and Lily worked frantically for four days, painting
and redecorating, while John stayed with a friend. When he came home the
cramped and dark rooms were at least clean.

Their rent was paid for two months in advance. Jessie had enough cash to
buy food for approximately the same period. She redoubled her efforts during
the weeks, writing dozens of letters to congressmen, to their old friends in
the Army and in the Cabinet, setting up ever new plans and schemes to secure
for John even the simplest kind of appointment, to help push through Congress the bill necessary to repay them for Black Point. Several times it
seemed as though she were to have success: John was proposed as governor
for various territories, as Indian commissioner for one of the western districts,
as collector or commissioner of the Land Office in San Francisco. The House
of Representatives passed a bill appropriating money for Black Point, but at
the last moment it was defeated in the Senate.

The two months drew to a close. Jessie was at her wit's end. Only once
before had she had to think about money, after their court-martial, when
they had had to borrow from Tom Benton in order to start a home in California. Jessie knew that if she appealed to her sisters or to their many friends
she could borrow money. But how could she ever repay it? Although she
had a fine gift for giving, she had no whit of talent for asking in return. She
would have preferred to die in their shabby and cramped house on Eighth
Street, die quietly and respectably, than go out and ask for alms.

Lily began disappearing shortly after luncheon each day, returning at five,
with her hands looking smudgy. Jessie asked only if she was working somewhere, and was satisfied with Lily's denial. After a couple of weeks, when
Lily brought an old typewriter into the house and spent several hours at it
each morning, Jessie realized that her daughter was attending a secretarial
school. She was proud of the matter-of-fact way in which Lily was going
about the task of preparing herself for any eventuality.

At the end of the two months she knew they would have to move out of
even this sordid little shelter. Where were they to go? How was she to break
the news to John? How was she to keep from the world the fact that General
John C. Fremont was destitute? In Monterey she had been distressed because
it was the accumulation of gold that had separated them; now it was the lack
of gold that would tear them apart.

As always, she contrived a way. Hannah Kirsten had been urging her to come for a visit to her home in upstate New York. John had a long-standing invitation from one of his officers of the Western Command to visit in Staten Island and talk over old army days. Lily was always welcome at her aunt Susie's in Boston.

As they sat over their last meager supper in the dark dining room, Jessie at last found the courage to say, "John, why don't we accept these invitations? Hannah has stayed with us so many times and is eager to have me visit her. You know how often Colonel Wadsworth has pleaded for you to pay him a visit. I think it would be good for you to be among old army friends again. Don't you think you might enjoy that for a time?"

John pushed aside his plate and reached for her hand across the table.

"Don't think I don't know what you've been doing, Jessie dear, or how desperately you've been trying. I have said little . . . for what could I say? I have brought us to this desperate situation, I alone . . . and yet I can see no way out of it . . . no possible help for us . . ."

She rose quickly, went to his side and kissed his eyelids.

"Now, darling," she cried, "it's only for a few weeks, then we'll be together again. An appointment will come through. Good times will come back, you will see. Haven't they always? Think how often we have reached bottom, only to begin the long climb up again. We have had so much from the world, John, so much happiness and success. Surely they have inured us to times of difficulty?"

He sat with his head down, gripping her hand tightly, unable to speak.

The next morning at a very early hour they walked down the three unpainted steps of their house, each with a suitcase in hand. At the bottom of the steps they turned to each other, mutely. To Jessie it seemed that nothing she had endured before, not even the death of young Benton, was as heartbreaking as this moment of separation. Her husband needed her now more desperately than he ever had before, yet of all the millions of dollars they had extracted from the Mariposa, she could not command a sufficient sum to stay by her husband's side, remain with him when he was crushed, ill and old-looking, suffering as only the fiercely proud man suffers. They had been separated on their twentieth anniversary because John had been at the head of his army, pursuing General Price, and she had been working at headquarters in St. Louis. In a few days they would be celebrating their thirty-second anniversary, but once again they would be apart.

"My dear," she murmured softly, "I was just thinking of what we told each other that night in the tent before Springfield. It's easy to speak of love in good times, in the wonderful years such as we had on the Mariposa and at Black Point and Pocaho. But now that we are to be separated I can think of nothing to say but that I love you, darling; I have loved you every hour, every day, in good times and bad. You have always made my life happy and beautiful; it is beautiful even now because I love you and because you love me. Be of good heart, think of me every moment, write to me every day; we will find a way, John. Haven't we always?"

The early-morning streets were deserted. The air was quiet. Behind the closed doors and shuttered windows of the houses the world still slept. They were alone, two little figures, old, white-haired, alone in the universe. Then suddenly they were locked securely in each other's arms, lips to lips, two tiny, forlorn figures which now, merged into one, made a large and great figure: the figure of love: indestructible: immortal.

7

She remained at Hannah Kirsten's for two months, walking a little in the afternoons along the river, listening to Hannah play the piano and sing. She had hoped that the rest and distance from the ordeal of watching the last dollars disappear might bring fresh ideas and fresh energy which would enable her to find some solution. At the end of two months she was further away than ever from an understanding of what to do, with a new despair because the passing hours had brought nothing but blankness. The deeply built ship that drove best under a stormy wind had lost its compass and rudder, was adrift, pounded by the ever mounting seas. John was not unhappy with his friend in Staten Island, yet he was growing restive as a guest. Many times she thought how senseless and chaotic was the pattern of social responsibility when a man like John Fremont, now in his sixties, who had contributed so much to the development of his country could be destitute, without being compensated for property that had been pre-empted, without the saving graciousness of a minor government job, without even a modest pension from the War Department which he had served so well for so many years.

She knew that a disinterested party might well say it was their own fault: they had made millions of dollars from the Mariposa, they had been among the powerful and wealthy ones of the earth, but they had been improvident. They had left the money slip through their hands, they had not protected themselves against age and vicissitude. What use to tell these people that if they had been content to live on the outpourings of the Mariposa their money would still be intact? What use to protest that their wealth had been poured into the radical though imperative idea of a transcontinental railroad, where it had vanished as so many other fortunes had and would vanish, to form a roadbed upon which ultimately a transcontinental railroad would be erected? What use to publicize the tens of thousands they had poured into public funds, worth-while movements and causes, money that had been given to individuals to help them out of difficulties or to achieve success? What use to cry out in anguish, If only we could get back a tithe of what we have given away, and what has been taken from us, we could live out the rest of our lives in decent comfort and self-respect?

Tired, discouraged, weak in spirit and body, she wondered what would happen to them if she continued in this state of lassitude. Her father had taught her that one must not worry about the future, for if it ever arrived one could face it with the same good judgment as in the past. That had held true for some thirty-two years of marriage; now her ability to face up to a situation had collapsed.

She had no way of knowing how long she might have remained in stunned apathy had not a telegram reached her from Staten Island with the information that John was ill with pneumonia. Instantly her mind flashed back to her own siege of pneumonia during the court-martial; she knew how easy it was to die in the grip of this malady. Without railroad tickets, without money, without plans, without anything except the knowledge that she must get to her husband at once, she began crushing her few clothes into a suitcase.

Hannah Kirsten was not the kind who comforted in words only: in a few moments Jessie found herself in the Kirsten carriage. Soon she and Hannah were in Colonel Wadsworth's home standing by the side of John's bed while the Staten Island physician explained that her husband's condition was delicate, that as soon as possible he should be taken to a mild climate for the winter, to some place like Nassau where he could recoup his strength.

Even as she stood by John's bedside gazing down into the thin, pale face of her husband, she knew what she would do to meet this situation. It was not something she had to think about; it did not take an hour or a day of sorting out plans and choosing the best; the precise knowledge of what she could and must do was suddenly there, alive and whole and ready to act upon. She told Hannah that she had to go to New York at once. In a few moments Hannah had put her on a ferry, assured her that she would remain in Staten Island to nurse John until she returned. She also promised to send Jessie a telegram at the Astor House each morning and evening.

Jessie's ferry reached New York at seven o'clock of a cold winter evening. The carriage sloshed its way through the snow-covered streets to the Astor House. She ate no supper, but undressed the moment she reached her room, stretched out in bed as cold and still as a corpse and fell asleep. She awakened at seven, bathed, creamed her face and combed her hair with the utmost care, then summoned the housekeeper and had her one purple silk dress sponged and ironed. At nine she had breakfast in the Astor House restaurant and rode to the office of the New York *Ledger*. She waited only an instant after her card had been sent in; Robert Bonner, the red-bearded Irishman who owned the *Ledger*, came out of his office, beamed at her while he wrung her hand, and then ushered her into a wood-panelled office with its great desk littered with scrambled manuscripts and a succession of evil-smelling pipes. Bonner's two passions were fast horses and provocative advertising copy; he and Lily had frequently raced the Fremont horses along the ridge above the Hudson.

In a voice well masked with confidence Jessie said, "Mr. Bonner, I have been thinking that some of my early experiences with Mr. Fremont, and some of my early travels, would make excellent articles for your readers."

Bonner nodded his head in a vigorous affirmative.

"Indeed I should think they would, Mrs. Fremont. What precisely did you have in mind?"

"Well, stories like my first crossing of Panama, when the route had just been opened and hundreds of Americans were stranded in Panama City; stories from our life in Monterey when California was being made into a state; the great fires and action of the Vigilantes in San Francisco; stories of how we were besieged by the Hornitas League in the Sierras. Or, in a different direction, my early memories of the White House, of the family life of the early presidents and their First Ladies."

"That material sounds fascinating, Mrs. Fremont."

Brusquely she asked, "How much will you pay for each story?"

Mr. Bonner was somewhat startled by this quick transition to the commercial aspect of their discussion.

"Why . . . ah . . . we can pay one hundred dollars apiece, Mrs. Fremont, always providing, of course, that the material works out well."

"Of course," agreed Jessie, standing up. "The stories will come out exceedingly well. Thank you, Mr. Bonner, and good day."

On the way back to the hotel she stopped at a stationery store where she bought pencils, erasers, pens, ink and many tablets of paper. By the time she reached her room she had reasoned that putting together the cost of steamship tickets to Nassau, hotel accommodations there, as well as medical care, the expenses would be at least a thousand dollars. In order to earn this much money she must write ten stories.

It was almost noon when she took off her hat and coat and spread out her writing materials on the desk. By six o'clock she had the first article, "Panama," complete and recopied. Hungry now, remembering that she had had nothing since breakfast, she had a light supper brought up to her room, then rested for an hour. Shortly before eight o'clock she sat down at her desk and began working on her second story. She was getting into the swing of it now and the writing came a little easier. By two in the morning "Besieged," the story of the Hornitas League, was completed and neatly recopied.

She slept from two-thirty until five-thirty. By the time she sent down for breakfast at eight-thirty she already had a rough draft of her third story. A telegram arrived from Hannah saying that John was making satisfactory progress. By one o'clock that night she had three more stories to add to the two she had done the day before. The following day she did another three, giving her a total of eight. She had had only a little over three hours' sleep the night before, so she slept from one until six in the morning. She awakened thinking, Only two more stories to go and then I'll have my thousand dollars. A reassuring telegram from Hannah cleared her mind for action.

When night fell, and she had her ten stories completed, she thought suddenly, I must not stop now; the thousand dollars may not be quite enough, I must give myself a little latitude. If I write one more . . .

The eleventh story came hard, not because her will was wearing out, but because the first great rush of material was beginning to slacken and she was growing a little hard pressed to think of a new subject. She finally decided upon "Family Life in the White House" and wrote it quickly, almost in a breath, completing it at midnight.

She stretched out fully dressed on the bed to rest for a few minutes; the next thing she knew it was morning. Once again she bathed, combed her hair, put on her purple dress and took a carriage up to the office of the *Ledger*. Mr. Bonner was a little puzzled at the purpose of her call. When she unwrapped the package she had been clutching under her arm, saying, "I have completed eleven stories," his eyes were wide with astonishment.

"Eleven stor . . . Why, Mrs. Fremont, I thought you would be weeks, even months, in the writing."

Realizing for the first time that an editor had every reason to be astonished at her procedure, Jessie asked in alarm, "But surely that will make no difference to you? You will find these stories well done . . . they revolve about the early frontier and pioneer periods . . ."

Bonner chuckled as he replied, "It's just that I'm overcome by your productivity. I have to browbeat most of my authors to get one story from them in five days, let alone eleven."

"Then could I have the money right away, Mr. Bonner? One hundred dollars a story, eleven hundred in all."

Mr. Bonner gaped at her. "Eleven hundred dollars," he murmured. "That's a lot of money."

"It's also a lot of stories."

"But you don't object if I read them?"

"Most assuredly not; go right ahead."

The editor, who had had no intention of reading manuscript with the author watching his every expression, gave a little sigh, picked up the first story. He scanned five of the articles in quick succession, making a correcting flick with his pencil here and there, lighting several half-smoked pipes in the process and giving out only an occasional grunt of satisfaction. At the end of the fifth manuscript he looked up and said, "Yes, these are well done; our subscribers will like them. Suppose I give you a check for five hundred dollars now, and the balance in a few days after I've had a chance to read the rest of the stories?"

"Excellent," she replied. "That will enable me to take General Fremont to Nassau. He is ill with pneumonia."

Robert Bonner rose, requested his bookkeeper to give Jessie a check, told her that he was certain the general would get well, and suggested that when she returned she come in to see him about further stories.

Walking quickly to the steamship offices, Jessie purchased her tickets for Nassau, then once again boarded the ferry for Staten Island.

8

John healed in the warmth of the Nassau sun. Jessie was so happy to be reunited with her husband that she almost believed the illness had been designed to bring them together again. When she thought back to the two terror-stricken months at Hannah's she could only imagine that she must have been as ill as John had been, and that now she had recovered from her mental and spiritual pneumonia. She knew that she had found a way for them to live again: after recovering from her fatigue of the four-day effort, hundreds of stories had come to mind.

She uttered thanks to Tom Benton for once again having saved their lives. Though she had been grateful for the editorial training he had given her from the age of twelve, she had never imagined that she would one day use this skill for making a living; now it had not only enabled her to save her husband's life but would make it possible for them to live on together through the years. A hundred times a day she blessed her father's memory, silently blessed her husband for having been willing to let her collaborate with him on the reports, thus giving her a trade which had rescued them both.

They took leisurely walks along the white beach, gathering shells and reminiscing of other days and other beaches: Siasconset, where they had refused the Democratic nomination, Black Point, where they had walked along the sands at the base of their cottage and watched the sun plunge into the Pacific. These good memories were as healing as the clear air and the bright sunshine; soon they were going out in a little boat for a day's fishing. Flesh came back to John's emaciated frame, color to his cheeks and a renewed sparkle to his eyes. It was then she had the courage to talk to him about their future.

"John, when I think back over our years it appears to me that our best hours and our best memories are tied up with the work we did together."

He stretched out lazily on the cushions on the bottom of the boat, adjusted the parasol to keep the sun off his face, then answered slowly, "Yes, the months when we collaborated on the reports . . . the campaign of 1856 . . . the Hundred Days in Missouri . . . they stand out in my mind like great peaks in the Rockies."

"Then, as soon as you feel strong enough, why couldn't we continue our collaboration? The editor wants more stories, and we write well together —at least you always said we did. You've had sufficient adventures and experience to provide the material for a hundred books, books I always thought you should write . . ."

"I'm no author, Jessie. Have you forgotten my nosebleed in the house on C Street?"

"Neither am I! But together we have always done good work. You supply the material, I'll set down the stories. Isn't that a fair arrangement?"

In the spring they returned to New York. Jessie located a modest cottage on Staten Island, right on the waterfront, and Lily was called home.

The series of articles in the *Ledger* had been well received. Robert Bonner asked for more, "Though not eleven at a time, my dear Mrs. Fremont, I beg of you!" Since she could write them far faster than the *Ledger* could use them, she went to visit the editors of *Harper's, Century* and *Wide Awake;* they had seen the stories in the *Ledger,* so it was not difficult to sell them.

The summer and fall months passed quickly and happily, with all three of the family sharing the work. John wrote out many pages of notes about the trails and the mountains and his early expeditions for Jessie's reference. She then wrote her stories in pencil. When she had finished a rough draft Lily transferred the material to the typewriter. They made only a modest living, but they were intensely happy, for they were all busy; Charlie had completed his first cruise successfully, and Frank was doing well in his studies at West Point. Lily assumed the management of the house and the family funds, and so Jessie was relieved of a task for which she cared little, freed to work three or four hours in the morning, to take long walks with John over the Island in the afternoons, watching the ships come in and out of New York Harbor as they had watched from their glassed-in porch at Black Point.

And at last, in 1878, President Hayes appointed John to be governor of the Territory of Arizona. The salary was only two thousand dollars a year, but there was great rejoicing in Jessie's heart, for it meant that once again John would be in the service of his country, that he would be restored to activity and position.

They made the trip overland to San Francisco in seven days, riding the railroad that had risen on the ashes of John Fremont's first effort. It was seventeen years since she had sailed out of the Golden Gate strait to join her husband who had just been appointed major general of the Western Command. San Francisco was now a thriving metropolis; there was little left to remind her of her first view of the city when she clambered down the side of the S.S. *Panama* in 1849 and was carried through the surf by a sailor. Knowing that their home on Black Point had been torn down, she refused John's offer to take her there.

They stayed in San Francisco only long enough to regain their land legs, then boarded the Southern Pacific train for Los Angeles. John insisted upon riding his wife up to Fort Hill, where he could show her the emplacement and the remains of the battery which he had erected to defend the Pueblo of Los Angeles in 1847. The train carried them from Los Angeles to Yuma, where they were met by three army ambulances, each drawn by six mules. Jessie, John and Lily rode in the first ambulance, crossing the Gila River with the water up to the hubs and camping the first night on the bank of the Colorado River. For Jessie this was like the early days in California; she only wished she could see Beale and old Knight come galloping across the desert.

Jessie and Lily went house hunting in Prescott, renting one made of pine and juniper planks, covered only by cotton sheets. The wood proved to be infested with vermin, so the two women removed the sheets and scoured the planks with boiling lye. Lily kept the house filled with wild flowers in the wet season, and yellow and dark red cactus blossoms in the dry. Jessie gave history classes to the school children every Friday; she took pride in watching Prescott grow into a fair-sized village with the erection of churches, a hospital and a few plastered homes. If the hamlet was crude, with wooden sidewalks lashed by dust storms, its adobe houses sometimes melting down in the fierce rainstorms, if it was a town just being born in a wild country in process of being converted from a territory to a state, had not all her life and her family's life been spent in just such surroundings? Was it not their pattern to live with such young towns as St. Louis, Washington, Monterey, San Francisco, Mariposa and now Prescott?

John's duties were light, more a matter of keeping good will than law and order, but unfortunately their house cost ninety dollars a month, the Chinese cook provided by a sympathetic aunt in Los Angeles cost forty dollars a month, and foods were three times as high as in New York or San Francisco. Jessie continued her writing, for the two-thousand-dollar salary barely covered their food and rent. They could not keep saddle horses, for hay was fifty dollars a ton, but the army post made their stables available to the governor. John and Lily spent their days in the saddle, riding across the desert. The high altitude did not agree with Jessie. She found it difficult to work, was frequently short of breath, and when she came in from a walk she would have to lie down at once. She did not tell them that her heart and lungs were acting strangely in this new country, or that the lassitude which prevented her from continuing her writing was caused by anything more than laziness or contentment.

She stood this sapping of her energies in silence for a full year, determined neither to give in nor to worry her family. Then one day John and Lily returned from a horseback ride to find her lying face down on the floor. When they had revived her and demanded to know what had happened, she did not feel that she could conceal her ailment any longer. John announced quickly that he would resign his governorship and take her back to Staten Island. Jessie glanced at her husband's sunburned face, radiating good health. She could not let him go back to hateful idleness and obscurity.

That evening she effected a compromise: she would return east; Lily would remain in Prescott to keep her father company. They would come east for vacations, and she would visit them in Prescott during the more favorable weather. Neither her husband nor her daughter wanted to let her go, but she convinced them that it was the best way out of a difficult situation.

It was the last she was to see of her husband or daughter for three solid years, for they never garnered sufficient spare cash for traveling or visits. Jessie lived alone in the cottage they had formerly occupied on Staten Island, writing stories and essays which were collected in book form under such titles as *Far West Sketches, A Year of American Travel, The Will and Way Stories, Souvenirs of My Time*. Her writings sold fairly well, not enough to give her any assurance for the future, but enough to make her life secure in the Staten Island bungalow and enable her to send a few dollars each month to Lily for the management of the Prescott house. She kept her living expenses low, wearing her old dresses until they were threadbare, rarely going to New York, avoiding all social affairs. Occasionally she was visited by Charlie, when he was in from a cruise, or by Frank, who was now a second lieutenant in the Army. Hannah Kirsten and others of her old friends came for several days at a time to keep her company.

Yet she was alone, always terribly alone. She recalled what Lily had said in their library at Pocaho about watching her mother crawl about the house like a stricken creature when her husband was away. In her mind she went back again and again to those years when John had been gone on his expeditions, when she had spent six months, a year, two years without him. When she struck a balance in the account books of her memory she saw that half of her married life had been spent in separation from her husband. These separations had been necessary, sometimes to their career, sometimes to the demands of John's roving nature; yet they had never been necessary to her. Having been separated from her husband for half her life was like having been married only half as long; and it was too late now to recapture those lost years, to live still again that half of the marriage that had been so cruelly wasted. She had been through so much, she was so much older that she imagined the ache would be less and the torture less. Yet the passage of the years had not made her better able to endure separation.

Time and again she decided to return to Arizona: better to be ill at John's side than to be in the best of physical health but spiritually half alive without him. At other times she determined to ask John to come back to Staten Island, but she remembered how happy he was as governor and knew she could not do it.

More severely than anything that happened in the three years of working alone and thinking alone, she was distressed at being by herself on her fifty-eighth birthday. She somehow felt sentimental about the occasion; she remembered how John had resisted his fortieth birthday in Paris, feeling that it was the fatal milestone to an explorer and trail blazer. It had taken her eighteen years longer to reach this frame of mind; up to this moment she had felt old only a few times in her life: at the Delaware Indian Reservation, on the sand dunes of San Francisco, in St. Louis after they had relinquished their command to General Hunter, during the two months she had visited Hannah Kirsten. But now, going into her fifty-eighth year, sitting despondently in her little cottage, her hair snow white even though her eyebrows were still thick and black, her face fuller than when she had been young, her skin lined, the hazel in her eyes having turned to a deep brown, her once full mouth drawn taut, all these told her that she had at last grown old.

In the spring of 1883 she received a telegram from John saying that he had resigned his position and was returning to Staten Island to be with her. Her eyes lighted with happiness, but at the same moment she began to worry about their finances. She was not able to write as consistently as she had over the years: she had poured out most of her experiences and the editors were now frequently rejecting the stories. She told herself that the return of her husband would bring her new strength and spirit, that they would somehow get on.

When John came home he seemed to her as young and handsome as she had known him in his youth. He had many business hopes: the development of mines in Arizona, the promoting of a short railroad to take the place of the stagecoaches, the irrigation of Imperial Valley in California for farm lands. He spent a number of weeks trying to promote his ventures in New York, but the eastern financial magnates were not interested; they had no desire to start pioneering enterprises with a seventy-year-old man; and so within a few months his enthusiasm for being back in the East had burned out.

For the next few years they were hard put to it for funds. There was little left in their modest cottage to suggest the grandeur of bygone days; a very few precious books, one or two paintings, souvenirs from the early expeditions, the presidential campaign of 1856, the Hundred Days. Jessie did not always know how Lily managed to secure enough money to meet their ordinary needs. From the amount of time she spent in her bedroom behind the closed door, working at the heavy typewriter, Jessie sometimes suspected that her daughter was doing outside typing jobs.

They were sitting before the living-room fireplace, reading Ulysses S. Grant's *Personal Memoirs,* when Jessie exclaimed:

"You know, John, these memoirs of Grant's are popular; they've sold a great many copies. Why don't you write your memoirs? If you could put down the full story of your expeditions and everything that you have done since 1840—what a magnificent story that would make!"

John's eyes gleamed, but he did not answer.

"Who but you can pick up all the countless fragments and tell the full truth, as Father did in his *Thirty Years in the United States Senate?*"

"Yes, I should like that," replied John slowly. "Do you think we can find a publisher?"

"I am certain we can. I will go into New York tomorrow and make the arrangements."

"We would have to go to Washington to live, you know. All of the documents are there, in the Library of Congress."

"We'll manage it. You will find it stimulating to be back in Washington again. It will help you to write the book."

The next morning she found that the publishers were not overly excited about the idea. They said they would like to see the manuscript when it was completed, but they would advance no money to get it written. The firm of Belford & Clarke seemed more enthusiastic about the venture; while they too refused to advance any money they were willing to sign a generous contract and publish the manuscript immediately upon completion. Jessie was relieved that she could take at least this much good news back to her husband. Yet how were they to live in Washington for the year that would be required to write the book? As she stood at the stub-nosed prow of the Staten Island ferryboat she knew that the answer was up to her. She must become fruitful once again.

A picture arose behind her eyes: she was in the library of the home on C Street on the morning that her husband had left on his first expedition. Tom Benton was saying, "No one has ever put together a story of American exploration . . . I think our people would enjoy that story, Jessie." She had been carrying Lily when her father had first put that idea in her mind; though forty-four years had passed since then, no one had yet popularized the full story of western exploration. Here it was, ready-made for her purposes!

She told John of the contract that was being written up, putting the best face she could upon the discouraging fact that no one would advance any money against royalties, and then sat down to earn the funds they would need for the year in Washington. She made a number of false starts, but by the second week she was writing easily and steadily, evolving twenty articles about American exploration and the lives of the explorers. Four of these the New York editors rejected. The other sixteen were sold. With this money she moved her family to Washington where they rented a house on Dupont Circle overlooking the parklike grounds of the British Legation.

She turned the front room of the second floor into a workroom, for there was a bow window facing east in which she placed John's desk and across from it a green leather table for herself. Lily set up her typewriter in an alcove. Jessie found it good to be hard at work with John again, rising at seven for tea and a roll, then writing until noon, stopping for a light meal, going back to her desk at one o'clock and not stopping until six. At John's request she wrote a short biography of her father to serve as an introduction, but for the main body of the long memoir she merely took dictation from John, content to make an occasional suggestion about material that should be included. As she finished the handwritten pages, Lily took them to her adjoining alcove where she typed them. A reporter from the Washington *Star* reported to his paper:

General Fremont is now seventy-four years old, but looks scarce sixty. His hair, short beard, and mustache are white, but his brown eyes are clear and bright as stars, and his complexion has the ruddy, healthy glow of childhood.

The year passed swiftly and happily, for they were enjoying this voyage backward into their glorious past. The present existed hardly at all for them. They could not get used to the changes in Washington. What Tom Benton had found to be a miasmic mudhole in 1820 had, in 1886, grown into a world metropolis with thousands of beautiful homes, parks and government buildings. Practically all the landmarks so dear to their early years were gone: the Benton home, Hassler's house with its observatory, the glassworks and the fields across which they had walked in the days before their marriage. Gone too were most of their friends, and Tom Benton's comrades of the Senate.

They planned to do the work in two volumes. The publishers had their agents in the field taking subscriptions, but few buyers were willing to part with twelve dollars in advance of publication. Jessie was confident that once the book was released, once it had been enthusiastically reviewed in the press, it would sell well.

The book was issued, but it did not sell at all. Jessie was hard pressed to understand why: she knew that it was too expensive, that much of the material had already been published in their earlier reports and was widely known, that the publishers were new in the field and not particularly astute; but all these things put together did not explain to her satisfaction why John Fremont's *Memoirs* did not sell. Somewhere in the back of her mind was the knowledge that the book had failed because history had passed John C. Fremont by; because he had lived beyond his times, even as her father had before him; that this was a new and young world, interested in other people and other things.

For their solid year of work they received nothing; the publishers lost money on the bulky, well-illustrated book, and Jessie learned too late that their contract paid no royalties until the publisher had taken out his costs. All during the year she had watched John working happily, often brilliant in his analysis of historical forces, a man as young and vital at seventy-four as he had been in the accomplishing at thirty-four. Now, with the volume a failure, earning them not a dollar for their long labors, making it impossible for them to carry on with the proposed second volume, John became ill. When the doctor told her that she must take him at once to a country where the climate was warmer and milder, she was faced with the same problem that she had met thirteen years before. But now there was no way to earn quickly the money to take him to Nassau. She must do something the Fremonts had never done before: she went to Collis P. Huntington, who was in Washington on business for his Southern Pacific Railroad. When she had told Huntington the circumstances he said at once:

"It must be California. You should have my private car, but it is already lent. I will come to your house this evening with the railroad tickets and the necessary letters to insure you a pleasant journey."

When Jessie showed Collis Huntington into John's bedroom that evening, and her husband learned the purpose of the visit, he became angry.

"You had no right to do this, Jessie," he said with tears in his eyes. "We have no way of paying Mr. Huntington back . . ."

Huntington said quietly, "General, aren't you forgetting that our railroad goes over your buried campfires and climbs many a grade you jogged over on a mule? I think we rather owe you this."

9

She rented a vine-covered redwood house on Oak Street in Los Angeles, set in the midst of a broad lawn with flowering shrubs. Here in the warmth of the California sunshine John recovered his health. They lived quietly, rarely leaving their own grounds, welcoming old friends who came each afternoon to tea. Jessie did no more writing, for she felt that she had told all of her stories; but when young historians such as Josiah Royce attacked John, calling him a political adventurer in California who had had no secret orders, branding him as a routine trail marker who had never done any exploring, she wrote passionate articles of defense which such magazines as *Century* published.

A little money came in from these articles; each of her two sons now sent a small monthly check; they lived in modest comfort. She never relaxed her efforts to push through Congress the bill for compensation for Black Point; and here in the quiet warmth of southern California she began her last campaign: to have John put on the Army's pension list in return for his years of service. Her new efforts seemed more promising than any had been before: a bill again passed the House to return them the purchase price of Black Point, the movement to grant John a major general's pension was meeting with favor.

John was growing increasingly restless. He had been evolving promotional schemes that he wanted to talk over with former business associates in New York; his presence in Washington would be helpful in having him put on the pension list and in getting the Black Point bill through the Senate. In the winter of 1889 Jessie reluctantly agreed that he should go east. She had watched his strength ebb away, for though at seventy-seven his mind seemed as vigorous as it always had been, she knew that his physical strength was brittle. She was uneasy at letting him out of her ministering hands, away from the brusque, efficient care of Lily, but to hold him against his wishes when he so urgently needed a sense of motion would hurt him more than the separation. He planned to be gone for two months; Jessie could not spare the money to accompany him.

She remained quietly in the little cottage, waiting for the mailman to come swinging down Oak Street, a tan leather pouch at his side, bringing her the daily packet of news from John. Though he was staying at a cheap boardinghouse in a run-down part of town instead of going to the Astor House or to the home of a friend, he was feeling well, was excited and pleased to be active again. At last in April, after he had been gone for five months, she received a letter telling her that Congress had granted him a lifetime pension of six thousand dollars a year, "in view of the services to his country rendered by John C. Fremont, administrator and soldier."

Jessie hugged the letter to her, reading it again and again. This was the best news she had received for a long time. The government was at last acknowledging its debt to John Fremont. Now they could spend their remaining years in peace and contentment, unharassed by financial worries. She saw from John's letter how much it had meant to him, how pleased he was at this avowal of the value of his services and the unanimous praise which the bill received in the nation's press. He was going to wind up some business affairs, then he would return to Los Angeles and his Jessie, and they never would be parted again.

But the weeks dragged on and still John did not come home. While she did not like to urge him too strongly to return so long as he felt he had things to do in New York, she grew uneasy.

Then suddenly, without warning, on a suffocatingly hot July morning, she received a telegram from Charlie who was on shore leave in Washington. It read:

FATHER IS ILL

She sat in a rocker under a live-oak tree in her front yard, unmoving, almost unbreathing. That he should be stricken in a bleak bedroom of a strange rooming house, without his wife to take care of him, without the family he had raised, the few beloved souvenirs of his life, this brought anguish.

Three hours later, just as the bells of a near-by church began to chime of noon, a second telegram was delivered from Charlie. It said:

FATHER IS DEAD

After a time she walked slowly into the house and sat down at her desk in the corner of the little living room, above which was the portrait of General John C. Fremont made during the Hundred Days. On the side wall above her chair was the oil portrait of herself, painted shortly after her marriage. She sat looking up at the two pictures, somehow unable to feel that John Fremont was dead at seventy-eight, while she was still alive. She was heartbroken that he had died away from her, alone, without the last comfort of his hand in hers.

When night came, when some of the numbness of grief had eased, she understood that this was no accident: this was the way John Fremont had wanted to die, alone, as he had somehow always been alone, this shy, reserved little man who for forty-five years had been seeking, through the blinding snows of the high Sierras, to find that uncharted pass. He had known during these past weeks that he was going to die; much as he had loved her for fifty years he had wanted to die alone, alone in a drab rooming-house bed, die as he had been born, an outcast, an illegitimate one . . .

And now, at last, she knew that she would never accomplish the task on which she had set out as a girl of seventeen. Married half a century, she still had not solved the enigma of John Fremont. In her love, in her devotion she had perhaps come closer than any other woman could have; and yet how much there was which would go down to the grave with him, unexplained.

She had thought of this as a failure in her marriage. Now she realized that no one can ever completely understand another human soul. What was important was not the whole and total finding, but the search, the sympathy, the ever present and loving desire to understand. That, in its last analysis, was what love was, when viewed over half a century: at first it was light-hearted romance, then it was physical mating, then it was ambition and work together, then it was raising a family and creating a home, then it was service in good and various causes, then it was a mature partnership in progress and accomplishment, failure and hardship. Yes, love changed subtly with the passage of the years, but lasting longest and having the deepest meaning, creating the finest hours and the finest years, was the search for understanding, the full and sympathetic understanding of another being, the most elusive and at the same time the most beautiful of all human accomplishments. This was marriage.

The ensuing days were difficult. It was not possible to bring John's body to California for burial, nor could she reach New York in time for the funeral. She sat quietly in her chair in the corner of the living room, rereading her husband's last loving messages to her while his son buried him on a hill overlooking the Hudson River and Pocaho. She had a sense of Lily hovering over her to protect her, masking her own grief, keeping at a distance, not wishing to intrude yet wanting to be at her elbow for the word of comfort or the helping hand whenever it might be needed.

She shed no tears, for she had no regrets; there was nothing she had left undone, no kindness, no act of love or faith or loyalty that had been lacking. There was nothing with which to reprove herself, nothing she would have done differently. She had given John Fremont all of her love and all of her life; she could now live serenely until it was her time to go. Their lives together had passed so quickly, there had been no time to pause, to linger over the moments as they went by. Now there would be time. She was glad there would be time to relive all her memories, to watch her life pass in review, to understand it more fully now that she could hold back the hours. She had lived with John a life of tumultuous action; now she would be able to relive it quietly, savoring the best that was in it.

She picked up a letter which Charlie had written to Lily, telling his sister how painless her father's last hours had been and how thankful they should be that his last few months were happy ones. Then, at the end of the letter, she saw something which held her eye:

Of what the effect is going to be on Mother, I don't dare think. And when I do think, I doubt whether the cruelest result would not be the kindest. They lived in each other, so that I don't think there is any life for the one left.

No, Charlie, she thought, you are wrong. I won't be unhappy. Your father is safe. There is no more poverty or uncertainty for him, no more humiliation or disappointment or change of fortune. Ah, Charlie, we have lived so long together—a full half-century; we have been so close that nothing can separate us now: surely nothing so inconclusive as death. Do you imagine that merely by leaving my side your father leaves me alone? How can I ever be alone, Charlie, I who have worked and loved and suffered and rejoiced with him through all the years? You are too young to know the value of memories, my son; memories are stronger than the living flesh. Your father has died, but not in me; as long as I remain on this earth he will never die. I have him with me as surely and as vividly as I had him sitting beside me at that first musicale at Miss English's Academy, or holding me in his arms at Harriet Bodisco's wedding; just as surely as I had him with me during all those long hard months when he was away on his expeditions. True, I suffered then, for I too was young, I had no way of knowing how long and good our life together would be. But now I know it in its full length and its full goodness; I have had the greatest happiness available to a woman: I have loved my husband always and unfailingly; my husband has loved me; and our marriage has remained firm and beautiful. Do you think that these things can be taken away from a woman of sixty-six, Charlie? Do you think that, no matter how long I live, there can conceivably be time enough to relive in memory all our wonderful years together?

Nor is my work done even yet, Charlie; already the critics are hovering over your father's accomplishments, waiting to attack him. But so long as I remain alive, Charlie—and that will be for many years—your father will never go undefended. I fought for him while he was alive, and I will fight for him a thousand times harder now.

Do not grieve for me, Charlie, any more than you would grieve for your father, who had a long and magnificent life. I will know what to do with my days; a good marriage never ends; it will fill my life just as beautifully as it has for the past fifty years, fill it until the day I die.

NOTE ON SOURCES

THE READER may have asked himself, "How much of this story is true?" Much of the dialogue had to be reimagined; in one or two instances I have portrayed an incident where I was convinced of its probability even though I could not document it, for example, the meeting of Jessie Fremont and Secretary George Bancroft in the Benton home before the conquest of California; I have taken an occasional minor liberty with time where the change could have no significance in history, for example, staging Harriet Williams' wedding a year later than it actually happened, in order that Jessie might attend it with Lieutenant Fremont; and I have omitted several unimportant fragments of the complete story. Aside from these technical liberties the book is true.

My main source was the writings of Jessie Fremont: her unpublished memoirs in the Bancroft Library of the University of California at Berkeley; her unpublished letters, as well as those of her father, her husband and her friends; her published books: *Souvenirs of My Time, Far West Sketches, A Year of American Travel, The Story of the Guard, The Will and the Way Stories;* and her many uncollected magazine articles. Her daughter's book, *Recollections of Elizabeth Benton Fremont*, gives many colorful pictures of their later life. Thomas Hart Benton's *Thirty Years in the United States Senate* provides rich source material for the political history of the times; of the three biographies already published about him, the ones by Theodore Roosevelt and Joseph M. Rogers are fragments; the one by William M. Meigs is a complete political biography but contains nothing of his personal life. Jessie Fremont's short biography of her father, which serves as a prologue to John C. Fremont's *Memoirs,* is sensitively done.

John C. Fremont, in addition to the reports of his expeditions, published *Memoirs of My Life.* Six biographies have been written about him; of these, three were campaign biographies written in 1856: *The Life, Explorations and Public Services of John Charles Fremont,* by Charles W. Upham; *The Life of Colonel John Charles Fremont,* by Samuel M. Smucker; *Memoir of the Life and Public Services of John Charles Fremont,* by John Bigelow, assisted by Jessie Fremont. The fourth campaign biography appeared serially in the New York *Tribune,* and then in pamphlet form, written by Horace Greeley and Thomas McElrath. Frederick S. Dellenbaugh's *Fremont and '49,* 1914, is an excellent account of the expeditions. *A Man Unafraid,* by Herbert Bashford and Harry Wagner, 1927, is eulogistic, while *John Charles Fremont,*

1930, by Cardinal Goodwin, is quarrelsome. Allan Nevins' *Fremont, Pathmarker of the West*, 1939, is complete, authentic and highly readable.

The only previous study of Jessie Fremont is *Jessie Benton Fremont*, by Catherine Coffin Phillips, privately printed by the John Henry Nash Press in San Francisco in 1935. Mrs. Phillips' book contains invaluable source material, for she knew Jessie Fremont during the latter years of Mrs. Fremont's life and collected a fine store of anecdotes. She also had access to a group of one hundred letters written by Jessie Fremont to Nellie Haskell Browne, which have now disappeared.

The article which first awakened my interest in Jessie Fremont was "Fremont and Jessie," by Robert L. Duffus in the *American Mercury* of November 1925.

A book of this type would be difficult to write were it not for the many fine volumes that have already been published by my fellow biographers. I take this means of expressing my gratitude and sincere admiration for their research:

The Life and Letters of George Bancroft, M. A. DeWolfe Howe.
The Francis Preston Blair Family in Politics, W. E. Smith.
The Life of James Buchanan, G. Ticknor Curtis.
Kit Carson, Stanley Vestal.
Horace Greeley, Don C. Seitz.
Bret Harte, Henry C. Merwin.
Bret Harte of the Old West, Alvin F. Harlow.
General Phillip Kearny, Thomas Kearny.
Thomas Starr King, C. W. Wendte.
Abraham Lincoln: A History, Volume IV, Nicolay and Hay.
The American Leonardo: The Life of Samuel F. B. Morse, Carleton Mabee.
Little Mac: The Life of General George B. McClellan, Clarence Edward Macartney.
Franklin Pierce, Roy Franklin Nichols.
James K. Polk, Andrew C. McLaughlin.
Winfield Scott, Charles Winslow Elliott.
Whittier, Bard of Freedom, Whitman Bennett.

Among the more important general books used were:

The Truth About Fremont, Ernest A. Wiltsee.
Fremont's Hundred Days, M. F. Hixon. (Photostatic copy of manuscript in New York Public Library.)
Thirty-First Star, James A. B. Scherer.
The Year of Decision, Bernard DeVoto.
A History of the Presidency, Edward Stanwood.
Senate Executive Document, No. 33, First Session, Vol. 5, which is the complete story of the court-martial.
History of California, H. H. Bancroft.

Incidents of Travel and Adventure in the Far West with Colonel Fremont's Last Expedition, S. N. Carvalho.

John C. Fremont and the Republican Party, Ruhl Jacob Bartlett.

The Eve of Conflict, George Fort Milton.

Reveille in Washington, Margaret Leech.

Among the source books used on early western exploring were:

The Adventures of Captain Bonneville, U.S.A., Washington Irving.

Journals, Lewis and Clark.

An Account of the Expeditions to the Sources of the Mississippi, Zebulon Pike.

Expedition through the Upper Mississippi, Henry Schoolcraft.

General survey books in the field include:

Southern Trails to California in 1849, Ralph Bieber.

The Ashley-Smith Explorations and the Discovery of a Central Route to the Pacific, H. C. Dale.

Breaking the Wilderness, Frederick Dellenbaugh.

The Road to Oregon, W. J. Ghent.

Wagons West, a Story of the Oregon Trail, Elizabeth Page.

A complete Fremont biography follows:

Decision of California Supreme Court—Fremont vs. Fowler.

"Origin of the Fremont Exploration," Jessie Fremont. *Century*, March 1891.

"How a Woman's Wit Saved California," J. Moody. *Hist. Soc. of So. Calif.*, Pub., Vol. 4, 1899.

The Daring Adventures of Kit Carson and Fremont—Diary. N.Y.: Hurst & Co., 1885.

The Life and Love of J. C. Fremont, Samuel M. Smucker. N.Y.: Muller, Orton & Mulligan, 1856.

The Mariposa Estate, John C. Fremont. London: 1861, Whittingham & Wilkins.

Fremont's memorial to Congress for his claim for reimbursement for beef cattle.

"Fremont in the Conquest of California," John Bidwell. *Century*, February 1891.

Biographical Sketch of Colonel Fremont. Anonymous.

"Fremont Anecdotes," George R. Stewart. Typewritten item, Bancroft Library.

"The Opening of the Mariposa Mining Region," C. G. Campton. Ph.D. thesis, Berkeley.

Sons of the Eagle, George Creel.

Life of J. C. Fremont, Greeley and McElrath.

Life of Major-General J. C. Fremont, James Magoon. London: Beadle & Co., 1863.

"Montgomery and Fremont," Josiah Royce. *Century*, March 1891.

"Fremont Had No Secret Instructions," George Tays. Typewritten item, Bancroft Library.

"Senator Benton Lays His Plans," Thomas Drew. *Calif. Hist. Soc.*, Vol. 13, No. 2.

Fremont Songs for the People, 1856.

The Fremont Songster, 1856.

Defence of Lieutenant Colonel J. C. Fremont before the Military Court-Martial, Washington, January, 1848. (Pamphlet.)

Fremont, the West's Greatest Adventurer, Allan Nevins.

Fremont, Pathmarker of the West, Allan Nevins.

Letters to the Editors of the *National Intelligencer*, J. C. Fremont.

Colonel Fremont's Private and Public Character Vindicated, James Buchanan.

Colonel Fremont's Religion. Anonymous.

McClellan and Fremont, Antietam.

Fremont's Hundred Days in Missouri, Francis Preston Blair.

General Fremont and the Injustice Done Him, W. Brotherhead.

Colonel Fremont not a Roman Catholic. Anonymous.

Fremont and McClellan, V. B. Denslow.

Facts and Figures for Fremont and Freedom. Anonymous.

Fremont: His Supporters and Their Record. Anonymous.

"Fremont and the North Americans," F. H. Harrington. *Am. Hist. Rev.*, 1939, Vol. 44.

The Fremont Estate, David Hoffman.

J. C. Fremont's Record: Proof of His Romanism, Proof of His Pro-slavery Acts. Anonymous.

"Some of the Romance of Fremont," E. M. James. *Overland*, 1931, Vol. 89.

"Concerning Fremont," Thomas Kearny. *Argonaut*, 1931, Vol. 109.

Reminiscences of the Fremont Campaign, E. P. Powell.

"The Blairs and Fremont," W. F. Smith. *Missouri Hist. Rev.*, 1929, Vol. 23.

"Polk and Fremont," R. R. Stenberg. *Pac. Hist. Rev.*, 1938, Vol. 7.

Case of General Fremont, J. Thomas.

Report on Memorial of John C. Fremont.

U. S. Senate Res. of Senate Pub. Rep. of J. C. Fremont.

U. S. War Claims at St. Louis Comm. on J. C. Fremont.

Who is John C. Fremont? Anonymous.

Manuscripts in the Bancroft Library:

Narrative of J. C. Fremont's Expedition to California in 1845–46, and Subsequent Events in California Down to 1853, Thomas B. Martin.

History of California as Dictated by Major Salvador Vallejo.

New Helvetia Diary of Events from 1845 to 1848, Swasey, Bidwell, Tooker, Sutter.

California, 1841–48, an Immigrant's Recollection of a Trip Across the Plains, John Bidwell.

Personal Reminiscences, General John A. Sutter.

Papers on the Bear Flag, Jacob P. Leese.

The Days of 1846, William Buldridge.

California in 1846, William Hargrave.

The Bear Flag Revolt, John Fowler.

Official Correspondence, Thomas S. Larkin.

Senator William Gwin's Manuscripts.

William M. Gwin, Expansionist, Hallie McPherson (in possession of Stanford Gwin of San Francisco).

Original Study of Albert Sidney Johnston, Henry Duque.

Life of Larking, R. L. Underhill of Berkeley (unpublished manuscript in possession of author).

Letters of Thomas Hart Benton to His Daughters.

Letters and Autobiographical Writings of Jessie Fremont.

Letters and Memoranda, John C. Fremont.

Memoires, Jessie Fremont.

Statement of William F. Swasey (Cals. manuscripts D. 200).

Statement on Conditions in 1848, Charles V. Gillespie.

Manuscripts in the Huntington Library:

The Leidesdorff Papers.

Fremont and the Conquest of California, Henry L. Oak.

Unpublished Notebook of 1848–1851 (7 vols.), Edward M. Kern.

Secret Affairs of the Mexican War, Jessie Fremont.

Fort Sutter Papers, Edward Kern.

Jessie Fremont (pamphlet), Thomas R. Bard.